C0-APZ-136

"E"
Is for
EVIDENCE

A Kinsey Millhone Mystery

SUE GRAFTON

BANTAM BOOKS

NEW YORK · TORONTO · LONDON · SYDNEY · AUCKLAND

For my two mothers, past and present:
Viv and Lillian

This edition contains the complete text
of the original hardcover edition.
NOT ONE WORD HAS BEEN OMITTED.

"E" IS FOR EVIDENCE

A Bantam Crime Line Book / published by arrangement with
Henry Holt and Company, Inc.

PRINTING HISTORY

Henry Holt edition published May 1988

Bantam edition / May 1989

CRIME LINE and the portrayal of a boxed "cl" are trademarks of Bantam Books, a division
of Bantam Doubleday Dell Publishing Group, Inc.

All rights reserved.
Copyright © 1988 by Sue Grafton.
Cover art copyright © 1989 by Roy Pendleton.
Library of Congress Catalog Card Number: 87-28100.
No part of this book may be reproduced or transmitted in any form or by any means,
electronic or mechanical, including photocopying, recording, or by any information
storage and retrieval system, without permission in writing from the publisher.
For information address:
Henry Holt and Company, Inc., 115 West 18th Street, New York, NY 10011.

If you purchased this book without a cover you should be aware that this book is stolen
property. It was reported as "unsold and destroyed" to the publisher and neither the
author nor the publisher has received any payment for this "stripped book."

ISBN 0-553-27955-6

Published simultaneously in the United States and Canada

Bantam Books are published by Bantam Books, a division of Bantam Doubleday Dell
Publishing Group, Inc. Its trademark, consisting of the words "Bantam Books" and the
portrayal of a rooster, is Registered in U.S. Patent and Trademark Office and in other
countries. Marca Registrada. Bantam Books, 666 Fifth Avenue, New York, New York 10103.

PRINTED IN THE UNITED STATES OF AMERICA

RAD   17   16   15   14

RAVE REVIEWS FOR KINSEY MILLHONE AND "E" IS FOR EVIDENCE

"THE BEST DETECTIVE FICTION I HAVE READ IN YEARS. . . . The plot is just fine and does what a plot ought to in a good detective novel: it keeps us turning pages and serves as a vehicle for the *really* interesting stuff, an unveiling of the characters' foibles by the worldy-wise but uncorrupt private eye. And this is where Sue Grafton shines. She has endowed Kinsey with that most important attribute of a fictional private eye, a distinct voice. . . . Her observations on the surrounding society are right on the money without being condescending. . . . Lord, how I like this Kinsey Millhone. May her practice flourish."
—Vincent Patrick, *The New York Times Book Review*

"A DELECTABLE DETECTIVE. . . . Grafton is a funny writer; her movements are crisp, her dialogue snappy and (though Kinsey denies it) her heroine has class."
—*Newsweek*

"KINSEY, AS ALWAYS, IS A DELIGHT. . . . Sharp, sassy, and straightforward."
—*Christian Science Monitor*

"GRAFTON HAS AN ACCURATE, WICKED EYE for California life-style and wisecracking Kinsey is an appealing, nonhackneyed female detective. . . . Readers will be glad that further letters of the alphabet await Grafton's imagination."
—*Publishers Weekly*

"AN UNFLAGGING PACE, skilled buildup of tension, lively characters, and Kinsey's offbeat charm make this yet another of the author's first-class entertainments."
—*Kirkus Reviews*

"EXCEPTIONALLY STRONG. . . . A crackling good story."
—*The Drood Review of Mystery*

" 'E' IS ALSO FOR EXCELLENT. . . . Grafton is an extremely clever plotter and Kinsey Millhone is a witty and gritty private eye. It will be a pleasure to read her from A to Z."
—*Cincinnati Post*

Bantam Crime Line Books by Sue Grafton
Ask your bookseller for the books you have missed

"A" IS FOR ALIBI
"B" IS FOR BURGLAR
"C" IS FOR CORPSE
"D" IS FOR DEADBEAT
"E" IS FOR EVIDENCE
"F" IS FOR FUGITIVE

The author wishes to acknowledge the invaluable assistance of the following people: Steven Humphrey; Jim Hetherington, President, and Dorcas Lube, Office Manager, Hetherington, Inc.; Bruce Boller, First Vice President, Institutional Services, Robert W. Baird, Inc.; Joyce Mackewich and Kim Nelson of Montgomery, Fansler & Carlson Insurance; Dennis W. Leski; William Pasich; Robert Snowball; Caroline Ware, Santa Barbara Travel; Elisa Moran, Santa Barbara County Registrar of Voters; Kathleen Hotchkiss, Culinary Alliance and Bartenders Local 498; Anne Reid; Frank and Florence Clark; Lynn Herold, Ph.D., Senior Criminalist, Department of Chief Medical Examiner-Coroner, Los Angeles County; George Donner, A-1 Tri-Counties Investigations; Detective Robert J. Lowry, Investigative Division, Santa Barbara Police Department; and Deputy Juan Tejeda, Santa Barbara County Sheriff's Department.

1

It was Monday, December 27, and I was sitting in my office, trying to get a fix on the mood I was in, which was bad, bad, bad, comprised of equal parts irritation and uneasiness. The irritation was generated by a bank notice I'd just received, one of those windowed numbers with a yellow carbon showing through. At first, I assumed I was overdrawn, but what I pulled out was a slip, dated Friday, December 24, showing a five-thousand-dollar deposit to my checking account.

"What the hell is this?" I said.

The account number was correct, but the deposit wasn't mine. In my experience, banks are the least helpful institutions on earth, and the notion of having to stop what I was doing to straighten out an error was nearly more than I could bear. I tossed the notice aside, trying to reclaim my concentration. I was getting ready to write up the preliminary report on an insurance case I'd been asked to look into, and Darcy, the secretary at California Fidelity, had just buzzed to say that Mac wanted the file on his desk right away. Mentally, I'd come up with a tart suggestion about what she could do with herself, but I'd kept my mouth shut, showing (I thought) admirable restraint.

I turned back to my portable Smith-Corona, inserting the proper form for a property-insurance-loss register. My nimble fingers were poised to type while I reviewed my notes. That's where I was stuck. Something was off and I couldn't figure out what it was. I glanced at the bank notice again.

Almost with an eye toward the comic relief, I called

the bank, hoping the diversion would help me focus on what was bothering me about the situation at Wood/Warren, a local company manufacturing hydrogen furnaces for industrial use. They'd had a fire out there on December 19 that had destroyed a warehouse.

"Mrs. Brunswick, Customer Service. May I help you?"

"Well, I hope so," I said. "I just received a notice saying I put five thousand dollars in my checking account last Friday and I didn't do that. Is there any way you can straighten it out?"

"May I have your name and account number, please?"

"Kinsey Millhone," I said, supplying my account number in slow, measured tones.

She put me on hold briefly while she called up the records on her computer terminal. Meanwhile, I listened to the bank's rendition of "Good King Wenceslas," which I've personally never understood. What's the Feast of Stephen?

Mrs. Brunswick clicked back in. "Miss Millhone, I'm not certain what the problem is, but we do show a cash deposit to this account number. Apparently, it was left in the night-deposit slot and posted over the weekend."

"You still have one of those night-deposit slots?" I asked with amazement.

"At our downtown branch, yes," she said.

"Well, there's some kind of mistake here. I've never even seen the night-deposit slot. I use my twenty-four-hour instant teller card if I need to transact bank business after hours. What do we do now?"

"I can track down a copy of the deposit slip," she said skeptically.

"Would you do that, please? Because I didn't make a deposit of any kind last Friday and certainly not five thousand dollars' worth. Maybe somebody transposed some numbers on the deposit slip or something, but the money sure doesn't belong to me."

She took my telephone number and said she'd get back to me. I could tell I was in for countless phone calls before the correction could be made. Suppose somebody was merrily writing checks against that five grand?

I went back to the task at hand, wishing I felt more

enlightened than I did. My mind kept jumping around. The file on the fire claim at Wood/Warren had actually come into my hands four days before, late Thursday, the 23rd. I'd been scheduled to have a farewell drink with my landlord, Henry Pitts, at four, and then take him out to the airport and put him on a plane. He was flying back to Michigan to spend the holidays with his family, some of whom are edging into their nineties with their vigor and good spirits still in evidence. Henry's pushing eighty-two, a mere kid, and he was about as excited as one at the prospect of the trip.

I was still at the office that afternoon with my paperwork caught up and some time to kill. I went out onto my second-floor balcony, peering off to my right at the V of Pacific Ocean visible at the foot of State Street, ten blocks down. This is Santa Teresa, California, ninety-five miles north of Los Angeles. Winter here is a grand affair, full of sunshine and mild temperatures, vibrant magenta bougainvillea, gentle winds, and palm trees waving fronds at the sea gulls as they wheel overhead.

The only signs of Christmas, two days away, were the garlands of tinsel strung along the main streets. The stores, of course, were packed with shoppers, and there was a trio of Salvation Army horn players tooting away at "Deck the Halls." In the interests of feeling jolly, I thought I'd better work out my strategy for the next two days.

Anyone who knows me will tell you that I cherish my unmarried state. I'm female, twice divorced, no kids, and no close family ties. I'm a private detective by trade. Usually I'm perfectly content to do what I do. There are times when I work long hours on a case and times when I'm on the road and times when I hole up in my tiny apartment and read books for days. When the holidays come around, however, I find that I have to exercise a certain cunning lest the absence of loved ones generate unruly depression. Thanksgiving had been a breeze. I spent the day with Henry and some pals of his, who'd cooked and sipped champagne and laughed and told tales about days long past, making me wish I were their age instead of my own, which is thirty-two.

Now Henry was leaving town, and even Rosie, who

runs the dingy neighborhood tavern where I often eat, was closing down until January 2, refusing to tell a soul what she meant to do with herself. Rosie is sixty-six, Hungarian, short, top-heavy, bossy, and often rude, so it wasn't as though I was worried I'd miss any touching heart-to-heart chats. The fact that she was closing her eatery was simply one more uncomfortable reminder that I was out there in the world all by myself and had best find a way to look after me.

At any rate, I'd glanced at my watch and decided I might as well head on home. I switched on the answering machine, grabbed my jacket and handbag, and was just locking up when Darcy Pascoe, the receptionist from the insurance company next door, popped her head in. I had worked for California Fidelity full time at one point, doing investigations on fire and wrongful death claims. Now the arrangement is informal. I'm more or less on call, doing a certain number of investigations for them, as needed, in exchange for downtown office space I couldn't otherwise afford.

"Oh, wow. I'm glad I caught you," Darcy said. "Mac told me to give you this."

She handed me a file, which I glanced at automatically. The blank form inside indicated that I was being asked to do a fire-scene inspection, the first in months.

"Mac did?" Mac is the CF vice-president. I couldn't imagine him handling routine paperwork.

"Well, actually, Mac gave it to Andy and Andy said I should give it to you."

There was a memo attached to the file cover, dated three days before and marked RUSH. Darcy caught my look and her cheeks tinted faintly.

"It was stuck under a big pile of stuff on my desk or I'd have gotten it to you sooner," she said. Darcy's in her late twenties and something of a flake. I crossed to my desk, tossing the file on top of some others I was working on. I'd catch it first thing in the morning. Darcy lingered in the doorway, guessing my intent.

"Is there any way you can get to that today? I know he's anxious to get somebody out there. Jewel was supposed to handle it, but she's taking two weeks off, so Mac said maybe you could do it instead."

"What's the claim?"

"A big warehouse fire out in Colgate. You probably heard it on the news."

I shook my head. "I've been down in L.A."

"Well, the newspaper clippings are in there, too. I guess they want someone out there superquick."

I was annoyed at the pressure, but I opened the manila folder again and checked the property-loss notice, which was posted on top. "Wood/Warren?" I said.

"You know the company?"

"I know the Woods. I went to high school with the youngest girl. We were in the same homeroom."

She looked relieved, as if I'd just solved a problem for her. "That's great. I'll tell Mac maybe you can get out there this afternoon."

"Darcy, would you knock that off? I've got to take somebody to the airport," I said. "Trust me. I'll make an appointment for the earliest possible moment."

"Oh. Well, I'll make a note then so they'll know you're taking care of it," she said. "I have to get back to the phones. Let me know when you have the report and I'll come pick it up."

"Terrific," I said. She must have decided she had pushed me far enough because she excused herself and disappeared in haste.

As soon as she left, just to get it over with, I put a call through to Wood/Warren and arranged to meet with the company president, Lance Wood, at 9:00 the next morning, Christmas Eve day.

Meanwhile, as it was 3:45, I tucked the file in my handbag, locked up, and headed down the back stairs to the lot where my VW was parked. I was home ten minutes later.

During our little pre-Christmas celebration, Henry gave me a new Len Deighton novel and I gave him a periwinkle-blue mohair muffler, which I had crocheted myself—a little-known talent of mine. We sat in his kitchen and ate half a pan of his homemade cinnamon rolls, drinking champagne out of the matching crystal flutes I'd given him the year before.

He took out his plane ticket and checked the departure time again, his cheeks flushed with anticipation. "I wish you'd come with me," he said. He had the muffler wrapped around his neck, the color setting off his eyes. His white hair was soft and brushed to one side, his lean face tanned from California sun.

"I wish I could, but I just picked up some work that'll get my rent paid," I said. "You can take lots of pictures and show 'em to me when you get back."

"What about Christmas Day? You're not going to be by yourself, I hope."

"Henry, would you quit worrying? I've got lots of friends." I'd probably spend the day alone, but I didn't want him to fret.

He raised a finger. "Hold on. I almost forgot. I have another little present for you." He crossed to the counter by the kitchen sink and picked up a clump of greenery in a little pot. He set it down in front of me, laughing when he saw the expression on my face. It looked like a fern and smelled like feet.

"It's an air fern," he said. "It just lives on air. You don't even have to water it."

I stared at the lacy fronds, which were a nearly luminous green and looked like something that might thrive in outer space. "No plant food?"

He shook his head. "Just let it sit."

"I don't have to worry about diffuse sunlight or pinching back?" I asked, tossing around some plant terms as if I knew what they meant. I'm notoriously bad with plants, and for years I've resisted any urge whatever to own one.

"Nothing. It's to keep you company. Put it on your desk. It'll jazz the place up a bit."

I held the little pot up and inspected the fern from all sides, experiencing this worrisome spark of possessiveness. I must be in worse shape than I thought, I thought.

Henry fished a set of keys out of his pocket and passed them over to me. "In case you need to get into my place," he said.

"Great. I'll bring in your mail and the papers. Is there

anything else you need done while you're gone? I can mow the grass."

"You don't need to do that. I've left you the number where I can be reached if the Big One hits. I can't think of anything else." The Big One he referred to was the major earthquake we'd all been expecting any day now since the last one in 1925.

He checked his watch. "We better get a move on. The airport is mobbed this time of year." His plane wasn't leaving until 7:00, which left us only an hour and a half to make the twenty-minute trip to the airport, but there wasn't any point in arguing. Sweet man. If he had to wait, he might as well do it out there, happily chatting with his fellow travelers.

I put on my jacket while Henry made a circuit of the house, taking a few seconds to turn the heat down, making sure the windows and doors were secured. He picked up his coat and his suitcase and we were on our way.

I was home again by 6:15, still feeling a bit of a lump in my throat. I hate to say goodbye to folks and I hate being left behind. It was getting dark by then and the air had a bite to it. I let myself into my place. My studio apartment was formerly Henry's single-car garage. It's approximately fifteen feet on a side, with a narrow extension on the right that serves as my kitchenette. I have laundry facilities and a compact bathroom. The space has been cleverly designed and apportioned to suggest the illusion of living room, dining room, and bedroom once I open my sofa bed. I have more than adequate storage space for the few things I possess.

Surveying my tiny kingdom usually fills me with satisfaction, but I was still battling a whisper of Yuletide depression, and the place seemed claustrophobic and bleak. I turned on some lights. I put the air fern on my desk. Ever hopeful, I checked my answering machine for messages, but there were none. The quiet was making me feel restless. I turned on the radio—Bing Crosby singing about a white Christmas just like the ones he used to know. I've never actually seen a white Christmas, but I got the gist. I turned the radio off.

I sat on a kitchen stool and monitored my vital signs. I

was hungry. One thing about living alone . . . you can eat any time you want. For dinner that night I made myself a sandwich of olive-pimento cheese on whole-wheat bread. It's a source of comfort to me that the brand of olive-pimento cheese I buy has tasted exactly the same since the first time I remembered eating it at the age of three and a half. Resolutely I veered off *that* subject, since it connected to my parents, who were killed when I was five. I cut the sandwich into four fingers, as I always did, poured myself a glass of white wine, and took my plate over to the couch, where I opened the book Henry had given me for Christmas. I checked the clock.

It was 7:00 P.M. This was going to be a very long two weeks.

2

The next morning, December 24, I jogged three miles, showered, ate a bowl of cereal, packed a canvas tote with supplies, and was heading toward Colgate by 8:45, a quick ten-mile drive. I'd reviewed the file over breakfast, and I was already puzzled about what the big rush was. The newspaper account indicated that the warehouse was gutted, but there was no telltale closing line about arson, investigations pending, or any speculation that the nature of the blaze was suspect. The fire-department report was included, and I'd read that twice. It all looked routine. Apparently the origin of the fire was a malfunction in the electrical system, which had simultaneously shorted out the sprinklers. Since the materials stored in the two-story structure were largely paper goods, the 2:00 A.M. fire had spread rapidly. According to the fire inspector at the scene, there was no sign of firetraps, no gasoline or other flammables, and no sign of obstacles placed so as to impede the work of the firemen. There was no indication that doors or windows had been left open to create favorable drafts and no other physical evidence of incendiary origin. I'd read dozens of reports just like this one. So what was the big deal here? I wondered. Maybe I was missing a crucial piece of information, but as far as I could see, this was a standard claim. I had to guess that somebody at Wood/Warren was putting the squeeze on California Fidelity for a speedy settlement, which might explain Andy's panic. He's a nail-biter by inclination, anxious for approval, worried about censure, in the middle of marital problems, from what I'd heard. He was probably the source of the

little note of hysteria that had crept into the case. Maybe
Mac was leaning on him, too.

Colgate is the bedroom community that adjoins Santa
Teresa, providing affordable housing for average working
folk. While new construction in Santa Teresa is closely
regulated by the Architectural Board of Review, building
in Colgate has proceeded according to no known plan,
though it leans toward the nondescript. There is one major
street lined with donut shops, hardware stores, fast-food
establishments, beauty salons, and furniture stores that
feature veneer and laminate, velour and Naugahyde.
From the main thoroughfare, tract homes stretch out in all
directions, housing styles appearing like concentric rings
on a tree stump, spiraling out decade by decade until the
new neighborhoods peter out into raw countryside, or
what's left of it. In isolated patches there are still signs of
the old citrus groves that once flourished there.

Wood/Warren was located on a side street that angled
back toward an abandoned drive-in theater that functions
as a permanent location for weekend swap sales. The
lawns of the neighboring manufacturing plants were a
close-clipped green, and the shrubs were trimmed into
perfect rectangles. I found a parking place out front and
locked up. The building was a compact story and a half of
stucco and fieldstone. The address of the warehouse itself
was two blocks away. I'd inspect the fire scene after I
talked to Lance Wood.

The reception area was small and plain, furnished
with a desk, a bookcase, and an enlarged photograph of the
FIFA 5000 Hydrogen/Vacuum Furnace, the mainstay of
the company fortunes. It looked like an oversized unit for
an efficiency kitchen, complete with stainless-steel counter
and built-in microwave. According to the data neatly
framed nearby, the front-loading FIFA 5000 provided five
thousand cubic inches of uniform hot zone for hydrogen or
vacuum brazing, for metallizing ceramics, or manufacturing ceramic-to-metal seals. I should have guessed.

Behind me, the receptionist was returning to her desk
with a fresh cup of coffee and a Styrofoam container that
smelled of sausage and eggs. The laminated plastic sign on
her desk indicated that her name was Heather. She was in

her twenties and apparently hadn't yet heard about the
hazards of cholesterol and fat. She would find the latter on
her fanny one day soon.

"May I help you?" Her smile was quick, exposing
braces on her teeth. Her complexion was still ruddy from
last night's application of an acne cure that so far hadn't
had much effect.

"I have an appointment with Lance Wood at nine," I
said. "I'm with California Fidelity Insurance."

Her smile faded slightly. "You're the arson investigator?"

"Well, I'm here on the fire claim," I said, wondering if
she mistakenly assumed that "arson" and "fire" were in-
terchangeable terms.

"Oh. Mr. Wood isn't in yet, but he should be here
momentarily," she said. The braces infused her speech
with a sibilance that amused her when she heard herself.
"Can I get you some coffee while you wait?"

I shook my head. There was one chair available and I
took a seat, amusing myself by leafing through a brochure
on the molybdenum work rack designed specifically for
metallizing alumina at 1450° C. in a bell-style hydrogen
furnace. These people had about as many laughs as I do at
home, where a prime source of entertainment is a text-
book on practical aspects of ballistics, firearms, and forensic techniques.

Through a doorway to my left, I could see some of the
office staff, casually dressed and busy, but glum. I didn't
pick up any sense of camaraderie among them, but maybe
hydrogen furnace-making doesn't generate the kind of
good-natured bantering I'm accustomed to with California
Fidelity. Two desks were unoccupied, bare of equipment
or accouterments.

Some attempt had been made to decorate for Christmas. There was an artificial tree across the room from me,
tall and skeletal, hung with multicolored ornaments.
There didn't seem to be any lights strung on the tree,
which gave it a lifeless air and only pointed up the unifor-
mity of the detachable limbs stuck into pre-bored holes in
the aluminum shaft. The effect was dispiriting. From the
information I'd been given, Wood/Warren grossed close to

fifteen million bucks a year, and I wondered why they wouldn't pop for a live pine.

Heather gave me a self-conscious smile and began to eat. Behind her was a bulletin board decorated with garlands of tinsel and covered with snapshots of the family and staff. H–A–P–P–Y H–O–L–I–D–A–Y–S was spelled out in jaunty store-bought silver letters.

"Mind if I look at that?" I asked, indicating the collage.

By then, she had a mouth full of breakfast croissant, but she managed assent, holding a hand in front of her mouth to spare me the sight of her masticated food. "Help yourself."

Most of the photographs were of company employees, some of whom I'd seen on the premises. Heather was featured in one, her fair hair much shorter, her face still framed in baby fat. The braces on her teeth probably represented the last vestige of her teens. Wood/Warren must have hired her right out of high school. In one photograph, four guys in company coveralls stood in a relaxed group on the front doorstep. Some of the shots were stiffly posed, but for the most part they seemed to capture an aura of goodwill I wasn't picking up on currently. The founder of the company, Linden "Woody" Wood, had died two years before, and I wondered if some of the joy had gone out of the place with his demise.

The Woods themselves formed the centerpiece in a studio portrait that looked like it was taken at the family home. Mrs. Wood was seated in a French Provincial chair. Linden stood with his hand resting on his wife's shoulder. The five grown children were ranged around their parents. Lance I'd never met before, but I knew Ash because I'd gone to high school with her. Olive, older by a year, had attended Santa Teresa High briefly, but had been sent off to a boarding school in her senior year. There was probably a minor scandal attached to that, but I wasn't sure what it was. The oldest of the five was Ebony, who by now must be nearly forty. I remembered hearing that she'd married some rich playboy and was living in France. The youngest was a son named Bass, not quite thirty, reckless, irresponsible, a failed actor and no-talent musician, living in New York City, the last I'd heard. I had met him briefly eight years before through my ex-husband, Daniel, a jazz pianist. Bass was the black sheep of the family. I wasn't sure what the story was on Lance.

Seated across his desk from him sixty-six minutes later, I began to pick up a few hints. Lance had breezed in at 9:30. The receptionist indicated who I was. He introduced himself and we shook hands. He said he had a quick phone call to make and then he'd be right with me. I said "Fine" and that was the last I saw of him until 10:06. By then, he'd shed his suit coat and loosened his tie along with the top button of his dress shirt. He was sitting with his feet up on the desk, his face oily-looking under the fluorescent lights. He must have been in his late thirties, but he wasn't aging well. Some combination of temper and discontent had etched lines near his mouth and spoiled the clear brown of his eyes, leaving an impression of a man beleaguered by the Fates. His hair was light brown, thinning on top, and combed straight back from his face. I thought the business about the phone call was bullshit. He struck me as the sort of man who pumped up his own sense of importance by making people wait. His smile was self-satisfied, and the energy he radiated was charged with tension.

"Sorry for the delay," he said. "What can I do for you?" He was tipped back in his swivel chair, his thighs splayed.

"I understand you filed a claim for a recent fire loss."

"That's right, and I hope you're not going to give me any static over that. Believe me, I'm not asking for anything I'm not entitled to."

I made a noncommittal murmur of some sort, hoping to conceal the fact that I'd gone on "fraud alert." Every insurance piker I'd ever met said just that, right down to the pious little toss of the head. I took out my tape recorder, flicked it on, and set it on the desk. "The company requires that I tape the interview," I said.

"That's fine."

I directed my next few remarks to the recorder, establishing my name, the fact that I worked for California Fidelity, the date and time of the interview, and the fact that I was speaking to Lance Wood in his capacity as president and CEO of Wood/Warren, the address of the company, and the nature of the loss.

"Mr. Wood, you do understand that this is being taped," I said for the benefit of the record.

"Yes."

"And do I have your permission to make this recording of the conversation we're about to have?"

"Yes, yes," he said, making that little rolling hand gesture that means "Let's get on with it."

I glanced down at the file. "Can you tell me the circumstances of the fire that occurred at the Wood/Warren warehouse at 606 Fairweather on December nineteenth of this year?"

He shifted impatiently. "Actually, I was out of town, but from what I'm told . . ." The telephone intercom buzzed and he snatched up the receiver, barking at it like a dog. "Yes?"

There was a pause. "Well, goddamn it, put her through." He gave me a quick look. "No, wait a minute, I'll take it out there." He put the phone down, excused himself brusquely, and left the room. I clicked off the recorder, mentally assessing the brief impression I'd had of him as he passed. He was getting heavy in the waist and his gabardine pants rode up unbecomingly, his shirt sticking to the center of his back. He smelled harshly of sweat—not that clean animal scent that comes from a hard workout, but the pungent, faintly repellant odor of stress. His complexion was sallow and he looked vaguely unhealthy.

I waited for fifteen minutes and then tiptoed to the door. The reception area was deserted. No sign of Lance Wood. No sign of Heather. I moved over to the door leading into the inner office. I caught a glimpse of someone passing into the rear of the building who looked very much like Ebony, but I couldn't be sure. A woman looked up at me. The name plate on her desk indicated that she was Ava Daugherty, the office manager. She was in her late forties, with a small, dusky face and a nose that looked as if it had been surgically tampered with. Her hair was short and black, with the glossy patina of hair spray. She was unhappy about something, possibly the fact that she'd just cracked one of her bright-red acrylic fingernails.

"I'm supposed to be meeting with Lance Wood, but he's disappeared. Do you know where he went?"

"He left the plant." She was licking the cracked nail experimentally, as if the chemistry of her saliva might serve as adhesive.

"He left?"

"That's what I said."

"Did he say how soon he'd be back?"

"Mr. Wood doesn't consult with me," she said snappishly. "If you'd like to leave your name, I'm sure he'll get back to you."

A voice cut in. "Something wrong?"

We both looked up to find a dark-haired man standing in the doorway behind me. Ava Daugherty's manner became somewhat less antagonistic. "This is the company vice-president," she said to me. And to him, "She's supposed to be in a meeting with Lance, but he left the plant."

"Terry Kohler," he said to me, holding out his hand. "I'm Lance Wood's brother-in-law."

"Kinsey Millhone, from California Fidelity," I said, shaking hands with him. "Nice to meet you." His grip was hard and hot. He was wiry, with a dark moustache and large, dark eyes that were full of intelligence. He must have been in his early forties. I wondered which sister he was married to.

"What's the problem? Something I can help you with?"

I told him briefly what I was doing there and the fact that Lance Wood had abandoned me without a word of explanation.

"Why don't I show you the warehouse?" he said. "At least you can go ahead and inspect the fire scene, which I'm assuming is one of your responsibilities."

"I'd appreciate that. Is anybody else out here authorized to give me the information I need?"

Terry Kohler and Ava Daugherty exchanged a look I couldn't decipher.

"You better wait for Lance," he said. "Hold on and I'll see if I can find out where he went." He moved toward the outer office.

Ava and I avoided small talk. She opened her top

right-hand drawer and took out a tube of Krazy Glue,
ignoring me pointedly as she snipped off the tip and
squeezed one clear drop on the cracked fingernail. She
frowned. A long dark hair was caught in the glue and I
watched her struggle to extract it.

Idly I tuned into the conversation behind me, three
engineers in a languid discussion about the problem before
them.

"Now maybe the calculation is off, but I don't think
so," one was saying.

"We'll find out," someone interjected. All three men
laughed.

"The question came up . . . oh, this has occurred to
me many times . . . What would it take to convert this to
a pulse power supply for the main hot cell?"

"Depends on what your pulsing frequency is."

"About ten hertz."

"Whoa."

"Anything that would allow you to modulate a signal
away that was being influenced by the juice going through
the susceptors. You know, power on for nine-tenths of a
second, off for a tenth. Take measurements . . ."

"Um—hum. On for a half a second, off for a tenth of a
second. You can't really do it easily, can you?"

"The PID controller could send the output that fast.
I'm not sure what that would do to the NCRs. To the VRT
setup itself, whether that would follow it . . ."

I tuned them out again. They could have been plotting the end of the world for all I knew.

It was another ten minutes before Terry Kohler reappeared. He was shaking his head in apparent exasperation.

"I don't know what's going on around here," he said.
"Lance had to go out on some emergency and Heather's
still away from her desk." He held up a key ring. "I'll take
you over to the warehouse. Tell Heather I've got these if
she shows up."

"I should get my camera," I said. "It's with my handbag."

He tagged along patiently while I moved back to
Lance Wood's office, where I retrieved the camera, tucked
my wallet in my tote, and left my handbag where it was.

Together we retraced a path through the reception room and the offices beyond. Nobody actually looked up as we passed, but curious gazes followed us in silence, like those portraits where the eyes seem to move.

The assembly work was done in a large, well-ventilated area in the back half of the building with walls of corrugated metal and a floor of concrete.

We paused only once while Terry introduced me to a man named John Salkowitz. "John's a chemical engineer and consulting associate," Terry said. "He's been with us since 'sixty-six. You have any questions about high-temperature processing, he's the man you want to ask."

Offhand, I couldn't think of one—except maybe about that pulse power supply for the main hot cell. That was a poser.

Terry was moving toward the rear door, and I trotted after him.

To the right, there was a double-wide rolling steel door that could be raised to accommodate incoming shipments or to load finished units ready for delivery. We went out into the alleyway, cutting through to the street beyond.

"Which of the Wood sisters are you married to?" I asked. "I went to high school with Ash."

"Olive," he said with a smile. "What's your name again?"

I told him and we chatted idly for the remainder of the short walk, dropping into silence only when the charred skeleton of the warehouse loomed into view.

3

It took me three hours to examine the fire scene. Terry went through the motions of unlocking the front door, though the gesture seemed ludicrous given the wreckage the fire had left. Most of the outer shell of the building remained upright, but the second story had collapsed into the first, leaving a nearly impenetrable mass of blackened rubble. The glass in the first-floor windows had been blown out by the heat. Metal pipes were exposed, many twisted by the weight of the walls tumbling inward. Whatever recognizable objects remained were reduced to their abstract shapes, robbed of color and detail.

When it became apparent that I was going to be there for a while, Terry excused himself and went back to the plant. Wood/Warren was closing early that day as it was Christmas Eve. He said if I was finished soon enough, I was welcome to stop by and have some punch and Christmas cookies. I had already taken out my measuring tape, notebook, sketch pad, and pencils, mentally laying out the order in which I intended to proceed. I thanked him, scarcely aware of his departure.

I circled the perimeter of the building, noting the areas of severest burning, checking the window frames on the first floor for signs of forced entry. I wasn't sure how quickly the salvage crew would be coming in, and since there was no apparent evidence of arson, I didn't feel California Fidelity could insist on a delay. Monday morning, I would do a background check on Lance Wood's financial situation just to make sure there wasn't any hidden profit motive for the fire itself . . . a mere formality in this case, since the fire chief had already ruled out arson in his report. Since this was probably the only chance we'd have to survey the premises, I photographed everything, taking two rolls of film, twenty-four exposures each.

As nearly as I could tell, the probable point of origin of the fire was somewhere in the north wall, which seemed consistent with the theory of an electrical malfunction. I'd have to check the wiring diagram from the original blueprints, but I suspected the fire chief had done just that in coming up with his analysis. The surface of charred wood bore the typical pattern of crevices known as "alligatoring," the deepest charring and the smallest check in the pattern localized in this rear portion of the building. Since hot gases rise and fire normally sweeps upward, it's usually possible to track the course of the flames, which will tend to rise until an obstacle is encountered, then project horizontally, seeking other vertical outlets.

Much of the interior had been reduced to ashes. The load-bearing walls remained, as black and brittle as cinder. Gingerly, I picked my way through the char-broiled junk, making a detailed map of the ruins, noting the degree of burning, general appearance, and carbonization of burned objects. Every surface I encountered had been painted with the black and ashen pallor of extreme heat. The stench was familiar: scorched wood, soot, the sodden odor of drenched insulation, the lingering chemical aroma of ordinary materials reduced to their elements. There was some other odor as well, which I noted, but couldn't identify. It was probably connected to materials stored there. When I'd called Lance Wood the day before, I'd requested a copy of the inventory sheets. I'd review those to see if I could pinpoint the source of the smell. I wasn't crazy about having to inspect the fire scene before I'd had a chance to interview him, but I didn't seem to have much choice, now that he'd disappeared. Maybe he'd be back for the office Christmas party and I could pin him down then about an appointment first thing Monday morning.

At 2:00 P.M., I packed my sketch pad away and brushed off my jeans. My tennis shoes were nearly white with ash, and I suspected that my face was smudged. Still, I was reasonably content with the job I'd done. Wood/Warren was going to have to get several contractors' estimates, and those would be submitted to CF along with my recommendation regarding payment of the claim. Using the standard rule, I was guessing five hundred thousand dollars replacement cost, with additional payment for the inventory loss.

The Christmas party was indeed in progress. The festivities were centered in the inner offices where a punch bowl had been set up on a drafting table. Desks had been cleared and were covered with platters of cold cuts, cheeses, and crackers, along with slices of fruitcake and homemade cookies. The company employees numbered about sixty, so the noise level was substantial, the general atmosphere getting looser and livelier as the champagne punch went down. Some sort of Reggae version of Christmas carols was being blasted through the intercom system.

There was still no sign of Lance Wood, but I spotted Heather on the far side of the room, her cheeks rosy with wassail. Terry Kohler caught my eye and shouldered his way in my direction. When he reached me, he leaned down close to my ear.

"We better get your handbag before this gets out of control," he said. I nodded vigorously and inched my way behind him through the reception area to Lance's office. The door was standing open and his desk was being used as a bar. Liquor bottles, ice, and plastic glasses were arranged across the surface, with several people helping themselves to both the booze and the comfort of the boss's furniture. My handbag had been tucked into a narrow slot between a file cabinet and a bookcase jammed with technical manuals. I put away my camera and sketch pad, hefting the bag onto my right shoulder. Terry offered to fetch me some punch, and after a moment of hesitation, I agreed. Hey, why not?

My first impulse was to leave as soon as I could gracefully extricate myself. I don't generally do well in group situations, and in this instance I didn't know a soul. What kept me was the sure knowledge that I had nowhere else to go. This might be the extent of my holiday celebration, and I thought I might as well enjoy it. I accepted some punch, helped myself to cheese and crackers, ate some

cookies with pink and green sugar on top, smiled pleasantly, and generally made myself amenable to anyone
within range. By 3:00, when the party was really getting
under way, I excused myself and headed out the door. I
had just reached the curb when I heard someone call my
name. I turned. Heather was moving down the walk behind me, holding out an envelope embossed with the
Wood/Warren logo.

"I'm glad I caught you," she said. "I think Mr. Wood
wanted you to have this before you left. He was called
away unexpectedly. This was in my out box."

"Thanks." I opened the flap and peered at the contents: inventory sheets. "Oh great," I said, amazed that
he'd remembered in the midst of his vanishing act. "I'll
call on Monday and set up a time to talk to him."

"Sorry about today," she said. "Merry Christmas!" She
waved and then moved back to the party. The door was
now propped open, cigarette smoke and noise spilling out
in equal parts. Ava Daugherty was watching us, her gaze
fixed with curiosity on the envelope Heather'd given me,
which I was just tucking into my handbag. I returned to
my car and drove back into town.

When I stopped by the office, I passed the darkened
glass doors of California Fidelity. Like many other businesses, CF had shut down early for Christmas Eve. I unlocked my door, tossed the file on my desk, and checked
for messages. I put a call through to the fire chief for a
quick verification of the information I had, but he, too, was
gone. I left my number and was told he probably wouldn't
return the call until Monday.

By 4:00, I was back in my apartment with the drawbridge pulled up. And that's where I stayed for the entire
weekend.

Christmas Day I spent alone, but not unhappily.

The day after that was Sunday. I tidied my apartment,
shopped for groceries, made pots of hot tea, and read.

Monday, December 27, I was back in harness again,
sitting at my desk in a poinky mood, trying to wrestle the
fire-scene inspection into a coherent narrative.

The phone rang. I was hoping it was Mrs. Brunswick at
the bank, calling back to tell me the five-thousand-dollar

snafu had been cleared up. "Millhone Investigations," I said.

"Oh hi, Kinsey. This is Darcy, next door. I just wondered when I could pop over and pick up that file."

"Darcy, it's only ten-fifteen! I'm working on it, okay?" Please note: I did not use the "F" word, as I know she takes offense.

"Well, you don't have to take that tone," she said. "I told Mac the report wouldn't be ready yet, but he says he wants to review the file first anyway."

"Review the file before what?"

"I don't know, Kinsey. How am I supposed to know? I called because there's a note in the action file on my desk."

"Oh, your 'action' file. You should have said so before. Come pick the damn thing up."

Ill temper and intuition are not a good mix. Whatever inconsistency was nagging at me, I could hardly get a fix on it with Darcy breathing down my neck. My first act that morning had been to fill out a form for the Insurance Crime Prevention Unit, asking for a computer check on Lance Wood. Maybe at some point in the past I'd come across a previous fire claim and that's what was bugging me. The computer check wouldn't come back for ten days, but at least I'd have covered my bases. I adjusted the tabs on my machine, typed in the name of the insured, the location, date, and time of loss.

When Darcy arrived to pick up the file, I spoke without looking up. "I dropped the film off at Speedee-Foto on my way in. They'll have prints for me by noon. I haven't had a chance to talk to Lance Wood or the fire chief yet."

"I'll tell Mac," she said, her tone cool.

Oh well, I thought. She's never been a pal of mine anyway.

As there was no slot or box where unspecified hunches could be typed in, I kept my report completely neutral. When I finished, I rolled it out of the machine, signed it, dated it, and set it aside. I had an hour before I could pick up the photographs, so I cleaned up the sketch of the warehouse layout and attached that to the report with a paper clip.

The phone rang. This time it was Andy. "Could you step into Mac's office for a few minutes?"

I quelled my irritation, thinking it best not to sass the CF claims manager. "Sure, but I won't have the pictures for another hour yet."

"We understand that. Just bring what you've got."

I hung up, gathered up the report and the sketch, locked the office behind me, and went next door. What's this "we" shit? I thought.

The minute I stepped into Mac's office, I knew something was wrong. I've know Maclin Voorhies since I started working for California Fidelity nearly ten years ago. He's in his sixties now, with a lean, dour face. He has sparse gray hair that stands out around his head like dandelion fuzz, big ears with drooping lobes, a bulbous nose, and small black eyes under unruly white brows. His body seems misshapen: long legs, short waist, narrow shoulders, arms too long for the average sleeve length. He's smart, capable, stingy with praise, humorless, and devoutly Catholic, which translates out to a thirty-five-year marriage and eight kids, all grown. I've never seen him smoke a cigar, but he's usually chewing on a stub, the resultant tobacco stains tarnishing his teeth to the color of old toilet bowls.

I took my cue not so much from his expression, which was no darker than usual, but from Andy's, standing just to his left. Andy and I don't get along that well under the best of circumstances. At forty-two, he's an ass-kisser, always trying to maneuver situations so that he can look good. He has a moon-shaped face and his collar looks too tight and everything else about him annoys me, too. Some people just affect me that way. At that moment he seemed both restless and smug, studiously avoiding eye contact.

Mac was leafing through the file. He glanced over at Andy with impatience. "Don't you have some work to do?"

"What? Oh sure. I thought you wanted me in this meeting."

"I'll take care of it. I'm sure you're overloaded as it is."

Andy murmured something that made it sound like leaving was his big idea. Mac shook his head and sighed slightly as the door closed. I watched him roll the cigar stub

from one corner of his mouth to the other. He looked up
with surprise, as if he'd just realized I was standing there.
"You want to fill me in on this?"

I told him what had transpired to date, sidestepping
the fact that the file had sat on Darcy's desk for three days
before it came to me. I wasn't necessarily protecting her.
In business, it's smarter not to bad-mouth the help. I told
him I had two rolls of film coming in, that there weren't
any estimates yet, but the claim looked routine as far as I
could see. I debated mention of my uneasiness, but discarded the idea even as I was speaking. I hadn't identified
what was bothering me and I felt it was wiser to stick to the
facts.

The frown on Mac's face formed about thirty seconds
into my recital, but what alarmed me was the silence that
fell when I was done. Mac is a man who fires questions.
Mac gives pop quizzes. He seldom sits and stares as he was
doing in this case.

"You want to tell me what this is about?" I asked.

"Did you see the note attached to the front of this
file?"

"What note? There wasn't any note," I said.

He held out a California Fidelity memo form, maybe
three inches by five, covered with Jewel's curlicue script.
"Kinsey . . . this one looks like a stinker. Sorry I don't
have time to fill you in, but the fire chief's report spells it
out. He said to call if he can give you any help. J."

"This wasn't attached to the file when it came to me."

"What about the fire department report? Wasn't that
in there?"

"Of course it was. That's the first thing I read."

Mac's expression was aggrieved. He handed me the
file, open to the fire-department report. I looked down at
the familiar STFD form. The incidental information was
just as I remembered. The narrative account I'd never
seen before. The fire chief, John Dudley, had summed up
his investigation with a no-nonsense statement of suspected arson. The newspaper clipping now attached to the
file ended with a line to the same effect.

I could feel my face heat, the icy itch of fear beginning
to assert itself. I said, "This isn't the report I saw." My voice

had dropped into a range I scarcely recognized. He held his hand out and I returned the file.

"I got a phone call this morning," he said. "Somebody says you're on the take."

I stared. "What?"

"You got anything to say?"

"That's absurd. Who called?"

"Let's not worry about that for the moment."

"Mac, come on. Somebody's accusing me of a criminal act and I want to know who it is."

He said nothing, but his face shut down in that stubborn way of his.

"All right, skip that," I said, yielding the point. I thought it was better to get the story out before I worried about the characters. "What did this unidentified caller say?"

He leaned back in his chair, studying the cold coin of ash on the end of his cigar. "Somebody saw you accept an envelope from Lance Wood's secretary," he said.

"Bullshit. When?"

"Last Friday."

I had a quick flash of Heather calling to me as I left the plant. "Those were inventory sheets. I asked Lance Wood to have them ready for me and he left 'em in his out box."

"What inventory sheets?"

"Right there in the file."

He shook his head, leafing through. From where I stood, I could see there were only two or three loose papers clipped in on one side. There was nothing resembling the inventory sheets I'd punched and inserted. He looked up at me. "What about the interview with Wood?"

"I haven't done that yet. An emergency came up and he disappeared. I'm supposed to set up an appointment with him for today."

"What time?"

"Well, I don't know. I haven't called him yet. I was trying to get the report typed up first." I couldn't seem to avoid the defensiveness in my tone.

"This the envelope?" Mac was holding the familiar envelope with the Wood/Warren logo, only now there was a message jotted on the front. "Hope this will suffice for now. Balance to follow as agreed."

"Goddamn it, Mac. You can't be serious! If I were taking a payoff, why would I leave that in the file?"

No answer. I tried again. "You really think Lance Wood paid me off?"

"I don't think anything except we better look into it. For your sake as well as ours . . ."

"If I took money, where'd it go?"

"I don't know, Kinsey. You tell me. If it was cash, it wouldn't be that hard to conceal."

"I'd have to be a fool! I'd have to be an idiot and so would he. If he's going to bribe me, do you think he'd be stupid enough to put the cash in an envelope and write a note to that effect! Mac, this whole thing has frame-up written all over it!"

"Why would anyone do that?" At this point, his manner wasn't accusatory. He seemed genuinely puzzled at the very idea. "Who would go to such lengths?"

"How do I know? Maybe I just got caught in the loop. Maybe Lance Wood is the target. You know I'd never do such a thing. I'll bring you my bank statements. You can scrutinize my accounts. Check under my mattress, for God's sake. . . ." I broke off in confusion.

I saw his mouth move, but I didn't hear the rest of what he said. I could feel the trap close and something suddenly made sense. In the morning mail, I'd gotten notice about five thousand dollars credited to my account. I think I knew now what that was about.

4

I packed up my personal belongings and my current files. California Fidelity had suspended our relationship until the Wood/Warren matter could be "straightened out," whatever that meant. I had until noon to clear the premises. I called the telephone company and asked to have calls forwarded to my home until further notice. I unplugged the answering machine and placed it on top of the last cardboard box, which I toted down the back steps to my car. I had been asked to turn in my office keys before I left, but I ignored the request. I had no intention of giving up access to five years' worth of business files. I didn't think Mac would press the point and I didn't think anyone would bother to have the locks changed. Screw 'em. I know how to pick most locks, anyway.

In the meantime, I was already analyzing the sequence of events. The Wood/Warren folder had been sitting on my desk the entire weekend so the fire department reports could have been switched at any point. I'd worked from notes that morning without reference to the file itself, so I had no way of knowing if the inventory sheets were in the file or not. I might not have registered the loss had I looked. My office door and the French doors opening out onto the balcony showed no signs of forced entry, but my handbag, along with my keys, had sat in Lance Wood's office for three hours on Friday. Anybody could have gotten into that bag and had duplicate keys made. My checkbook was there, too, and it didn't take a wizard to figure out how somebody could have lifted a deposit slip, filled it out, stuck it in an envelope with five grand, and put the whole of it in the night-deposit slot at my bank. Obviously my instant-teller card couldn't be used because my code number wasn't written down anyplace.

I drove out to Wood/Warren, my brain clicking away, fired by adrenaline. The moment I'd understood what was going on, the anger had passed and a chill of curiosity had settled in. I'd felt my emotions disconnect and my mind had cleared like a radio suddenly tuned to the right frequency. Someone had gone to a lot of trouble to discredit me. Insurance fraud is serious damn shit, punishable by two, three, or four years in the state prison. That wasn't going to happen to me, folks.

Heather stared at me, startled, as I moved through the Wood/Warren reception area, scarcely slowing my pace. "Is he in?"

She looked down at the appointment book with confusion. "Do you have an appointment this morning?"

"Now I do," I said. I knocked on the door once and went in. Lance was meeting with John Salkowitz, the chemical engineer I had been introduced to on my earlier visit. The two men were bending over a set of specs for an item that looked like a giant diaper pin.

"We need to talk," I said.

Lance took one look at my face and then flicked a signal to Salkowitz, indicating that they'd continue some other time.

I waited until the door closed and then leaned on Lance's desk. "Somebody's trying to shove one up our collective rear end," I said. I detailed the situation to him, citing chapter and verse in a way that left no room for argument. He got the point. Some of the color left his face.

He sank into his swivel chair. "Jesus," he said. "I don't believe it." I could see him computing possibilities the same way I had.

I drew up a chair and sat down. "What was the emergency that pulled you out of here so fast Friday afternoon?" I asked. "It has to be connected, doesn't it?"

"How so?"

"Because if I'd questioned you as I intended to, you probably would have mentioned arson, and then I'd have known the fire-department report was counterfeit."

"My housekeeper called. I'm in the middle of a nasty divorce and Gretchen showed up at the house with two burly guys and a moving van. By the time I got home, she'd cleared out the living room and was working on the den."

"Does she have the wherewithal to set up a deal like this?"

"Why would she do that? It's in her best interest to keep me alive and well and earning money hand over fist. Right now, she's collecting over six grand a month in temporary support. Insurance fraud is the last thing she'd want to stick me with. Besides, she's been in Tulsa since March of this year."

"Or so she claims," I said.

"The woman is a twit. If you knew her, you wouldn't suspect her of anything except licking a pencil point every time she has to write her name."

"Well, somebody sure wanted to blacken your name," I said.

"What makes you think it's me they're after? Why couldn't it be you?"

"Because no one could be sure I'd be called in on this. These fire claims are assigned almost randomly, according to who's free. If it's me they want, they'd have to go about it differently. They're not going to burn down your warehouse on the off-chance that I'll be called to investigate."

"I suppose not," he said.

"What about you? What's going on in your life, aside from the divorce?"

He picked up a pencil and began to loop it through his fingers, end over end, like a tiny baton. He watched its progress and then shot me an enigmatic look. "I have a sister who moved back here from Paris three months ago. Rumor has it she wants control of the plant."

"Is this Ebony?"

He seemed surprised. "You know her?"

"Not well, but I know who she is."

"She disapproves of the way I run things."

"Enough to do this?"

He stared at me for a moment and then reached for the phone. "I'd better call my attorney."

"You and me both," I said.
I left and headed back into town.

As far as I knew, the D.A.'s office hadn't been notified, and
no charges had been filed. A valid arrest warrant has to be
based on a complaint supported by facts showing, first of
all, that a crime has been committed, and second, that the
informer or his information is reliable. At this point, all
Mac had was an anonymous telephone call and some circumstantial evidence. He'd have to take action. If the accusation was correct, then CF had to be protected. My
guess was that he'd go back through my workload, case by
case, to see if there was any whisper of misconduct on my
part. He might also hire a private detective to look into the
affairs of Wood/Warren, Lance Wood, and possibly me—a
novel idea. I wondered how my life would hold up if it
were subjected to professional scrutiny. The five grand
would certainly come to light. I wasn't sure what to do
about that. The deposit was damning in itself, but if I tried
to move the money, it would look even worse.

I remember the rest of the day in fragments. I talked
to Lonnie Kingman, a criminal attorney I'd done some
work for in the past. He's in his early forties, with a face
like a boxer; beetle-browed, broken nose. His hair is
shaggy and his suits usually look too tight across the shoulder blades. He's about five foot four and probably weighs
two hundred and five. He lifts weights at the same gym I
do and I see him in there doing squats with three hundred
pounds of plates wobbling on either end of the bar like
water buckets. He graduated summa cum laude from Stanford Law School and he wears silk shirts with his monogram on the cuff.

Attorneys are the people who can say things in the
mildest of tones that make you want to shriek and rend
your clothes. Like doctors, they seem to feel obliged to
acquaint you with the full extent of the horror you could
face, given the current path your life is on. When I told
him what was happening, he tossed out two possible addi-
tions to the allegation of insurance fraud: that I'd be
named with Lance Wood as co-conspirator, and charged as

an aider and abettor to arson after the fact. And *that* was just what he came up with off the top of his head.

I could feel myself pale. "I don't want to hear this shit," I said.

He shrugged. "Well, it's what I'd go for if I were D.A.," he said offhandedly. "I could probably add a few counts once I had all the facts."

"Facts, my ass. I never saw Lance Wood before in my life."

"Sure, but can you prove it?"

"Of course not! How would I do that?"

Lonnie sighed like he was going to hate to see me in a shapeless prison dress.

"Goddamn it, Lonnie, how come the law always helps the other guy? I swear to God, every time I turn around, the bad guys win and the little guys bite the Big Wienie. What am I supposed to do?"

He smiled. "It's not as bad as all that," he said. "My advice is to keep away from Lance Wood."

"How? I can't just sit back and see what happens next. I want to know who set me up."

"I never said you couldn't look into it. You're an investigator. Go investigate. But I'd be careful if I were you. Insurance fraud is bad enough. You don't want to take the rap for something worse."

I was afraid to ask him what he meant.

I went home and unloaded the boxes full of office files. I took a few minutes to reword the message on my answering machine at home. I put a call through to Jonah Robb in Missing Persons at the Santa Teresa Police Department. As a lady in distress, I don't ordinarily call on men. I've been schooled in the notion that a woman, these days, saves herself, which I was willing to do if I could just figure out where to start.

I'd met Jonah six months before while I was working on a case. Our paths had crossed more than once, most recently in my bed. He's thirty-nine, blunt, nurturing, funny, confused, a tormented man with blue eyes, black hair, and a wife named Camilla who stalks out intermittently with his two little girls, whose names I repress. I had ignored the chemistry between us for as long as I could, too wise (said I) to get pulled into a dalliance with a married gent. And then one rainy night I'd run into him on my way home from a depressing interview with a hostile subject. Jonah and I started drinking margaritas in a bar near the beach. We danced to old Johnny Mathis tunes, talked, danced again, and ordered more drinks. Somewhere around "The Twelfth of Never," I lost track of my resolve and took him home with me. I never could resist the lyrics on that one.

We were currently at that stage in a new relationship where both parties are tentative, reluctant to presume, quick to feel injured, eager to know and be known as long as the true frailties of character are concealed. The risking felt good, and as a consequence the chemistry felt good, too. I smiled a lot when I thought of him and sometimes I laughed aloud, but the warmth was undercut by a curious pain. I've been married twice, done in more times than I care to admit. I'm not as trusting as I used to be and with good reason. Meanwhile, Jonah was in a constant state of upheaval according to the fluctuations in Camilla's moods. Her most recent claim was that she wanted an "open" marriage, his guess being that the sexual liberties were intended more for her than for him.

"Missing Persons. Sergeant Schiffman."

For an instant my mind went absolutely blank. "Rudy? This is Kinsey. Where's Jonah?"

"Oh, hi, Kinsey. He's out of town. Took his family skiing for the holidays. It came up kind of sudden, but I thought he said he'd let you know. He never called?"

"I guess not," I said. "Do you know when he's expected back?"

"Just a minute. Let me check." He put me on hold and I listened to the Norman Luboff Choir singing "Hark, the Herald Angels Sing." Christmas was over. Hadn't anybody heard? Rudy clicked back in. "Looks like January third. You want to leave a message?"

"Tell him I hung myself," I said and rang off.

I have to confess that in the privacy of my own home, I burst into tears and wept with frustration for six minutes flat. Then I went to work.

The only line of attack I could think of was through

Ash Wood. I hadn't spoken to her since high school, nearly fourteen years. I tried the directory. Her mother, Helen Wood, was listed and so was Lance, but there was no sign of Ash, which probably meant that she'd moved away or married. I tried the main house. A woman answered. I identified myself and told her I was trying to locate Ash. Often I tell lies in a situation like this, but the truth seemed expedient.

"Kinsey, is that really you? This is Ash. How are you?" she said. All the Wood girls have voices that sound the same; husky and low, underlaid with an accent nearly Southern in its tone. The inflection was distinct, not a drawl, but an indolence. Their mother was from Alabama, if my memory hadn't failed me.

"I can't believe my luck," I said. "How are you?"

"Well, darlin', we are in a world of hurt," she replied, "which is why I'm so glad to hear from you. Lance mentioned that he'd seen you at the plant last Friday. What's happening?"

"That's what I called to ask you."

"Oh Lord. I'd love to bring you up-to-date. Are you free for lunch by any chance?"

"For you . . . anything," I said.

She suggested the Edgewater Hotel at 12:30, which suited me. I'd have to change clothes first. My standard outfit consists of boots or tennis shoes, form-fitting jeans, and a tank top or a turtleneck, depending on the season. Sometimes I wear a windbreaker or a denim vest, and I've always got a large leather shoulder bag, which sometimes (but not often) contains my little .32. I was relatively certain Ashley wouldn't appear in public like this. I hauled out my all-purpose dress, panty hose, and low heels. One day soon, I gotta get myself something else to wear.

5

The Edgewater Hotel sits on twenty-three acres of ocean-front property, with lawns sweeping down to the sea. An access road cuts through, not ten feet from the surf, with a sea wall constructed of local sandstone. The architecture of the main building is Spanish, with massive white stucco walls, arched doorways, and deeply recessed windows. Horizontal lines of red tile define the roof. A glass-walled dining patio juts out in front, white umbrella tables sheltering the patrons from sunlight and buffeting sea winds. The grounds are landscaped with juniper and palm, hibiscus, bottle brush and fern, flower beds filled year round with gaudy annuals in hot pink, purple, and gold. The day was chill, the sky icy white and overcast. The drab olive-green surf was churned up by the outer fringes of a storm system that had passed us to the north.

The valet parking attendant was far too discreet to remark, even with a look, the battered state of my ancient car. I moved into the hotel lobby and down a wide corridor furnished with a series of overstuffed couches, interspersed with rubber plants. The ceiling overhead was wood-beamed, the walls tiled halfway up, sounds muffled by a runner of thick carpet patterned with flowers the size of dinner plates.

Ash had reserved a table in the main dining room. She was already seated, her face turned expectantly toward me as I approached. She looked much as she had in high school; pale-red hair, blue eyes set in a wide, friendly face mottled with freckles. Her teeth were very white and straight and her smile was engaging. I had forgotten how

34

casually she dressed. She was wearing a blue wool jumpsuit with a military cut, and over it a bulky white sheepskin vest. I thought, with regret, of my jeans and turtleneck.

She was still maybe twenty pounds overweight, and she moved with all the enthusiasm of an ungainly pup, leaping up to hug me when I arrived at the table. There had always been a guileless quality about her. Despite the fact she came from money, she had never been snobbish or affected. Where Olive had seemed reserved, and Ebony intimidating, Ash seemed utterly unselfconscious, one of those girls everybody liked. In our sophomore year, we had ended up sitting in adjoining homeroom seats and we'd often chatted companionably before classes began. Neither of us was a cheerleader, an honor student, or a candidate for prom queen. The friendship that sprang up between us, though genuine, was short-lived. I met her family. She met my aunt. I went to her house and thereafter neatly bypassed her coming to mine. While the Woods were always gracious to me, it was obvious that Ash functioned at the top of the social heap and I at the bottom. Eventually the disparity made me so uncomfortable that I let the contact lapse. If Ash was injured by the rejection, she did a good job of covering it. I felt guilty about her anyway and was relieved the next year when she sat somewhere else.

"Kinsey, you look great. I'm so glad you called. I ordered us a bottle of Chardonnay. I hope that's okay."

"Fine," I said, smiling. "You look just the same."

"Big rump, you mean," she said with a laugh. "You're just as thin as you always were, only I half expected you to show up in jeans. I don't believe I ever saw you in a dress."

"I thought I'd act like I had some class," I said. "How are you? When I didn't find you listed in the phone book, I thought you'd probably gotten married or left town."

"Actually, I've been gone for ten years and just got back. What about you? I can't believe you're a private detective. I always figured you'd end up in jail. You were such a rebel back then."

I laughed. I was a misfit in high school and hung out with guys known as "low-wallers" because they loitered along a low wall at the far end of the school grounds. "You remember Donan, the boy with the gold tooth who sat right in front of you in homeroom? He's an Ob-Gyn in town. Got his teeth fixed and went to med school."

Ash groaned, laughing. "God, that's one way to get your hand up a girl's skirt. What about the little swarthy one who sat next to you? He was funny. I liked him."

"He's still around. Bald now and overweight. He runs a liquor store up on the Bluffs. Who was that girlfriend of yours who used to shoplift? Francesca something."

"Palmer. She's living with a fellow in Santa Fe who designs furniture. I saw her about a year ago when I was passing through. God, she's still a klepto. Are you married?"

"Was." I held up two fingers to indicate the number of husbands who had come and gone.

"Children?" she asked.

"Oh God, no. Not me. You have any?"

"Sometimes I wish I did." Ash was watching me with shining eyes and somehow I knew anything I said would be fine with her.

"When did we see each other last? It's been years, hasn't it?" I asked.

She nodded. "Bass's twenty-first birthday party at the country club. You were with the most beautiful boy I ever saw in my life."

"Daniel," I said. "He was husband number two."

"What about number one? What was he like?"

"I better drink some first."

The waiter appeared with the wine, presenting the label for her inspection before he opened it. She waved aside the ritual of the sniffing of the cork and let him go ahead and pour for both of us. I noticed that the waiter was smiling to himself, probably charmed as most people are by Ash's breezy manner and her impatience with formality. He was tall and slim, maybe twenty-six years old, and he told us about the specials as if we might want to take notes. "The sea bass is being served today with a green chili *beurre blanc*, gently poached first with fresh tomatoes, cilantro, lemon, and white wine, garnished with jalapeños and accompanied by a pine-nut rice pilau. We're also offering a fillet of coho salmon . . ." Ash made little mewing sounds, interrupting now and then for clarification of some culinary subtlety.

I let her order for us. She knew all the waiters by name and ended up in a long chat with ours about what we should eat. She settled on steamed clams in a broth with Pernod, a salad of field greens lightly dressed, and said we'd think about dessert if we were good girls and cleaned our plates.

While we ate, I told her about my connection to Wood/Warren and the irregularities that had come to light.

"Oh, Kinsey. I feel awful. I hope Lance isn't responsible for the trouble you're in."

"Believe me, I do, too. What's the story on him? Is he the type to burn down the family warehouse?"

Ash didn't leap to his defense as I'd expected her to. "If he did, I don't think he'd snitch on himself," she said.

"Good point. Who'd go after him like that?"

"I don't know. That whole situation got very screwed up once Daddy died. He was crazy about the boys, but Bass was a dilettante and Lance raised hell half the time."

"I seem to remember that. Your father must have had conniption fits."

"Oh, he did. You know how straight he was. Daddy had real strong ideas about parenting, but most of them were wrong. He had no idea how to implement them anyway. He wanted to control and mold and dominate but he couldn't even do that very well. Kids just don't behave like company employees. Daddy thought he'd have more control at home, but the truth was, he had less. Both Lance and Bass were determined to thwart him. Bass never has straightened out."

"He's still in New York?"

"Oh, he comes home now and then—he was here for a week at Thanksgiving—but for the most part, he's gone. New York, Boston, London. He spent a year in Italy and swears he's going back. Much as I love him, he's a waste of time. I don't think he's ever going to get his act together. Of course, Lance was that way for years. They're both smart enough, but they always partied hard and Lance had a few scrapes with the law. It drove Daddy up the wall."

The clams arrived. Each of us was presented with a plate piled high with small, perfect shells, swaddled in cloth to keep the broth piping hot. She speared a tender button of clam flesh and placed it on her tongue, her eyes closing in a near-swoon as she swallowed. I watched her butter a crescent of French bread and dip it in the bowl, sopping up clam liquor. As she bit into it, she made a little sound low in her throat like something out of an X-rated video.

"Your lunch okay?" I asked dryly.

"Fine," she said. "Good." She realized belatedly that I was teasing her and she smiled, her cheeks tinted becomingly with pink. "Someone asked me once which I'd rather have—sex or a warm chocolate-chip cookie. I still can't decide."

"Go for the cookies. You can bake 'em yourself."

She wiped her mouth and took a sip of wine. "Anyway, about the last six or seven years, Lance took hold, more or less, and started showing an interest in the business. Daddy was thrilled. Wood/Warren was Daddy's life. He loved us, but he couldn't manage us the way he did the business. By the time Bass came along, the last in line, Daddy'd pretty much given up any hopes for a successor."

"What about Ebony?"

"Oh, she's been passionate about the company since she was a kid, but she didn't believe Daddy'd ever let her have a hand in it. He was old-fashioned. A man leaves his business to his oldest son. Period. He knew Ebony was smart, but he didn't think she was tough enough, and he didn't think she'd stay with it. Women get married and have babies and spend money. That was his attitude. Women join the country club and play tennis and golf. They don't go head-to-head with chemical engineers and systems analysts. She even went off to Cal Poly and started working on an engineering degree, but Daddy made it clear it wouldn't help her cause, so she went to Europe and got married instead."

"Thus fulfilling his prophecy," I said.

"That's right. Of course, at that point, Daddy did a turnaround and swore he'd have left her the company if she'd stuck it out. She hated him for that, and I didn't blame her a bit. He was a real shit sometimes."

"She's back now, isn't she?"

"Right. She got home in August, minus Julian, which is no big loss. He was a dud if I ever saw one. A real bore. I don't know how she put up with him."

"Lance says she wants to take over."

"I've heard that, too, though it's not anything she talks to me about. I get along with Ebony, but we're not real close."

"What about Olive? Is she interested?"

"Peripherally, I guess. She married one of the chemical engineers who worked for Daddy. He's vice-president now, but they met when she was still in college and he'd just hired on."

"Is that Terry Kohler?"

She nodded. "You met him?"

"When I was out there. What's he like?"

"Oh, I don't know. Smart. Moody. Intense. Pleasant enough, but sort of humorless. Good at what he does. Crazy about her, I must say. He worships the ground she walks on. 'Slavish' is the word."

"Lucky girl. Is he ambitious?"

"He used to be. He wanted to go out on his own at one point and form his own company, but I guess it didn't work out. He kind of lost heart after that, and I don't know . . . being married to the boss's daughter probably takes the heat off."

"How does he get along with Lance?"

"They clash now and then. Terry's easily offended. You know the type. He gets his nose bent out of shape at the least little thing."

"What about John Salkowitz?"

"He's a sweetie. He's what Daddy wanted Lance to be."

"You said Lance had a couple of scrapes with the law. What was that about?"

"He stole some things from the plant."

"Really. When was this?"

"In high school. He came up with a scheme to make some money, but it didn't work out. It was part of an economics class and I guess his grade depended on how well he did. When he realized his little enterprise was failing, he stole some equipment—nothing big—but he tried to sell it to a fence. The guy got uneasy and called the cops."

"Not too smart."

"That's what pissed Daddy off, I suspect."

"Did he press charges?"

"Are you kidding? Of course. He said that was the only way Lance would ever learn."

"And did he?"

"Well, he got in trouble again, if that's what you mean. Lots of times. Daddy finally threw his hands up and sent him off to boarding school."

The subject veered off. We finished lunch, chatting about other things. At two, Ash glanced at her watch. "Oh Lord. I've got to go. I promised Mother I'd take her shopping this afternoon. Come along if you like. I know she'd love to see you." She signaled for the check.

"I better take care of some other business first, but I do want to talk to her."

"Give us a call and come up to the house."

"Are you living there now?"

"Temporarily. I just bought a place of my own and I'm having some work done. I'll be staying with Mother for another six weeks."

When the check arrived, I reached for my handbag, but she waved me off. "I'll take care of it. I'll claim it as a business lunch and charge it off to the company. It's the least I can do with the bind you're in."

"Thanks," I said. I got Ebony's personal telephone number from her and we walked out together. I was relieved that the valet service brought her car first. I watched her pull away in a little red Alfa-Romeo. My car appeared. I tipped the fellow more than I should have and got in with care, humping myself onto the seat to avoid snagging my panty hose behind the knee. The valet slammed the door and I turned the key. Honest to God, it started right up and I felt a surge of pride. The damn thing is paid for and only costs me ten bucks a week in gas.

I drove home and let myself in the gate, steadfastly

disregarding the yawning air of emptiness about the place. The winter grass seemed ragged and the dead heads on the zinnias and marigolds had multiplied. Henry's house stood silent, his back door looking blank. Usually the scent of yeast or cinnamon lies on the air like a heady perfume. Henry's a retired commercial baker who can't quite give up his passion for kneading dough and proofing bread. If he isn't in the kitchen, I can usually find him on the patio, weeding the flower beds or stretched out on a chaise inventing crossword puzzles filled with convoluted puns.

I let myself into my apartment and changed back into jeans, my whole body sighing with relief. I hauled the mower out of the toolshed and had a run at the yard, and then I got down on my hands and knees and clipped all the dead blossoms from the beds. This was very boring. I put the lawn mower away. I went inside and typed up my notes. As long as I was investigating in my own behalf, I decided to do it properly. This was boring, too.

Since Rosie's was closed, I ate dinner at home, preparing a cheese-and-pickle sandwich, which entertained me no end.

I'd finished the Len Deighton and I didn't have anything else in the house to read, so I switched on my little portable television set.

Sometimes I wonder if my personal resources aren't wearing a little thin.

6

Tuesday morning, I went into the gym at 6:00 A.M. As I no longer had an office to go to, I could well have waited until later in the morning, but I like the place at that hour. It's quiet and half empty, so there's no competition for equipment. The free weights are neatly reracked. The mirrors are clean and the air doesn't smell like yesterday's sweat socks. Weight-lifting apparatus are a curious phenomenon —machines invented to replicate the backbreaking manual labor the Industrial Revolution relieved us of. Lifting weights is like a meditation: intermittent periods of concentrated activity, with intervals of rest. It's a good time for thinking, as one can do little else. I did ab crunches first; thirty-five, then thirty, then twenty-five. I adjusted the bench on one of the Nautilus machines and started doing seated military presses, three sets, ten reps each, using two plates. The guys lift anywhere from ten to twenty plates, but I work just as hard, and I'm not really preparing for the regional body-building championship.

I was thinking back over the details of the frame-up . . . a clever piece of work, dependent on a number of events coming together just as they had. The phone call to Mac must have come from Ava Daugherty, but who put her up to it? Surely she didn't cook up that trouble by herself. Someone had access to the Wood/Warren file, and while it was possible that the office keys had been lifted from my bag, who at Wood/Warren knew enough to make a mockup of a fire-department report? That must have been done by someone who knew the procedure at CF. Insurance investigations usually follow a format. An outsider simply couldn't guarantee that all the paper switching could be done in the necessary sequence. Darcy could have managed it. Andy might have, or even Mac. But why?

I worked through biceps and triceps. Since I jog six days a week, my prime interest in the gym is the three A's —arms, abs, and ass—a routine that takes forty-five minutes three times a week. I was finished by 7:15. I went home to shower and then I started out again, dressed in jeans, turtleneck, and boots. Darcy was due at work at 9:00, but I'd spotted her three days out of five having breakfast first, coffee and a Danish in the coffee shop across the street. She used the time to chitchat, read the newspaper, and do her nails.

There was no sign of her when I got there at 8:00. I bought a paper and settled into the back booth where she usually sits. Claudine came by and I ordered breakfast. At 8:12, Darcy came through the door in a lightweight wool coat. She stopped when she saw me, checked her stride, and slid into an empty booth halfway down. I picked up my coffee cup and joined her, loving the sour look that crossed her face when she realized what I was up to.

"Mind if I join you?" I asked.

"Well, actually, I'd prefer to have the time to myself," she said, avoiding my gaze.

Claudine arrived with a steaming plate of bacon and scrambled eggs, which she set down in front of me. Claudine is in her fifties, with a booming voice and calves knotted with varicose veins.

"Morning, Darcy. What'll you have today? We're out of cheese Danish, but I laid back a cherry in case you're interested."

"That's fine. And a small orange juice."

Claudine made a note and tucked her order pad in her apron pocket. "Just a second and I'll bring you a coffee cup." She was gone again before Darcy could protest. I could see her do a quick visual survey, looking for an empty seat. The place was filling up rapidly and it looked like she was trapped.

While I ate, I studied her in a manner that I hoped was disconcerting. She eased out of her coat, making a big deal out of standing up so she could fold it just so. She's one of those women a glamour magazine should "make-over" as a challenge to their in-house experts. She has baby-fine hair that defies styling, a high, bulging forehead, pale-blue eyes. Her skin is milky white and translucent, with a tracery of veins showing through like faded laundry marks. I'd heard Darcy's boyfriend was a mail carrier, dealing drugs on the side, and I wondered if he delivered junk mail and junk on the same run. I could tell I was ruining her day, which improved my appetite.

"I'm assuming you heard about the trouble I'm in."

"It'd be hard not to," she said.

I opened a plastic locket of grape jelly and spread half on a triangle of whole-wheat toast. "Got any ideas about who set me up?"

Claudine returned with a cup and saucer and the coffeepot. Darcy judiciously elected to refrain from comment until her cup was filled and mine had been topped off. When Claudine departed, Darcy's expression turned prim and her coloring altered like a mood ring, shifting down a grade from woeful to glum. Actually, the change was not unappealing. She's big on pastel shades, imagining, I suppose, that washed-out colors are somehow more flattering to her than bold ones. She wore a pale-yellow sweater about the hue of certain urine samples I've seen where the prognosis isn't keen. The pink in her cheeks gave her back an air of health.

She leaned forward. "I didn't do anything to you," she said.

"Great. Then maybe you can help."

"Mac told us specifically not to talk to you."

"How come?"

"Well, obviously, he doesn't want you to get information you're not supposed to have."

"Such as?"

"I'm not going to discuss it with you."

"Why don't I tell you my theory," I said sociably. I half expected her to stick her fingers in her ears and start singing aloud to drown me out, but I noticed that she was not completely uninterested and I took heart from that. "I suspect maybe Andy's at the bottom of this. I don't know what he's getting out of it, but it's probably some form of financial gain. Maybe somebody's throwing business his way, or giving him a kickback. Of course, it crossed my mind that it might be you, but I don't really think so at this point. I think if you'd done it you'd be friendly, to convince me of your goodwill, if nothing else."

Darcy opened a paper sugar packet and measured out half a teaspoon, which she stirred into her coffee. I went right on, talking aloud as if she were a pal of mine and meant to help.

"CF hires other outside investigators so I'm imagining that any one of us could have been implicated. It was just my dumb luck that I was up at bat. Not that Andy wouldn't take a certain satisfaction from the fact. He's never been fond of me and he always hated it that Mac let me have office space. Andy wanted to knock the wall out and take that corner for himself. At any rate, I have to assume Lance Wood is the real focus of the frame, though I don't know why yet. What I'll probably do is try working both sides of the street here and just see where all the paths intersect. Should be fun. I've never worked for me before and I'm looking forward to it. Cuts down on the paperwork."

I checked her reaction. Those pale eyes were focused on mine and I could see that her mental gears were engaged.

"Come on, Darcy. Help me out," I coaxed. "What do you have to lose?"

"You don't even like me."

"You don't like me either. What's that got to do with it? We both hate Andy. *That's* the point. The guy's a shitheel."

"Actually he is," she said.

"You don't think Mac had anything to do with it, do you?"

"Well, no."

"So who else could it be?"

She cleared her throat. "Andy has been hanging around my desk a lot."

Her voice was so low I had to lean forward. "Go on."

"It started the day Jewel left on vacation and Mac told

him to farm out her work. Andy was the one who suggested you for the Wood/Warren fire claim."

"He probably thought it'd be easier to pressure me."

Claudine brought Darcy's OJ and the cherry Danish. Darcy broke the Danish into small pieces, buttering each with care before she popped it in her mouth. Jesus, maybe I'd have one.

She was just warming up on the subject of Andy Motycka, who was apparently no fonder of her than he was of me. "What irritates me," she said, "is that I got in trouble with Mac because Andy said the file sat on my desk for three days before it got to you. That's an outright lie. Andy took it home with him. I saw him put it in his briefcase Tuesday when the fire-department report came in."

"Did you tell Mac that?"

"Well, no. Why bother? It sounds like I'm trying to defend myself by pushing all the blame off on him."

"You're right. I found myself in the same position," I said. "Look, if Andy falsified the fire-department report, he probably did the dirty work at home, don't you think?"

"Probably."

"So maybe we can turn up some proof if we look. I'll nose around at his place if you'll try his office."

"He moved, you know. He's not at the house. He and Janice are in the process of splitting up."

"He's getting divorced?"

"Oh, sure. It's been going on for months. She's hosing him, too."

"Really. Well, that's interesting. Where's he living?"

"One of those condos out near Sand Castle."

I'd seen the complex: one hundred and sixty units across from a public golf course called Sand Castle, out beyond Colgate in the little community of Elton. "What about his office? Is there any way you could check that out?"

Darcy smiled for the first time. "Sure. I'll do that. It would serve him right."

I got her home number and said I'd call later. I paid both checks and took off, figuring it wouldn't be a good idea to get caught in Darcy's company. While I was downtown, I hoofed it over to the credit bureau and had a discreet chat with a friend of mine who works as a key-punch operator. I'd done some work for her years before, checking into the background of a certain seedy gent who had hoped to relieve her of a burdensome savings account. She'd had the bucks in hand to pay me, but I sensed that both of us would benefit from a little bartering—"professional courtesies," as they're known. Now I check out any new fellow in her life and, in return, she pirates occasional confirmation copies of computer runs. One drawback is that I have to wait until a periodic updating of the master file is scheduled, which usually happens once a week. I asked her to give me anything she had on Lance Wood and she promised me something in a day. On an impulse, I asked her to check out Andy Motycka while she was at it. Financial information on Wood/Warren I'd have to get from the local equivalent of Dun & Bradstreet. My best source of information was going to be California Fidelity itself, for whom Lance Wood had no doubt filled out countless forms in applying for coverage. I was hoping I could enlist Darcy's aid again on that one. It was amazing to me how much more appealing she seemed now that she was on my team. I trotted back to pick up my car.

As I pulled out of the parking lot behind the building, Andy was just pulling in, pausing while the machine stamped and spat a ticket through the slot. He pretended he didn't see me.

I drove back to my apartment. I'd never paid much attention to the looming importance of the office in my life. I conduct maybe 40 percent of all business in my swivel chair, telephone in the crook of my neck, files close at hand. Sixty percent of the time I'm probably on the road, but I don't like feeling cut off from my reference points. It puts me at a subtle disadvantage.

It was only 10:05 and the day loomed ahead. Out of habit, I hauled out my little portable Smith-Corona and started typing up my notes. That done, I caught up with some filing, prepared some bills for a couple of outstanding accounts, and then tidied up my desk. I hate sitting around. Especially when I could be out getting into trouble. I gave Darcy a call at CF and got Andy's new address

and telephone number. She assured me he was sitting in
his office even as we spoke.

I dialed his apartment and was reassured to hear the
answering machine pick up. I changed into a pair of blue-
gray slacks with a pale stripe along the seam and a matching pale-blue shirt with Southern California Services
stitched around a patch on the sleeve. I added hard black
shoes left over from my days on traffic detail with the Santa
Teresa Police Department, tacked on a self-important key
ring with a long chain, and grabbed up a clipboard, my key
picks, and a set of master keys. I checked myself out in the
mirror. I looked like a uniformed public servant just about
to make a routine service check—of what, I wasn't sure. I
looked like I could read meters and make important notes.
I looked like I could verify downed lines and order up
repair crews on the mobile phone in my county-owned
maintenance vehicle. I hopped in my car and headed out
to Andy's condominium for a little B & E.

7

The Copse at Hurstbourne is one of those fancy-sounding titles for a brand-new tract of condominiums on the outskirts of town. "Copse" as in "a thicket of small trees." "Hurst" as in "hillock, knoll, or mound." And "bourne" as in "brook or stream." All of these geological and botanical wonders did seem to conjoin within the twenty parcels of the development, but it was hard to understand why it couldn't have just been called Shady Acres, which is what it was. Apparently people aren't willing to pay a hundred and fifty thousand dollars for a home that doesn't sound like it's part of an Anglo-Saxon land grant. These often quite utilitarian dwellings are never named after Jews or Mexicans. Try marketing Rancho Feinstein if you want to lose money in a hurry. Or Paco Sanchez Park. Middle-class Americans aspire to tone, which is equated, absurdly, with the British gentry. I had already passed Essex Hill, Stratford Heights, and Hampton Ridge.

The Copse at Hurstbourne was surrounded by a high wall of fieldstone, with an electronic gate meant to keep the riffraff out. The residents were listed on a mounted panel beside a telephone handset with push-buttons, and an intercom. Each occupant was assigned a personal entry code that one had to have in order to gain admittance. I know because I tried several sequences at random and got nowhere. I pulled over and waited until another car approached. The driver punched in his code. When the gate rolled back, I tucked my car in behind his and sailed through. No alarms went off. I wasn't set upon by dogs.

Security measures, like the property's pedigree, were largely in the mind of the marketing team.

There were maybe twenty buildings in all, eight units each, gray frame with white trim in a Cape Cod style, all angles, mullioned windows, and wooden balconies. Sycamore and eucalyptus trees still graced the terrain. Winding roads led in two directions, but it was clear that both came together in the same rear parking lot rimmed with carports. I found a visitor's space and pulled in, checking the building directory which sported a plot map of units.

Andy Motycka's was number 144, located, happily, at the far reaches of the property. I took my clipboard and a flashlight and tried to look as officious as I could. I passed the recreational facility, the spa, the laundry rooms, the gym, and the sales office. There were no signs of children. Judging from the number of empty carports, my guess was that many of the residents were off at work somewhere else. Wonderful. A band of thugs could probably sweep through and clean the place out in half a day.

I moved around some Cape Cod-style garbage bins and went up a set of outside stairs to the second floor of building number 18. The landing of the apartment next door to Andy's was attractively furnished with shoulder-high ficus and assorted potted plants. Andy's porchlet was bare. Not even a doormat. The drapes were open, and there were no interior lights on. No sound of a television set, stereo, or toilets flushing. I rang the bell. I waited a decent interval, easing back slightly so I could check for tenants on either side. No signs of activity. It looked like I had the building to myself.

The front-door lock was a Weiss. I sorted through my key picks and tried one or two without luck. Picking a lock is time-consuming shit and I didn't feel I could stand out there indefinitely. Someone might pass and wonder why I was jiggling that length of thin metal in the keyhole and cursing mildly to myself. On an impulse I raised my hand and felt along the top of the doorjamb. Andy'd left me his key. I let myself in.

I dearly love being in places I'm not supposed to be. I can empathize with cat burglars, housebreakers, and second-story men, experiencing, as I've heard some do, adrenaline raised to a nearly sexual pitch. My heart was thudding and I felt extraordinarily alert.

I did a quick walking survey, eyeballing the two bedrooms, walk-in closets and both bathrooms, just to determine that no one was tossing the apartment but me. In the master bedroom, I opened the sliding glass door and the screen. I went out on the balcony that connected the two bedrooms and devised an escape route in case Andy came home unexpectedly. Against the side wall, around the corner to the right, was an ornamental trellis with a newly planted bougainvillea at its base. In a pinch, I could scamper down like an orangutan and disappear.

I eased back into the apartment and began my search. Andy's bedroom floor was densely matted with dirty clothes, through which a narrow path had been cleared. I picked my way past socks, dress shirts, and boxer shorts in a variety of vulgar prints. In lieu of a chest of drawers, he kept his clean clothes in four dark-blue plastic stacking crates. His newfound bachelorhood must be taking him back to his college days. None of the bins contained anything of interest. I spent fifteen minutes sliding my hand into all the coat pockets on his hanging rod, but all I came up with were some woofies, a handkerchief full of old boogers, and a ticket for a batch of cleaning he hadn't yet retrieved. The second bedroom was smaller. Andy's bicycle was propped against one wall, the back tire flat. He had a rowing machine, eight cardboard moving boxes, unlabeled and still taped shut. I wondered how long he'd been separated.

I'd met Andy's wife, Janice, at a couple of California Fidelity office parties and hadn't thought much of her until I saw what she'd left him with. The lady had really done a thorough shakedown. Andy had always complained about her extravagance, making sure we all knew she shopped at the best stores in town. It was a measure of his success, of course, that she could charge with impunity. What was clear now was that she played for keeps. Andy'd been granted a card table, four aluminum lawn chairs with webbed seats, a mattress, and some flatwear with what must have been his mother's monogram. It looked like Janice had been sticking it in the dishwasher for years because the finish was dull and the silver plate was worn off the handles.

The kitchen cabinets held paper plates and insulated cups, along with a sorry assortment of canned goods. This guy ate worse than I did. Since the condos were brand-new, the appliances were up-to-date and immaculate: self-cleaning oven, big refrigerator (empty except for two six-packs of no-brand beer) with an ice-maker clattering away, dishwasher, microwave, disposal, trash compactor. The freezer was stacked with cartons of Lean Cuisine. He favored Spaghetti and Chicken Cacciatore. A bottle of aquavit lay on its side and he had a bag of frozen rock-hard Milky Way bars that were just an invitation to break off a tooth.

The dining area was actually a simple extension of the small living room, the kitchen separated by a pass-through with bi-fold shutters painted white. There was very little in the way of furnishings. The card table seemed to double as dining-room table and home office. The telephone sat there, plugged into the answering machine, which showed no messages. The surface was littered with typing supplies, but there was no typewriter in sight. His bottle of white-out was getting as sluggish as old nail polish. The wastebasket was empty.

I went back into the kitchen and slid open the compactor, which was loosely packed, but full. Gingerly, I rooted through, spotting crumpled sheets of paper about three layers down. I removed the liner and inserted a fresh one. I doubted Andy would remember whether he'd emptied his trash or not. He'd probably spent most of his married life being waited on hand and foot, and my guess was he took household chores for granted, as if the elves and fairies crept in at night and cleaned pee off the rim of the toilet bowl whenever he missed. I glanced at my watch. I'd been in the place thirty-five minutes and I didn't want to press my luck.

I closed and locked the sliding glass door again, made a final pass to see if I'd overlooked anything, and then let myself out the front, taking his trash bag with me.

By noon, I was home again, sitting on Henry's back

patio with Andy's garbage spread around me like a beggar's picnic. Actually, the debris was fairly benign and didn't make me feel I needed a tetanus booster just to sort through. He was heavy into pickles, olives, anchovies, jalapeño peppers, and other foodstuffs in which no germs could live. There were no coffee grounds or orange peels. No evidence whatever that he ate anything fresh. Lots of beer cans. There were six plastic Lean Cuisine pouches, layers of junk mail, six dunning notices rimmed in red or pink, a notice of a Toastmaster's roast of a local businessman, a flyer from a carwash, and a letter from Janice that must have left him incensed, as he had crumpled it into a tiny ball and bitten down on it. I could see the perfect impression of his teeth in the wadded paper. She was bugging him about a temporary support check that was late *again*, said she, underlined twice and bracketed with exclamation points.

At the bottom of the bag was the back end of a pad of checks, deposit slips still attached, with the name of Andy's bank and his checking-account number neatly printed thereon. I saved that for future reference. I had set aside the crumpled papers that were shoved into the bag halfway down. I smoothed them out now—six versions of a letter to someone he referred to variously as "angel," "beloved," "light of my life," "my darling," and "dearest one." He seemed to remember her anatomy in loving detail without much attention to her intellect. Her sexual enthusiasms still had him all aflame and had thus, apparently, impaired his typing skills—lots of strikeovers in the lines where he reviewed their "time together," which I gathered was on or about Christmas Eve. In recalling the experience, he seemed to struggle with a paucity of adjectives, but the verbs were clear enough.

"Well, Andy, you old devil," I murmured to myself.

He said he longed to have her suckle the something-something from his xxxxxxxx . . . all crossed out. My guess was that it was related to flower parts and that his botanical knowledge had failed him. Either that or the very idea had caused emotional dyslexia. Also, he couldn't quite decide what tone to take. He vacillated somewhere between groveling and reverential. He said several things about her breasts that made me wonder if she might benefit from surgical reduction. It was embarrassing reading, but I tried not to shrink from my responsibilities.

Having finished, I made a neat packet of all the papers. I'd make a separate holding file for them until I could decide if any might be of use. I shoved the trash back in the bag and tossed it in Henry's garbage can. I let myself into my apartment and checked my answering machine. There was one message.

"Hi, Kinsey. This is Ash. Listen, I talked to my mother yesterday about this business with Lance and she'd like to meet with you, if that's okay. Give me a call when you get in and we'll set something up. Maybe this afternoon sometime if that works for you. Thanks. Talk to you soon. Bye."

I tried the number at the house, but the line was busy. I changed into my jeans and made myself some lunch.

By the time I got through to Ash, her mother was resting and couldn't be disturbed, but I was invited to tea at 4:00.

I decided to drive up the pass to the gun club and practice target shooting with the little .32 I keep locked in my top desk drawer in an old sock. I shoved the gun, clip, and a box of fifty cartridges into a small canvas duffel and tucked it in the trunk of my car. I stopped for gas and then headed north on 101 to the junction of 154, following the steep road that zigzags up the mountainside. The day was chilly. We'd had several days of unexpected rain and the vegetation was a dark green, blending in the distance to an intense navy blue. The clouds overhead were a cottony white with ragged underpinnings, like the torn lining on the underside of an old box spring. As the road ascended, fog began to mass and dissipate, traffic slowing to accommodate the fluctuating visibility. I downshifted twice and pulled the heater on.

At the summit, I turned left onto a secondary road barely two lanes wide, which angled upward, twisting half a mile into back country. Massive boulders, mantled in dark-green moss, lined the road, where the overhanging trees blocked out the sun. The trunks of the live oaks were frosted with fungus the color of a greened-out copper roof. I could smell heather and bay laurel and the frail scent of woodsmoke drifting from the cabins tucked in along the ridge. Where the roadside dropped away, the canyons were blank with fog. The wide gate to the gun club was open and I drove the last several hundred yards, pulling into the gravel parking lot, deserted except for a lone station wagon. Aside from the man in charge, I was the only person there.

I paid my four bucks and followed him down to the cinder-block shed that housed the restrooms. He opened the padlock to the storage room and extracted an oblong of cardboard mounted on a piece of lathing, with a target stapled to it.

"Visibil'ty might be tough now in this fog," he warned.

"I'll chance it," I said.

He eyed me with misgivings, but finally handed over the target, a staple gun, and two additional targets.

I hadn't been up to the practice range for months, and it was nice to have the whole place to myself. The wind had picked up and mist was being blown across concrete bunkers like something in a horror movie. I set up the target at a range of twenty-five yards. I inserted soft plastic earplugs and then put on hearing protectors over that. All outside noises were damped down to a mild hush, my breathing audible in my own head as though I were swimming. I loaded eight cartridges into the clip of my .32 and began to fire. Each round sounded like a balloon popping somewhere close by, followed by the characteristic whiff of gunpowder I so love.

I moved up to the target and checked to see where I was hitting. High and left. I circled the first eight holes with a Magic Marker, went back to the bench rest and loaded the gun again. A sign just behind me read: "Guns as we use them here are a source of pleasure and entertainment, but one moment of carelessness or foolishness can bring it all to an end forever." Amen, I thought.

The hard-packed dirt just in front of me was as littered with shells as a battlefield. I saved my brass, collecting the casings after each firing, tucking them neatly back into the Styrofoam brick that cradled the live rounds.

By 3:15 I was cold, and most of my ammunition was gone. I can't claim that my little semiautomatic is wildly accurate at twenty-five yards, but at least I was feeling connected to the process again.

8

At 3:55, I was turning into the circular drive to the Wood family home, located on seven acres of land that sat on the bluffs overlooking the Pacific. Their fortunes on the rise, they'd moved since I'd last visited. This house was enormous, done in a French Baroque style—a two-story central structure flanked by two prominent tower wings. The stucco exterior was as smooth and white as frosting on a wedding cake, roofline and windows edged with plaster garlands, rosettes, and shell motifs that might have been piped out of a pastry tube. A brick walk led from the driveway around to the seaward-facing front of the house and up two steps to a wide uncovered brick porch. A series of arched French doors spanned the facade, which curved outward around a conservatory on one end and a gazebo on the other. A heavy black woman in a white uniform admitted me. I followed her, like a stray pup, across a foyer tiled in black and white marble squares.

"Mrs. Wood asked if you'd wait in the morning room," the maid said, without pausing for a reply. She departed on thick crepe soles that made no sound on the polished parquet floors.

Oh, sure, I thought, that's where I usually hang out at my place . . . the morning room, where else?

The walls were apricot, the ceiling a high dome of white. Large Boston ferns were arranged on stands between high curving windows through which light streamed. The furniture was French Provincial; round table, six chairs with cane backs. The circle of Persian carpeting was a pale blend of peach and green. I stood at one of the windows, looking out at the rolling sweep of the grounds (which is what rich people call their yards). The C-shape of the room cupped a view of the ocean in its lower curve and a view of the mountains in its hook so that the windows formed a cyclorama. Sky and sea, pines, a pie wedge of city, clouds spilling down the distant mountainside . . . all of it was perfectly framed, wheeling gulls picked out in white against the dark hills to the north.

What I love about the rich is the silence they live in— the sheer magnitude of space. Money buys light and high ceilings, six windows where one might actually do. There was no dust, no streaks on the glass, no scuff marks on the slender bowed legs of the matching French Provincial chairs. I heard a whisper of sound, and the maid returned with a rolling serving cart, loaded with a silver tea service, a plate of assorted tea sandwiches, and pastries the cook had probably whipped up that day.

"Mrs. Wood will be right with you," she said to me.

"Thanks," I said. "Uh, is there a lavatory close by?" "Bathroom" seemed like too crude a term.

"Yes, ma'am. Turn left into the foyer. Then it's the first door on the left."

I tiptoed to the loo and locked myself in, staring at my reflection in the mirror with despair. Of course, I was dressed wrong. I never could guess right when it came to clothes. I'd gone to the Edgewater Hotel in my all-purpose dress to eat lunch with Ashley, who'd worn an outfit suitable for bagging game. Now I had down-dressed to the point where I looked like a bum. I didn't know what I'd been thinking of. I knew the Woods had money. I'd just forgotten how much. The trouble with me is I have no class. I was raised in a two-bedroom stucco bungalow, maybe eight hundred and fifty square feet of space, if you counted the little screened-in utility porch. The yard was a tatty fringe of crabgrass surrounded by the kind of white picket fence you bought in sections and stuck in the ground where you would. My aunt's notion of "day-core" was a pink plastic flamingo standing on one foot, which I'd thought was pretty classy shit until I was twelve.

I blocked the bathroom out of my visual field, but not before I got a glimpse of marble, pale-blue porcelain, and gold-plated hardware. A shallow dish held six robin's-egg-sized ovals of soap that had never been touched before by human hands. I peed and then just ran my hands under the water and shook them off, not wanting to soil anything. The terry hand towels looked as though they'd just had the price tags removed from the rims. There were four guest towels laid out beside the basin like big decorative paper napkins, but I was way too smart to fall for that trick. Where would I put a used one afterward—in the trash? These people didn't make trash. I finished drying my hands on the backside of my jeans and returned to the morning room feeling damp around the rear. I didn't dare sit down.

Presently, Ash appeared with Mrs. Wood holding on to her arm. The woman walked slowly, with a halting gait, as if she'd been forced to ambulate with a pair of swim fins for shoes. I was startled to realize she must be in her early seventies, which meant that she'd had her children rather late. Seventy isn't that old out here. People in California seem to age at a different rate than the rest of the country. Maybe it's the passion for diet and exercise, maybe the popularity of cosmetic surgery. Or maybe we're afflicted with such a horror of aging that we've halted the process psychically. Mrs. Wood apparently hadn't developed the knack. The years had knocked her flat, leaving her knees weak and her hands atremble, a phenomenon that seemed to cause her bitter amusement. She appeared to watch her own progress as if she were having an out-of-body experience.

"Hello, Kinsey. It's been a long time," she said. She lifted her face to mine at that point, her gaze dark and snappish. Whatever energy had been drained from her limbs was being concentrated now in her eyes. She had high cheekbones and a strong chin. The skin hung from her face like tissue-thin kid leather, lined and seamed, yellowing with the years like a pair of cotillion gloves. Like Ashley, she was big: wide through the shoulders, thick through the waist. Like Ash, too, she might have been a redhead in her youth. Now her hair was a soft puff of white, gathered on top and secured by a series of tortoiseshell combs. Her clothes were beautifully made—a softly draped kimono of navy silk over a dark red silk wrap-around dress. Ashley helped her into a chair, pulling the tea cart within range so her mother could supervise the pouring of tea.

Ash glanced over at me. "Would you prefer sherry? The tea is Earl Grey."

"Tea's fine."

Ash poured three cups of tea while Helen selected a little plate of cookies and finger sandwiches for each of us. White bread spread with butter, sprigs of watercress peeping out. Wheat bread with curried chicken salad. Rye layered with herbed cream cheese and lox. There was something about the ritual attention to detail that made me realize neither of them cared what I was wearing or whether my social status was equivalent to theirs.

Ashley flashed me a smile when she handed me my tea. "Mother and I live for this," she said, dimples appearing.

"Oh, yes," Helen said, with a smile. "Food is my last great vice and I intend to sin incessantly as long as my palate holds out."

We munched and sipped tea and laughed and chatted about old times. Helen told me that both she and Woody had sprung from the commonplace. His father had owned a hardware store in town for years. Her father was a stonemason. Each had inherited a modest sum which they'd pooled to form Wood/Warren sometime in the forties. The money they'd amassed was all fun and games as far as they were concerned. Woody was dead serious about the running of the company, but the profits had seemed like a happy accident. Helen said he'd carried nearly two million dollars' worth of life insurance on himself, considering it a hot joke as it was the only investment he knew of with a guaranteed payoff.

At 5:00, Ash excused herself, leaving the two of us alone.

Helen's manner became brisk. "Now tell me about this business with Lance."

I brought her up-to-date. Ash had apparently filled her in, but Helen wanted to hear it all again from me.

"I want you to work for me," she said promptly when I finished.

"I can't do that, Helen. For starters, my attorney doesn't want me anywhere near Lance, and I certainly can't accept employment from the Wood family. It already looks like I'm being paid off."

"I want to know who's behind this," she said.

"So do I. But suppose it turns out to be one of you. I don't mean to offend, but we can't rule that out."

"Then we'd have to put a stop to it. I don't like underhanded dealings, especially when people outside the company are affected. Will you keep me informed?"

"If it's practical, of course. I'm willing to share anything I find. For once, I don't have a client to protect."

"Tell me how I can help."

"Fill me in on the details of Woody's will, if that's not too personal. How was his estate divided? Who controls the company?"

A flash of irritation crossed her face. "That was the only thing we argued about. He was determined to leave the business to Lance, which I didn't disagree with in principle. Of all the children, Lance seemed to be the best qualified to carry on once his father was gone. But I felt Woody should have given him the clout to go with it. Woody wouldn't do it. He absolutely refused to give him control."

"Meaning what?"

"Fifty-one percent of the stock, that's what. I said, 'Why give him the position if you won't give him the power to go along with it? Let the boy run it his way, for God's sake, you old goat!' But Woody wouldn't hear of it. Wouldn't even *consider* the possibility. I was livid, but that old fool wouldn't budge. Lord, he could be stubborn when he made his mind up."

"What was he so worried about?"

"He was afraid Lance would run the business into the ground. Lance's judgment *is* sometimes faulty. I'd be the first to admit it. He doesn't seem to have a feel for the market like Woody did. He doesn't have the relationships with suppliers or customers, not to mention employees. Lance is impetuous and he has very grandiose schemes

that never quite pan out. He's better now, but those last
few years before Woody died, Lance would go off on a tear,
all obsessed with some muddleheaded idea he'd got hold
of. While Woody was alive, he could rein him in, but he was
petrified that Lance would make a disastrous mistake."

"Why leave him the company in the first place? Why
not put someone he trusted at the helm?"

"I suggested that myself, but he wouldn't hear of it. It
had to be one of the boys, and Lance was the logical choice.
Bass was . . . well, you know Bass. He had no desire to
follow in Woody's footsteps unless they led straight to the
bank."

"What about Ebony? Ash mentioned she was interested."

"I suppose she was, but by the time Woody made out
this last will of his, she was off in Europe and showed no
signs of coming back."

"How was the stock divided?"

"Lance has forty-eight percent. I have nine, our attorney has three percent, and Ebony, Olive, Ash, and Bass
each have ten."

"An odd division, isn't it?"

"It's set up so Lance can't act alone. To make up a
majority, he has to persuade at least one of us that what
he's proposing makes good business sense. For the most
part he's free to do as he sees fit, but we can always rally
and outvote him in a pinch."

"That must drive him crazy."

"Oh, he hates it, but I must say I begin to see Woody's
point. Lance is young yet and he's not that experienced.
Let him get a few years under his belt and then we'll see
how things stand."

"Then the situation could change?"

"Well, yes, depending on what happens to my shares
when I die. Woody left that entirely up to me. All I have to
do is leave three shares to Lance. That would make him a
majority stockholder. No one could touch him."

"Sounds like the stuff of which soap operas are made."

"I can wield power like a man if it comes to that. Next
to eating, it's what I enjoy best." She glanced at the watch
that was pinned to her dress, then reached over to the wall

and pressed a button that apparently signaled the maid somewhere in the house. "Time for my swim. Would you care to join me? We have extra suits and I'd enjoy the company. I can still do a mile, but it bores me to death."

"Maybe another time. I tend to be a land animal, given my choice." I got up and shook her hand. "Tea was lovely. Thanks for the invitation."

"Come again, any time. Meanwhile, I'll see that Ebony and Olive give you any information you need."

"I'd appreciate that. I'll see myself out."

As I moved toward the foyer, the maid was returning with a portable wheelchair.

Behind her the front door opened, and Ebony came in. I hadn't seen her since I was seventeen. She must have been twenty-five then, which seemed very mature and sophisticated to me. She still had the power to intimidate. She was tall, rail-thin, high cheekbones, dark-red lipstick. Her hair was jet-black and pulled back dramatically, worn with a bow at her neck. She'd gone to Europe originally as a fashion model and she still walked like she was whipping down a runway. She'd been at Cal Poly for two years, had quit, had tried photography, dance, design school, and free-lance journalism before she turned to modeling. She'd been married maybe six years to a man whose name had recently been linked with Princess Caroline of Monaco. As far as I knew, Ebony had no children and, at forty, seemed an unlikely prospect for motherhood.

She paused when she caught sight of me, and for a moment I wasn't sure if she remembered who I was. She flicked me a chill smile and continued toward the stairs.

"Hello, Kinsey. Come upstairs. I think we should talk."

I followed her. She was wearing a wide-shouldered black suit, nipped in at the waist, a stark white shirt, knee-high glossy black boots with heels sharp enough to pierce a cheap floor covering. She smelled of a high-powered perfume, dark and intense, faintly unpleasant at close range. A trail of it wafted back at me like diesel fuel. This was going to give me a headache, I could tell. I was already annoyed by her attitude, which was peremptory at best.

The second floor was carpeted in pale beige, a wool pile so dense I felt as if we were slogging through dry sand.

The hallway was wide enough to accommodate a settee and a massive antique armoire. It surprised me somehow that she was living at home. Maybe, like Ash, she was here temporarily until she found a permanent residence somewhere else.

She opened a bedroom door and stepped back, waiting for me to pass in front of her. She should have been a school principal, I thought. With a tiny whip, she could have done a thriving trade in dominance. As soon as I'd entered the room, she closed the door and leaned against it, still holding onto the knob at the small of her back. Her complexion was fine, loose powder lending a matte finish to her face, like the pale cast of hoarfrost.

9

There was an alcove to the left, done up as a little sitting
room with a coffee table and two easy chairs. "Sit down,"
she said.

"Why don't you just tell me what you want and let's
get on with it?"

She shrugged and crossed the room. She leaned down
and plucked a cigarette from the crystal box on the coffee
table. She sat down in one of the upholstered chairs. She lit
her cigarette. She blew the smoke out. Every gesture was
separate and deliberate, designed to call maximum attention to herself.

I moved to the door and opened it. "Thanks for the
trip upstairs. It's been swell," I said, as I started out the
door.

"Kinsey, wait. Please."

I paused, looking back at her.

"I'm sorry. I apologize. I know I'm rude."

"I don't care if you're rude, Ebony. Just pick up the
pace a bit."

Her smile was wintry. "Please sit, if you would."

I sat down.

"Would you like a martini?" She set her burning cigarette in the ashtray and opened a small refrigerator unit
built into the coffee table. She extracted chilled glasses, a
jar of pitted green olives, and a bottle of gin. There was no
vermouth in sight. Her nails were so long they had to be
fake, but they allowed her to extract the olives without
getting her fingers wet. She inserted an acrylic tip and
pierced the olives one by one, lifting them out. I watched

her pour gin with a glint in her eye that suggested a thirst springing straight from her core.

She handed me a drink. "What happened with you and Lance?"

"Why do you ask?"

"Because I'm curious. The company's affected by whatever affects him. I want to know what's going on." She picked up her cigarette again and took a deep drag. I could tell the nicotine and alcohol were soothing some inner anxiety.

"He knows as much as I do. Why don't you ask him?"

"I thought you might tell me, as long as you're here."

"I'm not sure that's such a good idea. He seems to think you're part of it."

Her smile returned, but it held no mirth. "In this family, I'm not part of anything. I wish I were."

I felt another surge of impatience. I said, "Jesus, let's quit fencing. I hate conversations like this. Here's the deal. Someone set me up and I don't like it. I have no idea why and I don't much give a shit, but I'm going to find out who it was. At the moment I'm self-employed, so the only client I have to answer to is me. If you want information, hire a private detective. My services are spoken for."

Her expression hardened like plaster of Paris, dead white. I suspected if I reached out to touch her, her skin would have had the same catalytic heat. "I hoped you'd be reasonable."

"What for? I don't know what's going on, and what I've seen so far, I don't like. For all I know, you're at the bottom of this or you know who is."

"You don't mince words, do you?"

"Why should I mince words? I don't work for you."

"I made a simple inquiry. I can see you've decided to take offense." She stubbed out her cigarette at the halfway mark.

She was right. I was hot and I wasn't sure why. I took a deep breath and calmed myself. Not for her sake, but for mine. I tried again. "You're right. I'm out of line. I didn't think I was pissed off, but clearly I am. Somehow I've gotten caught up in family politics and that doesn't sit well with me."

"What makes you so sure it's family politics? Suppose it's someone outside the company?"

"Like who?"

"We have competitors like anybody else." She took a sip of her martini and I could see her savor the icy liquid as it flooded through her mouth. Her face was narrow, her features fine. Her skin was flawless and unlined, giving her the bland expression of a Madame Alexander doll. Either she'd already had plastic surgery or she'd somehow learned not to have the kinds of feelings that leave telltale marks. It was hard to imagine that she and Ash were sisters. Ash was earthy and open with a sunny disposition, generous, good-natured, easygoing, relaxed. Ebony was as lean as a whip, all edged—brittle, aloof, controlled, arrogant. It was possible, I thought, that the differences between them were related, in part, to their relative positions in the family constellation. Ebony was the oldest daughter, Ash the youngest. Woody and Helen had probably expected perfection of their first child. By the time they got down to Ash, and beyond her to Bass, they must have given up expecting anything.

Ebony touched the olive in her drink, turning it. She eased the fingernail into the hole and plucked it out, laying the green globe on her tongue. Her lips closed around her finger and she made a faint sucking noise. The gesture had obscene overtones and I wondered suddenly if she was coming on to me.

She said, "I don't suppose you'll tell me what Mother wanted."

I could feel my temper climb again. "Don't you people talk to each other? She invited me for tea. We had a few laughs about old times. I'm not going to run straight up here and spill it all to you. If you want to know what we talked about, ask her. When I find out what's going on, I'll be delighted to dump the whole thing in your lap. In the meantime, I don't think it's smart to run around telling everything I know."

Ebony was amused. I could see the corners of her mouth turning up.

I stopped what I was saying. "Have you got some kind of problem with that?"

She laughed. "I'm sorry. I don't mean to condescend, but you were always like this. All that energy. So fiery and defensive."

I stared at her, stumped for a response.

"You're a professional," she went on pleasantly. "I understand that. I'm not asking you to divulge any confidences. This is my family and I'm concerned about what goes on. That's my only point. If I can be of any help, just tell me how. If something you discover has a bearing on me, I'd like to hear about it. Is that so unreasonable?"

"Of course not. Sorry," I said. I circled back through our conversation, returning to something she'd said earlier. "You mentioned that the trouble might originate from someone outside the company. Were you talking in general or specific terms?"

She shrugged languidly. "General, really, though I do know of someone who hates us bitterly." She paused, as though trying to decide how to frame her explanation. "There was an engineer who worked for us for many years. A fellow named Hugh Case. Two years ago, a couple of months before my father died, as a matter of fact, he—um, killed himself."

"Was there a connection?"

She seemed faintly startled. "With Daddy's death? Oh, no, I'm sure not, but from what I'm told, Hugh's wife was convinced Lance was responsible."

"How so?"

"You'd have to ask someone else for the details. I was in Europe at the time, so I don't know much except that Hugh shut himself up in his garage and ran his car until he died of carbon monoxide poisoning." She paused to light another cigarette and then sat for a moment, using the spent match to rake the ash into a neat pile in the ashtray.

"His wife felt Lance drove him to it?"

"Not quite. She thought Lance murdered him."

"Oh, come on!"

"Well, he was the one who stood to benefit. There was a rumor floating around at the time that Hugh Case intended to leave Wood/Warren and start a company of his own in competition with us. He was in charge of research and development, and apparently he was on the track of a revolutionary new process. The desertion could have caused us serious harm. There are only fifteen or so companies nationwide in our line of work so the defection would have set us back."

"But that's ridiculous. A man doesn't get murdered because he wants to change jobs!"

Ebony arched an eyebrow delicately. "Unless it represents a crippling financial loss to the company he leaves."

"Ebony, I don't believe this. You'd sit there and say such a thing about your own brother?"

"Kinsey, I'm reporting what I heard. I never said *I* believed it, just that she did."

"The police must have investigated. What did they find?"

"I have no idea. You'd have to ask them."

"Believe me, I will. It may not connect, but it's worth checking out. What about Mrs. Case? Where is she at this point?"

"I heard she left town, but that might not be true. She was a bartender, of all things, in that cocktail lounge at the airport. Maybe they know where she went. Her name is Lyda Case. If she's remarried or gone back to her maiden name, I don't know how you'd track her down."

"Anybody else you can think of who might want to get to Lance?"

"Not really."

"What about you? I heard you were interested in the company. Isn't that why you came back?"

"In part. Lance has done some very foolish things since he took over. I decided it was time to come home and do what I could to protect my interests."

"Meaning what?"

"Meaning just what it sounds like. He's a menace. I'd like to get him out of there."

"So if he's charged with fraud, it won't break your heart."

"Not if he's guilty. It would serve him right. I'm after his job. I make no bones about it, but I certainly wouldn't need to go about it in an underhanded way, if that's what you're getting at," she said, almost playfully.

"I appreciate your candor," I said, though her attitude

irritated me. I'd expected her to be defensive. Instead, she was amused. Part of what offended me in Ebony was the hint of superiority that underscored everything she did. Ash had told me Ebony was always considered "fast." In high school, she'd been daring, a dazzler and wild, one of those girls who'd try anything once. At an age when everyone else was busy trying to conform, Ebony had done whatever suited her. "Smoked, sassed adults, and screwed around," was the way Ash put it. At seventeen she'd learned not to give a shit, and now she seemed indelibly imprinted with an air of disdain. Her power lay in the fact that she had no desire to please and she didn't care what your opinion of her was. Being with her was exhausting and I was suddenly too tired to press her about the little smile that played across her mouth.

It was 6:15. High tea wasn't doing much for someone with my low appetites. I was suddenly famished. Martinis give me a headache anyway and I knew I smelled of secondhand cigarette smoke.

I excused myself and headed home, stopping by McDonald's to chow down a quarter-pounder with cheese, large fries, and a Coke. This was no time to torment my cells with good nutrition, I thought. I finished up with one of those fried pies full of hot glue that burns the fuck out of your mouth. Pure heaven.

When I got back to my place, I experienced the same disconcerting melancholy I'd felt off and on since Henry got on the plane for Michigan. It's not my style to be lonely or to lament, even for a moment, my independent state. I like being single. I like being by myself. I find solitude healing and I have a dozen ways to feel amused. The problem was I couldn't think of one. I won't admit to depression, but I was in bed by 8:00 P.M. . . . not cool for a hard-assed private eye waging a one-woman war against the bad guys everywhere.

10

By 1:00 the next afternoon, I had tracked Lyda Case by telephone to a cocktail lounge at the Dallas/Fort Worth airport, where she was simultaneously tending bar and hanging up in my ear with a force that made me think I'd have to have my hearing rechecked. Last May I'd been compelled to shoot someone from the depths of a garbage bin and my ears have been hissing ever since. Lyda didn't help this . . . especially as she said a quite rude word to me before she smacked the phone down. I was deeply annoyed. It had taken me a bit of doing to locate her and she'd already hung up on me once that day.

I'd started at 10:00 A.M. with a call to the Culinary Alliance and Bartenders Local 498, which refused to tell me anything. I've noticed lately that organizations are getting surly about this sort of thing. It used to be you could ring them right up, tell a plausible tale, and get the information you wanted within a minute or two. Now you can't get names, addresses, or telephone numbers. You can't get service records, bank balances, or verification of employment. Half the time, you can't even get confirmation of the facts you already have. Don't even bother with the public schools, the Welfare Department, or the local jail. They won't tell you nothin'.

"That's privileged," they say. "Sorry, but that's an invasion of our client's privacy."

I hate that officious tone they take, all those clerks and receptionists. They *love* not telling you what you want to know. And they're smart. They don't fall for the same old

song and dance that worked a couple of years ago. It's too
aggravating for words.

I reverted to routine. When all else fails, try the
county clerk's office, the public library, or the DMV.
They'll help. Sometimes there's a small fee involved, but
who cares?

I whipped over to the library and checked back
through old telephone directories year by year until I
found Hugh and Lyda Case listed. I made a note of the
address and then switched to the crisscross and found out
who their neighbors had been two years back. I called one
after another, generally bullshitting my way down the
block. Finally, someone allowed as how Hugh had died and
they thought his widow moved to Dallas.

It worried me briefly that Lyda Case might be unlisted, but I dialed Information in Dallas and picked up a
home phone number right away. Hot damn, this was fun. I
tried the number and someone answered on the third ring.

"Hello."

"May I speak to Lyda Case?"

"This is she."

"Really?" I asked, amazed at my own cleverness.

"Who is this?" Her voice was flat.

I hadn't expected to get through to her and I hadn't
yet made up a suitable fib, so I was forced to tell the truth.
Big mistake. "My name is Kinsey Millhone. I'm a private
detective in Santa Teresa, California. . . ."

Bang. I lost some hearing in the mid-range. I called
back, but she refused to answer the phone.

At this point, I needed to know where she was employed and I couldn't afford to call every bar in the Dallas/
Fort Worth area, if indeed that's the sort of work she still
did. I tried Information again and picked up the telephone
number of the Hotel and Restaurant Employees Union
Local 353 in Dallas. I had my index finger poised to dial
when I realized I would need a ruse.

I sat and thought for a moment. It would help to have
Lyda Case's Social Security number, which might lend a
little air of credibility to my bogus pursuit. Never try to get
one of these from the Social Security Office. They're right
up there with banks in their devotion to thwarting you at

every turn. I was going to have to get the information through access to public records of some sort.

I grabbed my handbag, a jacket, and my car keys and headed over to the courthouse. The Registrar of Voters is located in the basement, down a flight of wide red-tile steps with a handrail made out of antique rope as big around as a boa constrictor.

I followed the signs down a short corridor to the right, pushing into the office through a glass door. Two clerks were working behind the counter, but no one paid any attention to me. There was a computer terminal on the counter and I typed in Lyda Case's name. I closed my eyes briefly, offering up a small prayer to whichever of the gods is in charge of bureaucracies. If Lyda had registered to vote any time in the last six years, the revised form wouldn't show her Social Security number. That question had been deleted in 1976.

The name flashed up, line after line of green print streaking out. Lyda Case had first registered to vote October 14, 1974. The number of the original affidavit was listed on the bottom line. I made a note of the number and gave it to the clerk who had approached when she saw I needed help.

She disappeared into a back corridor where the old files are kept. She returned a few minutes later with the affidavit in hand. Lyda Case's Social Security number was neatly filled in. As a bonus, I also picked up her date of birth. I started laughing at the sight of it. The clerk smiled and I knew from the look we exchanged that she felt as I did about some things. I love information. Sometimes I feel like an archaeologist, digging for facts, uncovering data with my wits and a pen. I made notes, humming to myself.

Now I could go to work.

I went home again and picked up the phone, redialing the Bartenders Local in Santa Teresa.

"Local Four-Ninety-eight," the woman said.

"Oh, hi," said I. "Who am I speaking to, please?"

"I'm the administrative assistant," she said primly. "Perhaps you'll identify yourself."

"Oh, sorry. Of course. This is Vicky with the Chamber of Commerce. I'm addressing invitations for the annual

Board of Supervisors dinner and I need your name, if you'd be so kind."

There was a dainty silence. "Rowena Feldstaff," she said, spelling it out for me carefully.

"Thank you."

I dialed Texas again. The phone on the other end rang four times while two women in teeny, tiny voices laughed about conditions in the Inky Void. Someone picked up.

"Hotel and Restaurant Employees Local Three-Five-Three. This is Mary Jane. Can I he'p you?" She had a soft voice and a mild Texas accent. She sounded like she was about twenty.

"You sure can, Mary Jane," I said. "This is Rowena Feldstaff in Santa Teresa, California. I'm the administrative assistant for Bartenders Local Four-Ninety-eight and I'm trying to do a status check on Lyda Case. That's C-A-S-E . . ." Then I rattled out her date of birth and her Social Security number, as though from records of my own.

"Can I have a number so I can call you back?" said the ever-cautious Mary Jane.

"Sure," I said and gave her my home phone.

Within minutes, my phone rang again. I answered as Bartenders Local 498, and Mary Jane very kindly gave me Lyda Case's current place of employment, along with the address and phone number. She was working at one of the cocktail lounges at the Dallas/Fort Worth airport.

I called the bar and one of the waitresses told me Lyda would be there at 3:00 Dallas time, which was 1:00 where I was.

At 1:00, I called back and lost another couple of decibels' worth of hearing. Whoo, that lady was quick. I'd have to walk around with a horn sticking out of my ear at this rate.

If I'd been working off an expense account, I'd have hied myself out to the Santa Teresa airport and jumped on a plane for Dallas. I can be pretty cavalier with someone else's money. My own, I think about first, as I'm very cheap.

I hopped in my car and drove over to the police station. Jonah Robb, my usual source of illicit information, was out of town. Sergeant Schiffman, sitting in for him, was not all that swift and didn't really like to bend the rules, so I bypassed him and went straight to Emerald, the black clerk in Records and Identification. Technically she's not supposed to give out the kind of information I needed, but she's usually willing to help if no one's around to catch her.

I leaned on the counter in the reception area, waiting while she finished typing a department memo. She took her time getting to me, probably sensing that I was up to no good. She's in her forties, with a medium complexion about the color of a cigar. Her hair is cut very short and it curls tensely around her head, a glistening, wet-looking black with gray frizz at the tips. She's probably fifty pounds overweight and it's all solidly packed into her waist, her belly, and her rump.

"Uh–uhn," she said to me as she approached. Her voice is higher than one would imagine for a woman her size, and it has a nasal cast to it, with just the faintest suggestion of a lisp. "What do you want? I'm almost afraid to ask."

She was wearing a regulation uniform, a navy-blue skirt and a white short-sleeved blouse that looked very stark and clean against the tobacco brown of her arms. The patch on her sleeve said Santa Teresa Police Department, but she's actually a civilian clerk.

"Hello, Emerald. How are you?"

"Busy. You better cut right down to what you want," she said.

"I need you to look something up for me."

"Again? I'm gonna get myself fired one of these days because of you. What is it?" Her tone was offset by a sly smile that touched off dimples in her cheeks.

"A suicide, two years back," I said. "The guy's name was Hugh Case."

She stared at me.

Uh–oh, I thought. "You know who I'm talking about?"

"Sure, I know. I'm surprised you don't."

"What's the deal? I assume it wasn't routine."

She laughed at that. "Oh, honey, no way. No way. Uh–un. Lieutenant Dolan still gets mad when he hears the name."

"How come?"

"How come? Because the evidence disappeared, that's how come. I know two people at St. Terry's got fired over that."

Santa Teresa Hospital, St. Terry's, is where the hospital morgue is located.

"What evidence came up missing?" I asked.

"Blood, urine, tissue samples, the works. His weren't the only specimens disappeared. The courier picked 'em up that day and took 'em out to County and that's the last anybody ever saw of the whole business."

"Jesus. What about the body? Why couldn't they just redo the work?"

Emerald shook her head. "Mr. Case'd been cremated by the time they found out the specimens were missing. Mrs. Case had the ashes what-do-you-call-'em . . . scattered at sea."

"Oh, shit, you're kidding."

"No ma'am. Autopsy'd been done and Dr. Yee already released the body to the mortuary. Mrs. Case didn't want any kind of funeral, so she gave the order to have him cremated. He was gone. People had a fit. Dr. Yee turned St. Terry's upside down. Nothing ever did show. Lieutenant Dolan was beside himself. Now I hear they got this whole new policy. Security's real tight."

"But what was the assumption? Was it an actual theft?"

"Don't ask me. Like I said, lot of other stuff disappeared at the same time so the hospital couldn't say what went on. It could have been a mistake. Somebody might have thrown all that stuff out by accident and then didn't want to admit it."

"Why was Dolan involved? I thought it was a suicide."

"You know nobody will make a determination on the manner and cause of death until the reports come back."

"Well, yeah," I said. "I just wondered if the lieutenant had any initial doubts."

"Lieutenant always has doubts. He'll have some more he catches you sniffin' around. Now I got work to do. And don't you tell nobody I told you this stuff."

I drove over to the Pathology Department at St. Terry's, where I had a quick chat with one of the lab techs I'd dealt with before. She confirmed what Emerald had told me, adding a few details about the mechanics of the episode. From what she said, a courier from the coroner's office did a daily run in a blood-transport vehicle, making a sweep of labs and law-enforcement agencies. Specimens to be picked up were sealed, labeled and placed in insulated cold packs, like picnic supplies. The "hamper" itself was stored in the lab refrigerator until the driver showed up. The lab tech would fetch the hamper. The courier would sign for the evidence and away he'd go. The Hugh Case "material," as she so fastidiously referred to it, was never seen again once it left the hospital lab. Whether it disappeared en route or after it was delivered to the coroner's lab, no one ever knew. The clerk at St. Terry's swore she gave it to the driver and she had a signed receipt to show for it. She assumed the hamper reached its destination as it had every day for years. The courier remembered putting it in the vehicle and assumed it was among the items delivered at the end of his run. It was only after some days had passed and Dr. Yee began to press for lab results on the toxicological tests that the disappearance came to light. By then, of course, as Emerald had indicated, Hugh Case's remains had been reduced to ashes and flung to the far winds.

I used one of the pay phones in the hospital lobby to call my travel agent and inquire about the next flight to Dallas. There was one seat left on the 3:00 shuttle from Santa Teresa to Los Angeles, arriving at LAX at 3:35. With a two-hour layover, I could pick up a United flight that would get me into Dallas that night at 10:35, CST. If Lyda clocked into the bar at 3:00 and worked an eight-hour shift, she should be getting off at 11:00. A delay at any point in the journey would get me there too late to connect with her. I couldn't get a flight back to Santa Teresa until morning anyway, because the airport here shuts down at 11 P.M. I was going to end up spending a night in Dallas in any event. The air fare itself was nearly two hundred bucks, and the notion of paying for a hotel room on top of that made me nearly giddy with anxiety. Of course, I could always sleep listing sideways in one of those molded-plastic airport chairs, but I didn't relish the idea. Also, I wasn't quite sure how I could contrive to eat on the ten bucks in cash I had on me. I probably couldn't even afford to retrieve my VW from the long-term parking lot when I got home again.

My travel agent, Lupe, was breathing patiently into my ear while I did these lightning-quick calculations.

"I don't want to bug you, Millhone, but you got about six minutes to make up your mind about this."

I glanced at my watch. It was 2:17. I said, "Oh hell, let's go for it."

"Done," she said.

She booked the seats. I charged the tickets to my United credit card which I had just gotten paid off. Curses, I thought, but it had to be done. Lupe said the tickets would be waiting for me at the ticket counter. I hung up, left the hospital, and headed out to the airport.

My handsome travel wardrobe that day consisted of my boots, my ratty jeans, and a cotton turtleneck, navy blue with the sleeves only slightly stretched out of shape. I had an old windbreaker in the back seat of my car. Happily, I hadn't used it recently to clean off my windshield. I also keep a small overnight case in the back seat, with a toothbrush and clean underwear.

I boarded the plane with twelve minutes to spare and tucked my overnight case under the seat in front of me. The aircraft was small and all fifteen seats were occupied. A hanging curtain separated the passengers from the cockpit. Since I was only two seats back, I could see the whole instrument panel, which didn't look any more complicated than the dashboard of a new Peugeot. When the flight attendant saw me rubbernecking, she pulled the curtain across the opening, as if the pilot and copilot were doing something up there we were better off not knowing about.

The engines sounded like lawn mowers and reminded me vaguely of the Saturday mornings of my youth when I would wake late to hear my aunt out cutting the grass. Over the din, the intercom system was worthless. I couldn't hear a word the pilot said, but I suspected he was reciting that alarming explanation of what to do in the "unlikely" event of a water landing. Most planes crash and burn on land. This was just something new to worry about. I didn't think my seat cushion was going to double as a flotation device of any kind. It was barely adequate to keep my rear end protected from the steel-reinforced framework of the seat itself. While the pilot droned on, I looked at the plastic card with its colorful cartoon depicting the aircraft. Someone had placed two X's on the diagram. One said, "You are here." A second X out on the wing tip said, "Toilet is here."

The flight only took thirty-five minutes so the flight attendant, who wore what looked like a Girl Scout uniform, didn't have time to serve us complimentary drinks. Instead, she whipped down the aisle, passing a little basket of Chiclets chewing gum in tiny boxes. I spent the flight time trying to get my ears to unpop, looking, I'm sure, like I was suffering from some kind of mechanical jaw disease.

My United flight left right on time. I sat in the no-smoking section being serenaded by a duet of crying babies. Lunch consisted of a fist of chicken breast on a pile of rice, covered with what looked like rubber cement. Dessert was a square of cake with a frosting that smelled like Coppertone. I ate every bite and tucked the cellophane-wrapped crackers in my purse. Who knew when I'd get to eat again.

Once we landed in Dallas, I grabbed up my belongings and eased my way toward the front of the plane as we waited for the jetway to thump against the door. The stewardess released us like a pack of noisy school kids and I dogtrotted toward the gate. By the time I actually hit the terminal, it was 10:55. The cocktail lounge I was looking for was in another satellite, typically about as far away as you could get. I started running, grateful, as usual, that I keep myself fit. I reached the bar at 11:02. Lyda Case had left. I'd missed her by five minutes and she wasn't scheduled to work again until the weekend. I won't repeat what I said.

11

I had Lyda paged. I had passed a Traveler's Aid station, an L-shaped desk, where the airline-terminal equivalent of a candy-striper was posted. This woman was in her fifties, with an amazingly homely face: gaunt and chinless, with one eye askew. She was wearing a Salvation Army uniform, complete with brass buttons and epaulets. I wasn't sure what the deal was. Maybe distraught mothers of lost toddlers and foreign-speaking persons in need of Kaopectate were meant to garner spiritual comfort along with the practical kind. She was just shutting down her station for the night, and at first she didn't seem to appreciate my request for help.

"Look," I said, "I just flew in from California to speak with a woman who's on her way out of the terminal. I've got to catch her before she hits the parking lot, and I have no idea which exit she's using. Is there any way to have her paged?"

The woman fixed me with the one eye while the other moved to the one-page directory she kept taped to her desk top. Without a word, she picked up the phone and dialed. "What's the name?" she asked.

"Lyda Case."

She repeated the name and within moments, I heard Lyda Case being paged to the Traveler's Aid station, terminal 2. I was profuse in my thanks, though she didn't seem to require much in the way of appreciation. She finished packing up and, with a brief word, departed.

I had no idea if Lyda Case would show. She might have been out of the building by the time her name was

called. Or she might have been too tired and cranky to
come back for any reason. On an impulse, I rounded the
desk and sat down in the chair. A man passed with a rolling
suitcase that trailed after him reluctantly, like a dog on its
way to the vet. I glanced at my watch. Twelve minutes had
passed. I checked the top desk drawer, which was unlocked. Pencils, pads of paper, tins of aspirin, cellophane-
wrapped tissue, a Spanish-language dictionary. I read the
list of useful phrases inside the back cover. *"Buenas
tardes,"* I murmured to myself. *"Buenas noches."* Good
nachos. I was starving to death.

"Somebody paging me? I heard my name on the pub-
lic-address system and it said to come here." The accent
was Texan. Lyda Case was standing with her weight on one
hip. Petite. No makeup. All freckles and frizzy hair. She
was dressed in dark slacks and a matching vest—one of
those all-purpose bartender uniforms that you can probably order wholesale from the factory. Her name was
machine-embroidered on her left breast. She had on a
diamond-crusted watch, and in her right hand she held
a lighted cigarette, which she dropped and crushed underfoot.

"What's the matter, baby? Did I come to the wrong
place?" Mid-thirties. Lively face. Straight little nose and a
sharp, defiant chin. Her smile revealed crooked eyeteeth
and gaps where her first molars should have been. Her
parents had never gone into debt for *her* orthodontia
work.

I got up and held my hand out. "Hello, Mrs. Case. How
are you?"

She allowed her hand to rest in mine briefly. Her eyes
were the haunting, surreal blue of contact lenses. Distrust
flickered across the surface. "I don't believe I know you."

"I called from California. You hung up on me twice."

The smile drained away. "I thought I made it clear I
wasn't interested. I hope you didn't fly all this way on my
account."

"Actually, I did. You'd just gone off duty when I got to
the lounge. I'm hoping you'll spare me a few minutes. Is
there some place we can go to talk?"

"This is called talkin' where I come from," she snapped.

"I meant, privately."

"What about?"

"I'm curious about your husband's death."

She stared at me. "You some kind of reporter?"

"Private detective."

"Oh, that's right. You mentioned that on the phone. Who all are you working for?"

"Myself at the moment. An insurance company before that. I was investigating a warehouse fire at Wood/Warren when Hugh's name came up. I thought you might fill me in on the circumstances of his death."

I could see her wrestling with herself, tempted by the subject. It was probably one of those repetitious nighttime tales we tell ourselves when sleep eludes us. Somehow I imagined there were grievances she recited endlessly as the hours dragged by from 2:00 to 3:00. Something in the brain comes alive at that hour and it's usually in a chatty mood.

"What's Hugh got to do with it?"

"Maybe nothing. I don't know. I thought it was odd his lab work disappeared."

"Why worry about it? No one else did."

"It's about time then, don't you think?"

She gave me a long look, sizing me up. Her expression changed from sullenness to simple impatience. "There's a bar down here. I got somebody waiting so I'll have to call home first. Thirty minutes. That's all you get. I worked my butt off today and I want to rest my dogs." She moved off and I followed, trotting to keep up.

We sat in captain's chairs at a table near the window. The night sky was thick with low clouds. I was startled to realize it was raining outside. The plate glass was streaked with drops blown sideways by a buffeting wind. The tarmac was as glossy as black oilcloth, with runway lights reflected in the mirrored surface of the apron, pebbled with raindrops. Three DC-10s were lined up at consecutive gates. The area swarmed with tow tractors, catering vehicles, boom trucks, and men in yellow slickers. A baggage trailer sped by, pulling a string of carts piled high with suitcases. As I watched, a canvas duffel tumbled onto the wet pavement, but no one seemed to notice. Somebody was going to spend an irritating hour filling out "Missing Baggage" claim forms tonight.

While Lyda went off to make her phone call, I ordered a spritzer for me and a Bloody Mary for her, at her request. She was gone a long time. The waitress brought the drinks, along with some Eagle Snack pretzels in a can. "Lyda wanted somethin' to snack on, so I brought you these," she said.

"Can we run a tab?"

"Sure thing. I'm Elsie. Give a holler if you need anything else."

Ground traffic was clearing and I saw the jetway retract from the side of the plane nearest us. On the runway beyond, an L-1011 lumbered by with a stripe of lighted windows along its length. The bar was beginning to empty, but the smoke still sat on the air like a visible smudge on a photograph. I heard high heels clopping toward the table, and Lyda was back. She'd peeled off her vest, and her white blouse was now unbuttoned to a point just between her breasts. Her chest was as freckled as a bird's egg and it made her look almost tanned.

"Sorry it took me so long," she said. "I got this roommate in the middle of a nervous breakdown, or so she thinks." She used her celery stalk to stir the pale cloud of vodka into the peppered tomato juice down below. Then she popped the top off the can of pretzels.

"Here, turn your hand up and lemme give you some," she said. I held my hand out and she filled my palm with tiny pretzels. They were shaped like Chinese pagodas encrusted with rock salt. Her hostility had vanished. I'd seen that before—people whose mistrust takes the form of aggressiveness at first, their resistance like a wall in which a sudden gate appears. She'd decided to talk to me and I suppose she saw no point in being rude. Besides, I was buying. With ten bucks in my pocket, I couldn't afford more than thirty minutes' worth of drinks anyway.

She had taken out a compact and she checked her makeup, frowning at herself. "God. I am such a mess." She plunked her bag up on the table and rooted through until she found a cosmetics pouch. She unzipped it and took out various items, and then proceeded to transform herself before my very eyes. She dotted her face with liquid foundation and smoothed it on, erasing freckles, lines, discolorations. She took out an eyeliner and inked in her upper and lower lids, then brushed her lashes with mascara. Her eyes seemed to leap into prominence. She dusted blusher high on each cheek, lined the contour of her mouth with dark red and then filled her lips in with a lighter shade. Less than two minutes passed, but by the time she glanced at me again, the rough edges were gone and she had all the glamour of a magazine ad. "What do you think?"

"I'm impressed."

"Oh, honey, I could make you over in a minute. You ought to do a little more with yourself. That hair of yours looks like a dog's back end."

I laughed. "We better get down to business if thirty minutes is all I get."

She waved dismissively. "Don't worry about that. I changed my mind. Betsy's workin' on an overdose and I don't feel like going home yet."

"Your roommate took an overdose?"

"She does that all the time, but she never can get it right. I think she got a little booklet from the Hemlock Society and takes half what she needs to do the job. Then I get home and have to deal with it. I truly hate paramedics trooping through my place after midnight. They're all twenty-six years old and so clean-cut it makes you sick. Lot of times she'll date one afterwards. She swears it's the only way to meet nurturing men."

I watched while she drained half her Bloody Mary. "Tell me about Hugh," I said.

She took out a pack of chewing gum and offered me a piece. When I shook my head, she unwrapped a stick and doubled it into her mouth, biting down. Then she lit a cigarette. I tried to imagine the combination . . . mint and smoke. It was an unpleasant notion even vicariously. She wadded up the gum wrapper and dropped it in the ashtray.

"I was just a kid when we met. Nineteen. Tending bar. I went out to California on the Greyhound bus the day I turned eighteen, and went to bartending school in Los Angeles. Cost me six hundred bucks. Might have been a rip-off. I did learn to mix drinks but I probably could have done that out of one of them little books. Anyway, I got this job at LAX and I've been working airport bars ever since. Don't ask me why. I just got stuck somehow. Hugh came in one night and we got talkin' and next thing I knew, we fell in love and got married. He was thirty-nine years old to my nineteen, and I was with him sixteen years. I knew that man. He didn't kill himself. He wouldn't do that to me."

"What makes you so sure?"

"What makes you sure the sun's coming up in the east ever' day? It just does, that's all, and you learn to count on that the way I learned to count on him."

"You think somebody killed him?"

" 'Course I do. Lance Wood did it, as sure as I'm sittin' here, but he's not going to admit it in a million years and neither will his family. Have you talked to them?"

"Some," I said. "I heard about Hugh's death for the first time yesterday."

"I always figured they paid off the cops to keep it hush. They got tons of money and they know ever'one in town. It was a cover-up."

"Lyda, these are honorable people you're talking about. They'd never tolerate murder and they wouldn't protect Lance if they thought he had anything to do with it."

"Boy, you're dumber than I am, if you believe that. I'm tellin' you it was murder. Why'd you fly all this way if you didn't think so yourself?"

"I don't know what to think. That's why I'm asking you."

"Well, it wasn't suicide. He wasn't depressed. He wasn't the suicidal type. Why would he do such a thing? That's just dumb. They knew him. They knew what kind of man he was."

I watched her carefully. "I heard he was planning to leave the company and start a business of his own."

"He talked about that. He talked about a lot of things. He worked for Woody fifteen years. Hugh was loyal as they come, but everybody knew the old man meant to leave the company to Lance. Hugh couldn't stand the idea. He said Lance was a boob and he didn't want to be around to watch him mess up."

"Did the two of them have words?"

"I don't know for sure. I know he gave notice and Woody talked him out of it. He'd just bid on a big government contract and he needed Hugh. I guess Hugh said he'd stay until word came through whether Woody got the bid or not. Two days later, I got home from work, opened the garage door, and there he was. It looked like he fell asleep in the car, but his skin was cherry red. I never will forget that."

"There's no way it could have been an accident?"

She leaned forward earnestly. "I said it once and I'll say it again. Hugh wouldn't kill himself. He didn't have a reason and he wasn't depressed."

"How do you know he wasn't holding something back?"

"I guess I don't, if you put it like that."

"The notion of murder doesn't make any sense. Lance wasn't even in charge at that point, and he wouldn't kill an employee just because the guy wants to move on. That's ludicrous."

Lyda shrugged, undismayed by my skepticism. "Maybe Lance worried Hugh would take the business with him when he went."

"Well, aside from the fact he wasn't gone yet, it still seems extreme."

She bristled slightly. "You asked for my opinion. I'm tellin' you what I think."

"I can see you believe it, but it's going to take more than that to talk me into it. If Hugh was murdered, it could have been someone else, couldn't it?"

"Of course it could. I believe it was Lance, but I can't *swear* to it. I don't have any proof, anyhow. Sometimes I think it's not worth foolin' with. It's over and done, so what difference does it make?"

I shifted the subject. "Why'd you have him cremated so fast?"

She stared at me. "Are you thinking *I* had a hand in it?"

"I'm just asking the questions. What do I know?"

"He *asked* to be cremated. It wasn't even my idea. He'd been dead for two days. The coroner released the body and the funeral director suggested we go ahead with it, so I took his advice. You can talk to him yourself if you don't believe me," she said. "Hugh was drugged. I'd bet money that's how they pulled it off. His lab work was stolen so nobody'd see the test results."

"Maybe he was drunk," I suggested. "He might have pulled into the garage and fallen asleep."

She shook her head. "He didn't drink. He'd given that up."

"Did he have a problem with alcohol?"

"Once upon a time, he did," she said. "We *met* in a bar. Two in the afternoon, in the middle of the week. He wasn't even travelin'. He just liked to come watch the planes, he said. I should have suspected right then, but you know what it's like when you fall in love. You see what you want to see. It took me years to figure out how far gone he was. Finally I said I'd leave him if he didn't straighten up. He went into this program . . . not AA, but something similar. He got sobered up and that's how he stayed."

"Is there a chance he'd gone back to drinking? It wouldn't be unheard of."

"Not with him on Antabuse. He'da been sick as a pup."

"You're sure he took the stuff?"

"I gave it to him myself. It was like a little game we played. Every morning with his orange juice. He held his hand out and I gave him his pill and watched him swallow it right down. He wanted me to see he didn't cheat. He swore, the day he quit drinking, he'd never go back to it."

"How many people knew about the Antabuse?"

"I don't know. He never made a big deal of it. If people around him were drinking, he just said 'No thanks.' "

"Tell me what was happening the week he died."

"Nothing. It seemed like an ordinary week to me. He talked to Woody. Two days later, he was dead. After the funeral, I packed up, put everything in a U-Haul, and hit the road for home. This is where I've been ever since."

"And there was nothing among his things to suggest what was going on? No letter? A note?"

She shook her head. "I went through his desk the day he died, and I didn't see a thing."

12

The flight home was uneventful. I'd spent an hour and a half with Lyda, and the rest of the night in the airport terminal with its red carpeting, high glass ceiling, real trees, and an actual bird that flew back and forth, chirping incessantly. It was sort of like camping out, only I was sitting upright and I didn't have any wienies to roast. I made notes of my conversation with Lyda, which I'd transcribe for the files when I got home. I was inclined to believe Hugh Case had been murdered, though I had no idea how, why, or by whom. I also tended to think his death was related to current events at Wood/Warren, though I couldn't imagine what the connection might be. Lyda had promised to get in touch if she remembered anything of note. All in all, it was not an unproductive trip. It had generated more questions than it answered, but that was fine with me. As long as there are threads to unravel, I'm in business. The frustration starts when all the leads dry up and the roads turn out to be dead ends. With Hugh Case, I felt like I'd just found one of the corner pieces of a jigsaw puzzle. I had no idea what the final picture would look like, but at least I had a place to start.

I boarded the plane at 4:30 A.M. and arrived at LAX at 5:45. I had to wait for a 7:00 A.M. shuttle to Santa Teresa, and by the time I dragged my sorry ass home, I was dead on my feet. I let into the apartment an hour later, checked for messages (none), pulled my boots off, and curled up in the folds of my quilt, fully dressed.

At approximately 9:02, there was a knock at my door. I staggered up out of sleep and shuffled to the door, drag-

89

ging my quilt behind me like a bridal train. My mouth tasted foul and my hair was standing straight up, as spiky as a punker's, only not as clean. I peered through the fish-eye, too clever to be caught unawares by an early-morning thug. Standing on my doorstep was my second ex-husband, Daniel Wade.

"Shit," I murmured. Briefly, I leaned my head against the door and then peeked again. All I could see in truncated form was his face in profile, blond hair curling around his head like an aura. Daniel Wade is quite possibly the most beautiful man I've ever seen—a bad sign. Beautiful men are usually either gay or impossibly narcissistic. (Sorry for the generalization, folks, but it's the truth.) I like a good face or an interesting face or a face with character, but not this sculpted perfection of his . . . the straight, well-proportioned nose, high cheekbones, strong jawline, sturdy chin. His hair was sun-bleached, his eyes a remarkable shade of blue, offset by dark lashes. His teeth were straight and very white, his smile slightly crooked. Get the picture, troops?

I opened the door. "Yes?"

"Hi."

"Hello." I gave him a rude stare, hoping he'd disappear. He's tall and slim and he can eat anything without gaining weight. He stood there in faded jeans and a dark-red sweatshirt with the sleeves pushed up. His skin had a golden sheen, tanned and windburned, so his cheeks glowed darkly. Just another boring California golden boy. The hair on his arms was bleached nearly white. His hands were tucked in his pockets, which was just as well. He's a jazz pianist with long, bony fingers. I fell in love with his hands first and then worked my way up.

"I've been in Florida." Good voice, too . . . just in case his other virtues fail to excite. Reedy and low. He sings like an angel, plays six instruments.

"What brought you back?"

"I don't know. Homesick, I guess. A friend of mine was heading this way so I tagged a ride. Did I wake you up?"

"No, I often walk around looking like this."

A slight smile here, perfectly timed. His manner seemed hesitant, which was unusual for him. He was searching the sight of me, looking (perhaps) for some evidence of the girl I used to be.

"I like the haircut," he said.

"Gee, this is fun. I like yours, too."

"I guess I caught you at a bad time. I'm sorry about that."

"Uh, Daniel, could we skip to the punch line here? I'm operating on an hour's sleep and I feel like shit."

It was clear he'd rehearsed this whole conversation, but in his mind my response was tender instead of downright rude. "I wanted you to know I'm clean," he said. "I have been for a year. No drugs. No drinking. It hasn't been easy, but I really have straightened up."

"Super. I'm thrilled. It's about bloody time."

"Could you knock off the sarcasm?"

"That's my natural way of speaking ever since you left. It's real popular with men."

He rocked slightly on his heels, looking off across the yard. "I guess people don't get a second chance with you."

I didn't bother to respond to that.

He tried a new tack. "Look. I have a therapist named Elise. She was the one who suggested I clean up the unfinished business in my life. She thought maybe you might benefit, too."

"Oh, hey. That's swell. Give me her address and I'll write her a bread-and-butter note."

"Can I come in?"

"Jesus Christ, Daniel, of course not! Don't you get it yet? I haven't seen you for eight years and it turns out that's not long enough."

"How can you be so hostile after all this time? I don't feel bad about you."

"Why would you feel bad? I didn't do anything to you!"

A look of injury crossed his face and his bewilderment seemed genuine. There's a certain class of people who will do you in and then remain completely mystified by the depth of your pain. He shifted his weight. This apparently wasn't going as he thought it would. He reached up to pick at a wood splinter in the door frame above my head. "I didn't think you'd be bitter. That's not like you, Kinsey. We had some good years."

"Year. Singular. Eleven months and six days, to be exact. You might move your hand before I slam the door on it."

He moved his hand.

I slammed the door and went back to bed.

After a few minutes, I heard the gate squeak.

I thrashed about for a while, but it was clear I wouldn't get back to sleep. I got up and brushed my teeth, showered, shampooed my hair, shaved my legs. I used to have fantasies about his showing up. I used to invent long monologues in which I poured out my sorrow and my rage. Now I was wishing he'd come back again so I could do a better job of it. Being rejected is burdensome that way. You're left with emotional baggage you unload on everyone else. It's not just the fact of betrayal, but the person you become . . . usually not very nice. Jonah had survived my tartness. He seemed to understand it had nothing to do with him. He was so blunt himself that a little rudeness didn't bother him. For my part, I really thought I'd made my peace with the past until I came face to face with it.

I called Olive Kohler and made an appointment to see her later in the day. Then I sat down at my desk and typed up my notes. At noon, I decided to get some errands done. Daniel was sitting in a car parked just behind mine. He was slouched down in the passenger seat, his booted feet propped up on the dashboard, a cowboy hat tilted over his face. The car was a ten-year-old Pinto, dark blue, dented, rusted, and stripped of its hubcaps. The sheepskin car-seat covers looked like badly matted dog. A decal on the bumper indicated that the car was from Rent-A-Ruin.

Daniel must have heard the gate squeak as I came out. He turned his head, pushing his hat back lazily. He sometimes affects that aw-shucks attitude. "Feeling better (Miss Kitty)?"

I unlocked my car and got in, started the engine and pulled away. I avoided the apartment for the rest of the day. I can't remember now half of what I did. Mostly I wasted time and resented the fact that I was not only out an office but banned from my own residence.

At 5:00, with the aid of a street map, I found the Kohlers' house on an obscure leafy lane in Montebello. The property was hidden by a ten-foot hedge, the driveway barred by an electronically controlled wrought-iron gate. I parked out on the street and let myself in through a wooden gate embedded in the shrubbery. The house was a two-story, English Tudor style, with a steeply pitched shingled roof, half-timbered gables, and a handsome pattern of vertical beams across the front. The lot was large, shaded with sycamores and eucalyptus trees as smooth and gray as bare concrete. Dark-green ivy seemed to grow everywhere. A gardener, a graduate of the Walt Disney school of landscape maintenance, was visible, trimming the shrubs into animal shapes.

The newspaper was resting on the doormat. I picked it up and then I rang the bell. I expected a maid, but Olive opened the door herself in a gray satin robe and low-heeled satin mules. I'd mostly seen those in Joan Crawford movies, and they looked like they'd be a trick to wear. I had brief visions of plopping around my apartment in backless bedroom slippers. Cigarette holder. Marcelled hair. I could have my eyebrows plucked back to ogee arches.

"Hello, Kinsey. Come in. Terry's on his way. I forgot we were due at a cocktail party at six." She stepped away from the door and I followed her in.

"We can do this another time if you like," I said. I handed her the paper.

"Thanks. No, no. This is fine. It's not for an hour anyway and the people don't live far. I've got to finish dressing, but we can talk in here." She glanced at the paper briefly and then tossed it on the hall table next to a pile of mail.

She clattered her way along the dark stone-tile hallway toward the master suite at the rear of the house. Olive was slim and blond, her shoulder-length hair blunt-cut and thick. I wondered sometimes if Ash was the only sister whose hair remained its natural shade. Olive's eyes were bright blue, her lashes black, her skin tone gold. She was thirty-three or so, not as brittle as Ebony, but with none of

Ash's warmth. She was talking back over her shoulder to me.

"I haven't seen you for ten years. What have you been up to?"

"Setting up my own agency," I said.

"Married? Kids?"

"No, on both counts. You have kids?"

She laughed. "God forbid."

The bedroom we entered was spacious. Beamed ceiling, big stone fireplace, French doors opening onto a walled-in patio where a small deck had been added on. I could see a round two-person hot tub, surrounded by ferns. A white Persian cat was curled up on a chaise, its face tucked into the circling plume of its tail.

The bedroom floor was polished teak with area rugs of a long white wool that probably came from yaks. The entire wall behind the bed was mirrored and I flashed on an image of Terry Kohler's sexual performances. What did Olive stare at, I wondered, while he watched himself? I glanced at the ceiling, checking to see if there was a cartoon tacked up there, like the one in my gynecologist's examining room: "Smile. It gives your face something to do!" This does not amuse.

I eased into an easy chair and watched while Olive moved into a walk-in closet the size of a two-car garage. Quickly she began to sort through a rack of evening clothes, rejecting sequined outfits, floor-length organza gowns, beaded jackets with long, matching skirts. I could see an assortment of shoes stacked in clear plastic boxes on the shelf overhead, and at one end of the rack, several fur coats of various lengths and types. She selected a knee-length cocktail dress with spaghetti straps and returned to the bedroom where she scrutinized her reflection. The dress was avocado green, infusing her skin with sallow undertones.

"What do you think?" she said, eyes still pinned to her own image in the glass.

"Makes you look green."

She stared at herself, squinting critically. "You're right. Here. You take this. I never liked it anyway." She tossed the dress on the bed.

"I don't wear clothes like that," I said uncomfortably.

"Take it. We'll have a New Year's Eve party and you can wear it then." She pulled out a black taffeta dress cut straight across the front. She stepped into it, then zipped it up the back in a motion that snapped everything into place. She was so slender I didn't see how the globelike breasts could possibly be hers. She looked like she'd had softballs surgically implanted on her chest. Hug a woman like that and she was bound to leave dents.

She sat down on the dressing-table bench and pulled on black panty hose, then slipped her feet into four-inch black spike heels. She looked gorgeous, all curves and flawless skin, the pale-blond hair brushing against her bare shoulders. She sorted through her jewelry box and selected clip-on diamond earrings shaped like delicate silver branches hung with sparkling fruit.

She returned to the closet and emerged in a soft, white fur coat the same length as the dress. When she pulled the coat around her, she looked like a flasher decked out in white fox.

She half-smiled when she caught my look. "I know what you're thinking, sweetie, but they were already dead when I got to the furrier's. Whether or not I bought the coat had no effect on their fates."

"If women didn't wear them, they wouldn't be killed in the first place," I said.

"Oh, bullshit. Don't kid yourself. In the wild, these animals get torn to shreds every day. Why not preserve the beauty, like a piece of art? The world's a vicious place. I don't pretend otherwise. And don't argue with me," she said, firmly. She pointed a finger. "You came to talk, so talk." She slipped the coat off and tossed it on the bed, then sat down on the bench and crossed her legs. She eased off one high heel and let her shoe flap against the bottom of her foot.

I said, "How much do you know about the situation at Wood/Warren?"

She gestured impatiently. "Business is a bore. I use that section of the paper to line the cat box."

"You have no interest in the family split?"

"What split? You mean with Lance? I have nothing

invested one way or the other. He and Ebony disagree. She wants me to vote with her. The way she explains it, it's to my advantage. Lance will have a fit, of course, but who gives a shit? He's had his chance."

"You're siding with her?"

"Who knows? Probably. She's smarter than he is and it's time for new blood. He's got his head in the toilet half the time."

"Meaning what?"

"Let me give you the lowdown on my brother, honey-bun. He's a salesman at heart. He can charm your socks off when it suits him. He's enthusiastic about anything that interests him, which isn't much. He has no head for figures. Absolutely none. He hates sitting in an office and he can't stand routine. He's good at generating business and lousy at follow-through. End transmission."

"You've seen this firsthand or is this Ebony's claim?"

"I hear about what happens at the plant every day. Terry's a workaholic and most of what he talks about is business."

"How do he and Lance get along?"

"They knock heads all the time. Terry's obsessive. It drives him crazy when people fuck up. Excuse the scientific term. Lance has poor judgment. Everyone knows that. Meet the woman he married if you have any doubts."

"What about the rest of the family? Can't they vote him out?"

"Nope. The rest of us combined only own forty-nine percent of the stock. Ebony wants to put the squeeze on him, but she can't actually force him out. She can bring him to heel, which I suspect is what she wants."

"I take it Bass isn't involved since he lives in New York."

"He shows up for board meetings occasionally. He enjoys playing mogul, but he's harmless enough. He and Lance are usually thick."

"Who will Ashley side with?"

"She could go either way. Obviously, Ebony's hoping she can persuade us all to mutiny."

"How does your mother feel? This couldn't sit well with her."

"She hates it. She wants Lance in charge. Not because he's good, but because it's less hassle."

"Do you think he's honest?"

"Lance? Are you kidding? No way."

"How do you and he get along?"

"I can't stand him. He's a very tense person and he's soooo paranoid. I hate to be around him. He gets on my nerves. He's my brother and I love him, don't get me wrong. I just don't like him much." She wrinkled her nose. "He always smells like garlic and sweat and that nasty Brut cologne. I don't know why men wear it. Such a turnoff."

"Have you heard any gossip about the warehouse blaze?"

"Just what Terry's told me. You know Lance borrowed money against the company two years ago and now he's losing his shirt. He'd love half a million bucks."

"Oh really. That's the first I heard of it."

She shrugged carelessly. "He went into the printing business, which is foolish in itself. I've heard printing and restaurants are the quickest way to go broke. He's lucky the warehouse burned down. Or is that the point?"

"Why don't you tell me?"

She rested her elbow on her knee and propped her chin up on her fist. "If you're looking for answers, I've just run out. I don't care about Lance. I don't care about Wood/Warren, to tell you the truth. Sometimes the politics amuse me in a soap-opera kind of way, like *Dynasty*, but it's still boring stuff."

"What *do* you care about?"

"Tennis. Travel. Clothes. Golf. What else is there?"

"Sounds like a fun life."

"Actually, it is. I entertain. I do charity work when I have the time. There are people who think I'm a spoiled, lazy bitch, but I have what I want. That's more than most can say. It's the have-nots who wreak havoc. I'm a real pussycat."

"You're fortunate."

"Like they say, there's no such thing as a free ride. I pay a price, believe me."

I could see what an exhausting proposition that must be.

We heard someone at the entrance, then footsteps along the hall. By the time Terry Kohler reached the bedroom door, he was already in the process of removing his coat and tie.

"Hello, Kinsey. Olive mentioned you'd be stopping by. Let me grab a quick shower and then we can talk." He looked at Olive. "Could you fetch us a drink?" he said, his tone peremptory.

She didn't exactly perk up and pant, but that's the impression she gave. Maybe her job was harder than I thought. I wouldn't do that for anyone.

13

I waited in the living room while Olive stepped into the kitchen. The place was handsome; beveled windowpanes, pecan paneling, a fieldstone fireplace, traditional furniture in damask and mahogany. Everything was rose and dusty pink. The room smelled faintly spicy, like carnations. I couldn't imagine the two of them sitting here doing anything. Aside from the conventional good taste, there was no indication that they listened to music or read books. No evidence of shared interests. There was a current copy of *Architectural Digest* on the coffee table, but it looked like a prop. I've never known rich people to read *Popular Mechanics*, *Family Circle*, or *Road & Track*. Come to think of it, I have no idea what they do at night.

Olive returned in ten minutes with a tray of hors d'oeuvres and a silver cooler with a wine bottle nestled in ice. Her entire manner had changed since Terry walked in the door. She still had an air of elegance, but her manner was tinged now with servitude. She fussed with small linen cocktail napkins, arranging them in a pattern near the serving plate she'd placed at one end of the coffee table. She'd prepared ripe figs stuffed with mascarpone cheese, triangles of phyllo, and chilled new potato halves topped with sour cream and caviar. If I called this my dinner, would all of my nutritional needs be met?

Olive crossed briskly to a sideboard and set out liquor bottles so we'd have a choice of drinks. The room was beginning to darken and she turned on two table lamps. The panels of her taffeta skirt made a silky scritching sound

99

every time she moved. Her legs were well muscled and the spike heels threw her calves into high relief.

I glanced over to see Terry standing in the doorway, freshly showered and dressed, his gaze lingering on the picture she presented. He caught my eye, smiling with the barest suggestion of proprietorship. He didn't look like an easy man to please.

"Gorgeous house," I said.

Olive looked over with a rare smile. "Thanks," she said.

"Have a seat," he said.

"I don't want to hold you up."

Terry waved dismissively, as if the pending conversation took precedence. The gesture had the same ingratiating effect as someone who tells his secretary to hold all the calls. It's probably bullshit . . . maybe no one ever calls anyway . . . but it gives the visitor a feeling of importance.

"He'd never pass up a chance to talk business," Olive said. She handed him a martini and then glanced at me. "What would you like?"

"The white wine, if I may."

While I looked on, she opened the bottle, pouring a glass for me and then one for herself. She handed me mine and then eased out of her shoes and took a seat on the couch, tucking her feet up under her. She seemed softer, less egotistical. The role of helpmeet suited her, which surprised me, somehow. She was a woman who had no apparent purpose beyond indulging herself and pampering "her man." The notion seemed outdated in a world of career women and supermoms.

Terry perched on the arm of the couch, staring at me with guarded interest. He took charge of the conversation, a move he must have been accustomed to. His dark eyes gave his narrow face a brooding look, but his manner was pleasant. He made only an occasional digital reference to the fact of his moustache. I've seen men who stroke their facial hair incessantly, as if it were the last remnant of a baby bunting, comforting and soft. "Lance says someone tried to frame you," he said. He ate a new-potato half and passed the plate to me.

"Looks that way," I said. I helped myself to a fig. Heaven on the tongue.

"What do you need from us?"

"For starters, I'm hoping you can fill me in on Ava Daugherty."

"Ava? Sure. What's she got to do with it?"

"She was there the day I did the fire-scene inspection. She also saw Heather give me the envelope full of inventory sheets, which have since disappeared."

His gaze shifted and I watched him compose his reply before he spoke. "As far as I know, Ava's straight as an arrow. Hardworking, honest, devoted to the company."

"What about Lance? How does she get along with him?"

"I've never heard them exchange a cross word. He's the one who hired her, as a matter of fact, when it was clear we needed an office manager."

"How long ago was that?"

"God, it must be two, three years now," he said. He looked down at Olive, sitting close by. "What's your impression? Am I reporting accurately?"

Olive shrugged. "Well, I wouldn't say she's crazy about him. She thinks he plays too much when he ought to be getting work done, but I don't think she'd devise any scheme to do him in." Olive passed the hors d'oeuvre tray to me. I thought it only gracious to sample something else so I selected a potato half and popped it in my mouth.

"Who might?" I asked, licking sour cream from my thumb. This shit was great. If they'd just leave the room for a minute, I'd have a go at the rest.

Both seemed to come up blank.

"Come on. He must have enemies. Somebody's gone to a lot of trouble over this," I said.

Terry said, "At the moment, I couldn't name one, but we can give it some thought. Maybe something will occur to us."

"What can you tell me about the Wood/Warren engineer who killed himself?"

"Hugh Case," Olive said.

Terry seemed surprised. "What brought that up? I just got a call from Lyda Case this afternoon."

"Really?" I said. "What did she have to say?"

"It wasn't what she said so much as her attitude. She was completely freaked out, screaming at the top of her lungs. Said his death was my fault."

Olive looked at him in disbelief. "Yours? What bullshit! Why would she say that?"

"I have no idea. She sounded drunk. Ranting and raving. Foulmouthed, shrill."

"That's curious," I said. "Is she here in town?"

Terry shook his head. "She didn't say. The call was long distance from the sound of it. Where's she live?"

"Dallas, I believe."

"I got the impression she intended to fly out. Do you want to talk to her if she shows up?"

"Yes, I'd like that," I said, careful to omit any reference to the fact that I'd met with her the night before. She hadn't seemed paranoid to me at all and she'd never mentioned Terry's name.

Olive stirred on the couch, shifting positions. "Just in time for New Year's. Everyone'll be here." She glanced at Terry. "Did I tell you Bass gets in tonight?"

A look of annoyance flashed across his face. "I thought he was broke. I hope you didn't pay his way."

"Me! Absolutely not. Ebony sends him money, but you wouldn't catch me doing it," she remarked. And then to me, "Bass and I had a falling-out at Thanksgiving and we haven't spoken since. He's got a big mouth in matters that are none of his business. I think he's loathsome, and he's just about that fond of me."

Terry glanced at his watch and I took that as my cue. "I should let you go if you've got a party," I said.

"I don't feel we've been any help," Olive said.

"Don't worry about it. I've got other sources. Just let me know if you come up with anything you think might pertain."

I left my card on the coffee table. Terry walked me to the door while Olive excused herself to fetch her coat. He watched her disappear into the bedroom. "I didn't want to mention this in front of her," he said, "but Lyda Case scared the shit out of me this afternoon."

"How so?"

"I don't want to make Olive nervous, but the woman threatened me. I don't think it has anything to do with Lance or I'd have said so up front. This is different. I don't know what it's about, but she really sounded cracked."

"What kind of threat?" I asked.

"Out of nowhere, she asked me how old I'd be on my next birthday. I didn't know what she was getting at, but when I told her I'd be forty-six, she said, 'Don't count on it.' And then she laughed like a fiend. Jesus, the sound made my blood run cold. I can't believe she was serious, but my God! What a thing to say."

"And you have no idea why she suddenly got in touch?"

"I haven't talked to her for years. Since Hugh died, I guess."

"I understand there's some question about the manner of his death."

"I've heard that too and I don't know what to think."

"How well did you know him?"

"I wouldn't say we were close, but I worked with him, oh, probably five years or so. He never struck me as the sort who'd commit suicide. Of course, you never know what someone under pressure will do."

"Pressure?"

"Lyda'd threatened to leave him. Hugh was a sweet guy, but he was terribly dependent on her and I think it just knocked the props out from under him."

"Why was she leaving? What was that about?"

"I wasn't privy to the details. Lance might know."

Olive reappeared, white fur coat across her shoulders, the green dress over her arm. Terry and I abandoned the topic of Lyda Case. He made no comment when she gave me the dress. Maybe Olive always gave away her clothes. The three of us left the house together, confining ourselves to small talk.

It was fully dark by then and the night was chilly. I turned on the heater in my car and drove to a pay phone in Montebello Village, putting a call in to Darcy at home. I wanted to stop off and see her before I went back to my place. But she told me Andy'd worked late, so she hadn't had a chance to search his office. She was going in early the next morning, and said she'd call if she came up with anything.

I hung up, realizing then how exhausted I felt. In addition to the jet lag, I was operating on a bad night's sleep, and the fragmentary nap I'd picked up this morning wasn't helping anything. I headed home. As I turned the corner onto my street, I spotted Daniel's rental car, still sitting at the curb in front of my apartment. I parked and got out. Even in the dark, I could see him slouched in the front seat, feet on the dash as they had been before. I was just opening the gate when he rolled down his window. "Can I talk to you?"

I felt something snappish rise up in me, but I forced it back down again. I don't like being bitchy, and I hated admitting to myself that he still had the power to distress. "All right," I said. I approached the car and halted about six feet away. "What is it?"

He unfolded himself and emerged from the car, leaning his elbows on the open car door. The pale glow from the street light gilded his cheekbones, touching off strands of silver in the cloud of blond hair.

"I'm in a bit of a bind," he said. His face was dappled with shadows that masked the remembered clear blue of his eyes. After eight years, it was amazingly painful just to be in his company.

I thought the safest course was to repeat information back to him without comment. "You're in a bind," I said. There was a brief silence wherein I assumed I was meant to quiz him on the nature of his problem. I clamped my teeth together, waiting patiently.

He smiled ruefully. "Don't worry. I'm not going to ask you for money and I'm not trying to get in your pants."

"This comes as a big relief, Daniel. What *do* you want?" The bitchy tone was already back, but I swear I couldn't help myself. There's nothing more infuriating than a man who's manipulated your emotions once and now thinks he can do it again. I could still remember the charge that ran between us early in our relationship, sexual electricity infusing the very air we breathed. It had taken years for me to realize that I had generated most of it myself out of my own neediness. Maybe that's what was making me so churlish in retrospect. I was still chafing at myself for what a fool I'd been.

"I need a place to stash my gear," he said.

"What gear?"

He shrugged. "I got a two-thousand-dollar acoustic guitar I can't leave because the trunk lock is busted on the rental car I picked up. It'll get ripped off if it's in the back seat."

"You brought a guitar like that all the way from Florida?"

"I thought maybe I'd pick up a gig out here. I could use the bucks."

"What happened to your friend? I thought you got a ride with someone. Why not take it to his place? Or is it a woman? I guess I never asked you that."

"Well, no, it's a guy," he said. "The problem is, he doesn't actually live here in town. He was just passing through on his way to San Francisco and he won't be back till late on Sunday. That's why I had to rent a car of my own."

"Where are you staying? Don't you have a place?"

"I'm working on that. The town's booked solid because of the holidays. Meantime, I can't even pull into a gas station to take a leak without hauling everything in with me. It's just for a couple of days."

I stared at him. "You always do things like this, you know that? You're always in a bind, shifting your weight from foot to foot, hoping someone'll bail you out of the hole you're in. Try the Rescue Mission. Pick up a woman. That shouldn't be so tough. Or sell the damn thing. Why is it up to me?"

"It's not up to you," he said mildly. "It's a simple favor. What's the big deal?"

I ran out of steam. We'd had this same exchange a hundred times and he'd never heard me before. I might as well save my breath. I might as well give him what he wanted and get it over with. It was probably just an elaborate excuse to prolong our contact. "Never mind," I said. "No big deal. You can park the damn thing in a corner until Sunday and then I want it out of here."

"Sure. No problem. Thanks."

"I'm warning you, Daniel. If you've got a stash anywhere within six blocks of here, I'll call the cops."

"I'm clean. I told you that. You can look for yourself."

"Skip it," I said. I knew him well enough to know he wouldn't bluff on that, because he knew *me* well enough to know I'd have him thrown in the slammer if I caught him.

14

I took a couple of Tylenols and slept like a stone—deep, dreamless sleep that soothed my frazzled nerves and restored my good spirits. I was up at 6:00, ready to jog as usual. There was no sign of Daniel parked at my curb. I did a perfunctory stretch against the fence post and headed toward Cabana Boulevard.

The run felt great. The sky was a pearl gray streaked with pink. To my right, a dark-gray surf boomed against the hard-packed sand, leaving snowy froth in its wake. The wharf was mirrored in the glistening pools that remained when the waves receded. The sea seemed to shush the birds that shrieked overhead. This was the last day of the year and I ran with a sense of optimism the new year always brings. I'd find a way to sort it all out: Lance, Mac's suspicions about me, even Daniel's sudden appearance on my doorstep. I was alive and healthy, physically fit. Rosie's would open again on Monday. Henry would be home in another six days. I had the sassy green dress Olive had given me, and maybe a New Year's invitation if she came through as hoped. I did my three miles and slowed to a walk, cooling off as I headed home.

I showered and dressed in jeans as usual, savoring the morning at home. By then it was 7:00—too early for phone calls. I ate my cereal and read the *L.A. Times* over two cups of coffee. Daniel's guitar sat in the corner in mute testimony to his renewed presence in my life, but I ignored it for the most part.

Darcy called at 7:35 from California Fidelity. She'd done a thorough search. Andy's office was clean.

"Shit," I said. "What about a typewriter? I was hoping we could get a match on the phony fire department report, but I didn't find one at his apartment."

"Maybe he keeps it in the trunk of his car."

"Oh, I like that. I'll see if I can find a way to check that out. In the meantime, keep an eye peeled. Maybe something will surface. Andy's gotta be tied into this business somehow. It would help a lot to know who he knows at Wood/Warren. Did you go through his Rolodex?"

"That won't help. He knows all those guys because that was his account. He's bound to have the number handy. I'll check it out, though. Maybe something else will come to light." She clicked off.

At 8:00, I put a call through to Lyda Case in Texas. Her roommate said she was out of town, maybe in California, but she wasn't sure. I left my number and asked her to have Lyda get in touch with me if she called home.

I called my pal at the credit bureau, but she was out until Monday. I had the feeling the rest of the day was going to come down about the same way. It was New Year's Eve day. As with Christmas Eve, businesses were closing early, people taking off at noon. Olive called me at 10:00 to say that she was indeed putting together an impromptu cocktail party. "It's mostly family and a few close friends. Half the people I called already had plans. Are you free? We'd love to have you, if you're not already tied up."

"Of course I'm not," I said. "I'd love to come." I hated to sound so eager, but in truth I was. I didn't want to spend this New Year's Eve alone. I was worried Daniel might start looking too good. "Can I bring anything?"

"Actually I could use some help," she said. "I gave the housekeeper the weekend off, so I'm throwing the whole thing together by myself. I can always use an extra set of hands."

"Well, I'm not a cook, but I can sure chop and stir. What time?"

"Four-thirty? I'll be back from the supermarket by then. Ash said she'd come about five to help, too. Everybody else will be coming about seven. We'll keep going till the food and alcohol give out."

"Great," I said. "And the green dress will be okay?"

"It better be. I'm giving this party so you can wear the damn thing."

I put a call through to Lance. I didn't like initiating the contact with him, but I had to hear his version of the situation with Hugh Case. As soon as he was on the line, I told him what I'd heard. The silence was weighty. "Lance?"

"I'm here," he said. He sighed heavily. "Jesus, I don't know how to deal with this. What the hell is going on? I heard rumors back then she thought I had something to do with his death. It's not true. It's completely untrue, but I don't have a way of proving it. Why would I do that? What could I possibly gain by killing him?"

"Wasn't he leaving the company?"

"Absolutely not. He talked about quitting. He said he wanted to start a company of his own. He even gave notice, but hell, Dad called him in and they had a long talk. Dad offered to make him a vice-president. Gave him a big raise and he was happy as a clam."

"When was this?"

"I don't know. A couple of days before he died."

"Didn't that strike you as peculiar?"

"Sure it did. She swore he didn't kill himself and I agreed. He wasn't the depressive type and he'd just made a hell of a deal for himself. Somehow she got it in her head that I killed the man. I wouldn't harm a soul. You gotta believe me. Somebody's working very hard to get me put away."

"Speaking of which, have you heard anything from California Fidelity?"

His tone changed. "Yeah, yesterday. They're turning everything over to the cops."

I could feel my stomach clench. "Really? Do they have enough to make a case?"

"I don't know. I hope not. Look, I need to talk to you privately and I can't do it here. It's important. Is there any way we can meet?"

I told him I'd be at Olive's later and we agreed to talk then. I wasn't anxious to be seen in his company, but he seemed insistent, and at that point, I didn't see how things could get worse. I wasn't guilty of conspiracy and I was

tired of acting like I was. Worry was sitting on my chest like
a weight, leaden and oppressive. I had to do something to
get my mind off things.

I went out and bought a pair of high heels, anxiety
translating into excitement as the day progressed. Being
isolated that week had made me aware that I do have a few
social impulses—buried deep, perhaps, under layers of
caution, but part of me nevertheless. This was like dress-up
time with the big kids, and I was looking forward to it. I'd
begun to feel very charitable about Olive, whose life-style
only yesterday had seemed superficial and self-indulgent.
Who was I to judge? It was none of my business how she
made her peace with the world. She'd fashioned a life out
of tennis and shopping, but she managed to do occasional
charity work, which was more than I could claim. She was
right about one thing: the harm in the world is done by
those who feel disenfranchised and abused. Contented
people (as a rule) don't kite checks, rob banks, or kill their
fellow citizens.

I thought about going to the gym, but decided to bag
that idea. I hadn't done a workout since Tuesday, but I just
didn't give a damn. I puttered and napped through the
middle of the day.

At 3:00 I took a long bubble bath . . . well, I used
dishwashing liquid, but it did foam right up. I washed my
hair and combed it for a change. I did some stuff to my face
that passed for makeup in my book, and then wiggled into
underwear and panty hose. The dress was grand, and it fit
like a charm, rustling the same way Olive's had the night
before. I'd never had a role model for this female stuff.
After my parents' death when I was five, I'd been raised by
a maiden aunt, no expert herself at things feminine. I'd
spent the days of my childhood with cap guns and books,
learning self-sufficiency, which loomed large with her. By
the time I reached junior high I was a complete misfit, and
by high school I'd thrown in my lot with some bad-ass boys
who cussed and smoked dope, two things I mastered at an
early age. In spite of the fact that I'm a social oaf, my aunt
instilled a solid set of values, which prevailed in the end.
By the time I graduated, I'd straightened up my act and
now I'm a model citizen, give or take a civil code or two. At

heart, I've always been a prissy little moralist. Private investigation is just my way of acting out.

By 4:30, I was standing on the Kohlers' doorstep, listening to the door chime echo through the house. It didn't look as if anyone was there. There was mail jammed in the box, the newspaper and a brown paper-wrapped parcel on the mat. I peered into one of the long glass panels on either side of the front door. The foyer was dark and no lights were showing at the rear of the house. Olive probably wasn't home from the supermarket yet. The cat appeared from around the side of the house with her long white coat and flat face. Somehow she seemed like a girl to me, but what do I know? I said some cat-type things. She appeared unimpressed.

I heard a car horn toot. The electronic gate was rolled back from the driveway and a white Mercedes 380 SL pulled in. Olive waved and I moved toward the parking pad. She got out of the car and moved around to the rear, looking very classy in her white fur coat.

"Sorry I'm late. Have you been here long?"

"Five minutes."

She opened the trunk and picked up one grocery bag, then struggled to lift a second.

"Here, let me help with that."

"Oh, thanks. Terry should be right behind me with the liquor."

I took the bag, snagging up another one while I was at it. There were two more in the trunk and another two bags visible in the front seat. "God, how many people did you invite?"

"Just forty or so. It should be fun. Let's get these in and we'll have Terry bring the rest. We've got a ton of work to do."

She moved toward the front door while I brought up the rear. There was a crunch of tires on gravel and Terry pulled into the drive in a silver-gray Mercedes sedan. Must be nice, I thought. The gate rolled shut. I waited while Olive emptied the mailbox and shoved the stack of envelopes in the top of her grocery bag. She picked up the newspaper and tucked that in, too, then grabbed the parcel.

"You need help? I can take something else."

"I got it." She laid the parcel across the bag, securing it with her chin while she fumbled for her house key.

The cat was sauntering toward the driveway, plumed tail aloft. I heard the clink of liquor bottles as Terry set his bags down on the concrete. He began to coil up a garden hose the yardman had left on the walk.

"Break your neck on this thing," he said. Olive got the door open and gave it a push. The telephone started to ring. I glanced back as she tossed the parcel toward the hall table.

What happened next was too swift to absorb. There was a flash of light, a great burst that filled my visual field like a sun, followed by a huge cloud of white smoke. Shrapnel shot from a central point, spraying outward with a deadly velocity. A fireball seemed to curl across the threshold like a wall of water with a barrier removed, washing flames into the grass. Every blade of green in its path turned black. At the same time, I was lifted by a shattering low-frequency boom that hurtled me capriciously across the yard. I found myself sitting upright against a tree trunk like a rag doll, shoes gone, toes pointing straight up. I saw Olive fly past me as if she'd been yanked, tumbling in a high comic arc that carried her to the hedge and dropped her in a heap. My vision shimmered and cleared, a light show of the retina, accompanied by the breathless thumping of my heart. My brain, mute with wonder, failed to compute anything but the smell of black powder, pungent and harsh.

The explosion had deafened me, but I felt neither fear nor surprise. Emotions are dependent on comprehension, and while I registered the event, nothing made any sense. Had I died in that moment, I would not have felt the slightest shred of regret, and I understood how liberating sudden death must be. This was pure sensation with no judgment attached.

The front wall of the house was gone and a crater appeared where the hall table had been. The foyer was open to the air, surrounded by coronas of charred wood and plaster, burning merrily. Large flakes of pale blue and pale brown floated down like snow. Grocery items littered the entire yard, smelling of pickles, cocktail onions, and Scotch. I had taken in both sight and sound, but the apparatus of evaluation hadn't caught up with me yet. I had no idea what had happened. I couldn't remember what had transpired only moments before, or how this might relate to past events. Here we were in this new configuration, but how had it come to pass?

From the change in light, I guessed that my eyebrows and lashes must be gone and I was conscious of singed hair and flash burns. I put a hand up, amazed to find my limbs still functioning. I was bleeding from the nose, bleeding from both ears, where the pain was now excruciating. To my left, I could see Terry's mouth working, but no words were coming out. Something had struck him a glancing blow and blood poured down his face. He appeared to be in pain, but the movie was silent, sound reel flapping ineffectually. I turned to see where Olive was.

For one confused moment, I thought I saw a pile of torn foxes, their bloodied pelts confirming what she'd said the day before. It *is* true, I thought, these animals in the wild get ripped to shreds every day. The harsh splattering of red against the soft white fur seemed obscene and out of place. And then, of course, I understood what I was looking at. The blast had opened her body, exposing tangles of bloody flesh, yellow fat, and jagged bone along her backside. I closed my eyes. By then, the smell of black powder was overlaid with the scent of woodsmoke and cooked flesh. Carefully I pondered the current state of affairs.

Olive had to be dead, but Terry seemed okay, and I thought perhaps at some point he would come and help me up. No hurry, I thought. I'm comfy for now. The tree trunk provided back support, which helped, as I was tired. Idly, I wondered where my shoes had gone. I sensed movement, and when I opened my eyes again, confused faces were peering into mine. I couldn't think what to say. I'd already forgotten what was going on, except that I was cold.

Time must have passed. Men in yellow slickers pointed hoses at the house, swords of water cutting through the flames. Worried people crouched in front of me and worked their mouths some more. It was funny.

They didn't seem to realize they weren't saying anything. So solemn, so animated, and so intent. Lips and teeth moving to such purpose with no visible effect. And then I was on my back, looking up into tree branches that wobbled through my visual field as I was borne away. I closed my eyes again, wishing that the reeling of the world would stop before I got sick. In spite of the fire, I was shivering.

15

Gradually my hearing returned, pale voices in the distance coming nearer until I understood that it was someone bending over me. Daniel, as radiant as an archangel, appeared above me. The sight of him was baffling, and I felt an incredible urge to put a hand to my forehead, like a movie heroine recovering from a swoon, murmuring, Where am I? I was probably dead. Surely, hell is having your former spouse that close again . . . flirting with a nurse. Ah, I thought, a clue. I was in a hospital bed. She was standing to his right, in polyester white, a vestal virgin with a bedpan, her gaze fixed on his perfect features in profile. I'd forgotten how cunning he was at that sort of thing. While he feigned grave concern for me, he was actually casting backward with his little sexual net, enveloping her in a fine web of pheromones. I moved my lips and he leaned closer. He said, "I think she's conscious."

"I'll get the doctor," the nurse said. She disappeared.

Daniel stroked my hair. "What is it, babe? Are you in pain?"

I licked my lips. "Asshole," I said, but it came out all garbled and I wasn't sure he got the drift. I vowed, in that moment, to get well enough to throw him out. I closed my eyes.

I remembered the flash, the deafening bang, Olive flying past me like a mannequin. She had looked unreal, arms crooked, legs askew, as lumpen as a sandbag flung through the air, landing with a sodden thump.

Olive must be dead. There wasn't any way to mend the parts of her turned inside out by the blast.

I remembered Terry with the blood gushing down his face. Was he dead, too? I looked at Daniel, wondering how bad it was.

Daniel sensed my question. "You're fine, Kin. Everything's okay. You're in the hospital and Terry's here, too," he said. And after a hesitation, "Olive didn't make it."

I closed my eyes again, hoping he'd go away.

I concentrated on my various body parts, hoping that all of them could be accounted for. Many treasured portions of my anatomy hurt. I thought at first I was in some sort of bed restraint, but it turned out to be an immobilizing combination of bruises, whiplash, IV fluids, painkillers, and pressure dressings on the areas where I had suffered burns. Given the fact that I'd been standing ten feet away from Olive, my injuries turned out to be miraculously insignificant—contusions and abrasions, mild concussion, superficial burns on my extremities. I'd been hospitalized primarily for shock.

I was still confused about what had happened, but it didn't take a 160 IQ to figure out that something had gone boom in a big way. A gas explosion. More likely a bomb. The sound and the impact were both characteristic of low explosives. I know now, because I looked it up, that low explosives have velocities of 3,300 feet per second, which is much faster than the average person tends to move. That short trip from Olive's front porch to the tree base was as close to free flight as I was ever going to get.

The doctor came in. She was a plain woman with a good face and sense enough to ask Daniel to leave the room while she examined me. I liked her because she didn't lapse into a slack-jawed stupor at the sight of him. I watched her, as trusting as a child while she checked my vital signs. She must have been in her late thirties, with haphazard hair, no makeup, gray eyes that poured out compassion and intelligence. She held my hand, lacing her cool fingers through mine. "How are you feeling?"

Tears welled up. I saw my mother's face superimposed on hers, and I was four again, throat raw from a tonsillectomy. I'd forgotten what it was like to experience the warmth radiated by those who tend the sick. I was saturated by a tenderness I hadn't felt since my mother died. I don't take well to helplessness. I've worked hard in my life to deny neediness, and there I was, unable to sustain any pretense of toughness or competence. In some ways it came as a great relief to lie there in a puddle and give myself up to her nurturing.

By the time she'd finished checking me, I was somewhat more alert, anxious to get my bearings. I quizzed her in a foggy way, trying to get a fix on my current state.

She told me I was in a private room at St. Terry's, having been admitted, through Emergency, the night before. I remembered, in fragments, some of it: the high keening of sirens as the ambulance swayed around corners, the harsh white light above me in the Emergency Room, the murmurs of the medical personnel assigned to evaluate my injuries. I remembered how soothing it was when I was finally tucked into bed: clean, patched up, pumped full of medications, and feeling no pain. It was now mid-morning of New Year's Day. I was still groggy, and I discovered belatedly that I was dropping off to sleep without even being aware of it.

The next time I woke, the IV had been removed and the doctor had been replaced by a nurse's aide who helped me onto the bedpan, cleaned me up again, changed my gown, and put fresh sheets on the bed, cranking me into a sitting position so I could see the world. It was nearly noon. I was famished by then and wolfed down a dish of cherry Jell-O the aide rustled up from somewhere. That held me until the meal carts arrived on the floor. Daniel had gone down to the hospital cafeteria for lunch, and by the time he got back, I'd requested a "No Visitors" sign hung on the door.

The restrictions must not have applied to Lieutenant Dolan, however, because the next thing I knew, he was sitting in the chair, leafing through a magazine. He's in his fifties, a big, shambling man, with scuffed shoes and a lightweight beige suit. He looked exhausted from the horizontal lines across his forehead to his sagging jawline, which was ill-shaved. His thinning hair was rumpled. He had bags under his eyes and his color was bad. I had to guess that he'd been out late the night before, maybe looking forward to a day of football games on TV instead of interviewing me.

He looked up from his magazine and saw that I was awake. I've known Dolan for maybe five years, and while we respect each other, we're never at ease. He's in charge of the homicide detail of the Santa Teresa Police Department, and we sometimes cross swords. He's not fond of private investigators and I'm not fond of having to defend my occupational status. If I could find a way to avoid homicide cases, believe me, I would.

"You awake?" he said.

"More or less."

He set the magazine aside and got up, shoving his hands in his coat pockets while he stood by my bed. All my usual sassiness had been, quite literally, blown away. Lieutenant Dolan didn't seem to know how to handle me in my subdued state. "You feel well enough to talk about last night?"

"I think so."

"You remember what happened?"

"Some. There was an explosion and Olive was killed."

Dolan's mouth pulled down. "Died instantly. Her husband survived, but he's blanking on things. Doctor says it'll come back to him in a day or two. You got off light for someone standing right in the path."

"Bomb?"

"Package bomb. Black powder, we think. I have the bomb techs on it now, cataloguing evidence. What about the parcel? You see anything?"

"There was a package on the doorstep when I got there."

"What time was that?"

"Four-thirty. Little bit before. The Kohlers were having a New Year's Eve party and she asked me to help." I filled him in briefly on the circumstances of the party. I could feel myself reviving, my thoughts gradually becoming more coherent.

"Tell me what you remember about the parcel."

"There isn't much. I only glanced at it once. Brown paper. No string. Block lettering, done with a Magic Marker from the look of it. I saw it upside down."

"The address facing the door," he said. He took out a little spiral-bound notebook and a pen.

"Right."

"Who's it sent to?"

"Terry, I think. Not 'Mr. and Mrs.' because the line of print wasn't that long. Even upside down, I'd have noticed the 'O' in Olive's name."

He was jotting notes. "Return address?"

"Uhn–un. I don't remember any postmark either. There might have been a UPS number, but I didn't see one."

"You're doing pretty good," he said. "The regular mailman says he only delivered hand mail yesterday, no packages at all. UPS had no record of a delivery to that address. They didn't even have a truck in the area. You didn't see anyone leave the premises?"

I tried to think back, but I was drawing a blank. "Can't help you there. I don't remember anyone on foot. A car might have passed, but I can't picture it."

I closed my eyes, visualizing the porch. There were salmon begonias in big tubs along the front. "Oh, yeah. The newspaper was on the doormat. I don't know how far up the walk the paperboy comes, but he might have seen the parcel when he was doing his route."

He made another note. "We'll try that. What about dimensions?"

I could feel myself shrug. "Size of a shirt box. Bigger than a book. Nine by twelve inches by three. Was there anything left of it?"

"More than you'd think. We believe there was gift wrap under the brown mailing paper. Blue."

"Oh sure," I said, startled. "I remember seeing flakes of brown and blue. I thought it was snow, but it must have been paper particles." I remembered what Terry had said to me. "Something else," I said. "Terry was threatened. He talked about it when I was there the night before. He had a phone call at the plant from a woman named Lyda Case. She asked him when his birthday was and when he told her, she said he shouldn't count on it."

I filled him in on the rest, unburdening the sequence of events from the first. For once, I loved offloading the information on him. This was big time . . . the heavy hitters . . . more than I could deal with by myself. When it came down to bombs, I was out of my league. Lieutenant Dolan was scratching notes at a quick clip, his expression that mask of studied neutrality all cops tend to wear—taking in everything, giving nothing back. He talked as if he was already on the witness stand. "So there's a chance she's in Santa Teresa. Is that what you're saying?"

"I don't know. He seemed to think she was coming out, but he was pretty vague on that point. He's here, too?" I asked.

"This floor. Other end of the hall."

"You care if I talk to him?"

"No, not a bit. Might help jog his memory."

After Lieutenant Dolan left, I eased into a sitting position on the edge of the bed, feet dangling over the side. My head was pounding at the sudden exertion. I sat and waited for the light show inside my head to fade. I studied as much of my body as I could see.

My legs looked frail under the lightweight cotton of the hospital gown, which tied at the back and let in lots of air. The pattern of bruises across my front looked like someone had taken a powder puff and dusted me with purple talc. My hands were bandaged and I could see an aura of angry red flesh along my inner arms where the burns tapered off. I held onto the handrail and slid off the bed, supporting myself on the bed table. My legs were trembling. I could almost bet they didn't want me getting up this way. I didn't think it was such a hot idea myself, the more I thought of it. Nausea and clamminess were chiming in with the pounding in my head and a fuzzy darkness was gathering along the periphery of my vision. I wasn't going to win an award for this so I sat back down.

There was a tap at the door and the nurse came in. "Your husband's out here. He says he has to leave and he'd like to see you before he goes."

"He's not my husband," I said automatically.

She put her hands in the pockets of her uniform—a tunic over white pants, no cap. I only knew she was a nurse because her plastic name tag had an R.N. after her name, which was Sharie Wright. I studied her covertly, knowing how much Daniel liked women with names like that. Debbie and Tammie and Cindie. Candie loomed large in there, too. I guess Kinsey qualified, now that I thought of it. Kinsie. Infidelity reduces and diminishes, leaving nothing where you once had a sense of self-worth.

"He's been worried sick," she said. "I know it's none of my business, but he was here all night. I thought you should be aware." She saw that I was struggling to get settled in the bed and she gave me a hand. I guessed that she was twenty-six. I was twenty-three when I married him, twenty-four when he left. No explanation, no discussion. The divorce was no-fault, served up in record time.

"Is there a way I can get a wheelchair? There's someone down the hall I'd like to see. The man who was admitted at the same time I was."

"Mr. Kohler. He's in three-oh-six at the end of the hall."

"How's he doing?"

"Fine. He's going home this afternoon."

"The policeman who was here a little while ago wants me to talk to him."

"What about your husband? He said it would only take two minutes."

"He's not my husband," I said, parrotlike, "but sure. Send him in. After he goes, could you find me a wheelchair? If I try to walk, I'll fall on my puss and have to sue this outfit."

She didn't think I was amusing and she didn't like the reference to lawsuits. She went out without a word. My husband, I thought. I should live so long.

16

He looked tired—an improvement, I thought. Daniel stood by my hospital bed, showing every minute of his forty-two years. "I know this won't sit well with you," he said, "but the doctor says she won't let you go home unless you have someone to look after you."

A feeling very like panic crept up in my chest. "I'll be fine in a day. I don't need anyone looking after me. I hate that idea."

"Well, I knew you would. I'm telling you what she said."

"She didn't mention it to me."

"She never had a chance. You were half zonked. She said she'd talk to you about it next time she made her rounds."

"They can't keep me here. That's disgusting. I'll go nuts."

"I already told her that. I just wanted you to know I'd be willing to help. I could get you signed out of here and settled at home. I wouldn't actually have to stay on the premises. That place of yours looks too small for more than one person anyway. But I could at least check on you twice a day, make sure you have everything you need."

"Let me think about it," I said grudgingly. But I could already see the bind I was in. With Henry gone, Rosie on vacation, and Jonah out of town, I'd be on my own. Truly, I wasn't feeling that good. I just couldn't make my body do what I wanted it to. The elderly, the feeble, and the infirm must experience the same exasperation and bewilderment. For once, my determination had nothing whatever to do with my proficiency. It was exhausting to sit up, and I knew perfectly well I couldn't manage much at home. Staying here was out of the question. Hospitals are dangerous. People make mistakes. Wrong blood, wrong medication, wrong surgeries, wrong tests. I was checking out of this place "toot sweet."

Daniel ran his hand across the top of my head. "Do what you want. I'll be back later."

He was gone again before I could protest.

I buzzed the nurses' station on the intercom.

A hollow voice came on. "Yes?"

"Can Mr. Kohler in three-oh-six have visitors?"

"As far as I know he can." The nurse sounded like she was talking into an old tin can, coughs and rustling in the background.

"Can I get a wheelchair? I'd like to go down and see him."

It was twenty minutes before anybody managed to find me one. In the meantime, I became aware that I was struggling with a depression generated by Olive's death. It wasn't as if we had had a relationship, but she'd been around on the borders of my life for years. I'd first seen her in high school when I met Ashley, but she'd left just before our junior year began. After that she was more rumor than fact . . . the sister who was always off somewhere else: boarding school, Switzerland, skiing in Utah with friends. I don't think we'd exchanged more than superficial chat until two days before, and then I'd found my opinion of her undergoing a shift. Now, death had smashed her like a bug, the blow as abrupt as a fly being swatted on a windowsill. The effect was jarring and the emotional impact hadn't worn off. I found myself turning images in my mind, trying to absorb the finality. I hadn't been consulted in the matter and I hadn't agreed. Death is insulting, and I resented its sudden appearance, like an unannounced visit from a boorish relative. I suspected the knot in my chest would be there for a long time; not grief per se, but a hard fist of regret.

I wheeled myself down the corridor to room 306. The door was closed and Bass was standing in the hall. He turned his head idly as I approached. Bass had the smooth good looks of someone in an eighteenth-century oil painting. His face was oval, boyish, his brow unlined, his eyes a barren brown. His mouth was sensual, his manner superior. Put him in a satin vest, a waistcoat, breeches, and leggings, and he might have been Blue Boy, grown slightly decadent. His hair was fine and dark, receding at the temples, worn slightly long and rather wispy where it gathered in a point on his forehead. He should have had an Afghan at his side, some creature with silky ears and a long, aristocratic snout.

"Hello, Bass. I'm Kinsey Millhone. Do you remember me?"

"Of course," he said. He bent down then and gave my cheek a social buss, more noise than contact. His expression was bleak. There was a dead time in the air, one of those uncomfortable stretched moments when you struggle to find something to say. His sister was dead. This was hardly the time for effusiveness, but I was puzzled by the awkwardness of our encounter.

"Where's Terry?"

He glanced at the door. "He's having his dressing changed. They should be done shortly. He's going home as soon as the doctor signs the release. How are you? We heard you were down the hall."

"I'm all right. I'm sorry about Olive," I said, and I truly was.

"God, this is all so screwed up. I don't know what's going on."

"How's your mother doing? Is she holding up all right?"

"She'll be okay. She's a tough old bird. She's taking it pretty hard, but she's got a spine of steel. Ash is destroyed. She's been leveled. She and Olive were always just like this," he said, holding up crossed fingers. "What about you? You look like you took a beating."

"I'm all right. This is the first time I've been out of bed and I feel like shit."

"You're lucky to be alive from what I hear."

"Lucky is right. I thought about picking the package up myself, but Olive's car pulled in and I went to help her with the groceries instead. Are you staying at your mother's?"

He nodded. "I got in Thursday night and then Olive called yesterday and said she was putting the party together. Seems like years ago. I was having a swim before I got dressed when Ebony showed up at the side of the pool. I couldn't figure out what was wrong with her. You know Eb. Always in control, never a hair out of place. Well, she looked like a wild woman. I pulled myself up on the side of the pool and she said a bomb had gone off at Olive's house and she was dead. I thought she was making the whole thing up. I laughed. It was so far-fetched, I couldn't help myself. She slapped the shit out of me and that's when I realized she was serious. What happened? Terry can't remember and the police won't tell us much."

I told him what I could, omitting the gruesome details of Olive's injuries. Even talking about it made me shake. I clamped my teeth shut, trying to relax. "Sorry," I said.

"It's my fault. I shouldn't have brought it up," he said. "I didn't mean to put you through it all again."

I shook my head. "That's fine. I'm okay. Nobody's told me much either. Honestly, I think it helps. The blanks are frustrating." I was looking for a narrative thread to hang fragments on. I'd lost the night. Everything from 4:30 on had been deleted from my memory bank.

He hesitated for a moment and then filled me in on events from his end. Ash had left. She was on her way to Olive's to help set up for the party. As soon as he heard about the explosion, he pulled some clothes on and he and Ebony jumped in the car. They arrived to find Terry being loaded into the ambulance. I was being bundled onto a stretcher, semiconscious. Olive was still lying near the shrubs, covered by a blanket.

Bass's recital of events was flat, like a news report. He was calm, his tone impersonal. He made no eye contact. I stared down the hall where a doctor with a somber expression was talking to an older couple sitting on a bench. The news must have been bad because the woman clutched and unclutched the purse in her lap.

I remembered then that I had seen Bass . . . one of the faces scrutinizing mine, bobbing above me like a balloon on a string. By then, shock had set in and I was shivering uncontrollably, in spite of the blankets they'd wrapped me in. I didn't remember Ebony. Maybe they had kept her out by the road, refusing to let her any closer to the carnage. The bomb had made tatters of Olive's flesh. Hunks of her body had been blown against the hedges, like clots of snow.

I put a hand against my face, feeling flushed with tears. Bass patted me awkwardly, murmuring nonsense, upset that he'd upset me, probably wondering how to get out of it. The emotion passed and I collected myself, taking a deep breath. "What about Terry's injuries?"

"Not bad. A cut on his forehead. Couple of cracked ribs where the blast knocked him into the garage. They wanted him in for observation, but he seems okay."

There was activity behind us and the door to Terry's room opened. A nurse came out bearing a stainless steel bowl full of soiled bandages. She seemed enveloped in aromas of denatured alcohol, tincture of iodine, and the distinctive smell of adhesive tape.

"You can go in now. Doctor said he can leave any time. We'll get a wheelchair for him when he's ready to go down."

Bass went in first. I wheeled myself in behind. A nurse's aide was straightening the bed table where the nurse had been working. Terry was sitting on the edge of the bed, buttoning up his shirt. I caught sight of his taped ribs through the loose flaps of his shirt and I looked away. His torso was stark white and hairless, his chest narrow and without musculature. Illness and injury seem so personal. I didn't want to know the details of his frailty.

He looked battered, with a dark track sketched along his forehead where the stitches had been put in. One wrist was bandaged, from cuts perhaps, or burns. His face was pale, his moustache stark, his dark hair disheveled. He seemed shrunken, as if Olive's death had diminished him.

Ebony appeared in the doorway, taking in the scene with a cursory glance. She hesitated, waiting for the aide to finish. The room seemed unbearably crowded. I needed fresh air.

"I'll come back in a minute," I murmured. I wheeled

myself out. Ebony followed me as far as the visitors' lounge, a small alcove with a green tweed couch, two matching chairs, an artificial palm, and an ashtray. She took a seat, searching through her handbag for her cigarettes. She lit one, sucking in smoke as if it were oxygen. She looked totally composed, but it was clear that the hospital atmosphere unsettled her. She picked a piece of lint from the lap of her skirt.

"I don't understand any of this," she said harshly. "Who'd want to kill Olive? She never did anything."

"Olive wasn't the target. It was Terry. The package with the bomb in it was addressed to him."

Ebony's gaze shot up to mine and hung there. A pale wash of pink appeared in the dead white of her face. The hand with the cigarette gave a lurch, almost of its own accord, and cigarette ash tumbled into her lap. She rose abruptly, brushing at it.

"That's ridiculous," she snapped. "The police said there was nothing left of the package once the bomb went off." She stubbed the cigarette out.

"Well, there was," I said. "Besides which, I saw it. Terry's name was printed on the front, not hers."

"I don't believe it." A wisp of smoke drifted up from the crushed cigarette stub. She snatched it up again, working the live ember out with her fingertips. She was shredding the remains of the cigarette. The strands of raw tobacco seemed obscene.

"I'm just telling you what I saw. Olive could have been the target, but the package was addressed to him."

"Bullshit! That *bastard*! Don't tell me Olive died because she picked it up instead of him!" Her eyes suffused with tears and she struggled for control. She got up, pacing with agitation.

I turned the wheelchair slightly, tracking her course. "What bastard, Ebony? Who are you referring to?"

She sat down abruptly, pressing the butts of both palms against her eyes. "No one. I'm sorry. I had no idea. I thought someone meant to kill her, which was horrible enough. But to die by mistake. My God! At least she didn't suffer. They swear she died instantly." She sobbed once.

She formed a tent of her hands, breathing hard into her palms.

"Do you know who killed her?"

"Of course not! Absolutely not! What kind of monster do you think I am? My own sister . . ." Her tone of outrage fell away and she wept earnestly. I wanted to believe her, but I couldn't be sure. I was tired, too close to events to sort out the false from the true. She lifted her face, which was washed with tears.

"Olive said she wasn't going to vote with you," I said, trying the possibility on her for size.

"You're such a bitch!" she shrieked at me. "How dare you! Get away from me!"

Bass appeared in the archway, his gaze turning to mine quizzically. I jammed backward on the push rim, pivoting in the wheelchair. I pushed myself down the corridor, passing a room where someone was calling for help in a low, hopeless tone. A clear plastic tube trailed from under the sheet to a gallon jug of urine under the bed. It looked like lemonade.

Olive usually brought the mail in. I'd seen her toss it on the hall table carelessly the day before. She might have been the intended victim even if the package *was* addressed to him. I really couldn't remember what she'd told me about who she was siding with in the power play between Ebony and Lance. Maybe he did it as a means of persuading the others to fall in line.

Darcy was waiting in my room when I got back. "Andy's gone," she said.

17

I eased myself back into bed while Darcy filled me in on the details. Andy had come whipping into the office at about 10:00 the day before. Mac had insisted on keeping office hours until 5:00, despite the fact that it was New Year's Eve day. Andy had a lunch meeting scheduled as well as a 2:00 appointment with one of the company vice-presidents. Darcy said Andy was in panic mode. She tried to give him his phone messages, but he cut her dead, hurried into his office, and began to load his personal items into his briefcase, along with his Rolodex. Next thing she knew, he was gone.

"It was too weird for words," she said. "He's never done anything like that before. And why the Rolodex? I'd already been through it and I didn't find a thing, but what made him think of that?"

"Maybe he's psychic."

"He'd have to be. Anyway, we didn't see him again for the rest of the day, so after work I hopped in my car and drove out to his place."

"You went all the way out to Elton?"

"Well, yeah. I just didn't like his attitude. He really had his undies in a bundle and I wanted to know what it was about. I didn't see his car parked anywhere near his apartment, so I went up and peeked in his front window. The place was a pigsty and all the furniture was gone. Maybe a card table in the living room, but that was it."

"That's all he's got," I said. "It looks like Janice took him for a bundle and she's clamoring for more."

"She can clamor all she wants, Kinsey, the man is

gone. His next-door neighbor saw me peering in the window and he came out and asked me what I was up to. I told him the truth. I said I worked with Andy and we were worried because he left the office in a snit without telling us what to do about his appointments. This guy claims he saw Andy going down the steps yesterday morning with two big suitcases banging against his legs. This was maybe nine-thirty, something like that. He must have come straight to the office, packed up his stuff, and taken off. I called his place every couple of hours last night and again this morning. All I get is his machine."

I thought about it briefly. "Did the newspapers carry an account of Olive's death?"

"Not till this morning and he was gone by then."

I could feel a surge of energy, part restlessness, part dread. I pushed the covers back and swung my legs over the side of the bed. "I've gotta get out of here."

"Are you supposed to be up?"

"Sure. No problem. Check the closet and see if Daniel brought me any clothes." The green cocktail dress was gone, probably dissected by a pair of surgical scissors in the emergency room the night before, along with my tatty underwear.

"It's empty, except for this," she said. She held up my handbag.

"Great. We're in business. As long as I've got my keys, I can get some clothes when I get home. I assume you've got a car here."

"Can you leave without a doctor's permission?"

"I got it. She told Daniel I could go as long as he looked in on me, which he said he would."

Darcy studied me uncertainly, probably guessing what I said was part fib.

"God, don't worry about it, Darcy. It's not against the law to check out of a hospital. It's not a prison sentence. I'm a volunteer," I said.

"What about your bill?"

"Would you quit being such a stickler? My insurance pays for this so I don't owe them anything. They've got my address. They'll find me if they need to."

Darcy was clearly unconvinced, but she shrugged and

helped me into the wheelchair, pushing me down the corridor toward the elevators. One of the nurse's aides stared at us as we went by, but I gave her a little wave and she apparently decided she didn't need to concern herself.

When we got downstairs, Darcy lent me her coat and left me in the glass foyer while she went to fetch the car. There I sat in my borrowed coat and little paper slippers, handbag in my lap. If my doctor walked by, I wasn't sure what I'd do. People passing through the foyer gave me cursory glances, but nobody said a word. Being sick is bullshit. I had work to do.

By 3:15 I was letting myself into my apartment, which already seemed to have the musty smell of neglect. I'd been gone one day, but it felt like weeks. Darcy came in behind me, her expression tinged with guilt when she saw that I was still shaky on my feet. I perched on the couch, momentarily clammy, and then set about getting dressed.

"What next?" she asked.

I was easing into my blue jeans. "Let's go into the office and see if Andy left anything behind," I said. I pulled on a sweatshirt and went into the bathroom, where I brushed my teeth. My reflection in the bathroom mirror showed a face marked by astonishment where my eyebrows used to be. My cheeks looked sunburned. I could see a few scrapes and bruises, but it was no big deal. I kind of liked having frizz across the front where my hair once was. I opened the medicine cabinet and took out my trusty nail scissors. I clipped the tape off my right arm and unwound the gauze, inspecting what was underneath. Looked okay to me. Burns do better in the open air, anyway. I took a painkiller just in case, and then waved dismissively at the sight of myself. I was fine.

I snagged the file folder I'd made after raiding Andy's trash. I put on some sweatsocks and tennis shoes, grabbing a jacket just before I locked up again. Santa Teresa usually gets chilly once the sun goes down and I wasn't sure how long I'd be gone.

Outside, it felt more like August than January. The sky was clear, the sun high overhead. There was no breeze at all, and the sidewalks were functioning like solar panels, absorbing the sunlight, throwing off heat. There was no sign of Daniel, for which I was grateful. He would no doubt have disapproved of my hospital defection. I spotted my little VW parked two doors down and I was glad somebody'd had the foresight to drive it back to my place. I wasn't up to driving yet, but it was nice to know the car was there.

Darcy drove us over to the office. There was scarcely any traffic. The whole downtown area seemed deserted, as if in the wake of nuclear attack. The parking lot was empty, except for a series of beer bottles clustered near the kiosk, the dregs of a New Year's Eve revelry.

We went up the back stairs. "You know what bothers me?" I asked Darcy as we climbed.

She unlocked the door to the building, glancing back at me. "What's that?"

"Well, suppose we assume Andy's guilty of conspiracy in this. It does look that way even though we don't have proof at this point, right?"

"I'd say so."

"I can't figure out why he agreed to it. We're talking major insurance fraud. He gets caught, it's his livelihood. So what's in it for him?"

"It has to be a payoff," Darcy said. "If Janice hosed him, he's probably desperate for cash."

"Maybe," I said. "It means somebody knew him well enough to think he'd tumble to a bribe. Andy's always been a jerk, but I never really thought of him as dishonest."

We'd reached the glass doors of California Fidelity. "What are you saying?" she asked as she unlocked the door and let us in. She flipped the overhead lights on and tossed her handbag on a chair.

"I don't really know. I'm wondering if something else was going on, I guess. He's in a perfect position to fiddle with the claim forms, but it's still a big risk. And why the panic? What went wrong?"

"He probably didn't count on Olive getting killed. That's gotta fit in somewhere," she said.

We went into Andy's office. Darcy watched with interest as I went through a systematic search. It looked like his business files were still intact, but all of his personal effects had been removed: the photograph of his kids that had sat on his desk, his leather-bound appointment calendar, address book, Rolodex, even the framed APSCRAP and MDRT awards he'd gotten some years before. He'd left a studio portrait of Janice, a five-by-seven color head shot, showing bouffant blond hair, a heart-shaped face, and a pointed chin. She did have a spiteful look about her, even grinning at the camera. Andy had blackened one front tooth and penned in some handsome hairs growing out of her nose. By widening her nostrils slightly, he'd created a piggy effect. The ever-mature Andy Motycka expressing his opinion of his ex-wife.

I sat in his swivel chair and surveyed the place, wondering how I was going to get a line on him. Where would he go and why take off like that? Had he made the bomb? Darcy was quiet, not wanting to interrupt my thought processes, such as they were.

"You have a number for Janice?" I asked.

"Yeah, at my desk. You want me to call and see if she knows where he is?"

"Let's do that. Make up an excuse if you can, and don't give anything away. If she doesn't know he's skipped out, let's don't tip it at this point."

"Right," Darcy said. She moved out to the reception area. I picked up the file I'd brought and pulled out all the papers. It was clear that Andy was in serious financial straits. Between Janice's harangue over the late support check, and the pink- and red-rimmed dunning notices, it was safe to assume that the pressure was on. I reread the various versions of his love letter to his inamorata. That must have been quite a Christmas eve they'd had. Maybe he'd run away with her.

Andy's calendar pad still sat at the uppermost edge of his blotter, two date sheets side by side, connected by arched clips that allowed the pages to lie flat. He'd taken his leather month-by-month appointment book, but he'd left this behind. Apparently he made a habit of noting appointments on both places so his secretary could keep track of his whereabouts. I leafed back through the week, day by day. On Friday, December 24, he'd circled 9:00 P.M. and penciled in the initial L. Was this his beloved? I worked my way back through the last six months. The initial cropped up at irregular intervals, with no pattern that I could discern.

I went out to the reception area, taking the calendar pad and the file folder with me.

Darcy was on the phone, in the midst of a chat with Janice, from what I gathered.

"Uh–hun. Well, I wouldn't know anything about that. I don't know him all that well. Uh–hun. What's your attorney telling you? I guess that's true, but I don't know what good it would do you. Look, I'm going to have to run, Janice. I've got somebody standing here waiting to use the phone. Uh–hun, I'd appreciate that and I'll let you know what we hear on this end. I'm sure he just went off for the weekend and forgot to mention it. Thanks much. You too. Bye-bye. Right."

Darcy replaced the receiver and let out a deep breath. "Good God, that woman can talk! It's lucky I called when I did because I got an earful. She's p.o.'d. He was supposed to come by last night and pick the kids up and he never showed. She was all set to go out and had to cancel her plans. No call, no apologies, nothing. She's convinced he's skipped town and she's all set to call the cops."

"Wouldn't do any good unless he's been missing seventy-two hours," I said. "He's probably shacked up somewhere with this bimbo he's so crazy about." I showed Darcy the letters I'd picked out of his trash.

It was wonderful watching her expression shift from amusement to distaste. "Oh God, would you let him suckle your hmphm-hmph?"

"Only if I doused it with arsenic first."

Darcy's brow wrinkled. "Her bazookas must be huge. He couldn't think what to compare 'em to."

I looked over her shoulder. "Well, 'footballs,' but he crossed that out. Probably didn't seem romantic."

Darcy shoved the papers back in the file. "That was titillating stuff. Oh, bad joke. Now what?"

"I don't know. He took his address book with him, but

I do have this." I flipped through the calendar pad and showed her the penciled initials scattered through the months. I could see Darcy's mental wheels start to turn.

"Wonder if she ever called him here," she said. "She must have, don't you think?"

She opened her top right-hand desk drawer and took out the log for incoming telephone calls. It was a carbonless system with a permanent record in yellow overlaid by white perforated originals. If a call came in for someone out of the office, she made a note of the date and time, the caller, and the return number, checking off one of the responses to the right, "Please call," "Will call back," or "Message." The top slip was then torn out and given to the relevant recipient. Darcy turned back to December 1.

It didn't take us long to find her. By comparing the log of Andy's calls with the calendar pad, we came up with one repeat caller who left a number, but no name, always a day or two prior to Andy's assignations . . . if indeed that's what they were.

"Do you keep crisscross around here?" I asked.

"I don't think so. We used to have one, but I haven't seen it for months."

"I've got last year's in my office. Let's see who's listed at this number. We better hope it's not a business."

I pulled my keys out of my handbag as Darcy followed me.

"You were supposed to turn those keys in," she said in mild reproof.

"Oh really? I didn't know that."

I unlocked my office door and moved to the file cabinet, pulling the crisscross from the bottom drawer. The number, at least the year before, belonged to last name, Wilding, first name Lorraine.

"You think it's her?" Darcy asked.

"I know a good way to find out," I said. The address listed was only two blocks from my apartment, down near the beach.

"Are you sure you're okay? I don't think you should be running around like this."

"Don't sweat it. I'm fine," I said. The truth was, I wasn't feeling all that terrific, but I didn't want to lay my little head down until a few questions had been answered first. I was running on adrenaline—not a bad source of energy. When it ran out, of course, you were up shit creek, but for the time being it seemed better to be on the move.

18

I had Darcy drop me off. In an interview situation I prefer to work alone, especially when I'm not quite sure who I'm dealing with. People are easier to manage one on one; there's more room to ad-lib and more room to negotiate.

The apartment building was Spanish style, probably dating from the thirties. The red-tile roof had aged to the color of rust and the stucco had mellowed from stark white to cream. There were clumps of beaky-looking bird of paradise plants in front. A towering, sixty-foot pine tree enveloped the yard in shade. Bougainvillea was massed at the roofline, a tumble of magenta blossoms that spread out along the gutters and trailed like Spanish moss. Wood shutters, painted dark brown, flanked the windows. The loggia was chilly and smelled of damp earth.

I knocked at apartment D. There was no sign of Andy's car on the street, but there was still a possibility that he was here. I had no idea what I'd say if he appeared at the door. It was nearly six and I could smell someone's supper in the making, something with onions and celery and butter. The door opened and I felt a little lurch of surprise. Andy's ex-wife was staring out at me.

"Janice?" I said, with disbelief.

"I'm Lorraine," she said. "You must be looking for my sister."

Once she spoke, the resemblance began to fade. She had to be in her mid-forties, her good looks just beginning to dehydrate. She had Janice's blond hair and the same pointed chin, but her eyes were bigger and her mouth was more generous. So was her body. She was my height, prob-

ably ten pounds heavier, and I could see where she carried
the excess. Her eyes were brown and she'd lined them
with black, adding false lashes as dense as paintbrushes.
She wore snug white twill shorts and a halter top. Her legs
had been shapely once, but the muscles had taken on that
stringy look that connotes no exercise. Her tan looked like
the comprehensive sort you acquire at a tanning salon—
the electric beach.

Andy must have been in heaven. I've known men who
fall in love with the same type of woman over and over
again, but the similarities are usually not so obvious. She
looked hauntingly like Janice. The difference was that Lorraine was voluptuous where the former Mrs. Motycka
tended toward the small, the dry, and the mean. Judging
from Andy's letter, Lorraine was freer with her affections
than Janice ever was. She did things to him that made his
syntax turn to hiccups. I wondered if his affair with Lorraine came before or after his divorce. Either way, the
liaison was dangerous. If Janice found out about it, she
would extract a pretty price. It crossed my mind briefly
that someone might have used this as leverage to secure
his cooperation.

"I'm looking for Andy," I said.

"Who?"

"Andy Motycka, your brother-in-law. I'm from the insurance company where he works."

"Why look at me? He and Janice are divorced."

"He gave me this address in case I ever needed to get
in touch."

"He did?"

"Why else would I be here?"

She looked at me with suspicion. "How well do you
know Janice?"

I shrugged. "I don't really. I used to see her at company parties before they split. When you first opened the
door, I thought it was her, you look so much alike."

She took that in and digested it. "What do you want
Andy for?"

"He disappeared yesterday and no one seems to know
where he went. Did he say anything to you?"

"Not really."

"Mind if I come in? Maybe we can figure what's happening."

"All right," she said reluctantly. "I suppose that's okay. He never told me he gave anyone this address."

She stepped back and I followed her into the apartment. A small tiled entry dropped down two steps into a large living room. The apartment looked as if it had been furnished from a rental company. Everything was new, handsome, and impersonal. A foot-high live spruce decked with candy canes sat on the glass-and-brass coffee table, but that was the only indication that Christmas had come and gone.

Lorraine flicked the television off and motioned me to a chair. The upholstery had the tough, rubbery feel of Scotchgarding. Neither tears, blood, or spilled booze could penetrate such a finish. She sat down, giving the crotch of her shorts a pull so the inseam wouldn't bury itself in her private parts. "How'd you say you know Andy? Do you work for him?"

"Not really for him, but the same company. When did you see him last?"

"Three days ago. I talked to him on the phone Thursday night. He was taking his kids on New Year's Eve so I wasn't going to see him till late tomorrow anyway, but he always calls, regardless of what's going on. When I didn't hear by this morning, I drove out to his place, but there's no sign of him. Why would you need him New Year's Day?"

I stuck as close to the truth as I could, filling her in on the fact that he'd departed Friday morning without giving any indication where he meant to go. "We need one of the files. Do you know anything about the claim he was working on? There was a fire out at Wood/Warren about a week ago and I think he was doing some of the paperwork."

There was a startled silence and the barriers shot up again. "Excuse me?"

"Did he mention that to you?"

"What'd you say your name was?"

"Darcy. I'm the receptionist. I think I've talked to you a couple of times on the phone."

Her manner became formal, circumspect. "I see. Well,

Darcy, he doesn't talk to me about his work. I know he loves the company and he's fine at what he does."

"Oh, absolutely," said I. "And he's very well liked, which is why we were concerned when he went off without a word. We thought maybe some kind of family matter came up. He didn't say anything about going out of town for a few days?"

She shook her head.

Judging from her attitude, I was almost certain she knew about the scam. I was equally certain she'd never give a hint of confirmation.

She said, "I wish I could help you, but he never said a word to me. In fact, I'd appreciate a call myself when the man turns up. I don't like to have to sit here and fret."

"I don't blame you," I said. "You can reach me at this number if you need to, and I'll check back with you if I hear anything." I jotted down Darcy's name and my telephone number.

"I hope nothing's wrong." This seemed like the first sincere comment she'd made.

"I'm sure not," I said. Personally, I was betting something had scared the hell out of him and he'd taken off.

She'd had a few minutes now to focus on my browless, burned face. "Uh, I hope this doesn't seem rude, but were you in some kind of accident?"

"A gas heater blew up in my face," I said. She made some sympathetic noises and I hoped the lie wouldn't come back to haunt me. "Well, I'm sorry I had to bother you on a holiday. I'll let you know if we hear from him." I got up and she rose as well, crossing with me to the front door.

I walked home through streets beginning to darken, though it was not quite 5:00. The winter sun had sunk and the air temperature was dropping with it. I was exhausted, secretly wishing I could check back into the hospital for the night. Something about the clean white sheets seemed inviting. I was hungry, too, and for once would have welcomed something more nutritious than peanut butter and crackers, which was what I was looking forward to.

Daniel's car was parked at the curb out in front of my apartment. I peered in, half expecting to find him asleep on the back seat. I went in through the gate and around the side of the building to Henry's backyard. Daniel was sitting on the cinder-block wall that separated Henry's lot from our neighbor to the right. Daniel, his elbows on his knees, was blowing a low, mournful tune on an alto harmonica. With the cowboy boots, the jeans, and a blue-denim jacket, he might have been out on the range.

" 'Bout time you got home," he remarked. He tucked the harmonica in his pocket and got up.

"I had work to do."

"You're always working. You should take better care of yourself."

I unlocked my front door and went in, flipping on the light. I slung my handbag on a chair and sank down on the couch. Daniel moved into my kitchenette and opened the refrigerator.

"Don't you ever grocery-shop?"

"What for? I'm never home."

"Lord." He took out a stub of butter, some eggs, and a packet of cheese so old it looked like dark plastic around the edge. While I watched, he searched my kitchen cabinets, assembling miscellaneous foodstuffs. I slouched down on my spine, leaning my head against the back of the couch with my feet propped up on the ottoman. I was fresh out of snappy talk and I couldn't conjure up a shred of anger. This was a man I'd loved once, and though the feelings were gone, a certain familiarity remained.

"How come this place smells like feet?" he said idly. He was already chopping onions, his fingers nimble. He played piano the same way, with a careless expertise.

"It's my air fern. Somebody gave it to me as a pet."

He picked up the tag end of a pound of bacon, sniffing suspiciously at the contents. "Stiff as beef jerky."

"Lasts longer that way," I said.

He shrugged and extracted the three remaining pieces of bacon, which he dropped into the skillet with a clinking sound. "God, one thing about giving up dope, food never has tasted right," he said. "Smoke dope, you're always eating the best meal you ever had. Helps when you're broke or on the road."

"You really gave up the hard stuff?"

" 'Fraid so," he said. "Gave up cigarettes, gave up coffee. I do drink a beer now and then, though I notice you don't have any. I used to go to AA meetings five times a week, but that talk of a higher power got to me in the end. There isn't any power higher than heroin, you can take my word for it."

I could feel myself drifting off. He was humming to himself, a melody dimly remembered, that blended with the scent of bacon and eggs. What could smell better than supper being cooked by someone else?

He shook me gently and I woke to find an omelet on a warmed plate being placed in my lap. I roused myself, suddenly famished again.

Daniel sat cross-legged on the floor, forking up eggs while he talked. "Who lives in the house?"

"My landlord, Henry Pitts. He's off in Michigan."

"You got something goin' with him?"

I paused between bites. "The man is eighty-one."

"He have a piano?"

"Actually, I think he does. An upright, probably out of tune. His wife used to play."

"I'd like to try it, if there's a way to get in. You think he'd care?"

"Not at all. I've got a key. You mean tonight?"

"Tomorrow. I gotta be somewhere in a bit."

The way the light fell on his face, I could see the lines near his eyes. Daniel had lived hard and he wasn't aging well. He looked haggard, a gauntness beginning to emerge. "I can't believe you're a private detective," he said. "Seems weird to me."

"It's not that different from being a cop," I said. "I'm not part of the bureaucracy, that's all. Don't wear a uniform or punch a time clock. I get paid more, but not as regularly."

"A bit more dangerous, isn't it? I don't remember anyone ever tried to blow you up back then."

"Well, they sure tried everything else. Traffic detail, every time you pull someone over, you wonder if the car's stolen, if the driver's got a gun. Domestic violence is worse. People drinking, doing drugs. Half the time they'd just as soon waste you as one another. Knock on the door, you never know what you're dealing with."

"How'd you get involved in a homicide?"

"It didn't start out like that. You know the family, by the way," I said.

"I do?"

"The Woods. Remember Bass Wood?"

He hesitated. "Vaguely."

"His sister Olive is the one who died."

Daniel set his plate down. "The Kohler woman is *his* sister? I had no idea. What the hell is going on?"

I sketched it out for him, telling him what I knew. If I have a client, I won't talk about a case, but I couldn't see the harm here. Just me. It felt good, giving me a chance to theorize to some extent. Daniel was a good audience, asking just the right questions. It felt like old times, the good times, when we talked on for hours about whatever suited us.

Finally a silence fell. I was cold and feeling tense. I reached for the quilt and covered my feet. "Why'd you leave me, Daniel? I never have understood."

He kept his tone light. "It wasn't you, babe. It wasn't anything personal."

"Was there someone else?"

He shifted uneasily, tapping with the fork on the edge of his dinner plate. He set the utensil aside. He stretched his legs out in front of him and leaned back on his elbows. "I wish I knew what to tell you, Kinsey. It wasn't that I didn't want you. I wanted something else more, that's all."

"What?"

He scanned my face. "Anything. Everything. Whatever came down the pike."

"You don't have a conscience, do you?"

He broke off eye contact. "No. That's why we were such a mismatch. I don't have any conscience and you have too much."

"No, not so. If I had a conscience, I wouldn't tell so many lies."

"Ah, right. The lies. I remember. That was the one thing we had in common," he said. His gaze came up to mine. I was chilled by the look in his eyes, clear and empty.

I could remember wanting him. I could remember looking at his face, wondering if there could ever be a man more beautiful. For some reason I never expect the people I know to have any talent or ability. I'd been introduced to Daniel and dismissed him until the moment I heard him play. Then I did a long double-take, astonished, and I was hooked. There just wasn't any place to go from there. Daniel was married to his music, to freedom, to drugs, and briefly, to me. I was about that far down on the list.

I stirred restlessly. A palpable sexual vapor seemed to rise from his skin, drifting across to me like the scent of woodsmoke half a mile away. It's a strange phenomenon, but true, that in sleeping with men, none of the old rules apply to a man you've slept with before. Operant conditioning. The man had trained me well. Even after eight years, he could still do what he did best . . . seduce. I cleared my throat, struggling to break the spell. "What's the story on your therapist?"

"No story. She's a shrink. She thinks she can fix me."

"And this is part of it? Making peace with me?"

"We all have delusions. That's one of hers."

"Is she in love with you?"

"I doubt it."

"Must be early in the game," I said.

The dimple appeared and a smile flashed across his face, but it was mirthless, evasive, and I wondered if I hadn't touched on some pain of his. Now, he was the restless one, glancing at his watch.

"I got to get," he said abruptly. He gathered both plates and the silverware, toting dishes to the kitchen. He'd cleaned up while he cooked, an old habit of his, so he didn't have much to do. By 7:00, he was gone. I heard the thunder and rattle of his car as he started it and pulled away.

The apartment seemed dark. Extraordinarily quiet.

I locked up. I took a bath, keeping the water away from my burns. I closed myself into the folds of my quilt and turned out the light. Being with him had brought back the pain in fossil form, evidence of ancient emotional life, embedded now in rock. I studied the sensations as I would some extinct subspecies, for the curiosity, if nothing more.

Being married to a doper is as close to loneliness as you can get. Add to that his chronic infidelity and you've got a lot of sleepless nights on your hands. There are certain men who rove, men who prowl the night, who simply don't show up for hours on end. Lying in bed, you tell yourself you're worried that he's wrecked the car again, that he's drunk or in jail. You tell yourself you're worried he's been rolled, mugged, or maimed, that he's overdosed. What really worries you is he might be with someone else. The hours creep by. From time to time, you hear a car approaching, but it's never his. By 4:00 A.M., it's a toss-up which is uppermost in your mind—wishing he would come home or wishing he were dead.

Daniel Wade was the one who taught me how to value solitude. What I endure now doesn't hold a candle to what I endured with him.

19

The memorial service for Olive was held at 2:00 P.M. on Sunday at the Unitarian Church, a spartan ceremony in a setting stripped of excess. Attendance was limited to family and a few close friends. There were lots of flowers, but no casket in evidence. The floors were red tile, glossy and cold. The pews were carved and polished wood, without cushions. The lofty ceiling of the church lent a sense of airiness, but the space was curiously devoid of ornamentation and there were no religious icons at all. Even the stained-glass windows were a plain cream with the barest suggestion of green vines curling around the edges. The Unitarians apparently don't hold with zealousness, piety, confession, penance, or atonement. Jesus and God were never mentioned, nor did the word "amen" cross anybody's lips. Instead of scriptures, there were readings from Bertrand Russell and Kahlil Gibran. A man with a flute played several mournful classical tunes and ended with a number that sounded suspiciously like "Send In the Clowns." There was no eulogy, but the minister chatted about Olive in the most conversational of tones, inviting those congregated to stand up and share recollections of her. No one had the nerve. I sat near the back in my all-purpose dress, not wanting to intrude. I noticed that several people nudged one another and turned to look at me, as if I'd achieved celebrity status by being blown up with her. Ebony, Lance, and Bass remained perfectly composed. Ash wept, as did her mother. Terry sat alone in the front row, leaning forward, head in his hands. The whole group didn't occupy more than about the first five rows.

Afterward we assembled in the small garden court-yard outside, where we were served champagne and finger sandwiches. The occasion was polite and circumspect. The afternoon was hot. The sun was bright. The garden itself was gaudy with annuals, gold, orange, purple, and red marching along the white stucco wall that enclosed the churchyard. The stone-and-tile fountain plashed softly, a breeze occasionally blowing spray out onto the surrounding paving stones.

I moved among the mourners, saying little, picking up fragments of conversation. Some were discussing the stock market, some their recent travels, one the divorce of a mutual acquaintance who'd been married twenty-six years. Of those who thought to talk about Olive Wood Kohler, the themes seemed to be equally divided between conventional sentiment and cattiness.

". . . he'll never recover from the loss, you know. She was everything to him . . ."

". . . paid seven thousand dollars for that coat . . ."

". . . shocked . . . couldn't believe it when Ruth called me . . ."

". . . poor thing. He worshiped the ground she walked on, though I never could quite see it myself . . ."

". . . tragedy . . . so young . . ."

". . . well, I always wondered about that, as narrow as she was through the chest. Who did the work?"

I found Ash sitting on a poured-concrete bench near the chapel door. She looked drawn and pale, her pale-red hair glinting with strands of premature gray. The dress she wore was a dark wool, loosely cut, the short sleeves making her upper arms seem as shapeless as bread dough. In another few years she'd have that matronly look that women sometimes get, rushing into middle age just to get it over with. I sat down beside her. She held out her hand and we sat there together like grade-school kids on a field trip. "Line up in twos and no talking." Life itself is a peculiar outing. Sometimes I still feel like I need a note from my mother.

I scanned the crowd. "What happened to Ebony? I don't see her."

"She left just after the service. God, she's so cold. She sat there like a stone, never cried a tear."

"Bass says she was a mess when she first heard the news. Now she's got herself under control, which is probably much closer to the way she lives. Were she and Olive close?"

"I always thought so. Now I'm not so sure."

"Come on, Ashley. People deal with grief differently. You never really know what goes on," I said. "I went to a funeral once where a woman laughed so hard she wet her pants. Her only son had died in a car accident. Later, she was hospitalized for depression, but if you'd seen her then, you never would have guessed."

"I suppose." She let her gaze drift across the courtyard. "Terry got another phone call from that woman."

"Lyda Case?"

"I guess that's the one. Whoever threatened him."

"Did he call the police?"

"I doubt it. It came up a little while ago, before we left the house to come here. He probably hasn't had a chance."

I spotted Terry talking to the minister. As if on cue, he turned and looked at me. I touched Ash's arm. "I'll be right back," I said.

Terry murmured something and broke away, moving toward me. Looking at him was like looking in my mirror . . . the same bruises, same haunted look about the eyes. We were as bonded as lovers after the trauma we'd been through. No one could know what it was like in that moment when the bomb went off. "How are you?" he said, his voice low.

"Ash says Lyda Case called."

Terry took my arm and steered me toward the entrance to the social hall. "She's here in town. She wants to meet with me."

"Bullshit. No way," I whispered hoarsely.

Terry looked at me uneasily. "I know it sounds crazy, but she says she has some information that could be of help."

"I'm sure she does. It's probably in a box and goes boom when you pick it up."

"I asked her about that. She swears she didn't have anything to do with Olive's death."

"And you believed her?"

"I guess I did in a way."

"Hey, you were the one who told me about the threat. She scared the life out of you and here she is again. If you won't call Lieutenant Dolan, I will."

I thought he would argue, but he sighed once. "All right. I know it's the only thing that makes any sense. I've just been in such a fog."

"Where's she staying?"

"She didn't say. She wants to meet at the bird refuge at six. Would you be willing to come? She asked for you by name."

"Why me?"

"I don't know. She said you flew to Texas to talk to her. I can't believe you didn't mention that when the subject came up."

"Sorry. I guess I should have. That was early in the week. I was trying to get a line on Hugh Case, to see how his death fits in."

"And?"

"I'm not sure yet. I'd be very surprised if it didn't connect. I just can't figure out how."

Terry gave me a skeptical look. "It's never been proven he was murdered, has it?"

"Well, that's true," I said. "It just seems highly unlikely that the lab work would disappear unless somebody meant to conceal the evidence. Maybe it's the same person with a different motive this time."

"What makes you say that? Carbon-monoxide poisoning is about as far away from bombs as you can get. Wouldn't the guy use the same method if it worked so well the first time?"

I shrugged. "I don't know. If it were me, I'd do whatever was expedient. The point is, this is not something we should fool around with on our own."

I saw Terry's gaze focus on something behind me. I turned to see Bass. He looked old. Everybody had aged in the wake of Olive's death, but on Bass the lines of weariness were the least flattering—something puffy about the eyes, something pouty about the mouth. He had one of those boyish faces that didn't lend itself to deep emotion. On him, sorrow looked like a form of petulance. "I'm taking Mother home," he said.

"I'll be right there," Terry said. Bass moved away and Terry turned back to me. "Do you want to call Lieutenant Dolan or should I?"

"I'll do it," I said. "If there's any problem, I'll let you know. Otherwise, I'll meet you down at the bird refuge at six."

I was home by 3:35, but it took me almost an hour to track down the lieutenant, who was certainly interested in having a chat with Lyda Case. He said he'd be there at 5:00 in an unmarked car, on the off-chance that she was feeling truly skittish about contact with the police. I changed into jeans and a sweatshirt and pulled on my tennis shoes. I was tired, and the residual pain from my injuries was like a slow leak from a tire, depleting. Over the course of the day, I could feel myself go flat. In some ways I shared Terry's sentiments. It was hard to believe Lyda was responsible for the package bomb, let alone her husband's death two years before. In spite of her accusations and the veiled threat to Terry, she didn't seem like the homicidal type, for whatever that's worth. I've been surprised by killers again and again, and I try not to generalize, but there it was. Maybe she was just what she claimed to be . . . someone with information that might be of help.

By the time I reached the meeting place, the sun was almost down. The bird refuge is a landscaped preserve near the beach, established to protect geese, swans, and other fowl. The forty-three-acre property abuts the zoo and consists of an irregular-shaped freshwater lagoon, surrounded by a wide lane of clipped grass through which a bike trail runs. There's a small parking lot at one end where parents bring little children with their plastic bags of old popcorn and stale bread. Male pigeons puff and posture in jerky pursuit of their inattentive female counterparts who manage to strut along just one step away from conception.

I pulled into the lot and parked. I got out of my car. Sea gulls swirled and settled in an oddly choreographed dance of their own. Geese honked along the shore in search of crumbs while the ducks paddled through the still waters, sending out ripples around them. The sky was a deepening gray, the ruffled silver surface of the lagoon reflecting the rising wind.

I was glad when Lieutenant Dolan's car pulled in beside mine. We chatted idly until Terry appeared, and then the three of us waited. Lyda Case never showed. At 8:15, we finally gave it up. Terry took Dolan's number and said he'd be in touch if he heard from her. It was a bit of a letdown, as all three of us had hoped for a break in the case. Terry seemed grateful for the activity and I had to guess that it was going to be hard for him to spend his first night alone. He'd been in the hospital Friday night and with his mother-in-law on Saturday while the bomb squad finished their crime-scene investigation and a work crew came in to board up the front wall of the house.

My own sense of melancholy had returned in full force. Funerals and the new year are a bad mix. The painkillers I'd been taking dulled my mental processes and left me feeling somewhat disconnected from reality. I needed companionship. I wanted lights and noise and a good dinner somewhere with a decent glass of wine and talk of anything except death. I fancied myself an independent soul, but I could see how easily my attachments could form.

I drove home hoping Daniel would appear again. With him, you never knew. The day he walked out of the marriage eight years before, he hadn't even left a note. He didn't like to deal with anger or recrimination. He said it bummed him out to be around people who were sad, depressed, or upset. His strategy was to let other people cope with unpleasantness. I'd seen him do it with his family, with old friends, with gigs that no longer interested him. One day he wasn't there, and you might not see him for two years. By then, you couldn't even remember why you'd been so pissed off.

Sometimes, as in my case, there'd be some residual rage, which Daniel usually found puzzling. Strong emotion is hard to sustain in the face of bafflement. You run out of things to say. Most of the time, in the old days, he was stoned anyway, so confronting him was about as productive as trying to discipline a cat for spraying on the drapes. He didn't "get it." Fury didn't make any sense to him. He couldn't see the connection between his behavior and the wrath that was generated as a consequence. What the man did really well was play. He was a free spirit, whimsical, inventive, tireless, sweet. Jazz piano, sex, travel, parties, he was wonderful at those . . . until he got bored, of course, or until reality surfaced, and then he was gone. I had never been taught how to play, so I learned a lot from him. I'm just not sure it was anything I really needed to know.

I found a parking spot six doors away. Daniel's car was parked in front of my place. He was leaning against the fender. There was a paper bag with twine handles near his feet, a baguette of French bread sticking out of it like a baseball bat.

"I thought you might be gone by today," I said.

"I talked to my friend. It looks like I'll be here a couple days more."

"You find a place to stay?"

"I hope so. There's a little motel here in the neighborhood that will have a room free later. Some folks are checking out."

"That's nice. You can reclaim your stuff."

"I'll do that as soon as I know for sure."

"What's that?" I said, pointing at the baguette.

He looked down at the sack, his gaze following mine. "Picnic," he said. "I thought I'd play the piano some, too."

"How long have you been here?"

"Since six," he said. "You feel all right? You look beat."

"I am. Come on in. I hope you have wine. I could use some."

He pushed away from the car, toting the bag as he followed me through the gate. We ended up at Henry's, sitting on the floor in his living room. Daniel had bought twenty-five votive candles and he arranged those around the room until I felt like I was sitting in the middle of a birthday cake. We had wine, pâté, cheeses, French bread, cold salads, fresh raspberries, and sugar cookies the size of Frisbees. I stretched out afterward in a food-induced reverie while Daniel played the piano. Daniel didn't play music so much as he discovered it, calling up melodies, pursuing them across the keys, embroidering, embellishing. His background was in classical piano, so he warmed up with Chopin, Liszt, the intricacies of Bach, drifting over into improvisation without effort.

Daniel stopped abruptly.

I opened my eyes and looked at him.

His expression was pained. He touched at the keyboard carelessly, a sour chord. "It's gone. I don't have it anymore. I gave up drugs and the music went with 'em."

I sat up. "What are you talking about?"

"Just what I said. It was the choice I had to make, but it's all bullshit. I can live without drugs, babe, but not without music. I'm not made that way."

"It sounded fine. It was beautiful."

"What do you know, Kinsey? You don't know anything. That was all technique. Mechanics. I got no soul. The only time music works is when I'm burning with smack, flying. This is nothing. Half-life. The other is better . . . when I'm on fire like that and give it all away. You can't hold back. It's all or nothin'."

I could feel my body grow still. "What are you saying?" Dumb question. I knew.

His eyes glowed and he pinched his thumb and index finger together near his lips, sucking in air. It was the gesture he always used when he was about to roll a joint. He looked down at the crook of his elbow and made a fist lovingly.

"Don't do that," I said.

"Why not?"

"It'll kill you."

He shrugged. "Why can't I live the way I want? I'm the devil. I'm bad. You should know that by now. There isn't anything I wouldn't do just for the hell of it . . . just to stay *awake*. Fuck. I'd like to fly again, you know? I'd like to feel good. I'll tell you something about being straight . . . it's a goddamn drag. I don't know how you put up with it. I don't know how you keep from hangin' yourself."

I crumpled up paper napkins and stuffed them in the sack, gathered paper plates, plastic ware, the empty wine bottle, cardboard containers. He sat on the piano bench, his hands held loosely in his lap. I doubted he'd live to see forty-three.

"Is that why you came back?" I asked. "To lay this on me. What do you want, permission? Approval?"

"Yeah, I'd like that."

I started blowing out candles, darkness gathering like smoke around the edges of the room. You can't argue with people who fall in love with death. "Get out of my life, Daniel. Would you just do that?"

20

I got up Monday morning at 6:00 and did a slow, agonizing five-mile jog. I was in bad shape and I had no business being out there at all, but I couldn't help myself. This had to be the worst Christmas I'd ever spent and the new year wasn't shaping up all that great as far as I could see. It was now January 3, and I wanted my life back the way it was. With luck, Rosie would reopen later in the day, and maybe Jonah would return from Idaho. Henry was flying home on Friday. I recited my blessings to myself as I ran, ignoring the fact that my body hurt, that I had no office at the moment, and a cloud of suspicion was still hanging over my head.

The sky was clear, a torpid breeze picking up. The day seemed unseasonably warm even at that hour, and I wondered if we were experiencing Santa Ana conditions, winds gusting in from the desert, hot drafts like the blast from an oven. It was the wrong time of year for it, but the air had that dry, dusty feel to it. The sweat on my face evaporated almost at once and my T-shirt was clinging to my back like a hot, soggy rag. By the time I got back to my neighborhood, I felt I'd blown some of the tension away. Kinsey Millhone, perpetual optimist. I jogged all the way to Henry's gate and took a few minutes walking back and forth, catching my breath, cooling down. Daniel's car was gone. In its place was a vehicle I hadn't seen before—a compact, judging from the shape, anonymous under a pale-blue cotton car cover. Off-street parking in the area is restricted and garages are rare. If I ever got a new car, I'd have to invest in a cover myself. I leaned against the fence, stretching my hamstrings dutifully before I went in to shower.

Lance Wood called me at 8:00. The background noise was that hollow combination of traffic and enclosure that suggests a phone booth.

"Where are you?" I asked, as soon as he'd identified himself.

"On a street corner in Colgate. I think my phone at work is tapped," he said.

"Have you had it checked?"

"Well, I'm not really sure how to go about it and I feel like a fool asking the phone company to come out."

"I'll bet," I said. "That's like asking the fox to secure the henhouse. What makes you think you've got a tap?"

"Odd stuff. I'll have a conversation and the next thing I know, something I've said is all over the place. I'm not talking about office gossip. It's something more insidious than that, like comments I've made to out-of-state customers that people here would have no way of knowing."

"Could it be a simple case of someone listening in? A lot of employees have access to the phones out there."

"Not my private line. It isn't like anything we do is top secret, but we all say things we'd rather not have spread around. Someone's making me look very bad. Is there some way you can check it out?"

"I can try," I said. "What about the phone itself? Have you tried unscrewing the mouthpiece?"

"Sure, but I don't know what the inside of a receiver's supposed to look like. I'm not picking up any odd noises or clicks, I will say that."

"You wouldn't if the tap is set up properly. It'd be virtually undetectable. Of course, it might not be that at all," I said. "Maybe the office itself is bugged."

"In which case, what? Is that something you can spot?"

"Sometimes, with luck. It's also possible to buy an electronic device that will scan for bugs. I'll see if I can locate one before I come out. Give me a couple of hours and I'll meet you at the plant. I've got some other things I probably ought to take care of first."

"Right. Thanks."

I took the next hour to type up my notes, clipping the newspaper article about the explosion to include with my files. I tried Lyda Case's telephone number in Texas on the off chance that her roommate had heard from her. It would help if I knew how to find her here in Santa Teresa.

At 9:10, my phone rang. It was Darcy calling from California Fidelity and talking as if she had a hand cupped over the mouthpiece. "Big trouble," she said.

I could feel my heart sink. "Now what?"

"If I change the subject abruptly, you'll know Mac walked in," she murmured. "I overheard a conversation between him and Jewel. He says someone tipped the cops about the warehouse inventory. It looks like Lance Wood moved all the merchandise to another location before his warehouse burned down. The inventory he claimed reimbursement for was all worthless junk."

"That's bullshit," I said. "I saw some of it myself. I must have gone through five or six boxes when I inspected the place."

"Well, I guess he had a few real boxes seeded in among the fake. He's going to be charged, Kinsey. Arson and fraud, and you're being named as co-conspirator. Mac turned everything over to the D.A. this morning. I thought you'd like to know in case you need to talk to an attorney."

"What's the timetable? Do you know?"

"Mr. Motycka isn't in today, but I can leave a message on his desk," she said.

"Is that Mac?"

"He didn't say exactly, but we're expecting him some time today. Uh—hun. Yes, I'll do that. All right, thanks," she said and hung up.

I put a call through to Lonnie Kingman and alerted him. He said he'd check with the D.A.'s office and find out if a warrant was being issued. His advice was to surrender voluntarily, thus avoiding the ignominy and uncertainty of a public arrest.

"Jesus, I can't believe this is happening," I said.

"Well, it hasn't yet. Don't worry about it until I tell you to," he said.

I grabbed my handbag and car keys and headed out the door. I had disconnected my emotions again. There was no point in letting anxiety get in my way. I hopped in my car and drove over to an electrical-supply place on Granita. My knowledge of electronic surveillance was bound to be out-of-date, limited to information picked up in a crash course at the Police Academy nearly ten years before. The advances in miniaturization since then had probably revolutionized the field, but I suspected the basics were always going to be the same. Microphone, transmitter, recorder of some type, probably voice-activated these days. The planting can be done by a technician disguised as any commonly seen service person: telephone lineman, meter reader, cable-television installer. Electronic surveillance is expensive, illegal unless authorized by the court, and looks a lot easier on television than it is in real life. Bug detection is another matter altogether. It was always possible, of course, that Lance Wood was imagining the whole thing, but I doubted it.

The small all-band receiver I bought was about the size of a portable radio. While not truly all-band, it was sufficient to cover most bugging frequencies—30–50 MHz and 88–108 MHz. If the bug in his office was wired, I was going to have to find the wire myself, but if the bug was wireless, the receiver would start emitting a high-pitched squeal when it was within range.

I drove out to Colgate with my windows rolled down, parched air whipping through the interior of the VW like a convection oven. The weather forecaster on the car radio seemed as baffled as I was. It felt like August, asphalt shimmering in the heat. January in Santa Teresa is usually our best month. Everything is green, flowers in full bloom, the temperatures in the low seventies, mild and pleasant. The time-and-temp sign on the bank building was showing 89 degrees and it wasn't yet noon.

I parked in front of Wood/Warren and went in. Lance came out of his office in a wilted shirt with the sleeves rolled up.

"Do we need to watch what we say once we go in there?" he asked, indicating the office door.

"I don't think so. Let's let 'em know we're hot on the trail. Maybe it'll shake 'em up."

Before we started work, I did a quick check of both

interior and exterior office walls on the off-chance that someone had installed a spike mike, a small probe that can be inserted between the studs, or hidden in a hollow door, the door panel itself serving as a diaphragm to transmit sound. Lance's office was located in the right-front corner of the building. The construction on those two sides was block and fieldstone, which didn't lend itself to easy installation. Somebody would have had to drill through solid rock. Inside, one office wall was contiguous with the reception area, where the pickup unit would have been difficult to conceal. The fourth wall was clean.

Company employees watched the two of us incuriously as we moved through the preliminary phases of the search. If anyone was worried about surveillance equipment coming to light, there was no indication of it.

We went into the office. I examined the telephone first, taking the plate off the bottom, unscrewing the mouth and ear pieces. As far as I could tell, the instrument was clean.

"I take it it's not the phone," Lance said, watching me.

"Who knows? The bug might be downstream," I said. "I don't have any way to find out if somebody's tapped into the line at the pole. We'll have to operate on the premise that the bug's somewhere in the room. It's just a matter of coming up with it."

"What exactly are we looking for?" Lance asked.

I shrugged. "Microphone, transmitter. If you're being spied on by the FBI or the CIA, we probably won't find anything. I'm assuming those guys are good. On the other hand, if your eavesdropper's an amateur, the device might be fairly crude."

"What's that thing?"

"My handy little all-band receiver," I said. "This should pick up any sound being transmitted by the bug in a feedback loop that'll result in a high-pitched squeal. We'll try this first, and if nothing comes to light, we'll take the office apart item by item."

I flipped the receiver on and began to work my way through the popular bugging frequencies, moving around the office like someone dowsing for water. Nothing.

I tucked the debugger in the outside pocket of my

handbag and started searching in earnest, working my way around the periphery of the room, then toward the center in an imaginary grid pattern that covered every square foot.

Nothing.

I stood for a moment, perplexed, my eye traveling along the ceiling, down the walls, along the baseboard. Where was the sucker? I felt my attention tugged by the phone jack just to the right of the door. There was no telephone cord coming from it.

"What's that?"

"What? Oh. I had the jack moved when I changed the office around. The telephone used to be over there."

I got down on my hands and knees and inspected the jack. It looked okay. I took out my screwdriver and popped off the cover. A small section of the baseboard had been cut away. Tucked into the space was a microcassette recorder about the size of a deck of playing cards.

"Hello," I said. The tape gave a half-turn and stopped. I moved the microsensor button away from the voice-activated setting and placed the recorder on his desk. Lance sank heavily into his swivel chair. He and I exchanged a long look.

"Why?" he said, baffled.

"I don't know. You tell me."

He shook his head. "I can't even think where to start. I don't have enemies as far as I know."

"Apparently you do. And it isn't just you. Hugh Case is dead and Terry *would* have been if he'd picked up that package instead of Olive. What do the three of you have in common?"

"Nothing, I swear. We're all connected to Wood/Warren, but none of us even do the same kind of work. We make hydrogen furnaces. That's all we do. And Hugh died two years ago. Why then? If somebody wants control of the company, why kill off the key personnel?"

"Maybe that's not the motive. It could be something wholly unrelated to the work. Give it some thought. I'll talk to Terry and have him do the same. Maybe there's something you've overlooked."

"There must be," he said, his face florid with heat and

tension. He pushed at the tape recorder with one finger. "Thanks for this."

"Be careful. There could be another one. Maybe this one was planted someplace obvious to distract us from the other." I picked up my handbag and started toward the door, pausing at the threshold. "Get in touch if you think of anything. And if you hear from Lyda Case, let me know."

As I passed through the reception area, I did a detour to the right. This was the office where the engineers had their drafting tables. John Salkowitz glanced up at me from the rough diagram he was working on. "Can I help you?"

"Is Ava Daugherty here someplace?"

"She just left. She had some errands to run, but she should be right back."

I took out my business card and placed it on her desk. "Have her get in touch with me, if you would."

"Will do."

I was home again by 3:00, feeling hot and grimy from crawling the perimeter of Lance's office, peering under things. I let myself into my apartment and tossed my handbag on the couch. A piercing shriek started up and I jumped a foot, grabbing up my bag. I snatched the debugger out of the outside compartment and flipped the switch off. Jesus Christ, I'd scared myself to death! The silence was wonderful. I stood there, heart pounding, enjoying the air conditioning the sudden sweat had generated. I patted myself on the chest and blew out a big breath. I shook my head and moved into the kitchenette. I felt dry, longing for a beer. The apartment was as close and muggy as a sauna. I checked the refrigerator. I didn't even have a can of Diet Pepsi.

And then I paused, my head swiveling slowly toward the room behind me. I closed the refrigerator door and moved back to the couch. I picked up the debugger and flipped it on again, sweeping the room. The high-pitched squeal cut through the silence like a burglar alarm.

I crossed to the corner and stood there, looking down. I hunkered on my heels, running a hand carefully into the sound hole in Daniel's guitar. The tiny transmitter, no bigger than a matchbox, was affixed to the body of the instrument with tape. A chill started at the base of my spine and raced up my body. Daniel was somehow connected to the case.

21

It took me nearly two hours to find the voice-activated tape recorder which turned out to be hidden on the sun porch that formerly connected my converted garage apartment to the main house. I wasn't sure how Daniel had gotten in. Perhaps he'd picked the lock, as I would have in his place. The tape was new, which meant he must have been there fairly recently, pulling out the old tape, inserting this one. I couldn't even remember what was going on when he had first appeared. It was appalling now to think of all the telephone conversations he must have picked up in the last few days. Even messages coming in on my answering machine would have been recorded and passed on, not to mention the lengthy discussion I'd had with him about the case itself. He'd been so interested, so astute in the questions he asked. I'd felt so gratified by his attention. Looking back, I could see that in his own way he'd tried to warn me. All that talk about what a liar he was. Had every word he said to me been false? I sat on my back step, turning the situation over in my mind. Who had put Daniel up to it? Lyda Case perhaps, or maybe Ebony. One or the other of them might have run into Daniel, the amoral, the promiscuous, bored and at loose ends, restless and sick of life. What difference would it make to him who he betrayed? He'd done me in before. One more time couldn't matter in the grand scheme of things. It was staggering to think of all the information that must have been passed down the line, just by listening in, just by assembling my end of telephone conversations. Maybe that's how Andy Motycka had figured out Darcy and I were onto

him. *Something* had caused him to cut and run. Olive's
death hadn't hit the papers until the day *after* he disappeared. Had he known what was going to happen? I had to
find Daniel.

I gathered up his guitar, the transmitter, and the tape
recorder, shoving everything in the back seat of the car,
and then I started cruising the neighborhood, looking for
his Rent-A-Ruin. I live one block from the beach in an area
made up of motels and vintage California bungalows. I
started at Cabana Boulevard and circled each block,
checking the cars at every motel, scanning the restaurant
parking lots along the beach. There was no sign of him.
He'd probably lied about where he was staying, along with
everything else.

At 5:00, I finally gave up and went home. As usual, I
was forced to park several doors away. The intense heat of
day was yielding to balminess and it felt like we were in for
a warm night ahead. The sun had begun to drop and the
combination of January twilight and the summery temperature was disconcerting and set my teeth on edge. I was
turning in at my gate when I picked up the smell. Dead
dog, I thought. Something fetid and rotten. I looked back
at the street, thinking I'd spot some poor flattened creature on the pavement. Instead my attention was caught by
the vehicle shrouded by the blue cotton car cover right out
in front. I hesitated for a moment and then retraced my
steps. The smell was stronger. Saliva began to collect involuntarily on the floor of my mouth. I swallowed, tears welling briefly, a fear reaction of mine. Gingerly, I lifted the
car cover, pulling it up off the hood so that I could peer in
through the windshield.

I jerked my hand away, making one of those sounds
that has no translation in human speech.

Leaning against the window on the passenger side was
the bloated face of Lyda Case, eyes bulging, tongue as fat
and round and dark as a parakeet's, protruding slightly
beyond puffy darkened lips. A scarf gaily printed with a
surfing motif was nearly buried in the swollen flesh of her
neck. I pulled the cover back over the windshield and
went straight to my phone where I dialed 911 and reported the body. My voice sounded low and emotionless,

but my hands were shaking badly. The sight of Lyda's face still danced in the air, a vision of death, wed to the smell of putrescence. The dispatcher assured me someone was on the way.

I went back out to the street. I sat on the curb to wait for the cops, guarding Lyda's body like some old loyal pooch. I don't think four minutes had passed before the black-and-white came barreling around the corner. I got up and moved to the street, holding an arm up like a crossing guard.

The two uniformed police who emerged were familiar, Pettigrew and Gutierrez, male and female. I knew they'd seen worse than Lyda Case . . . what beat cop hasn't? . . . but there was something repellent about the spectacle of this death. It looked like she'd been positioned so as to maximize the horror. The message was for me . . . mockery and macabre arrogance, an escalation of the terms between this killer and me. I hadn't taken Olive's death personally. I'd felt the loss, but I didn't believe I'd been targeted in any way. My presence there when the bomb went off was purely circumstantial. This was different. This was aimed at me. Someone knew where I lived. Someone had made very special arrangements to get her here.

The next two hours were filled with police routine, comforting procedures, as formalized as a dance. All of the responsibility belonged to someone else. Lieutenant Dolan appeared. I answered questions. The car turned out to be another rental, Hertz this time instead of Rent-A-Ruin. I'd first seen it this morning, as nearly as I could remember. No, I'd never seen it before. No, I hadn't seen any strangers in the area. Yes, I knew who she was, but she hadn't been in touch. No, I had no idea when or why she'd come to town except that she'd told Terry Kohler she had information for him. Dolan had waited with us at the bird refuge so he knew she hadn't showed up. She was probably already dead by then, her flesh beginning to bake in the toaster oven of the locked car.

Out of the corner of my eye, I watched the medical examiner do his preliminary examination of the body. The car doors were hanging open, the neighborhood perfumed

by the stink of the corpse. By that time it was fully dark and
neighbors were giving the crime scene a wide berth,
watching from porches all up and down the street. Some
were still in work clothes. Many held handkerchiefs to
their faces, filtering the smell. The police personnel working directly with the body wore protective masks. Lights
had been set up and the fingerprint technicians were going over every inch of the dark-blue car with white powder and brushes. Door handles, windows, dash, steering
wheel, steering column, plastic seat covers. Since the
rental car was probably cleaned up between uses, there
was a good chance that any prints lifted would be significant. Easy to match, at any rate.

Pettigrew had gone into my apartment to contact the
Hertz manager by phone.

Lyda was zipped into a body bag. The gases that had
collected under her skin made her look like she'd suddenly
gained fifty pounds, and for a moment, grotesquely, I worried she would burst. I got up abruptly and went inside. I
poured myself a glass of wine and chugged it down like
water. Officer Pettigrew finished his conversation and
hung up the phone.

"I'm going in to take a shower if no one objects." I
didn't wait for an answer. I grabbed a plastic garbage bag
from the kitchen, closed myself into the bathroom and
stripped, dropping every article of clothing, including my
shoes, into the bag. I tied it shut and set it outside the
bathroom door. I showered. I shampooed my hair. When I
was done, I wrapped myself in a towel, searching my face
in the mirror for reassurance. I couldn't shake the images.
Lyda's features seemed to be superimposed on my own,
the stench of her competing with the scent of shampoo
and soap. Never had my own mortality seemed so immediate. My ego recoiled, incapable of contemplating its own
surcease. There's nothing so astonishing or insulting to a
soul as the suggestion that a day might come when it would
not "be." Thus springs religion with comforts I couldn't
accept.

By 9:00 the neighborhood had cleared again. Several
prints, including a partial palm, had been lifted from the
car, which had then been towed to the impound lot. The

Hertz manager had appeared on the scene and the finger-print technician had taken a set of his prints, as well as mine, for comparison. The crime-scene investigators would dust and vacuum the car like a crew of charwomen and then they'd begin the painstaking business of analyzing trace evidence.

In the meantime, I was too restless to stay at home. Any sense of refuge and safety I felt had been obliterated by the angle of Lyda's face, tilted so she seemed to be watching my gate. I hunched myself into a windbreaker and grabbed my handbag, depositing the sackful of fouled clothes in Henry's trash can on my way out. I cruised the neighborhood again, looking for Daniel's car, covering the same restaurant parking lots, the same motels. I still had his guitar in the back seat and I didn't think he'd skip out of town without retrieving it.

I hit pay dirt at the Beach View, which in fact only had a view of the backside of the adjacent motel. Daniel's ratty rented vehicle was parked in front of room 16, ground floor, rear. Parked beside it was a little red Alfa-Romeo convertible. Uneasily I turned to stare at it as I pulled in. I locked my car, pausing to check the glove compartment in the Alfa for the owner registration slip. Not surprisingly, the car belonged to Ashley Wood. My, my, my.

I knocked on Daniel's door. I could see that the lights were on, but there was a long wait. I was beginning to think they might have gone off somewhere on foot when the door opened and Daniel peered out. He was barefoot and shirtless, but he'd pulled on a pair of faded jeans. He looked slim-hipped and bronzed, his blond hair tousled as if he'd been asleep. His cheeks were flushed and the lines had been eased from around his eyes. He looked ten years younger, the haggard cast to his face magically erased. If he was surprised to see me, he gave no indication of it.

"Mind if I come in?" I asked.

He hesitated slightly and then stepped aside. I moved into the room, noting with grim amusement that the bathroom door was shut. The musky smell of sex still hung in the air like ozone after a rainstorm.

"I have your guitar in my car."

"You didn't have to do that. I told you I'd pick it up."

"It's no problem. I wanted to talk to you again, any-way." I strolled around the room, noting the roach clip, the darkened stub of a joint in the ashtray. "God, you got right to it, didn't you?" I remarked.

His gaze was watchful. He knew me well enough to realize I was in a mean mood. He said, "What's on your mind? I'm kind of tied up right now."

I smiled, wondering if he meant that literally. Bond-age had never been part of his sexual repertoire, but who knew how Ash's taste ran? "I found the transmitter. The tape recorder's in the car along with the guitar. I thought I might dump it all off the pier, but I'm too nice. I give you credit for balls, Daniel. It took a lot of fuckin' nerve to come waltzing back in my life and betray me again."

His expression altered, but at least he had the decency not to deny anything.

I moved to the bathroom door and opened it.

Bass was standing there. Something like pain shot through me, followed by the cessation of all feeling. Even rage was washed away in that moment of recognition. I thought about the last time I'd seen them together . . . Bass's twenty-first birthday party at the country club. Dan-iel's jazz combo had played for the occasion and I'd been invited, too, since I knew Ash. Two weeks later, Daniel was gone, without so much as a by-your-leave. I was looking at the reason. Who, I wondered, had seduced whom. Daniel was older than Bass by thirteen years, but that wasn't necessarily relevant. Not that it mattered anyway. Passion had ionized all the air in the room. I felt nearly giddy as I drank it in.

Bass had a towel wrapped around his waist. I found myself checking out the body Daniel found preferable to mine. Bass was pale, narrow through the chest, but he carried himself with perfect composure as he brushed by me.

"Hello, Kinsey." He paused at the ashtray and picked up the roach. He tilted his head, lighting it with a dispos-able Bic. He took a hit and held it out to Daniel, who declined with a slight shake of his head. The two men locked eyes, exchanging a look so filled with tenderness I had to drop my gaze.

Bass glanced over at me. "What brings you here?"

"Lyda Case is dead."

"Who?"

"Come on, Bass. Don't give me that shit. She was married to Hugh Case, who worked for Wood/Warren. Surely, you haven't forgotten him so soon."

Bass set the roach aside and moved to the bed. He stretched out, crossing his arms behind his head. The hair in his armpits was silky and black and I could see bite marks in the crook of his neck. When he spoke, his tone was mild and relaxed. "No need to get ugly. I haven't been around for years. This has nothing to do with me," he said. "You're the one."

"*I* am? That's bullshit! I got backed into this business because of California Fidelity."

"So I heard. The D.A.'s office got in touch with Mother. You're being charged with insurance fraud."

"And you believe that," I said flatly.

"Hey, I can understand it. Lance got his tit in a wringer and needed some cash. Burning the warehouse was better than a bank loan. All he needed was a little help from you."

"Oh, really? You seem well informed for someone who's been gone. Who fills you in?"

"What's it to you?"

"You can't believe everything you hear, Bass. Sometimes you can't even believe your eyes. There's something going on here, and none of us has been smart enough to figure out what it is."

"I'm sure you'll come up with something. I understand you're very good at what you do."

I looked at Daniel. "How did you get sucked into this, or is that a bad choice of words?"

Daniel seemed uncertain how to reply so Bass answered for him. "We had to know what was going on. Obviously, you weren't going to tell us so we had to take steps." He paused to shrug. "We'll be turning the tapes over to the D.A., of course."

"Oh shit, yes. Of course. We who?"

"I'd rather not discuss that, in case you're inclined to retaliate," Bass said. "The point is, I knew Daniel and he knew you and it seemed like the logical way to gather information."

"And Andy Motycka? How does he fit in?"

"I don't know all the details on that. Why don't you tell me?"

"Well, I don't know the details either, Bass. My guess is that somebody pressured Andy into it. Maybe he got nervous when he found out that Darcy and I were onto him. Or maybe he got wind of Olive's death and felt like it was more than he had bargained for. Anyway, it looks like he's left town unless he's been murdered, too. Doesn't it bother you that Lyda Case died?"

"Why should it? I never knew the lady personally. Sure, I'm sorry she died, but I didn't have anything to do with it."

"How do you know you aren't next, Bass? Or maybe Daniel here? If you're not concerned about Olive, at least give some thought to your own vulnerability. You're dealing with someone who has less and less to lose."

"What makes you think he knows who it is?" Daniel said.

"What makes you think he doesn't?" I snapped.

22

When I got home, I turned on all of Henry's exterior lights, flooding his yard like a prison compound. I checked locks on all his doors and windows first and then secured my own. I cleaned and checked my little semiautomatic, loading eight cartridges into the magazine. It worried me that the sights were off. A gun is no protection if you can't control what it does. I stuck it in my handbag. I was going to have to leave it at a gun shop in the morning. Grimly I wondered if a gunsmith supplied loaners.

I brushed my teeth and washed my face, then surveyed my various burns, bruises, and minor cuts. I felt like shit, but I decided it was better to bypass the pain medication. I was afraid of sleeping deeply on the off-chance that someone might have a go at me. I was afraid, too, that Lyda Case might appear in my dreams unannounced.

I watched the digital clock flick its way through the night. Outside, the wind was hot and dry, teasing the palm fronds into rattling conspiracies. The air in my apartment seemed stifling, sounds muffled by the heat. Twice I got up and moved silently into the bathroom where I stood in the shadows of the bathtub, peering out of the window. The tree branches bucked in the wind. Leaves scuttled along the street. Dust was funneled up out of nowhere into whirling spirals. Once a car passed slowly, its headlights fanning up against my ceiling. I pictured Daniel sheltered in the protective curve of Bass's body and I envied them their security. In the dead of night, personal safety seems more important than propriety.

I slept, finally, as the darkness was lifting to the soft

gray of dawn. The wind had died and the ensuing silence
was just as unsettling as the erratic creak of the live oak in
my neighbor's yard. I woke at 8:15 with a start, disoriented
by the sense of the day gone all wrong. I wanted to talk to
Ava at Wood/Warren as soon as the plant opened, which
meant I'd have to skip my run. I was going to have to live
with the brooding dread that was circulating through my
bones. Exercise sweeps that away as nothing else can.
Without the jog, I suspected the anxiety would accumulate. I dragged myself into the shower, then dressed and
made a quick pot of coffee, double-strength, which I
poured into a thermos and sipped as I drove the ten miles
to Colgate.

Lance wasn't expected until after 10:00, and Terry
was on a leave of absence, but Ava was at her desk, looking
dark and sour. She'd had her cracked nail repaired and the
color had shifted from harsh red to a mauve, with a chev-
ron of dark maroon painted on each fingertip. Her outfit
was purple jersey with a cross-chest bandolier of red, altogether dazzling, I thought.

"I left my business card yesterday. I was hoping you'd
call," I said, taking a seat in the metal chair beside her
desk.

"I'm sorry. We were swamped with work." She focused a look on me. All the flint was gone and worry had
taken its place. The lady was in a mood to talk. She said, "I
heard about Lyda Case on the radio this morning. I don't
understand what's going on."

"Did you know Lyda?"

"Not really. I'd only talked to her a couple of times on
the phone, but I was married to a man who killed himself. I
know how devastating that can be."

"Especially when there was no way to have it verified," I said. "You did know all his lab work disappeared
within days."

"Well, I heard that, but I wasn't sure it was true. Suicide is sometimes hard to accept. People make things up
without even meaning to. What happened to Lyda? The
radio didn't say much except that her body'd been found. I
can't tell you how shocked I was. It's horrible."

I told her the details, sparing little. Ordinarily I'd

downplay the particulars, not wanting to pander to the public appetite for the gruesome specifics of violent death. With Ava, I felt the reality of the situation might loosen her tongue. She listened to me with distaste, her dark eyes filling with anxiety.

"Do you mind if I smoke?" she said.

"Not at all. Go ahead."

She opened the bottom drawer of her desk and pulled out her handbag. Her hands were trembling as she shook a Winston from the pack and lit it. "I've been trying to quit, but I just can't help myself. I stopped at the drugstore and picked up a pack on the way to work. I smoked two in the car." She took a deep drag. One of the engineers peered around from his drafting table as the smoke drifted toward him. She had her back turned so she missed the look of annoyance that crossed his face.

"Let's go back to Hugh's death," I said.

"I can't help you much with that. I'd only been with the company a few weeks before he died, so I hardly knew the man."

"Was there an office manager before you?"

Ava shook her head. "I was the first, which meant the office was a mess. Nobody did a thing. Filing alone was piled up to here. There was just one secretary. Heather was the receptionist, but all the day-to-day business was handled by Woody himself, or one of the engineers. It took me six months to get things squared away. Engineers may be obsessive, but not when it comes to paperwork." She took another drag, then tapped the small accumulation of ash from the end of her cigarette.

"What was the atmosphere like at the time? Was it tense? Was anybody caught up in an office dispute? A feud of any kind?"

"Not that I ever heard. Woody bid on a government contract and we were trying to get organized for that. . . ."

"Which entailed what?"

"Routine office procedure. Forms to be filled out, clearances, that kind of thing."

"What happened to the bid?"

"Nothing. The whole thing fell through. Woody had a heart attack, and after he died, Lance let the matter drop."

"What was it they were bidding on? I wonder if that ties in."

"I don't remember what it was. Hold on. I'll ask." Ava turned and scanned the room. John Salkowitz was passing through, blueprint in hand, apparently on his way to the rear of the plant. "John? Could I ask you about something over here?"

He detoured toward us, his expression clouding with concern when he caught sight of me. "What's the story on Lyda Case? My wife just called and said she heard about her on the news."

I gave him the shorthand version, putting it together with the question at hand. "I'm still trying to figure out how it ties into this business with Lance. There's gotta be a connection somewhere."

"He's not seriously being accused of insurance fraud, is he?"

"Looks that way. Along with me, I might add."

"Appalling," he said. "Well. I don't see how it could have any bearing on the contract we bid on, but I'll fill you in. We get a little trade paper called *Commerce Daily*, published by the government. It was Hugh's job to check it for any contract available for bid that might apply to us. He found one under heating equipment, requesting bids on a furnace for processing beryllium, which is used in the making of nuclear bombs and rocket fuel. It's hazardous work. We'd have had to build in a whole new venting system to accommodate CAL-OSHA, but if we got it, we'd have been in a position to bid on future contracts. Woody felt it was worth the expense of retooling. Not all of us agreed with him, but he was a shrewd man and you had to trust his instincts. Anyway, that's what we were going after."

"What would it have been worth to the company?"

"Quarter million bucks. Half a million maybe. More, of course, in the long run, if we bid on future work."

"What was the status of the bid when Hugh died?"

"I don't know. I guess we were gearing up. I know he'd gone down to the Federal Building in Los Angeles to pick up all the paperwork. Since it was the Department of

Defense, we were going to need a company clearance, plus individual clearances. Hugh's death really didn't have much effect, but when Woody died on top of that, we lost heart."

"Could the company have handled the work with both men gone?"

"Probably, but of course Lance was just taking over, getting his feet wet. I guess we dropped the ball, but that's all it amounted to. We weren't out anything. We might not have been low bidder anyway, so it's all speculative."

"What about bids since?"

"That's an aspect of the business we haven't paid much attention to. We're on overload half the time as it is."

I looked at him, truly stumped. "And you don't think it's relevant?"

"If it is, I don't see how."

"Thanks for your time, at any rate. I may need to get back to you."

"Sure thing," he said.

Ava and I chatted a while longer, but the conversation seemed unproductive, except for one minor point. She mentioned, in passing, that Ebony had attended the memorial services for Hugh Case.

"I thought she was in Europe, married to some playboy named Julian."

"She was, but they came back to the States to visit every six months or so."

"How long had she been in town? Do you have any idea?"

Her look was blank. "Can't help you there. I was too new myself to sort out what was normal in that family."

"Maybe I can check it out," I said. "Thanks for your help."

Driving back into town, I was kicking myself. I'd falsely assumed that neither Ebony nor Bass could have been tied in to Hugh's death as both of them were out of the picture at the time—Ebony in Europe, Bass in New York. Now I wasn't sure. I stopped at a public phone booth and called the Woods' house. The maid answered. I was willing to talk to just about any member of the family, but that turned out to be problematic. Mrs. Wood was resting and had asked not to be disturbed. Ebony and Ashley had gone to the Santa Teresa Monument Company to look at memorial tablets for Miss Olive's gravesite. Bass was due back at any minute. Did I care to leave my name and number? I decided to hold off on that. I said I'd call again later and hung up without identifying myself. I hauled more change from my handbag and tried Darcy at the office. She had nothing new to report. I brought her up-to-date and we commiserated briefly on the blanks we were drawing. She said she'd leave word on my answering machine if anything developed. Fat chance, I thought.

I returned to my car and sat there at the curb. I poured the rest of the hot coffee into the thermos lid, sipping it with care. I was getting closer to the truth. I could feel it in my bones. I felt like I was circling, the orbits getting tighter as I approached the central point. Sometimes all it took was one tiny nudge and everything fell into place. But the balance was delicate, and if I pushed too hard, I might barge right past the obvious.

I didn't have that many trees to shake. I screwed the lid on the thermos and tossed it in the back seat. I started up the car and drove back into town again. Maybe Andy's mistress had heard from him. That might help. Fifteen minutes later, I was standing at her door, knocking politely. I wasn't sure if she worked or not. She was home, but when she opened the door, she didn't seem that thrilled to see me.

"Hi," said I. "I'm still looking for Andy and I wondered if you'd heard from him."

She shook her head. Some people think they can lie to me that way, without forming the actual falsehood with their lips. It's apparently part of an inner conviction that if they don't speak the lie aloud, they won't burn in hell.

"He never checked in to let you know he was okay?"

"I just said that, didn't I?"

"Seems odd to me," I remarked. "I half expected him to drop you a note, or make a quick phone call."

"Sorry," she said.

There was a tiny silence wherein she was hoping to close the door and be done with me.

"How'd he get that account anyway?" I asked.

"What account?"

"Wood/Warren. Did he know Lance pretty well or was it someone else in the family?"

"I have no idea. Anyway, he's the claims manager. I don't know that he sold the policy in the first place."

"Oh. Somehow I thought he did. I thought I saw that somewhere on one of the forms we processed. Maybe it was his account before he got promoted to claims manager."

"Are you through asking questions?" she said snappishly.

"Uh, well, actually I'm not. Did Andy know any of the Woods personally? I don't think you told me that."

"How do I know who he knew?"

"Just thought I'd take a flyer," I said. "It puzzles me that you're not worried about him. The man's been gone, what, four days? I'd be frantic."

"I guess that's the difference between us," she said.

"Maybe I'll check out at his place again. You never know. He might have stopped back at the apartment to pick up his clothes and his mail."

She just stared at me. There didn't seem a lot left to say.

"Well, off I go," I said, cheerfully. "You've really been a peach."

Her goodbye was brief. Two words, one of which started with the letter "F." Her mama apparently hadn't taught her to be ladylike any more than mine had taught me. I decided to drive back out to Andy's place because, frankly, I couldn't think what else to do.

23

I headed out to the condominium complex where Andy lived, thrilled that I wasn't going to have to type up a report on the day's events. The truth was, I had no plan afoot, no strategy whatever for wrapping this business up. I didn't have a clue to what was going on. I was driving randomly from one side of the city to the other, hoping that I could shake something loose. I was also avoiding my apartment, picturing the gendarmes at my door with a warrant for my arrest. Andy represented one of the missing links. Someone had designed an elaborate scheme to discredit Lance and eliminate two key engineers at Wood/ Warren. Andy had facilitated the frame-up, but once Olive was blown to kingdom come, he must have decided to blow town himself. If I could pinpoint the connection between Andy Motycka and the person who'd suckered him into it, then maybe I could figure out what the payoff was.

The electronic gates at The Copse stood open, and I passed through without attracting armed guards or vicious dogs. A tall, fair-haired woman in a jumpsuit was walking an apricot poodle, but she scarcely looked at me. I parked my car in the slot Andy had left in the wake of his departure. I trotted up to the second-floor landing and let myself in with the front-door key, which I knew from past experience he kept hidden on the cornice above the front door. I confess I sniffed the air apprehensively as I let myself in, mindful that Andy might have ended up in the same state as Lyda Case. The apartment smelled benign and the dust that had settled on the empty bookshelves attested to the fact that no one had been here for days.

I did a quick pass through the apartment to make sure
it was unoccupied. I opened the rear sliding-glass door,
peered into each bedroom, then returned to the living
room, where I drew the front drapes. I moved through the
daylight gloom with curiosity. Andy lived on such spartan
terms that his place had looked abandoned even when he
was in residence. Now, however, the emptiness had the
aura of a vacant lot, the wall-to-wall carpeting littered with
paper scraps. In situations like this, I always long for the
obvious—cryptic messages, motel receipts, annotated itin-
eraries indicating where the missing might have gone. The
various bits of paper on Andy's floor were none of the
above and I was no wiser for having crawled around on my
hands and knees reading them. The business of private
investigation is fraught with indignities.

The medicine cabinet in his bathroom had been
cleared out. Shampoo, deodorant, and shaving gear were
gone. Wherever he was, he'd be clean-shaven and smell
good. In his bedroom, all of the dirty clothes were gone
and the blue plastic crates had been emptied of their contents. One tatty pair of boxer shorts remained, wild with
fuchsia exclamation marks. I'm always amazed by men's
underwear. Who could guess such things by looking at
their sober three-piece suits? He'd left behind his bicycle,
rowing machine, and the remaining moving cartons.
There were still a few poorly folded sheets in the linen
closet, one package of pizza rolls in the freezer. He'd taken
the bottle of aquavit and the Milky Way bars, perhaps
anticipating his life on the road as an endless round of
sugar and alcohol abuse.

The card table was still in place, the answering machine on top, aluminum lawn chairs pulled up as if he'd
had dinner guests for a banquet of Lean Cuisine. I sat
down, propped my feet up on the adjacent chair and
surveyed Andy's makeshift office. There were still some
pencils, a scratch pad, gummy white-out, unpaid bills. His
answering machine turned out to be a duplicate of mine. I
reached over and flipped open the side panel where the
"oft-dialed" numbers were penned in. Of the sixteen
spaces allotted, only six were filled. Andy was real imagina-

tive. Fire, Police, California Fidelity, his ex-wife, a liquor store, and a pizza joint with free delivery.

I stared at the display on the answering machine, thinking about the features on this model. Carefully I pressed the asterisk button to the left of 0. On my machine, the * redials the last number called. With a flurry of notes up and down the scale, the machine redialed, the number displayed in green. It was vaguely familiar and I made a note of it. The line began to ring. Three times. Four.

Someone picked up. There was a whir and a pause as a machine on the far end of the line came to life.

"Hello. This is Olive Kohler at 555-3282. Sorry we're not here to take your call. I'm out at the supermarket at the moment, but I should be home at four-thirty or so. If you'll leave your number and a message, I'll get back to you as soon as I return. If you're calling with confirmations for the New Year's Party, just leave your name and we'll see you this evening. 'Bye for now."

I could feel my heart thump. No one had changed the message since Olive's death, and there she was again, perpetually hung up in New Year's Eve day, leaving a verbal note before she went off to shop for the party that would never take place.

Perversely, I pressed the asterisk again. Four rings, and Olive picked up, her voice sounding hollow, but full of life. She was still going out to shop for the New Year's party, still requesting the caller's name, telephone number, and a message. " 'Bye for now," she said. I knew if I called a hundred times, she'd still be saying " 'Bye for now" without ever knowing how final that farewell would be.

Andy's last phone call had been to her, but what did it mean? A tiny jolt of memory shot through me. I saw Olive unlock the front door, her arms loaded with groceries, the package bomb, addressed to Terry, resting on top. As the door swung open, the telephone had rung and that's why she'd tossed the package in such haste. Maybe Andy knew the package was waiting on the doorstep and had called to warn them off.

I closed up Andy's apartment, got in my car, and headed back to town, detouring en route to wolf down a fast-food lunch. The Kohlers' house was the next logical stop, but as I turned into the lane, I noticed a whisper of anxiety. I had not, of course, been to the house since the bomb went off and I was not eager to live through the trauma again. I parked in front and gingerly stepped through the gap in the hedge where the gate had been. Only the posts remained now, the hardware twisted where the force of the bomb had wrenched the heavy wooden gate from its hinges. In places the blast had left the shrubbery completely bald.

I approached the house. Plywood sheets and two-by-fours had been nailed across the yawning opening where the front door had been. One of the columns supporting the porch roof had been snapped in two and a clumsy six-by-six had been rigged up in its place. The walkway was scorched, grass sparse and blackened. Sawhorses and warning signs cautioned folks to use the rear. I could still detect the faint briny smell of the cocktail onions that had littered the yard like pearls.

I felt my gaze drawn irresistibly to the spot where Olive had lain in a tumbled, bloody heap. I remembered then how I'd offered to carry the package for her since her arms were loaded with grocery bags. Her casual refusal had saved me. Death sometimes passes us by that way, with a wink, a nod, and an impish promise to return for us at another time. I wondered if Terry felt the same guilt I did that she'd died in our stead.

I was holding my breath, and I shook my arms out like a runner in the middle of a race, moving then toward the rear of the house. I knocked at the back door, cupping my hand against the glass to see if Terry or the housekeeper was home. There was no sign of anyone. I waited, then knocked again. In the lower right-hand corner of the kitchen window there was an alarm-company decal that said "Armed Response" across the bottom. I stepped back so I could scan the area. There was a red light showing on the alarm panel to the right, indicating that the system was armed. If the light was green, any burglar would know it was safe to start work. I took a business card from my handbag and sketched a quick note, asking Terry to call

me when he got home. I got in my car again and drove to
the Woods'. For all I knew, he was still there.

Early-afternoon sunlight poured down on the house
with its dazzling white facade. The grass was newly cut, as
short and densely green as wool-pile carpeting. Beyond
the bluffs, the ocean was an intense navy blue, the surface
feathered with whitecaps that suggested a strong wind
coming off the water. The hot desert wind was blowing at
my back, and the palms tossed restlessly where the two
met. Ash's little red sports car was parked in the circular
driveway, along with a BMW. There was no sign of Terry's
Mercedes. I walked around the house to the long, low
brick porch on the seaward side and rang the bell.

The maid let me in and left me in the foyer while she
went to fetch Miss Ebony. I had asked for Ash, but I was
willing to take pot luck. I wished fervently that I had a
theory, but this was still a fishing expedition. I couldn't be
far from understanding the truth, but I had no clear concept what the revelation might be. Under the circumstances, all I knew to do is persist, plowing through. Bass
was the only member of the family I was hoping to avoid.
Not that it made any difference at that point, but pride is
pride. Who wants to make small talk with your ex-spouse's
lover? I had to be careful that my sense of injury didn't get
in the way of spotting his role in this.

"Hello, Kinsey."

Ebony was standing at the bottom of the stairs, her
pale oval face as smooth as an egg, expressionless, composed. She was wearing a shirtwaist dress of black silk that
emphasized her wide shoulders and slim hips, the long
shapely legs. Her red spike heels must have added five
inches to her height. Her hair was skinned back from the
taut bones of her face. A swath of blusher on each cheek
suggested high stress instead of the good health it was
meant to convey. In the family mythology, she was the
thrill-seeker, addicted to the sort of treacherous hobbies
that can spell early death: sky-diving, helicopter skiing,
climbing the sheer faces of impossible cliffs. In the family
dynamic, maybe she'd been designated to live recklessly,
just as Bass lived with vanity, idleness, and self-indulgence.

I said, "I thought we should talk."

"About what?"

"Olive's death. Lyda Case is dead, too."

"Bass told me that."

My smile had a bitter feeling to it. "Ah. Bass. How did he get involved? Somehow I get the feeling you might have put a call through to him in New York."

"That's right."

"Dirty pool, Ebony."

She shrugged, undismayed. "It's your own damn fault."

"*My* fault?"

"I asked you what was going on and you wouldn't say. It's my family, Kinsey. I have a right to know."

"I see. And who thought about bringing Daniel into it?"

"I did, but Bass was the one who tracked him down. He and Daniel had an affair years ago, until Bass broke it off. There was unfinished business between them. Daniel was more than happy to accommodate him in the hopes of rekindling the fires."

"Selling me out in the process," I said.

She smiled slightly, but her gaze was intent. "You didn't have to agree, you know. You must have had some unfinished business of your own or you wouldn't have been suckered in so easily."

"True," I said. "That was smart. God, he nicked right in there and gave you everything, didn't he?"

"Not quite."

"Oh? Something missing? Some little piece of the scheme incomplete?"

"We still don't know who killed Olive."

"Or Lyda Case," I said, "though the motive was probably not the same. I suspect she somehow figured out what was going on. Maybe she went back through Hugh's papers and came up with something significant."

"Like what?"

"Hey, if I knew that, I'd probably know who killed her, wouldn't I?"

Ebony stirred restlessly. "I have things to do. Why don't you tell me what you want."

"Well, let's see. Just in rambling around town, it occurred to me that it might help to find out who inherits Olive's stock."

"Stock?"

"Her ten voting shares. Surely, those wouldn't be left to someone outside the family. So who'd she leave 'em to?"

For the first time she was genuinely flustered and the color in her cheeks seemed real. "What difference does it make? The bomb was meant for Terry. Olive died by mistake, didn't she?"

"I don't know. Did she?" I snapped back. "Who stands to benefit? You? Lance?"

"Ash," came the voice. "Olive left all her stock to her sister Ashley." Mrs. Wood had appeared in the upstairs hall. I looked up to see her clinging to the rail, the walker close by, her whole body trembling with exertion.

"Mother, you don't have to concern yourself with this."

"I think I do. Come to my room, Kinsey." Mrs. Wood disappeared.

I glanced at Ebony and then pushed past her and went up the stairs.

24

We sat in her room near French doors that opened onto a balcony facing the sea. Sheer curtains were pulled across the doorway, billowing lazily in a wind that smelled of salt. The bedroom suite was dark and old, a clumsy assortment of pieces she and Woody must have salvaged from their early married years: a dresser with chipped veneer, matching misshapen lamps with dark-red silk shades. I was reminded of thrift-store windows filled with other people's junk. Nothing in the room would qualify as "collectible," much less antique.

She sat in a rocker upholstered in horsehair, frayed and shiny, picking at the fabric on the arms of the chair. She looked awful. The skin on her face had been blanched by Olive's death and her cheeks were mottled with liver spots and threaded with visible capillaries. She looked as though she'd lost weight in the last few days, the flesh hanging in pleats along her upper arms, her bones rising to the surface like a living lesson in anatomy. Even her gums had shrunk away from her teeth, the aging process suddenly as visible as in time-lapse photography. She seemed weighed down with some as yet unidentified emotion that left her eyes red-rimmed and lusterless. I didn't think she'd survive it, whatever it was.

She had clumped her way back to her room with the aid of her walker, which she kept close to her, holding on to it with one trembling hand.

I sat in a hard-backed chair near hers, my voice low. "You know what's going on, don't you?" I said.

"I think so. I should have spoken up sooner, but I so

hoped my suspicions were groundless. I thought we'd buried the past. I thought we'd moved on, but we haven't. There's so much shame in the world as it is. Why add to it?" Her voice quavered and her lips trembled as she spoke. She paused, struggling with some inner admonition. "I promised Woody I wouldn't speak of it again."

"You have to, Helen. People are dying."

For a moment, her dark eyes sparked to life. "I know that," she snapped. The energy was short-lived, a match flaring out. "You do the best you can," she went on. "You try to do what's right. Things happen and you salvage what's left."

"Nobody's blaming you."

"I blame myself. It's my fault. I should have said something the minute things began to go wrong. I knew the connection, but I didn't want to believe it, fool that I am."

"Is this related to Woody?"

She shook her head.

"Who then?"

"Lance," she whispered. "It started with him."

"Lance?" I said, disconcerted. It was the last name I expected to hear.

"You'd think the past could be diffused . . . that it wouldn't have the power to affect us so long after the fact."

"How far back does this go?"

"Seventeen years, almost to the day." She clamped her mouth shut, then shook her head again. "Lance was a hellion in his teens, rebellious and secretive. He and Woody clashed incessantly, but boys do that. Lance was at an age when *of course* he had to assert himself."

"Ash says he had a couple of scrapes with the law back then."

She stirred impatiently. "He was constantly in trouble. 'Acting out' they call it now, but I didn't think he was a bad boy. I still don't. He had a troubled adolescence. . . ." She broke off, taking a deep breath. "I don't mean to belabor the point. What's done is done. Woody finally sent him off to military school, and after that he went into the army. We hardly saw him until he came home that Christmas on leave. He seemed fine by then. Grown up. Mature. Calm and pleasant and civil to us both. He became interested in the company. He talked about settling down and learning the business. Woody was thrilled." She fumbled in her pocket for a handkerchief, which she pressed to her lips, blotting the film of perspiration that had formed like dew.

So far she wasn't telling me a thing I didn't already know. "What happened?"

"That year . . . when Lance came home and things were going so well . . . that year . . . it was New Year's Day. I remember how happy I was things were off to such a good start. Then Bass came to us with the most preposterous tale. Somehow, in my heart, I suppose I've always blamed him. He spoiled everything. I've never really forgiven him, though it was hardly his fault. Bass was thirteen then. Sly. He knew about wickedness even at that age and he enjoyed it all so very much."

Still does, I thought. "What did he tell you?"

"He said he'd walked in on Lance. He came straight to us with that sneaky look in his eyes, pretending to be so upset when he knew exactly what he was about. At first, Woody didn't believe a word of it."

"He walked in on Lance doing what?"

There was a silence and then she pushed on, her voice dropping so low I was forced to lean closer. "With Olive," she whispered. "Lance and Olive. In her room on the bed. She was sixteen and so beautiful. I thought I'd die of the shame and embarrassment, the loathing at what was going on. Woody was crazed. He was in a towering rage. Lance swore it was innocent, that Bass misunderstood, but that was nonsense. Absurd to think we'd believe any such thing. Woody beat Lance to within an inch of his life. A fearful beating. I thought he'd kill him. Lance swore it only happened once. He swore he'd never lay another hand on her and he honored that. I know he did."

"That's when Olive was sent away to boarding school," I said.

Helen nodded.

"Who else knew about the incident?"

"No one. Just the five of us. Lance and Olive, Bass and Woody and me. Ebony was off in Europe. Ash knew something dreadful had happened, but she never knew what it was."

There was a silence. Helen smoothed the frayed fabric on the arm of the rocker where she'd picked strands loose. She glanced at me. Her expression seemed tinged with guilt, like an old dog that's piddled somewhere you haven't discovered yet. There was more, something she didn't want to own up to.

"What's the rest?" I asked. "What else?"

She shook her head, her cheeks turning pink in patches.

"Just tell me, Helen. It can't matter now."

"Yes, it does," she whispered. She'd begun to weep. I could see her clamp down, forcing her feelings back into the box she'd kept them in all these years.

I waited so long that I didn't think she meant to finish. Her hands began to shake in a separate dance of their own, a jitterbug of anxiety.

Finally she spoke. "Lance was lying about the two of them. It had gone on for years. Woody never knew, but I suspected as much."

"You suspected Lance was abusing her and you never interfered?"

"What could I say? I had no proof. I kept them away from each other whenever I could. He'd go off to summer camp. She'd stay with friends of ours in Maine. I never left them alone in the house. I hoped it was a phase, something that would disappear of its own accord. I thought if I called attention to it . . . I don't know what I thought. It was so unspeakable. A mother doesn't sit a boy down and discuss such things. I didn't want to pry, and Olive denied the slightest suggestion that anything was amiss. If she'd come to me, I'd have stepped in. Of course I would, but she never said a word. She might have been the one who initiated the contact for all I knew."

"How long did this go on?" I was having a hard time keeping the judgment out of my voice, afraid if she sensed the full range of my outrage, she'd clam up.

"Lance was obsessed with her almost from infancy. He was five when she was born and I was so relieved, you see, that he didn't resent her. It was just him and Ebony until Olive came along. He'd been the baby so I was delighted he seemed taken with her. It must have started as childish curiosity and advanced to something else. It did end once they were discovered. They could hardly tolerate each other's company these past few years, but by then the damage had been done. She had terrible problems."

"Sexual problems, I'd assume."

Helen nodded, cheeks coloring. "She also suffered deep depressions that would go on for months. All she did was run, run, run. Anything to escape the feelings. Play and spend. Spend and play. That's how she lived."

Rapidly I sorted through all the things I'd been told, processing the trivia I'd picked up in passing. "Olive said she and Bass had a falling-out when he was home for Thanksgiving. What was that about?"

"Something silly. I don't even remember now what the subject matter was. One of those ridiculous spats people get into when they've drunk too much. Bass was furious and wanted to get back at her, but it wasn't *about* anything. Petty temper, that's all."

I watched her carefully, making my mind a blank, trying to let the sense of this filter in. It had started with Lance, with Wood/Warren, talk of a takeover, evidence of insurance fraud. Someone had set Lance up and I'd been caught in the same trap. When Olive died, I'd assumed it was business-related, an accident. It was meant to look like that, but it wasn't. I felt the answer leap at me, so obvious once I knew what had gone on. "Oh shit," I said. "Bass told Terry, didn't he?"

"I think so," she said, almost inaudibly. "I don't think Terry's like the rest of us. He's not a well man. He doesn't seem right to me. Even when they met, he seemed 'off' somehow, but he was crazy about Olive. . . ."

"'Obsessed' is the word I've heard applied," I broke in. "That he worshiped the ground she walked on."

"Oh, he adored her, there's no doubt of that. It was just what she needed and I thought it would all work out. She had such a low opinion of herself all her life. She couldn't seem to sustain a relationship until Terry came along. I thought she deserved a little happiness."

"You mean because she was 'damaged goods,' don't you? Tainted by what Lance had done."

"Well, she *was* tainted. Who knows what bestial appetites Lance had wakened in her?"

"That was hardly *her* fault."

"Of course not, but what nice boy was ever going to look at her if the truth came out? Terry seemed like a godsend."

"So the two of you decided not to say anything to him."

"We never spoke of it between us," she said tartly, "so we could hardly speak of it to him. Why stir up trouble when everything was going so well?"

I got up abruptly and went to the phone, dialing Lieutenant Dolan's number at the Santa Teresa PD. The clerk said she'd put me through and I waited for Dolan's line to ring. Helen was right. What was done was done. There wasn't any point in blaming Bass. If anything, the blame lay with Helen and Woody. Olive died because Helen was too bloody polite to deal with the truth.

"Where's Terry now?" I said to Helen over my shoulder.

She was weeping openly. It seemed a little late for tears, but I didn't say so. "He was here a short while ago. He's on his way home."

When Dolan answered, I identified myself and laid it out for him, chapter and verse.

"I'll have him picked up for questioning," Dolan said. "We'll get a warrant so we can search the premises. He put that bomb together somewhere."

"He might have assembled it at work."

"We'll check that," he said. "Hang on." He put his hand across the mouth of the receiver and I could hear him issue an order to someone else in the room. He came back on the line. "Let me tell you what we have on this end. We got a match on the prints we lifted from the rental car Lyda Case was found in. They belong to a fellow named Chris Emms, who was charged with the murder of his foster mother twenty years ago. Blew her up with a package bomb he sent through the mail. The jury brought in a verdict of temporary insanity."

"Oh geez, I get it. No prison for him."

"Right. He was committed to the state hospital at Camarillo and escaped after eighteen months."

"And he was never picked up?"

"He's been free as a bird. I just talked to one of the staff docs and they're hunting up the old records to see what else they have on him."

"Was he really nuts or faking it?"

"Anybody who does what he did is nuts."

"Will you let the family know as soon as he's in custody?"

"Will do. I'll send somebody over in the meantime just in case he decides to come back."

"You better beef up security at Wood/Warren, too. He may make a try for Lance."

"Right," Dolan said. He broke off the connection.

I left Helen huddled in the rocker. I went downstairs, looking for Ebony, and told her what was going on. When I let myself out, she was on her way upstairs to see her mother. I couldn't imagine what they'd talk about. I had a flash of Olive sailing through the air, flying to oblivion. I just couldn't shake the image. I drove home feeling low, my perpetual state these days. I get tired of digging around in other people's dirty laundry. I'm sick of knowing more about them than I should. The past is never nice. The secrets never have to do with acts of benevolence or good deeds suddenly coming to light. Nothing's ever resolved with a handshake or a heart-to-heart talk. So often, humankind just seems tacky to me, and I don't know what the rest of us are supposed to do in response.

Under the bandages, my burns were chafed and fiery hot, throbbing dully. I glanced at myself in the rearview mirror. With my hair singed across the front and my eyebrows gone, I looked startled somehow, as if unprepared for the sudden conclusion to the case at this point. Quite true. I hadn't had time to process events. I thought about Daniel and Bass. Mentally I had to close the door on them, but it felt like unfinished business, and I didn't like that. I wanted closure, surcease. I wanted peace of mind again.

I pushed through the gate, pulling mail out of the box as I passed. I let myself into my place, and slung my handbag on the couch. I felt a desperate need to take a bath,

symbolic as it was. It was only 4:00 in the afternoon, but I
was going to scrub up and then go pound on Rosie's door. It
was Tuesday and she was bound to be back in business by
now. My neighborhood tavern usually opens at 5:00, but
maybe I could sweet-talk her into letting me in early. I
needed a heavy Hungarian dinner, a glass of white wine,
and someone to fuss at me like a mother.

I paused at my desk and checked my answering machine. There were no messages. The mail was dull. Belatedly, I registered the fact that my bathroom door was
closed. I hadn't left it that way. I never do. My apartment is
small and the light from the bathroom window helps illuminate the place. I turned my head and I could feel the
hair rise on the back of my neck. The knob rotated and the
door swung open. That portion of the room was in shadow
at that hour of day, but I could see him standing there. My
spinal column turned to ice, the chill radiating outward to
my limbs, which I couldn't will to move. Terry emerged
from the bathroom and circled the couch. In his right hand
he had a gun pointed right at my gut. I felt my hands rise
automatically, palms up, the classic posture of submission
guns seem to inspire.

Terry said, "Oops, you caught me. I expected to be
gone by the time you got home."

"What are you doing here?"

"I brought you a present." He made a gesture toward
the kitchenette.

Trancelike, I turned to see what he was pointing to.
On the counter was a shoe box wrapped in Christmas
paper, white HO HO HO's emblazoned on a dark-green
background with a cartoon Santa swinging from each O. A
preformed red satin bow was stuck to the lid. Surprise,
surprise. Terry Kohler wanted me to have a box of death.

"Nice," I managed, though my mouth was dry.

"Aren't you going to open it?"

I shook my head. "I think I'll just leave it where it is.
I'd hate to give it a bump."

"This one's on a timer."

I managed to loosen my jaw, but I couldn't form any
words. Where had I put my gun? My mind was washed
absolutely blank. I reached for the edge of my desk, sup-

porting myself with my fingertips. Bombs are loud. The end is quick. I cleared my throat. "Sorry to interrupt you," I said. "Don't stick around on my account."

"I can stay for a minute. We could have a little chat."

"Why kill me?"

"It seemed like a good idea," he said mildly. "I thought you might like to go out with a bang, as opposed to a you-know-what."

"I'm surprised you didn't try for Lance."

"I have a package just like it in the car for him."

Probably in the bottom of my handbag, I thought. I'd meant to take it to the gun shop. Had I stuck it in the briefcase in the back seat of my car? If so, it was still out there and my ass was grass. "Do you mind if I sit?"

He did a quick survey of the area, making sure there weren't any rifles, bullwhips, or butcher knives within range. "Go ahead."

I moved to the couch and sank down without taking my eyes off him. He pulled my desk chair closer and sat down, crossing his legs. He was a nice-looking man, dark and lean, on the slight side. There was nothing in his manner to indicate how nuts he was. How nuts is he? I thought. How far gone? How amenable to reasoning? Would I trade my life for bizarre sexual favors if he asked? Oh sure, why not?

I was having trouble appraising the situation. I was home where I should have been safe. It wasn't even dark out. I really needed to pee, but it sounded like a ploy. And honest to god, I was embarrassed to make the request. It seemed advisable to try opening a dialogue, one of those conversations designed to ingratiate. "What's the timetable here?"

He glanced at his watch. "Ten minutes, more or less. The bomb should go off at four-thirty. I was worried you wouldn't get home in time," he said. "I can reset it, but I don't want to mess the wrapping paper up."

"I can understand that," I said. I checked the clock on my desk. 4:22. I could feel my adrenal gland squirt some juice into my veins. Terry didn't seem concerned. "You seem calm enough," I remarked.

He smiled. "I'm not going to be around when the damn thing goes off. They're dangerous."

"How can you keep me here? You'll have to shoot me first."

"I'll tie you up. I have some rope." I could see then that he had a coil of clothesline he'd tossed on the kitchen floor.

"You think of everything," I said. I wanted him to talk. I didn't want him to tie me up because then I'd be dead for sure. There wasn't going to be any way to hump and thump my way out. No broken glass by which I could saw through my ropes. No knives, no tricks, no miracles. "What if it goes off prematurely?"

"Too bad," he said with mockery, "but you know what Dylan Thomas said. 'After the first death, there is no other.'"

"How does Hugh Case fit in? Do you mind if I ask? I just want to know for the sake of it."

"I don't mind. We don't have anything else to talk about. Hugh was made the security officer after Woody bid on a government contract. We were all going to have to have clearances, but the guy went overboard. Forms, interviews, all these questions. He really took himself seriously. At first I thought it was all a game, but gradually I realized he was coming up with too many penetrating questions. He knew. Of course, he wanted my fingerprints. I stalled as long as possible, but I couldn't refuse. I had to kill him before he told Woody all the sordid details."

"About your mother."

"Foster mother," he corrected.

"Wouldn't somebody else have come up with the same information?"

"I'd figured a way around it, but I needed him out of the way for it to work."

"But you don't know that he was actually onto you."

"Oh, but I do and he was. I destroyed the file he kept at work, but he had a duplicate at home. Talk about a breach of security," he said. "That came to light just recently."

"Lyda found it."

"Now that was your fault. After you flew to Texas, she

went through the papers she'd packed up and came across all the data on Chris Emms. She had no idea who he was, but she figured it was someone at the plant. She called me from Dallas and said she had some information Hugh had unearthed. I told her I'd be happy to take a look at it and help her figure out what to do with it. She made me promise not to mention it to Lance since she was so suspicious of him anyway."

"Nice," I said. "And the threat from her . . . you just made that up?"

"Yep."

"And the day we waited at the bird refuge, she was already dead out in front?"

"Righty-o," he said.

"How'd you kill Hugh?"

Terry shrugged indifferently. "Chloral hydrate. Then I strolled in and stole his blood and urine samples so it couldn't be traced."

"Takes nerve," I said.

"It had to be done and I knew I was right. I couldn't have him upsetting my life. What made me so mad afterwards, of course, is it was all for nothing. Olive had a past just as bad as mine. I didn't need to protect myself at all. I could have traded her, tit for tat, if she'd leveled with me."

"You must feel better now that she's gone. She's been paid in full, hasn't she?"

His face clouded. "I should have killed Lance and left her alive. I could have made her life miserable."

"I thought you'd already done that."

"Well, yes, but she didn't suffer nearly enough. And now she's off the hook."

"She did love you," I said.

"So what?"

"So nothing. I guess love doesn't count for much with you." I felt my eyes stray to the clock. 4:25.

"Not when it's based on lies and deceit," he said piously. "She should have told me the truth. She never shared the facts. She let me go right on believing our sex life was all my fault. She made me think I was inadequate when all the time it was her. Sometimes I think about him with his mouth all over her, feeding like a leech, sucking at her everywhere. Disgusting," he said.

"That was a long time ago."

"Not long enough."

"What about Andy Motycka? How'd you persuade him to help?"

"Money and threats. The carrot and the stick. Janice was hosing him for every cent he had. I paid him ten grand. Every time he got nervous, I reminded him that I'd be happy to tell Janice about Lorraine if he tried to back out."

"How'd you find out about her?"

"We've all known each other for years. The four of us went to UCST together before he and Janice got married. This was after I conjured up my new identity, of course. Once I settled on the frame-up, it didn't take much to figure out he was in the perfect position to assist me."

"Did you kill him too?"

"I wish I had. He ducked out on me, but I'll find a way to lure him back. He's not very smart."

Even with the tinnitus I suffer, I could have sworn I could hear the package bomb ticking merrily. I wet my lips. "Is there really a clock in there? Is that how it works?"

He glanced over at the kitchen counter. "It's not a complicated device. The one for Olive was more elaborate, but I had to make sure it would detonate on impact."

"It's amazing I wasn't killed then."

"Might have simplified things," he said.

I remembered then how he'd bent to recoil the hose lying on the walk. Any excuse to hang back out of range. I was beginning to feel strangely free. The time left was brief, but it was beginning to stretch and sag like a long strand of chewing gum. It seemed absurd to think I'd spend the last minutes of my life discussing trivial points with the man who was going to do me in. Oh hell, why not, you know? I flashed again to my brief flight off the front of Olive's porch while she soared beyond me like a bird. A death like that barely registers. What scared me was surviving, maimed and burned, living long enough to feel the loss of self. Time to make a move, I thought, regardless of the consequences. Once your life is threatened, what else do you have to lose?

I reached for my handbag. "I've got some tranqs in my bag. Do you mind?"

He seemed startled, waving his gun at me. "Leave it where it is."

"I'm a wreck, Terry. I really need a Valium. Then you can tie me up."

"No," he said peevishly. "Don't touch it. I mean it!"

"Come on. Indulge me. It's a small request."

I pulled the bag over and unzipped the top, rooting through the contents until I located the crosshatched ivory handle of my beloved .32 and eased the safety off. He couldn't believe I'd disobey him, but he couldn't seem to think what to do.

As he rose to his feet, I fired through the bottom of the handbag at a range of ten feet without any visible effect. He did jump as if I'd tossed hot gravy on his pants, but I didn't see blood and he didn't topple to the floor as I'd sincerely prayed he would. Instead, he roared to life, coming at me like a mad dog. I pulled the gun out of my purse to fire again, but he was on me, taking me with him to the floor. I saw his fist come at me, and I jerked to the right. The blow landed on my left ear, which rang with pain. I scrambled up, grabbing at the couch for support. I had no idea where my gun had gone, but he was aiming his at me. I snatched up my handbag and swung it. I caught him in the head. The momentum knocked him sideways.

He was blocking my passage to the front door, so I veered the other way, and raced into the bathroom. I slammed the door after me, turned the lock, and hit the floor. He fired twice, bullets zinging through the door like bees. There was no way out. The bathroom window was right in the line of fire and I couldn't see anything to defend myself with. He started kicking at the door, savage blows that splintered the wood on impact. I saw his foot come through the panel and he kicked again. His hand shot through the hole and he fumbled for the lock. I jerked the lid off the toilet tank and cracked him a blow. I heard him yelp and he snatched his hand back through the hole. He fired again, screaming obscenities. Suddenly his face

appeared in the gap, eyes roving wildly as he searched for
my location. The nose of the gun peered at me. All I could
think to do was to protect myself with the tank lid, holding
it in front of me like a shield. The bullet slammed into it
with a clang, the impact fierce enough to jolt the lid right
out of my hands, breaking it in two. Terry started kicking
at the door again, but the blows were losing force.

On the other side, I heard him fall heavily. I froze,
astonished, gasping for breath. There wasn't time to wait
to see if he was faking it. I flipped the lock, shoving at the
door, which I couldn't budge. I dropped to my knees and
peered at him through the panel. He was flat on his back,
his shirt front drenched in red. Apparently I'd wounded
him the first time I fired, but it had taken him this long to
go down. Blood seeped from him like a slow leak from a
worn tire. His chest was still heaving. Above his stertorous
breathing I could hear the package ticking like a grandfather clock.

"Get out of the doorway! Terry, move!"

He was unresponsive. The clock on my desk said 4:29.

I shoved as hard as I could, but there was no budging
him. I had to get out of there. Frantically I glanced around
the room and then grabbed up one half of the broken toilet
tank. I smashed at the window. Glass showered out into
the front yard, leaving fangs of glass in the frame. I
grabbed a towel and wedged it over the glass-ragged sill as
I boosted myself up.

The boom from the explosion propelled me through
the window, like Superman in full flight. I landed on the
grass with a whunk that knocked the wind right out of me.
For a moment, I felt the panic of paralysis, wondering if I'd
ever breathe again. Debris was raining down around me. I
saw a hunk of the roof hover briefly above me, like a UFO.
Then it began to tumble and bounce down through the
intervening branches of a tree. A cloud of white smoke
drifted into view and began to disperse. I angled my gaze
up to the wall behind me, which seemed to be intact. My
sofa bed was sitting in the driveway with the cushions
askew. Perched on the arm was my perky green air fern
looking like it had hopped up there by itself. I knew the
whole front wall of my apartment would be gone, the

interior a shambles, all my possessions destroyed. Lucky I don't have much in this world, I thought.

I was temporarily deaf again, but I was getting used to it. Eventually, with effort, I roused myself and went back inside to see if there was anything of Terry left.

Epilogue

Henry Pitts came home to find a crater where his rental unit had been. He was more distressed about my troubles in his absence than any damage to his property, which was covered by insurance. He has big plans now about building a new studio for me and he's already conferring with an architect. I managed to salvage a few articles of clothing, among them my all-purpose dress and my favorite vest. What could I complain about? As soon as I was on my feet again, I went back to work. Mac arranged for California Fidelity to refurbish my office as a way of making amends for my temporary suspension. Andy Motycka was fired and criminal charges were filed against him. The D.A.'s office probably whited my name out and typed his in its place. Within two days of the explosion, Daniel left with Bass. I can't say I felt much. After all I'd been through, his betrayal seemed beside the point.

In surveying the situation, there was only one other matter that needed cleaning up. I conferred with Lieutenant Dolan in private about the five thousand dollars Terry'd deposited to my account. He advised me to keep my mouth shut, which I did.

Respectfully submitted,
Kinsey Millhone

ABOUT THE AUTHOR

SUE GRAFTON has written novels, articles, short fiction, a screenplay, and numerous teleplays. She has also lectured on writing at colleges and conferences in Southern California and the Midwest. Her first mystery, 'A' IS FOR ALIBI, won an award from the Cloak and Clue Society of Wisconsin. 'B' IS FOR BURGLAR won both the Anthony and the Shamus awards for best novel of 1985, and 'C' IS FOR CORPSE won the Anthony Award for Best Novel in 1986. ''The Parker Shotgun'' won a Macavity Award from the Mystery Readers of America and an Anthony for Best Short Story of 1986. Grafton, who was born in Louisville, Kentucky, now lives in Southern California with her husband, Steven Humphrey.

Sue Grafton's

Kinsey Millhone is

"A refreshing heroine."
—*The Washington Post Book World*

"The best new private eye."
—*The Detroit News*

"A stand-out specimen of the new female operatives."
—*Philadelphia Inquirer*

"The gutsiest, grittiest female operative going."
—*Daily News*, New York

❑ "A" IS FOR ALIBI   27991-2 $5.99/$6.99 in Canada

❑ "B" IS FOR BURGLAR   28034-1 $5.99/$6.99 in Canada

❑ "C" IS FOR CORPSE   28036-8 $5.99/$6.99 in Canada

❑ "D" IS FOR DEADBEAT   27163-6 $5.99/$6.99 in Canada

❑ "E" IS FOR EVIDENCE   27955-6 $5.99/$6.99 in Canada

❑ "F" IS FOR FUGITIVE   28478-9 $5.99/$6.99 in Canada

"Once a fan reads one of Grafton's alphabetically titled detective novels, he or she will not rest until all the others are found."—*Los Angeles Herald Examiner*

Available at your local bookstore or use this page to order.

Send to: Bantam Books, Dept. BD 26
          2451 S. Wolf Road
          Des Plaines, IL 60018

Please send me the items I have checked above. I am enclosing $_____ (please add $2.50 to cover postage and handling). Send check or money order, no cash or C.O.D.'s, please.

Mr./Ms._____

Address_____

City/State_____Zip_____

Please allow four to six weeks for delivery.

Prices and availability subject to change without notice. BD 26 3/92

MORE RAVE REVIEWS FOR
KINSEY MILLHONE
AND
"D" IS FOR DEADBEAT

"One of the things that makes Sue Grafton's Kinsey Millhone series so unfailingly entertaining is
Millhone's character. She's the last one to cultivate eccentricities in the Nero Wolfe manner, and
her unsentimental, loner's-eye view of herself and
the world keeps her feet on the ground. But her
cases often get messy because she feels things
strongly. This happens again, more satisfyingly
than ever, in *"D" is for Deadbeat*."

—*The Detroit News*

"Kinsey Millhone has the characteristic persist-
ence of the good private eye who won't be
deterred from digging out the truth. With skill,
Grafton keeps not only her appealing detective but
her readers on edge to know more."

—*Ms. magazine*

"Taut prose and controlled plotting make Grafton
an outstanding writer of hardboiled detective stories. Social awareness and human weakness play a
great part in the Millhone books, which always
manage to finish with a heart-stopping climax.
Well done indeed."

—*Library Journal*

Bantam Crime Line Books by Sue Grafton
Ask your bookseller for the books you have missed

"A" IS FOR ALIBI
"B" IS FOR BURGLAR
"C" IS FOR CORPSE
"D" IS FOR DEADBEAT
"E" IS FOR EVIDENCE
"F" IS FOR FUGITIVE

"D" is for Deadbeat

A Kinsey Millhone Mystery

SUE GRAFTON

BANTAM BOOKS

NEW YORK • TORONTO • LONDON • SYDNEY • AUCKLAND

*This edition contains the complete text
of the original hardcover edition.*
NOT ONE WORD HAS BEEN OMITTED.

"D" IS FOR DEADBEAT

*A Bantam Crime Line Book / published by arrangement with
Henry Holt and Company, Inc.*

PRINTING HISTORY
Henry Holt edition published May 1987
Bantam edition / June 1988

CRIME LINE *and the portrayal of a boxed "cl" are trademarks of Bantam Books, a division
of Bantam Doubleday Dell Publishing Group, Inc.*

All rights reserved.
Copyright © 1987 by Sue Grafton.
Cover art copyright © 1988 by Roy Pendleton.
Library of Congress Catalog Card Number: 86-25843.
*No part of this book may be reproduced or transmitted in any form or by any means,
electronic or mechanical, including photocopying, recording, or by any information
storage and retrieval system, without permission in writing from the publisher.*
For information address:
Henry Holt and Company, Inc., 115 West 18th Street, New York, NY 10011.

If you purchased this book without a cover you should be aware that this book is stolen
property. It was reported as "unsold and destroyed" to the publisher and neither the
author nor the publisher has received any payment for this "stripped book."

ISBN 0-553-27163-6

Published simultaneously in the United States and Canada

*Bantam Books are published by Bantam Books, a division of Bantam Doubleday Dell
Publishing Group, Inc. Its trademark, consisting of the words "Bantam Books" and the
portrayal of a rooster, is Registered in U.S. Patent and Trademark Office and in other
countries. Marca Registrada. Bantam Books, 666 Fifth Avenue, New York, New York 10103.*

PRINTED IN THE UNITED STATES OF AMERICA

OPM   24   23   22   21   20   19   18   17

For my sister, Ann,
and the memories of Maple Hill.

The author wishes to acknowledge the invaluable assistance of the following people: Steven Humphrey, Florence Clark, Joyce Mackewich, Steve Stafford, Bob Ericson, Ann Hunnicutt, Charles and Mary Pope of the Rescue Mission, Michael Thompson of the Santa Barbara Probation Department, Michelle Bores and Bob Brandenburg of the Santa Barbara Harbor Master's Office, Mary Louise Days of the Santa Barbara Building Department, and Gerald Dow, Crime Analyst, Santa Barbara Police Department.

"D" is Deadbeat

1

Later, I found out his name was John Daggett, but that's not how he introduced himself the day he walked into my office. Even at the time, I sensed that something was off, but I couldn't figure out what it was. The job he hired me to do seemed simple enough, but then the bum tried to stiff me for my fee. When you're self-employed, you can't afford to let these things slide. Word gets out and first thing you know, everybody thinks you can be had. I went after him for the money and the next thing I knew, I was caught up in events I still haven't quite recovered from.

My name is Kinsey Millhone. I'm a private investigator, licensed by the state of California, operating a small office in Santa Teresa, which is where I've lived all my thirty-two years. I'm female, self-supporting, single now, having been married and divorced twice. I confess I'm sometimes testy, but for the most part I credit myself with an easygoing disposition, tempered (perhaps) by an exaggerated desire for independence. I'm also plagued with the sort of doggedness that makes private investigation a viable proposition for someone with a high school education, certification from the police academy, and a constitutional inability to work for anyone else. I pay my bills on time, obey most laws, and I feel that other people should do likewise . . . out of courtesy, if nothing else. I'm a purist when it comes to justice, but I'll lie at the drop of a hat. Inconsistency has never troubled me.

It was late October, the day before Halloween, and the weather was mimicking autumn in the Midwest—clear and sunny and cool. Driving into town, I could have sworn I smelled woodsmoke in the air and I half expected the leaves to be turning yellow and rust. All I actually saw were the same old palm trees, the same relentless green everywhere. The fires of summer had been contained and the rains hadn't started yet. It was a typical California *unseason*, but it *felt* like fall and I was responding with inordinate good cheer, thinking maybe I'd drive up the pass in the afternoon to the pistol range, which is what I do for laughs.

I'd come into the office that Saturday morning to take care of some bookkeeping chores—paying personal bills, getting out my statements for the month. I had my calculator out, a Redi-Receipt form in the typewriter, and four completed statements lined up, addressed and stamped, on the desk to my left. I was so intent on the task at hand that I didn't realize anyone was standing in the doorway until the man cleared his throat. I reacted with one of those little jumps you do when you open the evening paper and a spider runs out. He apparently found this amusing, but I was having to pat myself on the chest to get my heart rate down again.

"I'm Alvin Limardo," he said. "Sorry if I startled you."

"That's all right," I said, "I just had no idea you were standing there. Are you looking for me?"

"If you're Kinsey Millhone, I am."

I got up and shook hands with him across the desk and then suggested that he take a seat. My first fleeting impression had been that he was a derelict, but on second glance, I couldn't find anything in particular to support the idea.

He was in his fifties, too gaunt for good health. His face was long and narrow, his chin pronounced. His hair was an ash gray, clipped short, and he smelled of citrus cologne. His eyes were hazel, his gaze remote. The suit he wore was an odd shade of green. His hands seemed huge, fingers long and bony, the knuckles enlarged. The two inches of narrow wrist extending, cuffless, from his coat sleeves suggested shabbiness though his clothing didn't really look worn. He held a slip of paper which he'd folded twice, and he fiddled with that self-consciously.

"What can I do for you?" I asked.

"I'd like for you to deliver this." He smoothed out the piece of paper then and placed it on my desk. It was a cashier's check drawn on a Los Angeles bank, dated October 29, and made out to someone named Tony Gahan for twenty-five thousand dollars.

I tried not to appear as surprised as I felt. He didn't look like a man with money to spare. Maybe he'd borrowed the sum from Gahan and was paying it back. "You want to tell me what this is about?"

"He did me a favor. I want to say thanks. That's all it is."

"It must have been quite a favor," I said. "Do you mind if I ask what he did?"

"He showed me a kindness when I was down on my luck."

"What do you need me for?"

He smiled briefly. "An attorney would charge me a hundred and twenty dollars an hour to handle it. I'm assuming you'd charge considerably less."

"So would a messenger service," I said. "It's cheaper still if you do it yourself." I wasn't being a smart-mouth about it. I really didn't understand why he needed a private detective.

He cleared his throat. "I tried that, but I'm not entirely certain of Mr. Gahan's current address. At one

time, he lived on Stanley Place, but he's not there now. I
went by this morning and the house is empty. It looks
like it hasn't been lived in for a while. I want someone to
track him down and make sure he gets the money. If you
can estimate what that might run me, I'll pay you in
advance."

"That depends on how elusive Mr. Gahan turns out
to be. The credit bureau might have a current address,
or the DMV. A lot of inquiries can be done by phone, but
they still take time. At thirty bucks an hour, the fee does
mount up."

He took out a checkbook and began to write out a
check. "Two hundred dollars?"

"Let's make it four. I can always refund the balance
if the charges turn out to be less," I said. "In the
meantime, I've got a license to protect so this better be
on the up and up. I'd be happier if you'd tell me what's
going on."

This was where he hooked me, because what he said
was just offbeat enough to be convincing. Liar that I am,
it still didn't occur to me that there could be so much
falsehood mixed in with the truth.

"I got into trouble with the law awhile back and
served some time. Tony Gahan was helpful to me just
before I was arrested. He had no idea of my circumstances so he wasn't an accessory to anything, nor would
you be. I feel indebted."

"Why not take care of it yourself?"

He hesitated, almost shyly I thought. "It's sort of
like that Charles Dickens book, *Great Expectations.* He
might not like having a convicted felon for a benefactor.
People have strange ideas about ex-cons."

"What if he won't accept an anonymous donation?"

"You can return the check in that case and keep the
fee."

I shifted restlessly in my chair. What's wrong with

this picture, I asked myself. "Where'd you get the money if you've been in jail?"

"Santa Anita. I'm still on parole and I shouldn't be playing the ponies at all, but I find it hard to resist. That's why I'd like to pass the money on to you. I'm a gambling man. I can't have that kind of cash around or I'll piss it away, if you'll pardon my French." He closed his mouth then and looked at me, waiting to see what else I might ask. Clearly, he didn't want to volunteer more than was necessary to satisfy my qualms, but he seemed amazingly patient. I realized later, of course, that his tolerance was probably the function of his feeding me so much bullshit. He must have been entertained by the game he was playing. Lying is fun. I can do it all day myself.

"What was the felony?" I asked.

He dropped his gaze, addressing his reply to his oversized hands, which were folded in his lap. "I don't think that pertains. This money is clean and I came by it honestly. There's nothing illegal about the transaction if that's what's worrying you."

Of *course* it worried me, but I wondered if I was being too fastidious. There was nothing wrong with his request on the face of it. I chased the proposition around in my head with caution, wondering what Tony Gahan had done for Limardo that would net him this kind of payoff. None of my business, I supposed, as long as no laws had been broken in the process. Intuition was telling me to turn this guy down, but it happens that the rent on my apartment was due the next day. I had the money in my checking account, but it seemed providential to have a retainer drop in my lap unexpectedly. In any event, I didn't see a reason to refuse. "All right," I said.

He nodded once, pleased. "Good."

I sat and watched while he finished signing his name to the check. He tore it out and pushed it toward me, tucking the checkbook into the inner pocket of his suit coat. "My address and telephone number are on that in case you need to get in touch."

I pulled a standard contract form out of my desk drawer and took a few minutes to fill it in. I got his signature and then I made a note of Tony Gahan's last known address, a house in Colgate, the township just north of Santa Teresa. I was already feeling some low-level dread, wishing I hadn't agreed to do anything. Still, I'd committed myself, the contract was signed, and I figured I'd make the best of it. How much trouble could it be, thought I.

He stood up and I did too, moving with him as he walked toward the door. With both of us on our feet, I could see how much taller he was than I . . . maybe six-four to my five-foot-six. He paused with his hand on the knob, gazing down at me with the same remote stare.

"One other thing you might need to know about Tony Gahan," he said.

"What's that?"

"He's fifteen years old."

I stood there and watched Alvin Limardo move off down the hall. I should have called him back, folks. I should have known right then that it wasn't going to turn out well. Instead I closed the office door and returned to my desk. On impulse, I opened the French doors and went out on the balcony. I scanned the street below, but there was no sign of him. I shook my head, dissatisfied.

I locked the cashier's check in my file cabinet. When the bank opened on Monday, I'd put it in my safe deposit box until I located Tony Gahan and then turn it over to him. Fifteen?

At noon, I closed up the office and went down the back stairs to the parking lot, where I retrieved my VW, a decaying sedan with more rust than paint. This is not the sort of vehicle you'd choose for a car chase, but then

most of what a P.I. does for a living isn't that exciting
anyway. I'm sometimes reduced to serving process
papers, which gets hairy now and then, but much of the
time I do preemployment background checks, skip-
tracing, or case-and-trial preparation for a couple of
attorneys here in town. My office is provided by California Fidelity Insurance, a former employer of mine. The
company headquarters is right next door and I still do
sporadic investigations for them in exchange for a
modest two rooms (one inner, one outer) with a separate
entrance and a balcony overlooking State Street.

I went by the post office and dropped the mail in
the box and then I stopped by the bank and deposited
Alvin Limardo's four hundred dollars in my checking
account.

Four business days later, on a Thursday, I got a
letter from the bank, informing me that the check had
bounced. According to their records, Alvin Limardo
had closed out his account. In proof of this, I was
presented with the check itself stamped across the face
with the sort of officious looking purple ink that makes it
clear the bank is displeased.

So was I.

My account had been debited the four hundred
dollars and I was charged an additional three bucks,
apparently to remind me, in the future, not to deal with
deadbeats. I picked up the phone and called Alvin
Limardo's number in Los Angeles. A disconnect. I'd
been canny enough to ignore the search for Tony Gahan
until the check cleared, so it wasn't as if I'd done any
work to date. But how was I going to get the check
replaced? And what was I going to do with the twenty-
five grand in the meantime? By then, the cashier's check
was tucked away in my safe deposit box, but it was
useless to me and I didn't want to proceed with delivery
until I knew I'd be paid. In theory, I could have dropped
Alvin Limardo a note, but it might have come bouncing

back at me with all the jauntiness of his rubber check, and then where would I be? Crap. I was going to have to drive down to L.A. One thing I've learned about collections—the faster you move, the better your chances are.

I looked up his street address in my *Thomas Guide to Los Angeles Streets.* Even on the map, it didn't look like a nice neighborhood. I checked my watch. It was then 10:15. It was going to take me ninety minutes to reach L.A., probably another hour to locate Limardo, chew him out, get the check replaced, and grab a bite of lunch. Then I'd have to drive ninety minutes back, which would put me in the office again at 3:30 or 4:00. Well, that wasn't too bad. It was tedious, but necessary, so I decided I might as well quit bellyaching and get on with it.

By 10:30, I'd gassed up my car and I was on the road.

2

I left the Ventura Freeway at Sherman Oaks, taking the San Diego Freeway south as far as Venice Boulevard. I exited, turning right at the bottom of the off-ramp. According to my calculations, the address I wanted was somewhere close. I doubled back toward Sawtelle, the street that hugs the freeway on a parallel route.

Once I saw the building, I realized that I'd spotted the rear of it from the freeway as I passed. It was painted the color of Pepto-Bismol and sported a sagging banner of Day-Glo orange that said NOW RENTING. The building was separated from the roadway by a concrete rain wash and protected from speeding vehicles by a ten-foot cinderblock wall sprayed with messages for passing motorists. Spiky weeds had sprung up along the base of the wall and trash had accumulated like hanging ornaments in the few hearty bushes that managed to survive the gas fumes. I had noted the building because it seemed so typical of L.A.: bald, cheaply constructed, badly defaced. There was something meanspirited about its backside, and the entrance turned out to be worse.

The street was largely made up of California "bungalows," small two-bedroom houses of wood and stucco with ragged yards and no trees. Most of them had been painted in pastel hues, odd shades of turquoise

9

and mauve, suggestive of discount paints that hadn't quite covered the color underneath. I found a parking space across the street and locked my car, then crossed to the apartment complex.

The building was beginning to disintegrate. The stucco looked mealy and dry, the aluminum window frames pitted and buckling. The wrought-iron gate near the front had been pulled straight out of the supporting wall, leaving holes large enough to stick a fist into. Two apartments at street level were boarded up. The management had thoughtfully provided a number of garbage bins near the stairs, without (apparently) paying for adequate trash removal services. A big yellow dog was scratching through this pile of refuse with enthusiasm, though all he seemed to net for his efforts was a quarter moon of pizza. He trotted off, the rim of crust clenched in his jaws like a bone.

I moved into the shelter of the stairs. Most of the mailboxes had been ripped out and mail was scattered in the foyer like so much trash. According to the address on the face of the check, Limardo lived in apartment 26, which I surmised was somewhere above. There were apparently forty units, only a few marked with the occupants' names. That seemed curious to me. In Santa Teresa, the post office won't even deliver junk mail unless a box is provided, clearly marked, and in good repair. I pictured the postman, emptying out his mail pouch like a wastepaper basket, escaping on foot then before the inhabitants of the building swarmed over him like bugs.

The apartments were arranged in tiers around a courtyard "garden" of loose gravel, pink paving stones, and nut grass. I picked my way up the cracked concrete steps.

At the second-floor landing, a black man was seated in a rickety metal folding chair, whittling with a knife on a bar of Ivory soap. There was a magazine open on his lap to catch the shavings. He was heavyset and shapeless, maybe fifty years old, his short-cropped frizzy hair showing gray around his ears. His eyes were a muddy brown, the lid of one pulled askew by a vibrant track of stitches that cut down along his cheek.

He took me in at a glance, turning his attention then to the sculpture taking form in his hands. "You must be looking for Alvin Limardo," he said.

"That's right," I said, startled. "How'd you guess?"

He flashed a smile at me, showing perfect teeth, as snowy as the soap he carved. He tilted his face up at me, the injured eye creating the illusion of a wink. "Baby, you ain't live here. I know ever'body live here. And from the look on your face, you ain't thinkin' to rent. If you knew where you were going, you'd be headed straight there. Instead, you be lookin' all around like somethin' might jump out on you, including me," he said and then paused to survey me. "I'd say you do social work, parole, something like that. Maybe welfare."

"Not bad," I said. "But why Limardo? What made you think I was looking for him?"

He smiled then, his gums showing pink. "We *all* Alvin Limardo 'round here. It's a joke we play. Just a name we take when we jivin' folk. I been Alvin Limardo myself lass week at the food stamp line. He get welfare checks, disability, AFDC. Somebody show up lass week wid a warrant on him. I tole 'em, 'Alvin Limardo's done leff. He gone. Ain't nobody here by that name about now.' The Alvin Limardo you want . . . he be white or black?"

"White," I said and then described the man who'd come into my office on Saturday. The black man started nodding about halfway through, his knife blade still smoothing the surface of the soap. It looked like he'd carved a sow lying on her side with a litter of piglets scrambling over her to nurse. The whole of it couldn't have been more than four inches long.

"That's John Daggett. Whooee. He bad. He the one you want, but he gone for sure."

"Do you have any idea where he went?"

"Santa Teresa, I heard."

"Well, I know he was up there last Saturday. That's where I ran into him," I said. "Has he been back since then?"

The man's mouth drooped with skepticism. "I seen him on Monday and then he gone off again. Only other peoples must want him too. He ack like a man who's runnin' and don't want to be caught. What you want wid him?"

"He wrote me a bum check."

He shot me a look of astonishment. "You take a check from a man like that? Lord God, girl! What's the matter wid you?"

I had to laugh. "I know. It's my own damn fault. I thought maybe I could catch him before he skipped out permanently."

He shook his head, unable to sympathize. "Don't take nothin' from the likes of him. That's your first mistake. Comin' 'round this place may be the next."

"Is there anybody here who might know how to get in touch with him?"

He pointed the blade of his knife toward an apartment two doors down. "Axe Lovella. She might know. Then again, she might not."

"She's a friend of his?"

"Not hardly. She's his wife."

I felt somewhat more hopeful as I knocked at apartment 26. I was afraid he'd moved out altogether. The door was a hollowcore with a hole kicked into the bottom about shin high. The sliding glass window was open six inches, a fold of drapery sticking out. A crack ran diagonally across the pane, held together by a wide band of electrician's tape. I could smell something cooking inside, kale or collard greens, with a whisper of vinegar and bacon grease.

The door opened and a woman peered out at me. Her upper lip was puffy, like the kind of scrape children get falling off bicycles when they first learn to ride. Her left eye had been blackened not long ago and it was streaked now with midnight blue, the surrounding tissue a rainbow of green and yellow and gray. Her hair was the color of hay, parted in the middle and snagged up over each ear with a bobby pin. I couldn't even guess how old she might be. Younger than I expected, given John Daggett's age, which had to be fifty plus.

"Lovella Daggett?"

"That's right." She seemed reluctant to admit that much.

"I'm Kinsey Millhone. I'm looking for John."

She licked uneasily at her upper lip as if she was still unfamiliar with its new shape and size. Some of the scraped area had formed a scab, which resembled nothing so much as half a moustache. "He's not here. I don't know where he's at. What'd you want him for?"

"He hired me to do some work, but he paid me with a bum check. I was hoping we could get it straightened out."

She studied me while she processed the information. "Hired you to do what?"

"Deliver something."

She didn't believe a bit of that. "You a cop?"

"No."

"What are you, then?"

I showed her the photostat of my license by way of reply. She turned and walked away from the door, leaving it open behind her. I gathered this was her method of inviting me in.

I stepped into the living room and closed the door behind me. The carpeting was that green cotton shag so admired by apartment owners everywhere. The only

furniture in the room was a card table and two plain
wooden chairs. A six-foot rectangle of lighter carpeting
along one wall suggested that there'd once been a couch
on the spot, and a pattern of indentations in the rug
indicated the former presence of two heavy chairs and a
coffee table, arranged in what decorators refer to as "a
conversational grouping." Instead of conversation these
days, Daggett apparently got right down to busting her
chops, breaking anything else that came to hand. The
one lamp I saw had been snapped off at the socket and
the wires were hanging out like torn ligaments.

"Where'd the furniture go?"

"He hocked it all last week. Turns out he used the
payments for his bar bill. The car went before that. It
was a piece of junk, anyway, but I'd paid for it. You
ought to see what I've got for a bed these days. Some
peed-on old mattress he found out on the street."

There were two bar stools at the counter and I
perched on one, watching as Lovella ambled into the
small space that served as a kitchen. An aluminum
saucepan sat on a gas flame on the stove, the water in it
boiling furiously. On one of the other back burners,
there was a battered aluminum kettle filled with simmering greens.

Lovella wore blue jeans and a plain white tee shirt
wrong-side out, the Fruit of the Loom label visible at the
back of her neck. The bottom of the shirt had been
pulled tight and knotted to form a halter, leaving her
midriff bare. "You want coffee? I was just fixing some."

"Yes, please," I said.

She rinsed a cup under the hot water faucet and
gave it a quick swipe with a paper towel. She set it on the
counter and spooned instant coffee into it and then used
the same paper towel as a potholder when she reached
for the saucepan. The water sputtered against the edge
of the pan as she poured. She added water to a second
cup, gave a quick stir to the contents, and pushed it

toward me with the spoon still resting up against the rim.

"Daggett's a jerk. They should lock him up for life," she remarked, almost idly, I thought.

"Did he do that to you?" I asked, my gaze flicking across her bruised face.

She fixed a pair of dead gray eyes on me without bothering to reply. Up close, I could see that she wasn't much more than twenty-five. She leaned forward, resting her elbows on the counter, her coffee cup cradled in her hands. She wasn't wearing a bra and her breasts were big, as soft and droopy as balloons filled with water, her nipples pressing against the tee-shirt fabric like puckered knots. I wondered if she was a hooker. I'd known a few with the same careless sexuality—all surface, no feeling underneath.

"How long have you been married?"

"You care if I have a cigarette?"

"It's your place. You can do anything you want," I said.

That netted me a wan smile, the first I'd seen. She reached for a pack of Pall Mall 100s, flipped on the gas burner, and lit her cigarette from it, tilting her head so her hair wouldn't catch fire. She took a deep drag and exhaled it, blowing a cloud of smoke at me. "Six weeks," she said, answering my question belatedly. "We were pen pals after he got sent to San Luis. Wrote for a year and then I married him the minute he got out. Dumb? Jesus. Can you believe I did that?"

I shrugged noncommittally. She didn't really care if I believed it or not. "How'd you connect in the first place?"

"A buddy of his. Guy named Billy Polo I used to date. They'd sit and talk about women and my name came up. I guess Billy made me sound like real hot stuff, so Daggett got in touch."

I took a sip of my coffee. It had that flat, nearly sour

taste of instant, with tiny clumps of coffee powder floating at the edge. "Do you have any milk for this?"

"Oh, sure. Sorry," she said. She moved over to the refrigerator where she took out a small can of Carnation.

It wasn't quite what I had in mind, but I added some to my coffee, intrigued as evaporated milk rose to the surface in a series of white dots. I wondered if a fortune teller could read the pattern, like tea leaves. I thought I spied some indigestion in my future, but I wasn't sure.

"Daggett's a charmer when he wants," she said. "Give him a couple of drinks, though, and he's mean as a snake."

That was a story I'd heard before. "Why don't you leave?" said I, as I always do.

"Because he'd come after me is why," she said snappishly. "You don't know him. He'd kill me without giving it a second thought. Same thing if I called the cops. Talk back to that man and he'll punch your teeth down your throat. He hates women is what's the matter with him. Of course, when he sobers up, he can charm your socks off. Anyway, I'm hoping he's gone for good. He got a phone call Monday morning and he was out of here like a shot. I haven't heard from him since. Of course, the phone was disconnected yesterday so I don't know how he'd reach me even if he wanted to."

"Why don't you talk to his parole officer?"

"I guess I could," she said reluctantly. "He reports to the guy every time he turns around. For two days he had a job, but he quit that. Of course, he's not supposed to drink. I guess he tried to play by the rules at first, but it was too much."

"Why not get out while you have the chance?"

"And go where? I don't have a nickel to my name."

"There are shelters for battered women. Call the rape crisis center. They'll know."

She gestured dismissively. "Jesus, I love people like you. You ever had a guy punch you out?"

"Not one I was married to," I said. "I wouldn't put up with that shit."

"That's what I used to say, sister, but I'll tell you what. You don't get away as easy as all that. Not with a bastard like Daggett. He swears he'd follow me to the ends of the earth and he would."

"What was he in prison for?"

"He never said and I never asked. Which was also dumb. It didn't make any difference to me at first. He was fine for a couple weeks. Just like a kid, you know? And sweet? Lord, he trotted around after me like a puppy dog. We couldn't get enough of each other and it all seemed just like the letters we wrote. Then he got into the Jack Daniel's one night and the shit hit the fan."

"Did he ever mention the name Tony Gahan?"

"Nuh-uh. Who's he?"

"I'm not sure. Some kid he asked me to find."

"What'd he pay you with? Can I see the check?"

I took it out of my handbag and laid it on the counter. I thought it best not to mention the cashier's check. I didn't think she'd take kindly to his giving money away. "I understand Limardo is a fabricated name."

She studied the check. "Yeah, but Daggett did keep some money in this account. I think he cleaned it out just before he left." She took a drag of her cigarette as she handed back the check. I managed to turn my head before she blew smoke in my face again.

"That phone call he got Monday, what was it about? Do you know?"

"Beats me. I was off at the Laundromat. I got home and he was still on the phone, his face as gray as that dish rag. He hung up quick and then started shovin' stuff in a duffel. He turned the place upside down lookin' for his bank book. I was afraid he'd come after me, thinkin' I took it, but I guess he was too freaked out to worry about me."

"He told you that?"

"No, but he was cold sober and his hands were shaking *bad*."

"You have any idea where he might have gone?"

A look flashed through her eyes, some emotion she concealed by dropping her gaze. "He only had one friend and that was Billy Polo up in Santa Teresa. If he needed help, that's where he'd go. I think he used to have family up there too, but I don't know what happened to them. He never talked much about that."

"So Polo's out of prison?"

"I heard he got out just recently."

"Well, maybe I'll track him down since that's the only lead I have. In the meantime, would you find a phone and call me if you hear from either one?" I took out a business card and jotted my home address and phone on the back. "Call collect."

She looked at both sides of the card. "What do you think is goin' on?"

"I don't know and I don't much care. As soon as I run him down, I'll clean up this business and *bail out*."

3

As long as I was in the area, I went by the bank. The woman in charge of customer service couldn't have been less helpful. She was dark haired, in her early twenties, and new at the job I gathered because she greeted my every request with the haunted look of someone who isn't quite sure of the rules and therefore says no to everything. She would not verify "Alvin Limardo's" account number or the fact that the account had been closed. She would not tell me if there was, perhaps, another account in John Daggett's name. I knew there had to be a registered copy of the cashier's check itself, but she refused to verify the information he'd given at the time. I kept thinking there was some other tack I might take, especially with that much money at stake. Surely, the bank must care what happened to twenty-five thousand dollars. I stood at the counter and stared at the woman, and she stared back. Maybe she hadn't understood.

I took out the photostat of my license and pointed. "Look," I said, "You see this? I'm a private investigator. I've got a real problem here. I was hired to deliver a cashier's check, but now I can't find the man who gave it to me and I don't know the whereabouts of the person who's supposed to receive it and I'm just trying to get a lead so I can do what I was hired to do."

"I understand that," she said.

"But you won't give me any information, right?"

"It's against bank regulations."

"Isn't it against bank regulations for Alvin Limardo to write me a bad check?"

"Yes."

"Then what am I supposed to do with it?" I said. I really knew the answer . . . eat it, dum-dum . . . but I was feeling stubborn and perverse.

"Take him to small claims court," she said.

"But I can't find him. He can't be hauled into court if nobody knows where he is."

She stared at me blankly, offering no comment.

"What about the twenty-five thousand?" I said. "What am I supposed to do with that?"

"I have no idea."

I stared down at the desk. When I was in kindergarten, I was a biter and I still struggle with the urge. It just feels good, you know? "I want to speak to your supervisor."

"Mr. Stallings? He's gone for the day."

"Well, is there anybody else here who might give me some help on this?"

She shook her head. "I'm in charge of customer service."

"But you're not doing a thing. How can you call it customer service when you don't do shit?"

Her mouth turned prim. "Please don't use language like that around me. It's very offensive."

"What do I have to do to get help around here?"

"Do you have an account with us?"

"If I did, would you help?"

"Not with this. We're not supposed to divulge information about bank customers."

This was silly. I walked away from her desk. I wanted to make a withering remark, but I couldn't think of one. I knew I was just mad at myself for taking the job to begin with, but I was hoping to lay a little ire off on her . . . a pointless enterprise. I got back in my car and headed toward the freeway. When I reached Santa Teresa, it was 4:35. I bypassed the office altogether and went home. My disposition improved the minute I walked in. My apartment was once a single-car garage and consists now of one room, fifteen feet on a side, with a narrow extension on the right that serves as a kitchenette, separated from the living area by a counter. The space is arranged with cunning: a stackable washer-dryer tucked in beside the kitchenette, bookshelves, drawers and storage compartments built into the wall. It's tidy and self-contained and all of it suits me absolutely. I have a six-foot convertible sofa that I usually sleep on as is, a desk, a chair, an endtable, and plump pillows that serve as additional seating if anyone comes over to sit. My bathroom is one of those pre-formed fiberglass units with everything molded into it, including a towel bar, a soap holder, and a cutout for a window that looks out at the street. Sometimes I stand in the bathtub, elbows resting on the sill, and stare at passing cars, just thinking how lucky I am. I love being single. It's almost like being rich.

I dropped my handbag on the desk and hung my jacket on a peg. I sat on the couch and pulled off my boots, then padded over to the refrigerator and took out a bottle of white zinfandel and a corkscrew. At intervals, I try to behave like a person with class, which is to say I drink wine from a bottle instead of a cardboard box. I pulled the cork and poured myself a glass. I crossed to the desk, taking the telephone book from the top drawer, trailing telephone cord, directory, and wine glass over to the sofa. I set the wine glass on the endtable and thumbed through the book to see if Billy Polo was listed. Of course, he wasn't. I looked up the name Gahan. No dice. I drank some wine and tried to think what to do next.

On an impulse, I checked for the name Daggett. Lovella had mentioned that he once lived up here. Maybe he still had relatives in town.

There were four Daggetts listed. I started dialing them in order, saying the same thing each time. "Oh, hi. I'm trying to reach a John Daggett, who used to live in this area. Can you tell me if this is the correct number?"

On the first two calls, I drew a blank, but with the third, the man who answered responded to my query with one of those odd silences that indicate that information is being processed.

"What did you want with him?" he asked. He sounded like he was in his sixties, his phrasing tentative, alert to my response, but undecided how much he was willing to reveal.

He was certainly skipping right down to the tricky part. From everything I'd heard about Daggett, he was a bum, so I didn't dare claim to be a friend of his. If I admitted he owed me money, I was going to have the phone slammed down in my ear. Ordinarily, in a situation like this, I'd insinuate that I had money for *him*, but somehow I didn't think that would fly. People are getting wise to that shit.

I laid out the first lie that occurred to me. "Well, to tell you the truth," I said, "I've only met John once, but I'm trying to get in touch with a mutual acquaintance and I think John has his address and telephone number."

"Who were you looking to get in touch with?"

That caught me off-guard, as I hadn't made that part up yet. "Who? Um . . . Alvin Limardo. Has John ever mentioned Alvin?"

"No, I don't believe so. But, now, you may have the wrong party. The John Daggett that used to live here is currently in prison and he's been there, oh I'd say nearly two years." His manner suggested a man whose retirement has invested even a wrong number with some interesting possibilities. Still, it was clear I'd hit pay dirt.

"That's the one I'm talking about," I said. "He was up in San Luis Obispo."

"He still is."

"Oh, no. He's out. He was released six weeks ago."

"John? *No*, ma'am. He's still in prison and I hope he stays there. I don't mean to speak ill of the man, but you'll find he's what I call a problematic person."

"Problematic?"

"Well, yes. That's how I'd have to put it. John is the type of person that creates problems and usually of a quite serious nature."

"Oh, really," I said. "I didn't realize that." I loved it that this man was willing to chat. As long as I could keep him going, I might figure out how to get a bead on Daggett. I took a flyer. "Are you his brother?"

"I'm his brother-in-law, Eugene Nickerson."

"You must be married to his sister then," I said.

He laughed. "No, he's married to *my* sister. She was a Nickerson before she became a Daggett."

"You're Lovella's brother?" I was trying to picture siblings with a forty-year age span.

"No, Essie's."

I held the receiver away from my ear and stared at it. What was he talking about? "Wait a minute. I'm confused. Maybe we're *not* talking about the same man." I gave a quick verbal sketch of the John Daggett I'd met. I didn't see how there could be two, but there was something going on here.

"That's him all right. How did you say you knew him?"

"I met him last Saturday, right here in Santa Teresa."

The silence on the other end of the line was profound.

I finally broke into it. "Is there some way I might stop by so we can talk about this?"

"I think you'd best," he said. "What would your name be?"

"Kinsey Millhone."

He told me how to get to the place.

The house was white frame with a small wooden porch, tucked into the shadow of Capillo Hill on the west side of town. The street was abbreviated, only three houses on each side before the blacktop petered out into the gravel patch that formed a parking pad beside the Daggett residence. Beyond the house, the hill angled upward into sparse trees and underbrush. No sunlight whatever penetrated the yard. A sagging chicken wire fence cut along the lot lines. Bushes had been planted at intervals, but had failed to thrive, so that now there were only globes of dried twigs. The house had a hangdog look, like a stray being penned up until the dogcatcher comes.

I climbed the steep wooden steps and knocked. Eugene Nickerson opened the door. He was much as I had pictured him: in his sixties, of medium height, with wiry gray hair and eyebrows drawn together in a knot. His eyes were small and pale, his lashes nearly white. Narrow shoulders, thick waist, suspenders, flannel shirt. He carried a Bible in his left hand, his index finger closed between the covers, keeping his place.

Uh-oh, I thought.

"I'll have to ask your name again," he said as he admitted me. "My memory's not what it was."

I shook his hand. "Kinsey Millhone," I said. "Nice to meet you, Mr. Nickerson. I hope I didn't interrupt anything."

"Not at all. We're preparing for our Bible class. We usually get together on Wednesday nights, but our pastor has been down with the flu this week, so the

meeting was postponed. This is my sister, Essie Daggett.
John's wife," he said, indicating the woman seated on the
couch. "You can call me Eugene if you like," he added. I
smiled briefly in assent and then concentrated on her.

"Hello. How are you? I appreciate your letting me
stop by like this." I moved over and offered my hand.
She allowed a few fingers to rest in mine briefly. It was
like shaking hands with a Playtex rubber glove.

She was broad-faced and colorless, with graying
hair in an unbecoming cut and glasses with thick lenses
and heavy plastic frames. She had a wen on the right
side of her nose about the size of a kernel of popcorn.
Her lower jaw jutted forward aggressively, with protru-
sive cuspids on either side. She smelled virulently of
lilies of the valley.

Eugene indicated that I should have a seat, my
choice being the couch where Essie sat, or a Windsor
chair with one of the wooden spokes popped out. I
opted for the chair, sitting forward slightly so as not to
pop anything else. Eugene seated himself in a wicker
rocker that creaked under his weight. He took up the
narrow purple ribbon hanging out of the Bible and
marked his place, then set the book on the table in front
of him. Essie had said nothing, her gaze fixed on her
lap.

"May I get you a glass of water?" he asked. "We
don't hold with caffeinated beverages, but I'd be happy
to pour you some 7-Up, if you like."

"I'm fine, thanks," I said. I was seriously alarmed.
Being with devout Christians is like being with the very
rich. One senses that there are rules at work, some
strange etiquette that one might inadvertently breech. I
tried to hold bland and harmless thoughts, hoping I
wouldn't blurt out any four-letter words. How *could* John
Daggett be related to these two?

Eugene cleared his throat. "I was explaining to
Essie this confusion we're having over John Daggett's

whereabouts. Our understanding is that John is still
incarcerated, but now you seem to have a different point
of view."

"I'm as baffled as you are," I said. I was thinking
fast, wondering how much information I might elicit
without giving anything away. As bugged as I was with
Daggett, I still didn't feel I should be indiscreet. Not
only was there the issue of his being out on parole—
there was Lovella. I didn't want to be the one to spill the
beans about this new bride of his to a woman he was
apparently still married to. "Do you happen to have a
picture of him?" I asked. "I suppose it's possible the man
I talked to was simply claiming to be your brother-in-
law."

"I don't know," Eugene said, dubiously. "It surely
sounded like him from what you described."

Essie reached over and picked up a color studio
photograph in an ornate silver frame. "This was taken
on our thirty-fifth wedding anniversary," she said. Her
voice had a nasal cast and a grudging undertone. She
passed the photograph to her brother as though he'd
never seen it before and might like to have a peek.

"Shortly before John left for San Luis," Eugene
amended, passing the photo to me. His tone suggested
John was off on a business trip.

I studied the picture. It was Daggett all right,
looking as self-conscious as someone in one of those
booths where you dress up as a Confederate soldier or a
Victorian gent. His collar looked too tight, his hair too
slicked down with pomade. His face looked tight too, as
if any minute he might cut and run. Essie was seated
beside him, as placid as a blancmange. She was wearing
what looked like a crepe de chine dress in lilac, with
shoulder pads and glass buttons, a big orchid corsage
pinned to her left shoulder.

"Lovely," I murmured, feeling guilty and false. It
was a terrible picture. She looked like a bulldog and
John looked like he was suppressing a fart.

I handed the picture to Essie again. "What sort of crime did he commit?"

Essie inhaled audibly.

"We prefer not to speak of that," Eugene interjected smoothly. "Perhaps you should tell us of your own acquaintance with him."

"Well, of course, I don't know him well. I think I mentioned that on the phone. We have a mutual friend and he's the one I was hoping to get in touch with. John mentioned that he had family in this area and I just took a chance. I'm assuming you haven't spoken to him recently."

Essie shifted on the couch. "We stuck by him as long as we could. The pastor said in his opinion we'd done enough. We don't know what John might be wrestling with in the dark of his soul, but there's a limit to what others can *take*." The edge was there in her voice and I wondered what it was made of: rage, humiliation perhaps, the martyrdom of the meek at the hands of the wretched.

I said, "I gather John's been a bit of a trial."

Essie pressed her lips together, clutching her hands in her lap. "Well, it's just like the Bible says. '*Love* your enemies, *bless* them that curse you, do *good* to them that hate you, and pray for them which despitefully use you and persecute you'!" Her tone was accusatory. She began to rock with agitation.

Whoa, I thought, this lady's heat gauge has shot right up into the red.

Eugene creaked in his chair, snagging my attention with a gentle clearing of his throat. "You said you saw him on Saturday. May I ask what the occasion was?"

I realized then that I should have devoted a lot more time to the fib I'd told because I couldn't think how to respond, I was so unnerved by Essie Daggett's outburst that my mind went blank.

She leaned forward then. "Have you been saved?"

"Excuse me, what?" I said, squinting.

"Have you taken Jesus into your heart? Have you set aside *sin*? Have you *repented*? Have you been washed in the Blood of the *Lamb*?"

A spark of spit landed on my face, but I didn't dare react. "Not lately," I said. What is it about me that attracts women like this?

"Now Essie, I'm sure she didn't come by to ponder the state of her soul," Eugene said. He glanced at his watch. "My goodness, I believe it's time for your medication."

I took the opportunity to rise. "I don't want to take up any more of your time," I said, conversationally. "I really appreciate your help on this and if I need any more information, I'll give you a call." I fumbled in my handbag for a business card and left it on the table.

Essie had kicked into high gear by now. "'And they shall stone thee with stones, and *thrust* thee through with their swords. And they shall burn thine houses with fire, and execute judgments upon thee in the sight of many women; and I will cause thee to *cease* from playing harlot, and thou also shalt give no hire anymore . . .'"

"Well, okay now, thanks a lot," I called, easing toward the door. Eugene was patting Essie's hands, too distracted to worry about my departure.

I closed the door and trotted back to my car at a quick clip. It was getting dark and I didn't like the neighborhood.

4

Friday morning I got up at 6:00 and headed over to the beach for my run. For much of the summer, I'd been unable to jog because of an injury, but I'd been back at it for two months and I was feeling good. I've never rhapsodized about exercise and I'd avoid it if I could, but I notice the older I get, the more my body seems to soften, like butter left out at room temp. I don't like to watch my ass drop and my thighs spread outward like jodhpurs made of flesh. In the interest of tight-fitting jeans, my standard garb, I jog three miles a day on the bicycle path that winds along the beach front.

The dawn was laid out on the eastern skyline like water-colors on a matte board: cobalt blue, violet, and rose bleeding together in horizontal stripes. Clouds were visible out on the ocean, plump and dark, pushing the scent of distant seas toward the tumbling surf. It was cold and I ran as much to keep warm as I did to keep in shape.

I got back to my apartment at 6:25, showered, pulled on a pair of jeans, a sweater, and my boots, and then ate a bowl of cereal. I read the paper from front to back, noting with interest the weather map, which showed the radiating spiral of a storm sweeping toward us from Alaska. An 80 percent chance of showers was forecast for the afternoon, with scattered showers

through the weekend, clearing by Monday night. In
Santa Teresa, rain is not a common event, and it takes on
a festive air when it comes. My impulse, always, is to shut
myself inside and curl up with a good book. I'd just
picked up a new Len Deighton novel and I was looking
forward to reading it.

At 9:00, reluctantly, I dug out a windbreaker and
picked up my handbag, locked the apartment, and
headed over to the office. The sun was shining with a
brief show of warmth while the bank of charcoal clouds
crept in from the islands twenty-six miles out. I parked
in the lot and went up the back stairs, passing the glass
double doors of California Fidelity, where business was
already under way.

I unlocked my office and dropped my bag on the
chair. I really didn't have much to do. Maybe I'd put in a
little bit of work and then head home again.

My answering machine showed no messages. I
sorted through the mail from the day before and then
typed up the notes from my visit with Lovella Daggett,
Eugene Nickerson, and his sister, Essie. Since no one
seemed to know where John Daggett was, I decided I'd
try to get a line on Billy Polo instead. I was going to need
data for an effective paper search. I put a call through to
the Santa Teresa Police Department and asked to be
connected to Sergeant Robb.

I'd met Jonah back in June when I was working on a
missing persons case. His erratic marital status made a
relationship between us inadvisable from my point of
view, but I still eyed him with interest. He was what they
called Black Irish: dark-haired, blue-eyed, with (perhaps) a streak of masochism. I didn't know him well
enough to determine how much of his suffering was of
his own devising and I wasn't sure I wanted to find out.
Sometimes I think an unconsummated affair is the
wisest course, in any event. No hassles, no demands, no
disappointments, and both partners keep all their neu-

roses under wraps. Whatever the surface appearances, most human beings come equipped with convoluted emotional machinery. With intimacy, the wreckage starts to show, damage rendered in the course of passions colliding like freight trains on the same track. I'd had enough of that over the years. I wasn't in any better shape than he was, so why complicate life?

Two rings and the call was picked up.

"Missing Persons, Sergeant Robb."

"Hello, Jonah. It's Kinsey."

"Hey, babe," he said, "What can I do for you that's legal in this state?"

I smiled. "How about a field check on a couple of ex-cons?"

"Sure, no sweat," he said.

I gave him both names and what little information I had. He took it down and said he'd get back to me. He'd fill out a form and have the inquiry run through the National Crime Information Computer, a federal offense since I'm really not entitled to access. Generally, a private investigator has no more rights than the average citizen and relies on ingenuity, patience, and resourcefulness for facts that law enforcement agencies have available as a matter of course. It's a frustrating, but not impossible, state of affairs. I simply cultivate relationships with people plugged into the system at various points. I have contacts at the telephone company, the credit bureau, Southern California Gas, Southern Cal Edison, and the DMV. Occasionally I can make a raid on certain government offices, but only if I have something worthwhile to trade. As for information of a more personal sort, I can usually depend on people's tendencies to rat on one another at the drop of a hat.

I made up a check sheet for Billy Polo and went to work.

Knowing Jonah, he'd call Probation and pick up Polo's current address. In the meantime, I wanted to tag some bases of my own. A personal search always pays unexpected dividends. I didn't want to bypass the possibility of surprise, as that's half the fun. I knew Polo wasn't listed in the current phone book, but I tried information, thinking he might have had a phone put in. There was no new listing for him.

I put a call through to my pal at the utility company, inquiring about a possible service connection. Their records showed nothing. Apparently he hadn't applied for water, gas, or electricity in the area in his own name, but he could be renting a room somewhere, paying a flat rate, with utilities thrown in.

I put calls through to five or six fleabag hotels on lower State Street. Polo wasn't registered and nobody seemed to spark to the name. While I was at it, I tried John Daggett's name and got nowhere.

I knew I wouldn't get so much as a by-your-leave from the local Social Security office and I doubted I'd find Billy Polo's name among the voter registration files.

Which left what?

I checked my watch. Only thirty minutes had passed since I talked to Jonah. I wasn't sure how long it would take him to call back and I didn't want to waste time sitting around until I heard from him. I grabbed my windbreaker, locked the office, and went down the front stairs to State Street, walking two blocks over and two blocks up to the public library.

I found an empty table in the reference department and hauled out Santa Teresa telephone directories for the past five years, checking back year by year. Four books back, I found Polo. Great. I made a note of the Merced Street address, wondering if his prison sentence accounted for the absence of a listing since then.

I went over to the section on Santa Teresa history and pulled out the city directory for that year. In addition to an alphabetical listing by name, the city directory lists *addresses* alphabetically so that if you have

an address and want to know the resident, you can
thumb to the street and number and pick up the name
of the occupant and a telephone number. In the back
half, telephone numbers are listed sequentially. If all
you have is a telephone number, the city directory will
provide you with a name and address. By cross referenc-
ing the address, you can come up with the name again,
an occupation, and the names of neighbors all up and
down the same street. In ten minutes, I had a list of
seven people who had lived in range of Billy Polo on
Merced. By checking for those seven in the current
directory, I determined that two were still living there. I
jotted down both current telephone numbers, returned
the books to their proper places, and headed back
toward my office.

The sunlight, intermittent for the last hour, was
now largely blocked by incoming clouds which had
crowded out blue sky, leaving only an occasional patch,
like a hole in a blanket. The air was beginning to cool
rapidly, a damp breeze worrying at women's hems. I
looked toward the ocean and spotted that silent veil of
gray that betokens rain already falling some miles out. I
quickened my pace.

Once in my office again, I entered the new information in the file I'd opened. I was just on the verge of
closing up for the day when I heard a tap at the door. I
hesitated, then crossed to the door and peered out.

There was a woman standing in the corridor, late
thirties, expressionless and pale.

"Can I help you?" I said.

"I'm Barbara Daggett."

Quickly, I prayed this wasn't wife number three. I
tried the optimistic approach. "John Daggett's
daughter?"

"Yes."

She was one of those icy blondes, with skin as finely
textured as a percale bedsheet, tall, substantially built,

with short coarse hair fanning straight back from her
face. She had high cheekbones, a delicate brow, and her
father's piercing gaze. Her right eye was green, her left
eye blue. I'd seen a white cat like that once and it had
had the same disconcerting effect. She was wearing a
gray wool business suit and a prim, high-necked white
blouse with a froth of lace at the throat. Her heels were a
burgundy leather and matched her shoulder bag. She
looked like an attorney or a stockbroker, someone
accustomed to power.

"Come on in," I said, "I was trying to figure out how
to get in touch with him. I take it your mother told you I
stopped by."

I was making small talk. She wasn't having any of it.
She sat down, turning those riveting eyes on me as I
moved around to my side of the desk and took a seat. I
thought of offering her coffee, but I really didn't want
her to stay that long. Even the air around her seemed
chilly and I didn't like the way she looked at me. I
rocked back in my swivel chair. "What can I do for you?"

"I want to know why you're looking for my father."

I shrugged, underplaying it, sticking to the story I'd
started with. "I'm not really. I'm looking for a friend of
his."

"Why weren't we told Daddy was out of prison? My
mother's in a state of collapse. We had to call the doctor
and have her sedated."

"I'm sorry to hear that," I said.

Barbara Daggett crossed her legs and smoothed her
skirt, her movements agitated. "Sorry? You don't know
what this has done to her. She was just beginning to feel
safe. Now we find out he's in town somewhere and she's
very upset. I don't understand what's going on."

"Miss Daggett, I'm not a parole officer," I said. "I
don't know when he got out or why nobody notified you.
Your mother's problems didn't start yesterday."

A bit of color came to her cheeks. "That's true. Her

problems started the day she married him. He's ruined her life. He's ruined life for all of us."

"Are you referring to his drinking?"

She brushed right over that. "I want to know where he's staying. I have to talk to him."

"At the moment, I have no idea where he is. If I find him, I'll tell him you're interested. That's the best I can do."

"My uncle tells me you saw him on Saturday."

"Only briefly."

"What was he doing in town?"

"We didn't discuss that," I said.

"But what did you talk about? What possible business could he have had with a private detective?"

I had no intention of giving her information, so I tried her technique and ignored the question.

I pulled a legal pad over and picked up a pen. "Is there a number where you can be reached?"

She opened her handbag and took out a business card which she passed across the desk to me. Her office address was three blocks away on State and her title indicated that she was chairman and chief executive officer of a company called FMS.

As if in response to a question, she said, "I develop financial management software systems for manufacturing firms. That's my office number. I'm not listed in the book. If you need to reach me at home, this is the number."

"Sounds interesting," I remarked. "What's your background?"

"I have a math and chemistry degree from Stanford and a double masters in computer sciences and engineering from USC."

I felt my brows lift appreciatively. I couldn't see any evidence that Daggett had ruined *her* life, but I kept the observation to myself. There was clearly more to Barbara Daggett than her professional status indicated. Maybe she was one of those women who succeeds in business and fails in relationships with men. As I'd been accused of that myself, I decided not to make a judgment. Where is it written that being part of a couple is a measure of anything?

She glanced at her watch and stood up. "I have an appointment. Please let me know if you hear from him."

"May I ask what you want with him?"

"I've been urging Mother to file for divorce, but so far she's refused. Maybe I can persuade him instead."

"I'm surprised she didn't divorce him years ago."

Her smile was cold. "She says she married him 'for better or for worse.' To date, there hasn't been any 'better.' Maybe she's hoping for a taste of that before she gives up."

"What about his imprisonment? What was that for?"

Something flickered in her face and I thought at first she wouldn't answer me. "Vehicular manslaughter," she said, finally. "He was drunk and there was an accident. Five people were killed, two of them kids."

I couldn't think of a response and she didn't seem to expect one. She stood up, closed the conversation with a perfunctory handshake, and then she was gone. I could hear her high heels tapping away down the corridor.

5

By the time I closed up the office and got down to my car, the clouds overhead looked like dark gray vacuum cleaner fluff and the rain had begun to splatter the sidewalk with polka dots. I stuck Daggett's file on the passenger seat and backed out of my space, turning right from the parking lot onto Cannon, and right again onto Chapel. Three blocks up, I made a stop, ducking into the supermarket to pick up milk, Diet Pepsi, bread, eggs, and toilet paper. I was into my siege mentality, looking forward to ·pulling up the drawbridge and waiting out the rain. With luck, I wouldn't have to go out for days.

The phone was ringing as I let myself in. I put the grocery bag on the counter and snatched up the receiver.

"God, I was just about to give up," Jonah said. "I tried the office, but all I got was your answering machine."

"I closed up for the day. I can work at home if I'm in the mood, which I'm not. Have you seen the rain?"

"Rain? Oh yeah, so there is. I haven't even looked out the window since I got in. God, that's great," he said. "Listen, I have some of the information you're looking for and the rest will have to wait. Woody's got a priority request and I had to back off. I'm working tomorrow so I can pick it up then."

"You're working Saturday?"

"I'm filling in for Sobel. My good deed for the week," he said. "Got a pencil? Polo's the one I got a line on."

He rattled out Billy Polo's age, date of birth, height, weight, hair and eye color, his a.k.a., and a hasty rundown of his record, all of which I noted automatically. He'd picked up the name of Billy's parole officer, but the guy was out of the office and wouldn't be available until Monday afternoon.

"Thanks. In the meantime, I'm nosing around on my own," I said. "I bet I'll get a line on him before you do." He laughed and hung up.

I put groceries away and then sat down at my desk, hauling out the little portable Smith-Corona I keep in the knee hole. I consigned the data Jonah'd given me to index cards and then sat and stared at it. Billy Polo, born William Polokowski, was thirty years old, five-foot-eight, a hundred and sixty pounds, brown hair, brown eyes, no scars, tattoos, or "observable physical oddities." His rap sheet sounded like a pop quiz on the California Penal Code, with arrests that ranged from misdemeanors to felonies. Assault, forgery, receiving stolen property, grand theft, narcotics violations. Once he was even convicted of "injuring a public jail," a misdemeanor in this state. Had this occurred in the course of an escape attempt, the charge would have been bumped up to a felony. As it was, he'd probably been caught scratching naughty words on the jail house walls. A real champ, this one.

Apparently, Billy Polo was pretty shiftless when it came to breaking the law and had never even settled on an area of expertise. He'd been arrested sixteen times, with nine convictions, two acquittals, five dismissals. Twice, he'd been put on probation, but nothing seemed to have affected the nature of his behavior, which appeared nearly pathological in its thrust. The man was determined to screw up. Since the age of eighteen, he'd spent an accumulated nine years in jail. No telling what his juvenile record looked like. I assumed his acquaintance with John Daggett dated from his latest offense, an armed robbery conviction, for which he'd served two years and ten months at the California Men's Colony at San Luis Obispo, a medium security facility about ninety miles north of Santa Teresa.

I pulled out the telephone book again and checked for a listing under the name Polokowski. Nothing. God, why can't anything be simple in this business? Oh well. I wasn't going to worry about it for the moment.

By now, I could hear the rain tapping on the glass-enclosed breezeway that connects my place to Henry Pitt's house. He's my landlord and has been for nearly two years. In dry weather, he places an old Shaker cradle out there, filled with rising bread. When the sun is out, the space is like a solar oven, warm and sheltered, dough puffing up above the rim of the cradle like a feather pillow. He can proof twenty loaves at a time, then bake them in the big industrial-sized oven he had installed when he retired from commercial baking. Now he trades fresh bread and pastries for services in the neighborhood and stretches his Social Security payments by clipping coupons avidly. He picks up additional income constructing crossword puzzles which he sells to a couple of those pint-sized "magazines" you can purchase in a supermarket checkout line. Henry Pitts is eighty-one years old and everyone knows I'm half in love with him.

I considered popping over to see him, but even the fifty-foot walk seemed like too much to deal with in the wet. I put some tea water on and picked up my book, stretching out on the sofa with a quilt pulled over me. And that's how I spent the rest of the day.

During the night, the rain escalated and I woke up twice to hear it lashing at the windows. It sounded like somebody spraying the side of the place with a hose. At intervals, thunder rumbled in the distance and my windows flickered with blue light, tree branches illuminated briefly before the room went black again. It was clear I'd have to cancel my 6:00 A.M. run, an obligatory day off, so I burrowed into the depths of my quilt like a little animal, delighted at the idea of sleeping late.

I woke at 8:00, showered, dressed, and fixed myself a soft-boiled egg on toast with lots of Lawry's Seasoned Salt. I'm not going to give up salt. I don't care what they say.

Jonah called as I was washing my plate. He said, "Hey, guess what? Your friend Daggett showed."

I tucked the receiver into the crook of my neck, turning off the water and drying my hands. "What happened? Did he get picked up?"

"More or less. A scruffy drifter spotted him face down in the surf this morning, tangled up in a fishing net. A skiff washed ashore about two hundred yards away. We're pretty sure it connects."

"He died last night?"

"Looks like it. The coroner estimates he went into the water sometime between midnight and five A.M. We don't have a determination yet on the cause and manner of death. We'll know more after the autopsy's done, of course."

"How'd you find out it was him?"

"Fingerprints. He was over at the morgue listed as a John Doe until we ran the computer check. You want to take a look?"

"I'll be right there. What about next of kin? Have they been notified?"

"Yeah, the beat officer went over as soon as we made the I.D. You know the family?"

"Not well, but we've met. I wouldn't want to be quoted on this, but I think you'll find out he's a bigamist. There's a woman down in L.A. who also claims she's married to him."

"Cute. You better come talk to us when you leave St. Terry's," he said and hung up.

The Santa Teresa Police Department doesn't really have a morgue of its own. There's a coroner-sheriff, an elected officer in this county, but the actual forensic work is contracted out among various pathologists in the tri-county area. The morgue space itself is divided between Santa Teresa Hospital (commonly referred to as St. Terry's) and the former County General Hospital facility on the frontage road off 101. Daggett was apparently at St. Terry's, which was where I headed as soon as I'd rounded up my slicker, an umbrella, and my handbag.

The visitors' lot at the hospital was half empty. It was Saturday and doctors would probably be making rounds later in the day. The sky was thick with clouds and, high up, I could see the wind whipping through like a fan, blowing white mist across the gray. The pavement was littered with small branches, leaves plastered flat against the ground. Puddles had formed everywhere, pockmarked by the steady rainfall. I parked as close to the rear entrance as I could and then locked my car and made a dash for it.

"Kinsey!"

I turned as I reached the shelter of the building. Barbara Daggett hurried toward me from the far side of the lot, her umbrella tilted against the slant of the rain. She was wearing a raincoat and spike-heeled boots, her white-blonde hair forming a halo around her face. I held the door open for her and we ducked into the foyer.

"You heard about my father?"

"That's why I'm here. Do you know how it happened?"

"Not really. Uncle Eugene called me at eight-fifteen. I guess they tried to notify Mother and he interceded. The doctor has her so doped up it doesn't make any sense to tell her yet. He's worried about how she'll take it, as unstable as she is."

"Is your uncle coming down?"

She shook her head. "I said I'd do it. There's no doubt it's Daddy, but somebody has to sign for the body so the mortuary can come pick it up. Of course, they'll autopsy first. How did you find out?"

"Through a cop I know. I'd told him I was trying to get a line on your father, so he called me when they got a match on the fingerprints. Did you manage to locate him yesterday?"

"No, but it's clear someone did." She closed her umbrella and gave it a shake, then glanced at me. "Frankly, I'm assuming somebody killed him."

"Let's not be too quick off the mark," I said, though privately, I agreed.

The two of us moved through the inner door and into the corridor. The air was warmer here and smelled of latex paint.

"I want you to look into it for me, in any event," she said.

"Hey, listen. That's what the police are for. I don't have the scope for that. Why don't you wait and see what they have to say first?"

She studied me briefly and then moved on. "They don't give a damn what happened to him. Why would they care? He was a drunken bum."

"Oh come on. Cops don't have to *care*," I said. "If it's homicide, they have a job to do and they'll do it well."

When we reached the autopsy room, I knocked and a young black morgue attendant came out, dressed in surgical greens. His name tag indicated that his name was Hall Ingraham. He was lean, his skin the color of pecan wood with a high-gloss finish. His hair was

cropped close and gave him the look of a piece of
sculpture, his elongated face nearly stylized in its perfection.

"This is Barbara Daggett," I said.

He looked in her direction without meeting her
eyes. "You can wait right down here," he said. He moved
two doors down and we followed, pausing politely while
he unlocked a viewing room and ushered us in.

"It'll be just a minute," he said.

He disappeared and we took a seat. The room was
small, maybe nine by nine, with four blue molded-plastic
chairs hooked together at the base, a low wooden table
covered with old magazines, and a television screen
affixed, at an angle, up in one corner of the room. I saw
her gaze flick to it.

"Closed circuit," I said. "They'll show him up
there."

She picked up a magazine and began to flip
through it distractedly. "You never really told me why he
hired you," she said. An ad for pantyhose had apparently caught her eye and she studied it as if my reply were
of no particular concern.

I couldn't think of a reason not to tell her at this
point, but I noticed that I censored myself to some
extent, a habit of long standing. I like to hold something
back. Once information is out, it can't be recalled so it's
better to exercise caution before you flap your mouth.
"He wanted me to find a kid named Tony Gahan," I
said.

That remarkable two-toned gaze came up to meet
mine and I found myself trying to decide which eye
color I preferred. The green was more unusual, but the
blue was clear and stark. The two together presented a
contradiction, like the signal at a street corner, flashing
Walk and Don't Walk simultaneously.

"You know him?" I asked.

"His parents and a younger sister were the ones

killed in the accident, along with two other people in the car with them. What did Daddy want with him?"

"He said Tony Gahan helped him once when he was on the run from the cops. He wanted to thank him."

Her look was incredulous. "But that's bullshit!"

"So I gather," I said.

She might have pressed for more information, but the television screen flashed with snow at that moment and then flipped over to a closeup of John Daggett. He was lying on a gurney, a sheet neatly pulled up to his neck. He had the blank, plastic look that death sometimes brings, as if the human face were no more than an empty page on which the lines of emotion and experience are transcribed and then erased. He looked closer to twenty years old than fifty-five, with a stubble of beard and hair carelessly arranged. His face was unmarked.

Barbara stared at him, her lips parting, her face diffused with pink. Tears rose in her eyes and hung there, captured in the well of her lower lids. I looked away from her, unwilling to intrude any more than I had to. The morgue attendant's voice reached us through the intercom.

"Let me know when you're done."

Barbara turned away abruptly.

"Thank you. That's fine," I called. The television screen went dark.

Moments later, there was a tap at the door and he reappeared with a sealed manila envelope and a clipboard in hand.

"We'll need to know what arrangements you want made," he said. He was using that tone of studied neutrality I've heard before from those who deal with the bereaved. Its effect is impersonal and soothing, liberating one to transact business without intrusive emotionalism. He needn't have bothered. Barbara Daggett was a businesswoman, bred to that awesome poise that so unsettles men accustomed to female subservience. Her manner now was smooth and detached, her tone as impassive as his.

"I've talked to Wynington-Blake," she said, indicating one of the funeral homes in town. "If you'll notify them once the autopsy's done, they'll take care of everything. Is that form for me?"

He nodded and held the clipboard out to her with a pen attached. "A release for his personal effects," he said.

She dashed off a signature as if she were signing an autograph for a pesky fan. "When will you have the autopsy results?"

He handed her the envelope, which apparently contained Daggett's odds and ends. "Probably by late afternoon."

"Who's doing the post?" I asked.

"Dr. Yee. He's scheduled it for two-thirty."

Barbara Daggett glanced at me. "She's a private investigator. I want all information released to her. Will I need to sign a separate authorization for that?"

"I don't know. There's probably some procedure, but it's a new one on me. I can check into it and contact you later, if you like."

She slipped her business card under the clamp as she handed the clipboard back to him. "Do that."

His eyes met hers for the first time and I could see him register the oddity of the mismatched irises. She brushed past him, moving out of the room. He stared after her. The door closed.

I held my hand out. "I'm Kinsey Millhone, Mr. Ingraham."

He smiled for the first time. "Oh yeah. I heard about you from Kelly Borden. Nice to meet you."

Kelly Borden was a morgue attendant I'd met during a homicide investigation I'd worked on in August.

"Nice to meet you too," I said. "What's the story on this one?"

"I can't tell you much. They brought him in about seven, just as I was coming to work."

"Do you have any idea how long he'd been dead?"

"I don't know for sure, but it couldn't have been long. The body wasn't bloated and there wasn't any putrefaction. From what I've seen of drowning victims, I'd guess he went in the water late last night. Don't quote me on that. The watch he had on was stopped at two thirty-seven, but it could have been broken. It's a crummy watch and looks all beat up. It's in with his effects. Hell, what do I know? I'm just a flunkie, lowest of the low. Dr. Yee hates it if we talk to people like this."

"Believe me, I'm not going to say anything. I'm just asking for my own purposes. What about his clothing? How was he dressed?"

"Jacket, pants, shirt."

"Shoes and socks?"

"Well, shoes. He didn't have socks on and he didn't have a wallet or anything like that."

"Any signs of injury?"

"None that I've seen."

I couldn't think of anything else I wanted to ask for the moment so I thanked him and said I'd be in touch.

Then I went out to look for Barbara Daggett. If I was going to work for her, we needed to get business squared away.

6

I found her standing in the foyer, looking out at the parking lot. The rain was falling monotonously, occasional gusts of wind tossing the treetops. Cozy-looking lights were on in all the buildings that rimmed the parking lot, which only emphasized the dampness and the chill outside. A nurse, her white uniform flashing from the flaps of a dark blue raincoat, approached the doorway, leaping over puddles like a kid playing hopscotch. Her white hose were speckled with flesh-colored blotches where the rain had soaked through and the tops of her white shoes were spattered with mud. She reached the entrance and I held the door for her.

She flashed me a smile. "Whoo! Thanks. It's like an obstacle course out there." She shook the water from her raincoat and padded down the hallway, crepe soles leaving a pattern of damp footprints in her wake.

Barbara Daggett seemed rooted to the spot. "I have to go to Mother's," she said. "Somebody has to tell her." She turned and looked at me. "How much do you charge for your services?"

"Thirty an hour, plus expenses, which is standard for the area. If you're serious, I can drop a contract off at your office this afternoon."

"What about a retainer?"

I made a quick assessment. I usually ask for an

47

advance, especially in a situation like this, when I know I'll be talking to the cops. There's no concept of privilege between a P.I. and a client, but at least the front money makes it clear where my loyalties lie.

"Four hundred should cover it," I said. I wondered if the figure came to mind because of Daggett's bounced check. Oddly enough, I felt protective of him. He'd conned me—there was no doubt of that—but I *had* agreed to work for him, and in my mind, I still had a duty to discharge. Of course, I might not have felt as charitable if he were still alive, but the dead are defenseless, and somebody in this world has to look out for them.

"I'll have my secretary cut you a check first thing Monday morning," she said. She turned back, looking out the double doors into the gloom. She leaned her head against the glass.

"Are you okay?"

"You don't know how many times I've wished him dead," she said. "Have you ever dealt with an alcoholic?"

I shook my head.

"They're so maddening. I used to look at him and I was convinced he could quit drinking if he wanted to. I don't know how many times I talked to him, begging him to stop. I thought he didn't understand. I thought he just wasn't aware of what we were going through, my mother and me. I can remember the look he'd get in his eyes when he was drunk. Little pink piggy eyes. His whole body radiated this odor. Bourbon. God, I hate that stuff. He smelled like somebody'd dropped a bottle of Early Times down a heater vent . . . waves of smell. He reeked of it."

She looked over at me, her eyes dry and pitiless. "I'm thirty-four and I've hated him with every cell in my body for as long as I can remember. And now I'm stuck with it. He won, didn't he? He never changed, never straightened up, never gave us an inch. He was such a shitheel. It makes me want to smash this glass door out. I don't even know why I care how he died. I should be relieved, but I'm pissed. The irony is that he's probably still going to dominate my life."

"How so?"

"Look what he's done to me already. I think of him every time I have a drink. I think of him if I decide *not* to have a drink. If I even *meet* a man who drinks or if I see a bum on the street or smell bourbon, his face is the first thing that comes to mind. Oh God, and if I'm around someone who's had too much, I can't stand it. I disconnect. My life is filled with reminders of him. His apologies and his phony, wheedling charm, his boo-hooing when the booze got to him. The times he fell, the times he got put in jail, the times he spent every dime we had. When I was twelve, Mother got religion and I don't know which was worse. At least Daddy woke up most days in okay shape. She had Jesus for breakfast, lunch, and dinner. It was grotesque. And then there were the joys of being an only child."

She broke off abruptly and seemed to shake herself. "Oh hell. What difference does it make? I know I sound sorry for myself, but it's been such a bitch and there's no end in sight."

"Actually, you look like you've done pretty well," I said.

She turned her gaze back to the parking lot and I could see her faint, bitter smile reflected in the glass. "You know what they say about living well as the best revenge. I did well because it was the one defense I had. Escape has been the motivating force in my life. Getting away from him, getting away from her, putting that household behind me. The funny thing is, I haven't moved an inch, and the harder I run, the faster I keep slipping back to them. There are spiders that work like that. They bury themselves and create a little pocket of loose dirt. Then when their prey comes along, the soil gives way and the victim slides right down into the trap. There are laws for everything except the harm families do."

She turned, shoving her hands down in her raincoat pockets. She pushed the door open with her backside and a draft of cold air rushed in. "What about you? Are you leaving or will you stick around?"

"I guess I'll hit the office as long as I'm out," I said.

She pressed a button on the handle of her umbrella and it lifted into the open position with a muffled *thunk*. She held it for me and we walked toward my car together. The raindrops tapping on the umbrella fabric made a muted sound, like popcorn in a covered saucepan.

I unlocked my car and got in, while she moved off toward hers, calling back over her shoulder. "Try me at the office as soon as you hear anything. I should be there by two."

My office building was deserted. California Fidelity is closed on weekends so their offices were dark. I let myself in, picking up the batch of morning mail that had been shoved through the slot. There were no messages on my answering machine. I pulled a contract out of my top drawer and spent a few minutes filling in the blanks. I checked Barbara Daggett's business card to verify the address, then I locked up again and went down the front stairs.

I walked the three blocks and dropped the contract off at her office, then headed over to the police station on Floresta. The combination of the weekend and the bad weather lent the station much the same deserted air as my office building. Crime doesn't adhere to a forty-hour week, but there are days when even the criminals don't seem to feel like doing much. The linoleum showed a gridwork of wet footprints, like a pattern of dance steps too complex to learn. The air smelled of cigarette smoke and damp uniforms. I could see where someone had fashioned a folded newspaper into a rain hat and then abandoned it on the wooden bench just inside the door.

One of the clerks in the identification and records section buzzed Jonah and he came out to the locked foyer door and admitted me.

He wasn't looking good. During the summer, he'd shed an excess twenty pounds and he'd told me he was still working out at the gym, so it wasn't that. His dark hair seemed poorly trimmed and the lines around his eyes were pronounced. He also had that weary aura that unhappiness seems to breed.

"What happened to you?" I asked as we walked back to his office. He'd been reconciled with his wife since June, after a year's separation, and from what I'd gathered, it was not going well.

"She wants an open relationship," he remarked.

"Oh come *on*," I said, with disbelief.

That netted me a tired smile. "That's what the lady says." He held the door open for me and we passed into an L-shaped room, furnished with big wooden desks.

Missing Persons is included in Crimes Against Persons, which in turn is considered part of the Investigations Division, along with Crimes Against Property, Narcotics, and Special Investigations. The room was deserted at the moment, but people came and went at intervals. From the interview room off the inside corridor, I could hear the rise and fall of a shrill female voice and I guessed that an interrogation was under way. Jonah closed the hall door, automatically protective of department business.

He filled two Styrofoam cups with coffee and brought them over, handing me packets of Cremora and Equal. Just what I needed, a cup of hot chemicals. We went through the motions of doctoring the coffee, which smelled like it'd been on the burner too long.

I took a few minutes to lay out the Daggett

situation. At this point, we didn't have the results of the autopsy, so the idea of murder was purely theoretical. Still, I told Jonah what had gone on to date, detailing the principal characters. I was talking to him as a friend instead of a cop and he listened as an interested, but unofficial, party.

"So how long was he up here before he died?" Jonah asked.

"Since Monday presumably," I said. "It's possible he went somewhere else first, but Lovella seemed to think he'd head straight for Billy Polo if he needed help."

"Did that information on Polo do you any good?"

"Not yet, but it will. I'm just waiting to see what we've got on our hands before I proceed. Even if the death was accidental, I suspect Barbara Daggett will want me to look into it. I mean, for starters, what was he doing on a boat in a rainstorm? And where has he been all this time?"

"Where have *you* been?" Jonah asked.

I focused on him and realized he'd shifted the subject. "Who, me? I've been around."

He picked up a pencil and began to tap out a beat, like a man auditioning for a tiny blues band. He was giving me a look I'd seen before, full of heat and speculation. "Are you dating anyone?"

I shook my head, smiling slightly. "The only good men I know are married." I was being flirtatious and he seemed to like that.

His blue eyes locked into mine and the color rose in his face. "What do you do for sex?"

"Jog on the beach. How about you?"

He smiled, breaking off eye contact. "In other words, it's none of my business."

I laughed. "I'm not avoiding the question. I'm telling the truth."

"Really? That's funny. I always pictured you out raising hell."

"I did some of that years ago, but I can't stand it these days. Sex is a bonding process. I'm careful who I connect up with. Besides, you don't know what the marketplace is like. A one-night stand is more like a wrestling match with a couple of quick take-downs. Talk about demoralizing. I'd rather be alone."

"I know what you mean. I was out there hustling some the year she was gone, but I never got the hang of it. I'd go in a bar and some babe would sidle up to me, but I never made the right moves. Couple of times, women told me I was rude when I just thought I was making small talk."

"It's worse if you're successful at it," I said. "Be grateful you never learned the gamesmanship. I know a couple of guys on the circuit and they're hard as nails, you know? Unhappy. Hostile toward women. They get laid, but that's about all they get."

Behind him, Lieutenant Becker came in and took a seat at a desk across the room. Jonah's pencil tapping started again and then stopped. He tossed it aside and rocked back in his chair.

"I wish life were simple," he said.

I kept my tone of voice mild. "Life *is* simple. You're the one making things complex. You were doing great without Camilla, as far as I could see. She crooks her finger, though, and you go running back. And now you can't figure out what went wrong. Quit acting like a victim when you did it to yourself."

This time he laughed. "God, Kinsey. Why don't you just say what's on your mind."

"Well, I don't understand voluntary suffering. If you're unhappy, change something. If you can't make it work, then bail out. What's the big deal?"

"Is that what you did?"

"Not quite. I dumped the first and the second one dumped me. With both, I did my share of suffering, but when I look back on it, I can't understand why I endured so long. It was dumb. It was a big waste of time and cost me a lot."

"I've never even heard you mention those guys."

"Yeah, well I'll tell you about them sometime."

"You want to have a drink when I get off work?"

I looked at him briefly and then shook my head. "We'd end up in bed, Jonah."

"That's the point, isn't it?" He smiled and did a Groucho Marx wiggle with his eyebrows.

I laughed and turned the subject back to Daggett as I got up. "Call me when Dr. Yee has results on the post."

"I'll call for more than that."

"Get your life squared away first."

When I left, he was still staring after me, and it was all I could do to get out of there. I had this troubling urge to gallop over and leap onto his lap, laughing while I covered his face with licks, but I didn't think the department would ever be the same. As I glanced back, I could see Becker giving us a speculative look while he pretended to check his "in" box.

7

Daggett's death was ruled accidental. Jonah called me at home at 4:00 to give me the news. I'd spent the afternoon again wrapped up in a quilt, hoping to finish the book. I'd just put on a fresh pot of coffee and I was scurrying back under the covers as the phone rang. When he told me, I was puzzled, but I wasn't convinced. I kept waiting for the punchline, but there wasn't one.

"I don't get it," I said. "Does Yee know the background on this?"

"Babe, Daggett's blood alcohol was point three-five. You're talking acute ethanol intoxication, almost coma stage."

"And that was the cause of death?"

"Well no, he drowned, but Yee says there's no evidence of foul play. None. Daggett went out in a boat, got tangled up in a fishing net, and fell overboard, too drunk to save himself."

"Bullshit!"

"Kinsey, some people die accidentally. It's a fact."

"I don't believe it. Not this one."

"The crime scene investigation unit didn't find a thing. Not even a *hint*. What can I say? You know these guys. They're as good as they come. If you think it's murder, come up with some evidence. In the meantime, we're calling it an accident. As far as we're concerned, the case is closed."

"What was he doing dead drunk in a boat?" I asked. "The man was broke and it was raining cats and dogs. Who'd he rent the boat from?"

I could hear Jonah sigh. "He didn't. Apparently, he took a little ten-foot skiff from its mooring off the dock at Marina One. The harbor master identified the boat and you can see where the line was cut."

"Where'd they find it?"

"On the beach near the pier. There weren't any usable prints."

"I don't like it."

"Look, I know what you're saying and you've got a point. I tend to agree, if that makes you feel any better, but who's asking us? Look at it as a gift. If the death is ruled a homicide, you can't get near it. This way, you've got carte blanche . . . within limits, of course."

"Does Dolan know I'm interested?" Lieutenant Dolan was an assistant division commander and an old antagonist of mine. He hated private investigators getting involved in police business.

"The case is Feldman's. He won't give a shit. You want me to talk to him?"

"Yeah, do that," I said. "And clear it with Dolan, while you're at it. I'm tired of getting my hand smacked."

"Okay. I'll get back to you first thing Monday then," Jonah said. "In the meantime, let me know if anything turns up."

"Right. Thanks."

I put a call through to Barbara Daggett, repeating the information I'd just received. When I finished, she was silent.

"What do you think?" she asked, finally.

"Let's put it this way. *I'm* not satisfied, but it's your money. If you like, I can nose around for a couple of days and if nothing turns up, we'll dump the whole business and you'll just have to live with it."

"What are the odds?"

"I have no idea. All I know to do is pick up a thread and see where it leads. We may come up with six dead ends, but at least you'll know we gave it a shot."

"Let's do it."

"Great. I'll be in touch."

I pushed the quilt aside and got up. I hoped Billy Polo was still around. I didn't know where else to start.

I unplugged the coffeepot, poured the balance of the coffee into a thermos, and then made myself a peanut butter and dill pickle sandwich, which I put in a brown paper bag like a school kid. I had just about that same feeling in my gut too . . . the dull dread I'd experienced when I was eight, trudging off to Woodrow Wilson Elementary. I didn't want to go out in the rain. I didn't want to connect up with Billy Polo, who was probably a creep. He sounded like one of the sixth-grade boys I'd been so fearful of . . . lawless, out of control, and mean.

I searched through my closet until I found my slicker and an umbrella. I left my warm apartment behind and drove over to Billy Polo's old address on Merced. It was 4:15 and getting prematurely dark. The neighborhood had probably been charming once, but it was gradually being overtaken by apartment buildings and was now no more than a hapless mix of the down-at-the-heel and the bland. The little gingerbread structures were wedged between three-story stucco boxes with tenant parking underneath and everywhere there was evidence of the same tasteless disregard for history.

I parked under a pepper tree, using the overhanging branches as brief shelter while I put up my umbrella. I checked the names and house numbers of the two former neighbors, hoping one of them could give me a lead on Polo's current whereabouts.

The first door I knocked on was answered by an elderly woman in a wheelchair, her legs wrapped in Ace bandages and stuffed into lace-up shoes with slices cut out of the sides to accommodate her bunions. I stood on her leaky front porch, talking to her through the screen door, which she kept latched. She had a vague recollection of Billy, but had no idea what had happened to him or where he'd gone. She did direct me to a little rental unit at the rear of the property next door. This was not one of the addresses I'd picked up from the city directory. She said Billy's family had lived in the front house, while the rear was still occupied by an old gent named Talbot, who had been there for the last thirty years. I thanked her and picked my way down the rain-slicked stairs and back along the driveway.

The front unit must have been one of the early houses in the area—a story and a half of white frame, with a peaked roof, two dormers, and a front porch that was screened in now and furnished with junk. I could see the coils on the backside of an old refrigerator and beside it, what looked like a pillar of milk cartons, filled with paperback books. Hydrangeas and bougainvillea grew together in a tangle along the side of the house and the runoff from the rain gutter threw a gush of water out on the drive, forcing me to cut wide to the right.

The rear unit looked like it was originally a tool shed, with a lean-to attached to the left side and a tiny carport on the right. There was no car visible and most of the sheltered space was taken up by a cord of firewood, stacked against the wall. There was room left for a bicycle maybe, but not much else.

The structure was white frame, propped up on cinderblocks, with a window on either side of a central door, and a tiny chimney poking up through the roof. It looked like the drawing we all did in grade school, even to the smoke curling up from the chimney pipe.

I knocked and the door was opened by a wizened

old man with no teeth. His mouth was a wide line barely separating the tip of his nose from the upward thrust of his chin. When he caught sight of me and realized that I was no one he knew, he left the doorway briefly and returned with his dentures, smiling slightly as he shifted them into place. His false teeth made a crunching sound like a horse chewing on a bit. He looked to be in his seventies, frail, his pale skin speckled with red and blue. His white hair was brushed into a pompadour in front, shaggy over his ears and touching his collar in the back. He wore a shirt that looked soft from years of washing and a cardigan sweater that probably belonged to a woman at some point. The buttons were rhinestone and the buttonholes were on the wrong side. He smoothed his hair back with a trembling hand and waited to see what I could possibly want.

"Are you Mr. Talbot?"

"Depends on who's asking," he said.

"I'm Kinsey Millhone. The woman next door suggested that I talk to you. I'm looking for Billy Polo. His family lived in that front house about five years ago."

"I know Billy quite well. Why are you looking for him?"

"I need some information about a friend of his," I said and then gave him a brief explanation. I couldn't see any reason to prevaricate so I simply stated my purpose and left it at that.

He blinked at me. "Billy Polo's a very bad fella. I wonder if you're aware of that." His voice was powdery and I noticed that he had a tremor, his head oscillating as he spoke. I guessed that he suffered from some form of parkinsonism.

"Yeah, I am. I heard he was up at the California Men's Colony until recently. I think that's where he met the man I'm referring to. Do you have any idea how I might reach him?"

"Well, you know, his mother is the one who owned

that place," he said, nodding toward the front house. "She sold it about two years ago when she remarried."

"Is she still here in town?"

"Yes, and I believe she's living on Tranvia. Her married name is Christopher. Just a minute and I'll give you the address." He shuffled away and a few moments later was back with a small address book in hand. "She's a lovely woman. Sends me a card every year at Christmastime. Yes, here it is. Bertha Christopher. Goes by the nickname of Betty. If you chance to see her, I wish you'd give her my best."

"I'll do that, Mr. Talbot. Thanks so much."

Tranvia turned out to be a wide, treeless street off Milagro on the east side of town, a neighborhood of one-story frame houses on small lots, with chicken wire fences, unruly head-high poinsettia bushes pelted by the rain, and soggy children's toys abandoned in driveways paved with parallel strips of concrete. The level of maintenance here seemed erratic, but the address I now had for Bertha Christopher showed one of the better-kept houses on the block, mustard-colored with dark brown trim. I parked my VW on the opposite side of the street, about fifty yards away, so I could sit and watch the place inconspicuously. Most of the parked cars were crummy so mine fit right in.

It was now after 5:00 and the light was fading fast, the chill in the air more pronounced. The rain had eased somewhat so I left my umbrella where it was. I grabbed my yellow slicker and slipped into it, pulling up the hood. I locked the car and crossed the street, splashing through puddles that darkened the leather of my boots. The rain drummed against the fabric of the slicker with a pocking sound that made me feel like I was in a pup tent.

The Christopher property was surrounded by a low rock wall, constructed with sandstone boulders the size of cantaloupes, held together with concrete. A row of hanging planters screened the front windows from the street and a set of glass windchimes, suspended in one corner of the porch, tinkled with the wind. There were two lightweight aluminum lawn chairs arranged on either side of a metal table. Everything was soggy and smelled of wet grass.

There was no doorbell, but I tapped on the pane of glass in the front door, cupping a hand so I could peer in. The interior was in shadow, no lights showing from the rear of the house. I moved to the porch rail and checked the adjacent houses, both of which were dark. My guess was that many of these people were off at work. After a few minutes, I went back to my car.

I started the engine and ran the heater for a while, fogging up the windows until I could barely see. I rubbed a clear spot in the middle of the windshield and then sat and stared. Streetlights came on. At 5:45, I ate my sandwich just for something to do. At 6:15, I drank some coffee and flipped on my car radio, listening to a talk-show host interview a psychic. Fifteen minutes later, right after the 6:30 news, a car approached and slowed, turning into the Christophers' driveway.

A woman got out, dimly illuminated by the street light. She paused as if to raise her umbrella and then apparently decided to make a dash for it. I watched her scuttle up the driveway and around toward the back of the house. Moments later, the lights went on in sequence . . . first the rear left room, probably a kitchen, then the living room, and finally the front porch light. I gave her a few minutes to get her coat hung up and then I returned to her front door.

I knocked again. I could see her peer into the hallway from the rear of the house and then approach the front door. She stared at me blankly, then leaned her head close to the glass for a better look.

She appeared to be in her fifties, with a sallow complexion and a deeply creased face. Her hair was too

uniform a shade to be a natural brown. She wore it
parted on the side with big puffy bangs across her lined
forehead. Her eyes were the size and color of old
pennies and her makeup looked like it needed renewing
at this hour of the day. She wore a uniform I'd seen
before, brown pants and a brown-and-yellow-checked
tunic. I couldn't place the outfit offhand.

"Yes?" she called through the glass.

I raised my voice against the sound of the rain. "I'm
looking for Billy. Is he back yet?"

"He don't live here, hon, but he said he'd be by at
eight o'clock. Who are you?"

I picked a name at random. "Charlene. Are you his
mother?"

"Charlene who?"

"A friend of his said I should look him up if I was
ever in Santa Teresa. Is he at work?"

She gave me an odd look, as if the notion of Billy
working had never crossed her mind. "He's out checking
the used car lots for an automobile."

She had one of those faces that seemed tantalizingly
familiar and it dawned on me, belatedly, that she was a
checker at the supermarket where I shop now and then.
We'd even chatted idly about the fact that I was a P.I. I
eased back out of the porch light, hoping she hadn't
recognized me at the same time I recognized her. I held
the corner of the slicker up as though to shield my face
from the wind.

She seemed to pick up on the fact that something
odd was going on. "What'd you want him for?"

I ignored that, pretending I couldn't hear. "Why
don't I come back when he gets home?" I hollered. "Just
tell him Charlene stopped by and I'll catch up with him
when I can."

"Well, all right," she said reluctantly. I gave her a
casual wave as I turned. I went down the porch steps
and into the dark, aware that she was peering after me

suspiciously. I must have disappeared from her field of vision then because she turned the porch light off.

I got back in my car with one of those quick, involuntary shudders that racks you from head to toe. When I caught up with Billy, I might well admit who I was and what I wanted with him, but for the moment, I didn't want to tip my hand. I checked my watch and settled in, prepared to wait. Already, it was feeling like a long night.

8

Four hours passed. The rain stopped. It became apparent that Billy was not only late, but possibly not coming at all. Maybe he'd bought a car and hightailed it out of town, or maybe at some point he'd phoned his mother and decided to skip the visit when he heard about "Charlene." I finished all the coffee in the thermos, my brain fairly crackling from caffeine. If I smoked cigarettes, I could have gone through a pack. Instead, I listened to eight more installments of the news, the farm report, and an hour of Hispanic music. I pondered the possibility of learning the Spanish language by simply listening to these gut-wrenching tunes. I thought about Jonah and the husbands I'd known. Surely, if my heart broke again, it would sound just like this, though for all I knew, the lyrics were about cut worms and inguinal hernias, matters only made soulful through soaring harmonies. Altogether, I came perilously close to boring myself insensible with my own mental processes, so it was with real relief that I saw the car approach and pull into the curb in front of the house across the street. It looked like a 1967 Chevrolet, white, with a temporary registration sticker on the windshield. I couldn't tell much about the guy who got out, but I watched with interest as he took the porch steps in two bounds and rang the bell.

   Betty Christopher came to the door to let him in.
The two of them disappeared. A moment later, shadows
wavered against the kitchen light. I figured they'd sit
down for a couple of beers and a heart-to-heart talk.
The next thing I knew, however, the front door opened
again and he came out. I slipped down on the car seat
until my eyes were level with the bottom of the window.
The cloud cover was still heavy, obscuring the moon,
and the cars along the curb created deeper shadows still.
He stared out at the street, taking in the line of parked
cars one by one. I felt my heart start to thump as I
watched him come down the steps and head in my
direction.
   He paused in the middle of the street. He moved
over to a van parked two cars away from mine. He
flicked on a flashlight and opened the door on the
driver's side, apparently to check the registration. I lost
sight of him. Moments went by. I watched the shadows,
wondering if he'd crept around the other side and was
coming up on my right. I heard a muffled sound as he
closed the door to the van. The beam from his flashlight
swept over the car in front of me and flashed across my
windshield, the light too diffused by the time it reached
me to illuminate much. He flicked it off. He waited,
scanning the street on both sides. Apparently, he decided there was nothing to worry about. He crossed back
to the house. As he reached the porch, she came out,
clutching a robe around her. They talked for a few
minutes and then he got in his car and took off. The
minute she went inside, I started the VW and did a big
U-turn, following. I hoped this wasn't all some elaborate
ruse to flush me into the open.
   He had already made a left turn and then a right by
the time I caught sight of him two blocks ahead of me.
We were driving along the back streets with no traffic
lights at all and only an occasional stop sign to slow our
progress. I had to close the gap or risk losing him. A

"one-man" tail is nearly pointless unless you know who
you're following and where he's going to begin with. At
this hour, there were very few cars on the road, and if he
drove far, he'd realize the presence of my VW was no
accident.

I thought he was headed toward the freeway, but
before he reached the northbound on-ramp, he slowed
and made a right-hand turn. By then, I was only half a
block back so I whipped over to the curb and parked,
killing the engine. I locked the car and took off on foot,
heading diagonally across the corner lot at a dead run. I
caught sight of his taillights half a block ahead. The car
was making a left-hand turn into a shabby trailer park.

Puente is a narrow street that parallels Highway 101
on the east side of town, with the trailer park itself
squeezed into the space between the two roadways,
screened off from the highway by a ten-foot board fence
and masses of oleander. I was covering ground at a
quick clip. The houses I passed were dark, driveways
crowded with old cars, most of them sporting dents. The
street lighting here was poor, but ahead of me I caught
traces of light from the trailer park, which was strung
with small multicolored bulbs.

By the time I got to the entrance, there was no sign
of the Chevrolet, but the place was small and I didn't
think the car would be hard to spot. The road twisting
through the trailer park was two lanes wide. The
blacktop still glistened from the rain and water was
dripping from the eucalyptus trees that towered at
intervals. There were signs posted everywhere: SLOW.
SPEED BUMPS. TENANT PARKING ONLY. DO NOT BLOCK
DRIVEWAY.

Most of the trailers were "single-wides," fifteen to
twenty feet long, the kind that once upon a time you
could actually hitch to your car and travel in. Nomad,
Airstream, and Concord seemed to predominate. Each
had a numbered cardboard sign in the window, indicat-

ing the number of the lot on which it sat. Some were
moored in narrow patches of grass, temporary camper
spaces for RVs passing through, but many were permanent and, by the look of them, had been there for years.
The lots were stingy squares of poured concrete, surrounded by sections of white picket fence two feet high,
or separated from one another by sagging lengths of
bamboo matting. The yards, when they existed, harbored an assortment of plastic deer and flamingos.

It was almost eleven and many of the trailers were
dark. Occasionally, I could see the blue-gray flicker of a
TV set. I found the Chevrolet, hood warm, the engine
still ticking, parked beside a dark green battered trailer
with a torn awning and half the aluminum skirting
ripped away. From inside, I could hear the dull thump
of rock and roll music being played too loudly in too
small a space.

The trailer windows were ovals of hot yellow light,
positioned about a foot higher than eye level. I edged
around to the right-hand side, easing in as close as I
could, checking the area to see if any of the neighbors
had spotted me. The trailer next door had a FOR RENT
sign taped to the siding, and the one across the lane had
the curtains pulled. I turned back to the window and got
up on tiptoe, peering in. The window was opened
slightly and the air seeping out was hot and smelled of
fried onions. The curtains consisted of old cotton dish
towels, with a brass rod threaded through one end,
hanging crookedly enough to provide a clear view of
Billy Polo and the woman he was talking to. They were
both seated at a flop-down table in the galley, drinking
beer, mouths working, words inaudible in the thumping
din of music. The interior of the trailer was a depressing
collage of cheap paneled walls, dirty dishes, junk, torn
upholstery, newspapers, and canned goods stacked on
counter tops. A bumper sticker pasted above the front
door said, I'VE BEEN TO ALL 48 STATES!

There was a small black-and-white television set perched on a cardboard box, tuned to what looked like the tag end of a prime-time private-eye show. The action was speeding up. A car careened out of control, flipping end over end before it went off a cliff, exploding in midair. The picture cut to two men in an office, one talking on the phone. Neither Billy nor his companion seemed to be watching and the music must have made it impossible for them to hear the dialogue anyway.

I could feel a cramp forming in my right calf. I cast about for something to stand on to ease the strain. The yard next door was a jungle of overgrown shrubs, the parking space choked with discards. There was a set of detached wooden steps tucked up under the trailer door. I blundered through the bushes, my jeans and boots getting drenched in the process. I was counting on the thunder of music to cover the sound of my labors as I hefted the box steps, tramped back through the shrubs, and set the steps under the window.

Cautiously, I mounted, peering in again. Billy Polo had a surprisingly boyish face for a man who'd lived his thirty years as a thug. His hair was dark, a curly mass standing out around his face. His nose was small, his mouth generous, and he had a dimple in his chin that looked like a puncture wound. He wasn't a big man, but he had a wiry musculature that suggested strength. There was something manic about him, a hint of tension in his gestures. His eyes were restless and he tended to stare off to one side when he spoke, as if direct eye contact made him anxious.

The woman was in her early twenties, with a wide mouth, strong chin, and a pug nose that looked as if it was made of putty. She wore no makeup and her fair hair was dense, a series of tight ripples that she wore shoulder length, brittle and illcut. Her skin was very pale, mottled with freckles. She was wearing a man's oversized silk bathrobe and apparently nursing a cold.

She kept a wad of Kleenex in her pocket which she honked into from time to time. She was so close to me I could see the chapping where the frequent blowing had reddened her nose and upper lip. I wondered if she was an old girlfriend of Billy's. There was no overt sexuality in the way they related to one another, but there was a curious intimacy. An old love affair gone flat perhaps.

The continuous rock and roll music was driving me nuts. I was never going to hear what they were saying with that stuff booming out all over the place. I got down off the steps and went around the other side of the trailer to the front door. The window to the right was wide open, though the curtains were pinned shut.

I waited until there was a brief pause between cuts. I took a deep breath and pounded on the door. "Hey! Could you cut the goddamn noise," I yelled. "We're tryin' to get some sleep over here!"

From inside the trailer, the woman hollered, "Sorry!" The music ceased abruptly and I went back around to the other side to see how much of their conversation I could pick up.

The quiet was divine. The volume on the television set must have been turned all the way down, because the string of commercials that now appeared was antic with silence and I could actually catch snatches of what they were saying, though they mumbled unmercifully.

". . . course, she's going to say that. What did you expect?" she said.

"I don't like the pressure. I don't like havin' her on my back . . ." He said something else I couldn't make out.

"What difference does it make? Nobody forced her. Shit, she's free, white, and twenty-one . . . the point is . . . getting into . . . just so she doesn't think . . . the whole thing, right?"

Her voice had dropped and when Billy answered,

he had one hand across his mouth so I couldn't understand him at all. He was only half attentive anyway, talking to her with his gaze straying to the television picture. It must have been 11:00 because the local news came on. There was the usual lead-in, a long shot of the news desk with two male newscasters, one black, one white, like a matched set, sitting there in suits. Both looked properly solemn. The camera cut to a head shot of the black man. A photograph of John Daggett appeared briefly behind him. There was a quick shot of the beach. It took me a moment to realize that it must have been the spot where Daggett's body had been found. In the background, I could see the mouth of the harbor and the dredge.

Billy jerked upright, grabbing the woman's arm. She swiveled around to see what he was pointing to. The announcer talked on, smoothly moving the top sheet of paper aside. The camera cut to the co-anchor and the picture shifted to a still shot of a local waste disposal site.

Billy and the woman traded a long, anxious look. Billy started cracking his knuckles. "Christ!"

The woman snatched up the paper and tossed it at him. "I told you it was him the minute I read some bum washed up on the beach. Goddamn it, Billy! Everything with you comes down to the same old bullshit. You think you're so smart. You got all the angles covered. Oh sure. Turns out you don't even know what you're talking about!"

"They don't even know we knew him. How would they know that?"

She gave him a scornful look, exasperated that he'd try to defend himself. "Give the cops some credit! They probably identified him by his fingerprints, right? So they know he was up in San Luis. It's not going to take a genius to figure out you were up there with him. Next thing we know somebody's coming around knocking at the door. 'When'd you last see this guy?' Shit like that."

He got up abruptly. He crossed to a kitchen cabinet and opened it. "You got any Black Jack?"

"No, I don't have any Black Jack. You drank it all last night."

"Get some clothes on. Let's go over to the Hub."

"Billy, I've got a cold! I'm not going out at this hour. You go. Why do you need a drink anyway?"

He reached for his jacket, hunching into it. "You have any cash? All I got on me is a buck."

"Get a job. Pay your own way. I'm tired of givin' you money."

"I said you'd get it back. What are you worried about? Come on, come on," he said, snapping his fingers impatiently.

She took her time about it, but she did root through her purse, coming up with a crumpled five-dollar bill, which he took without comment.

"Are you crashing here?" she asked.

"I don't know yet. Probably. Don't lock up."

"Well, just keep it down, okay? I feel like hell and I don't want to be woke up."

He put his hands on her arms. "Hey," he said. "Cool it. You worry too much."

"You know what your problem is? You think all you have to do is say shit like that and it's all okay. The world doesn't work that way. It never did."

"Yeah, well there's always a first time. Your problem is you're a pessimist. . . ."

At that point, I figured I'd better cut out and head back to my car. I eased down off my perch, debating briefly about whether I should move the steps or leave them there. Better to move them. I hefted them, swiftly pushing through the undergrowth to a cleared space where the junk was stacked up. I set the box down and then took off through the darkened trailer park and out to the street.

I jogged to my car, started it, and did another

U-turn, anticipating that Billy would head back the same way he came. Sure enough, in my rearview mirror I saw the Chevrolet make a left turn onto the main thoroughfare, coming up behind me. He followed me for a block and a half, tailgating, a real A-type. With an impatient toot of the horn, he passed me, squealed into another left-hand turn, and zoomed off toward Milagro. I knew where he was headed so I took my time. There's a bar called the Hub about three blocks up. I walked into the place maybe ten minutes after he did. He'd already bought his Jack Daniel's, which he was nursing while he played pool.

9

The Hub is a bar with all the ambience of a converted warehouse. The space is too vast for camaraderie, the air too chill for relaxation. The ceiling is high, painted black, and covered with a gridwork of pipes and electrical conduits. The tables in the main room are sparse, the walls lined with old black-and-white photographs of the bar and its various clientele over the years. Through a wide archway is a smaller room with four pool tables. The juke box is massive, outlined in bands of yellow, green, and cherry red, with bubbles blipping through the seams. The place was curiously empty for a Saturday night. A Willie Nelson single was playing, but it wasn't one I knew.

I was the only woman in the bar and I could sense the male attention shift to me with a bristling caution. I paused, feeling sniffed at, as if I were a dog in an alien neighborhood. Cigarette smoke hung in the air, and the men with their pool cues were caught in the hazy light, bent above the tables in silhouette. I identified Billy Polo by the great puff of hair around his head. Upright, he was taller than I'd pictured him, with wide, hard shoulders and slim hips. He was playing pool with a Mexican kid, maybe twenty-two, with a gaunt face, tattooed arms, and a strip of pinched-looking chest which was visible in the gap of the Hawaiian shirt he wore unbuttoned to the waist. He sported maybe six chest hairs in a shallow depression in the middle of his sternum.

I crossed to the table and stood there, waiting for Billy to finish his game. He glanced at me with disinterest and lined up the cue ball with the six ball, which he smacked smartly into a side pocket. He moved around the table without pause, lining up the two ball which he fired like a shot into the corner pocket. He chalked his cue, eyeing the three ball. He tested an angle and rejected it, leaning into the table then with a shot that sent the three ball rocketing into the side pocket, while the five ball glanced off the side, rolled into range of the corner pocket, hung there, and finally dropped in. A trace of a smile crossed Billy's face, but he didn't look up.

Meanwhile, the Mexican kid stood there and grinned at me, leaning on his cue stick. He mouthed, "I love you." One of his front teeth was rimmed in gold, like a picture frame, and there was a smudge of blue chalk near his chin. Behind him, Billy cleaned up the table and put his cue stick back in the rack on the wall. As he passed, he plucked a twenty from the kid's shirt pocket and tucked it into his own. Then, with his face averted, he said, "You the chick came looking for me at my mom's house earlier?"

"That's right. I'm a friend of John Daggett's."

He cocked his head, squinting, his right hand cupped behind his ear. "Who?"

I smiled lazily. We were apparently playing charades. I raised my voice, enunciating. "Daggett. John."

"Oh, yeah, him. How's he doing these days?" He started snapping his fingers lightly to the music, which had switched from Willie Nelson to a George Benson tune.

"He's dead."

I have to credit him. He did a nice imitation of casual surprise, not overdoing it. "You're shittin' me. Daggett's dead? Too bad. What happened to the dude, heart attack?"

"Drowned. It just happened last night, down at the marina." I wagged a thumb over my shoulder in the direction of the beach so he'd know which marina I meant.

"Here in town? Hey, that's tough. I didn't know that. He was in L.A. last I heard."

"I'm surprised you didn't see it on the news."

"Yeah, well I never pay attention to that shit, you know? Bums me out. I got better things to do with my time."

His eyes were all over the place and his body was half turned away. I had to guess that he was busy trying to figure out who I was and what I was up to. He flicked a look at me. "I'm sorry. I didn't catch your name."

"Kinsey Millhone."

He studied me fleetingly. "I thought my mom said the name was Charlene."

I shook my head. "I don't know where she got that."

"And you do what?"

"Basic research. I free-lance. What's that got to do with it?"

"You don't look like a friend of Daggett's. He was kind of a lowlife. You got too much class for a scumbag like him."

"I didn't say we were close. I met him recently through a friend of a friend."

"Why tell me about it? I don't give a damn."

"I'm sorry to hear that. Daggett said if anything happened to him, I should talk to you."

"Me? Naww," he said with disbelief. "That's fuckin' weird. You must have got me mixed up with somebody else. I mean, I knew Daggett, but I didn't *know* him, you dig?"

"That's funny. He told me you were the best of friends."

He smiled and shook his head. "Old Daggett gave you a bum steer, baby doll. I don't know nothin' about it. I don't even remember when I saw him last. Long time."

"What was the occasion?"

He glanced at the Mexican kid who was eavesdropping shamelessly. "Catch you later, man," he said to him. Then under his breath, with contempt, he said, "Paco." Apparently, this was a generic insult that applied to all Hispanics.

He touched my elbow, steering me into the other room. "These beaners are all the same," he confided. "Think they know how to play pool, but they can't do shit. I don't like talking personal in front of spics. Can I buy you a beer?"

"Sure."

He indicated an empty table and held a chair out for me. I hung my slicker over the back and sat down. He caught the bartender's eye and held up two fingers. The bartender pulled out two bottles of beer which he opened and set on the bar.

Billy said, "You want anything else? Potato chips? They make real nice french fries. Kinda greasy, but good."

I shook my head, watching him with interest. At close range, he had a curious charisma . . . a crude sexuality that he probably wasn't even aware of. I meet men like that occasionally and I'm always startled by the phenomenon.

He ambled over and picked up the beers, dropping a couple of crumpled bills on the bar. He said something to the bartender and then waited while the guy placed a glass upside down on each bottle, shooting a smirk in my direction.

He came back to the table and sat down. "Jesus, ask for a glass in this place and they act like you're puttin' on airs. Bunch of bohunks. I only hang out here because I got a sister works here three nights a week."

Ah, I thought, the woman in the trailer.

He poured one of the beers and pushed it over to me, taking his time then as he poured his own. His eyes were deepset, and he had dimples that formed a crease on either side of his mouth. "Look," he said, "I can see you got your mind made up I know something I don't. The truth is, I didn't like Daggett much and I don't think he liked me. Where you got this yarn about me bein' some pal of his, I don't know, but it wasn't from him."

"You called him Monday morning, didn't you?"

"Nuh-uh. Not me. Why would I call him?"

I went on as though he hadn't said anything. "I don't know what you told him, but he was scared."

"Sorry I can't help you out. Must have been somebody else. What was he doin' up here anyway?"

"I don't know. His body washed up in the surf this morning. I thought maybe you could fill me in on the rest. Do you have any idea where he was last night?"

"Nope. Not a clue." He'd gotten interested in a speck of dust in the foam on his beer and he had to pick that out.

"When did you see him last? I don't think you said."

His tone became facetious. "Geez, I don't have my Day-Timer with me. Otherwise, I could pin it down. We might've had lunch at some little out of the way place, just him and me."

"San Luis perhaps?"

There was a slight pause and his smile dimmed a couple of watts. "I was at San Luis with him," he said, cautiously. "Me and thirty-seven hundred other guys. So what?"

"I thought maybe you'd kept in touch."

"I can tell you didn't know Daggett too good. Being with him is like walking around with dog-do on your shoe, you know? It's not something you'd seek out."

"Who else did he know here in town?"

"Can't help you there. It's not my week to keep track."

"What about your sister? Did he know her?"

"Coral? No way. She don't hang out with bums like that. I'd break her neck. I don't get why you're goin' on and on about this. I told you I don't know nothin'. I didn't see him, didn't hear from him. Why can't you just take my word for it?"

"Because I don't think you're telling the truth."

"Says who? I mean, you came lookin' for me, remember? I don't have to talk to you. I'm doin' you a favor. I don't know who you are. I don't even know what the fuck you're up to."

I shook my head, smiling slightly. "God, Billy. Such foul talk. I didn't think you dealt with women that way. I'm shocked."

"Now you're makin' fun of me, right?" He scrutinized my face. "You some kind of cop?"

I ran my thumbnail down the bottle, snagging an accordion strip of label, which I picked off. "Actually I am."

He snorted. Now he'd heard everything. "Come on. Like what," he said.

"I'm a private investigator."

"Bullshit."

"It's a fact."

He tipped back in his chair, amused that I'd try to lay such a line on him. "Jesus, you're too much. Who do you think you're talkin' to? I might have been born at night, but it wasn't *last* night. I know the private eyes around town and you ain't one, so try somethin' else."

I laughed. "All right, I'm not. Maybe I'm just a nosy chick looking into the death of a man I once met."

"Now, that I'd buy, but it still don't explain why you're crankin' on my case."

"You introduced him to Lovella, didn't you?"

That stopped him momentarily. "You know Lovella?"

"Sure. I met her down in L.A. She has an apartment on Sawtelle."

"When was this?"

"Day before yesterday."

"No foolin'. And she told you to look me up?"

"How else would I know where you were?"

He stared at me, going through some sort of mental debate.

I thought a little coaxing might loosen his tongue. "Are you aware that Daggett's been beating the shit out of her?"

That made him restless and his eyes dropped away from mine. "Yeah, well Lovella's a big girl. She has to learn how to take care of herself."

"Why don't you help her out?"

He smiled bitterly. "I know people who'd laugh at the notion of me helping anyone," he said. "Besides, she's tough. You don't want to underestimate that one, I'm tellin' you."

"You've known her a long time, haven't you?"

His knee had started to jump. "Seven years, eight. I met her when she was seventeen. We lived together for a while, but it didn't work out. We used to knock heads too much. She's a bullheaded bitch, but I loved her a lot. Then I got busted on a burglary rap and me and her, hell, I don't know what it was. We wrote to each other for a while, but you can't go back to something once it's dead, you know? Anyway, now we're friends, I guess. At least I dig her. I don't know how she feels about me."

"Have you seen her recently?"

The knee stopped. "No, I haven't seen her recently," he said. "What about you? Why'd you go down there?"

"I was looking for Daggett. The phone was disconnected."

"What exactly did she say?"

I shrugged. "Nothing much. I wasn't there long and she wasn't feeling that good. She was nursing a big black eye."

"Jesus," he said. He rocked back in his chair. "Tell me something. How come women do that? Let guys punch 'em out?"

"I have no idea."

He drained his beer glass and set it down. "I bet you don't take crap from anyone, am I right?"

"We all take crap from someone," I said.

Billy got up. "Sorry to cut this off, but I gotta split." He turned, tucking his shirt down into his pants more securely. His body language said he'd already taken off and hoped his clothing would catch up with him by the time he hit the street.

I got up, reaching for my slicker. "You're not leaving town, are you?"

"What business is it of yours?"

"It doesn't seem like a good idea with Daggett's death hanging fire. Suppose the cops want to talk to you."

"About what?"

"Where you were last night, for starters."

His tone rose. "Where *I* was? What are you talkin' about?"

"They might want to know about the connection between Daggett and you."

"What connection? That's a crock. I don't know where you come up with that."

"It's not me you have to worry about. It's the cops who count."

"What cops?"

I shook my head. "You know who your friendly local cops are," I said. "If somebody puts a bug in the wrong ear, you'll be sitting in the hot seat."

He was all outrage. "Why would you do that to me?"

"Because you're not leveling with me, William."

"I *am* leveling with you! I've told you everything I know."

"I don't think so. I think you knew about Daggett's death. I think you saw him this week."

He put his hands on his hips and looked off across the room, shaking his head. "Man, this is all I need. This is no lie. I've been straight. I'm minding my own business, doing like I been told. I didn't even know the dude was up here."

"You can stick to your story if you like," I said, "but I'll give you a word of advice. I've got the license number of that car you bought. You bolt and I'm calling Lieutenant Dolan down at Homicide."

He seemed as much puzzled as dismayed. "What is this? A shakedown? Is that what this is about?"

"What's to shake? You don't have a cent. I want information, that's all."

"I don't *have* any information. How many times I gotta tell you that?"

"Look," I said patiently. "Why don't I let you think about the situation and then we can talk again."

"Why don't you go fuck yourself!"

I put my slicker on, tucking the strap of my handbag over my shoulder. "Thanks for the beer. I'll buy yours next time."

He made an exaggerated gesture of dismissal, too

pissed off to reply. He headed toward the door and I watched him go. I glanced at my watch. It was well after midnight and I was exhausted. My head was starting to ache and I knew everything about me smelled like stale cigarette smoke. I wanted to go home, strip down, shower, and then crawl into the folds of my quilt. Instead, I took a deep breath and went after him.

10

I gave him a good head start, then followed him back to the trailer. The temperature felt like it had dropped into the fifties. The eucalyptus trees were still tossing occasional showers at me when the wind cut through, but for the most part, the night was clear. Above me, I could see pale puffs of rain clouds receding, wide patches of starry sky breaking through. I parked half a block away and padded into the park on foot as I had before. Billy's car was parked beside the trailer. I was getting bored, but I had to be certain he wasn't heading off to consult with some confederate I didn't know about.

The same lights were on in the galley, but a dim light now glowed at the rear of the trailer, where I imagined the bedroom to be. I picked my way through the bushes to that end. Curtains were pulled across the windows, but the venting system was piping a murmured conversation right out through a mesh-covered opening. I hunkered down by the torn skirting, leaning my head against the aluminum. I could smell cigarette smoke, which I guessed was Coral's.

". . . want to know why she showed up now," she was saying. "That's what we have to worry about. For all we know, they're in it together."

"Yeah, but doin' what? That's what I can't figure out."

"When'd she say she'd get in touch?"

"She didn't. Said I should think about the situation. Jesus. How'd she get a bead on the Chevy so fast? That's what bugs me. I had that car two hours."

"Maybe she followed you, dimwit."

The silence was profound. "Goddamn it," he said.

I heard footsteps thump toward the front of the trailer. By the time the door banged open I was easing my way around the end. I peered out into the carport. The nose of the Chevy was about six feet away, the space on either side of it crowded with junk.

The door to the trailer had been flung open. Light poured out, washing as far as the point where the asphalt began. With a quick look over my shoulder, I waded into the refuse, picking my way around to the far side of the car, where I crouched, listening intently. Sometimes I feel like I spend half my life this way. I heard Billy fumble his way around the bedroom end of the trailer just as I had.

"Jesus!" he hissed.

Coral peered out the side window, whispering hoarsely. "What's wrong?"

"Shut up! Nothing. I banged my goddamn shin on the trailer hitch. Why don't you clean up this crap?"

My sentiments exactly.

Coral laughed and the curtain dropped back into place.

Billy appeared again at the far end of the carport, rubbing his left shin. He did a quick visual survey, apparently convinced by then there wasn't anybody lurking about the premises. He shook his head and thumped up the steps, banging the door shut behind him. The carport went dark. I let out my breath.

I could hear them murmuring together, but by then I didn't really care what else they discussed. As soon as I was convinced it was safe, I crept out of the driveway and headed for my car.

Sunday morning was overcast. The very air looked gray, and dampness seemed to rise up out of the earth like a mist. I went through my usual morning routine, getting a three-mile run in before the skies opened up again. At 9:00, I put a call through to Barbara Daggett at home. I brought her up to date, filling her in on my night's activities.

"What now?" she asked.

"I'm going to let Billy Polo stew for a day or two and then get back to him."

"What makes you think he won't skip?"

"Well, he *is* on parole and I'm hoping he won't want to mess that up. Besides, it feels like a waste of money to pay me to sit there all day."

"I thought you said he was the only lead you had."

"Maybe not," I said cautiously. "I've been thinking about Tony Gahan and the other people killed in the accident."

"Tony Gahan?" she said with surprise. "How could he be involved in this?"

"I don't know. Your father hired me originally to track him down. Maybe he found the kid himself and that's where he was early in the week."

"But Kinsey, why would Daddy want to track him down? That boy must hate his guts. His whole family was wiped out."

"That's my point."

"Oh."

"Do you have any idea how to locate him? Your father had an address on Stanley Place, but the house was apparently empty. I can't find a Gahan listed in the telephone book."

"He lives with his aunt now, I think, somewhere in Colgate. Let me see if I've got an address."

Colgate is the bedroom community, attached to Santa Teresa like a double star. The two are just about the same size, but Santa Teresa has all the character and Colgate has the affordable housing, along with hardware stores, paint companies, bowling alleys, and drive-in theaters. Colgate is the Frostee-Freeze capital of the world.

There was a pause and I could hear pages rattle. She came back on the line. "My mistake. They live near the Museum. Her last name is Westfall. Ramona."

"I wonder why your father didn't know about her."

"I don't know. She was there for the trial. I do remember that, because someone pointed her out to me. I wrote her a note afterwards, saying that of course we'd do anything we could to help, but I never heard back."

"You know anything else about her? Is she married, for instance?"

"I think so, yes. Her husband manufactures industrial supplies or something like that. Actually, now that I think about it, she *was* working at that kitchenware place on Capilla because I spotted her when I was in there shopping a couple of months ago. Maybe you could catch her this afternoon if she still works there."

"On Sunday?"

"Sure, they're open from twelve to five."

"I'll try her first and see how far I get," I said. "What about your mother? How's she holding up?"

"Surprisingly well. Turns out she handles death like a champ. If it's covered in the Bible, she trots out all the appropriate attitudes and goes through the sequence automatically. I thought she'd flip out, but it seems to have put her back on her feet. She's got church women sitting with her, and the pastor's there. The kitchen table's stacked with tuna casseroles and chocolate cakes. I don't know how long it will last, but for now, she's in her element."

"When's the funeral?"

"Tuesday afternoon. The body's been transported to the mortuary. I think they said he'd be ready for viewing early this afternoon. Are you coming by?"

"Yes, I think I will. I can tell you then if I've talked to this Westfall woman or the kid."

Jorden's is a gourmet cook's fantasy, with every imaginable food preparation device. Rack after rack of cookware, utensils, cookbooks, linens, spices, coffees, and condiments; chafing dishes, wicker baskets, exotic vinegars and oils, knives, baking pans, glassware. I stood in the entrance for a moment, amazed by the number and variety of food-related implements. Pasta machines, cappuccino makers, food warmers, coffee grinders, ice cream freezers, food processors. The air smelled of chocolate and made me wish I had a mother. I spotted three saleswomen, all wearing wraparound aprons made of mattress ticking, with the store's name embroidered in maroon across the bib.

I asked for Ramona Westfall and was directed toward the rear aisle. She was apparently doing a shelf count. I found her perched on a small wooden stool, clipboard in hand, checking off items on a list that included most of the non-electrical gadgets. She was sorting through a bin of what looked like small stainless steel sliding boards with a blade across the center that would slice your tiny ass off.

"What are those?" I asked.

She glanced up at me with a pleasant smile. She appeared to be in her late forties, with short, pale sandy hair streaked with gray, hazel eyes peering at me over a pair of half-glasses which she wore low on her nose. She used little if any makeup, and even seated, I could tell she was small and slim. Under the apron, she wore a white, long-sleeved blouse with a Peter Pan collar, a gray tweed skirt, hose, and penny loafers.

"That's a mandoline. It's made in West Germany."

"I thought a mandolin was a musical instrument."

"The spelling's different. This is for slicing raw vegetables. You can waffle-cut or julienne."

"Really?" I said. I had sudden visions of homemade French fries and cole slaw, neither of which I've ever prepared. "How much is that?"

"A hundred and ten dollars. With the slicing guard, it's one thirty-eight. Would you like a demonstration?"

I shook my head, unwilling to spend that much money on behalf of a potato. She got to her feet, smoothing the front of her apron. She was half a head shorter than I and smelled like a perfume sample I'd gotten in the mail the week before. Lavender and crushed jasmine. I was impressed with the price of the stuff, if not the scent. I stuck it in a drawer and I'm assailed with the fragrance now every time I pull out fresh underwear.

"You're Ramona Westfall, aren't you?"

Her smile was modified to a look of expectancy. "That's right. Have we met?"

I shook my head. "I'm Kinsey Millhone. I'm a private investigator here in town."

"Is there something I can help you with?"

"I'm looking for Tony Gahan. I understand you're his aunt."

"Tony? Good heavens, what for?"

"I was asked to locate him on a personal matter. I didn't know how else to get in touch with him."

"What personal matter? I don't understand."

"I was asked to deliver something to him. A check from a man who's recently deceased."

She looked at me blankly for a moment and then I saw recognition leap into her eyes. "You're referring to John Daggett, aren't you? Someone told me it was on the news last night. I assumed he was still in prison."

"He's been out for six weeks."

Her face flooded with color. "Well, isn't that typical," she snapped. "Five people dead and he's back on the streets."

"Not quite," I said. "Could we go someplace and talk?"

"About what? About my sister? She was thirty-eight, a beautiful person. She was decapitated when he ran a stoplight and plowed into them. Her husband was killed. Tony's sister was crushed. She was six, just a baby. . . ." She bit off her sentence abruptly, suddenly aware that her voice had risen. Nearby, several people paused, looking over at us.

"Who were the others? Did you know them?" I asked.

"You're the detective. You figure it out."

In the next aisle, a dark-haired woman in a striped apron caught her eye. She didn't open her mouth, but her expression said, "Is everything all right?"

"I'm taking a break," Ramona said to her. "I'll be in the back room if Tricia's looking for me."

The dark-haired woman glanced at me briefly and then dropped her gaze. Ramona was moving toward a doorway on the far side of the room. I followed. The other customers had lost interest, but I had a feeling that I'd be facing an unpleasant scene.

By the time I entered the back room, Ramona was fumbling in her handbag with shaking hands. She opened a zippered compartment and took out a vial of pills. She extracted a tablet and broke it in half, downing it with a slug of cold coffee from a white mug with her name on the side. On second thought, she took the second half of the tablet as well.

I said, "Look, I'm sorry to have to bring this up . . ."

"Don't apologize," she spat. "It doesn't do any good." She searched through the bag and came up with a hard pack of Winston's. She pulled out a cigarette and tamped it repeatedly on her thumbnail, then lit it with a

Bic disposable lighter she'd tucked in her apron pocket. She hugged her waist with her left arm, propping the right elbow on it so she could hold the cigarette near her face. Her eyes seemed to have darkened and she fixed me with a blank, rude stare. "What is it you want?"

I could feel my face warm. Somehow the money was suddenly beside the point and seemed like too paltry a sum in any event. "I have a cashier's check for Tony. John Daggett asked me to deliver it."

Her smile was supercilious. "Oh, a *check*. Well, how much is it for? Is it per *head* or some sort of lump sum payment by the carload?"

"Mrs. Westfall," I said patiently.

"You can call me Ramona, dear, since the subject matter's so intimate. We're talking about the people I loved best in this world." She took a deep drag of her cigarette and blew smoke toward the ceiling.

I clamped down on my temper, controlling my response. "I understand that the subject is painful," I said. "I know there's no way to compensate for what happened, but John Daggett was making a gesture, and regardless of your opinion of him, it's possible that Tony might have a use for the money."

"We provide for him very nicely, thanks. We don't need anything from John Daggett *or* his daughter or from *you*."

I plowed on, heading into the face of her wrath like a swimmer through churning surf. "Let me just say something first. Daggett came to me last week with a cashier's check made out to Tony."

She started to speak, but I held up one hand. "Please," I said.

She subsided, allowing me to continue.

"I put the check in a safe deposit box until I could figure out how to deliver it, as agreed. You can toss it in the trash for all I care, but I'd like to do what I said I'd do, which is to see that Tony Gahan gets it. In theory, it's

Tony's to do with as he sees fit, so I'd appreciate it if you'd talk to him before you do anything else."

She thought about that one, her eyes locked on mine. "How much?"

"Twenty-five thousand. That's a good chunk of education for Tony, or a trip abroad. . . ."

"I get the point," she cut in. "Now maybe you'll allow me to have my say. That boy has been with us for almost three years now. He's fifteen years old and I don't think he's slept a full eight hours since the accident. He has migraines, he bites his nails. His grades are poor, school attendance is *shit*. We're talking about a kid with an I.Q. right off the charts. He's a wreck and John Daggett did that to him. There's no way . . . no *way* anyone can ever make up to Tony for what that man did."

"I understand that."

"No, you don't." Her eyes filled suddenly with tears. She was silent, hands shaking again so badly now that she could scarcely get the Winston to her lips. She managed to take another drag, fighting for control. The silence lengthened. She seemed to shudder and I could almost see the tranquilizer kick in. She turned away abruptly, dropped the cigarette, and stepped on it. "Give me a number where I can reach you. I'll talk to my husband and see what he says."

I handed her my card, taking a moment to jot down my home address and telephone number on the back, in case she needed to reach me there.

11

After I left Ramona Westfall, I stopped by my apartment and changed into pantyhose, low heels, and my all-purpose dress. This garment, which I've owned for five years, is made of some magic fabric that doesn't wilt, wrinkle, or show dirt. It can be squashed down to the size of a rain hat and shoved in the bottom of my handbag without harm. It can also be rinsed out in any bathroom sink and hung to dry overnight. It's black, lightweight, has long sleeves, zips up the back, and should probably be "accessorized," a women's clothing concept I've never understood. I wear the dress "as is" and it always looks okay to me. Once in a while I see this look of recognition in someone's eye, but maybe it's just a moment of surprise at seeing me in something other than jeans and boots.

The Wynington-Blake Mortuary—Burials, Cremation, and Shipping, Serving All Faiths—is located on the east side of town on a shady side street with ample parking. It was originally built as a residence and retains the feeling of a substantial single-family dwelling. Now, of course, the entire first floor has been converted into the equivalent of six spacious living rooms, each furnished with metal folding chairs and labeled with some serene-sounding word.

The gentleman who greeted me, a Mr. Sharonson, wore a subdued navy blue suit, a neutral expression, and used a public library voice. John Daggett was laid out in "Meditation," which was just down the corridor and to my left. The family, he murmured, was in the Sunrise Chapel if I cared to wait. I signed in. Mr. Sharonson removed himself discreetly and I was left to do as I pleased. The room was rimmed with chairs, the casket at the apex. There were two sprays of white gladioli that looked somehow like pristine fakes provided by the mortuary, instead of wreaths sent by those who mourned Daggett's passing. Organ music was being piped in, a nearly subliminal auditory cue meant to trigger thoughts about the brevity of life.

I tiptoed across the room to have a peek at him. The color and texture of Daggett's skin looked about like a Betsy-Wetsy doll I'd had as a kid. His features had a flattened appearance, which I suspected was a side effect of the autopsy process. Peel somebody's face back and it's hard to line it all up again. Daggett's nose looked crooked, like a pillowcase put on with the seam slightly skewed.

I was aware of a rustling behind me and Barbara Daggett appeared on my right. We stood together for a moment without a word. I don't know why people stand and study the dead that way. It makes about as much sense as paying homage to the cardboard box your favorite shoes once came in. Finally, she murmured something and turned away, moving toward the entrance where Eugene Nickerson and Essie Daggett were just coming in through the archway.

Essie was wearing a dark navy dress of rayon jersey, her massive arms dimpled with pale flesh. Her hair looked freshly "done," puffed and thick, sprayed into a turban of undulating gray. Eugene, in a dark suit, steered her by the elbow, working her arm as if it were the rudder on a ship. She took one look at the casket and her wide knees buckled. Barbara and Eugene caught her before she actually hit the floor. They guided her to an upholstered chair and lowered her into the seat. She fumbled for a handkerchief, which she pressed to her mouth as if she meant to chloroform herself.

"Sweet Jesus Lord," she mewed, her eyes turned up piteously. "Lamb of God . . ." Eugene began to pat at her hand and Barbara sat down beside her, putting one arm around her protectively.

"You want me to bring her some water?" I asked.

Barbara nodded and I moved toward the doorway. Mr. Sharonson had sensed the disturbance and had appeared, his face forming a question. I passed the request along and he nodded. He left the room and I returned to Mrs. Daggett's side. She was having a pretty good time by now, rolling her head back and forth, reciting scriptures in a high-pitched voice. Barbara and Eugene were working to restrain her and I gathered that Essie had expressed a strong desire to fling herself into the coffin with her beloved. I might have given her a boost myself.

Mr. Sharonson returned with a paper envelope full of water, which Barbara took, holding it to Essie's lips. She jerked her head back, unwilling to accept even this small measure of solace. "By night on my bed, I sought him whom my soul loveth," she warbled. "I sought him, but I found him not. I will rise now, and go about the city in the streets, and in the broad ways I will seek him whom my soul loveth. The watchmen that go about the city found me . . . Lord in Heaven . . . O God. . . ."

With surprise, I realized she was quoting fragments from the Song of Solomon, which I recognized from my old Methodist Sunday School days. Little kids were never allowed to read that part of the Bible as it was considered too smutty, but I was real interested in the idea of a man with legs like pillars of marble set upon sockets of fine gold. There was some talk of swords and thighs that caught my attention too. I believe I lasted three Sundays before my aunt was asked to take me down the street to the Presbyterians.

Essie was rapidly losing control, whipping herself into such an agitated state that Eugene and Mr. Sharonson had to assist her to her feet and help her out of the room. I could hear her cries becoming feebler as she was moved down the hall. Barbara rubbed her face wearily. "Oh God. Count on Mother," she said. "How has your day been?"

I sat down beside her. "This doesn't seem like the best time to talk," I said.

"Oh, don't worry about it. She'll calm down. This is the first she's seen of him. There's some kind of lounge upstairs. She can rest for a while and she'll be fine. What about Ramona Westfall? Did you talk to her?"

I filled her in on my brief interview, bringing the subject around to my real question at this point, which had to do with the two other victims in the accident. Barbara closed her eyes, the matter clearly causing her pain.

"One was a little friend of Hilary Gahan's. Her name was Megan Smith. I'm sure her parents are still in the area. I'll check the address and telephone number when I get home. Her father's name is Wayne. I forget the name of the street, but it's probably listed."

I took my notebook out and jotted the name down. "And the fifth?"

"Some kid who'd bummed a ride with them. They picked him up at the on-ramp to the freeway to give him a lift into town."

"What was his name?"

"Doug Polokowski."

I stared at her. "You're kidding."

"Why? Do you know him?"

"Polokowski is Billy Polo's real last name. It's on his rap sheet."

"You think they're related?"

"They'd almost have to be. There's only one Polokowski family in town. It's got to be a cousin or a brother, *something*."

"But I thought Billy Polo was supposed to be Daddy's best friend. That doesn't make sense."

Mr. Sharonson returned to the room and caught her eye. "Your mother is asking for you, Miss Daggett."

"You go ahead," I said. "I've got plenty to work on at this point. I'll call you later at home."

Barbara followed Mr. Sharonson while I headed out to the foyer and hustled up a telephone book. Wayne and Marilyn Smith were listed on Tupelo Drive out in Colgate, right around the corner from Stanley Place, if my memory served me correctly. I considered calling first, but I was curious what the reaction would be to the fact of Daggett's death, if the news hadn't already reached them. I stopped to get gas in the VW and then headed out to the freeway.

The Smiths' house was the single odd one in a twelve-block radius of identical tract homes and I guessed that theirs was the original farmhouse at the heart of what had once been a citrus grove. I could still spot orange trees in irregular rows, broken up now by winding roads, fenced lots, and an elementary school. The Smiths' mailbox was a small replica of the house and the street number was gouged out of a thick plank of pine, stained dark and hung above the porch steps. The house itself was a two-story white frame with tall, narrow windows and a slate roof. A sprawling vegetable garden stretched out behind the house, with the garage beyond that. A tire swing hung by a rope from a sycamore that grew in the yard. Orange trees extended on all sides, looking twisted and barren, their producing years long past. It was probably cheaper to leave them there than to tear them out. An assortment of boys' bicycles in a rack on the porch suggested the presence of male offspring or an in-progress meeting of a cycling club.

The bell consisted of a metal twist in the middle of the door. I cranked it once and it trilled harshly. As with the Christopher house, the upper portion of the door was glass, allowing me a glimpse of the interior—high ceilings, waxed pine floors, a scattering of rag rugs, and Early American antiques that looked authentic to my untrained eye. The walls were covered with patchwork quilts, the colors washed out to pale shades of mauve and blue. Numerous children's jackets hung from a row of pegs to the left, rainboots lined up underneath.

A woman in jeans and an oversized white shirt trotted down the stairs, trailing one hand along the banister. She gave me a quick smile and opened the front door.

"Oh hi. Are you Larry's mom?" She read instantly from my expression that I hadn't the faintest idea what she was talking about. She gave a quick laugh. "I guess not. The boys got back from the movie half an hour ago and we've been waiting for Larry's mother to pick him up. Sorry."

"That's all right. I'm Kinsey Millhone," I said. "I'm a private investigator here in town." I handed her my card.

"Can I help you with something?" She was in her mid-thirties, her blonde hair pulled straight back from her face in a clumsy knot. She was dark-eyed, with the tanned good looks of someone who works outdoors. I imagined her to be the kind of mother who forbade her children to eat refined sugar and supervised the television shows they watched. Whether such vigilance pays off or not, I'm never sure. I tend to place kids in a class with dogs, preferring the quiet, the smart, and the well trained.

"John Daggett was killed here in town Friday night," I said.

Something flickered across her face, but maybe it was just the realization that a painful subject was coming up again. "I hadn't heard about that. What happened?"

"He fell out of a boat and drowned."

She thought about that briefly. "Well, that's not too bad. Drowning's supposed to be fairly easy, isn't it?" Her tone of voice was light, her expression pleasant. It took me a minute to realize the savagery of the sentiment. I wondered what kind of torture she'd wished on him.

"Most of us don't get to choose our death," I said.

"My daughter certainly didn't," she said tartly. "Was it an accident or did someone give him a nice push?"

"That's what I'm trying to find out," I said. "I heard he came up from L.A. on Monday, but nobody seems to know where he spent the week."

"Not here, I can assure you. If Wayne so much as set eyes on him, he'd have. . . ." The words tapered off to a faint smile and her tone became almost bantering. "I was going to say, he'd have killed him, but I didn't mean that literally. Or maybe I did. I guess I shouldn't speak for Wayne."

"What about you? When did you see him last?"

"I have no idea. Two years ago at least."

"At the trial?"

She shook her head. "I wasn't there. Wayne sat in for a day, but he couldn't take it after that. He talked to Barbara Daggett once, I think, but I'm sure there's been nothing since. I'm assuming somehow that the man was murdered. Is that what you're getting at?"

"It's possible. The police don't seem to think so, but

I'm hoping they'll revise their opinion if I can come up with some evidence. I get the impression a lot of people wanted Daggett dead."

"Well, I sure did. I'm thrilled to hear the news. Somebody should have killed him at birth," she said. "Would you like to come in? I don't know what I can tell you, but we might as well be comfortable." She glanced at my business card again, double-checking the name and then tucking it in her shirt pocket.

She held the door and I passed over the threshold, pausing to see where she meant for us to go. She led me into the living room.

"You and your husband were home Friday night?"

"Why? Are we suspects?"

"There isn't even a formal investigation yet," I said.

"I was here. Wayne was working late. He's a C.P.A."

She indicated a chair and I sat down. She took a seat on the couch, her manner relaxed. She was wearing a thin gold bracelet on her right wrist and she began to turn that, straightening a kink in the chain. "Did you ever meet John Daggett yourself?" she asked.

"Once. He came to my office a week ago Saturday."

"Ah. Out on parole, no doubt. He must have served his ten minutes."

I made no comment, so she went on.

"What was he doing in Santa Teresa? Returning to the scene of the slaughter?"

"He was trying to locate Tony Gahan."

This seemed to amuse her. "To what end? It's probably none of my business, but I'm curious."

I was discomfited by her attitude, which seemed an odd mix of the wrathful and the jocular. "I'm not really sure what his intentions were," I said carefully. "The story he told me wasn't true anyway, so it's probably not worth repeating. I gathered he wanted to make restitution."

Her smile faded, dark eyes boring into mine with a look that chilled me. "There's no such thing as 'restitution' for what that man did. Megan died horribly. Five-and-a-half years old. Has anyone given you the details?"

"I have the newspaper clippings in the car. I talked to Ramona Westfall too, and she filled me in," I said, lying through my teeth. I didn't want to hear about Megan's death. I didn't think I could bear it, whatever it was. "Have you kept in touch with the other families?"

For a moment, I didn't think I could distract her. She was going to sit there and tell me some blood-curdling tale that I was never going to forget. Cruel images seemed to play across her face. She faltered and her expression underwent that transformation that precedes tears—her nose reddening, mouth changing shape, lines drawing down on either side. Then her self-control descended and she looked at me with clouded eyes. "I'm sorry. What?"

"I was wondering if you'd talked to the others recently. Mrs. Westfall or the Polokowskis."

"I've hardly even talked to Wayne. Megan's death has just about done us in."

"What about your other children? How are they handling it?"

"Better than we are, certainly. People always say, 'Well, you still have the boys.' But it doesn't work that way. It's not like you can substitute one child for another." Belatedly, she took out a Kleenex and blew her nose.

"I'm sorry I had to bring it all up again," I said. "I've never had children, but I can't imagine anything more painful than losing one."

Her smile returned, fleeting and bitter. "I'll tell you what's worse. Knowing there's a man out there doing a few months in jail for 'vehicular manslaughter' when he murdered five people. Do you know how many times he got picked up for drunk driving before that accident? Fifteen. He paid a few fines. He got his hand smacked. Once he did thirty days, but most of the time. . . ." She broke off, then changed her tone. "Oh hell. What difference does it make? Nothing changes anyway and it never ends. I'll tell Wayne you stopped by. Maybe he knows where Daggett was."

12

I sat in the car and shuddered. I couldn't think when an interview had made me feel so tense. Daggett *had* to have been murdered. I just didn't see how it could come down any other way. What I couldn't figure out was how to get my thinking straight. Usually the morality of homicide seems clear to me. Whatever the shortcomings of the victim, murder is wrong and the penalties levied against the perpetrator had better be substantial to balance out the gravity of the crime. In this case, that seemed like a simplistic point of view. It was *Daggett* who had caused the world to tilt on its axis. Because of him, five people had died, so that his death, whatever the instrument, was swinging the planet upright again, restoring a moral order of sorts. At the moment, I still didn't know whether his desire to make restitution was sincere or part of some elaborate con. All I knew was that I'd been caught up in the loop and I had a part to play, though I had no idea yet what it was.

I started the car and headed back to my place. The sky was clouding over again. It was after 5:00 and a premature twilight already seemed to be spilling down the mountainside. I pulled up in front of my apartment and switched off the ignition. I glanced over at my windows, which were dark. I was feeling edgy and I wasn't ready to go home yet. On impulse, I started the

car again and headed for the beach, drawn by the scent
of salt in the air. Maybe a walk would ease my restlessness.

I pulled into one of the municipal lots and parked,
slipping out of my shoes and pantyhose, which I tossed
in the back seat along with my handbag. I zipped up my
windbreaker and locked the car, tucking my keys in my
jacket pocket as I crossed the bike path to the beach.
The ocean was silver, but the breaking waves were a
muddy brown and the sand along the surf line was
peppered with rocks. This was the winter beach, dark
boulders having surfaced with the shifting coastal sands.
Gulls hovered overhead, eyeing the thundering waves
for signs of edible sea life.

I walked along the wet sand with a buffeting wind at
my back. A windsurfer clung to the crossbar on a bright
green sail, arching himself against the force of the wind,
his board streaking toward the beach. Two big fishing
boats were chugging into the marina. Everywhere there
was the sense of urgency and threat—the torn white of
storm surf, the darkening gray of the sky. Across the
harbor, the ocean drove at the shore without pity,
pounding at the breakwater with a grudging monotony.
A rocketing spray shot straight up on impact, fanning
along the seawall. I could almost hear the splats as
successive waves hit the concrete walkway on the landward side.

I passed the entrance to the wharf. Ahead the beach
widened, curving left toward the marina where the bare
masts of sailboats tilted in the wind like metronomes.
The sand was softer here, deeper too, so that walking
became a labor. I turned and walked backwards for a
few steps, trying to get my bearings. Somewhere along
this part of the beach was the spot where Daggett's body
had been found. A brief glimpse of the site had
appeared on the newscast and I was hoping now to get a
fix on the place. I thought it was probably this side of the

boat launch. Ahead and to my right was the kiddie park
with its playground equipment and a fenced-in area
with a wading pool.

The newscast had shown a portion of the dredge in
the background, intersected by the breakwater and a
line of rocks. I trudged on until I had the three lined up
in the same configuration. The dry sand was trampled
and there were signs that vehicles had crossed the beach.
Where waves slapped against the shore, all traces of
activity had been erased. The crime scene investigators
had, no doubt, done at least a cursory search. I scanned
the area without any expectation of finding "evidence."
If you murder a man by tossing him, dead drunk, out of
a rowboat, there aren't any telltale clues to dispose of
afterward. The boat itself had been left to drift and,
from what Jonah said, must have washed ashore closer
to the pier.

I drank in the heady perfume of the sea, watching
the restless surge of the waves, turning myself slowly
until the ocean was at my back and I was staring at the
line of motels across the boulevard. Daggett had apparently died sometime between midnight and 5:00 A.M. I
wondered if it would be productive to canvas the
neighborhood for witnesses. It was possible, of course,
that Daggett had actually cut the line on the skiff
himself, rowing out of the harbor alone. With a 0.35
blood alcohol level, it seemed unlikely. By the time blood
alcohol concentrations reach 0.40 percent, a drunk is
essentially in a state of deep anesthesia, incapable of
anything so athletic as working an oar. He might have
maneuvered his way out of the harbor first and *then* sat
in the bobbing boat, drinking himself insensible, but I
couldn't picture that. I kept visualizing somebody with
him . . . waiting, watching . . . finally hefting his feet
and toppling him backwards. "A lesson in the back flip,
Daggett. Oh shit, you blew it. Too bad, sucker. You die."

Getting him in the boat in the first place might have

been a trick, as drunk as he was, but the rest of it must have been a snap.

I glanced to my right. An old bum with a shopping cart was picking through a trash container. I crossed the sand, heading toward him. As I approached, I could see that his skin was nearly gray with accumulated filth, tanned by the wind, with an overlay of rosiness from recent sunburn or Mogen David wine . . . Mad Dog 20–20, as it's better known among the scruffy drifters. He looked in his seventies and was bulked up by layers of clothing. He wore a watch cap, his gray hair hanging out of it like mop strings. He smelled as musky as an old buffalo. The odor radiated from his body in nearly visible wavy lines, like a cartoon rendition of a skunk.

"Hello," I said.

He went about his business, ignoring me. He pulled out a pair of spike heels, inspecting them briefly before he tucked them into one of his plastic trash bags. A two-day-old newspaper didn't interest him. Beer cans? Yes, he seemed to like those. A Kentucky Fried Chicken barrel was a reject. A skirt? He held it up with a critical eye and then shoved it into the trash bag with the shoes. Someone had discarded a plastic beach ball with a hole punched in it. The old man set that aside.

"Did you hear about the guy they found in the surf yesterday?" I asked. No response. I felt like an apparition, calling to him from the netherworld. I raised my voice. "I heard somebody down here spotted him and called the cops. Do you happen to know who?"

I guess he didn't care to discuss it. He resolutely avoided eye contact. I didn't have my handbag with me so I didn't have a business card or even a dollar bill as a letter of reference. I had no choice but to let it drop. I moved away. By then, he had worked his way down in the bin, his head almost out of sight. So much for my interviewing techniques.

By the time I got back to the parking lot, the light

had faded, so I registered the fact that something was wrong long before I realized what it was. The door on the passenger side of my car was ajar. I stopped in my tracks.

"Oh no," I said.

I approached with caution, as if the vehicle might be booby-trapped. It looked like someone had run a coathanger in through the wind-wing in an attempt to jimmy the lock. Failing that, the shitheel had simply smashed the window out on the passenger side and had opened the door. The glove compartment hung open, the contents spilling out across the front seat. My handbag was missing. *That* generated a flash of irritation, swiftly followed by dread. I jerked the seat forward and hauled out my briefcase. The strap that secured the opening had been cut and my gun was gone.

"Oh nooo," I wailed. I gave vent to a string of expletives. In high school, I had hung out with some bad-ass boys who taught me to cuss to perfection. I tried some combinations I hadn't thought of in years. I was mad at myself for leaving the stuff in plain sight on the seat and mad at the jerk who ripped me off. Mine was one of the last cars left in the lot and had probably stood out like a beacon. I slammed the car door shut and headed off across the street, still barefoot, gesturing and muttering to myself like a mental case. I didn't even have the spare change to call the cops.

There was a hamburger stand close by and I conned the fry cook into making the call for me. Then I went back and waited until the black-and-white arrived. The beat officers, Pettigrew and Gutierrez (Gerald and Maria, respectively), I'd encountered some months before when they made an arrest in my neighborhood.

She took the report now, while he made sympathetic noises. Somehow the two of them managed to console me insofar as that was possible, calling for a crime scene investigator who obligingly came out and dusted for prints. We all knew it was pointless, but it made me feel better. Pettigrew said he'd check the computer for the serial number on my gun, which was registered, thank God. Maybe it would turn up later in a pawn shop and I'd get it back.

I love my little semiautomatic, which I've had for years . . . a gift from the aunt who raised me after my parents' death. That gun was my legacy, representing the odd bond between us. She'd taught me to shoot when I was eight. She had never married, never had children of her own. With me, she'd exercised her many odd notions about the formation of female character. Firing a handgun, she felt, would teach me to appreciate both safety and accuracy. It would also help me develop good hand-eye coordination, which she thought was useful. She'd taught me to knit and crochet so that I'd learn patience and an eye for detail. She'd refused to teach me to cook as she felt it was boring and would only make me fat. Cussing was okay around the house, though we were expected to monitor our language in the company of those who might take offense. Exercise was important. Fashion was not. Reading was essential. Two out of three illnesses would cure themselves, said she, so doctors could generally be ignored except in case of accident. On the other hand, there was no excuse for having bad teeth, though she viewed dentists as the persons who came up with ludicrous schemes for the human mouth. Drilling out all of your old fillings and replacing them with gold, was one. She had dozens of these precepts and most are still with me.

Rule Number One, first and foremost, above and beyond all else, was financial independence. A woman should never, never, never be financially dependent on anyone, especially a man, because the minute you were dependent, you could be abused. Financially dependent persons (the young, the old, the indigent) were inevitably treated badly and had no recourse. A woman should *always* have recourse. My aunt believed that every woman should develop marketable skills, and the more money she was paid for them the better. Any feminine pursuit that did not have as its ultimate goal increased self-sufficiency could be disregarded. "How to Get Your Man" didn't even appear on the list.

When I was in high school, she'd called Home Ec "Home Ick" and applauded when I got a D. She thought it would make a lot more sense if the boys took Home Ec and the girls took Auto Mechanics and Wood Shop. Make no mistake about it, she liked (some) men a lot, but she wasn't interested in tending to one like a charwoman or a nurse. She was nobody's mother, said she, not even mine, and she didn't intend to behave like one. All of which constitutes a long-winded account of why I wanted my gun back, but there it is. I didn't have to explain any of this to G. Pettigrew or M. Gutierrez. They both knew I'd been a cop for two years and they both understood the value of a gun.

By the time everyone left the parking lot, it was fully dark and starting to rain again. Oh perfect.

I drove home and started making out a list of items I'd have to replace, including my driver's license, gasoline charge card, checkbook, and God knows what else. While I was at it, I looked up three "800" numbers, phoning in the loss of my credit cards from the Xerox copy I keep in my file drawer at home. I'd only been carrying about twenty bucks in cash, but I resented the loss. It was all too irritating to contemplate for long. I showered, pulled on jeans, boots, and a sweater, and headed up to Rosie's for a bite to eat.

Rosie's is the tavern in my neighborhood, run by herself, a Hungarian woman in her sixties, short and top-heavy, with dyed red hair that recently had looked like a cross between terra cotta floor tile and canned pumpkin pie filling. Rosie is an autocrat—outspoken, overbearing, suspicious of strangers. She cooks like a dream when it suits her, but she usually wants to dictate what you should eat at any given meal. She's protective, sometimes generous, often irritating. Like your best friend's cranky grandmother, she's someone you endure for the sake of peace. I hang out at her establishment because it's unpretentious and it's only half a block away from my place. Rosie apparently feels that my patronage entitles her to boss me around . . . which is generally true.

That night when I walked in, she took one look at my face and poured me a glass of white wine from her personal supply. I moved to my favorite booth at the rear. The backs are high, cut from construction grade plywood and stained dark, with side pieces shaped like the curve of a wingback chair. Within moments, Rosie materialized at the table and set the glass of wine in front of me.

"Somebody just busted out the window of my car and stole everything I hold dear, including my gun," I said.

"I've got some *sóska leves* for you," she announced. "And after that, you gonna have a salad made with celery root, some chicken paprikas, some of Henry's good rolls, cabbage strudel, and deep-fried cherries if you're good and clean up your plate. It's on the house, on account of your troubles, only think about this one thing while you eat. If you had a good man in your life, this would never happen to you and that's all I'm gonna say."

I laughed for the first time in days.

13

The next morning, Monday, I began the laborious process of replacing the contents of my handbag. I hit the DMV first, since the offices opened at 8:00 A.M. I set in motion the paperwork for a new driver's license, paying three dollars for a duplicate. The minute the bank opened, I closed out my checking account and opened a new one. I stopped by the apartment then and put a call through to Sacramento to the Bureau of Collection and Investigative Services, Department of Consumer Affairs, requesting application for a certified replacement for my private investigator's registration card. I armed myself with a batch of business cards from my ready supply and hunted up an old handbag to use until I could buy a new one. I drove over to the drugstore and made purchases to replace at least a few of the odds and ends I carry with me as a matter of course, birth control pills being one. At some point, I'd have to have my car window replaced, too. Irksome, all of it.

I didn't reach the office until almost noon and the message light on my answering machine was blinking insistently. I tossed the morning mail aside and punched the playback button as I passed the desk, listening to the caller as I opened the French doors to let in some fresh air.

"Miss Millhone, this is Ferrin Westfall at 555-6790. My wife and I have discussed your request to speak with our nephew, Tony, and if you'll get in touch, we'll see what we can work out. Please understand, we don't want the boy upset. We trust you'll conduct whatever business you have with him discreetly." There was a click, breaking the connection. His tone had been cold, perfectly suited to his formal, well-organized speaking voice. No "uh"s, no hesitations, no hiccups in the presentation. I lifted my brows appreciatively. Tony Gahan was in capable hands. Poor kid.

I made myself a pot of coffee and waited until I'd downed half a cup before I returned the call. The phone rang twice.

"Good morning. PFC," the woman said.

PFC turned out to be Perforated Formanek Corporation, a supplier of industrial abrasives, grinders, clamps, epoxy, cutters, end mills, and precision tools. I know this because I asked and she recited the entire inventory in a sing-song tone, thinking perhaps that I was in the market for one of the above. I asked to speak to Ferrin Westfall and was thanked for my request.

There was a click. "Westfall," said he.

I identified myself. There was a silence, meant (perhaps) to intimidate. I resisted the urge to rush in with a lot of unnecessary chatter, allowing the pause to go on for as long as it suited him.

Finally, he said, "We'll see that Tony's available this evening between seven and eight if that's acceptable." He gave me the address.

"Fine," I said. "Thank you." Ass, I added mentally. Then I hung up.

I tipped back in my swivel chair and propped my feet up. So far, it was a crummy day. I wanted my handbag back. I wanted my gun. I wanted to get on with life and quit wasting time with all this clerical nonsense. I glanced out at the balcony. At least it wasn't raining at the moment. I pulled the mail over and started going through it. Most of it was junk.

I was feeling restless again, thinking about John Daggett and his boat trip across the harbor. Yesterday, at the beach, the notion of canvassing the neighborhood for witnesses had seemed pointless. Now I wasn't so sure. Somebody might have seen him. Public drunkenness is usually conspicuous, especially at an hour when not many people are about. Weekend guests at the beach motels had probably checked out by now, but it might still be worth a shot. I grabbed my jacket and my car keys, locked the office, and headed down the back stairs.

My VW was looking worse every time I turned around. It's fourteen years old, an oxidized beige model with dents. Now the window was smashed out on the passenger side. Not a class act by any stretch of the imagination, but it was paid for. Every time I think about a new car, it makes my stomach do a flip-flop. I don't want to be saddled with car payments, a jump in insurance premiums, and hefty registration fees. My current registration costs me twenty-five dollars a year, which suits me just fine. I turned the ignition key and the engine fired right up. I patted the dashboard and backed out of the space, taking State Street south toward the beach.

I parked on Cabana, just across from the entrance to the wharf. There are eight motels strung out along the boulevard, none with rooms for under sixty dollars a night. This was the "off" season and there were still no vacancies. I started with the first, the Sea Voyager, where I identified myself to the manager, found out who'd been working the night desk the previous Friday, jotted down the name, and left my card with a handwritten note on the back. As with many other aspects of the job I do, this door-to-door inquiry requires dogged patience and a fondness for repetition that doesn't really come naturally. The effort has to be made, however, on the off chance that someone, somewhere can fill in a detail that might help. Having worked my way to the last motel, I returned to my car and headed on down the boulevard toward the marina, half a mile away.

I parked this time near the Naval Reserve Building, in the lot adjacent to the harbor. There didn't seem to be much foot traffic in the area. The sky was overcast, the air heavy with the staunch smells of fresh fish and diesel fuel. I ambled along the walk that skirts the waterfront, with its eighty-four acres of slips for eleven hundred boats. A wooden pier, two lanes wide, juts out into the water topped with a crane and pulleys for hoisting boats. I could see the fuel dock and the city guest dock, where two men were securing the lines on a big power boat that they'd apparently just brought in.

On my right, there was a row of waterfront businesses—a fish market with a seafood restaurant above, a shop selling marine and fishing supplies, a commercial diving center, two yacht brokers. The building fronts are all weathered gray wood, with bright royal blue awnings that echo the blue canvas sail covers on boats all through the harbor. For a moment, I paused before a plate glass window, scanning the snapshots of boats for sale—catamarans, luxury cabin cruisers, sailboats designed to sleep six. There's a small population of "live-aboards" in the harbor—people who actually use their boats as a primary residence. The idea is mildly appealing to me, though I wonder about the reality of chemical toilets in the dead of night and showering in marina restrooms. I crossed the walk and leaned on the iron railing, looking out across the airy forest of bare boat masts.

The water itself was dark hunter green. Big rocks were submerged in the gloomy depths, looking like sunken ruins. Few fish were visible. I spotted two little crabs scuttling along the boulders at the water's edge,

but for the most part, the shallows seemed cold and
sterile, empty of sea life. A beer bottle rested on a shelf
of sand and mud. Two harbor patrol boats were moored
not far away.

I spotted a line of skiffs tied up at one of the docks
below and my interest perked up. Four of the marinas
are kept locked and can only be entered with a card key
issued by the Harbor Master's Office, but this one was
accessible to the public. I moved down the ramp for a
closer look. There were maybe twenty-five small skiffs,
wood and fiberglass, most of them eight to ten feet long.
I had no way of knowing if one of these was the boat
Daggett had taken, but this much seemed clear: if you
cut the line on one of these boats, you'd have to row it
out around the end of the dock and through the harbor.
There was no current here and a boat left to drift would
simply bump aimlessly against the pilings without going
anyplace.

I went up the ramp again and turned left along the
walkway until I reached Marina One. At the bottom of
the ramp, I could see the chain-link fence and locked
gate. I loitered on the walk, keeping an eye on passersby.
Finally, a middle-aged man approached, his card key in
one hand, a bag of groceries in the other. He was trim
and muscular, tanned to the color of rawhide. He wore
Bermuda shorts, Topsiders, and a loose cotton sweater, a
mat of graying chest hairs visible in the V.

"Excuse me," I said. "Do you live down there?"

He paused, looking at me with curiosity. "Yes." His
face was as lined as a crumpled brown grocery bag
pressed into service again.

"Do you mind if I follow you out onto Marina One?
I'm trying to get a line on the man who washed up on
the beach Saturday."

"Sure, come on. I heard about that. The skiff he
stole belongs to a friend of mine. By the way, I'm Aaron.
You are?"

"Kinsey Millhone," I said, trotting down the ramp after him. "How long have you lived down here?"

"Six months. My wife and I split up and she kept the house. Nice change, boat life. Lot of nice people. You a cop?"

"Private investigator," I said. "What sort of work do you do?"

"Real estate," he said. "How'd you get into it?" He inserted his card and pushed the gate open. He held it while I passed through. I paused on the other side so he could lead the way.

"I was hired by the dead man's daughter," I said.

"I meant how'd you get into investigative work."

"Oh. I used to be a cop, but I didn't like it much. The law enforcement part of it was fine, but not the bureaucracy. Now I'm self-employed. I'm happier that way."

We passed a cloud of sea gulls converging rapidly on an object bobbing in the water. The screeches from the birds were attracting gulls from a quarter of a mile away, streaking through the air like missiles.

"Avocado," Aaron said idly. "The gulls love them. This is me." He had paused near a thirty-seven-foot twin-diesel trawler, a Chris-Craft, with a flying bridge.

"God, it's a beautiful boat."

"You like it? I can sleep eight," he said, pleased. He hopped down into the cockpit and turned, holding a hand out to me. "Pop your boots off and you can come on board and take a look around. Want a drink?"

"I better not, thanks. I've got a lot of ground to cover yet. Is there any way you can introduce me to the guy whose skiff was stolen?"

Aaron shrugged. "Can't help you there. He's out on a fishing boat all day, but I can give him your name and telephone number if you like. I think the police impounded the skiff, so if you want to see that, you better talk to them."

I didn't expect anything to come of it, but I thought I'd leave the door open just in case. I took out a business card, jotting down my home number on the back before I passed it on to him. "Have him give me a call if he knows anything," I said.

"I'll tell you who you might want to talk to. Go down here six slips and see if that guy's in. *The Seascape* is the name of the boat. His is Phillip Rosen. He knows all the gossip down here. Maybe he can help."

"Thanks."

The Seascape was a twenty-four-foot Flicka, a gaff-rigged sloop with a twenty-foot mast, teak deck, and a fiberglass hull that mimicked wood.

I tapped on the cabin roof, calling a hello toward the open doorway. Phillip Rosen appeared, ducking his head as he came up from down below. His emerging was like a visual joke: he was one of the tallest men I'd seen except on a basketball court. He was probably six-foot-ten and built on a grand scale—big hands and feet, big head with a full head of red hair, a big face with red beard and moustache, bare-chested and barefoot. Except for the ragged blue jean cut-offs, he looked like a Viking reincarnated cruelly into a vessel unworthy of him. I introduced myself, mentioning that Aaron had suggested that I talk to him. I told him briefly what I wanted.

"Well, I didn't see them, but a friend of mine did. She was coming down here to meet me and passed 'em in the parking lot. Man and a woman. She said the old guy was drunk as a skunk, staggering all over the place. The little gal with him had a hell of a time trying to keep him upright."

"Do you have any idea what she looked like?"

"Nope. Dinah never said. I can give you her number though, if you want to ask her about it yourself."

"I'd like that," I said. "What time was this?"

"I'd say two-fifteen. Dinah's a waitress over at the Wharf and she gets off at two. I know she didn't close up that night and it only takes five minutes to get here. Shoot, if she walked on water, she could skip across the harbor in the time it takes her to get to the parking lot."

"Is she at work now by any chance?"

"Monday afternoon? Could be. I never heard what her schedule was this week, but you can always try. She'd be up in the cocktail lounge. A redhead. You can't miss her if she's there."

Which turned out to be true. I drove the half mile from the marina to the wharf, leaving my car with the valet who handles restaurant parking. Then I went up the outside staircase to the wooden deck above. Dinah was crossing from the bar to a table in the corner, balancing a tray of margaritas. Her hair was more orange than red, too carroty a shade to be anything but natural. She was probably six feet tall in heels, wearing dark mesh hose, and a navy blue "sailor" suit with a skirt that skimmed her crotch. She had a little sailor cap pinned to her head and an air about her that suggested she'd known starboard from port since the day she reached puberty.

I waited until she'd served the drinks and was on her way back to the bar. "Dinah?"

She looked at me quizzically. Up close, I could see the overlay of pale red freckles on her face and a long, narrow nose. She wore false eyelashes, like a series of commas encircling her pale hazel eyes, lending her a look of startlement. I gave her a brief rundown, patiently repeating myself. "I know who the old guy is," I said. "What I'm trying to get a fix on is the woman he was with."

Dinah shrugged. "Well, I can't tell you much. I just saw them as I went past. I mean, the marina's got *some* lights, but not that great. Plus, it was raining like a son of a bitch."

"How old would you say she was?"

"On the young side. Twenties, maybe. Blonde. Not real big, at least compared to him."

"Long hair? Short? Buxom? Flat-chested?"

"The build, I don't know. She was wearing a raincoat. Some kind of coat, anyway. Hair was maybe shoulder length, not a lot of curl. Kind of bushy."

"Pretty?"

She thought briefly. "God, all I remember thinking was there was something off, you know? For starters, he was such a mess. I could smell him ten feet away. Bourbon fumes. Phew! Actually, I kind of thought she might be a hooker on the verge of rolling him. I nearly said something to her, but then I decided it was none of my business. He was having a great old time, but you know how it is. Drunk as he was, she really could have ripped him off."

"Yeah, well, she did. *Dead* is about as ripped off as you can get."

14

By the time I pulled out of the restaurant parking lot, it was 2:00 and the air felt dank. Or maybe it was only the shadowy image of Daggett's companion that chilled me. I'd been half convinced there was someone with him that night and now I had confirmation—not proof of murder, surely, but some sense of the events leading up to his death, a tantalizing glimpse of his consort, that "other" whose ghostly passage I tracked.

From Dinah's description, Lovella Daggett was the first name that popped into my head. Her trashy blonde looks had made me think she was hooking when I met her in L.A. On the other hand, most of the women I'd run across to date were on the young side and fair-haired—Barbara Daggett, Billy Polo's sister Coral, Ramona Westfall, even Marilyn Smith, the mother of the other dead child. I'd have to start pinning people down as to their whereabouts the night of the murder, a tricky matter as I had no way to coerce a reply. Cops have some leverage. A P.I. has none.

In the meantime, I went by the bank and removed the cashier's check from my safe deposit box. I ducked into a coffee shop and grabbed a quick lunch, then spent the afternoon in the office catching up on paperwork. At 5:00, I locked up and went home, puttering around

until 6:30 when I left for Ferrin and Ramona Westfall's
house to meet Tony Gahan.

The Westfalls lived in an area called the Close, a
deadend street lined with live oaks over near the
Natural History Museum. I drove through stone gates
into the dim hush of privacy. There are only eight
homes on the cul-de-sac, all Victorian, completely restored, immaculately kept. The neighborhood looks,
even now, like a small, rural community inexplicably
lifted out of the past. The properties are surrounded by
low walls of fieldstone, the lots overgrown with bamboo,
pampas grass, and fern. It was fully dark by then and
the Close was wreathed in mist. The vegetation was
dense, intensely scented, and lush from the recent rain.
There was only one street light, its pale globe obscured
by the branches of a tree.

I found the number I was looking for and parked
on the street, picking my way up the path to the front.
The house was a putty-colored, one-story wood frame
with a wide porch, white shutters and trim. The porch
furniture was white wicker with cushions covered in a
white-and-putty print. Two Victorian wicker plant
stands held massive Boston ferns. All too perfect for my
taste.

I rang the bell, refusing to peer in through the
etched glass oval in the door. I suspected the interior
was going to look like something out of *House and Garden*
magazine, an elegant blend of the old, the new, and the
offbeat. Of course, my perception was probably colored
by Ferrin Westfall's curt treatment of me and Ramona's
outright hostility. I'm not above holding grudges.

Ramona Westfall came to the door and admitted
me. I kept my tone pleasant, but I didn't fall all over
myself admiring the place, which, at a glance, did
appear to be flawlessly done. She showed me into the
front parlor and removed herself, closing the oak-
paneled sliding doors behind her. I waited, staring

resolutely at the floor. I could hear murmuring in the hall. After a moment, the doors slid open and a man entered, introducing himself as Ferrin Westfall . . . as if I hadn't guessed. We shook hands.

He was tall and slim, with a cold, handsome face and silver hair. His eyes were a dark green, as empty of warmth as the harbor. There were hints of something submerged in the depths, but no signs of life. He wore charcoal gray pants and a soft gray cashmere sweater that fairly begged to be stroked. He indicated that I should have a seat, which I did.

He surveyed me for a moment, taking in the boots, the faded jeans, the wool sweater beginning to pill at the elbows. I was determined not to let his disapproval get through to me, but it required an effort on my part. I stared at him impassively and warded off his withering assessment by picturing him on the toilet with his knickers down around his ankles.

Finally, he said, "Tony will be out in a moment. Ramona's told me about the check. I wonder if I might examine it."

I removed the check from my jeans pocket and smoothed it out, passing it to him for his inspection. I wondered if he thought it was forged, stolen, or in some way counterfeit. He scrutinized it, fore and aft, and returned it, apparently satisfied that it was legitimate.

"Why did Mr. Daggett come to you with this?" he asked.

"I'm not really sure," I said. "He told me he'd tried to find Tony at an old address. When he had no luck, he asked me to track him down and deliver it."

"Do you know how he acquired the money?"

Again, I found myself feeling protective. It was really none of this man's business. He probably wanted to assure himself that Daggett hadn't come by the money through some tacky enterprise—drugs, prostitutes, selling dogs and kitty cats to labs for medical experiments.

"He won it at the track," I said. Personally, I hadn't quite believed this part of Daggett's tale, but I didn't mind if Ferrin Westfall got sucked in. He didn't seem any more convinced than I. He shifted the subject.

"Would you prefer to be alone with Tony?"

I was surprised at the offer. "Yes, I would. I'd really like to go off somewhere with him and have a Coke."

"I suppose that would be all right, as long as you don't keep him too long. This is a school night."

"Sure. That's very nice of you."

There was a tap at the door. Mr. Westfall rose and crossed the room. "This will be Tony," he said.

The doors slid back and Tony Gahan came in. He looked like an immature fifteen. He was maybe five-foot-six, a hundred and twenty-five pounds. His uncle introduced me. I proferred my hand and we fumbled through a handshake. Tony's eyes were dark, his hair a medium brown, attractively cut, which struck me as odd. Most of the high school kids I've seen lately look like they're being treated for the same scalp disease. I suspected Tony's hairstyle was a concession to Ferrin Westfall's notions of good taste and I wondered how that sat with him.

His manner was anxious. He seemed like a kid trying desperately to please. He shot a cautious look at his uncle, searching for visual cues as to what was expected of him and how he was meant to behave. It was painful to watch.

"Miss Millhone would like to take you out for a Coke, so she can talk to you," Mr. Westfall said.

"How come?" he croaked. Tony looked like he was going to drop dead on the spot and I remembered in a flash how much I'd hated eating and drinking in the presence of strange adults when I was his age. Meals represent a series of traps when you haven't yet mastered the appropriate social skills. I hated adding to his distress, but I was convinced I'd never have a decent conversation with him in this house.

"She'll explain all that," Mr. Westfall said. "Obviously, you're not required to go. If you'd prefer to stay here, simply say so."

Tony seemed unable to get a reading from his uncle's statement, which was neutral on the surface, but contained some tricky side notes. It was the word "simply" that tripped him, I thought, and the "obviously" didn't help.

Tony glanced at me with a half shrug. "It's okay, I guess. Like, right now?"

Mr. Westfall nodded. "It won't be for long. You'll need a jacket, of course."

Tony moved out into the hall and I followed, waiting until he found his jacket in the hall closet.

At fifteen, I thought he could probably figure out if he needed a jacket or not, but neither of them consulted me on the subject. I opened the front door and held it while he went out. Mr. Westfall watched us for a moment and then closed the door behind us. God, it was just like a date. I nearly swore I'd have him home by 10:00. Absurd.

We made our way down the path in the dark. "You go to Santa Teresa High School?"

"Right."

"What year?"

"Sophomore."

We got in the car. Tony tried to roll down the smashed window on his side without much success. A shard of glass tinkled down into the door frame. He finally gave up.

"What happened to this?"

"I was careless," I said, and let it go at that.

I did a U-turn in the lane and I headed for the Clockworks on State Street, a teen hangout generally regarded as seedy, unclean, and corrupt, which it

is . . . a training ground for junior thugs. Kids come
here (stoned, no doubt) to drink Cokes, smoke clove
cigarettes, and behave like bad-asses. I'd been introduced to the place by a seventeen-year-old pink-
haired dope dealer named Mike, who made more
money than I did. I hadn't seen him since June, but I
tend to look for him around town.

We parked in a small lot out back and went in
through the rear entrance. The place is long and
narrow, painted charcoal gray, the high ceiling rimmed
with pink and purple neon. A series of mobiles, looking
like big black clock gears, revolve in the smoky air. The
noise level, on weekends, is deafening, the music so loud
it makes the floor vibrate. On week nights, it's quiet and
oddly intimate. We found a table and I went over to the
counter to pick up a couple of Cokes. There was a tap on
my shoulder and I turned to find Mike standing there. I
felt a rush of warmth. "I was just thinking about you!" I
said. "How are you?"

A pink tint crept across his cheeks and he gave me a
slow seductive smile. "I'm okay. What are you doin' these
days?"

"Nothing much," I said. "Great hair." Formerly,
he'd sported a Mohawk, a great cockscomb of pink
down the center of his head, with the sides shaved close.
Now it was arranged in a series of purple spurts, each
clump held together with a rubber band, the feathery
tips bleached white. Aside from the hair, he was a good-
looking kid, clear skin, green eyes, good teeth.

I said, "Actually, I'm about to have a talk with that
guy over there . . . a schoolmate of yours."

"Yeah?" He turned and gave Tony a cursory inspection.

"You know him?"

"I've seen him. He doesn't hang out with the kind of
people I do." His gaze returned to Tony and I thought
he was going to say more, but he let it pass.

"What are you up to?" I asked. "Still dealing?"

"Who me? Hey, no. I told you I'd quit," he said, sounding faintly righteous. The look in his eyes, of course, suggested just the opposite. If he was doing something illegal, I didn't want to know about it anyway, so I bypassed the subject.

"What about school? You graduate this year?"

"June. I got college applications out and everything."

"Really?" I couldn't tell if he was putting me on or not.

He caught the look. "I get good grades," he protested. "I'm not just your average high school dunce, you know. The bucks I got, I could go anyplace I want. That's what private enterprise is about."

I had to laugh. "For sure," I said. The "bar maid" set two Cokes on the counter and I paid her. "I have to get back to my date."

"Nice seeing you," he said. "You ought to come in sometime and talk to me."

"Maybe I'll do that," I said. I smiled at him, mentally shaking my head. Flirtatious little shit. I moved over to the table where Tony was sitting. I handed him a Coke and sat down.

"You know that guy?" Tony asked cautiously.

"Who, Mike? Yes, I know him."

Tony's eyes strayed to Mike and back again, resting on my face with something close to respect. Maybe I wasn't such a geek after all.

"Did your uncle tell you what this is about?" I asked.

"Some. He said the accident and that old drunk."

"You feel okay discussing it?"

He shrugged by way of reply, avoiding eye contact.

"I take it you weren't in the car," I said.

He smoothed the front of his hair to the side. "Uh-uh. Me and my mom got into this argument. They were going to my granny's for this Easter egg hunt and I didn't want to go."

"Your grandmother's still in town someplace?"

He shifted in his chair. "In a rest home. She had a stroke."

"She's your mother's mother?" I didn't care particularly about any of this. I was just hoping the kid would relax and open up.

"Yeah."

"What's it like living with your aunt and uncle?"

"Fine. No big deal. He comes down on my case all the time, but she's nice."

"She said you were having some problems at school."

"So?"

"Just curious. She says you're very smart and your grades are in the toilet. I wondered what that was about."

"It's about school sucks," he said. "It's about I don't like people butting into my fuckin' business."

"Really," I said. I took a sip of Coke. His hostility was like a sewer backing up and I thought I'd give the efflux a chance to subside. I didn't care if he cussed. I could outcuss him any day of the week.

When I didn't react, he filled the silence. "I'm trying to get my grades pulled up," he said somewhat grudgingly. "I had to take all this bullshit math and chemistry. That's why I didn't do good."

"What's your preference? English? Art?"

He hesitated. "You some kind of shrink?"

"No. I'm a private investigator. I assumed you knew that."

He stared at me. "I don't get it. What's this got to do with the accident?"

I took out the check and laid it on the table. "The man responsible wanted me to look you up and give you this."

He picked the check up and glanced at it.

"It's a cashier's check for twenty-five thousand dollars," I said.

"What for?"

"I'm not really sure. I think John Daggett was hoping to make restitution for what he did."

Tony's confusion was clear and so was the anger that accompanied it. "I don't want this," he said. "Why give it to me? Megan Smith died too, you know, and so did that other guy, Doug. Are they gettin' money too, or just me?"

"Just you, as far as I know."

"Take it back then. I don't want it. I hate that old bastard." He tossed the check on the table and gave it a push.

"Look. Now just wait and let me say something first. It's your choice. Honestly. It's up to you. Your aunt was offended by the offer and I understand that. No one can force you to accept the money if you don't want it. But just hear me out, okay?"

Tony was staring off across the room, his face set.

I lowered my voice. "Tony, it's true John Daggett was a drunk, and maybe he was a totally worthless human being, but he did something he felt bad about and I think he was trying to make up for it. Give him credit for that much and don't say no without giving it consideration first."

"I don't *want* money for what he did."

"I'm not done yet. Just let me finish this."

His mouth trembled. He made a dash at his eyes with the sleeve of his jacket, but he didn't get up and walk away.

"People make mistakes," I said. "People do things they never meant to do. He didn't kill anyone deliberately . . ."

"He's a fuckin' drunk! He was out on the fuckin' street at fuckin' nine in the morning. Dad and Mom and

Hilary . . ." His voice broke and he fought for control. "I don't want anything from him. I hate his guts and I don't want his crummy check."

"Why don't you cash it and give it all away?"

"No! You take it. Give it back to him. Tell him I said he could get fucked."

"I can't. He's dead. He was killed Friday night."

"Good. I'm glad. I hope somebody cut his heart out. He deserved it."

"Maybe so. But it's still possible that he felt something for you and wanted to give you back some of what he took away."

"Like what? It's done. They're all dead."

"But you're not, Tony. You have to find a way to get on with life . . ."

"Hey! I'm doing that, okay? But I don't have to listen to this bullshit! You said what you had to say and now I want to go home."

He got up, radiating rage, his whole body stiff. He moved swiftly toward the rear entrance, knocking chairs aside. I snatched up the check and followed.

When I reached the parking lot, he was kick-boxing the remaining glass out of the smashed window of my car. I started to protest and then I stopped myself.

Oh why not, I thought. I had to replace the damn thing anyway. I stood and watched him without a word. When he was done, he leaned against the car and wept.

15

By the time I got Tony home again, he was calm, shut down, as if nothing out of the ordinary had occurred. I pulled up in front of the house. He got out, slammed the door, and headed up the path without a word. I was reasonably certain he wouldn't mention his outburst to his aunt and uncle, which was fortunate as I'd sworn I could talk to him without his getting upset. I was, of course, still in possession of Daggett's check, wondering if I'd be toting it around for life, trying in vain to get someone to take it off my hands.

When I got back to my place, I spent twenty minutes unloading my VW. While I tend to maintain an admirable level of tidiness in the apartment, my organizational skills have never extended to my car. The back seat is usually crowded with files, law books, my briefcase, piles of miscellaneous clothing—shoes, pantyhose, jackets, hats, some of which I use as "disguises" in the various aspects of my trade.

I packed everything in a cardboard box and then proceeded around to the backyard where the entrance to my apartment is located. I opened the padlock on the storage bin attached to the service porch and stowed the box, snapping the padlock into place again.

As I reached my door, a dark shape loomed out of the shadows. "Kinsey?"

I jumped, realizing belatedly that it was Billy Polo. I couldn't distinguish his features in the dark, but his voice was distinctly his own.

"Oh Jesus, what are you doing here?" I said.

"Hey, I'm sorry. I didn't mean to scare you. I wanted to talk to you."

I was still trying to recover from the jolt he'd given me, my temper rising belatedly. "How'd you know where to find me?"

"I looked you up in the telephone book."

"My home address isn't in the book."

"Yeah, I know. I tried your office first. You weren't in, so I asked next door at that insurance place."

"California Fidelity gave you my home address?" I said. "Who'd you talk to?" I didn't believe for a minute that CF would release that kind of information to him.

"I didn't get her name. I told her I was a client and it was urgent."

"Bullshit."

"No, it's the truth. She only gave it to me because I leaned on her."

I could tell he wasn't going to budge on the point, so I let it pass. "All right, what is it?" I said. I knew I sounded cranky, but I didn't like his coming to my place and I didn't believe his tale about how he found out where it was.

"We're just gonna stand around out here?"

"That's right, Billy. Now get on with it."

"Well, you don't have to get so huffy."

"Huffy! What the hell are you talking about? You loom up out of the dark and scare me half to death! I don't know you from Jack the Ripper so why should I invite you in?"

"Okay, okay."

"Just say what you have to say. I'm beat."

He did some fidgeting around . . . for effect, I

thought. Finally, he said, "I talked to my sister, Coral, and she told me I should be straight with you."

"Oh goody, what a treat. Straight about what?"

"Daggett," he mumbled. "He did get in touch."

"When was this?"

"Last Monday when he got to town."

"He called you?"

"Yeah, that's right."

"How'd he know where you were?"

"He tried my mom's house and talked to her. I wasn't home at the time, so she got his number and I called him back."

"Where'd he call from?"

"I don't know for sure. Some dive. There was all this noise in the background. He was drunk and I figured he must have parked himself in the first bar he found."

"What time of day was this?"

"Maybe eight at night. Around in there."

"Go on."

"He said he was scared and needed help. Somebody called him down in Los Angeles and told him he was dead meat on account of a scam he pulled up in prison just before he got out."

"What scam?"

"I don't know all the details. What I heard was his cellmate got snuffed and Daggett helped himself to a big wad of cash the guy had hidden in his bunk."

"How much?"

"Nearly thirty grand. It was some kind of drug deal went sour, which is why the guy got killed in the first place. Daggett walked off with the whole stash and somebody wanted it back. They were comin' after him. At least that's what they told him."

"Who?"

"I don't want to mention names. I got a fair idea and I could find out for sure if I wanted to, but I don't like puttin' my neck in a noose unless I have to. The point is I shined him on. I wasn't going to help that old coot. No way. He got himself in a hole, let him get himself out. I didn't want to be involved. Not with those guys after him. I'm too fond of my health."

"So what happened? You talked on the phone and that was it?"

"Well, no. I met him for a drink. Coral said I should level with you about that."

"Really," I said. "What for?"

"In case something came up later. She didn't want it to look like I was holding out."

"So you think they caught up with him?"

"He's dead, ain't he?"

"Proving what?"

"Don't ask me. I mean, all I know is what Daggett said. He was on the run and he thought I'd help."

"How?"

"A place to hide."

"When did you meet with him?"

"Not till Thursday. I was tied up."

"Pressing social engagements, no doubt."

"Hey, I was looking for work. I'm on parole and I got requirements to meet."

"You didn't see him Friday?"

"Uh-uh. I just saw him once and that was Thursday night."

"What'd he do in the meantime?"

"I don't know. He never said."

"Where'd you meet him?"

"At the bar where Coral works."

"Ah, now I see. She got worried I'd ask around and somebody'd say they saw you with him."

"Well, yeah. Coral don't like me to mess with the law, especially with me on parole anyway."

"How come it took the bad guys so long to catch up with him? He's been out of prison for six weeks."

"Maybe they didn't figure it was him at first. Daggett wasn't the brightest guy, you know. He never did nothin' right in his life. They prob'bly figured he was too dumb to stick his hand in a mattress and walk off with the cash."

"Did Daggett have the money with him when you talked to him?"

"Are you kidding? He tried to borrow ten bucks from me," Billy said, aggrieved.

"What was the deal?" I asked. "If he gave the money back, they'd let him off the hook?"

"Probably not. I doubt that."

"So do I," I said. "How do you think Lovella figures into this?"

"She doesn't. It's got nothing to do with her."

"I wouldn't be too sure about that. Somebody saw Daggett down at the marina last Friday night, dead drunk, in the company of a trashy-looking blonde."

Even in the dark, I could tell Billy Polo was staring at me.

"A blonde?"

"That's right. She was on the young side from what I was told. He was staggering, and she had to work to keep him on his feet."

"I don't know nothin' about that."

"Neither do I, but it sure sounded like Lovella to me."

"Ask her about it then."

"I intend to," I said. "So what happens next?"

"About what?"

"The thirty thousand, for starters. With Daggett dead, does the money go back to the guys who were after him?"

"If they found it, I guess it does," he said, uncomfortably.

"What if they didn't find it?"

Billy hesitated. "Well, I guess if it's stashed somewhere, it'd belong to his widow, wouldn't it? Part of his estate?"

I was beginning to get the drift here, but I wondered if he did. "You mean Essie?"

"Who?"

"Daggett's widow, Essie."

"He's divorced from her," Billy said.

"I don't think so. At least not as far as the law is concerned."

"He's married to Lovella," he said.

"Not legally."

"You're shittin' me."

"Come to the funeral tomorrow and see for yourself."

"This Essie has the money?"

"No, but I know where it is. Twenty-five thousand of it, at any rate."

"Where?" he said, with disbelief.

"In my pocket, sweetheart, in the form of a cashier's check made out to Tony Gahan. You remember, Tony, don't you?"

Dead silence.

I lowered my voice. "You want to tell me who Doug Polokowski is?"

Billy Polo turned and walked away.

I stood there for a moment and then followed reluctantly, still pondering the fact that he had my home address. Last time I'd talked to him, he didn't even buy the fact that I was a private investigator. Now suddenly he was seeking me out, having confidential chats about Daggett on my front step. It didn't add up.

I heard his car door slam as I reached the street. I hung back in the shadows, watching as he swung the Chevrolet out of a parking place four doors down. He gunned it, speeding off toward the beach. I debated about whether to pursue him, but I couldn't bear the thought of lurking about outside Coral's trailer again.

Enough of that stuff. I turned back and let myself into
my apartment. I kept thinking about the fact that my car
was broken into, my handbag stolen, along with all of
my personal identification. Had Billy Polo done that? Is
that how he came up with my home address? I couldn't
figure out how he'd tracked me to the beach in the first
place, but it would explain how he knew where to find
me now.

I was sure he was maneuvering, but I couldn't
figure out what he'd hoped to get. Why the yarn about
Daggett and the bad guys in jail? It did fit with some of
the facts, but it didn't have that nice, untidy ring of
truth.

I hauled out a stack of index cards and wrote it all
down anyway. Maybe it would make sense later, when
other information came to light. It was 10:00 by the time
I finished. I pulled the white wine out of the refrigerator, wiggled the cork loose, and poured myself a
glass. I stripped my clothes off, turned the lights out,
and toted the wine into the bathroom where I set it on
the window sill in the bathtub and stared out at the
darkened street. There's a streetlight out there, buried
in the branches of a jacaranda tree, largely denuded
now by the rain. The window was half opened and a
damp slat of night wind wafted in, chilly and secretive. I
could hear rain begin to rattle on my composition roof. I
was restless. When I was a young girl, maybe twelve or
so, I wandered the streets on nights like this, barefoot, in
a raincoat, feeling anxious and strange. I don't think my
aunt knew about my nocturnal excursions, but maybe
she did. She had a reckless streak of her own and she
may have honored mine. I was thinking a lot about her,
of late, perhaps because of Tony. His family had been
wiped out in a car accident, just as mine had, and he was
being raised now by an aunt. Sometimes, I had to admit
to myself . . . especially on nights like this . . . that
the death of my parents may not have been as tragic as it

seemed. My aunt, for all her failings, was a perfect guardian for me . . . brazen, remote, eccentric, independent. Had my parents lived, my life would have taken an altogether different route. There was no doubt of that in my mind. I like my history just as it is, but there was something else going on as well.

Looking back on the evening, I realized how much I'd identified with Tony's kicking my car window out. The rage and defiance were hypnotic and touched off deep feelings of my own. Daggett's funeral was coming up the next afternoon and that touched off something else . . . old sorrows, good friends gone down into the earth. Sometimes I picture death as a wide stone staircase, filled with a silent procession of those being led away. I see death too often to worry about it much, but I miss the departed and I wonder if I'll be docile when my turn comes.

I finished my wine and went to bed, sliding naked into the warm folds of my quilt.

16

The dawn was accompanied by drizzle, dark gray sky gradually shading to a cold white light. Ordinarily, I don't run in the rain, but I hadn't slept well and I needed to clear away the dregs of nagging anxiety. I wasn't even sure what I was worried about. Sometimes I awaken uncomfortably aware of a low-level dread humming in my gut. Running is the only relief I can find short of drink and drugs, which at 6:00 A.M. don't appeal.

I pulled on a sweat suit and hit the bike path, jogging a mile and a half to the recreation center. The palm trees along the boulevard had shed dried fronds in the wind and they lay on the grass like soggy feathers. The ocean was silver, the surf rustling mildly like a taffeta skirt with a ruffle of white. The beach was a drab brown, populated by sea gulls snatching at sand fleas. Pigeons lifted in a cloud, looking on. I have to admit I'm not an outdoor person at heart. I'm always aware that under the spritely twitter of birds, bones are being crunched and ribbons of flesh are being stripped away, all of it the work of bright-eyed creatures without feeling or conscience. I don't look to Nature for comfort or serenity.

Traffic was light. There were no other joggers. I

passed the public restrooms, housed in a cinderblock building painted flesh pink, where two bums huddled with a shopping cart. One I recognized from two nights before and he watched me now, indifferently. His friend was curled up under a cardboard comforter, looking like a pile of old rags. I reached the turnaround and ran the mile and a half back. By the time I got home, my Etonics were soaked, my sweat pants were darkened by the drizzle, and the mist had beaded in my hair like a net of seed pearls. I took a long hot shower, optimism returning now that I was safely home again.

After breakfast, I tidied up and then checked my automobile insurance policy and determined that the replacement of my car window was covered, after a fifty-dollar deductible. At 8:30, I started soliciting estimates from auto glass shops, trying to persuade someone to work me in before noon that day. I zipped myself into my all-purpose dress again, resurrected a decent-looking black leather shoulder bag that I use for "formal" wear and filled it with essentials, including the accursed cashier's check.

I dropped the car off at an auto glass shop not far from my office and hoofed it the rest of the way to work. Even with low-heeled pumps, my feet hurt and my pantyhose made me feel like I was walking around with a hot, moist hand in my crotch.

I let myself into the office and initiated my usual morning routines. The phone rang as I was plugging in the coffeepot.

"Miss Millhone, this is Ramona Westfall."

"Oh hello," I said. "How are you?" Secretly, my stomach did a little twist and I wondered if Tony Gahan had told her about his freak-out at the Clockworks the night before.

"I'm fine," she said. "I'm calling because there's

something I'd like to discuss with you and I hoped you
might have some time free this morning."

"Well, my schedule's clear, but I don't have a car.
Can you come down here?"

"Yes, of course. I'd prefer that anyway. Is ten
convenient? It's short notice, I know."

I glanced at my watch. Twenty minutes. "That's
fine," I said. She made some good-bye noises and clicked
off. I depressed the line and then put a call through to
Barbara Daggett at her mother's house to verify the time
of the funeral. She was unavailable to come to the
phone, but Eugene Nickerson told me the services were
at 2:00 and I said I'd be there.

I took a few minutes to open my mail from the day
before, posting a couple of checks to accounts receivable, then made a quick call to my insurance agent,
giving her the sketchy details about my car window. I'd
no more than put the phone down when it rang again.

"Kinsey, this is Barbara Daggett. Something's come
up. When I arrived here this morning, there was some
woman sitting on the porch steps who says she's Daddy's
wife."

"Oh God. Lovella."

"You know about her?"

"I met her last week when I was down in L.A.,
trying to get a line on your father's whereabouts."

"And you knew about this claim of hers?"

"I never heard the details, but I gathered they were
living in some kind of common-law relationship."

"Kinsey, she has a marriage certificate. I saw it
myself. Why didn't you tell me what was going on? I was
speechless. She stood out on the front porch, screaming
bloody murder until I finally had to call the police. I
can't believe you didn't at least *mention* it."

"When was I supposed to do that? At the morgue?

Over at the funeral home with your mother in a state of collapse?"

"You could have called me, Kinsey. Any time. You could have come to my office to discuss it."

"Barbara, I could have done half a dozen things, but I didn't. Frankly, I was feeling protective of your father and I was hoping you wouldn't have to find out about this 'alleged' marriage. That certificate could be a fake. The whole thing could be trumped up, and if not, you've still got problems enough without adding bigamy to his list of personal failings."

"That isn't yours to decide. Now Mother wants to know what the ruckus was about and I have no idea what to say."

"Well, I can see why you're upset, but I'm not sure I'd do it any differently."

"I can't believe you'd take that attitude! I don't appreciate being kept in the dark," she said. "I hired you to investigate and I expect you to pass on whatever comes to light."

"Your father hired me long before you did," I said.

That silenced her for a moment and then she took off again. "To do what? You never did specify."

"Of course I didn't. He talked to me confidentially. It was all bullshit, but it's still not mine to flap around. I couldn't stay in business if I blabbed all the information that came my way."

"I'm his daughter. I have a right to know. Especially if my father's a *bigamist*. What else am I paying you for?"

"You might be paying me to exercise a little judgment of my own," I said. "Come on, Barbara. Be reasonable. Suppose I'd told you. What purpose would that have served? If your parents are still legally married, Lovella has no claim whatever and, for all I know, she's perfectly aware of that. Why add to your grief when she might well have slunk away without a word?"

"How did she know he died in the first place?"

"Not from me, I can tell you that. I'm not an idiot. The last thing in the world I wanted was her up here camping out on your doorstep. Maybe she read it in the paper. Maybe she heard it on the news."

She murmured something, temporarily mollified.

"What happened when the cops got there?" I asked.

There was another pause while she debated whether to move on or continue berating me. I sensed that she enjoyed chewing people out and it was hard for her to give up the opportunity. From my point of view, she wasn't paying me enough to take much guff. A little bit, perhaps. I probably should have told her.

"The two officers took her aside and had a talk with her. She left a few minutes ago."

"Well, if she shows up again, I'll take care of it," I said.

"Again? Why would she do that?"

I remembered then that aside from the matter of her father's apparent bigamy, I hadn't told her about the infamous twenty-five thousand dollars, which Billy Polo assumed was part of Daggett's "estate." Maybe Lovella had come up here to collect. "I think we better have a chat soon," I said.

"Why? Is there something *else*?"

I looked up. Ramona Westfall was standing in my doorway. "There's always something else," I said. "That's what makes life so much fun. I've got someone here. I'll talk to you this afternoon."

I hung up and rose to my feet, shaking hands with Mrs. Westfall across the desk. I invited her to take a seat and then poured coffee for us both, using social ritual as a way of setting her at ease, or so I hoped.

She was looking drawn, the fine skin under her

mild eyes smudged with fatigue. She wore a tan poplin shirtwaist with shoulder epaulets and carried a mesh-and-canvas handbag that looked like it could be packed for a quick safari somewhere. Her pale hair had the sheen of a Breck shampoo ad in a magazine. I tried to picture her in a raincoat, lurching around the marina with Daggett's arm draped over her shoulder. Could she have flipped him, ass over teakettle, right out of that skiff? Hey, sure. Why not?

She stared at me uneasily, reaching out automatically to straighten some items on my desk. She lined up three pencils with the points facing me, like little ground-to-air missiles, and then she cleared her throat.

"Well. We were wondering. Tony never said anything so we thought perhaps we should ask you about it. Did you tell Tony about the money when you talked to him last night?"

"Sure," I said. "Not that it did any good. I got nowhere. He was adamant. He wouldn't even discuss it."

She colored slightly. "We're thinking to take it," she said. "Ferrin and I talked about it last night while Tony was out with you and we're beginning to believe we should put the money in a trustee account for him . . . at least until he's eighteen and really has a sense of what he might do with it."

"What brought about the change?"

"Oh everything, I guess. We've been in family counseling and the therapist keeps hoping we can work through some of the anger and the grief. He feels Tony's migraines are stress-related in part, a sort of index of his unwillingness . . . or maybe inability is a better word . . . to process his loss. I've been wondering how much I've contributed to that. I haven't dealt with Abby's death that well and it can't have helped him." She paused and then shook her head slightly as though embarrassed. "I know it's a reversal. I suppose we've been unnecessarily rude to you and I'm sorry."

"You don't have to apologize," I said. "Personally, I'd be delighted to have you take the check. At least then I could feel I'd discharged my responsibilities. If you change your mind later, you can always donate the money to a worthy cause. There are lots of those around."

"What about his family? Daggett's. They may feel they're entitled to the money, don't you think? I mean, I wouldn't want to take it if there are going to be any legal ramifications."

"You'd have to talk to an attorney about that," I said. "The check is made out to Tony, and Daggett hired me to deliver it to him. I don't think there's any question about his intention. There may be other legal issues I don't know about, but you're certainly welcome to talk to someone first." Secretly, I wanted her to take the damn thing and be done with it.

She stared at the floor for a moment. "Tony said . . . last night he mentioned that he might want to go to the funeral. Do you think he should? I mean, does that seem like a good idea to you?"

"I don't know, Mrs. Westfall. That's way out of my line. Why don't you ask his therapist?"

"I tried, but he's out of town until tomorrow. I don't want Tony any more upset than he is."

"He's going to feel what he feels. You can't control that. Maybe it's something he has to go through."

"That's what Ferrin says, but I'm not sure."

"What's the story on the migraines? How long has that been going on?"

"Since the accident. He had one last night as a matter of fact. It's not your fault," she added hastily. "His head started bothering him about an hour after he got home. He threw up every twenty minutes or so from midnight until almost four A.M. We finally had to take him over to the emergency room at St. Terry's. They gave him a shot and that put him out, but he woke up a little while ago and he's talking now about going to the funeral. Did he mention it to you?"

"Not at all. I told him Daggett was dead, but he didn't react much at the time, except to say he was glad. Is he well enough to go?"

"He will be, I think. The migraines are odd. One minute you think he's never going to pull out of it and the next minute he's on his feet and starving to death. It happened last Friday night."

"Friday?" I said. The night of Daggett's death.

"That episode wasn't quite as bad. When he came home from school, he knew he was on the verge of a headache. We tried to get some medication down him to head it off, but no luck. Anyway, he pulled out of it after a while and I ended up fixing him two meatloaf sandwiches in the kitchen at two A.M. He was fine. Of course, he had another headache on Tuesday, and then the one last night. Two the week before that. Ferrin thinks maybe his going to the funeral will have some symbolic significance. You know, finish it off for him and set him free."

"That's always possible."

"Would Barbara Daggett object?"

"I don't see why she would," I said. "I suspect she feels as guilty as her father did, and she's offered to help."

"I guess I'll see how he's doing when I get home, then," she said. She glanced at her watch. "I better go."

"Let me give you the check." I pulled my handbag out of the bottom drawer and took out the check, which I passed across the desk to her. As her husband had done the night before, she smoothed out the folds, looking at it closely as if it might be some preposterous fake. She folded it up again and slipped it in her bag as she got to her feet. She hadn't touched her mug of coffee. I hadn't drunk mine either.

I told her the time and place of the services and walked her to the door. After she left, I sat down at my desk again, reviewing everything she'd said. At some point, I wanted to take Tony Gahan aside and see if he could verify her presence at the house the night Daggett died. It was hard to picture her as a killer, but I'd been fooled before.

17

John Daggett's funeral service took place in the sanctuary of some obscure outpost of the Christian church. The building itself was a one-story yellow stucco, devoid of ornament, located just off the free-way—the sort of chapel you glimpse through the bushes when you're going someplace else. I arrived late. I'd retrieved my VW from the auto glass shop at 1:45 after countless delays, and I confess I'd spent a few contented moments cranking my new car window up and down. The drizzle was beginning to turn serious and I was heartened by the notion that it wouldn't blow straight in on me.

When I reached the gravel parking lot beside the church, there were already fifty cars jammed into space for thirty-five. Some vehicles had nosed out into the vacant lot next door and some hugged the fence along the frontage road. I was forced to pass the place, snag a spot at the end of a long line of cars, and walk back. I could already hear electronic organ music thumping out in a style better suited to a skating rink than a house of God. I noticed from the sign out front that the minister was called a pastor instead of "Reverend" and I wondered if that was significant. Pastor Howard Bowen. The church name was composed of a long string of words and reminded me uneasily of the outfit that distributes pamphlets door-to-door. I hoped they weren't keen on converts.

Mr. Sharonson, from Wynington-Blake, was standing by himself on the low front steps and he gave me a pained look as he passed me a mimeographed copy of the program with a hand-drawn lily on the front. His manner suggested that the services were spiritually second-rate, this being the K mart of churches.

I went in. An usher peeled a metal folding chair from a stack near the door and flipped it open for me. The congregation had risen to its feet to sing so I stood in the back row, wedged in among other late arrivals. The woman on my left offered to share her hymnal and I took my half, my gaze sliding over the page in haste. They were on verse four of a ditty that went on and on about blood and sin. I made some mouth noises which I hoped were being lost in the general din. Aside from the fact I don't believe in this stuff, I don't sing too good and I was worried I might be denounced on both counts.

Way up at the front, I thought I spotted Barbara Daggett's blonde head, but I didn't see anyone else I knew. We sat down with a rustle of clothing and the scrape of metal chair legs. While Pastor Bowen, in a matte black suit, talked about what wretches we were, I stared at the brown vinyl tile floor and studied the staunch row of stained glass windows which depicted forms of spiritual torment that made me squirm. Already, I could feel a burgeoning urge to repent.

I could see Daggett's casket up by the altar, looking somehow like one of those boxes magicians use when they cut folk in half. I checked my program. We'd whipped through the opening prayer and the invocation, and now that we'd dispensed with the first hymn, we were apparently settling in for an energetic discourse on the temptations of the flesh, which put me in mind of the numerous and varied occasions on which I'd succumbed. That was entertaining.

Pastor Bowen was in his sixties, balding, a small man with a tight round face, who looked like he would suffer from denture breath. He'd chosen as his subject matter a passage from Deuteronomy: "The Lord shall smite thee in the knees, and in the legs, with a sore botch that cannot be healed, from the sole of thy foot unto the top of thy head," and I heard more on that subject than I thought possible without falling asleep. I was curious what he could find to say about John Daggett, whose transgressions were many and whose repentances were few, but he managed to tie Daggett's passing into "He shall lend to thee, and thou shalt not lend to him; he shall be the head, and thou shalt be the tail," and sailed right into an all-encompassing prayer.

When we stood for the final hymn, I felt someone's eyes on me and I looked over to spot Marilyn Smith two rows down, in the company of a man I assumed to be her husband, Wayne. She was wearing red. I wondered if she would leap up and do a tap dance on the coffin lid. The congregation by now was really getting into the spirit of things and hosannas were being called out on all sides, accompanied by amens, huzzahs, and much rending and tearing of clothes. I wanted to excuse myself, but I didn't dare. This was beginning to feel like soul-aerobics.

The woman next to me began to sway, her eyes closed, while she hooted out an occasional "Yes, Lord." I'm not given to this sort of orthodox public outburst and I commenced to edge my way to the door. I could see now that the minister, doing what looked like deltoid releases, was leading his merry band of church elders in the equivalent of a canonical conga line with Essie Daggett bringing up the rear.

At the exit, I came face to face with Billy Polo and his sister, Coral. He took me by the arm and pulled me aside as the service drew to a close behind me and people began to crowd through the door. Essie Daggett

was wailing, nearly borne aloft like a football coach after
a big win. Barbara Daggett and Eugene Nickerson had
arranged themselves on either side, giving her what
protection they could. For some reason, the other
mourners were reaching out to touch and pat and grasp
at Essie, as if her grief lent her healing powers.

The pallbearers came last, pulling the coffin along
on a rolling cart instead of toting it. None of the six of
them appeared to be under sixty-five and Wynington-
Blake may have worried that they'd collapse, or topple
their cargo right out into the aisle. As it was, the cart
seemed to have one errant wheel which caused it to
meander, squeaking energetically. The coffin, as though
with a will of its own, headed for the chairs first on one
side and then the other. I could see the pallbearers
struggle to maintain mournful expressions while cor-
recting its course, dragging it up the aisle like a stubborn
dog.

I caught sight of Tony Gahan briefly, but he was
gone again before I could speak to him. The hearse
pulled up in front and the coffin was angled down the
low steps and into the rear. Behind it, the limousine
pulled up and Essie was helped into the back seat. She
was wearing a black suit, with a broad-brimmed black
straw hat, swathed in veiling. She looked more like a
beekeeper than anything else. Stung by the Holy Spirit,
I thought. Barbara Daggett wore a charcoal gray suit
and black pumps, her two-toned eyes looking almost
electric in the pale oval of her face. The rain was falling
steadily and Mr. Sharonson was distributing big black
umbrellas as people ducked off the porch and hurried
to the parking lot.

Cars were being started simultaneously in a rumble
of exhaust fumes, gravel popping as we pulled out onto
the frontage road and began the slow procession to the
cemetery, maybe two miles away. Again, we parked in a
long line, car doors slamming as we crossed the soggy

grass. This was apparently a fairly new cemetery, with few trees—a wide flat field planted to an odd crop. The headstones were square cut and low, without any of the worn beauty of stone angels or granite lambs. The grounds were well kept, but consisted primarily of asphalt roadways winding among sections of burial plots that had apparently been sold "pre-need." I wondered if cemeteries, like golf courses, had to be designed by experts for maximum aesthetic effect. This one felt like a cut-rate country club, low membership fees for the upstart dead. The rich and respectable were buried someplace else and John Daggett couldn't possibly qualify for inclusion among them.

Wynington-Blake had set up a canopy over the grave itself and, nearby, a second larger one with folding chairs arranged under it. No one seemed to know who was supposed to go where and there was a bit of milling around. Essie and Barbara Daggett were led into the big tent and placed in the front row, with Eugene Nickerson on one side and a fat woman on the other in a set of four folding chairs connected at the base. The back legs were already beginning to sink into the rain-softened soil, tilting the four of them backward at a slight angle. I had a brief image of them trapped like that, staring at the tent top, legs dangling, unable to right themselves again. Why is it that grief always seems edged with absurdity?

I eased over to one side, under shelter, but remained standing. Most of the mourners appeared to be elderly and (perhaps) needed folding chairs more than I. It looked like the entire church membership had turned out in Essie Daggett's behalf.

Pastor Bowen had declined a raincoat and he stood now in the open air, rain collecting on his balding head, waiting patiently for everyone to get settled. At this range, I saw evidence of a hearing aid tucked into the tiny ear cave on his right. Idly, he fiddled with the device, keeping his expression benign so as not to call attention to himself. I wondered if the battery was shorting out from the damp. I could see him tap on the aid with his index finger, flinching then as though it had suddenly barked to life again.

On the far side of the tent, I saw Marilyn and Wayne Smith, and behind them Tony Gahan, accompanied by his aunt Ramona. He looked like the perfect prep school gentleman in gray wool slacks, white shirt, navy blazer, rep tie. As though sensing that he was being watched, his eyes strayed to mine, his expression as empty as a robot's. If he was expunging raw hate or an old sorrow, there was no sign of it. Billy Polo and his sister stood outside the tent in the rain, sharing an umbrella. Coral looked miserable. She was apparently still caught up in the throes of a cold, clutching a fistful of Kleenex. She belonged in bed with a flannel rag on her chest reeking of Vick's Vaporub. Billy seemed restless, scanning the crowd with care. I followed his gaze, wondering if he was looking for someone in particular.

"Dear friends," the minister said in a powdery voice. "We are gathered here on the sad occasion of John Daggett's death, to witness his return to the earth from which he was formed, to acknowledge his passing, to celebrate his entry into the presence of our Lord Jesus. John Daggett has left us. He is free now of the cares and worries of this life, free of sin, free of his burdens, free of blame. . . ."

From somewhere near the back, a woman hollered out "Yes, Lord!" and a second woman yelled out "Buulllshiit!" in just about the same tone. The minister, not hearing that well, apparently took both as spiritual punctuation marks, Biblical whoopees to incite him to greater eloquence. He raised his voice, closing his eyes as he began quoting admonitions against sin, filth, defiled flesh, lasciviousness, and corruption.

"John Daggett was the biggest asshole who ever
lived so get it straight!" came the jeering voice again.
Heads whipped around. Lovella had gotten to her feet
near the back. The people turned to stare, their faces
blank with amazement.

She was drunk. She had the little bitty pink eyes that
suggest some high-grade marijuana toked up in addition to the booze. Her left eye was still slightly puffy, but
the bruising had lightened up to a mild yellow on that
side and she looked more like she was suffering from an
allergy than a rap up the side of the head from the dead
man. Her hair was the same blonde bush I remembered,
her mouth a slash of dark red. She'd been weeping
copiously and her mascara was speckled under her
lower lids like soot. Her skin was splotchy, her nose hot
pink and running. For the occasion she'd chosen a black
sequined cocktail dress, low cut. Her breasts looked
almost transparent and bulged out like condoms in-
flated as a joke. I couldn't tell if she was weeping out of
rage or grief and I didn't think this crowd was prepared
to deal with either one.

I was already headed toward the rear. Out of the
corner of my eye, I saw Billy Polo make a beeline toward
her on the far side of the tent. The minister had figured
out by now that she was not on his team and he shot a
baffled look at Mr. Sharonson, who motioned the ushers
to take charge. We all reached her just about at the same
time. Billy grabbed her from behind, pinning her arms
back. Lovella flung him off, kicking like a mule, yelling
"Fuck-heads! You scum-sucking hypocrites!" One usher
snagged her by the hair and the other took her feet. She
shrieked and struggled as they carried her toward the
road. I followed, glancing back briefly. Barbara Daggett
was obscured by the mourners who'd stood up for a
better look, but I saw that Marilyn Smith was loving
every trashy minute of Lovella's performance.

By the time I reached Lovella, she was lying in the

front seat of Billy Polo's Chevrolet, hands covering her
face as she wept. The doors were open on both sides of
the car and Billy knelt by her head, shushing and
soothing her, smoothing her rain-tangled hair. The two
ushers exchanged a look, apparently satisfied that she
was under control at that point. Billy bristled at their
intrusion.

"I got her, man. Just bug off. She's cool."

Coral came around the car and stood behind him,
holding the umbrella. She seemed embarrassed by
Billy's behavior, uncomfortable in the presence of Lovella's excess. The three of them formed an odd unit and I
got the distinct impression that the connection between
them was more recent than Billy'd led me to believe.

The graveside service, I gathered, was drawing to a
close. From the tent came the thin, discordant voices of
the mourners as they joined in an a cappella hymn.
Lovella's sobs had taken on the intensity of a child's—
artless, unself-conscious. Was she truly grieving for
Daggett or was something else going on?

"What's the story, Billy?" I said.

"No story," he said gruffly.

"Something's going on. How'd she find out about
his death? From you?"

Billy laid his face against her hair, ignoring me.

Coral shifted her gaze to mine. "He doesn't know
anything."

"How about you, Coral? You want to talk about it?"

Billy shot her a warning look and she shook her
head.

Murmurs and activity from the tent. The crowd was
breaking up and people were beginning to move toward
us.

"Watch your head. I'm closing the car doors," Billy
said to Lovella. He shut the door on the driver's side and
moved around the front to catch the door on the
passenger side. He paused with his hand on the handle,

waiting for her to pull her knees up to make clearance. Idly, he surveyed the mourners still huddled under the cover of the tent. As the crowd shifted, I saw his gaze flicker. "Who's that?"

He was looking at a small group formed by Ramona Westfall, Tony, and the Smiths. The three adults were talking while Tony, his hands in his pockets, passed his shoe over the rung of a folding chair, scraping the mud from the sole. Barbara Daggett was just behind him, in conversation with someone else. I identified everyone by name. I thought Wayne was the one who seemed to hold his attention, but I wasn't positive. It might have been Marilyn.

"How come the Westfalls showed up for this?"

"Maybe the same reason you did."

"You don't know why I came," he said. He was agitated, jingling the car keys, his gaze drifting back to the mourners.

"Maybe you'll tell me one of these days."

His smirk said don't count on it. He signaled to Coral and she got in the back seat. He got in the car and started it, pulling out then without a backwards glance.

18

Barbara Daggett invited me back to her mother's house after the funeral, but I declined. I couldn't handle another emotional circus act. After I've spent a certain amount of time in the company of others, I need an intermission anyway. I retreated to my office and sat there with the lights out. It was only 4:00, but dark clouds were massing again as though for attack. I slipped my shoes off and put my feet up, clutching my jacket around me for warmth. John Daggett was in the ground now and the world was moving on. I wondered what would happen if we left it at that. I didn't think Barbara Daggett gave a damn about seeing justice done, whatever that consisted of. I hadn't come up with much. I thought I was on the right track, but I wasn't sure I really wanted an answer to the question Daggett's death had posed. Maybe it was better to forget this one, turn it under again like top soil, worms and all. The cops didn't consider it a homicide anyway and I knew I could talk Barbara Daggett out of pursuing the point. What was there to be gained? I wasn't in the business of avenging Daggett's death. Then what was I uneasy about? It was the only time in recent memory that I'd wanted to drop a case. Usually I'm dogged, but this time I wanted out. I think I could have talked myself into it if nothing else had occurred. As it happened, my phone rang about ten minutes later, nudging me into action again. I took my feet off the desk for form's sake and picked up on the first ring. "Millhone."

A young-sounding man said hesitantly: "Is this the office or an answering service?"

"The office."

"Is this Kinsey Millhone?"

"Yes. Can I help you?"

"Yeah, well my boss gave me this number. Mr. Donagle at the Spindrift Motel? He said you had some questions about Friday night. I think maybe I saw that guy you were asking about."

I reached for a lined yellow pad and a pen. "Great. I appreciate your getting in touch. Could you tell me your name first?"

"Paul Fisk," he said. "I read in the paper some guy drowned and it just sure seemed like an odd coincidence, but I didn't know if I should say anything or not."

"You saw him Friday night?"

"Well, I think it was him. This was about quarter of two, something like that. I'm on night desk and sometimes I step outside for some air, just to keep myself awake." He paused and I could hear him shift gears. "This is confidential, isn't it?"

"Of course. Strictly between us. Why? Did your girlfriend stop by or something like that?"

His laugh was nervous. "Naw, sometimes I smoke a little weed is all. Place gets boring at two A.M., so that's how I get through. Get loaded and watch old black-and-white movies on this little TV I got. I hope you don't have a problem with that."

"Hey, it's your business, not mine. How long have you worked at the Spindrift?"

"Just since March. It's not a great job, but I don't want to get fired. I'm trying to get myself out of debt and I need the bucks."

"I hear you," I said. "Tell me about Friday night."

"Well, I was on the porch and this drunk went by. It was raining pretty hard so I didn't get a real good look at him at the time, but when I saw the news, the age and stuff seemed pretty close."

"Did you see the picture of him by any chance?"

"Just a glimpse on TV, but I wasn't paying much attention so I couldn't say for sure it was him. I guess I should have called the cops, but I didn't have anything much to report and I was afraid it'd come out about the . . . about that other stuff."

"What was he doing, the drunk?"

"Nothing much. It was him and this girl. She had him by the arm. You know, kind of propped up. They were laughing like crazy, wandering all over the place on account of his being so screwed up. Alcohol'll do that, you know. Bad stuff. Not like weed," he said.

I bypassed the sales pitch. "What about the woman? Did you get a good look at her?"

"Not really. Not to describe."

"What about hair, clothing, things like that?"

"I noticed some. She had these real spiky heels and a raincoat, a skirt, and let's see . . . a shirt with this sweater over it. Like, what do you call 'em, preppies wear."

"A crewneck?"

"Yeah. Same color green as the skirt."

"You saw all that in the dark?"

"It's not that dark there," he said. "There's a streetlight right out front. The two of them fell down in a heap they were laughing so hard. She got up first and kind of looked down to see if her stockings were torn. He just lay there in a puddle on his back till she helped' him up."

"Did they see you?"

"I don't think so. I was standing in the shadows of this overhang, keeping out of the wet. I never saw 'em look my way."

"What happened after the fall?"

"They just went on toward the marina."

"Did you hear them say anything?"

"Not really. It sounded like she was teasing him about falling down, but other than that nothing in particular."

"Could they have had a car?"

"I don't think so. Anyway, not that I saw."

"What if they'd parked it in that municipal lot across the street?"

"I guess they could have, but I don't know why they'd walk to the marina in weather like that. Seems like if they had a car it'd be easier to drive and then park it down there."

"Unless he was too drunk. He'd had his driver's license yanked too."

"She could have driven. She was half sober at least."

"You've got a point there," I said. "What about public transportation? Could they have come by bus or cab?"

"I guess, except the buses don't run that late. A cab maybe. That'd make sense."

I was jotting down information as he gave it to me. "This is great. What's your home phone in case I need to get in touch?"

He gave me the number and then said, "I usually work eleven to seven on weekdays."

I made a quick note. "Do you think you'd recognize the girl if you saw her again?"

"I don't know. Probably. Do you know who she is?"

"Not yet. I'm working on that."

"Well, I wish you luck. You think this'll help?"

"I hope so. Thanks for calling. I really appreciate it."

"Sure thing, and if you catch up with her, let me know. Maybe you can do like a police lineup or something like that."

"Great and thanks."

He clicked off and I finished making notes, adding this information to what I had. Dinah had spotted Daggett and the girl at 2:15 and Paul Fisk's sighting placed them right on Cabana thirty minutes before. I wondered where they'd been before that. If they'd arrived by cab, had she taken one home from the marina afterward? I didn't get it. Most killers don't take taxis to and from. It isn't good criminal etiquette.

I hauled out the telephone book and turned to the Yellow Pages to look up cab companies. Fortunately, Santa Teresa is a small town and there aren't that many. Aside from a couple of airport and touring services, there were six listed. I dialed each in turn, patiently explaining who I was and inquiring about a 2:00 A.M. Saturday fare with a Cabana Boulevard drop off. I was also asking about a pickup anywhere in that vicinity sometime between 3:00 and 6:00 A.M. According to the morgue attendant, the watch Daggett had been wearing was frozen at 2:37, but anybody could have jimmied that, breaking the watch to pinpoint the time, then attaching it to his wrist before he was dumped. If she'd left the boat and swum ashore or rowed to the wharf and abandoned it there, it was still going to take her a little time to organize herself for the cab ride home.

All the previous week's trip sheets, of course, had been filed and there were some heavy sighs and grumblings all around at the notion of having to look them up. Ron Coachella, the dispatcher for Tip Top, was the only cheerful soul in the lot, primarily because he'd done a records search for me once before with good results. I couldn't talk anyone into doing the file check right then, so I left my name and number and a promise that I'd call again. "Whoopee-do," said one.

While I was talking, I'd been doodling on the legal pad, running my pencil around idly so that the line formed a maze. I circled the note about the green skirt.

Hadn't that old bum pulled a pair of spike heels and a green skirt out of a trash bin at the beach? I remembered his shoving discarded clothing into one of the plastic bags he kept in his shopping cart. Hers? Surely she hadn't made her way home in the buff. She did have the raincoat, but I wondered if she might have had a change of clothes stashed somewhere too. She'd sure gone to a lot of trouble if she were setting Daggett up. This didn't look like an impulsive act, done in the heat of the moment. Had she had help? Someone who picked her up afterward? If the cab companies didn't come up with a record of a fare, I'd have to consider the possibility of an accomplice.

In the meantime, I thought I'd better head down to the beach and look for my scruffy drifter friend. I'd seen him that morning near the public restrooms when I did my run. I tore the sheet off the legal pad and folded it, shoving it in my pocket as I grabbed up my handbag, locked the office, and headed down the back stairs to my car.

It was now nearly quarter to five, getting chillier by the minute, but at least it was dry temporarily. I cruised along Cabana, peering from my car window. There weren't many people at the beach. A couple of power walkers. A guy with a dog. The boulevard seemed deserted. I doubled back, heading toward my place, passing the wharf on the left and the string of motels across the street. Just beyond the boat launch and kiddie pool, I pulled up at a stoplight, scanning the park on the opposite corner. I could see the band shell where bums sometimes took refuge, but I didn't see any squatters. Where were all the transients?

I circled back, passing the train station. It occurred to me that this was probably the bums' dinner hour. I cut over another block and a half and sure enough, there they were—fifty or so on a quick count, lined up outside the Redemption Mission. The fellow I was looking for

was near the end of the line, along with his pal. There
was no sign of their shopping carts, which I thought of
as a matched set of movable metal luggage, the derelict's
Louis Vuitton. I slowed, looking for a place to park.

The neighborhood is characterized by light industry, factory outlets, welding shops, and quonset huts
where auto body repair work is done. I found a parking
spot in front of a place that made custom surfboards. I
pulled in, watching in my rearview mirror until the
group outside the mission had shuffled in. I locked the
car then and crossed the street.

The Redemption Mission looks like it's made out of
papier-mâché, a two-story oblong of fakey-looking fieldstone, with ivy clinging to one end. The roofline is as
crenellated as a castle's, the "moat" a wide band of
asphalt paving. City fire codes apparently necessitated
the addition of fire escapes that angle down the building
now on all sides, looking somehow more perilous than
the possibility of fire. The property is considered prime
real estate and I wondered who would house the poor if
the bed space were bought out from under them. For
most of the year, the climate in this part of California is
mild enough to allow the drifters to sleep outdoors,
which they seem to prefer. Seasonally, however, there
are weeks of rain . . . even occasionally someone with a
butcher knife intent on slitting their throats. The
mission offers safe sleeping for the night, three hot
meals a day, and a place to roll cigarettes out of the wind.

I picked up cooking odors as I approached—bulk
hamburger with chili seasoning. As usual, I couldn't
remember eating lunch and here it was nearly din-
nertime again. The sign outside indicated prayer services at 7:00 every night and Hot Showers & Shaves on
Mondays, Wednesdays, and Saturdays. I stepped inside.
The walls were painted glossy beige on top and shoe
brown below. Hand-lettered signs pointed me to the

dining room and chapel on the left. I followed the low
murmur of conversation and the clatter of silverware.

On the right, through a doorway, I spotted the
dining room—long metal folding tables covered with
paper, metal folding chairs filled with men. Nobody
paid any attention to me. I could see serving plates
stacked high with soft white bread, bowls of applesauce
sprinkled with cinnamon, salads of iceberg lettuce that
glistened with bottled dressing. The table seated twenty,
already bent to their evening meal of chili served over
elbow macaroni. Another fifteen or twenty men sat
obediently in the "chapel" to my left, which consisted of
a lectern, an old upright piano, orange molded plastic
chairs, and an imposing cross on the wall.

The scruffy drifter I was looking for sat in the back
row with his friend. Slogans everywhere assured me that
Jesus cared, and that certainly seemed true here. What
impressed me most was the fact that Redemption
Mission (according to the wall signs) was supported by
private donations, with little or no connection to the
government.

"May I help you?"

The man who'd approached me was in his sixties,
heavyset, clean-shaven, wearing a red short-sleeved
cotton shirt and baggy pants. He had one normal arm
and one that ended at the elbow in a twist of flesh like
the curled top of a Mr. Softee ice cream cone. I wanted
to introduce myself, shaking hands, but the stump was
on the right and I didn't have the nerve. I took out a
business card instead, handing it to him.

"I wonder if I might have a word with one of your
clients?"

His beefy brow furrowed. "What's this about?"

"Well, I think he retrieved some articles I'm looking
for from a trash can at the beach. I want to find out if he
still has them in his cart. It will only take a minute."

"You see him in here?"

I indicated the one who interested me.

"You'll have to talk to the both of them," the man said. "Delphi's the fellow you want, but he don't talk. His buddy does all the talking. His name is Clare. I'll bring them out if you'll wait out there in the corridor. They got their shopping carts on the back patio. I'd go easy about them carts. They get a might possessive of their treasures sometimes."

I thanked him and retraced my steps, lingering in the entranceway until Delphi and Clare appeared. Delphi had shed some of his overcoats, but he wore the same dark watch cap and his skin had the same dusky red tone. His friend Clare was tall and gaunt with a very pink tongue that crept out of his mouth through the gap left by his missing front teeth. His hair was a silky white, rather sparse, his arms long and stringy, hands huge. Delphi made no eye contact at all, but Clare turned out to have some residual charm, left over perhaps from the days before he started to drink.

I explained who I was and what I was looking for. I saw Delphi look at Clare with the haunted subservience of a dog accustomed to being hit. Clare may have been the only human being in the world who didn't frighten or abuse him and he evidently depended on Clare to handle interactions of this kind.

"Yep. I know the ones. High heels in black suede. Green wool skirt. Delphi here was pleased. Usually it's slim pickin's around that bin. Aluminum cans is about the best you can hope for, but he got lucky, I guess."

"Does he still have the items?"

The tongue crept out with a crafty life of its own, so pink it looked like Clare had been sucking red hots. "I can ask," he said.

"Would you do that?"

Clare turned to Delphi. "What do you think, Delphi? Shall we give this little gal what she wants? Up to you."

Delphi gave no evidence whatever of hearing, absorbing, or assenting. Clare waited a decent interval.

"Now that's tough," Clare said to me. "That was his best day and he likes that green skirt."

"I could reimburse him," I said tentatively. I didn't want to insult these guys.

Out came the tongue, like some shy creature peering from its lair. Delphi's hearing seemed to improve. He shifted slightly. I left Clare to translate this movement into dollars and cents.

"A twenty might cover it," Clare said at length.

I only had a twenty on me, but I took it out of the zippered compartment in my black handbag. I offered it to Delphi. Clare interceded. "Hold that until we've done our business. Let's step outside."

I filed after them along a short corridor to a back exit that opened on a small concrete patio surrounded on three sides by an openwork fence made of lathing. Someone had "landscaped" the entire area in annuals planted in coffee cans and big industrial-sized containers that had held green beans and applesauce. Delphi stood by, looking on anxiously, while Clare pawed through one of the shopping carts. He seemed to know exactly where the shoes and skirt were located, whisking them out in no time flat. He passed them over to me and I handed him the twenty. It felt somehow like an illicit drug sale and I had visions of them buying a jug of Mad Dog 20–20 after I'd left. Clare held the bill up for Delphi to inspect, then he glanced at me.

"Don't you worry. We'll put this in the collection plate," Clare said. "Delphi and me have give up drink." I thought Clare seemed happier about it than Delphi did.

19

My dinner that night was cheese and crackers, with a side of chili peppers just to keep my mouth awake. I'd changed out of my all-purpose dress into a tee shirt, jeans, and fuzzy slippers. I ate sitting at my desk, with a Diet Pepsi on the rocks. I studied the skirt and shoes. I tried the right shoe on. Too wide for me. The back of the heel was scuffed, the toe narrowing to a bunion-producing point. The manufacturer's name on the inner sole had been blurred by sweat. A pair of Odor-eaters wouldn't have been out of line here. The skirt was a bit more informative, size 8, a brand I'd seen at the Village Store and the Post & Rail. Even the lining was in good shape, though wrinkled in a manner that suggested a recent soaking. I touched my tongue to the fabric. Salt. I checked the inseam pockets, which were empty. No cleaner's marks. I thought about the women connected, even peripherally, with Daggett's death. The skirt might fit any one of them, except for Barbara Daggett maybe, who was big-boned and didn't seem like the type for the preppy look, especially in green. Ramona Westfall was a good candidate. Marilyn Smith, perhaps. Lovella Daggett or Billy's sister, Coral, could probably both wear an 8, but the style seemed wrong . . . unless the outfit had been lifted from a Salvation Army donation box. Maybe in the morning I'd stop by a couple of clothing stores

and see if any of the salesclerks recognized the skirt. Fat
chance, I thought. A better plan would be to show it,
along with the shoes, to all five women and see if anyone
would admit ownership. Unlikely under the circumstances. Too bad I couldn't do a little breaking and
entering. The matching green sweater might come to
light in someone's dresser drawer.

I padded into the kitchen and rinsed my plate.
Eating alone is one of the few drawbacks to single life.
I've read those articles that claim you should prepare
food just as carefully for yourself as you would for
company. Which is why I do cheese and crackers. I don't
cook. My notion of setting an elegant table is you don't
leave the knife sticking out of the mayonnaise jar. Since
I usually work while I eat, there isn't any point in
candlelight. If I'm not working, I have *Time* magazine
propped up against a stack of files and I read it back to
front as I munch, starting with the sections on books and
cinema, losing interest by the time I reach Economy &
Business.

At 9:02, my phone rang. It was the night dispatcher
for Tip Top Cab Company, a fellow who identified
himself as Chuck. I could hear the two-way radio
squawking in the background.

"I got this note from Ron says to call you," said he.
"He pulled the trip sheets for last Friday night and said
to give you the information you were asking about, but
I'm not really sure what you want."

I filled him in and waited briefly while he ran his
eye down the sheet. "Oh yeah. I guess this is it. He's got
it circled right here. It was my fare. That's probably why
he asked me to call. Friday night, one twenty-three . . .
well, you'd call that early Saturday. I dropped a couple
off at State and Cabana. Man and a woman. I figured
they were booked into a motel down there."

"I've heard the man was drunk."

"Oh yeah, very. Looked like she'd been drinking

too, but not like him. He was a mess. I mean, this guy
smelled to high heaven. Stunk up the whole back seat
and I got a pretty fair tolerance for that kind of thing."

"What about her? Can you tell me anything?"

"Can't help you on that. It was late and dark and
raining to beat the band. I just took 'em where they
said."

"Did you talk to them?"

"Nope. I'm not the kind of cabbie engages in small
talk with a fare. Most people aren't interested and I get
sick of repeating myself. Politics, weather, baseball
scores. It's all bull. They don't want to talk to me and I
don't want to talk to them. I mean, if they ask me
something I'm polite, don't get me wrong, but I can't
manufacture chitchat to save my neck."

"What about the two of them? They talk to each
other?"

"Who knows? I tuned 'em out."

God, this was no help at all. "You remember
anything else?"

"Not offhand. I'll give it some thought, but it wasn't
any big deal. Sorry I can't be a help."

"Well, at least you've verified a hunch of mine and I
appreciate that. Thanks for your time."

"No problem."

"Oh, one more thing. Where'd the fare originate?"

"Now *that* I got. You know that sleazeball bar on
Milagro? That place. I picked 'em up at the Hub."

I sat and stared at the phone for a moment after he
hung up. I felt like I was running a reel of film
backwards, frame by frame. Daggett left the Hub Friday
night in the company of a blonde. They apparently had
a lot of drinks, a lot of laughs, staggered around in the
rain together, fell down, and picked themselves up
again. And little by little, block by block, she was steering
him toward the marina, herding him toward the boat,
guiding him out into the harbor on the last short ride of

his life. She must have had a heart of stone and steadier nerves than mine.

I made some quick notes and tossed the index cards in the top drawer of my desk. I kicked off my slippers and laced up my tennies, then pulled on a sweatshirt. I snatched up the skirt and shoes, my handbag, and car keys and locked up, heading out to the VW. I'd start with Coral first. Maybe she'd know if Lovella was still in town. I was remembering now the fragment of conversation I'd overheard the night I eavesdropped on Billy and Coral. She'd been talking to Billy then about some woman. I couldn't remember exactly what she'd said, but I did remember that. Maybe Coral had seen the woman I was looking for.

When I reached the trailer park, I found the trailer dimly lighted, as if someone had gone out and left a lamp burning to keep the burglars at bay. Billy's Chevrolet was in the carport, the hood cold to the touch. I knocked on the door. After a moment, I heard footsteps bumping toward the front.

"Yeah?" Billy's muffled voice came through the door.

"It's Kinsey," I said. "Is Coral here?"

"Uh-uh. She's at work."

"Can I talk to you?"

He hesitated. "About what?"

"Friday night. It won't take long."

There was a pause. "Wait a sec. Let me throw some clothes on."

Moments later, he opened the door and let me in. He had pulled on a pair of jeans. Aside from that, he was barefoot and naked to the waist. His dark hair was tousled. He looked like he hadn't worked out recently, but his arms and chest were still well developed, overlaid by a fine mat of dark hair.

The trailer was disordered—newspapers, magazines, dinner dishes for two still out on the table, the counters covered with canned goods, cracker boxes, bags of flour, sugar, and corn meal. There wasn't a clear surface anywhere and no place to sit. The air was dense, smelling faintly of fresh cigarette smoke.

"Sorry to disturb you," I said. He looked like he'd been screwing his brains out and I wondered who was in the bedroom. "You have company?"

He glanced toward the rear, his dimples surfacing. "No, I don't. Why, are you interested?"

I smiled and shook my head, at the same time caught up in a flash fantasy of me and Billy Polo tangled up in sheets that smelled like him, musky and warm. His skin exuded a masculine perfume that conjured up images of all the trashy things we might do if the barriers went down. I kept my expression neutral, but I could feel my face tint with pink. "I have some questions I was hoping Coral might help me with."

"So you said. Try the Hub. She'll be there till closing time."

I laid the skirt and shoes across the television set, which was the only bare surface I could find. "Do you know if these are hers?"

He glanced at the items, too canny to bite. "Where'd you get 'em?"

"A friend of a friend. I thought you might know whose they were."

"I thought this was supposed to be about Friday night."

"It is. I talked to a cabbie who picked Daggett up at the Hub Friday night and dropped him off down near the wharf."

"I'll bite. So what?"

"A blonde was with him. The cabbie took them both. I figure she met him at the Hub, so I thought Coral might have had a look at her."

Billy knew something. I could see it in his face. He was processing the information, trying to decide what it meant.

I was getting impatient. "Goddamn it, Billy, level with me!"

"I am!"

"No, you're not. You've been lying to me since the first time you ever opened your mouth."

"I have not," he said hotly. "Name one thing."

"Let's start with Doug Polokowski. What's your relation to him? Brother?"

He was silent. I stared at him, waiting him out.

"Half-brother," he said grudgingly.

"Go on."

His tone of voice dropped, apparently with embarrassment. "My mom and dad split up, but they were still legally married when she got pregnant by somebody else. I was ten and I hated the whole idea. I started gettin' in trouble right about then so I spent half my time in Juvenile Hall anyway, which suited me just fine. She finally had me declared a whaddyou call 'em. . . ."

"An out-of-control minor?"

"Yeah, one of them. Big deal. I didn't give a fat rat's ass. Let her dump us. Let her have a bunch more kids. She didn't have any more sense than that, then to hell with her."

"So you and Doug were never close?"

"Hardly. I used to see him now and then when I'd come home but we didn't have much of a relationship."

"What about you and your mother?"

"We're okay. I got over it some. After Doug got killed, we did better. Sometimes it happens that way."

"But you must have known Daggett was responsible."

"Sure I knew. Of course I did. Mom wrote and told me he was bein' sent up to San Luis. At first, I thought I'd get even with him. For her sake, if nothin' else. But it didn't work out like that. He was too pathetic. Know what I mean? Hell, I ended up almost feeling sorry for him. I despised him for the whiny little fucker that he was, but I couldn't leave him alone. It's like I had to torment him. I liked to watch him squirm, which maybe makes me weird but it don't make me a killer. I never murdered anybody in my life."

"What about Coral? Where was she in all this?"

"Hey, you ask her."

"Could she have been the one with Daggett that night? It sounds like Lovella to me, but I can't be sure."

"Why ask me? I wasn't there."

"Did Coral mention it?"

"I don't want to talk about this," he said, irritably.

"Come on. You talked to Daggett Thursday night. Did he mention this woman?"

"We didn't talk about women," Billy said. He began to snap the fingers of his right hand against his left palm, making a soft, hollow pop. I could feel myself going into a terrier pup mode, worrying the issue like a rawhide bone, knotted on both ends.

"He must have known who she was," I said. "She didn't just materialize out of the blue. She set him up. She knew what she was doing. It must have been a very carefully thought-out plan."

The popping sound stopped and Billy's tone took on a crafty note. "Maybe she was connected to the guys who wanted their money back," he said.

I looked at him with interest. That really hadn't occurred to me, but it didn't sound bad. "Did you tip them off?"

"Listen, babe, I'm not a killer and I'm not a snitch. If Daggett had a beef with somebody, that was his lookout, you know?"

"Then what's the debate? I don't understand what you're holding back."

He sighed and ran a hand through his hair. "Lay off, okay? I don't know nothin' else so just leave it alone."

"Come on, Billy. What's the rest of it?" I snapped.

"Oh, shit. It wasn't Thursday," he blurted out. "I met Daggett Tuesday night and that's when he asked me to help him out."

"So he could hide from the guys at San Luis," I said, making sure I was following.

"Well, yeah. I mean, they'd called him Monday morning and that's why he'd hightailed it up here. We talked on the phone late Monday. He was drunk. I didn't feel like putting myself out. I'd just got home and I was bushed so I said I'd meet him the next night."

"At the Hub?"

"Right."

"Which is what you did," I said, easing him along.

"Sure, we met and talked some. He was already in a panic so I kind of fanned the flames, just twitting him. There's no harm in that."

"Why lie about it? Why didn't you tell me this to begin with?" I was crowding him, but I thought it was time to persist.

"It didn't look right somehow. I didn't want my name tied to his. Thursday night sounded better. Like I wasn't all that hot to talk to him. You know, like I didn't rush right out. I can't explain it any better than that."

It was just lame enough to make sense to me. I said, "All right. I'll buy it for now. Then what?"

"That's all it was. That's the last I saw of him. He came in again Friday night and Coral spotted him, so she called me, but by the time I got there, he'd left."

"With the woman?"

"Yeah, right."

"So Coral did see her."

"Sure, but she didn't know who she was. She thought it was some babe hittin' on him, like a whore, something like that. The chick was buyin' him all these drinks and Daggett was lappin' 'em up. Coral got kind of worried. Not that either of us really gave a shit, but you know how it is. You don't want to see a guy get taken, even if you don't like him much."

"Especially if you've heard he's got thirty thousand dollars on him, right?" I said.

"It wasn't thirty. You said so yourself. It was twenty-five." Billy was apparently feeling churlish now that he'd opened up. "Anyway, what are you goin' on and on about? I told you everything I know."

"What about Coral? If you lied, maybe she's been lying too."

"She wouldn't do that."

"What'd she say when you got there?"

The look on Billy's face altered slightly and I thought I'd hit on something. I just didn't know what. My mind leapt ahead. "Did Coral *follow* them?" I asked.

"Of course not."

"What'd she say then?"

"Coral wasn't feeling so hot," he replied, uneasily.

"So she'd what, gone home?"

"Not really. She was coming down with this cold and she'd taken a cold cap. She was feeling zonked so she went back in the office and lay down on the couch. The bartender thought she'd left. I get there and I'm pissed because I can't find her, I can't find Daggett. I don't know what's goin' on. I hang around for a while and then I come back here, thinking she's home. Only she's not. It was a fuck-up, that's all. She was at the Hub the whole time."

"What time did she get home?"

"I don't know. Late. Three o'clock. She had to wait till the owner closed out the register and then he gave her a lift partway so she had to walk six blocks in the rain. She's been sick as a dog ever since."

I stared at him, blinking, while the wheels went round and round. I was picturing her at the wharf with Daggett and the fit was nice.

"Why look at me like that?" he said.

"Let me say this. I'm just thinking out loud," I said. "It could have been Coral, couldn't it? The blonde who left the Hub with him? That's what's been worrying you all this time."

"No, uh-uh. No way," he said. His eyes had settled on me with fascination. He didn't like the line I was taking, but he'd probably thought about it himself.

"You only have her word for the fact that this other woman even exists," I said.

"The cabbie saw her."

"But it could have been Coral. She might have been the one buying Daggett all those drinks. He knew who she was and he trusted her too, because of you. She could have called the cab and then left with him. Maybe the reason the bartender thought she was gone was because he saw her leave."

"Get the hell out of here," Billy whispered.

His face had darkened and I saw his muscles tense. I'd been so caught up in my own speculation I hadn't been paying attention to the effect on him. I picked up the skirt and shoes, keeping an eye on him while I edged toward the door. He leaned over and opened it for me abruptly.

I had barely cleared the steps when the door slammed behind me hard. He shoved the curtain aside, staring at me belligerently as I backed out of the carport. The minute the curtain dropped, I cut around to the trailer window where I'd spied on him before. The louvers were closed, but the curtain on that side gaped open enough to allow me a truncated view.

Billy had sunk down on the couch with his head in his hands. He looked up. The woman who'd been in the back bedroom had now emerged and she leaned against the wall while she lit another cigarette. I could see a portion of her heavy thighs and the hem of a shortie nightgown in pale yellow nylon. Like a drowning man, Billy reached for her and pulled her close, burying his

face between her breasts. Lovella. He began to nuzzle at
her nipples through the nylon top, making wet spots.
She stared down at him with that look new mothers have
when they suckle an infant in public. Lazily, she leaned
over and stubbed out her cigarette on a dinner plate,
then wound her fingers into his hair. He grabbed her at
the knees and lowered her to the floor, pushing her
gown up around her waist. Down, down, down, he went.

I headed over to the Hub.

20

It looked like another slow night at the Hub. The rain had picked up again and business was off. The roof was leaking in two places and someone had put out galvanized pails to catch the drips . . . one on the bar, one by the ladies' room. The place, at its best, was populated by neighborhood drinkers—old women with fat ankles in heavy sweaters who started at 2:00 in the afternoon and consumed beer steadily until closing time, men with nasal voices and grating laughs whose noses were bulbous and sunburned from alcohol. The pool players were usually young Mexicans who smoked until their teeth turned yellow and squabbled among themselves like pups. That night the pool room was deserted and the green felt table tops seemed to glow as though lighted from within. I counted four customers in all and one was asleep with his head on his arms. The jukebox was suffering from some mechanical quirk that gave the music a warbling, underwater quality.

I approached the bar, where Coral was perched on a high-backed stool with a Naugahyde top. She was wearing a Western-cut shirt with a silver thread running through the brown plaid, tight jeans rolled up at the ankles, and heels with short white socks. She must have recognized me from the funeral because when I asked if

176

I could talk to her, she hopped down without a word and went around to the other side of the bar.

"You want something to drink?"

"A wine spritzer. Thanks," I said.

She poured a spritzer for me and pulled a draft beer for herself. We took a booth at the back so she could keep her eye on the clientele in case someone needed service. Up close, her hair looked so bushy and dry I worried about spontaneous combustion. Her makeup was too harsh for her fair coloring and her front teeth were decayed around the edges, as if she'd been eating Oreo cookies. Her cold must have been at its worst. Her forehead was lined and her eyes half squinted, like a magazine ad for sinus medication. Her nose was so stopped up she was forced to breathe through her mouth. In spite of all that, she managed to smoke, lighting up a Virginia Slim the minute we sat down.

"You should be home in bed," I said, and then wondered why I'd suggested such a thing. Billy and Lovella were currently back there groveling around on the floor, probably causing the trailer to thump on its foundations. Who could sleep with that stuff going on?

Coral put her cigarette down and took out a Kleenex to blow her nose. I've always wondered where people learn their nose-blowing techniques. She favored the double-digit method, placing a tissue over her hands, sticking the knuckles on both index fingers up her nostrils, rotating them vigorously after each honk. I kept my eyes averted until she was done, wondering idly if she was aware of Lovella's current whereabouts.

"What's the story on Lovella? She seemed distraught at the funeral."

Coral paused in her endeavors and looked at me. Belatedly, I realized she probably didn't know what the

word distraught meant. I could see her put the defini-
tion together.

"She's fine. She had no idea they weren't legally
married to each other. That's why she fell apart. Freaked
her out." She gave her nose a final Roto-rooting and
took up her cigarette again with a sniff.

"You'd think she'd be relieved," I said. "From what
I hear, he beat the shit out of her."

"Not at first. She was crazy about him when he first
got out. Still is, actually."

"That's probably why she called him the world's
biggest asshole at the funeral," I remarked.

Coral looked at me for a moment and then
shrugged noncommittally. She was smarter than Billy,
but not by much. I had the same feeling here that I'd
had with him. I was tapping into a matter they'd hoped
to bury, but I didn't know enough to pursue the point.

I tried fishing. "I thought Lovella and Billy had a
thing at one time."

"Years ago. When she was seventeen. Doesn't count
for shit."

"She told me Billy set her up with Daggett."

"Yeah, more or less. He talked to Daggett about her
and Daggett wrote and asked if they could be pen pals."

"Too bad he never mentioned his wife," I said. "I do
want to talk to Lovella, so when you see her please tell
her to get in touch." I gave her a business card with my
office number on it, which she acknowledged with a
shrug.

"I won't see Lovella," she said.

"That's what you think," said I.

Coral's attention strayed to the bartender who was
holding a finger aloft. "Hang on."

She crossed to the bar where she picked up a couple
of mixed drinks and delivered them to the one other

table that was occupied. I tried to picture her flipping
Daggett backwards out of a rowboat, but I couldn't quite
make it stick. She fit the description, but there was
something missing.

When she got back to the booth, I held up the high
heels. "These yours?"

"I don't wear suede," she said flatly.

I loved it. Like suede was against her personal dress
code. "What about the skirt?"

She took a final drag of the cigarette and crushed it
in the metal ashtray, blowing out a mouthful of smoke.
"Nope. Whose is it?"

"I think the blonde who killed Daggett wore it
Friday night. Billy says she picked him up in here."

Belatedly, she focused on the skirt. "Yeah, that's
right. I saw her," she said, as if cued.

"Does this look like the skirt she wore?"

"It could be."

"You know who she is?"

"Uh-uh."

"I don't mean to be rude about this, Coral, but I
could use a little help. We're talking murder."

"I've been all tore up about it too," she said, bored.

"Don't you give a shit about any of this?"

"Are you kidding? Why should I care about Daggett? He was scum."

"What about the blonde? Do you remember anything about her?"

Coral shook another cigarette out of the pack.
"Why don't you give it a rest, kid. You don't have the
right to ask us any of this shit. You're not a cop."

"I can ask anything I want," I said, mildly. "I can't
force you to answer, but I can always ask."

She stirred with agitation, shifting in her seat.
"Know what? I don't like you," she said. "People like you
make me sick."

"Oh really. People like what?"

She took her time extracting a paper match from a packet, scratching the tip across the striking area until it flared. She lit her cigarette. The match made a tiny tinkling sound when she dropped it in the ashtray. She rested her chin on her palm and smiled at me unpleasantly. I wanted her to get her teeth fixed so she'd be prettier. "I bet you've had it real easy, haven't you?" she said, her voice heavy with sarcasm.

"Extremely."

"Nice white-collar middle-class home. The whole mommy-hubby trip. Bet you had little brothers and sisters. Nice little fluffy white dog . . ."

"This is amazing," I said.

"Two cars. Maybe a cleaning woman once a week. I never went to college. I never had a daddy giving me all the advantages."

"Well, that explains it then," I said. "I did meet your mom, you know. She looks like someone who's worked hard all her life. Too bad you don't appreciate the effort she made in your behalf."

"What effort? She works in a supermarket checkout line," Coral said.

"Oh, I see. You think she should do something classy like you."

"I'm sure not going to do *this* for life, if that's what you think."

"What happened to your father? Where was he in all this?"

"Who knows? He bugged out a long time ago."

"Leaving her with kids to raise by herself?"

"Skip it. I don't even know why I brought it up. Maybe you should get to the point and let me get back to work."

"Tell me about Doug."

"None of your business." She slid out of the booth. "Time's up," she said, and walked away. God, and here I was being friendly.

I picked up the shoes and skirt and dropped a couple of bucks on the table. I moved to the entranceway, pausing in the shelter of the doorway before I stepped out into the rain. It was 10:17 and there was no traffic on Milagro. The street was shiny black and the rain, as it struck the pavement, made a noise like bacon sizzling in a pan. A mist drifted up from the manhole covers that dotted the block, and the gutters gushed in a widening stream where water boiled back out of the storm drains.

I was restless, not ready to pack it in for the night. I thought about stopping by Rosie's, but it would probably look just like the Hub—smoky, drab, depressing. At least the air outside, though chilly, had the sweet, flowery scent of wet concrete. I started the car and did a U-turn, heading toward the beach, my windshield stippled with rain.

At Cabana, I turned right, driving along the boulevard. On my left, even without a moon visible, the surf churned with a dull gray glow, folding back on itself with a thundering monotony. Out in the ocean, I could see the lights on the oil derricks winking through the mist. I'd pulled up at a stoplight when I heard a car horn toot behind me. I checked my rearview mirror. A little red Honda was pulling over into the lane to my right. It was Jonah, apparently heading home just as I was. He made a cranking motion. I leaned over and rolled the window down on the passenger side.

"Can I buy you a drink?"

"Sure. Where?"

He pointed at the Crow's Nest to his right, a restaurant with exterior lights still burning. The light

changed and he took off. I followed, pulling into the lot
behind him. We parked side by side. He got out first,
hunching against the rain while he opened an umbrella
and came around to my door. We huddled together and
puddle hopped our way to the front entrance. He held
the door and I ducked inside, holding it for him then
while he lowered the umbrella and gave it a quick shake.

The interior of the Crow's Nest was done in a
halfhearted nautical theme which consisted primarily of
fishing nets and rigging draped along the rafters and
mariner's charts sealed into the table tops under a half-
inch of polyurethane. The restaurant section was closed,
but the bar seemed to be doing all right. I could see
maybe ten tables occupied. The level of conversation
was low and the lighting was discreet, augmented by fat
round jars where candles glowed through orange glass.
Jonah steered us past a small dance floor toward a table
in the corner. The place had an aura of edgy excitement. We were protected by the weather, drawn together like the random souls stranded in an airport
between flights.

The waitress appeared and Jonah glanced at me.

"You decide," I said.

"Two margaritas. Cuervo Gold, Grand Marnier,
shaken, no salt," he said. She nodded and moved off.

"Very impressive," I said.

"I thought you'd like that. What brings you out?"

"Daggett, of course." I filled him in, realizing as I
summed it up that I'd had just about as much of Billy
Polo and his ilk as I could take for one night.

"Let's don't talk about him," I said when I was done.
"Tell me what you're working on."

"Hey, no way. I'm here to relax."

The waitress brought our drinks and we paused
briefly while she dipped neatly, knees together, and

placed a cocktail napkin in front of each of us, along with our drinks. She was dressed like a boatswain except that her high-cut white pants were spandex and her buns hung out the back. I wondered how long uniforms like that would last if the night manager was required to squeeze his hairy fanny into one.

When the waitress left, Jonah touched his glass to mine. "To rainy nights," he said. We drank. The tequila had a little "wow" effect as it went down and I had to pat myself on the chest. Jonah smiled, enjoying my discomfiture.

"What brings you out so late?" I asked.

"Catching up on paperwork. Also, avoiding the house. Camilla's sister came down from Idaho for a week. The two of them are probably drinking wine and carving me up like a roast."

"Her sister doesn't like you, I take it."

"She thinks I'm a dud. Camilla came from money. Deirdre doesn't think either one of them should take up with guys on salary, for God's sake. And a cop? It's all too bourgeois. God, I gotta watch myself here. All I do is complain about life on the home front. I'm beginning to sound like Dempsey."

I smiled. Lieutenant Dempsey had worked Narcotics for years, a miserably married man whose days were spent complaining about his lot. His wife had finally died and he'd turned around and married a woman just like her. He'd taken early retirement and the two of them had gone off in an RV. His postcards to the department were amusing, but left people uncomfortable, like a stand-up comic making mean-spirited jokes at a spouse's expense.

Conversation dwindled. The background music was a tape of old Johnny Mathis tunes and the lyrics suggested an era when falling in love wasn't complicated by herpes, fear of AIDS, multiple marriages, spousal support, feminism, the sexual revolution, the Bomb, the Pill, approval of one's therapist, or the specter of children on alternate weekends.

Jonah was looking good. The combination of shadow and candlelight washed the lines out of his face, and heightened the blue of his eyes. His hair looked very dark and the rain had made it look silkier. He wore a white shirt, opened at the neck, sleeves rolled up, his forearms crosshatched with dark hair. There's usually a current running between us, generated I suppose by whatever primal urges keep the human race reproducing itself. Most of the time, the chemistry is kept in check by a bone-deep caution on my part, ambivalence about his marital status, by circumstance, by his own uneasiness, by the knowledge on both our parts that once certain lines are crossed, there's no going back and no way to predict the consequences.

We ordered a second round of drinks, and then a third. We slow danced, not saying a word. Jonah smelled of soap and his jaw line was smooth and sometimes he hummed with a rumbling I hadn't heard since I sat on my father's lap as a very young child, listening to him read to me before I knew what words meant. I thought about Billy Polo lowering Lovella to the trailer floor. The image was haunting because it spoke so eloquently of his need. I was always such a stoic, so careful not to make mistakes. Sometimes I wonder what the difference is between being cautious and being dead. I thought about rain and how nice it is to sink down on clean sheets. I pulled my head back and Jonah looked down at me quizzically.

"This is all Billy Polo's fault," I said.

He smiled. "What is?"

I studied him for a moment. "What would Camilla do if you didn't come home tonight?"

His smile faded and his eyes got that look. "She's the one who's talking about an open relationship," he said.

I laughed. "I'll bet that applies to her, not you."

"Not anymore," he said.

His kiss seemed familiar.

We left soon afterward.

21

I drove to the office at 9:00. The rain clouds were hunched above the mountains moving north, while above, the sky was the blue white of bleached denim. The city seemed to be in sharp focus, as if seen through new prescription lenses. I opened the French doors and stood on the balcony, raising my arms and doing one of those little butt wiggles so favored by the football set. *That* for you, Camilla Robb, I thought, and then I laughed and went and had a look at myself in the mirror, mugging shamelessly. Amazing Grace. I looked just like myself. Where tears erase the self, good sex transforms and I was feeling energized.

I put the coffee on and got to work, typing up my case notes, detailing the conversations I'd had with Billy and Coral. Cops and private eyes are always caught up in paperwork. Written records have to be kept of everything, with events set out so that anyone who comes along afterward will have a clear and comprehensive résumé of the investigation to that point. Since a private eye also bills for services, I have to keep track of my hours and expenses, submitting statements periodically so I can make sure I get paid. I prefer fieldwork; I suspect we all do. If I'd wanted to spend my days in an office, I'd have studied to be an underwriter for the

insurance company next door. Their work seems boring
80 percent of the time while mine only bores me about
one hour out of every ten.

At 9:30, I touched base with Barbara Daggett by
phone, giving her a verbal update to match the written
account I was putting in the mail to her. The duplication
of effort wasn't really necessary, but I did it anyway.
What the hell, it was her money. She was entitled to the
best service she could get. After that, I did some filing,
then locked up again, taking the green skirt and heels
with me down the back stairs to my car, heading out to
Marilyn Smith's. I was beginning to feel like the prince
in search of Cinderella, shoe in hand.

I took the highway north, driving in the newly
washed air. Colgate is only a fifteen-minute drive, but it
gave me a chance to think about events of the night
before. Jonah had turned out to be a clown in bed . . .
funny and inventive. We'd behaved like bad kids, eating
snacks, telling ghost stories, returning now and then to a
lovemaking which was, at the same time, intense and
comfortable. I wondered if I'd known him in another
life. I wondered if I'd know him again. He was so
generous and affectionate, so amazed at being with
someone who didn't criticize or withhold, who didn't
withdraw from his touch as though from a slug's. I
couldn't imagine where we'd go from here and I didn't
want to start worrying. I'm capable of screwing things
up by trying to solve all the problems in advance instead
of simply taking care of issues as they surface.

I missed my off-ramp, of course. I caught sight of it
as I sped by, cursing good-naturedly as I took the next
exit and circled back.

By the time I reached Wayne and Marilyn Smith's
house, it was nearly 10:00. The bicycles that had been
parked on the porch were gone. The orange trees,

though nearly leafless with age, still carried the aura of ripe fruit, a faint perfume spilling out of the surrounding groves. I parked my car in the gravel drive behind a compact station wagon I assumed belonged to her. A peek into the rear, as I passed, revealed a gummy detritus of fast-food containers, softball equipment, school papers, and dog hair.

I cranked the bell. The entrance hall was deserted, but a golden retriever bounded toward the front door, toenails ticking against the bare floors as it skittered to a stop, barking joyfully. The dog's entire body waggled like a fish on a hook.

"Can I help you?"

Startled, I glanced to my right. Marilyn Smith was standing at the bottom of the porch steps in a tee shirt, drenched jeans, and a straw hat. She wore goatskin gardening gloves and bright yellow plastic clogs that were spattered with mud. When she realized it was me, her expression changed from pleasant inquiry to a barely disguised distaste.

"I'm working in the garden," she said, as if I hadn't guessed. "If you want to talk you'll have to come out there."

I followed her across the rain-saturated lawn. She tapped a muddy trowel against her thigh, distractedly.

"I saw you at the funeral," I remarked.

"Wayne insisted," she said tersely, then looked over her shoulder at me. "Who was the drunk woman? I liked her."

"Lovella Daggett. She thought she was married to him, but it turned out the warranty hadn't run out on his first wife."

When we reached the vegetable patch, she waded between two dripping rows of vines. The garden was in its winter phase—broccoli, cauliflower, dark squashes tucked into a spray of wide leaves. She'd been weeding. I could see the trampled-looking spikes scattered here and there. Farther down the row, there was evidence that the earth had been turned, heavy clods piled up near a shallow excavation site.

"Too wet for weeding, isn't it?"

"The soil here has a high clay content. Once it dries out, it's impossible," she said.

She shucked the gardening gloves and began to tear widths from an old pillow case, tying back the masses of sweet pea plants that had drooped in the rain. The strips of white rag contrasted brightly with the lime green of the plants. I held up the skirt and shoes I'd brought.

"Recognize these?"

She scarcely looked at the articles, but the chilly smile appeared. "Is that what the killer wore?"

"Could be."

"You've made progress since I saw you last. Three days ago, you weren't even certain it was murder."

"That's how I earn my pay," I said.

"Maybe Lovella killed him when she found out he was a bigamist."

"Always possible," I said, "though you still haven't said for sure where you were that night."

"Oh, but I did. I was here. Wayne was at the office and neither of us has corroborating witnesses." She was using that bantering tone again, mild and mocking.

"I'd like to talk to him."

"Make an appointment. He's in the book. Go down to the office. The Granger Building on State."

"Marilyn, I'm not your enemy."

"You are if I killed him," she replied.

"Ah, yes. In that case, I would be."

She tore off another strip of pillow case, the width

of cotton dangling from her hand like something limp with death. "Sounds like you have suspects. Too bad you're short on proof."

"But I do have someone who saw her and that should help, don't you think? This is just preliminary work, narrowing the field," I said. It was bullshit, of course. I wasn't sure the motel clerk could identify anybody in the dark.

Her smile dimmed by a watt. "I don't want to talk to you anymore," she whispered.

I raised my hands, as if she'd pulled a gun. "I'm gone," I said, "but I have to warn you, I'm persistent. You'll find it unsettling, I suspect."

I kept my eyes on her as I moved away. I'd seen the muddy hoe she was using and I thought it best not to turn my back.

I cruised by the Westfalls on my way into town. I was going to have to show the skirt to Barbara Daggett at some point, but the Close was on my way. The low fieldstone wall surrounding the place was still a dark gray from the passing rain. I drove through the gates and parked along the road as I had before, pulling over into dense ivy. By day, the eight Victorian houses were enveloped in shade, sunlight scarcely penetrating the branches of the trees. I locked the car and picked my way up the path to the front steps. In the yard, the trunks of the live oak were frosted with a fungus as green as the oxidized copper on a roof. Tall palms punctuated the corners of the house. The air felt cool and moist in the wake of the storm.

The front door was ajar. The view from the hallway was a straight shot through to the kitchen and I could see that the back door was open too, the screen door unlatched. A portable radio sat on the counter and music blasted out, the *1812 Overture*. I rang the bell, but the sound was lost against the booming of cannons as the last movement rose to a thunder pitch.

I left the front porch and walked around to the back, peering in. Like the rest of the house, the kitchen had been redone, the owners opting here to modernize, though the Victorian character had been retained. There was a small floral print paper on the walls, lots of wicker, oak, and fern. The cabinet doors had been replaced with leaded glass, but the appliances were all strictly up-to-date.

There was no one in the room. A door on the left was open, the oblong of shadow suggesting that the basement stairs must be located just beyond. Two brown grocery bags sat on the kitchen table and it looked like someone had been interrupted in the course of unloading them. There was an electric percolator plugged into the outlet on the stove. While I was watching, the ready-light went on. Belatedly, I picked up the smell of hot coffee.

The music ended and the FM announcer made his concluding remarks about the piece, then introduced a Brahms concerto in E minor. I knocked on the frame of the screen door, hoping someone would hear me before the music started up again. Ramona appeared from the depths of the basement. She was wearing a six-gore wool skirt in a muted gray plaid, with a line of dark maroon running through it. Her pullover sweater was dark maroon, with a white blouse under it, the collar pinned sedately at the throat by an antique brooch. For effect, I decided not to mention the heels and wool skirt I'd brought.

"Tony?" she said. "Oh, it's you."

She had an armload of ragged blue bath towels which she dumped on a chair. "I thought I heard someone knock. I couldn't see who it was through the

screen." She turned the radio off as she passed and then
she opened the screen door to admit me.

"Tony's bringing groceries in from the garage. We
just got back from the market. Have a seat. Would you
like a cup of coffee? The pot's fresh."

"Yes, please. That's nice." I moved the pile of rags
out of the chair and sat down, putting the skirt and
shoes on the table in front of me. I saw her eyes stray to
them, but she made no comment.

"Isn't this a school day for him?" I asked.

"They're giving the sophomores some sort of ac-
ademic placement tests. He finished early so they let him
go. He's got an appointment with his therapist shortly
anyway."

I watched her move about the kitchen, fetching
cups and saucers. She had one of those hairstyles that
settle into perfect shape with a flick of the head. I
butcher my own at six-week intervals with a pair of nail
scissors and a two-way mirror, causing salon stylists to
pale when they see me. "Who *did* that to you?" they
always ask. I wanted perfect waves like hers, but I didn't
think I could achieve the effect.

Ramona poured two cups of coffee. "There's something I probably should have mentioned before," she
said. She took a ceramic pitcher from the cupboard and
filled it with milk, realizing then that I was waiting for
her to continue. Her smile was thin. "John Daggett
called here Monday night, asking to talk to Tony. I took
his number, but Ferrin and I decided it wasn't a good
idea. It might not matter much at this point, but I
thought you should be aware."

"What made you think of it?"

She hesitated. "I came across the number on the
pad by the phone. I'd forgotten all about it."

I could feel a tingle at the back of my neck—that

clammy feeling you get when your body overloads on sugar. Something was off here, but I wasn't sure what it was.

"Why bring it up now?" I asked.

"I thought you were tracking his activities early in the week."

"I wasn't aware that I'd told you that."

Her cheeks tinted. "Marilyn Smith called me. She mentioned it."

"How'd Daggett know where to reach you? When I talked to him on Saturday, he had no idea where Tony was and he certainly didn't have your name or number."

"I don't know how he got it," she said. "What difference does it make?"

"How do I know you didn't make a date to meet him Friday night?"

"Why would I do that?" she said.

I stared at her. A millisecond later she realized what I was getting at.

"But I was here Friday night."

"I haven't heard that verified so far."

"That's ridiculous! Ask Tony. He knows I was here. You can check it out yourself."

"I intend to," I said.

Tony thumped up the wooden porch steps, armed with two more grocery bags, his attention diverted as he groped for the screen door handle, missing twice. "Aunt Ramona, can you give me a hand with this?"

She crossed to the door and held it open. Tony spotted me and the green skirt at just about the same time and I saw his gaze jump to his aunt's face quizzically. Her expression was neutral, but she busied herself right away, pushing canned goods aside so he could set one bag on the table top. The second bag she took herself and placed on the counter. She sorted through and lifted out a carton of ice cream. "I better get this put away," she murmured. She crossed to the freezer.

"What are you doing here?" Tony said to me.

"I was curious how you were feeling. Your aunt mentioned that you had a migraine Monday night."

"I feel okay."

"What'd you think about the funeral?"

"Bunch of freaks," he said.

"Let's get these unloaded, dear," his aunt said. The two of them began to put groceries away while I sipped my coffee. I couldn't tell if she was deliberately distracting him or not, but that was the effect.

"You need some help?" I asked.

"We can manage," she murmured.

"Who was that lady who went nuts?" Tony asked. Lovella had made a big impression on everyone.

Ramona held up a soft drink in a big plastic bottle. "Stick this in the refrigerator while you're there," she said.

She released the bottle an instant before he'd gotten a good grip on it and he had to scramble to catch it before it toppled to the floor. Had she done that deliberately? He was waiting for my reply so I gave him a brief rendition of the tale. It was gossip, in some ways, but he was as animated as I'd seen him and I hoped to keep his attention.

"I don't mean to interrupt, but Tony does have homework to take care of. Finish your coffee, of course," she said. Her tone suggested that I suck it right down and scram.

"I'm due back at the office anyway," I said, getting up. I looked at Tony. "Could you walk me to my car?"

He glanced at Ramona, whose gaze dropped away from his. She didn't protest. He ducked his head in assent.

He held the door for me while I gathered the skirt and shoes and turned back to her. "I nearly forgot. Are these yours, by any chance?"

"I'm sure not," she said to me, and then to him, "Don't be long."

He looked like he was on the verge of saying something, but he shrugged instead. He followed me out on the porch and down the steps. I led the way as we circled the house. The path to the street was paved with stepping-stones spaced oddly, so that I had to watch my feet to gauge the distances.

"I have a question," I said as we reached the car.

He was watching me warily by then, interested but on guard.

"I was curious about the migraine you had Friday night. Do you remember how long that one lasted?"

"Friday night?" His voice had a croak in it from surprise.

"That's right. Didn't you have a migraine that night?"

"I guess."

"Think back," I said. "Take your time."

He seemed uncomfortable, casting about for some visual clue. I'd seen him do this before, reading body language so he could adjust his response to whatever was expected of him. I waited in silence, letting his anxiety accumulate.

"I think that's the day I got one. When I came home from school," he said, "but then it cleared."

"What time was that?"

"Real late. After midnight. Maybe two . . . two-thirty, something like that."

"How'd you happen to notice the time?"

"Aunt Ramona made me a couple of sandwiches in the kitchen. It was a real bad headache and I'd been throwing up for hours so I never had dinner. I was starving. I must have looked at the kitchen clock."

"What kind of sandwiches?"

"What?"

"I was wondering what kind she made."

His gaze hung on mine. The seconds ticked away. "Meatloaf," he said.

"Thanks," I said. "That helps."

I opened the VW on the driver's side, tossing skirt and shoes on the passenger seat as I got in. His version was roughly the same as his aunt's, but I could have sworn the "meatloaf" was a wild guess.

I started the car and did a U-turn, heading toward the gates. I caught a glimpse of him in the rearview mirror, already moving toward the house.

22

It's a fact of life that when a case won't break, you have to go through the motions anyway, stirring up the waters, rattling all the cages at the zoo. To that end, on my way into town I did a long detour that included a stop at the trailer park, in hopes that Lovella would still be there. It was obvious to me, as I'm not a fool, that toting a green wool skirt and a pair of black suede heels all over town was a pointless enterprise. No one was going to claim them and if someone did, so what? The articles proved nothing. No one was going to break down sobbing and confess at the mere sight of them. The pop quiz was simply my way of putting them all on notice, making the rounds one more time to announce that I was still on the job and making progress, however insignificant it might appear.

I knocked at the trailer door, but got no response. I jotted a note on the back of a business card, indicating that Lovella should call. I tucked it in the doorjamb, went back to my car, and headed for town.

Wayne Smith's office was located on the seventh floor of the Granger Building in downtown Santa Teresa. Aside from the clock tower on the courthouse, the Granger is just about the only structure on State Street that's more than two stories high. Part of the charm of the downtown area is its low-slung look. The flavor, for the most part, is Spanish. Even the trash containers are faced with stucco and rimmed with decorative tile. The telephone booths look like small adobe huts and if you can ignore the fact that the bums use them for urinals, the effect is quaint. There are flowering shrubs along the walk, jacaranda trees, and palms. Low ornamental stucco walls widen in places to form benches for weary shoppers. Everything is clean, well kept, pleasing to the eye.

The Granger Building looks just like hundreds of office buildings constructed in the twenties—yellow brick, symmetrical narrow windows banded with granite friezes, topped by a steeply pitched roof with matching gables. Along the roofline, just below the cornice, there are decorative marble torches affixed to the wall with inexplicable half shells mounted underneath. The style is an anomaly in this town, falling as it does between the Spanish, the Victorian, and the pointless. Still, the building is a landmark, housing a movie theater, a jeweler's, and seven stories of office space.

I checked the wall directory in the marble foyer for Wayne Smith's suite number, which turned out to be 702. Two elevators serviced the building and one was out of order, the doors standing open, the housing mechanism in plain view. It's not a good idea to scrutinize such things. When you see how elevators actually work, you realize how improbable the whole scheme is . . . raising and lowering a roomful of people on a few long wires. Ridiculous.

A fellow in coveralls stood there, mopping his face with a red bandanna.

"How's it going?" I asked, while I waited for the other elevator doors to open.

He shook his head. "Always something, isn't it? Last week it was that one wouldn't work."

The doors slid open and I stepped in, pressing seven. The doors closed and nothing happened for a

while. Finally, with a jolt, the elevator began its ascent,
stopping at the seventh floor. There was another inter-
minable delay. I pressed the "DOOR OPEN" button. No
dice. I tried to guess how long I could survive on just
that one ratty piece of chewing gum at the bottom of my
handbag. I banged the button with the flat of my hand
and the doors slid open.

The corridor was narrow and dimly illuminated, as
there was only one exterior window, located at the far
end of the hall. Four dark, wood-paneled doors opened
off each side, with the names of the professional tenants
in gold-leaf lettering that looked as if it had been there
since the building went up. There was no activity that I
could perceive, no sounds, no muffled telephones ringing. Wayne Smith, C.P.A., was the first door on the right.
I pictured a receptionist in a small waiting area, so I
simply turned the knob and walked in without knocking. There was only one large room, tawny daylight
filtering in through drawn window shades. Wayne Smith
was lying on the floor with his legs propped up on the
seat of his swivel chair. He turned and looked at me.

"Oh sorry! I thought there'd be a waiting room," I
said. "Are you okay?"

"Sure. Come on in," he said. "I was resting my
back." He removed his legs from the chair, apparently in
some pain. He rolled over on his side and eased himself
into an upright position, wincing as he did. "You're
Kinsey Millhone. Marilyn pointed you out at the funeral
yesterday."

I watched him, wondering if I should lend him a
hand. "What'd you do to yourself?"

"My back went out on me. Hurts like a son of a
bitch," he said. Once he was on his feet, he dug a fist into
the small of his back, twisting one shoulder slightly as if
to ease a cramp. He had a runner's body—lean, stringy
muscles, narrow through the chest. He looked older
than his wife, maybe late forties while I pegged her in

her early thirties. His hair was light, worn in a crewcut, like something out of a 1950s high school annual. I wondered if he'd been in the military at some point. The hairstyle suggested that he was hung up in the past, his persona fixed perhaps by some significant event. His eyes were pale and his face was very lined. He moved to the windows and raised all three shades. The room became unbearably bright.

"Have a seat," he said.

I had a choice between a daybed and a molded plastic chair with a bucket seat. I took the chair, doing a surreptitious visual survey while he lowered himself into his swivel chair as though into a steaming sitz bath. He had six metal bookcases that looked like they were made of Erector sets, loosely bolted and sagging slightly from the weight of all the manuals. Brown accordion file cases were stacked up everywhere, his desk top virtually invisible. Correspondence was piled on the floor near his chair, government pamphlets and tax law updates stacked on the window sill. This was not a man you'd want to depend on if you were facing an I.R.S. audit. He looked like the sort who might put you there.

"I just talked to Marilyn. She said you came by the house. We're puzzled by your interest in us."

"Barbara Daggett hired me to investigate her father's death. I'm interested in everyone."

"But why talk to us? We haven't seen the man in years."

"He didn't get in touch last week?"

"Why would he do that?"

"He was looking for Tony Gahan. I thought he might have tried to get a line on him through you."

The phone rang and he reached for it, conducting a business-related conversation while I studied him. He wore chinos, just a wee bit too short, and his socks were the clinging nylon sort that probably went up to his knees. He switched to his good-bye tone, trying to close out his conversation. "Uh-huh, uh-huh. Okay, great. That's fine. We'll do that. I got the forms right here. Deadline is the end of the month. Swell."

He hung up with an exasperated shake of his head.

"Anyway," he said, as a way of getting back to the subject at hand.

"Yeah, right. Anyway," I said, "I don't suppose you remember where you were Friday night."

"I was here, doing quarterly reports."

"And Marilyn was home with the kids?"

He sat and stared at me, a smile flickering off and on. "Are you implying that we might have had a hand in John Daggett's death?"

"Someone did," I said.

He laughed, running a hand across his crewcut as if checking to see if he needed a trim. "Miss Millhone, you've got a hell of a nerve," he said. "The newscast said it was an accident."

I smiled. "The cops still think so. I disagree. I think a lot of people wanted Daggett dead. You and Marilyn are among them."

"But we wouldn't do a thing like that. You can't be serious. I despised the man, no doubt about that, but we're not going to go out and track a man down and kill him. Good God."

I kept my tone light. "But you did have the motive and you had the opportunity."

"You can't hang anything on that. We're decent people. We don't even get parking tickets. John Daggett must have had a lot of enemies."

I shrugged by way of agreement. "The Westfalls," I said. "Billy Polo and his sister, Coral. Apparently, some prison thugs."

"What about that woman who set up such a howl at the funeral?" he said. "She looked like a pretty good candidate to me."

"I've talked to her."

"Well, you better go back and talk to her again. You're wasting time with us. Nobody's going to be arrested on the basis of 'motive' and 'opportunity.'"

"Then you don't have anything to worry about."

He shook his head, his skepticism evident. "Well. I can see you have your work cut out for you. I'd appreciate it if you'd lay off Marilyn in this. She's had trouble enough."

"I gathered as much." I got up. "Thanks for your time. I hope I won't have to bother you again." I moved toward the door.

"I hope so too."

"You know, if you did kill him, or if you know who killed him, I'll find out. Another few days and I'm going to the cops anyway. They'll scrutinize that alibi of yours like you wouldn't believe."

He held his hands out, palms up. "We're innocent until proven otherwise," he said, smiling boyishly.

23

Waiting for the elevator, I replayed the conversation, trying to figure out what I'd missed. On the surface, there was nothing wrong with his response, but I felt irritated and uneasy, maybe just because I wasn't getting anyplace. I banged on the DOWN button. "Come on," I said. The elevator door opened partway. Impatiently, I shoved it back and got on. The doors closed and the elevator descended one floor before it stopped again. The doors opened. Tony Gahan was standing in the corridor, a shopping bag in hand. He seemed as surprised to see me as I was to see him.

"What are you doing here?" he said. He got on the elevator and we descended.

"I had to see someone upstairs," I said. "What about you?"

"A shrink appointment. He's been out of town and now his return flight was delayed. His secretary's supposed to pick him up in an hour so she said to come back at five."

We reached the lobby.

"How are you getting home? Need a ride?" I asked.

He shook his head. "I'm going to hang around down here." He gestured vaguely at the video arcade across the street where some high school kids were horsing around.

"See you later then," I said.

We parted company and I returned to the parking lot behind the building. I got in my car and circled the four blocks to the lot behind my office where I parked. For the time being, I left the skirt and shoes in the backseat.

There were no messages on my answering machine, but the mail was in and I sorted through that, wondering what else to do with myself. Actually, I realized I was exhausted, the emotional charge from Jonah having drained away. I'm not used to drinking that much, for starters, and I tend, being single, to get a lot more sleep. He'd left at 5:00, before it was light, and I'd managed maybe an hour's worth of shut-eye before I'd finally gotten up, jogged, showered, and fixed myself a bite to eat.

I tilted back in my swivel chair and propped my feet up on the desk, hoping no one would begrudge me a snooze. The next time I was aware of anything, the clock hands had dissolved magically from 12:10 to 2:50 and my head was pounding. I staggered to my feet and trotted down the hall to the ladies' room. I peed, washed my hands and face, rinsed my mouth out, and stared at myself in the mirror. My hair was mashed flat in the back and standing straight up everywhere else. The flourescent light in the room made my skin look sickly. Was this the consequence of illicit sex with a married man? "Well, I soitonly hope so," I said. I ducked my head under the faucet and then dried my hair with eight rounds of hot air from a wall-mounted machine that had been installed (the sign said) to help protect me from the dangers of diseases that might be transmitted through paper towel litter. Idly, I wondered what diseases they were worried about. Typhus? Diphtheria?

I could hear my office phone from halfway down the hall and I started to run. I snagged it on the sixth ring, snatching up the receiver with a winded hello.

"This is Lovella," the glum voice said. "I got this note to call you."

I took a deep breath, inventing as I went along. "Right," I said. "I thought we should touch base. We really haven't talked since I saw you in L.A." I sidled around my desk and sat down, still trying to catch my breath.

"I'm mad at you, Kinsey," she said. "Why didn't you tell me you had Daggett's money?"

"To what end? I had a cashier's check, but it wasn't made out to you. So why mention it?"

"Because I'm standing around telling you I'm married to a guy who'd just as soon kill me as look at me and you're telling me to call the rape crisis center, some bullshit like that. And all the time, Daggett had thousands of dollars."

"But he stole the money. Didn't Billy tell you that?"

"I don't care where it came from. I'd just like to have a little something for myself. Now he's dead and she gets everything."

"Who, Essie?"

"Her and that daughter."

"Oh come on, Lovella. He couldn't have left them enough to worry about."

"More than he left me," she said. "If I'd known about the money, I might have talked him out of some."

"Yeah, right. As generous as he was," I said drily. "If you'd gotten your hands on it, you might be dead now instead of him. Unless Billy's been lying to me about the punks from San Luis who were after him." I'd never really taken that story seriously, but maybe it was time I did.

She was silent. I could practically hear her shifting gears. "All I know is I think you're a shit and he was too."

"I'm sorry you feel that way, Lovella. John hired me, and my first loyalty was to him . . . misguided, as it

turned out, but that's where I was coming from. You
want to vent a little more on the subject before we turn
to something else?"

"Yeah. I should have got the money, not someone
else. I was the one who got banged around. I still got two
cracked ribs and an eye looks like it's all sunk in on one
side from the bruise."

"Is that why you freaked out at the funeral?"

Her tone of voice became tempered with sheepish-
ness. "I'm sorry I did that, but I couldn't help myself. I'd
been sittin' in some bar drinkin' Bloody Marys since ten
o'clock and I guess I got outta hand. But it bugged me,
all that Bible talk. Daggett never went to church a day in
his life and it didn't seem right. And that old fat-ass
claimed she was married to him? I couldn't believe my
eyes. She looked like a bulldog."

I had to laugh. "Maybe he didn't marry her for her
looks," I said.

"Well, I hope not."

"When did you see him last?"

"At the funeral home, where else?"

"Before that, I mean."

"Day he left L.A.," she said. "Week ago Monday. I
never saw him after he took off."

"I thought maybe you hopped a bus on Thursday
after I left."

"Well, I didn't."

"But you could have, couldn't you?"

"What for? I didn't even know where he went."

"But Billy did. You could have come up to Coral's
last week. You might have met him at the Hub Friday
night and bought him a couple of drinks."

Her laugh was sour. "You can't pin that on me. If
that was me, how come Coral didn't recognize me, huh?"

"For all I know, she did. You're friends. Maybe she
just kept her mouth shut."

"Why would she do that?"

"Maybe she wanted to help you out."

"Coral doesn't even like me. She thinks I'm a slut so why would she help me?"

"She might've had reasons of her own."

"I didn't kill him, Kinsey, if that's what you're getting at."

"That's what everyone says. You're all wide-eyed and innocent. Daggett was murdered and nobody's guilty. Amazing."

"You don't have to take my word for it. Ask Billy. Once he gets back, he can tell you who it was for sure, anyway."

"Oh hey, sounds great. How's he going to manage that?"

There was a pause, as if she'd said something she really wasn't authorized to say. "He thought he recognized somebody at the funeral and then he figured out where he'd seen 'em before," she said reluctantly.

I blinked at the telephone receiver. In a quick flash, I remembered Billy's staring at the little group formed by the Westfalls, Barbara Daggett, and the Smiths. "I don't understand. What's he up to?"

"He set up a meeting," she said. "He wants to find out if his theory's right and then he said he'd call you."

"He's going to *meet* with her?"

"That's what I said, isn't it?"

"He shouldn't be doing that by himself. Why didn't he notify the police?"

"Because he doesn't want to make a fool of himself in front of them. Suppose he's wrong? He doesn't have any proof, anyway. Just a hunch is all and even that's not a hundred percent."

"Do you have any idea who he was talking about?"

"Uh-uh. He wouldn't tell, but he was pretty happy with himself. He said we might get some money after all."

Oh God, I thought, not blackmail. I could feel my

heart sink. Billy Polo wasn't smart enough to pull that off. He'd blow it like he did every other crime he tried. "Where's the meeting taking place?"

"What makes you ask?" she said, turning cagey.

"Because I want to go!"

"I don't think I should tell."

"Lovella, don't do this to me."

"Well, he didn't say I could."

"You've told me this much. Why not the rest? He could be in trouble."

She hesitated, mulling it over. "Down at the beach somewhere. He's not dumb, you know. He made sure it was public. He figured in broad daylight, there wouldn't be any problem, especially with other people around."

"Which beach?"

"What if he gets mad at me?"

"I'll square it with him myself," I said. "I will *swear* I forced the information out of you."

"He's not going to like it if you show up and spoil everything."

"I won't spoil it. I'll lurk in the background and make sure he's okay. That's all I'm talking about."

Silence. She was so slow I thought I'd scream. "Look at it this way," I said. "He might be happy for the help. What if he needs backup?"

"Billy wouldn't need back up from a *woman*."

I closed my eyes, trying to keep my temper in check. "Just give me a hint, Lovella, or I'll come over to the trailer and rip your heart out by the roots." That, she heard.

"You better never tell him I told," she warned.

"Cross my heart and hope to die. Now come on."

"I think it's that parking lot near the boat launch. . . ."

I banged the phone down and snagged my hand-bag. I locked the office in haste and ran down the hall, going down the back stairs two and three at a time. I'd

had to park my car at the far end of the lot and once I
got to the pay booth, there were three other cars in front
of mine. "Come on, come on," I murmured, banging on
the steering wheel.

Finally, it was my turn. I showed the attendant my
parking permit and shot through the gate as soon as the
bar went up.

Chapel is one way, heading up from the beach, so I
had to turn right, take a left, and hit the one-way street
going down again. I caught the light wrong at 101 so
that delayed me. I didn't want to miss this one. I didn't
want to show up two minutes late and miss the only
chance I might have. I pictured a citizen's arrest . . .
me and Billy Polo saving the day.

The light turned green and I crossed the highway.
Two blocks more and I reached Cabana where I took a
right turn. The entrance to the lot I wanted was all the
way around the bend near Santa Teresa City College. I
got a ticket from the machine and threaded my way
along the perimeter of the lot. I scanned the parked
cars, hoping for a glimpse of Billy's white Chevy. The
marina was on my right, the sun reflecting starkly from
the white sails of a stately boat as it glided out of the
harbor. The boat launch itself was at the very end of the
parking lot, through a second parking gate. I pulled a
second ticket and the arm went up. I found a slot and
left my car, proceeding on foot.

Four joggers passed me. There were people on the
boat dock, people on the walk, people by the snack shop
and the public restrooms. I broke into a trot, searching
the landscape ahead of me for some sign of Billy or the
blonde. I heard three hollow pops in quick succession
dead ahead. I ran. No one else was reacting, but I could
have sworn it was the sound of shots.

I reached the boat launch, where the parking lot
slants down into the water. There was no one in sight.
No one running, no one leaving the scene in haste. The

air was still, the water lapping softly at the asphalt. Two
pontoon piers extend into the water about thirty feet,
but both were empty, no boats or pedestrians in sight. I
did a three-sixty turn, surveying every foot of the area.
And then I spotted him. He was lying on his side by a
boat trailer, one arm caught under him awkwardly. He
struggled, gasping, and turned himself over on his back.
I crossed the macadam rapidly.

A man in cutoffs had come out of a snack shop and
he peered at me as I went past. "Is that guy okay?"

"Call the cops. Get an ambulance," I snapped.

I knelt beside Billy, angling so he could see me. "It's
me," I said. "Don't panic. You'll be fine. We'll have help
here in a second."

Billy's eyes strayed to mine. His face was gray and
there was a widening puddle of quite red blood spreading out under him. I took his hand and held it. A crowd
was beginning to collect, people running from all
directions. I could hear them buzzing at my back.

Somebody handed me a beach towel. "You want to
cover him with this?"

I grabbed the towel. I let go of him long enough to
unbutton his shirt, opening it so I could see what I was
dealing with. There was a hole in his belly. He must have
been shot from behind, because what I was looking at
was an exit wound, ragged, welling with blood. The slug
must have severed the abdominal aorta. A coil of his
lower intestine was visible, gray and glistening, bulging
through the hole. I could feel my hands start to shake,
but I kept my expression neutral. He was watching me,
trying to read my face. I made a pad of the towel,
pressing it against the wound to staunch the flow of
blood.

He groaned, breathing rapidly. He had one hand
resting on his chest and his fingers fluttered. I took his
hand again, squeezing hard.

He tilted his head. "Where's . . . my leg? I can't feel nothin' down there."

I glanced down at his right knee. The pantleg looked like it had caught on a nail. Blood and bone seemed to blossom through the tear.

"Don't sweat it. They can fix that. You'll be fine," I said. I didn't mention the blood soaking through the towel. I thought he probably knew about that.

"I'm gut-shot."

"I know. Relax. It's not bad. The ambulance is on its way."

The hand I held was icy, his fingers pale. There were questions I should have asked, but I didn't. I couldn't. You don't intrude on someone's dying with a bullshit interrogation like you're some kind of pro. This was just me and him and nothing else entered into it.

I studied his face, sending love through my eyes, willing him to live. His hair looked curlier than I remembered it. With my free hand, I moved it away from his forehead. Sweat beaded on his upper lip.

"I'm goin' . . . I can feel myself goin' out . . ." He clutched my hand convulsively, bucking against a surge of pain.

"Take it easy. You'll be fine."

He began to hyperventilate and then his struggle subsided. I could see the life drain away, see it all fade— color, energy, awareness, pain. Death comes in a gathering cloud that settles like a veil. Billy Polo sighed, his gaze still pinned on my face. His hand relaxed in mine, but I held on.

24

I sat on the curb near the snack shop and stared at the asphalt. The proprietor had brought me a can of Coke and I held the cold metal against my temple. I felt sick, but there wasn't anything wrong with me. Lieutenant Feldman had appeared and he was hunkered over Billy's body, talking to the lab guys, who were bagging his hands. The ambulance had backed around and waited with its doors open, as if to shield the body from the public view. Two black-and-whites were parked nearby, radios providing a squawking counterpoint to the murmurs of the gathering crowd. Violent death is a spectator sport and I could hear them trading comments about the way the final quarter had been played. They weren't being cruel, just curious. Maybe it was good for them to see how grotesque homicide really is.

The beat officers, Gutierrez and Pettigrew, had arrived within minutes of Billy's demise and they'd radioed for the CSI unit. The two of them would probably drive over to the trailer park to break the news to Coral and Lovella. I felt I should ride along, but I couldn't bring myself to volunteer yet. I'd go, but for the moment, I was having trouble coping with the fact of Billy's death. It had happened so fast. It was so irrevocable. I found it hard to accept that we couldn't rewind the tape and play the last fifteen minutes differently. I would arrive earlier. I would warn him off and he could walk away unharmed. He'd tell me his theory and then I'd buy him the beer I'd promised him that first night at the Hub.

Feldman appeared. I found myself staring at his pantlegs, unable to look up. He lit a cigarette and came down to my level, perching on the curb. I hugged my knees, feeling numb. I barely know the man, but what I've seen of him I've always liked. He looks like a cross between a Jew and an Indian—a large flat face, high cheekbones, a big hooked nose. He's a big man, probably forty-five, with a cop haircut, cop clothes, a deep rumbling voice. "You want to bring me up to speed on this?" he said.

It was the act of opening my mouth to speak that brought the tears. I held myself in check, willing them back. I shook my head, struggling with the nearly overwhelming rush of regret. He handed me a handkerchief and I pressed it to my eyes, then folded it, addressing my remarks to the oblong of white cotton. There was an "F" embroidered in one corner with a thread coming loose.

"Sorry," I murmured.

"That's okay. Take your time."

"He was such a screw-up," I said. "I guess that's what gets me. He thought he was so smart and so tough."

I paused. "I guess you never know which people will affect your life," I said.

"He never said who shot him?"

I shook my head. "I didn't ask. I didn't want the last minutes of his life taken up with that stuff. I'm sorry."

"Well, he might not have said anyway. What was the setup?"

I started talking, saying anything that came to mind. He let me ramble till I finally took control of myself and began to lay it out systematically. After

hundreds of reports, I know the drill. I cited chapter
and verse while he nodded, making notes in a battered
black notebook.

When I finished, he tucked his ballpoint pen away
and shoved the notebook back into the inside pocket of
his suitcoat. He got up and I rose with him, automatically.

"What next?" I asked.

"Actually, I got Daggett's file sitting on my desk," he
said. "Robb told me you tagged it a homicide and I
thought I'd take a look. We had a double killing, one of
those execution-style shootings, up on the Bluffs late
yesterday and we've had to put a lot of manpower on
that one, so I haven't had a chance as yet. It'd help if you
came down to the station and talked to Lieutenant
Dolan yourself."

"Let me see Billy's sister first," I said. "This is the
second brother she's lost in the whole Daggett mess."

"You don't think there's any chance she's the one
who plugged him?"

I shook my head. "I thought she might connect to
Daggett's death, but I can't picture her involved in this.
Unless I'm missing something big. For one thing, he
wouldn't have to meet her out in public like this. It was
someone at the funeral, I'm almost sure."

"Make a list and we'll take it from there," he said.

I nodded. "I can also stop by the office and make
some copies of my file reports. And Lovella may know
more than she's told us so far." It felt good, turning
everything over to him. He could have it all. Essie and
Lovella and the Smiths.

Pettigrew approached, holding a small plastic Ziploc bag by one corner. In it were three empty brass
casings. "We found these over by that pickup truck.
We're sealing off the whole parking lot until the guys
have a chance to go over it."

I said, "You might check the trash bins. That's

where I found the skirt and shoes after Daggett was killed."

Feldman nodded, then gave the shells a cursory look. "Thirty-twos," he remarked.

I felt a cold arrow shoot up my spine. My mouth went dry. "My thirty-two was stolen from my car a few days ago," I said. "Gutierrez took the report."

"A lot of thirty-twos around, but we'll keep that in mind," Feldman said to me, and then to Pettigrew, "Let's hustle these folk out of here. And be polite."

Pettigrew moved away and Feldman turned to study me. "Are you all right?"

I nodded, wishing I could sit down again, afraid once I did I'd be stuck.

"Anything you want to add before I let you go?"

I closed my eyes for a moment, thinking back. I know the snapping sound a .32 makes when fired and the shots I'd heard weren't like that. "The shots," I said. "They sounded odd to me. Hollow. More like a pop than a bang."

"A silencer?"

"I've never heard one except on TV," I said, sheepishly.

"I'll have the lab take a look at the slugs, though I don't know where anybody'd get a silencer in this town." He made another quick note in his book.

"You can probably order one from the back of a magazine," I said.

"Ain't that the truth."

The photographer was snapping pictures and I could see Feldman's gaze flick in that direction. "Let me tend to this guy. He's new. I want to make sure he covers everything I need."

He excused himself and crossed to Billy's body where he engaged in a conversation with the forensic photographer, using gestures to describe the various angles he wanted.

Maria Gutierrez came up to me. "We're going out to the trailer park. Gerry said you might want to come."

"I'll follow in my car," I said. "You know where it is?"

"We know the park. We can meet you there if you want."

"I'm going to see if Billy's car is here in the lot. I'll be along shortly, but don't wait on my account."

"Right," she said.

I watched them pull out and then I worked my way through the lot, checking the vehicles in the area adjacent to the boat launch. I spotted the Chevy three rows from the entrance, tucked between two RV's. The temporary sticker was still on the windshield. The windows were down. I stuck my head in without touching anything. The car looked clean to me. Nothing in the front seat. Nothing in the back. I went around to the passenger window and peered in, checking the floorboards from that side. I don't even know what I was hoping for. A hint, some suggestion of where we might go from here. It looked as if Feldman might initiate a formal investigation after all, and glad as I was to turn it over to him, I still couldn't quite let go.

I stopped by my car and picked up the skirt and shoes, which I handed over to Lieutenant Feldman. I told him where to find Billy's car and then I finally got back in mine and took off. In my heart, I knew I'd been stalling to allow Pettigrew and Gutierrez a chance to deliver the news of Billy's death. That has to be the worst moment in anybody's life, finding two uniformed cops at your door, their expressions somber, voices grave.

By the time I got to the trailer park, the word had apparently spread. By some telepathic process, people were collecting in twos and threes, all staring at the trailer uncomfortably, chatting in low tones. The trailer door was closed and I heard nothing as I approached, but my appearance had generated conversation at my back.

A fellow stepped forward. "You a family friend? Because she's had bad news. I wasn't sure if you were aware," he said.

"I was there," I said. "She knows me. How long ago did the officers leave?"

"Two minutes. They were real good about it . . . talked to her a long time, making sure she was all right. I'm Fritzy Roderick. I manage the park," he said, offering me his hand.

"Kinsey Millhone," I said. "Is anybody with her now?"

"I don't believe so, and we haven't heard a peep. We were just talking among ourselves here . . . the neighbors and all . . . wondering if someone ought to sit with her."

"Is Lovella in there?"

"I don't know the name. Is she a relative?"

"Billy's ex-girlfriend," I said. "Let me see if I can find out what's going on. If she needs anything, I'll let you know."

"I'd appreciate that. We'd like to help any way we can."

I knocked at the trailer door, uncertain what to expect. Coral opened it a crack and when she saw it was me, she let me in. Her eyes were reddened, but she seemed in control. She sat down on a kitchen chair and picked up her cigarette, giving the ash a flick. I sat down on the banquette.

"I'm sorry about Billy," I said.

She glanced at me briefly. "Did he know?"

"I think so. When I found him, he was already in shock and fading fast. I don't think he suffered much if that's what you're asking."

"I'll have to tell Mom. The two cops who came said they'd do it, but I said no." Her voice trailed off, hoarse from grief or the head cold. "He always knew he'd die young, you know? Like when we'd see old people on the street, crippled or feeble. He said he'd never end up like them. I used to beg him to straighten up his act, but he had to do everything his way." She lapsed into silence.

"Where's Lovella?"

"I don't know," Coral said. "The trailer was empty when I got here."

"Coral, I wish you'd fill me in. I need to know what was going on. Billy told me three different versions of the same tale."

"Why look at me? I don't know anything."

"But you know more than I do."

"That wouldn't take much."

"Level with me. Please. Billy's dead now. There's nothing left to protect. Is there?"

She stared at the floor for a moment and then she sighed and stubbed out her cigarette. She got up and started clearing the table, running water in the tiny stainless steel kitchen sink. She squirted in Ivory Liquid, dropping silverware and plates into the mounting suds, talking in a low monotone as she worked. "Billy was already up at San Luis when Daggett got there. Daggett had no idea Doug was related to us, so Billy struck up an acquaintance. We were both of us bitter as hell."

"Billy told me he and Doug were never close."

"Bullshit. He just told you that so you wouldn't suspect him. The three of us were always thick as thieves."

"So you did intend to kill him," I said.

"I don't know. We just wanted to make him pay. We wanted to punish him. We figured we'd find a way once we got close. Then Daggett's cellmate died and he got all that money."

"And you thought that would compensate?"

"Not me. I knew I'd never be happy till the day Daggett died, but I couldn't do it myself. I mean, kill someone in cold blood. Billy was the one who said the money would help. We couldn't bring Doug back, but at least we'd have something. He always knew Daggett lifted the cash, but he didn't think he'd get away with it. Daggett gets out of prison and sure enough, he's home free. He starts throwin' money around. Lovella calls Billy and we decide to go for it."

"So the guys up at San Luis never did figure it out," I said.

"Nope. Once Billy saw Daggett was in the clear, we decided to rip him off."

"And Lovella was part of it?"

Coral nodded, rinsing a plate, which she placed in the dish rack. "They got married the same week he got out, which suited us just fine. We figured if she didn't talk him out of it, she could steal it. . . ."

"And failing that, what?"

"We never meant to kill anyone," she said. "We just wanted the money. We didn't have much time anyway because he'd already spent part of it. He went through five grand before we could bat an eye and we knew if we didn't move fast, he'd blow the whole wad."

"You didn't realize he intended to give the rest of it to Tony Gahan?"

"Of course not," she said with energy. "Billy couldn't believe it when you told him about that. We thought most of it was still around somewhere. We thought we could still get our hands on it."

I watched her face, trying to compute the information she was giving me. "You mean you set Daggett up with Lovella so you could con him out of twenty-five thousand bucks?"

"That's right," she said.

"You were splitting it three ways! That's a little over eight grand apiece."

"So?"

"Coral, eight grand is nothing."

"Bullshit, it's nothing! Do you know what I could do with eight grand? How much do you have? Do you have eight grand?"

"No."

"So, all right. Don't tell me it's nothing."

"All right. It's a fortune," I said. "What went wrong?"

"Nothing at first. Billy called him up and said the guys at San Luis heard about the money and they wanted it back. He told Daggett they were coming after him, so that's when Daggett split."

"How'd you know he'd hightail it up here?"

"Billy told Daggett he'd help him out," she said with a shrug. "And then when Daggett got into town, Billy started working on him, trying to get him to fork it over to us. He said he'd act as a go-between, smooth it all over and get him off the hook."

"He'd already given it to me at that point, right?"

"Sure, but we didn't know that. He acted like he still had it handy. He acted like he might turn it over to Billy, but that was all crap. Of course, he was drunk all the time by then."

"So he was conning you while you conned him."

"He was just stringing us along!" she said indignantly. "Billy met him Tuesday night and Daggett was real cagey. Said he needed time to get his hands on it. He said he'd bring it in Thursday night, so Billy met him at the Hub again, only Daggett said he needed one more day. Billy really laid into him. He said these guys were getting very pissed and might kill Daggett anyway, whether he gave 'em the money or not. Daggett got real nervous and swore he'd have it the next night, which was Friday."

"The night he died."

"Right. I was working that night, and I was supposed to keep an eye on him, which I did. Billy decided to come late, just to make him sweat, and before I knew what was happening this woman showed up and started buying him drinks. You know the rest."

"Billy told me you took some kind of cold cap and crashed in the back room. Was that true?"

"I was just laying low," she said. "When I saw Daggett leave, I knew Billy'd have a fit. I already felt bad enough without putting up with his bullshit."

"And Billy finally figured out who she was?"

"I don't know. I guess. I wasn't here this morning, so I don't know what he was up to."

"Look. I have to go down to the police station and tell Lieutenant Dolan what's been going on. If Lovella comes back, please tell her it's urgent that she get in touch. Will you do that?"

Coral wedged the last clean dish against the pile in the rack. She filled a glass with water and poured it over the lot of them, rinsing off the few remaining suds. She turned to look at me with a gaze that chilled. "Do you think she killed Billy?"

"I don't know."

"Will you tell me if you find out it's her?"

"Coral, if she did it, she's dangerous. I don't want you in the middle of this."

"But will you tell me?"

I hesitated. "Yes."

"Thank you."

25

I had a brief chat with the manager of the trailer park. I gave him my card and asked him to call me if Lovella came back. I didn't really trust Coral to do it. The last I saw of him, he was tapping at her door. I got in my car and headed over to the police station. I asked for Lieutenant Dolan at the desk, but he and Feldman were in a section meeting. The clerk buzzed Jonah for me and he came as far as the locked door, admitting me into the corridor beyond. Both of us were circumspect—pleasant, noncommittal. No one observing us could have guessed that mere hours ago, we'd been cavorting stark naked on my Wonder Woman sheets.

"What happened when you got home?" I asked.

"Nothing. Everybody was asleep," he said. "We have something in the lab you might want to see." He moved down the hall to the right and I followed. He looked back at me. "Feldman had the guys check the trash bins at your suggestion. We think we found the silencer."

"You did?" I said, startled.

He opened the half-door into the crime lab, holding it for me as I passed in front of him. The lab tech was out, but I could see Billy's bloody shirt, tagged, on the counter, along with an object I couldn't at first identify.

"What's that," I said. "Is *that* it?" What I was looking

at was a large plastic soft drink bottle, painted black, lying on its side with a hole visible in the bottom.

"A disposable silencer. Handmade. A sound suppressor, in effect. It's been wiped clean of prints," Jonah said.

"I don't understand how it works."

"I had to have Krueger explain it to me. The bottle's filled with rags. Take a look. The barrel of the gun is usually wrapped with tape and the bottle affixed to it with a one-inch hose clamp. The soda bottle has a reinforced bottom, but it's only effective for a few shots because the noise level increases each time as the exit hole gets larger. Obviously, the device works best at close range."

"God, Jonah. How do people know about these things? I never heard of it."

He picked up a paperbound booklet from the counter behind me, flipping through it carelessly so I could see. Every page was filled with diagrams and photographs, illustrating how disposable silencers could be made out of common household objects. "This is from a gun shop down in Los Angeles," he said. "You ought to see what you can do with a length of window screen or a pile of old bottle caps."

"Jesus."

Lieutenant Becker stuck his head in the door. "Line one for you," he said to Jonah and then disappeared. Jonah glanced at the lab phone, but the call hadn't been transferred.

"Let me take this and I'll be right back," Jonah said. "Hang on."

"Right," I murmured. I leaned toward the silencer, trying to remember where I'd seen something similar. Through the hole in the bottom, I caught a glimpse of the blue terrycloth filling the interior. When I realized what it was, my mental process clicked in, and the interior machinery fired up. I knew.

I straightened up and crossed to the door, checking the corridor, which was empty. I headed for my car. I could still see Ramona Westfall coming up the basement stairs with an armload of ragged blue bath towels, which she'd dumped on the chair. The plastic bottle had been filled with a soft drink which she nearly dropped as she passed it to Tony to refrigerate.

I stopped by the office long enough to try the Westfall's number. The phone rang four times and then the machine clicked in.

"Hello. This is Ramona Westfall. Neither Ferrin nor I can come to the phone right now, but if you'll leave your name, telephone number, and a brief message, we'll get back to you as soon as possible. Thank you." I hung up at the sound of the tone.

I checked my watch. It was 4:45. I had no idea where Ramona was, but Tony had a 5:00 appointment just a few blocks away. If I could intercept him, I could lean on him some about her alibi since he represented the only confirmation she had. How had she pulled it off? He had to be on heavy medication for the migraine, so she might have slipped out while he was sleeping, adjusting the kitchen clock when she got back so she'd be covered for the time of Daggett's death. Once she was home again, Tony had wakened—she'd probably made sure of that so she'd have someone to corroborate the time. She'd fixed the sandwiches, chatting pleasantly while he ate, and as soon as he went back to bed, she changed the clock again. Or maybe it wasn't even as complicated as that. Maybe the watch Daggett wore had been set for 2:37 and then submerged. She could have killed him earlier and been home by 2:00. Tony may have realized what she'd done and tried to shield her when he understood how close my investigation was bringing me. It was also possible that he was in cahoots with her, but I hoped that wasn't the case.

I locked my office and went down the front stairs,

trotting up State Street on foot. The Granger Building was only three blocks up and it made more sense than hopping in my car and driving all the way around to the parking lot behind the building. Tony might still be hanging out at the arcade across the street. I had to get him before she had a chance to intercept. I didn't want him going home. She had to realize things were getting hot, especially since I'd shown up at the house with the shoes and skirt. All I needed from him was an indication I was on the right track and then I'd call Feldman. I thought about the Close, which I knew would be gloomy with the gathering twilight. I didn't want to go back there unless I had to.

I checked the arcade. Tony was at the rear, on the right-hand side, playing a video game. He was concentrating fully and I didn't think he was aware of me. I waited, watching small creatures being blasted off the screen. His scores weren't that good and I was tempted to have a try at it myself. The creatures suddenly froze into place, random weapons firing off here and there without regard to his manipulations. He looked up. "Oh hi."

"I need to talk to you," I said.

His eyes moved to the clock. "I got an appointment in five minutes. Can it wait?"

"I'll walk you over. We can talk on the way."

He picked up his package and we moved out to the street. The fading afternoon sun seemed bright after the darkness of the arcade. Even so, the fog was rolling in, November twilight beginning to descend. I punched the button at the crosswalk and we waited for the light to change. "Last Friday . . . the night Daggett died, do you remember where your uncle was?"

"Sure. Milwaukee, on a business trip."

"Are you on medication for the migraines?"

"Well, yeah. Tylenol with codeine. Compazine if I'm throwing up. How come?"

"Is it possible your aunt went out while you slept?"

"No. I don't know. I don't understand what you're getting at," he said.

I thought he was stalling, but I kept my mouth shut. We'd reached the Granger Building and Tony moved into the lobby ahead of me.

The elevator that had been out of order was now in operation, but the other one was immobilized, doors open, the housing visible, two sawhorses in front of the opening with a warning sign.

Tony was watching me warily. "Did she say she went out?"

"She claims she was home with you."

"So?"

"Come on, Tony. You're the only alibi she has. If you were zonked on medication, how do you know where she was?"

He pressed the elevator button.

The doors opened and we got on. The doors closed without incident and we went up to six. I checked his face as we stepped into the hallway. He was clearly conflicted, but I didn't want to press just yet. We headed down the corridor toward the suite his psychiatrist apparently occupied.

"Is there anything you want to talk about?" I asked.

"No," he said, his voice breaking with indignation. "You're crazy if you think she had anything to do with it."

"Maybe you can explain that to Feldman. He's in charge of the case."

"I'm not talking to the cops about her," Tony said. He tried the office door and found it locked. "Shit, he's not here."

There was a note taped to the door. He reached up to snatch the piece of paper, turning the movement into an abrupt shove. Next thing I knew, I was on my hands and knees and he'd taken off. He banged on the elevator

button and then veered right. I was up and running
when I heard the door leading to the stairway slam back
against the wall. I ran, banging into the stairwell only
seconds after he did. He was already heading up.

"Tony! Come on. Don't do this."

He was moving fast, his footsteps scratching on the
concrete stairs. His labored breathing echoed against
the walls as he went up. I don't keep fit for nothin', folks.
He had youth on me, but I was in good shape. I flung
my bag aside and grabbed the rail, starting up after him,
mounting the steps two at a time. I peered upward as I
ran, trying to catch sight of him. He reached the seventh
floor and kept on going. How many floors did this
building have?

"Tony. Goddamn it! Wait up! What are you doing?"

I heard another door bang up there. I stepped up
my pace.

I reached the landing at the top. The elevator
repairman had apparently left the door to the attic
unlocked and Tony had shot through the gap, slamming
the door behind him. I snatched the handle, half expecting to find it locked. The door flew open and I pushed
through, pausing on the threshold. The space was dim
and hot and dry, largely empty except for a small door
opening off to my right where the elevator brake,
sheave, and drive motors were located. I ducked my
head into the cramped space briefly, but it appeared to
be empty. I pulled out and peered around. The roof was
another twenty feet up, the rafters steeply pitched,
timbers forming a ninety-degree angle where they met.

Silence. I could see a square of light on the floor
and I looked up. A wooden ladder was affixed to the
wall to my right. At the top, a trap door was open and
waning daylight filtered down. I scanned the attic.
There was an electrical panel sitting on some boxes. It
looked like some kind of old light board from the
theater on the ground floor. For some reason, there was

a massive papier-mâché bird standing to one side . . . a blue jay, wearing a painted business suit. Wooden chairs were stacked, seat to seat, to my left.

"Tony?"

I put a hand on one of the ladder rungs. He might well be hiding somewhere, waiting for me to head up to the roof so he could ease out and down the steps again. I started up, climbing maybe ten feet so I could survey the attic from a better vantage point. There was no movement, no sound of breathing. I looked up again and started climbing cautiously. I'm not afraid of heights, but I'm not fond of them either. Still, the ladder seemed secure and I couldn't figure out where else he might be.

When I got to the top, I pulled myself into a sitting position and peered around. The trap came out in a small alcove, hidden behind an ornamental pediment, with a matching pediment halfway down the length of the roof. From the ground, the two of them had always looked strictly decorative, but I could see now that one disguised a brace of air vents. There was only a very narrow walkway around the perimeter of the roof, protected by a short parapet. The steep pitch of the roof would make navigating hazardous.

I peered down into the attic, hoping to see Tony dart out of hiding and into the stairwell. There was no sign of him up here, unless he'd eased around to the far side. Gingerly, I got to my feet, positioning myself between the nearly vertical roofline on my left and the ankle-high parapet on my right. I was actually walking in a metal rain gutter that popped and creaked under my weight. I didn't like the sound. It suggested that any minute now the metal would buckle, toppling me off the side.

I glanced down eight floors to the street, which didn't seem that far away. The buildings across from me were two stories high and lent a comforting illusion of proximity, but pedestrians still seemed dwarfed by the height. The streetlights had come on, and the traffic below was thinning. To my right, half a block away, the bell tower at the Axminster Theater was lighted from within, the arches bathed in tawny gold and warm blue. The drop had to be eighty feet. I tried to remember the velocity of a falling object. Something-something per foot per second was as close as I could come, but I knew the end result would be an incredible splat. I paused where I was and raised my voice. "Tony!"

I caught a flash of movement out of the corner of my eye and my heart flew into my throat. The plastic bag he'd been carrying was eddying downward, floating lazily. Coming from where? I peered over the parapet. I could see one of the niches that cut into the wall just below the cornice molding. The frieze that banded the building had always looked like marble from the street, but I could see now that it was molded plaster, the niche itself down about four feet and to the left. A half shell extended out maybe fifteen inches at the bottom edge and it held what was probably meant to be some sort of lamp with a torch flame, all molded plaster like the frieze. Tony was sitting there, his face turned up to mine. He'd climbed over the edge and he was now perched in the shallow ornamental niche, his arm locked around the torch, legs dangling. He'd taken a wig out of the bag he carried, donning it, looking up at me with a curious light in his eyes.

I was looking at the blonde who'd killed Daggett.

For a moment, we stared at each other, saying nothing. He had the cocky look of a ten-year-old defying his mom, but under the bravado I sensed a kid who was hoping someone would step in and save him from himself.

I put a hand on the pediment to steady myself. "You coming up or shall I come down?" I kept my tone matter-of-fact, but my mouth was dry.

"I'll be going down in a minute."

"Maybe we could talk about that," I said.

"It's too late," he said, smiling impishly. "I'm poised for flight."

"Will you wait there until I reach you?"

"No grabbing," he warned.

"I won't grab."

My palms were damp and I wiped them on my jeans.

I squatted, turning to face the roof, extending a foot tentatively down along the frieze. I glanced down, trying to find some purchase. Garlands of pineapple, grapes, and fig leaves formed a bas relief design that wound across the face of the building. "How'd you do this?" I asked.

"I didn't think about it. I just did it. You don't have to come down. It won't help."

"I just don't want to talk to you hanging over the edge," I said, lying through my teeth. I was hoping to get close enough to nab him, ignoring visions of grappling with him at that height. I steadied myself, tucking a toe into the shallow crevice formed by a curling vine. The niche was only four feet away. At ground level, I wouldn't have given it a thought.

I sensed that he was watching me, but I didn't dare look. I held onto the parapet, lowering my left foot.

He said, "You're not going to talk me out of this."

"I just want to hear your side of it," I said.

"Okay."

"You won't try to kill me, will you?" I asked.

"Why would I? You never did anything to me."

"I'm glad you recognize that. Now I feel really confident." I heard him laugh lightly at my tone.

I've seen magazine pictures of a man who can climb a vertical cliff face in a pair of tennis shoes, holding himself with the tips of his fingers tucked into small cracks that he discovers as he ascends. This has always seemed like a ludicrous pursuit and I usually flip to an article that makes more sense. The sight of the photographs makes me hyperventilate, especially the ones taken from his vantage point, staring down into some yawning crevasse. Maybe, if the truth be known, I'm more anxious about heights than I let on.

I allowed my right foot to inch down again as far as the lip of the niche. I found a handhold, down and to the right. Felt like a pineapple, but I wasn't sure. Pinning my safety to a phony piece of fruit. I had to be nuts.

The hardest part was actually letting go of the coping once my foot was resting safely in the recess. I had to bend my knees, turning slightly to the right, sinking little by little until I could take a seat. Tony, ever gallant, actually gave me a hand, steadying me until I eased down next to him. I'm not a brave soul. I'm really not. I just didn't want him flying off the side of that building while I looked on. I locked my left arm around the torch, just below his, holding onto my wrist with my right hand. I could feel sweat trickle down my sides.

"I hate this," I said. I was winded, not from effort but from apprehension.

"It's not bad. Just don't look down."

Of course I did. The minute he said that I had an irresistible desire to peek. I was hoping somebody would spot us, like they always do on TV. Then the cops would come with nets and the fire engines would arrive and somebody would talk him out of this. I'm an organism of the earth, a Taurus. I was never born of air, of water, or of fire. I'm a creature of gravity and I could feel the ground whisper. The same thing happens to me in old hotels when I'm staying on the twenty-second floor. I open a window and want to fling myself out.

"Oh, Jesus. This is such a bad idea," I said.

"For you maybe. Not for me."

I tried to think back to my short life as a cop and the standard procedure for dealing with potential suicides.

Stall for time was the first rule. I didn't recall anything about hanging your ass off the side of a building, but here I was. I said, "What's the story, babe. You want to tell me what's been going on?"

"There's not much to it. Daggett called the house on Monday. Aunt Ramona made a note of the number so I called him back. I dreamed about killing him. I couldn't wait. I had fantasies for months, every night before I went to sleep. I wanted to catch him with a wire around his neck and twist till it bit into his windpipe and his tongue bugged out. It doesn't take that long. I forget what that's called now . . ."

"Garroting," I supplied.

"Yeah, I would have liked that, but then I figured it was better if it looked like an accident because that way I could get away with it."

"Why'd he call?"

"I don't know," Tony said uncomfortably. "He was drunk and blubbering, said he was sorry and wanted to make it up to me for what he did. I go, 'Fine. Why don't we meet and talk?' And he goes, 'It would mean so much to me, son.'" Tony was acting out the parts, using a quavering falsetto for Daggett. "So then I tell him I'll meet him the next night at this bar he's calling from, the Hub, which didn't give me much time to put together this getup."

"Was that Ramona's skirt?"

"Nah, I got it at the Salvation Army thrift store for a buck. The sweater was another fifty cents and the shoes were two bucks."

"Where'd the sweater go?"

"I tossed it in another trash can a block away from the first. I thought it would all end up at the dump."

"What about the wig?"

"That was Aunt Ramona's from years ago. She didn't even know it was gone."

"Why'd you keep it?"

"I don't know. I was going to put it back in her closet where I got it, in case I needed it again. I had it on at the beach, but then I remembered Billy already knew who I was." He broke off, obviously confused. "I might have told my shrink about the whole thing if he'd been here. Anyway, the wig's expensive. This is real hair."

"The color's nice too," I said. I mean, where else could I go with this? Even Tony recognized the absurdity and he flashed me a look.

"You're humoring me, right?"

"Of course I'm humoring you!" I snapped. "I didn't come down here so we could have an argument."

He did a half shrug, smiling sheepishly.

I said, "Did you actually meet him there Tuesday night?"

"Not really. I went. I had it all worked out by then, only when I walk in, he's sittin' at this table talking to some guy. Turned out to be Billy Polo, but I didn't know it at the time. Billy was sitting in this booth with his back to the door. I saw Daggett, but I didn't realize he had company till I was right there in front of him. I veer off the minute I spot Billy, but by then he's had a good look at me. I'm not worried. I figure I'll never see him again anyway. I hang around for a while but they're really into it. I can tell Billy's leaning all over him and isn't likely to let up so I take a hike and go home."

"Was this one of the nights you had a migraine?"

"Yeah," he said. "I mean, some are real and some are fake, but I have to have a pattern, know what I mean? So I can come and go as I please."

"How'd you get down to the Hub, by cab?"

"My bike. The night I killed him, I rode down and left it at the marina and then I called a cab from a pay phone and took it over to the Hub."

"How'd you know he'd show up?"

"Because he called again and I said I'd be there."

"He never twigged to the fact that you'd showed up the first time in drag?"

"How was he going to know? He hadn't seen me since way before the trial. I was twelve, thirteen, something like that, a fat boy back then. I figured even if he guessed, I'd do it anyway, kill his ass . . . and once he was dead, who would know?"

"What went wrong?"

His brow furrowed. "I don't know. Well, I do. The plan went fine. It was something else." His eyes met mine and he looked every bit of fifteen, the blonde wig adding softness and dimension to a face that was nearly formless with youth. I could see how he'd pass as a woman, slim, with a clear complexion, sweet smile on his wide mouth. He looked down at the street and for a moment I thought he meant to swing out into space.

"When I was eight, I had these pet mice," he said. "Really sweet. I kept 'em in this cage with a wheel and a water bottle hanging upside down. Mom didn't think I'd take care of 'em but I did. I'd cut up strips of paper in the bottom of the cage so they could nest. Anyway, the girl mouse had these babies. They couldn't have been as long as this." He was indicating the end of his little finger. "Bald," he went on. "Just little bitty old things. We had to go out of town one weekend and when we got back the cat had tried to get in the cage. Knocked it off the desk and everything. The mice were gone. Probably the cat got 'em except for this one that had been laying in all these paper shreds. Well, the water had spilled so the paper was damp and the little thing must have had pneumonia or something because it was panting, like it couldn't breathe good. I tried to keep it warm. I watched it for hours and it just kept getting worse and worse so I decided I better . . . you know, do away with it. So it wouldn't suffer anymore."

He leaned forward, swinging his feet back and forth.

"Don't do that," I murmured anxiously. "Finish the story. I want to know what happened next."

He looked over at me then, his tone of voice mild. "I tossed it in the toilet. That's the only way I could think of to kill it. I couldn't crush it, so I just figured I'd flush it away. The little thing was half dead anyway and I thought I'd be doing it a favor, putting it out of its misery. But before I could do it, that little tiny hairless baby started struggling. You could tell it was in a total panic, trying to get out of there, like it knew what was happening . . ." He paused, dashing at his eyes. "Daggett did that and now I can't get away from the look on his face, you know? I see it all day long. He knew. Which was fine with me. I wanted that. I wanted him to know it was me and his life wasn't worth two cents. I just didn't think he'd care. He was a drunk and a bum and he killed all those people. He should have died. He shoulda been glad to go. I was putting him out of his misery, you know? So why'd he have to make it so hard?"

He fell silent and then he let out a deep breath. "Anyway, that's how that went. I can't sleep anymore. I dream about that stuff. Makes me sick."

"What about Billy? I assume he figured it out when he saw you at the funeral."

"Yeah. That was weird. He didn't give a shit about Daggett, but he felt like he should get part of the money if he kept his mouth shut. I would have given him all of it, but I didn't believe him. You should have seen him. Swaggering around, making all these threats. I figured he'd start bragging one night about what he knew and there I'd be."

The edge of the niche was beginning to cut into my rear end. I was hanging on so tightly that my arm was getting numb, but I didn't dare ease up. I couldn't figure out how to get us out of this, but I knew I'd better start talking fast.

"I killed a man once," I said. I meant to say more,

but that's all I could get out. I clamped my teeth
together, trying to force the feelings back down where
I'd been keeping them. It surprised me that after all this
time, it was still so painful to think about.

"On purpose?"

I shook my head. "Self-defense, but dead is dead."

His smile was sweet. "You can always come with
me."

"Don't say that. I'm not going to jump and I don't
want you to either. You're fifteen years old. There are
lots of other ways out."

"I don't think so."

"Your parents have money. They could hire Melvin
Belli if they wanted to."

"My parents are dead."

"Well, the Westfalls, then. You know what I mean."

"But Kinsey, I murdered two people and it's first
degree because I looked it up. How'm I gonna get away
with that?"

"The way half the killers in this country do," I said
with energy. "Hell, if Ted Bundy's still alive, why
shouldn't you be?"

"Who's he?"

"Never mind. Someone who did a lot worse than
you."

He thought for a moment. "I don't think it would
work. I hurt too bad and I don't see the point."

"There isn't a point. That's the part you invent."

"Could you do me a favor."

"All right. What's that?"

"Could you tell my aunt I said good-bye? I meant to
write her a note, but I didn't have a chance."

"Goddamn it, Tony! Don't do this. She's had enough
pain."

"I know," he said, "but she's got my Uncle Ferrin
and they'll be okay. They never really knew what to do
with me anyway."

"Oh, I see. You've got this all worked out."

"Well, yeah, I do. I've been reading up on this stuff and it's no big deal. Kids kill themselves all the time."

I hung my head, almost incapable of framing a response. "Tony, listen," I said finally. "What you're talking about is dumb and it doesn't make any sense. Do you have any idea how crummy life seemed when I was your age? I cried all the time and I felt like shit. I was ugly. I was skinny. I was lonely. I was mad. I never thought I'd pull out of it, but I did. Life is hard. Life hurts. So what? You tough it out. You get through and then you'll feel good again, I swear to God."

He tilted his head, watching me intently. "I don't think so. Not for me. I'm in too deep. I can't bear any more. It's too much."

"Tony, there are days when none of us can bear it, but the good comes around again. Happiness is seasonal, like anything else. Wait it out. There are people who love you. People who can help."

He shook his head. "I can't do that. It's kind of like I made a deal with myself to go through with this. She'll understand."

I could feel my temper snapping. "You want me to tell her that? You took a flying leap because you made a fucking *deal* with yourself?" His face clouded with uncertainty. I pressed on in a softer tone. "You want me to tell her we sat up here like this and I couldn't talk you out of it? I can't let you do it. You'll break her heart."

He looked down at his lap, his eyes remote, face coloring up the way boys do in lieu of tears. "It doesn't have anything to do with her. Tell her it was me and she did just great. I love her a lot, but it's my life, you know?"

I was silent for a moment, trying to figure out where to go next.

His face brightened and he held up an index finger. "I nearly forgot. I have a present for you." He shifted, letting go of the torch with a move that made me snatch at him instinctively. He laughed at that. "Take it easy. I'm just reaching in the waistband of my jeans."

I looked to see what he'd produced. My .32 lay across his palm. He held his hand out so I could take it, realizing belatedly that I couldn't free up a hand to reach for it.

"That's okay. I'll put it right here," he said kindly. He set it in the niche, behind the ornamental torch I was clinging to.

"How'd you get it?" Stalling, stalling.

"Same way I did everything else. I used my head. You put your home address on that business card you gave Aunt Ramona, so I rode over on my bike and waited till you got home. I was going to introduce myself, you know, and act like this real polite kid with good manners and a nifty haircut and stuff like that. Real innocent. I wasn't sure how much you knew and I thought maybe I could steer you off. I saw the car and you almost stopped, but then you took off again. I had to pedal my ass off to keep up with you and then you parked at the beach and I saw a chance to go through your stuff."

"You killed Billy with that?"

"Yeah. It was handy and I needed something quick."

"How'd you know about disposable silencers?"

"Some kid at school. I can make a pipe bomb too," he said. Then he sighed. "I gotta go soon. Time's nearly up."

I glanced down at the street. It was really getting dark up here, but the sidewalk was bright, the arcade across the way lit up like a movie house. Two people on the far side of the street had spotted us, but I could tell they hadn't figured out what was going on. A stunt? A movie being shot? I looked at Tony, but he didn't seem to be aware. My heart began to bang again and it made my chest feel tight and hot.

"I'm getting tired," I said casually. "I may go back up, but I need some help. Can you give me a hand?"

"Sure," he said. And then he paused, his whole body alert. "This isn't a trick, is it?"

"No," I said, but I could hear my voice shake and the lie cut my tongue like a razor blade. I've always lied with ease and grace, with ingenuity and conviction and I couldn't get this one out. I saw him make a move. I grabbed him, hanging on for dear life, but all he had to do was give his arm a quick twist and my hand came loose. I reached again, but it was too late. I saw him push out, lifting off. For a moment, he seemed to hover there, like a leaf, and then he disappeared from my line of sight. I didn't look down again after that.

I thought I heard a siren wailing, but the sound was mine.

I billed Barbara Daggett for $1,040.00, which she paid by return mail. It's nearly Christmas now and I haven't slept well for six weeks. I've thought a lot about Daggett and I've changed my mind about one thing. I suspect he knew what was going on. From a distance, Tony might have passed for a woman, but up close, he looked exactly what he was . . . a young kid playing dress-up, smart beyond his years, but not wise enough by half. I don't think Daggett was fooled. Why he went along with the game, I'm not sure. If he believed what Billy'd told him, he must have figured he was dead either way. Maybe he felt he owed Tony that last sacrifice. I'll never know, but it makes more sense to me that way. Some debts of the human soul are so enormous only life itself is sufficient forfeit. Perhaps in this case, all of the accounts are now paid in full . . . except mine.

—Respectfully submitted,
Kinsey Millhone

ABOUT THE AUTHOR

SUE GRAFTON has written novels, articles, short fiction, a screenplay, and numerous teleplays. She has also lectured on writing at colleges and conferences in Southern California and the Midwest. Her first mystery, 'A' IS FOR ALIBI, won an award from the Cloak and Clue Society of Wisconsin. 'B' IS FOR BURGLAR won both the Anthony and the Shamus awards for best novel of 1985, and 'C' IS FOR CORPSE won the Anthony Award for Best Novel in 1986. "The Parker Shotgun" won a Macavity Award from the Mystery Readers of America and an Anthony for Best Short Story of 1986. Grafton, who was born in Louisville, Kentucky, now lives in Southern California with her husband, Steven Humphrey.

Sue Grafton's

Kinsey Millhone is

"A refreshing heroine."
—*The Washington Post Book World*

"The best new private eye."
—*The Detroit News*

"A stand-out specimen of the new female operatives."
—*Philadelphia Inquirer*

"The gutsiest, grittiest female operative going."
—*Daily News*, New York

❑ "A" IS FOR ALIBI	27991-2	$5.99/$6.99 in Canada
❑ "B" IS FOR BURGLAR	28034-1	$5.99/$6.99 in Canada
❑ "C" IS FOR CORPSE	28036-8	$5.99/$6.99 in Canada
❑ "D" IS FOR DEADBEAT	27163-6	$5.99/$6.99 in Canada
❑ "E" IS FOR EVIDENCE	27955-6	$5.99/$6.99 in Canada
❑ "F" IS FOR FUGITIVE	28478-9	$5.99/$6.99 in Canada

"Once a fan reads one of Grafton's alphabetically titled detective novels, he or she will not rest until all the others are found."—*Los Angeles Herald Examiner*

Available at your local bookstore or use this page to order.

Send to: Bantam Books, Dept. BD 26
2451 S. Wolf Road
Des Plaines, IL 60018

Please send me the items I have checked above. I am enclosing $_____$ (please add $2.50 to cover postage and handling). Send check or money order, no cash or C.O.D.'s, please.

Mr./Ms._____

Address_____

City/State_____Zip_____

Please allow four to six weeks for delivery.

Prices and availability subject to change without notice. BD 26 3/92

REX STOUT'S NERO WOLFE

A master of the form, Rex Stout is one of America's greatest mystery writers and Nero Wolfe is one of the greatest fictional detectives of all time. Together, they have entertained and puzzled millions of fans.

THE REX STOUT LIBRARY

An ongoing program dedicated to making available the complete set of Nero Wolfe mysteries, these special collector's editions will feature new introductions by today's best writers and never-before-published memorabilia from the life of Rex Stout.

❑ **Fer-de-Lance,** Introduction by Loren D. Estleman
   27819-3 $4.99/$5.99 in Canada
❑ **The League of Frightened Men,** Introduction by Robert Goldsborough 25933-4 $4.99/$5.99 in Canada
❑ **The Rubber Band,** Introduction by Nelson DeMille
   25550-9 $4.99/$5.99 in Canada
❑ **The Red Box,** Introduction by Carolyn G. Hart
   24919-3 $4.99/$5.99 in Canada
❑ **Where There's a Will,** Introduction by Dean R. Koontz
   29591-8 $4.99/$5.99 in Canada
❑ **The Final Deduction,** Introduction by Andrew M. Greeley
   25254-2 $4.99/$5.99 in Canada
❑ **The Hand in the Glove,** Introduction by Marcia Muller
   22857-9 $4.99/$5.99 in Canada
❑ **Black Orchids,** Introduction by Lawrence Block
   25719-6 $4.99/$5.99 in Canada
❑ **The Doorbell Rang,** Introduction by Stuart Kaminsky
   23721-7 $4.99/$5.99 in Canada
❑ **If Death Ever Slept,** Introduction by Robert B. Parker
   23649-0 $4.99/$5.99 in Canada

Available at your local bookstore or use this page to order.
Send to: Bantam Books, Dept. BD 17
              2451 S. Wolf Road
              Des Plaines, IL 60018
Please send me the items I have checked above. I am enclosing
$_____ (please add $2.50 to cover postage and handling). Send
check or money order, no cash or C.O.D.'s, please.

Mr./Ms._____

Address_____

City/State_____Zip_____
Please allow four to six weeks for delivery.
Prices and availability subject to change without notice.   BD 17 7/92

Girlfriend of the Corpse

I scurried after Carrie, catching the door as she passed into the corridor.

"Who else was Bobby hanging out with back then?" I asked. "Just give me a couple of names. I gotta have something to go on."

She paused, glancing back at me. "Try a kid named Gus. I don't know his last name, but he works at the skate-rental place down at the beach. He's an old high school buddy and I think Bobby trusted him."

"What were the other things? You said you got pregnant among other things."

Her smile was tense. "God, you are so persistent. Bobby was in love with someone else. I have no idea who, so don't bother to ask. If I'd known about the other woman I'd have broken off our relationship long before. As it was, I didn't hear about her until I told him I was pregnant. I thought at first he might marry me, but when he told me he was seriously involved with someone else, I knew what I had to do. To his credit, he did feel terrible about the bind I was in and he did as much as he could. There was nothing cheap about Bobby and he really was a sweet guy at heart."

She started to move away and I caught her by the arm, thinking rapidly. "Carrie, I don't suppose he gave you a little red address book, did he?"

"All he gave me was a heartache," she said and walked off without looking back.

CRIME LINE Bantam Crime Line Books offer the finest in
classic and modern American mysteries.
Ask your bookseller for the books you have missed.

REX STOUT
The Black Mountain
Broken Vase
Death of a Dude
Death Times Three
Fer-de-Lance
The Final Deduction
Gambit
Plot It Yourself
The Rubber Band
Some Buried Caesar
Three for the Chair
Too Many Cooks

MAX ALLAN COLLINS
The Dark City
Bullet Proof
Butcher's Dozen
coming soon:
Neon Mirage

LOREN ESTLEMAN
Peeper

Whiskey River

DICK LUPOFF
The Comic Book Killer

MEG O'BRIEN
The Daphne Decisions
coming soon:
Salmon in the Soup

VIRGINIA ANDERSON
Blood Lies
King of the Roses

WILLIAM MURRAY
When the Fat Man Sings
The King of the Nightcap
coming soon:
The Getaway Blues

EUGENE IZZI
King of the Hustlers
The Prime Roll
Invasions

GLORIA DANK
Friends Till the End
Going Out in Style

JEFFERY DEAVER
Manhattan Is My Beat
coming soon:
Death of a Blue Movie Star

ROBERT GOLDSBOROUGH
Murder in E Minor
Death on Deadline
The Bloodied Ivy
The Last Coincidence
coming soon:
Fade to Black

SUE GRAFTON
"A" Is for Alibi
"B" Is for Burglar
"C" Is for Corpse
"D" Is for Deadbeat
"E" Is for Evidence
"F" Is for Fugitive

DAVID LINDSEY
In the Lake of the Moon

CAROLYN G. HART
Design for Murder
Death on Demand
Something Wicked
Honeymoon with Murder
A Little Class on Murder

ANNETTE MEYERS
The Big Killing
coming soon:
Tender Death

ROB KANTNER
Dirty Work
The Back-Door Man
Hell's Only Half Full
coming soon:
Made in Detroit

ROBERT CRAIS
The Monkey's Raincoat
Stalking the Angel

KEITH PETERSON
The Trapdoor
There Fell a Shadow
The Rain
Rough Justice

DAVID HANDLER
The Man Who Died Laughing
The Man Who Lived by Night
coming soon:
The Man Who Would be
F. Scott Fitzgerald

JERRY OSTER
Club Dead
Internal Affairs

BENJAMIN M. SCHUTZ
A Tax in Blood
Embrace the Wolf
The Things We Do for Love

"C"
is for
CORPSE

A Kinsey Millhone Mystery

SUE GRAFTON

BANTAM BOOKS
NEW YORK • TORONTO • LONDON • SYDNEY • AUCKLAND

This edition contains the complete text
of the original hardcover edition.
NOT ONE WORD HAS BEEN OMITTED.

"C" IS FOR CORPSE

A Bantam Book / published by arrangement with
Henry Holt and Company, Inc.

PRINTING HISTORY

Henry Holt edition published May 1986
Bantam edition / May 1987

"Ac-cent-tchu-ate the Positive" by Harold Arlen
and Johnny Mercer
© 1944 Harwin Music Co. © renewed 1972 Harwin Music Co.
International copyright secured.
All rights reserved. Used by permission.
"Someone to Watch Over Me" by George and Ira Gershwin
© 1926 (renewed) WB Music Corp.
All rights reserved. Used by permission.

All rights reserved.
Copyright © 1986 by Sue Grafton.
Cover art copyright © 1987 by Bantam Books.
Library of Congress Catalog Card Number: 85-24797.
No part of this book may be reproduced or transmitted
in any form or by any means, electronic or mechanical,
including photocopying, recording, or by any information
storage and retrieval system, without permission in
writing from the publisher.
For information address: Henry Holt and Company, Inc.,
115 West 18th Street, New York, NY 10011.

ISBN 0-553-28036-8

Published simultaneously in the United States and Canada

Bantam Books are published by Bantam Books, a division of Bantam
Doubleday Dell Publishing Group, Inc. Its trademark, consisting of the
words "Bantam Books" and the portrayal of a rooster, is Registered in U.S.
Patent and Trademark Office and in other countries. Marca Registrada.
Bantam Books, 666 Fifth Avenue, New York, New York 10103.

PRINTED IN THE UNITED STATES OF AMERICA

OPM   30 29 28 27 26 25 24 23 22 21

For the children who chose me:
Leslie, Jay, and Jamie

The author wishes to acknowledge the invaluable assistance of the following people: Steven Humphrey; Sam Chirman, M.D., and Betty Johnson of the Rehabilitation Group of Santa Barbara; David Dallmeyer, R.P.T.; Deputies Tom Nelson and Juan Tejeda of the Santa Barbara County Sheriff's Department; C. Robert Dambacher, Chief of Investigations, Los Angeles County Medical Examiner–Coroner; Andrew H. Bliss, Director of Medical Records, LAC-USC Medical Center; Delbert Dickson, M.D.; R. W. Olson, M.D.; Peg Ortigiesen; Barbara Stephans; Billie Moore Squires; H. F. Richards; Michael Burridge; Midge Hayes and Adelaide Gest of the Santa Barbara Public Library; and Michael Fitzmorris of Security Services Unlimited, Inc.

1

I met Bobby Callahan on Monday of that week. By Thursday, he was dead. He was convinced someone was trying to kill him and it turned out to be true, but none of us figured it out in time to save him. I've never worked for a dead man before and I hope I won't have to do it again. This report is for him, for whatever it's worth.

My name is Kinsey Millhone. I'm a licensed private investigator, doing business in Santa Teresa, California, which is ninety-five miles north of Los Angeles. I'm thirty-two years old, twice divorced. I like being alone and I suspect my independence suits me better than it should. Bobby challenged that. I don't know quite how or why. He was only twenty-three years old. I wasn't romantically involved with him in any sense of the word, but I did care and his death served to remind me, like a custard pie in the face, that life is sometimes one big savage joke. Not funny "ha ha," but cruel, like those gags sixth-graders have been telling since the world began.

It was August and I'd been working out at Santa Teresa Fitness, trying to remedy the residual effects of a broken left arm. The days were hot, filled with relentless sunshine and clear skies. I was feeling cranky and bored, doing pushdowns and curls and wrist rolls. I'd just worked two cases back-to-back and I'd sustained more damage than a fractured humerus. I was feeling emotionally battered and I needed a rest. Fortunately, my bank account was fat and I knew I could afford to take two months off. At the same time, the idleness was making me restless and the physical-therapy regimen was driving me nuts.

Santa Teresa Fitness is a real no-nonsense place: the brand X of health clubs. No Jacuzzi, no sauna, no music

piped in. Just mirrored walls, body-building equipment
and industrial-grade carpeting the color of asphalt. The
whole twenty-eight-hundred square feet of space smells
like men's jockstraps.

I'd arrive at eight in the morning, three days a week, and
warm up for fifteen minutes, then launch into a series of
exercises designed to strengthen and condition my left deltoid, pectoralis major, biceps, triceps, and anything else
that had gone awry since I'd had the snot beaten out of me
and had intersected the flight path of a .22 slug. The
orthopedist had prescribed six weeks of physical therapy
and so far, I'd done three. There was nothing for it but to
work my way patiently from one machine to the next. I was
usually the only woman in the place at that hour and I
tended to distract myself from the pain, sweat, and nausea
by checking out men's bodies while they were checking out
mine.

Bobby Callahan came in at the same time I did. I wasn't
sure what had happened to him, but whatever it was, it had
hurt. He was probably just short of six feet tall, with a football player's physique: big head, thick neck, brawny shoulders, heavy legs. Now the shaggy blond head was held to
one side, the left half of his face pulled down in a permanent grimace. His mouth leaked saliva as though he'd just
been shot up with Novocain and couldn't quite feel his own
lips. He tended to hold his left arm up against his waist and
he usually carried a folded white handkerchief that he used
to mop up his chin. There was a terrible welt of dark red
across the bridge of his nose, a second across his chest, and
his knees were crisscrossed with scars as though a swords-
man had slashed at him. He walked with a lilting gait, his
left Achilles tendon apparently shortened, pulling his left
heel up. Working out must have cost him everything he
had, yet he never failed to appear. There was a doggedness
about him that I admired. I watched him with interest,
ashamed of my own interior complaints. Clearly, I could
recover from my injuries while he could not. I didn't feel
sorry for him, but I did feel curious.

That Monday morning was the first time we'd been alone
together in the gym. He was doing leg curls, facedown on
the bench next to mine, his attention turned inward. I had

shifted over to the leg-press machine, just for variety. I weigh 118 and I only have so much upper body I can rehabilitate. I hadn't gotten back into jogging since the injury, so I figured a few leg presses would serve me right. I was only doing 120 pounds, but it hurt anyway. To distract myself, I was playing a little game wherein I tried to determine which apparatus I hated most. The leg-curl machine he was using was a good candidate. I watched him do a set of twelve repetitions and then start all over again.

"I hear you're a private detective," he said without missing a beat. "That true?" There was a slight drag to his voice, but he covered it pretty well.

"Yes. Are you in the market for one?"

"Matter of fact, I am. Somebody tried to kill me."

"Looks like they didn't miss by much. When was this?"

"Nine months ago."

"Why you?"

"Don't know."

The backs of his thighs were bulging, his hamstrings taut as guy wires. Sweat poured off his face. Without even thinking about it, I counted reps with him. Six, seven, eight.

"I hate that machine," I remarked.

He smiled. "Hurts like a son of a bitch, doesn't it?"

"How'd it happen?"

"I was driving up the pass with a buddy of mine late at night. Some car came up and started ramming us from behind. When we got to the bridge just over the crest of the hill, I lost it and we went off. Rick was killed. He bailed out and the car rolled over on him. I should have been killed too. Longest ten seconds of my life, you know?"

"I bet." The bridge he'd soared off spanned a rocky, scrub-choked canyon, four hundred feet deep, a favorite jumping-off spot for suicide attempts. Actually, I'd never heard of anyone surviving that drop. "You're doing great," I said. "You've been working your butt off."

"What else can I do? Just after the accident, they told me I'd never walk. Said I'd never do anything."

"Who said?"

"Family doctor. Some old hack. My mom fired him on the spot and called in an orthopedic specialist. He brought me back. I was out at Rehab for eight months and now I'm doing this. What happened to you?"

"Some asshole shot me in the arm."

Bobby laughed. It was a wonderful snuffling sound. He finished the last rep and propped himself up on his elbows.

He said, "I got four machines to go and then let's bug out. By the way, I'm Bobby Callahan."

"Kinsey Millhone."

He held his hand out and we shook, sealing an unspoken bargain. I knew even then I'd work for him whatever the circumstances.

We ate lunch in a health-food café, one of those places specializing in cunning imitation meat patties that never fool anyone. I don't understand the point myself. It seems to me a vegetarian would be just as repelled by something that *looked* like minced cow parts. Bobby ordered a bean-and-cheese burrito the size of a rolled-up gym towel, smothered in guacamole and sour cream. I opted for stir-fried veggies and brown rice with a glass of white wine of some indeterminate jug sort.

Eating, for Bobby, was the same laborious process as working out, but his single-minded attention to the task allowed me to study him at close range. His hair was sun-bleached and coarse, his eyes brown with the kind of lashes most women have to buy in a box. The left half of his face was inanimate, but he had a strong chin, accentuated by a scar like a rising moon. My guess was that his teeth had been driven through his lower lip at some point during the punishing descent into that ravine. How he'd lived through it all was anybody's guess.

He glanced up. He knew I'd been staring, but he didn't object.

"You're lucky to be alive," I said.

"I'll tell you the worst of it. Big hunks of my brain are gone, you know?" The drag in his speech was back, as though the very subject affected his voice. "I was in a coma for two weeks, and when I came out, I didn't know what the fuck was going on. I still don't. But I can remember how I used to be and that's what hurts. I was smart, Kinsey. I knew a lot. I could concentrate and I used to have ideas. My mind would make these magic little leaps. You know what I mean?"

I nodded. I knew about minds making magic little leaps.

He went on. "Now I got gaps and spaces. Holes. I've lost big pieces of my past. They don't exist anymore." He paused to dab impatiently at his chin, then shot a bitter glance at the handkerchief. "Jesus, bad enough that I drool. If I'd always been like this, I wouldn't know the difference and it wouldn't bug me so much. I'd assume everybody had a brain that felt like mine. But I was quick once. I know that. I was an A student, on my way to medical school. Now all I do is work out. I'm just trying to regain enough coordination so I can go to the fuckin' toilet by myself. When I'm not in the gym, I see this shrink named Kleinert and try to come to terms with the rest of it."

There were sudden tears in his eyes and he paused, fighting for control. He took a deep breath and shook his head abruptly. When he spoke again, his voice was full of self-loathing.

"So. That's how I spent my summer vacation. How about you?"

"You're convinced it was a murder attempt? Why couldn't it have been some prankster or a drunk?"

He thought for a moment. "I knew the car. At least I think I did. Obviously, I don't anymore, but it seems like . . . at the time, I recognized the vehicle."

"But not the driver?"

He shook his head. "Couldn't tell you now. Maybe I knew then, maybe not."

"Male? Female?" I asked.

"Nuh-un. That's gone, too."

"How do you know Rick wasn't meant to be the victim instead of you?"

He pushed his plate away and signaled for coffee. He was struggling. "I knew something. Something had happened and I figured it out. I remember that much. I can even remember knowing I was in trouble. I was scared. I just don't remember why."

"What about Rick? Was he part of it?"

"I don't think it had anything to do with him. I couldn't swear to it, but I'm almost positive."

"What about your destination that night? Does that tie in somehow?"

Bobby glanced up. The waitress was standing at his elbow with a coffeepot. He waited until she'd poured coffee for both of us. She departed and he smiled uneasily. "I don't know who my enemies are, you know? I don't know if people around me know this 'thing' I've forgotten about. I don't want anyone to overhear what I say . . . just in case. I know I'm paranoid, but I can't help it."

His gaze followed the waitress as she moved back toward the kitchen. She put the coffeepot back on the unit and picked up an order at the window, glancing back at him. She was young and she seemed to know we were talking about her. Bobby dabbed at his chin again as an afterthought. "We were on our way up to Stage Coach Tavern. There's usually a bluegrass band up there and Rick and I wanted to hear them." He shrugged. "There might have been more to it, but I don't think so."

"What was going on in your life at that point?"

"I'd just graduated from UC Santa Teresa. I had this part-time job at St. Terry's, waiting to hear if I was accepted for med school."

Santa Teresa Hospital had been called St. Terry's ever since I could remember. "Wasn't it late in the year for that? I thought med-school candidates applied during the winter and got replies back by spring."

"Well, actually I *had* applied and didn't get in, so I was trying again."

"What kind of work were you doing at St. Terry's?"

"I was a 'floater,' really. I did all kinds of things. For a while, I worked Admissions, typing up papers before patients came in. I'd call and get preliminary data, insurance coverage, stuff like that. Then for a while, I worked in Medical Records filing charts until I got bored. Last job I had was clerk-typist in Pathology. Worked for Dr. Fraker. He was neat. He let me do lab tests sometimes. You know, just simple stuff."

"It doesn't sound like hazardous work," I said. "What about the university? Could the jeopardy you were in be traced back to the school somehow? Faculty? Studies?

Some kind of extracurricular activity you'd been involved in?"

He was shaking his head, apparently drawing a blank. "I don't see how. I'd been out since June. Accident was November."

"But your feeling is that you were the only one who knew this piece of information, whatever it was."

His gaze traveled around the café and then came back to me. "I guess. Me and whoever tried to kill me to shut me up."

I sat and stared at him for a while, trying to get a fix on the situation. I stirred what was probably raw milk into my coffee. Health-food enthusiasts like eating microbes and things like that. "Do you have any sense at all of how long you'd known this thing? Because I'm wondering . . . if it was potentially so dangerous . . . why you didn't spill the beans right away."

He was looking at me with interest. "Like what? To the cops or something like that?"

"Sure. If you stumbled across a theft of some kind, or you found out someone was a Russian spy . . ." I was rattling off possibilities as they occurred to me. "Or you uncovered a plot to assassinate the President . . ."

"Why wouldn't I have picked up the first telephone I came to and called for help?"

"Right."

He was quiet. "Maybe I did that. Maybe . . . shit, Kinsey, I don't know. You don't know how frustrated I get. Early on, those first two, three months in the hospital, all I could think about was the pain. It took everything I had to stay alive. I didn't think about the accident at all. But little by little, as I got better, I started going back to it, trying to remember what happened. Especially when they told me Rick was dead. I didn't find out about that for weeks. I guess they were worried I'd blame myself and it would slow my recovery. I did feel sick about it once I heard. What if I was drunk and just ran us off the road? I had to find out what went on or I knew I'd go crazy on top of everything else. Anyway, that's when I began to piece together this other stuff."

"Maybe the rest of it will come back to you if you've re-membered this much."

"But that's just it," he said. "What if it does come back? I figure the only thing keeping me alive right now is the fact that I can't remember any more of it."

His voice had risen and he paused, gaze flicking off to one side. His anxiety was infectious and I felt myself glancing around as he had, wanting to keep my voice low so our conversation couldn't be overheard.

"Have you actually been threatened since this whole thing came up?" I asked.

"No. Un-un."

"No anonymous letters or strange phone calls?"

He was shaking his head. "But I *am* in danger. I know I am. I've been feeling this way for weeks. I need help."

"Have you tried the cops?"

"Sure, I've tried. As far as they're concerned, it was an accident. They have no evidence a crime was committed. Well, hit-and-run. They know somebody rear-ended me and forced me off the bridge, but premeditated murder? Come on. And even if they believed me, they don't have manpower to assign. I'm just an ordinary citizen. I'm not entitled to police protection twenty-four hours a day."

"Maybe you should hire a bodyguard—"

"Screw that! It's you I want."

"Bobby, I'm not saying I won't help you. Of course I will. I'm just talking about your options. It sounds like you need more than me."

He leaned forward, his manner intense. "Just get to the bottom of this. Tell me what's going on. I want to know why somebody's after me and I want them stopped. Then I won't need the cops or a bodyguard or anything else." He clamped his mouth shut, agitated. He rocked back.

"Fuck it," he said. He shifted restlessly and got up. He pulled a twenty out of his wallet and tossed it on the table. He started for the door with that lilting gait, his limp more pronounced than I'd seen it. I grabbed my handbag and caught up with him.

"God, slow down. Let's go back to my office and we'll type up a contract."

He held the door open for me and I went out.

"I hope you can afford my services," I said back over my shoulder.

He smiled faintly. "Don't sweat it."

We turned left, moving toward the parking lot.

"Sorry I lost my temper," he murmured.

"Quit that. I don't give a shit."

"I wasn't sure you'd take me seriously," he said.

"Why wouldn't I?"

"My family thinks I've got a screw loose."

"Yeah, well that's why you hired me instead of them."

"Thanks," he whispered. He tucked his hand through my arm and I glanced over at him. His face was suffused with pink and there were tears in his eyes. He dashed at them carelessly, not looking at me. For the first time, I realized how young he was. God, he was just a kid, banged up, bewildered, scared to death.

We walked back to my car slowly and I was conscious of the stares of the curious, faces averted with pity and uneasiness. It made me want to punch somebody out.

2

By two o'clock that afternoon, the contract was signed,
Bobby had given me a two-thousand-dollar advance against
fees, and I was dropping him off outside the gym, where
he'd left his BMW before lunch. His disability entitled him
to the handicapped slot, but I noticed he hadn't used it.
Maybe someone else was parked there when he arrived, or
maybe, obstinately, he preferred to walk the extra twenty
yards.

I leaned across the front seat as he got out. "Who's your
attorney?" I asked. He held the door open on the passenger
side, his head tilted so he could look in at me.

"Varden Talbot of Talbot and Smith. Why? You want to
talk to him?"

"Ask him if he'd have copies of the police reports released
to me. It would save me a lot of time."

"O.K. I'll do that."

"Oh, and I should probably start with your immediate
family. They might have a theory or two about what's going
on. Why don't I give you a call later and find out when
people are free?"

Bobby made a face. On the way to my office, he'd told me
his disabilities had forced him to move back into the family
home temporarily, which didn't sit well with him. His parents had divorced some years ago and his mother had remarried, in fact, this was marriage number three.
Apparently, Bobby didn't get along with his current stepfather, but he had a seventeen-year-old stepsister named
Kitty whom he seemed to like. I wanted to talk to all three.
Most of my investigations start with paperwork, but this
one felt different from the outset.

"I have a better idea," Bobby said. "Stop by the house this afternoon. Mom's having some people in for drinks around five. My stepfather's birthday. It'll give you a chance to meet everyone."

I hesitated. "You sure it'll be all right? She might not want me barging in on a special occasion like that."

"It's fine. I'll tell her you're coming. She won't care. Got a pencil? I'll give you directions."

I rooted through my handbag for a pen and my notebook and jotted down the details. "I'll be there about six," I said.

"Great." He slammed the car door and moved off.

I watched him hobble as far as his car and then I headed for home.

I live in what was once a single-car garage, converted now to a two-hundred-dollar-a-month studio apartment maybe fifteen feet square, which serves as living room, bedroom, kitchen, bathroom, closet, and laundry room. All of my possessions are multipurpose and petite. I have a combination refrigerator, sink, and stovette, a doll-sized stacking washer/dryer unit, a sofa that becomes a bed (though I seldom bother to unfold it), and a desk that I sometimes use as a dining-room table. I tend to be work-oriented and my living quarters seem to have shrunk, year by year, to this miniature state. For a while, I lived in a trailer, but that began to feel too opulent. I'm often out of town and I object to spending money for space I don't use. It's possible that one day I'll reduce my personal requirements to a sleeping bag that I can toss in the backseat of my car, thus eliminating altogether the need for paying rent. As it is, my wants are few. I don't have pets or houseplants. I do have friends, but I don't entertain. If I have any hobbies at all, they consist of cleaning my little semi-automatic and reading up on evidential documents. I'm not exactly a bundle of laughs, but I do pay my bills, keep a little money tucked away, and provide myself with medical insurance to cover the hazards of my trade. I like my life as it is, though I try not to boast overmuch about the fact. About every six or eight months, I run into a man who astounds me sexually, but between escapades, I'm celibate, which I don't think is any big deal. After two unsuccessful marriages, I find myself keeping my guard up, along with my underpants.

My apartment is located on a modest palm-lined street a block from the beach and it's owned by a man named Henry Pitts, who lives in the main house on the property. Henry is eighty-one years old, a retired baker who supplements his income now by turning out breads and pastries that he trades with local merchants for goods and services. He caters tea parties for the little old ladies in the neighborhood, and in his spare time, he writes crossword puzzles that are a bitch to figure out. He's a very handsome man: tall, lean, and tanned, with shocking-white hair that looks as soft as baby fuzz, a thin aristocratic face. His eyes are a violet-blue, the color of ground morning glories, and they radiate intelligence. He's caring, compassionate, and sweet. It shouldn't have surprised me, therefore, to find him in the company of the "babe" who was having mint juleps with him in the garden when I got home.

I had parked my car out front as usual, and I was heading around to the back, where my entrance is located. My apartment faces the rear and looks out onto a picturesque little bit of scenery. Henry has a patch of grass back there, a weeping willow, rosebushes, two dwarf citrus trees, and a small flagstone patio. He was just coming out of his own back door with a serving tray when he caught sight of me.

"Oh, Kinsey. Well, good. Come on over here. There's someone I want you to meet," he said.

My glance followed his and I saw a woman stretched out on one of the lounge chairs. She must have been in her sixties, plump, with a crown of dyed brown curls. Her face was as lined as soft leather and she used makeup skillfully. It was her eyes that bothered me: a velvety brown, quite large, and, just for a moment, poisonous.

Henry set the tray down on a round metal table between the chairs. "This is Lila Sams," he said, then nodded at me. "My tenant, Kinsey Millhone. Lila's just moved to Santa Teresa. She's renting a room from Mrs. Lowenstein down the street."

She held out a hand with a clatter of red plastic bracelets, moving as though she meant to struggle to her feet.

I crossed the patio. "Don't get up," I said. "Welcome to the neighborhood." I shook hands with her, smiling sociably. Her return smile erased the chill from her gaze and I

found myself doing a mental doubletake, wondering if I'd
misinterpreted. "What part of the country are you from?"

"Here, there, and everywhere," she said, glancing slyly
at Henry. "I wasn't sure how long I'd stay, but Henry makes
it seem veerry niiice."

She wore a low-cut cotton sundress, a bright green-and-
yellow geometric print on a white background. Her breasts
looked like two five-pound flour sacks from which some of
the contents had spilled. Her excess weight was carried in
her chest and waist, her hefty hips and thighs tapering to a
decent set of calves and quite dainty feet. She wore red
canvas wedgies and fat red plastic button earrings. As with a
painting, I found my gaze traveling right back around to the
place where it began. I wanted to make eye contact again,
but she was surveying the tray Henry held out to her.

"Oh my. Well, what's all this? Aren't you a sweetie pie!"

Henry had prepared a plate of canapés. He's one of those
people who can whip into the kitchen and create a gourmet
snack out of canned goods from the back of the cupboard.
All I have at the back of my kitchen cupboard is an old box
of cornmeal with bugs.

Lila's red fingernails formed a tiny crane. She lifted a canapé and conveyed it to her mouth. It looked like a toast
round with a bite of smoked salmon and a dab of dilled
mayonnaise. "Mmm, that's *wonderful*," she said, mouth
full, and then licked her fingertips, one by one. She wore
several crusty diamond rings, the stones clotted together
with rubies, and a square-cut emerald the size of a postage
stamp, with diamonds on either side. Henry offered me the
plate of canapés. "Why don't you try one of these while I fix
you a mint julep?"

I shook my head. "I better not. I may try to jog and then I
have work to do."

"Kinsey's a private detective," he said to her.

Lila's eyes got big and she blinked in wonderment. "Oh
my goodness. Well, how interesting!" She spoke effusively,
implying more enthusiasm than etiquette required. I wasn't
nearly that thrilled with her and I'm sure she sensed it. I
like older women as a rule. I like almost all women, as a
matter of fact. I find them open and confiding by nature,
amusingly candid when it comes to talk of men. This one

was of the old school: giddy and flirtatious. She'd despised me on sight.

She looked at Henry and patted the chaise pad. "Now, you sit down here, you bad boy. I won't have you waiting on me hand and foot. Can you believe it, Kinsey? All he's done this afternoon is fetch me this, fetch me that." She bent over the canapé plate, enthralled. "Now, what is this one?"

I glanced at Henry, half expecting him to shoot me a pained look, but he had settled on the chaise as commanded, peering over at the plate. "That's smoked oyster. And that's a little cream cheese and chutney. You'll like that one. Here."

He was apparently about to hand-feed her, but she smacked at him ineffectually.

"Quit that. You take one for yourself. You are spoiling the life out of me, and what's more, you're going to make me get fat!"

I could feel my face set with discomfort, watching their two heads bent together. Henry is fifty years older than I am and our relationship has always been completely decorous, but I wondered if this was how he felt on those rare occasions in the past when he'd spotted some guy rolling out of my place at six A.M.

"Talk to you later, Henry," I said, moving toward my front door. I don't even think he heard me.

I changed into a tank top and a pair of cutoffs, laced up my running shoes, and then slipped out again without calling attention to myself. I walked briskly one block over to Cabana, the wide boulevard that parallels the beach, and broke into a trot. The day was hot and there was no cloud cover at all. It was now three o'clock and even the surf seemed sluggish. The breeze fanning in off the ocean was dense with brine and the beach was littered with debris. I don't even know why I was bothering to run. I was out of shape, huffing and puffing, my lungs on fire within the first quarter-mile. My left arm ached and my legs felt like wood. I always run when I'm working and I guess that's why I did it that day. I ran because it was time to run and because I needed to shake the rust and stiffness from my joints. As dutiful as I am about jogging, I've never been a big fan of exercise. I just can't think of any other way to feel good.

The first mile was pure pain and I hated every minute of it. Mile two, I could feel the endorphins kick in, and by mile three, I'd found my pace and might have gone on forever. I checked my running watch. It was 3:33. I never said I was swift. I slowed to a walk, pouring sweat. I would pay for this on the morrow, I was relatively sure, but for the moment, I felt loose, my muscles soft and warm. I used the walk home to cool down.

By the time I reached my place again, evaporating sweat had left me chilled and I was looking forward to a hot shower. The patio was deserted, empty mint-julep glasses sitting side by side. Henry's back door was closed and the window shades were drawn. I let myself into my place with the key I carry tied to my shoelace.

I washed my hair and shaved my legs, slipped into a robe, and puttered around for a while, tidying up the kitchen, cleaning off my desk. Finally, I donned a pair of pants, tunic top, sandals, and cologne. At 5:45, I grabbed my big leather handbag and went out again, locking up.

I checked the directions to Bobby's house and turned left on Cabana toward the bird refuge, following the road as it wound into Montebello, which is rumored to have more millionaires per square mile than any other community in the country. I don't know if that's true or not. The residents of Montebello are a mixed lot. Though the big estates are interspersed now with middle-class homes, the overall impression is of money, carefully cultivated and preserved, vintage elegance harking back to a time when wealth was handled with discretion and material display reserved for one's financial peers. The rich, these days, are merely gaudy imitators of their early California counterparts. Montebello does have its "slums," a curious string of clapboard shacks that sell for $140,000 apiece.

The address Bobby'd given me was off West Glen, a narrow road shaded by eucalyptus and sycamore, lined with low walls of hand-hewn stone that curve back toward mansions too remote to be seen by passing motorists. An occasional gatehouse hints at the stately digs beyond, but for the most part West Glen seems to wander through groves of live oak with nothing more on its mind than dappled sunshine, the scent of French lavender, and bumblebees droning

among hot-pink geraniums. It was six now and wouldn't get
dark for another two hours or so.

I spotted the number I was looking for and turned into a
driveway, slowing. To my right were three white stucco cottages, looking like something the three little pigs might
have built. I peered through the windshield, but couldn't
see a parking place. I rolled forward, hoping there would be
a parking pad somewhere around the bend coming up. I
glanced back over my shoulder, wondering why there
weren't any other cars in sight, and wondering which of the
little bungalows belonged to Bobby's folks. I felt a brief moment of uneasiness. He *had* said this afternoon, hadn't
he? I could just picture myself arriving on the wrong
day. I shrugged. Oh, well. I'd suffered worse embarrass-
ments in my life, though for the moment, I couldn't think of
one. I rounded the curve, looking for a place to pull in.
Involuntarily, I slammed on the brakes, skidding to a stop.
"Holy shit!" I whispered.

The lane had opened out into a large paved courtyard.
Just ahead I saw a house. Somehow, in my gut, I knew
Bobby Callahan lived here, not in one of those homey little
snuggeries up front. Those were probably servants' quarters. This was the real thing.

The house was the size of the junior high school I'd attended and had probably been designed by the same architect, a man named Dwight Costigan, dead now, who had
revitalized Santa Teresa single-handedly during the forty-
odd years he worked. The style, if I'm not mistaken, is
Spanish Revival. I have tended, I confess, to sneer at white
stucco walls and red tile roofs. I've been contemptuous of
arches and bougainvillea, distressed beams and balconies,
but I had never seen them put together quite like this.

The central portion of the house was two stories high,
flanked by two cloistered arcades. Arch after arch after
arch, supported by graceful columns. There were clusters
of airy palms, sculptured portals, tracery windows. There
was even a bell tower, like an old mission church. Hadn't
Kim Novak been pushed out of something similar? The
place looked like a cross between a monastery and a movie
set. Four Mercedes were parked in the courtyard like a

glossy ad campaign, and a fountain in the center shot a stream of water fifteen feet high.

I pulled in as far to the right as I could get and parked, then looked down at what I had on. The pants, I saw now, had a stain on one knee that I could only conceal if I held myself in a continual crouch so the tunic would hang down that far. The tunic itself wasn't bad: black gauzy stuff with a low square neck, long sleeves, and a matching tie belt. For a moment, I considered driving home again to change clothes. Then, it occurred to me that I didn't have anything at home that looked any better than this. I torqued myself around to the backseat, sorting through the incredible collection of odds and ends I keep back there. I drive a VW, one of those nondescript beige sedans, great for surveillance work in most neighborhoods. Around here, I could see I'd need to hire a stretch limo. The gardeners probably drove Volvos.

I pushed aside the law books, file boxes, tool kit, the briefcase where I keep my gun locked. Ah, just what I was looking for: an old pair of pantyhose, useful as a filter in an emergency. On the floor, I found a pair of black spike heels I'd bought when I'd intended to pass myself off as a hooker in a tacky part of Los Angeles. When I'd gotten there, of course, I'd discovered that all the whores looked like college girls, so I'd abandoned the disguise.

I tossed the sandals I was wearing into the backseat and hunched my long pants off. I wiggled into the pantyhose, did a spit polish on the pumps, and slipped into those. I took the self-belt off the tunic and tied it around my neck in an exotic knot. In the bottom of my handbag, I found an eyeliner pencil and some blusher and I did a quick makeover, tilting the rearview mirror so I could see myself. I thought I looked weird, but how would they know? Except for Bobby, none of them had ever seen me before. I hoped.

I got out of the car and steadied myself. I hadn't worn heels this high since I'd played dress-up in my aunt's cast-offs when I was in first grade. Beltless, the tunic hit me midthigh, the lightweight fabric clinging to my hips. If I walked in front of a light, they'd see my bikini underpants, but so what? If I couldn't afford to dress well, at least I could provide a distraction from the fact. I took a deep breath and clattered my way toward the door.

3

I rang the bell. I could hear it echo through the house. In due course, the door was opened by a black maid in a white uniform like a nurse's aide's. I wanted to fall into her arms and be dragged off to the infirmary, my feet hurt so bad, but I mentioned my name instead and murmured that Bobby Callahan expected me.

"Yes, Miss Millhone. Won't you come in, please?"

She stepped aside and I moved into the hallway. The ceiling in the entryway was two stories high, light filtering down through a series of windows that followed the line of the wide stone stairs curving up to the left. The floor was tile, a soft red, polished to a satiny sheen. There were runners of Persian carpeting in faded patterns. Tapestries hung from ornamental wrought-iron rods that looked like antique weaponry. The air temperature was perfect, cool and still, scented by a massive floral arrangement on a heavy side table to my right. I felt like I was in a museum.

The maid led me down the hallway to a living room so large the group of people at the far end seemed constructed on a smaller scale than I. The stone fireplace must have been ten feet wide and a good twelve feet high, with an opening big enough to roast an ox in. The furniture looked comfortable; nothing fussy or small. The couches, four of them, seemed substantial, and the chairs were large and overstuffed, with wide arms, reminding me somehow of first-class seats on an airplane. There was no particular color scheme and I wondered if it was only the middle class that ran out and hired someone to make everything match.

I caught sight of Bobby and, mercifully, he lumbered in my direction. He had apparently divined from my expression that I was ill-prepared for this whole pageant.

"I should have warned you. I'm sorry," he said. "Let me get you a drink. What would you like? We've got white wine, but if I tell you what it is, you'll think we're showing off."

"Wine is perfect," I said. "I'm crazy about the show-off kind."

Another maid, not the one who opened the door, but one especially trained for living rooms, anticipated Bobby's needs, approaching with glasses of wine already poured. I was really hoping I wouldn't disgrace myself by spilling a drink down my front or catching a heel on the rug. He handed me a glass of wine and I took a sip.

"Did you grow up in this place?" I asked. It was difficult to picture binkies, Johnny-Jump-Ups, and Tonka trucks in a room that looked like the nave of a church. I suddenly tuned in to what was happening in my mouth. This wine was going to ruin me for the stuff in a cardboard box, which is what I usually drink.

"Actually, I did," he said, looking around with interest now, as though the incongruity had just occurred to him. "I had a nanny, of course."

"Oh sure, why not? What do your parents do? Or should I guess."

Bobby gave me a lopsided smile and dabbed at his chin, almost sheepishly, I thought. "My grandfather, my mother's father, founded a big chemical company at the turn of the century. I guess they ended up patenting half the products essential to civilization. Douches and mouthwashes and birth-control devices. A lot of over-the-counter drugs, too. Solvents, alloys, industrial products. The list goes on for a bit."

"Brothers? Sisters?"

"Just me."

"Where's your father at this point?"

"Tibet. He's taken to mountain climbing of late. Last year, he lived in an ashram in India. His soul is evolving at a pace with his VISA bill."

I cupped a hand to my ear. "Do I detect some hostility?"

Bobby shrugged. "He can afford to dabble in the Great Mysteries because of the settlement he got from my mother when they divorced. He pretends it's a great spiritual jour-

ney when he's really just indulging himself. Actually, I felt
O.K. about him until he came back just after the accident.
He used to sit by my bedside and smile at me benevolently,
explaining that being crippled must be something I was
having to sort through in this life." He looked at me with an
odd smile. "Know what he said when he heard Rick was
dead? 'That's nice. That means he's finished his work.' I got
so upset Dr. Kleinert refused to let him visit anymore, so he
went off to hike the Himalayas. We don't hear from him
much, but it's just as well, I guess."

Bobby broke off. For a moment, tears swam in his eyes
and he fought for control. He stared off toward a cluster of
people near the fireplace and I followed his gaze. There
were only ten or so on a quick count.

"Which one is your mother?"

"The woman in the cream-colored outfit. The guy standing just behind her is my stepfather, Derek. They've been
married three years, but I don't think it's working out."

"How come?"

Bobby seemed to consider several replies, but he finally
settled for a slight head shake and silence. He looked back
at me. "You ready to meet them?"

"Tell me about the other people first." I was stalling, but I
couldn't help myself.

He surveyed the group. "Some, I forget. That woman in
blue I don't know at all. The tall fellow with gray hair is Dr.
Fraker. He's the pathologist I was working for before the
accident. He's married to the redhead talking to my mom.
My mother's on the board of trustees for St. Terry's so she
knows all these medical types. The balding, heavyset man
is Dr. Metcalf and the guy he's talking to is Dr. Kleinert."

"Your psychiatrist?"

"Right. He thinks I'm crazy, but that's all right because he
thinks he can fix me." Bitterness had crept into his voice
and I was acutely aware of the level of rage he must be
dealing with day by day.

As though on cue, Dr. Kleinert turned and stared at us
and then his eyes slid away. He looked like he was in his
early forties with thin, wavy gray hair and a sorrowful expression.

Bobby smirked. "I told him I was hiring a private detective, but I don't think he's figured out yet that it's you or he'd have come down here to have a little chat to straighten us out."

"What about your stepsister? Where is she?"

"Probably in her room. She's not very sociable."

"And who's the little blonde?"

"My mother's best friend. She's a surgical nurse. Come on," he said impatiently. "You 'might as well take the plunge."

I followed Bobby, keeping pace with him as he hobbled down the room toward the fireplace, where people had congregated. His mother watched us approach, the two women with her pausing in the middle of their conversation to see what had engaged her attention.

She looked young to be the mother of a twenty-three-year-old, lean, with narrow hips and long legs. Her hair was a thick glossy bush of pale fawn brown, not quite shoulder-length. Her eyes were small and deep-set, her face narrow, mouth wide. Her hands were elegant, her fingers long and thin. She wore a cream-colored silk blouse and a full linen skirt nipped in at the waist. Her jewelry was gold, delicate chains at her wrist and throat. The gaze she turned on Bobby was intense and I thought I could feel the pain with which she regarded his crippled form. She looked from him to me, smiling politely.

She moved forward, holding out her hand. "I'm Glen Callahan. You must be Kinsey Millhone. Bobby said you'd be stopping by." Her voice was low and throaty. "I'll give you a chance to enjoy yourself. We'll talk in a bit."

I shook hands with her, startled how bony and warm her hand felt in mine. Her grip was iron.

She glanced at the woman to her right, introducing me. "This is Nola Fraker."

"Hi, how are you?" I said as we shook hands.

"And Sufi Daniels."

Murmured pleasantries were exchanged. Nola was a red-head, with clear, fine-textured skin, and luminous blue eyes, wearing a dark red jumpsuit that left her arms bare and a deep V of naked flesh visible from throat to waist. Already, I didn't want her to bend down or make any sudden moves. I had the feeling I knew her from somewhere. Possibly I'd seen her picture in the society section or something of that sort. Reminder bells went off, at any rate, and I wondered what the story was.

The other woman, Sufi, was small and somewhat misshapen, thick through the trunk, her back hunched. She wore a mauve velour sweatsuit that looked like she'd never sweated in it. Her blond hair was thin and fine, worn too long, I thought, to be flattering.

After a decent interval, the three of them resumed their conversation, much to my relief. I hadn't the faintest idea what to say to them. Nola was talking about a thirty-dollar fabric remnant she was whipping up to wear to a wine-tasting down in Los Angeles. "I checked all the shops in Montebello, but it was ridiculous! I wouldn't pay four bills for an outfit. I wouldn't even pay *two*," she said with energy.

That surprised me. She looked like a woman who enjoyed extravagance. Unless I just make up things like that. My notion of women with money is that they drive to Beverly Hills to have their legs waxed, charge a bauble or two on Rodeo Drive, and then go to charity luncheons at $1,500 a plate. I couldn't picture Nola Fraker pawing through the bargain bin at our local Stretch N' Sew. Maybe she'd been poor as a young girl and couldn't get used to being a doctor's wife.

Bobby took my arm and steered me toward the men. He introduced me to his stepfather, Derek Wenner, and then in quick succession to Drs. Fraker, Metcalf, and Kleinert. Before I knew what to think, he was hustling me toward the hallway. "Let's go upstairs. We'll find Kitty and then I'll show you the rest of the house."

"Bobby, I want to talk to those people!" I said.

"No, you don't. They're dull and they don't know anything."

As we passed a side table, I started to set my wineglass down, but he shook his head. "Bring it with you."

He grabbed a full bottle of wine out of a silver cooler and tucked it under his arm. He was really moving at a fair clip, limp and all, and I could hear my high heels clip-clopping along inelegantly as we moved toward the foyer. I paused for a moment to slip my shoes off, and then I caught up with him. Something about Bobby's attitude made me want to laugh. He was accustomed to doing exactly as he pleased among people I'd been taught to respect. My aunt would have been impressed by the company, but Bobby didn't seem to be.

We went up the stairs, Bobby pulling himself along by the smooth stone banister.

"Your mother doesn't use the name Wenner?" I asked, as I followed him.

"Nope. Callahan is her maiden name as a matter of fact. I changed mine to Callahan when she and my father divorced."

"That's unusual, isn't it?"

"Doesn't seem that way to me. He's a jerk. This way, I don't have to be connected to him any more than she does."

The gallery at the top formed a semicircle with wings branching out on either side. We passed through an archway to the right and into a wide corridor with rooms opening off at intervals. Most of the doors were closed. Daylight was beginning to fade and the upstairs was gloomy. I once conducted a homicide investigation at an exclusive girls' school that had this same air to it. The house felt as if it had been converted to institutional use, someplace impersonal and chill. Bobby knocked at the third door down on the right.

"Kitty?"

"Just a minute," she called.

He flashed me a smile. "She'll be stoned."

Hey, why not? I thought with a shrug. Seventeen.

The door opened and she looked out, gaze shifting from Bobby to me with suspicion. "Who's this?"

"Come on, Kitty. Would you knock that shit off?"

She moved away from the door indifferently. Bobby and I went in and he closed the door behind us. She was anoretic; tall and painfully thin, with knees and elbow joints standing out like Tinkertoys. Her face was gaunt. She was barefoot, wearing shorts and a white tube top that looked about as big as a man's crew sock, one size fits all.

"What are *you* looking at?" she said. She didn't seem to expect an answer so I didn't bother with one. She flopped down on an unmade king-sized bed, staring at me as she took up a cigarette and lit it. Her nails were bitten to the quick. The room had been painted black and looked like a parody of an adolescent girl's room. There were lots of posters and stuffed animals but all of them had a nightmare quality. The posters were of rock groups in tartish makeup, sinister and sneering, depicted in vignettes largely hostile toward women. The stuffed animals ran more to satyrs than Winnie-the-Pooh. The air was scented with eau de dope and my guess was she'd smoked so much grass in there, you could bury your nose in the bedcovers and get high.

Bobby apparently enjoyed her antagonism. He pulled a chair over for me, dumping clothes on the floor unceremoniously. I sat down and he stretched out on the foot of the bed, circling her left ankle with one hand. His fingers overlapped as if he were holding her wrist instead. It reminded me of Hansel and Gretel. Maybe Kitty was worried that if she got fat, they'd put her in the cooking pot. I thought they'd put her in a grave long before that point and it was frightening. She leaned back on both elbows, smiling at me faintly down the length of her long, frail legs. All the veins were visible, like an anatomical diagram with a celluloid overlay. I could see how the bones were strung together in her feet, her toes looking almost prehensile.

"So what's going on downstairs?" she said to Bobby, her gaze still pinned on me. Her speech was ever so slightly slurred and her eyes seemed to swim in and out of focus. I wondered if she was drunk or had just popped some pills.

"They're standing around sucking up booze as usual. Speaking of which, I brought us wine," he said. "Got a glass?"

She leaned over to her bed-table and sorted through the mess, coming up with a tumbler with something sticky and green in the bottom: absinthe or crème de menthe. She held the glass out to him. The wine he poured into it became tainted with the remnants of liqueur.

"So, who's the chick?"

I loathe being called a chick.

Bobby laughed. "Oh God, I'm sorry. This is Kinsey. She's the private detective I told you about."

"I should've figured as much." Her eyes came back to mine, her pupils so dilated I couldn't tell what color the irises were. "So how do you like our little sideshow? Bobby and I are the family freaks. What a pair, right?"

This child was getting on my nerves. She wasn't smart enough or quick enough to pull off the tough air she was affecting, and the strain was evident, like watching a stand-up comic with second-rate gags.

Bobby cut in smoothly. "Dr. Kleinert's downstairs."

"Ah, Dr. Destructo. What did you think of him?" She took a drag of her cigarette, feigning nonchalance, but I sensed that she was genuinely curious about my response.

"I didn't talk to him," I said. "Bobby wanted me to meet you first."

She stared at me and I stared back. I remembered doing this sort of stuff in sixth grade with my mortal enemy, Tommy Jancko. I forget now why we disliked each other, but stare contests were definitely the weapons of choice.

She looked back at Bobby. "He wants me hospitalized. D'I tell you that?"

"You going?"

"Hey, no *way*! Get all those needles stuck in me? Uh-un, no thanks. I'm not interested." She swung her long legs over the side of the bed and got up. She crossed the room to a low dressing table with a gilt-edged mirror above it. She studied her face, glancing back at me. "You think I look thin?"

"Very."

"Really?" She seemed fascinated by the notion, turning slightly so she could see her own flat behind. She studied her face again, watching herself take a drag of her cigarette. She did a quick shrug. Everything looked fine to her.

"Could we talk about this murder attempt?" I said.

She padded back to the bed and flopped down again. "Somebody's after him. Definitely," she said. She stubbed out her cigarette, with a yawn.

"What makes you say that?"

"The vibes."

"Aside from the vibes," I said.

"Oh balls, you don't believe us either," she said. She turned sideways and settled against the pillows, folding an arm under her head.

"Is someone after you too?"

"Nun-un. I don't think so. Just him."

"But why would someone do that? I'm not saying I don't believe you. I'm looking for a place to start and I want to hear what you have to say."

"I'd have to think about it some," she said and then she was quiet.

It took me a few minutes to realize she'd passed out. Jesus, what was she on?

4

I waited in the hallway, shoes in hand, while Bobby covered her with a blanket and tiptoed out of the room, closing the door gently.

"What's the story?" I said.

"She's O.K. She was just up late last night."

"What are you talking about? She's half dead!"

He shifted uneasily. "You really think so?"

"Bobby, would you *look* at her? She's a skeleton. She's doing drugs, alcohol, cigarettes. You know she's smoking dope on top of that. How's she going to survive?"

"I don't know. I guess I didn't think she was that bad off," he said. He was not only young, he was *naïve*, or maybe she'd been going under so gradually that he couldn't see the shape she was in.

"How long has she been anoretic?"

"Since Rick died, I guess. Maybe some before that. He was her boyfriend and she took it pretty hard."

"Is that what Kleinert's seeing her for? The anorexia?"

"I guess. I never really asked. She was a patient of his before I started seeing him."

A voice cut in. "Is there some problem?"

Derek Wenner was approaching from the gallery, highball in hand. He was a man who'd been good-looking once. Of medium height, fair-haired, his gray eyes magnified by glasses with steel-blue frames. He was in his late forties now, by a charitable estimate, a solid thirty pounds overweight. He had the puffy, florid complexion of a man who drinks too much and his hairline had receded in a wide U that left a runner of thinning hair down the center, clipped short and brushed to one side. The excess pounds had given him a double chin and a wide neck that made the collar of his dress shirt seem tight. His pleated gabardine pants looked expensive and so did his loafers, which were tan and white, with vents cut into the leather. He'd been wearing a sport coat earlier, but he'd taken it off, along with his tie. He unbuttoned his collar with relief.

"What's going on? Where's Kitty? Your mother wants to know why she hasn't joined us."

Bobby seemed embarrassed. "I don't know. She was talking to us and she fell asleep."

"Fell asleep" seemed a bit understated to me. Kitty's face had been the color of a plastic ring I sent away for once as a kid. The ring was white, but if you held it to the light for a while and then cupped your hand over it, it glowed faintly green. This, to me, did not connote good health.

"Hell, I better talk to her," he said. I had to guess he'd had his hands full with her. He opened the door and went into Kitty's room.

Bobby gave me a look that was part dismay and part anxiety. I glanced in through the open door. Derek put his drink on the table and sat down on Kitty's bed.

"Kitty?"

He put a hand on her shoulder and shook her gently. There was no response. "Hey, come on, honey. Wake up."

He shot me a worried look.

He gave Kitty a rough shake. "Hey, come on. Wake up."

"You want me to get one of the doctors from downstairs?" I said. He shook her again. I didn't wait for a response.

I slipped my shoes on and left my handbag by the door, heading for the stairs.

When I reached the living room, Glen Callahan glanced over at me, apparently sensing that something was wrong.

She moved forward. "Where's Bobby?"

"Upstairs with Kitty. I think it might be smart to have somebody take a look at her. She passed out and your husband's having trouble rousing her."

"I'll get Leo."

I watched while she approached Dr. Kleinert, murmuring to him. He glanced over at me and then he excused himself from his conversation. The three of us went upstairs.

Bobby had joined Derek at Kitty's bedside, his face creased with concern. Derek was trying to pull Kitty into a sitting position, but she slumped to one side. Dr. Kleinert moved forward swiftly and pushed both men out of the way. He did a quick check of her vital signs, pulling a penlight out of the inside breast pocket of his suit. Her pupils had contracted down to pinpoints, and from where I stood, the green eyes looked milky and lifeless, apparently responding little to the light he flashed first in one, then the other. Her breathing was slow and shallow, her muscles flaccid. Dr. Kleinert reached for the telephone, which was sitting on the floor near the bed, and dialed 911.

Glen remained in the doorway. "What is it?"

Kleinert ignored her, apparently talking to the emergency dispatcher.

"This is Dr. Leo Kleinert. I'm going to need an ambulance out on West Glen Road in Montebello. I've got a patient suffering from barbiturate poisoning." He gave the address and a brief set of instructions about how to reach the place. He hung up and looked at Bobby. "You have any idea what she took?"

Bobby shook his head.

Derek responded, addressing the remark to Glen. "She was fine half an hour ago. I talked to her myself."

"Oh Derek. For God's sake," she said with annoyance.

Kleinert reached over and opened the bed-table drawer. He sorted through some junk and then hesitated, pulling out a stash of pills that would have felled an elephant. They were in a Ziploc bag, maybe two hundred capsules: Nembutals, Seconals, blue-and-orange Tuinals, Placidyls, Quaaludes, like colorful supplies for some exotic cottage industry.

Kleinert's expression was despairing. He looked up at Derek, holding the bag by one corner. Exhibit A in a trial that had been going on for some time by my guess.

"What are those things?" Derek said. "How'd she get them?"

Kleinert shook her head. "Let's get people out of here and then we'll worry about that."

Glen Callahan had already turned and left the room and I could hear her heels clipping purposefully toward the

stairs. Bobby took my arm and the two of us moved out into
the hallway.

Derek was apparently still having trouble believing this
was happening. "Is she going to be O.K.?"

Dr. Kleinert murmured a reply, but I couldn't hear what
it was.

Bobby steered me into a room across the hall and closed
the door. "Let's stay out of the way. We'll go downstairs in a
bit." He rubbed at the fingers of his bad hand as if it were a
talisman. The drag in his voice was back.

The room was large, with deep-set windows looking out
onto the rear of the property. The wall-to-wall carpeting was
white, a dense cut-pile so recently vacuumed that I could
see Bobby's footprints in places. His double bed seemed
diminutive in a room that was probably thirty feet square,
with a large dressing room opening off to the left and what
was apparently a bathroom beyond that. A television set
rested on an antique pine blanket-chest at the foot of the
bed. On the wall to my right was a long built-in desk with a
white Formica surface. An IBM Selectric II and the keyboard, monitor, and printer for a home computer were
lined up along its length. The bookshelves were white Formica too, filled almost exclusively with medical texts. There
was a sitting area in the far corner: two overstuffed chairs
and an ottoman covered in a plaid fabric of rust, white, and
slate blue. The coffee table, reading lamp, books and magazines stacked nearby suggested that this was where Bobby
spent his leisure time.

He went to an intercom on the wall and pressed a button.
"Callie, we're starving up here. Could you send us a tray?
There are two of us and we'll need some white wine too."

I could hear a hollow clattering in the background: dishes
being loaded into the dishwasher. "Yes, Mr. Bobby. I'll have
Alicia bring something up."

"Thank you."

He limped over to one of the chairs and sat down. "I eat
when I'm anxious. I've always done that. Come sit down.
Shit, I hate this house. I used to love it. When I was a kid, it
was great. Places to run. Places to hide. A yard that went on
forever. Now it feels like a cocoon. Insulated. But it doesn't
keep bad stuff out. It feels cold. Are you cold?"

"I'm fine," I said.

I sat down in the other chair. He pushed the ottoman over and I put my feet up. I wondered what it must be like to live in a house like this where all of your needs were tended to, where someone else was responsible for grocery shopping and food preparation, cleaning, trash removal, landscape maintenance. What did it leave you free to do?

"What's it like coming from money like this? I can't even imagine it."

He hesitated, lifting his head.

In the distance, we could hear the ambulance approach, the siren reaching a crescendo and then winding down abruptly with a whine of regret. He glanced at me, dabbing self-consciously at his chin. "You think we're spoiled?" The two halves of his face seemed to give contradictory messages: one animated, one dead.

"How do I know? You live a lot better than most," I said.

"Hey, we do our share. My mother does a lot of fund raising for local charities and she's on the board for the art museum and the historical society. I don't know about Derek. He plays golf and hangs out at the club. Well, that's not fair. He has some investments he looks after, which is how they met. He was the executor for the trust my grandfather left me. Once he and Mom got married, he left the bank. Anyway, they support a lot of causes so it's not like they're just self-indulgent, grinding the poor underfoot. My mother launched the Santa Teresa Girls' Club just about single-handedly. The Rape Crisis Center too."

"What about Kitty? What does she do with herself besides get loaded?"

He looked at me carefully. "Don't make judgments. You don't know what any of us has been through."

"You're right. I'm sorry. I didn't mean to sound quite so righteous. Is she in private school?"

He shook his head. "Not anymore. They moved her over to Santa Teresa High School this year. Anything to try to get her straightened out."

He stared at the door uneasily. The house was so solidly constructed there was no way to tell if the paramedics had come upstairs yet.

I crossed the room and opened the door a crack. They were just coming out of Kitty's room with the portable gurney, its wheels swiveling like a grocery cart's as they angled her into the hall. She was covered with a blanket, so frail that she scarcely formed a mound. One thin arm was extended outside the covers. They'd started an I.V., a plastic bag of some clear solution held aloft by one of the paramedics. Oxygen was being administered through a nose cone. Dr. Kleinert moved toward the stairs ahead of them and Derek brought up the rear, hands shoved awkwardly in his pockets, his face pale. He seemed out of place and ineffectual, pausing when he caught sight of me.

"I'm going to follow in my car," he said, though no one had asked. "Tell Bobby we'll be at St. Terry's."

I felt sorry for him. The scene was like something out of a TV series, the medical personnel very deadpan and businesslike. This was his daughter being taken away and she might actually die, but no one seemed to be addressing the possibility. There was no sign of Bobby's mother, no sign of the people who'd come for drinks. Everything felt ill-planned somehow, like an elaborate entertainment that was falling flat. "You want us to come, too?" I asked.

Derek shook his head. "Let my wife know where I am," he said. "I'll call as soon as I know what's going on."

"Good luck," I said, and he flashed me a weak smile as if good luck was not something he'd had much experience with.

I watched the procession disappear down the stairs. I closed the door to Bobby's room. I started to say something, but Bobby cut me off.

"I heard," he said.

"Why isn't your mother involved in this? Are she and Kitty on the outs or what?"

"Jesus, it's all too complicated to explain. Mom washed her hands of Kitty after the last incident, which isn't as heartless as it sounds. Early on, she did what she could, but I guess it was just one crisis after another. That's part of the reason she and Derek are having such a tough time."

"What's the other part?"

His look was bleak. Clearly, he felt he was equally to blame.

There was a tap at the door and a Chicano woman with her hair in a braid appeared with a tray. Her face was expressionless and she made no eye contact. If she knew what was happening, she gave no indication of it. She fussed around for a bit with cloth napkins and cutlery. I almost expected her to present a room-service check to be signed off with a tip added in.

"Thanks, Alicia," Bobby said.

She murmured something and departed. I felt uncomfortable that it was all so impersonal. I wanted to ask her if her feet hurt like mine, or if she had a family we could talk about. I wanted her to voice curiosity or dismay about the people she worked for, carted away on stretchers at odd hours of the day. Instead, Bobby poured the wine and we ate.

The meal was like something out of a magazine. Plump quartered chicken served cold with a mustard sauce, tiny flaky tarts filled with spinach and a smoky cheddar cheese, clusters of grapes and sprigs of parsley tucked here and there. Two small china bowls with lids held an icy tomato soup with fresh dill clipped across the surface and a little dollop of crème fraîche. We finished with a plate of tiny decorated cookies. Did these people eat like this every day? Bobby never batted an eye. I don't know what I expected him to do. He couldn't squeal with excitement every time a supper tray showed up, but I was impressed and I guess I wanted him to marvel, as I did, so I wouldn't feel like such a rube.

By the time we went downstairs, it was nearly eight and the guests were gone. The house seemed deserted, except for the two maids who were tidying up the living room in silence as we passed. Bobby led us to a heavy oak-paneled door across the wide hall. He knocked and there was a murmured response. We went into a small den, where Glen Callahan was seated with a book, a wineglass on the end table at her right hand. She'd changed into chocolate-brown wool slacks and a matching cashmere pullover. A fire burned in a copper grate. The walls were painted tomato red, with matching red drapes drawn against the chill dusk. In Santa Teresa, most nights are cold regardless of the month. This room felt cozy, an intimate retreat from the rest of the house with its high ceilings and chalk-white stucco walls.

Bobby sat down in the chair across from his mother. "Has Derek called yet?"

She closed her book and set it aside. "A few minutes ago. She's pulled out of it. She had her stomach pumped and they'll be admitting her as soon as she's out of emergency. Derek will stay until the papers have been signed."

I glanced at Bobby. He lowered his face into his hands and sighed once with relief, a sound like a low note on a bagpipe. He shook his head, staring down at the floor.

Glen studied him. "You're exhausted. Why don't you go on to bed? I'll want to talk to Kinsey alone anyway."

"All right. I might as well," he said. The slur in his voice had become pronounced and I could see now that the fine muscles near his eyes were being tugged, as though stimulated electrically. Fatigue apparently exacerbated his disability. He got up and crossed to her chair. Glen took his face in her hands and stared at him intently.

"I'll let you know if there's any change in Kitty's condition," she murmured. "I don't want you to worry. Sleep well."

He nodded, laying the good side of his face near hers. He moved toward the door. "I'll call you in the morning," he said to me, then let himself out. I could hear his dragging gait for a moment in the hallway and then it faded from hearing.

5

I sat in the chair Bobby had vacated. The down-filled cushion was still warm, contoured to the shape of his body. Glen was watching me, formulating, I gathered, an opinion of me. By lamplight, I could see that her hair color was the handiwork of an expert who'd matched it almost exactly to the mild brown of her eyes. Everything about her was beautifully coordinated: makeup, clothing, accessories. She was apparently a person who paid attention to detail and her taste was impeccable.

"I'm sorry you had to see us like this."

"I'm not sure I ever see people at their best," I said. "It gives me a rather skewed impression of humankind. Will he be paying my bills or will you?"

The question caused her to focus on me with interest and I guessed that she brought a considerable intelligence to any matter involving money. She raised an eyebrow ever so slightly.

"He will. He came into his trust when he was twenty-one. Why do you ask?"

"I like to know who I'm reporting to," I said. "What's your feeling about his claim that someone's trying to kill him?"

She took a moment to respond, shrugging delicately. "It's possible. The police seem convinced that someone forced him off that bridge. Whether it was premeditated, I have no idea." Her voice was distinct, low, and intense.

"From what Bobby says, it's been a long nine months."

She ran a thumbnail along her pantleg, directing her comments to the crease. "I don't know how we survived it. He's my only child, the light of my life."

She paused, smiling slightly to herself, and then looked up at me with an unexpected shyness. "I know all mothers

must talk like this, but he was special. He really was. Even
from infancy. Smart, alert, sociable, quick. And gorgeous.
Such a beautiful little boy, easygoing and affectionate,
funny. He was magical.

"The night of the accident, the police came to the house.
They weren't able to notify us until four in the morning
because the car wasn't discovered for a while and then it
took hours to get the two boys up the side of the mountain.
Rick died instantly, of course."

She broke off and I thought at first she'd lost her train of
thought. "Anyway. The doorbell rang. Derek went down,
and when he didn't come back, I grabbed a robe and went
down myself. I saw two policemen in the foyer. I thought
they'd come to tell us there was a burglary in the neighborhood or an accident on the road out front. Derek turned
around and he had this awful look on his face. He said,
'Glen, it's Bobby.' I thought my heart had stopped."

She looked up at me and her eyes were luminous with
tears. She laced her fingers together, making a steeple of
her two index fingers, which she rested against her lips. "I
thought he was dead. I thought they'd come to tell me he'd
died. I felt a spurt of ice, like I'd been stabbed. It started in
my heart and spread through my body 'til my teeth chat-
tered. He was at St. Terry's by then. All we knew at that
point was he was still alive, but barely. When we got to the
hospital, the doctor didn't give us any hope at all. None.
They told us there were extensive injuries. Brain damage
and so many broken bones. They said he'd never recover,
that he'd be a vegetable if he survived. I was dying. I died
because Bobby was dying and it went on for days. I never
left his side. I was crazy, screaming at everyone, nurses,
doctors . . ."

Her gaze flattened and she lifted an index finger, like a
teacher who wants to make a point very clear. "I'll tell you
what I learned," she said carefully. "I understood I couldn't
buy Bobby's life. Money can't buy life, but it can buy anything else you want. I'd never used money that way, which
seems odd to me now. My parents had money. My parents'
parents had money. I've always understood the power of
money, but I'd never wielded it with quite such effect. He
had the best of everything. The best! Nothing was spared.

And he pulled out of it. Having endured so much, I'd hate to think someone did it deliberately. To all intents and purposes, Bobby's life is ruined. He'll be all right and we'll find a way for him to live productively, but only because we're in a position to make that happen. The losses are incalculable. It's miraculous he's come this far."

"You have any theories about why someone might try to kill him?"

She shook her head.

"You said Bobby has his own money. Who benefits if he dies?"

"You'd have to ask him that. He has a will, I'm sure, and we've discussed his leaving his money to various charities . . . unless of course, he marries and has legitimate heirs of his own. You think money might be the motive?"

I shrugged. "I tend to look at that first, especially in a situation like this when it sounds like there's a lot."

"What else could it be? What could anyone have against him?"

"People murder for absurd reasons. Someone gets into a rage over something and retaliates. People get jealous or want to defend themselves from a real or imagined attack. Or they've done something wrong and they kill to cover it up. Sometimes it doesn't even make that much sense. Maybe Bobby cut someone off in a lane change that night and the driver followed him all the way up the pass. People go nuts in cars. I take it he wasn't in the middle of a hassle with anyone?"

"Not that I was aware of."

"Nobody mad at him? A girl friend maybe?"

"I doubt it. He was going with someone at the time, but it was a fairly casual relationship from what I could tell. Once this happened, we didn't see much of her. Of course, Bobby changed. You don't come that close to death without paying a penalty. Violent death is like a monster. The closer you get to it, the more damage you sustain . . . if you survive at all. Bobby's had to pull himself out of the grave, step by step. He's different now. He's looked into the monster's face. You can see the claw marks on his body everywhere."

I glanced away from her. It was true. Bobby looked like he had been attacked: torn and broken and mauled. Violent death leaves an aura, like an energy field that repels the observer. I've never looked at a homicide victim yet without a quick recoil. Even photographs of the dead chill and repulse me.

I shifted back to the matter at hand. "Bobby said he was working for Dr. Fraker at the time."

"That's right. Jim Fraker's been a friend of mine for years. That's why Bobby was hired at St. Terry's, as a matter of fact. As a favor to me."

"How long had he worked there?"

"At the hospital itself, maybe four months. He'd been working for Jim in Pathology for two months, I think."

"And what did he actually do?"

"Cleaned equipment, ran errands, answered the phone. It was all routine. They'd taught him to do a few lab tests and sometimes he monitored machinery, but I can't imagine his job entailed anything that would endanger his life."

"He had his degree from UCST by then, I gather," I said, repeating what Bobby'd told me.

"That's right. He was working temporarily, hoping to get accepted to med school. His first applications had been turned down."

"How come?"

"Oh, he got cocky and only applied to about five schools. He'd always been an excellent student and he'd never failed at anything in his life. He miscalculated. Med schools are ferociously competitive and he simply didn't get accepted to the ones he tried for. It set him back on his heels for a time, but he'd rallied, I think. I know he felt the job with Dr. Fraker was valuable, because it gave him some exposure to disciplines he wouldn't otherwise have known about until much later in the game."

"What else was going on in his life at that point?"

"Not a lot. He went to work. He dated. He did some weight lifting, surfed now and then. He went to movies, went out to dinner with us. It all seemed very ordinary at the time and it seems very ordinary looking back."

There was another avenue I needed to explore and I wondered how she would react. "Were he and Kitty involved with one another sexually?"

"Ah. Well, I can't really answer that. I have no idea."

"But it's possible."

"I suppose so, though I don't think it's likely. Derek and I have been together since she was thirteen. Bobby was eighteen, nineteen, something like that. Out of the house at any rate. I do think Kitty was smitten with him. I don't know how he felt about her, but I can't believe a thirteen-year-old would interest him in the least."

"She's grown up pretty fast from what I've seen."

She crossed her legs restlessly, wrapping one around the other. "I don't understand why you're pursuing this point."

"I need to know what was going on. He was anxious about her tonight and more than relieved when he found out she was all right. I wondered how deep the connections ran."

"Oh. I see. A lot of his emotionalism is the aftermath of the accident. From what I'm told, it's not uncommon for people who've suffered head injury. He's moody now. Impatient. And he overreacts. He weeps easily and he gets very frustrated with himself."

"Is part of that the memory loss?"

"Yes," she said. "What makes it hard is he can never predict where the losses will occur. Sometimes he can remember the most inconsequential things, then he'll turn around and forget his own birthdate. Or he'll blank out on someone altogether, maybe someone he's known all his life. That's one of the reasons he's seeing Leo Kleinert. To help him cope with the personality changes."

"He told me Kitty was seeing Dr. Kleinert, too. Was that for the anorexia?"

"Kitty's been impossible from the first."

"Well, I gathered that much. What was it about?"

"Ask Derek. I'm the wrong person to consult about her. I did try, but I don't give a damn anymore. Even this business tonight. I know it sounds cruel, but I can't take it seriously. She does it to herself. It's her life. Let her do anything she wants as long as it doesn't affect the rest of us. She can drop dead for all I care."

"It looks like her behavior affects you whether you like it or not," I ventured carefully. This was clearly touchy stuff and I didn't want to antagonize her.

"I'm afraid that's true, but I've had it. Something's got to change. I'm tired of playing games and I'm sick of watching her manipulate Derek."

I shifted the subject slightly, probing a question I'd been curious about. "You think the drugs were actually hers?"

"Of course. She's been stoned since she walked in my front door. It's been such a bone of contention between Derek and me I can hardly speak of it. She's ruining our relationship." She closed her mouth and composed herself, then said, "What makes you put it that way?"

"About the drugs? It seems odd to me, that's all," I said. "I can't believe she'd leave them in her bed-table drawer in a Ziploc bag for starters and I can't believe she'd have pills in that quantity. Do you know what that stuff is worth?"

"She has an allowance of two hundred dollars a month," Glen said crisply. "I've argued and cajoled until I'm blue in the face, but what's the point? Derek insists. The money comes out of his own account."

"Even so, it's pretty high-level stuff. She'd have to have an incredible connection somewhere."

"I'm sure Kitty has her little ways."

I let the subject pass and made a mental note for myself. I'd recently made the acquaintance of one of Santa Teresa High School's more enterprising drug dealers and he might be able to identify her source. He might even *be* her source, for all I knew. He'd promised me he'd shut down his operation, but that was like a wino promising to buy a sandwich with the dollar you'd donated in good faith. Who were we trying to kid here?

"Maybe we should let it go for now," I said. "I'm sure this day has seemed long enough. I'd like to have the name and telephone number of Bobby's old girl friend if you have it, and I'll probably want to talk to Rick's parents, too. Can you tell me how to get in touch with them?"

"I'll give you both numbers," she said. She got up and crossed to a little antique rosewood desk with pigeonholes and tiny drawers along the top. She opened one of the large drawers below and took out a monogrammed leather address book.

"Beautiful desk," I murmured. This was like telling the Queen of England she has nice jewels.

"Thank you," Glen said idly, while she leafed through the address book. "I bought it at an auction in London last year. I'd hesitate to tell you how much I paid for it."

"Oh, give it a whirl," I said, fascinated. I was getting giddy hanging out with these people.

"Twenty-six thousand dollars," she murmured, running a finger down the page.

I could feel myself shrug philosophically. Hey, big deal. Twenty-six grand was as nothing to her. I wondered what she paid for underwear. I wondered what she paid for *cars*.

"Here it is." She scribbled the information on a scratch pad and tore off a leaf, which she passed to me.

"You'll find Rick's parents rather difficult, I suspect," she said.

"How so?"

"Because they blame Bobby for his death."

"How does he handle that?"

"Not well. Sometimes I think he believes it himself, which is all the more reason to get to the bottom of this."

"Can I ask you one more thing?"

"Of course."

"Is it 'Glen' as in 'West Glen'?"

"The other way around," she said. "I wasn't named for the road. The road was named for me."

By the time I got back in my car, I had a lot of information to digest. It was 9:30, fully dark, and too chilly for a black gauze tunic that ended six inches above my knees. I took a few minutes to wiggle out of my pantyhose and hunch into my long pants. I dropped the high heels into the backseat and pulled on my sandals again, then started the car and put it in reverse. I backed around in a semicircle, looking for a way out. I spotted the second arm of the drive and followed it, catching a glimpse of the rear of the house. There were four illuminated terraces, each with a reflecting pool, shimmering black by night, probably giving back sequential images of the mountains by day, like a series of overlapping photographs.

I reached West Glen and turned left, heading toward town. There'd been no indication that Derek had gotten home and I thought I'd try to catch him at St. Terry's before he left. Idly, I wondered what it'd be like to have a city street named after me. Kinsey Avenue. Kinsey Road. Not bad. I figured I could learn to live with the tribute if it came my way.

6

Santa Teresa Hospital, by night, looks like an enormous art deco wedding cake, iced with exterior lights: three tiers of creamy white, with a square piece missing in front where the entranceway has been cut out. Visiting hours must have been over because I found a parking space right across the street. I locked my car, crossed, and headed up the circular driveway. There was a large portico and covered walk leading up to double doors that shushed open as I approached. Inside, the lobby lights had been dimmed like the interior of an airplane on a night flight. To my left was the deserted coffee shop, one waitress still at work, dressed in a white uniform almost like a nurse's. To my right was the gift shop with a window display done up with the hospital equivalent of naughty lingerie. The whole place smelled like cold carnations in a florist's refrigerated case.

The decor had been designed to soothe and pacify, especially over in the area marked "cashier." I moved to the information desk, where a woman who resembled my old third-grade teacher sat in a pink-striped pinafore with an expectant look on her face.

"Hi," said I. "Can you tell me if Kitty Wenner's been admitted? She was brought into the emergency room a little while ago."

"Well, now let me just check," she said.

I noticed that her name tag read "Roberta Choat, Volunteer." It sounded like one of a series of novels for young girls that was now sorely out of date. Roberta must have been in her sixties and she had all sorts of good-conduct medals pinned to her bib.

"Here it is. That's Katherine Wenner. She's on Three South. You just walk down this corridor and around these elevators to the bank on the far side. Third floor, and you'll be turning to your left. But now, that's a locked psychiatric ward and I don't know that you'll be able to see her. Visiting hours are over, you know. Are you family?"

"I'm her sister," I said easily.

"Well now, dear, why don't you repeat that to the charge nurse up on the floor and maybe she'll believe you," Roberta Choat said just as easily.

"I hope so," I said. It was actually Derek I wanted to see.

I moved down the corridor, as instructed, and rounded the elevators to the bank on the far side. Sure enough, there was a sign that read SOUTH WING, which I found·reassuring. I punched the "up" button and the doors opened instantly. A man entered the elevator behind me and then hesitated, eyeing me as if I were the kind of person he'd read about in a rape-prevention pamphlet. He punched "2" and then stayed close to the control panel until he reached his floor and exited.

The south wing looked better than most of the hotels where I've stayed. Of course, it was also more expensive and offered many personal services that didn't interest me, autopsy being one. The lights were all on and the carpet was a blaze of burnt orange, the walls hung with Van Gogh reproductions; a curious choice for the psycho ward, if you ask me.

Derek Wenner was sitting in a visitors' lounge just outside a set of double doors that had small windows embedded with chicken wire and a sign reading PLEASE RING FOR ADMITTANCE with a buzzer underneath.

He was smoking a cigarette, an issue of *National Geographic* open on his lap. He glanced at me blankly when I sat down next to him.

"How's Kitty?" I said.

He started slightly. "Oh. Sorry. I didn't recognize you when you came around the corner. She's better. They just brought her up and they're getting her settled. I'll have a chance to see her in a bit." His glance strayed toward the elevators. "Glen didn't come down with you by any chance, did she?"

I shook my head, watching a mixture of relief and momentary hope fade out of his face.

"Don't tell her you caught me with a cigarette," he said, sheepishly. "She made me quit last March. I'll toss these out before I go home tonight. It's just with Kitty so sick and then all this stuff—" He broke off with a shrug.

I didn't have the heart to tell him he reeked of tobacco. Glen would have to be comatose not to notice it.

"What brings you down here?" he asked.

"I don't know. Bobby went off to bed and I talked to Glen for a while. I just thought I'd stop by and see what was happening with Kitty."

He smiled, not quite sure what to make of it. "I was just sitting here thinking how much this felt like the night she was born. Waiting out in the lounge for hours, wondering how it was all going to come out. They didn't let fathers in the delivery room in those days, you know. Now, I understand, they practically insist."

"What happened to her mother?"

"She drank herself to death when Kitty was five."

He lapsed into silence. I couldn't think of a comment that didn't seem either trivial or beside the point. I watched him put out his cigarette. He worked the hot ember loose, leaving an empty socket like a pulled tooth.

Finally, I said, "Is she being admitted to Detox?"

"Actually, this is the psychiatric ward. I think the detoxification unit is separate. Leo wants to get her stabilized and then do an evaluation before he does anything. Right now, she's a little bit out of control."

He shook his head, pulling at his double chin. "God, I don't know what to do with her. Glen's probably told you what a source of friction it's been."

"Her drug use?"

"Oh, that and her grades, her hours, the drop in her weight. That's been a nightmare. I think she's down to ninety-seven pounds at this point."

"So maybe this is where she needs to be," I said.

One of the double doors opened and a nurse peered out. She wore jeans and a T-shirt. No cap, but she did wear a nursing pin and a name tag that I couldn't read from where I sat. Her hair was ill-dyed, a stade of orange I'd only seen before in marigolds, but her smile was quick and pleasant.

"Mr. Wenner? Would you like to follow me, please?"

Derek got up with a glance at me. "You want to wait? It won't be long. Leo said five minutes was all he'd permit, given the shape she's in. I could buy you a cup of coffee or a drink as soon as I'm done."

"All right. That's nice. I'll be out here."

He nodded and moved off with the nurse. For one brief moment, as they passed into the ward, I could hear Kitty delivering some high-decibel curses of a quite imaginative sort. Then the door closed and the key turned resoundingly in the lock. No one on 3 South was going to sleep tonight. I picked up the *National Geographic* magazine and stared at a series of time-lapse photographs of a blowhole in Yosemite.

Fifteen minutes later, Derek and I were seated in a motel bar half a block away from the hospital. The Plantación is a rogue of a drinking establishment that looks as if it's crept to its present location from some other part of town. The motel itself was apparently built with an eye to sheltering the relatives of the ill and infirm who come to St. Terry's for treatment from small towns nearby. The bar was added as an afterthought, in violation of God knows what city codes, as it is smack in the middle of the residential neighborhood. Of course, the area by now has been infiltrated by medical buildings, clinics, convalescent homes, pharmacies, and various other suppliers to the health-care industry, including a mortuary two blocks away to service folk when all else fails. Maybe the city planning commission decided, at some point, to help ease the pain by making eighty-six-proof alcohol available along with the other kind.

The interior is narrow and dark, with a diorama of a banana plantation that extends behind the bar in the space that usually supports a long mirror, liquor bottles, and a neon beer sign. Instead, arranged as though on a small lighted stage, scale-model banana palms are laid out in orderly rows and tiny mechanized laborers go about the business of harvesting fruit in a series of vignettes. All of the workers appear to be Mexican, including the tiny carved woman who arrives with a water barrel and a dipper just as the noon whistle blows. One man waves from a treetop while a wee wooden dog barks and wags its tail.

Derek and I sat at the bar for a while, scarcely speaking, we were so taken by the scene. Even the bartender, who must have seen it hundreds of times, paused to watch while the mechanical mule pulled a load of bananas around the bend and another cart took its place. Not surprisingly, the house specialties run to cuba libres and banana daiquiris, but no one cares if you order something adult. Derek had a Beefeater martini and I had a glass of white wine that made my lips pull together like a drawstring purse. I'd watched the bartender pour it from a gallon jug that ran about three bucks at any Stop N' Go. The label was from one of those wineries the grape pickers are always striking and I pondered the possibility that they'd peed on the crop to retaliate for unfair labor practices.

"What do you think about this business with Bobby?" I said to Derek when I finally got my mouth unpuckered.

"His claim about a murder attempt? God, I don't know. It sounds pretty farfetched to me. He and his mother seem to believe it, but I can't figure out why anybody'd do such a thing."

"What about money?"

"Money?"

"I've been wondering who benefits financially if Bobby dies. I asked Glen the same thing."

Derek began to stroke his double chin. The excess weight made him look as if he had one normal-sized face superimposed on a much larger one. The jowls were just leftover flesh hanging out the sides. "It'd be a fairly conspicuous motive, I should think," he said. He wore the skeptical look of a man in a stage play: an exaggerated effect for the audience twenty-five rows back.

"Yeah, well forcing him off the bridge was conspicuous too. Of course, if he'd died in the wreck, nobody would have known the difference," I said. "Cars go off the pass every six months or so anyway because people take the curves too fast, so it could have been passed off as a single-car accident. There might have been some damage to the rear bumper where the other driver made contact, but by the time they'd hauled Bobby's car up the mountain, I don't think anybody would have suspected what really occurred. I take it there weren't any witnesses."

"No, and I'm not sure you can count on what Bobby says."

"Meaning what?"

"Well, he obviously has a vested interest in having someone else to blame. The kid doesn't want to own up to the fact that he'd been drinking. He always drove too fast anyway. His best friend gets killed. Rick was Kitty's boyfriend, you know, and his death threw her for a loop. I don't mean to cast doubt on Bobby's version of the story, but it's always struck me as self-serving to some extent."

I studied Derek's face, wondering at the change in his tone of voice. It was an interesting theory and I got the impression that he'd been thinking about it for some time. He seemed uncomfortable, though, pretending to be casual and objective when, in fact, he was undermining Bobby's credibility. I was sure he hadn't dared mention his idea to Glen. "You're saying Bobby made it up?"

"I didn't say *that*," he replied evasively. "I think *he* believes it, but then it gets him off the hook, doesn't it?" His eyes slid away from mine and he signaled to the bartender for a repeat, then glanced back at me. "You ready for another one?"

"Sure, why not?" I hadn't actually finished the wine I had, but I hoped he'd be more at ease if he thought I was matching him drink for drink. Martinis will make you say anything and I was curious what might come out once his tongue was loosened. I could already see that look in his eyes, something slithery and pink that hints of alcoholic tendencies. He fumbled in his shirt pocket and took out the pack of cigarettes, his gaze riveted to the diorama. A tiny mechanical Mexican with a machete was climbing up the tree again. Derek lit a cigarette without looking at it and the gesture took on a curious air, as if it couldn't count against him if he ignored it himself. He was probably the kind of person who eats while watching TV and tops off his Scotch so it will always look as though he is only having one.

"How was Kitty when you saw her? You haven't said."

"She was . . . you know, she was upset, I guess, to find herself hospitalized, but I told her . . . I said, 'Now look, kid. You're just going to have to shape up.'" Derek had shifted into his parental persona and he seemed uncomfortable with that, too. I could just imagine how effective he'd been to date.

"Glen didn't seem very sympathetic," I said.

"Well, no. I can't blame her for that, but then Kitty's had it rough and I don't think Glen understands the toll it can take on a kid like her. Bobby's had every advantage money could buy. Why shouldn't he have it made? I tell you what bothers me. I mean, anything Bobby does is excused. Anything Kitty does is the crime of the century. Bobby's screwed up. Don't kid yourself. But when he fouls up, Glen can always find a way to rationalize what he's done. Know what I mean?"

I shrugged noncommittally. "I don't know what he's done."

The drinks arrived and Derek took a sip from his as though he tasted martinis for a living. He nodded judiciously and set the glass down with care in the center of his cocktail napkin. He touched a knuckle to the corners of his mouth. His movements were becoming liquid and his eyes were beginning to slide around in their sockets like marbles in oil. Kitty had apparently gotten crocked in exactly the same way, only on downers instead of gin.

The bartender took a couple of beers out of the cooler and moved down to the other end of the bar to serve a customer.

Derek's voice dropped. "This is just between you and me and the lamppost," he said. "But the kid's been cited twice on drunk-driving raps and he got some little gal knocked up over a year ago. Glen wants to treat it like youthful hijinks— boys will be boys and all that sort of crap—but let Kitty cross the line once and all hell breaks loose."

I was beginning to see why Bobby thought their marriage wouldn't last. We were playing hardball here, parent vs. parent in the semifinals. Derek tried on a smile that was meant to charm, shifting over to neutral ground.

"So where do you start on a thing like this?" he asked.

"I don't know yet. Usually I nose around, do a background check, uncover a thread, and follow where it leads." I looked at him, watching while he nodded as though I'd actually said something significant.

"Well, I wish you luck. Bobby's a good kid, but there's a lot going on. More to that kid than meets the eye," he said with a knowing look. His speech wasn't slurred, but the consonants were getting soft. The winsome smile flickered back with its sly message. His whole manner implied that he could have said plenty, but discretion held him back. I didn't take him seriously. He was doing some kind of maneuvering, apparently unaware of how transparent he was. I took a sip of wine, wondering if there was anything else I might learn from him.

Derek glanced at his watch. "I better get home. Face the music." He tossed the rest of his martini back and eased himself off the barstool. He pulled out his wallet and sorted through several layers of bills until he found a five and a ten, which he placed on the bar.

"Will Glen be mad?"

He smiled to himself as if he were considering a number of replies. "Glen is always mad these days. It's been a hell of a birthday, I can tell you that."

"Maybe next year will be better. Thanks for the drinks."

"Thanks for coming down here. I appreciate your concern. If I can do anything to help you, you just let me know."

We walked the half-block to my car and then parted company. I watched him in my rearview mirror as he ambled toward the visitors' parking lot on the far side of the hospital. I suspected he was pretending more motor control than he actually had. We'd only been in the Plantación for thirty minutes and I'd watched him down two martinis. I started my car and did a U-turn, pulling up next to him. I leaned across the seat and opened the door on the passenger side. "Why don't I give you a lift?"

"Oh no, I'm fine," he said. He stood for a moment, his body swaying slightly. I could see the message being relayed through his central nervous system. He cocked his head, frowning, and then he got into my car and pulled the door shut. "I got problems enough, right?"

"Right," I said.

7

By the time I got into the office the next morning at nine, Bobby's attorney had forwarded copies of the initial accident report, along with notes from the follow-up investigation and numerous eight-by-ten color photographs that showed in glossy detail just how thoroughly demolished Bobby's car had been and just how dead Rick Bergen had become as a result. His body had been found, crushed and mangled, halfway down the slope. I recoiled from the sight as though a bright light had been flashed in my face, a shock of revulsion running down my frame. I had to steel myself to look again so that I could study the details dispassionately. There was something about the way the police photographer's lights had been rigged against the harsh dark of night that made the death seem garish, like a low-budget horror move that was real short on plot. I shuffled through the series until I found photographs of the accident scene itself.

Bobby's Porsche had taken out a big section of guardrail, had sheared off a scrub oak at its base, scarred boulders, and dug a long trench through the underbrush, apparently flipping over five or six times before it came to rest at the bottom of the ravine in a crumpled mass of twisted metal and shattered glass. There were several views of the car, front and rear, showing its position relative to various landmarks in the terrain and then the close-ups of Bobby before the ambulance crew had removed him from the wreckage. "Oh shit," I breathed. I put the whole stack down for a moment and put a hand across my eyes. I hadn't even had my coffee yet and there I was looking at human bodies turned inside out on impact.

I opened the French doors and went out on the balcony and sucked in some fresh air. Below me, State Street was orderly and quiet. Traffic was light and pedestrians obeyed the signals as if they were appearing in an educational film instructing grade-school kids how to conduct themselves on city streets. I watched all the healthy people walk up and down with their limbs intact and the flesh still covering their bones. The sun was shining and the palm trees weren't even stirred by a breeze. Everything looked so ordinary, but only for the moment and only as far as I could see. Death could pop up anytime, a jarring jack-in-the-box with a fixed, bloody grin.

I went back inside and made a pot of coffee and then sat down at my desk, going through the photographs again and taking time now to study the police reports. A copy of the postmortem examination on Rick Bergen had been included and I noticed that it had been conducted by Jim Fraker, whose responsibilities at St. Terry's apparently extended to such services. Santa Teresa is too small a town to pay for its own police morgue and its own medical examiner, so the work is contracted out.

The report Dr. Fraker had dictated effectively reduced Rick's death to observations about the craniocerebral trauma he'd sustained, with a catalogue of abrasions, contusions, small-intestine avulsions, mesenteric lacerations, and sufficient skeletal damage to certify Rick's crossing of the River Styx.

I hauled out my typewriter and opened a file for Bobby Callahan, feeling soothed and comforted as I translated all the unsettling facts into a terse account of events to date. I logged in his check, made a note of the receipt number, and filed the copy of the contract he'd signed. I typed in the names and addresses of Rick Bergen's parents and Bobby's ex–girl ,friend, along with a list of those present at Glen Callahan's house the night before. I didn't speculate. I didn't editorialize. I just typed it all out and used my two-hole punch at the top of the paper, which I then clamped into a folder and placed in my file cabinet.

That done, I glanced at my watch. Ten-twenty. Bobby's physical-therapy regimen was parceled out into daily stints, while mine was set up for Mondays, Wednesdays, and Fridays. It was possible he was still at the gym. I closed up the office and went down the back steps to the lot, where I keep my car parked. I headed toward Santa Teresa Fitness, gassing up on the way, and caught Bobby just as he was coming out of the building. His hair was still damp from the shower and the scent of Coast soap radiated from his skin. Despite the facial paralysis, the crippled left arm, and the limp, something of the original Bobby Callahan shone through, young and strong, with the blond good looks of a California surfer. I'd seen pictures of him broken, and by comparison, he now seemed miraculously whole, even with the scars still etched on his face like tattoos done by an amateur. When he saw me, he smiled crookedly, dabbing automatically at his chin. "I didn't expect to see you here this morning," he said.

"How was your workout?"

He tilted from side to side, indicating so-so. I tucked my arm through his.

"I have a request, but you don't have to agree," I said.

"What's that?"

I hesitated for a moment. "I want you to go up the pass with me and show me where the car went off."

The smile faded. He glanced away from me and launched into motion again, moving toward his car with that lilting gait. "All right, but I want to stop by and see Kitty first."

"Is she allowed to have visitors?"

"I can talk my way in," he said. "People don't like to deal with cripples, so I can usually get anything I want."

"Spoiled," I said.

"Take any advantage you can," he replied sheepishly.

"You want to drive?"

He shook his head. "Let's drop my car off at the house and take yours."

I parked in the visitor's lot at St. Terry's and waited in the car while he went in to see Kitty. I imagined she'd be back on her feet by now, still pissed off, and raising hell on the ward. Not anything I wanted to face. I hope to talk to her again in a couple of days, but I preferred to give her time to settle down. I flipped on the car radio, tapping on the steering wheel in time to the music. Two nurses passed through the parking lot in white uniforms, white shoes and hose, with dark blue capes that looked like something left over from World War I. In due course, Bobby emerged from the building and hobbled across the parking lot, his expression preoccupied. He got into the car. I flipped the radio off and started the engine, backing out of the slot.

"Everything okay?"

"Yeah, sure."

He was quiet as I headed across town and turned left onto the secondary road that cuts along the back side of Santa Teresa at the base of the foothills. The sky was a flat blue and cloudless, looking like semigloss paint that had been applied with a roller. It was hot, and the hills were brown and dry, laid out like a pile of kindling. The long grasses near the road had bleached out to a pale gold, and once in a while, I caught sight of lizards perched up on big rocks, looking as gray and still as twigs.

The road twisted, two lanes of blacktop angling back and forth up the side of the mountain. I downshifted twice and my little VW still complained of the climb.

"I thought I remembered something," Bobby said after a while. "But I can't seem to pin it down. That's why I had to see Kitty."

"What kind of thing?"

"I had an address book. One of those small leather-bound types about the size of a playing card. Cheap. Red. I gave it to someone for safekeeping and now I have no idea who." He paused, shaking his head with puzzlement.

"You don't remember why it was important?"

"No. I remember feeling anxious about it, thinking I better not have it in my possession because it was dangerous to me, so I passed it on. At the time—and I remember this part clearly—I figured I could retrieve it later." He shrugged, snorting derisively. "So much for that."

"Was this before the accident or afterwards?"

"Don't know. I just remember giving it to someone."

"Wouldn't it be dangerous to whoever you gave it to?"

"I don't think so. God." He slid down on his spine so he could rest his head on the back of the seat. He peered through the windshield, following the line of gray hills up to the left where the pass cuts through at the crest. "I *hate* this feeling. I hate knowing I once knew something and having no access to it. It's just an image with nothing attached to it. There aren't any memory cues so I have no way to place it in time. It's like pieces of a jigsaw puzzle with a whole hunk knocked off on the floor."

"But how does it work when you forget like that? Is there any retrieving the information or is it just gone?"

"Oh, sometimes it'll come back, but usually it's blank . . . like a hole in the bottom of a box. Whatever used to be there has spilled out along the way."

"What made you think of it in the first place?"

"I don't know. I was looking through a desk drawer and came across the red leather memo pad that was part of the same set. Suddenly, I got this flash." He fell silent. I glanced over at him and realized how tense he was. He was massaging his bad hand, milking the fingers as if they were long rubber teats.

"Kitty didn't know anything about it?"

He shook his head.

"How's she doing?"

"She's up and around. I guess Derek's going over to see her later on. . . ." He paused. We were reaching the crest of the hill and a muscle near his left eye had started to jump.

"Are you going to be all right with this?" I asked.

He was staring intently at the side of the road. "Just up here. Slow down and pull over if you can."

I checked my rearview mirror. There were three cars behind me, but the road was narrowing from three lanes to two. I eased over to the right and found a gravel shoulder where I could park. The bridge, with its low concrete guardrails, was about ten yards ahead. Bobby sat there, staring to his right.

Where the road descends from the summit, the whole valley opens out, hills sweeping back as far as the eye can see to a range of lavender mountains pasted against the rim of the sky. The August heat shimmered in silence. The land seemed vast and primitive, looking as it must have looked for thousands of years. In the distance, live oaks dotted the landscape, as shaggy and dark and hunched as buffalo.

There'd been no rain for months and the vista seemed chalky and pale, the color washed out.

Closer to us, the roadside dropped away into the treacherous canyon that had nearly marked Bobby's death nine months ago. A length of metal railing had been replaced, but where the bridge began, there was still a chunk of concrete missing.

"The other car started ramming us from behind just as we came over the rim of the hill," he said. I thought he meant to continue, so I waited.

He walked forward a few feet, gravel crunching under his shoes. He was clearly uneasy as he peered down the rocky slope. I looked back over my shoulder at the few cars passing. No one paid the slightest attention to us.

I studied the scene, picking out one of the scarred boulders I'd seen in the photograph, and farther down, the raw, jagged stump where a scrub oak had been snapped off at the base. I knew the Santa Teresa police had swept the area clean of debris from the accident, so there was no need to whip out a magnifying glass or creep around picking fibers from the underbrush.

Bobby turned to me. "Have you ever been close to death?"

"Yes."

"I remember thinking, 'This is it. I'm gone.' I disconnected. I felt like a plant ripped up by the roots. Airborne." He stopped. "And then I was cold and everything hurt and people were talking to me and I couldn't understand a word they said. That was in the hospital and two weeks had passed. I've wondered since then if that's how newborn babies feel. Bewildered like that and disoriented. Helpless. It was such a struggle to stay in touch with the world. Sending down new roots. I knew I could choose. I was barely attached, barely tethered, and I could feel how easy it'd be just to let go like a balloon and sail away."

"But you hung on."

"Hey, my mother willed it. Every time I opened my eyes, I saw her face. And when I closed my eyes, I heard her voice. She'd say, 'We're going to make it, Bobby. We're going to do this, you and I.'"

He was silent again. I thought, Jesus, what must it be like to have a mother who could love you that way? My parents had died when I was five, in a freak car accident. We'd been on a Sunday outing, driving up to Lompoc, when a huge boulder tumbled down the mountain and smashed through the windshield. My father had died instantly and we'd crashed. I'd been in the backseat, thrust down against the floorboards on impact, wedged in by the crushed frame. My mother had lingered, moaning and crying, sinking into a silence finally that I sensed was ominous and forever. It had taken them hours to extract me from the wreckage, trapped there with the dead whom I loved who had left me for all time. After that, I was raised by a no-nonsense aunt who had done her best, who had loved me deeply, but with a matter-of-factness that had failed to nourish some part of me.

Bobby had been infused with a love of such magnitude that it had brought him back from the grave. It was odd, when he was so broken, that I experienced an envy that made tears well up in my eyes. I felt a laugh burble and he turned a puzzled glance on me.

I took out a Kleenex and blew my nose. "I just realized how much I envy you," I said.

He smiled ruefully. "That's a first."

We got back in the car. There'd been no blinding recall, no sudden recollection of forgotten facts, but I'd seen the miry pit into which he had been flung and I'd felt the bond between us strengthened.

"Have you been up here since the accident?"

"No. I never had the nerve and no one ever suggested it. Made me sweat."

I started the car. "How about a beer?"

"How about a bourbon on the rocks?"

We went to the Stage Coach Tavern, just off the main road, and talked for the rest of the afternoon.

8

When I dropped him off at his house at five, he hesitated as he got out of the car, pausing as he'd done before with his hand on the door, peering back in at me.

"Know what I like about you?" he said.

"What," I said.

"When I'm with you, I don't feel self-conscious or like I'm crippled or ugly. I don't know how you do that, but it's nice."

I looked at him for a moment, feeling oddly self-conscious myself. "I'll tell you. You remind me of a birthday present somebody's sent through the mail. The paper's torn and the box is damaged, but there's still something terrific in there. I enjoy your company."

A half-smile formed and disappeared. He glanced over at the house and then back to me. He had something else on his mind, but he seemed embarrassed to admit to it.

"What," I coaxed.

He tilted his head and the look in his eyes was one I knew. "If I were O.K. . . . . if I'd been whole, would you have thought about having a relationship with me? I mean, boy-girl type?"

"You want the truth?"

"Only if it's flattering."

I laughed. "The truth is if I'd run into you before the accident, I'd have been intimidated. You're too good-looking, too rich, and too young. So I gotta say no. If you were 'whole,' as you put it, I probably wouldn't have known you at all. You're really not my type, you know?"

"What is your type?"

"I haven't figured that out yet."

57

He looked at me for a minute with a quizzical smile forming.

"Would you just say what's on your mind?" I said.

"How can you turn it around and make me feel good that I'm deformed?"

"Oh God, you're not deformed. Now, quit that! I'll talk to you later."

He smiled and slammed the car door, moving back then so I could make the turn-around and head out the far side of the driveway.

I drove back to my place. It was only 5:15. I still had time to get a run in, though I wondered at the wisdom of it. Bobby and I had spent the better part of the day drinking beer and bourbon and bad Chablis, gnawing barbecued spareribs and sourdough bread tough enough to tug your dentures out. I was really more in the mood for a nap than a run, but I thought the self-discipline would serve me right.

I changed into my running clothes and did three miles while I went through the mental gymnastics of getting the case organized. It felt like iffy stuff and I wasn't quite sure where to start. I thought I better check with Dr. Fraker in the Pathology Department at St. Terry's first, maybe pop in and see Kitty at the same time, and then try the newspaper morgue and go through the tedious business of checking back through local news prior to the accident just to see what was going on at the time. Maybe some event then current would shed light on Bobby's claim that someone had tried to murder him.

I went over to Rosie's at seven for a glass of wine. I was feeling restless and I wondered if Bobby hadn't set something in motion somehow. It was nice having someone to pal around with, nice to while away an afternoon in good company, nice to have someone whose face I looked forward to seeing. I wasn't sure how to categorize our relationship. My affection for him wasn't maternal in any way. Sisterly, perhaps. He seemed like a good friend and I felt for him all the admiration one feels for a good friend. He was fun, and being with him was peaceful. I'd been alone for so long that a relationship of any kind seemed like seductive stuff.

I snagged a glass of wine at the bar and then I sat in the back booth and surveyed the place. For a Tuesday night, there was a lively crowd, which is to say, two guys arguing nasally at the bar, and an old couple from the neighborhood sharing a big plate of pancakes layered with ham. Rosie remained at the bar with a cigarette, smoke drifting up around her head in a halo of nicotine and hair spray. She's in her sixties, Hungarian and bossy, a creature of muumuus and dyed auburn tresses, which she wears parted down the center and plastered into place with sprays that have sat on the grocery-store shelves since the beehive hairdo bumbled out of fashion in 1966. Rosie has a long nose, a short upper lip, eyes that she pencils into narrow, suspicious-looking slits. She's short, top-heavy, and opinionated. Also she pouts, which in a woman her age is ludicrous, but effective. Half the time, I don't like her much, but she never ceases to fascinate.

Her establishment has the same crude but cranky appeal. The bar extends along the left wall with a stuffed marlin arched above it that I suspect was never really alive. A big color TV sits on the far end of the bar, sound off, images dancing about like transmissions from another planet where life is vibrant and lunatic. The place always smells of beer, cigarette smoke, and cooking grease that should have been thrown out last week. There are six or seven tables in the center of the room surrounded by chrome-and-plastic chairs out of somebody's 1940s dinette set. The eight booths along the right wall have been fashioned out of plywood and stained the color of walnut, complete with tasteless suggestions carved in by ruffians who apparently had had a go at the ladies' room, too. It's possible that Rosie doesn't read English well enough to divine the true meaning of these primitive slogans. It's also possible that they express her sentiments exactly. Hard to know with her.

I glanced over at her and discovered that she was sitting bolt upright and very still, squinting narrowly at the front door. I followed her gaze. Henry had just come in with his new lady friend, Lila Sams. Rosie's antennae had apparently gone up automatically, like My Favorite Martian in drag. Henry found a table that seemed reasonably clean and pulled out a chair. Lila sat down and settled her big plastic bag on her lap like a small dog. She was wearing a bright cotton dress in a snazzy print, bold red poppies on a

ground of blue, and her hair looked as if it had been poufed
at the beauty parlor that very afternoon. Henry sat down,
glancing back at the booth, where he knows I usually sit. I
gave a little finger wave and he waved back. Lila's head
swiveled in my direction and her smile took on a look of
false delight.

Rosie, meanwhile, had set her evening paper aside and
had left her stool, gliding through the bar like a shark. I
could only surmise that she and Lila had met before. I
looked on with interest. This might be almost as entertaining as *Godzilla Meets Bambi*, at my local cinema. From my
vantage point, of course, the whole encounter took place in
pantomime.

Rosie had her order pad out. She stood and stared at
Henry, behaving as though he were alone, which is exactly
how she treats me when I come in with a friend. Rosie
doesn't speak to strangers. She doesn't make eye contact
with anyone she hasn't known for some time. This is especially true when the "anyones" are women. Lila was all
aflutter. Henry conferred with her and ordered for them
both. Much discussion ensued. I gathered that Lila had
made some request that didn't suit Rosie's notion of
gourmet Hungarian cuisine. Maybe Lila wanted the peppers left out or something roasted instead of fried. Lila
looked like the sort of woman who'd have lots of dietary
taboos. Rosie only had the one. You ate it the way she served
it or you went somewhere else. Lila apparently couldn't believe that she couldn't be catered to. Shrill and quarrelsome
noises arose, all Lila's. Rosie didn't say a word. It was her
place. She could do anything she wanted to. The two men
at the bar who'd been arguing about politics turned to
watch the show. The couple eating the sonkás palacsinta
paused simultaneously, forks in midair.

Lila flounced her chair back. I thought for a minute she
meant to hit Rosie with her purse. Instead, she delivered
what looked like a scathing remark and marched toward the
door with Henry scrambling after her. Rosie remained unruffled, smiling secretly as cats do in the midst of mouse
dreams. The customers in the place, all five of us, got very
quiet, tending studiously to our own private thoughts lest
Rosie turn on us inexplicably and eighty-six us for life.

Twenty minutes passed before Rosie found an excuse to head my way. My wineglass was empty and she was bringing me a refill with unheard-of good grace. She set the second glass on the table and then folded her hands in front of her, wiggling slightly in place. She does this when she wants your attention or feels you haven't lauded her with quite enough praise for some culinary accomplishment.

"Looks like you took care of *her*," I remarked.

"Is vulgar woman. Terrible creature. She was in once before and I don't like her a bit. Henry must be crazy nuts to come in my place with a hussy like that. Who is she?"

I shrugged. "Listen, all I know is her name is Lila Sams. She's renting a room from Mrs. Lowenstein and Henry seems to be smitten."

"I'm gonna smitten her if she comes in here again! She got something funny with her eyes." Rosie screwed her face up and did an imitation of Lila that made me laugh. Rosie's generally a humorless person and I had no idea her powers of observation were so keen, let alone her ability to mimic. She was dead serious, of course. She drew herself together. "What's she want with him anyway?"

"What makes you think she wants anything? Maybe the two of them are just interested in a little companionship. Henry's very handsome, if you ask me."

"I didn't ask you! He's very handsome. He's good fellow too. So why does he need companionship with that little snake?"

"Like they say, Rosie, there's no accounting for taste. Maybe she has redeeming qualities that aren't immediately evident."

"Oh no. Not her. She's up to something no good. I'm gonna talk to Mrs. Lowenstein. What's the matter with her, renting to a woman like that?"

I rather wondered about that myself, walking the half-block home. Mrs. Lowenstein is a widow who owns considerable property in the neighborhood. I couldn't believe she needed the money and I was curious how Lila Sams had arrived at her doorstep.

When I got back to my place, Henry's kitchen light was on and I could hear the muffled sounds of Lila's voice, shrill and inconsolable. The encounter with Rosie had apparently

upset her thoroughly and all of Henry's murmured reas-
surances were doing no good. I unlocked my door and let
myself in, effectively shutting out the noise.

I read for an hour—six thrilling chapters from a book on
burglary and theft—and went to bed early, wrapping myself
up in my quilt. I turned off the light and lay there for a
while in the dark. I could have sworn I still heard the faint
rise and fall of Lila's wine, circling my ear like a mosquito. I
couldn't distinguish the words, but the tone was clear . . .
contentious and ill-humored. Maybe Henry would realize
she was not as nice as she pretended to be. Maybe not,
though. I'm always startled at what fools men and women
make of themselves in the pursuit of sex.

I woke at seven, had a cup of coffee while I read the paper, and then headed over to Santa Teresa Fitness for my
Wednesday workout. I was feeling stronger and the two
days of jogging had left my legs aching pleasantly. The
morning was clear, not yet hot, the sky was blank as a canvas
being prepared for paint. The parking lot at the gym was
almost full and I snagged the one empty space. I spotted
Bobby's car two slots over and I smiled, looking forward to
seeing him.

The gym was surprisingly populated for the middle of the
week, with five or six two-hundred-and-eighty-pound guys
lifting weights, two women in tights on the Nautilus equipment, and a trainer supervising the workout of a young
actress whose rear end was spreading out like slowly melt-
ing candle wax. I caught sight of Bobby doing bench presses
on a Universal machine near the far wall. He'd apparently
been there for a while because his T-shirt was ringed with
sweat and his blond hair had separated into damp strands. I
didn't want to interrupt him so I simply stashed my gym
bag and and got down to business myself.

I started my workout with some bicep curls, using dumb-
bells with hardly any weight, beginning to concentrate as I
warmed up. By now, I knew my routine and I had to fight a
certain mounting impatience. I'm not a process person. I
like goals and closure, the arrival instead of the journey itself. Repetition makes me rebellious. How I manage to jog
from day to day I'm never sure. I proceeded to wrist curls,
mentally leaping ahead through my routine, wishing I was

at the end of it instead of two exercises in. Maybe Bobby and I could have lunch again if he was free.

I heard a clatter and then a thump and looked up in time to see that he'd lost his balance and stumbled against a stack of five-pound plates. It was clear he hadn't hurt himself, but he seemed to catch sight of me for the first time and his embarrassment was acute. He flushed, trying to scramble to his feet again. One of the guys at the next machine leaned over casually and gave him an assist. He steadied himself self-consciously, waving aside any further help. He limped over to the leg-press machine, his air brusque and withdrawn. I went on working out as though I hadn't seen anything, but I kept a discreet eye on him. Even at that distance, I could see that his mood was dark, his face tense. A couple of people sent looks in his direction that spoke of pity, veiled as concern. He mopped at his chin, his attention turned inward. His left leg was going into muscle spasms of some sort and he clutched at his knee with frustration. The leg was like a separate creature, jumping fitfully, defying containment or control. Bobby groaned, pounding angrily at his own flesh as though he might subdue it with his fist. I struggled with an impulse to cross the room, but I knew it would only make things worse. He'd been pushing himself and his body was vibrating with fatigue. Just as suddenly as it had begun, the spasm seemed to fade. He dashed at his eyes, keeping his head low. As soon as he was able to walk again, he snatched up a towel and headed for the locker room, abandoning the rest of his regimen.

I hurried through the rest of my workout and showered as quickly as I could. I expected to find his car gone, but it was still parked in the slot where I'd seen it. Bobby sat with his arms encircling the steering wheel, his head resting on his arms, his shoulders convulsing with dry, hacking sobs. I hesitated for a moment and then approached the car on the passenger side. I got in and closed the door and sat there with him until he was done. I didn't have any comfort for him. There wasn't anything I could do. I had no way to address his pain or his despair and my only hope was to let him know by my presence that I did feel for him and I did care.

It passed by degrees, and when it was over, he dried his eyes with a towel and blew his nose, keeping his face averted.

"You want to go have some coffee?"

He shook his head. "Just leave me alone, O.K.?" he said.

"I got time," I said.

"Maybe I'll call you later."

"All right. I'll go ahead and take care of some business and maybe we can connect up this afternoon. You need anything in the meantime?"

"No." The tone was dull, his manner listless now.

"Bobby—"

"No! Just get the fuck away from me and leave me alone. I don't need your help."

I opened the car door. "I'll check back with you," I said. "Take care."

He reached over and grabbed the door handle, slamming it shut. He started the engine with a roar, and I stepped aside, as he backed out of the slot with a squeal of tires and shot out of the parking lot without a backward glance.

That was the last I ever saw of him.

9

The Pathology Department at St. Terry's is located below
ground in the heart of a maze of small offices. Miles of corridors branch out in all directions, connecting the non-
medical departments charged with the actual running of the
facility: maintenance, housekeeping, engineering, plant
operations. Where the floors above are renovated and taste-
fully done, the decor down here runs to brown vinyl tile
and glossy paint the color of vanished bones. The air smells
hot and dry and certain open doorways reveal glimpses of
ominous machinery and electrical ducts as big as sewer
pipes.

There was a steady flow of pedestrian traffic that day, people in hospital uniforms, as pale and expressionless as residents of an underground city, starved for sunlight. The
Pathology Department itself was a pleasant contrast: spacious, well lighted, handsomely appointed in royal blue and
gray, with fifty to sixty lab technicians working to accommodate the blood, bone, and tissue specimens that filtered
down from above. The computerized equipment seemed to
click, hum, and whir: efficiency augmented by an army of
experts. Noise was muted, telephones pinging daintily
against the artificial air. Even the typewriters seemed to be
muffled, recording discreetly the secrets of the human condition. There was order, proficiency, and calm, the sense
that here, at least, the pain and indignation of illness was
under control. Death was being held at bay, measured, cali-
brated, and analyzed. Where it had claimed a victory, the
same crew of specialists dissected the results and fed them
into the machinery. Paper poured out in a long road, paved
with hieroglyphics. I stood in the doorway for a moment,

struck by the scene. These were microscope detectives, pursuing killers of another order than those I hunted down.

"May I help you?"

I glanced over at the receptionist, who was watching me.

"I'm looking for Dr. Fraker. Do you know if he's here?"

"Should be. Down this aisle to the first left, then left again and you can ask somebody back there."

I found him in a modular compartment lined with bookshelves, furnished with a desk, a swivel chair, plants, and graphic art. He was tipped back in his chair, his feet propped up on the edge of his deck, leafing through a medical book the size of the *Oxford English Dictionary*. He had a pair of rimless bifocals in one hand, chewing on one of the stems as he read. He was substantially built—wide shoulders, heavy thighs. His hair was a thick, silvery white, his skin the warm tone of a flesh-colored crayon. Age had given his face a softly crumpled look, like a freshly laundered cotton sheet that needs to be starched and ironed. He wore surgical greens with matching booties.

"Dr. Fraker?"

He glanced up at me and his gray eyes registered recognition. He pointed a finger. "Bobby Callahan's friend."

"That's right. I wondered if I could talk to you."

"Sure, absolutely. Come on in."

He got to his feet and we shook hands. He indicated the chair near his desk and I sat down.

"We can make an appointment to talk later if I've caught you at a bad time," I said.

"Not at all. What can I do for you? Glen told me Bobby hired someone to look into the accident."

"He's convinced it was a murder attempt. Hit and run. Has he talked to you about that?"

Dr. Fraker shook his head. "I haven't seen him for months except for Monday night. Murder. Do the police agree?"

"I don't know yet. I've got a copy of the accident report and as nearly as I can tell, they don't have much to go on. There weren't any witnesses and I don't think they found much evidence at the scene."

"That's unusual, isn't it?"

"Well, there's usually *something* to go on. Broken glass, skid marks, transfer traces on the victim's vehicle. Maybe the guy jumped out of his car and swept up all the soil and paint flecks, I don't know. I do trust Bobby's intuition on this. He says he was in danger. He just can't remember why."

Dr. Fraker seemed to consider that briefly and then shifted in his seat. "I'd be inclined to believe him myself. He's a bright boy. He was a gifted student, too. It's a damn shame there's so little left of that. What's he think is going on?"

"He hasn't any idea and, as he points out, the minute he remembers, he's in more trouble than he is now. He suspects somebody's still after him."

He cleaned his glasses with a handkerchief, contemplating the matter. He was a man apparently accustomed to dealing with puzzles, but I imagined his solutions were derived from symptoms instead of circumstances. Diseases don't require an underlying motivation in the same way homicide does.

He shook his head slightly, his eyes meeting mine. "Odd. The whole thing's a little bit out of my range." He put his glasses on, turning businesslike. "Well. We better figure out what's going on, then. What do you need from me?"

I shrugged. "All I know to do is start back at square one and see if I can determine what kind of trouble he was in. He'd worked for you for what? Two months?"

"About that. He started in September, I believe. I can have Marcy look that up if you want exact dates."

"I gather he was hired here because of your relationship with his mother."

"Well, yes and no. We generally have a slot available for a premed student. It just happened that Bobby filled the bill in this case. Glen Callahan's a very big cheese around here, but we wouldn't have hired him if he'd been a dud. Can I get you some coffee? I'm about to have some."

"All right, sure."

He leaned sideways slightly, calling to the secretary, whose desk was in his line of sight. "Marcy? Can we get some coffee in here, please?"

To me, he said, "You take cream and sugar?"

"Black is fine."

"Both black," he called out.

There was no reply, but I assumed it was being taken care of. He turned his attention back to me. "Sorry to interrupt."

"That's all right. Did he have desk space down here?"

"He had a desk up front, but that was cleared out, oh, I'd say within a day of the accident. Nobody thought he'd survive, you know, and we had to bring somebody else in pretty quickly. This place is a madhouse most of the time."

"What happened to his things?"

"I dropped them by the house myself. There wasn't much, but we put what we came across in a cardboard box and I passed it on to Derek. I don't know what he did with it, if anything. Glen was at the hospital twenty-four hours a day at that point."

"Do you remember what was in it?"

"His desk? Odds and ends. Office things."

I made a note to myself to check for the box. I supposed there was a chance it was still at the house somewhere. "Can you walk me through Bobby's day and show me what sorts of things he did?"

"Sure. Actually, he divided his time between the lab and the morgue out in the old county medical facility on Frontage Road. I've got to make a run out there anyway and you can ride along if you like, or follow in your car if that's easier."

"I thought the morgue was here."

"We've got a small one here, just off the autopsy room. We've got another morgue out there."

"I didn't realize there was more than one."

"We needed the added space for the contract work we do. St. Terry's maintains a few offices out there, too."

"Really. I didn't think that old county building was still in use."

"Oh yes. There's a private radiology group that works out there, and we've got storage rooms for medical records. It's a bit of a hodgepodge, but I don't know what we'd do without it."

He glanced over as Marcy came in with two mugs, her gaze carefully affixed to the surface of the coffee, which was threatening to slop over the sides. She was young, dark-haired, no makeup. She looked like the sort of person you'd want holding your hand if the lab techs did something excruciating.

"Thank you, Marcy. Just on the edge of the desk here is fine."

She set the mugs down and gave me a quick smile on her way out.

Dr. Fraker and I discussed the office procedures while we drank the coffee and then he took me on a tour of the lab, explaining Bobby's various responsibilities, all of which seemed routine and not very important at that. I made a note of the names of a couple of his co-workers, thinking I might talk to them at a later date.

I waited while he took care of a few details and signed out, telling Marcy where he'd be.

I followed him to the freeway in my car, heading toward the former county hospital. The complex was visible from the highway: a sprawling labyrinth of yellowing stucco and red tile roofs that had turned nearly rust-brown with age. We passed it, took the next off-ramp, and circled back along Frontage Road, turning left into the main driveway.

County General had once been a flourishing medical facility, designed to serve the entire Santa Teresa community. It was secondarily earmarked as the treatment center for the indigent, funded through various social-service agencies. As the years passed, it came to be associated with the underprivileged: welfare recipients, illegal aliens, and all the unfortunate victims of Saturday-night crime sprees. Gradually, County General was shunned by both the middle class and the well-to-do. Once MediCal and Medicare came into effect, even the poor opted for St. Terry's and other local private hospitals, turning this place into a ghost town.

There was a sprinkling of cars in the parking lot. Temporary wooden signs shaped like arrows directed the visitor to Medical Records, nursing offices, Radiology, the morgue, and departments representing obscure branches of medicine.

Dr. Fraker parked his car and I pulled into the slot next to his. He got out, locked up, and waited while I did the same. A modest attempt was being made to maintain the grounds, but the driveway itself was cracked, coarse weeds beginning to sprout through the asphalt. The two of us headed toward the main entrance without saying much. He seemed to take the place for granted, but I found it all vaguely unsettling. The architecture was, of coarse, of the usual Spanish styling: wide porches along the front, deeply recessed windows faced with wrought-iron bars.

We went in, pausing in a spacious lobby. It was clear that over the years some attempt had been made to "modernize" the place. Fluorescent lighting was now tucked up against the high ceilings, throwing down illumination too diffuse to satisfy. Once-grand anterooms had been partitioned off. Counters had been built across two of the interior arches but there was no furniture in the reception area and no one awaiting admission. The very air was permeated with the smell of abandonment and neglect. From the far end of the dim hallway to our right, I could hear a typewriter clacking, but it sounded like an old manual, operated by an amateur. There was no other indication of occupancy.

Dr. Fraker gave me a perfunctory tour. According to him, Bobby had made the round-trip as needed between this place and St. Terry's, picking up inactive files for patients readmitted to the hospital after an interval of years, hand-delivering X rays and autopsy reports. Old charts were automatically retired to the storage facilities out here. Of course, most data was kept on computer now, but there was still a backlog of paper that had to be warehoused somewhere. Bobby apparently also did some moonlighting out here, taking the graveyard shift for morgue attendants who were out sick or on vacation. Dr. Fraker indicated that this was largely a babysitting function, but that Bobby had put in a considerable number of hours during the two months he was on the job.

We were on our way downstairs by then, descending a wide staircase of red Spanish tile, our footsteps resounding at a hollow, mismatched pace. Because the hospital is constructed against a hillside, the rear of the building is below ground, while the front portion looks out onto paths partially overgrown with shrubs. It was darker down here, as though the utilities had been cut back for the sake of economy. The temperature was cool and the air was scented with formaldehyde, that acrid deodorant for the deceased. An arrow on the wall pointed us to Autopsy. I began to armor myself against the images my senses were conjuring up.

Dr. Fraker opened the door with its frosted-glass panel. I didn't actually hesitate before entering, but I did do a quick visual scan to assure myself that we weren't interrupting some guy with a boning knife filleting a corpse. Dr. Fraker seemed to sense my apprehension and he touched at my elbow briefly.

"There's nothing scheduled," he said and led the way.

I smiled uneasily and followed. At first glance, the place seemed deserted. I noted walls of apple-green ceramic tile, long stainless-steel counters with lots of drawer space. This was like a high-tech kitchen in a decorator magazine, complete with a stainless-steel island in the middle that sported its own wide sink, tall crook-necked faucets, a hanging scale, and drainboard. I felt my mouth set in distaste. I knew what was prepared here and it wasn't food.

A swinging door on the far side of the room was pushed open and a young man in surgical greens backed in, pulling a gurney after him. The body on the cart was wrapped in a dense, tawny plastic that obscured age and sex. A toe tag was visible and I could see a portion of the dark head, blank face swaddled in plastic like a mummy's. It reminded me vaguely of the caution spelled out now on dry cleaners' bags: "WARNING: To avoid danger of suffocation, keep away from babies and children. Do not use in cribs, beds, carriages, or playpens. This bag is not a toy." I averted my gaze, taking in a deep breath then just to prove I could.

Dr. Fraker introduced me to the attendant, whose name was Kelly Borden. He was in his thirties, big and soft-bodied, with fuzzy, prematurely graying hair pulled back in a fat braid that extended halfway down his back. He had a beard, a handlebar mustache, mild eyes, and a wristwatch that looked like it would keep time on the ocean floor.

"Kinsey's a private investigator looking into Bobby Callahan's accident," Dr. Fraker said.

Kelly nodded, his expression neutral. He rolled the gurney over to what looked like a big refrigerator case and eased it in beside a second gurney, also occupied. Roommates, I guessed.

Dr. Fraker looked back at me. "I've got some things to take care of upstairs. Why don't I leave you two alone and you can ask him anything you want. Kelly worked with him. Maybe he can fill you in and then we can talk again, when you see what's what."

"Great," I said.

10

Once Dr. Fraker left, Kelly Borden got out a spray bottle of disinfectant that he began to squirt on the stainless-steel counters, wiping everything down methodically. I wasn't sure he really needed to do it, but it allowed him to keep his eyes averted. It was a polite way of ignoring me, but I didn't object. I used the time to circle the room, peering into glass-fronted cabinets filled with scalpels, forceps, and grim little hacksaws.

"I thought there'd be more bodies," I said.

"In there."

I glanced over at the door he'd come through. "Can I look?"

He shrugged.

I crossed and opened the door, which had a temperature gauge beside it reading forty degrees. The room, about the size of my apartment, was lined with fiberglass pallets arranged in tiers like bizarre bunk beds. There were eight bodies in evidence, most wrapped in the same yellowing plastic, through which I could discern, in some cases, arms and legs and seeping injuries, blood and body fluids condensing on the surface of the plastic wrap. Two bodies were covered with sheets. An old woman, lying on the pallet nearest me, was naked, as still as wood and looking faintly dehydrated. A dramatic Y-shaped cut had been made down the middle of her body, sewn back in big clumsy stitches, like a chicken, stuffed and trussed. Her breasts were splayed outward like old beanbags and her pubic area was almost as hairless as a young girl's. I wanted to cover her, but what was the point? She was beyond cold, beyond pain, modesty, or sex. I watched her chest, but there was no reassuring rise and fall. Death was beginning to seem like a parlor trick—how long can you hold your breath? I felt myself breathing deeply again, not wanting to participate. I closed the door, stepping back into the warmth of the autopsy room. "How many can you accommodate?"

"Fifty, maybe, in a pinch. I've never seen more than eight or so."

"I thought most people went straight to a mortuary."

"They do if they've died of natural causes. We get everything else. Homicide victims, suicides, accidents, any death of a suspicious or unusual nature. Most of those are autopsied and then released to a mortuary in a relatively short period of time. Of the ten we have on hand, some are indigents. A couple of 'em are John Does we're holding in hopes we'll get a positive I.D. Sometimes burial arrangements are pending so we hold a body for the next of kin. Two we've had around for years. Franklin and Eleanor. Like mascots."

I crossed my arms, feeling chilled, shifting the subject back to the living. "Do you know Bobby very well?" I asked. I turned and leaned against the wall, watching him polish the faucet handles on the stainless-steel sink.

"I hardly know him at all. We worked different shifts."

"How long have you worked out here?"

"Five years."

"What else do you do with your time?"

He paused, looking up at me. He didn't seem to like the personal questions, but he was too polite to say so. "I'm a musician. I play jazz guitar."

I stared at him for a minute, hesitating. "Have you ever heard of Daniel Wade?"

"Sure. He was a local jazz pianist. Everybody's heard of him. He hasn't been around town in years, though. He a friend of yours?"

I moved away from the wall, taking up my rounds. "I was married to him once."

"*Married* to him?"

"That's right." There were some jars filled with a brackish liquid in which body parts were marinating. I wondered if there might be a pickled heart tucked in among all the livers, kidneys, and spleens.

Kelly went back to his work. "Incredible musician," he remarked in a tone of voice that was part caution, part respect.

"That he is," I said, smiling at the irony. I never talked about this stuff and it seemed odd to be doing it in an autopsy room to a morgue attendant in surgical greens.

"What happened to him?" Kelly asked.

"Nothing. He was in New York last I heard. Still playing his music, still on drugs."

He shook his head. "God, the talent that guy has. I never really knew him, but I used to see him every chance I got. I can't understand why he never got anywhere."

"The world is full of talented people."

"Yeah, but he's smarter than most. At least from what I heard."

"Too bad I wasn't as smart as he was. I could have saved myself a lot of grief," I said. Actually, the marriage, though brief, had been the best few months of my life. Daniel had the face of an angel back then . . . clear blue eyes, a cloud of yellow curls. He always reminded me of some artist's rendering of a Catholic saint—lean and beautiful, ascetic-looking, with elegant hands and an unassuming air. He exuded innocence. He just couldn't be faithful, couldn't lay off the drugs, couldn't stay in one place. He was wild and funny and corrupt, and if he came back today, I can't swear I'd turn him down, whatever he asked.

I let the conversation lapse and Kelly, prompted by the silence, finally spoke up.

"What's Bobby doing these days?"

I glanced back at him. He had perched himself on a tall wooden stool, the rag and disinfectant on the counter to his left.

"He's still trying to get his life back together," I said. "He works out every day. I don't know what else he does with his time. I don't suppose you have any idea what was going on back then, do you?"

"What difference does it make at this point?"

"He says he was in some kind of danger, but his memory's shot. Until I fill in the gaps, he's probably still in trouble."

"How come?"

"If somebody tried to kill him once, they may try again."

"Why haven't they done that so far?"

"I don't know. Maybe they think they're safe."

He looked at me. "That's weird."

"He never confided in you?"

Kelly shrugged, his manner ever so slightly guarded again. "We only worked together a couple of times. I was off on vacation for part of the time he was here, and the rest of it, I was on days while he did graveyard shift."

"Is there any chance he might have left a small red leather address book out here?"

"I doubt it. None of us even have lockers for our stuff."

I took a business card out of my wallet. "Will you give me a call if you have any ideas? I'd like to know what was going on back then and I know Bobby'd appreciate some help."

"Sure."

I went in search of Dr. Fraker, passing Nuclear Medicine, the nursing offices, and the offices of a group of local radiologists, all in the basement. I ran into Fraker just as he was coming downstairs again.

"All through?" he said.

"Yes, are you?"

"I've got a 'post' at noon, but we can find an empty office and talk if you like."

I shook my head. "I don't have any other questions for the moment. I may want to check back with you at some point."

"Absolutely. Just give me a call."

"Thanks. I'll do that."

I sat in my car in the parking lot, making notes on some three-by-five index cards I keep in the glove compartment: date, time, and names of the two people I'd talked to. I thought Dr. Fraker was a good resource, even though the interview with him hadn't yielded much. Kelly Borden hadn't been much help either, but at least it was an avenue I'd explored. Sometimes the noes are just as important as the yeses because they represent cul-de-sacs, allowing you to narrow your field of inquiry until you stumble into the heart of the maze. In this case, I had no idea where that might lie or what might be hidden there. I checked my watch. It was 11:45 and I thought about lunch. I have a hard time eating meals when I should. Either I'm not hungry when I'm supposed to be or I'm hungry and not in a place where I can stop and eat. It becomes a weight-control maneuver, but I'm not sure it's good for my health. I started my car and headed toward town.

I went back to the health-food restaurant where Bobby and I had eaten lunch on Monday. I was really hoping to run into him, but he was nowhere in sight. I ordered a longevity salad that was supposed to take care of 100 percent of my nutritional needs for life. What the waitress brought me was a plate piled with weeds and seeds, topped with a zesty pink dressing with specks. It didn't taste nearly as yummy as a Quarter Pounder with cheese, but I did feel virtuous, knowing I had all that chlorophyll coursing through my veins.

When I got back in my car, I checked my teeth in the rearview mirror to make sure they weren't flecked with alfalfa sprouts. I prefer not to interview people looking like I've just been grazing out in some field. I leafed through my notebook for Rick Bergen's parents' address and then I hauled out a city map. I had no idea where Turquesa Road was. I finally spotted it, a street about the size of an ingrown hair, off an equally obscure lane in the foothills that stretch across the back of town.

The house was staunch and plain, all upright lines, with a driveway so steep that I avoided it altogether and squeezed my car in along the ice plant growing below. A bald cinderblock wall prevented the hillside from tumbling into the road and gave the impression of a series of barricades as it zigzagged up to the front. Once I reached the porch, the view was spectacular, a wide-angle shot of Santa Teresa from end to end with the ocean beyond. A hang-glider hovered high up to my right, sailing in lazy circles toward the beach. The day was full of hard sunlight, meager clouds looking like white foam just beginning to evaporate. It was dead quiet. No traffic, no sense of neighbors nearby. I could see a rooftop or two but there was no feeling of people. The landscaping was sparse, composed of drought-tolerant plants: pyracantha, wisteria, and succulents.

I rang the bell. The man who came to the door was short, tense, unshaven.

"Mr. Bergen?"

"That's right."

I handed him my business card. "I'm Kinsey Millhone. Bobby Callahan hired me to look into the accident last—"

"What for?"

I made eye contact. His were small and blue, red-rimmed. His cheeks were prickly with a two-day growth of beard that made him look like a cactus. He was a man in his fifties, radiating the smell of beer and sweat. His hair was thinning and combed straight back from his face. He wore pants that looked like he'd retrieved them from a Salvation Army box and a T-shirt that read "Life's a bitch. Then you die." His arms were soft and shapeless, but his gut protruded like a basketball pumped to maximum pressure per square inch. I wanted to respond in the same rude tone he was using with me, but I curbed my tongue. This man had lost a son. Nobody said he had to be polite.

"He thinks the accident was an attempt on his life," I said.

"Bullshit. I don't mean to be rude to you, lady, but let me fill you in. Bobby Callahan is a rich kid. He's spoiled, irresponsible, and self-indulgent. He fuckin' drank too much and he ran off the road, killing my son, who was incidentally his best friend. Anything else you've heard is horseshit."

"I'm not so sure of that," I said.

"Well, I am and I'm telling you straight. Check the police reports. It's all there. Have you seen 'em?"

"I got copies yesterday from Bobby's attorney," I said.

"No physical evidence, right? You got Bobby's claim someone ran him off the road, but you got nothing to substantiate a word he says, which in my mind makes his story pure crap."

"The police seem to believe him."

"You think they can't be bought off? You think the cops can't be persuaded by a few bucks?"

"Not in this town," I said. This man had really put me on the defensive and I didn't like the way I was handling myself.

"Says who?"

"Mr. Bergen, I know a lot of the local police. I've worked with them—" It sounded lame, but I was sincere.

He interrupted again, saying, "Nuts!" He made a dismissive gesture, turning his head with disgust. "I got no time for this. Maybe my wife'll talk to you."

"I'd rather talk to you," I said. He seemed surprised by that, as though no one ever preferred to talk to him.

"Forget it. Ricky's dead. It's all over with."

"Suppose it's not? What if Bobby's really telling the truth and it wasn't his fault?"

"What's it to me in any event? I don't give a good goddamn about him."

I nearly replied, but I shut my mouth instead, trusting some other instinct. I didn't want to get caught up in endless petty arguments that would only serve to keep this man inflamed. His agitation was profound, but I suspected that there was an ebb and flow to it. "May I have ten minutes of your time?"

He thought about it for a moment and then agreed with an air of annoyance. "Christ, come on in. I'm havin' my lunch. Reva's gone anyway."

He walked away from the door, leaving it up to me to close it after us and follow him through the house, which was drably carpeted and smelled as if it had been closed up. Window shades were drawn against the afternoon sun and the light in the house had an amber cast. I received a brief impression of overscaled furniture: two matching recliners covered in green plastic, and an eight-foot sectional sofa with an afghan on one end, occupied by a big black dog.

The kitchen was done in thirty-year-old linoleum with cabinets painted an intense shade of pink. The appliances made the room look like an illustration from an old issue of *Ladies' Home Journal*. There was a small built-in breakfast nook with newspapers piled up on one bench, and a narrow wooden table with a permanent centerpiece composed of sugar bowl, paper-napkin dispenser, salt and pepper shakers shaped like ducks, a mustard jar, ketchup bottle, and a bottle of A-1 Sauce. I could see his sandwich preparations laid out too: an assortment of processed cheese slices and a lunchmeat laced with olives and ominous chunks of animal snout.

He sat down and motioned me into the bench across from him. I shoved aside some of the newspapers and took a seat.

He was already slathering Miracle Whip on that brand of soft white bread that can double as a foam sponge. I kept my eyes discreetly averted as if he were engaged in pornographic practices. He laid a thin slice of onion on the bread and then peeled the cellophane wrap from the cheese, finishing with layers of lettuce, dill pickles, mustard, and meat. He looked up at me belatedly. "You hungry?"

"Starved," I said. I'd eaten a mere thirty minutes before and it wasn't my fault if I was hungry again. The way I looked at it, the sandwich was filled with preservatives, which might be just what I needed to keep my body from going bad. He cut the first masterpiece diagonally, passing half to me, and then he made a second sandwich more lavish than the first and cut that one, too. I watched him patiently, like a well-trained dog, until he gave the signal to eat.

For three minutes, we sat in silence, wolfing down lunch. He popped open a beer for me and a second one for himself. I despise Miracle Whip but, in this instance, it seemed like a gourmet sauce. The bread was so soft our fingertips left dents near the crust.

Between bites, I dabbed the corners of my mouth with a paper napkin. "I don't know your first name," I said.

"Phil. What kind of name is Kinsey?"

"My mother's maiden name."

And that was the extent of the social niceties until we'd both pushed our plates back with a sigh of relief.

11

After lunch, we sat out on the deck in painted metal porch chairs pockmarked with rust. The deck was actually a shelf of poured concrete, forming the roof of the garage, which had been carved into the hillside. Wooden planters filled with annuals formed a low protective barrier around the perimeter. A mild breeze was picking up, offsetting the heavy blanket of sunshine that settled on my arms. Phil's belligerence was gone. He'd been pacified perhaps by the many chemicals in his lunch, but more likely by the two beers and the prospect of the cigar he was clipping with a pocket guillotine. He plucked a big wooden kitchen match from a can next to his chair and bent down, using the surface of the deck to scratch it into life. He puffed on the cigar until it drew fully, then shook the match out and dropped it in a flat tin ashtray. For a moment, we both sat and stared out at the ocean.

The view was like a mural painted on a blue backdrop. The islands in the channel looked grim and deserted, twenty-six miles out. On the mainland, the small beaches were faintly visible, the surf like a tiny ruffle of white lace. The palm trees looked no bigger than fledgling asparagus. I could pick out a few landmarks: the courthouse, the high school, a big Catholic church, a theater, the one office building downtown over three stories high. From this vantage point, there was no evidence of the Victorian influence or any of the later architectural styles that blended now with the Spanish.

This house, he told me, had been finished in the summer of 1950. He and his wife, Reva, had just bought the place when the Korean War broke out. He'd been drafted and had gone off two days after they moved in, leaving Reva with stacks of cardboard boxes to unpack, returning four-teen months later with a service-related disability. He didn't specify what it was and I didn't ask, but he had apparently only worked sporadically since his medical discharge. They'd had five children and Rick had been the youngest. The others were scattered now through the Southwest.

"What was he like?" I asked. I wasn't sure he'd answer. The silence stretched on and I wondered if perhaps it might have been the wrong question. I hated to spoil whatever sense of camaraderie we'd established.

He shook his head finally. "I don't know how to answer that," he said. "He was one of those kids you think you're never going to have a minute's trouble with. Always sunny, did things without being told, good grades in school. Then when he was sixteen or so—his last year in high school—he seemed to lose his footing. He graduated all right, but he didn't seem to know what to do with himself. He was drifting. Had the grades for college and God knows I'd have found the money someplace, but it didn't interest him. Nothing did. Oh, he worked, but it never amounted to a hill of beans."

"Was he doing drugs?"

"I don't think so. At least there was never any sign of it that I could see. The kid drank a lot. Reva thought it was that, but I don't know. He did like to party. He was out 'til all hours, slept the weekends away, hung out with kids like Bobby Callahan, way above us socially. Then he started dating Bobby's stepsister, Kitty. Christ, that girl was trouble the day she was born. By then, I was sick of putting up with him. If he didn't want to be part of the family, fine. Go somewhere else, though, earn your own keep. Don't think you can use this place to get meals and laundry done." He paused, looking over at me. "Was I wrong? I'm asking you."

"I don't know," I said. "How can you answer a question like that anyway? Kids get off-course and then they straighten out. Half the time, it doesn't have anything to do with parents. Who knows what it is?"

He was silent, staring out at the horizon, his lips encir-cling the cigar like a hose coupling. He sucked in some nicotine, then blew out a cloud of smoke. "Sometimes I wonder how bright he was. Maybe he should have seen a therapist, but how did I know? That's what Reva says now. What's a psychiatrist going to do with a kid who has no ambition?"

I didn't have a response to any of this so I made sympathetic sounds and let it go at that.

Brief silence. He said, "I hear Bobby's all messed up."

His tone was hesitant, a guarded inquiry about a hated rival. He must have wished Bobby dead a hundred times, cursing his good fortune at having survived.

"I'm not sure he wouldn't trade places with Rick if he could," I said, feeling my way. I didn't want to set off a fresh surge of agitation, but I didn't want him harboring the notion that Bobby was somehow "luckier" than Rick. Bobby was working his ass off to make life all right, but it was a struggle.

Below us, an old pale blue Ford rattled into view, spewing exhaust. The driver swung wide around my car and paused, apparently activating an automatic garage door. The car nosed out of sight beneath us and, moments later, I heard the muffled sound of the car door slamming.

"That's my wife," Phil said, as the garage-door mechanism ground under our feet.

Reva Bergen trudged up the steep walk, burdened with grocery sacks. I noted with curiosity that Phil made no move to assist her. She caught sight of us as she reached the porch. She hesitated, her face a perfect blank. Even at that distance, her gaze had an unfocused quality that seemed more pronounced when she finally came out of the back door, moments later, to join us. She was a dishwater blonde with that washed-out look women sometimes acquire in their fifties. Her eyes were small, nearly lashless. Pale eyebrows, pale skin. She was frail and bony, her hands looking as clumsy as gardening gloves on her narrow wrists. The two of them seemed so entirely unsuited to each other that I quickly discarded the unbidden image of their marital bed.

Phil explained who I was and the fact that I was investigating the accident in which Rick had been killed.

Her smile was mean. "Bobby's conscience bothering him?"

Phil interceded before I could frame a response. "Come on, Reva. What harm can it do? You said yourself the police—"

She turned abruptly and went back inside. Phil shoved his hands down in his pockets with embarrassment. "Nuts. She's been like that ever since it happened. Things set her off. I haven't been a joy to live with myself, but this thing has torn her heart out."

"I should be on my way," I said. "But I would like for you to do one thing if you would. I've been trying to figure out what could possibly have been going on back then and I'm not having much luck so far. Did Rick give you any indication that Bobby was in trouble or upset? Or that he might have had some kind of problem himself?"

He shook his head. "Rick's whole life was a problem to me, but it didn't have anything to do with the accident. I'll ask Reva, though, and see if she knows anything."

"Thanks," I said. I shook his hand and then fished a card out of my bag so he'd know how to get in touch with me.

He walked me down to the road and I thanked him again for lunch. As I got in my car, I glanced up. Reva was standing on the porch, staring down at us.

I headed back into town. I stopped by the office to check my answering machine for messages (none) and my mail, which was all junk. I made a fresh pot of coffee and hauled out my portable typewriter, detailing the notes on my investigation to that point. It was painstaking stuff, given the fact that I'd turned up absolutely nothing. Still, Bobby was entitled to know how I'd spent my time and at thirty bucks an hour, he was entitled to know where the money went.

At three o'clock, I locked the office and walked over to the public library, which was two blocks over and two blocks up. I went downstairs to the periodicals room and asked for the previous September's newspapers, now consigned to microfilm. I found a machine and sat down, threading in the first reel. The print was white on black, all of the photographs looking like negatives. I had no idea what I might spot so I was forced to skim every page. Current events, national news, local political issues, fire, crime, storm systems, folks being born and dying and getting divorced. I read the lost-and-found column, the personals, society, sports. The mechanism for advancing the film was somehow out of whack, so that paragraphs jerked onto the nine-by-twelve screen with the focus slightly skewed, generating a motion sickness of sorts. Around me, people were browsing among the magazines or were seated in low chairs, reading newspapers attached to upright wooden lances. The only sounds in the room were the drone of the machine I was using, an occasional cough, and the rustle of newsprint.

I managed to check the papers for the first six days of September before my resolve faltered. I'd have to do this in small doses. My neck felt stiff and my head was starting to ache. A glance at my watch showed that it was nearly five and I was bored to death. I made a note of the last date I'd scanned and then I fled into the late-afternoon sunshine. I walked back to my office building and retrieved my car from the parking lot without going upstairs.

On the way home, I stopped off at the supermarket for milk, bread, and toilet paper, doing a quick tour with my cart. There was so much lyrical music playing overhead, I felt like the heroine in a romantic comedy. Once I'd found what I needed, I moved to the express lane, twelve items or less. There were five of us in line, all surreptitiously counting the contents of each other's carts. The man in front of me had a head too small for the size of his face, like an underinflated balloon. He had a little girl with him, maybe four years old, wearing a brand-new dress several sizes too big. Something about it spelled "poor," but I don't know why. It made her look like a midget; waistline at her hips, the hem down around her ankles. She held the man's hand with perfect trust, giving me a shy smile so filled with pride that I found myself smiling back.

I was tired by the time I got home and my left arm ached. There are days when I scarcely remember the injury, other days when I feel drained by a constant dull pain. I decided to skip my run. To hell with it. I took a couple of Tylenol with codeine, kicked my shoes off, and crawled into the folds of my quilt. I was still there when the phone rang. I awoke with a start, reaching automatically for the receiver. My apartment was dark. The unexpected shrill blast of sound had sent a jolt of adrenaline through me and my heart was pounding. I glanced at the clock with uneasiness. Eleven-fifteen.

I mumbled hello, rubbing a hand across my face and through my hair.

"Kinsey, it's Derek Wenner. Have you heard?"

"Derek, I'm sound asleep."

"Bobby's dead."

"What?"

"I guess he'd been drinking, though we're not even sure of that at this point. His car went off the road and smashed into a tree on West Glen. I thought you'd want to know."

"What?" I knew I was repeating myself, but I couldn't understand what he was talking about.

"Bobby's been killed in a car accident."

"But when?" I don't know why it mattered. I was just asking questions because I couldn't cope with the information any other way.

"A little after ten. He was dead by the time they got him to St. Terry's. I have to go down and identify him, but there doesn't seem to be any doubt."

"Can I do anything?"

He seemed to hesitate. "Well, actually, maybe you could. I tried to reach Sufi, but I guess she's out. Dr. Metcalf's service is tracking him down, so he'll probably be here in a bit. I wonder if you could sit with Glen in the meantime. That way, I can head on over to the hospital and see what's going on."

"I'll be right there," I said and hung up.

I washed my face and brushed my teeth. I was talking to myself the whole time, but I didn't feel anything. All my inner processes seemed to be suspended temporarily while my brain struggled with the facts. The information kept bounding back. No way. Nuh-un. How could Bobby be gone? Not true.

I grabbed a jacket, my handbag, and my keys. I locked up, got in my car, started the engine, pulled out. I felt like a well-programmed robot. When I turned onto West Glen Road, I saw the emergency vehicles and I could feel a chill tickle at the base of my spine. It was just at the big bend, a blind corner near the "slums." The ambulance was already gone, but patrol cars were still there, radios squawking in the night air. Bystanders stood on the side of the road in the dark while the tree he'd hit was washed with high-intensity floodlights, the raw gash in the trunk looking like a fatal wound in itself. His BMW was just being removed by a tow truck. The scene looked, oddly, like a location for a movie being shot. I slowed, turning to peer at the site with an eerie feeling of detachment. I didn't want to add to the confusion and I was worried about Glen, so I drove on. A little voice murmured, "Bobby's dead." A second voice said, "Oh no, let's don't do that. I don't want that to be true, O.K.?"

I pulled into the narrow drive, following it until it opened out into the empty courtyard. The entire house was blazing with lights as if a massive party were in progress, but there was no sound and not a soul in sight, no cars visible. I parked and moved toward the entrance. One of the maids, like an electronic sensing device, opened the door as I approached. She stepped back, admitting me without comment.

"Where's Mrs. Callahan?"

She closed the door and started down the hall. I followed. She tapped at the door to Glen's study and then turned the knob and stepped back again, letting me pass into the room.

Glen was dressed in a pale pink robe, huddled in one of the wing-back chairs, knees drawn up. She raised her face, which was swollen and waterlogged. It looked as if all of her emotional pipes had burst, eyes spilling over, cheeks washed with tears, her nose running. Even her hair was damp. For a moment, still in disbelief, I stood there and looked at her and she looked at me and then she lowered her face again, extending her hand. I crossed and knelt by her chair. I took her hand—small and cold—and pressed it against my cheek.

"Oh Glen, I'm sorry. I'm so sorry," I whispered.

She was nodding acknowledgment, making a low sound in her throat, not even a clearly articulated cry. It was a sound more primitive than that. She started to speak, but she could only manage a sort of dragged-out, stuttering phrase, sub-English, devoid of sense. What difference did it make what she said? It was done and nothing could change it. She began to cry as children cry, deep, shuddering sobs that went on and on. I clung to her hand, offering her a mooring line in that churning sea of grief.

Finally, I could feel the turbulence pass like a battering rain cloud moving on. The spasms subsided. She let go of me and leaned back, taking in a deep breath. She took out a handkerchief and pressed it against her eyes, then blew her nose. She paused, apparently looking inward, much in the way one does at the end of an attack of hiccups.

She sighed. "Oh *God*, how will I get through this?" she said, and the tears welled up again, sp shing down her face. She regained control after a moment and went through the mop-up process again, shaking her head. "Jesus. Shit. I don't think I can do this, Kinsey. You know? It's just too hard and I don't have that kind of strength."

"You want me to call anyone?"

"No, not now. It's too late and what's the point? In the morning, I'll have Derek get in touch with Sufi. She'll come."

"What about Kleinert? You want me to let him know?"

She shook her head. "Bobby couldn't stand him. Just let it be. He'll find out soon enough. Is Derek back?" Her tone was anxious now, her face tense.

"I don't think so. You want a drink?"

"No, but help yourself if you like. The liquor's in there."

"Maybe later." I wanted something, but I wasn't sure what it was. Not a drink. I was afraid alcohol would eat through the thin veneer of self-control. The last thing in the world she needed was to have to turn around and comfort me. I sat down in the chair across from her and an image flashed into my mind. I remembered Bobby bending down to say good night to her just two nights ago. He had turned automatically so he could offer her the good side of his face. It had been one of his last night's sleep on this earth, but neither of them had known that, nor had I. I glanced up at her and she was looking at me as if she knew what was going on in my head. I glanced away, but not quickly enough. Something in her face spilled over me like light through a swinging door. Sorrow shot through the gap, catching me off-guard, and I burst into tears.

12

Everything happens for a reason, but that doesn't mean there's a point. The next few days were a nightmare, the more so as mine was only a peripheral role in the pageantry of Bobby's death. Because I'd appeared in the first moments of her grief, Glen Callahan seemed to fix on me, as though I might provide a solace for her pain.

Dr. Kleinert agreed to release Kitty until after the burial, and an attempt was made to reach Bobby's natural father overseas, but he never responded and nobody seemed to care. Meanwhile, hundreds of people streamed through the funeral home: Bobby's friends, old high-school classmates, family friends and business associates, all the town dignitaries, members of the various boards Glen served on. The Who's Who of Santa Teresa. After that first night, Glen was totally composed—calm, gracious, tending to every detail of Bobby's funeral. It would be done properly. It would be done in the best of taste. I would be on hand throughout.

I had thought Derek and Kitty would resent my constant presence, but both seemed relieved. Glen's single-mindedness must have been a frightening prospect to them.

Glen ordered Bobby's casket closed, but I saw him for a moment at the funeral home after his body had been "prepared." In some ways, I needed that glimpse to convince myself that he was really dead. God, the stillness of the flesh when life has gone. Glen stood there beside me, her gaze fixed on Bobby's face, her own expression as blank and inanimate as his. Something had left her with his death. She was unflinching, but her grip on my arm tightened as the lid to the casket was closed.

"Good-bye, baby," she whispered. "I love you."

I turned away quickly.

Derek approached from behind and I saw him move as though to touch her. She didn't turn her head, but she radiated a rage so limitless that he kept his distance, intimidated by the force of it. Kitty stood against the back wall, stony, her face blotchy from tears wept in solitude. Somehow I suspected that she and her father wouldn't remain in Glen's life for long. Bobby's death had accelerated the household decay. Glen seemed impatient to be alone, intolerant of the requirements of ordinary intercourse. They were takers. She had nothing left to give. I scarcely knew the woman, but it seemed clear to me that she was suddenly operating by another set of premises. Derek watched her uneasily, sensing, perhaps, that he wasn't part of this new scheme, whatever it was.

Bobby was buried on Saturday. The church services were mercifully short. Glen had selected the music and a few passages from various non-Biblical sources. I took my cue from her, surviving the eulogy by neatly disconnecting myself from what was said. I wasn't going to deal with Bobby's death today. I wasn't going to lose control in a public setting like this. Even so, there were moments when I could feel my face heat up and my eyes blur with tears. It was more than this loss. It was all death, every loss—my parents, my aunt.

The funeral cortege must have been ten blocks long, cruising across the city at a measured pace. At every intersection, traffic had been forced to stop as we rolled by, and I could see the comments in the faces we passed. "Ooo, a funeral. Wonder whose." "Gorgeous day for it." "God, look at all the cars." "Come on, come on. Get out of the way."

We wound into the cemetery, as green and carefully landscaped as a housing tract. Headstones stretched out in all directions, a varied display, like a stonecutter's yard filled with samples of his work. There were intermittent evergreens, clusters of eucalyptus and sycamore. The cemetery parcels were sectioned off by low walls of shrubbery and on a plot map probably had names like Serenity and Heavenly Meadows.

We parked and everyone trooped across the newly trimmed grass. It felt like an elementary-school outing: everyone on their best behavior, nobody quite sure what to do next. There were occasional murmured conversations, but for the most part, we were silent. Mortuary personnel, in dark suits, escorted us to our seats like ushers at a wedding.

The day was hot, the afternoon sunlight intense. There was a breeze that rustled the treetops and lifted the canvas tent flaps flirtatiously. We sat dutifully while the minister conducted the final rites. I felt better out here and I realized it was the absence of organ music that made the graveside ceremony less potent. Even the most banal of church hymns can rip your heart out at times like this. I preferred the sound of wind.

Bobby's casket was a massive affair of glossy walnut and brass, like an oversized blanket chest too large for the space allotted. Apparently, the casket would fit down into the vault especially purchased to house it underground. There was some kind of complex mechanism set up above the grave site that would eventually be used to lower the casket into the hole, but I gathered that was done at some later time.

Funeral styles had evolved since my parents were buried and I wondered, idly, what had dictated the change. Technology, no doubt. Maybe death was tidier these days and easier to regulate. Graves were dug by machinery, which carved out a neat pit surmounted now by this low-slung contraption on which the casket rested. No more of this horseshit with the loved ones flinging themselves into the grave. With this new apparatus in place, you'd have to get down on your belly and leopard-crawl into the hole, which robbed the gesture of its theatrical effect.

Off to one side among the mourners, I saw Phil and Reva Bergen. He seemed upset, but she was impassive. Her gaze drifted from the minister's face to mine and she stared at me flatly. Behind them, I thought I saw Kelly Borden, but I couldn't be sure. I shifted in my chair, hoping to make eye contact, but the face was gone. The crowd began to disperse and I was startled to realize it was over. The minister, in his black robes, gave Glen a solemn look, but she ignored him and moved toward the limousine. Derek, in a show of good manners, lingered long enough to exchange a few remarks.

Kitty was already in the backseat when we reached the limo. I would have bet money she was high on something. Her cheeks were flushed and her eyes were feverishly bright, her hands restless in her lap, plucking at her black cotton skirt. The outfit she'd elected to wear had an outlandish gypsy air to it, the black cotton top composed of tiers of ruffles, embroidered in garish shades of turquoise and red. Glen had blinked lazily when she'd first set eyes on Kitty and an almost imperceptible smile had hovered on her lips before she turned her attention to something else. She'd apparently decided not to make an issue of it. Kitty's manner had been defiant, but with no resistance on Glen's part the juice had drained out of the drama before she'd even launched into the first art.

I was standing by the limo when I saw Derek approach. He climbed into the backseat and pulled down one of the collapsible camp stools, reaching to pull the door shut.

"Leave it open," Glen murmured.

The limo driver was still nowhere in sight. There was a delay while people took their places in the vehicles parked along the road. Others were milling around on the grass to no apparent purpose.

Derek tried to catch Glen's eye. "Well, I thought that went very well."

Glen turned pointedly and peered out of the far window. When your only child has been killed, who really gives a shit?

Kitty took out a cigarette and lit it. Her hands looked like birds' claws, the skin almost scaly. The elasticized neckline of her blouse revealed a chest so thin that her sternum and costal cartilages were outlined like one of those joke T-shirts.

Derek made a face as the smell of smoke filled the backseat. "Jesus, Kitty, put that out. For Christ's sake!"

"Oh, leave her alone," Glen said, dully. Kitty seemed surprised by the unexpected support, but she stubbed out the cigarette anyway.

The driver appeared and closed the door on Derek's side, then moved around the rear of the limousine and slid in under the steering wheel. I moved on toward my car as he pulled away.

*   *   *

The mood was much lighter once we got to the house. People seemed to shrug death aside, comforted by good wine and lavish hors d'oeuvres. I don't know why death still generates these little têtes-à-têtes. Everything else has been modernized, but some vestige of the wake remains. There must have been two hundred people crowded into the living room and hall, but it all seemed O.K. It was filler, just something to smooth the awkward transition from the funeral to the bone-crushing sleep that was bound to come afterward.

I recognized most of the people who'd been at Derek's birthday gathering that past Monday night: Dr. Fraker and his wife, Nola; Dr. Kleinert and a rather plain woman whom I assumed was Mrs. K.; the other doctor who'd been present, Metcalf, in conversation with Marcy, who had worked with Bobby briefly in the Pathology Department. I snagged a glass of wine and inched my way across the room to Fraker's side. He and Kleinert had their heads bent together and they paused as I approached.

"Hi," I said, suddenly self-conscious. Maybe this wasn't such a hot idea. I took a sip of wine, noting the look that passed between them. I guess they decided I could be privy to their discussion, because Fraker picked up where he'd left off.

"Anyway, I won't be doing the microscopic until Monday, but from the gross, it looks like the immediate cause of death was a ruptured aortic valve."

Kleinert said, "From impact with the steering wheel."

Fraker nodded, taking a sip of wine. The explanation of his findings continued almost as though he were dictating it all over again. "The sternum and multiple ribs were fractured and the ascending aorta was incompletely torn just above the superior border of the valve cusps. Additionally, there was a left hemothorax of eight hundred cc and a massive aortic adventitial hemorrhage."

Kleinert's expression indicated that he was following. The whole thing sounded sickening to me and I didn't even know what it meant.

"What about the blood alcohol?" Kleinert asked.

Fraker shrugged. "That was negative. He wasn't drunk.

We should have the rest of the results this afternoon, but I don't think we're going to find anything. I could be surprised, of course."

"Well, if you're right about the CSF blockage, a seizure was probably inevitable. Bernie warned him to watch for the symptoms," Kleinert said. His face was long and etched with a look of permanent sorrow. If I had emotional problems and needed a shrink, I didn't think it would help me to look at a face like that week after week. I'd want somebody with some energy, pizzazz, somebody with a little hope.

"Bobby had a seizure?" I asked. It was clear by now that they were discussing his autopsy results. Fraker must have realized I didn't have any idea what they were actually saying, because he offered a translation.

"We think Bobby may have been suffering from a complication of the original head injury. Sometimes, a blockage develops in the normal flow of cerebrospinal fluid. Intracranial pressure builds up and part of the brain starts to atrophy, resulting in posttraumatic epilepsy."

"And that's why he ran off the road?"

"In my opinion, yes," Fraker said. "I can't state this categorically, but he'd probably been experiencing headaches, anxiety, irritability perhaps."

Kleinert cut in again. "I saw him at seven, seven fifteen, something like that. He was terribly depressed."

"Maybe he suspected what was going on," Fraker was saying.

"Too bad he didn't speak up then, if that's the case."

The murmuring between them continued while I tried to take in the implications.

"Is there any way a seizure like that could have been drug-induced?" I asked.

"Sure, it's possible. Toxicology reports aren't comprehensive and the analyses' results depend on what's asked for. There are several hundred drugs which could affect a person with a predisposition to seizures. Realistically, it isn't possible to screen for all of them," Fraker said.

Kleinert shifted restlessly. "Actually, after what he went through, it's a wonder he survived as long as he did. We tried to spare Glen, but I think we've all been worried that something like this might occur."

There didn't seem to be anything left to say on the subject.

Kleinert finally turned to Fraker. "Have you eaten yet? Ann and I are going out for supper if you and Nola want to join us."

Fraker declined the invitation, but he did need his wineglass filled and I could see him eyeing the crowd for some sign of his wife. Both doctors excused themselves.

I stood there, unsettled, reviewing the facts. Theoretically, Bobby Callahan had died of natural causes, but in fact, he'd died as a consequence of injuries received in the accident nine months ago, which he, at least, believed was a murder attempt. As nearly as I could remember, California law provides that "a killing is murder or manslaughter if the party dies within three years and a day after the stroke is received or the cause of death is administered." So the truth was, he was murdered and it didn't make any difference at all if he died that night or last week. At the moment, of course, I didn't have any proof. I did still have the bulk of the money Bobby had paid me and a clear set of instructions from him, so I was still in business if I wanted to be.

Mentally, I got up and dusted myself off. It was time to put grief aside and get back to work. I set my wineglass down and had a brief word with Glen to let her know where I'd be and then I went upstairs and systematically searched Bobby's room. I wanted that little red book.

13

I was operating, of course, on the hope that Bobby had hidden the address book somewhere on the premises. He said he remembered giving the book to someone, but that might not be true. There was no way I could search the entire house, but I could certainly comb a couple of places. Glen's study, maybe Kitty's room. It was quiet upstairs and I was glad to be alone for a while. I searched for an hour and a half and came up with nothing. I wasn't discouraged. In some odd way, I was heartened. Maybe Bobby's memory had served him correctly.

At six, I wandered out into the corridor. I leaned my elbows on the balustrade that circled the landing and listened for sounds filtering up from below. Apparently, the crowd had diminished considerably. I heard smatterings of laughter, an occasional light conversational swell, but it sounded like most of the guests had departed. I retraced my steps and tapped on Kitty's door.

Muffled response. "Who is it?"

"It's me. Kinsey," I said to the blank door. After a moment, I heard the lock retracted, but she didn't actually let me in.

Instead, she hollered, "Enter!"

Lord, she was tedious. I entered.

The room had been tidied and the bed was made, I'm sure through no effort of hers. She looked as if she'd been crying. Her nose was reddened, her makeup smeared. She was, of course, doing drugs. She had gotten out a mirror and a razor blade and was laying out a couple of lines of coke. There was a half-filled wineglass on the bed table.

"I feel like shit," she said. She had exchanged her gypsy outfit for a raw silk kimono in a lush shade of green with butterflies embroidered on the back and sleeves. Her arms were so thin she looked like a praying mantis, her green eyes aglitter.

"When are you due back at St. Terry's?" I asked.

She paused to blow her nose, not wanting to screw up her high. "Who knows?" she said, glumly. "Tonight, I guess. At least I'll have a chance to pack some of my own clothes to take with me. Shit, I ended up on the psycho ward with *nothing*."

"Why do you do this stuff, Kitty? You're playing right into Kleinert's hands."

"Terrific. I didn't know you came up here to lecture me."

"I came up to search Bobby's room. I'm looking for the little red address book he asked you about last Tuesday. I don't suppose you have any idea where it might be."

"Nope." She bent over, using a rolled-up dollar bill like a straw, her nostril forming a little vacuum cleaner. I watched the coke fly up her nose, like a magic trick.

"Can you think who he might have given it to?"

"Nuh-un." She sat back on the bed, pinching her nose shut. She wet her index finger and cleaned the surface of the mirror, running her fingertip across her gums then, like a remedy for teething pains. She reached for her wineglass and settled back against the bed pillows, lighting a cigarette.

"God, that's great," I said. "You're tagging all the bases today. Do a little coke, knock back some wine, cigarettes. They're going to have to run you through Detox before you hit Three South again." I knew I was baiting her, but she got on my nerves and I was spoiling for a fight, which I suspected would feel better than grief.

"Fuck you," she said, bored.

"Mind if I sit down?" I asked.

She gestured permission and I perched on the edge of the bed, looking around with interest.

"What happened to your stash?" I asked.

"What stash?"

"The one you kept in there," I said, indicating the bed table drawer.

She stared. "I never kept a *stash* in there."

I loved the little note of righteous indignation. "That's funny," I said. "I saw Dr. Kleinert pull a whole Ziploc bag full of pills out of there."

"When?" she said in disbelief.

"Monday night when they carted you away. Quaaludes, Placidyls, Tuinals, the works." Actually, I didn't really believe the pills were hers, but I was curious to hear what she had to say.

She stared at me for a moment more, then eased out a mouthful of smoke, which she neatly channeled up her nose. "I don't do any of those," she said.

"What'd you take Monday night?"

"Valium. Prescription."

"Dr. Kleinert gave you a prescription for Valium?" I asked.

She got up with annoyance and started pacing the room. "I don't need your bullshit, Kinsey. My stepbrother was buried today in case your memory's short. I got other things on my mind."

"Were you involved with Bobby?"

"No, I wasn't 'involved' with Bobby. What do you mean, like some kind of sexual thing? Like was I having an *affair*?"

"Yeah, like that."

"God, you are so imaginative. For your information, I didn't even think about him that way."

"Maybe he thought about you that way."

She stopped pacing. "Says who?"

"Just a theory of mine. You know he loved you. Why wouldn't he have sexual feelings as well?"

"Oh come on. Did Bobby say that?"

"No, but I saw his reaction the night you were hospitalized. I didn't think it was strictly brotherly love I was looking at. In fact, I asked Glen about it at the time, but she said she didn't think there was anything going on."

"Well, there wasn't."

"Too bad. Maybe you could have saved each other."

She rolled her eyes, giving me a look—God, adults are such geeks!—but she was restless and distracted. She located an ashtray on the chest of drawers and stubbed out her cigarette. She lifted the lid to a music box and let a few notes of "Lara's Theme" escape before she snapped it shut again. When she looked at me again, she had tears in her eyes and she seemed embarrassed by that.

She pushed away from the chest of drawers. "I gotta pack my stuff."

She went into the closet and hauled out a canvas duffel. She opened her top dresser drawer and snatched up a stack of underpants, which she shoved into the duffel. She bumped the drawer shut and opened the next one, grabbing T-shirts, jeans, socks.

I got up and moved to the door, turning back with my hand on the knob. "Nothing lasts, you know. Not even misery."

"Yeah, sure. Especially not mine. What do you think I do drugs for, my health?"

"You're tough, right?"

"Shit, why don't you go work in a rescue mission? You got the line down pat."

"One day some happiness is going to come into your life in spite of you. You ought to keep yourself alive so you can enjoy it."

"Sorry. No sale. I'm not interested."

I shrugged. "So die. It won't be that big a deal. It sure won't be the loss that Bobby's death was. So far, you haven't given the world a thing."

I opened the door.

I heard her bump a drawer shut. "Hey, Kinsey?"

I looked back at her. Her smirk was almost self-mocking, but not quite.

"Want to do a line of coke? My treat."

I left the room, closing the door quietly. I felt like slamming it, but what would be the point?

I went down to the living room. I was hungry and I needed a glass of wine. There were only five or six people left. Sufi sat next to Glen on one of the sofas. I didn't recognize anybody else. I crossed to the buffet table that had been set up on the far side of the room. The Chicano maid, Alicia, was rearranging a platter of shrimp, consolidating hors d'oeuvres so the plates wouldn't look all ratty and half eaten. God, there was a lot to this business of being rich. It had never occurred to me. I thought you just invited people over and turned 'em loose, but I could see now that entertaining requires all kinds of subtle monitoring.

I filled a plate and picked up a fresh glass of wine. I chose a seat close enough to the others so I wouldn't seem rude, but far enough away so I wouldn't have to talk to anyone. I have a shy streak that surfaces in situations like this. I'd rather have chatted with some hooker down on lower State Street than try to exchange pleasantries with this crew. What could we possibly have discussed? They were talking about long-term paper. I took a bite of salmon mousse and tried to keep an interested look on my face, like maybe I had a lot of long-term paper I was hoping to unloaad. Such a nuisance, that shit, isn't it?

I felt a light touch on my arm and glanced over to see Sufi Daniels easing into the chair next to mine.

"Glen tells me Bobby was very fond of you," she said.

"I hope so. I liked him."

Sufi stared at me. I kept eating because I couldn't think what else to say. She was wearing an odd outfit: a long black dress of some silky material with a matching jacket over it. I assumed it was meant to disguise her misshapen form with its slightly hunched back, but it made her look as if she were about to perform with some big philharmonic orchestra. Her hair was the same lank, pale mess it had been when I met her the first time and her makeup was inexpert. She couldn't have been more different from Glen Callahan. Her manner was faintly patronizing, like she was just on the verge of slipping me a couple of bucks for my services. I might have been short with her, but there was always the chance that she had Bobby's little red book.

"How do you know Glen?" I asked, taking a sip of wine. I set the glass down on the floor near my chair and forked up some cold shrimp in a spicy sauce. Sufi's gaze flicked over to Glen and then back.

"We met in school."

"You've been friends a long time."

"Yes, we have."

I nodded, swallowing. "You must have been around when Bobby was born," I remarked, just to keep things going.

"Yes."

Shit, this is fun, I thought. "Were you close to him?"

"I liked him, but I can't say we were close. Why?"

I retrieved my wine and took a sip. "He gave someone a little red book. I'm trying to figure out who."

"What sort of book?"

I shrugged. "Addresses, telephone numbers. Small, bound in red leather, from what he said."

She suddenly began to blink at me. "You're not still investigating," she said. It wasn't a question. It was a statement tinged with disbelief.

"Why not?"

"Well, the boy is dead. What difference could any of it possibly make?"

"If he was murdered, it makes a difference to me," I said.

"If he was murdered, it's a matter for the police."

I smiled. "The cops around here love my help."

Sufi looked over at Glen, lowering her voice. "I'm sure she wouldn't want this pursued."

"She didn't hire me. Bobby did. Anyway, why do you care?"

She seemed to catch the danger in my tone, but it didn't worry her much. She smiled thinly, still superior.

"Of course. I didn't mean to interfere," she murmured. "I just wasn't sure what your plans were and I didn't want Glen upset."

I was supposed to make comforting noises back to her, but I just sat there and stared. A bit of color rose in her cheeks.

"Well. It's been nice seeing you again." She got up and wandered over to one of the remaining guests, engaging in conversation with a pointed turning of her back. I shrugged to myself. I wasn't sure what she'd been up to. I didn't care either, unless it pertained to the case. I glanced over at her, speculating.

Soon after, almost at a signal, people started getting into their good-bye behavior. Glen stood by the archway to the living room, being hugged, having her hands pressed in sympathy. Everyone said the same thing. "You know we love you, sweetie. Now you let us know if we can do anything."

She said "I will" and got hugged again.

Sufi was the one who actually walked them to the door.

I was on the verge of following when Glen caught my eye.
"I'd like to talk to you if you can stay on for a while."

"Sure," I said. I realized for the first time that I hadn't
seen Derek for hours. "Where's Derek?"

"Taking Kitty back to St. Terry's." She sank into one of the
couches, slouching down so she could rest her head on the
back. "Would you like a drink?"

"Actually, I could use one. Shall I fix you one while I'm at
it?"

"God, I'd love it. There's a liquor cabinet in my den if
we're low out here. Make it Scotch. Lots of ice, please."

I crossed the hall and went into the den, fetching an old-
fashioned glass and the bottle of Cutty Sark. When I
reached the living room again, Sufi was back and the house
was mantled in that dull quiet that follows too much noise.

There was an ice bucket on the end of the buffet table and
I plopped a couple of cubes into the glass with a set of those
sterling-silver ice tongs that look somehow like dinosaur
claws. It made me feel sophisticated, like I was in a 1940s
movie wearing a suit with shoulder pads and stockings with
a line up the back.

"You must be exhausted," Sufi was murmuring. "Why
don't I get you into bed before I take off?"

Glen smiled wearily. "No, that's all right. You go ahead."

Sufi had no other choice but to bend down and give Glen
a buss and then find her purse. I handed Glen the glass
with ice, pouring Scotch into it. Sufi made her final
farewells and then left the room with a cautionary look at
me. A few moments later, I heard the front door shut.

I pulled a chair over and sat down, propping my feet up
on the couch, cataloguing my current state. The small of my
back ached, my left arm ached. I finished off the wine in my
glass and added Cutty Sark.

Glen took a long swallow of hers. "I saw you talking to
Jim. What did he have to say?"

"He thinks Bobby had a seizure and that's why he ran off
the road. Some kind of epilepsy from his head injuries in
the first accident."

"Meaning what?"

"Well, as far as I'm concerned, it means if *that* accident
was really a murder attempt, it finally paid dividends."

Her face was blank. She dropped her gaze. "What will you do now?"

"Hey, listen. I still have money left from the retainer Bobby gave me. I'll work 'til I find out who killed him."

She met my eyes and the look she gave me was curious. "Why would you do that?"

"To settle accounts. I believe in clearing the ledger, don't you?"

"Oh yes," she said.

We stared at each other for a moment and then she raised her glass. I lifted mine and we drank.

When Derek came in, the two of them went upstairs and, with Glen's permission, I spent the next three hours in a fruitless search of her den and Kitty's room. Then I let myself out and went home.

14

By Monday morning at eight o'clock I was in the gym again, working out. I felt like I'd been to the moon and back. Without even thinking about it, I looked for Bobby, realizing a millisecond later that he was gone and wasn't ever going to be there again. It didn't sit well with me. Missing someone is a vague, unpleasant sensation, like gnawing anxiety. It isn't as concrete as grief, but it's just as pervasive and there's no escaping it. I kept moving, working out hard, as though physical pain might blot out its emotional counterpart. I filled every minute with activity and I suppose it worked. In some ways, it's like rubbing Ben-Gay on a sore back. You want to believe it's doing you some good, but you can't think why it would. It's better than nothing, but it's no cure.

I showered, got dressed, and headed over to the office. I hadn't been there since Wednesday afternoon. There was several days' mail piled up and I tossed it on the desk. The message light on my answering machine was blinking, but I had other things to attend to first. I opened the French doors and let some fresh air circulate, then made a pot of coffee for myself. I checked the half-and-half in my little refrigerator, sniffing at the carton spout. Borderline. I'd have to replace that soon. When the coffee was done, I found a clean mug and filled it. The half-and-half formed an ominous pattern on the surface, but it tasted O.K. Some days I drink my coffee black, some days with cream for the comfort of it. I sat down in my swivel chair and propped my feet up, punching the replay button on the answering machine.

The tape rewound itself and Bobby came on. I felt a chilly finger touch the nape of my neck when I realized who it was.

"Hi, Kinsey. This is Bobby. I'm sorry I was such a jerk a little while ago. I know you were just trying to cheer me up. One thing came to me. I know this doesn't make much sense, but I thought I'd pass it on anyway. I think the name Blackman ties into this. Somebody Blackman. I don't know if that's who I gave the little red book to or the guy who's after me. Could be it's nothing the way my brain scrambles things. Anyway, we can put our heads together later and see if it means anything. I've got some stuff to do and then I have to see Kleinert. I'll try to get back to you. Maybe we can have a drink or something later tonight. Bye for now, kid. Watch your backside."

I flipped the machine off and stared at it.

I reached in my top drawer for the telephone book and hauled it out. There was one Blackman listed, an S. No address. Probably a woman trying to avoid obscene phone calls. I believe in trying for the obvious first. I mean, why not? Maybe Sarah, or Susan, or Sandra Blackman knew Bobby and had his little red book, or maybe he'd told her exactly what was going on and I could wrap the whole thing up with one phone call. The number was a disconnect. I tried it again, just to double-check. The same recording clicked in again. I made a note. The number might still pertain. Maybe S. Blackman had left town or died mysteriously.

I punched the replay button, just to hear Bobby's voice again. I was feeling restless, wondering how to get down to brass tacks on this thing. I checked back through Bobby's file. I hadn't yet talked to his former girl friend, Carrie St. Cloud, and that seemed like a reasonable possibility. Glen had told me she dropped out of the picture after the accident, but she might remember something from that period. I tried the number Glen had given me and had a brief chat with Carrie's mother, explaining who I was and why I wanted to get in touch with her. Carrie had apparently moved out of the family home a year ago and into a little apartment of her own that she shared with a roommate. She was working full-time now as an aerobics instructor at a studio on Chapel. I made a note of the two addresses, her work and home, and thanked the woman. I set my mug aside, unplugged the coffeepot, locked the office, and trotted down the back stairs.

The day was overcast, the sky a low ceiling of white. A pale gray haze seemed to permeate the streets with chill air. After the insufferable heat of the last few weeks, it seemed odd. The weather in Santa Teresa has been straying from the norm of late. It used to be that you could count on clear sunny skies and a tamed and temperate sea, with maybe a few clouds massing behind the mountains more for the visual effect than anything else. The rains came dutifully in January, two weeks of constant downpour, after which the countryside turned emerald green, bougainvillea and cape honeysuckle exploding across the face of the town like gaudy makeup. Nowadays, there are enexplicable rains in April and October, chilly days like this in August when the temperature should be eighty-five degrees. The shift is baffling, the sort of climatic alteration associated with the eruption of South Sea volcanoes and rumors about the ozone being penetrated by hair sprays.

The studio was only half a block away, housed in a former racquetball club that had gone belly-up once the passion for racquetball had passed. With aerobics coming in, it made perfect sense to convert all those plain narrow rooms with hardwood floors into little fat-burning ovens for women who yearned to be lean and fit. I asked if Carrie was teaching and the woman at the desk pointed mutely toward the source of the deafening music that made further conversation unlikely at best. I followed the end of her finger and rounded the corner. On my right, there was a waist-high wall overlooking an aerobics class in full swing one floor below.

The acoustics were grim. I watched from the observer's gallery while the music blasted. Carrie hollered out encouragement and fifteen of the best-looking female bodies in town exercised with a fanaticism I'd seldom seen. Apparently, I'd caught the class at its apex. They were doing buttocks lifts that looked obscene: women groaning on the floor in frosted, skintight leotards, doing hip thrusts and bun squeezes as if unseen partners were grinding away at them in unison.

Carrie St. Cloud was a surprise. Her name suggested a second runner-up for a Junior Miss pageant, or maybe a budding actress whose real name is Wanda Maxine Smith. I had pictured run-of-the-mill California good looks, the trim surfer's body, blond hair, dazzling white teeth, maybe a little tendency to tap dance. She was none of these things.

She couldn't have been more than twenty-two with a body builder's musculature and dark hair to her waist. Her face was strong, like Greek statuary, with a full mouth, rounded chin. The leotard she wore was a pale yellow Spandex, defining the wide shoulders and lean hips of a gymnast. If she had an ounce of fat on her, I didn't spy it anyplace. She had no breasts to speak of, but the effect was intensely female anyway. This was no beach bunny. She took herself seriously, and she knew what fitness was about, breezing through the exercises without even breathing hard. Every other woman in the place was in pain. It made me grateful that all I have to do is jog three miles a day. I'm never going to look as good as she, but it didn't seem like a bad trade.

Carrie took the class through cool-down, a slow stretch, and a couple of yoga moves and then let them sprawl on the floor like casualties on a battlefield. She turned the music off, grabbed a towel, and buried her face in it, moving out of the room through a doorway just below me. I found the stairs and headed down, catching her at the water fountain just outside the locker rooms. Her hair fell across her shoulders like a nun's veil and she had to gather it in a knot and hold it to one side so she could drink without getting it wet.

"Carrie?"

She straightened up, blotting a trickle of sweat with the sleeve of her leotard, the towel around her neck now, like a fighter just out of the ring. "That's right."

I told her who I was and what I was doing and then asked her if we could talk about Bobby Callahan.

"All right, but we'll have to do it while I clean up. I have to be somewhere at noon."

I followed her through a door and into the locker room. The floor plan was open, with a counter on the right that circled the perimeter about halfway, banks of metal lockers, a line of hair dryers mounted on the wall. The tile was a pristine white and the place was spotless, with benches anchored to the floor, mirrors everywhere. I could hear showers running somewhere out of sight to my left. Women were beginning to straggle in from the class and the level of laughter, I knew, would rise as the room filled.

Carrie kicked off her shoes and peeled her leotard down like a banana skin. I busied myself looking for a place to perch. As a rule, I don't interview naked ladies in a roomful of chattering strippers. I noticed that they smelled just like the guys at Santa Teresa Fitness and I thought that was nice.

I waited while she tucked her hair up under a plastic cap and went into the showers. In the meantime, women paraded back and forth in various stages of undress. It was a comforting sight. So many versions of the female breast, of buttocks and bellies and pubic nests, endless repetitions of the same forms. These women seemed to feel good about themselves and there was a camaraderie among them that I enjoyed.

Carrie returned from showering, wrapped in a towel. She pulled her shower cap off and gave her dark mane a toss. She began to dry herself off, talking to me over her shoulder.

"I thought about coming to the funeral, but I just couldn't handle it. Did you go?"

"Yeah, I went. I hadn't known Bobby long, but it was tough. You were dating him when he had the accident, weren't you?"

"Actually, we'd just broken up. We dated two years and then things went sour. I got pregnant, among other things, and that was the end of it. He paid for the abortion, but we weren't seeing much of each other by then. I did feel terrible when he got hurt, but I stayed away. I know people thought I was a real cold fish, but what could I do? It was over. I couldn't see hovering around him loyally just so I'd look good."

"Did you hear any talk about the accident?"

"Just that someone ran him off the road."

"You have any idea who it might have been or why?"

She sat down on a bench and hauled a foot up, drying carefully between her toes. "Well, yes and no. Not who really, but I know something was going on with him. He didn't confide much by then, but he did go with me when I had the abortion and he stayed real close for a couple of days." She switched feet, bending to inspect her toes. "I worry about athlete's foot," she murmured. "Sorry."

She tossed the towel aside and got up, crossing to a locker, taking out clothes. She glanced at me. "I'm just trying to say this right because I don't really have any facts. Just an impression. I remember him saying some friend of his was in trouble and I had the feeling it was blackmail."

"Blackmail?"

"Well, yes, but not in any ordinary sense. I mean, I don't think there was money changing hands or anything like that. It wasn't sinister cloak-and-dagger stuff. Somebody had something on somebody else and it was pretty serious. I gathered he'd been trying to help and he'd just figured out how to do it. . . ." She pulled on her underpants and then an undershirt. I guess she figured her breasts weren't big enough to worry with a bra.

"When was this?" I asked. "Do you remember the date?"

"Well, I know I had the abortion on November sixteenth and he stayed with me that night. The accident was the day after that, I think, the night of the seventeenth, so it was all in that same week."

"I've been going through the newspaper starting in September, thinking maybe he was caught up in something public. Did you get *any* impression of the arena where all this was taking place? I mean, I don't even know what to look for."

She shook her head. "I have no idea. Really. I'm sorry, but I couldn't even make a guess."

"You think Rick Bergen was the friend in trouble?"

"I doubt it. I knew Rick. I think Bobby would have told me if it had been Rick."

"Somebody at work?"

"Look, I just can't help you with that," she said impatiently. "He was being very tight-lipped and I wasn't in a mood to pry. I was just glad the abortion was over with. I was taking pain-killers anyway so I slept a lot and the rest was a blur. He was just talking for the sake of it, to take my mind off things and maybe a little bit from nerves."

"Does the name Blackman mean anything to you?"

"I don't think so."

She pulled on a pair of sweatpants and slipped her feet into some thongs. She bent at the waist, flipped her hair across one shoulder, and gave it a couple of whacks with a hairbrush, then grabbed up her shoulder bag, moving toward the door. I had to do a quick two-step to catch up with her. I didn't think she'd finished dressing but I could see now that this was all she intended to wear. Sweatpants and an undershirt? She was going to freeze once she got outside. I scurried after her, catching the door as she passed into the corridor.

"Who else was he hanging out with back then?" I asked, trotting up the stairs to the main entrance with her. "Just give me a couple of names. I gotta have something to go on."

She paused, glancing back at me. "Try a kid named Gus. I don't know his last name, but he works at that skate-rental place down at the beach. He's an old high-school buddy and I think Bobby trusted him. Maybe he'll know what it's about."

"What were the other things? You said you got pregnant 'among other things.'"

Her smile was tense. "God, you are so persistent. He was in love with someone else. I have no idea who, so don't bother to ask. If I'd known about the other woman I'd have broken off our relationship long before. As it was, I didn't hear about her until I told him I was pregnant. I thought at first he might marry me, but when he told me he was seriously involved with someone else, I knew what I had to do. To his credit, he did feel terrible about the bind I was in and he did as much as he could. There was nothing cheap about Bobby and he really was a sweet guy at heart."

She started to move away and I caught her by the arm, thinking rapidly. "Carrie, is there a chance that the friend in trouble and the woman he was involved with were one and the same person?"

"How do I know?"

"I don't suppose he gave you a little red address book, did he?"

"All he gave me was heartache," she said and walked off without looking back.

15

The skate-rental shack is a dark green box just off a parking lot near the wharf. For three bucks, you can rent roller skates for an hour, with kneepads, elbow pads, and wrist braces thrown in without charge so you won't sue them later for the harm you might do yourself.

Bobby's taste in friends was hard to predict. Gus looked like the sort of fellow if you saw on a street corner, you'd reach over casually and make sure your car doors were locked. He must have been Bobby's age, but he was sunken-chested and frail, and his color was bad. His hair was dark brown and he was struggling to grow a mustache that only made him look like a fugitive. I'd seen mug shots of felons I'd trust before him.

I had introduced myself and ascertained that this was indeed Bobby's friend, when a blonde with flyaway hair and long tanned legs came up to turn in a pair of skates. I watched their interchange. Despite my first impression, Gus had a nice way about him. His manner was mildly flirtatious and he had a tendency to glance in my direction, showing off, I suspect. I waited, looking on while he calculated how much she owed him. He returned her street shoes and I.D. and she hopped over to a bench to put on her tennies. Gus waited until she was gone before he spoke.

"I saw you at the funeral," he said shyly when he turned back to me. "You were sitting near Mrs. Callahan."

"I don't remember seeing you," I said. "Did you come to the house afterwards?"

He shook his head, coloring. "I wasn't feeling too good."

"I don't think there's any way to feel good about that."

"Not when your buddy dies," he said. His voice carried a barely perceptible quaver. He turned away, making a big display of shoving the shoe skates back into the proper slot on the shelf.

"Have you been sick?" I asked.

He seemed to debate for just an instant and then said, "I got Crohn's disease. You know what that is?"

"No."

"Inflammatory bowel disease. Everything goes right through me. I can't keep weight on. Run a fever half the time. Stomach hurts. 'Etiology unknown,' which means they don't know what causes it or where it comes from. I've had it almost two years and it's got me down. I can't keep a real job, so I do this."

"Is that something you recover from?"

"I guess so. In time. That's what they say, at any rate."

"Well, I'm sorry you're suffering. It sounds grim."

"You don't know the half of it. Anyway, Bobby cheered me up. He was in such bad shape himself, we'd get laughin' sometimes. I miss him. When I heard he died, I almost gave up, but then this little voice said, 'Aw Gus, get up off your dead ass and get on with it . . . this isn't the end of the world, so don't be a jerk.'" He shook his head. "It was Bobby, I swear. Sounded just like him. So I got up off my dead ass. Are you looking into his death?"

I nodded, glancing over as a couple of kids approached to rent skates.

Gus conducted some business and came back to me, apologizing for the interruption. It was summer and despite the uncharacteristic chill in the air, the tourists were swarming the beaches. I asked him if he had any idea what Bobby was involved in. He moved uneasily, glancing off across the street.

"I got an idea, but I don't know what to say. I mean, if Bobby didn't tell you, why should I?"

"He couldn't remember. That's what he hired me for. He thought he was in danger and he wanted me to find out what was going on."

"So maybe it's best to just leave it be."

"Leave what be?"

"Look, I don't know anything for sure. Just what Bobby said."

"What are you worried about?"

He shifted his gaze. "I don't know. Let me think about it
some. Honest, I don't know much, but I don't want to talk
about it unless it feels right. You know what I mean?"

I conceded the point. You can always push people
around, but it's not a good idea. Better to let them volunteer information for reasons of their own. You get more that
way.

"I hope you'll give me a call," I said. "If I don't hear from
you, I might have to come back and make a pest of myself."
I took a card out and laid it on the counter.

He smiled, apparently feeling guilty for holding out. "You
can skate for nothing if you want. It's good exercise."

"Some other time," I said. "Thanks."

He watched me until I pulled out of the parking lot, turning left. In the rearview mirror, I could see him scratching
at his mustache with the corner of my business card. I
hoped I'd hear from him.

In the meantime, I decided to see if I could lay my hands
on the cardboard box the lab had packed up after Bobby's
accident. I drove over to the house. Glen had apparently
flown up to San Francisco for the day, but Derek was home
and I told him what I needed.

His look was skeptical. "I remember the box, but I'm not
sure where it went. Probably out in the garage, if you want
to have a look."

He closed the front door behind him and the two of us
crossed the courtyard to the three-car garage that stretched
out at one end of the house. There were storage bins built
into the back wall. None of them was locked, but most were
stacked top to bottom with boxes that looked as if they'd
been on the premises since the year oughty-ought.

I spotted a carton that seemed to be a good bet. It was
shoved against the back wall under a workbench, marked
"disposable syringes" with the name of the medical supplier
and a torn shipping label addressed to Santa Teresa Hospital Pathology Department. We hauled it out and opened it.
The contents looked like Bobby's, but were disappointing
nevertheless. No little red book, no reference to anybody
named Blackman, no clippings, no cryptic notes, no personal correspondence. There were some medical books,
two technical manuals for radiology equipment, and office

supplies of the most benign sort. What was I going to do
with a box of paper clips and two ballpoint pens?

"It doesn't look like much," Derek remarked.

"It doesn't look like *anything*," I replied. "You mind if I
take it with me anyway? I may want to check through it
again."

"No, go right ahead. Here let me get that." I stepped
back obligingly and let him heft the box up off the floor and
carry it to my car. I could have done it, but it seemed important to him, so why hassle? He shoved some stuff aside and
we wrestled the box into the backseat. I told him I'd be in
touch and then I took off.

I went back to my place and changed into my running
clothes. I was just locking up when Henry came around the
corner with Lila Sams. They were walking hip to hip, arms
entwined. He was a good foot taller than she and lean in all
the places she was plump. He looked flushed with happiness, that special aura people take on when they've just
fallen in love. He was wearing pale blue brushed denim
pants and a pale blue shirt that made his blue eyes look
nearly luminous. His hair looked freshly cut and my guess
was he'd actually had someone "style" it this time. Lila's
smile tensed somewhat when she caught sight of me, but
she recovered her composure, laughing girlishly.

"Oh Kinsey, now look what he's gone and done," she said
and held her hand out. She was sporting a big square-cut
diamond that I hoped was some gaudy fake.

"God, it's gorgeous. What's the occasion?" I asked, heart
sinking. Surely, they weren't engaged. She was so wrong for
him, so giddy and false, while he was genuine.

"Just celebrating the fact that we met," Henry said with a
glance at her. "What was it, a month ago? Six weeks?"

"Well, naughty you," she said with a playful stamp of her
little foot. "I have half a mind to make you take this right
back. We met June twelfth. It was Moza's birthday and I'd
just moved in. You catered that tea she gave and you've
spoiled me rotten ever since." She lowered her voice then
to its most confidential pitch. "Isn't he awful?"

I don't know how to talk to people this way, exchanging
pointless banter. I could feel my smile becoming self-con-

scious but I couldn't make it go away. "I think he's great," I
said, sounding somehow lame and inept.

"Well, of course he's great," she said in a flash. "Why
wouldn't he be? He's such an innocent, anyone can take
advantage of him."

Her tone was suddenly quarrelsome, as though I'd insulted him. I could feel the warning signals clanging away
like crazy, but I still couldn't guess what was coming. She
was wagging a finger at me, red painted nails piercing the
air near my face. "You, for one, you bad girl. I told Henry
and I'll say it right to your face, the rent you pay is a scandal
and you know perfectly well you've been robbing him
blind."

"What?"

She narrowed her eyes, pushing her face toward mine.
"Now don't you play dumb with me. Two hundred dollars a
month! My stars. Do you know what studio apartments are
renting for in this neighborhood? Three hundred. That's a
hundred dollars you take away from him every time you
write him a check. Disgraceful. It's just a disgrace!"

"Oh now, Lila," Henry broke in. He seemed nonplussed
that she'd launched into this, but it was clearly something
they'd discussed. "Let's don't get into this now. She's on her
way out."

"You can spare a few minutes, I'm sure," she said with a
glittering look at me.

"Sure," I said faintly and then glanced at him. "Have you
been unhappy with me?" I felt the same sick combination of
heat and cold that Chinese-food syndrome produces. Did
he really feel I'd been cheating him?

Lila cut in again, answering before he could even open
his mouth. "Let's not put Henry on the spot," she said. "He
thinks the world of you, which is why he hasn't had the
heart to speak up. You're the one I'd like to spank. How
could you take an old softie like Henry and twist him
around your finger that way? You should be ashamed."

"I wouldn't take advantage of Henry."

"But you already have. How long have you been living
here at that same ridiculous rent? A year? Fifteen months?
Don't tell me it never occurred to you that you were getting

this place dirt-cheap! Because if you say that, I'll have to call you a liar right to your face and embarrass us both."

I could feel my mouth open, but I couldn't say a word.

"We can talk about this later," Henry murmured, taking her by the arm. He was steering her around me, but her eyes were still fixed on mine and her neck and cheeks were now blotchy with rage. I turned and stared as he moved her toward his back stairs. She was already starting to protest in the same irrational tone I'd heard the other night. Was the woman nuts?

When the door closed behind them, my heart began to thump and I realized I was damp with sweat. I tied my door key to my shoelace and then I took off, breaking into a trot long before I'd had a chance to warm up. I ran, putting distance between us.

I did three miles and then walked back to my place, letting myself in. Henry's back shades were down and his windows were shut. The rear of his house looked blank and uninviting, like a beachfront park after closing time.

I showered and threw some clothes on, and then took off, fleeing the premises. I still felt stung, but I was getting in touch with some anger too. What business was it of hers anyway? And why hadn't Henry leapt to my defense?

When I pushed into Rosie's, it was late afternoon and there wasn't a soul in sight. The restaurant was gloomy and smelled of last night's cigarette smoke. The TV set on the bar was turned off and the chairs were still upside down on the tabletops, like a troupe of acrobats doing tricks. I crossed to the rear and opened the swinging door to the kitchen. Rosie glanced up at me, startled. She was sitting on a tall wooden stool with a cleaver in her hand, chopping leeks. She hated anyone intruding on her kitchen, probably because she violated health codes.

"What happened?" she said when she saw my face.

"I had an encounter with Henry's lady friend," I replied.

"Ah," she said. She whacked a leek with the cleaver, sending hunks flying. "She don't come in here. She knows better."

"Rosie, the woman is crazy as a loon. You should have heard her the other night after you tangled with her. She ranted and raved for hours. Now she's accusing me of cheating Henry on the rent."

"Take a seat. I got some vodka somewhere." She crossed to the cabinet above the sink and stood on tippytoe, tilting a vodka bottle into reach. She broke the seal and poured me a hit in a coffee cup. She shrugged then poured herself one too. We drank and I could feel the blood rush back to my face.

I said, "Woo!" involuntarily. My esophagus felt scorched and I could sense the contours of my stomach outlined in alcohol. I always pictured my stomach much lower down than that. Weird. Rosie placed the chopped leeks in a bowl and rinsed the cleaver at the sink before she turned back to me.

"You got twenty cents? Give me two dimes," she said, holding a hand out. I fished around in my handbag, coming up with some loose change. Rosie took it and crossed to the pay phone on the wall. Everybody has to use that pay phone, even her.

"Who are you calling? You're not calling Henry," I said, with alarm.

"Ssss!" She held a hand up, shushing me, her eyes focusing in the way people do when someone picks up the phone on the other end. Her voice got musical and syrupy.

"Hello, dear. This is Rosie. What are you doing right this minute. Uh-hun, well I think you better get over here. We have a little matter to discuss."

She clunked the receiver down without waiting for a response and then she fixed me with a satisfied look. "Mrs. Lowenstein is coming over for a chat."

Moza Lowenstein sat on the chrome-and-plastic chair that I'd brought in from the bar. She is a large woman with hair the color of a cast-iron skillet, worn in braids wrapped around her head. There are strands of silver threaded through like tinsel, and her face, with its pale powder, has the soft look of a marshmallow. Generally, she likes to hold on to something when she talks to Rosie: a bouquet of pencils, a wooden spoon, any talisman to ward off attack. Today, it was the dish towel she'd brought with her. Apparently, Rosie had interrupted her in the middle of some chore and she'd hurried right over, as bid. She's afraid of Rosie, as anyone with good sense would be. Rosie launched right in, skipping all the niceties.

"Who is this Lila Sams?" Rosie said. She took up her cleaver and began to pound on some veal, making Moza flinch.

Her voice, when she found it, was trembly and soft. "I don't really know. She came to my door, she said in response to an ad in the paper, but it was all a mistake. I didn't have a room for rent and I told her as much. Well, the poor thing burst into tears and what was I to do? I had to ask her in for a cup of tea."

Rosie paused to stare in disbelief. "And then you rented her a room?"

Moza folded the towel, forming a lobster shape like a napkin in a fancy restaurant. "Well, no. I told her she could stay with me until she found a place, but she insisted that she pay her own way. She didn't want to be indebted, she said."

"That's called room rent. That's what that is," Rosie snapped.

"Well, yes. If you want to *put* it that way."

"Where does this woman come from?"

Moza flapped the towel out and dabbed it against her upper lip, blotting sweat. She laid it out on her lap and pressed it with her hand, keeping her fingers together in a wedge like an iron. I saw Rosie's flinty gaze follow every movement and I thought she might give Moza's hand a smack with the cleaver. Moza must have thought so too because she quit fiddling with the towel and looked up at Rosie with guilt. "What?"

Rosie enunciated carefully, as though speaking to an alien. "Where does Lila Sams come from?"

"A little town in Idaho."

"*What* little town?"

"Well, I don't know," Moza said defensively.

"You have a woman living in your house and you don't know what town she comes from?"

"What difference does it make?"

"And you don't know what difference it makes?" Rosie stared at her with exaggerated astonishment. Moza broke eye contact and folded the towel into a bishop's miter.

"You do me a favor and you find out," Rosie said. "Can you manage that?"

"I'll try," Moza said. "But she doesn't like people prying. She told me that and she was quite definite."

"I'm very definite too. I'm definite about I don't like this lady and I want to know what she's up to. You find out where she comes from and Kinsey can take care of the rest. And I don't have to tell you, Moza, I don't want Lila Sams to know. You understand?"

Moza looked cornered. I could see her debate, trying to decide which was worse: infuriating Rosie or getting caught spying on Lila Sams. It was going to be a close contest, but I knew who I was betting on.

16

I went back to my office late in the day and typed up my notes. There wasn't much, but I don't like to get behind. With Bobby dead, I intended to write regular reports and submit itemized bills at intervals, even if it was just to myself. I had tucked his file back in the drawer and I was tidying up my desk when there was a tap at the door and Derek Wenner peered in.

He said, "Oh. Hello. I was hoping I'd catch you here."

"Hi, Derek. Come on in," I said.

He stood for a moment, undecided, his gaze tracing the perimeters of my small office space. "Somehow I didn't picture this," he said. "Nice. I mean, it's small, but efficient. Uh, how'd you do with Bobby's box? Any luck?"

"I haven't had a chance to look closely. I've been doing other things. Have a seat."

He pulled a chair up and sat down, still looking around. He was wearing a golf shirt, white pants, and two-tone shoes. "So this is it, huh?"

This was his version of small talk, I assumed. I sat down and let him ramble briefly. He seemed anxious and I couldn't imagine what had brought him in. We made mouth noises at each other, demonstrating goodwill. I'd just seen him a few hours earlier and we didn't have that much to talk about.

"How's Glen doing?" I asked.

"Good," he nodded. "She's doing pretty well. God, I don't know how she's gotten through, but you know she's made of substantial stuff." He tended to speak in doubtful tones, as if he weren't absolutely certain he was telling the truth.

He cleared his throat and the timbre of his voice changed.

"Say, I'll tell you why I stopped in," he said. "Bobby's attorney gave me a call a little while ago just to talk about the terms of Bobby's will. Do you know Varden Talbot?"

"We've never met. He sent me copies of the reports on Bobby's accident, but that's the extent of it."

"Smart fellow," Derek said. He was stalling. I thought I better goose him along or this could take all day.

"What'd he have to say?"

Derek's expression was a wonderful combination of uneasiness and disbelief. "Well, that's the amazing thing," he said. "From what he indicated, I guess my daughter inher-. its the bulk of Bobby's money."

It took me a moment to compute the fact that the daughter he referred to was Kitty Wenner, cokehead, currently residing in the psycho ward at St. Terry's. "Kitty?" I said.

He shifted in his seat. "I was surprised too, of course. From what Varden tells me, Bobby made out a will when he came into his inheritance three years ago. At that point, he left everything to Kitty. Then sometime after the accident, he added a codicil, so that a little money would go to Rick's parents as well."

I was about to say "Rick's parents?" as if I were suffering from echolalia, but I clamped my mouth shut and let him continue.

"Glen won't be back until late, so she's not aware of it. I'd imagine she'll want to talk to Varden in the morning. He said he'd make a copy of the will and send it over to the house. He's going to go ahead and file it for probate."

"And this is the first anybody's heard of it?"

"As far as I know." He went on talking while I tried to figure out what it meant. Money, as a motive, always seems so direct. Find out who benefits financially and start from there. Kitty Wenner. Phil and Reva Bergen.

"Excuse me," I said, cutting in. "Just how much money are we talking about?"

Derek paused to run a hand up along his jaw, as though deciding if he was due for a shave. "Well, a hundred grand to Rick's parents and gee, I don't know. Kitty probably stands to gain a couple mill. Now, you're going to have inheritance tax . . ."

All of the little zeros began to dance in my head like sugar plums. "Hundred grand" and "couple mill," as in a hundred thousand dollars and two million of them. I just sat and blinked at him. Why had he come in here to tell me this stuff?

"What's the catch?" I asked.

"What?"

"I'm just wondering why you're telling me about it. Is there some problem?"

"I guess I'm worried about Glen's reaction. You know how she feels about Kitty."

I shrugged. "It was Bobby's money to do with as he saw fit. How could she object?"

"You don't think she'd contest it?"

"Derek, I can't speculate about what Glen might do. Talk to her."

"Well, I guess I will when she gets back."

"I'm assuming the money was put in some kind of trust fund since Kitty's just seventeen. Who was named executor? You?"

"No, no. The bank. I don't think Bobby had a very high opinion of me. To tell you the truth, I'm a little worried about how this might look. Bobby claims someone's trying to kill him and then it turns out Kitty inherits all this money when he dies."

"I'm sure the police will have a chat with her."

"But you don't think she had anything to do with Bobby's accident, do you?"

Ah, the subtext of his visit.

I said, "Frankly, I'd find it hard to believe, but Homicide might see it differently. They might also want to take a look at you while they're at it."

"Me?!" He managed to pack a lot of punctuation into one syllable.

"What if something happens to Kitty? Who gets the money then? She's not exactly in the best of health."

He looked at me uncomfortably, probably wishing he'd never come in. He must have harbored the vague notion that I could reassure him. Instead, I'd only broadened the basis for his anxieties. He wound up the conversation and got up moments later, telling me he'd be in touch. When he turned to go, I could see that the golf shirt was sticking to his back and I could smell the tension in his sweat.

"Oh, Derek," I called after him. "Does the name Blackman mean anything to you?"

"Not that I know. Why?"

"Just curious. I appreciate your coming in," I said. "If you find out anything else, please let me know."

"I will."

Once he was gone, I put in a quick call to a friend of mine at the telephone company and asked about S. Blackman. He said he'd check into it and call me back. I went down to the parking lot and hauled out the cardboard box I'd picked up from Bobby's garage. I went back up to the office and checked the contents, taking the items out one by one. It was all just as I remembered it: a couple of radiology manuals, some medical texts, paper clips, ballpoint pens, scratch pads. Nothing of significance that I could see. I hauled the box back out and shoved it into the backseat again, thinking I'd drop it back at Bobby's house next time I was there.

What to try next? I couldn't think of a thing.

I went home.

As I pulled into a parking place out front, I found myself scanning the walk for signs of Lila Sams. For a woman I'd only seen three or four times in my life, she was looming large, spoiling any sense of serenity I'd come to attach to the notion of "home." I locked my car and went around to the backyard, glancing at the rear of Henry's house to see if he was there. The back door was open and I caught the spicy scent of yeast and cinnamon through the screen. I peered in and spotted Henry sitting at the table with a coffee mug and the afternoon paper in front of him.

"Henry?"

He looked up. "Well, Kinsey. There you are." He came over and unlatched the screen, holding the door open for me. "Come in, come in. Would you like some coffee? I've got a pan of sweet rolls coming out in a minute."

I entered hesitantly, still half expecting Lila Sams to jump out like a tarantula. "I didn't want to interrupt anything," I said. "Is Lila here?"

"No, no. She had some business to take care of, but she
should be back by six. I'm taking her out to dinner tonight.
We have reservations at the Crystal Palace."

"Oh, wow, impressive," I said. Henry pulled a chair out
for me and then poured me some coffee while I looked
around. Lila had apparently taken her fine hand to the
place. The curtains were new: avocado green cotton with a
print of salt and pepper shakers, vegetable clusters, and
wooden spoons, tied back with green bows. There were
matching placemats and napkins, with accessories in a con-
trasting pumpkin shade. There was a new trivet on the
counter with a homely saying in wrought-iron curlicue. I
thought it said, "God Bless Our Biscuits," but that couldn't
have been right.

"You've fixed the place up," I said.

His face brightened and he looked around. "You like it? It
was Lila's idea. I tell you, the woman has made such a difference in my life."

"Well, that's good. I'm glad to hear that," I said.

"She's made me feel . . . I don't know, *vital* is the word I
guess. Ready to start all over again."

I wondered if he was going to pass right over her accusations about my cheating him. He got up and opened the
oven door, checking the sweet rolls, which he apparently
decided were not quite done. He shoved them back and
shut the oven, leaving the pumpkin-colored mitt on his
right hand like a boxing glove.

I shifted uncomfortably on the stool where I was
perched. "I thought maybe you and I should have a talk
about Lila's accusations about the rent."

"Oh, don't worry about it," he said. "She was just in one
of her moods."

"But Henry, I don't want you to feel like I'm cheating
you. Don't you think we should get that ironed out?"

"No. Piffle. I don't feel you're cheating me."

"But she does."

"No no, not at all. You misunderstood."

"Misunderstood?" I said incredulously.

"Look, this is all my fault and I'm sorry I didn't get it
straightened out at the time. Lila flew off the handle and
she realizes that. In fact, I'm sure she means to apologize.

She and I had a long talk about it afterwards and I know she felt bad. It had nothing to do with you personally. She's a little high-strung, but she's just the dearest woman you'll ever meet. Once you get to know her, you'll see what a wonderful person she is."

"I hope so," I said. "What worried me is that she and Rosie had that tiff and then she took off after me. I wasn't sure what was going on."

Henry laughed. "Well, I wouldn't take that too seriously. You know Rosie. She gets into tiffs with everyone. Lila's fine. She's got a heart of gold and she's just as loyal as a little pup."

"I just don't want to see you going off the deep end," I said. It was one of those sayings that doesn't really mean anything but somehow it seemed to apply.

"No need to worry about that," he said mildly. "I've been around a long time, you know, and I haven't gone off the deep end yet."

He checked the sweet rolls again, and this time, he took them out and put the pan on the trivet to cool. He glanced over at me. "I haven't had a chance to tell you. She and I are going into a real-estate venture together."

"Oh really?"

"Which is how the subject of your rent came up in the first place. Rental income affects the overall value of the property and that was her main concern. She said she didn't mean to interfere in our relationship at all. She's hard-headed when it comes to business but she didn't want to look like she was butting in."

"What kind of real-estate venture?"

"Well, she owns some property she's going to put up as collateral, and with this place thrown in, we'll just about have the down payment on the property we want."

"Something here in town?"

"I better not say. She swore me to secrecy. I mean, it's not firm yet anyway, but I'll tell you about it when we get the deal put together. It should be happening in the next couple of days. I had to swear I'd keep mum."

"I don't understand," I said. "You're selling your house?"

"I can't even begin to understand the details. Too complicated for me," he said.

"I wasn't aware that she was involved in real estate."

"Oh, she's been doing this sort of thing for years. She was married to some big wheeler-dealer in New Mexico, and when he died, he left her very well off. She's got a bundle. Does real-estate investments almost as a hobby, she says."

"And she's from New Mexico? I thought someone told me it was Idaho."

"Oh, she's lived everywhere. She's a gypsy at heart. She's even talking me into it. You know, just take off into the sunset. Big RV and a map of the States. Go where the road takes us. I feel like she's added twenty years to my life."

I wanted to question him more closely, but I heard Lila's "yoo hoo" at the screen door and her face appeared, wreathed in saucy curls. She put a hand to her cheek when she saw me, turning all sheepish and coy.

"Oh, Kinsey. I bet I know just what you're doing here," she said. She came into the kitchen and paused for a moment, hands clasped in front of her as though she might drop to her knees in prayer. "Now don't say a word until I get this out," she went on. She paused to peer over at Henry. "Oh Henry, you did tell her how sorry I was to fuss at her that way." She was using a special "little" voice.

Henry put an arm around her, giving her a squeeze. "I've already explained and I'm sure she understands," he said. "I don't want you to worry any more about that."

"But I do worry, Puddy, and I won't feel right about it 'til I tell her myself."

Puddy?

She came over to the stool where I was perched and took my right hand, pressing it between her own.

"I am so sorry. I tell you I am so apologetic for what I said to you and I beg your forgiveness." Her tone was contrite and I thought Puddy was going to get all choked up. She was making deep eye contact with me and a couple of her rings were digging into my fingers rather painfully. She had apparently turned the ring around so that the stones were palm inward, producing maximum effect as she tightened her grip.

I said, "Oh, that's all right. Don't think another thing about it. I'm sure I won't."

Just to show her what a brick I was, I got up and put my left arm around her just the way Henry had. I gave her the same little squeeze, easing my foot across the toe of her right shoe and leaning forward slightly. She pulled back from the waist, but I managed to keep my foot where it was so that we were standing hip to hip. We locked eyes for a moment. She gave me a gooey smile and then eased her grip. I shifted my weight from her foot, but not before two coins of color had appeared high up on her cheeks like a cockatiel.

Puddy seemed pleased that we'd come to this new understanding and I was too. I made my excuses and departed soon after that. Lila had stopped looking at me altogether by then and I noticed that she had sat down abruptly, easing off one shoe.

17

I let myself into my apartment and poured a glass of wine and then I made myself a sandwich with creamed cheese and thinly sliced cucumbers and onions on dark bread. I cut it in half and used a piece of paper toweling as a combination napkin and dinner plate, toting sandwich and wineglass into the bathroom. I opened my bathroom window a crack and ate standing in the tub, peering out at intervals to see if Henry and Lila were departing for their dinner date. At 6:45, they came around the corner of the building and Henry unlocked his car, opening the door for her on the passenger side. I eased into an upright position, ducking back out of sight until I heard him start the car and pull away.

I'd finished dinner by then and I had nothing to do in the way of dishes except to wad up my paper towel and throw it in the trash, feeling inordinately pleased with myself. I traded my sandals for tennis shoes, grabbed up my master keys, my key picks, penknife, and a flashlight, then headed down the block to Moza Lowenstein's house, where I rang the bell. She peered out of the side window at me in perplexity, the opened the door.

"I couldn't think who it was at this hour," she said. "I thought Lila must be coming back for something she forgot."

I don't ordinarily visit Moza and I could tell she was wondering what I was doing on her doorstep. She moved back and admitted me, smiling timidly. The television was tuned to a rerun of "M.A.S.H.," helicopters whipping up a cloud of dust.

"I thought I'd do a little background check on Lila Sams," I said, while "Suicide Is Painless" played merrily.

"Oh, but she's just gone out," Moza said in haste. It was already occurring to her that I was up to no good and I guess she thought she could head me off.

"Is this her room back here?" I asked, moving into the corridor. I knew Moza's bedroom was the one at the end of the hall to the left. I figured Lila's must be the former "spare" room.

Moza lumbered after me. She's a big woman, suffering from some condition that makes her feet swell. Her expression was a cross between pain and bewilderment.

I tried the knob. Lila's door was locked.

"You can't go in there."

"Really?"

She was looking fearful by now and she didn't seem reassured by the sight of the master key I was easing into the keyhole. This was a simple house lock requiring only a skeleton key, several styles of which I had on a ring.

"You don't understand," she said again. "That's locked."

"No, it's not. See?" I opened the door and Moza put a hand on her heart.

"She'll come back," she said with a quaking voice.

"Moza, I'm not going to take anything," I said. "I will work with great care and she'll never know I was here. Why don't you sit out there in the living room and keep an eye open, just in case? O.K.?"

"She'll be so angry if she finds out I let you in," she said to me. Her eyes were as mournful now as a basset hound's.

"But she won't find out, so there's nothing to worry about. By the way, did you ever find out what little town in Idaho she's from?"

"Dickey is what she told me."

"Oh good. I appreciate that. She never mentioned living in New Mexico, did she?"

Moza shook her head and began to pat her chest as if she were burping herself. "Please hurry," she said. "I don't know what I'd do if she came back."

I wasn't sure myself.

I eased into the room and closed the door, flipping on the light. On the other side of the door, I heard Moza shuffling back toward the front of the house, murmuring to herself.

The room was furnished with an ancient wood-veneer bedroom suite that I doubt could be called "antique." The pieces looked like the ones I've seen out on thrift-shop sidewalks in downtown Los Angeles: creaky, misshapen, smelling oddly of wet ash. There was a chiffonier, matching bedtables, a dressing table with a round mirror set between banks of drawers. The bed frame was iron, painted a flaking white, and the spread was chenille in a dusty rose with fringe on the sides. The wallpaper was a tumble of floral bouquets, mauve and pale rose on a gray background. There were several sepia photographs of a man whom I imagined was Mr. Lowenstein; someone, at any rate, who favored hair slicked down with water and spectacles with round gold rims. He appeared to be in his twenties, smooth and pretty with a solemn mouth pulled over slightly protruding teeth. The studio had tinted his cheeks a pinkish tone, slightly at odds with the rest of the photo, but the effect was nice. I'd heard that Moza was widowed in 1945. I would have loved seeing a picture of her in those days. Almost reluctantly, I turned back to the task at hand.

Three narrow windows were locked on the inside, shades drawn. I moved over and peered out of one, catching a glimpse of backyard through screens rusted into the old wooden frames. I checked my watch. It was only seven. They'd be gone, at the very least, an hour, and I didn't think I needed to provide myself an emergency exit. On the other hand, there isn't any point in being dumb about these things. I went back to the door and opened it, leaving it ajar. Moza had turned off the TV set and I pictured her peeking through the front curtain, heart in her throat, which is about where mine was.

It was still light outside, but the room was gloomy even with the overhead light on. I started with the chiffonier. I did a preliminary survey, using my flashlight to check for any crude attempts at security. Sure enough, Lila had booby-trapped a couple of drawers by affixing a strand of hair slyly across the crack. I removed these beauties and placed them carefully on the hand-crocheted runner on top.

The first drawer contained a jumble of jewelry, several belts coiled together, embroidered handkerchiefs, a watch case, hairpins, a few stray buttons, and two pairs of white cotton gloves. I stared for a long time, without touching anything, wondering why any of it warranted a protective strand of hair. Actually, anybody snooping in Lila's things would probably start here and work down, so maybe it was just a ready reference on her part, a checkpoint each time she returned to her room. I tried the next drawer, which was filled with neat piles of nylon underpants in a quite large old-lady style. I ran an experimental finger down between the stacks, being careful not to disturb the order. I couldn't feel anything significant; no handgun, no unidentifiable boxes or bumps.

On an impulse, I opened the first drawer again and peered up at the underside. Nothing taped to the bottom. I pulled the whole drawer out and checked along the back. Hello! Score one for my team. There was an envelope encased in plastic, sealed flat against the back panel of the drawer and secured by masking tape on all four sides. I took out my penknife and slid the small blade under one corner of the tape, peeling it up so I could remove the envelope from the plastic housing. In it was an Idaho driver's license in the name of Delilah Sampson. The woman had a real biblical sense of humor here. I made a note of the address, date of birth, height, weight, hair and eye color, much of which seemed to apply to the woman I knew as Lila Sams. God, I had really hit pay dirt. I slipped the license back into the envelope, returned the envelope to its hiding place, and pressed the masking tape securely against the wood. I squinted critically at my handiwork. Looked untouched to me, unless she'd powdered everything with some kind of tricky dust that would dye my hands bright red the instant I washed them again. Wouldn't that be a bitch!

The back of the second drawer was also being used as a little safe-deposit box, containing a stack of credit cards and yet another driver's license. The name on this one was Delia Sims, with an address in Las Cruces, New Mexico, and a date of birth that matched the first. Again, I made a note of the details and carefully returned the document to its hiding place. I replaced the drawer, glancing quickly at my watch. Seven thirty-two. I was still O.K., but I had a lot of ground to cover yet. I continued my search, working with delicacy, leaving the contents of each drawer undisturbed.

When I finished with the chiffonier, I retrieved the two hairs and moored them across the drawer cracks again.

The dressing table revealed nothing and the bed-tables were unremarkable. I went through the closet, checking coat pockets, suitcases, handbags, and shoe boxes, one of which still contained the receipt for the red wedgies she'd been wearing the first time we met. There was a credit-card slip stapled to the receipt and I tucked both in my pocket for later inspection. There was nothing under the bed, nothing stashed behind the chiffonier. I was checking back to see if I'd missed anything when I heard a peculiar warbling from the living room.

"Kinsey, they're back!" Moza wailed, her voice hoarse with dread. From out on the street, I caught the muffled thump of a car door slamming.

"Thanks," I said. Adrenaline flooded through me like water through a storm drain and I could have sworn my heart was boinging up against my tank top as in a cartoon. I did a hasty visual canvas. Everything looked O.K. I reached the door to the hallway, eased out, and pulled it shut behind me, snatching the ring of skeleton keys out of my jeans pocket. The flashlight. Shit! I'd left it on the dressing table.

Murmurs at the front door. Lila and Henry. Moza was making nice, asking about dinner. I yanked the door open and did a running tiptoe to the dressing table, snagged the flashlight, and bounded, like a silent gazelle, back to the door again. I tucked the flashlight up under my arm and prayed that I was inserting the proper key into the lock. A twist to the left and I heard the latch slide into the hole. I turned the key back quietly, extracting it with shaking hands, careful not to let the keys jingle together noisily. I glanced back over my shoulder, at the same time looking for an escape route.

The hallway extended about three feet to the right, where the archway to the living room cut through. At the extreme end of the hall was Moza's bedroom. To my left, there was an alcove for the telephone, a closet, the bathroom, and the kitchen, with an archway to the dining room visible beyond that. The dining room, in turn, opened into the living room again. If they were heading back this way, I had to guess they'd come straight through the archway to my right. I took two giant steps to the left and slipped into the bathroom. The minute I did it, I knew I'd made a bad choice. I should have tried the kitchen, with its outside exit. This was a dead end.

There was a separate shower to my immediate left with an opaque glass door, bathtub adjacent. To my right was a pedestal sink, and next to it, the toilet. The only window in the room was small and probably hadn't been opened in years. By now, I could hear voices growing louder as Lila moved into the hall. I stepped into the enclosed shower and pulled the door shut. I didn't dare latch it. I was certain the distinct sound of the metallic click would carry, alerting her to my presence. I set the flashlight down and held on to the door from the inside, bracing my fingers against the tile. I sank down to a crouch, thinking that if someone came in, I'd be less conspicuous if I was hunkered down. The voices in the hall bumbled on and I heard Lila unlock her bedroom door.

The shower was still damp from recent use, scented with Zest soap. A washrag hanging over the cold-water knob dripped intermittently on my shoulder. I listened intently, but I couldn't hear much. In situations like this, you have to get into the Zen of hiding. Otherwise your knees ache, your leg muscles go into spasms, and pretty soon you lose all sense of caution and just want to leap out, shrieking, regardless of the consequence. I leaned my face on my right arm, looking inward. I could still taste the onion from my sandwich. I was longing to clear my throat. Also I needed to pee. I hoped I wouldn't get caught, because I was going to feel like such an ass if Lila or Henry whipped open the shower door and found me crouching there. I didn't even bother to think up an explanation. There wasn't one.

I lifted my head. Voices in the hall. Lila had come out of her room, locking it after her. Maybe she'd gone in to make sure the hairs were in place. I wondered if I should have confiscated the duplicate licenses while I had the chance. No, better that I left them where they were.

Suddenly the bathroom door flew back and Lila's voice echoed against the bathroom walls like a bullhorn. My heart leapt into action so fast it was like being flung in an icy swimming pool. She was right on the other side of the shower door, her plump form vaguely defined through the milky glass. I closed my eyes like a kid, willing myself invisible.

"I'll be right there, dearie love," she sang from two feet away.

She crossed to the john and I heard the rustle of her polyester dress and the snap of her girdle as she struggled with it.

Please God, I thought, don't let her decide to take an impromptu shower or a dump. My tension level was so high that I was bound to sneeze or cough or groan or cackle maniacally. I willed myself into a hypnotic state, feeling my armpits dampen with sweat.

The toilet flushed. Lila took forever putting herself back together again. Rustle, pop, snap. I heard her jiggle the handle when the toilet continued to run. She washed her hands, the faucet squeaking as she turned it off. How long could she drag this out? Finally, she moved toward the bathroom door and opened it, and then she was gone, footsteps receding toward the living room. Yakety-yak, chit chat, soft laughter, good-bye sounds, and the front door closed.

I stayed exactly where I was until I heard Moza in the hall.

"Kinsey? They're gone. Are you still here?"

I let out the breath I'd been holding and stood up, shoving my flashlight into my back pocket. This is not a dignified way to make a living, I thought. Hell, I wasn't even getting paid for this. I peered out of the shower door, making sure I hadn't been set up in some elaborate ruse. The house felt quiet except for Moza, who was opening the broom-closet door, still whispering, "Kinsey?"

"I'm in here," I said, voice booming.

I went out into the hall. Moza was so thrilled we hadn't been caught that she couldn't even get mad at me. She leaned against the wall, fanning herself. I figured I better get out of there before they came back for something else, taking ten more years off my projected life-span.

"You're terrific," I murmured. "I'm indebted for life. I'll buy you dinner at Rosie's."

I moved through the kitchen, peering out the back door before I exited. It was fully dark by then, but I made sure the street was deserted before I stepped out of the shadow of Moza's house. Then I walked the half-block toward home laughing to myself. Actually, it's fun to horse around with danger. It's fun to snoop in people's dresser drawers. I might have turned to burgling houses if law enforcement hadn't beckoned to me first. With Lila, I was finally beginning to take control of a situation I didn't like and the surge of power made me feel nearly giddy with relief. I wasn't sure what she was up to, but I intended to find out.

18

When I was safely back in my apartment again, I took out the credit-card receipt I'd lifted from Lila's shoe box. The date on it was May 25 and the store was located in Las Cruces. The credit-card imprint read "Delia Sims." In the box marked "phone number," someone had obligingly penned in a phone number. I hauled out my telephone book and looked up the area code for Las Cruces. Five-oh-five. I picked up the receiver and dialed the number, wondering as I heard it ring on the far end just what I intended to say.

"Hello?" Man's voice. Middle-aged. No accent.

"Oh hello," I said smoothly. "I wonder if I might speak to Delia Sims."

There was a moment of silence. "Hang on."

A palm was secured across the mouthpiece and I could hear muffled conversation in the background.

The receiver was apparently taken over by someone else, because a new voice inquired, "May I help you?"

This one was female and I couldn't classify the age.

"Delia?" I said.

"Who is this, please?" The tone was guarded, as though the call might be obscene.

"Oh, sorry," I said. "This is Lucy Stansbury. That's not you, is it, Delia? It doesn't sound like your voice."

"This is a friend of Delia's. She not here at the moment. Was there something I might help you with?"

"Well, I hope so," I said, mind racing. "Actually, I'm calling from California. I just met Delia recently and she left some of her things in the backseat of my car. I couldn't figure out any other way to reach her except to try this number, which was on a credit-card receipt for a purchase

136

she made in Las Cruces. Is she still in California or is she home again?"

"Just a minute."

Again, a palm across the mouthpiece and the drone of conversation in the background. The woman came back on the line.

"Why don't you give me your name and number and I'll have her get back to you?"

"Oh sure, that's fine," I said. I gave her my name again, spelling it out laboriously and then I made up a telephone number with the area code for Los Angeles. "You want me to mail this stuff back to her or just hang on to it? I'd feel bad if I thought she didn't realize where she'd left it."

"What exactly did she leave?"

"Well, most of it's just clothes. A summer dress I know she's fond of, but I don't guess that matters much. I do have that ring of hers with the square-cut emerald and the little diamond baguettes," I said, describing the ring I'd seen Lila wearing that first afternoon in Henry's garden. "Do you expect her back soon?"

After the barest hesitation, the woman's chill reply came. "Who is this?"

I hung up. So much for trying to fool the folks in Las Cruces. I couldn't imagine what she was up to, but I sure didn't like the notion of this real-estate venture she'd proposed to Henry. He was so smitten, she could probably talk him into anything. She was moving quickly too, and I thought I better come up with some answers before she took him for all he was worth. I reached for a pile of blank index cards in my top desk drawer, and when the phone rang moments later, I jumped. Shit, could someone have put a trace on the call that fast? Surely not.

I lifted the receiver with caution, listening for the white noise of a long-distance connection. There was none.

"Hello?"

"Miss Millhone?" Male. The voice sounded familiar, though I couldn't for the moment figure out who it was. Music blasting in the background was forcing him to yell, and I found myself yelling too.

"This is she."

"This is Gus," he hollered, "Bobby's friend from the skate-rental place."

"Oh, it's you. Hello. I'm glad you called. I hope you have some information for me. I could sure use the help."

"Well, I've been thinking about Bobby and I guess I owe him that much. I should have spoken up this afternoon."

"Don't worry about it. I appreciate your getting back to me. You want to get together or just talk on the phone?"

"Either way is fine. One thing I wanted to mention—and I don't know if this would be a help or not—but Bobby gave me this address book you might want to take a look at. Did he ever talk to you about that?"

"Of course he did. I've been turning the town upside down looking for that thing," I said. "Where are you?"

He gave me an address on Granizo and I said I'd be right there. I hung up the phone and grabbed my handbag and car keys.

Gus's neighborhood was poorly lighted and the yards were flat patches of dirt, graced with occasional palm trees. The cars parked along the curbs were primer-painted low riders with bald tires and ominous dents. My VW fit right in. About every third property boasted a brand-new chain link fence, erected to corral God knows what kind of beast. As I passed one house, I heard something that sounded ugly and snappish scramble forward to the length of its choke chain, whimpering hoarsely when it couldn't quite get to me. I picked up my pace.

Gus lived in a tiny frame cottage in a U-shaped courtyard ringed with cottages. I passed through an ornamental entranceway with the street number in wrought iron arched across it in a rainbow shape. There were eight units altogether, three on each side of a central walkway and two at the end. All were cream-colored and even in the darkness looked drab with soot. I identified Gus's place because the music thundering out was the same stuff I'd heard on the phone. Up close, it didn't sound as good. His front drape consisted of a bedsheet slung over a curtain rod and the knob on his screen was an empty wooden spool on a nail. I had to wait for a brief silence between cuts to pound on the doorframe. The music started up again with a vengeance, but he'd apparently caught my knock.

"Yo!" he called. He opened the door and held the screen for me. I stepped into the room, assaulted by heat, loud rock, and the strong smell of catbox.

"Can you turn that shit down?" I yelled.

He nodded, moving to the stereo, which he flicked off. "Sorry," he said sheepishly. "Have a seat."

His place was about half the size of mine and jammed with twice the furniture. King-sized bed, a big chest of drawers in pecan-wood plastic laminate, the stereo cabinet, sagging brick-and-board bookcases, two upholstered chairs with shredded sides, a space heater, and one of those units the size of a television console, housing sink, stove, and refrigerator. The bathroom was separated from the main room by a panel of material hanging on a length of twine. The room's two lamps were draped with red terry-cloth towels that muted their two-hundred-and-fifty-watt bulbs to a rosy glow. Both chairs were filled with cats, which he seemed to notice about the same time I did.

He gathered one batch of them up by the armload as if they were old clothes and I sat down in the space he had cleared. As soon as he tossed the cats on the bed, they made their way back to their original places. One of them kneaded my lap as if it were a hunk of bread dough and then curled up when he was satisfied with the job he'd done. Another one crowded in beside me and a third one settled on the arm of the chair. They seemed to eye each other, trying to figure out who had the best deal. They appeared to be full-grown and probably from the same litter, as they all sported thick tortoiseshell coats and heads the size of softballs. There were two adolescent cats curled up in the other chair, a buff and a black, tangled together like mismatched socks. A sixth cat emerged from under the bed and paused, pointing each hind foot in turn. Gus watched this feline activity with a shy smile, his face flushed with pride.

"Aren't they great?" he said. "I just never get tired of these little peckerheads. At night, they pile on the bed with me like a quilt. I got one sleeps on my pillow with his feet in my hair. I can kiss their little faces anytime I want." He snatched one up and cradled it like a baby, an indignity the cat endured with surprising passivity.

"How many do you have?"

"Six right now, but Luci Baines and Lynda Bird are both pregnant. I don't know what I'm gonna do about that."

"Maybe you could get them fixed," I said helpfully.

"Well, after this batch is born, I guess I should. I'm real good at finding homes for the kittens, though, and they're always so sweet."

I wanted to mention how good they smelled too, but I didn't have the heart for sarcasm when he was clearly so crazy about his brood. There he was, looking like a police artist's composite of a sex killer, making a fool of himself over this collection of domesticated furs.

"I guess I should have spoken up sooner about this stuff," he was saying. "I don't know what got into me." He crossed to the bookshelf and sorted through the mess on top, coming up with an address book about the size of a playing card, which he held out to me.

I took it, leafing through. "What's the significance? Did Bobby fill you in?"

"Well no. He told me to keep it and he said it was important, but he didn't explain. I just assumed it must be a list or a code, *some* kind of information he had, but I don't know what."

"When did he give you this?"

"I don't remember exactly. It was sometime before the accident. He stopped over one day and gave it to me and asked me if I'd just hold on to it for him, so I said sure. I'd forgotten all about it until you brought it up."

I checked the index tab for *B*. There wasn't a Blackman listed there, but I did find the name penciled inside the back cover, with a seven-digit number beside it. No area code indicated, so it was probably local, though I didn't think it matched the number for S. Blackman I'd found in the telephone book.

"What did he actually say at the time?" I asked. I knew I was repeating myself, but I kept hoping to solicit some indication of Bobby's intent.

"Nothing really. He wanted me to hang on to it is all. He didn't tell you either, huh?"

I shook my head. "He couldn't remember. He knew it was important, but he had no idea why. Have you ever heard the name Blackman? S. Blackman? Anybody Blackman?"

"Nope." The cat was squirming and he put it down.

"I understand Bobby had fallen in love with someone. I wonder if it might have been this S. Blackman."

"If it was, he didn't tell me. A couple of times he did meet some woman down at the beach. Right out in that parking lot by the skate shack."

"Before the accident or afterwards?"

"Before. He'd sit in his Porsche and wait and she'd pull in and then they'd talk."

"He never introduced you or mentioned who she was?"

"I know what she looked like but not her name. I saw 'em go in the coffee shop once and she was built odd, you know? Kind of like a Munchkin. I couldn't figure that out. Bobby was a good-lookin' guy and he always hung out with these real foxy chicks, but she was a dog."

"Blond wispy hair? Maybe forty-five?"

"I never saw her up close so I don't know about her age, but the hair sounds right. She drives this Mercedes I see around now and then. Dark green with a beige interior. Looks like a 'fifty-five or 'fifty-six, but it's in great shape."

I glanced through the address book again. Sufi's address and telephone number were listed under the D's.

Had he been having an affair with *her*? It seemed so unlikely. Bobby had been twenty-three years old and, as Gus said, a good-looking kid. Carrie St. Cloud had mentioned a blackmailing scheme, but if Sufi was being blackmailed by someone, why would she turn to him for help? Surely it wasn't a matter of her blackmailing *him*. Whatever it was, it gave me a lead and I was grateful for that. I tucked the book in my handbag and looked up. Gus was watching me with amusement.

"God, you should see your face. I could really watch the old wheels turn," he said.

"Things are beginning to happen and I like that," I said. "Listen, this has been a big help. I don't know what it means yet, but believe me, I'll figure it out."

"I hope so. I'm just sorry I didn't speak up when you asked. If there's anything else I can do, just let me know."

"Thanks," I said. I shifted the cat off my lap and got up, shaking hands with him.

I went out to my car, brushing at my jeans, picking cat hair off my lip. It was now ten o'clock at night and I should have headed home, but I was feeling wired. The episode at Moza's and the sudden appearance of Bobby's address book were acting on me like a stimulant. I wanted to talk to Sufi. Maybe I'd stop by her place. If she was up, we could have a little chat. She'd tried once to steer me away from this investigation and I wondered now what that was about.

19

I pulled into the shadows across the street from Sufi's place on Haughland Road in the heart of Santa Teresa. For the most part, the houses I had passed were two-story frame-and-stone on large lots complete with junipers and oaks. Many lawns sported the ubiquitous California crop of alarm-company signs, warning of silent surveillance and armed patrols.

Sufi's yard was darkened by the interlacing tree branches overhead, the property stretching back in a tangle of shrubs and surrounded by a picket fence with wide pales. The house was done in a dark shingle siding, possibly a muted brown or green, though it was hard to tell which at this hour of the night. The side porch was narrow and deeply recessed with no exterior light visible. A dark green Mercedes was parked in the drive to the left.

It was a quiet neighborhood. The sidewalks were deserted and there was no traffic. I got out of my car and crossed to the front of the house. Up close, I could see that the place was massive, the kind being converted now to bed-and-breakfast establishments with odd names: The Gull and Satchel, The Blue Tern, The Quackery. They're all over town these days: renovated Victorian mansions impossibly quaint, where for ninety bucks a night, you can sleep in a bed with a fake brass frame and struggle, the next morning, with a freshly baked croissant that will drop pastry flakes in your lap like dandruff.

From the look of it, Sufi's was still a single-family dwelling, but it had a shabby air. Maybe, like many single women her age, she'd reached that point where the absence of a man translates out to dripping faucets and rain gutters in need of repair. A single woman my age would haul out a crescent wrench or shinny up the down spout, feeling that odd joyousness that comes with self-sufficiency. Sufi had let her property decline to a state of lingering disrepair and it made me wonder what she did with her salary. I thought surgical nurses made good money.

At the rear of the house, there was a glass-enclosed porch, the windows flickering with the blue/gray reflections of a television set. I fumbled my way up several crumbling concrete steps and tapped on the door. After a moment, the porch light came on and Sufi looked through the curtain.

"Hi, it's me," I said. "Can I talk to you?"

She leaned closer to the glass, peering around, apparently checking to see whether I was accompanied by roving bands of thugs.

She opened the door in her robe and slippers, clutching the lapels together at her throat, one arm circling her waist. "Oh my God, you scared me to death," she said. "What are you doing here at this hour? Is something wrong?"

"Not at all. Sorry to alarm you. I was in the neighborhood and I needed to talk to you. Can I come in?"

"I was on my way to bed."

"We can talk out here on the porch, then."

She gave me a grudging look, stepping back reluctantly so I could enter. She was half a head shorter than I and her blond hair was so thin, I could see stretches of scalp underneath. I hadn't pegged her as the type who'd lounge around in a slinky peach satin wrapper and matching mules with dandelion fuzz across the instep. This was hotsy-totsy stuff. I wanted to say, "Hubba-hubba" but I was afraid she'd take offense.

Once inside, I took a quick mental picture and stored it away for future assessment. The room was cluttered, disorganized, and probably unclean judging from the used dishes piled here and there, the dead flowers in a vase, and the wastebasket spilling trash out onto the floor. The water in the bottom of the vase was cloudy with bacteria and probably smelled like the last stages of some disease. There was a crumpled cellophane packet on the arm of the easy chair and I saw that she'd been sneaking Ding Dongs. A *Reader's Digest* condensed book was open facedown on the ottoman. The place smelled like pepperoni pizza, some of which I spied sitting in a box on top of the television set. The heat from the circuitry was keeping it warm, the scent of oregano and mozzarella cheese mingling with the odor of hot cardboard. God, I thought, when did I last eat?

"You live alone?" I asked.

She looked at me as if I were casing the joint. "What of it?"

"I've been assuming you were single. I just realized no one had ever really said as much."

"It's very late to be doing a survey," she said tartly. "What did you want?"

I find it so liberating when other people are rude. It makes me feel mild and lazy and mean. I smiled at her. "I found Bobby's address book."

"Why tell me?"

"I was curious about your relationship with him."

"I didn't have a relationship with him."

"That's not what I hear."

"Well, you heard wrong. Of course I *knew* him. He was Glen's only child and she and I are best friends and have been for years. Aside from that, Bobby and I didn't have that much to say to one another."

"Why'd you need to meet him down at the beach, then?"

"I never 'met' Bobby at the beach," she snapped.

"Somebody saw you with him on more than one occasion."

She hesitated. "Maybe I ran into him once or twice. What's wrong with that? I used to see him at the hospital, too."

"I wondered what you talked about, that's all."

"I'm sure we talked about lots of things," she said. I could see her shifting gears, trying another tack. Some of the huffiness dropped away. She'd apparently decided to roll out the charm. "God, I don't know what's the matter with me. I'm sorry if I sounded rude. As long as you're here, you might as well sit down. I have wine chilled if you want some."

"I'd like that. Thanks."

She left the room, probably grateful for the chance to stall while she figured out how to cover her tracks. For my part, I was delighted with the opportunity to nose around. I crossed in haste to the easy chair, checking the table beside it. The top was littered with things I didn't want to touch. I eased the drawer open. The interior looked like a catchall for household fallout. Batteries, candles, an extension cord, receipts, rubber bands, packets of matches, two buttons, a sewing kit, pencils, junk mail, a dinner fork, a stapler gun—all of it surrounded by accumulated grit. I ran a hand down along the chair cushion and came up with a nickel, which I left there. I heard the chirp of a wine cork in the kitchen and the tinkle of wineglasses as she removed them from a cabinet. The glass rims began to clink together as she moved back toward the TV room. I abandoned my search and perched myself casually on the arm of the couch.

I was trying to think of something nice to say about her house, but I was secretly worried about my tetanus shots being out of date. This was the kind of place if you had to use the john, you'd want to put paper down on the seat. "Quite a house," I remarked.

Sufi made a face. "The cleaning lady comes tomorrow," she said. "Not that she does much. She worked for my parents for years and I don't have the heart to let her go."

"Do they live with you?"

She shook her head. "Dead. Cancer."

"Both of them?"

"That's the way it goes," she said with a shrug.

So much for family sentiment.

She poured a glass of wine and handed it to me. I could tell from the label, it was the same ultra-crummy stuff I drank before I got into the boxed brand with the picture of a phony-looking vineyard on the front. Clearly, neither of us had the budget or the palate for anything decent.

She settled into the easy chair, wineglass in hand. The change in her manner was conspicuous. She must have come up with a good one while she was gone.

She took a sip of wine, staring at me over the rim of her glass. "Have you talked to Derek lately?" she asked.

"He stopped by my office this afternoon."

"He moved out. When Glen got back from San Francisco this evening, she had the maid pack his bags and put them out in the driveway. Then she changed the locks."

"My, my," I said, "I wonder what brought that on."

"You'd be smart to talk to him before you worry about me."

"Why's that?"

"He had a motive for killing Bobby. I didn't, if that's what you're getting at."

"What motive are you referring to?"

"Glen discovered he'd taken out a big life-insurance policy on Bobby eighteen months ago."

"What?" My wineglass tipped and wine slopped out on my hand. I couldn't disguise the fact that I was startled, but I didn't like the smug look that crossed her face in response.

"Oh yes. The insurance company tracked her down to ask for a copy of the death certificate. I guess the agent read about Bobby in the paper and remembered the name. That's how Glen found out."

"I thought you couldn't take out a policy on someone without their signature."

"Technically, that's true, but it can be done."

I busied myself wiping up spilled wine with a tissue. In the midst of the mop-up procedure, I realized, like a cartoon light bulb going on overhead, that she felt an intense dislike for Derek. "What's the story?" I asked.

"Derek got caught with his pants down," she said. "His claim is that he got the policy ages ago after Bobby'd totaled his car a couple of times. He thought Bobby would self-destruct. You know the type. One accident after another until the kid winds up dead. It becomes a socially acceptable form of suicide. Personally, I'm not sure Derek was that far off. Bobby drank like a fish and I'm sure he did drugs. He and Kitty were both a mess. Rich and spoiled and self-indulgent—"

"Be careful what you say here, Sufi. I liked Bobby Callahan. I think he had guts."

"I think we're all aware of that," she said. She was using that superior tone of voice that drove me mad, but I couldn't afford to react at this point. She crossed her legs, swinging one foot. The dandelion fuzz on that slipper undulated as the air passed over it. "You may not like it, but it *is* the truth. And that's not all of it. Word has it that Derek took out a policy on Kitty too."

"For how much?"

"Half a million bucks on each."

"Come on, Sufi. That doesn't make any sense. Derek wouldn't kill his own daughter."

"Kitty isn't dead, though, is she?"

"But why would he kill Bobby? He'd have to be nuts. The first thing the cops are going to do is turn around and look at him."

"Kinsey," she said patiently. "Nobody ever said Derek had brains. He's an idiot. A fool."

"He's not that big a fool," I said. "How could he hope to get away with it?"

"Nobody's got any proof that he did anything. There never was any evidence from the first accident and Jim Fraker seems to think this one came about because Bobby had a seizure first. How can they pin that on Derek?"

"But why would he do it? He's got money."

"*Glen's* got money. Derek doesn't have a dime. He'd go for anything that would get him out from under her. Don't you know that?"

All I could do was stare at her, running the information through my mental computer. She took another sip of wine and smiled at me, loving the effect she'd produced.

Finally, I said, "I just don't believe it."

"You can believe anything you like. All I'm saying is you better check that out before you do anything else."

"You don't like Derek, do you?"

"Of course not. I think he's the biggest ass who ever lived. I don't know what Glen saw in him in the first place. He's poor. He's dumb. He's pompous. And those are his *good* qualities," she said with energy. "Aside from all that, he's ruthless."

"He doesn't seem ruthless to me," I said.

"You haven't known him as long as I have. He's a man who'd do anything for money and I suspect he's got lots he's not anxious to discuss. Doesn't he strike you as a man with a past?"

"Like what?"

"I'm not sure. But I'd be willing to bet you his buffoonery is just a cover for something else."

"Are you saying Glen's been hoodwinked? She seems smarter than that."

"She's smart about everything but men. This is her third time around, you know, and Bobby's father was a mess. Husband number two I don't know about. She was living in Europe when she married him and it didn't last long."

"Let's get back to you for a minute. The day of Bobby's funeral, I got the impression you were trying to steer me away from the investigation. Now you're giving me leads. Why the switch?"

She had to stop and pay attention to the tie on her robe, though she was talking to me the whole time. "I guess I thought you'd be prolonging Glen's pain and heartache," she said, looking up at me then. "It's clear now that nothing I say is going to dissuade you in any event, so I might as well tell you what I know."

"Why'd you meet Bobby down at the beach? What was going on?"

"Oh, poo. Nothing," she said. "I ran into him a couple of times and he wanted to bitch about Derek. Bobby couldn't stand him either and he knew I made a good audience. That's all it amounted to."

"Why didn't you say that in the first place?"

"I'm not accountable to you. You show up at my door uninvited and quiz me about all this bullshit. It's none of your business so why should I answer to you? I don't think you know how you come off sometimes."

I felt myself flush at the well-placed insult. I drank the last of my wine. I was having trouble believing her story about meeting Bobby, but it was clear I wasn't going to get much more out of her. I decided to drop it for the moment, but it didn't sit well with me. If she'd only been listening to his complaints, why not just say so to begin with?

A glance at my watch showed that it was just after eleven and I decided to try to catch Glen at home. I excused myself abruptly and got out. I'm sure the haste of my departure wasn't lost on her.

There are times when things begin to break by sheer dint of dumb luck. I don't pretend to take credit for what happened next. By the time I got to my little VW, I realized how chilly it was. I hopped in and shut the door, locking it as is my habit, and then I turned and started rooting around in my junky backseat for a sweatshirt I'd tossed back there.

I'd just laid my hands on it and I was in the process of hauling it out from under a pile of books when I heard a car start
up. I glanced to my right. Sufi's Mercedes was being backed
out of the driveway. I did a quick surface dive, disappearing
from view. I wasn't sure if she knew my car or not, but she
must have assumed I was gone because she pulled straight
off. As soon as she did, I rolled into the driver's seat, fumbling for my keys. I started the car and did a quick U-turn,
catching a glimpse of her taillights as she hung a right,
heading toward State Street.

She couldn't have had time enough to change her
clothes. At best, she might have thrown a coat over her satin
lounging outfit. Who did she know well enough to visit unannounced in a Jean Harlow getup at this hour of the night?
I couldn't wait to see.

20

In Santa Teresa, the rich are divided into two cliques: half live in Montebello, half in Horton Ravine. Montebello is the old money, Horton Ravine, the new. Both communities have acres of old trees, bridle paths, and country clubs requiring proper sponsorship and entrance fees of twenty-five grand. Both communities discourage fundamentalist churches, tacky yard ornaments, and door-to-door sales. Sufi was headed for Horton Ravine.

As she passed through the main gates on Los Piratas, she slowed to thirty miles an hour, reluctant perhaps to get picked up for speeding while dressed like a call girl on her way to a john. I slowed my car at a pace with hers, hanging back as far as I could. I was worried about having to pursue her along miles of winding road, but she surprised me by turning into one of the first driveways on the right. The house was set back about a hundred yards, a one-story California "bungalow": maybe five bedrooms, four thousand square feet, not remarkable to look at, but expensive nevertheless. The property was probably five acres all told, surrounded by an ornamental split-rail fence, with rambling roses laid along its length. Exterior lights had come on when Sufi's Mercedes reached the house. She got out of the car in a blur of peach satin and mink, moving toward the front door, which opened and swallowed her up.

I had passed the house by then. I drove on as far as the first road on the right, where I did a turnaround, dousing my headlights as I drifted back. I parked my car on the berm on the left-hand side, hugging some shrubs. The area was shrouded in darkness, no streetlights at all. Across from me, the tag end of the golf course was visible and the narrow artificial lake that served as a water hazard. Moonlight glimmered on the surface of the lake, making it as glossy as a remnant of gray silk.

I removed the flashlight from the glove compartment and got out of my car, picking my way carefully through the tall grass growing by the road. It was thick and wet, soaking my tennis shoes and the legs of my jeans.

I reached the driveway. There wasn't any name on the mailbox, but I noted the numbers. I could always stop by my office and check my crisscross directory if I needed to. I had gone about halfway up the drive when I heard a dog barking at the house. I had no idea what kind it was, but it sounded big—one of those dogs that knows how to bark from its balls—deep, businesslike barks, suggestive of sharp teeth and a bad attitude. Furthermore, that sucker had picked up my scent and was anxious to make contact. There was no way I could creep any closer without alerting the occupants of the house. They were probably already wondering what was making Old Dog Tray wet himself with excitement. For all I knew, they'd release him from his three-eighths-inch chain and send him flying down the driveway after me, toenails scratching along the blacktop. I've been chased by dogs before and it's not that much fun.

I reversed my course and got back in the car. Common sense is no disgrace in the private-eye trade. I watched the house for an hour, but there was no sign of activity. I was getting tired and this felt like a waste of time. Finally, I started the engine and eased the car into gear, not flipping on my headlights until I was out through the gate again.

By the time I got home, I was exhausted. I made a few quick notes and packed it in for the night. It was nearly one o'clock when I finally turned out the light. I got up at six and did a three-mile run just to get my head on straight. Then I sped through my morning ablutions, grabbed an apple, and arrived at the office by seven. It was Tuesday and I was thankful I wasn't scheduled for physical therapy that day. Now that I thought about it, my arm was feeling pretty good, or maybe the fact that I was involved in an investigation distracted me from whatever pain or immobility remained.

There were no messages on my answering machine and no mail that needed dealing with from the day before. I hauled out my crisscross and checked the house numbers on Los Piratas. Well, well. I should have guessed. Fraker, James and Nola. I wondered which of them Sufi had gone to see and why the rush. It was possible, of course, that she'd consulted with both, but I couldn't quite picture that. Could Nola be the woman Bobby'd fallen in love with? I couldn't see how Dr. Fraker tied into this, but something was sure going on.

I took out Bobby's address book and tried the number for Blackman. I got a recorded message from that woman who sounds like the fairy godmother in a Walt Disney cartoon. "We're sorry, but the number you've dialed cannot be connected in the eight-oh-five area code. Please check the number and dial again. Thank you." I tried the codes for surrounding areas. No luck. I spent a long time looking through the other entries in the book. If all else failed, I'd have to sit here and contact each person in turn, but it seemed like a tiresome prospect and not necessarily productive. In the meantime, what?

It was too early in the morning to make house calls, but it occurred to me that a visit to Kitty might make sense. She was still at St. Terry's and, given hospital routine, she'd probably been rousted out of bed at dawn. I hadn't seen her for days anyway and she might be of help.

The chill of the day before was gone. The air was clear and the sun was already intense. I slid my VW into the last available space in the vistors' lot and went around to the front entrance. The information desk in the lobby was deserted but the hospital itself was in full swing. The coffee shop was jammed, the scent of cholesterol and caffeine wafting irresistibly through the open doorway. Lights were on in the gift shop. The cashier's office was busy, filled with young female clerks preparing final bills as if this were some grand hotel nearing check-out time. There was an aura of excitement—medical personnel gearing up for birth and death and complex surgeries, cracked bones and breakdowns and drug overdoses . . . a hundred life-threatening episodes any given day of the week. And through it all the insidious sexuality that made it the stuff of soaps.

I went up to the third floor, turning left when I got off the elevators near 3 South. The big double doors were locked, as usual. I pushed the buzzer. After a moment, a heavyset black woman in jeans and a royal blue T-shirt rattled some keys and opened the door a crack. She wore a nursy no-nonsense watch and those shoes with two-inch crepe soles designed to offset fallen arches and varicose veins. She had startling hazel eyes and a face that radiated competence. Her white plastic tag indicated that her name was Natalie Jacks, LVN. I showed Ms. Jacks the photostat of my license and asked if I could talk to Kitty Wenner, explaining that I was a friend of the family.

She looked my I.D. over carefully and finally stepped back to let me in.

She locked the door behind me and led the way down the corridor to a room near the end. I was sneaking peeks into rooms along the way. I don't know what I anticipated—women writhing and babbling to themselves, men imitating ex-Presidents and jungle beasts. Or the lot of them in a drug-induced stupor that would swell their tongues and make their eyes roll back in their heads. Instead, as I passed each door, I saw faces raised in curiosity toward mine, as if I were a new admission who might shriek or do birdcalls while I tore off my clothes. I couldn't see any difference between them and me, which I thought was worrisome.

Kitty was up and dressed, her hair still wet from a shower. She was stretched out on her bed, pillows propped up behind her, a breakfast tray on the bed-table next to her. She wore a silk caftan that drooped on her frame as if she were a coat hanger. Her breasts were no bigger than buttons on a couch and her arms were bare bones fleshed out with skin as thin as tissue paper. Her eyes were enormous and haunted, the shape of her skull so pronounced that she looked as if she were seventy. Sally Struthers could have used her picture in an ad for foster parenting.

"You got a visitor," Natalie said.

Kitty's eyes flicked to me, and for a moment, I could see how scared she was. She was dying. She had to know that. The energy was seeping out of her pores like sweat.

Natalie inspected the breakfast tray. "You know they're going to put you on an I.V. if you don't do better than this. I thought you had a contract with Dr. Kleinert."

"I *ate* some," Kitty said.

"Well, I'm not supposed to pester you, but he'll be doing rounds soon. Try picking away at this while you talk to her, O.K.? We're on your team, baby. Honestly."

Natalie gave us both a brief smile and left, moving into the room next door, where we could hear her talking to someone else.

Kitty's face was suffused with pink and she was fighting back tears. She reached for a cigarette and lit it, coughing some against the back of her bony hand. She shook her head, conjuring up a smile that had some sweetness to it. "God, I can't believe I got myself into this," she said, and then wistfully, "You think Glen might come see me?"

"I don't know. I may go over there after I talk to you. I'll mention it to her if you like."

"She kicked Daddy out."

"So I heard."

"She'll probably kick me out next."

I couldn't look at her anymore. Her longing for Glen was so tangible it hurt me to see it. I studied the breakfast tray: a fresh fruit cup, a blueberry muffin, a carton of strawberry yogurt, granola, orange juice, tea. There was no indication that she'd eaten any of it.

"You want some of that?" she asked.

"No way. You'll tell Kleinert you ate it."

Kitty had the good grace to blush, laughing uneasily.

"I don't understand why you don't eat," I said.

She made a face. "Everything just looks so gross. There's this girl two doors down and she was suffering from anorexia, you know? So they brought her in here and she finally started to eat? Now she looks like she's pregnant. She's still thin. She's just got half a basketball for a stomach. It's disgusting."

"So what? She's alive, isn't she?"

"I don't want to look like that. Nothing tastes good anyway and it just makes me throw up."

There was no point in pursuing the subject so I let it go, shifting over to something else instead. "Have you talked to your father since Glen kicked him out?"

Kitty shrugged. "He's here every day in the afternoon. He's moved into the Edgewater Hotel until he finds a place."

"Did he tell you about Bobby's will?"

"Some. He says Bobby left me all this money. Is that true?" Her tone was one of dismay as much as anything.

"As far as I know, it is."

"But why would he do that?"

"Maybe he felt like he messed up your life and wanted to do right by you. Derek tells me he left some money to Rick's parents too. Or maybe he considered it a little incentive for you to get your shit together for a change."

"I never made any deals with him."

"I don't think he meant to make a 'deal.'"

"Well, I don't like to feel controlled."

"Kitty, I think you've demonstrated the fact that you can't be controlled. We're all getting that message loud and clear. Bobby loved you."

"Who asked him to? Sometimes I wasn't even nice to him. And I didn't exactly have his best interests at heart."

"Meaning what?"

"Nothing. Skip it. I wish he hadn't left me anything is all. It makes me feel crummy."

"I don't know what to tell you," I said.

"Well, I never asked him for a thing." Her tone was argumentative, but I couldn't understand what her position was.

"What's bothering you?"

"Nothing."

"What's all the fretting about, then?"

"I'm not fretting! God. Why should I fret? He did it so he'd feel good, right? It had nothing to do with me."

"It had *something* to do with you or he'd have left the money to someone else."

She started gnawing on her thumbnail, temporarily abandoning the cigarette, which sat on the lip of the ashtray and sent up a tiny trail of smoke like an Indian signal on a distant mountaintop. Her mood was getting dark. I wasn't sure why she was so upset at the notion of two million dollars being dumped in her lap, but I didn't want to alienate her. I wanted information. I shifted the subject again. "What about the insurance your father took out on Bobby's life? Did he mention that?"

"Yeah. That's weird. He does stuff like that, and later, he can't understand why people get upset. He doesn't see anything wrong with it at all. To him, it just makes sense. Bobby'd cracked up his car once or twice so Daddy just figured if he died, somebody might as well benefit. I guess that's why Glen threw him out, huh?"

"I think that's a safe bet. She'd never tolerate his profiting from Bobby's death. My God, it was the worst possible move he could have made as far as she's concerned. Besides which, it sets him up as a murder suspect."

"My father wouldn't kill anyone!"

"That's what he says about you."

"Well, it's true. I didn't have any reason to want Bobby dead. Neither of us did. I didn't even know about the money and I don't want it anyway."

"Money might not be the motive," I said. "It's an obvious place to start, but it doesn't necessarily go anywhere."

"But you don't think Daddy did it, do you?"

"I haven't made up my mind about that yet. I'm still trying to figure out what Bobby was up to and I need to fill in some gaps. Something was going on back then and I can't get a line on it. What was his relationship to Sufi? You have any idea?"

Kitty picked up her cigarette, averting her gaze. She took a moment to tap the ash from the end, and then she took a last, deep drag and put it out. Her nails were bitten down so far the pads of the fingers seemed like little round balls.

She was debating something with herself. I kept my mouth shut and gave her some room. "She was a contact," she said finally, her voice low. "Bobby was doing this investigation or something for somebody else."

"Who?"

"I don't know."

"It had to be the Frakers, right? I talked to Sufi last night, and the minute I left, she hightailed it over to their place. She was in there so long, I finally had to go home."

Kitty's eyes came up to mine. "I don't know for sure what it was."

"But how'd he get into it? What was it about?"

"All I know is he told me he was looking for something and he got the job out at the morgue so he could search at night."

"Medical records? Something stored out there?"

Her face closed down again and she shrugged.

"But Kitty, when you realized someone was trying to kill him, didn't you figure it was connected to that?"

She was chewing on her thumbnail in earnest by now. I saw her eyes flick and I turned around. Dr. Kleinert was standing in the doorway, staring at her. When he realized I'd seen him, he looked over at me. His smile seemed forced and it was not full of merriment.

"Well. I didn't know you were entertaining this morning," he said to her. Then briefly to me, "What brings you in so bright and early?"

"I just stopped by on my way to Glen's. I've been trying to persuade Kitty to eat," I said.

"No need for that," he said easily. "This young lady has an agreement with me." He gave a practiced glance at his watch, adjusting the face of it on his wrist before it disappeared up his cuff again. "I hope you'll excuse us. I have other patients to see and my time is limited."

"I'm on my way out," I said. I glanced at Kitty. "I may give you a call in a little while. I'll see if Glen can stop in to visit you."

"Great," she said. "Thanks."

I waved and moved out of the room, wondering how long he'd been standing there and how much he'd heard. I was trying to remember what Carrie St. Cloud had said. She'd told me Bobby was involved in some kind of blackmail scheme, but not the usual kind with money changing hands. Something else. "Somebody had something on some friend of his and he was trying to help out," was the way she'd put it as nearly as I could remember. If it was extortion, why didn't he go to the police? And why was it up to him to do anything?

I got back in my car and headed out to Glen's place.

21

It was just after nine when I pulled into Glen's driveway. The courtyard was deserted. The fountain sent up a column of water fifteen feet high, cascading back on itself in a tumble of pale green and white. I could hear a power mower whining from one of the terraces in the rear and rainbirds were jetting a fine spray into the giant fern, dappled with sunlight, that bordered the gravel walks. The air seemed tropical, scented with jasmine.

I rang the bell and one of the maids admitted me. I asked for Glen and she murmured something in Spanish, raising her eyes to the second floor. I gathered that Glen was upstairs.

The door to Bobby's room was open and she was seated in one of his easy chairs, hands in her lap, her face impassive. When she caught sight of me, she smiled almost imperceptibly. She was looking drawn, dark lines etched under her eyes. Her makeup was subtle, but it only seemed to emphasize the pallor in her cheeks. She wore a knit dress in a shade of red too harsh for her. "Hello, Kinsey. Come sit down," she said.

I sat in the matching plaid chair. "How are you doing?"

"Not that well. I find myself spending much of the day up here. Just sitting. Waiting for Bobby."

Her eyes strayed to mine. "I don't mean that literally, of course. I'm far too rational a person to believe the dead return. I keep thinking there's something more, that it can't be over yet. Do you know what I mean?"

"No. Not quite."

She stared at the floor, apparently consulting her inner voices. "Part of it is a feeling of betrayal, I think. I was brave and I did everything I was supposed to. I was a trouper and now I want the payoff. But the only reward that interests me is having Bobby back. So I wait." Her gaze moved around the room as if she were taking a series of photographs. Her manner seemed very flat to me, despite the emotional content of her speech. It was curious, like talking to a robot. She said human things, but mechanically. "You see that?"

I followed her eyes. Bobby's footprints were still visible on the white carpeting.

"I won't let them vacuum in here," she said. "I know it's stupid. I don't want to turn into one of those dreadful women who erect a shrine for the dead, keeping everything just as it was. But I don't want him erased. I don't want him wiped out like that. I don't even want to go through his belongings."

"There's no need to do anything yet, is there?"

"No. I guess not. I don't know what I'll do with the room anyway. I have dozens and they're all empty. It's not like I need to convert it into a sewing room or a studio."

"Are you taking care of yourself otherwise?"

"Oh, yes. I know enough to do that. I feel like grief is an illness I can't recover from. What worries me is I notice there's a certain attraction to the process that's hard to give up. It's painful, but at least it allows me to feel close to him. Once in a while, I catch myself thinking of something else and then I feel guilty. It seems disloyal not to hurt, disloyal to forget even for a moment that he's gone."

"Don't get mean with yourself and suffer more than you have to," I said.

"I know. I'm trying to wean myself. Every day I mourn a little less. Like giving up cigarettes. In the meantime, I pretend to be a whole person, but I'm not. I wish I could think of something that would heal me. Ah, God, I shouldn't go on and on about it. It's like someone who's had a heart attack or major surgery. It's all I can talk about. So self-centered."

Again, she paused and then she seemed to remember polite behavior. She looked at me. "What have you been doing?"

"I went over to St. Terry's this morning to see Kitty."

"Oh?" Glen's expression was devoid of interest.

"Is there any chance you might stop by to see her?"

"Absolutely none. For one thing, I'm furious that she's alive while Bobby's not. I hate it that he left her all that money. As far as I'm concerned, she's grasping, self-destructive, manipulative—" She broke off, closing her mouth. She was silent for a moment. "Sorry. I don't mean to be so vehement. I never liked her. Just because she's in trouble now doesn't change anything. She's done it to herself. She thought there'd always be someone who'd bail her out, but it won't be me. And Derek's not capable of it."

"I heard he left."

She stirred restlessly. "We had a terrible fight. I didn't think I'd ever get him out of here. I finally had to call one of the gardeners. I despise him. Truly. It makes me sick to think he was ever in my bed. I don't know which is worse . . . the fact that he took out that ghoulish policy on Bobby's life or the fact that he hadn't the faintest sense how despicable it was."

"Can he collect?"

"He seems to think so, but I intend to fight him every step of the way. I've put the insurance company on notice and I've contacted a firm of lawyers in L.A. I want him out of my life. I don't really care what it costs, though the less of mine he gets the better. Fortunately, we signed premarital agreements, though he swears he'll challenge me on that if I thwart his insurance claim."

"Jesus, you're really drawing up battle lines."

She rubbed her forehead wearily. "God, it was horrible. I called Varden to see if I can get a restraining order out on him. It's lucky there wasn't a gun in the house or one of us would be dead."

I was silent.

After a moment, she seemed to collect herself. "I don't mean to sound so crazy. Everything I say comes out so manic somehow. Anyway. Enough of that. I'm sure you didn't come here to listen to me rave. Would you like some coffee?"

"No thanks. I just wanted to touch base with you and bring you up to date. Most of this has to do with Bobby, so if you don't want to talk about it now, I can stop back another time."

"No, no. That's fine. Maybe it will give me something new to think about. I do want you to find out who killed him. It may be the only form of relief I can look forward to. What have you come up with so far?"

"Not a lot. I'm putting it together piece by piece and I'm not really sure of my facts. For one thing, I may have people lying to me, but since I don't really know the truth, I can't be sure," I said.

"I understand."

I hestitated, oddly reluctant to pass on my conjecture. It felt intrusive to speculate about his past, in poor taste somehow to discuss the intimate details of his life with the woman who was trying so hard to cope with his death. "I think Bobby was having an affair."

"That's not surprising. I think I mentioned that he was dating someone."

"Not her. Nola."

She stared at me as though waiting for the punch line. Finally, she said, "You can't be serious."

"From what I've heard, Bobby was having an affair with someone and he fell in love. That's why he broke up with Carrie St. Cloud in the first place. I have reason to believe it was Nola Fraker, though I haven't confirmed it yet."

"I don't like that. I hope that's not true."

"I don't know what to tell you. It seems to fit the facts."

"I thought you said he was in love with Kitty."

"Maybe not 'in love.' I think he loved her a lot. That doesn't mean he acted on it. She claims there was nothing going on between them and I tend to believe her. If they'd had a sexual relationship, I'm sure you'd have been the first to know—for the shock value if nothing else. You know how she is. She's obviously immature and confused and he was certainly aware of your attitude toward her. Anyway, whatever he felt for her wouldn't have precluded an involvement with someone else."

"But Nola's happily married. She and Jim have been here dozens of times. There was never even a hint of anything between her and Bobby."

"I hear what you're saying, Glen, but that's the way the game is played. You're having a clandestine affair. You and your lover end up at the same social event and walk around

chatting politely, ignoring each other . . . but not too pointedly because that would be conspicuous. Sly little hand
touches by the punch bowl, secret glances across the room.
It's a big hot joke and later you giggle about it in bed like a
couple of kids because you put one over on the grown-ups."

"But why Nola? The whole idea is ludicrous."

"Not at all. She's a beautiful woman. Maybe they ran into
each other and suddenly the spark was there. Or maybe
they'd been eyeing each other for years. Actually, it must
have started last summer because I don't think his relationship to her could have overlapped his to Carrie by
much. He didn't strike me as the type who'd have two affairs running at the same time."

Glenn's expression changed and she glanced at me with
apparent discomfort.

"What?"

"I just remembered. Derek and I were in Europe for two
months last summer. When we got back, I noticed we were
suddenly seeing more of the Frakers, but I shrugged it off.
You know how it is. Sometimes you see a lot of another
couple and then they drop out of your life for a while. I just
can't believe she'd do that to me or to Jim. It makes me feel
like a jealous spouse. Like I've been duped."

"But Glen, come on. Maybe it was the best thing that
ever happened to him. Maybe it helped him grow up some.
Who knows? Bobby was a good kid. What difference could
it possibly make at this point anyway?" I said. It felt mean
but I didn't want her getting into this bullshit of denying
who he was and what he did.

Her cheeks had taken on a tint of pink and she turned a
cold eye toward me. "I get the message. I still don't understand why you're telling me this."

"Because it's not up to me to shield you from the truth."

"It's not up to you to carry tales either."

"Yes. All right. You're right about that. I'm not into gossip
for the sake of it. There's a chance that it's tied up with
Bobby's death."

"How?"

"I'll get to that, but I have to have your assurances first
that this won't go any further."

"What's the connection?"

"Glen, you're not listening. I'll tell you as much as I can, but I can't tell you everything and I don't want you flying off the handle. If you turn around and repeat this to anyone, you could be putting both of us in jeopardy."

Her eyes came into focus and I felt she was finally taking in what I was saying. "I'm sorry. Of course. I won't say a word to anyone."

I told her briefly about Bobby's last message on my answering machine, and about the blackmail scheme, which I still didn't understand. I deleted mention of Sufi's part in all of this because I was still worried Glen would take matters into her own hands and do something dumb. She seemed volatile right now, unstable, like a vial of nitroglycerin. One minor bump and she might blow.

"I do need your help," I said when I finished.

"Doing what?"

"I want to talk to Nola. So far I still don't have confirmation on this and if I call or stop by out of a clear blue sky, it's going to scare the shit out of her. I'd like you to call her and see if you can set something up."

"For when?"

"This morning if possible."

"What would you want me to say to her?"

"Tell her the truth. Tell her I'm looking into Bobby's death, that we think he may have been involved with some woman last summer, and since you were gone, you thought maybe she might have seen him around with someone. Ask her if she'd mind talking to me."

"Won't she suspect? Surely, she'll figure out that you're onto her."

"Well, for starters, I could be wrong. Maybe it's not her. That's what I'm trying to determine. If she's innocent, she won't care one way or the other. And if she's not, let her cook up a cover so she'll feel secure. I don't care. The point is, she won't have the balls to shut the door in my face, which is what she'd probably do if I went over there unannounced."

She considered briefly. "All right."

She got up and crossed to the telephone on the night stand, punching in Nola's number from memory. She handled the request as deftly as anything I'd ever heard, and I could see how good she must be at fund raising. Nola couldn't have been nicer or more cooperative and in fifteen minutes I was on my way back to Horton Ravine.

By day, I could see that the Frakers' house was pale yellow with a shake roof. I went up the driveway and pulled onto the parking pad to the left of the house, where a dark maroon BMW and a silver Mercedes were parked. As I was not feeling suicidal, I leaned out of my car window, looking for the dog. Rover or Fido, whatever his name was, turned out to be a great dane with rubbery black-rimmed lips, complete with strings of slobber hanging down. From that distance, I swear it looked like his collar was studded with spikes. His food dish was a wide aluminum bowl with bite marks around the rim.

I got out of the car cautiously. He ran up to the fence and started barking bad breath in my direction. He stood up on his hind legs, his front paws tucked over the gate. His dick looked like a hot dog in a long, furry bun and he wagged it at me like a guy who's just stepped out of a phone booth to open his raincoat.

I was just on the verge of insulting him when I realized that Nola had come out on the porch behind me.

"Don't mind him," she said. She was wearing another jump suit, this one black, with spike heels that made her half a head taller than me.

"Nice pup," I remarked. People always love it when you say their dogs are nice. Just shows you how out of touch they are.

"Thanks. Come on in. I have something to do first, but you can wait in the den."

22

The interior of the Fraker house was cool and spare; gleaming dark wood floors, white walls, bare windows, fresh flowers. The furniture was upholstered in white linen and the den into which Nola ushered me was lined with books. She excused herself and I heard her high heels tap-tap-tapping away down the hall.

It's never a good idea to leave me in a room by myself. I'm an incurable snoop and I search automatically. Having been raised from the age of five by an unmarried aunt, I spent a lot of time as a child in the homes of her friends, most of whom had no children of their own. I was told to keep quiet and amuse myself, which I managed in the first five minutes with the latest in an endless series of coloring books we brought with us when visiting. The problem was that I was terrible at keeping in the lines and the pictures always seemed dumb to me—little children frolicking with dogs and visiting farms. I didn't like to color chickens or hogs, so I learned to search. In this manner, I discovered people's hidden lives—the prescriptions in the medicine cabinets, tubes of jelly in bed-table drawers, cash reserves in the back of coat closets, startling sex manuals and marital artifacts between the mattress and box springs. Of course, I could never quiz my aunt afterward about the extraordinary-looking objects I came across because I wasn't supposed to know about them in the first place. Fascinated, I would wander into the kitchen, where the adults in those days seemed to congregate, drinking highballs and talking about achingly dull things like politics and sports, and I would stare at women named Bernice and Mildred whose husbands were named Stanley and Edgar, and I would wonder who did what with the long doodad with the battery stuck in one end. It was not a flashlight. That much I knew. Early on, I discerned the sometimes remarkable distinction between public appearances and private tastes. These were the people my aunt forbade me to swear in front of no matter how we talked at home. Some of the phrases she used, I thought might have application here, but I could never confirm this. The whole process of education for me was learning the proper words to attach to things I already knew.

The Frakers' den exhibited a shocking lack of hiding places. No drawers, no cabinets, no end tables with cupboards underneath. The two chairs were chrome with leather straps. The coffee table was glass with narrow chrome legs, sporting a decanter of brandy and two snifters on a tray. There wasn't even a carpet to peek under. Jesus, what kind of people were they? I was reduced to touring the bookshelves, trying to divine their hobbies and avocations from the volumes on hand.

People do tend to hang on to hardbacked books, and I could see that Nola had gone through interior design, gourmet cooking, gardening, needlework, and personal beauty hints. What caught my attention, however, were the two shelves lined with books on architecture. What was that about? Surely, neither she nor Dr. Fraker was commissioned to design buildings in their spare time. I took out an oversized volume called *Architectural Graphic Standards* and checked the flyleaf. The engraved bookplate showed a lithograph of a seated cat staring at a fish in a bowl. Under the Ex Libris, the name Dwight Costigan was scratched in a masculine hand. A reminder bell tinkled at the back of my brain. I thought he was the architect who designed Glen's house. A borrowed book? I checked three more in rapid succession. All of them were "from the library of" Dwight Costigan. That was odd. Why here?

I heard Nola tapping back in my direction and I slipped the book into place, then eased over to the window and acted as though I'd occupied my time by looking out. She came into the den with a smile that went on and off again like a loose connection. "Sorry you had to wait. Have a seat."

I hadn't really given a lot of thought to how I was going to handle this. Every time I rehearse these little playlets in advance, I'm brilliant and the other characters say exactly what I want to hear. In reality, nobody gets it right, including me, so why worry about it before the fact?

I sat down in one of the chrome-and-leather chairs, hoping I wouldn't get lodged in the straps. She sat down on the edge of a white linen love seat, resting one hand gracefully on the surface of the glass coffee table in an attitude that suggested serenity, except that she was leaving little pads of perspiration at her fingertips. I took in the sight of her at a quick glance. Slim, long-legged, with those perfect apple-sized breasts. Her hair was a paid-for shade of red, framing her face in a tumble of soft waves. Blue eyes, flawless skin. She had that clear ageless look that comes with first-rate cosmetic surgery, and the black jumpsuit she wore emphasized her lush body without being vulgar or crass. Her manner was solemn and sincere, and struck me as false.

"What can I help you with?" she asked.

I had a split second in which to make a judgment. Could Bobby Callahan *truly* have gotten involved with a woman as phony as this? Oh hell, who was I trying to kid? Of course!

I gave her a fifteen-watt smile, resting my chin on my fist. "Well, I have a little problem, Nola. May I call you Nola?"

"Certainly. Glen mentioned you were investigating Bobby's death."

"That's true. Actually Bobby just hired me a week ago and I feel like I ought to give him his money's worth."

"Oh. I thought maybe there was something wrong and that was why you were looking into it."

"There might be. I don't know yet."

"But shouldn't the police be doing that?"

"I'm sure they are. I'm conducting a . . . you know, an auxiliary investigation, just in case they're on the wrong track."

"Well, I hope somebody figures it out. Poor kid. We all feel so bad for Glen. Are you having any luck?"

"As a matter of fact, I am. Somebody told me half the story and all I have to do is figure out the rest."

"It sounds like you're doing pretty well, then." She hesitated delicately. "What kind of story?"

I suspect she didn't really want to ask, but the nature of the conversation dictated that she must. She was pretending to cooperate so, of course, she had to feign interest in a subject she'd probably prefer to ignore.

I let a moment pass while I stared down at the tabletop. I thought it lent a note of credibility to the lie I was about to tell. I looked back at her, making significant eye contact. "Bobby told me he was in love with you."

"With me?"

"That's what he said."

The eyes blinked. The smile went off and on. "Well, I'm astonished. I mean, it's very flattering and I always thought he was a sweet kid, but really!"

"I didn't find it that astonishing."

Her laugh conveyed a wonderful combination of innocence and disbelief. "Oh, for heaven's sake. I'm married. And I'm twelve years older than he is."

Shit, she was quick—shaving years off her age without pausing to count on her fingers or anything. I'm not that fast at subtraction so it's probably fortunate that I don't lie about how old I am.

I smiled slightly. She was pissing me off and I found myself using a mild, deadly tone. "Age doesn't matter. Bobby's dead now. He's older than God. He's as old as anybody's ever going to get."

She stared at me, cuing in to the fact that I was mad. "You don't have to get nasty about it. I can't help it if Bobby Callahan decided he was in love with me. So the kid had a crush on me. So what?"

"So the kid had an *affair* with you, Nola. That's what. You got your tit in a wringer and the kid was helping you out. The *kid* was murdered because of you, ass eyes. Now, shall we quit bullshitting each other and get down to business on this or shall I call Lieutenant Dolan down at Homicide and let him have a chat with you?"

"I don't know what you're talking about," she snapped. She got up, but I was already on my feet and I clamped a hand around that dainty wrist so fast she gasped. She gave a little jerk and I released her, but I could feel myself expand with anger like a hot-air balloon.

"I'm telling you, Nola. You've got a choice. You tell me what was going on or I'm going to start leaning on you. In fact, I may do that anyway. I'll whip on down to the courthouse and I'll start going through public records and newspaper accounts and police files until I get a little background information on you and then I'm going to figure out what you're hiding and *then* I'm going to find a way to stick it to you so bad you'll wish you'd blabbed the whole story out right here."

That's when I got the jolt. In the back of my brain, I heard a sound like a parachute catching air. Thwunk . . . it opened up. It was one of those extraordinary moments when automatic recall clicks in and a piece of information pops up like a flash card. It must have been the adrenaline pumping through my head because I suddenly retrieved some data from my memory bank and it appeared on my mental screen just as clear as could be . . . not the whole of it, but enough. "Wait a minute. I know who you are. You were married to Dwight Costigan. I knew I'd seen you somewhere. Your picture was in all the papers."

Her face drained of color. "That has nothing to do with this," she said.

I laughed, primarily because sudden recollection does that to me. A mental leap has a little chemical component to it that gives a quick rush.

"Oh come on," I said. "It does connect. I don't know how yet, but it's all the same tale, isn't it?"

She sank back down on the love seat, one hand reaching for the glass tabletop to steady herself. She breathed deeply, trying to relax. "You would do well to let this pass," she said, not looking at me.

"Are you nuts?" I said. "Are you out of your tiny mind? Bobby Callahan hired me because he thought somebody was trying to kill him and he was right. He's dead now and he's got no way to rectify the situation, but *I* do and if you think I'll back off this sucker, you don't know me."

She was shaking her head. All the beauty was gone and what remained seemed drab. She looked, then, like we all look in fluorescent lighting—tired, sallow, shopworn. Her voice was low. "I'll tell you what I can. And then I beg you to drop the investigation. I mean that. For your own good. I did have an affair with Bobby." She paused, searching for the path she wanted to take. "He was a wonderful person. He really was. I was crazy about him. He was so uncomplicated and he had no history. He was just young and healthy, vigorous. God. He was twenty-three. Even the sight of his *skin*. He was like a—" Her eyes came up to mine and she broke off with embarrassment, a smile forming and faltering, this time from some emotion I couldn't read . . . pain or tenderness, perhaps.

I eased into the chair carefully, hoping I wouldn't spoil the mood.

"When you're that age," she said, "you still think things can be made right. You still think you can have anything you want. You think life's simple, that you only have to do one or two little things and it will all turn around. I told him it wasn't like that for me, but he had a streak of gallantry in him. Sweet fool."

She was silent for a long time.

"'Sweet fool,' what?" I said quietly.

"Well, he died for it, of course. I can't tell you the guilt I've felt. . . ." She trailed off and she looked away.

"Tell me the front end. How does Dwight fit in? He was shot, right?"

"Dwight was much older than I. Forty-five when we were married. I was twenty-two. It was a good marriage . . . up to a point at any rate. He adored me. I admired him. He did incredible things for this town."

"He designed Glen's house, didn't he?"

"Not really. His father was the original architect when the house was built back in the twenties. Dwight did the restoration," she said. "I think I need a drink. Do you want one?"

"Sure, that's fine," I said.

She reached for the brandy decanter, removing the heavy glass stopper. She laid the neck of the decanter against the edge of one of the snifters, but her hands were shaking so badly I thought she'd crack the glass. I reached over and took the bottle from her, pouring her a stiff shot. I poured myself one too, though at ten in the morning, it was the last thing I wanted. She gave hers a perfunctory swirl and we both drank. I swallowed and my mouth came open automatically as if I'd just risen to the surface of a swimming pool. This was clearly fine stuff, but I didn't think I'd need my teeth cleaned for a *year*. I watched her calm herself, taking a deep breath or two.

I was trying desperately to recall the accounts I'd read of the incident in which Costigan was killed. It must have been five or six years ago. As nearly as I could remember, someone had broken into their Montebello house one night and had shot Dwight to death after a struggle in the bedroom. I'd been off in Houston for a client so I hadn't followed the events very closely, but as far as I knew, it was still sitting on the books as an unsolved homicide.

"What happened?" I asked.

"Don't ask and don't interfere. I pleaded with Bobby to let it go, but he wouldn't listen and it cost him his life. The past is the past. It's over and done with and I'm the only one paying for it now. Forget it. I don't care, and if you're smart, you won't either."

"You know I can't do that. Tell me what went on."

"What for? It won't change anything."

"Nola, I'm going to find out whether you tell me or not. If you lay it out for me maybe it won't have to go any further than this. Maybe I'll understand and agree to drop the whole thing. I'm not unreasonable, but you've gotta play fair."

I could see the indecision written in her face. She said, "Oh God," and put her head down for a moment. She looked at me with anxiety. "We're talking about a lunatic. Someone so crazy. You'd have to swear . . . you'd have to promise to back off."

"I can't make a promise like that and you know it. Tell me the story and then we'll figure out what has to be done."

"I've never told anyone except Bobby and look what happened to him."

"What about Sufi? She knows, doesn't she?"

She blinked at me, momentarily startled at the mention of Sufi's name. She looked away from me. "No, not at all. I'm sure she doesn't know what's going on. Why would she?" The answer seemed too hesitant to be convincing, but I let it pass for the time being. Could Sufi be blackmailing her?

"Well, *somebody* else knows," I said. "From what I gather, you're being blackmailed and that's what Bobby was trying to stop. What's the deal? What does this person have on you? What kind of leverage?"

I let the silence stretch, watching as she struggled with her need to unload.

Finally, she started talking, her voice so low I was forced to lean forward so I could hear her. "We'd been married nearly fifteen years. Dwight was on medication for high blood pressure and it made him impotent. We'd never had a highly charged sex life anyway. I got restless and found . . . someone else."

"A lover."

She nodded, eyes closed as if the recollection hurt her. "Dwight walked in on us one night in bed. He was crazed. He got a gun from the study and came back and there was a struggle."

I caught the sound of footsteps coming down the hall. I glanced toward the door and she did too, her voice becoming urgent.

"Don't breathe a word of this. Please."

"Trust me, I won't. What's the rest?"

She hesitated. "I shot Dwight. It was an accident, but somebody has the gun with my fingerprints on it."

"And that's what Bobby was searching for?"

She nodded almost imperceptibly.

"But who has it? Your ex-lover?"

Nola raised a finger to her lips. There was a tap at the door and Dr. Fraker stuck his head in, apparently surprised to see me sitting there. "Oh, hi, Kinsey. Is that your car in the drive? I was just about to take off, and I couldn't figure out who was here."

"I stopped by to talk to Nola about Glen," I said. "I don't think she's doing too well and I was wondering if we shouldn't work out some arrangement to take turns spending time with her now that Derek's gone."

He shook his head regretfully. "Dr. Kleinert told me she'd kicked him out. Damn shame. Not that I have any use for him myself, but she's got her share of trouble right now. I hate to see her saddled with something else."

"Me, too," I said. "Do you need me to move my car?"

"No, that's fine," he said, looking over at Nola. "I've got some work to do at the hospital, but I shouldn't be back too late. Do we have dinner plans?"

She smiled pleasantly, though she had to clear her throat before she could speak. "I thought we'd eat here if that's all right with you."

"Sure, it's fine. Well. I'll let you two hatch your little schemes. Nice to see you, Kinsey."

"Actually we're finished," Nola said, getting up.

"Oh, well good," he said, "I'll walk you out."

I knew she was just using his appearance as a way to terminate the conversation, but I couldn't think of any delaying tactics, especially with the two of them standing there looking at me.

We exchanged brief good-byes and then Dr. Fraker held the door for me and I left the den. As I glanced back, I could see that Nola's expression was tinged with anxiety, and I suspected she was wishing she'd kept her secret to herself. She had a lot at stake: freedom, money, status, respectability. She was vulnerable to anyone who knew what I now knew. I wondered how desperate she was to hang on to what she had and what kind of payment had been extracted from her as a result.

23

I went into the office. There was a pile of mail on the floor under the door slot. I gathered that up and tossed it on my desk, opening the French doors to let in some fresh air. The message light on my answering machine was blinking. I sat down and pressed the playback button.

The message was from my friend at the telephone company with a report on the disconnect for S. Blackman, whose full name was Sebastian S., male, age sixty-six, with a forwarding address in Tempe, Arizona. Well, that didn't sound very promising. If all else failed, I could double back and check that out to see if there was any tie to Bobby. Somehow I doubted it. I made a note in his file. There was a certain security in having it all committed to paper. At least that way, if anything happened to me, someone could come along afterward and pick up the thread—a grim notion, but not unrealistic given Bobby's fate.

I spent the next hour and a half going through my mail, catching up on my bookkeeping. A couple of checks had come in and I entered those in accounts receivable, making out a deposit slip. One statement had been shipped back to me unopened, marked "Addressee Unknown. Return to Sender" with a big purple finger pointing right at me. God, a deadbeat. I hated getting stung for services rendered. I'd done some good work for that guy, too. I'd known he was a slow pay, but I didn't think he'd actually stiff me for my fee. I set it aside. I'd have to track him down when I had some time.

It was almost noon by then and I glanced at the phone. I knew there was a call I should make and I picked up the receiver, punching in the number before I lost my nerve.

"Santa Teresa Police Department. Deputy Collins."

"I'd like to speak to Sergeant Robb in Missing Persons."

"Just a moment. I'll connect you."

My heart was thudding in a way that made my armpits damp.

I'd run into Jonah while I was investigating the disappearance of a woman named Elaine Boldt. He was a nice guy with a bland face, maybe twenty pounds overweight, amusing, direct, a bit of a rebel, pirating copies of some homicide reports for me against all the rules. He'd been married for years to his junior-high-school sweetheart, who'd abandoned him a year ago, departing with his two daughters, and leaving him with a freezer full of crappy dinners that she'd done up herself. He hadn't been flashy but I don't look for that anyway and I'd liked him a lot. We'd never been lovers, but he'd exhibited a bit of healthy male interest and I'd taken a dim view of it when he went back to his wife. Face it, I was miffed, and I'd kept my distance from him ever since.

"Robb here."

"Jesus," I said, "I haven't even talked to you yet and I'm already pissed."

I could hear him hesitate. "Kinsey, is that you?"

I laughed. "Yes, it's me and I just figured out how frosted I am."

He knew exactly what I was talking about. "God. I know, babe. What a load of pig swill that was. I've thought about you so often."

I was saying "uh-hun, uh-hun" in what I hoped was my most skeptical tone. "How's Camilla?"

He sighed and I could almost see him run a hand through his hair. "About the same. She treats me like dirt. I don't know why I let her back in my life."

"Must be nice to have the girls home though, isn't it?"

"Well, yeah, that's true," he said. "And we're seeing a counselor. Not them. Me and her."

"Maybe that will help."

"Maybe it won't." He caught himself and changed his tone. "Ah. Well. I shouldn't complain. I guess I did it to myself. I'm just sorry it ended up affecting you."

"Don't worry about it. I'm a big girl. Besides, I've got a way for you to redeem yourself. I thought maybe I could buy you lunch today and pick your brain."

"Sure. I'd love it, only lunch is on me. It'll help assuage my guilt. How you like that 'assuage' stuff? That's the word of the day on my vocabulary calendar. Yesterday was 'ineluctable.' I never did figure out how to sneak that one in. Where do you want to go? You name the place."

"Oh, let's keep it simple. I don't want to spend a lot of time on social niceties."

"How about the courthouse? I'll pick up some sandwiches and we can eat on the lawn."

"God, right out in public. Won't the department talk?"

"I hope so. Maybe Camilla will get wind of it and leave me again."

"See you at twelve-thirty."

"Is there something you want me to research in the meantime?"

"Oh right. Good point." I gave him a quick synopsis of the Costigan shooting, leaving Nola Fraker out of it. I'd decide later how much of the story I could trust him with. For now, I fed him the public version and asked if he could take a peek at the files.

"I have a vague recollection of that one. Let me see what I can dig up."

"And one more thing if you would," I said. "Could you run a check through NCIC on a woman named Lila Sams?" I gave him her two a.k.a.'s, Delia Sims and Delilah Sampson, the birthdate I'd taken off the driver's license, and the additional information I had in my notes.

"Right. Got it. I'll do what I can. See you shortly," he said and hung up.

It had occurred to me that if Lila was running some kind of scam on Henry, she might well have a prior record. There was no way I'd have access to the National Crime Information Center except through an authorized law-enforcement agency. Jonah could have the name run through the computer and get feedback in minutes and at least then I'd know if my instincts were accurate.

I tidied up my office, grabbed the bank deposit, and locked up, going next door for a few minutes to chat with Vera Lipton, one of the claims adjusters for California Fidelity Insurance. I stopped off at the bank on the way over to the courthouse, depositing most of the money to savings, with enough to my checking account to cover current expenses.

The day, which had started out on preheat, was cranked up to broil by now. The sidewalks shimmered and the palms looked bleached out by the sun. Where occasional potholes in the street had been filled, the asphalt was as soft and grainy as cookie dough.

The Santa Teresa Courthouse looks like a Moorish castle: hand-carved wooden doors, towers, and wrought-iron balconies. Inside, there's so much mosaic tile on the walls, it looks like someone's covered them with patchwork quilts. One courtroom sports a cycloramic mural that depicts the settling of Santa Teresa by the early Spanish missionaries. It's sort of the Walt Disney version of what really went on as the artist has omitted the introduction of syphilis and the corruption of the Indians. I prefer it myself, if the truth be known. It would be hard to concentrate on justice if you had to stare up at some poor bunch of Indians in the last stages of paresis.

I cut through the great archway toward the sunken gardens in the rear. There were about two dozen people scattered across the lawn, some eating lunch, some napping or taking in the sun. Idly, I catalogued the merits of a good-looking man coming toward me in a pale blue short-sleeved shirt. I was doing one of those visual surveys that starts at the bottom and moves up. Uh-hun, nice hips, dressing left . . . uh-hun, flat belly, great arms, I thought. He'd almost reached me when I checked out the face and realized it was Jonah.

I hadn't seen him since June. Apparently the diet and his weight-lifting regimen had worked like a charm. His face, which in the past I'd labeled "harmless," was now nicely honed. His dark hair was longer and he'd picked up a tan so that his blue eyes now blazed in a face the color of maple sugar.

"Oh, God," I said, stopping dead in my tracks. "You look great."

He flashed me a smile, loving it. "You think so? Thanks. I must have lost twenty pounds since I saw you last."

"How'd you do it? Hard work?"

"Yeah, I did a little work."

He stood and stared at me and I stared back. He was exuding pheromones like a musky aftershave and I could feel my body chemistry start to shift. Mentally, I shook myself. I didn't need this. The only thing worse than a man just out of a marriage is a man who's still *in* one.

"I heard you got shot," he said.

"A mere .22, which hardly counts. I got beat up too, and that's what hurt. I don't know how guys put up with that shit," I said. I rubbed at the bridge of my nose ruefully. "Broke my schnoz."

He reached out impulsively and ran a finger down my nose. "Looks O.K. to me."

"Thanks," I said. "It still blows pretty good."

We endured one of those awkward pauses that had always punctuated our relationship.

I shifted my bag from one shoulder to the other, just for something to do. "What'd you bring?" I said, indicating the paper sack he held.

He glanced down. "Oh, yeah. I forgot. Uh, subs and Pepsis and Famous Amos cookies."

"We could even eat," I said.

He didn't move. He shook his head. "Kinsey, I don't remember going through this before," he said. "Why don't we fuckin' skip lunch and go over there behind that bush?"

I laughed, because I'd just had this quick flash of something hot and nasty that I don't care to repeat. I tucked my hand through his arm. "You're cute."

"I don't want to hear about cute."

We went down the wide stone steps and headed toward the far side of the courthouse lawn, where shaggy evergreens shade the grass. We sat down, distracted by the business of eating lunch. Pepsis were opened and lettuce fell out of sandwiches and we exchanged paper napkins and murmured about how good it all was. By the time we finished eating, we'd recovered some professional composure and conducted most of our remaining conversation like adults instead of sex-starved kids.

He shoved his empty Pepsi can in the sack. "I'll tell you the scuttlebutt on that Costigan shooting. The guy I talked to used to work Homicide and he says he always thought it was the wife. It was one of those situations where the whole story stank, you know? She claimed some guy broke in, husband gets a gun, big struggle, boom! The gun goes off and hubby's dead. Intruder runs away and she calls the cops, distraught victim of a random burglary attempt. Well, it didn't look right, but she stuck to her guns. Hired some hotshot lawyer right off the bat and wouldn't say a word until he got there. You know how it goes. 'Sorry my client can't answer this.' 'Sorry I won't let her respond to that.' Nobody believed a word she said, but she never broke down and in the end there wasn't any proof. No evidence, no informant, no weapon, no witness. End of tale. I hope you're not working for her because if you are, you're screwed."

I shook my head. "I'm looking into Bobby Callahan's death," I said. "I think he was murdered and I think it connects back to Dwight Costigan." I sketched the whole story out for him, avoiding his gaze. We were stretched out in the grass by then and I kept having these images of sexual misbehavior that I didn't think would serve. I plowed right ahead, talking more than I should have just to create a diversion.

"God, you come up with something on the Costigan killing and Lieutenant Dolan's gonna crochet you a watch," he said.

"What about Lila Sams?"

He held a finger up. "I was saving the best for last," he said. "I ran a field check on her and came up with a hit. This lady has a string of wants and warrants as long as your arm. Priors going back to 1968."

"What for?"

"Fraud, obtaining property by false pretenses, larceny by trick and device. She's been passing bad paper, too. She's got six outstanding warrants on her even as we speak. Well, wait. Take a look for yourself. I brought the print-out."

He held out the computer print-out and I took it. Why didn't I feel more elated at the notion of nailing her? Because it would break Henry's heart and I didn't want to take responsibility for that. I ran an eye down the sheet. "Can I keep this?"

"Sure, but don't jump up and down like that. Calm yourself," he said. "I take it you know where she is."

I looked over at him with a weak smile. "Probably sitting in my backyard drinking iced tea," I said. "My landlord is head over heels in love with her and I suspect she's on the verge of taking him for everything he's worth."

"Talk to Whiteside in Fraud and he'll have her picked up."

"I think I better talk to Rosie first."

"That old bag who runs the dive down the street from you? What's she got to do with it?"

"Oh, neither one of us can stand Lila. Rosie wanted me to do the background check for the aggravation if nothing else. We needed to know where she was coming from."

"So now you know. What's the problem?"

"I don't know. It just feels crummy somehow, but I'll figure it out. I don't want to rush into anything I'll regret."

There was a momentary silence and then Jonah gave my shirt a tug. "You been up to the shooting range lately?"

"Not since we were there together," I said.

"You want to go up there sometime?"

"Jonah, we can't do that."

"Why not?"

"Because it might feel like a date and confuse us both."

"Come on. I thought we were friends."

"We are. We just can't hang out together."

"Why not?"

"Because you're too good-looking and I'm too smart," I said tartly.

"We're back to Camilla again, right?"

"Right. I'm not going to interfere with that. You've been with her a long time."

"I tell you something. I'm still kicking myself. I could have gone to the other junior high school, you know? Seventh grade. How did I know I was making a decision that would haunt me in middle-age?"

I laughed. "Life is full of that stuff. You had to choose between metal or woodshop, right? You could have turned out to be an auto mechanic. Instead you're a cop. You know what my choices were? Child psychology or home ec. I didn't give a shit about either one."

"I wish I hadn't seen you again."

I could feel my smile fade. "Well, I'm sorry for that. It was my fault." I could tell we'd been looking at each other too long, so I got up, brushing grass off my jeans. "I have to go."

He got up too and we said some good-bye things. We parted company shortly thereafter. I walked backward for a few steps, watching him head back to the station. Then I continued on toward my office, turning my attention back to the matter of Henry Pitts. I realized then that there wasn't any point in talking to Rosie about it. Of course I'd have to tell the cops where Lila was. She'd been a con for nearly twenty years and she wasn't going to reform and make Henry a happy man in the twilight of their days. She was going to cheat him silly, thus breaking his heart anyway. What difference did it make how she got caught or who turned her in? Better to do it now before she took every cent he had.

I'd been walking rapidly, head down, but when I got to the corner of Floresta and Anaconda, I did an abrupt left and headed for the police station.

24

I was at the police station for an hour and forty-five minutes. Fortunately, the Missing Persons Department and Fraud were nowhere near each other so I didn't have to worry about running into Jonah again. First, Whiteside was at lunch and then he had a quick meeting to attend. Then when I explained the situation to him, he had to place a call to a county in northern New Mexico where three of the warrants had been issued. While he was waiting for a response to that inquiry, he contacted the county sheriff in some little town up near San Francisco, trying to get confirmation on a no-bail warrant that originated in Marin. The charge on the fifth warrant in Boise, Idaho, turned out to be a misdemeanor and the fraud detective said he couldn't afford to come get her in any event. The sixth warrant, in Twin Falls, had been recalled for reasons unspecified. So far, Lila Sams was home free.

At 3:20, Marin County finally returned Whiteside's call, confirming the no-bail warrant and indicating that they'd have someone pick her up once they knew she was actually in custody. Their cooperation was largely due to the fact that one of their deputies was vacationing in Santa Teresa anyway and had agreed to accompany her back to Marin. Whiteside said as soon as a telexed copy of the warrant came through, he'd send the beat officer over to make the arrest. He didn't really have to have the warrant in hand, but I think he'd sensed by now that she was slippery. I gave him Moza's address, my address, and a thorough description of Lila Sams.

It was 3:40 by the time I got home. Henry was sitting on a chaise in the backyard, surrounded by books. He looked up from his legal pad as I came around the corner.

"Oh, it's you," he said. "I thought it might be Lila. She said she'd stop in and say good-bye before she took off."

That caught me by surprise. "She's leaving?"

"Well, she's not really 'leaving.' She's going to Las Cruces for a few days, but she hopes to be back by the end of the week. I guess a little problem came up on some property she owns and she has to get things squared away. It's a darn nuisance, but what can you do?"

"She's not gone already, though, is she?"

He checked his watch. "I can't imagine she would be. Her plane takes off about five. She said she had to go to the title company and then she'd toss a few things in a suitcase. Did you want to talk to her?"

I shook my head, unable to say yet what needed to be said. I could see that he was mapping out a new crossword puzzle, jotting down preliminary notes. At the top of the page, he'd written two titles, "Elementary, Dear Watson!" and "Home Sweet Holmes."

He smiled shyly when he saw me take note. "This one's for the Sherlockeans in the crowd," he said. He set the legal pad aside, as though self-conscious at having someone watch him work. "Well, now, how are things with you?"

He seemed so innocent, nothing more on his mind than his passion for words. How could she deceive a man like that?

"Something's come up I think you ought to know about," I said. I unfolded the computer print-out and handed it to him.

He looked down at it. "What's this?"

Lila's name apparently caught his eye then, because his gaze settled on the page. His face lost animation as he assimilated the facts. When he finished reading, he gestured aimlessly. He was silent for a moment and then he glanced up at me. "Well. Makes me look like a fool, doesn't it?"

"Come on, Henry. Don't talk like that. I don't think so at all. You took a risk and she brought you some happiness. Hey, so later it turns out she's a crook. That's not your fault."

He stared at the paper like a kid just learning to sound out words. "What made you check into it?"

I thought there might be a tactful explanation, but nothing occurred to me. "I didn't like her much, to tell you the truth. I guess I felt protective, especially when you talked about doing business with her. I just didn't think she was on the level and it turns out she's not. You haven't given her any money, have you?"

He folded the print-out. "I closed out one of my accounts this morning."

"How much?"

"Twenty thousand in cash," he said. "Lila said she'd deposit it to an escrow account at the title company. The bank manager urged me to reconsider, but I thought he was simply being conservative. I see now, he was not." His manner had become very formal and it nearly broke my heart.

"I'm going down to Moza's to see if I can intercept her before she takes off. You want to come?"

He shook his head, his eyes bright. I turned on my heel and moved off at a quick clip.

I trotted the half-block to Moza's. A taxicab was cruising at half speed, the driver scanning house numbers. The two of us reached Moza's at just about the same time. He pulled over to the curb. I crossed to the passenger side, peering into the open window. He had a face like a beachball made of flesh.

"You the one wanted a cab?"

"Uh, sure. Lila Sams?"

He checked his trip sheet. "Right. You got any bags you need help with?"

"Actually, I don't need the cab. A neighbor said she'd run me out to the airport. I called back, but I guess the dispatcher didn't head you off in time. Sorry."

He gave me a look, then heaved an exasperated sigh, making a big display of crossing the address off his sheet. He shifted gears with annoyance, pulling away from the curb with a shake of his head. God, he could go on stage with an act like that.

I crossed Moza's yard at an angle and took the porch steps two at a time. She was holding the screen door open, looking out anxiously at the departing taxi. "What did you say to him? That was Lila's cab. She has to get to the airport."

"Really? He told me he had the wrong address. He was looking for Zollinger, one street over, I think."

"I better try another company. She ordered a cab thirty minutes ago. She's going to miss her plane."

"Maybe I can help," I said. "Is she in here?"

"You're not going to cause any trouble, Kinsey. I won't have that."

"I'm not causing trouble," I said. I moved through the living room and into the hall. The door to Lila's room was open.

The place had been stripped of personal possessions. One of the drawers where she'd concealed a phony I.D. was sitting on top of the chest of drawers, its back panel bare. She'd left the masking tape in a wad like a hunk of chewing gum. One suitcase was packed and sat near the door. Another was open on the bed, half filled, and beside it was a white plastic purse.

Lila had her back to me, bending over to remove a stack of folded clothes from one of the dressing-table drawers. The polyester pantsuit she wore was not very flattering. From the rear, her ass looked like two hanging foam-rubber hams. She caught sight of me as she turned. "Oh! You scared me. I thought it was Moza. What can I do for you?"

"I heard you were leaving. I thought maybe I could help."

Uncertainty flickered in her eyes. Her abrupt departure was probably at the urging of her cohorts in Las Cruces, alerted by my phone call of the night before. She might have suspected it was me, but she couldn't be sure. For my part, I was just hoping to stall until the cops showed up. I had no intention of confronting her. For all I knew, she might whip out a little two-shot Derringer or fly at me with some kind of old-lady karate-type move that would take me right out.

She checked her watch. It was now almost 4:00. It took twenty minutes to get to the airport and she'd have to be there by 4:30 or risk losing her seat. That gave her ten minutes. "Oh dear. Well, I don't know why my taxi isn't here. I might need a ride to the airport, if you could do that," she said.

"No problem," I said. "My car's right down the street. Henry said you'd be stopping by his place anyway to say good-bye."

"Of course I am, if I have time. He's such a sweetie." She finished laying in the armload of clothes and I could see her look around the room to see if she'd missed anything.

"Did you leave anything in the bathroom? Shampoo? Hand laundry?"

"Oh, I believe I did. I'll be right back." She moved past me, heading for the bathroom.

I waited until she rounded the corner and then reached over and opened her purse. Inside was a fat manila envelope with Henry's name penciled on the front. I took off the rubber band and checked the contents. Cash. I closed her purse again and tucked the envelope into the waistband of my jeans at the small of my back. I figured Henry was never going to press charges and I hated to see his savings confiscated and itemized as police property. No telling when he'd get it back. I was just adjusting my T-shirt over the bulge when she returned, toting shampoo, shower cap, hand lotion. She tucked them in around the sides of her folded clothes and closed up the suitcase, snapping the locks shut.

"Here, I'll get it," I said. I hauled that suitcase off the bed and picked up the other one, moving out into the hall like a pack mule. Moza was standing there, wringing out an imaginary dish towel in her anxiety.

"I can take one of those," she said.

"I got it."

I headed for the door, with Moza and Lila bringing up the rear. I certainly hoped the cops would show. Lila and Moza were saying those last-minute things to one another, Lila faking it out the whole time. She was taking off. She was gone. She had no intention of coming back.

As we reached the front, Moza moved ahead so she could hold the screen door open for me. A black-and-white patrol car had just pulled up in front. I was afraid if Lila spotted them too soon, she'd bolt for the rear.

"Did you get that pair of shoes under the bed?" I asked over my shoulder. I paused in the doorway, blocking her view.

"I don't know. I just looked and I didn't see any."

"You probably got them, then," I said.

"No, no. I better check." She hurried toward the bedroom while I set the two suitcases on the porch.

Moza, meanwhile, was staring at the street with puzzlement. Two uniformed officers were coming up the walk, one
male, one female, both bareheaded, in short-sleeved shirts.
In Santa Teresa, there's been a move afoot to divest the police of their authoritarian images, but these two managed to
seem ominous anyway. Moza probably thought she'd violated some civil code—grass too long, TV too loud.

I left her to have a little conversation with them while I
herded Lila up this way, so she wouldn't spot the cops and
try slipping out the back. "Lila, your ride's here," I called.

"Well thank heaven for that," she said, as she came
through the living room. "I didn't find anything under the
bed, but I'd left my ticket right up on the chest, so it's lucky
I went back."

As she reached the front door, I eased behind her. She
glanced up, catching sight of the officers.

The guy, according to his name tag, was G. Pettigrew. He
was black, maybe in his thirties, with big arms and a barrel
chest. His partner, M. Gutierrez, looked almost as hefty as
he.

Pettigrew's eyes settled on Lila. "Are you Lila Sams?"

"Yes." She loaded that one syllable with puzzlement,
blinking at him. Her body seemed to change so that she
looked older and more squat.

"Could you step out onto the porch, please?"

"Of course, but I can't think what this is about." Lila
made a move toward her purse, but Gutierrez intercepted,
checking the contents quickly for weapons.

Pettigrew told Lila she was under arrest, reciting her
rights to her from a card he held. I could tell he'd done it all
a hundred times and didn't really need the cue, but he read
it anyway so there wouldn't be any question later.

"Could you turn around and face the wall, please?"

Lila did as she was told and Gutierrez did a pat-down,
then snapped on a pair of handcuffs. Lila was starting to
wail pitifully. "But what have I done? I haven't done anything. This is all a terrible mistake." Her desperation
seemed to set Moza off.

"What's going on, officer?" Moza said. "This woman is my tenant. She hasn't done anything wrong."

"Ma'am, we'd appreciate it if you'd step back, please. Mrs. Sams is entitled to contact an attorney when we get downtown." Pettigrew touched at Lila's elbow, but she pulled away, her voice rising to a shrill pitch.

"Help! Oh no! Let go of me. Help!"

The two officers took control of her, one on either side, moving her off the porch at a businesslike pace, but Lila's shrieks were beginning to bring curious neighbors out onto their porches. She went limp, sagging heavily between them, craning her face toward Moza with a piteous cry. They hustled her into the squad car, picking her feet up to deposit her in the rear. Lila somehow conveyed the impression that this was a Gestapo arrest, that she was being hauled off by the Nazis and might never be heard from again. Shaking his head, Officer Pettigrew gathered up her belongings, which were now strewn along the walk. He tucked her suitcases in the trunk.

The man next door apparently felt called upon to intercede and I saw him in conversation with Pettigrew while Gutierrez called in to the station and Lila thrashed about, flinging herself at the mesh that separated her from Gutierrez in the front seat. Finally Pettigrew got in the car on the driver's side, slamming the door shut, and they pulled away.

Moza was dead white and she turned a stricken face to me. "This was your doing! What in heaven's name were you thinking of? The poor woman."

But I'd caught sight of Henry half a block away. Even at that distance, his face seemed blank with disbelief, his body tense. "I'll talk to you later, Moza," I said and headed toward him.

25

By the time I reached my place, Henry was nowhere in sight. I pulled the envelope out of my waistband and knocked on his back door. He opened it. I held the envelope up and he took it, glancing at the contents. He gave me a searching look, but I didn't explain how I'd come by it and he didn't ask.

"Thank you."

"We'll talk later," I said, and he closed the door again, but not before I caught a glimpse of his kitchen counter. He had gotten out the sugar canister and a new blue-and-white sack of flour, turning to the activity he knew best while he worked through his pain. I felt awful for him but I had to let him sort it out for himself. God, it was all so unpleasant. In the meantime, I had to get back to work.

I let myself into my apartment and got out the telephone book, looking for Kelly Borden. If Bobby'd been searching for the gun out at the old county building, I wanted to have a crack at it too and I thought maybe Kelly could tell me where to start. No sign of him in the telephone book. I tried to find the number for the former medical facility, but there wasn't a listing for it and the information operator was being obtuse, pretending she had no idea what I was talking about. If he worked a seven-to-three shift, he'd be gone anyway. Shit. I looked up the number of Santa Teresa Hospital and put a call in to Dr. Fraker. His secretary, Marcy, told me he was "away from his desk" (meaning in the men's room), but would be back shortly. I told her I needed to talk to Kelly Borden and asked for his address and telephone number.

"Gee, I don't know," she said. "Dr. Fraker probably wouldn't mind my giving you the information, but I'm not really supposed to do it without his O.K."

"Look, I've got some errands to run anyway so why don't I stop by. It'll take me ten minutes," I said. "Just make sure he doesn't leave work before I get there."

I drove over to St. Terry's. Parking turned out to be a trick and I had to leave my car three blocks away, which was okay with me because I had to stop at a drugstore. I went in through the back entrance, following varicolored lines on the floor, as though on my way to Oz. Finally, I reached a set of elevators and took one down to the basement.

By the time I reached Pathology, Dr. Fraker was off again, but Marcy had told him I was coming and he'd instructed her to forward me, like a piece of mail. I trailed after her through the lab and finally came across him in surgical greens, standing at a stainless-steel counter with a sink, disposal, and hanging scales. He was apparently about to launch into some procedure and I was sorry I had to interrupt.

"I really didn't mean to disturb you," I said. "All I need is Kelly Borden's address and telephone number."

"Pull up a chair," he said, indicating a wooden stool at one end of the counter. And then to Marcy, "Why don't you look up the information for Kinsey and I'll keep her amused in the meantime."

As soon as she departed, I pulled the stool over and perched.

For the first time, I cued in to what Fraker was actually doing. He was wearing surgical gloves, scalpel in hand. There was a white plastic carton on the counter, a one-pint size, like the kind used for chicken livers in the meat section of the supermarket. As I watched, he dumped out a glistening blob of organs, which he began to sort through with a pair of long tweezers. Against my will, I felt my gaze fix on this small pile of human flesh. Our entire conversation was conducted while he trimmed off snippets from each of several organs.

I could feel my lips purse in distaste. "What are those?"

His expression was mild, impersonal, and amused. He used the tweezers to point, touching each of several hunks in turn. I half expected the little morsels to draw away from his probing, like live slugs, but none of them moved. "Well, let's see. That's a heart. Liver. Lung. Spleen. Gall bladder.

This fella died suddenly during surgery and nobody can figure out what his problem was."

"And you can? Just from doing that?"

"Well, not always, but I think we'll come up with something in this case," he said.

I didn't think I'd ever look at stew meat in quite the same way. I couldn't take my eyes away from his dicing process and I couldn't get it through my head that these had once been functioning parts of a human being. If he was aware of my fascination, he didn't give any indication of it and I tried to be as nonchalant about the whole deal as he was.

He glanced over at me. "How does Kelly Borden figure into this?"

"I'm not sure," I said. "Sometimes I have to look at things that end up having no connection whatever to a case. Maybe it's the same as what you do—inspecting all the pieces of the puzzle until you come up with a theory."

"I suspect this is a lot more scientific than what you do," he remarked.

"Oh, no doubt about it," I said. "But I'll tell you one advantage I have."

He paused, looking over at me again, but with the first genuine interest I'd seen.

"I know the man whose death I'm dealing with and I have a personal stake in the outcome. I think he was murdered and it pisses me off. Disease is neutral. Homicide's not."

"I think your feeling for Bobby is coloring your judgment. His death was accidental."

"Maybe. Or maybe I can persuade Homicide that he died as a result of a murder attempt nine months ago."

"If you can prove that," he said. "So far I gather you don't have much to go on, which is where your work differs from mine. I can probably come up with something conclusive here and I won't have to leave the room."

"I do envy you that," I said. "I mean, I don't doubt Bobby was killed, but I don't have any idea who did it and I may never have any evidence."

"Then I have it all over you," he said. "For the most part, I deal in certainty. Once in a while, I'm stumped, but not often."

"You're lucky."

Marcy returned with Kelly's address and telephone number on a slip of paper, which she handed to me.

"I prefer to think I'm talented," he was saying wryly. "I better not keep you in any case. Let me know how it comes out."

"I'll do that. Thanks for this," I said, holding up the slip of paper.

It was now five o'clock. I found a pay phone in an offshoot of one of the hospital corridors and tried Kelly's number.

He picked up on the third ring. I identified myself, reminding him of Dr. Fraker's introduction.

"I know who you are."

"Listen," I said, "could I stop by and talk to you? There's something I need to check out."

He seemed to hesitate at first. "Sure, O.K. You know where I am?"

Kelly's apartment was on the west side of town, not far from St. Terry's. I trotted back to my car and drove over to an address on Castle. I parked in front of a frame duplex and walked down a long driveway to a small wooden outbuilding at the rear of the property. His place, like mine, had probably been a garage at one time.

As I rounded some shrubs, I spotted him sitting on his front step, smoking a joint. He wore jeans and a leather vest over a plaid shirt, feet bare. His hair was pulled back in the same neat braid, beard and mustache looking grayer somehow than I remembered. He seemed very mellow, except for his eyes, which were aquamarine and impossible to read. He held the joint out to me, but I declined with a shake of my head.

"Didn't I see you at Bobby's funeral?" I asked.

"Might have. I saw you." His eyes settled on me with a disconcerting gaze. Where had I seen that color before? In a swimming pool where a dead man was floating like a lily pad. That had been four years ago, one of the first investigations I ever did.

"Chair over there if you have time to sit." He managed to get this sentence out while holding his breath, dope smoke locked in his lungs.

I glanced around and spotted an old wooden lawn chair, which I dragged over to the step. Then I took the address

book out of my handbag and passed it to him, open to the
back cover. "Any idea who this is? It's not a local number."

He glanced at the penciled entry and then gave me a
quick look. "You tried calling?"

"Sure. I also tried the only Blackman listed in the book.
It's a disconnect. Why? Do you know who it is?"

"I know the number, but it's not a telephone listing.
Bobby moved the hyphen over."

"What's it for? I don't understand."

"These first two digits indicate Santa Teresa County. Last
five are the morgue code. This is the I.D. number on a
body we got in storage. I told you we had two that had been
out there for years. This is Franklin."

"But why list it under Blackman?"

Kelly smiled at me, taking a long pull off his joint before
he spoke. "Franklin's black. He's a black man. Maybe it was
Bobby's joke."

"Are you sure?"

"Reasonably sure. You can check it yourself if you don't
believe me."

"I think he was searching for a handgun out there. Would
you have any idea where he might have started?"

"Nope. Place is big. They must have eighty, ninety rooms
out there that haven't been used in years. Could be anywhere. Bobby would have worked his shift by himself. He
had the run of the building as long as no one found out he
was away from his work."

"Well. I guess I'll just have to wing it. I appreciate your
help."

"No problem."

I went back to my office. Kelly Borden had told me that a
kid named Alfie Leadbetter would be working the three-to-
eleven shift at the morgue. The guy was a friend of his and
he said he'd call ahead and let him know I was coming out.

I hauled out my typewriter again and made some notes.
What was this? What did the corpse of a black man have to
do with the murder of Dwight Costigan and the blackmailing of his former wife?

The phone rang and I picked it up like an automaton, my
mind on the problem at hand. "Yes?"

"Kinsey?"

"Speaking."

"I wasn't sure that was you. This is Jonah. You always answer that way?"

I focused. "God, sorry. What can I do for you?"

"I heard about something I thought might interest you. You know that Callahan accident?"

"Sure. What about it?"

"I just ran into the guy who works Traffic and he says the lab boys went over the car this afternoon. The brake lines were cut just as clean as you please. They transferred the whole case to Homicide."

I could feel myself doing the same kind of mental double take I'd done just minutes before when I finally heard what the name Blackman meant. "What?"

"Your friend Bobby Callahan was murdered," Jonah said patiently. "The brake lines on his car had been cut, which means all the brake fluid ran out, which means he crashed into that tree because he rounded the curve with no way to slow down."

"I thought the autopsy showed he had a stroke."

"Maybe he did when he realized what was happening. That's not inconsistent as far as I can tell."

"Oh, you're right." For a moment I just breathed in Jonah's ear. "How long would that take?"

"What, cutting the brake lines or the fluid running out?"

"Both, now that you mention it."

"Oh, probably five minutes to cut the lines. That's no big deal if you know where to look. The other depends. He probably could have driven the car for a little while, pumped the brakes once or twice. Next thing he knew, he'd have tried 'em and boom, gone."

"So it happened that night? Whoever cut the lines?"

"Had to. The kid couldn't have driven far."

I was dead silent, thinking of the message Bobby'd left on my machine. He'd seen Kleinert the night he died. I remember Kleinert mentioning it too.

"You there?"

"I don't know what it means, Jonah," I said. "This case is starting to break and I just can't figure out what's going on."

"You want me to come over and we'll talk it out?"

"Not, not yet. I need to be by myself. Let me call you later when I have more to go on."

"Sure. You've got my home number, haven't you?"

"Better give it to me again," I said and jotted it down.

"Now, listen," he said to me. "Swear to me you won't do anything stupid."

"How can I do anything stupid? I don't even know what's going on," I said. "Besides, 'stupid' is after the fact. I always feel smart when I think things up."

"God damn it, you know what I'm talking about."

I laughed. "You're right. I know. And believe me, I'll call you if anything comes up. Honestly, my sole object in life is to protect my own ass."

"Well," he said grudgingly. "That's good to hear, but I doubt it."

We said our good-byes and he hung up. I left my hand on the receiver.

I tried Glen's number. I felt she should have the information and I couldn't be sure the cops would bring her up to date, especially since, at this point, they probably didn't have any more answers than I did.

She picked up the phone and I told her what was going on, including the business about Blackman in Bobby's address book. Of necessity, I told her as much as I knew about the blackmailing business. Hell, why not? This was no time to keep secrets. She already knew that Nola and Bobby were lovers. She might as well understand what he had undertaken in Nola's behalf. I even took the liberty of mentioning Sufi's involvement, though I still wasn't sure about that. I suspected that she was a go-between, ferrying messages between Nola and Bobby, counseling Bobby, perhaps, when his passion clashed with his youthful impatience.

She was quiet for a moment in the same way I had been. "What happens now?"

"I'll talk to Homicide tomorrow and tell them everything I know. They can handle it after that."

"Be careful in the meantime," she said.

"No sweat."

26

There was still an hour and a half of daylight left when I reached the old county medical complex. From the number of parking spaces available, it was clear that most of the offices were closed, personnel gone for the day. Kelly had told me there was a second parking lot around the side that was used by the janitorial staff at night. I didn't see any reason to park that far away. I pulled into a slot as close to the entrance as I could get, noting with interest that there was a bicycle chained to a rack just off to my left. It was a banged-up old Schwinn with fat tires and a fake license plate wired onto the rear, reading "Alfie." Kelly had told me the building was generally locked up by seven, but that I could buzz in and Alfie would buzz back to admit me.

I grabbed my flashlight and my key picks, pausing to pull a sweatshirt over my tank top. I remembered the building as chilly, even more so, I imagined, if I was there after sunset. I locked my car and headed for the entrance.

I paused at the double doors in front and pressed a bell to my right. After a moment, the door buzzed back, releasing the lock, and I went in. The lobby was already accumulating shadows and reminded me vaguely of an abandoned train station in a futuristic movie. It had that same air of vintage elegance: inlaid marble floors, high ceilings, beautiful woodwork of buffed oak. The few remaining fixtures must have been there since the twenties, when the place was built.

I crossed the lobby, glancing idly at the wall directory as I passed. Almost subliminally, a name caught my eye. I paused and looked again. Leo Kleinert had an office out here, which I hadn't realized before. Had Bobby driven this far for weekly psychiatric sessions? Seemed a bit out of the way. I went downstairs, footsteps scratching on the tile steps. As before, I could feel the temperature dropping, like a descent into the waters of a lake. Down here, it was gloomier, but the glass door to the morgue was lighted, a bright rectangle in the gathering darkness of the hall. I checked my watch. It wasn't even 7:15.

I tapped on the glass for form's sake and then tried the knob. It was unlocked. I opened the door and peered in.

"Hello?"

There was no one in evidence, but that had happened to me before when Dr. Fraker and I had visited. Maybe Alfie was in the refrigerated storage room where the bodies were kept.

"Heellloo!"

No response. He'd buzzed me in, so he had to be around here someplace.

I closed the door behind me. The fluorescent lighting was harsh, giving the illusion of winter sunlight. There was a door to my left. I crossed and knocked before I opened it to find an empty office with a dark brown Naugahyde couch. Maybe the guy on the graveyard shift snagged some shut-eye in here when nothing else was going on. There was a desk and a swivel chair. The outside of the window was covered with ornamental wrought-iron burglar bars, the daylight blocked out by a mass of unruly shrubs. I closed the door and moved over to the refrigerated room where the bodies were kept, peering in.

No Alfie in sight. Inside, the light was constant, occupants laid out on blue fiberglass berths, engaged in their eternal, motionless naps, some wrapped in sheets, some in plastic, necks and ankles wound with what looked like masking tape. Somehow, it reminded me of quiet time at summer camp.

I returned to the main room and sat for a while, staring at the autopsy table. My customary procedure would have been to snoop into every cabinet, drawer, and storage bin, but it felt disrespectful here. Or maybe I was afraid I'd stumble onto something grotesque: trays of dentures, a Mason jar chock-full of floating eyeballs. I don't know what I thought I'd see. I shifted restlessly. I felt as if I were wasting time. I went to the door and looked out into the hall, tilting my head to listen. Nothing.

"Alfie?" I called. I listened again, then shrugged and closed the door. It occurred to me that as long as I was there, I could at least verify that the number Bobby'd written down was, in fact, the same as the number on Franklin's toe tag. That wouldn't do any harm. I took the address book out of my handbag and turned to the penciled entry on the back cover. I went into the cold-storage room again, moving from body to body, checking I.D. tags. This was like some kind of bargain-basement sale only nothing was marked down.

When I got to the third body, the numbers matched. Kelly was right. Bobby'd shifted the hyphen over so the seven-digit code looked like a telephone number. I stared at the body, or what I could see of it. The plastic that Franklin was wrapped in was transparent but yellowing, as though stained with nicotine. Through the swaddling, I could see that he was a middle-aged black man of medium height, slim, with a face of stone. Why was this corpse significant? I was feeling anxious. I figured Alfie would be back shortly and I really didn't want to be caught nosing around in here. I went back to my chair.

Coming out of the cold-storage room was like leaving an air-conditioned theater. It made the autopsy room feel balmy by comparison. I was getting itchy to explore. I couldn't help myself. I was irritated that no one was there to help me and feeling edgy from the quiet. This was not a fun place. Ordinarily, I don't hang out in morgues and it was making me tense.

Just to soothe my nerves, I peered into a drawer, testing the contents against the grisly images I'd conjured up. This one contained scratch pads, order blanks, and miscellaneous paper supplies. Reassured, I tried the next drawer: small vials of several drugs, the names of which I did not recognize. I was warming up here and I checked on down the line. Everything appeared to be related to the business of dissecting the dead; not surprising, given the locale, but not very enlightening.

I straightened up and looked around the room. Where were the files? Didn't anybody keep records around this place? Somebody had mentioned that there were medical charts stored out here, but where? This floor? Somewhere on one of the floors above? I didn't relish the idea of creeping through the empty building by myself. I'd been picturing Alfie Leadbetter at my side, telling me what was accessible and where I might start. I'd even pictured slipping him a twenty-dollar bill if that's what it took to enlist his aid.

I glanced at my watch. I'd now been here forty-five minutes and I wanted some results. I grabbed my handbag and went out in the hall, looking in both directions. It was getting darker down here, although I could see through a window at the end of the hall that it was still light outside. I found a wall switch and flipped on the lights and then I wandered along the corridor, reading the small white signs mounted above each office door. The radiology offices were right next to the morgue. Beyond that, Nuclear Medicine, and nursing offices. I wondered if Sufi Daniels had occasion to come out here.

Something was beginning to stir at the back of my brain. I was thinking about the cardboard box full of Bobby's belongings. What was in it? Medical texts and office supplies and two radiology manuals. What was he actually doing with those? He hadn't even been a medical student and I couldn't think why he'd need the manuals for equipment he might not be using for years, if ever. He'd indicated no particular interest in radiology.

I went upstairs. It wouldn't hurt to look at that stuff again. When I reached the front entrance, I slipped off my sweatshirt and wedged it in the opening. I could push the door open with no problem, but I didn't want the lock snapping shut behind me as I went out. I crossed to my car and unlocked it, wrestling the carton out the backseat. I removed the two radiology books and leafed through them quickly. These were technical manuals for specific equipment, information about the various gauges and dials and switches, with a lot of esoteric talk about exposures, rads, and roentgens. At the top of one page was a penciled number, like a doodle, surrounded by curlicues. Franklin's again. The sight of the now familiar seven-digit code

seemed eerie, like the sound of Bobby's voice on my answering machine five days after he died.

I tucked the two manuals under my arm and locked my
car again, leaving the box on the front seat. Slowly, I returned to the building. I let myself in, pausing to pull on
my sweatshirt. As long as I was on the first floor, I did a
superficial survey. I kept thinking it was medical records I
was looking for, the handgun tucked down in a banker's box
packed with old charts. This had been a working hospital at
one time and there had to be a records department somewhere. Where else would old charts be kept? If my memory
of St. Terry's served me, the Medical Records Department
was fairly centrally located so that doctors and other authorized personnel would have easy access.

Not many offices on this floor appeared to be occupied. I
tried door handles randomly. Most were locked. I rounded
the corner at the end of the hall and there it was, "Medical
Records" painted above a set of double doors in a faded
scrawl. I could see now that many of the old departments
were similarly marked: florid lettering on a painted scroll,
as though by declaration of the conquistadors.

I tried the knob, expecting to have to experiment with
my key picks. Instead, the door swung open with a low-
pitched creak that might have been contrived by a special-
effects man. Waning daylight filtered in. The room yawned
before me, barren, stripped of everything. No file cabinets,
no furniture, no fixtures. A crumpled cigarette pack, some
loose boards, and a couple of bent nails were scattered
across the floor. This department had literally been dismantled at some point and God only knew where the old
records were now. It was possible they were somewhere in
one of the abandoned hospital rooms above, but I really
didn't want to go up there by myself. I'd promised Jonah I
wouldn't be stupid and I was trying to be a good scout on
that score. Besides, something else was nagging at me.

I returned to the stairs, descending. What was that little
voice in the back of my head murmuring? It was like a radio
playing in the next room. I could pick up only a faint phrase
now and then.

When I reached the basement, I crossed to the radiology
office and tried the knob. Locked. I got out my key picks

and played around for a while. This was one of those "burglar-proof" locks that *can* be picked, but it really is a pain in the ass. Still, I wanted to see what was in there and I worked patiently. I was using a set of rocker picks, with random depth cuts spaced along the top, the back side of each pick ground to an oval. The whole idea is that with enough different cut combinations, together with an applied rocking motion, somewhere along the way all the pins will, by chance, be raised to the shear line at the same time, popping the lock.

Like hiding, the only way to approach the whole process is to give oneself up to it. I stood there for maybe twenty minutes, easing the pick forward, rocking it, applying slight pressure when I felt movement of any sort. Lo and behold, the sucker gave way and I let out a little exclamation of delight. "Oh, wow. Hey, that's great." It's this sort of shit that makes my job fun. Also illegal, but who was going to tell?

I eased into the office. I flipped the overhead light on. It looked like ordinary office space. Typewriters and telephones and file cabinets, plants on the desks, pictures on the walls. There was a small reception area where I imagined patients seated, waiting to be called for their X rays. I wandered through some of the rooms in the rear, picturing the procedures for chest X rays and mammograms, upper G.I. series. I stood in front of the machines and opened one of the manuals I'd brought in from the car.

I checked the diagrams against the various dials and gauges on the X-ray equipment itself. It was a match, more or less. Maybe some variation according to year, make, or model of the actual machinery installed. Some of it looked like the stuff of science fiction. Massive nose cone on a swinging arm. I stood there, manual open in my arms, pages pressed to my chest while I stared at the table and the lead apron that looked like a baby bib for a giant. I thought about the X rays I'd had taken of my left arm two months ago, just after I'd been shot.

It wasn't as if the idea came to me all at once. It formed around me, like fairy dust, gradually taking shape. Bobby had been out here all by himself, just like this. Night after night, searching for the handgun that had Nola's fingerprints on it. He knew who had hidden it, so he must have formed some kind of theory about the hiding place. I had to guess that he'd found the gun and that's why he was killed. Maybe he'd actually retrieved it, but I didn't think so. I'd been operating on the assumption that it was still hidden out here and that still seemed like a good bet. He'd made some little notes to himself, doodling the I.D. number of a corpse in his little red book and again in the pages of a radiology manual he'd acquired.

The phrases running through my head began to connect. Maybe you should X-ray the corpse, said I to myself. Maybe that's what Bobby did and maybe that's why he made the penciled notation in the radiology book. Maybe the gun is *inside* the corpse. I thought about it briefly, but I couldn't see why I shouldn't give it a try. The worst that could happen (aside from my getting caught) was that I'd be wasting time and making a colossal fool of myself. This would not be a first.

I left my handbag and the manuals on one of the X-ray tables and went next door to the morgue. In the refrigerated storage room, I spotted a gurney against the right wall. I was on automatic pilot by now, simply doing what I knew had to be done. There was still no sign of Alfie Leadbetter and no one was going to help me. I might be wrong, so maybe it was just as well that no one knew what I was up to. The building was deserted. It was early yet. Even if I fumbled the X-ray procedure, it couldn't hurt the dead man.

I rolled the gurney over to the fiberglass bunk where the body lay. I pretended I was a morgue attendant. I pretended I was an X-ray technician or a nurse, some thoroughly professional person with a job to do.

"Sorry to disturb you, Frank," I said, "but you have to go next door for some tests. You're not looking so good."

Tentatively, I reached out and eased a hand under Franklin's neck and knees and pulled, slipping him from his resting place onto the gurney. He was surprisingly light, and cold to the touch, about the consistency of a package of raw chicken breasts just out of the fridge. God, I thought, why do I plague myself with these domestic images? I'd never be motivated to learn to cook at this rate.

It took incredible maneuvering to get the gurney through the morgue and out into the corridor, then into the reception area of the radiology offices and into one of the X-ray rooms in the rear. I lined the gurney up parallel to the X-ray table and shoved the body into place. I raised and lowered the nose cone a couple of times experimentally, sliding it along its overhead track until it was right over Franklin's abdomen. At some point, I was going to have to figure out how far away from the body it should be. Meanwhile, since I intended to take some pictures, I thought I better find some film of some kind.

I looked through the four cabinets in the room and found nothing. I circled the room. There was a shallow cupboard mounted on the wall, like a fuse box with double doors. A strip of masking tape was pasted on one side, with the word *exposed* printed on it in ballpoint pen. A second strip of tape said *unexposed*. I opened that door. There were film cassettes of varying sizes lined up like serving trays. I took one out.

I went over to the table and studied the layout of the machinery. I didn't see any way to slide the cassette into the apparatus above the table, but there was a sliding tray in the table itself, just under the padded edge. I pulled it out and inserted the cassette. I hoped I had guessed right about which side should be up. Looked right to me. Maybe I could fashion a whole new career out of this.

I figured Franklin didn't need protecting, so I picked up the full-length lead apron and put it on myself, feeling somehow like the goalie in a hockey match. Actually, I'd never seen an X-ray technician running around in one of these things, but it made me feel secure. I pointed the nose cone at Franklin's belly, about three feet up, and then went behind the screen in one corner of the room.

I checked the manual again, leafing through until I found diagrams that seemed relevant. There were numerous gauges with little arrow-shaped pointers at rest, ready to whip into the green zone, the yellow, or the red at the flick of a switch. There was a lever on the right marked "power supply," which I flipped to the "on" position. Nothing went on. A puzzlement. I flipped it off and then checked the wall to my left. There were two breaker boxes with big switches that I shifted from "off" to "on." There was a murmur of power being generated. I flipped the power supply lever to "on" again. The machine came on. I smiled. That was great.

I studied the panel in front of me. There was a timer that would apparently have to be set on a scale from 1/120 of a second to six seconds. A gauge for kilovolts. One marked "milliamperes." God, three rows of lighted green squares to choose from. I started with a midrange setting on everything, figuring I could use one gauge as a control and adjust the other two in some sort of rotating system. In between, I would check my results on the finished film and see what kind of picture I was getting.

I peered around the screen. "O.K., Frank, take a deep breath and hold."

Well, at least he got the "holding" part right.

I pressed the switch on the handgrip. I heard a brief bzzt. Cautiously, I came out from behind the screen as though X rays might still be flying around the room. I crossed to the table and removed the cassette. Now what? There had to be some kind of developing process, but it didn't appear to be in here. I left the machine on and carried the cassette with me, checking into rooms nearby.

Two doors away, I found what looked right to me. On the wall was a flow chart, giving the step-by-step procedure for developing plates. I could get a job out here after this.

Again, it was necessary to switch the power on. After that, I worked in the dull red glow of the safelights, squinting my way through the process slowly. I filled the wall-mounted tank with water as specified. I flipped the cassette over and unlatched the back, removing the film, which I eased into the tray. It disappeared into the machine with a sound.

Shoot, where'd it go? I couldn't see anything in the room that looked like it would produce a piece of processed film. I felt like a puppy learning what happens when a ball rolls under the couch. I left the room and went next door. The hind end of the automatic developer was there, looking like a big Xerox machine with a slot. I waited. A minute and a half later, a finished piece of film slid out. I looked at it. Pitch black. Shit. What had I done wrong? How could it be overexposed when I'd been so careful? I stared at the developer. The lid was open a crack. I peered at it. Experimentally, I gave it a push. It snapped shut. Maybe that would do it.

I went back into the other room and got a second cassette out and went through the entire process again. Two rounds later, I found what I was looking for. The overall quality of the picture was poor, but the image was distinct. In the center of Franklin's belly was the solid white silhouette of a handgun. It looked like a large-frame automatic, arranged at an angle, maybe to accommodate his skeletal structure or internal organs. There was something unnerving about the sight. I rolled up the X ray and put a rubber band around it. Time to get out of here.

Hastily, I shut down the machinery and shifted Franklin onto the cart for the ride back to the morgue, turning off lights and locking up the office in my wake.

I navigated the gurney back through the hall and into the morgue. I was easing Franklin onto his berth again when something caught my eye. I glanced over at the next tier of bunks. A man's hand was resting just about at eye level and it didn't look right. The bodies I'd seen had been deadly pale, the flesh like a doll's skin, rubbery and unreal. This hand seemed too pink. I could see now that the body itself was only loosely covered with plastic sheeting. Had it been there before? I moved closer, reaching out hesitantly. I think I made that little humming sound you make when you're close to a shriek, but haven't yet committed yourself.

Tentatively, I lifted the plastic away from the face. Male, white, in his twenties. There was no pulse evident but that was probably because there was a ligature wound around his neck so tightly that it had all but disappeared, sinking into the flesh until his tongue bugged out. The body was cool, but not cold. I stopped breathing. I thought my heart would stop as well. I was reasonably sure I'd just made the acquaintance of Alfie Leadbetter, newly deceased. At that instant I wasn't as worried about who had killed him as who had buzzed the door open to let me in. I didn't think it was Alf. I suddenly suspected that I'd been cruising around that deserted building in the company of a killer who was undoubtedly still there, waiting to see what I was up to, wait-

ing to do to me what had been done to the hapless morgue
attendant who'd gotten in the way.

I backed out of the room as fast as I could, my heart banging away, sending sick spurts of fear through my electrified
frame. The morgue was reassuringly bright, but so deadly
still.

Mentally, I traced an escape route, wondering what
choices I had. The windows down here were covered with
burglar bars too narrow to slip through. The exterior doors
were heavy glass, embedded with wire that I might or
might not be able to penetrate. I certainly wasn't going to
smash through them without calling attention to myself. I'd
have to try for the stairs, pushing out of the same double
doors I'd come through in the first place, though the idea of
even going out into the *hall* at this point was nearly more
than I could bear.

Somewhere above me, a door slammed and I jumped. I
heard someone coming down the stairs, whistling aimlessly.
A security guard? Someone coming back after work? I absolutely could not move. It was too late for action, too late for
escape, and there was no place to hide. Transfixed, I stared
at the door as footsteps approached. Someone paused in the
corridor, singing the first few snatches of "Someone to
Watch over Me." The knob turned and Dr. Fraker came in,
glancing up, startled, at the sight of me.

"Oh! Hello. I didn't expect to see you here," he said. "I
thought you were off talking to Kelly."

I let out a breath and found my voice. "I did that. A little
while ago."

"Jesus, what's wrong? You're as white as a ghost."

I shook my head. "I was just on my way out when I heard
the door slam. You scared the shit out of me." My voice
cracked in the middle of the sentence as if I'd just reached
puberty.

"Sorry. I didn't mean to spook you like that." He had on
his surgical greens. I watched him cross the counter and
open a drawer, taking out instruments. From the next
drawer down, he took out a vial and a syringe.

"Listen, we've got a problem," I said.

"Oh really. What's that?" Dr. Fraker turned to smile at
me and Nola's line popped into my head. "We're talking

about a lunatic. Someone so crazy," she had whispered. Dr. Fraker's eyes were fixed on mine as he filled the syringe. The penny dropped. She hadn't wanted to stay *in* the marriage. She had wanted *out*. Bobby Callahan in his naïveté had thought he could help.

It was there in his face and the lazy way he moved. This man meant to kill me. Judging from the tools he'd assembled, he had all of the equipment he needed—nice table with a drain, hacksaws, scalpels, a working disposal just under the sink. He knew anatomy too, all the tendons and ligaments. I pictured a turkey wing, how you have to bend it backward to ease the blade into that joint.

I usually cry when I'm scared and I could feel tears well up. Not sorrow, but horror. Given all the lies I'd told in my life, right then I couldn't think of one. My mind was empty of thought. There I stood with the X ray in my hand, the truth, I'm sure, written all over my face. My only hope was to act before he did and move twice as fast.

I dove for the door, fumbling with the knob. I yanked it open and ran for the stairs, taking two at a time, then three, looking back with a moan of raw fear. He was coming out of the door, syringe held loosely in one hand. What scared me was that he was moving slowly, as if he had all the time in the world. He'd taken up the song lyric where he left off, a sort of tuneless rendition that didn't do the Gershwins justice.

"Like a little lamb who's lost in the wood . . . I know I could always be good . . . to one who'll watch over me . . ."

I reached the top of the stairs. What did he know that I didn't know? Why did he feel that this leisurely pace would suit when I was flying toward the entrance? I lowered a shoulder and slammed up against the double doors, but neither gave way. I rammed them again. The entranceway, locked like this, formed a small cul-de-sac. If I gave him time to reach the corridor, I'd have no way out. I reached the hall just as he got to the top of the stairs.

Chit, chit. I could hear his footsteps scratch on the tile while he sang on.

"Although he may not be the man some girls think of as handsome, to my heart he'll carry the key . . ."

Still taking his time. I wanted to scream, but what was the point? The building was empty. It was locked up tight. Dark except for the pale light filtering in from the parking lot. I needed a weapon. Dr. Fraker had his little syringe filled with whatever he meant to pop me with. He was a big guy too, and once he made contact, I was in trouble.

I flew down the hall to the old medical-records room and slammed the door back on its hinge. I snatched up a two-by-four, still running, and headed back out into the corridor, racing for the far end. There had to be stairs. There had to be windows to smash, *some* way out.

Behind me, from a man who couldn't even carry a tune, I heard . . . *"Won't you tell him please to put on some speed, follow my lead, oh how I need, someone to watch over me . . ."*

I reached the stairwell and headed up, beginning to analyze the situation as I ran. At this rate, he could chase me all over the building. I'd soon be exhausted and he wouldn't even be breaking a sweat. Not a good idea, this form of pursuit. I reached the landing and snatched for the door. Locked. There was just one more floor. Was I being trapped or herded? In either case, I had the feeling he was in charge, that he'd set this all up in advance.

He was just coming into the stairwell below me as I took to the stairs again, heading toward the third floor, the two-by-four clutched in my hot little hand. I didn't like this. The door at the third floor flew back at a touch and I stepped into the darkened hall. I took off to my right, forcing myself to slow my pace. I was out of breath from climbing the stairs, bathed in sweat. I considered searching out a place to hide, but my choices were limited. There were rooms opening off on either side of me, but I was afraid I was going to get cornered in one. All he had to do was check each one in turn and pretty soon he'd figure out where I was. Also I hate hiding. It turns me into a six-year-old and I'm sick of that. I wanted to be on my feet, in motion, taking action instead of crouching down with my hands held over my face hoping God had rendered me transparent.

I made another right-hand turn. Behind me, I heard the door to the third-floor landing slam shut. I spotted an elevator halfway down the corridor on the right-hand side. I sprinted, and when I reached it, pounded on the "down" button with my palm.

Dr. Fraker had just taken up a new tune, this time whistling the first few bars of "I Don't Stand a Ghost of a Chance with You." Was this man sick or what?

I banged on the button again, listening fervently as the elevator cable whirred softly on the other side of the door. I looked to my right. There he came, his surgical greens showing up as a pale glow in the shadows. I heard the mechanism stop. He seemed to be moving faster, but he was still twenty yards away from me. The elevator doors slid open. Oh fuck!

I stepped forward just as I flashed on the fact that there was nothing there except a yawning shaft and a gust of cold air wafting up from below. I caught myself half a second from tumbling into that pitch-black hole. A low cry escaped me as I caught at the doorframe, swinging out over the pit for an instant before I managed to right myself. I stumbled backward to safety but I'd lost my purchase. I was down and the two-by-four flew out of my hand, skittering off. I flipped over on my hands and knees scrambling toward it.

He had caught up to me by then and he grabbed me by the hair, hauling me upright just as my hand closed around the board. I swung it up, whacking at him. I made contact but the angle was awkward and there was no force behind the blow. I felt the sting of the needle in my left thigh. Both of us barked out a sound at the same time. Mine was a shrill yelp of pain and surprise, his the low grunt as the impact from the two-by-four registered. I had the advantage of a split second and I took it, lashing out with a side kick that caught him in the shin. No good, too low. The wisdom of self-defense would have it that there's no point in simply inflecting pain on your attacker. It'll just piss him off. Unless I could disable him, I didn't have a chance.

He grabbed at me from behind. I snapped my left elbow back, but again I was slightly off the mark. I pushed at him, kicking repeatedly at his shin until he backed off, breathing hard. I cracked him one across the shoulder with the two-by-four and ran, pounding down the hall. I stumbled briefly, but regained my footing. I felt as if I'd stepped in a hole, and it occurred to me belatedly that whatever he'd injected me with was taking effect. My left leg was feeling wobbly, my kneecap loose, both feet going numb. The same fear that had sent adrenaline coursing through my body was speeding some drug on its way. Like snakebite. They say you shouldn't run.

I glanced back. He was clutching his shoulder, just beginning to move in my direction, coming slowly again. He didn't seem worried that I'd get away, so I had to guess that he had jammed the door to the stairwell as he came through. Either that or he knew that the shit he'd popped me with would soon knock me out. I was losing contact with my extremities and I could scarcely sense my own grip on the board. A chill was seeping from my skin toward my core as if I were being put through a quick-freeze process for shipping to God knows where. I was working as hard as I could, but the darkness had become gelatinous and I felt slow. Time was grinding down too as my body labored against the drug. My mind was working, but I felt myself distracted by the odd sensations I experienced.

Oh, the bothersome details that finally fall into place like a little right-brain joke. It did come to me, in a flash, like a bubble through my veins, that Fraker was the one supplying Kitty with drugs, probably in exchange for information about Bobby's search for the gun. The stash in her bed-table drawer was a plant. He'd been there that night. Maybe he thought it was time to take her out, lest she in her guilt admit to her own duplicity where Bobby was concerned.

The distance to the corner of the hallway had been extended. I'd been running forever. The simple commands I was managing to send to my body were taking too long and I was losing the feedback system that records a response. Was I, in fact, running? Was I going anywhere? Sound was being stretched out, the echo of my own footsteps coming belatedly. I felt as if I were bounding down a corridor with a floor like a trampoline. Flash number two. Fraker had rigged the autopsy report. No seizure. He'd cut the brake lines. Too bad I hadn't figured it out before now. God, what a dummy I was.

I reached the corner slowing, and I could feel my body folding down on itself. As I rounded the corner, I had to pause. I propped myself against the wall, working to breathe. I had to clear my head. Stay upright. I had to lift my arms if I could. Time had begun to stretch out like taffy, long strands, sticky, hard to manage.

He was singing again, treating me to some oldies but goodies in his own private hit parade. He'd moved on now to "Accentuate the positive . . . eliminate the negative" . . . vowels dragged out like a phonograph record slowing when the power shuts off.

Even the voice in my own brain got hollow and remote. Crouch, Kinsey, it said.

I thought I might be crouching but I couldn't tell anymore where my legs were or my hips or much of my spine. My arms were feeling heavy and I wondered if my elbows were bent.

Batter up, the voice said and I believed, but couldn't have sworn to the fact, that I was drawing the two-by-four back, elbow crooked as my aunt had taught me long long ago.

Day was passing into night, life into death.

Fraker's voice droned out the song. "*Acceeennntuate the pooosssitive, eeeellliiiimindaate the neeegatiiiive . . .*"

When he came around the corner, I stepped into the swing, the two-by-four aimed straight at his face. I could see the board begin its march through space, like a series of time-lapse photographs, light against dark, closing down the distance. I felt the board connect with a sweet popping sound.

It was out of the ball park and I went down with the roar of the crowd in my ears.

Epilogue

They told me later, though I remember little of it, that I managed to make my way down to the morgue, where I dialed 911, mumbling a message that brought the cops. What comes back to me most clearly is the hangover I endured after the cocktail of barbiturates I was injected with. I woke in a hospital bed, as sick as a dog. But even with a pounding head, retching into a kidney-shaped plastic basin, I was glad to be among the living.

Glen spoiled me silly and everyone came to see me, including Jonah, Rosie, Gus, and Henry, bearing hot cross buns. Lila, he said, had written to him from a jail up north, but he didn't bother to reply. Glen never relented in her determination to reject both Derek and Kitty, but I introduced Kitty Wenner to Gus. Last I heard, they were dating and Kitty was cleaning up her act. Both had gained weight.

Dr. Fraker is currently out on bail, awaiting trial on charges of attempted murder and two counts of first-degree murder. Nola pleaded guilty to voluntary manslaughter, but served no time. When I got back to the office, I typed up my report, submitting a bill for thirty-three hours, plus mileage; a total I rounded off to an even $1000. The balance of Bobby's advance I returned to Varden Talbot's office to be factored into his estate. The rest of the report is a personal letter. Much of my last message to Bobby is devoted to the simple fact that I miss him. I hope, wherever he may be, that he sails among the angels, untethered and at peace.

—Respectfully submitted,
Kinsey Millhone

ABOUT THE AUTHOR

SUE GRAFTON has written novels, articles, short fiction, a screenplay, and numerous teleplays. She has also lectured on writing at colleges and conferences in Southern California and the Midwest. Her first mystery, 'A' IS FOR ALIBI, won an award from the Cloak and Clue Society of Wisconsin. 'B' IS FOR BURGLAR won both the Anthony and the Shamus awards for best novel of 1985, and 'C' IS FOR CORPSE won the Anthony Award for Best Novel in 1986. "The Parker Shotgun" won a Macavity Award from the Mystery Readers of America and an Anthony for Best Short Story of 1986. Grafton, who was born in Louisville, Kentucky, now lives in Southern California with her husband, Steven Humphrey.

Sue Grafton's

Kinsey Millhone is

"A refreshing heroine."
—*The Washington Post Book World*

"The best new private eye."
—*The Detroit News*

"A stand-out specimen of the new female operatives."
—*Philadelphia Inquirer*

"The gutsiest, grittiest female operative going."
—*Daily News,* New York

☐ "A" IS FOR ALIBI   27991-2 $5.99/$6.99 in Canada

☐ "B" IS FOR BURGLAR   28034-1 $5.99/$6.99 in Canada

☐ "C" IS FOR CORPSE   28036-8 $5.99/$6.99 in Canada

☐ "D" IS FOR DEADBEAT   27163-6 $5.99/$6.99 in Canada

☐ "E" IS FOR EVIDENCE   27955-6 $5.99/$6.99 in Canada

☐ "F" IS FOR FUGITIVE   28478-9 $5.99/$6.99 in Canada

"Once a fan reads one of Grafton's alphabetically titled detective novels, he or she will not rest until all the others are found."—*Los Angeles Herald Examiner*

Available at your local bookstore or use this page to order.
Send to: Bantam Books, Dept. BD 26
           2451 S. Wolf Road
           Des Plaines, IL 60018

Please send me the items I have checked above. I am enclosing
$_____ (please add $2.50 to cover postage and handling).
Send check or money order, no cash or C.O.D.'s, please.

Mr./Ms._____

Address_____

City/State_____ Zip_____

Please allow four to six weeks for delivery.
Prices and availability subject to change without notice.   BD 26 3/92

REX STOUT'S NERO WOLFE

A master of the form, Rex Stout is one of America's greatest mystery writers and Nero Wolfe is one of the greatest fictional detectives of all time. Together, they have entertained and puzzled millions of fans.

THE REX STOUT LIBRARY

An ongoing program dedicated to making available the complete set of Nero Wolfe mysteries, these special collector's editions will feature new introductions by today's best writers and never-before-published memorabilia from the life of Rex Stout.

- ☐ **Fer-de-Lance**, Introduction by Loren D. Estleman
  27819-3 $4.99/$5.99 in Canada
- ☐ **The League of Frightened Men**, Introduction by Robert Goldsborough 25933-4 $4.99/$5.99 in Canada
- ☐ **The Rubber Band**, Introduction by Nelson DeMille
  25550-9 $4.99/$5.99 in Canada
- ☐ **The Red Box**, Introduction by Carolyn G. Hart
  24919-3 $4.99/$5.99 in Canada
- ☐ **Where There's a Will**, Introduction by Dean R. Koontz
  29591-8 $4.99/$5.99 in Canada
- ☐ **The Final Deduction**, Introduction by Andrew M. Greeley
  25254-2 $4.99/$5.99 in Canada
- ☐ **The Hand in the Glove**, Introduction by Marcia Muller
  22857-9 $4.99/$5.99 in Canada
- ☐ **Black Orchids**, Introduction by Lawrence Block
  25719-6 $4.99/$5.99 in Canada
- ☐ **The Doorbell Rang**, Introduction by Stuart Kaminsky
  23721-7 $4.99/$5.99 in Canada
- ☐ **If Death Ever Slept**, Introduction by Robert B. Parker
  23649-0 $4.99/$5.99 in Canada

Available at your local bookstore or use this page to order.
Send to: Bantam Books, Dept. BD 17
           2451 S. Wolf Road
           Des Plaines, IL 60018

Please send me the items I have checked above. I am enclosing $_____ (please add $2.50 to cover postage and handling). Send check or money order, no cash or C.O.D.'s, please.

Mr./Ms._____

Address_____

City/State_____ Zip_____
Please allow four to six weeks for delivery.
Prices and availability subject to change without notice.   BD 17 7/92

HAPPIER DAYS

I took the elevator down to Tillie's and asked her if she had any photographs of Elaine. She disappeared in the direction of the den and after a few minutes returned with a Polaroid snapshot.

"This was taken last fall," Tillie said. "That's Elaine on the left."

"Who's the other woman?"

"Marty Grice, a neighbor of ours. Now that was an awful thing. She was killed . . . oh gosh, I guess six months back."

"What happened to her?"

"Well, they think she interrupted a burglar breaking into the house. I guess he killed her on the spot."

"That's too bad. Do you mind if I keep this?"

"Go right ahead."

I glanced at it again. The image was faintly disturbing, capturing a moment not long ago when both women grinned with such ease. Now, one was dead and the other missing. I didn't like that combination at all.

CRIME LINE

Bantam Crime Line Books offer the finest in classic and modern American mysteries. Ask your bookseller for the books you have missed.

REX STOUT
The Black Mountain
Broken Vase
Death of a Dude
Death Times Three
Fer-de-Lance
The Final Deduction
Gambit
Plot It Yourself
The Rubber Band
Some Buried Caesar
Three for the Chair
Too Many Cooks

MAX ALLAN COLLINS
The Dark City
Bullet Proof
Butcher's Dozen
coming soon:
Neon Mirage

LOREN ESTLEMAN
Peeper

Whiskey River

DICK LUPOFF
The Comic Book Killer

MEG O'BRIEN
The Daphne Decisions
coming soon:
Salmon in the Soup

VIRGINIA ANDERSON
Blood Lies
King of the Roses

WILLIAM MURRAY
When the Fat Man Sings
The King of the Nightcap
coming soon:
The Getaway Blues

EUGENE IZZI
King of the Hustlers
The Prime Roll
Invasions

GLORIA DANK
Friends Till the End
Going Out in Style

JEFFERY DEAVER
Manhattan Is My Beat
coming soon:
Death of a Blue Movie Star

ROBERT GOLDSBOROUGH
Murder in E Minor
Death on Deadline
The Bloodied Ivy
The Last Coincidence
coming soon:
Fade to Black

SUE GRAFTON
"A" Is for Alibi
"B" Is for Burglar
"C" Is for Corpse
"D" Is for Deadbeat
"E" Is for Evidence
"F" Is for Fugitive

DAVID LINDSEY
In the Lake of the Moon

CAROLYN G. HART
Design for Murder
Death on Demand
Something Wicked
Honeymoon with Murder
A Little Class on Murder

ANNETTE MEYERS
The Big Killing
coming soon:
Tender Death

ROB KANTNER
Dirty Work
The Back-Door Man
Hell's Only Half Full
coming soon:
Made in Detroit

ROBERT CRAIS
The Monkey's Raincoat
Stalking the Angel

KEITH PETERSON
The Trapdoor
There Fell a Shadow
The Rain
Rough Justice

DAVID HANDLER
The Man Who Died Laughing
The Man Who Lived by Night
coming soon:
The Man Who Would be
F. Scott Fitzgerald

JERRY OSTER
Club Dead
Internal Affairs

BENJAMIN M. SCHUTZ
A Tax in Blood
Embrace the Wolf
The Things We Do for Love

"B"
is for
BURGLAR

SUE GRAFTON

BANTAM BOOKS
NEW YORK • TORONTO • LONDON • SYDNEY • AUCKLAND

This edition contains the complete text
of the original hardcover edition.
NOT ONE WORD HAS BEEN OMITTED.

"B" IS FOR BURGLAR

A Bantam Book / published by arrangement with
Holt, Rinehart & Winston

PRINTING HISTORY

Holt, Rinehart & Winston edition published June 1985
Bantam edition / October 1986

All rights reserved.
Copyright © 1985 by Sue Grafton.
Cover art copyright © 1986 by Bantam Books.
Library of Congress Catalog Card Number: 84-22378.
No part of this book may be reproduced or transmitted
in any form or by any means, electronic or mechanical,
including photocopying, recording, or by any information
storage and retrieval system, without permission in
writing from the publisher.
For information address: Holt, Rinehart & Winston,
6277 Sea Harbor Dr., Orlando, FL 32821.

ISBN 0-553-28034-1

Published simultaneously in the United States and Canada

Bantam Books are published by Bantam Books, a division of Bantam
Doubleday Dell Publishing Group, Inc. Its trademark, consisting of the
words "Bantam Books" and the portrayal of a rooster, is Registered in U.S.
Patent and Trademark Office and in other countries. Marca Registrada.
Bantam Books, 666 Fifth Avenue, New York, New York 10103.

PRINTED IN THE UNITED STATES OF AMERICA

OPM   29 28 27 26 25 24 23 22 21

For Steven,
who sees me through.

The author wishes to acknowledge the invaluable assistance of the following people: Steven Humphrey; John Carroll; Brenda Harman, D.D.S.; Billie Moore Squires; De De La Fond; William Fezler, Ph.D.; Sydney Baumgartner; Frank E. Sincavage, Milton Weintraub; Jay Schmidt; Judy Cooley; Bill Pronzini and Marcia Muller; and Joe Driscoll of Driscoll and Associates Investigations, Columbus, Ohio.

Prologue

After it's over, of course, you want to kick yourself for all the things you didn't see at the time. The Had-I-But-Known school of private investigation perhaps. My name is Kinsey Millhone and most of my reports begin the same way. I start by asserting who I am and what I do, as though by stating the same few basic facts I can make sense out of everything that comes afterward.

This is what's true of me in brief. I'm female, age thirty-two, single, self-employed. I went through the police academy when I was twenty, joining Santa Teresa Police Department on graduation. I don't even remember now how I pictured the job before I took it on. I must have had vague, idealistic notions of law and order, the good guys versus the bad, with occasional court appearances in which I'd be asked to testify as to which was which. In my view, the bad guys would all go to jail, thus making it safe for the rest of us to carry on. After a while, I realized how naïve I was. I was frustrated at the restrictions and frustrated because back then, policewomen were viewed with a mixture of curiosity and scorn. I didn't want to spend my days defending myself against "good-natured" insults, or having to prove how tough I was again and again. I wasn't getting paid enough to deal with all that grief, so I got out.

For two years, I tried an assortment of occupations, but none had the same pull. Whatever else is true of police work, it does entail the intermittent sick thrill of life on the edge. I was hooked on the adrenal rush, and I couldn't go back to the commonplace.

Eventually, I joined a small firm of private investigators

and spent another two years learning the business, after which I opened an office of my own, duly licensed and bonded. I've been at it for five years, supporting myself in a modest way. I'm wiser now than I used to be and I'm more experienced, but the fact remains that when a client sits down in the chair across the desk from me, I never know what's going to happen next.

1

I'd been in the office no more than twenty minutes that morning. I'd opened the French doors out onto the second-floor balcony to let in some fresh air and I'd put on the coffee pot. It was June in Santa Teresa, which means chill morning fog and hazy afternoons. It wasn't nine o'clock yet. I was just sorting through the mail from the day before when I heard a tap at the door and a woman breezed in.

"Oh good. You're here," she said. "You must be Kinsey Millhone. I'm Beverly Danziger."

We shook hands and she promptly sat down and started rooting through her bag. She found a pack of filter-tipped cigarettes and shook one out.

"I hope you don't mind if I smoke," she said, lighting up without waiting for a response. She inhaled and then extinguished the match with a mouthful of smoke, idly searching about for an ashtray. I took one from the top of my file cabinet, dusted it off, and passed it over to her, offering her coffee at the same time.

"Oh sure, why not?" she said with a laugh, "I'm already hyper this morning so I might as well. I just drove up from Los Angeles, right through the rush-hour traffic. Gawd!"

I poured her a mug of coffee, doing a quick visual survey. She was in her late thirties by my guess; petite, energetic, well groomed. Her hair was a glossy black and quite straight. The cut was angular and perfectly layered so that it framed her small face like a bathing cap. She had bright blue eyes, black lashes, a clear complexion with just a hint of blusher high on each cheekbone. She wore a boat-necked sweater in a pale blue cotton knit, and a pale blue poplin skirt. The bag she carried was quality leather, soft and supple, with a

3

number of zippered compartments containing God knows what. Her nails were long and tapered, painted a rosy pink and she wore a wedding ring studded with rubies. She projected self-confidence and a certain careless attention to style, conservatively packaged like the complimentary gift wrap in a classy department store.

She shook her head to the offer of cream and sugar so I added half-and-half to my own mug and got down to business.

"What can I help you with?"

"I'm hoping you can locate my sister for me," she said.

She was searching through her handbag again. She took out her address book, a rosewood pen-and-pencil set, and a long white envelope, which she placed on the edge of my desk. I'd never seen anyone so self-absorbed, but it wasn't unattractive stuff. She gave me a quick smile then, as though she knew that. She opened the address book and turned it so that it faced me, pointing to one of the entries with a rosy fingertip.

"You'll want to make a note of the address and telephone number," she said. "Her name is Elaine Boldt. She has a condo on Via Madrina and that second one is her address in Florida. She spends several months a year down in Boca."

I was feeling somewhat puzzled, but I noted the addresses while she took a legal-looking document out of the long white envelope. She studied it briefly, as though the contents might have changed since she'd last seen it.

"How long has she been missing?" I asked.

Beverly Danziger gave me an uncomfortable look. "Well, I don't know if she's 'missing' exactly. I just don't know where she is and I've got to get these papers signed. I know it sounds dumb. She's only entitled to a ninth interest and it probably won't come to more than two or three thousand dollars, but the money can't be distributed until we have her notarized signature. Here, you can see for yourself."

I took the document and read through the contents. It had been drawn up by a firm of attorneys in Columbus, Ohio, and it was full of whereases, adjudgeds, ordereds, and whatnots, which added up to the fact that a man named Sidney Rowan had died and the various people listed were entitled to portions of his estate. Beverly Danziger was the third party listed, with a Los Angeles address, and Elaine Boldt was fourth, with an address here in Santa Teresa.

"Sidney Rowan was some kind of cousin," she went on

garrulously. "I don't believe I ever met the man, but I got this notice and I assume Elaine got one too. I signed the form and got it notarized and sent off and then didn't think any more about it. You can see from the cover letter that this all took place six months ago. Then, lo and behold I got a call last week from the attorney . . . what's his name again?"

I glanced at the document. "Wender," I said.

"Oh, that's right. I don't know why I keep blocking that. Anyway, Mr. Wender's office called to say they'd never heard from Elaine. Naturally, I assumed she'd gone off to Florida as usual and just hadn't bothered to have her mail sent, so I got in touch with the manager of her condominium here. She hasn't heard from Elaine in months. Well, she did at first, but not recently."

"Have you tried calling the Florida number?"

"From what I understand, the attorney tried several times. Apparently, she had a friend staying with her and Mr. Wender left his name and number, but Elaine never called back. Tillie had about the same luck."

"Tillie?"

"The woman who manages the building here where Elaine has her permanent residence. Tillie's been forwarding the mail and she says Elaine usually drops her a little note every other week or so, but she hasn't heard anything since March. Frankly, it's a nuisance more than anything else, but I don't have time to track her down myself." Beverly took a final drag of the cigarette and stubbed it out with a series of pecking motions.

I was still taking notes, but I suppose the skepticism was showing in my face.

"What's the matter? Isn't this the sort of work you do?"

"Sure, but I charge thirty dollars an hour, plus expenses. If there's only two or three thousand dollars involved, I wonder if it's going to be worth it to you."

"Oh, I fully intend to have the estate reimburse me out of Elaine's share since she caused all this trouble to begin with. I mean, everything's come to a screeching halt until her signature can be obtained. I must say it's typical of the way she's behaved all her life."

"Suppose I end up flying down to Florida to look for her? Even if I only charge you half my usual hourly rate for travel time, it'll cost a fortune. Look, Mrs. Danziger—"

"Beverly, please."

"All right, Beverly. I don't want to discourage your business, but in all honesty it sounds like something you could handle yourself. I'd even be happy to suggest some ways to go about it."

Beverly gave me a smile then, but it had a hard edge to it and I realized, at long last, that she was used to getting her way. Her eyes had widened to a china glaze, as blue and unyielding as glass. The black lashes blinked mechanically.

"Elaine and I are not on the best of terms," she said smoothly. "I feel I've already devoted quite enough time to this, but I promised Mr. Wender I'd find her so the estate can be settled. He's under pressure from the other heirs and he's putting pressure on me. I can give you an advance if you like."

She was back in her bag again, coming up with a checkbook this time. She uncapped the rosewood pen and stared at me.

"Will seven hundred and fifty dollars suffice?"

I reached into my bottom drawer. "I'll draw up a contract."

I walked the check over to the bank and then I retrieved my car from the lot behind the office and drove over to Elaine Boldt's address on Via Madrina. It wasn't far from the downtown area.

I figured this was a routine matter I could settle in a day or two and I was thinking with regret that I'd probably end up refunding half the money I'd just deposited. Not that I was doing much else anyway—things were slow.

The neighborhood Elaine Boldt lived in was composed of modest 1930s bungalows mixed with occasional apartment complexes. So far, the little frame and stucco cottages were predominant but the properties were being converted to commercial use one by one. Chiropractors were moving in, and cut-rate dentists who were willing to give you twilight sleep so you could have your teeth cleaned without cringing. ONE-DAY DENTURES—CREDIT. It was worrisome. What did they do to you if you missed a payment on your upper plate? The area was still largely intact—old-age pensioners stubbornly propping up their hydrangea bushes—but real-estate syndicates would eventually mow them all down. There's a lot of money in Santa Teresa and much of it is devoted to maintaining a certain "look" to the town. There are no flashing neon signs, no slums, no fume-spewing manufacturing complexes to blight the landscape. Everything is stucco, red tile roofs, bougain-villea, distressed beams, adobe brick walls, arched windows, palm trees, balconies, ferns, fountains, paseos, and flowers in bloom. Historical restorations abound. It's all oddly unsettling—so lush and refined that it ruins you for anyplace else.

When I reached Mrs. Boldt's address, I parked my car out front and locked it, taking a few minutes then to survey the premises. The condominium was a curiosity. The building itself was shaped like a horseshoe with broad arms opening onto the street; three stories high, parking level underneath, a strange combination of modern and mock-Spanish. There were arches and balconies along the front, with tall wrought-iron gates sweeping inward to a palm-planted courtyard, but the sides and back of the building were flat and unadorned, as though the architect had applied a Mediterranean veneer to a plain plywood box, adding a lip of red tile at the top to suggest an entire roof when there was none. Even the palms looked like cardboard cutouts, propped up with sticks.

I passed through the courtyard and found myself in a glass-enclosed lobby with a row of mailboxes and door buzz-ers on the right. On my left, through another set of glass doors, apparently kept locked, I could see a set of elevator doors and an exit leading to a set of fire stairs. Huge potted plants had been artfully arranged throughout the entrance-way. Straight ahead, a door led out into a patio where I caught sight of a pool surrounded by bright yellow canvas deck chairs. I checked the tenants' names, which were punched out on strips of plastic tape and pasted alongside each apart-ment buzzer. There were twenty-four units. The manager, Tillie Ahlberg, occupied apartment 1. An "E. Boldt" was listed at apartment 9, which I guessed was on the second floor.

"I gave "E. Boldt" a buzz first. For all I knew, she'd answer on the intercom and then my job would. be done. Stranger things had happened and I didn't want to make a fool of myself looking high and low for a lady who might well by now be at home. There was no response so I tried Tillie Ahlberg.

After ten seconds, her voice crackled into the intercom as though the sound were being transmitted from outer space. "Yes?"

I placed my mouth near the box, raising my voice slightly. "Mrs. Ahlberg, my name is Kinsey Millhone. I'm a private detective here in town. Elaine Boldt's sister asked me to see if I could locate her and I wondered if I might talk to you."

There was a moment of white noise and then a reluctant reply.

"Well. I suppose. I was on my way out, but I guess ten minutes won't hurt. I'm on the ground floor. Come through the door to the right of the elevator and it's down at the end of the hall to the left." The buzzer sounded and I pushed through the glass doors.

Tillie Ahlberg had left her front door ajar while she collected a lightweight jacket, her purse, and a collapsible shopping cart that rested against the hall table. I tapped on the doorframe and she appeared from my left. I caught a glimpse of a refrigerator and a portion of kitchen counter.

Tillie Ahlberg was probably in her sixties, with apricot-tinted hair in a permanent wave that looked as if it had just been done. The curl must have been a little frizzier than she liked because she was pulling on a crocheted cotton cap. An unruly fringe of apricot hair was still peeking out, like Ronald McDonald's, and she was in the process of tucking it away. Her eyes were hazel and there was a powdery patina of pale ginger freckles on her face. She wore a shapeless skirt, hose, and running shoes, and she looked like she was capable of covering ground when she wanted to.

"I hope I didn't seem unsociable," she said comfortably. "But if I don't get to the market first thing in the morning, I lose heart."

"It shouldn't take long anyway," I said. "Can you tell me when you last heard from Mrs. Boldt? Is she Miss or Mrs.?"

"Mrs. She's a widow, though she's only forty-three years old. She was married to a man who had a string of manufacturing plants down south. As I understand it, he dropped dead of a heart attack three years ago and left her a bundle. That's when she bought this place. Here, have a seat if you like."

Tillie moved off to the right, leading the way into a living room furnished with antique reproductions. A gauzy golden light came through the pale yellow sheers and I could still smell the remnants of breakfast: bacon and coffee and something laced with cinnamon.

Having established that she was in a hurry, she seemed ready to give me as much time as I wanted. She sat down on an ottoman and I took a wooden rocking chair.

"I understand she's usually in Florida this time of year," I said.

"Well, yes. She's got another condominium down there. In Boca Raton, wherever that is. Near Fort Lauderdale, I guess. I've never been to Florida myself, so these towns are all just names to me. Anyhow, she usually goes down around the first of February and comes back to California late July or early August. She likes the heat, she says."

"And you forward mail to her while she's gone?"

Tillie nodded. "I do that about once a week in batches, depending on how much has accumulated. Then she sends me back a note every couple of weeks. A postcard, you know, just to say hi and how the weather is and if she needs someone let in to clean the drapes or something of that nature. This year she wrote me through the first of March and since then I haven't heard a word. Now, that's not like her a bit."

"Do you still have the postcards by any chance?"

"No, I just threw 'em out like I always do. I'm not much for collecting things like that. There's too much paper piling up in the world if you ask me. I read 'em and tossed 'em and never thought a thing of it."

"She didn't mention taking a side trip or anything like that?"

"Not a word. Of course, it's none of my business in the first place."

"Did she seem distressed?"

Tillie smiled ruefully. "Well, it's hard to seem upset on the message side of a postcard, you know. There isn't but that much room. She sounded fine to me."

"Do you have any guesses about where she might be?"

"Not a one. All I know is it's not like her not to write. I tried calling four or five times. Once some woman friend of hers answered but she was real abrupt and after that, there wasn't anything at all."

"Who was the friend? Anyone you knew?"

"No, but now I don't know who she knows in Boca. It could have been anyone. I didn't make a note of the name and wouldn't know it if you said it to me right this minute."

"What about the mail she's been getting? Are her bills still coming in?"

She shrugged at that. "It looks that way to me. I haven't paid much attention. I just shipped on whatever came in. I do have a few I was about to forward if you'd like to see them." She got up and crossed to an oak secretary, opening one of the glass doors by turning the key in the lock. She took out a short stack of envelopes and sorted through them, then handed them to me. "This is the kind of thing she usually gets."

I did the same quick sorting job. Visa, MasterCard, Saks Fifth Avenue. A furrier named Jacques with an address in Boca Raton. A bill from a John Pickett, D.D.S., Inc., right around the corner on Arbol. No personal letters at all.

"Does she pay utility bills from here too?" I asked.

"I already sent those this month."

"Could she have been arrested?"

That sparked a laugh. "Oh no. Not her. She wasn't anything like that. She didn't drive a car, you know, but she wasn't the type to get so much as a jaywalking ticket."

"Accident? Illness? Drink? Drugs?" I felt like a doctor interviewing a patient for an annual physical.

Tillie's expression was skeptical. "She could be in the hospital I suppose, but surely she would have let us know. I find it very peculiar to tell you the truth. If that sister of hers hadn't come along, I might have gotten in touch with the police myself. There's just something not right."

"But there are lots of explanations for where she might be," I said. "She's an adult. Apparently she's got money and no pressing business. She really doesn't have to notify anybody of her whereabouts if she doesn't want to. She might be on a cruise. Or maybe she's taken a lover and absconded with him. Maybe she and this girl friend of hers took off on a toot. It might never occur to her that anyone was trying to get in touch."

"That's why I haven't really done anything so far, but it doesn't sit well with me. I don't think she'd leave without a word to anyone."

"Well, let me look into it. I don't want to hold you up right now, but I'll want to see her apartment at some point," I said. I got up and Tillie rose automatically. I shook her hand and thanked her for her help.

"Hang on to the mail for the time being, if you would," I said. "I'm going to chase down some other possibilities, but I'll get back to you in a day or two and let you know what I've come up with. I don't think there's any reason to worry."

"I hope not," Tillie said. "She's a wonderful person."

I gave Tillie my card before we parted company. I wasn't worried yet myself, but my curiosity had been aroused and I was eager to get on with it.

2

On the way back to the office, I stopped off at the public library. I went to the reference department and pulled the city directory for Boca Raton, checking the address I had for Elaine Boldt against the addresses listed. Sure enough, she was there with a telephone number that matched the one I'd been given. I noted the names of several other owners of adjacent condominiums, jotting down telephone numbers. There seemed to be a number of buildings in the same complex and I guessed that it was an entire "planned community." There was a general sales office, a telephone number for tennis courts, a health spa, and a recreational facility. I made notes of everything just to save myself a possible trip back.

When I reached the office, I opened a file on Elaine Boldt, logging the time I'd put in so far and the information I had. I tried the Florida number, letting it ring maybe thirty times without luck, and then I put in a call to the sales office of the Boca Raton condominium. They gave me the name of the resident manager in Elaine Boldt's building, a Roland Makowski, apartment 101, who picked up on the first ring.

"Makowski here."

I told him as briefly as possible who I was and why I was trying to get in touch with Elaine Boldt.

"She didn't come down this year," he said. "She's usually here about this time, but I guess she had a change of plans."

"Are you sure?"

"Well, I haven't seen her. I've been up and down and around this building day in and day out and I never laid eyes on her. That's all I know. I guess she could be here if she's always someplace where I'm not," he said. "That friend of

12

hers, Pat, is here, but Mrs. Boldt went off someplace else is
what I was told. Maybe she could tell you where. I just
bumped into her hanging towels out on the rail which we
don't allow. The balcony's not a drying rack and I told her as
much. She kinda went off in a huff."

"Can you tell me her last name?"

"What?"

"Can you tell me Pat's last name? Mrs. Boldt's friend."

"Oh. Yes."

I waited a moment. "I've got a pencil and paper," I said.

"Oh. It's Usher. Like in a movie theater. She's sublet, she
said. What's your name again?"

I gave him my name again and my office number in case he
wanted to get in touch. It was not a satisfactory conversation.
Pat Usher seemed to be the only link to Elaine Boldt's
whereabouts and I thought it essential to talk to her as soon
as possible.

I put in another call to Elaine's Florida number, letting it
ring until *I* got annoyed with the sound. Nothing. If Pat
Usher was still in the apartment, she was resolutely refusing
to answer the phone.

I checked the list I'd made of neighboring apartments and
tried the telephone number of a Robert Perreti, who apparently lived right next door. No answer. I tried the number for
the neighbor on the other side, dutifully letting the phone
ring ten times as the telephone company advises us. At long
last, someone answered—a very old someone by the sound of
her.

"Yes?" She sounded as if she were feeble and might want to
weep. I found myself speaking loudly and carefully as though
to the hearing-impaired.

"Mrs. Ochsner?"

"Yes."

"My name is Kinsey Millhone. I'm calling from California
and I'm trying to reach the woman who's staying next door to
you in apartment 315. Do you happen to know if she's in?
I've just called and I let the phone ring about thirty times
with no luck."

"Do you have a hearing problem?" she asked me. "You're
speaking very loudly, you know."

I laughed, bringing my tone down into a normal range.
"I'm sorry," I said. "I wasn't sure how well you could hear
me."

"Oh, I can hear perfectly. I'm eighty-eight years old and I can't walk a step without help, but there's nothing wrong with my ears. I counted every one of those thirty rings through the wall and I thought I'd go crazy if it went on much longer."

"Has Pat Usher stepped out? I was just on the line to the building manager and he said she was there."

"Oh, she's there all right. I know she is because she slammed the door not moments ago. What was it you wanted, if it's not too impertinent of me to ask?"

"Well, actually I'm trying to locate Elaine Boldt, but I understand she didn't make it down this year."

"That's true and I was awfully disappointed. She's part of a bridge foursome when Mrs. Wink and Ida Rittenhouse are here and we count on her. We haven't been able to play a hand since last Christmas and it's made Ida very cranky if you want to know the truth."

"Do you have any idea where Mrs. Boldt might be?"

"No, I don't and I suspect the woman in there is on her way out. The condominium bylaws don't permit sublets and I was surprised that Elaine agreed to it. We've complained aplenty to the association and I believe Mr. Makowski has asked her to vacate. The woman has her back up, of course, claiming her agreement with Elaine covers through the end of June. If you want to have a conversation with her yourself, you'd do well to get down here soon. I saw her bringing up some cartons from the liquor store and I believe . . . well, I should say I *hope* she's packing up even as we speak."

"Thanks. I may do that. You've been a big help. If I get down there, I'll stop by."

"I don't suppose you play bridge, do you, dear? We've been reduced to playing hearts now for the last six months and Ida's developing quite a mean mouth. Mrs. Wink and I can't take too much more of this."

"Well, I've never played but maybe I could give it a try," I said.

"A penny a point," she said brusquely, and I laughed.

I put in a call to Tillie. She sounded out of breath, as though she'd had to run for the phone.

"Hi, Tillie," I said. "It's me again. Kinsey."

"I just got back from the market," she panted. "Hang on until I catch my breath. Whew! What can I do for you?"

"I think I better go ahead and take a look at Elaine's apartment."

"Why? What's going on?"

"Well, the people in Florida say she's not there, so I'm hoping we can figure out where else she might have gone. If I come back over there, could you let me in?"

"I guess so. I'm not doing anything except unloading groceries and that won't take but two shakes."

When I reached the condominium again, I called her on the intercom and she buzzed me through and then met me at the elevator door with a key to Elaine's apartment. I told her the details of my conversation with Elaine's building manager down in Florida, filling her in as we rode up to the second floor.

"You mean nobody down there has seen her at all? Well, something's wrong then," she said. "Definitely. I know she left and I know she fully intended to go down to Florida. I was looking out the window when the cab pulled up out front and gave a toot and she got in. She had on her good fur coat and that fur turban that matched. She was traveling at night, which she didn't like to do, but then she wasn't feeling good and she thought the change in climate might help."

"She was sick?"

"Oh, you know. Her sinuses were acting up and she'd had that awful head cold or allergy or whatever it was. I don't mean to criticize, but she was a bit of a hypochondriac. She called me and said she'd decided to go ahead and fly on down, almost on the spur of the moment. She wasn't really scheduled to go for nearly two weeks, but then the doctor said it might do her good and I guess she booked the first flight she could get."

"Do you know if she used a travel agent?"

"I'm almost sure she did. Probably one close by. Since she didn't drive, she liked to deal with businesses within walking distance where she could. Here it is."

Tillie had paused outside of apartment 9, which was on the second floor, directly above hers. She unlocked the door and then followed me in.

The apartment was dim, drapes drawn, the air dry and still. Tillie crossed the living room and opened the drapes.

"Nobody's been in since she left?" I asked. "Cleaning lady? Tradesmen?"

"Not as far as I know."

Both of us seemed to be using our public-library tones, but there's something unsettling about being in someone else's place when you're not supposed to be. I could feel a low-level electrical current surging through my gut.

We did a quick tour together and Tillie said it looked all right to her. Nothing unusual. Nothing out of place. She left then and I went through on my own, taking my time so I could do it right.

This was a corner apartment, second-floor front, with windows running along two sides. I took a minute to stare down at the street. There were no cars passing. A boy with a Mohawk haircut was leaning up against a parked car directly below. The sides of his head were shaved to a preexecution gray and the strip of hair that remained stood up like a dry brush in the center divider of a highway. It was dyed a shade of pink that I hadn't seen since hot pants went out of style. He looked to be sixteen or seventeen, wearing a pair of bright red parachute pants tucked down into combat boots, and an orange tank top with a slogan on the front that I couldn't read from where I stood. I watched him roll and light a joint.

I moved to the side windows which looked down at an angle through the ground-floor windows of the small frame house next door. The roof had been gnawed by fire, the eaves of the house showing through like the frail bones of an overcooked fish. The door was boarded up, the glass broken out of the windows, apparently by the heat. A FOR SALE sign was jammed into the dead grass like a flimsy headstone. Not much of a view for a condominium that I estimated must have cost Elaine more than a hundred thousand dollars. I shrugged to myself and went into the kitchen.

The counters and appliances gleamed. The floor had apparently been washed and waxed. The cupboards were neatly stacked with canned goods, including some 9-Lives Beef and Liver Platter. The refrigerator was empty, except for the usual door full of olives and pickles and mustards and jams. The electric stove had been unplugged, the cord dangling across the clockface, which read 8:20. An empty brown paper sack had been inserted in the plastic wastebasket under the sink, a cuff neatly turned down at the top. It looked as if Elaine Boldt had systematically prepared the apartment for a long absence.

I left the kitchen and wandered out into the entrance hall. The layout seemed to be a duplicate of Tillie's apartment downstairs. I moved down a short corridor, glancing to my right into a small bathroom with a sink shaped like a sunken marble shell, gold-plated fixtures, gold-flecked mirrored tiles on one wall. The small wicker wastebasket under the sink was empty except for a delicate gray-brown clump of hair clinging to the side like the light matting when a hairbrush has been cleaned.

Across from the bathroom was a small den, with a desk, a television set, an easy chair, and a sofa bed. The desk drawers contained the usual assortment of pens, paper clips, note cards, and files, which for the moment I saw no reason to examine more closely. I did come across her social-security card and I made a note of the number. I left the den and moved into a master suite with an adjoining bathroom.

The bedroom was gloomy with the drapes pulled, but again everything seemed in order. To the right, there was a walk-in closet large enough to rent out. Some of the hangers were empty and I could see gaps in the articles lined up on the shelves where she'd probably packed an item. A small suit-case was still tucked down in one corner, one of the expensive designer types covered with somebody else's name all done in curlicues.

I checked dresser drawers randomly. Some still contained wool sweaters in plastic cleaner's bags. A few were empty except for a sachet or two left behind like tiny scented pillows. Lingerie. A few pieces of costume jewelry.

The master bath was spacious and orderly, the medicine cabinet stripped of all but a few over-the-counter remedies. I moved back to the door and stood there for a moment, surveying the bedroom. There was nothing to suggest foul play or haste, burglary, vandalism, illness, suicide, drunken-ness, drug abuse, confusion, or recent occupancy. Even the faint powdering of household dust on the glossy surfaces seemed undisturbed.

I left, locking the door behind me. I took the elevator down to Tillie's and asked her if she had any photographs of Elaine.

"Not that I know," she said, "but I can describe her if you like. She's just about my size, which would make her five foot five, a hundred and thirty pounds. She has streaked blond hair which she wears pulled back. Blue eyes." Tillie stopped.

"Oh wait, maybe I do have a picture. I just remembered one. Hold on."

She disappeared in the direction of the den and after a few moments returned with a Polaroid snapshot that she handed to me. The picture had an orange cast to it and seemed sticky to the touch. Two women stood in the courtyard, a full-length shot, taken from perhaps twenty feet back. One I guessed immediately was Elaine, smiling happily, trim and elegant in a pair of well-cut slacks. The other woman was thick through the middle, with blue plastic eyeglass frames and a hairdo that looked as if it could be removed intact. She appeared to be in her forties, squinting into the sun self-consciously.

"This was taken last fall," Tillie said. "That's Elaine on the left."

"Who's the other woman?"

"Marty Grice, a neighbor of ours. Now that was an awful thing. She was killed . . . oh gosh, I guess six months back. It doesn't seem that long ago."

"What happened to her?"

"Well, they think she interrupted a burglar breaking into the house. I guess he killed her on the spot and then tried to burn the place down to cover it up. It was horrible. You might have read about it in the paper."

I shook my head. There are long periods when I don't read the paper at all, but I remembered the house next door with its charred roof and windows broken out. "That's too bad," I said. "Do you mind if I keep this?"

"Go right ahead."

I glanced at it again. The image was faintly disturbing, capturing a moment not that long ago when both women grinned with such ease, unaware that anything unpleasant lay ahead. Now, one was dead and the other missing. I didn't like that combination at all.

"Were Elaine and this woman good friends?" I asked.

"Not really. They played bridge together now and then, but they didn't socialize aside from that. Elaine is a bit standoffish where most people are concerned. Actually, Marty used to get a little snippy about Elaine's attitude. Not that she ever said anything much about it to me, but I can remember her being a bit snide once in a while. Elaine does treat herself well—there's no doubt about *that*—and she tends to be insensitive to the idea that people really can't afford to live as well as she does. That fur coat of hers is a case in point. She knew Leonard and Marty were in financial straits, but she'd wear the coat over there to play bridge. To Marty, that was just like waving a red flag in front of a bull."

"That's the same coat she was wearing when you saw her last?"

"Yes, indeed. A twelve-thousand-dollar lynx fur coat with a matching hat."

"Wow," I said.

"Oh, it's beautiful. I'd give my eyeteeth to have a coat like that."

"Can you remember anything else about her departure that night?"

"I can't say that I do. She was carrying some sort of luggage—I guess a carry-on—and the cab driver brought down the rest."

"Do you remember what cab company?"

"I really didn't pay much attention at the time, but she usually called City Cab or Green Stripe, sometimes Tip Top, though she didn't like them much. I wish I could be more help. I mean, if she left here on her way to Florida and never got there, where did she end up?"

"That's what I want to know," I said.

I gave Tillie what I hoped was a reassuring smile, but I was feeling uneasy.

I went back to the office and did a quick calculation of the expenses I'd run up so far; maybe seventy-five bucks for the time spent with Tillie and the time going through Elaine's apartment, plus the time in the library and on the telephone and the long-distance charges. I've known P.I.s who conduct entire investigations on the phone, but I don't think it's smart. Unless you're dealing with people face-to-face, there are too many ways to be deceived and too many things to miss.

I called a travel agent and got myself booked round-trip to Miami. The fare was ninety-nine bucks each way if I flew in the dead of night and didn't eat, drink, or go to the john. I also reserved a cheap rental car on the far end.

My plane didn't leave for hours yet, so I went home and got in a three-mile jog, then stuck a toothbrush and tooth-paste in my purse and called it packing. At some point, I was going to have to track down Elaine's travel agent and find out what airline she had taken and whether perhaps she'd booked herself through to Mexico or the Caribbean. In the meantime, I hoped I could catch Elaine's friend in Florida before she flew the coop, taking with her my only link to Elaine's whereabouts.

3

It was still dark when the plane touched down in Miami at 4:45 A.M. The airport was sparsely populated at that hour, the lighting as subdued as a funeral home's. In the baggage claim area, stacks of abandoned suitcases were piled together in shadowy glass-fronted cabinets. All the airport shops were closed. Travelers slept here and there on the unyielding plastic seats, resting their heads on bulging canvas totes, their jackets hunched up over their shoulders. The intercom paged a passenger to the white courtesy telephone, but the name was garbled and I didn't think anyone would respond. I had only managed to sleep for about an hour on the plane and I felt rumpled and out of sorts.

I picked up my rental car and a sheet map and by 5:15 was headed north on U.S. 1. Twenty miles to Fort Lauderdale, another fifteen to Boca Raton. Dawn was turning the sky a pearly translucent gray and clouds were piled up like heads of cauliflower in a roadside stand. The land on either side of the highway was flat, with white sand creeping up to the edges of the road. Patches of saw grass and stunted cypress cut into the horizon and Spanish moss hung from the trees like tattered rags. The air was already moist and balmy and the streaks of orange from the rising sun hinted at a hot day to come. To kill some time, I stopped at a fast-food place and ate some brown and yellow things that I washed down with a carton of orange juice. All of it tasted like something the astronauts would have to reconstitute.

By the time I reached the community where Elaine Boldt had her Florida condominium, it was nearly seven o'clock and the sprinkler system was sending out jets of water across the closely clipped grass. There were six or seven buildings of poured concrete, each three stories high, with screened-in porches punctuating the low clean lines. Hibiscus bushes added touches of bright red and pink. I circled through the area, driving slowly along the wide avenues that curved back as far as the tennis courts. Each building seemed to have its own swimming pool cradled close and there were already people stretched out on plastic chaise longues sunning themselves. I spotted the street number I was looking for and pulled into a small parking lot out in front. The manager's apartment was on the ground floor, the front door standing open, the screen door secured against the onslaught of big Florida bugs that were already making warning sounds in the grass.

I knocked against the aluminum frame.

"I'm right here." It was a woman's voice, disconcertingly close.

I cupped one hand, shading my eyes so that I could see who I was talking to through the screen door.

"Is Mr. Makowski here?"

The woman seemed to materialize on the other side, her face level with my knees.

"Hold on. I've been doing my sit-ups and I can't get to my feet yet. Lord, that hurts." She hauled herself into a kneeling position, clinging to the arm of a chair. "Makowski's off fixing the toilet in 208. What can I do you for?"

"I'm trying to get in touch with Elaine Boldt. Do you have any idea where she might be?"

"You that investigator who called from California?"

"Yes, that's me. I thought I should talk to someone down here and see if I could get a lead on her. Did she leave a forwarding address?"

"Nope. I wish I could help you out, but I don't know much more than you do. Here, come on in." She lurched to her feet and held the screen door open. "I'm Charmaine Makowski, or what's left of her. Do you exercise?"

"Well, I jog, but that's about it," I said.

"Good for you. Don't ever do sit-ups. That's my advice. I do a hundred a day and it always hurts." She was still winded, her cheeks tinted pink from the effort. She was in her late forties, wearing a bright yellow sweat suit, her belly protruding in pregnancy. She looked like a ripe Florida grapefruit.

"You got it," she said. "Another one of life's little jokes. I thought it was a tumor 'til it started to kick. Know what that is?"

She was pointing to a bump just below her waist. "That's what a belly button looks like turned inside out. It's embarrassing. Makowski and I didn't think we could have any kids. I'm almost fifty and he's sixty-five. Oh hell, what difference does it make? It's more fun than menopause, I guess. Have you talked to that woman up in 315? Her name is Pat Usher, but you probably know that. She claims Elaine let her sublet, but I doubt that."

"What's the story on that? Mrs. Boldt never talked to you about the arrangement?"

"Nope. Not a word. All I know is this Usher woman showed up a few months ago and moved in. At first nobody objected because we all just figured it was a two-week visit or something like that. People in the building can have any kind of company they want for short periods of time, but the rules say you can't sublet. Prospective buyers are screened real carefully and if we allowed sublets it would just be an invitation for any Tom, Dick, or Harry to move in here. The whole community would start to deteriorate. Anyway, after a month, Makowski went up to have a little chat with her and she claims she paid Elaine for six months and doesn't intend to move. It's driving Makowski around the bend."

"Does she have a signed lease?"

"She has a receipt showing she's paid Elaine some money, but it doesn't say for what. Makowski's had her served with an eviction notice, but she's taking her sweet time getting out. You haven't met her yet, I take it."

"I'm just on my way up. Do you know if she's in?"

"Probably. She doesn't go out much except to the pool to work on her tan. Tell her 'drop dead' from the management."

Three-fifteen was located on the third floor in the crook of the L-shaped building. Even before I rang the bell, I had the feeling that I was being inspected through the fish-eye spy hole in the middle of the door. After a moment, the door opened to the width of the burglar chain, but no face appeared.

"Pat Usher?"

"Yes."

"My name is Kinsey Millhone. I'm an investigator from California. I'm trying to locate Elaine Boldt."

"What for?" Her tone was flat, guarded, no lilt at all and no graciousness.

"Her sister's been trying to get in touch with her to sign a legal document. Can you tell me where she is?"

There was a cautious silence. "Are you here to serve me papers?"

"No." I took out the photostatic copy of my license and passed it through the crack. The license disappeared smoothly, like a bank card being sucked into an instant-cash machine. After an interval, it came back.

"Just a minute. I'll see if I can find her address."

She left the door ajar, still secured by the chain. I felt a little flash of hope. Maybe I was making progress. If I could track Elaine down in another day or two, I'd feel pretty smug, which sometimes counts as much as money whatever business you're in. I waited, staring down at the welcome mat. The letter *B* was defined in dark bristles, surrounded by bristles in a lighter shade. Did they have enough mud in Florida to justify a mat like that? It was coarse enough to rip the bottom of your shoe off. I glanced to my left. Just off the balcony, I could see palm trees with little beaded skirts near the top. Pat Usher was back, still talking through the crack.

"I must have thrown it out. She was in Sarasota last I heard."

Already, I was tired of talking to the door and I felt a surge of irritation. "Do you mind if I come in? It's about the settlement on somebody's estate. She could pick up two or three thousand dollars if I can just get her signature." Appeal to greed, I thought. Appeal to the secret yearning for a windfall. Sometimes I use it as a ploy when I am tracking down a deadbeat who's run out on a bill. This time it was even true, so my voice had this wonderful sincere ring to it.

"Did the manager send you up here?"

"Come on, would you quit being paranoid? I'm looking for Elaine and I want to talk to you. You're the only person so far who seems to have any idea where she is."

Silence. She was pondering this as though it were an I.Q. test and she could pad the results. I had to struggle with the urge to bite. This was the only lead I had and I didn't want to blow it.

"All right," she said reluctantly, "let me get some clothes on first."

When she finally opened the door, she was wearing a float,

one of those gauzy print caftans you slip over your head when you're too lazy to put on your underpants. She had adhesive tape across her nose. Her eyes were puffy and circled with bruises that were fading from blue to green. She had a strip of clear tape under each eye and her tan had dimmed to a sallow hue that made her look like she had a mild case of hepatitis.

"I was in a car accident and broke my nose," she said. "I don't like for people to see me like this."

She moved away from the door, the caftan sailing out behind her as though there were a breeze. I followed her in, closing the door behind me. The place was done in rattan and pastels and smelled faintly of mildew. Sliding glass doors on one side of the living room opened out onto the screened-in porch, beyond which there were only lush green treetops visible and clouds piling up like a bubble bath.

She took a cigarette out of a lead crystal box on the coffee table and lit it with a matching table lighter that actually worked. She sat down on the couch, propping her bare feet up on the edge of the table. Her soles were gray.

"Sit down if you want."

Her eyes were an eerie, electric green, tinted by contact lenses I had to guess. Her hair was a tawny shade, with a luster I've never been able to coax out of mine. She stared at me with interest now, her manner fairly amused. "Whose estate is it?"

She had this way of asking certain questions with no tilt at the end, soliciting information by making flat statements that I was supposed to respond to. Odd. It made me wary somehow and I found myself taking care with what I said.

"A cousin, apparently. Someone in Ohio."

"Isn't it a bit radical to hire a private detective so you can hand out three thousand bucks?"

"There are other inheritors involved," I said.

"You have some kind of form you want her to sign."

"I want to talk to her first. People are worried because they haven't heard from her. I'd like to include something in my report about where she's been."

"Oh my God, now we got a report. She was restless. She's been traveling. What's the big deal?"

"Do you mind if I ask you about your relationship with her?"

"No, I don't mind. We're friends. I've known her for years.

She came down to Florida this time and she wanted some company."

"When was this?"

"Middle of January. Something like that." She paused, watching the ash on her cigarette. Her eyes came up to mine again, her expression remote.

"And you've been staying here ever since?"

"Sure, why not? I'd just lost the lease on my place and she said I could move in."

"Why'd she take off?"

"You'd have to ask her that."

"When did you last hear from her?"

"Two weeks ago, something like that."

"And she was in Sarasota then?"

"That's right. Staying with some people she met."

"Can you tell me who?"

"Look, she wanted me to keep her company, not baby-sit. It's none of my business who she hangs out with, so I don't ask."

I felt as if we were playing a parlor game that I couldn't possibly win. Pat Usher was having a better time than I was too, and I resented that. I went at it again. Was it Mrs. Peacock in the library with the rope?

"Can you tell me anything else you think might help?"

"I wasn't aware I'd helped so far," she said with a smirk.

"I was trying an optimistic approach," I snapped.

She shrugged. "Sorry to dim your little ray of hope. I've told you everything I know."

"I guess we'll have to let it go at that. I'll leave you my card. If she calls again, would you have her contact me?"

"Hey, sure. No sweat."

I took a card out of my wallet and put it on the table as I got up. "I understand you're getting some hassles from people here."

"Can you believe that? I mean, what's it to them? I've paid my rent. No parties, no loud music. I hang my laundry out and the manager comes unglued. Threw a fit. I don't get it."

She got to her feet and led me to the door. The caftan billowing out behind her made her seem like a larger woman than she was. As I went past the kitchen, I caught sight of some cardboard boxes stacked up near the sink. She turned and followed my gaze.

"I'll probably find a motel close by if it comes to that. The last thing in the world I need is the sheriff on my case. That's who I thought you were, as a matter of fact. They got women sheriffs these days, did you know that? Sheriffettes."

"So I've heard."

"What about you?" she asked. "How'd you become a detective. That's a weird way to make a living, isn't it?"

She was becoming real chatty now that I was on my way out and I wondered if I might pump her for more information. She seemed eager to prolong the contact, like someone who's been cooped up too long with a pack of preschool kids.

"I sort of backed into detective work," I said, "but it beats selling shoes. You don't work yourself?"

"Not me. I'm retired. I don't ever want to work again."

"You're lucky. I don't have much choice. If I don't work, I don't eat."

She smiled for the first time. "I used to spend my life waiting for a break. Then I figured out I better make my own luck, you know what I mean? Nobody gives you nothing in this world, that's for sure."

I feigned agreement, glancing down toward the parking lot.

"I better be on my way," I said. "But could I ask you one more thing?"

"Like what."

"Do you know Elaine's other friends? There must be someone who knows how to get in touch with her, don't you think?"

"I'm the wrong one to ask," she said. "She used to visit me down in Lauderdale, so I don't know friends of hers up here."

"How'd you connect up this time? I understand she flew down almost on impulse."

She seemed momentarily perplexed at that, but regained her composure. "Yeah, that's right, she did. She called me from the airport in Miami and then picked me up on her way through."

"In a rented car?"

"Yeah. An Oldsmobile Cutlass. White."

"How long was she here then before she took off?"

Pat shrugged again. "I don't know. Not long. A couple of days, I guess."

"Did she seem at all nervous or upset?"

She became faintly irritated at that. "Wait a minute. What are you getting at? Maybe I could come up with something if I knew what was on your mind."

"I'm not sure," I said mildly. "I'm just fishing around, trying to figure out what's going on. The people who know her in Santa Teresa think it's unusual that she'd disappear without a word."

"But she told *me*. I've been telling you that. What is she, some kind of kid that she has to call home all the time and tell someone where she is and what time she's getting in? What's the problem?"

"There isn't one. Her sister wants her to get in touch. That's all it amounts to."

"Yeah, all right. I get touchy now and then. I've been under a lot of pressure and I don't mean to take it out on you. She'll probably call at some point and I'll give her your name and number, okay?"

"Great. I'd appreciate that."

I held out my hand and she shook it briefly. Her fingers were dry and cold.

"It's been nice talking to you," I said.

"You too," she replied.

I hesitated, glancing back at her. "If you do move into a motel, how will Elaine know where to reach you?"

The smirk was back, but there was something else in her eyes. "How about I'll leave a forwarding address with Makowski, my friendly building manager downstairs. That way you'll know how to reach me too. Will that do the trick?"

"Probably so. Thanks much."

4

I moved off toward the stairs. I could feel her eyes on my back and then I heard the door close. I continued on down to the parking lot and got in my car and drove off. I wanted to talk to Mrs. Ochsner in the next apartment, but I thought it was better to wait. Something about Pat Usher bothered me. It was not just the fact that some of what she'd told me was untrue. I'm a born liar myself and I know how it's done. You stick as close to the truth as you can. You pretend to volunteer a few bits of information, but the facts are all carefully selected for effect. Pat's problem was that she was having to wing far too much and she'd started to embroider where she should have kept her mouth shut. That business about Elaine Boldt picking her up in Fort Lauderdale in a rented white Cutlass was crap. Elaine didn't drive. Tillie had told me that. At the moment, I couldn't figure out why Pat had lied about it, but it must have been significant. What really bothered me about her was that she had no class and it struck me as odd that Elaine Boldt had chosen her for a friend. From what Tillie and Beverly told me, I had the feeling Elaine was a bit of a snob and Pat Usher didn't seem quite glossy enough to satisfy.

I found a drugstore half a block away and bought two packs of index cards so I could make some notes and then I put in a call to Mrs. Ochsner in 317. Finally, she picked up.

"Hello?"

I identified myself and told her where I was. "I've just been up there talking to Pat Usher and I don't want her to know that I'm talking to you. Is there some way we can get together?"

"Well, what fun," Mrs. Ochsner said. "What shall we do? I

could take the elevator down to the laundry room. It's right near the parking lot, you know, and you could pick me up."

"Let's do that," I said. "I'll swing by in ten minutes."

"Make it fifteen. I'm slower than you think."

The woman whom I helped into the front seat of the car had hobbled out of the laundry room with a cane. She was small, with a dowager's hump the size of a backpack and off-white hair that stood out around her head like dandelion fuzz. Her face was as soft and withered as an apple doll and arthritis had twisted her hands into grotesque shapes, as though she intended to make geese heads in shadow on the wall. She was wearing a housedress that seemed to hang on her bony frame and her ankles were wrapped in Ace bandages. She had two garments over her left arm.

"I want to drop these off at the cleaner's," she said. "You can run them in. I want to stop by the market, too. I'm out of my cereal and half-and-half." Her manner was energetic, her voice wavering but excited.

I went around to my side of the car and got in. I started the car, glancing at the third floor to make sure Pat Usher wasn't standing there watching us. I pulled out. Mrs. Ochsner peered at me avidly.

"You don't look at all like you sounded on the phone," she said. "I thought you'd be blond with blue eyes. What are they, gray?"

"Hazel," I said. I lowered my sunglasses so she could see for herself. "Where's the cleaner's from here?"

"Right next door to that drugstore you telephoned from. What do you call that haircut?"

I glanced at myself in the rearview mirror. "I guess I don't call it anything. I do that myself with nail scissors every six weeks. I keep my hair short because I don't like to fool with it. Why, do you think it looks bad?"

"I don't know yet. It probably suits, but I don't know you well enough to say. What about me? Do I look like I sound?"

I glanced over at her. "You sound like a hell-raiser on the phone."

"I was when I was your age. Now, I have to be careful I'm not just written off as a crank like Ida. All my dear friends died and I got stuck with the crabby ones. What kind of luck are you having with Elaine?"

"Not a lot. Pat Usher says she was actually in Boca for a couple of days and then took off again."

"No, she wasn't."

"Are you sure?"

"Of course I am. She always knocked on the wall when she got in. It was like a little code. She's been doing it for years. She'd come over within the hour and make arrangements to play bridge with us because she knew how much it meant."

I parked in front of the cleaner's and picked up the two dresses she'd placed over the seat. "I'll be right back," I said.

I took care of both errands while Mrs. Ochsner waited and then we sat in the car and talked. I filled her in on my conversation with Pat Usher.

"What do you think of her?" I asked.

"She's too aggressive," Mrs. Ochsner said. "She tried to cultivate me at first, you know. Sometimes I'd sit out on the balcony in the sun and she'd talk to me. She always had that sooty smell people get when they smoke too much."

"What'd you talk about?"

"Well, it wasn't culture, I'll tell you that. She talked about food most of the time, but I never saw her put anything in her mouth except cigarettes and Fresca. She drank pop incessantly and that mouth of hers flapped all the time. So self-centered. I don't believe she ever asked me one word about myself. It simply never occurred to her. I was bored to death, of course, and began to avoid her whenever I could. Now she's rude because she knows I disapprove of her. Insecure people have a special sensitivity for anything that finally confirms their own low opinion of themselves."

"Did she mention Elaine?"

"Oh yes. She said Elaine was off on a trip, which struck me as odd. I'd never known her to come down here only to go someplace else. What would be the point?"

"Can you tell me who else Elaine might have kept in touch with? Any other friends or relatives down here?"

"I'll have to think about that. I don't know of anyone offhand. I assume that most of her good friends are in California, since that's where she lives most of the time."

We talked on for a while, but mostly about other things. At 11:15, I thanked her and took her back to the parking lot, gave her my business card so she could call me if she needed to, and then watched her hobble to the elevator. Her gait was irregular, like a marionette's being worked from above by strings. She waved to me with her cane and I waved back. She hadn't told me much, but I was hoping she'd be able to report on what was happening here after I flew back.

I drove out to the beach and sat in the parking lot with my index cards, making notes of everything I could remember about my search to this point. It took an hour and my hand was cramped, but I needed to get it down while the details were fresh. When I finished, I took my shoes off and locked the car, walking the beach. It was too hot to jog and the lack of sleep had left me torpid anyway. The breeze coming in off the ocean was dense with the smell of salt. The surf seemed to roll in at half speed and there were no whitecaps. The ocean was a luminous blue and the sand was littered with exotic shells. All I'd ever seen on the California beaches were tangles of kelp and occasional Coke-bottle bottoms worn smooth by the sea. I longed to stretch out on the beach and nap in the hot sun, but I had to be on my way.

I ate lunch at a roadside stand built of pink cinder block while a radio station blared out Spanish-language programs as foreign to me as the food. I feasted on black-bean soup and a bolsa—a sort of pouch made of pastry holding a spicy ground meat. By four o'clock that afternoon, I was on a plane, headed for California. I'd been in Florida for less than twelve hours and I wondered if I was any closer to finding Elaine Boldt. It was possible that Pat Usher was being straight with me when she claimed Elaine was in Sarasota, but I doubted it. In any event, I was anxious to get home and I slept like the dead until the plane reached LAX.

When I got to the office at nine the next morning, I filled out a routine form for the Driver's License Records at the Department of Motor Vehicles in Tallahassee, Florida, and a second form for Sacramento on the off-chance that Elaine might have been issued a driver's license in her own name sometime in the last six months. I also sent similar requests to the Vehicle Registration Records in both places, not so much with the expectation of the inquiries paying off, but just to cover my bets. I stuck all four envelopes in my out box and then I pulled out the phone book and started checking addresses for travel agents located within walking distance of Elaine's condominium. I was hoping to establish her travel arrangements and find out if a plane ticket had been used. So far, I had only Pat Usher's word that Elaine had ever arrived in Miami. Maybe she never even reached the airport in Santa Teresa, or maybe she got off the plane at some point en route. In any event, I was going to have to check it out item by item. I felt as if I were on an assembly line, inspecting reality with a jeweler's loupe. There's no place in a P.I.'s life for impatience, faintheartedness, or sloppiness. I understand the same qualifications apply for housewives.

Most of my investigations proceed just like this. Endless notes, endless sources checked and rechecked, pursuing leads that sometimes go no place. Usually, I start in the same place, plodding along methodically, never knowing at first what might be significant. It's all detail; facts accumulated painstakingly.

It's hard to remain anonymous these days. Information is available on just about anyone: credit files on microfiche, service records, lawsuits, marriages, divorces, wills, births, deaths, licenses, permits, vehicles registered. If you want to remain invisible, pay cash for everything and if you err, don't get caught. Otherwise, any good P.I. or even a curious and persistent private citizen can find you out. It amazes me that the average person isn't more paranoid. Most of our personal data is a matter of public record. All you have to know is how to look it up. What your state and city government don't have on file, your next-door neighbor will usually share without so much as a dollar changing hands. If there was no way to get a line on Elaine Boldt directly, I'd try an oblique approach. She'd left for Boca two weeks early, traveling at night, which, according to Tillie, was something she didn't like to do. She'd told Tillie she was ill, leaving town on doctor's orders, but at this point, there was no verification of that claim. Elaine might have lied to Tillie. Tillie might be lying to me. For all I knew Elaine had left the country, planting Pat Usher behind her to promulgate the notion that she was in Sarasota instead. I hadn't any idea why she'd do such a thing, but then I had a lot of ground to cover yet.

Having narrowed the list of travel agencies to six possibilities, I put in a call to Beverly Danziger and filled her in on my excursion to Florida. I wanted to bring her up to date even though the trip hadn't netted me much. I also had a couple of questions for her.

"What about family?" I asked. "Are your parents alive?"

"Oh, they've both been gone for years. We were never a

close-knit family in the first place. I don't even think there were uncles or cousins she'd kept in touch with."

"What about jobs? What sort of work has she done?"

Beverly laughed at that. "You must not have a clear sense of Elaine quite yet. Elaine never lifted a finger in her life."

"But she does have a social-security card," I said. "If she's worked at all, it gives me one more avenue to pursue. For all we know, she's waiting tables someplace for a lark."

"Well, I don't think she's ever had a job, and if she did, it's not something she'd ever do again," Beverly said primly. "Elaine was spoiled. She felt she should be handed everything and what she wasn't handed, she took right out from under your nose anyway."

I really wasn't much in the mood to listen to Beverly unload past grievances. "Look, let's skip to the bottom line here. I think we ought to file a missing persons report. That way we can open up the scope of this thing. It should also eliminate some possibilities and believe me, at this point, everything helps."

The silence was so complete, I thought she'd hung up on me.

"Hello?"

"No, I'm here," she said. "I just don't understand why you want to talk to the *police* of all people."

"Because it's the next logical step. She may well be somewhere in Florida, but suppose she's not. At the moment, we only have Pat Usher's word for that. Why not get some broadscale coverage? Let the cops put out an APB. Let the Boca Raton P.D. get some sort of inquiry routed through Sarasota and see what they come up with. They can circulate a description through the state and local police down there and at least determine that she's not ill or dead or under arrest."

"Dead?"

"Hey, I'm sorry. I know it sounds alarming, and it may be nothing like that, but the cops will have access to information I just can't get."

"I don't believe this. I just wanted her signature. I hired you because I thought it would be the quickest way to find her. I don't think it's really a police matter. I mean, I simply don't want you to do that."

"All right. What, then? You can't ask me to find your sister for you and then start cutting off lines of inquiry."

"I don't see why not if I don't think it's appropriate. I don't see why you can't just let it go at this."

This time I was silent, wondering at the nature of her uneasiness. "Beverly, did I miss something here? Are you telling me to drop it?"

"Well, I don't know. Let me think about it and I'll call you back. I just didn't think it would be a problem and I'm not sure I want you to go on with this. Maybe Mr. Wender can proceed without her. Maybe he can find some loophole that will let him hold out only her portion of the estate until she turns up."

"You didn't seem to feel that way two days ago," I said.

"Maybe I made a mistake," she said. "Let's just don't worry about it right now, okay? I'll be in touch if I want you to go on with it. In the meantime, why don't you send me a report and an itemized bill of some kind? I'll have to talk to my husband about what to do from here."

"All right," I said with puzzlement, "but I have to tell you, I'm worried."

"Well, don't be," she said and the phone clicked in my ear.

I stared at the receiver. Now what was all that about? Her anxiety had been unmistakable, but I couldn't ignore the message. She hadn't fired me outright, but she'd put me on hold and I wasn't technically supposed to proceed without her instructions to do so.

Reluctantly, I went back through my index cards and typed up a report. I was stalling for time and I knew it, but I wasn't ready to let go. I put a carbon in my files and slipped the original in an envelope, which I addressed to Beverly, enclosing an itemization of my expenses to that point. Beyond the seven-hundred-and-fifty-dollar retainer she'd given me, she'd authorized an additional two hundred and fifty dollars for a total "not to exceed one thousand dollars without further written notice"—which was contractual double-talk for the fact that so far, we were covered. With the plane fare, the rental car, long-distance calls, and approximately thirty hours of my time, the charges came to $996 plus change. She owed me two hundred and forty-six bucks. I suspected she'd pay me off and wash her hands of it. My guess was that she'd enjoyed hiring a detective, officiously stirring up trouble for Elaine, who'd annoyed her by not signing on the dotted line as she'd been asked. Now suddenly, she must have realized that she'd opened up a big can of worms.

I locked up the office and dropped the report in a mailbox on my way home. Elaine Boldt was still among the missing and that didn't sit well with me.

5

My phone rang at 2:08 A.M. I picked up the receiver automatically, my brain still blank with sleep.

"Kinsey Millhone." The voice was male and the tone was neutral, like someone reading at random from a telephone book. Somehow I knew it was a cop. They all sound like that.

"Yes. Who's this?"

"Miss Millhone, this is Patrolman Benedict of the Santa Teresa Police Department. We've been called on a 594 at 2097 Via Madrina, apartment 1, and a Mrs. Tillie Ahlberg is asking for you. Would it be possible for you to lend some assistance? We have a policewoman with her, but she's asked for you specifically and we'd appreciate it if you could respond."

I raised up on one elbow, a few brain cells switching to ignition. "What's a 594?" I said. "Malicious mischief?"

"Yes ma'am."

It was clear Patrolman Benedict didn't want to risk anything by rushing right in with a lot of facts.

"Is Tillie okay?" I asked.

"Yes ma'am. She's unharmed, but she's upset. We don't mean to disturb you, but the lieutenant okayed us to get in touch."

"I'll be there in five minutes," I said and hung up.

I pushed the quilt back and grabbed for my jeans and sweatshirt, pulling on boots without ever getting up off the couch. I usually sleep naked in a fold of quilt because it's so much easier than opening the sofa bed. I went into the bathroom, brushed my teeth and splashed water on my face, combing my unruly hair with my fingers as I snatched up my keys and moved to the car. I was wide awake by now, wondering what kind of 594 we were talking about. Tillie

Ahlberg was clearly not the perpetrator or she'd have called an attorney instead.

The night air was cold and the fog had rolled in off the beach and halfway across town, filling the empty streets with a fine mist. Stoplights blinked dutifully from red to green to red again, but there was no traffic and I ran the lights every chance I got. There was a black-and-white parked out in front of 2097 and the lights in Tillie's ground-floor apartment were all on, but things seemed quiet; no flashing red lights, no neighbors gathered on the sidewalk. I announced myself on the intercom and somebody buzzed me in. I pushed through the door to the right of the elevator and moved quickly down the corridor to Tillie's apartment at the end. Several people in robes and pajamas stood in the hall near the door, but a patrolman in uniform was encouraging them to go on back to bed. When he spotted me, he approached, hands on his hips as though he didn't know what else to do with them. He looked like he'd probably still be asked for his I.D. when he ordered a drink, but up close I could see signs of age: fine lines near his eyes, a slight loosening of the taut skin along his jaw. His eyes were old and I knew he'd already seen more of the human condition than he could assimilate.

I held out my hand. "Are you Benedict?"

"Yes ma'am," he said, shaking hands with me. "You're Miss Millhone, I take it. Nice to meet you. We appreciate this." His grip was firm, but brief. He nodded toward the door to Tillie's apartment, which stood ajar. "You can go on in if you want. Officer Redfern is with her, taking down particulars."

I thanked him and moved into the apartment, glancing to my right. The living room looked like something left in the path of a tornado. I stopped and stared for a moment. Vandalism in a place like this? I moved into the kitchen. Tillie was sitting at the table with her hands tucked between her knees, the freckles standing out on her pale face like red pepper flakes. A uniformed policewoman, maybe forty years old, was seated at the table taking notes. She had short-cropped blond hair and a birthmark like a patch of rose petals on one cheek. Her name tag identified her as Isabelle Redfern and she talked to Tillie in low, earnest tones like someone trying to persuade a flier not to leap off a bridge.

When Tillie caught sight of me, tears spilled out of her eyes and she began to shake, as though my appearance were tacit permission to fall apart. I knelt down beside her, taking her hands. "Hey, it's okay," I said, "what's going on?"

She tried to speak, but nothing came out at first except a wheezing sound like someone stepping on a rubber duck. Finally, she managed to choke out a response. "Someone broke in. I woke up and saw this woman standing in the door to my room. My God, I thought my heart would stop. I couldn't even move I was so terrified. And then . . . and then, she started . . . it was like this hissing sound and she ran in the living room and started tearing everything up. . . ." Tillie put a handkerchief over her mouth and nose, closing her eyes. Officer Redfern and I exchanged a look. Bizarre stuff. I put my arm around Tillie's shoulders, giving her a little shake.

"Come on, Tillie," I said, "it's over now and you're safe."

"I was so scared. I was so scared. I thought she was going to kill me. She was like a maniac, like a totally crazy person, panting and hissing and crashing around. I slammed the bedroom door shut and locked it and then dialed 911. Next thing I knew it got quiet, but I didn't open up the door until the police got here."

"That's great. You did great. Look, I know you were scared, but you did it just right and now it's okay."

The policewoman leaned forward. "Did you get a good look at this woman?"

Tillie shook her head, beginning to shake again.

This time the policewoman took Tillie's hands. "Take a couple of deep breaths. Just relax. It's over now and everything's fine. Breathe deeply. Come on. Do you have any tranquilizers on hand or alcohol of some kind?"

I got up and moved over to the kitchen cabinets, opening doors at random, but there didn't seem to be any liquor at all. I found a bottle of vanilla extract and poured the contents into a jelly glass. Tillie downed it without even looking.

She began to breathe deeply, calming herself. "I never saw her before in my life," she said in somewhat more ordered tones. "She was crazy. A lunatic. I don't even know how she got in." She paused. The air smelled like cookies.

The policewoman looked up from her notes. "Mrs. Ahlberg, there was no sign of forced entry. It had to be someone who had a key. Have you given a key to anyone in the past? Maybe someone who was house-sitting? Someone who watered your plants when you were away?"

At first Tillie shook her head and then she stopped and shot a look at me, her eyes filled with sudden alarm.

"Elaine. She's the only one who ever had one." She turned to the policewoman. "My neighbor in the apartment right above me. I gave her a key last fall when I took a little trip to San Diego."

I took over then, filling in the rest; Elaine's apparent disappearance and her sister's hiring me.

Officer Redfern got up. "Hold on. I want Benedict to hear this."

It was 3:30 in the morning by the time Redfern and Benedict were finished, and Tillie was exhausted. They asked her to come down to the station later that morning to sign a statement and in the meantime, I said I'd stay with her until she had herself under control again.

When the cops finally left, Tillie and I sat and stared at each other wearily.

"Could it have been Elaine?" I asked.

"I don't know," she said. "I don't think so, but it was dark and I wasn't thinking straight."

"What about her sister? Did you ever meet Beverly Danziger? Or a woman named Pat Usher?"

Tillie shook her head mutely. Her face was still as pale as a dinner plate and there were dark circles under her eyes. She anchored her hands between her knees again, tension humming through her like a wind across guitar strings.

I moved into the living room and surveyed the damage more closely. The big glass-fronted secretary had been tipped over and lay facedown on the coffee table, which looked to have collapsed on impact. The couch had been slashed, the foam hanging out now like pale flesh. Drapes were torn down. Windows had been broken, lamps and magazines and flowerpots flung together in a heap of pottery shards and water and paper pulp. This was what insanity looked like when it was on the loose. That or unbridled rage, I thought. This had to be connected to Elaine's disappearance. There was no way I'd believe it was an independent event, coincidental to my search for her. I wondered if there was a way to find out where Beverly Danziger had been tonight. With her porcelain good looks and her blinking china blue eyes, it was hard to picture her loping around all looney-tunes, but how did I know for sure? Maybe she'd driven up to Santa Teresa the first time on an institutional pass.

I tried to imagine what it would be like to wake in the dead of night to some hissing female on the rampage. An involuntary shiver took me and I went back into the kitchen. Tillie hadn't moved, but her eyes came up to my face with a look of dependency.

'Let's get it cleaned up," I said. "We're neither of us going to sleep anyway and you shouldn't have to do this by yourself. Where do you keep your dustpan and broom?"

She pointed to the utility room and then with a sigh she got to her feet and we went to work.

When order had been restored, I told Tillie I wanted the key to Elaine's apartment. "What for?" she asked apprehensively.

"I want to check it out. Maybe she's up there."

"I'll come with you," she volunteered promptly. I wondered vaguely if she was going to follow me around for life like Yogi Bear and Boo-Boo. Still, I gave her a quick hug and told her to wait a minute while I made a quick trip to my VW. She shook her head and followed me outside.

I took my semi-automatic out of the glove compartment, hefting it in my hand. It was a nondescript .32 with a cross-hatched ivory grip and a clip that would hold eight rounds. The life of a private eye is short on gun battles, long on basic research, but there are times when a ballpoint pen just doesn't get it. I had visions of some deranged female flying out of the darkness at me like a bat. A .32 may not have much stopping power, but it can sure slow you down. I wedged the gun in the back of my jeans and headed back to the elevator with Tillie at my heels.

"I thought it was against the law to carry a concealed weapon like that," she said uneasily.

"That's why I have a permit," I said.

"But I always heard handguns were so dangerous."

"Of course they're dangerous! That's the point. What do you want me to do? Go in there with a hunk of rolled-up newspaper?"

She was still giving that one some thought when we reached the second floor. I took out the automatic and eased the safety off, pulling back the slide on the barrel to cock it. I slipped the key to Elaine's lock and then I opened the door and let it swing back. Tillie was holding on to my sleeve like a little kid. I waited a moment, staring into the gloomy interior

with my heart thumping. There was no sound...no movement inside. I felt for the light switch and flipped it on,
peering around the doorframe quickly. Nothing. I indicated
that Tillie was to wait where she was and I moved through
the apartment quietly, turning lights as I went, using a
modified version of my best junior G-man stance every time I
entered a room. As far as I could tell, there was no sign that
anyone had been there. I checked the closets and took a
quick peek under the bed and then sighed, realizing that I'd
been holding my breath. I went back to the front door and
had Tillie come in, closing and locking it behind us. I moved
back down the hallway to the den.

I went through Elaine's desk quickly, checking her files. In
the third drawer down, I found her passport and flipped
through the pages. It was still valid, but it hadn't been used
since a trip to Cozumel one April three years back. I tucked
the passport in my back pocket. If she was still around, I
didn't want her using her passport to slip out of the country.
There was something else knocking around in the back of my
head, but I couldn't figure out what it was. I shrugged to
myself, assuming it would surface in due course.

I deposited Tillie at her door.

"Look," I said, "when you have a chance, take a careful
look around and see if anything's missing. When you go down
to the police station, they'll want a list of stolen property if
you know of any. Do you carry any homeowner's insurance
that might cover the damages?"

"I don't know," she said, "I guess I can check. Would you
like some tea?" Her expression was wistful and she clung to
my hand.

"Tillie, I wish I could, but I've got to go. I know you're
uneasy, but you'll be okay. Is there somebody in the building
who can keep you company?"

"Maybe the woman in apartment 6. I know she's up early.
I'll try her. And thanks, Kinsey. I mean that."

"Don't worry about it. I was glad to help. I'll talk to you
later. Get some sleep if you can."

I left her looking after me plaintively as I headed toward
the lobby. I got in the car and tucked the gun in the glove
compartment again, and then I headed for my place. My
head was full of questions, but I was too tired to think. By the
time I crept back in the folds of my quilt, the sky was a

predawn gray and an enterprising rooster somewhere in my neighborhood was heralding the day.

The phone shrilled again at 8:00 A.M. I'd just reached that wonderful heavy stage of sleep where your nervous system turns to lead and you feel like some kind of magnetic force has just fused you to the bed. Consistently waking someone from a sleep like that could generate psychosis in two days.

"What," I mumbled. I could hear static in the line, but nothing else. Oh goody, maybe I'd been wakened by a long-distance obscene phone caller. "Hello?"

"Oh, that's you! I thought I'd dialed the number wrong. This is Julia Ochsner down in Florida. Did I wake you up?"

"Don't worry about it," I said. "I thought I just saw you. What's happening?"

"I've come across some information I thought you might like to have. It looks like that woman next door was telling the truth when she told you Elaine flew down here in January, at least as far as Miami."

"Really?" I said, sitting up. "What makes you say that?"

"I found the plane ticket in the garbage," she said with satisfaction. "You'll never believe what I did. She was packing up to go and she'd set several boxes full of discards and trash out. I'd been down to the manager's apartment and on my way back I spotted the ticket. It was right near the top, shoved down half out of sight, and I wanted to see whose it was. I didn't think I could come right out and ask her so I waited until she made a trip down to the parking lot with a load of clothes and I just scampered out there and stole it."

"You scampered?" I said, with disbelief.

"Well, it wasn't 'scampering' exactly. More like a fast creep. I don't think she even missed it."

"Julia, what made you do that? Suppose she'd caught you!"

"What do I care? I'm having a ball. When I got back, I had to go lie down I was laughing so hard!"

"Yeah, well you'll never guess what's happened here," I said. "I got fired."

"Fired?"

"More or less. Elaine's sister told me to lay off for the time being. She got nervous when I told her I thought we should file a missing persons report with the cops."

"I don't understand. Why would she object?"

"Beats me. When did Elaine leave Santa Teresa? Do you have the date?"

"It looks like January ninth. The return was left open."

"Well, that helps some. Why don't you drop that in the mail to me if it's not too much trouble. Beverly may back down yet."

"But that's ridiculous! What if Elaine's in trouble?"

"What can I do? I'm paid to follow instructions. I can't just bop around doing anything I please."

"What if I hired you myself?"

I hesitated, taken aback by the idea but not opposed to it.

"I don't know. That could get sticky. I suppose I could terminate my relationship with her, but there's no way I could release information to you that I'd uncovered for her. You and I would have to start from scratch."

"But she couldn't *prevent* me from hiring you, could she? I mean, once you've settled your account with her?"

"God, it's too early in the morning for me to worry about this stuff, but I'll mull it over and see what I can come up with. As far as I know, I could turn around and work for you, as long as it doesn't represent any conflict of interest. I'd have to advise her what's going on, but I don't see how she could interfere."

"Good, then do it."

"Are you sure you want to spend your money that way?"

"Of course I am. I have lots of it and I want to know what's happened to Elaine. Besides, I'm having the time of my life! Just tell me what we do next."

"All right. Let me nose around some and I'll call you back. And Julia, in the meantime, would you watch out for yourself?" I said, but she just laughed.

6

I stayed in the shower until the hot water ran out and then I got dressed, pulling on jeans and a cotton sweater, zipping boots up to my knees. I plopped on a soft leather hat with a wide brim and studied the effect in the bathroom mirror. It would do.

I headed for the office first and wrote a letter to Beverly Danziger, terminating our professional relationship. I was pretty sure she'd be thoroughly disconcerted by that and it gave me a nice feeling. I went next door to the offices of California Fidelity Insurance and made a photocopy of my itemized bill to her, marked it "final," and tucked it in with the letter and a copy of my final report. Then I headed over to the police station on Floresta and talked to a Sergeant Jonah Robb about a missing persons report on Elaine Boldt, watching his fingers fly across the keys as he typed the information I gave him on the form.

He looked like he was in his late thirties, his body compact in his uniform. He was maybe twenty pounds overweight, not an unattractive amount, but something he'd have to cope with soon. Dark hair trimmed very short, smooth rounded face, a dent in his left ring finger where he'd recently worn a wedding ring. He shot a look at me at that point. Blue eyes flecked with green.

"Anything you want to add to this?"

"Her next-door neighbor down in Florida is sending me a plane ticket she apparently used. I'll take a look at it and see if it tells us anything else. A friend of hers named Pat Usher swears up and down she spent a couple of days with Elaine Boldt before she went off to Sarasota, but I don't believe much of what she says."

45

"She'll probably show up. They usually do." He took a file folder out and inserted a clamp. "You used to be a cop, didn't you?"

"Briefly," I said. "But I couldn't make it work. Too rebellious I guess. What about you? How long have you been on the force?"

"Eight years. I was a detail man before that. Sold drugs for Smith, Kline, and French. I got tired of driving around in a late-model car, hitting up on doctors. It was all hype anyway. Just like selling anything else. Sickness is big business." He looked down at his hands, then back at me. "Well. Anyway, I hope you find your lady. We'll do what we can."

"Thanks," I said, "I'll give you a call later in the week."

I picked up my bag and moved toward the door.

"Hey," he said.

I looked back.

"I like the hat."

I smiled.

As I passed the front counter on my way out, I caught sight of Lieutenant Dolan in Identification and Records, talking to a young black clerk in uniform. His glance slid past me and then came back with a look of recognition. He broke off his conversation with her and ambled over to the counter. Lieutenant Dolan is in his fifties, with a square, baggy face and a bald spot he tries to disguise with tricky arrangements of what hair remains. It's the only evidence of any vanity on his part and it cheers me up somehow. I imagine him standing in front of his bathroom mirror every morning, trying to cope with the creeping expanse of naked scalp. He was wearing rimless bifocals, apparently new, because he couldn't quite get me in range. He peered at me first from above the little half-moons and then from below. Finally, he slipped the glasses off and tucked them in the pocket of his rumpled gray suit.

"Hello, Kinsey. I haven't see you since the shooting. How are you doing with that?"

I felt myself flush with discomfort. I'd killed someone in the course of an investigation two weeks before and I was studiously avoiding the subject. The moment he mentioned it I realized how completely I'd willed it away. It hadn't even crossed my mind and his reference to it seemed as startling as that dream where you find yourself stark-naked in a public place.

"I'm fine," I said briefly, breaking off eye contact. In a flash, I saw the beach at night, that slat of light when the big trash bin I was hiding in was opened and I looked up. My little semiautomatic had jumped in my hand like some kind of reflex test and I'd squeezed off more rounds than were really necessary for getting the job done. The blast in that confined space had been deafening and my ears had been ringing ever since, a high-pitched hiss like gas escaping from a faulty valve. In a flash, the image was gone again and Lieutenant Dolan was standing there, maybe wishing he'd kept his mouth shut judging from the look on his face.

My relationship to Con Dolan has always been adversarial, remote, based on grudging mutual respect. He doesn't like private investigators as a rule. He feels we should mind our own business, whatever *that* is, and leave law enforcement to professionals like him. My fantasy has always been that one day we'll sit down and exchange criminal gossip like little old ladies, but now that he'd introduced a personal note, I could feel myself withdraw, disconcerted by the shift. When I met his eyes again, his gaze was flat, his expression bland.

I shook my head. "Sorry," I said, "you took me by surprise. I guess I haven't quite sorted it through." Actually what took me by surprise was realizing I'd killed someone and didn't much care. No, that wasn't true. I did care, but if my life was threatened, I knew I'd do it again. I'd always believed I was a good person. Now I didn't know what "good" meant. Surely good people didn't kill other human beings, so where did that put me?

He said, "What are you doing down here?"

I shook my head again slightly and focused on the subject at hand. "I just filed a missing persons report for a client," I said. I hesitated, wondering if he'd encountered Elaine during his investigation of the incident next door. "Did you handle the Grice homicide back in January of this year?"

He stared at me, his face closing up like sea anemone. Apparently he had. "What about it?"

"I wondered if you interviewed a woman named Elaine Boldt. She lives in the condominium next door."

"I remember the name," he said carefully. "I spoke to her myself by phone. She was supposed to come down and talk to us, but I don't think she ever showed up. She your client?"

"She's the one I'm looking for."

"How long she been gone?"

I detailed the information I had and I could see him run through the possibilities in the same way I had. In Santa Teresa County, some four thousand persons, male and female, are reporting missing every year. Most are found again but a few remain somewhere out in the ether.

He shoved his hands down in his pockets, rocking on his heels. "When she does turn up, tell her I want her down here for an interview," he said.

I was startled. "That case hasn't been wrapped up yet?"

"No, and I won't discuss it with you either. Department policy," he said. His favorite phrase.

"Jesus, Lieutenant Dolan. Big deal. Who asked you?" I knew he was protecting the integrity of his case, but I get tired of his being such a tight-ass. He thinks he is entitled to any information I have, while he never gives me a thing. I was hot and he knew it.

He smiled at me. "I just thought I'd head off that tendency of yours to stick your nose where it doesn't belong."

"I'll help you out sometime too," I said. "And meanwhile, if you want to talk to Elaine Boldt, you can find her yourself."

I pushed away from the counter, heading toward the exit.

"Well, you don't need to take that attitude," he called. I glanced back. He was looking entirely too self-satisfied for my taste.

"Right," I said and pushed on out the double doors.

I came out of the police station into the flat overcast day and stood for a moment, collecting myself. The man gets to me. No doubt about it. I took a deep breath.

The temperature was in the mid-sixties. Pale remnants of sunlight shone through the clouds, tinting the neighborhood with lemon-colored light. The shrubbery had taken on a chartreuse glow and the grass seemed dry and artificial from the lack of moisture. It hadn't rained for weeks and the month of June had been a monotonous succession of foggy mornings, hazy afternoons, and chilly nights. Actually, Lieutenant Dolan had opened up a possibility and I wondered if Elaine's departure was coincidental with the murder of Marty Grice or connected in some way. If the vandalism at Tillie's was related, why not this? Could she have taken off to avoid the lieutenant's questioning? I thought it might help to pin down some dates.

I headed over to the newspaper office six blocks away and asked the clerk in the newspaper morgue to track down the file clips on Marty Grice's death. There was only one clip, a small article, maybe two inches long, stuck back on page eight of local news, dated January 4.

BURGLAR KILLS HOUSEWIFE, THEN BURNS BODY, POLICE SAY

A Santa Teresa housewife was bludgeoned to death during an apparent burglary in her west-side residence early last night. According to homicide detectives, Martha Renée Grice, 45, of 2095 Via Madrina, was struck repeatedly with a blunt instrument and doused with flammable liquid. The victim's body was discovered, badly burned, in the foyer of the partially destroyed single-family dwelling after Santa Teresa fire fighters battled the blaze for thirty minutes. The fire was first spotted by neighbors at 9:55 P.M. Two adjacent homes were evacuated, but no other injuries were reported. Details of the arson were withheld pending further investigation.

The crime seemed pretty spectacular to get such small play. Maybe the cops hadn't had much to go on and had tried to minimize the coverage. That might explain Dolan's attitude. Maybe he wasn't being uncooperative. Maybe he had no evidence. Nothing makes a cop any tighter than that. I took down the pertinent information in my notebook and then I walked over to the public library and checked the Santa Teresa city directory that had come out last spring. Martha Grice was listed at 2095 Via Madrina along with a Leonard Grice, bldg. contrctr. I assumed he was the husband. The newspaper account had made no mention of him and I wondered where he'd been when the whole thing went down. The directory listed the neighbors next door at 2093 as Orris and May Snyder. His occupation was "retired" but the directory didn't say from what. I jotted down the names and the telephone number. It might be interesting to see if I could find what went on and whether Elaine might have seen something she didn't want to talk about. The more I thought about it, the better I liked that idea. It gave me a whole new line to pursue.

I retrieved my car from the lot behind my office and circled back around to Via Madrina. It was now twelve o'clock straight up and high-school students were spilling out onto the streets; girls in jeans, short white socks and high heels, guys in chinos and flannel shirts. The wholesome California sorts outnumbered the punkers about three to one, but most of them looked like they'd been dressed out of ragbags. Some kids were wearing outrageous designer jumpsuits and some wore whole outfits in camouflage fabric as though prepared for an air attack. About half the girls sported three to four earrings per ear. In hairstyles, they seemed to fancy the wet look, or ponytails sticking up out of the sides of their heads like waterspouts.

As I pulled up in front of the condominium, a cluster of six girls were clumping down the sidewalk, smoking clove-scented cigarettes. Shoulder pads and green nail polish, dark red lipstick. They looked like they were on their way to a USO dance in 1943.

I caught just a fragment of their conversation.

"So I'm all 'What the fuck did you think I was talking about, dick-head?!' and he goes like 'Hey, well, I never did anything to you, bitch, so I don't know what your problem is.'"

I smiled to myself, and then looked over at the Grice house with interest. It was white frame, a story and a half, with a squat L-shaped porch across the front, resting on fat red-brick pillars topped with short pyramids of wood. It looked as if it had been jacked up somehow and might, at any moment, collapse. Most of the porch roof had burned away. The yard was scrappy and a row of pale pink-and-blue hydrangea bushes crowded the porch, still looking browned and wilted from the fire, though new growth was bravely showing through. The front window frames on the first floor were capped with lintels of black soot where the fire had licked the framing. A sign had been posted warning trespassers away. I wondered if the salvage crew had already gone in to clean up. I was hoping not, but I was probably out of luck on that. I wanted to see the house as it had been on the night of the fire. I also wanted to chat with Leonard Grice, but there was no indication whatever that the house was inhabited. Even from the street, I could still pick up the six-month-old cologne of charred wood and grinding damp where the firemen's hoses had penetrated every seam and crevice.

As I headed toward Elaine's condominium, I spotted someone coming out of a small wooden utility shed in the Grices' backyard. I paused to watch. A kid, maybe seventeen. He had a Mohawk haircut, three inches of what looked like bright pink hay with a path mown on either side. He had his head down, his hands shoved into the pockets of his army fatigues. With a start, I realized I'd seen him before—from Elaine's front window the first time I searched her place. He'd been standing in the street below, rolling a joint at a leisurely pace. Now what was he up to? I veered, picking up my pace so my path would intersect his just about at the property line.

"Hello," I said.

He looked up at me, startled, flashing the sort of polite smile kids reserve for adults. "Hi."

His face didn't match the rest of him. His eyes were deepset, a jade green set off by dark lashes and dark eyebrows that feathered together at the bridge of his nose. His skin was clear, his smile engaging, slightly snaggle-toothed. He had a dimple in his left cheek. He glanced to one side, moving past me. I reached out and caught him by the sleeve.

"Can I talk to you?"

He looked at me and then quickly back over his shoulder. "You talking to me?"

"Yes. I saw you coming out of that shed back there. You live around here?"

"What? Oh. Sure, couple of blocks away. This is my Uncle Leonard's house. I'm supposed to check and make sure nobody's bothering his stuff." His voice was light, almost feminine.

"What stuff is that?"

The jade-green eyes had settled on me with curiosity. He smiled and his whole face brightened. "You a cop or something?"

"Private investigator," I said. "My name is Kinsey Millhone."

"Wow, that's great," he said. "I'm Mike. You guarding the place or something like that?"

I shook my head. "I'm looking into another matter, but I heard about the fire. Your aunt was the one who was killed?"

The smile flickered. "Yeah, right. Jesus, that was terrible. I mean, her and me were never close, but my uncle really got messed up over that. He's a fuckin' basket case. Oh. Sorry 'bout that," he said sheepishly. "He's like vegged out or something, staying with this other aunt of mine."

"Can you tell me how to get in touch with him?"

"Well, my aunt's name is Lily Howe. I don't remember the number offhand, or I'd help you out."

He was beginning to blush and the effect was odd. Pink hair, green eyes, rosy cheeks, green army fatigues. He looked like a birthday cake, innocent and festive somehow. He ran a hand across his hair, which was standing straight up on top like a whisk broom.

I wondered why he was so ill at ease. "What were you doing back there?"

He glanced back at the shed with an embarrassed shrug. "I was checking the padlock. I get like really paranoid, you know? I mean, the guy pays me ten bucks a month and I like to do right by him. Did you want something else? Because I have to go grab some lunch and get back to class, okay?"

"Sure. Maybe I'll see you later."

"Right. That'd be great. Anytime." He smiled at me again and then moved away, walking backward at first, his eyes latched to mine, turning finally so that I was watching the narrow back and slim hips. There was something disturbing about him, but I couldn't think what it was. Something didn't jibe. That goody-two-shoes helpfulness and the look in his eyes. Artless and cunning...a kid whose conscience is clear because he doesn't have one. Maybe I'd check him out too, as long as I was at it. I went into the condominium courtyard.

7

I found Tillie spraying down the walk, a rolling tumble of
leaves and debris pushed along by the force of the jet. Water
dripped from the feather palms, the rubbery scent of hose
mingling with the odor of wet earth. Stepping-stones were
tucked in among the giant ferns, though why anyone would
want to walk back in there was beyond me. It looked like a
shadowy haven for daddy longlegs. Tillie smiled when she
saw me and released the trigger nozzle, shutting off the spray.
She was wearing jeans and a T-shirt, her spare form giving
her a girlish look even in her sixties.

"Did you ever get any sleep?" I asked.

"No, and I'm not going to stay in that apartment 'til the
windows are fixed. I may have an alarm system put in too. I
came out here just to busy myself. Hosing the walks is
restful, don't you think? It's one of the pleasures of adult-
hood. When I was a kid, my dad never would let me have a
turn."

"Have you been down to the police station yet?"

"Oh, I'll go in a bit, but I don't look forward to it."

"I went by a little while ago and filed a missing persons
report on Elaine."

"What'd they say?"

I shrugged. "Nothing much. They'll do what they can. I
ran into a homicide detective who worked on Marty Grice's
murder. He says Elaine was supposed to come in for an
interview and never showed up. Do you remember how soon
afterward she went to Florida?"

"Well, I'm not sure. It was that same week. I do know that
much. She was terribly upset about the murder and that's
one reason she left. I thought I mentioned that."

"You said she was sick."

"She was, but she always seemed to have something wrong with her. She said the murder had her crazy with anxiety. She thought getting out of town would help. Hang on," Tillie said. She went into the bushes and turned off the water at the faucet, using the last of the water pressure to empty the hose before she coiled it up again. She emerged from the shrubbery, wiping her damp hands on her jeans. "Are you thinking she knew something about Marty's death?"

"I think it's worth looking into," I said. "Her side window looks right down into the Grices' entryway. Maybe she saw the burglar."

Tillie made a skeptical face. "In the dark?"

I shrugged. "It doesn't seem likely, does it, but I don't know what else to think."

"But why wouldn't she have gone to the police if she knew who it was?"

"Who knows? Maybe she wasn't thinking straight. People panic. They don't like to get involved in these things. Maybe she felt she was in jeopardy herself."

"Well, she *was* nervous," Tillie said. "But then we were all a bundle of nerves that week. You want to come in?"

"Actually I do. I think I ought to take a look at those bills of hers. At least we can see how recently she's used her charge accounts and where she was at the time. Has anything else come in?"

"Just a couple of things. I'll show you what I've got."

I followed Tillie through the lobby and into the corridor beyond.

She unlocked her front door and moved into the living room, crossing to the secretary. Since the glass had been broken out of the doors, there was no need to unlock anything, but I saw her hesitate, nonplussed, putting an index finger on the side of her cheek like someone posing for a photograph. "Now, that's odd."

"What?" I asked. I crossed to the secretary and looked in. We'd replaced the tumble of books the night before, and there was nothing else on the shelves now except a small brass elephant and a framed snapshot of a puppy with a stick in its mouth.

"I don't see Elaine's bills and they should be there," she said. "Now, isn't that strange." She glanced at the shelves again and then opened the drawers one by one, sorting through the contents.

She moved into the kitchen and dug into the big black plastic bag where we had dumped all the broken glass and debris the night before. There was no sign of them.

"Kinsey, they were in the secretary yesterday. I saw them myself. Where could they have gone?"

She looked up at me. It didn't take a massive leap of intelligence to arrive at the obvious possibility.

"Could *she* have taken them?" Tillie asked. "That woman who broke in last night? Is that what she was really up to?"

"Tillie, I don't know. Something about it bothered me at the time," I said. "It didn't make sense to think someone would break in while you were here just to tear the place apart. Are you sure you saw them yesterday?"

"Of course. I put the new batch of bills with the other ones on the shelf. They were right here. And I don't remember seeing them at all when we cleaned up. Do you?"

I thought back, chasing it around in my memory. I'd only seen the bills once, the first time I'd talked to her. But why would someone bother to steal them? It didn't make sense.

"Maybe she deliberately scared the pants off you to keep you out of the way while she searched the place," I said.

"Well, she sure had the right idea. I wouldn't have come out of my room on a dare! But why would she do that? I don't understand."

"I don't either. I can always get duplicates of the bills, but it's going to be a pain in the ass and I'd rather not do it if I don't have to."

"I want to know who has a key to my apartment. That makes my blood run cold."

"I don't blame you. Listen, Tillie. Nothing makes me crazier than sixteen unanswered questions in a row. I'm going to see what I can find out about this murder next door. It has to be connected somehow. Have you talked to Leonard Grice recently?"

"Oh, he hasn't been there since it happened," she said. "I haven't seen him at any rate."

"What about the Snyders on the other side? Do you think they could be of any help?"

"They might. Do you want me to talk to them?"

"No, don't worry about it. I'll check with them myself. Just one more thing. Leonard Grice has a nephew . . . a kid with a pink Mohawk."

"Mike."

"Yeah, him. Is there any chance he might have been the person who broke in last night? I just talked to him outside and he's not a big guy. He might well have looked like a woman in the dark."

"I don't think so," she said, skepticism plain. "I couldn't swear to it, but I don't think it was him."

"Well. Just a thought. I don't like to make assumptions about gender. It really could have been anyone. I'm going to go next door and see what the Snyders have to say. You take care of yourself."

The house at 2093 was similar in feeling to the house that burned . . . the same-size lot, same ill proportions, the same white frame and red brick. The brick itself was roughly textured, a cunning imitation of fired clay. There was a FOR SALE sign out front with a banner pasted across it boasting SOLD! as though an auction had been enacted just before I started up the walk. A large tree shaded the yard down to a chill, and dark ivy choked the trunk, spreading out in all directions in a dense mat that nearly smothered the walk. I went up the porch steps and knocked on the aluminum screen door. The front door had a big glass panel in it, blocked by a sheer white curtain stretched between two rods. After a moment, someone moved the curtain aside and peered out.

"Mr. Snyder?"

The curtain was released and the door opened a crack. The man appeared to be in his seventies, corpulent and benign. Old age had given him back his baby fat and the same look of grave curiosity.

I held out a business card. "My name is Kinsey Millhone. Could I have a few minutes of your time? I'm trying to track down Elaine Boldt, who lives in that big condominium over there, and Tillie Ahlberg suggested I talk to you. Can you help me out?"

Mr. Snyder released the catch on the screen door. "I'll do what I can. Come on in." He held the screen door open and I followed him inside. The house was as dark as the inside of a soup can and smelled of cooked celery.

From the rear of the house, a shrill voice called out.

"What's that? Who all is out there, Orris?"

"Someone Tillie sent!"

"Who?"

"Hold on a minute," he said to me, "she's deaf as a yard of grass. Take a seat."

Mr. Snyder lumbered toward the back. I perched on an upholstered chair with wooden arms. The fabric was a dark maroon plush with a high-low pattern of foliage, some nondescript sort that I'd never seen in real life. The seat was sprung; all hard edges and the smell of dust. There was a matching couch stacked with newspapers and a low mahogany coffee table with an inset of oval glass barely visible for all the paraphernalia on top: dog-eared paperbacks, plastic flowers in a ceramic vase shaped like two mice in an upright embrace, a bronze version of praying hands, six pencils with erasers chewed off, pill bottles, and a tumbler that had apparently held hot milk which had left a lacy pattern on the sides of the glass like baby's breath. There was also an inexplicable pile of pancakes wrapped in cellophane. I leaned forward, squinting. It was a candle. Mr. Snyder could have moved the entire table outside and called it a yard sale.

From the back end of the house, I could hear his exasperated explanation to his wife. "It's nobody selling anything," he snapped. "It's some woman Tillie sent, says she's looking for Mrs. Boldt. Boldt!! That widda woman lived upstairs of Tillie, the one played cards with Leonard and Martha now and again."

There was a feeble interjection and then his voice dropped.

"No, you don't need to come out! Just keep set. I'll take care of it."

He reappeared, shaking his head, his jowls flushed. His chest was sunken into his swollen waistline. He'd had to belt his pants below his big belly and his cuffs drooped at the ankles. He hitched at them irritably, apparently convinced he'd lose them if he didn't hang on. He wore slippers without socks and all the hair had been worn away from his ankles, which were narrow and white, like soup bones.

"Switch on that light there," he said to me. "She likes to pinch on util'ties. Half the time, I can't see a thing."

I reached over to the floor lamp and pulled the chain. A forty-watt bulb came on, buzzing faintly, not illuminating much. I could hear a steady thump and shuffling in the hall. Mrs. Snyder appeared, moving a walker in front of her.

She was small and frail and her jaw worked incessantly. She stared intently at the hardwood floor and her feet made a sticky sound as she walked, as though the floor had been shellacked and had never dried properly. She paused, hanging on to her walker with shaking hands. I stood up, projecting my voice.

"Would you like to sit here?" I asked her.

She surveyed the wall with rheumy eyes, trying to discover the source of the sound. Her head was small, like a little pumpkin off the vine too long, looking shrunken from some interior softening. Her eyes were narrow inverted V's and one tooth protruded from her lower gum like a candle wick. She seemed confused.

"What?" she said, but the question had a hopeless ring to it. I didn't think anybody answered her these days.

Snyder waved at me impatiently. "She's fine. Just leave her be. Doctor wants her on her feet more anyway," he said.

I watched her uncomfortably. She continued to stand there, looking puzzled and dismayed, like a baby who's learned how to pull itself up on the sides of a crib, but hasn't figured out how to sit down again.

Mr. Snyder ignored her, settling on the couch with his knees spread. His belly filled the space between his legs like a duffel bag, as cumbersome on him as a clown suit with a false front. He put his hands on his knees, giving me his full attention as though I might be soliciting his entire history for inclusion on "This Is Your Life."

"We been in this house forty year," he said. "Bought it back in nineteen and forty-three for four thousand dollar. Bet you never heard of a house that cheap. Now it's worth one hunnert and fifteen thousand. Just the lot we're settin' on. That don't even count the house. They can knock this place down and build anything they want. Hell, she can't even get that walker into the commode. Now Leonard, next door, nearly sold his house for a hunnert and thirty-five, had it in escroll and everything and then the deal fell out. That about done him in. He's the one I feel sorry for. House burnt. Wife dead. You know what the kids these days would say ... his carnal was bad."

He went right on talking while I took mental notes. This was better than I'd hoped. I had thought I'd have to tell a few fibs, leading the conversation around judiciously from Elaine's whereabouts to the subject of the murder next door, but here sat Orris Snyder giving testimony extemporaneously. I realized he'd stopped. He was looking at me.

"You've sold this house? I saw the sign out front."

"Sold," he said with satisfaction. "We can move us up to that retirement place when the kids get everything here packed up. We've got a regular reservation. We're on the list and everything. She's old. She doesn't even know where she is half the time. Fire broke out in this place, she'd lay there and cook."

I glanced at his wife, who had apparently locked her knees. I was worried she would pass out, but he didn't seem to give it much thought. She might as well have been a hall tree.

Snyder went on as though prompted by questions from an unseen audience. "Yessir, I sold it. She like to have a fit, but the house is in my name and I own it free and clear. Paid four thousand dollar. Now I call that a profit, wouldn't you?"

"That's not bad," I said. I glanced over at his wife again. Her legs had begun to tremble.

"Why don't you get on back to bed, May?" he said and then looked at me with a disapproving shake of his head. "She can't hear good. Hearing comes and goes. Got tintypes of the ear and all she can see is living shapes. She got the leg of that walker hung up on the broom-closet door last week and stood there for forty-six minutes before she got loose. Old fool."

"You want me to help you get her back to bed?" I asked.

Snyder floundered on the couch, turning himself sideways so he could get up. He pushed himself to his feet and then went over to her and shouted in her face. "Go lay down awhile, May, and then I'll get you some snackin' cake," he said.

She stared steadfastly at his neck, but I could have sworn she knew exactly what he was talking about and was just feeling stubborn and morose.

"Why did you put the light on? I thought it was day," she said.

"It only cost five cent to run that bulb," he said.

"What?"

"I said it's pitch-black night outside and you got to go to bed!" he hollered.

"Well," she said, "I think I might in that case."

Laboriously, she thumped the walker around, navigating

with effort. Her eyes slid past me and she seemed suddenly to discern me in the haze.

"Who's that?"

"It's some woman," Snyder broke in. "I was telling her of Leonard's back luck."

"Did you tell her what I heard that night? Tell about the hammering kept me awake. Hanging pictures . . . bang, bang, bang. I had to take a pill it made my head hurt so bad."

"That wasn't the same night, May. How many times I told you that? It couldn't have been because he wasn't home and he's the one did that kind of thing. Burglars don't hang pictures."

He looked over at me then, twirling his index finger beside his temple to indicate that she was rattlebrained.

"Banged and banged," she said, but she was only muttering to herself as she thunked away, moving the walker in front of her like a clothes rack.

"She hasn't a faculty left," he said to me over his shoulder. "Pees on herself half the time. I had to move every stick of dining-room furniture out and put her bed in there right where the sideboard stood. I told her I'd outlive her the day I married her. She gets on my nerves. She did back then too. I'd just as soon live with a side of meat."

"Who's at the door?" she said insistently.

"Nobody. I'm talkin' to myself," he said.

He shuffled into the hallway behind her. His hovering had a tender quality about it in spite of what he said. In any event, she didn't seem aware of his aggravation or his minor tyrannies. I wondered if he'd stood there and timed her for the forty-six minutes while she struggled with the broom-closet door. Is that what marriages finally come down to? I've seen old couples toddle down the street together holding hands and I've always looked on faintly misty-eyed, but maybe it is all the same clash of wills behind closed doors. I've been married twice myself and both ended in divorce. I berate myself for that sometimes but now I'm not sure. Maybe I haven't made such a bad trade-off. Personally, I'd rather grow old alone than in the company of anyone I've met so far. I don't experience myself as lonely, incomplete, or unfulfilled, but I don't talk about that much. It seems to piss people off—especially men.

8

Mr. Snyder returned to the living room and sat down heavily on the couch. "Now then."

"What can you tell me about that fire next door?" I asked. "I saw the place. It looks awful."

He nodded, preparing himself as though for a television interview, staring straight ahead. "Well now, the fire engine woke me up ten o'clock at night. Two of 'em. I don't sleep good anyhow and I heard the siren come right up here close so I got up and went out. Neighbors was runnin' from ever' which way. Black smoke outen that house like you never saw. These firemen, they bashed their way in and pretty soon flames et up the front porch. Whole backside got saved. They found Marty, that was Leonard's wife, layin' on the floor. It'd be right about over there," he said, pointing toward the front door. "I never seen her myself, but Tillie said she was charred head to foot. Just a bunch of stumps, like a piece of wood."

"Oh really. Tillie didn't mention that to me."

"She seen the smoke and called right up. Nine-one-one it was. I was sound to sleep. Woke up when the fire engine come blastin' down the road. I thought they'd go right on by, but then I seen the lights and I got up and put a robe on and went out. Poor Leonard wasn't even home. He drove up about the time they got the fire out. Collapsed right on the street when he heard she was dead. I never saw a man so tore up. My wife, May, she never woke up at all. She'd tooken a pill and she's deaf as a broom anyway. You've seen that yourself. Fire broke out here, she'd been roast pork."

"What time was it when Mr. Grice got home?"

"I don't know the exact time. Fifteen, twenty minutes after

the fire engines come as best I recollect. He was out to dinner with his sister as I hear tell and he comes home to find his own wife dead. His knees give out and down he went. Right on the sidewalk with me standin' not this far away. Turned white and dropped like a big hand had give him a thump and knocked him out. It was the awfullest thing you ever saw. They brought her out zipped up in a plastic sack—"

"How'd Tillie happen to see her?" I interrupted. "I mean, if she was zipped up in a body bag?"

"Oh, that Tillie, she sees everything. Ask her. She prob'ly pushed through when the door got bashed in and seen the body for herself. Makes me sick to think of it."

"I understand Leonard's been staying with his sister since then."

"That's what I heard, too. Her name is Howe. Lives on Carolina. It's in the book if you want to get in touch."

"Good. I'll try to see him this afternoon. I'm hoping he can tell me something about where Mrs. Boldt might have gone."

I got up and held out my hand. "You've been a big help."

Mr. Snyder struggled to his feet and shook my hand, walking to the door with me.

I looked over at him with curiosity. "What do you think your wife was referring to when she mentioned the hammering that night? Do you have any idea what she meant?"

He waved impatiently. "She don't know what she's talkin' about. She got that all confused."

I shrugged. "Well, I hope Mr. Grice is doing all right at any rate. Did he have good insurance coverage? That would be a big help, I'm sure."

He shook his head, pulling at his chin. "I don't think he come out too good on that. Him and me has the same insurance comp'ny, but his policy didn't amount to much as I understand it. Between the fire and his wife's being gone now, he's about ruined. He collects disability for a bad back, you know, and she was sole support."

"God, that's terrible. I'm sorry to hear that," I said, and then took a chance. "What insurance company?"

"California Fidelity."

Ahh. I felt my little heart go pitty-pat. This was the first break I'd had. I worked for them.

California Fidelity Insurance is a small company that handles all the ordinary coverage: life and health, homeowner's, auto, and some commercial lines, with branches in San Francisco, Pasadena, and Palm Springs. Santa Teresa is the home office, occupying the second floor of a three-story building on State Street, which cuts straight through the heart of town. My corner consists of two rooms—one inner, one outer—with a separate entrance. Early in my career, I worked for CFI, doing insurance investigations on fire and wrongful-death claims. Now that I'm out on my own, we maintain a loose association. I cover certain inquiries for them every month in exchange for office space.

I let myself into the office now and checked the answering machine. The light was blinking, but the tape was blank except for some hissing and a couple of high-pitched beeps. For a while, I had a live answering service, but the messages were usually botched. I didn't think prospective clients were that keen to confide their troubles to some twenty-year-old telephone operator who could barely spell, let alone keep the numbers straight. An answering machine is irritating, but at least it tells the caller than I am female and I pick up on the second ring. The mail wasn't in yet, so I went next door to talk to Vera Lipton, one of the California Fidelity claims adjusters.

Vera's office is located in the center of a warren of cubicles separating adjusters. Each small space is equipped with a desk, a rolling file, two chairs and a telephone, rather like a little bookie joint. Vera's niche is identifiable by the pall of smoke hovering above the shoulder-high partitions. She's the only one in the company who smokes and she does so with vigor, piling up stained white filter tips like ampules of distilled nicotine. She's also addicted to Coca-Cola and she usually has a row of empty bottles marching around her desk, accumulating them at the rate of one every hour. She's thirty-six, single, and she collects men with ease, though none of them seems to suit her. I peered into her cubicle.

"What'd you do to your hair?" I asked when I caught sight of it.

"I was up all night. It's a wig," she said. She stuck a fresh cigarette between her teeth, biting gently while she lit up. I've always admired her smoking style. It's jaunty and sophisticated, dainty and tough. She pointed to the wig, which was streaked with blond, a wind-blown effect.

"I'm thinking of dyeing my hair this shade. I haven't been a blond for months."

"I like it," I said. Her usual color was auburn, a mix of several Clairol offerings that varied in hues from Sparkling Sherry to Flame. Her glasses today had tortoiseshell rims and big round lenses tinted the color of iced tea. She wore glasses so well it made other women wish their eyesight would fail.

"You must have a new man in your life," I said.

Vera shrugged dismissively, shaking her head. "I got two actually, but I wasn't up doing what you think. I read a book on how the new technology works. Lasers and analog-to-digital converters. I got curious about electricity yesterday, you know? Turns out nobody really knows what it is, which is worrisome if you ask me. Great terminology though. 'Pulse amplitude' and 'oscillation.' Maybe I'll run into a guy I can say that to. What's with you? You want a Coke?"

She had already opened her bottom file drawer where she kept a little cooler packed with ice. She pulled out a Coke in a bottle about the size of a Playtex nurser, and uncapped it by wedging it under the metal drawer handle and giving a quick downward snap. She proffered the bottle, but I shook my head and she drank it down herself. "Have a seat," she said then and set the bottle on the desk top with a thunk.

I moved aside a stack of files and sat down in the extra chair. "What do you know about a woman named Marty Grice who was murdered six months ago? I heard she was insured through CFI."

Vera touched daintily at the corners of her mouth with her thumb and index finger. "Sure, I was assigned to that one. I went out and took a look at the place two days after it happened. God, what a mess. I don't have the proof of loss yet, but Pam Sharkey said she'd get it to me in the next couple of weeks."

"She's the agent on it?"

Vera nodded, taking a drag of her cigarette. She blew the smoke straight up. "The big life-insurance policy lapsed, but there was a little twenty-five-hundred-dollar policy in effect. That's probably not enough to bury a dog these days. There's also a homeowner's for the fire loss, but the guy was desperately underinsured. Pam swears up and down she advised him to upgrade, but he didn't want to be saddled with the added expense. You know how people get. They try to save six bucks and end up blowing two-three hundred thousand when the bottom drops out." She tapped the cigarette on the lip of the empty Coke bottle, neatly knocking the ash into it.

"Why's the settlement taking so long?"

Vera's mouth turned down and she lowered one eyelid—a gesture that conveyed the message "big deal," though I don't know how. "Who knows?" she said. "The guy's got a year to file the claim. Pam says he's been a basket case since his wife died. He can hardly manage to sign his own name."

"Did she leave a will?"

"Not that I heard. The whole thing's been sitting in probate court for the last five months or so, in any event. What's your interest in it? Are you looking into her death?"

"Not really. I'm looking for a woman who lived next door when it happened. She left town a couple of days afterward and hasn't been seen since then by the people who count. I keep thinking there's a connection. I was hoping you'd tell me there was a great big policy in effect."

"The cops had the same idea. Your buddy Lieutenant Dolan was over here practically sitting in my lap for days. I kept saying, 'Forget it! The guy's broke. He's not going to net a dime.' I guess I finally convinced him because I haven't heard from him since. What are you thinking, that Grice and this doll next door were in cahoots?"

"It did cross my mind. I haven't met him yet and I have no idea whether there could have been a relationship between them, but it does look suspect. From what I'm told, she left town abruptly and she was upset. My first instinct was that maybe she'd seen something and took off to avoid getting caught up in it."

"Maybe so." Vera sounded dubious.

"But you don't believe it."

"I'm just looking at his end. If the guy killed his wife for fun and profit, he sure went about it wrong. Why let a policy lapse like that? If he were smart, he'd have jacked the face value up two-three years ago, let enough time pass so it didn't look too obvious and then . . . whap, his wife is dead and he collects. If he killed her with no payoff, he's an idiot."

"Unless he just wanted her out of his way. Maybe that was all he cared about. Maybe letting the policy lapse was a ploy."

"Hey, listen, what do I know? I'm not a homicide dick."

"Me neither. I'm just trying to figure out why this woman disappeared and where she might have gone. Even if you're right and Grice had nothing to do with it, she still might have witnessed something. This burglar business sounds too tidy for words."

Vera smiled cynically. "Hell, maybe she did it herself."

"God, you're more suspicious than I am."

"Well, you want Grice's number? I got it somewhere here." Vera paused to toss the tag end of her cigarette into the Coke bottle. There was a quick spitting sound as the ember touched the thimbleful of Coke that remained. She extracted a file from the bottom of a stack and found the telephone number and the address.

"Thanks," I said.

She gave me a speculative look. "You interested in an unemployed aerospace engineer? He's got bucks. He invented some little dingus they use now in all the satellites."

"How come you don't want him?" I asked. Vera tended to offer up her rejects like hostess gifts.

She made a face. "He was fine for a while, but now he's on a health kick. Started taking algae pills. I don't want to kiss a man who eats pond scum. I thought you might not object since you live so clean. Maybe you two could jog together and nibble dried seaweed snacks. If you're interested, he's yours."

"You're too good to me," I said. "I'll keep an eye out. I might run into someone who's up for him."

"You're way too picky about men, Kinsey," she said reprovingly.

"*I'm* picky?! What about you?"

Vera stuck another cigarette between her teeth and I watched her flick a tiny gold lighter into play before she spoke.

"I figure guys are like Whitman's Samplers. I like to take a little bite out of each and then move on before the whole box gets stale."

9

It was 1:30 by now and as nearly as I could remember, I hadn't eaten lunch. I pulled into a fast-food restaurant, parked, and went in. I could have hollered my order into a clown's mouth and eaten in the car as I drove, but I wanted to show I had class. I wolfed down a cheeseburger, fries, and a Coke for a dollar sixty-nine and was back on the streets again in seven minutes flat.

The house where Leonard Grice was supposedly staying was located in a dingy tract of houses just off the freeway, a neighborhood of winding streets that had been named after states, starting with the East Coast. I rambled down Maine, Massachusetts, New York, and Rhode Island Drives, getting stuck in tricky cul-de-sacs where Vermont and New Jersey turned into dead ends. It looked like the builder had gotten as far as Colorado Avenue before the money ran out or his knowledge of geography failed. There was a long stretch of vacant lots with stakes visible at intervals, each tied with a little white rag to mark off the undeveloped parcels of land.

Most of the houses had gone up in the fifties. The trees had flourished, overpowering the small lots. The houses were alternately pale pink and pale green stucco, mirror images of one another like a whole tray of loaf cakes on a bakery shelf. All had the same rock-covered roofs, as though some volcano nearby had erupted, raining down a thin debris. The whole tract seemed dominated by wide-mouthed garages and I was subjected to untidy views of lawn equipment and camper shells, toys, tools, dusty luggage, banged-up refrigerators. There were surprisingly few cars visible and the impression I got was of a community abandoned in the wake of some natural disaster. Maybe a plague had passed this way or maybe toxic wastes had risen up through the soil, killing all the dogs and cats and burning holes in children's feet. At the intersection of Maryland and Virginia, I turned right.

On Carolina, a few enterprising souls had faced their homes with fieldstone or cedar shingle, and some had opted for an Oriental effect—trellises of plywood with geometric cutouts that were meant to look Chinese, the roof corners tilted up for that gala 1950s pagoda look. Compared to more recent tracts on the outskirts of Santa Teresa, these houses were shabby and the evidence of poor construction floated on the surface like chicken fat on homemade soup. There were cracks in the stucco, window shutters askew. The veneer on the front doors was peeling off in strips. Even the drapes were hung crookedly and I could imagine bathroom plaster bulging out in places, faucet handles frozen with rust.

The Howes had traded their front lawn for a rock garden, apparently burying the scruffy grass under tons of sand, topped with gravel beds in shades of mauve and green. I could still see a strip of black plastic "mulch" peeping out around the edge where some attempt had been made to suppress the weeds. The Bermuda grass had risen to the challenge and it was snaking its way through the gravel at a leisurely pace. There was a birdbath tucked among the succulents and a poured-concrete squirrel seemed to pop up out of the cactus in an attitude of perpetual, stony optimism. I doubted there was a live squirrel within blocks.

I parked the car and walked up to the house, taking the clipboard I keep in the backseat of my car. The Howes' garage door was closed, making the place look blank and unoccupied. The long, low line of the porch was obscured with ivy, looking picturesque, but capable, I knew, of lifting the roof right off. The drapes were closed. I rang the bell, but there was no reassuring "ding-dong" within. A minute passed. I knocked.

The woman who came to the door was subdued, her faded blue eyes searching my face hesitantly.

"Mrs. Howe?"

"I'm Mrs. Howe," she said.

It felt like Lesson One on a foreign-language record. There were dark circles under her eyes and her voice was as flat and dry as a cracker.

"I understand Leonard Grice is staying here. Is that correct?"

"Yes."

I held my clipboard up. "I'm from the insurance company and I wonder if I might have a word with him." It's a marvel God doesn't reach right down and rip my tongue out by the roots for the lies I tell.

"Leonard's taking a rest. Why don't you come back another time." She was closing the door.

"I'll just take a minute," I said quickly. I stuck the clipboard into the crack. She'd never get the door shut that way.

She paused. "The doctor still has him on sedatives." A non sequitur but the point was clear.

"I see. Well, of course, I wouldn't want to disturb him, but I'd really like to see him, as long as I've driven all the way out here." I tried to sound winsome, but apparently failed.

She stared at me stubbornly and I could see the color rise in her face. She glanced sideways as though she were consulting an invisible companion. Abruptly, she moved back and let me into the house with the attitude of someone using the *f* word under her breath. Her hair was gray, shoulder-length and thin, turned under in a tight pageboy. She had bangs along her forehead in a hairstyle I hadn't seen since those June Allyson movies where she was so loving and so long-suffering. Mrs. Howe wore a plain white blouse and a sensible charcoal-gray wool skirt. She was chunky through the waist. What is it about middle age that makes a woman's body mimic pregnancy?

"I'll see if he'll talk to you," she said and left the room.

I waited just inside the front door, taking in with a quick glance the cotton shag carpeting, brick fireplace painted white, an oil painting above it of waves crashing on rocks. She'd apparently used the painting as the focal point of her decorating scheme because the couch and wing chairs were upholstered in the same passionate shade of turquoise, in a fabric that looked faintly damp. I hated this part of my job—asserting myself persistently into somebody else's pain and grief, violating privacy. I felt like a door-to-door salesman, pushing unwanted sets of nature encyclopedias complete with fake walnut case. I also hated myself vaguely for being judgmental. What did I know about hairstyles anyway? What did I know about waves crashing on rocks? Maybe the turquoise said exactly what she'd meant to say about the room.

When Leonard Grice appeared, I could feel my heart sink. He didn't look like a man who'd murdered his wife, as much as that theory appealed to me. He was probably in his early fifties, but he moved like an old man. He was not bad-looking, but his face was pallid, cheeks sunken as though he'd recently lost some weight. His manner was vacant and he held his hands in front of him when he walked as though he were blindfolded. He had all the airs of a man who has stumbled painfully over something in the dark and wants to be certain he doesn't get caught by surprise again. It was possible, of course, that he'd killed her and was consumed now by guilt and remorse, but the killers I've run into in my brief career are either cheerful or matter-of-fact, like they can't understand what all the fuss is about.

Leonard's sister walked beside him, her hand near his elbow, watching where he placed his feet. She eased him toward a chair and shot me a look, clearly hoping I was satisfied at the trouble I'd caused. I did feel crummy, I'll confess.

He sat down. He seemed to be coming to life, reaching automatically for a pack of Camels in his shirt pocket while Mrs. Howe perched on the edge of the couch.

"Sorry to have to bother you," I said, "but I've just been talking to the adjuster at California Fidelity and there were a few details we wanted to clarify. Do you mind answering some questions for me?"

"He can hardly afford not to cooperate with the insurance company," she interjected peevishly.

Leonard cleared his throat, striking a match twice without effect against a paper matchbook. His hands were trembling and I wasn't sure he'd ever manage to match the flame to the end of his cigarette even if he could conjure one up. Mrs. Howe reached over, took the packet, and struck the match for him. He inhaled deeply.

"You'll have to pardon me," he said, "the doctor has me on some medicine that does this to me. I'm on disability for my back. What is it exactly that you want?"

"I've just recently been assigned to this case and I thought it might be helpful to hear your own account of what happened that night."

"What on earth for!" Mrs. Howe said.

"That's all right, Lily," he broke in, "I don't mind. I'm sure she's got her reasons for wanting to know." His voice was stronger now, dispelling the original impression of feebleness.

He took a deep drag of his cigarette, letting it rest in the fork between his index and third fingers.

"My sister's widowed," he said, as though that might explain her belligerence. "Mr. Howe died of a heart attack eighteen months ago. After that, Marty and I got in the habit of taking Lil out to dinner every week. Mostly it was a way to keep up with each other and visit back and forth. Well that night, Marty planned to go as usual, but she said she felt like she was coming down with the flu, so at the last minute she decided to stay home. It was Lil's birthday and Marty was disappointed because she knew we were going to have a little cake brought to the table and waiters singing . . . you know how they do. She wanted to see the look on Lily's face. Anyway, she felt if she wasn't well, she might spoil everybody's evening so she didn't go." He paused, taking a deep drag of his cigarette. He'd accumulated a long ash and Lily pushed an ashtray toward him just as it tumbled.

"Did you tend to go out the same night of the week each time?" I asked.

He nodded. "Tuesdays as a rule."

I made a note dutifully on the legal pad on my clipboard. I hoped I looked like I had some legitimate reason to be asking all this stuff. I pretended to consult a form or two, flipping back a page. I thought the clipboard was a nice touch. I guess Lily did too. She peered over, wanting to see me write down something she said too.

"That's the best night for me," she ventured. "I get my hair done on Tuesdays and I like to go out when it's looking nice."

"Hair on Tues.," I wrote. "How many people knew you went out on Tuesday nights?"

Leonard's eyes slid over to mine with a curious look. The medication had opened his pupils to the full, perfect black holes that looked like they'd been made with a paper punch. "Pardon?"

"I wondered how many people knew about your nights out. If the intruder was someone you knew, he might have thought she'd be out with you as usual."

His expression flickered with uncertainty. "I don't understand what this has to do with the insurance claim," he said.

I had to be careful how I framed my reply because he'd put his finger on the flaw in my charade. My questions had nothing to do with anything except trying to figure out if

Elaine could have seen a murder. So far, I didn't even know
what had actually happened that night and I was trying to
weasel the information out of him. Lieutenant Dolan wasn't
going to tell me, that was for sure.

I smiled briefly, keeping my tone light. "Naturally we're
interested in seeing this crime solved," I said. "We may need
a determination on the case before the claim is paid."   •

Lily glanced at Leonard and then back to me, alerted by
his wariness. "What kind of 'determination'?" she asked. "I
don't understand what you mean."

Leonard shifted back to his original attitude. "Now, Lil, it
can only help," he said. "The insurance company wants to get
to the bottom of this just like we do. The police haven't done
anything on it for months." He glanced at me again. "You'll
have to pardon Lil. . . ."

She flashed him a look. "Don't apologize for me when I'm
sitting right here," she snapped. "You're too trusting, Leonard.
That's what's wrong with you. Marty was the same way. If
she'd been a little more cautious, she might be alive today!"

She faltered, clamping her mouth shut, then surprised me
by filling in some details. "She was on the phone to me that
night and someone came to the door. She rang off to see who
it was."

He chimed in. "The police said it's possible she knew the
person, or it might have been someone off the street. Police
said a lot of times a burglar rings the bell if the lights are on.
If someone answers the door, he can act like he's got the
wrong address. Nobody answers, he might go ahead and
break in."

"Were there signs of a struggle?"

"I don't think so," Leonard said. "Not that I ever heard. I
went through the house myself, but I couldn't see anything
missing."

I looked back at Lily. "What had she called about?" I
asked. "Or did you call her?"

"I called her myself when we got in," she said. "We got
back here a little later than we thought and Leonard didn't
want her to worry."

"And she sounded all right when you talked to her?"

Lily nodded. "She sounded fine. She sounded just like she
always did. Leonard talked to her for a bit and then I got back
on with her and we were just winding down when she said
there was someone at the door and she had to go see who it

was. I was going to offer to stay on the line, but we were done anyway so I just said good-bye and hung up."

Leonard pulled a handkerchief out of his pants pocket and pressed it to his eyes. His hands had begun to shake badly and there was a tremor in his voice. "I don't even know what her last moments were like. Police said the guy must have hit her square in the face with a baseball bat, something that size. She must have been terrified—"

He broke off.

I could feel myself squirm, but I didn't say anything. What actually occurred to me, as tacky as it sounds, is that a baseball bat in the face doesn't leave time to feel much of anything. Crack! You're gone. No terror, no pain. Just lights out, home run.

Lily reached over and place her hand on his. "They were married twenty-two years."

"Good years too," he said, his tone almost argumentative. "We never went to bed mad. That was a rule we made early. Anytime we had a quarrel, we got it settled. She was a fine woman. Smarter than me and I'm not ashamed to admit it."

Tears glittered in his eyes, but I felt oddly removed, like the only sober person at a party full of drunks.

"Did the police mention any possibility of witnesses? Someone who might have seen or heard something that night?"

He shook his head, mopping at his eyes. "No. I don't think so. I never heard that."

"Possibly someone in the building next door?" I suggested. "Or someone passing by? I understand you've got people across the street from you too. You'd think someone would have noticed *something*."

He blew his nose, recovering his composure. "I don't think so. Police never said anything to us."

"Well, I've taken up enough of your time and I'm sorry I've caused you so much distress. I'd like to go through the house and assess the fire damage if you don't mind. One of our adjusters has already been through, but I'll need to see for myself so I can make my report."

He nodded. "My neighbor has a key. Orris Snyder right next door. You go knock on his door and tell him I said it was all right."

I got up and held my hand out to him. "Thanks for talking to me."

Leonard got to his feet automatically and shook my hand. His grip was solid, his flesh almost feverishly hot.

"By the way," I said as if it had just occurred to me, "have you heard from Elaine Boldt lately?"

He focused on me, apparently perplexed by the reference. "Elaine? No, why?"

"I was trying to get in touch with her on another matter and I realized she lived in that condominium right next door," I replied with ease. "Someone mentioned that she was a friend of yours."

"That's right. We used to play bridge together before Marty died. I haven't talked to her for months. She's usually in Florida this time of year, I believe."

"Oh, that's right. I think somebody else mentioned that. Well, maybe she'll call when she gets back," I said. "Thanks again."

By the time I got back out to my car again, both my armpits were ringed with sweat.

10

It was now nearly three o'clock and I was feeling frazzled. I'd been up since two A.M. with just a brief time-out for sleep at dawn before the long-distance call from Mrs. Ochsner had wakened me. I couldn't face the office again, so I headed for my apartment and changed into my running clothes. I use the word *apartment* here in its loosest sense. Actually I live in a converted one-car garage, maybe fifteen feet square, tricked out as living room, bedroom, kitchen, bathroom, closet, and laundry facility. I've always liked living in small spaces. For months as a child, just after my parents were killed, I spent my spare time in a cardboard box that I filled with pillows and pretended was a sailing vessel on its way to some new land. It doesn't take an analyst to interpret this excursion on my part, but it's carried over into my adult life, manifesting itself now in all sorts of things. I drive small cars and I favor "littleness" in any form, so this place suits me exactly. For two hundred dollars a month I have everything I want, including a debonair eighty-one-year-old landlord named Henry Pitts.

I peered in his back window on my way out, and spotted him in the kitchen rolling out puff pastry dough. He's a former commercial baker who supplements his social security these days doing up breads and sweets, which he sells to or trades with local merchants. I tapped on the glass and he motioned me in. Henry is what I like to think of as an octogenarian "hunk," tall and lean with close-cropped white hair and eyes that are periwinkle blue, full of curiosity. Age has boiled him down to a concentrate, all male, compassionate and prudent and wry. I can't say that the years have invested him with spirituality, or infused him with any special

75

wisdom, second sight, profundity, or depth. I mean, let's not overstate the case here. He was smart enough when he first started out and age hasn't diminished that a whit. Despite the fifty years' difference in our ages, there's nothing of the pundit in his attitude toward me, and nothing (I hope) of the postulant in my attitude toward him. We simply eye one another across that half a century with a lively and considerable sexual interest that neither of us would *dream* of acting out.

That afternoon, he was wearing a red rag around his head pirate-style, his tanned forearms bare and powdered with flour, his fingers as long and nimble as a monkey's as he gathered the dough and turned it halfway. He was using a length of chilled pipe as a rolling pin and he paused to flour it while he worked, coaxing the pastry into a rectangle.

I perched up on a wooden stool and retied my shoes. "You making napoleons?"

He nodded. "I'm catering a tea for someone up the street. What are you up to, besides a run?"

I filled him in briefly on my search for Elaine Boldt while he folded the dough in thirds and wrapped it, returning it to the refrigerator. When I got to the part about Marty Grice, I saw his brows shoot up.

"Stay away from it. Take my advice and leave it to the homicide detectives. You're a fool if you get involved in that end of it."

"But what if she saw who killed Marty? What if that's why she took off?"

"Then let her come forward with the information. It's not up to you. If Lieutenant Dolan catches you messing around with his case, he'll have your rear end."

"Actually, that's true," I said ruefully. "But how can I back off? I'm running out of places to look."

"Who says she's lost? What makes you think she's not down in Sarasota someplace lapping up gin and tonic on the beach?"

"Because somebody would have heard from her. I mean, I don't know if she's up to something or maybe in big trouble herself, but until she shows up I'm going to beat the bushes and bang on pans and see if I can run her to ground."

"Make-work," he said. "You're chasing your own tail."

"Well, that's probably true, but I gotta do something."

Henry gave me a skeptical look. He opened a bag of sugar and weighed out a mound. "You need a dog."

"No, I don't. And what's that got to do with it? I hate dogs."

"You need protection. That business at the beach would never have happened if you'd had a Doberman."

That again. God, even my recent brush with death had taken place in a garbage bin... someplace small and cozy with me sobbing like a kid.

"I was thinking about that stuff today and you want to know the truth? All this talk about women being nurturing is crap. We're being sold a bill of goods so we can be kept in line by men. If someone came after me today, I'd do it again, only this time I don't think I'd hesitate."

Henry didn't seem impressed. "I'm sorry to hear that. I hope you haven't started a trend."

"I mean it. I'm tired of feeling helpless and afraid," I said.

Henry puffed his cheeks up and blew a raspberry, giving me a bored look. Big talk, his face said, but you don't fool me a bit. He cracked an egg on the counter and opened it up with one hand, letting the white slip through his fingers into a cup. He put the yolk in a bowl and took up another egg, repeating the process with his eyes pinned on me.

He said, "So defend yourself. Who's arguing with that? But you can drop the rhetoric. It's bullshit. Killing is killing and you better take a look at what you did."

"I know," I said, with less energy. The look in his eyes was making me squirm and I wasn't all that crazy about his tone. "Look, maybe I haven't really dealt with that. I just don't want to be a victim anymore. I'm sick of it."

Henry cradled the bowl in his arms, whisking the eggs with a practiced ease. When I do that, the eggs always slop out the side.

He said, "When were you ever a victim? You don't have to justify yourself to me. You did what you did. Just don't try to turn it into a philosophical statement, because it doesn't ring true. It's not as if you made a rational decision after months contemplating the facts. You killed somebody in the heat of the moment. It's not a platform for a political campaign and it's not a turning point in your intellectual life."

I smiled at him tentatively. "I'm still a good person, aren't I?" I didn't like the wistful tone. I meant to show him I was a grown-up, coping with the truth. Until the words came out of my mouth, I hadn't even known I felt so unsure.

He didn't smile back. His eyes rested on my face for a

moment and then dropped back to the eggs. "What happened to you doesn't change that, Kinsey, but you have to keep it straight. Blow somebody's brains out and you don't brush that off. And you don't try to turn it into an intellectual stance."

"No, you don't," I said uneasily. I had a quick flash of the face that peered into the garbage bin just before I fired. By some remarkable distortion, I could have sworn I saw how the first bullet stretched the flesh like elastic before smashing through. I shook the image away and hopped down. "I have to run," I said, feeling anxious.

I left the kitchen without glancing back, but I know what the look was on Henry's face. Caution and sorrow and pain.

Once outside, I had to put it out of my mind again. Back the subject went, into its own little box. I did a quick stretch, concentrating on my hamstrings. I don't run fast enough or far enough to justify much of a warm-up. Other joggers, I know, would argue with that, citing injuries that result from insufficient stretching before a run, but I find exercise loathsome enough without adding contortions up front. For a time, I tried it, dutifully lying on my back in the grass with one leg straight out and the other cocked sideways toward my waist as though broken at the hip. I could never get up afterward unless I flopped about like a bug and I finally decided it was worth a possible groin-muscle pull to avoid the indignity. I've never been injured running anyway. I've never thrilled to it either. I'm still waiting for the rumored "euphoria" that apparently infuses everyone but me. I headed over to the boulevard at a brisk walk, keeping my mind blank.

I generally do three miles, jogging along the bicycle path that borders the beach. The walkway is stenciled with odd cartoons at intervals and I watch for those, counting off the quarter-miles. The tracks of some improbable bird, the mark of a single fat tire that crosses the concrete and disappears into the sand. There are usually tramps on the beach; some who camp there permanently, others in transit, their sleeping bags arranged under the palm trees like large green larvae or the skins shed by some night-stirring beast.

That afternoon the air seemed heavy and chill, the ocean sluggish. The cloud cover was beginning to break up, but the visible sky was a pale washed-out blue and there was no real sign of sun. Out on the water a speedboat ran a course parallel to the beach and the path of the wake was like a spinning ribbon of silver winding along behind. On the

landward side, the mountains were dark green. At this distance, the low-growing vegetation looked like soft suede, with
rock face showing through along the ridges as though the nap
had worn away from hard use.

I did the turnaround at East Beach and ran the mile and a
half back, then walked the block to my apartment as a
cool-down. I'm big on cool-downs. I showered and dressed
again and then hopped in my car and headed up to Pam
Sharkey's office on Chapel. Pam was the insurance agent
who'd written up the policies for Leonard Grice and I wanted
to probe that issue before I set it aside. I trust Vera, but I
don't like taking people's word for things. Maybe Grice had
taken out a massive policy from some other company. How
did I know?

The Valdez Building is located at the corner of Chapel and
Feria, a Spanish word meaning "fair." I only know that
because I looked it up. I've been thinking I should take a
Spanish class one of these days, but I haven't gotten around
to it yet. I can say *taco* and *gracias* but I'm real short on
verbs. The Valdez is typical of the architecture in this town:
two stories of white stucco with a red tile roof, big arches,
windows faced with wrought-iron gratings. There are azure
blue awnings and the landscaping consists of small plots of
perfect grass. Palm trees grace the courtyard and there's a
fountain capped by a small naked boy doing something wicked with a fish.

Pam Sharkey's office is on the first floor and sports the
same network of cubicles I'd seen at California Fidelity.
Nothing architecturally innovative for the insurance game
these days. It must be like doing business in a series of
playpens. The company she works for, Lambeth and Creek, is
an independent agency that writes policies for a number of
companies, CFI being one. I'd only dealt with Pam once,
when I was bird-dogging an errant husband. His wife, my
client, was in the process of divorcing him and was hoping for
evidence of his philandering as a negotiating tool when it
came down to the settlement. Pam had taken offense, not
because I'd uncovered her affair with the man, but because
I'd turned up two other women involved with him at the
same time. None of this was ever brought up in court, of
course, but her name was prominent in my report. She had
never forgiven me for knowing too much. Santa Teresa is a
small town and our paths cross now and then. We're polite to

one another, but the civilities are undercut with spite on her part and sly amusement on mine.

Pam is petite, a bristly little chihuahua of a human being. She's the only woman I ever met who claims to be ten years older than she actually is so that everyone will tell her how young she looks. On that basis, she swears she's thirty-eight. Her face is small, her skin dusky and she applies pancake makeup in varying shades in a vain attempt to add "planes" to her cheeks. I got news for her. There's no way to disguise the bags under your eyes by the skillful use of "cover." From most angles anybody with a brain can see the bags sitting right there, only looking phantom white instead of gray. Who's fooled by this? Why not go for the dark circles and at least look exotic and worldly-wise . . . Anna Magnani, Jeanne Moreau, Simone Signoret perhaps. Pam had also taken lately to a permanent wave, so her pale brown hair looked frizzy and unkempt, a style apparently billed as "the bedroom look." That afternoon she was done up in a little hunting outfit: a hacking jacket, brown knickers, pink hose and low heels with buckles. The only hunting she did was in singles bars, bagging one-night stands as though the season were nearly over and her license about to expire. Well, wait a minute here. I can see I've been unfair about this. I don't like Pam any more than she likes me. Every time I see her, it makes me feel petty and mean—not my favorite way to experience myself. Maybe she avoids me for the same reason.

Her cubicle is near the front—a status symbol, I think. She caught sight of me and busied herself with papers and files. By the time I'd made my way over to her desk, she was on the phone. She must have been talking to a man because her manner was flirtatious. She touched herself everywhere as she talked, rolling a lock of hair around her finger, checking an earring, stroking the lapel of her jacket. She wore a series of gold necklaces and those got a workout too. Sometimes she'd rub her chin with a loop of gold chain, uttering a carefree, trilling laugh she must have practiced late at night. She glanced at me, feigning surprise, holding up a palm to indicate that I'd have to wait.

She turned away from me in her swivel chair, completing the telephone exchange with a murmured intimacy of some sort. On top of a stack of files on her desk, I could see a copy of *Cosmo*, offering articles on the G spot, cosmetic breast surgery, and social rape.

Pam hung up at long last and swiveled back, all the animation leaving her face. No point in wasting the whole show on me. "Something I can help you with, Kinsey?"

"I understand you wrote a couple of policies for Leonard and Marty Grice."

"That's right."

I smiled slightly. "Could you tell me the status of the paperwork at this point?"

Pam broke eye contact, going through another quick digital survey: earring, hair, lapel. She took up a loop of gold chain, running her index finger back and forth on it until I worried she'd saw right through the skin. She wanted to tell me Leonard Grice was none of my business, but she knew I did occasional work for California Fidelity.

"What's the problem?"

"No problem," I said. "Vera Lipton's wondering about the claim on the fire loss and I need to know if there were any other policies in effect."

"Now, wait a minute. Leonard Grice is a very dear man and he's been through a terrible six months. If California Fidelity intends to make trouble, Vera better deal directly with me."

"Who said anything about trouble? Vera can't even process the claim until the proof of loss is in."

"That goes without saying, Kinsey," she said. "I still don't see what this has to do with you."

I could feel my smile begin to set like a pan of fudge. I leaned forward, left hand flat on the desk, right hand resting on my hip. I thought it was time to clarify our relationship.

"Not that it's any of your business, Pam, but I'm in the middle of a big investigation adjunctive to this. You don't have to cooperate, but I'm just going to turn around and present a court order to the supervisor here and somebody's going to come down on you like a ton of bricks for all the trouble it'll cause. Now is that how you want to proceed on this or what?"

Under the pancake makeup, she began to show signs of sunburn. "I hope you don't think you can intimidate me," she said.

"Absolutely not." I shut my mouth then and let her assimilate the threat. I thought it sounded pretty good.

She took up a stack of papers and rapped them on the desk, aligning the edges. "Leonard Grice was insured through

California Fidelity Life and California Fidelity Casualty Insurance. He collected twenty-five hundred dollars for the life insurance and he'll get twenty-five thousand for the structural damage to the house. The contents were uninsured."

"Why only twenty-five for the house? I thought that place was worth over a hundred grand? He won't have enough money to do the repairs, will he?"

"When he bought the place in 1962, it was worth twenty-five thousand and that's what he insured it for. He never increased the coverage and he hasn't taken out any other policies. Personally, I don't see how he can do anything with the house. It's a complete loss, which I think is what's broken him."

Now that she'd told me, I felt guilty for all the macho bullshit I'd laid on her.

"Thanks. That's a big help," I said. "Uh... by the way, Vera wanted me to ask if you'd be interested in meeting an unattached aerospace engineer with bucks."

A wonderful look of uncertainty crossed her face: suspicion, sexual hunger, greed. Was I offering her a cookie or a flat brown turd on a plate? I knew what was going through her head. In Santa Teresa, a single man is on the market maybe ten days before someone snaps him up.

She shot me a worried look. "What's wrong with him? Why didn't you take him first?"

"I just came off a relationship," I said, "I'm in retreat." Which was true.

"Maybe I'll give Vera a buzz," she said faintly.

"Great. Thanks again for the information," I said and I gave her a little wave as I moved away from her desk. With my luck, she'd fall in love with the guy and want me to be a bridesmaid. Then I'd be stuck with one of those dumb dresses with a hunk of flounce on the hip. When I glanced back at her, she seemed to have shrunk and I felt a twinge. She wasn't so bad.

11

I ate dinner that night at Rosie's, a little place half a block down from my apartment. It's a cross between a neighborhood bar and an old-fashioned beanery, sandwiched between a Laundromat on the corner and an appliance repair shop that a man named McPherson operates out of his house. All three of these businesses have been in operation for over twenty-five years and are now, in theory, illegal, representing zoning violations of a profound and offensive sort, at least to people who live somewhere else. Every other year, some overzealous citizen gets a bug up his butt and goes before the city council denouncing the outrage of this breach of residential integrity. In the off years, I think money changes hands.

Rosie herself is probably sixty-five, Hungarian, short, and top-heavy, a creature of muumuus and hennaed hair growing low on her forehead. She wears lipstick in a burnt-orange shade that usually exceeds the actual shape of her mouth, giving the impression that she once had a much larger set of lips. She uses a brown eyebrow pencil lavishly, making her eyes look stern and reproachful. The tip of her nose comes close to meeting her upper lip.

I sat down in my usual booth near the back. There was a mimeographed menu sheet slipped into a clear plastic cover stuck between the ketchup bottle and the napkin box. The selections were typed in pale purple like those notices they used to send home with us when we were in grade school. Most of the items were written in Hungarian; words with lots of accent marks and z's and double dots, suggesting that the dishes would be fierce and emphatic.

Rosie marched over, pad and pencil poised, her manner withdrawn. She was feeling offended about something, but I wasn't sure yet what I'd done. She snatched the menu out of my hand and put it back, writing out the order without consulting me. If you don't like the way the place is run, you go somewhere else. She finished writing and squinted at the pad, checking the results. She wouldn't quite meet my eyes.

"You didn't come in for a week so I figured you was mad at me," she said. "I bet you been eating junk, right? Don't answer that. I don't want to hear. You don't owe me an apology. You just lucky I give you something decent. Here's what you gonna get."

She consulted the pad again with a critical eye, reading the order to me then with interest as though it were news to her too.

"Green pepper salad. Fantastic. The best. I made it myself so I know it's done right. Olive oil, vinegar, little pinch of sugar. Forget the bread, I'm out. Henry didn't bring fresh today so what do I know? He could be mad at me too. How do I know what I did? Nobody tells me these things. Then I give you sour oxtail stew."

She crossed that off. "Too much grease. Is no good for you. Instead I give you tejfeles sult ponty, some nice pike I bake in cream, and if you clean your plate, I could give you deep-fried cherries if I think you deserve it, which you don't. The wine I'm gonna bring with the flatware. Is Austrian, but okay."

She marched away then, her back straight, her hair the color of dried tangerine peels. Her rudeness sometimes has an eccentric charm to it, but it's just as often simply irritating, something you have to endure if you want to eat Rosie's meals. Some nights I can't tolerate verbal abuse at the end of the day, preferring instead the impersonal mechanics of a drive-in restaurant or the peace and quiet of a peanut butter and dill pickle sandwich at home.

That night Rosie's was deserted, looking drab and not quite clean. The walls are paneled in construction-grade plywood sheets, stained dark, with a matte finish of cooking fumes and cigarette smoke. The lighting is wrong—too pale, too generalized—so that the few patrons who do wander in look sallow and unwell. A television set on the bar usually flashes colored images with no sound, and a marlin arched above it looks like it's fashioned of plaster of Paris and dusted with soot. I'm embarrassed to say how much I like the place. It will never be a tourist attraction. It will never be a singles bar. No one will ever "discover" it or award it even half a star. It will always smell like spilled beer, paprika, and hot grease. It's a place where I can eat by myself and not even have to take a book along in order to avoid unwelcome company. A man would have to worry about any woman he could pick up in a dive like this.

The front door opened and the old crone who lives across the street came in, followed by Jonah Robb, whom I'd talked to that morning in Missing Persons. I almost didn't recognize him at first in his civilian clothes. He wore jeans, a gray tweed jacket, and brown desert boots. His shirt looked new, the package folds still evident, the collar tightly starched and stiff. He carried himself like a man with a shoulder holster tucked up under his left arm. He had apparently come in to look for me because he headed straight for my table and sat down.

I said, "Hello. Have a seat."

"I heard you hung out in here," he said. He glanced around and his brows gave a little lift as though the rumor were true but hard to believe. "Does the Health Department know about this place?"

I laughed.

Rosie, coming out of the kitchen, caught sight of Jonah and stopped dead in her tracks, retreating as though she'd been yanked backward by a rope.

He looked over his shoulder to see if he'd missed something. "What's the matter? Could she tell I was a cop? Has she got a problem with that?"

"She's checking her makeup. There's a mirror just inside the kitchen door," I said.

Rosie appeared again, simpering coquettishly as she brought my silverware and plunked it down on the table tightly bound in a paper napkin.

"You never said you was entertaining," she murmured. "Does you friend intend to have a little bite to eat? Some liquid refreshment perhaps? Beer, wine, a mixed drink?"

"Beer sounds good," he said. "What do you have on tap?"

Rosie folded her hands and regarded me with interest. She never deals directly with a stranger so we were forced to go through this little playlet in which I interpreted as though suddenly employed by the U.N.

"You still have Mich on tap?" I asked.

"Of course. Why would I have anything else?"

I looked at Jonah and he nodded assent. "I think we'll have a Mich then. Are you eating? The food's great."

"Fine with me," he said. "What do you recommend?"

"Why don't you just double the order, Rosie? Could you do that for us?"

"Of course." She glanced at him with sly approval. "I had no idea," she said. I could feel her mentally nudge me with one elbow. I knew what her appraisal consisted of. She favored weight in men. She favored dark hair and easygoing attitudes. She moved away from the table then, artfully leaving us alone. She isn't nearly as gracious when I come in with women friends.

"What brings you here?" I said.

"Idleness. Curiosity. I did a background check on you to save us talking about all the stupid stuff."

"So we could get right down to what?" I asked.

"You think I'm on the make or something?"

"Sure," I said. "New shirt. No wedding ring. I bet your wife left you week before last and you shaved less than an hour ago. The cologne isn't even dry on the side of your neck."

He laughed. He had a harmless face and good teeth. He leaned forward on his elbows. "Hers's how it went," he said. "I met her when I was thirteen and I was with her from that time to this. I think she grew up and I never could, at least not with her. I don't know what to do with myself. Actually she's been gone for a year. It just *feels* like a week. You're the first woman I've looked at since she went off."

"Where'd she go?"

"Idaho. She took the kids. Two," he said as though he knew I'd ask that next. "One girl ten, another one eight. Courtney and Ashley. I'd have named 'em something else. Sara and Diane, Patti and Jill, something like that. I don't even understand girls. I don't even know what they think about. I really love my kids, but from the day they were born it was like they were in this exclusive little club with my wife. I couldn't seem to get a membership no matter what I did."

"What was your wife's name?"

"Camilla. Shit. She ripped my heart out by the roots. I put on thirty pounds this year."

"Time to take it off," I said.

"Time to do a lot of things."

Rosie came back to the table with a beer for him and a glass of white table wine for me. Did I know this story or what? Men just out of marriages are a mess and I was a mess myself. I already knew all the pain, uncertainty and mismanaged emotions. Even Rosie sensed it wasn't going to fly. She looked at me like she couldn't figure out how I'd blown it so fast. When she left, I got back to the subject at hand.

"I'm not doing all that well myself," I said.

"So I heard. I thought we could help each other out."

"That's not how it works."

"You want to go up to the pistol range and shoot sometime?"

I laughed. I couldn't help myself. He was all over the place. "Sure. We could do that. What kind of gun do you have?"

"Colt Python with a six-inch barrel. It'll take a .38 or a .357 magnum cartridge. Usually I just wear a Trooper MK III but I had a chance to pick up the Python and I couldn't pass it up. Four hundred bucks. You've been married twice? I don't see how you could bring yourself to do that. I mean, Jesus. I thought marriage was a real commitment. Like souls, you know, fused all through eternity and shit like that."

"Four hundred bucks is a steal. How'd you pull that off?" I squinted at him. "What is it, are you Catholic or something?"

"No, just dumb I guess. I got my notions of romance out of ladies' magazines in the beauty shop my mother ran when I was growing up. The gun I got from Dave Whitaker's estate. His widow hates guns and never liked it that he got into 'em so she unloaded his collection first chance she got. I'd have paid the going rate, but she wouldn't hear of it. Do you know her? Bess Whitaker?"

I shook my head.

He glanced up then as Rosie put a plate down in front of each of us. I could tell by his look that he hadn't expected green peppers with a vinaigrette, even with little curlicues of parsley tucked here and there.

Usually Rosie waited until I tasted a dish and gave elaborate restaurant-reviewer-type raves, but this time she seemed to think better of it. As soon as she left, Jonah leaned forward.

"What is this shit?"

"Just eat."

"Kinsey, for the last ten years I been eating with kids who sit and pick all the onions and mushrooms out. I don't know how to eat if it's not made with Hamburger Helper."

"You're in for a big surprise," I said. "What have you been eating for the year since your wife left?"

"She put up all these dinners in the deep freeze. Every night I thaw one and stick it in the oven at three-fifty for an hour. I guess she went to a garage sale and bought up a bunch of those TV dinner tins with the little compartments. She wanted me to eat well-balanced meals even though she was fucking me over financially."

I lowered my fork and looked at him, trying to picture someone freezing up 365 dinners so she could bug out. This was the woman he apparently imagined mating with for life, like owls.

He was eating his first bite of pepper salad, his eyes turning inward. His facial expression suggested that the pepper was sitting in the middle of his tongue while he made chewing motions around it. I do that myself with those mashed candied sweet potatoes people insist on at Thanksgiving time. Why would anyone put a marshmallow on a vegetable? Would I put licorice on asparagus, or jelly beans on Brussels sprouts? The very idea makes my mouth purse.

Jonah nodded philosophically to himself and began to fork up the pepper salad with gusto. It must have been at least as tasty as the shit Camilla cooked for him. I pictured tray after tray of frozen tuna casserole with crushed potato chips, with maybe frozen peas in one compartment, carrot coins in the next. I bet she left him six-packs of canned fruit cocktail for dessert. He was looking at me.

He said, "What's the matter? Why do you have that look on your face?"

I shrugged. "Marriage is a mystery."

"I'll second that," he said. "By the way, how's your case shaping up?"

"Well, I'm still nosing around," I said. "Right now, I'm making a little side investigation into an unsolved murder. Her next-door neighbor was killed the same week she left."

"That doesn't sound good. What's the connection?"

"I don't know yet. Maybe none. It just struck me as an interesting sequence of events that Marty Grice was murdered and Elaine Boldt disappeared within days of it."

"Was there a positive I.D.?"

"On Marty? I have no idea. Dolan's getting really anal-retentive about that stuff. He won't tell me a thing."

"Why not take a look at the files?"

"Oh come on. He's not going to let me see the files."

"So don't ask him. Ask me. I can make copies if you tell me what you want."

"Jonah, he would fire your ass. You would never work again. You'd have to sell shoes for the rest of your life."

"Why would he have to know?"

"How could you get away with it? He knows everything."

"*Bull*shit. The files are kept over in Identification and Records. I'll bet he's got a second set in his office so he probably never even looks at the originals. I'll just wait 'til he's out and Xerox whatever you need. Then I'll put it back."

"Don't you have to sign 'em out?"

He gave me a look then like I was probably the kind of person who never parked in a red zone. Actually, for someone to whom lying comes so easily, I get anxious about vehicle codes and overdue library books. Violations of the public trust. Oh hey, once in a while I might pick a lock illegally, but not if I think there's a chance I'll get *caught*. The idea of sneaking official documents out of the police station made my stomach squeeze down like I was on the verge of getting a tetanus shot.

"Oh wow, don't do that," I said. "You can't."

"What do you mean, I 'can't.' Of course I can. What do you want to see? Autopsy? Incident report? Follow-up interviews? Lab reports?"

"That'd be great. That would really help."

I looked up guiltily. Rosie was standing there waiting to pick up our salad plates. I leaned back in the booth and waited until both had been removed. "Look, I'd never ask you to do such a thing—"

"You didn't ask. I volunteered. Quit being such a candy ass. You can turn around and do me a favor sometime."

"But Jonah, he really is a nut about department leaks. You know how he gets. Please don't put yourself in jeopardy."

"Don't sweat it. Homicide detectives are full of crap sometimes. You're not going to blow his case for him. He probably doesn't even have a case, so what's to worry about?"

After dinner, he walked me back over to my place. It was only 8:15, but I had work to do and he really seemed a bit relieved that the contact between us wasn't going to be prolonged or intimate. As soon as I heard his footsteps retreat, I turned the outside lights off, sat down at my desk with some index cards and caught up with my notes.

I checked back through the cards I'd filled out before and tacked them up on the big bulletin board above my desk. I stood there for a long time, reading card after card, hoping for a flash of enlightenment. Only one curious note emerged. I'd been very meticulous about writing down every single item I remembered from my first search of Elaine's apartment. I do that routinely almost like a little game I play with myself to test my memory. In the kitchen cabinet, she'd had some cans of cat food. 9-Lives Beef and Liver Platter, said the note. Now it seemed out of place to me. What cat?

12

At nine the next morning, I drove over to Via Madrina. Tillie didn't answer my buzz so I stood for a minute, surveying the list of tenants' names on the directory. There was a Wm. Hoover in apartment 10, right next door to Elaine's. I gave him a buzz.

The intercom came to life. "Yes?"

"Mr. Hoover? This is Kinsey Millhone. I'm a private detective here in town and I'm looking for Elaine Boldt. Would you mind if I asked you a couple of questions?"

"You mean, right this minute?"

"Well, yes, if you wouldn't mind. I stopped by to talk to the building manager, but she's not here."

I could hear a murmur of conversation and then the door buzzed at me by way of consent. I had to jump to catch it while the lock would still open. I took the elevator up a floor. Apartment 10 was just across from me when the elevator door slid open. Hoover was standing in the hall in a short blue terry-cloth robe with snags. I estimated his age at thirty-four, thirty-five. He was slight, maybe five foot six, with slim, muscular legs faintly matted with down. His dark hair was tousled and he looked as if he hadn't shaved for two days. His eyes were still baggy from sleep.

"Oh God, I woke you up," I said. "I hate to do that to people."

"No, I've been up," he said. He ran a hand across his hair, scratching the back of his head while he yawned. I had to clamp my teeth so I wouldn't yawn in response. Barefoot, he moved back into the apartment and I followed him.

"I just put some coffee on. It'll be ready in a sec. Come on in and have a seat." His voice was light and reedy.

He indicated the kitchen to the right. His apartment was the flip image of Elaine's and my guess was that their two master bedrooms shared a wall. I glanced at the living room which, like hers, opened off the entryway and also looked down on the Grices' property next door. Where Elaine's apartment had a view of the street, this one didn't have much to recommend it—only a glimpse of the mountains off to the left, partially obscured by the two rows of Italian stone pines that grow along Via Madrina.

Hoover adjusted his short robe and sat down on a kitchen chair, crossing his legs. His knees were cute. "What's your name again? I'm sorry, I'm still half-unconscious."

"Kinsey Millhone," I said. The kitchen smelled of brewing coffee and the fumes of unbrushed teeth. His, not mine. He reached for a slim brown cigarette and lit it, hoping perhaps to mask his morning mouth with something worse. His eyes were a mild tobacco brown, his lashes sparse, face lean. He regarded me with all the boredom of a boa constrictor after a heavy meal of groundhog. The percolator gave a few last burps and subsided while he reached for two big blue-and-white mugs. One had an overall design of bunny rabbits humping. The other portrayed elephants similarly occupied. I tried not to look. The thing I've worried about for years is how dinosaurs mated, especially those great big spiny ones. Someone told me once they did it in water, which helped support all that weight, but I find it hard to believe dinosaurs were that smart. It didn't seem likely with those tiny pinched heads. I shook myself back to reality.

"What do you call yourself? William? Bill?"

"Wim," he said. He fetched a carton of milk from the refrigerator and found a spoon for the sugar bowl. I added milk to my coffee and watched with interest while he added two heaping tablespoons of sugar to his. He caught my look.

"I'm trying to gain a little weight," he said. "I know the sugar's bad for my teeth, but I've been doing up these torturous protein drinks in the morning—you know the kind— with egg and banana and wheat germ thrown in. Ugh. The aftertaste just cannot be disguised. Besides, I hate to eat before two in the afternoon so I guess I should resign myself to being thin. Anyway, that's why I load up my coffee. I figure anything's bound to help. You look a little on the Twiggy side yourself."

"I run every day and I forget to eat." I sipped my coffee, which was scented faintly with mint. It was really very good.

"How well did you know Elaine?" I asked.

"We spoke when we ran into one another in the hall," he said. "We've been neighbors for years. Why do you want her? Did she run out on her bills?"

I told him briefly about her apparent absence, adding that the explanation didn't have to be sinister, but that it was puzzling nevertheless. "Do you remember when you saw her last?"

"Not really. Sometime before she went off. Christmas, I guess. No, I take that back. I did see her New Year's Eve. She said she was staying home."

"Do you happen to know if she had a cat?"

"Oh sure. Gorgeous thing. A massive gray Persian named Mingus. He was actually my cat originally, but I was hardly ever home and I thought he should have company so I gave him to her. He was just a kitten at the time. I had no idea he'd turn out to be such a beauty or I never would have given him up. I mean, I've kicked myself ever since, but what can one do? A deal's a deal."

"What was the deal?"

He shrugged indifferently. "I made her swear she'd never change his name. Charlie Mingus. After the jazz pianist. Also she had to promise not to leave him by himself, or what was the point in giving him away? I might as well have kept him myself."

Wim took a careful drag of his cigarette, resting his elbow on the kitchen table. I could hear the shower running somewhere in the back of the apartment.

"Did she take him with her to Florida every year?"

"Oh sure. Sometimes right up in the cabin if the airline had the space. She said he loved it down there, thought he owned the place." He picked up a napkin and folded it in half.

"Well, it's curious he hasn't shown up someplace."

"He's probably still with her, wherever she is."

"Did you talk to her after that murder next door?"

Wim shook his head, neatly flicking ash into the folded napkin. "I did talk to the police, or rather they talked to me. My living-room windows look right down on that house and they were interested in what I could have seen. Which was nothing, I might add. That detective was the biggest macho asshole I've ever met and I didn't appreciate his antagonistic attitude. Can I warm that up for you?"

He got up and fetched the coffee.

I nodded and he topped off both our mugs, pouring from a thermos. The sound of running water had abruptly ceased and Wim took note of it, just as I did. He went back to the sink and extinguished his cigarette by running it under the tap and then he tossed it in the trash. He got out a frying pan and took a package of bacon from the refrigerator. "I'd offer you breakfast, but I don't have enough unless you want to join me in a protein drink. I'm going to make that up in a minute, disgusting as it is. I'm doing real food for a friend of mine."

"I've got to go shortly anyway," I said, getting up.

He waved at me impatiently. "Sit down, sit down. Finish your coffee at any rate. You might as well ask whatever you want as long as you're here."

"What about a vet for the cat? Did she have someone in the neighborhood?"

Wim peeled off three strips of bacon and laid them in the pan, flipping on the gas. He leaned over, peering at the low blue flame. He had to tug his robe down in back.

He said, "There's a cat clinic around the corner on Serenata Street. She used to take Ming over in one of those cat carriers, howling like a coyote. He hated the vet."

"You have any guesses about where Elaine might be?"

"What about her sister? Maybe she's gone down to L.A. to see her."

"The sister was the one who hired me in the first place," I said. "She hasn't seen Elaine in years."

Wim looked up sharply from the bacon pan and laughed. "What a crock of shit! Who told you that? I met her up here myself not six months back."

"You met Beverly?"

"Sure," he said. He took a fork and pushed the bacon strips in the pan. He went back to the refrigerator and got out three eggs. I was starving to death just watching this stuff.

He continued chattily. "She was maybe four years younger than Elaine. Black hair, cut gamin-style, exquisite skin." He looked at me. "Am I right or am I not?"

"Sounds like the woman I met," I said. "But I wonder why she lied to me."

"I can probably guess," he said. He tore off some paper

toweling and folded it, putting it near the frying pan. "They had that nasty falling-out, you know, at Christmastime. Beverly probably doesn't want the word to get out. They positively shrieked and threw things, doors slamming. Oh my God! And the language they used. It was obscene. I had no idea Elaine could swear like that, though I must say the other one was worse."

"What was it about?"

"A man, of course. What else do any of us fuss about?"

"You have any idea who it was?"

"Nope. Frankly, I suspect Elaine's one of those women who's secretly thrilled with widowhood. She gets a lot of sympathy, tons of freedom. She has all that money and no one to hassle with. Why cut some guy in on a deal like that? She's better off by herself."

"Why quarrel with Beverly if that's the case?"

"Who knows? Maybe they just thought it was fun."

I finished my coffee and got up then. "I better scoot. I don't want to interrupt your breakfast, but I may want to get back to you. Are you listed in the book?"

"Of course. I do work... tending bar at the Edgewood Hotel near the beach. You know the place?"

"I can't afford it, but I know which one you mean."

"Pop in and visit sometime. I'm there from six until closing every night except Monday. I'll buy you a drink."

"Thanks, Wim. I'll do that. I appreciate your help. The coffee was a treat."

"Anytime," he said.

I let myself out, catching a glimpse of Wim's breakfast mate, who looked like something out of *Gentlemen's Quarterly*: sultry eyes, a perfect jawline, collarless shirt, and an Italian cashmere sweater tossed across his shoulders with the sleeves folded into a knot in front.

In the kitchen, Wim had started to sing a version of "The Man I Love." His singing voice sounded just like Marlene Dietrich's.

When I reached the lobby I ran into Tillie, who was pushing a wire cart in front of her like a stroller. It was loaded with brown paper bags.

"I feel like I go to the market twice a day," she said. "Are you here looking for me?"

"Yes, but when you weren't in, I went up and had a brief

chat with Wim instead. I didn't realize Elaine Boldt had a cat."

"Oh, she's had Ming for years. I don't know why I didn't think to mention that. I wonder what she did with him?"

"You said she had some carry-on luggage that night going out to the cab. Could it have been Mingus in the cat carrier?"

"Well, it must have been. It was certainly big enough and she did take the cat with her everywhere she went. I guess he's missing too. Isn't that what you're getting at?"

"I don't know yet, but probably. Too bad he's not suffering from some rare cat disease so I could track him down through a veterinarian someplace," I said.

She shook her head. "Can't help you there. He's in good health, as far as I ever knew. He'd be easy to recognize. Big old gray long-haired thing. He must have weighed almost twenty pounds."

"Was he purebred?"

"No and she'd had him neutered early on, so he wasn't used for breeding purposes or anything like that."

"Well," I said, "I may as well start checking up on him too, since I don't have anything else at this point. Did you talk to the police yesterday?"

"Oh yes, and told 'em we thought the woman might have stolen Elaine's bills when she broke in. The officer looked at me like he thought I was nuts, but he did write it down."

"I'll tell you something else Wim brought up. He swears Elaine's sister Beverly was up here at Christmastime and got into a big fight with her. Were you aware of that?"

"No I wasn't, and Elaine never mentioned anything about it either," she said, shifting restlessly. "I've got to go in, Kinsey. I've got some sherbet that'll leak right out if I don't pop it in the freezer soon."

"All right. I'll get back to you later if I need anything else," I said. "Thanks, Tillie."

Tillie went on through the lobby, lugging her grocery cart and I went back to my car and unlocked it. I glanced over at the Grices' house as usual, my attention drawn almost irresistibly to that half-charred ruin where the murder had taken place. On impulse, I locked my car again and trotted up to the Snyders' front door. He must have spotted me through the window because the door opened just as I raised my hand to knock. He stepped out on the porch.

"I saw you coming up the walk. You're the one was here yesterday," he said. "I don't remember your name."

"Kinsey Millhone. I talked to Mr. Grice out at his sister's house yesterday. He said you had a key to his place and would let me in so I could take a look around."

"Yes, that's right. I got it here somewhere." Mr. Snyder seemed to frisk himself and then fished a key ring out of his pocket. He sorted through the keys.

"This's it," he said. He wrestled the key off the ring and handed it to me. "That's to the back door. Front's all boarded up as you can see. For a time there, they had the whole place cordovaned off 'til them fellas from the crime-scene unit could go over everything."

From the rear, I heard, "What is it, Orris? Who's that you're talking to?"

"Hold your horses! Y'old coot. I got to go," he said, his jowls atremble.

"I'll bring this back when I'm done," I said, but he was already lumbering off toward the back of the house in a snit. I thought she could hear remarkably well for someone he claimed was as deaf as a loaf of bread.

I cut across the Snyders' yard, the ivy rustling under my feet. The Grices' front lawn was dead from neglect and the sidewalk was littered with debris. It didn't look as if it had been cleaned up since the fire trucks departed, and I was crossing my fingers that the salvage crew had never gone in to clear the place out. I went around the side, passing the padlocked double doors that were slanted up against the house and led down into the basement. At the rear of the house, I climbed five crumbling steps onto a small back porch. The back door had a big glass window in the upper half and I could see into the kitchen through ruffled curtains that were dingy now and hung crookedly.

I unlocked the door and let myself in. For once, I was in luck. The floor was covered with rubble, but the furniture was still in place; kitchen table filthy, chairs knocked askew. I left the door open behind me and surveyed the room. There were dishes on the counter, shelves of canned goods visible through an open pantry door. I was feeling a faint thrill of uneasiness as I always do in situations like these.

The house smelled richly of scorched wood and there was a heavy layer of soot on everything. The kitchen walls were gray with smoke and my shoes made a gritty sound as I

moved through the hallway, crushing broken glass to a sugary
consistency underfoot. As nearly as I could tell, the interior
of the Grices' house was laid out like the Snyders' house next
door and I could identify what I guessed was the dining room
just off the kitchen, with a blackened swinging door between.
This must be the counterpart to the room in the Snyders'
house that Orris had now outfitted as a bedroom for his wife.
There was a half-bath across the hall, just the toilet and sink.
The old linoleum had blistered and buckled, showing blackened
floorboards beneath. The window in the hallway was broken
now, but it looked out onto a narrow walkway between the
two houses and right into May Snyder's converted bedroom.
I could see her clearly, lying on a hospital bed that had been
cranked up to a forty-five-degree angle. She seemed to be
asleep, looking small and shrunken under a white counter-
pane. I moved away from the window and down the hall
toward the living room.

The fire had leached the color out of everything and it
looked now like a black-and-white photograph. The char
patterns—like dark stretches of alligator hide—covered doorframes and window sashes. The destruction became more
pronounced as I moved toward the front of the house. As I
passed the stairs leading to the half-story up above, I could
see where the flames had chewed the treads and part of the
wooden banister. The wallpaper in the stairwell was as tattered and inky as an old treasure map.

I moved on, trying to get my bearings. There was an
ominous patch of missing floorboards near the front door
where I imagined Marty Grice's body had been found. Flames
had eaten up the walls, leaving pipes and blackened beams
exposed. Across the floor here, and extending back down the
hall and up the stairs, there were irregular burned trails
where an accelerant of some kind had been splashed. I
bypassed the gaping hole in the floor and peered into the
living room, which looked as if it had been outfitted with
avant-garde "works of furniture" made entirely of charcoal
briquettes. Two chairs and a couch were still arranged in a
conversational grouping, but the fire had gnawed the upholstery right down to the bare springs. All that remained of the
coffee table was a burned frame.

I went back to the stairs and crept up with care. The fire
had taken the bedroom in whimsical bites, leaving a stack of
paperback books untouched while the footstool nearby had

been almost completely consumed. The bed was still made, but the room had been drenched by the fire hoses and smelled now of rotting carpet fiber and soggy wallpaper, mildewed blankets, singed clothing, and clumps of insulation that had boiled out through the fire-bared lath and plaster here and there. On the bed table, there was a framed photograph of Leonard with an appointment card for a teeth cleaning and exam tucked in the edge of the glass.

I moved the card aside, peering closely at Leonard's face. I thought about the snapshot I'd seen of Marty. Such a dumpy little thing: overweight, plastic eyeglass frames, a hairdo that looked like a wig. Leonard was much more attractive and in happier times presented a trim appearance, a rather distinguished face, graying hair, a steady gaze. His shoulders were rounded, possibly because of his back problems, but it gave the impression of something weak or apologetic in his nature. I wondered if Elaine Boldt had found him appealing. Could she have come between these two?

I put the picture back and picked my way down the stairs. As I moved along the hall toward the kitchen, I noticed a door ajar and I pushed it open gingerly. Before me yawned the basement, looking like a vast, black pit. Shit. In the interest of being thorough, I knew I'd have to check it out. I made a face to myself and went out to my car to get the flashlight out of the glove compartment.

13

The basement stairs were intact. The fire had apparently been contained before it reached this far. The damage to the rooms above seemed to be the result of some accelerant that had ensured at least a superficial combustion throughout the house. The beam from my flashlight cut through the dark, illuminating a narrow, moving path filled with things I didn't want to touch. I reached the bottom of the stairs. There wasn't a lot of headroom. The house was more than forty years old and the foundation was dank and spider-pocked. The air felt dense, like the atmosphere in a greenhouse, except that everything down here was dead, exuding that fenny perfume of old fire and old damp, abandonment and rot.

I angled the light along the joists, tracing the beams to the hole where daylight spilled down. Had the floor burned through and the body tumbled into the basement? I moved closer, craning to see better. The edges of the hole looked cut to me. Maybe the fire inspector had taken samples of the boards for lab tests. To my left, I could see the furnace, a silent squat bulge of gray, with sooty ducting extending in all directions. The floor was hard-packed dirt and cracked concrete, the entire space filled with junk. Paint cans and old window screens were stacked up under the stairs and there was an ancient galvanized sink in the corner, the pipes corroded away.

I toured the perimeter, poking the light into spaces where eight-legged creatures skittered away from me, horrified. Later I was glad I'd been such a conscientious little bun, but at the time, I only wanted to get out of there as quickly as I could. An empty house always seems to make those noises that have you wondering if an ax murderer is creeping through the premises in search of prey. I shone the flashlight over to the far wall where the stairs jutted up a short distance to the bolted double doors leading out to the side yard. Daylight slanted through the cracks but the smell of fresh air didn't sift down this far. I knew the double doors were padlocked on the outside, but the wood was old and crumbly and didn't seem that secure. From what Lily Howe had said, the burglar hadn't even bothered with breaking and entering. He'd marched right up to the front door and rung the bell. Had they struggled? Had he panicked when she opened the door and killed her instantly? The intruder might have been a woman, of course, especially if the weapon had actually been a baseball bat. Ever since Title IX, women have become more adept at the sportier side arms; death by discus, javelin, shot put, bow and arrow, hockey puck . . . the possibilities are endless, one would think.

I moved back toward the stairs shivering involuntarily with the darkness at my back. I took the steps two at a time, nearly knocking myself out when I banged into a crossbeam. I cursed soundly to myself, bursting out of the basement and into the hall again as though pursued. Something feathery caught my eye and when I realized it was a delicate centipede whiffling down my front, I did this erratic quick dance step, brushing my shirt like I'd suddenly burst into flames. God, the things I do for money, I thought savagely. I went out the back door, locking it behind me, and sat down on the porch steps. My breathing finally slowed, but it took me a few more minutes to regain my composure.

In the meantime, I had a chance to check the backyard. I don't know what I was looking for or what I thought I might find after six months. There were only overgrown bushes and weeds, a little orange tree crippled by the lack of water and covered with hard fruit turning brown because it hadn't been picked. The shed was one of those prefabricated metal jobs you can order through the Sears catalogue and put up anywhere. It was secured by a nice big fat padlock that looked sturdy enough. I cross the yard and inspected it. It was actually a simple warded lock I thought I could open in a few minutes, but I didn't have my little double-headed pick key with me and I wasn't crazy about the idea of standing out there fiddling with a padlock in broad daylight. Better I should come back when the sun went down and find out what

Grice or his nephew kept in there. Old lawn furniture was my guess, but one can never be sure.

I took the house key back to Mr. Snyder and then got in my car and headed over to the office. I let myself in and made a pot of coffee. The mail wasn't in yet and there were no messages on my machine. I opened the French doors and stood out on the balcony. Where the fuck was Elaine Boldt? And where was Elaine Boldt's pussycat? I was running out of things to do and places to look. I typed up a contract for Julia Ochsner to sign and stuck that in my out box. When the coffee was ready, I poured myself some and sat down in my swivel chair and swiveled. When in doubt, I thought, it's best to fall back on routine.

I made a long-distance telephone call to a newspaper in Boca Raton, and another call to a paper in Sarasota, placing classified ads in the personals columns of each. "Anybody knowing the whereabouts of Elaine Boldt, female, Caucasian, age 43..." etc. "Please contact..." with my name, address, and phone number and an invitation to call collect.

That felt productive. What else? I swiveled some more and then put a call through to Mrs. Ochsner. She was on my mind anyway.

"Hello?" she said, picking up at long last. Her voice was tremulous, but held a note of anticipation, as though despite the fact she was eighty-eight, anyone might be calling and anything might come to pass. I hoped I'd always feel that way myself. At the moment, I wasn't so optimistic.

"Hi, Julia. This is Kinsey out in California."

"Just a minute, dear, and I'll turn the television down. I'm watching my program."

"You want me to call you back in a bit? I hate to interrupt."

"No, no. I'd prefer talking to you. Hold on."

Some moments passed and I heard the volume of the background noise reduced to silence. Julia was apparently creeping back to the phone as fast as she could. I waited. Finally she picked up the receiver again. "I kept the picture on," she said, out of breath, "though it just looks like one big blur from across the room. How are you?"

"Frustrated at the moment," I said. "I'm running out of things to do, but I wanted to ask you about Elaine's cat. I don't suppose you've seen Mingus in the last six months, have you?"

"Oh goodness, no. I hadn't even thought about him. If she's gone, he'd have to be missing too, I suppose."

"Well, it looks that way. The building manager here says she left that night with what looked like a cat carrier, so if she actually got to Florida, I'm assuming she'd have had him with her."

"I'd be willing to swear he never got here any more than she did, but I could check with vets and kennels in the area," Julia said. "Maybe she boarded him out for some reason."

"Could you do that? It would really save me some time. I don't know that you'll turn up anything, but at least we'll know we tried. I'm going to see if I can trace the taxicab she took and find out if she had the cat with her when she went to the airport. Did Pat Usher ever mention him?"

"Not that I recall. She's gone, you know. Moved out lock, stock, and barrel."

"Oh, really? Well, I'm not surprised, but I would like to know where she is. Could you get her forwarding address from the Makowskis? I'll call you back in a day or two, but don't you dare call Pat yourself. I don't want her to know you're involved. I may need you to do some more snooping later and I don't want your cover blown." I added, "How are things with you otherwise?"

"Oh, I'm fine, Kinsey. You needn't worry about me. I don't suppose you'd consider a partnership after we wrap this one up."

"I've had worse offers in my day," I said.

Julia laughed. "I'm going to start reading Mickey Spillane just to get in shape. I don't know a lot of rude words, you know."

"I think I've got us covered on that score. I'll talk to you later. Let me know if you come up with anything startling in the meantime. Oh—and I'm shipping you a contract for your signature. We might as well do this right."

"Roger. Over and out," she said and hung up.

I left my vintage VW in the parking lot behind the office and walked over to the Tip Top Cab Company on Delgado. The business office is located in a narrow strip of stores best noted for their liquidation sales: a constant round of discount shoes, car stereos, lunch counters, and motorcycle shops with an occasional beauty salon or a "fast-foto" establishment. It is not a desirable location. The one-way street runs the wrong way.

The parking lot is too small and apparently the owner of the
building, while not exacting outrageous rents, is also content
to let the premises languish under worn paint and tatty
carpeting.

Tip Top was jammed between a Humane Society Thrift
Shop and a Big N' Tall Men's Shop with a suit in the window
designed for the steroid enthusiast. The office itself was long
and narrow, partitioned across the middle with a plywood
wall with a door cut into it. The place was furnished like
some kid's hideout, complete with two broken-down couches
and a table with one short leg. There were drawings and
hand-lettered signs Scotch-taped to the walls, trash piled up
in one corner, dog-eared copies of *Road and Track* magazine
in an irregular tier by the front door. The bucket seat from a
car was propped against the far wall, tan upholstery slashed
in one spot and mended with old Band-Aids covered with
stars. The dispatcher was perched on a stool, leaning one
elbow on a counter as littered as a workbench. He was
probably twenty-five with curly black hair and a small dark
mustache. He wore chinos, a pale blue T-shirt with a faded
decal of the Grateful Dead, and a visor that made his hair
stick up on the sides. The shortwave radio squawked
incomprehensibly and he took up the mike.

"Seven-oh," eh said, his eyes immediately focusing on the
map of the city affixed to the wall above the counter. I saw a
butt-filled ashtray, an aspirin bottle, a cardboard calendar
from Our Lady of Sorrows Church, a fan belt, plastic packets
of ketchup, and a big penciled note that read "Has Anybody
Seen My Red Flash Lite?" Tacked to the wall there was a list
of addresses for customers who'd passed bad checks and those
in the habit of calling more than one cab to see who could get
there first.

There was a short burst of squawking and the dispatcher
moved a round magnet from one part of the map to another.
It looked like he was playing a board game all by himself.

He rotated toward me on the stool. "Yes ma'am."

I held out my hand. "I'm Kinsey Millhone," I said. He
seemed slightly disconcerted at the notion of shaking hands,
but he covered himself and gamely obliged.

"Ron Coachello."

I took out my wallet and showed him my identification. "I
wonder if you could check some records for me."

His eyes were very dark and bright and his look said that

he could check anything he wanted if it suited him. "What's the skinny?"

I gave him the *Reader's Digest* condensed version of the tale, complete with Elaine Boldt's local address and the approximate time the taxi'd been there. "Can you go back to January ninth of this year and see if Tip Top picked up the fare? It might have been City Cab or Green Stripe. I've got some questions for the driver."

He shrugged. "Sure. It might take a day. I got that stuff at home. I don't keep it down here. Why don't I give you a call, or better yet, you buzz me back? How's that?"

The phone rang and he took a call, logging it in. Then he took up the mike and pressed the button. "Six-eight." He cocked his head, listening idly. There was static, then a squawk.

"Four-oh-two-nine Orion," he said and clicked off. I gave him my card. He glanced at it with curiosity as if he'd never known a woman with a business card before. The radio suddenly came to life again and he turned back, taking up the mike. I waved to him and he waved back over his shoulder at me.

I went through exactly the same procedure with the other two cab companies, which were fortunately within walking distance of one another. By the time I repeated the same story twice more I felt like I was suffering from a bad case of tongue flop.

When I got into the office, there was a message from Jonah Robb on my machine.

"Ah, yeah, Kinsey. This if Officer Robb on that...ah...issue we discussed. I wonder if you could give me a call sometime ...ah...this afternoon and we'll find a way to get together on it. It's now Friday and it's...ah...twelve-ten P.M. Talk to you soon. Okay. Thanks." The number he left was for the police station, with the extension for Missing Persons.

I called him back, identifying myself as soon as he came on the line. "I understand you have some information for me."

"Right," he said. "You want to stop by my place later on?"

"I could do that," I said. I took down his address and we settled on 8:15, bypassing dinner. I didn't think we should get into any little domestic numbers at this point. I thanked him for his help and rang off.

I couldn't for the life of me think of anything else to do on the case that afternoon so I locked the office and headed for

home. It was only 1:20 and since I'd accomplished so little at
work, I felt morally obliged to be useful at my place. I
washed the cup and saucer and plate that were sitting in the
sink and left them in the rack to dry until I needed them
again. I put a load of towels in the washer and then scoured
the bathroom and kitchen sinks, took out the trash, and
vacuumed a path around the furniture. Now and then, I
actually move things and suck up all the woofies underneath,
but today it was sufficient to have a few vacuum-cleaner
tracks here and there and the apartment smelling of that
peculiar cross between hot machine oil and cooked dust. I do
love tidiness. When you live by yourself, you can either get
all piggy or pick up as you go, which is what I prefer. There's
nothing more depressing than coming home at the end of a
long day to a place that looks like it's just been tossed by the
mob.

I changed into my sweat pants and did three miles with
energy to burn. This was one of those rare days when the run
seemed inexplicably grand.

I came home, showered, washed my hair, napped, got
dressed, sneaked in a little grocery shopping, and then I sat
down at my desk and worked on note cards while I drank a
glass of white wine and ate a warm, sliced-hard-boiled-egg
sandwich with loads of Best Food's mayo and salt, nearly
swooning at the taste.

At eight, I snatched up a jacket, my handbag, and my key
pick and hopped in my car, heading over to Cabana Boulevard, the wide avenue that parallels the beach. I turned
right. Jonah lived in an odd little tract of houses off Primave-
ra, maybe a mile away. I passed the marina, then Ludlow
Beach, glancing to my left. Even in the gathering twilight, I
could identify the big trash bin where death had almost
caught up with me two weeks before. I wondered how long it
would take before I could pass that area without unconsciously
glancing left, without taking just that one peek at the place
where I'd thought my life would end. The beach seemed to
glow with the last light of day and the sky was a silver gray
layered with pink and lavender, deepening to dark magenta
where the near hills intersected the view. Out on the ocean,
the islands retained a magical hot gold light where lingering
rivulets of sunlight formed a shimmering pool.

I went up the hill, passing Sea Shore Park, turning right
then into a tangle of streets across the boulevard. The prox-

imity to the Pacific meant too much chill fog and corrosive salt air, but there was an elementary school close by. For Jonah, who had had a family to support on a cop's salary, the neighborhood was affordable, but by no means grand.

I found the street number I was looking for and pulled into the driveway. The porch light was on and the yard looked well kept. The house was a ranch-style stucco painted slate blue with dark blue trim. I guessed there would be three bedrooms with maybe a patio in back. I rang the doorbell and Jonah came to the door. He wore jeans and an L. L. Bean Oxford-cloth dress shirt with a pink pinstripe. He carried a beer bottle loosely by the neck, motioning me in with a glance at his watch.

"God, you're prompt," he said.

"Well, you're not far away. I just live at the bottom of the hill."

"I know. You want me to take that?"

He was holding his hand up for the jacket, which I shed and handed to him, along with my handbag. He tossed both unceremoniously into a chair.

For a minute neither of us could think of anything to say. He took a sip of beer. I put my hands in my back pockets. Why did this feel so awkward? It reminded me of those awful junior-high-school dates where you got driven to the movies by somebody's mother and you never knew what to talk about.

I glanced around. "Nice house," I remarked.

"Come on. I'll show you around."

I followed while he talked back over his shoulder at me.

"It was a shit heap when we first moved in. The guy'd been renting it out to these weirdos who kept a ferret in the closet and never flushed the toilet because it was against their religious beliefs. You've probably seen 'em around town. Barefoot with these red and yellow rags around their heads and outfits like something out of the Old Testament. He said they hardly ever paid their rent, but every time he came to hassle them about it, they'd start humming and hold his hand, making significant eye contact. You want some wine? I bought you some high-class stuff—no twist-off cap."

I smiled. "I'm flattered."

We detoured into the kitchen and he opened a bottle of

white wine for me, pouring it into a wineglass that still had
the price tag on the bottom. He grinned sheepishly when he
saw it.

"All I had was plastic glasses the kids used to use in the
backyard," he said. "This is the kitchen."

"I kind of figured that."

It was a nice house. I don't know what I expected, but
someone had made good choices. The whole place had a
stripped-down feeling: bare, gleaming wood floors, furniture
with simple lines, clean surfaces. Why had Camilla left this?
What else was she looking for?

He showed me three bedrooms, two baths, a deck out back
and a small yard enclosed by a vine-covered stucco wall.

"I'll tell you the truth," he said. "When she walked out, I
packed up all her stuff and had the Salvation Army come take
it away. I wasn't going to sit around looking at her little
artsy-fartsy geegaws. I kept the kids' rooms intact. Maybe
she'll get tired of them like she got tired of me and send them
back, but *her* stuff I don't need. She was royally irritated
when she heard, but what was I supposed to do?" He
shrugged, standing there holding the beer bottle by the
neck.

His face was beginning to take form now that I'd seen him
twice. Before, I'd only registered qualities like "bland" and
"harmless." I'd been aware of the extra weight he carried, a
personality made up of something nice mixed with something
droll. He was direct and I responded to that, but he also had
a trait I'd noticed in certain cops before: bemused self-
assurance, as if he were looking at the world from a long way
back but it was all okay with him. Clearly, Camilla still
loomed large in his life and he smiled every time he talked
about her, not with affection, but to cover his wrath. I
thought he needed to go through a few more women before
he got down to me.

"What is that? What's that look?" he asked.

I smiled. "Beware of dog," I said. I'm not sure if I was
talking about him or me.

He smiled too, but he knew what I meant. "I got the stuff
in here."

He pointed toward the dining-room table in an alcove just
off the living room.

I sat down in a hot circle of light, feeling like a glutton with
a napkin tucked under my chin and a knife and fork upright

in each fist. Along with the reports he'd Xeroxed, he'd also managed to slip me some duplicate photographs. I was going to see the aftermath of the crime with my own eyes and I could hardly wait.

14

I read through everything quickly, just to get an overview, and then I went back and noted the details that interested me. The official version of the story, as much as I knew it, and the interviews with Leonard Grice, his sister Lily, neighbors, the fire inspector, and the first police officer on the scene more or less spelled out events in the same way I'd been told. Leonard and Marty were scheduled to go out for their traditional Tuesday-night dinner with Leonard's widowed sister, Mrs. Howe. Marty wasn't feeling well and canceled out at the last minute. Leonard and Lily went out as planned and got back to the Howes' at about nine P.M., at which point a call was put through to Marty to let her know they were home. Both Mr. Grice and his sister spoke to Marty and she finally terminated the call in order to respond to a knock at the door. According to both Lily and Leonard, they had a cup of coffee and chatted for a bit. He left at approximately ten o'clock, arriving at Via Madrina twenty-some minutes later to find that his house had burned. By then, the blaze had been brought under control and his wife's body was being removed from the partially destroyed residence. He collapsed and was revived by paramedics at the scene. Tillie Ahlberg was the one who'd spotted the smoke and she'd turned in an alarm at 9:55. Two units had responded within minutes, but the blaze was such that entry couldn't be effected through the front door. Firemen had broken in through the rear, extinguishing the fire after thirty minutes or so. The body was discovered in the entryway and removed to the morgue.

Identification had been established by full-mouth X rays supplied by Marty's local dentist and through an examination of stomach contents. She'd apparently mentioned to Leonard on the phone that she'd fixed herself some canned tomato soup and a tuna sandwich. The empty cans were found in the kitchen wastebasket. The time of death had more or less been fixed in a narrow framework between the time of the telephone call and the time the fire alarm had been turned in.

I read through the autopsy report, mentally summing up a lot of technical details. The pathologist reported no carbon granules deposited in the bronchial passages or lungs and no carbon monoxide in the blood or other tissues. It was therefore determined that she had been dead when the fire broke out. Additional lab tests had revealed no alcohol, chloroform, drugs, or poisons in the system. The cause of death was attributed to multiple skull fractures apparently caused by repeated blows with a blunt instrument. Because of the nature of the wounds, the pathologist estimated the object to be some four to five inches in width, speculating that it might have been a two-by-four wielded with great force, a baseball bat, or some kind of club, possibly metal. The murder weapon had never been found. Unless, of course, it was a big old board burned up in the fire, but there was no evidence to support that possibility.

The arson investigators didn't seem to have any doubts that the fire had been deliberately set. Lab tests showed traces of kerosene in the floorboards. Charring patterns throughout the house had borne this out. They'd seen the same blackened splash marks and the same liquid trails that I'd spotted when I went through the house earlier. They'd also used some sophisticated methods of verifying the point of origin and the course the fire had taken as it burned. Leonard Grice had been questioned about the kerosene and he said he'd been storing a quantity in the basement for use in two lamps and a cooking stove that he and Marty took on camping trips, which accounted for the intruder's having had access to a flammable liquid. It looked as if the burglar had come with a weapon in hand, but without any intention of burning the place down. The fire was apparently an afterthought, a hastily concocted plan to conceal the bludgeoning of Marty Grice. So far there was nothing to suggest that anybody knew she'd be there, so the cops were having a hard time imagining that the murder had been planned in advance.

There was no evidence that a time-delay device had been employed, which ruled out the possibility that Grice had rigged the fire before he left. Grice's nephew, Mike, had been questioned and cleared. He'd been seen by numerous impartial witnesses in a hangout called The Clockworks in downtown Santa Teresa during the critical period when experts speculated that the fire had been set. There were no other suspects and no other witnesses. Any other hard evidence including fingerprints had been destroyed by the fire. Elaine Boldt's name was on a list of persons to be interviewed and there was a note that Lieutenant Dolan had contacted her by telephone on the fifth. He'd made an appointment to see her on January 10, but she'd never appeared. According to the information I had, she'd left for Florida the night before.

One entry, appearing in the middle of a typed report, interested me considerably. According to a deputy at the police department, a call had come in at 9:06 on the night of the murder that might well have been placed by Marty Grice. The caller had been female, in a panic, and had blurted out a cry for help before the phone went dead. Since the call was placed to the police station instead of 911, the deputy had no way of getting a fix on the address from which the call had originated. She'd made a note of it, however, and when the murder came to light, she'd reported it to Dolan, who had included it in his report. He'd questioned Grice about that too. If it *was* Marty, why would she have called the station instead of dialing 911? Leonard had pointed out that he and Marty had a telephone answering machine with a rapid-dial function. She'd entered the telephone numbers of both the police department and the fire department. The answering machine was found, undamaged, on a table in the rear of the hallway with the numbers neatly printed on the index. It looked as if Marty had had some warning of the attack and had been able to reach the telephone, calling out at least part of a distress signal before she'd been killed. If she'd actually placed the call, it pinpointed the time of death at 9:06 or soon afterward.

For a moment, I harbored the fleeting hope that Leonard Grice might still be implicated. After all, as nearly as I could tell, the police had only Lily's word for the fact that he was still at her place at that time. I was speculating that he might have come home early, killed Marty, started the fire, and then parked around the block until the appropriate moment to arrive. If he and his sister were in cahoots, they could both simply maintain afterward that he'd been with her. I was out of luck on that one. Three interviews down, there was a short paragraph detailing a conversation that Dolan had had with some of Lily's neighbors who'd stopped by unexpectedly at nine P.M. to drop off a birthday present. The husband and wife both reported independently that Leonard was there and hadn't left for home until approximately ten. The time was noted because they'd been trying to persuade him to stay for a television program that came on at ten. It turned out to be a rerun and since he was anxious to get home to his wife anyway, he'd left.

Well, shit, I thought.

Now, why was this making me feel so cross? Ah, well, because I wanted Leonard Grice to be guilty of something. Murder, conspiracy to murder, accessory to murder. I was fond of the idea for tidiness' sake—for statistical purposes, if nothing else. California has over three thousand homicide victims annually, and of those, fully two-thirds are slain by friends, acquaintances, or relatives, which makes you wonder if you might be better off as a friendless orphan in this state. The point is, when a murder goes down, the chances are good that someone near and dear has had a hand in it.

I thought about that, reluctant to give it up. Could Grice have hired someone to kill his wife? It was always possible, of course, but it was hard to see what he might have gained. The police, not being ignorant buffoons, had pursued the line as well, but had come up with nothing. No moneys unaccounted for, no meetings with unsavory characters, no apparent motive, no visible benefit.

Which brought me back to Elaine Boldt. Could she have been involved in Marty Grice's death? Most of what I'd learned about her cried out a big resounding "no." There really wasn't a hint that she'd been attached to Leonard romantically or any other way, except as an occasional bridge partner. I didn't think Marty Grice had been killed for messing up a small slam, but with bridge partners one can never tell. Wim Hoover had mentioned that Elaine and Beverly had quarreled about a man at Christmastime, but it was hard to picture the two of them in an arm wrestle over Leonard Grice. I kept coming back to the same suspicion—that Elaine knew something or had seen something related to Marty's murder and had left town to avoid the scrutiny of the Santa Teresa police.

I turned my attention to the photographs, neatly disconnecting my brain. I needed to know how things had looked and I couldn't afford to react emotionally. Violent death is repellent. My first impulse, always, is to turn abruptly away, to shield my soul from the sight, but this was the only tangible record of that event and I had to see for myself. I turned a cold eye to the first black-and-white photograph. The color pictures would be worse and I thought I'd start with the "easy" ones.

Jonah cleared his throat. I looked up.

"I'm going to have to turn in," he said. "I'm beat."

"You are?" I glanced at my watch, startled. It was 10:45. I'd been sitting there for more than two hours without moving.

"I'm sorry," I said. "I had no idea I'd been here that long."

"That's okay. I got up at five this morning to work out and I need some shut-eye. You can take that stuff if you like. Of course, if Dolan ever catches you with it, I'll deny everything and throw you to the wolves, but aside from that, I hope it helps."

"Thanks. It's already helped." I shoved the photographs and reports into a big manila envelope and tucked that, in turn, in my handbag.

I drove home, disturbed. Even now, there was an image of Marty's body graven behind my eyes: features blurred by charring, mouth open, lying in a circle of ash like a pile of gray confetti. The heat had caused the tendons in her arms to retract, pulling her fists up into a pugilistic pose. It was her last fight and she had lost, but I didn't think it was over yet.

I willed the image away, running back over what I'd learned to that point. One little detail still bothered me. Was it possible that May Snyder had been accurate when she talked about the bang-bang-bang of hammering that night? If so, what in the world could it have been?

I was almost home again when I remembered the shed in the Grices' backyard. I slammed the brakes on and hung a hard left, heading across town.

Via Madrina was dark, heavily overhung by Italian stone pines. There wasn't much traffic at that hour. The night sky was hazy and though the moon was full, the light that filtered down was partially blocked by the condominium next door. I parked and got a little penlight out of the glove compartment. I pulled on a pair of rubber gloves and locked my car, heading up the Grices' front walk. I cut around the side of the house, my tennis shoes making no sound at all on the concrete.

In my jacket pocket I fingered the key pick, shaped like a flattened metal mandolin. I had a set of five picks with me on a key ring and a second more elaborate set at home in a nice leather case. They'd been given to me by a nonresidential burglar who was currently serving ten months in the county jail. Last time he'd been caught, he'd hired me to keep an eye on his wife, whom he believed was misbehaving with the guy next door. Actually, she hadn't been doing anything and he was so grateful for the good news that he gave me the key picks and taught me how to use them. He'd paid me some cash too, but then it turned out he'd stolen it and he had to ask for it back when the judge ordered him to make restitution.

It was chilly and there was a frisky little breeze making breathy sounds in the pine boughs. The house behind the Grices' had canvas awnings that were snapping like sails, and the hollow sigh of dry grass gave the whole enterprise an eerie ambiance of its own. I was feeling jumpy anyway because I'd just been looking at pictures of a charbroiled corpse, and here I was, about to do a little breaking-and-entering number that could land me in jail and cause my license to be snatched away. If the next-door neighbors set up a howl and the cops arrived on the scene, what was I going to say? Why was I doing it anyway? Ah, because I wanted to know what was in this wee metal house and I couldn't figure out how else to get in.

I fixed a tiny beam of light on the bottom of the padlock. In the diagram my burglar friend had drawn of a lock like this, there is a flat, hairpin spring that latches into notches in the shackle. Usually only the tip of the key actuates the spring, so it was a question of figuring out which of my picks would spread the latch apart, releasing the mechanism. In truth, I could have tried a paper clip with a small L bent on one end but that was the shape of the first pick I used and the padlock wouldn't budge. I tried the next pick which had an H shape in the point. Nope. I tried the third, working it carefully. The lock popped open in my hand. I checked my watch. A minute and a half. I get a bit vain about these things.

The shed door made a wrenching sound when I opened it and I stood for a moment, heart thudding in my throat. I heard a motorcycle putter past in the street but I didn't pay much attention to it because I had just understood Mike's custodial relationship to his uncle's property. In the shed, along with the stack of clay pots, the hand-push lawn mover, and a weed whacker were six shelves crammed with illegal drugs: Mason jars full of reds and dexies, yellow jackets, rainbows and sopers . . . along with some fat plastic packets of grass and hashish. Well, this was all just too yummy for words. I didn't think Leonard Grice was the druggist, but I was willing to bet money his nephew had invested heavily in this little portable Rexall. I was so enamored of my discovery that I didn't know he was behind me until he let out an astonished "hey!"

I jumped back and whipped around, suppressing a shriek. I found myself face-to-face with the kid, his green eyes glowing in the dark like a cat's. He was as startled to see me as I was to see him. Fortunately, neither of us was armed or we might have had a quick duel, doing each other a lot of needless harm.

"What are you *doing*?" he said. He sounded outraged, as if he couldn't believe this was happening. His Mohawk was beginning to grow out and the wind was making it lean slightly to the left like a field of tall grass in one of those old commercials for Kotex. He had on a black leather motorcycle jacket and a rhinestone earring. His boots were knee-high and made of plastic scored to resemble cobra skin only looking more like psoriasis. It was hard to take this lad seriously, but in some odd way I did. I closed the shed door and snapped the padlock into place. What could *he* prove?

"I got curious about what you were doing back here so I thought I'd take a peek."

"You mean you just broke in?" he said. His voice had that adolescent crack left over from puberty and his cheeks were hot pink. "You can't do that!"

"Mike, sweetie, I just did," I said. "You're in big trouble."

He stared at me for a moment, his expression blank. "You gonna call the cops?"

"Shit yes!"

"But what you did is just as much against the law as this," he said. I could tell he was one of those bright boys accustomed to arguing righteously with adults.

"Oh crap," I said, "wise up. I'm not going to stand out here and argue the California penal code with you. You're dealing drugs. The cops aren't going to care what I was up to. Maybe

I was passing by and thought you were breaking in yourself. You're out of business, kiddo."

His eyes took on a shrewd look and he changed his tack. "Well now, wait a minute. Don't go so fast. Why can't we talk about this?"

"Sure, why not? What's to say?"

I could practically see his brain cells scurry around forming a new thought. He was no fool, but he still surprised me with the line he took. "Are you looking into Aunt Marty's death? Is that why you're here?"

Aunt Marty. Nice touch, I thought. I smiled briefly.

"Not quite, but that's close enough."

He glanced off toward the street, then down at the toe of his cobra boot. "Because I got something... you know, like some information about that."

"What kind of information?"

"Something I never told the cops. So maybe we could make a trade," he said. He stuck his hands in his jacket pockets looking back at me. His face was innocent, his complexion clear, the look in his eyes so pure I'd have given him my firstborn if I'd had one. The little smile that crossed his face was engaging and I wondered how much money he'd made selling dope to his high-school friends. And I wondered if he was going to end up with a bullet in his head for cheating someone higher up in the scheme of things. I was interested in what he had to say and he knew it. I had to make quick peace with my own corruption and it wasn't that hard to do. Times like this, I know I've been in the business too long.

"What kind of trade?"

"Just give me time to clear this stuff out before you tell anyone. I was about to lay off anyway because the narcs have some undercover agents at our school and I thought I'd cool it 'til the pressure's off."

We're not talking permanent reform here, folks. We're talking simple expediency, but at least the kid wasn't trying to con me... too much.

We looked at each other and something shifted. I knew I could rail and stomp and threaten him. I knew I could be pious and moralistic and disapproving and it wouldn't change a thing. He knew the score as well as I did and what we had to offer each other might not be a bad bet on either side.

"All right, you got it," I said.

"Let's go somewhere and talk," he said. "I'm freezin' my nuts off."

It bothered me to realize that I'd started to like him just a little bit.

15

We went to The Clockworks on State Street; he on his motorcycle, with me following in my car. The place is a teen hangout and looks like something out of a rock video; a long, narrow room painted charcoal gray with a high ceiling and the lighting done in pink and purple neon tubing. The whole of it resembles the interior of a clock in abstract and futuristic forms. There are mobiles looking like big black gears suspended from the ceiling, the smoke in the air moving them in slow circles. There are four small tables near the door and on the left are what look like shelves at chest height in a series of standing-room-only booths where couples can neck while drinking soda pop. The menu posted on the wall is larded with side orders like dinner salad and garlic toast that kids can snack on, paying seventy-five cents for the privilege of taking up table space for hours at a time. You can also buy two kinds of beer and a house chablis if you are old enough and have tangible proof. It was now nearly midnight and there were only two other people in the place, but the owner apparently knew Mike and his gaze slid over to me appraisingly. I tried to look like I was not Mike's date. I didn't mind a May/December romance now and then, but a seventeen-year-old is pushing it some. Also I'm not clear on the etiquette of making deals with junior dope peddlers. Who pays for the drinks? I didn't want his self-image to suffer.

"What do you want?" he asked, moving toward the counter.

"Chablis is fine," I said. He was already pulling his wallet out so I let him pay. He probably made thirty grand a year selling grass and pills. The owner looked over at me again and I waved my I.D. at him casually, indicating that he could card me, but he'd be wasting a trip across the room.

Mike came back with a plastic glass of white wine for me
and a soft drink for himself. He sat down, surveying the place
for narcs in disguise. He seemed strangely mature and I was
having trouble dealing with the incongruity of a kid who
looked like a Boy Scout and behaved like a Mafia management trainee. He turned toward me then, resting both
elbows on the table. He'd taken up a sugar packet from the
container on the table and he tapped it and turned it restlessly,
addressing most of what he had to say to the trivia question
printed on the back.

"Okay. Here's what happened," he said, "and I'm tellin'
you the truth. For one thing, I didn't stash at Uncle Leonard
and Aunt Marty's until after she got killed and he moved out.
Once the cops got done and everything, it occurred to me the
utility shed was perfect so I moved some stuff in. Anyway, I
went by the house the night she got killed. . . ."

"Did she know you were coming?"

"Nuh-uh, I'm getting to that. I mean, I knew they went
out on Tuesday nights and I thought they'd be gone. Like,
you know, if I was hard up and needed some bucks or
something, I might cruise by and pick up some loose change.
They kept cash around—not a lot, but enough. Or sometimes
I'd take something I could unload somewhere else. Nothing
they'd miss and nobody'd ever said anything about it so I
figured they hadn't tipped to it yet. Anyway what happened
was I went over there that night thinking the place would be
empty, but when I got there the door was open—"

"The door was standing open?"

He shook his head. "I just kind of turned the knob and it
was unlocked. When I stuck my head in I knew something
weird was going on. . . ."

I waited, watching him uneasily.

He cleared his throat, looking over his shoulder at the front
entrance. His voice dropped.

"I think the guy was still there, you know? The light was
on in the basement and I could hear someone knocking
around down there and there was this rug in the hall, like an
area rug that had been thrown over something. I saw a hand
sticking out with blood on it. Man, I took off."

"You're pretty sure she was dead at that point?"

He nodded, hanging his head. He ran a hand along the
pink center divider of hair, looking off to one side. "I should've
called the cops. I knew I should, but the whole thing really

freaked me out. I hate that shit. And what was I supposed to do? I couldn't tell the cops anything and I didn't want 'em looking at *me*, so I just kept my mouth shut. I mean, I couldn't see what difference it made. I didn't see who did it or anything like that."

"Do you remember anything else? A car parked out front..."

"I don't know. I didn't stay long. I took one look at that shit and I was gone. I could smell all these gasoline fumes or something and..."

He hesitated briefly. "Wait a minute, yeah, there was a brown grocery bag in the hall too. I don't know what it was doing there. I mean, I didn't know what the fuck was happening, so I just backed away real quiet and came on down here and made sure people saw me."

I took a sip of wine, running through his story. The chablis tasted like fermented grapefruit juice. "Tell me about the grocery bag. Was it empty, full, crumpled?"

"It had stuff in it, I think. I mean, I didn't see anything in particular. It was one of those brown paper bags from Alpha Beta, standing just inside the door to the right."

"Did it look like she'd been shopping? Is that what you're trying to say?"

He shrugged. "It just looked like junk, I guess. I don't know. Maybe it belonged to whoever was down in the basement."

"Too bad you didn't make an anonymous call to the cops. Maybe they could have gotten there before the place went up in smoke."

"Yeah, I know. I thought about that later and I was bummed I didn't do that, but I wasn't thinking straight."

He polished off his soft drink and rattled the ice in the cup, tilting a cube into his mouth. I could hear the ice crunching in his teeth. It sounded like a horse chewing on a bit.

"Do you remember anything else?"

"No, I guess that's it. Once I figured out what was going on, I back out of there and hightailed it down here as fast as I could."

"You have any idea what time it was?"

"Nuh-un, not exactly. It was quarter of nine when I got here and it probably took me ten minutes on the motorcycle by the time I found a place to park and all like that. I had to walk the sucker for two blocks so nobody would hear me start it up. It was probably eight-thirty or something like that when I left Uncle Leonard's house."

I shook my head. "Not eight-thirty. You must mean nine-thirty. She wasn't killed until after nine."

He took the cup away from his mouth, looking at me with puzzlement. "She wasn't?"

"Your uncle and Mrs. Howe both say they talked to her at nine and the cops took a call they think was your aunt at nine-oh-six."

"Well, maybe I got it wrong then because I thought it was quarter of nine when I got here. I looked at the clock when I walked in and then I turned around and asked this buddy of mine what time it was and he checked his watch."

"I'll see if I can check that out," I said. "By the way, how's Leonard related to you?"

"My dad and him are brothers. Dad's the youngest in his family."

"So Lily Howe is their sister."

"Something like that."

The purple neon tubes began to blink out in succession and the pink ones went dark after that. The owner of the place called over to the table. "Closing down in ten minutes, Mike. Sorry to break it up."

"That's okay. Thanks, man."

We got up, moving toward the back entrance. He was not much taller than I and I wondered if we looked like brother and sister or mother and son. I didn't say anything else until we got to the parking lot.

"You have any theories about who killed your aunt?"

"No, do you?"

I shook my head. "I'd get that shed cleaned out if I were you."

"Yeah, sure. That was the deal, wasn't it?"

He got on his cycle and did one of those jumps to start it up. "Hey, you know what? I don't remember your name."

I gave him my card, then got in my VW. He waited to make sure I was under way and then he roared off.

I intended to let the case sit for the weekend because I wasn't sure what else to do. Saturday morning, I went over the police reports again at home, added note cards to my collection up on the bulletin board, but for the time being, I simply had to sit it out. Come Monday, it was possible I'd get a response from the classified ads I'd placed in the Florida papers or maybe I'd hear from the DMV in Tallahassee or Sacramento. I was still waiting for the plane ticket Julia Ochsner had mailed, hoping it would give me information of some kind. If nothing new came to light, I was going to have to start all over again and see if I could develop a few new leads. I still had local vets to check, trying to get a rundown on the cat.

I took a few minutes to do recalls on the three cab companies. The dispatcher I'd talked to at Green Stripe said he hadn't had a chance to dig through his files yet. The owner of City Cab had looked and found nothing and Ron Coachella at Tip Top wasn't in yet, but the dispatcher on duty said he'd be in shortly. So much for that.

I went down to the office. I hadn't meant to, but I couldn't help myself. I was feeling itchy and restless and dissatisfied. I don't like not succeeding at things. California Fidelity was closed for the weekend. I unlocked my door and picked up the mail that had been shoved through the slot. There was an envelope with Julia Ochsner's return address on it. I tossed it on the desk while I checked my messages. There was only one and it had apparently just come in.

"Hello, Kinsey. This is Ron Coachella over at the cab company? I got the information you want. Tip Top did pick up the fare at 2097 Via Madrina . . . let's see—on January the ninth at ten-fourteen P.M. Driver's name was Nelson Acquistapace at 555-6317. I told him you'd be in touch. I've got the trip sheet down here and you're welcome to stop by and pick up a copy so he can look at it. Twenty bucks might help his memory, if you know what I mean. Aside from that, just remember . . . 'If you want the top ride in town, call Tip Top,' " he sang and hung up.

I smiled, making a note of the driver's name and number. I put on a pot of coffee and opened the note from Julia. Her handwriting was of the old school, surprisingly firm, a clear cursive with grand flourishes and well-formed capital letters. She said she was enclosing the ticket, that the June rains were in full force, and that Charmaine Makowski had given birth to a nine-pound nine-ounce boy the night before and wanted everyone to know that she never expected to sit down again. Charmaine and Roland had not yet named the child but were accepting suggestions. Julia said that most of the appellations proffered so far were not fit to repeat. Julia thought it was a hoot. Warmest regards, said she.

I studied the ticket, which was tucked in a TWA folder. It looked like it had been generated at the Santa Teresa airport, round-trip from Santa Teresa to LAX and from LAX to Miami. All four flight coupons had been removed but the carbon remained. The ticket had been paid for by credit card. Four flight coupons torn out. Now, that was interesting. Had she come back to town at some point? If so, why had the carbon been down in Boca Raton in Pat Usher's trash? I went back to my list of travel agents, trying to figure out which one Elaine Boldt ordinarily used. I decided on Santa Teresa Travel which has an office within easy walking distance of the condominium on Via Madrina. It was just a guess, but I had to start someplace. I put in a call, but there was no answer and I assumed the agency was shut down for the weekend.

I made a list of leads to pursue on Monday. I checked the ticket again. I didn't see any indication that she'd had the cat in tow, but I wasn't sure how that worked. Did kitty cats get tickets like everybody else? I'd have to ask. There were some luggage tags still stapled to the back of the folder, but that doesn't mean much. At the airport here in town, you can pick up your bags without anybody verifying the tags. I remembered Elaine's luggage as fairly distinctive anyway, dark red leather with the designer signature writ large on the fabric trim. I'd priced that stuff once and decided to open a Keogh account instead.

I put a call through to Nelson Acquistapace, the Tip Top cab driver. He was home in bed with a head cold, but said Ron had told him what I needed. He had to pause and blow his nose twice. "Why don't you pick up the trip sheet and bring it over here? I'm on Delgado, just half a block down from Tip Top," he said. "I'll be outside around in back."

I picked up the trip sheet and arrived at his place by 9:35. I found him sitting in the backyard of a white frame bungalow tucked into a jungle of overgrown pittosporum bushes. He was lying on a hammock in a freestanding metal frame in the only patch of sunlight. The rest of the property was in deep shade, rather chilly and uninviting. He looked to be in his sixties, balding, heavyset in a dark green velour bathrobe. He had a square of pink sprigged flannel on his chest and he smelled like Vicks VapoRub. He'd set up a small metal table with his cold remedies, a box of Kleenex, an empty juice glass, and some crossword-puzzle books that I recognized.

"I know the guy who writes those puzzles," I said. "He's my landlord."

His eyebrows shot up. "This guy lives in town here? He's a whiz! He drives me up the wall with these things. Look at this one. Eighteenth-Century English Novelists and he includes all their books and their characters and everything. I had to go read Henry Fielding and Laurence Sterne and people I never even heard about just to get through the thing. It's better than a college education. I'm tellin' you. What is he, some kind of professor?"

I shook my head, feeling absurdly proud. You'd have thought Henry was a rock star the way this guy was reacting. "He used to run that little bakery at the corner of State and Purdue. He started doing the crossword puzzles when he retired."

"Is that right? You sure it's the same guy? Henry Pitts?"

I laughed. "Sure I'm sure. He tries those things out on me all the time. I don't think I've ever finished one yet."

"You tell him I want to meet him sometime. He has a very twisted sense of humor, but I like that. He did one all made up of botanical oddities, remember that? I went crazy. I was up all night. I can't believe the guy lives here in Santa Teresa. I thought he was a full professor at MIT, someplace like that."

"I'll tell him you said that. He'll be thrilled to hear he has a fan."

"You tell him to stop by here anytime. Tell him Nelson Acquistapace is at his service. He needs a cab, just call Tip Top and ask for me."

"I'll do that," I said.

"You got the trip sheet? Ron said you were looking for some lady who disappeared. Is that right?"

I took the trip sheet out of my purse and passed it over to him.

"Don't get too close, sweetheart," he said. He took a handkerchief out of his robe pocket and dusted his nose with it, honking into it before he put it back. He unfolded the sheet, holding it at arm's length to look at it. "I left my glasses inside. Which one?"

I pointed to the Via Madrina address.

"Yeah, I remember her, I think. I took her to the airport

and dropped her off. I remember she was picking up that last flight from here to L.A. Where was she going, I forget now."

"Miami, Florida."

"Yeah, that's right. I remember now."

He was studying the trip sheet as though it were a pack of Tarot cards in some tricky configuration. "You know what this is?" He was tapping the paper. "You want to know why this fare is so high? Look at that. Sixteen bucks. It doesn't cost that much to go from Via Madrina to the airport. She made a stop and had me wait maybe fifteen minutes with the meter running. An intermediate stop. Now, just let me think where it was. Not far. Some place on Chapel. Okay, yeah, I got it now. That clinic down near the freeway."

"A clinic?" That took me by surprise.

"Yeah, you know. An emergency facility. For the cat. She dropped him off for some kind of emergency treatment and then she got back in the cab and we took off."

"I don't suppose you actually saw her get on the plane, did you?"

"Sure. I was done for the night. You can see for yourself from the trip sheet. She was my last fare so I went upstairs to the airport bar and had a couple of beers out on the patio. I told her I was gonna be up there so she even turned around and waved at me when she was walkin' out to the plane."

"Was she alone?"

"As far as I could tell."

"Had you ever picked her up before?"

"Not me. I just moved up here from L.A. in November last year. This is paradise. I love this town."

"Well," I said, "I appreciate your help. At least, we know she got on the plane. I guess now the question is, did she ever reach Boca Raton?"

"That's where she said she was going," he said, "though I tell you somethin'. With that fur coat, I told her she ought to head someplace cold. Get some use out of it. She laughed."

I felt myself hit the pause button mentally, a quick freeze frame. It was odd, that image, and it bothered me. I pictured Elaine Boldt with her fur coat and turban, on her way to warmth and sunshine, waving back over her shoulder to the taxi driver who'd taken her to the airport. It was disturbing somehow, that last glimpse of her, and I realized that until now I hadn't really pictured that at all. I'd been weighing the possibility that she was on the run, but in my heart of hearts,

I'd pictured her dead. I'd kept thinking that whoever killed Marty Grice killed her too. I just couldn't figure out why. Now the uncertainty had crept in again. Something was off, but I couldn't figure out what it was.

16

Well, at least now I had a tiny mission in life. When I left Nelson, he was taking his temperature with a digital thermometer, confessing sheepishly a secret addiction to gadgets like that. I wished him a speedy recovery and hopped in my car, circling back around to Chapel.

The veterinary clinic is a small box of glass and cinderblock painted the color of window putty and tucked into the dead end formed when Highway 101 was cut through. I love that whole series of dead-end streets—relics of the town as it used to be, a refreshing departure from the pervading Spanish look. The small frame houses in that neighborhood are actually Victorian cottages built for the working class, with hand-turned porch rails, exotic trim, wooden shutters, and peaked roofs. They look like shabby antiques now, but it's still possible to imagine a day when they were newly constructed and covered with fresh paint, the full-grown trees no more than slender saplings planted in the midst of newly seeded lawns. The town then must have been dirt roads and carriages. I'm not above wishing more of it remained.

I parked in the lot behind the clinic and went in through the back door. I could hear dogs barking hoarsely somewhere in the rear; shrill cries for mercy, freedom, and relief. There were only two animals in the waiting room, both bored-looking cats who had formed themselves into bolster pillows. Their humans spoke to them in what was apparently cat-English, using high-pitched voices that made my own head hurt. Now and then when some dog set up a howl in the back, one or the other of the cats would appear to smile faintly.

There must have been two vets working because both cats

got called at the same time and were carted off down the hall, leaving me alone with the receptionist behind the counter. She was in her late twenties, blue-eyed, pale, with an Alice-in-Wonderland blue ribbon across her straight blond hair. Her name tag read "Emily."

"May I help you?"

She spoke as though she'd never progressed beyond the age of six; a breathy, wispy tone, softly modulated, perhaps especially cultivated to soothe distressed beasts. Occasionally I run into women who talk like that and it's always puzzling, this perpetual girlhood in a world where the rest of us are struggling to grow up.

Dealing with her made me feel like a linebacker. "I wonder if you could give me some information."

"Well, I'll try," she whispered. Her voice was sweet and musical, her manner submissive.

I was going to show her the photostat of my P.I. license but I worried that it would seem brutal and coarse. I decided to hold off on that and whip it out if I had to turn the screws.

"Back in January, a woman brought a cat into the clinic for some kind of emergency treatment and I want to find out if she ever came back to pick it up."

"I can check our records if you like. Can you tell me the name, please?"

"Well, the woman's name was Elaine Boldt. The cat was Mingus. It would have been the night of January ninth."

Two patches of mild pink appeared on her cheeks and she licked her lips, staring at me fixedly. I wondered if she'd sold the cat to a vivisectionist.

"What happened?" I asked. "Do you know which one I'm talking about?"

"Well yes, I know which one. He was here for *weeks*," she said. Her speech had taken on a nasal cast, coming out through her nostrils now as though by ventriloquist. She wasn't exactly whining, but it was the tone of voice I've heard kids use in department stores when their moms accuse them of misbehavior and threaten to jerk their arms off. It was clear she was feeling defensive about something, but I wasn't sure quite what. She reached for a small tin box and walked her fingers through a file of index cards. She pulled out the record, snapping it onto the countertop self-righteously.

"She only paid three weeks' board and care and she never responded to any of our postcards or calls, so in

February the doctors said we'd have to make other arrangements because our space is so limited." She was really
working herself into a snit here.

"Emily," I said patiently. "Is that your name, or somebody
else's tag?"

"It's Emily."

"I really don't care where the cat is. I just need to know if
the woman came back."

"Oh. No, she didn't."

"What happened to the cat? I'm just curious."

She stared at me for a moment, her chin coming up. She
brushed her hair back across her shoulder with a flip of her
hand. "I adopted him. He's really a fabulous cat and I just
couldn't turn him over to the pound."

"That's fine. Hey, that's great. I've heard he was terrific
and I'm glad you found a place for him. Enjoy. I will take
your secret with me to the grave. If the woman shows up,
though, would you let me know?" I put my card on the
counter. She read it and nodded without another word.

"Thanks."

I went back to the office. I thought I better give Julia
Ochsner a call and tell her I'd located the cat, thus saving her
an unnecessary canvass of Boca kennels and vets. I left my car
in the parking lot out back and came up the rear stairs. When
I reached my office there was a man standing in the corridor,
scribbling a message on a scrap of paper.

"Can I help you?"

"I don't know. Are you Kinsey Millhone?" His smile seemed
superior and his attitude amused, as though he had a piece of
information too precious to share.

"Yes."

"I'm Aubrey Danziger."

It took me a second to compute the name. "Beverly's
husband?"

"Right," he said and then gave a little laugh in the back of
his throat. So far, I didn't think either one of us had much
cause for merriment. He was tall, maybe six foot two, with a
smooth, thin face. He had very dark hair, lank, looking as if it
would be silky to the touch, brown eyes, an arrogant mouth.
He was wearing a pale gray three-piece suit. He looked like a
riverboat gambler, a dandy, a "swell," if such persons exist in
this day and age.

"What can I do for you?"

I put my key in the lock, opened the door, and went in. He followed, surveying the premises with the sort of look that told me he was pricing the furniture, calculating my overhead, estimating my quarterly taxes, and wondering why his wife hadn't hired a high-class outfit.

I sat down behind my desk and watched him while he took a seat and crossed his legs. Nice, sharp crease in the pants, nice narrow ankle, Italian leather pumps with a narrow polished toe. I caught sight of his snow-white shirt cuff, his initials—AND—in a pale blue monogram, hand-done no doubt. He was smiling at me faintly, watching me watch him. He took a flat cigarette case out of his inside jacket pocket and extracted a slim, black cigarette that he tamped on the case and then stuck in his mouth, flicking a lighter that shot out a jet of fire I thought might set his hair ablaze. He had elegant hands and his fingernails were beautifully manicured, with clear polish on each tip. I confess I was sore amazed at the sight, amazed by the scent of him that was wafting across the desk at me; probably one of those men's designer aftershaves called Rogue or Magnum. He studied the ember on his cigarette and then fixed me with a look. His eyes reminded me of hard clay, flat brown with no warmth and no energy.

I didn't offer him coffee. I pushed the ashtray toward him as I'd done with his wife. The smoke from his cigarette smelled like a smothered campfire and I knew it would linger long after he'd driven back to Los Angeles.

"Beverly got your letter," he said. "She was upset. I thought maybe I should drive up here and have a chat."

"Why didn't she come herself?" I said. "She can talk."

That amused him. "Beverly doesn't care for scenes. She asked me to handle it for her."

"I'm not crazy about scenes myself, but I don't see the problem here. She asked me to look for her sister. I'm doing that. She wanted to dictate the terms and I decided I should work for someone else."

"No, no, no. You misunderstood. She didn't want to terminate the relationship. She simply didn't want you to go to Missing Persons with it."

"But I disagreed with her. And I didn't think it was nice to take her money when I was ignoring her advice." I tried a noncommittal smile on him, swiveling slightly in my chair. "Was there something else?" I asked. I felt certain he was angling around for something. He didn't have to drive ninety miles for this.

He shifted in his chair, trying a friendlier tone. "I can tell we've gotten off on the wrong foot here," he said. "I'd like to know what you've found out about my sister-in-law. If I've pissed you off, I'd like to apologize. Oh. And you might be interested in this."

He took a folded paper from his jacket pocket and passed it across the desk to me. For a moment, I thought it was going to be an address or a telephone number, some scrap of information that might really help. It was a check for the $246.19 Beverly owed me. He made it seem like some kind of bribe and I didn't like that. I took the money anyway. I knew the difference whether he did or not.

"I sent Beverly a copy of my report two days ago. If you want to know what I've come up with, why not ask her?"

"I've read the report. I'd like to know what you've found out since then if you're willing to share that."

"Well, I'm not. I don't mean to sound surly about this, but any information I have belongs to my current employer and that's confidential. I'll tell you this much. I did go to the cops and they're circulating a description of her, but that's only been a couple of days and so far they haven't come up with anything. You want to answer a question for me?"

"Not really," he said, but he laughed. I was beginning to realize that his manner was probably born of discomfort, so I plowed ahead anyway.

"Beverly told me she hadn't seen her sister for three years, but a neighbor of Elaine's claims she was not only up here at Christmas, but the two had a knock-down-drag-out fight. Is that true?"

"Well, yeah, probably." His tone was softening and he seemed less aloof. He took a final drag of his cigarette and pinched the ember loose from the end. "To tell you the truth, I've been concerned that Beverly's somehow involved in this."

"How so?"

He'd stopped looking at me now. He rolled the tag end of his cigarette between his fingers until nothing was left but a small pile of tobacco shreds and a scrap of black paper. "She's got a drinking problem. She's had it for some time, though you'd probably never guess. She's one of those people who might not have a drink for six months, then . . . boom, she's off on a three-day drunk. Sometimes a binge lasts longer than that. I think that's what happened in December." He looked at me then and most of the pomposity had dropped away. This was a man in pain.

"Do you know what they quarreled about?"

"I have a fair idea."

"Was it you?" I asked.

He focused on me suddenly, with the first real life in his eyes. "What made you say that?"

"The neighbor said they probably quarreled about a man. You were the only one I knew about. You want to buy me lunch?"

We went to a cocktail lounge called Jay's just around the corner. It's very dark, with massive art deco booths in pale gray leather and black onyx tables that look like small free-form pools. The surface of them is so shiny you can almost see your reflection, like some kind of commercial for liquid diswashing detergent. The walls are padded with gray suede and the carpet underfoot is tricked out with matting so thick you feel as if you're walking on sand. The whole place comes close to a sensory-deprivation tank, dim and hushed, but the drinks are huge and the bartender puts together incredible hot pastrami sandwiches on rye. I can't afford the place myself, but it felt like the perfect setting for Aubrey Danziger. He looked like he could pay the tab.

"What sort of work do you do?" I asked when we were seated.

Before he could answer, the waitress appeared. I suggested two pastrami sandwiches and two martinis. That look of secret amusement returned to his face but he agreed with a careless shrug. I didn't think he was accustomed to women ordering for him, but there didn't seem to be any harmful side effects. I felt like this was my show and I wanted to work the lights. I knew we'd get blasted, but I thought it might take the high gloss off the man and humanize him some.

When the waitress left, he answered my question. "I don't work," he said, "I own things. I put together real-estate syndicates. We buy land and put up office buildings and shopping malls, sometimes condominiums." He paused, as though he could have said a lot more, but had decided that much would suffice. He took out his cigarette case again and held it out to me. I declined and he lit another slim black cigarette.

He tilted his head. "What'd I do that pissed you off? That happens to me all the time." The superior smile was back but this time I didn't take offense. Maybe that's just the way his face worked.

"You seem arrogant and you're way too slick," I said. "You keep smiling like you know something I don't."

"I've had a lot of money for a long time, so I feel slick. Actually, it amuses me to think about a girl detective. That's half the reason I drove up here."

"What's the other half?"

He hesitated, debating whether to say it. He took a long drag of his cigarette. "I don't trust Beverly's account of what went on. She's devious and she manipulates. I like to double-check."

"Are you talking about her transactions with me or hers with Elaine?"

"Oh, I know about her transactions with Elaine. She can't stand Elaine. She also can't leave her alone. Have you ever hated anybody that way?"

I smiled slightly. "Not recently. I guess I have in my day."

"It's like Bev has to know about Elaine and if she hears something good, it pisses her off. And if she hears something bad, she's satisfied, but it's never enough."

"What was she doing up here at Christmastime?"

The martinis arrived and Aubrey took a long sip of his before he answered. Mine was silky and cold with that whisper of vermouth that makes me shudder automatically. I always eat the olive early because it blends so nicely with the taste of gin.

He caught sight of the shiver. "I can leave the room if you want to be alone with that."

I laughed. "I can't help it. I never drink these things, but Jesus Lord, what a rush. I can already feel the hangover forming."

"Hell, it's Saturday. Take the day off. I didn't think I'd catch you in your office at all. I was going to leave you a note and then nose around seeing if I could find out something about Elaine myself."

"I take it you're as puzzled as everybody else about where she might be."

He shook his head slightly. "I think she's dead. I think Bev killed her."

That got my attention at any rate. "Why would she do that?"

Again, the long hesitation. He looked off across the room, checking the premises, doing some kind of mental arithmetic as though in placing a dollar value on his surroundings, he'd know where he stood. His eyes slid back to me and the smile hovered on his mouth. "She found out I'd had an affair with Elaine. It was my own damn fault. The IRS is auditing my tax returns from three years back and, like a fool, I asked Beverly to dig up some canceled checks and credit-card receipts. She figured out I'd been in Cozumel right at the same time Elaine went down there after Max died. I'd told her I was off on a business trip.

"Anyway, I got home from the office that day and she flew at me in such a rage it's a wonder I got out alive. Of course, she'd been drinking. Any excuse to sock down the sauce. She took a pair of kitchen shears and stabbed me right in the neck. Caught me right here. Just above the collarbone. The only thing that saved me was my collar and tie and maybe the fact that I have my shirts done with heavy starch."

He laughed, shaking his head uncomfortably at the recollection. "When that didn't work, she got me in the arm. Fourteen stitches. I bled all over the place. When she drinks, it's like Jekyll and Hyde. When she doesn't drink, she's not too bad... bitchy and hard as nails, but she isn't nuts."

"How'd you get involved with Elaine? What was that about?"

"Oh hell, I don't know. It was stupid on my part. I guess I'd had the hots for her for years. She's a beautiful woman. She does tend to be self-involved and self-indulgent but that only made her harder to resist. Her husband had just died and she was a mess. What started out as brotherly concern turned into unbridled lust, like something off the back of a paperback novel. I've strayed before, but never like that. I don't shit in my own Post Toasties as the old saying goes. This time I blew it."

"How long did it last?"

"Until she disappeared. Bev isn't aware of that. I told her it was over after six weeks and she bought it because that's what she wanted to believe."

"And she found out about it this past Christmas?"

He nodded and then caught the waitress's attention, glancing over at me. "You ready for another one?"

"Sure."

He held up two fingers like a victory sign and the waitress moved over to the bar. "Yeah, she found out right about then. She tore into me and then jumped straight in the car and drove up here. I got a call through to Elaine to warn her, so we could at least get our stories straight, but I'm not really sure what was said between them. I didn't talk to her after that and I never saw her again."

"What'd she say when you told her?"

"Well, she wasn't crazy about the idea that Bev knew, but there wasn't anything she could do about it. She said she'd handle it."

The martinis arrived, along with the sandwiches, and we stopped talking for a while in order to eat. He was opening up a whole new possibility and I had a lot of questions to ask.

17

"What's your theory about what went on?" I asked when we'd finished lunch. "I mean, as nearly as I can tell, Elaine was in Santa Teresa until the night of January ninth. That was a Monday. I've tracked her from her apartment to the airport and I've got a witness who saw her get on the plane. I've got someone else who claims she arrived in Miami and drove up through Fort Lauderdale to Boca. Now, this person swears she was in Boca briefly and then took off again and was last heard from in Sarasota where she's supposedly staying with friends. I have a hard time believing that last bit, but it's what I've been told. When could Beverly have killed her and where?"

"Maybe she followed her to Florida. She was off on one of her benders just after New Year's. She was gone for ten days and came home a mess. I'd never seen her so bad. She wouldn't say a word about where she'd been or what had happened. I had a business deal I had to close in New York that week so I got her settled and then I took off. I was out of town until the following Friday. She could have been anywhere while I was gone. Suppose she followed Elaine to Florida and killed her the first chance she had? She flies home afterward and who's the wiser?"

"I can't believe you're serious," I said. "Do you have any evidence? Do you have anything that links Beverly even superficially with Elaine's disappearance?"

He shook his head. "Look, I know I'm fishing here and I could be completely off base. I hope like hell I am. I probably shouldn't have said anything. . . ."

I could feel myself getting restless, trying to make sense of what he had said. "Why would Beverly have hired me if she'd killed Elaine?"

"Maybe she wanted to make it look good. The business about the cousin's estate was legitimate. The notice arrives in the mail and now what's she going to do? Suppose she knows Elaine is strolling along the bottom of the ocean in a pair of concrete shoes. She has to go through the motions, doesn't she? She can't ignore the situation because somebody's going to wonder why she doesn't show more concern. So she drives up here and hires you."

I looked at him skeptically. "Only then she panics when I say I'm going to the police."

"Right. And then she figures she better cover for that so she talks to me."

I finished my martini, thinking about what he'd said. It was very elaborate and I didn't like that. Still, I had to concede that it was possible. I made concentric circles on the tabletop with the bottom of my glass. I was thinking about the break-in at Tillie's place. "Where was she Wednesday night?"

He drew a blank. "I don't know. What do you mean?"

"I'm wondering where she was Wednesday night and early Thursday morning of this week. Was she with you?"

He frowned. "No. I flew to Atlanta Monday night and came back yesterday. What's the deal?"

I thought I should keep the details to myself for the time being. I shrugged. "There was an incident up here. Did you call her from Atlanta on either of those days?"

"I didn't call her at all. We used to do that when I was off on business trips. Talk back and forth long-distance. Now it's a relief to be away." He took a sip of his drink, watching me above the rim of the glass. "You don't believe any of this, do you?"

"It doesn't make any difference what I believe," I said. "I'm trying to find out what's true. So far it's all speculation."

He shook his head. "I know I don't have any concrete proof, but I felt like I had to tell someone. It's been bugging the shit out of me."

"I'll tell you what's bugging me," I said. "How can you live with someone you suspect of murder?"

He stared down at the table for a moment and the smile when it came was tainted with the old arrogance. I thought he was going to answer me, but the silence stretched and

finally he simply lit another cigarette and signaled for the
check.

I called Jonah in the middle of the afternoon. The encounter
with Aubrey Danziger had depressed me, and the two martinis at lunch had left me with a nagging pain between the
eyes. I needed air and sunshine and activity.

"You want to go up to the firing range and shoot?" I said
when Jonah got on the line.

"Where are you?"

"I'm at the office, but I'm on my way home to pick up some
ammo."

"Swing by and pick me up too," he said.

I smiled when I hung up the phone. Good.

The clouds hung above the mountains like puffs of white
smoke left in the wake of a giant old-fashioned choo-choo
train. We took the old road up through the pass, my VW
making high-pitched complaints until I shifted from third
gear to second and finally into first. The road twisted up
through sage and mountain lilac. As we approached, the dark
green of the distant vegetation separated into discreet shrubs
clinging obstinately to the slopes. There were very few trees.
Steep expanses of California buckwheat were visible on the
right, interspersed with the bright little orange faces of
monkey flower and the hot pink of prickly phlox. The poison
oak was thriving, its lush growth almost overwhelming the
silvery leaves of the mugwort which grew alongside it and is
its antidote.

As we reached the summit, I glanced to my left. The
elevation here was about twenty-five hundred feet and the
ocean seemed to hover in the distance like a gray haze
blending into the gray of the sky. The coastline stretched as
far as the eye could see and the town of Santa Teresa looked
as insubstantial as an aerial photo. From this perspective, the
mountain ridge seemed to plunge into the Pacific, appearing
again in four rugged peaks that formed the offshore islands.
The sun up here was hot and the volatile oils, exuded by the
underbrush, scented the still air with camphor. There were
occasional manzanita trees along the slope, still stripped
down to spare, misshapen black forms by the fire that had
swept through two years back. Everything that grows up here
longs to burn; seed coats broken only by intense heat,

germinating then when the rains come again. It's not a cycle that concedes much to human intervention.

The narrow road to the firing range veered off to the left just at the mountain's crest, climbing at an angle through huge sandstone boulders that looked as light and fake as a movie set. I pulled into the dirt and gravel parking area and Jonah and I got out of the car, taking guns and ammo from the backseat. I don't think we'd exchanged six words the entire thirty-minute trip, but the silence was restful.

We paid our fees and tucked little wads of foam in our ears to muffle the sound. I had also brought along a headset, like earmuffs, for additional protection. My hearing had already sustained some damage that I was hoping wasn't going to be permanent. With the plugs in place, I could hear the air going in and out of my own nose, a phenomenon I didn't pay much attention to ordinarily. I like the quiet. At the core of it, I could hear my own heart, like someone thumping on a plaster wall two floors below.

We moved up to the range, roof overhead like a carport extending fifteen feet on either side of us. Only one man was shooting and he had an H&K .45 competition pistol that Jonah coveted the minute he laid eyes on it. The two of them talked about the adjustable trigger and adjustable sights while I inserted eight rounds of reloads into the magazine of my little gun. I inherited this no-brand semiautomatic from the very proper maiden aunt who raised me after my parents died. She'd taught me to knit and crochet when I was six, and when I was eight, she'd brought me up here and taught me to target-shoot, bracing my arms on a wooden ironing board that she kept in the trunk of her car. I had fallen in love with the smell of gunpowder when I first came to live with her. I'd sit out on her concrete porch steps with a strip of caps and a hammer, patiently banging away until each snapped out its load of perfume. The porch steps would be littered afterward with bits of red paper and gray spots of burned powder the size of the buckle holes in a belt. I guess she decided after two years of my incessant hammering that she might as well school me in the real thing.

Jonah had brought both his Colts and I fired a few rounds from each, but they felt like too much gun for me. The walnut grip on the Trooper handled like big hunk of petrified wood and the four-inch barrel made sighting a bitch. The gun bucked in my hand like that quick, automatic kick when a doctor taps on your knee, and each time the gun bucked a whiff of gunpowder blew back at me. I did slightly better with the Python, but it was still a distinct and familiar treat when I took up my .32 again, like holding hands with an old friend.

At five, we packed up our gear and headed over to the old stagecoach tavern, tucked into a shady hollow not far from the range. We had beer and bread and baked beans and talked about nothing in particular.

"How's your case going?" he asked me. "You turned up anything yet?"

I shook my head. "I've got some things I may want to talk to you about at some point, but not for now."

"You sound bummed out," he said.

I smiled. "I always do this to myself. I want quick results. If I don't get things wrapped up in two days, I get depressed. What about you? Are you okay?"

He shrugged. "I miss my kids. I used to spend Saturdays with them. It was nice you called. Gave me something to do besides mope."

"Yeah, you can watch *me* mope," I said.

He patted my hand on the table and squeezed it lightly. The gesture was brief and compassionate and I squeezed back.

I dropped him off at his place again at 7:30 or so and went home. I was tired of worrying about Elaine Boldt so I sat on the couch and cleaned my gun, taking in the smell of oil, finding it restful to dismantle and wipe and put it all back together again. After that, I stripped my clothes off and wrapped up in my quilt, reading a book about fingerprint mechanics until I fell asleep.

Monday morning, I stopped by Santa Teresa Travel on my way into the office and talked to an agent named Lupe who looked like an interesting mix of Chicano and black, slim as a cat. She was in her twenties, with tawny skin and dark frizzy hair with a faint golden cast, cut close to the shape of her head. She wore small rectangular glasses and a smart navy blue pantsuit with a striped tie. I showed her the ticket carbon and told her what I was looking for. My guess was correct. Elaine had been a regular client of theirs for the past several years, though Lupe seemed puzzled by the carbon. She pulled the glasses down low on her nose and looked at me. Her eyes were a flat gold, like a lemur's, and it gave her face an exotic quality. Puffy mouth, small straight nose. She had fingernails that were long and curved and looked as tough as horn. Maybe she had been some kind of burrowing creature in another life. She pushed the glasses back into place again thoughtfully.

"Well, I don't know what to think," she said. "She always bought her tickets through us, but this one was purchased at the airport." She touched at one corner of the carbon, turning the ticket around so I could see the face of it. It reminded me. of those teachers in grade school who somehow managed to read a picture book while holding it forward and to one side. "These numbers indicate that it was generated by the airline and paid for by credit card."

"What kind of credit card?"

"American Express. She usually uses that for travel, but I tell you what's odd. She'd made reservations for . . . wait a minute. Let me check." Lupe typed some numbers into her computer terminal, nails tap-dancing across the keys. The computer fired out line after line of green print-like tracers. She studied the screen.

"She was scheduled to fly out of LAX, first class, on February third, with a return 3 August and those tickets were paid for."

"I hear she left on the spur of the moment," I said. "If she set up the reservations over the weekend, she'd have had to go through the airlines, wouldn't she?"

"Sure, but she wouldn't just forget about the tickets she had. Hold on a sec and I'll see if she ever picked 'em up. She could have traded 'em in."

She got up and moved over to the file cabinet on the far wall, sorting through her files. She pulled out a packet and handed it to me. It was a set of tickets and an itinerary, tucked into a travel folder from the agency. Elaine's name was neatly typed across the front.

"That's a thousand dollars' worth of tickets," Lupe said. "You'd think she'd have called us and had 'em cashed in when she got to Boca."

I felt a chill. "I'm not sure she got there," I said. I sat for a full minute with the unused tickets in my hand. What was this? I reached into my purse and pulled out the original TWA folder Julia Ochsner had mailed to me. On the back flap, there were the four luggage tags sequentially numbered and still stapled firmly in place. Lupe was watching me.

I was thinking about my own quick flight to Miami, getting off the plane at 4:45 in the morning, passing the glass-fronted cases where abandoned suitcases were stacked.

"I want you to call Miami International for me," I said slowly. "Let's put in a claim for lost baggage and see if we come up with anything."

"You lost some bags?"

"Yeah, four of 'em. Red leather with gray fabric bindings. Hard-sided, graduated sizes, and my guess is that one is a hanging bag. These are the tags for them." I pushed the folder across the desk, and she wrote the numbers down.

I gave her my business card and she said she'd be in touch as soon as she heard anything.

"One more question," I said. "Was that flight she took non-stop?"

Lupe glanced at the carbon and shook her head. "That's the red-eye. She'd have had a layover and a change of planes in St. Louis."

"Thanks."

When I got to the office, the message light on my answering machine was blinking. I pressed the playback button.

It was my punker friend, Mike. "Hey, Kinsey? Oh shit, a machine. Well never mind. I'll call you back, okay? Oh. This is Mike and there's just something I want to talk to you about, but I have a class right now. Anyway, I'll call back later. Okay? Bye."

I made a note. The timer on the machine indicated that he'd called at 7:42 A.M. Maybe he'd try again at noon. I wished he'd left me a number.

I put in a call to Jonah and told him about Elaine's stopover. "Could you circulate a description of her through the St. Louis police?"

"Sure. You think that's where she is?"

"I hope."

I intended to sit and chat with him, but I didn't have the chance. There was a quick knock and my office door flew open. Beverly Danziger stood on the threshold and she looked pissed off. I told Jonah I'd get back to him and hung up, turning my attention to Beverly.

18

"You goddamn bitch!" She slammed the door behind her, eyes flashing.

I'm not real fond of being addressed like that. I could feel the heat rise in my cheeks, my temper climbing automatically. I wondered if she was going to challenge me to hand-to-hand combat. I gave her a slow smile just to show her I wasn't impressed with the histrionics.

"What's the problem, Beverly?" I sounded like a smart aleck even to myself and I thought I better cast about for something to smite her with if she came flying across the desk at me. All I spotted was an unsharpened pencil and a Rolodex.

She put her hands on her hips. "What the fuck did you contact Aubrey for? How dare you! How fucking *dare* you!!"

"I didn't contact Aubrey. He got in touch with me."

"I hired you. *I* did. You had no right to talk to him and no right to discuss my business behind my own back! You know what I'm going to do? I'm going to sue you for this!"

I wasn't worried she'd sue me. I was worried she'd pull a pair of scissors out of her purse and cut me up like patches for a quilt.

By now, she was leaning over my desk, stabbing a pointed index finger into my face. Shout lines appeared to come out of her mouth as in a cartoon. She thrust her chin forward, cheeks pink, bubbles collecting in the corner of her mouth. I wanted to slap the shit out of her, but I didn't think it'd be smart. She was beginning to hyperventilate, chest heaving. And then her mouth began to tremble and the fiery blue eyes filled with tears. She sobbed once. She dropped her handbag and put both hands to her face like a little kid. Was this woman nuts or what?

"Sit down," I said. "Have a cigarette. What's going on?"

I glanced down at the ashtray. Aubrey's telltale pile of shredded tobacco and a scrap of black paper were still sitting in my ashtray. Discreetly, I removed it, tipping the contents into my trash. She sat down abruptly, her anger gone, some deep-seated grief having taken its place. I'm sorry to report myself unmoved. I can be a coldhearted little thing.

While she wept, I made coffee. My office door opened a crack and Vera peered in, making eye contact. She'd apparently heard the ruckus and wanted to make sure I was all right. I lifted my eyebrows in a quick facial shrug and she disappeared. Beverly fished out a Kleenex and pinched it across the bridge of her nose, pressing her eyes as though to extract the last few tears. Her porcelain complexion was now mottled and her glossy black hair had taken on a stringy look, like a fur muff left out in the rain.

"I'm sorry," she breathed, "I know I shouldn't have done that. He's making me crazy. He's driving me absolutely insane. He's such a son of a bitch. I just hate his *guts*!"

"Take it easy, Beverly. You want some coffee?"

She nodded. She got a compact out of her bag and checked her eye makeup, mopping up a run of mascara with Kleenex folded over her finger. Then she tucked the compact away and blew her nose without making a sound. It was just a sort of squeezing process. She opened her bag again and searched for her cigarettes and matches. Her hands were shaking, but the minute she got her cigarette lighted, all the tension seemed to leave her body. She inhaled deeply as though she were taking in ether before surgery. I wish cigarettes felt that good to me. Every time I've had a drag, my mouth has tasted like a cross between charred sticks and spoiled eggs. It's made my breath smell about that good too, I'm sure. My office was now looking like the fog had rolled in.

She began to shake her head hopelessly. "You have no idea what I've been through," she said.

"Look," I said, "just to set the record straight—"

"I know you didn't do anything. It's not your fault." Her eyes filled with tears briefly. "I should be used to it by now, I guess."

"Used to what?"

She began to fold the Kleenex in her lap. She recited

slowly, fighting for control, sentences punctuated with silences and little humming noises when the weeping closed off her throat. "He...um...goes around to people. And he tells them...um...that I drink and sometimes he claims I'm a nymphomaniac or he says I'm undergoing shock treatments. Whatever occurs to him. Whatever he thinks will do the most harm."

I wasn't sure what to do with this. He *had* told me she was an alcoholic. He'd told me she went off on three-day toots. He'd told me she attacked him with a pair of scissors and had possibly murdered her sister in revenge for an affair he was having with her. Now here she sat, sobbing her tiny heart out, claiming that he was the perpetrator of this weird pathological stuff. Which of them was I to believe? She composed herself, giving her nose the old silent squeeze. She looked at me, the whites of her eyes now tinted with pink.

"Didn't he tell you something like that?" she asked.

"I think he was just concerned about Elaine," I said, trying to hedge until I could decide what to do. "We really didn't discuss anything personal so don't worry about that. How did you find out he'd been up here?"

"Something came up in conversation," she said. "I don't even remember what. That's how he handles these things. He gives me these *clues*. He leaves the evidence around and waits for me to discover it. And if I don't stumble across it accidentally, he points me right to it and then sits back and pretends to be contrite and amazed."

I was just about to say, "Like his affair with Elaine," but it suddenly occurred to me that it might not even be true, or if true, that she might not actually know about it. "Like what, for example?" I said.

"He had an affair with Elaine. He was fucking around with my only sister. God, I can't believe he did that to me. I didn't doubt *she'd* do it. She was always jealous. She'd take anything she could. But *him*. I felt like such a fool. He was off balling her the minute Max died and I was such a dunce I didn't figure it out for years! It took me *years*."

She did one of those bubbling laughs, filled more with hysteria than mirth. "Poor Aubrey. He must have been at his wit's end trying to get me to pick up on that. He finally cooked up this absurd tale about the IRS auditing his taxes. I told him the accountant could take care of it, but he said

Harvey wanted us to go through the canceled checks and
credit-card receipts. So like a dodo I did it and there it was."

"Why don't you leave?" I asked. "I don't understand why
you stay in a relationship like that." I always say the same
thing. Every time I hear a tale like this. Drunkenness,
beatings, infidelity, and verbal abuse. I just don't get it. Why
do people put up with it? I had said it to Aubrey so I figured
I might as well say it to her too. The marriage was a mess and
regardless of where the truth lay, these two people were
miserable. Was misery the point?

"Oh, I don't know. Part of it's the money, I guess." she said.

"Screw the money. This is a community-property state."

"That's what I mean," she said. "He'll walk away with half
of everything I have and it just seems so unfair."

I looked at her blankly. "The money's yours?"

"Well of course it's mine, " she said, and then her expression changed. "He told you it was his, didn't he?"

I shrugged uncomfortably. "More or less. He told me he
put together real-estate syndicates."

She was startled for an instant and then she laughed.

She started to cough, patting her chest. She stubbed out
her cigarette, pecking it in the bottom of the ashtray. Smoke
was streaming out of her nostrils as though her brain had
caught fire. She was shaking her head, smile fading. "Sorry,
but that's a new one on me. I should have guessed. What else
did he say?"

I held a hand up in protest. "Hey," I said. "Enough. I don't
want to play this game. I don't know what your problems are
and I don't care. . . ."

"You're right, you're right. God, we must seem like lunatics to you. I'm sorry you got sucked in. It's not your concern.
It's mine. How much do I owe you for your time?" She was
rooting through her handbag for her checkbook and her
famous rosewood pen-and-pencil set.

I could feel my temper on the rise again.

"I don't want any money from you. Don't be absurd. Why
don't you give me some straight answers for a change?"

She blinked at me, the china blue eyes glazing over like ice
on a pond. "About what?"

"Elaine's neighbor claims you were up here at Christmas
and the two of you had a big fight. You told me you hadn't
seen her for years. Now which is it?"

She stalled, reaching for another cigarette so she'd have time to frame a reply.

I headed her off. "Come on, Beverly. Just tell me the truth. Were you up here or not?"

She took out a packet of matches and removed a match, scratching it repeatedly across the packet without effect. She tossed that one, a dud apparently, into the ashtray and took out a second match. This time, she managed to light her cigarette. "I did come up," she said carefully. She tapped the lighted cigarette on the lip of the ashtray as though to remove an ash when there was none yet.

I was going to scream if she did any more shit with that cigarette. "Did you quarrel with her or didn't you?"

She switched to her officious tone, mouth going all prim. "Kinsey, I had just found out about the affair. Of course we quarreled. That's exactly what Aubrey had in mind, I'm sure. What would you have done?"

"What difference does it make? I'm not married to him so who gives a damn what I'd have done! I want to know why you lied to me."

She stared at the desk, her face taking on a stubborn look.

I tried another tack. "Why'd you call me off? Why wouldn't you let me contact the police?"

She smoked for a moment and I thought at first she didn't intend to answer that question either. "I was worried he'd done something."

I stared a her.

She caught my look and leaned forward earnestly.

"He's crazy. He is a truly crazy man and I was worried that he'd . . . I don't know . . . I suppose I was worried he'd killed her."

"All the more reason to call the police. Isn't it?"

"You don't understand. I couldn't turn the police loose on this. That's why I hired you in the first place. When this whole business came up about the will, I didn't think anything of it. It was such a minor matter. I just assumed she'd signed the paper and sent it to the attorney. And then when I realized no one had heard from her, it occurred to me that something might be wrong. I don't even know what I thought it was."

"But when I mentioned she might be dead, the penny dropped, right?" I sounded bored. I sounded contemptuous too.

She shifted uncomfortably. "Before that. I guess I'd just never really put it in words until you said it and then I realized I better reassess the situation before I agreed to anything."

"What makes you think Aubrey's involved?"

"That day... when I drove up here and Elaine and I had words... she told me that the affair had been going on for years. She'd finally figured out that Aubrey was a psychopath and she was trying to break it off." She paused and the blue eyes came up to mine. "You don't understand about Aubrey yet. You don't know what he's like. You just don't *leave* him. You just don't break it off. I've threatened to do that myself. Don't think it hasn't occurred to me. But I'd never make it. I don't know what he'd do, but I'd never get away from him. Never. He'd follow me to the ends of the earth and bring me back, only then he'd really make me pay."

"Bev, I've got to tell you I'm having trouble with this," I said.

"That's because you fell for it. He came waltzing up here and he laid a number on you. He conned you good and now you can't bear to admit you've been had. He's done it before. He does it to everyone. The man is certifiably insane. He was in Camarillo for years until Reagan became governor. Remember that? He cut the state budget and turned them all out in the streets. Aubrey Danziger came home at that point and my life has been hell ever since."

I picked up a pencil and tapped on the edge of the desk, then tossed it aside. "I'll tell you the truth. I want to find Elaine. That's all I want to do. I'm like a terrier pup. Somebody tells me to do something and it gets done. I'll worry the damn thing to death. I'm going to find out what happened to her and where she's been all these months. And you better hope it doesn't lead back to you."

She got up. She picked up her bag and leaned on my desk. "And you better hope it doesn't lead back to Aubrey, my dear!" she spat.

And then she was gone, leaving behind her the faint aura of whiskey that I'd just caught on her breath.

I hauled out my typewriter and wrote a detailed report for Julia, itemizing expenses for the last couple of days. I needed time to assimilate what Beverly had told me about Aubrey. It was like the paradox of the jungle tribes where one always lies and the other always tells the truth. How could one ever

determine which was which? Aubrey had told me Beverly
was Mr. Hyde when she drank. She had told me he was
certifiably mad, but she'd apparently been drinking when she
said so. I hadn't the faintest idea which of them was on the
level and I wasn't sure how to find out. I didn't even know if
it mattered. Was Elaine Boldt really dead? It had certainly
crossed my mind more than once, but I hadn't imagined that
Beverly or Aubrey might be at the heart of it. I'd been
looking in the opposite direction, assuming somehow that
Elaine's disappearance was linked to the murder of Marty
Grice. Now I'd have to go back and take another look.

I went home at lunchtime and did a run. I knew I was just
treading water at this point, but in some ways I had to wait it
out. Something would break. Some piece of information
would come to light. In the meantime, I was feeling tense
and I needed to work that off. The run was a bad one and that
put me in a foul mood. I picked up a stitch in my side at the
end of the first mile. I thought I could shake it. I tried
digging my fingers in, bending at the waist, thinking that if it
was a muscle cramp it might ease. No deal. Then I tried
expelling breath after breath, again bending from the waist.
The pain was no worse, but it didn't go away either. Finally, I
slowed to a walk until it subsided, but the minute I started to
jog again, my side seized up, stopping me in my tracks. I'd
reached the turnaround by then, but running seemed futile
so I walked the entire mile and a half back to my place,
cursing to myself. I hadn't even broken a sweat, and my
frustration, instead of dissipating, had doubled.

I showered and dressed again. I didn't want to go back to
the office, but I forced myself. I was going to have to start all
over again, go back to the beginning and cast a new set of
lines in the water to see if I could get a bite somewhere. I
had just about used up my whole bag of tricks, but there had
to be something else.

When I let myself into the office, I saw the message light
blinking on my machine. I opened the French doors to let
some air in and then punched playback.

"Hi, Kinsey. This is Lupe, over at Santa Teresa Travel. It
looks like you hit the jackpot on that luggage trace. I put a
call through to Baggage Claim at TWA and had the agent
check it out. The four bags were sitting right there. He said

he could put 'em on a plane this afternoon if you like. Could you call me back and let me know what you want to do?"

I snapped the machine off and shook both fists in the air, mouthing "All riiight!" to myself with a big grin. I put a call through to Jonah first and told him what was going on. I was jazzed. It was the first good news I'd had since I tracked down the cat. "What should I do, Jonah? Am I going to need some kind of court order to open those bags?"

"Screw that. Look, you have the claim tags, don't you?"

"Sure, I've got 'em right here."

"Then go down to Florida and pick up the bags."

"Why not just have them flown out?"

"Suppose she's *in* one," he said.

That certainly conjured up an image I didn't like. I could feel myself squirm. "Don't you think someone would have *noticed* by now? You know, an odor . . . something dripping out the side?"

"Hey, we found a body once had been in the trunk of a car for six months. Someone had shoved a high heel down some whore's throat and she ended up mummified. Don't ask me how or why, but she didn't decompose at all. She just dried up. She looked like a big leather doll."

"Maybe I'll get on a plane," I said.

By ten o'clock that night, I was back in the air again.

19

It was drizzling and the temperature was already in the seventies at 4:56 A.M. EST when we touched down. It was still dark outside, but the airport was filled with the flat light and artificial chill of a space station orbiting a hundred and ten miles out. Dawn travelers walked purposefully down deserted corridors while doors shushed open and shut automatically and the paging system seemed to drone on and on without hope of response. For all I knew, the whole operation was mechanical, running itself at that hour without any help from humankind.

The TWA baggage-service office didn't open until nine, so I had time to kill. I hadn't brought any luggage of my own, just a big canvas bag where I kept a toothbrush and all the odds and ends of ordinary life, including clean underpants. I never go anywhere without a toothbrush and clean underpants. I went into the women's room to freshen up. I washed my face and ran my wet fingers through my hair, noting how sallow my skin looked with the fluorescent lights overhead. There was a woman behind me, changing the diaper on one of those oversized babies who looks like a solemn adult with flushed cheeks. The child kept his eyes pinned on me gravely while his mother attended to him. Sometimes cats look at me that way, as though we're foreign agents sending silent signals to one another in an out of the way meeting place.

I paused at a stand and picked up a newspaper. There was a coffee shop open and I bought scrambled eggs, bacon, toast, and juice, taking my time about breakfast while I read a human-interest story about a man who'd left all his money to a mynah bird. I can't cope with the front section before seven A.M.

At quarter to nine, having walked the airport from end to

end twice, I stationed myself near Baggage Claim with a portable cart I'd rented for a buck. I could see Elaine's bags, neatly lined up at on end of the locked glass-fronted cabinets. It looked as if someone had hauled them out from the bottom of the pile in readiness. Finally, a middle-aged man in a TWA uniform, with a big set of jangling keys, unlocked the small cubicle and started turning on lights. It looked like the opening curtain of a one-act play with a modest set.

I presented myself and the baggage-claim tags and then followed him out to the storage cabinets and waited while he extracted the suitcases and stacked them on the cart. I expected him to ask for identification, but apparently he didn't care who I was. Maybe abandoned bags are like litters of unwanted kittens. He was just grateful to have someone take them off his hands.

When the Penny-Car Rental desk opened, I rented a compact car. I had given Julia a call the night before so she knew I was flying in. All I needed to do now was find the highway again and drive north. Once outside, I pushed the cart toward the slot where the rental car was parked. The drizzle settled on my skin like a layer of silk. The morning air was hot and close, smelling of rain and jet exhaust. I loaded the bags in the trunk of the car and headed toward Boca. It wasn't until I reached the condominium parking lot, unloading the suitcases one by one, that I realized all four were locked and I had no key. Well, how very cute. Maybe Julia would have a plan. I lugged them over to the elevator and went up to the third floor, hauling them to Julia's front door in two trips.

I knocked and waited a long interval while Julia thumped her way to the front door with her cane, calling encouragement.

"I'm coming. Don't give up. Six more feet to go and I'm bearing down hard."

On my side of the door, I smiled, peering over at Elaine's apartment. There was no sign of life. Even the welcome mat had been taken inside or thrown out, leaving a square of fine sand that had filtered through the bristles.

Julia's door opened. The dowager's hump sat between her shoulder blades like a weight, forcing her to bend with its burden. She seemed to be staring at my waist, tilting her head of dandelion fuzz to one side so she could peer up at me. Her skin seemed as sheer as rubber, pulled over her hands like surgical gloves. I could see veins and broken capillaries, her knuckles as knotted as rope. Age was making her transparent, crushing her from both ends like a can of soda pop.

"Well, Kinsey! I knew that was you. I've been awake since six this morning, looking forward to this. Come on in."

She hobbled to one side, making way for me. I set the four suitcases inside the door and closed it after me. She tapped one with her cane. "I recognize those."

"Unfortunately, they're locked."

Each of the four bags apparently had a combination lock, the numbers arranged on a dial embedded in the metal catch.

"We'll have to do some detective work," she said with satisfaction. "You want coffee first? How was your flight?"

"I'd love some," I said. "The flight wasn't bad."

Julia's apartment was crowded with antiques: a peculiar mix of Victorian pieces and Oriental furnishings. There was a huge carved cherry sideboard with a marble top, a black horsehair sofa, an intricate ivory screen, jade figures, a platform rocker, two cinnabar lamps, Persian rugs, a pier-glass mirror in a dark mahogany frame, a piano with a fringed shawl across the top, lace curtains, wall hangings of embroidered silk. A big portable television set with a twenty-five-inch screen loomed on the far side of the room surrounded by family photographs in heavy silver frames. The television set was turned off, its blank gray face oddly compelling in a room so filled with memorabilia. The only sound in the apartment was the steady ticking of a grandfather clock that sounded like someone tapping on Formica with a set of drumsticks.

I moved out to the kitchen, poured coffee for us both, and carried it back to the living room, the cups rattling slightly in the saucers like the tremor of a minor California earthquake. "Are these family antiques? Some of the pieces are beautiful."

Julia smiled, waggling her cane. "I'm the last person alive in my family so I've inherited all this by default. I was the youngest in a family of eleven children and my mother said I was fractious. She always swore I'd never get a thing, but I just kept my mouth shut and waited it out. Sure enough, she died, my father died. I had eight sisters and two brothers and they all died. Little by little, it all drifted down to me, though I hardly have a place to put anything at this point. Eventually you have to give it all away. You start with a ten-room house and finally you find yourself stranded in a nursing home with space for one night table and a candlestick. Not that I intend to let that happen to me."

"You've got a ways to go yet anyway from what I can see."

"Well, I hope so. I'm going to hold out as long as I can and then I'll lock and bar the door and do myself in, if nature doesn't take me first. I'm hoping I'll die in my bed one night. It's the bed I was born in and I think it'd be nice to end up there. Have you a large family?"

"No, just me. I was raised by an aunt, but she died ten years ago."

"Well then, we're in the same boat. Restful, isn't it."

"That's one way to put it," I said.

"I came from a family of shriekers and face slappers. They all threw things. Glasses, plates, tables, chairs, anything that came to hand. The air was always filled with flying missiles—objects rocketing from one end of the room to the other with howls on contact. This was mostly girls, you know, but all of us had deadly aim. I had a sister knock me out of my high chair once with a grapefruit thrown like a curve ball, oatmeal flying everywhere. Eulalie, her name was. Now that I look back on it, I see we were common as mud, but effective. We all got what we wanted in life and no one ever accused us of being helpless or fainthearted. Well now. Let's tackle those bags. If worse comes to worst, we can always hurl them off the balcony. I'm sure they'll open when they hit the pavement down below."

We approached the problem as though it were a code to be broken. Julia's theory, which proved to be correct, was that Elaine would have come up with a combination of numbers she already had in her life somewhere. Her street address, zip code, telephone number, social security, birthdate. Each of us chose one group of digits and started to work on separate bags. I hit it the third time around with the last four numbers on her social-security card. All four suitcases were coded with the same number, which simplified the task.

We opened them on the living-room floor. They were filled with exactly what one would expect: clothing, cosmetics, costume jewelry, shampoo, deodorant, slippers, bathing suit, but packed in a jumble the way they do in movies when the wife leaves the husband in the middle of a vicious snit. The hangers were still on the hanging clothes, garments folded over and bunched in, with the shoes tossed on top. It looked as if drawers had been turned upside down and emptied into the largest of the bags. Julia had hobbled over to the rocker and she sat there now, propping herself up with her cane as though she were a unwieldy plant. I sat down on the horse-hair sofa, staring at the suitcases. I looked at Julia uneasily.

"I don't like this," I said. "From what I know of Elaine, she was almost compulsively neat. You should have seen the way she left her place . . . everything just so . . . clean, tidy, tucked in. Does she strike you as the type who'd pack this way?"

"Not unless she were in a fearful hurry," Julia said.

"Well actually, she might have been, but I still don't think she'd pack like this."

"What's on your mind? What do you think it means?"

I told her about the double set of plane tickets and the layover in St. Louis and any other facts I thought might pertain. It was nice to have someone to try ideas on. Julia was bright and she liked to pick at knots the same way I did.

"I'm not convinced she ever got here," I said. "We only have Pat Usher's word for it anyway and neither of us set much store by that. Maybe she got off the plane in St. Louis for some reason."

"Without her luggage? And you said she left her passport behind too, so what could she have done with herself?"

"Well, she did have that lynx coat," I said, "which she could have pawned or sold." I had one of those little nagging thoughts on the subject, but I couldn't bring it into focus for the moment.

Julia waved dismissively. "I don't believe she'd sell her coat, Kinsey. Why would she do that? She has lots of money. Stocks, bonds, mutual funds. She wouldn't need to pawn anything."

I chewed on that one. She was right, of course. "I keep wondering if she's dead. The luggage got here, but maybe she never made it. Maybe she's in a morgue somewhere with a tag on her toe."

"You think someone lured her off the plane and killed her?"

I wagged my head back and forth, not wholly convinced. "I don't know. It's possible. It's also possible she never made the trip at all."

"I thought you told me someone saw her get on the plane. The cab driver you talked about."

"That wasn't really a positive identification. I mean, a cab driver picks up a fare and the woman claims she's Elaine Boldt. He never saw her before in his life, so who knows? He just takes her word for it, like we all do. How do you know I'm

Kinsey Millhone? Because I say I am. Someone might have posed as her just to establish a trail."

"What for?"

"Well now, *that* I don't know. We've got a couple of women who might have pulled it off. Her sister Beverly for one."

"And Pat Usher for another," Julia said.

"Pat did benefit from Elaine's being off the scene. She gets a rent-free condo in Boca for months."

"That's the first time I ever heard of anyone murdered for room and board," she said tartly.

I smiled. I knew we were floundering, but maybe we'd stumble onto something. I could have used a break at that point. "Did Pat ever leave that forwarding address she promised?"

Julia shook her head. "Charmaine says she left one, but it was humbug. She packed and took off the same day you were here and nobody's seen her since."

"Oh shit. I knew she'd do that."

"Well, it wasn't anything you could have prevented," she said charitably.

I leaned my head back against the sofa frame, playing mind games. "It could have been Beverly too, you know. Maybe Bev bumped her off in the ladies' room at the St. Louis airport."

"Or killed her in Santa Teresa and impersonated her from that point on. Maybe she was the one who packed the bags and took the plane."

"Try it the other way," I said. "Think about Pat. I mean, what if Pat Usher were a stranger to Elaine, just someone she met on the plane. Maybe they started talking and Pat realized—" I dropped that idea when I saw the expression on Julia's face. "It does sound pretty lame," I said.

"Oh, well—no harm done in speculating. Maybe Pat knew her in Santa Teresa and followed her from there."

I ran that around in my head. "Well, yeah. I guess it could be. Tillie says she heard from Elaine—at least, she assumed it was Elaine—by postcard until March, but I guess somebody could have faked that too."

I filled her in on my conversations with Aubrey and Beverly and right in the middle of it, my memory kicked in; one of those wonderful little mental jolts, like a quick electrical shock when a plug's gone bad. "Oh wait, I just remembered something. Elaine got a bill from some furrier here in

Boca. What if we could track him down and find out if he's
seen the coat? That might give us a lead."

"What furrier? We have quite a few."

"I'd have to check with Tillie. Can I make a call to
California? If we can track down the coat, maybe we can get a
line on her."

Julia wagged the cane toward the telephone. Within minutes, I'd gotten Tillie on the line and told her what I needed.

"Well, you know that bill got stolen along with the rest, but
I just got another one. Hold on and I'll see what it says." She
put the receiver down and went to fetch the mail.

She got back on the line. "She's being dunned. It's a
second overdue notice from a place called Jacques—seventy-
six dollars for storage and two hundred dollars for having the
coat recut. Wonder why she'd do that? There's a little happy
face drawn by hand: 'Thanks for your business'—followed by a
sad face: 'Hope the delay in payment is just an oversight.' A
few more bills have come in too. Let me see what those look
like."

I could hear Tillie ripping open envelopes on her end of
the line.

"Oops. Well, these are all overdue. It looks like she's run
up a lot of charges. Let's see. Oh my. Visa, MasterCard. The
last date on these is about ten days ago, but I guess that was
just the end of the billing period. They're asking her not to
use her cards until she's paid the balances down."

"Does it indicate where she was when the purchases were
made? Was she in Florida somewhere?"

"Yes, it looks like Boca Raton and Miami for the most part,
but you can check them yourself when you get back. Now
that I've had the locks changed, they should be safe."

"Thanks, Tillie. Can you give me the furrier's address?"

I made a note of it and got directions from Julia. I left her
and went back down to the parking lot. The sky was an
ominous gray and thunder rumbled in the distance like mov-
ers rolling a piano down a wooden ramp. It was hot and still,
the light a harsh white, making the grass turn phosphorescent
green. I was hoping I could take care of business before the
downpour caught up with me.

Jacques was located in the middle of an elegant shopping
plaza, shaded with latticework overhead and planted with
delicate birches in big pale blue urns. Tiny Italian lights had

been threaded through the branches, and in the prestorm gloom they twinkled like an early Christmas. The storefronts were done in a dove-gray granite and the pigeons strutting across the pavement looked as if they'd been placed there purely for their decorative effect. Even the sound they made was refined, a low, churring murmur that rode on the morning air like cash being riffled in a merchant's hands.

The window display at Jacques had been artfully done. A golden sable coat had been tossed carelessly across a dune of fine white sand against a sky-blue backdrop. Tufts of sea oats were growing on the crest of the sand and a hermit crab had crossed the surface, leaving a narrow track that looked like an embroidery stitch. It was like a little moment frozen in time: a woman—someone reckless and rich—had come down to the shore, had shrugged aside this luscious fur so that she could plunge naked into the sea—or perhaps she was making love to someone on the far side of the dune. Standing there, I could have sworn I saw the grasses bending in a nonexistent wind and I could almost smell the trail of perfume she'd left in her wake.

I pushed the door open and went in. If I'd had money and believed in wearing furry creatures on my back, I'd have laid down thousands in that place.

20

The interior was done in muted blues with a glittering chandelier dominating the high-ceilinged space. Chamber music echoed through the room as though there might be a string quartet sawing somewhere out of sight. Chippendale chairs were arranged in gracious conversational groupings and massive gilt-edged mirrors lined the walls. The only detail that spoiled an otherwise perfect eighteenth-century drawing-room was the little camera up in one corner monitoring my every move. I wasn't sure why. There wasn't a fur in sight and the furniture was probably nailed to the floor. I shoved my hands down in my back pockets just to show I knew how to behave myself. I caught sight of my reflection. There I stood in that rococo setting, in faded jeans and a tank top, looking like something deposited in error by a time machine. I flexed, wondering if I should start lifting weights again. The bicep made my right arm look like a snake that had recently eaten something very small, like a wad of socks.

"Yes?"

I turned around. The man who stood there looked as out of place as I did. He was huge, maybe three hundred pounds, wearing a caftan that made him look like a pop-open tent with a built-in aluminum frame. He was in his sixties with a face that needed to be taken up. His eyelids drooped and he had a sagging mouth and a big double chin. What was left of his hair had slipped down around his ears. I wasn't certain, but I thought he made a rude noise under his skirt.

"I'd like to talk to you about a past-due account," I said.

"I got a bookkeeper handles that. She's out."

"Someone left a twelve-thousand-dollar lynx coat here to be cleaned and recut. She never paid her bill."

"So?"

This guy didn't have to get by on good looks alone. He was gracious too.

"Is Jacques here?" I asked.

"That's who you're talking to. I'm Jack. Who are you?"

"Kinsey Millhone," I said. I took out a card and handed it to him. "I'm a private investigator from California."

"No fooling," he said. He stared at the card and then at me. He glanced around suspiciously like this might be a "Candid Camera" gag. "What do you want with me?"

"I'm looking for information about the woman who brought the coat in."

"You got a subpoena?"

"No."

"You got the money she owes?"

"No."

"Then what are you bothering me for? I don't have time for this. I got work to do."

"Mind if I talk to you while you do it?"

He stared at me. His breathing made that wheezing sound that fat people sometimes make. "Yeah, sure. Why not? Suit yourself."

I followed him into the big cluttered back room, taking in his scent. He smelled like something that spent the winter in a cave.

"How long have you been cutting fur?" I asked.

He turned and looked at me as if I were speaking in tongues.

"Since I was ten," he said finally. "My father cut fur and his father before him."

He indicated a stool and I sat, setting my big canvas handbag at my feet. There was a long worktable to my right, with a coarse brown-paper pattern laid out on it. The right front portion of a mink coat had been put together and he was apparently still working on it. The wall on the left was lined with hanging paper patterns and there were various quite ancient-looking sewing machines to my right. Every available surface was covered with pelts, scraps, unfinished coats, books, magazines, boxes, catalogues. Two dress forms stood side by side, like twins posing self-consciously for a photograph. The place reminded me of a shoe-repair shop, all leather smell and machinery and the feel of craftsmanship. He took up the coat and examined it closely, then reached for a cutting device with a nasty curved blade. He glanced up at me. His eyes were the same shade of brown as the mink.

"So what do you want to know?"

"You remember the woman?"

"I know the coat. Naturally, I remember the woman who brought it in. Mrs. Boldt, right?"

"That's right. Can you tell me when you saw her last?"

He dropped his gaze back to the fur. He made a cut. He crossed to one of the machines, motioning me to follow. He sat down on a stool and began to sew. I could see now that what had looked at first like an old-fashioned Singer was actually a machine especially designed for the stitching of fur. He lined up the two cut pieces vertically, fur-side in, and caught them in the grip of two flat metal disks, like large silver dollars set rim to rim. The machine whipped the leather edges together with an overhand stitch while he deftly tucked the fur out of the way so it wouldn't get caught in the seam. The whole maneuver took about ten seconds. He spread the seam, smoothing it with his thumb on the backside. There were maybe sixty similar cuts in the leather, a quarter-inch apart. I wanted to ask him what he was doing, but I didn't want to distract him.

"She came in in March and said she wanted to sell the coat."

"How'd you know it was really hers?"

"Because I asked for some identification and the bill of sale." The irritable tone was back, but I ignored it.

"Did she say why she was selling it?"

"Said she was bored with it. She wanted mink, maybe blond, so I offered her credit against something in the store, but she said she wanted the cash, so I told her I'd see what I could do. I wasn't that anxious to pay cash for a used coat. Ordinarily, I don't deal in secondhand fur. There's no market for it here and it's a pain in the ass."

"I take it you made an exception for her."

"Well yeah, I did. The thing is, this lynx coat was in perfect condition and my wife's been after me to get her one for years. She's already got five coats, but when this one came in, I thought . . . what the hell? Make the old broad happy. What's it to me? Mrs. Boldt and I haggled and I finally got the coat for five thousand, which was a good deal for both of us, especially since I got the matching hat. I told her she'd have to pay to have the coat cleaned and recut."

"Why recut?"

"My wife is on the down side of five feet. She's four foot eleven, if you want her exact height, but don't ever tell her I told you that. She considers it some kind of birth defect. You ever noticed that? Short women get that way. From the time they're teenagers, they start wearing funny shoes, trying to look like tall people when they're not. Know what she finally did? Learned to roller skate. She said it was the only time she really felt like a real human being. Anyway, I thought I'd give her this lynx. Gorgeous. You know the coat?"

I shook my head. "I've never seen it."

"Hey, come on. You ought to take a look. I've got it right back here. I haven't cut it yet."

He moved toward the rear and I trotted obediently behind. He opened the massive metal door to his vault. Cold air wafted out as though from a meat locker. There were fur coats hanging on both sides in double racks, sleeves almost touching, like hundreds of women lined up with their backs to us. He moved down the aisle checking coats as he went, wheezing from the effort. He really needed to lose some weight. His breathing sounded like someone sitting down on a leather couch and it couldn't connote good health.

He took a fur down off the top rack and we moved back out of the cold-storage room, the door shutting behind us with a clang. He held Elaine Boldt's coat up for me to inspect. The lynx was two shades—white and gray in a luscious blend, with the pelts arranged so that each panel ended in a tapering point at the hem. He must have guessed from the look on my face that I'd never seen a coat that expensive close up.

"Here. Try it on," he said.

I hesitated for a moment and then eased into the coat. I pulled it around me and looked at myself in the mirror. The coat hung almost to my shins, the shoulders protruding like protection pads for some strange new sport.

"I look like the Abominable Snowman," I said.

"You look great," he said. He looked from me to the image in the mirror. "So we take it in a little bit. Shorten the sleeves. Or maybe you'd look better in fox if this doesn't suit."

I laughed. "On my income, I think it's high-class to have a sweatshirt with a zipper up the front." I took the coat off and handed it to him, getting back to the subject. "Why'd you pay her for the coat before she paid you? Why not deduct your costs from the five grand and give her a check for the balance?"

"The bookkeeper wanted it the other way. Don't ask me why. Anyhow, it's not going to cost that much to clean the coat, and the alterations I'm doing myself, so what's it to me? I got a good deal. Adele probably bugged her for payment as a matter of course, but I can't get that upset over the whole thing."

While he returned the coat to cold storage, I went over to my bag and took out the Polaroid picture of Elaine and Marty that Tillie Ahlberg had given me.

When he came back out, I showed it to him. "Is this the woman you dealt with?"

He glanced at it briefly and gave it back.

"Nuh-un. I never saw either one of those women before in my life," he said.

"What did she look like?"

"How do I know? I only saw her once."

"Young, old? Short, tall? Fat, thin?"

"Yeah, about like that. She was middle-aged and she had blondish hair. And she wore a muumuu and chain-smoked. I wouldn't let her come back here because I don't like the smoke around my skins."

"What kind of identification did she have?"

"You know. The usual stuff. Driver's license. Check guarantee card. Credit cards. You gonna tell me the coat was stolen? Because I don't want to hear it."

"I don't think 'stolen' quite covers it," I said. "I suspect someone's been borrowing Elaine Boldt's identity. I'm just not sure where she is in the meantime. If I were you, I'd leave the coat intact until we figure out what's going on."

My last glimpse of him, he was pulling unhappily at the wattles on his neck and he didn't offer to accompany me to the door.

I went out into the oppressive Florida humidity. The cloud cover felt like a premature twilight and the first of several big raindrops had begun to splatter against the hot pavement. I scurried to my car, half-ducking as though I could avoid getting wet by shrinking myself to half my size. I thought about Jack's description of the woman who'd called herself Elaine Boldt. He'd seen the snapshot of Elaine and he'd sworn it wasn't her. It had to be Pat Usher as nearly as I could tell. I ran back through my encounter with her: her attitude of wary amusement, the questions about Elaine she'd fielded, the mixture of lies and truth she'd told. Had she simply stepped into someone else's shoes? She'd been staying in Elaine's condominium, but how had she acquired the lynx coat if not from Elaine? If she was the one running up charges on Elaine's credit cards, she had to be sure somehow that Elaine wouldn't catch her at it. It seemed to me she could only pull that off if she knew Elaine was dead, which had been my suspicion for days now anyway. There might be some other explanation, I supposed, but nothing that tied everything together so neatly.

The rain was coming down hard now, the windshield wipers on my rental car flapping back and forth like metronomes, doing little more than smearing the windshield with a thin film of grime. I found a phone booth and placed a credit-card call to Jonah at the Santa Teresa P.D. The connection was bad and we could barely hear each other over the static on the line, but I did manage to holler out what I needed, asking him if he'd expedite the request form I'd sent to the DMV in Tallahassee. A driver's license was the one thing Pat Usher would have had to come up with, since Elaine had none, but it wouldn't have been that hard to falsify. All she had to do was apply in Elaine Boldt's name, pass the test, and wait for the license to arrive in the mail. In some states, you could walk out of the Department of Motor Vehicles with license in hand within minutes of taking the test—at least for a renewal. I wasn't sure what the procedure was in Florida. Jonah said he'd put a call through to Tallahassee and get back to me. I expected to be in Santa Teresa again by the next day, so I said I'd call him when I got in.

In the meantime, I drove back to the condominium and had a brief chat with Roland Makowski, the building manager, who confirmed what I'd already heard through Julia. Pat Usher had departed, bag and baggage, the same day I'd spoken to her. She'd dutifully left a forwarding address—some motel down near the beach—but when Roland tried to get in touch, he'd found out it didn't exist. I asked him why he'd wanted to contact her. He said she'd taken a dump in the swimming pool as a parting gesture and then scrawled her name across the concrete in spray paint.

"She did what?" I asked.

"You heard right," he said. "She left a turd the size of a

Polish sausage floating right in the pool. I had to have the whole thing drained and sanitized and I got people who still won't go in. That woman is demented and you know what pissed her off? I told her she couldn't hang her towels over the balcony rail! You should have seen her reaction. She was in such a rage her eyes rolled back in her head and she started to pant. She scared the hell out of me. She's *sick*."

I blinked at him. "She panted?"

"She was almost foaming at the mouth."

I thought about Tillie's night visitor. "I think we better take a look at Elaine's apartment," I said flatly.

The stench came at us like a wall the minute the door was opened. The destruction was systematic and complete. There was fecal matter smeared everywhere and the couch and chairs had been slashed with murderous intent. It was clear that she'd gone about it quietly. Unlike Tillie's apartment, no glass had been broken and no furniture overturned. What she'd done instead was to open all the canned goods and pour the contents on the carpeting. She'd ground in crackers and dried pasta, jams, spices, coffee, vinegar, soups, moldering fruit, adding contributions from her own intestinal tract. The whole sick stew had been sitting there for days and the Florida heat and humidity had cooked the mess to a boiling foment of fungus and rot. The packages of once frozen meat that she'd torn open and tossed into the thick of it were full of wiggling life of their own that I didn't care to inspect. Big flies buzzed around malevolently, their glittering fluorescent heads like beacons.

Roland was speechless at first and when I turned he had tears in his eyes. "Well, we're never going to get this cleaned up," he said.

"Don't do it yourselves," I said automatically. "Hire someone else. Maybe your insurance will cover it. In the meantime, you better call the cops."

He nodded and swallowed hard while he backed out the door so that I was left to search the apartment by myself. I had to be very careful where I put my feet and I made a little mental note never to chide Pat Usher for anything. As far as I was concerned, she could hang her towels anyplace she pleased.

21

With the cops on the way, I didn't have much time. I picked my way through the apartment, gingerly opening drawers with a hankie across my fingertips out of respect for latent prints. I did a superficial run-through and came up with nothing, which didn't surprise me. She'd stripped the place. All of the drawers and closets were empty. She hadn't left so much as a tube of toothpaste behind. By now, she could be anyplace, but I had a feeling I knew where she was. I suspected she'd used the last two flight coupons for a return trip to Santa Teresa.

I closed the place up again and went next door to tell Julia what was going on. It was two-thirty in the afternoon and I had a four o'clock plane to catch with almost an hour of driving just to get to the airport. The sky was miraculously clear again, the air smelling damp and sweet, sidewalks steaming. I loaded Elaine's suitcases back in the rental car and took off, promising to call Julia as soon as I learned anything new. This case was going to break for me. I could feel it in my bones. I'd been on it a week now and I had smoked Pat Usher out of hiding. I wasn't sure what she'd done to Elaine or why, but she was on the run now and I wasn't far behind. We were circling right back to Santa Teresa where the whole thing had begun.

When I reached the airport in Miami, I returned the rental car and picked up my seat assignment at the TWA counter, checking the four bags through to Santa Teresa. I got on the plane with six minutes to spare. I was beginning to feel a low-level anxiety, the sort of sensation you experience when you know you're having major surgery in a week. There was no immediate danger, but my mind kept leaping into the uncertain future with a churning dread. Pat Usher and I were on a collision course and I wasn't sure I could handle the impact.

With the three-hour time difference, I felt like I got back to California roughly one hour after I left Florida and my body had trouble dealing with that. I had to wait an hour at LAX to catch the short hop to Santa Teresa, but even so it was only seven in the evening when I got home, toting Elaine's bags with me like a packhorse. It was still light outside, but I was exhausted. I'd never eaten lunch and all I'd had on the plane were some square things wrapped in cellophane that I was almost too tired to pick open. It was one of those lurching flights with sudden inexplicable drops in altitude that make napping tough. Most of us were too worried about how they'd collect and identify all the body parts once we'd crashed and burned. Some woman behind me had two kids of the whining and screeching sort and she spent most of the flight having long ineffectual chats with them about their behavior. "Kyle, honey, 'member Mommy told you she didn't want you to bite Brett because that hurts Brett. Now, how would you like it if Mommy bit you?" I thought a quick chop in the ear would go a long way toward parent effectiveness training, but she never consulted me.

At any rate, when I got home, I headed straight for the couch and fell asleep, still in my clothes. Which is why it took me until morning to figure out that somebody had been in my apartment searching discreetly for God knows what. I got up at eight and did a run, came home, showered, and dressed. I sat down at my desk and started to unlock the top drawer. It's a standard-issue desk with a lock on the top drawer that controls the bank of drawers to the right. Somebody had apparently slipped a knife blade into the lock and jimmied it open. The realization that someone had been there made the nape of my neck feel like I'd just applied an ice pack.

I pushed back from the desk and got up, turning abruptly so that I could survey the room. I checked the front door, but there was no indication that anyone had tampered with the double-key dead bolt. It was possible that someone had made a duplicate of the key, though, and I'd have to have the lock replaced. I've never worried about security, and I don't run around doing tricky things to assume that my domain is

inviolate—no talcum powder on the floor near the entranceway, no single strands of hair affixed across the window crack.
I resented the fact I was going to have to deal with this
break-in, surrendering a sense of safety I'd always taken for
granted. I checked the windows, moving carefully around the
perimeter of the room. Nothing. I went into the bathroom
and examined the window there. Someone had used a glass
cutter to make a small square opening just above the lock.
Electrical tape had evidently been used to eliminate any
sound of breaking glass. Where the strips of tape had been
peeled off, I could still see remnants of adhesive. The aluminum screen was skewed in one corner. It had probably been
popped out and then put back. The job had been cleverly
done, set up in such a way that I might not have discovered it
for weeks. The hole was large enough to allow someone to
unlock the window, sliding it up to permit ingress and egress.
There's a curtain at that window and with the panels in place,
the small hole in the glass wasn't even visible.

I went back into the other room and did a thorough search.
Nothing seemed to be missing. I could see that someone had
eased sly fingers between my folded clothes in the chest of
drawers, had deftly gone through the files, leaving everything
much as it had been, but with faint disarrangements here and
there. I hated it. I hated the cunning and the care with which
it had all been done, the satisfaction somebody must have felt
at pulling it off. And what was the point? For the life of me, I
couldn't see that anything was gone. I didn't own anything of
value and the files themselves were not worth much. Most of
the ones I kept at home had been closed out anyway and my
notes on Elaine Boldt were at the office. What else did I have
that someone might want? What worried me too was the
suspicion that this might be Pat Usher's handiwork. Somehow
she seemed much more dangerous if, along with savagery,
she was also capable of craftiness and stealth.

I called a locksmith and made an appointment to have her
come out later in the day to change all the locks. I could
replace the window glass myself. I did some quick measurements and then headed out to the street. Fortunately, no one
had broken into my car, but I didn't like the idea that
someone might try that too. I took my .32 out of the glove
compartment and tucked it into the waistband of my jeans at
the small of my back. I was going to have to lock it in my
office file cabinet and leave it there for the time being. I was

relatively certain that my office was secure. Since I'm on the second floor with a balcony right out in plain view, I didn't think anyone would risk a break-in from that vantage point. The building is kept locked at night and the door from the hallway is solid oak two inches thick with a double-key dead bolt that could only be breached if the lock itself were cored out with a power saw. Still, I was feeling apprehensive when I pulled into the parking lot behind the office and I ended up taking the back stairs two at a time. I didn't relax until I unlocked the office door and saw for myself that no one had been there.

I put the gun away and took out the file on Elaine Boldt. I typed up additional notes, bringing everything up to date. Inwardly, I was still fuming that someone had been in my apartment. I should have called the police and reported it, but I didn't want to stop for that. I tried to concentrate on the matter at hand. I had a lot of unanswered questions and I wasn't even sure which ones mattered at this point. Why, for instance, had Pat Usher closed up shop so abruptly in Boca after my first trip down there? I had to guess that once she knew I was looking for Elaine, she'd had to scuttle her plans. I was assuming, of course, that she'd headed to Santa Teresa and that it was she who'd broken into Tillie's apartment and stolen that stack of bills. But to what end? The bills had continued to arrive and if pertinent information might be gleaned from inspecting them, all we had to do was wait for the next batch.

Then I had Mike's account of what he saw on the night of his aunt's murder. I still wasn't sure how that fit in, if indeed it did. The fact remained that his estimate of the time of Marty Grice's death differed by thirty minutes from the time her husband and sister-in-law claimed they'd spoken to her. Were Leonard and Lily in cahoots?

There was still the minor matter of May Snyder next door who'd reported the sound of hammering at the Grices' house that night. Orris swore she was deaf and had it all confused with something else, but I wasn't quite willing to write her off like that.

When the phone rang, I jumped, snatching up the receiver automatically. It was Jonah. He didn't even bother to identify himself. All he said was, "I've got a response from the DMV in Tallahassee. You want to take a look?"

"I'll be right there," I said and hung up, heading out.

*   *   *

Jonah was waiting for me in the small reception area as I came into the police station and he walked me through the locked doors to the corridor leading back to Missing Persons.

"How'd you get the information so fast?" I asked. He held the gate open for me and I passed into the bullpen, where he had his desk.

He smiled faintly. "That's why cops are so much better at this business than private eyes," he said. "We've got access to information you can't even touch."

"Listen, *I* was the one who put in the original request! It's public record. I can't get it as fast as you can, but I was on the right track and you know it."

"Don't get so hot," he said. "I was just ragging you."

"Very cute. Lemme see it," I said, holding my hand out. He passed me a computer printout, a magnetic image of a driver's license issued to Elaine Boldt in January, with the Florida condominium address. I stared at the picture of the woman staring back at me and uttered a quick, involuntary "ah!" I knew the face. It was Pat Usher: same green eyes, same tawny hair. There were a few glaring differences. I'd seen her after an automobile accident, when her face was still a bit bruised and swollen. The resemblance was clear enough, though. Hot damn.

"I got her," I said. "Hey wow, I got her!"

"Got who?"

"I don't really know yet. She calls herself Pat Usher, but she probably made that up. I'll bet you money Elaine Boldt is dead. Pat had to know that or she never would have had the nerve to apply for a driver's license in Elaine Boldt's name. She's been living in Elaine's apartment ever since she disappeared. She's used her credit cards and probably helped herself to any bank accounts. Shit. Let's run a check on her through NCIC. Can we do that?" The National Crime Information Center might well turn up identification on Pat Usher in seconds.

"Computer's down. I just tried. I'm surprised you didn't ask me to do that before."

"Jonah, I didn't have the right data before. I had a name but no numerical identifier. Now I've got a birthdate. Can I have a copy of this?"

"That's yours," he said mildly. "I've got one for my files. What makes you think the birthdate is legitimate?"

"I'm just crossing my fingers on that. Even if she faked a name, it'd make sense for her to use her own birthdate. She might be forced to fabricate a lot of other stuff so why falsify this? She's smart. She wouldn't work harder than she had to."

I studied the printout, turning it toward the light. "Look at that. They marked the box that says 'corrective lenses.' Terrific. She has to wear glasses when she drives. It's great, isn't it? Look at all the information we have. Height, weight. God, she looks tired in this picture. And look how fat she is. Check the *bags* underneath her eyes. Oh boy, you should've heard her when I talked to her down there. So *smug*...."

He'd perched himself up on the edge of the desk and he was smiling at me, apparently amused by my excitement. "Well, I'm glad I could help," he said. "I'm gonna be out of town for a couple of days so it's lucky that came through when it did."

For the first time, I really focused on his face. His smile was slightly fixed and his posture had a self-conscious quality. "You're taking some time off?" I asked.

"Well yeah, something like that. Camilla's got a problem with one of the kids and I thought I better go straighten it out. It's no big deal, but you know how it is."

I looked at him, computing backward from what he'd said. Camilla had called and snapped her fingers. He was taking off like a shot. The kids, my foot. "What's going on?" I said.

He gestured casually and told me some long tale about bed-wetting and nightmares and visits to a child psychiatrist who'd recommended a session with the whole family. I said, uh-huh, uh-huh, not even tuning into which girl it was. I'd forgotten what their names were. Oh yeah, Courtney and something.

"I'll be back on Saturday and I'll give you a buzz. Maybe we can go back up and shoot some," he said and smiled again.

"Great. That'd be fun," I said, smiling back. I almost suggested that he bring a blowup of Camilla for a target, but I kept my mouth shut. I felt a tiny little moment of regret, which amazed me no end. I hadn't even gone to bed with this man...hadn't even *thought* of it. (Well, hardly.) But I'd forgotten what it's like with married men, how married they are even when the ex is somewhere else...*especially* when the ex is somewhere else. I didn't think she'd filed papers yet, which made the whole thing much simpler. He was running out of frozen dinners anyway, and by now she'd probably figured out how slim the choices were out there in Singlesland.

I suddenly felt myself growing self-conscious too. "Well. I better get on with this. Thanks a lot. You've been a big help."

"Hey, anytime," he said. "Spillman's gonna be on the desk while I'm gone if you need anything. I'll brief him so he knows the scoop, but I want you to take care of yourself." He pointed a finger at me as though it were a gun.

"Don't worry about it. I don't take chances if I don't have to," I said. "I hope things work out up north. I'll talk to you when you get back."

"Absolutely. Let's do that. Good luck."

"Same to you. Tell the kids I said hi."

That was dumb. I'd never met them and I couldn't think what the other one's name was in any event. Sarah?

I pushed through the gate.

"Hey, Kinsey?"

I looked back.

"Where's that hat of yours? I liked that. You should wear it all the time."

I smiled and waved and went on out. I didn't need advice on how to dress.

22

It was midmorning and I was suddenly starving to death. I left my car in front of the police station where it was parked and walked over to a little hole-in-the-wall called The Egg and I. I ordered my standard breakfast of bacon, scrambled eggs, toast, jelly, and orange juice, with coffee throughout. It's the only meal I'm consistently fond of as it contains every element I crave: caffeine, salt, sugar, cholesterol, and fat. How can one resist? In California, with all the health nuts around, the very act of eating such a meal is regarded as a suicide attempt.

I read the paper while I ate, catching up on local events. I had just gotten down to the second piece of rye toast when Pam Sharkey walked in with Daryl Hobbs, the manager at Lambeth and Creek. She caught sight of me and I waved. I didn't give it everything I had. It was a casual offhand wave to indicate that I was a good joe and wasn't going to lord it over her just because I bested her last time we met. Her expression faltered and she broke off eye contact, passing my table without a word. The snub was so pronounced that even Daryl seemed embarrassed. I was puzzled, but not cut to the quick, shrugging to myself philosophically. Maybe the aerospace engineer had turned out to be a jerk.

When I finished breakfast, I paid the check and retrieved my car, popping over to the office to drop off the data I'd picked up from Jonah. I was unlocking my door when Vera stepped out into the corridor from California Fidelity.

"Can I talk to you?" she said.

"Sure. Come on it." I pushed the office door open and she followed me in. "How are you?" I said, thinking this was a social call. She tucked a strand of auburn hair behind her ear, looking at me through the big pale blue-tinted lenses that made her eyes seem large and grave.

"Uh, listen. Just a word to the wise," she said uncomfortably. "All hell's broken loose over that Leonard Grice business."

I blinked at her. "Like what?"

"Pam Sharkey must have called him after you talked to her. I don't know what she said to him, but he's all up in arms. He'd hired an attorney who fired off a letter to CFI threatening to sue us within an inch of our lives. We're talking millions."

"For what?"

"They're claiming slander, defamation of character, breach of contract, harassment. Andy's livid. He says he had no idea you were involved. He says you weren't authorized by California Fidelity or anybody else to go out there and ask questions . . . blah, blah, blah. You know how Andy gets when he's on his high horse. He wants to see you the minute you come in."

"What *is* this? Leonard Grice hasn't even filed a claim!"

"Guess again. He submitted forms first thing Monday morning and he wants his money right now. The lawsuit was filed on top of that. Andy's over there processing papers as fast as he can and he's pissed. He's told Mac he thinks we should terminate the whole arrangement with you after the jeopardy you put us in. The rest of us think he's being a complete horse's ass, but I thought you should know what's going on."

"What's the total on the claim itself?"

"Twenty-five grand for the fire damage. That's the face value on the homeowner's policy and he has his losses itemized down to the penny. The life insurance isn't at issue. I think he's already collected some dinky little policy on her life—twenty-five hundred—and our records show he was paid that months ago. Kinsey, he's out for bear and you're it. Andy's looking for someone to point a finger at so Mac doesn't point a finger at him."

"Shit," I said. I couldn't think of anything else to say. The last thing in the world I needed right now was a dressing down by Andy Montycka, the CFI claims manager. Andy's in his forties, conservative and insecure, a man whose prime obsessions are biting his fingernails and not making waves.

"You want me to tell him you haven't come in?" she asked.

"Yeah, do that for me, if you would. Just let me check my

phone messages and I'll disappear," I said. I unlocked the file
and took out the folder on Elaine Boldt, looking back at Vera.
"I'll tell you something, Vera. This is hot. Leonard Grice has
had six months to file a claim, but he hasn't lifted a finger.
Now, all of the sudden, he's putting pressure on the insurance company to pay off. I'd like to know what prompted
him."

"Hey, I gotta scoot before they come looking for me," Vera
said. "Just don't cross Andy's path today or you'll pay for it."

I thanked her for the warning and told her I'd be in touch.
She eased out into the hallway again, closing the door behind
her. Belatedly, I felt my cheeks flush and my heart begin to
thump. I got sent down to the principal's office once in first
grade for passing notes in class and I've never recovered from
the horror of it. I was guilty as charged, but I'd never been in
trouble in my life. There I was, a timid little child with
skinny legs, so stricken with fear that I left the school and
went home in tears. My aunt marched me right back and
read everybody out while I sat on a little wooden chair in the
hall and prayed for death. It's hard to keep passing myself off
as a grown-up when a piece of me is still six years old and
utterly at the mercy of authority.

A glance at my answering machine showed no messages. I
locked up again and went down the front way so that I could
avoid passing the glass double doors of California Fidelity. I
got back in my car and drove over to Elaine's old condominium. I wanted to have a brief talk with Tillie and let her know
what was happening. I was turning right on Via Madrina
when I glanced in the rearview mirror and realized there was
some guy on a motorcycle roaring right up my tailpipe. I
eased over slightly to let him pass and glanced back again. He
was beeping away at me frantically. What had I done, run
over his dog? I pulled over to the curb and he pulled up
behind me, turning his bike off and booting his kickstand into
place. He was wearing a shiny black jumpsuit, black gloves
and boots, and a black helmet with a smoky face guard. I got
out of my car and walked back toward him, watching him
peel his helmet off as he approached. Oh hell, it was Mike. I
should have guessed. The pink of his Mohawk seemed to be
fading and I wondered whether he did his touch-ups with Rit
dye, food coloring, or cooked beets. He was irked.

"God, I been honking at you for blocks! How come you

never called me back? I left a message on your machine on Monday," he said.

"Sorry. I didn't realize it was you back there. I thought you said you were going to call *me*."

"Well, I tried to, but I kept getting your machine so I gave up. Where were you?"

"Out of town. I just got back last night. Why? What's happening?"

He pulled his motorcycle gloves off and tucked them in his helmet, which he cradled in the crook of his arm. "I think my Uncle Leonard has a girl friend. I just thought you might like to know."

"Oh really? How'd you find out about that?"

"I was moving that . . . uh . . . stash out of the shed at his old place and I saw him go into the building next door."

"The condo?"

"Well yeah, I guess that's what it is. That big apartment building."

"When was this?"

"Sunday night. That's why I called you so early Monday morning. At first, I wasn't sure it was him. I kind of *thought* it was his car pulling up out front but it was almost dark and I couldn't see that good. I figured he was coming over to the house for something and I was shovin' shit in my duffel bag like crazy. Man, I didn't know how I was going to explain what I was up to. Finally I was in such a panic, I whipped into the shed and pulled the door shut and watched through the crack. He ended up going over there instead."

"What makes you think he has a girl friend, though?"

"Because I saw him with her. I didn't have anything else to do, so I went across the street and hid behind a tree and waited until they came out. He was only in there five or ten minutes and then the lights went out, second floor left. Pretty soon they came out and shoved some stuff in the trunk and got in the car."

"Did you get a good look at her?"

"Not really. It was hard to see 'em from where I was and they were walking kind of fast. Then when they got in the car they were all over each other. He nearly jumped her bones right there in the front seat. It was kind of weird. I mean, you usually don't see people that age making out, you know what I mean? And anyway, I never thought about him like that. I figured he was just some old dried-out fart who couldn't even get it up. I didn't think he had it in him."

"Mike, the man is probably fifty-two years old. Would you knock that off! What did she look like? Had you ever seen her before?"

Mike held his hand up to his chin. "She came up to about here on him. I noticed that. She had her hair tied back with a scarf—like a babushka or whatever you call 'em. I don't think I'd seen her before. I mean, it wasn't like I thought, Oh yeah, there's old what's-her-face or anything like that. She was just some babe."

"Look, do me a favor. Go find a pencil and paper and write all this down while it's fresh in your mind. Make a note of the date and time and anything else you remember. You don't have to say what you were doing around here. You can always claim you came over to check on the house or something. Will you do that?"

"Okay, sure. What are you going to do?"

"I haven't made that part up yet," I said.

I got back in my car, and five minutes later I was being buzzed through from the lobby to Tillie's apartment.

She was waiting for me at the door and I followed her into the living room. She was wearing a pair of spectacles low on her nose and she peered at me over the rims. She took a seat in the rocker and picked up some needlework. It looked like a hunk of upholstery fabric printed with a scene of mountains and forest, deer grazing here and there, a stream gushing down through some rocks. She had wads of cotton and she was shoving them into the back of the cloth with a crochet hook. The deer were puffed out into three dimensions, surrounded by stitching, to produce a quilted effect.

"What *is* that?" I asked, sitting down. "Are you stuffing it?"

She smiled faintly. She'd finally let her new permanent wave have its way and her head was a nest of tight, frizzy curls the color of apricots. "That's right, I am. It's called trapunto. When I finish, I'll have it blocked and framed. I do it for the church bazaar in the fall. This is cotton I save out of the tops of pill bottles, so next time you open some Tylenol or cold caps, you keep the packing for me. Sit down. I haven't seen you for days. What have you been up to?"

I gave her a summary of events since Friday, which was when I had seen her last. I did some censoring. I told her how I'd found the cat, but deleted the stash of drugs Mike

kept in the shed next door. I told her about Aubrey Danziger
and my confrontation later with Beverly, the suitcases, the
trip to Florida, the threatened lawsuit, and Mike's tale about
Leonard Grice having a girl friend upstairs. That made her
take her glasses off and click the stems against the frames.

"I don't believe it," she said flatly. "Mike must have been
high."

"Well, of course he was high, Tillie, but a little grass isn't
going to make him hallucinate."

"Then he's inventing it."

"I'm just telling you what he told me," I said.

"Well, who in the world could it be? I'd be willing to
guarantee Leonard wasn't having an affair with any tenant of
mine! And from his description, it would have been Elaine's
apartment, and that's simply impossible."

"Oh come on, Tillie. Don't be naïve. It's the perfect
setup. Why couldn't he have a woman over here?"

"Because there's no one in the building who fits that
description."

"What about the woman in apartment 6? The one you
thought might be up early the day your place got broken
into."

"She's seventy-five."

"But you have lots of other tenants."

"Young married couples. Kinsey, I have more single *men*
who'd go for Leonard than I do single women."

"I'd buy that too. What about Elaine? Why couldn't it be
her?"

Tillie shook her head stubbornly.

"What about yourself?"

Tillie laughed and patted herself on the chest. "Well, I'm
flattered. I'd like to believe I'm still capable of hip-grinding
out on the street, but he's not exactly my type. Besides, Mike
knows me. He'd have recognized me even in the dark."

I conceded that one. I truly couldn't picture Tillie in a
liplock with Leonard Grice. It just didn't parse.

"What *about* Elaine?" I persisted. "What if she and Leonard
had a thing going and decided to eliminate his wife? She does
the deed while he's off at his sister's place that night. She
takes off for Florida a few days later and then lays low for the
next six months, waiting for him to get his affairs in order so
they can run away together into the sunset. Once they realize

I'm on to something, they step up the pace so they can blow town."

Tillie stared at me for a long time. "Then who is Pat Usher?"

I shrugged again. "Maybe they enlisted her help and she's covering for them."

"But who broke in here and why? I thought you were convinced Pat Usher did that."

I could feel myself getting exasperated. "I don't have all the answers, Tillie! I'm just telling you it's possible that he had some little tootsie stashed over here. Maybe it *was* Pat."

She didn't say a word. She just put her glasses back on and started stuffing the mountain with cotton, making it bulge like Mount St. Helens before it blew.

"Can I have the key to the apartment upstairs?"

"Of course," she said. "I'll go too."

She put down her needlework and went over to the secretary, taking a set of keys out of the drawer. She handed me a bunch of bills while she was at it and I stuffed them in the back pocket of my jeans. It reminded me vaguely of something, but I couldn't think what.

She locked her apartment and we headed for the elevator.

"You haven't heard anyone walking around overhead?"

She looked back at me. "Not at all, but this place is well built and someone could be upstairs without my hearing them. You really believe he was keeping someone up there?"

"It does make sense," I said. "With Elaine off the scene, it's a perfect little love nest. Maybe Pat Usher found a way to get in. I'm sure she's somewhere here in town. If she had access to Elaine's place in Florida, why not this one too? By the way, were you here Sunday night?"

She shook her head. "I was at a church social and didn't get home until shortly after ten."

The elevator door opened at the second floor and Tillie moved down the corridor to the left, talking to me over her shoulder. She reached Elaine's front door and turned the key in the lock.

"I can't believe anyone's been here," she said as we went in.

She was wrong, of course. Wim Hoover, the tenant from number 10, was sprawled in the entryway with a bullet hole just behind his right ear. The air smelled of stale cigarette smoke and the fetid perfume wafting up from his souring flesh. He'd been dead for at least three days.

Tillie paled and went down to her place to call the police.

23

As is my usual habit, I did a quick tour of the place while Tillie called the cops. I had cautioned her to keep my name out of it because I didn't want to have to stop and take one of Lieutenant Dolan's famous pop quizzes. I was already in trouble with California Fidelity and I couldn't take on Dolan as well. The place smelled so foul that I didn't think Tillie would have any trouble explaining what had brought her up here to investigate.

I didn't have to be Sherlock Holmes to figure out that Pat Usher had been in residence. She'd made no attempt to disguise her presence. The gauzy float I'd seen her wear in Boca Raton was now tossed carelessly across Elaine's unmade bed. She'd apparently helped herself to whatever suited her—food, clothing, cosmetics. There were dirty dishes everywhere, ashtrays filled to the brim, trash spilling out of the brown paper bag with its neatly cuffed top. The crime-scene unit was going to have a ball with this place, but what interested me was the den. All the desk drawers had been opened, the contents scattered furiously, file folders ripped in half. It looked like Pat Usher's usual rage and impatience. I wondered what she'd been looking for and whether she'd found it. I didn't touch a thing. It had been maybe five minutes since Tillie went downstairs and I thought I better scram. I didn't want to be anywhere in the neighborhood when the black-and-whites came screaming into view.

I paused in the foyer and looked down at Wim. He was lying facedown, one hand tucked under his cheek as though he meant to nap. His flesh was swollen, the skin darkening, the bullet hole as tidy as the eyelet for a shoelace. The gun was probably a .22—not a lethal weapon as a rule, but let a slug ricochet around inside a human skull and it could turn brains into scrambled eggs in no time flat. Poor Wim. I wondered why she'd killed him. There wasn't any doubt in my mind it was Pat. Had she killed Marty Grice as well? The autopsy hadn't shown any gunshot wounds, only the repeated blows of an unidentified blunt instrument. What was the weapon, and where?

I went down on the elevator and left the building without talking to Tillie again. I unlocked my car and got in, suddenly aware of the crackle of paper in my jeans pocket. I pulled out the bunch of bills Tillie had given me and let out an involuntary "ooohh." It had just dawned on me what Pat Usher might have been looking for upstairs. Elaine's passport. I had come across it myself the second time I searched the place and I'd stuck it in the back pocket of my jeans. I couldn't remember taking it into the office, so it must be somewhere in my apartment. Had Pat broken in to look for it? If she'd found it, she was probably already on a plane headed into the great beyond. On the other hand, Leonard hadn't collected his insurance money yet, so maybe the two of them were still somewhere in town.

I started the car and pulled out, determined to clear the neighborhood before the cops showed up. I was thinking hard. Pat and Leonard must have eliminated Marty first, then disposed of Elaine Boldt, maybe because she'd guessed what was going on. In any event, it must have opened up a whole new possibility. They had now gained entrance to her properties and all of her bank accounts, helping themselves to her credit while Leonard waited the requisite six months for Marty's estate to clear. The payoff there probably wasn't large, but add it to Elaine Boldt's assets and the profits began to mount. Once Leonard had acquired sole possession of the property on Via Madrina, he could sell it off for a hundred and fifteen thousand. The lot was probably worth more with the house gone anyway. In the meantime, all he had to do was pose as the grief-stricken spouse, feigning disinterest in the proceeds. Not only did he garner sympathy, but he deflected attention from his true motivation, which was monetary from the get-go. The scheme might have gone off without a hitch except that Beverly Danziger showed up, needing a routine signature on a minor document. Pat's claim about Elaine being off in Sarasota with friends simply wouldn't bear up under close scrutiny because Elaine's whereabouts couldn't really be accounted for. But how was I going to prove any of this? I was speculating like crazy, probably making a few wrong guesses here and there, but even if I had it right on the nose, I'd have to come up with some kind of concrete evidence to take to the police.

In the meantime, Leonard had effectively blocked my path, putting me in check at least where the insurance company was concerned. I didn't dare go back and question *him* again and I knew I'd better be careful about any inquiries I made in the world at large. Any line I pursued was going to be interpreted as slander, harassment, or defamation from his point of view. What had I gotten myself into? Leonard Grice and Pat Usher would have to stonewall my investigation or the whole operation would come tumbling down around their ears.

I stopped off at the hardware store to pick up a pane of glass and then went back to my place. I had to find Elaine's passport. I checked the trash bags, behind couch cushions, under furniture, and all the other niches where I tend to tuck odds and ends. I didn't remember filing it and it hadn't occurred to me to hide it. I knew I hadn't thrown it out, which meant it had to be here somewhere. I kept standing there, doing a 360 degree turn, surveying every corner of the room—desk top, bookcase, coffee table, the small counter that separates the kitchenette.

I went out to the car and looked in the glove compartment, map pocket, down behind the seat, sun visor, briefcase, jacket pocket—shit. I went back into my apartment and started all over again. Where had I put the damn thing? It *might* be at the office. I decided to try there after CF had closed up and Andy Montycka had gone home. God, what did he know anyway? I was beginning to unravel the knots and I only hoped I could finish before he got nervous and paid off the claim.

I checked my watch. It was a little after one and I had the locksmith coming at four. I sat down at my desk and hauled out my file on Elaine Boldt. Maybe there was something I'd overlooked. I baited my hook and started to cast about randomly. I felt like I'd been through my notes a hundred times and I couldn't believe anything new would surface. I went back and read every report I had. I tacked all my index cards to the bulletin board, first in order, then haphazardly just to see if any contradictions would appear. I reread all the material Jonah had photocopied from the homicide files and I studied glossy eight-by-tens of the murder scene until I knew every detail by heart. How had Marty been killed? A "blunt instrument" could mean just about anything.

A lot of things were bothering me—minor questions buzzing around at the back of my brain like a swarm of gnats. I had begun to believe that if Elaine was dead, she'd been killed fairly early on. I had no proof yet but I suspected that Pat Usher had masqueraded as Elaine and had staged that whole bogus departure for Florida as a sleight of hand, laying a false trail to create the illusion that Elaine was alive and well and on her way out of town when, in fact, she was already dead. But if she'd been killed in Santa Teresa, where was the body? Disposing of a corpse is no mean feat. Fling one in the ocean and it swells up and floats right back. Toss it in the bushes and a jogger will stumble across it by six A.M. What else do you do with one? You bury it. Maybe the body was concealed in the Grices' basement. I remembered the floor down the—cracked concrete and hard-packed dirt—and I thought, now that might explain why Leonard had never had the salvage crew come in. When I'd first searched the Grices' house I'd just been grateful for my good luck, but even at the time it had seemed almost too good to be true. Maybe Leonard didn't want the demolition experts knocking around down there.

Pat Usher bothered me too. Jonah hadn't had a chance to run a check on her through the National Crime Information Center because the computer had been down. By now he'd left for Idaho, but maybe I could have Spillman run the name for me to see what he could come up with. I didn't think Pat Usher was her real name, but it might show up as an alias—*if* she had a criminal record, which was uncertain at this point. I took out a legal pad and made myself a note. Maybe with some judicious backtracking, I could figure out who she was and how she'd gotten involved with Leonard Grice.

I sorted through the new stack of Elaine's bills that Tillie had given me, tossing out the few pieces of junk mail. I came across an appointment reminder from a dentist in the neighborhood and tossed that aside. Elaine Boldt didn't drive and I knew she patronized businesses within walking distance of her condominium. I remembered in the first batch of bills I'd seen, there was a bill from the same dentist. John Pickett, D.D.S., Inc. Where else had I run into him? I leafed back

through the material from the homicide file, running my eye
down each page. Ah. No wonder the name rang a bell. He
was the dentist who supplied the full mouth X rays used to
identify Marty Grice. There was a knock at the door and I
looked up, startled. It was already four o'clock.

I glanced out through the little fish-eye peephole and
opened the door. The locksmith was young, maybe twenty-
two. She flashed me a smile that featured nice white teeth.

"Oh hi," she said, "I'm Becky. Is this the right place? I
tried up front and the old guy said I probably wanted you."

"Yes, that's right," I said, "come on in."

She was taller than I and very thin, with long bare arms
and blue jeans that hung on her narrow hips. She had a
carpenter's belt slung around her waist, a hammer hanging
down like a gun in a holster. Her fair hair was cut short with a
boyish cowlick across the front. Freckles, blue eyes, pale
lashes, no makeup, all the gawkiness of an adolescent. She
had an athlete's no-nonsense good looks and she smelled of
Ivory soap.

I moved toward the bathroom. "The window's in here. I
want some kind of heavy-duty hardware installed that can't be
breached."

Her eyes lit up when she saw the cut in the glass. "Gee,
not bad. Slick job, huh. You want to put new locks on the
other windows or just this?"

"I want new locks on everything including my desk. Can
you rekey the dead bolt?"

"Sure. I can do anything you want. If you got glass, I'll
reglaze the window for you too. I love doing things like that."

I left her to install the heavy-duty hardware. Belatedly, I
snatched up several articles of dirty clothing strewn about my
living room. There's nothing like an outsider's idle glance to
make you conscious of your own environment. I chucked two
beach towels, a sweatshirt, and a dark cotton sundress on top
of some other stuff in the washing machine. I tend to use my
washer as a dirty-clothes hamper anyway since I'm pinched
for space. I tossed in a cup of detergent. I cranked the dial
around to permanent press, just to keep the cycle short, and
I was on the verge of popping the door shut again when I
spotted Elaine's passport poking up out of the back pocket of
a pair of blue jeans. I think I must have hooted my surprise
because Becky stuck her head out of the bathroom door.

"Did you call me?"

"No, that's all right. I just found something I'd been looking for."

"Oh. Okay. Good for you." She went back to work. I put the passport at the back of my bottom desk drawer and locked it. Thank God I have the passport, I thought. Thank God it had turned up. It was like a talisman, a good omen. Cheered, I decided I might as well type up my notes, so I hauled out my little portable typewriter and set it up. I could hear Becky thumping around with the window, and after a few minutes, she stuck her head out of the bathroom again.

"Hey, Kinsey? This thing is all gimmicked up. You want me to fix it?"

"Sure, why not?" I said. "If you get the window to work right, I've got some other things you can take care of too."

"Hey, great," she said and disappeared again.

I could hear a big wrenching noise as she pried the window frame away. It was worrisome. All that pep and enthusiasm. I thought I heard something crack.

"Don't worry about the noise," she called out. "I saw my dad do this once and it's a snap."

After a moment, she passed through the room, tiptoeing elaborately, finger to her lips. "Sorry to disturb your work. I have to go out to the truck and get some line. You go right ahead," she murmured. She was speaking in a hoarse whisper as though it would be less intrusive if she used a softer tone.

I rolled my eyes heavenward and went on typing. Three minutes later, she came back to the front door and tapped. I had to get up to let her in. She apologized again briefly and went back into the bathroom where she settled in. I did a cover letter for Julia and caught up with my accounting. Becky was in the other room going bang-bang-bang with her trusty hammer.

After a few minutes, she appeared again. "All done. Want to come try it?"

"Just a minute," I said. I finished typing the envelope and got up, moving into the bathroom. I wondered if this was what it felt like to have a little kid around the house. Noise, interruptions, the constant bid for attention. Even the average mother amazes me. God, what fortitude.

"Look at this," she said happily. She raised the window. Before, it had been like lifting a fifty-pound weight. It would stick midway and then shriek, flying up unexpectedly, glass nearly cracking as it whacked into the frame. To lower the

window, I practically had to hang by my hands, humping it
down inch by inch. Most of the time I just left it shut. Now it
slid up without a hitch.

She stepped back so I could try it. I reached over and
lowered it, apparently unprepared for the improvement because the window dropped so fast, it made the window
weights thump against the studs in the wall.

Becky laughed. "I told you it worked."

I was staring from her to the window frame. Two ideas had
popped into my head simultaneously. I was thinking about
Dr. Pickett and the dental X rays and about May Snyder's
claim that she heard someone going bang-bang-bang the
night Marty died.

"I have to go someplace," I said. "Are you nearly done?"

She laughed again; that uneasy, false merriment that bur-
bles out when you think you're dealing with someone who's
come unhinged. "Well, no. I thought you said you had other
things you wanted me to do."

"Tomorrow. Or maybe the next day," I said. I was moving
her toward the door, reaching for my handbag.

Becky allowed herself to be pushed along.

"Did I say something?" she asked.

"We'll talk about it tomorrow," I said. "I really appreciate
your help."

I drove back to Elaine Boldt's neighborhood and circled
the block, looking for Dr. Pickett's office on Arbol. I'd seen it
before; one of those one-story clapboard cottages once so
prevalent in the neighborhood. Most of them had been
converted into branch offices for real-estate companies and
antiques stores that looked like someone's tiny, crowded
living space with a sign hung out front.

Dr. Pickett had paved over some flowerbeds to create a
little parking lot. There was only one car out back: a 1972
Buick with a vanity plate that read: FALS TTH. I pulled in beside
it and locked my car, moving around the front and up to the
porch. The sign on the door said PLEASE WALK IN, so I did.

The interior felt distinctly like my old grade school: varnished
wood floors and the smell of vegetable soup. I could hear
someone clattering around out in the kitchen. There was a
radio on out there, tuned to a country-music station. A
scarred wooden desk was angled across the entry hall with a
little bell and a sign that said PLEASE RING FOR SERVICE. I tapped
on the bell.

To my right was a waiting room with Danish-modern plastic couches and low tables done in wood laminate. The magazines were lined up precisely, but I suspected the subscriptions had run out. I spotted an issue of *Life* with "Starlet Janice Rule" on the front. A partition had been put up between the reception area and Dr. Pickett's examining room. Through the open door, I caught sight of an old-fashioned dental chair with a black plastic seat and a white porcelain spitting sink. The instrument tray was round and apparently swiveled on a metal arm. The surface was protected with white paper, like a placemat, and the instruments were lined up on it like something out of a dental museum. I was certainly thrilled that I didn't need my teeth cleaned right then.

To my left, along the wall, were some battered wooden file cabinets. Unattended. I could hear the devil call out to me. Dutifully, I rang the bell again, the country music wailed right on. I knew the tune and the lyrics routinely broke my heart.

There were little brass frames on the front of each file cabinet into which hand-lettered white cards had been slipped. A-C read the first. D-F read the next. You can't lock those old files, you know. Well, sometimes you can, but not these. I was going to have to go through such a long song and dance too, I thought. And I might be on the wrong track, which would just waste everybody's time including my own. I only hesitated because the courts are real fussy about the integrity of evidence. You're not supposed to run around stealing information that you later hope to offer up as "Prosecution's Exhibits A & B." The cops are supposed to acquire all that stuff, tag it, initial it, and keep meticulous records about who's had access to it and where it's been. Chain of evidence, it's called. I mean, I read all this stuff and I know.

I called "Yoo-Hoo!" and waited, wondering if "yoo-hoo," like "mama" and "dada," was one of those phrases that crop up in most languages. If nobody responded in the next ten seconds, I was going to cheat.

24

Mrs. Dr. Pickett appeared. At least, I assumed it was she. She was stout, with a big round face, rimless glasses, and a soft pug nose. The dress she wore was a navy blue nylon jersey with a print of tiny white arrows flying off in all directions. Her hair was pulled up to the top of her head and secured with a rubber band, curls cascading as though from a little fountain. She had on a wide white apron with a bib front and she smoothed the lap of the fabric down self-consciously.

"Well now, I thought I heard someone out here, but I don't believe I know your name," she said. Her voice was honeyed, tinted with faint southern overtones.

I had one split second in which to decide whether to tell the truth. I held my hand out and gave her my name. "I'm a private detective," I said.

"Is that right?" she said, wide-eyed. "What in the world can I do for you?"

"Well, I'm not sure yet." I said. "Are you Mrs. Pickett?"

"Yes, I am," she said. "I hope you're not investigatin' John." Her voice rode up and down musically, infused with drama.

I shook my head. "I'm looking into the death of a woman who lived here in the neighborhood...."

"And I bet you're talkin' about Marty Grice."

"That's right," I said.

"Aw, and wadn't that the awfullest thing? I can't tell you how upset I was when I heard about that. Nice woman like her to meet up with such a fate. But now idn't that just the way."

"Terrible," I said.

"And you know what? They never did catch whoever did it."

"She was a patient of Dr. Pickett's, wasn't she?"

"She sure was. And a sweeter person you couldn't hope to meet. You know, she used to stop in here all the time. She'd set right there and we'd have us a chat. When my arthritis was actin' up, she'd help out with the phones and what not. I never saw John so upset as when we had to go out there and identify the remains. I don't believe he slept for a week."

"Was he the one who took the dental X rays during the autopsy?"

"The pathologist did that. John hand-carried the X rays he'd done in the office and they compared 'em right on the spot. There wasn't any doubt, of course. It was just a formality, is what they told us. He'd taken those X rays not six weeks before she died. I felt so sorry for that husband of hers I just thought I'd choke. We went over to the funeral too, you know, and I made the awfullest fool of myself that ever was. Cried like a baby and John did too. Oh, but now he's the one you'll want to talk to, I'm sure. This is his day off, but he should be home soon. He's out runnin' some errands. You can wait if you like or come back later on."

"You can probably help me as well as he could," I said.

"Well, I'll do what I can," she said dubiously. "I'm no expert, but I've assisted him all our married life. He's often said I could probably fill a tooth as well as he could, but now I don't like that Novocain. I won't fool with needles. It makes my hands turn to ice and I get all goose-bumpy on my arms." She rubbed her arms, giving a mock shiver to illustrate how upsetting it was. "Anyway, you go on and ask what you want. I don't mean to interrupt."

"I understand Dr. Pickett had a patient named Elaine Boldt," I said. "Could you check your records and tell me when she came in last?"

"The name sounds familiar, but I can't say I know her offhand. She wouldn't be anyone regular, I will say that, because I'd know her if she'd been here more than once." She leaned closer to me. "I don't suppose you're allowed to tell me how this applies," she said in a confidential tone.

"No, I'm not," I said, "but they were friends. Mrs. Boldt lived right next door to Mrs. Grice."

Mrs. Pickett nodded slightly, giving her eyebrows a lift as though she got the drift and wouldn't repeat a word of it. She went over to the file cabinets and pulled open the top drawer. I was right next to her. I wondered if she'd mind my looking over her shoulder, but she didn't seem to object. The drawer was packed so tightly she could barely squeeze her fingers in. She started reciting the names on the tags.

"Let's see. Bassage, Berlin, Bewley, Bevis . . . Uh oh, looka here now. That's out of place," she said. She switched the two files around and started where she'd left off. "Birch, Blackmar, Blount. I have Boles. Is that the name you gave?"

"No, Boldt," I said. "B-o-l-d-t. I know you billed her once and I just saw a reminder for a six-month checkup."

"I believe you're right. I wrote that recall card myself and I remember now. Via Madrina, wadn't it?" She looked back into the file drawer, checking a few folders forward and a few folders back. "I bet you for some reason he's got that on his desk," she said. 'You come on in here and we'll take a look."

I followed her down a short hallway and into a small office on the left that had probably once been a powder room. Dr. Pickett's desk was stacked with files and his wife put her hands on her hips as though she'd never laid eyes on such a sight.

"Oh my stars. Now if that's not a mess." She began to check through the nearest pile.

"Why would he have it on his desk?" I asked.

"We might have had a request for dental records is all I can think of," she said. "Sometimes patients transfer out of state."

"You want me to help?"

"I sure do, hon. This might take all day at this rate."

I pitched in, riffling through the stack nearest me, then rechecking the pile she'd done to make sure she hadn't overlooked anything. There was no Elaine Boldt.

"I got one more place," she said. She held a finger up and marched us back to the front desk where she opened the top desk drawer and reached for a small gray metal file box. "This is the recall file. If she got a notice, she'd be in this box. I don't guess she gave any hint when she might have been in."

"Nope," I said. "I'd guess December, though, if she just got a six-months' notice."

Mrs. Pickett gave me an appreciative glance. "Good point. I guess that's why you're a detective instead of me. All right, let's see what December looks like." She sorted through about fifteen cards. Already, I was worried about Dr. Pickett's annual income if he saw fewer patients than one a day.

"Light month," I remarked, watching her.

"He's semiretired," she said, absorbed in her hunt. "He still takes care of these old people in the neighborhood, but he tries to limit his practice. He's got varicose veins worse than me and his doctor doesn't want him on his feet all day. We get out and walk every chance we get. Keeps the circulation up. Here it is." She held an index card up, handing it to me with a mixture of triumph and relief. They might be near retirement age, but the office was still well run.

I studied the card. All it had on it was Elaine Boldt's name and address and the date she'd been in. December 28. Was I on the right track? I turned the notion over in my mind.

"Marty Grice would have come in first," I said, "and then recommended Dr. Pickett to Elaine."

"That's not hard to verify," Mrs. Pickett said. "See? On the back of the card, I have that line says 'referred by' and here's Mrs. Grice's name sure enough. Actually, we do that so if folks skip out on their bill, we have some way to trace back."

"Could I see Marty's chart?" I asked.

"Well, I don't see why not."

She went back to the file cabinet and pulled a slim folder out of the drawer marked G-I and passed it to me. Marty's name was neatly typed across the tag on the top. I opened the file. There were three sheets inside. The first was a medical questionnaire, asking for information about medications, known allergies, and past illnesses. Marty had completed the form and signed it, automatically authorizing "all necessary dental services." The second was a dental history inquiring about root canals, bleeding gums, occasional bad breath, and grinding or clenching of teeth. The third sheet contained information about treatment actually rendered, with a line drawing of the top and bottom rows of teeth laid out like a Mercator projection, current fillings marked in ballpoint pen. Marty's name was neatly typed on the top line. Below were Dr. Pickett's brief handwritten notes. A routine visit. She'd had her teeth cleaned. There were apparently no dental caries. X rays had been done and she was scheduled to return in June. I stared at it for a long time, running the whole sequence of events through my head. Everything seemed to be in order except for the date: December 28. I moved over to the window and held the chart to the light. I could feel a chill smile forming because somehow I'd

known it would come down like that. I just hadn't believed I
would actually find the proof. Yet here it was. Someone had
neatly whited out the name originally typed in and typed
Marty's name right over it. I ran my finger across the top
line, feeling for the name typed underneath as though it were
done in Braille. Elaine Boldt's name was visible as a faint
imprint under the name Marty Grice. The last few pieces
were falling into place. I was certain hers were the charred
remains recovered from the Grices' house that night. I closed
my eyes. It suddenly seemed very strange. I'd been tracking
Elaine for ten days without realizing I'd already seen her in a
photograph in the homicide file, burned beyond recognition.
Marty Grice was alive and I suspected that she and Pat Usher
were one and the same. There were details to nail down yet,
but I had a very good idea how the murder had been set up.

"Are you feelin' all right?"

"I'm fine," I said briefly.

"Did you want to talk to John?"

"Not right now, but at some point, yes. You've been a big
help, Mrs. Pickett. Thanks."

"Well, I don't know what I did, but you're certainly welcome."

I shook her hand, dimly aware of the mystified gaze that
followed me as I left. I got in my car and sat there, trying to
figure out what to do next. Jesus, how had they assured that
the stomach contents would match? That must have been a
slick one. The autopsy report indicated the blood type was
O-positive, the most common type, so that was easy enough.
Marty and Elaine were close in height. It wasn't as though
the murder victim was completely unknown. Everyone assumed
it was Marty, and the dental X rays had simply been used to
confirm her identity. There was no reason to imagine that the
dead woman was anyone else. Leonard and his sister had
talked to her on the phone at nine and Lily claimed Marty
had hung up to go answer the door. The call to the police
station was a little flourish someone thought up for the effect.
Mike was right about the time. At 8:30 that night, there *was*
a woman's body wrapped up in a rug. It just wasn't his aunt.
Elaine must have been bludgeoned to death sometime earlier, with enough of her jaw and teeth left intact to make
identification possible. So many things were suddenly falling
into place. Wim Hoover must have recognized Marty going
in or out of Elaine's apartment. Marty or Leonard apparently
got to him before he got to a phone.

I started the car and pulled out of the lot, turning left. I headed over to the police station and parked out front in a fifteen-minute green zone across the street. Once inside the station, I stopped at the counter on the left. Beyond the counter, there was a doorway leading back into the squad room.

Some cop in plainclothes I'd never laid eyes on spotted me standing there as he passed the door. He paused.

"You need some help?"

"I'm looking for Lieutenant Dolan."

"Let me check. I was just back there and I didn't see him."

He disappeared. I waited, glancing over my shoulder into Identification and Records. The black clerk was the only one there and she was typing away like crazy. I kept going back over it in my mind. It was so clear now how it all fit. Marty Grice had gone to Florida and lived in Elaine's apartment. It wasn't hard to figure out what she'd done. Lost some weight. Had her hair restyled and dyed. No one down there knew her from Adam so it wasn't as if she had to hide. She probably just got herself spiffied up once she had Elaine's bucks to do it with. I thought back to my encounter with her: the bruised, puffy face, the tape across her nose. She hadn't been in any automobile accident. She'd had cosmetic surgery—a new face to go along with her new identity. She'd told me herself that she was "retired" and didn't expect to work another day in her life. She and Leonard had fallen on hard times and there sat Elaine Boldt with money to burn and a tendency to indulge herself. How Marty must have seethed at the sight. Murder had been an equalizing force, with grand larceny providing a pension fund after the fact. Now all she had to do was wait until Leonard freed up and the two were set. It was Dolan's case. If the murder weapon turned up, I thought he'd have enough evidence to act on. For now, at least I could tell him what was happening. I didn't think it was smart to keep it to myself.

The plainclothesman returned. "He's gone for the day. Is there something I can help you with?"

"Gone?" I said. I bit back my customary expletive but inside my head, I was saying, "Shit!"

"I'll be in touch first thing in the morning."

"Sure. You want to leave him a note?"

I took one of my cards out and gave it to him. "Just tell him I'll stop by and fill him in."

"Will do," he said.

I went back to my car and took off. I had a theory about where the murder weapon was, but I wanted to talk to Lily Howe first. If she'd figured out what was going on, she'd be in danger. I glanced down at my watch. It was 6:15. I spotted a pay phone at a gas station and pulled in. My heart had begun to thud with dread. I didn't want Mike in jeopardy. If he realized his aunt was alive, he'd be in trouble too. Hell, we all were. My hands were trembling as I paged through the telephone book, feverishly scanning for the other Grice listings. I found a Horace Grice on Anaconda, which looked like a good bet, and then had to scramble around in the bottom of my handbag for twenty cents. I dialed, holding my breath while the phone rang once, twice, four times, six. I let twelve rings go by and then I put the receiver back. I ripped the page out of the phone book and shoved it into my bag, hoping I'd have an opportunity to call again.

I got back in my car and headed out to Lily Howe's place. Where were Leonard and Marty at this point? Could they have skipped or was it possible they were still together somewhere in town—at Lily Howe's perhaps? I missed Carolina Avenue and had to circle back, peering at house numbers as I passed. I spotted the Howes' residence and slowed, much to the annoyance of the people in the car behind me. I drove on by and did a turnaround in a driveway six doors down. As I pulled in to the curb to park, my heart gave a lurch. Leonard and his lady friend had just pulled into Lily's drive.

I slouched down in my seat abruptly, banging one knee on the dashboard. Oh jeez, that hurt! I eased up slightly, peering over the edge of the steering wheel. They apparently hadn't paid any attention to me because they were both getting out of the car, moving toward Lily's front door with nary a backward glance. They knocked and she opened the door for them without any exclamation of surprise, horror, shock, or dismay. I wondered how long she'd known that Marty was alive. Had she been in league with them from the beginning? I watched the house uneasily. As long as Leonard was there, I was reasonably certain that Lily was safe, but I didn't think Marty would be at all inclined to leave Lily Howe alive when they went off. I was going to have to do a little hovering over Lily Howe, playing guardian angel to her whether she knew it or not.

25

I sat there while an incredibly painful, probably permanent bruise formed on my knee, trying to figure out what I should do next. I didn't want to leave the scene now that I had the enemy in range. There wasn't a public phone within miles, and who was I going to call anyway? I thought about getting out of the car and creeping up to the house, but I've never had very good results with that sort of thing. There are never windows open where you want them to be. On the few occasions when I've managed to eavesdrop, the subject matter has always been irrelevant. People just don't sit around verbalizing the pertinent details of recent crimes. Peer over a windowsill and chances are you're going to watch the villains play Crazy Eights. I've never seen anyone dismember the body or divvy up the bank heist. I decided to stay in my car and wait.

There's nothing as conspicuous as someone sitting alone in a parked car in a residential neighborhood. With any luck, some worried homeowner would spot me and call the cops and then I could have a nice chat with someone in uniform. Mentally, I organized a condensed version of the murder plot so I could tell it succinctly when the time came. The house was quiet. An hour and forty-five minutes passed and the gathering darkness gradually reduced visibility to mush. Lights in houses all up and down the street came on, including Lily Howe's. Somebody sprayed the neighborhood with barbecue cologne. I was hungry and I wanted to take a leak and I couldn't decide if I should risk squatting down behind someone's bush. I don't feel I suffer from penis envy, but in moments like this, I do yearn for the anatomical advantages.

At 9:23, Lily's front door opened and Leonard and Marty

came out. I leaned forward, squinting. There weren't any
lingering farewells. The two of them got in the car, slammed
the doors, and backed out of the drive. I waited until their
car had disappeared and then approached the house. The
porch light had gone off. I knocked. There was a moment of
silence and then I heard the chain slide into place. Lily had
read all the manuals on rape prevention. Good for her.

"Who is it?" came the muffled voice from inside.

I reduced my voice to a whisper. "It's me. I forgot my
handbag."

The burglar chain slid back and Lily opened the door a
crack. I pushed forward so fast, the door almost broke her
nose. There was a clunk and she cried out, but by then I'd
closed the door behind me again.

"We have to talk," I said.

She had a hand to her face and tears had risen in her eyes,
not because of any damage I'd done, but because she was
upset to begin with. "She said she'd kill me if I said anything."

"She's going to kill you anyway, you twit. What do you
think—she's going to walk off and leave you around to spill
the beans? Did she tell you what she did to Wim Hoover?
She put a bullet right behind his ear. You're dog meat. You
don't stand a chance."

Lily paled. A sob broke the surface like a bubble of air
from the bottom of a pond, and then she seemed to collect
herself. She closed her eyes and shook her head, like a
prisoner faced with the rack. She didn't care what I did to
her, she was not going to talk.

"God damn it! Tell me what's going on!"

Her expression hardened and I got a sudden glimpse of
what she must have been like as a kid. Leonard's sister knew
how to deal with bullies like me. She became stubborn,
passive, a defensive stance she'd apparently perfected over
the years as a way of warding off attack. She simply withdrew,
pulling in on herself like a mollusk. She must have been
threatened routinely as a child with everything from tetanus
shots if she didn't wash her hands every time she peed, to
police arrest if she didn't look both ways before she crossed
the street. Instead of learning the rules, she'd learned to
disappear.

To my amazement, she crossed to one of the turquoise
chairs and sat down without another word. She picked up the
remote control and flicked the television on, moving through

six channels until she found a sitcom she liked. She was going to tune me out. I went over to the chair and hunkered beside her, talking earnestly while she kept her face to the screen. She watched intently as a buxom platinum blonde in a tank top proceeded to put together a birthday cake.

"Mrs. Howe, I'm not sure you understand what's going on here. Your sister-in-law has killed two people and no one seems to be aware of it but us."

Flour puffed up in a big cloud, obscuring the blonde's baby face. Befuddled, she'd apparently used baking powder *and* yeast, causing the dry flour to explode. The laugh track was cranked up to "hilarious." Oh that gal! Wasn't she a screech! Lily smiled faintly, reminded perhaps of baking disasters of her own.

I touched her arm. "We're running out of time, Lil, because know what? I think Marty Grice is going to double back and kill us too. She'll have to."

No response. Maybe what I said had no more reality for her than this bimbo with the birthday cake. She was cracking eggs now, getting splatted in the face with yolks. Simple laws of nature were being violated here and she was the butt of the joke. In walked the husband. His mouth fell open at the mess she'd made. New paroxysms of laughter erupted. I wondered if anything in the real world had ever struck me with such force.

I said, "Where did they go just now? Are they leaving town?"

Lily laughed aloud. The blonde had turned the mixing bowl upside down on her husband's head. She showed *him*. A few bars of the show's dizzy theme song played and the station cut away to the commercial. I reached over and pressed the volume button, extinguishing the sound. In silence, a dog skidded across the linoleum with a can of chopped liver in pursuit.

"Hey," I said, "Leonard's in trouble. Are you going to help him or not?"

She glanced over at me, and I saw her lips move. I leaned closer.

"Excuse me. What?"

The strain was showing in her face and her eyes seemed unfocused. She watched me with all the concentration of a drunk, dependent and out of control. "Leonard never hurt anyone," she said. "He had no idea what she was doing 'til it was too late."

I thought about Mike's report of Leonard's passion for his wife. I didn't see him as an innocent victim in all of this, but I kept my big mouth shut. "As long as he knows anything, he's in danger. If you'll tell me where they're going, I can get him out of it."

She spoke in a whisper. "Just to Los Angeles 'til the new passport for Marty comes through, and then they're flying to South America." Her eyes filled with tears. "I might never see him again," she said. "And we were always so close. I can't turn him in. I can't betray him, don't you see?"

"You're trying to do what's best for him, Lily. He'll understand."

"It's been awful. It's been a nightmare. When you showed up, I thought he'd die of fright. He nearly had a heart attack and that's when she came back. She thinks you took Elaine's passport and she's furious at the delay. He's afraid of her. He's always been frightened by the fits she throws. . . ."

"Of course he has. I'm afraid of her myself. She's nuts. Do they have the bags in the car with them?"

She was breaking down now, caving in. The notion of Leonard's desertion caused too much pain and the image of packed suitcases cracked her heart. It was all too much. What difference did any of it make now that he was leaving her?

"They've gone off to pack," she said. Her voice came out in a gasp and her nose had started to run. "That's were they went. The motel out by the pass and then the house. They fought about it, but she wouldn't leave it behind, because it was evidence."

"Leave what?"

"The . . . uh . . . you know . . ."

"The murder weapon?"

Lily nodded and nodded again. I didn't think she could stop. It was as if the cords in her neck had come loose and her head was destined to wag indefinitely. She looked like one of those bobble-head dogs people have perched up in the back windows of their cars.

"Lily, listen to me. I want you to call the police. Go to a neighbor's house and stay there until somebody comes. Do you understand? Come on. Do you need anything? A sweater, a handbag?" I wanted to scream at her to hurry, but I didn't dare.

She was looking at me with washed-out, worried blue eyes, her gaze as trusting as a dog's. I got her to her feet and flipped the TV off, and then bundled her out the front. I scanned the street, but there was no one in sight. I couldn't believe Leonard would let Marty hurt her, but we all knew who was in charge. In some ways I felt as if I was wasting time, but I had to make sure Lily Howe was safe. We went up to the first house that showed a light, a cedar-shingle place two doors down.

I rang the bell. Some man opened the door and I pushed her forward, explaining that there was trouble and she needed some help. I urged Lily to call the cops and then I left. I wasn't sure if she'd do it or not.

I got in my car and squealed out, burning rubber as I skidded around the corner two blocks down. I drove tensely, sliding through stop signs, bypassing traffic any way I could. I had to get to the house before they did. I got stuck at a light and used the time to paw through my glove compartment, looking for the flashlight. I pulled it out and checked the batteries. They seemed fine. The signal changed to green and I took off again.

Belatedly, I realized my gun was still locked in the file cabinet at the office. I nearly slammed the brakes on and went back for it, but I didn't have time. If they went to the motel first, packed, checked out, and loaded the car up, I might have time to get to the murder weapon before they did. If they beat me to the punch, I was going to head straight for Tillie's and call the police. I had no intention of taking on Marty Grice all by myself.

I could feel a big rush of adrenaline and my neurons fired up, completing a circuit with a joyous leap. An answer to an old question popped into my head and I suddenly knew how they'd maneuvered the stomach contents. Marty had stolen Elaine's kitchen trash. It wasn't any more complicated than that. The brown grocery bag Mike had seen in the hall was Elaine Boldt's garbage, containing the empty tuna can and the soup can that comprised her supper that night. Marty had had hours to set it up and I could visualize the scenario as though I had powers of clairvoyance. Leonard went out to dinner with Lily and Marty gave Elaine a call, inviting her over on some casual pretext. Elaine stopped by and at some point was bashed in the face until dead. Marty took the keys and went over to Elaine's as soon as it was dark. She retrieved the kitchen garbage and took it back to her house, leaving it in the hall for a minute while she went down to the basement for the kerosene. That's when Mike had appeared, opening the front door and closing it again when he realized that something was desperately wrong. Marty finished dousing the place with kerosene and sat back to wait for Leonard's prearranged call at nine, reporting by phone what Elaine had eaten so he could later mention it to the police. A tuna sandwich and tomato soup. Maybe Marty stuck the leftovers on her own refrigerator shelf so it would all tally up and look legitimate. Marty set the fire and then slipped over to Elaine's where she holed up in comfort until her flight to Florida the following Monday night. My guess was that she'd dyed her hair before she left and I suspected that the fine clump of gray-brown hair I'd seen in Elaine's bathroom wastebasket during my initial search was, in fact, additional evidence that Marty Grice had been there.

I reached the Grices' house and pulled up across the street, taking a moment to study the house and yard. In the darkness, the fire damage was hidden, but the place still exuded that aura of ruin and abandonment. There was no sign of the car out front. No lights anywhere in the house. No pedestrians on the street.

I left the keys in the ignition and got out of the car, leaving the door ajar. I wanted to be able to ease back in and take off without a lot of fumbling around, if it came to that. I opened the trunk and took out the tools I thought I'd need. As soon as I determined that nobody was coming, I crossed the street and cut through the Grices' side yard.

I moved quietly along the walk, surveying windows as I passed. Most of the windows at the front of the house had been broken out by the fire and boarded back up again, but there were two near the back of the house that were still intact. I chose one and jimmied it open. It was pitch-black, and the neighborhood was quiet except for crickets chirring in the grass. I knew I should give myself an escape route, but I couldn't take the chance. If the two of them showed up, they'd spot any open windows or doors. I'd just have to work fast and hope my guess about the murder weapon was correct. I didn't have time for mistakes.

I climbed into the kitchen and pulled the window shut. The floor crackled with broken glass as I passed through. My flashlight streaked across blackened doorframes, smoke-tinged walls, into a hallway dense with shadow. I held my breath, listening. The silence was flat, one-dimensional. The electricity was turned off and I missed the soft hum of machinery. No refrigerator, no furnace, no wall clock, no water heater ticking from the other room. Some vague phrase about the silence of the tomb came to mind, but I pushed it away.

I moved forward, startled as a shard of glass popped underfoot. Was someone moving around upstairs? I swung the light across the ceiling, half expecting footsteps to appear up there like visible dents. The imagination has primitive, cartoonlike qualities, as any child can testify. I moved again. There was some illumination farther on, a pale light spilling in from the house next door. I paused at the window that looked directly into the living room across the way. Mr. Snyder was watching a television show, images flickering silently. The only other window on this side of the house was a small one just off the kitchen near the rear. I had a theory now about the banging May Snyder heard that night and I was about to test it out. I glanced toward the room where she slept, but it was already dark. I wondered if that's what old age is about—sleeping longer and longer hours until one day you simply don't bother to wake.

I ran my fingers along the window frame, shining the light across the fire-warped paint, a shriveled and puckered white, like dead skin. I could see where the wood had been damaged before. I could see where it had been secured with nails again: bang-bang-bang. I propped the flashlight on the window sill. It took me a few minutes to get the flashlight angled properly so I could see what I was doing and still have both hands free to work. I edged the narrow curve of the crowbar into the window frame and pried it loose with a crack so deafening it made my heart skip. I believed Elaine had been killed with a sash weight that had been tucked back in the window frame and nailed into place. The notion had come to me in one of those flashes of insight when I heard the weights in my own bathroom window thump dully against the studs.

It was nice. It had a certain domestic tidiness about it that Marty must have liked. If the house had burned down entirely that night, then who would ever have figured it out? The bulldozers would have mowed down what was left of the house, rubble loaded into high-siders, hauled off to the dump. Even now, even as it was, who was going to know? In a way, she was foolish to come back for it. Why not just leave it where it was? She was being pushed into a panic, probably anxious to tie up loose ends so that she could feel safe wherever she went. They might catch her, but what could they prove? The murder weapon probably had her prints all over it. Maybe it still bore strands of Elaine's hair or fragments of broken teeth and bones, microscopic particles of flesh. I wondered what she planned to do with the grisly thing. Bury it somewhere perhaps . . . toss it off the end of a pier. I jammed a big screwdriver into the tight crack between the framing and the strip of wood that held it in place. Window parts must have names, I thought, but I didn't know what they were. I was just imitating Becky's carpentry. The result was the same. I had the frame dismantled, exposing both sets of weights, the cord connecting them, and the pulleys that regulated the raising and lowering of the sash. I hauled both sets into view, four weights all together, careful not to touch anything. Shit, prints weren't going to show up on these things. The metal was covered with a thin film of sawdust and grime. Moisture in the wall had generated so much rust that any latent prints had probably been obliterated now. It wasn't going to help that six months had passed. Flecks of dried blood would still show up on a microscopic exam, but I wasn't sure what else. I shone the flashlight along the sash. At the tip were two glinting blond hairs caught in a knot of dark brown. I could feel my lips purse with distaste.

I eased a small plastic Baggie over the tip and secured it with tape. I advanced the blade in the utility knife I'd brought with me and slashed through the cords, clanging the weights together inadvertently as I lowered them into a big plastic bag. Lieutenant Dolan and his trusty crime-scene crew would have fits if they saw me manhandling evidence this way, but I didn't have any choice. I tossed the utility knife in the plastic bag along with the rest of my tools, plastic rustling with my every move—which is why I didn't hear Leonard and Marty until they had already reached the back steps.

26

The key rattled in the lock and my head whipped up. Fear shot through me like a jolt of electricity and my heart started thudding so hard it made my whole neck pulse. My single advantage was that I knew about them before they knew about me. I snatched up the flashlight, tucking the plastic-wrapped packet of weights under my arm. I was already on the move, assessing my options with a brain that felt slow and cold, as though plunged in an icy surf. My temptation was to head up to the second floor, but I scotched the impulse. There was no cover up there and no access to the roof.

I eased to my left, toward the kitchen, my hearing opened to the full. I could pick up low conversational tones out there. They were probably trying to get their bearings just shining a flashlight here and there. If Marty hadn't been in the house since the night of the fire, she might be reacting to the damage, momentarily repelled as I had been by the charring, decay, and ruin. They hadn't figured it out yet, but soon they would. The minute they saw that window frame, they'd start looking for me.

The basement door was ajar, a vertical black slot against the gloom of the hallway. I allowed myself one flicker of light from the flashlight and slipped through the crack, descending as quickly as I could without making noise. I knew the slanted basement doors leading out to the side yard were padlocked shut, but at least I'd find someplace to hide down there. I hoped.

Down I went, pausing at the bottom of the stairs so that I could orient myself. Above me, I heard the snap and crunch of footsteps. It was pitch-bloody-black where I was. It felt like the darkness was lying on the surface of my eyes, a thick, black mask that no light could penetrate. I had to risk the flashlight again. Even after so short a time, I felt myself recoil from the glare, turning my head abruptly to shield my eyes. I blinked, willing my eyes to adapt. Oh God, how was I going to get out of this?

I did a quick search, raking the beam in a 360-degree arc. I had to hide the sash weights and there wasn't much time. They might catch me, but I didn't want them to get their hands on the murder weapon, which is exactly what they'd come to fetch. I crossed to the furnace which stood massive and dead, looking somehow as ominous as a tank down there. I eased the door open and shoved the weights in, jamming the packet down between the outer wall and the housing for the gas jets. The hinge gave a harsh shriek as I pushed the door shut. I froze, glancing up automatically, as though I might make a visual assessment of how far the sound had carried.

Silence overhead. They had to be in the hall by now, had to have seen the damage I'd left. Now they were listening for me as I listened for them. In the dark of an old house like this, sound can be as deceptive as the voice of a ventriloquist.

Frantically, I scanned for someplace to hide. Every nook and cranny I spotted was too small or too shallow to do me any good. Overhead, a floorboard creaked. It wasn't going to take them long. There were two of them. They'd split up. One would go upstairs and one would come down.

I cut left, tiptoeing across the basement to the short concrete stairwell that led to the outside world. I crouched and crept upward, squeezing into the narrow space at the top. My hunched back was right up against the wood doors, my legs drawn up under me. With the electricity shut down in the house, they'd be forced to search by flashlight and maybe they'd miss me. I hoped I'd be hard to spot wedged up here, but I couldn't be sure. In the meantime, the only thing that separated me from freedom was that slanted expanse of wood at my back. I could smell the damp night air through the cracks. The sweet scent of the jasmine near the house blended unpleasantly with the musk of soot and old paint. My heart was pounding in my chest, anxiety flying through me with such force that my lungs hurt. I held the flashlight like a club and stilled my breathing to some infinitesimal sibilance.

I became aware of a hard knot pressing into my thigh. Car

keys. I shifted my weight, extending my right leg with care, reluctant to allow so much as a whisper of tennis shoe on gritty concrete step. I placed the flashlight ever so carefully on the stair below me and inched the keys out, holding onto the bunch to prevent their jingling together. Attached to my key ring was a small ornamental metal disk, maybe the size of a fifty-cent piece with no rim, the closest thing to a tool I had access to at this point. I thought with longing of the utility knife, the crowbar, and hammer wrapped in plastic and wedged down in the furnace along with the weights. I ran my left hand up along the wood just above my head, feeling for the hinge. It was shaped like an airplane wing, maybe six inches long, and flat. The screws protruded unevenly, some loosened with age, some gone.

I tried using the edge of the disk like a screwdriver, but the heads of the screws had been painted over and the groove was too shallow now to afford any leverage. I hunched, pushing up. I sensed a little give. Hands shaking with hope, I sorted through the keys, picking out the VW key, which was longer than the rest. I eased it between the hinge and the wood and applied a slight pressure. The hinge yielded a bit. If I could work a little slack into the hinge, maybe the door could be forced up and wrenched free. I pried at it, pressing my lips tight to keep from wheezing with the effort.

I paused. All I could hear was my own breathing, labored now as I struggled to loosen the hinge. The wood was pine, old and rotting and soft. I shifted my weight again, trying to give myself more room to work. The basement door creaked.

I heard the soft scratch of a shoe on the basement stair.

And then I heard the panting and I knew who it was. Slowly I turned my head to the right. I could see the dim yellow glow from a flashlight, one of those big jobs the size of a lunchbox, throwing out a wide square beam of light. The batteries were weak, washing back only pale illumination. Even so, I recognized the woman I'd met in Florida. Pat Usher... Marty Grice. She wasn't looking good. The tawny hair seemed lifeless and her eyes were in deep shadow, cheekbones exaggerated by the angle of the light. She swung the beam to the far wall. I held my breath, wondering if there was any chance whatever she'd bypass my hiding place. She moved out of my line of sight for a moment. I didn't dare move. The tension made my bones ache. I could feel my legs start to shake, that uncontrollable trembling made up of stress and muscle cramp and the need to move. It was the drive toward flight turned inward, my body locked in place with no hope of relief. The flashlight beam made a slow turn in my direction, illuminating item by item everything in its path. She was going to pick me up any second and I did the only thing I could. I launched myself upward like a surfacing whale, pushing the locked doors with such force that they nearly sprung apart. I simply didn't have enough purchase and she was too quick. I strained, shoving upward again.

She must have crossed the room like a shot. My upward motion had taken me almost into an upright position, the doors bulging outward with a cracking sound. My feet were snatched out from under me and I went down, cracking my head on the concrete step. Her flashlight had careened off to one side, its fading beam aimed ineffectually now at the wall, the light as pointless as a television picture after sign-off. In the thick dark of the basement, there was just enough illumination to work to my disadvantage.

I scrambled sideways, pushing to my feet again. She flew at me, nearly climbing my frame, her arms locked around my head. I staggered backward, thrown off-balance by the sudden weight. I tried to heave her sideways, skinning her off by bashing with her into the stairs. She was on me like an octopus—tentacles, suckers, and ravaging mouth. I was going down. I tried driving into her with my elbow, but there was no way to connect with enough force to do her any harm. I got one hand up, grabbing her by the hair, tucking forward abruptly so that her own weight carried her to the concrete with a soft grunt.

I caught a quick impression of weaponry, warned by a whistling sound, but not soon enough to duck. I heard a sickening crack on impact. She'd come up with what looked like an ax handle, wielded with such force that I felt no pain at all at first. It was like that interval between lightning and thunder, and I wondered if there was some way to gauge the intensity of pain by how many seconds it took to register on the uncomprehending brain. The ax handle came whistling up at me again, and this time I got a hand up, protecting my face, taking the blow on my forearm. I didn't even associate the cracking sound with the pain that shuddered up my frame. My mouth came open, but no sound emerged. She drove down at me again, her eyes bright, her mouth pulled back in something that would pass for a smile among lunatics.

I hunched, taking the blow on the shoulder this time. The pain was like heat licking up my side. My fingers closed around the handrail. I hung on to the stairs for dear life. A bright cloud was reducing my vision to a pinpoint, and I knew once the aperture closed I was dead. I sucked air in, shaking my head, noting with relief that the dark flooded back.

I pulled my right fist back. With a low cry, I pushed off, driving forward with everything I had. I connected, and the blow rang all the way back down my arm. I felt the pain arc from my battered knuckles to her face, and she made a low sound I liked. She staggered back and I launched myself at her, getting a headlock on her that closed her throat. I swung her sideways, keeping her off-balance, moving backward at the same time so she couldn't get her feet under her. She was being hanged by the force of her own weight. I braced myself then and concentrated on narrowing the V of my arm where her neck was caught. I heard a loud pop, and for a moment, I thought I'd broken her neck. She sagged to the floor. I released my hold to keep from being pulled down on top of her. I looked down at her blankly and then looked up. Leonard was standing there with a .22 that was now aimed at me.

Marty was wheezing. "You shot me, you fool." Her voice was hoarse.

Leonard's gaze shifted to her with dumb amazement.

I stepped back. The slug had caught her in the side; not a fatal wound but one that had taught her a little respect. She was on her knees, clutching at herself. She hurt and she made little mews of outrage and pain.

I was winded, still heaving for air, but I felt the strange exhilaration of victory. I had almost killed her. I'd been seconds away from converting her live body to a quite corpselike state. Leonard couldn't shoot straight, so he'd felled her himself, thus spoiling the fun, but the battle had been mine. I wanted to laugh, until I caught the look on his face.

The craziness that had consumed me for the last few minutes drained away, and I realized my troubles were starting all over again. I was dead on my feet. Somehow, I'd taken a blow right across the mouth and I was tasting blood. I felt gingerly to see if a tooth was broken, but everything seemed to be intact. It was a dumb time to worry about the possibility of a cap, but that's what I did.

I was trying to pay attention, but it was very hard. I had this weird desire to grovel around on the floor with Marty, the two of us snuffling like wounded animals looking for a way to crawl off and hide. I would have to go after Leonard soon. Already too much time had passed, and I knew I was losing ground.

He was staring at me without expression. I didn't know how to read him anyway.

"Come on, Leonard. Let's pack it in."

He said nothing. I tried to keep my tone conversational, as if I spent part of every day talking guys out of shooting me dead.

"I'm tired and it's late. Let's go home. She needs help."

Wrong move. Marty seemed to rouse herself, focusing on him. She didn't represent any kind of threat at this point, but he was teetering on the brink, maybe testing, as I had, the odd new sensation that death-dealing brought.

"Shoot the bitch," she gasped at him. "Shoot!"

I used every last ounce of strength I had, pulling myself together. He fired at me as I moved forward, but by then I was carried along by my own momentum. I yelled, *"No!"* and kicked him in the kneecap so hard I heard it crack. He dropped, warbling with pain like some kind of weird songbird. The gun skittered off across the floor. I thought Marty would try for it, but she only stared, making no move at all as I bent to retrieve it. I released the cylinder and popped it out. There were four more live rounds in the chamber. I snapped it back and made sure the safety was off, turning so that I could keep them both in my line of fire. Leonard was sitting up now, rocking back and forth. He looked at me with momentary venom.

I extended the gun, aiming at his face. "I'll kill your ass if you move, Leonard. I've had a lot of practice of late and I'll drill you right between the eyes."

Marty started to cry. It was an odd sound, like an infant with colic. Leonard leaned over and put his arm around her protectively.

In that moment, I wished there was someone to comfort me. My left arm was hanging like a piece of wood with a loose connecting pin. I glanced down and saw blood spreading out across my sleeve from a rip the size of a pea. The sucker *shot* me, I thought with astonishment. I steadied the gun in my good hand and started yelling for help. It was May Snyder who finally heard me and called the cops.

Epilogue

I've been in the hospital now for two days with my left arm in a cast. There's an orthopedist coming in this afternoon to assess the X rays and figure out what kind of rehabilitation I'll need once I get out of here. I've talked to Julia Ochsner by phone and she's invited me to recuperate at her place down in Florida. She promises sunshine and rest, but I suspect she sees it as a chance to set me up as a fourth for bridge. My final bill came to $1,987.35 but she says she won't pay me until I arrive on her doorstep. You gotta watch out for little old ladies—they're tough—which is more than I can say for myself. I hurt just about every place there is. I look in the mirror and I see someone else's face: puffy mouth, bruised cheeks, the bridge of my nose looking flat. I'm feeling some other kind of pain as well and I don't know quite what that's made of. I'm closing the file, but the story's not over yet. We'll have to wait and see what the courts do now, and I've learned to be cautious about that. In the meantime, I stare out the window at the palms and wonder how many times I'll dance with death before the orchestra packs it in for the night.

—Respectfully submitted,
Kinsey Millhone

ABOUT THE AUTHOR

SUE GRAFTON has written novels, articles, short
fiction, a screenplay, and numerous teleplays. She
has also lectured on writing at colleges and conferences in Southern California and the Midwest. Her
first mystery, 'A' IS FOR ALIBI, won an award
from the Cloak and Clue Society of Wisconsin. 'B'
IS FOR BURGLAR won both the Anthony and the
Shamus awards for best novel of 1985, and 'C' IS
FOR CORPSE won the Anthony Award for Best
Novel in 1986. "The Parker Shotgun" won a Macavity Award from the Mystery Readers of America
and an Anthony for Best Short Story of 1986.
Grafton, who was born in Louisville, Kentucky,
now lives in Southern California with her husband,
Steven Humphrey.

Sue Grafton's

Kinsey Millhone is

"A refreshing heroine."
—*The Washington Post Book World*

"The best new private eye."
—*The Detroit News*

"A stand-out specimen of the new female operatives."
—*Philadelphia Inquirer*

"The gutsiest, grittiest female operative going."
—*Daily News*, New York

❏ "A" IS FOR ALIBI	27991-2	$5.99/$6.99 in Canada
❏ "B" IS FOR BURGLAR	28034-1	$5.99/$6.99 in Canada
❏ "C" IS FOR CORPSE	28036-8	$5.99/$6.99 in Canada
❏ "D" IS FOR DEADBEAT	27163-6	$5.99/$6.99 in Canada
❏ "E" IS FOR EVIDENCE	27955-6	$5.99/$6.99 in Canada
❏ "F" IS FOR FUGITIVE	28478-9	$5.99/$6.99 in Canada

"Once a fan reads one of Grafton's alphabetically titled detective novels, he or she will not rest until all the others are found."—*Los Angeles Herald Examiner*

Available at your local bookstore or use this page to order.

Send to: Bantam Books, Dept. BD 26
2451 S. Wolf Road
Des Plaines, IL 60018

Please send me the items I have checked above. I am enclosing
$_____ (please add $2.50 to cover postage and handling).
Send check or money order, no cash or C.O.D.'s, please.

Mr./Ms._____

Address_____

City/State_____Zip_____

Please allow four to six weeks for delivery.

Prices and availability subject to change without notice. BD 26 3/92

REX STOUT'S NERO WOLFE

A master of the form, Rex Stout is one of America's greatest mystery writers and Nero Wolfe is one of the greatest fictional detectives of all time. Together, they have entertained and puzzled millions of fans.

THE REX STOUT LIBRARY

An ongoing program dedicated to making available the complete set of Nero Wolfe mysteries, these special collector's editions will feature new introductions by today's best writers and never-before-published memorabilia from the life of Rex Stout.

❏ **Fer-de-Lance,** Introduction by Loren D. Estleman
  27819-3 $4.99/$5.99 in Canada
❏ **The League of Frightened Men,** Introduction by Robert
  Goldsborough 25933-4 $4.99/$5.99 in Canada
❏ **The Rubber Band,** Introduction by Nelson DeMille
  25550-9 $4.99/$5.99 in Canada
❏ **The Red Box,** Introduction by Carolyn G. Hart
  24919-3 $4.99/$5.99 in Canada
❏ **Where There's a Will,** Introduction by Dean R. Koontz
  29591-8 $4.99/$5.99 in Canada
❏ **The Final Deduction,** Introduction by Andrew M. Greeley
  25254-2 $4.99/$5.99 in Canada
❏ **The Hand in the Glove,** Introduction by Marcia Muller
  22857-9 $4.99/$5.99 in Canada
❏ **Black Orchids,** Introduction by Lawrence Block
  25719-6 $4.99/$5.99 in Canada
❏ **The Doorbell Rang,** Introduction by Stuart Kaminsky
  23721-7 $4.99/$5.99 in Canada
❏ **If Death Ever Slept,** Introduction by Robert B. Parker
  23649-0 $4.99/$5.99 in Canada

Available at your local bookstore or use this page to order.
Send to: Bantam Books, Dept. BD 17
          2451 S. Wolf Road
          Des Plaines, IL 60018
Please send me the items I have checked above. I am enclosing
$_____ (please add $2.50 to cover postage and handling). Send
check or money order, no cash or C.O.D.'s, please.

Mr./Ms._____

Address_____

City/State_____Zip_____
Please allow four to six weeks for delivery.
Prices and availability subject to change without notice.   BD 17 7/92

FOR EIGHT YEARS, NOTHING HAD HAPPENED AND NOW IT WAS ALL BEGINNING AGAIN . . .

If Nikki was innocent, then someone had been sitting pretty all this time, someone in danger of exposure. I saw, for an instant, the look that had flashed in Nikki's eyes, unreasoning malevolence, a harsh irrational rage. She had set this all in motion. There were pieces missing yet but they would fall into place and then maybe the whole of it would make sense. Assuming I lived long enough myself to figure it out. . . .

"A" IS FOR ALIBI

"Smart, well-paced, and very funny."
—*Newsweek*

"A vibrant debut."
—*Chicago Sun-Times*

CRIME LINE Bantam Crime Line Books offer the finest in classic and modern American mysteries. Ask your bookseller for the books you have missed.

REX STOUT
The Black Mountain
Broken Vase
Death of a Dude
Death Times Three
Fer-de-Lance
The Final Deduction
Gambit
Plot It Yourself
The Rubber Band
Some Buried Caesar
Three for the Chair
Too Many Cooks

MAX ALLAN COLLINS
The Dark City
Bullet Proof
Butcher's Dozen
coming soon:
Neon Mirage

LOREN ESTLEMAN
Peeper

Whiskey River

DICK LUPOFF
The Comic Book Killer

MEG O'BRIEN
The Daphne Decisions
coming soon:
Salmon in the Soup

VIRGINIA ANDERSON
Blood Lies
King of the Roses

WILLIAM MURRAY
When the Fat Man Sings
The King of the Nightcap
coming soon:
The Getaway Blues

EUGENE IZZI
King of the Hustlers
The Prime Roll
Invasions

GLORIA DANK
Friends Till the End
Going Out in Style

JEFFERY DEAVER
Manhattan Is My Beat
coming soon:
Death of a Blue Movie Star

ROBERT GOLDSBOROUGH
Murder in E Minor
Death on Deadline
The Bloodied Ivy
The Last Coincidence
coming soon:
Fade to Black

SUE GRAFTON
"A" Is for Alibi
"B" Is for Burglar
"C" Is for Corpse
"D" Is for Deadbeat
"E" Is for Evidence
"F" Is for Fugitive

DAVID LINDSEY
In the Lake of the Moon

CAROLYN G. HART
Design for Murder
Death on Demand
Something Wicked
Honeymoon with Murder
A Little Class on Murder

ANNETTE MEYERS
The Big Killing
coming soon:
Tender Death

ROB KANTNER
Dirty Work
The Back-Door Man
Hell's Only Half Full
coming soon:
Made in Detroit

ROBERT CRAIS
The Monkey's Raincoat
Stalking the Angel

KEITH PETERSON
The Trapdoor
There Fell a Shadow
The Rain
Rough Justice

DAVID HANDLER
The Man Who Died Laughing
The Man Who Lived by Night
coming soon:
The Man Who Would be
F. Scott Fitzgerald

JERRY OSTER
Club Dead
Internal Affairs

BENJAMIN M. SCHUTZ
A Tax in Blood
Embrace the Wolf
The Things We Do for Love

"A" IS FOR ALIBI

A KINSEY MILLHONE MYSTERY

BY
SUE
GRAFTON

CRIME LINE ™

BANTAM BOOKS
NEW YORK · TORONTO · LONDON · SYDNEY · AUCKLAND

*This edition contains the complete text
of the original hardcover edition.*
NOT ONE WORD HAS BEEN OMITTED.

"A" IS FOR ALIBI
*A Bantam Book / published by arrangement with
Holt, Rinehart & Winston*

PRINTING HISTORY

*Holt, Rinehart & Winston edition published April 1982
Bantam edition / July 1987*

*All rights reserved.
Copyright © 1982 by Sue Grafton.
Cover art copyright © 1987 by Bantam Books.
Library of Congress Catalog Card Number: 81-7128.
No part of this book may be reproduced or transmitted
in any form or by any means, electronic or mechanical,
including photocopying, recording, or by any information
storage and retrieval system, without permission in
writing from the publisher.
For information address: Holt, Rinehart & Winston,
6277 Sea Harbor Dr., Orlando, FL 32821.*

ISBN 0-553-27991-2

Published simultaneously in the United States and Canada

*Bantam Books are published by Bantam Books, a division of Bantam
Doubleday Dell Publishing Group, Inc. Its trademark, consisting of the
words "Bantam Books" and the portrayal of a rooster, is Registered in U.S.
Patent and Trademark Office and in other countries. Marca Registrada.
Bantam Books, 666 Fifth Avenue, New York, New York 10103.*

PRINTED IN THE UNITED STATES OF AMERICA

OPM   29 28 27 26 25 24 23 21

For my father,
CHIP GRAFTON,
who set me on this path

The author wishes to acknowledge the invaluable assistance of the following people: Steven Humphrey, Roger Long, Alan Tivoli, Barbara Stephans, Marlin D. Ketter of Investigations Unlimited and Joe Driscoll of Driscoll and Associates Investigations, both of Columbus, Ohio, and William Christensen, Police Captain, City of Santa Barbara.

1

My name is Kinsey Millhone. I'm a private investigator, licensed by the state of California. I'm thirty-two years old, twice divorced, no kids. The day before yesterday I killed someone and the fact weighs heavily on my mind. I'm a nice person and I have a lot of friends. My apartment is small but I like living in a cramped space. I've lived in trailers most of my life, but lately they've been getting too elaborate for my taste, so now I live in one room, a "bachelorette." I don't have pets. I don't have houseplants. I spend a lot of time on the road and I don't like leaving things behind. Aside from the hazards of my profession, my life has always been ordinary, uneventful, and good. Killing someone feels odd to me and I haven't quite sorted it through. I've already given a statement to the police, which I initialed page by page and then signed. I filled out a similar report for the office files. The language in both documents is neutral, the terminology oblique, and neither says quite enough.

Nikki Fife first came to my office three weeks ago. I occupy one small corner of a large suite of offices that house the California Fidelity Insurance Company, for whom I once worked. Our connection now is rather loose. I do a certain number of investigations for them in exchange for two rooms with a separate entrance and a small balcony overlooking the main street of Santa Teresa. I have an answering service to pick up calls when I'm out and I keep my own books. I don't earn a lot of money but I make ends meet.

I'd been out for most of the morning, only stopping by the office to pick up my camera. Nikki Fife was standing in the corridor outside my office door. I'd never really met her but I'd been present at her trial eight years before when she was convicted of murdering her husband, Laurence, a prominent divorce attorney here in town. Nikki was in her late twenties then, with striking white-blonde hair, dark eyes, and flawless skin. Her lean face had filled out some, probably the result of prison food with its high starch content, but she still had the ethereal look that had made the accusation of murder seem so incongruous at the time. Her hair had grown out now to its natural shade, a brown so pale that it appeared nearly colorless. She was maybe thirty-five, thirty-six, and the years at the California Institute for Women had left no visible lines.

I didn't say anything at first; just opened the door and let her in.

"You know who I am," she said.

"I worked for your husband a couple of times."

She studied me carefully. "Was that the extent of it?"

I knew what she meant. "I was also there in court when you were being tried," I said. "But if you're asking if I was involved with him personally, the answer is no. He wasn't my type. No offense. Would you like coffee?"

She nodded, relaxing almost imperceptibly. I pulled the coffeepot from the bottom of the file cabinet and filled it from the Sparkletts water bottle behind the door. I liked it that she didn't protest the trouble I was going to. I put in a filter paper and ground coffee and plugged in the pot. The gurgling sound was comforting, like the pump in an aquarium.

Nikki sat very still, almost as though her emotional gears had been disengaged. She had no nervous mannerisms, didn't smoke or twist her hair. I sat down in my swivel chair.

"When were you released?"

"A week ago."

"What's freedom feel like?"

She shrugged. "It feels good, I guess, but I can survive the other way too. Better than you'd think."

I took a small carton of half-and-half out of the little refrigerator to my right. I keep clean mugs on top and I turned one over for each of us, filling them when the coffee was done. Nikki took hers with a murmured thanks.

"Maybe you've heard this one before," she went on, "but I didn't kill Laurence and I want you to find out who did."

"Why wait this long? You could have initiated an investigation from prison and maybe saved yourself some time."

She smiled faintly. "I've been claiming I was innocent for years. Who'd believe me? The minute I was indicted, I lost my credibility. I want that back. And I want to know who did me in."

I had thought her eyes were dark but I could see now that they were a metallic gray. Her look was level, flattened-out, as though some interior light were growing dim. She seemed to be a lady without much hope. I had never believed she was guilty myself but I couldn't remember what had made me so sure. She seemed passionless and I couldn't imagine her caring enough about anything to kill.

"You want to fill me in?"

She took a sip of coffee and then set the mug on the edge of my desk.

"I was married to Laurence for four years, a little more than that. He was unfaithful after the first six months. I don't know why it came as such a shock. Actually, that's how I got involved with him . . . when he was with his first wife, being unfaithful to her with me. There's a sort of egotism attached to being a mistress, I suppose. Anyway, I never expected to be in her shoes and I didn't like it much."

"According to the prosecutor, that's why you killed him."

"Look, they needed a conviction. I was it," she said with the first sign of energy. "I've just spent the last eight years with killers of one kind or another and believe me, the motive isn't apathy. You kill people you hate or you kill in rage or you kill to get even, but you don't kill someone you're indifferent to. By the time Laurence died, I didn't give a damn about him. I fell out of love with him the first time I found out about the other women. It took me a while to get it all out of my system . . ."

"And that's what the diary was all about?" I asked.

"Sure I kept track at first. I detailed every infidelity. I listened in on phone calls. I followed him around town. Then he started being more cautious about the whole thing and I started losing interest. I just didn't give a shit."

A flush had crept up to her cheeks and I gave her a moment to compose herself. "I know it looked like I killed him out of jealousy or rage, but I didn't care about that stuff. By the time he died, I just wanted to get on with my own life. I was going back to school, minding my own business. He went his way and I went mine . . ." Her voice trailed off.

"Who do you think killed him?"

"I think a lot of people wanted to. Whether they did or not is another matter. I mean, I could make a couple of educated guesses but I don't have proof of anything. Which is why I'm here."

"Why come to me?"

She flushed again slightly. "I tried the two big agencies in town and they turned me down. I came across your name in Laurence's old Rolodex. I thought there was a certain kind of irony hiring someone he had once hired himself. I did check you out. With Con Dolan down at Homicide."

I frowned. "It was his case, wasn't it?"

Nikki nodded. "Yes it was. He said you had a good memory. I don't like having to explain everything from scratch."

"What about Dolan? Does he think you're innocent?"

"I doubt it, but then again, I did my time so what's it to him?"

I studied her for a moment. She was forthright and what she said made sense. Laurence Fife had been a difficult man. I hadn't been all that fond of him myself. If she was guilty, I couldn't see why she would stir it all up again. Her ordeal was over now and her so-called debt to society had been taken off the books except for whatever remaining parole she had to serve.

"Let me think about it some," I said. "I can get in touch with you later today and let you know."

"I'd appreciate that. I do have money. Whatever it takes."

"I don't want to be paid to rehash old business, Mrs. Fife. Even if we find out who did it, we have to make it stick and that could be tough after all this time. I'd like to check back through the files and see how it looks."

She took a manila folder out of her big leather bag. "I have some newspaper clippings. I can leave those with you if you like. That's the number where I can be reached."

We shook hands. Hers was cool and slight but her grip was strong. "Call me Nikki. Please."

"I'll be in touch," I said.

I had to go take some photographs of a crack in a sidewalk for an insurance claim and I left the office shortly after she did, taking my VW out the freeway. I like my cars cramped and this one was filled with files and law books, a briefcase where I keep my little automatic, cardboard boxes, and a case of motor oil given to me by a client. He'd been cheated by two con artists who had "allowed" him to invest two grand in their oil company. The motor oil was real enough but it wasn't theirs; just some Sears thirty-weight with new labels pasted on. It had taken me a day and a half to track them down. In addition to the junk, I keep a packed overnight case back there, too, for God knows what emergency. I wouldn't work for anyone who wanted me *that* fast. It just makes me feel secure to have a nightgown, toothbrush, and fresh underwear at hand. I have my little quirks I guess. The VW's a '68, one of those vague beige models with assorted dents. It needs a tune-up but I never have time.

I thought about Nikki as I drove. I had tossed the manila folder full of clippings on the passenger seat but I really didn't need to look at them. Laurence Fife had done a lot of divorce work and he had a reputation as a killer in court. He was cold, methodical, and unscrupulous, taking any advantage he could. In California, as in many states, the only grounds for divorce are irreconcilable differences or incurable insanity, which eliminates the trumped-up adultery charges that were the mainstay of divorce attorneys and private eyes in the old days. There is still the question of property settlements and custody—money and children—and Laurence Fife could get his clients anything. Most of them were women. Out of court, he had a reputation as a killer of another kind and the rumor was that he had mended many a broken heart in that difficult period between interlocutory and final decrees.

I had found him shrewd, nearly humorless, but exact; an easy man to work for because his instructions were clear and he paid in advance. A lot of people apparently hated him: men for the price he extracted, women for the betrayal of their trust. He was thirty-nine years old when he died. That Nikki was accused, tried, and convicted was just a piece of bad luck. Except for cases that clearly involve a homicidal maniac, the police like to believe murders are committed by those we know and love, and most of the time they're right—a chilling thought when you sit down to dinner with a family of five. All those potential killers passing their plates.

As nearly as I could remember, Laurence Fife had been having drinks with his law partner, Charlie Scorsoni, the night of his murder. Nikki was at a meeting of the Junior League. She got home before Laurence, who arrived about midnight. He was taking medication for numerous allergies and before he went to bed, he downed his usual capsule. Within two hours, he was awake—nauseated, vomiting, doubled over with violent stomach cramps. By morning, he was dead. An autopsy and lab tests showed that he'd died as a result of ingesting oleander, ground to a fine powder and substituted for the medication in the capsule he took: not a masterly plot, but one employed to good effect. Oleander is a common California shrub. There was one in the Fife's backyard as a matter of fact. Nikki's fingerprints were found on the vial along with his. A diary was discovered among her possessions, certain entries detailing the fact that she'd found out about his adulteries and was bitterly angry and hurt, contemplating divorce. The District Attorney established quite nicely that no one divorced Laurence Fife without penalty. He'd been married and divorced once before and though another attorney had handled his case, his impact was evident. He obtained custody of his children and he managed to come out ahead financially. The state of California is scrupulous in its division of assets, but Laurence Fife had a way of maneuvering monies so that even a fifty-fifty split gave him the lion's share. It looked as if Nikki Fife knew better than to try disentangling herself from him legally and had sought other means.

She had motive. She had access. The grand jury heard the evidence and returned an indictment. Once she got into court, it was simply a question of who could persuade twelve citizens of what. Apparently the D.A. had done his homework. Nikki hired Wilfred Brentnell from Los Angeles: a legal whiz with a reputation as the patron saint of lost causes. In some sense, it was almost like admitting her guilt. The whole trial had a sensational air. Nikki was young. She was pretty. She was born with money. The public was curious and the town was small. It was all too good to miss.

2

Santa Teresa is a Southern California town of eighty thousand, artfully arranged between the Sierra Madres and the Pacific Ocean—a haven for the abject rich. The public buildings look like old Spanish missions, the private homes look like magazine illustrations, the palm trees are trimmed of unsightly brown fronds, and the marina is as perfect as a picture postcard with the blue-gray hills forming a backdrop and white boats bobbing in the sunlight. Most of the downtown area consists of two- and three-story structures of white stucco and red tile, with wide soft curves and trellises wound with gaudy maroon bougainvillea. Even the frame bungalows of the poor could hardly be called squalid.

The police department is located near the heart of town on a side street lined with cottages painted mint green with low stone walls and jacaranda trees dripping lavender blossoms. Winter in Southern California consists of an overcast and is heralded not by autumn but by fire. After the fire season come the mud slides. And then the status quo is restored and everything goes on as before. This was May.

After I dropped the roll of film off to be developed, I went into the Homicide Department to see Lieutenant Dolan. Con is in his late fifties with the aura of the unkempt: bags under his eyes, gray stubble or its illusion, a pouchy face, and hair that's been coated with some kind of men's product and combed across a shiny place on top. He looks like he would smell of Thunderbird and hang out under bridges throwing up on his own shoes. Which is not to say he isn't very sharp. Con Dolan is a lot smarter than the average thief. He and killers run about neck and neck. He catches them most of the time and only occasionally guesses wrong. Few people can outthink him and I'm not sure why this is true, except that his powers of concentration are profound and his memory clear and pitiless.

He knew why I was there and he motioned me back to his office without a word.

What Con Dolan calls an office would do for a secretary anywhere else. He doesn't like being shut away and he doesn't much care for privacy. He likes to conduct his business tipped back in his chair with his attention half-turned to what's going on around him. He picks up a lot of information like that and it saves him needless talk with his men. He knows when his detectives come and go and he knows who's been brought in for questioning and he knows when reports aren't being done on time and why.

"What can I do for you?" he said, but his tone didn't indicate any particular desire to help.

"I'd like to look at the files on Laurence Fife."

He arched an eyebrow at me ever so slightly. "It's against department policy. We're not running a public library here."

"I didn't ask to take them out. I just want to look. You've let me do that before."

"Once."

"I've given you information more times than that and you know it," I said. "Why hesitate on this?"

"That case is closed."

"Then you shouldn't have any objections. It's hardly an invasion of anyone's privacy."

His smile then was slow and humorless and he tapped a pencil idly, loving, I imagined, the power to turn me down cold. "She killed him, Kinsey. That's all there is to it."

"You told her to get in touch with me. Why bother with it if you don't have a doubt yourself?"

"My doubts have nothing to do with Laurence Fife," he said.

"What then?"

"There's more to this one than meets the eye," he said evasively. "Maybe we'd like to protect what we've got."

"Are 'we' keeping secrets?"

"Oh I got more secrets than you ever dreamed about," he said.

"Me too," I said. "Now why are we playing games?"

He gave me a look that might have been annoyance and

might have been something else. He's a hard man to read.
"You know how I feel about people like you."

"Look, as far as I'm concerned, we're in the same
business," I said. "I'm straight with you. I don't know what
kind of gripes you have with the other private investigators in
town, but I stay out of your way and I've got nothing but
respect for the job you do. I don't understand why we can't
cooperate with one another."

He stared at me for a moment, his mouth turning down
with resignation. "You'd get more out of me if you'd learn to
flirt," he said grudgingly.

"No I wouldn't. You think women are a pain in the ass. If I
flirted, you'd pat me on the head and make me go away."

He wouldn't take the bait on that one but he did reach over
and pick up the phone, dialing Identification and Records.

"This is Dolan. Have Emerald bring me the files on
Laurence Fife." He hung up and leaned back again, looking at
me with a mixture of speculation and distaste.

"I better not hear any complaints about the way you handle
this. If I get one call from anyone—and I'm talking about a
witness who feels harassed or anyone else, including my men
or anybody else's men—you're up shit creek. You got that?"

I held up three fingers beside my temple dutifully. "Scouts
honor."

"When were you ever a Scout?"

"Well, I was a Brownie once for almost a week," I said
sweetly. "We had to paint a rose on a hanky for Mother's Day
and I thought it was dumb so I quit."

He didn't smile. "You can use Lieutenant Becker's office,"
he said when the files arrived. "And stay out of trouble."

I went into Becker's office.

It took me two hours to sort through the mass of paperwork
but I began to see why Con had been reluctant to let me look
because just about the first thing that came to light was a series
of Telexes from the West Los Angeles Police Department about
a second homicide. At first, I thought it was a mistake—that
communiqués from another case had been inadvertently
sandwiched into the wrong file. But the details nearly leapt
off the page and the implications made my heart go pitty-pat.
An accountant named Libby Glass, Causasian, female, age

twenty-four, had died from ingesting ground oleander four days after Laurence Fife died. She had worked for Haycraft and McNiece, a business-management firm representing the interests of Laurence Fife's law firm. Now what the hell was that about?

I flipped through copies of investigators' reports, trying to piece together the story from terse departmental memorandums and penciled summations of telephone calls flying back and forth between the Santa Teresa and West Los Angeles police departments. One memo noted that the key to her apartment had been found on the key ring in Laurence Fife's office desk drawer. A lengthy interview with her parents didn't add anything. There was an interview with a surly sounding ex-boyfriend named Lyle Abernathy, who seemed convinced that she was romantically involved with a "certain unnamed Santa Teresa attorney," but no one had pinned it down much beyond that. Still, the connection was ominous enough and it looked like Nikki Fife's alleged jealous rage might have included the object of her husband's philanderings as well as the man himself. Except that there wasn't any proof.

I made notes, jotting down last-known addresses and telephone numbers for whatever good that might do after all these years, and then I pushed my chair back and went to the door. Con was talking to Lieutenant Becker but he must have known what I wanted because he excused himself, apparently satisfied that I hadn't missed the point. I leaned on the doorframe, waiting. He took his sweet time ambling over.

"You want to tell me what that was about?"

His expression was bemused but there was an air of bitterness about it. "We couldn't make it stick," he said flatly.

"You think Nikki killed her too?"

"I'd be willing to bet on it," he snapped.

"I take it the D.A. didn't see it that way."

He shrugged, shoving his hands in his pockets. "I can read the California Evidence Code as well as the next man. They called off my dogs."

"The stuff in the file was all circumstantial," I said.

"That's right."

I shut my mouth, staring off at a row of windows that badly

needed to be cleaned. I didn't like this little turn of events at all and he seemed to know that. He shifted his weight.

"I think I could have nailed her but the D.A. was in a big hurry and he didn't want to jeopardize his case. Bad politics. That's why you didn't like being a cop yourself, Kinsey. Working with a leash around your neck."

"I still don't like that," I said.

"Maybe that's why I'm helping you," he said and the look in his eyes was shrewd.

"What about follow-up?"

"Oh we did that. We worked on the Libby Glass angle for months, off and on. So did the West LAPD. We never turned up anything. No witnesses. No informants. No fingerprints that could have placed Nikki Fife at the scene. We couldn't even prove that Nikki *knew* Libby Glass."

"You think I'm going to help you make your case?"

"Well, I don't know about that," he said. "You might. Believe it or not, I don't think you're a bad investigator. Young yet, and sometimes off the wall, but basically honest at any rate. If you turn up evidence that points to Nikki, I don't think you'd hold that back now, would you?"

"*If* she did it."

"If she didn't, then you don't have anything to worry about."

"Con, if Nikki Fife has something to hide, why would she open this whole thing up again? She couldn't be that kind of fool. What could she possibly gain?"

"You tell me."

"Listen," I said, "I don't believe she killed Laurence in the first place so you're going to have a hell of a time persuading me she killed someone else as well."

The phone rang two desks over and Lieutenant Becker held up a finger, looking over at Con. He gave me a fleeting smile as he moved away.

"Have a good time," he said.

I scanned the file again quickly to make sure I hadn't overlooked anything and then I closed it up and left it on the desk. He was deep in conversation with Becker again when I passed the two of them and neither looked up at me. I was troubled by the idea of Libby Glass but I was also intrigued.

Maybe this was going to be more than a rehash of old business, maybe there was more to be turned up than a trail that was eight years cold.

By the time I got back to the office, it was 4:15 and I needed a drink. I got a bottle of chablis out of my little refrigerator and applied the corkscrew. The two coffee mugs were still sitting on my desk. I rinsed out both and filled mine with wine tart enough to make me shudder ever so slightly. I went out onto the second-floor balcony and looked down at State Street, which runs right up the middle of downtown Santa Teresa, eventually making a big curve to the left and turning into a street with another name. Even where I stood, there were Spanish tile and stucco arches and bougainvillea growing everywhere. Santa Teresa is the only town I ever heard of that made the main street narrower, planted trees instead of pulling them up, and constructed cunning telephone booths that look like small confessionals. I propped myself up on the waist-high ledge and sipped my wine. I could smell the ocean and I let my mind go blank, watching the pedestrians down below. I already knew that I would go to work for Nikki but I needed just these few moments for myself before I turned my attention to the job to be done.

At 5:00 I went home, calling the service before I left.

Of all the places I've lived in Santa Teresa, my current cubbyhole is the best. It's located on an unpretentious street that parallels the wide boulevard running along the beach. Most of the homes in the neighborhood are owned by retired folk whose memories of the town go back to the days when it was all citrus groves and resort hotels. My landlord, Henry Pitts, is a former commercial baker who makes a living now, at the age of eighty-one, by devising obnoxiously difficult cross-word puzzles, which he likes to try out on me. He is usually also in the process of making mammoth batches of bread, which he leaves to rise in an old Shaker cradle on the sunporch near my room. Henry trades bread and other baked goods to a nearby restaurant for his meals and he has also, of late, become quite crafty about clipping coupons, declaring that on a good day he can buy $50.00 worth of groceries for $6.98. Somehow these shopping expeditions seem to net him pairs of panty hose, which he gives to me. I am halfway in love with Henry Pitts.

The room itself is fifteen feet square, outfitted as living room, bedroom, kitchen, bathroom, closet, and laundry facility. Originally this was Henry's garage and I'm happy to say that it sports no stucco, red Spanish tile, or vines of any kind. It is made of aluminum siding and other wholly artificial products that are weather-resistant and never need paint. The architecture is completely nondescript. It is to this cozy den that I escape most days after work and it was from here that I called Nikki and asked her to meet me for a drink.

3

I do most of my hanging out in a neighborhood bar called Rosie's. It's the sort of place where you look to see if the chair needs brushing off before you sit down. The plastic seats have little rips in them that leave curls of nylon on the underside of your stockings and the tables have black Formica tops hand-etched with words like *hi*. To the left above the bar, there's a dusty marlin, and when people get drunk, Rosie lets them shoot rubber-tipped arrows at it with a toy gun, thus averting aggressions that might otherwise erupt into vicious barroom snits.

The place appeals to me for a couple of reasons. Not only is it close to my home but it is never attractive to tourists, which means that most of the time it's half-empty and perfect for private conversations. Then, too, Rosie's cooking is inventive, a sort of devil-may-care cuisine with a Hungarian twist. It is with Rosie that Henry Pitts barters baked goods, so I get to eat his breads and pies as a dividend. Rosie is in her sixties with a nose that almost meets her upper lip, a low forehead, and hair dyed a remarkable shade of rust, rather like the color of cheap redwood furniture. She also does tricky things with an eyebrow pencil that makes her eyes look small and suspect.

When Nikki walked in that night, she hesitated, scanning the place. Then she spotted me and moved through the empty tables to the booth where I usually sit. She slid in across from me and eased out of her jacket. Rosie ambled over, eyeing Nikki with uneasiness. Rosie is convinced that I do business with Mafia types and drug crazies and she was probably trying to determine the category into which Nikki Fife might fit.

"So are you eating something or what?" Rosie said, getting straight to the point.

I glanced at Nikki. "Have you had dinner?"

She shook her head. Rosie's eyes moved from Nikki to me as though I might be translating for a deaf-mute.

"What have you got tonight?"

"It's veal porkolt. Veal cubes, lotta onion, paprika, and tomato paste. You'll love it. You'll go nuts. It's the best kinda stew I make. Henry's rolls and everything, and on a plate I'm gonna put some good soft cheese and a coupla gherkins."

She was already writing the order down as she spoke, so it didn't require much from us in the way of consent. "You gonna have wine too. I'll pick the kind."

When Rosie had left, I related the information I'd picked up in the files about the murder of Libby Glass, including the telephone calls that had been traced to Laurence's home phone.

"Did you know about her?"

Nikki shook her head. "I heard the name but it was through my attorney, sometime during the trial, I think. I can't even remember now what was said."

"You never heard Laurence mention her? Never saw her name written down anyplace?"

"No little love notes if that's what you mean. He was meticulous about that sort of thing. He was once named as corespondent in a divorce action because of some letters he wrote and after that, he seldom put anything personal in writing. I usually knew when he was involved with someone but never because he left cryptic notes or telephone numbers on matchbook covers or anything like that."

I thought about that one for a minute. "What about phone bills though? Why leave those around?"

"He didn't," Nikki said. "All the bills were sent to the business-management firm in Los Angeles."

"And Libby Glass handled the account?"

"Apparently she did."

"So maybe he called her on business matters."

Nikki shrugged. She was a little less remote than she had been but I still had the feeling that she was one step removed from what was happening. "He was having an affair with *someone*."

"How do you know?"

"The hours he kept. The look on his face." She paused, apparently thinking back. "Sometimes he would smell of someone else's soap. I finally accused him of that and afterwards he had a shower installed at the office and used the same kind of soap there that we used at home."

"Did he see women down at the office?"

"Ask his partner," she said with the faintest tinge of bitterness. "Maybe he even screwed 'em on the office couch, I don't know. Anyway it was little things. It sounds stupid now, but once he came home and the edge of his sock was turned down. It was summer and he said he'd been out playing tennis. He had on tennis shorts and he'd worked up a sweat all right, but not out on a public court. I really zapped him that time."

"But what would he say when you confronted him?"

"He'd admit it sometimes. Why not? I didn't have any proof and adultery isn't grounds for divorce in this state anyway."

Rosie arrived with the wine and two paper napkins wrapped around some silverware. Nikki and I were both silent until she'd departed again.

"Why did you stay married to him if he was such a jerk?"

"Cowardice I guess," she said. "I would have divorced him eventually, but I had a lot at stake."

"Your son?"

"Yes." Her chin came up slightly, whether from pride of defensiveness I wasn't sure. "His name is Colin," she said. "He's twelve. I have him in a boarding school up near Monterey."

"You also had Laurence's kids living with you at the time, didn't you?"

"Yes, that's right. A boy and a girl, both in school."

"Where are they now?"

"I have no idea. His ex-wife is here in town. You might check with her if you're curious. I don't hear from them."

"Did they blame you for his death?"

She leaned forward, her manner intense. "Everyone blamed me. Everyone believed I was guilty. And now I take it Con Dolan thinks I killed Libby Glass too. Isn't that what you were getting at?"

"Who cares what Dolan thinks? I don't think you did it and I'm the one going to work on this thing. Which reminds me. We ought to get the financial end of it clarified. I charge thirty bucks an hour plus mileage. I'd like to have at least a grand up front. I'll send you an itemized accounting from week to week indicating what time I've put in doing what. Also, you have to understand that my services are not exclusive. I sometimes handle more than one case at a time."

Nikki was already reaching into her purse. She took out a checkbook and a pen. Even looking at it upside down, I could see that the check was for five thousand dollars. I admired the carelessness with which she dashed it off. She didn't even have to check her bank balance first. She pushed it across the table to me and I tucked it into my purse as though I disposed of such matters as casually as she.

Rosie appeared again, this time with our dinner. She put a plate down in front of each of us and then stood there until we began to eat. "Mmm, Rosie it's wonderful," I said.

She wiggled slightly in place, not yielding her ground.

"Maybe it don't suit your friend," she said, looking at me instead of Nikki.

"Marvelous," Nikki murmured. "Really it is."

"She loves it," I said. Rosie's gaze slid across to Nikki's face and she finally seemed satisfied that Nikki's appreciation of the dish was equaled only by my own.

I let the conversation wander while we ate. Between the good food and the wine, Nikki seemed to be letting down her guard. Under that cool, unruffled surface, signs of life were beginning to show, as though she were just wakening from a curse that had rendered her immobile for years.

"Where do you think I should start?" I asked.

"Well I don't know. I've always been curious about his secretary back then. Her name was Sharon Napier. She was already working for him when he and I met, but there was something not right about her, something in her attitude."

"Was she involved with him?"

"I don't think so. I really don't know what it was. I could just about guarantee they didn't have any sexual ties, but something had gone on. She was sometimes sarcastic with him, which Laurence never tolerated from anyone. The first time I heard her do it, I thought he'd cut her down, but he never batted an eye. She never took any guff from him at all, wouldn't stay late, wouldn't come in on weekends when he had a big case coming up. He never complained about her either, just went out and hired temporary help when he needed it. It wasn't like him, but when I asked him about it, he acted as if I were crazy, reading significance into the situation when there wasn't any. She was gorgeous, too, hardly the run-of-the-mill office type."

"Do you have any idea where she is now?"

Nikki shook her head. "She used to live up on Rivera but she's not there now. At least, she's not listed in the telephone book."

I made a note of her last-known address. "I take it you never knew her well."

Nikki shrugged. "We had the customary exchanges when I called the office but it was just routine stuff."

"What about friends of hers or places she might hang out?"

"I don't know. My guess is she lived way beyond her means. She traveled every chance she could and she dressed a lot better than I did back then."

"She testified at the trial, didn't she?"

"Yes, unfortunately. She'd been a witness to a couple of nasty quarrels I had with him and that didn't help."

"Well, it's worth looking into," I said. "I'll see if I can get a line on her. Is there anything else about him? Was he in the middle of any hassles when he died? Any kind of personal dispute or a big legal case?"

"Not that I knew. He was always in the middle of something big."

"Well, I think the first move is to talk to Charlie Scorsoni and see what he has to say. Then we'll figure it out from there."

I left money on the table for the dinner check and we walked out together. Nikki's car was parked close by, a dark green Oldsmobile ten years out of date. I waited until she'd pulled away and then I walked the half block to my place.

When I got in, I poured myself a glass of wine and sat down to organize the information I'd collected so far. I have a system of consigning data to three-by-five index cards. Most of my notes have to do with witnesses: who they are, how they're related to the investigation, dates of interviews, follow-up.

Some cards are background information I need to check out and some are notes about legal technicalities. The cards are an efficient way of storing facts for my written reports. I tack them up on a large bulletin board above my desk and stare at them, telling myself the story as I perceive it. Amazing contradictions will come to light, sudden gaps, questions I've overlooked.

I didn't have many cards for Nikki Fife and I made no attempt to assess the information I had. I didn't want to form a hypothesis too early for fear it would color the entire course of the investigation. It did seem clear that this was a murder where an alibi meant little or nothing. If you go to the trouble to substitute poison for the medication in someone's antihistamine capsules, all you have to do afterward is sit back and wait. Unless you want to risk killing off others in the household, you have to be sure that only your intended victim takes that particular prescription, but there are plenty of pills that would satisfy that requirement: blood-pressure medication, antibiotics, maybe even sleeping pills. It doesn't matter much as long as you have access to the supply. It might take your victim two days or two weeks but eventually he'd dose himself properly and you could probably even manufacture a reasonable facsimile of surprise and grief. The plan has a further advantage in that you don't actually have to be there to shoot, bludgeon, hack up, or manually strangle your intended. Even where the motivation to kill is overpowering, it'd be pretty distasteful (one would think) to watch somone's eyes bug out and listen to his or her last burbling cries. Also, when done in person there's always that unsettling chance that the tables might be turned and you'd wind up on a slab in the morgue yourself.

As methods go, this little oleander number was not half bad. In Santa Teresa, the shrub grows everywhere, sometimes ten feet tall with pink or white blossoms and handsome narrow leaves. You wouldn't need to bother with anything so blatant as buying rat poison in a town where there are clearly no rats, and you wouldn't have to sport a false mustache when you went into your local hardware store to ask for a garden pest control with no bitter aftertaste. In short, the method for killing

Laurence Fife, and apparently Libby Glass as well, was inexpensive, accessible, and easy to use. I did have a couple of questions and I made notes of those before I turned out the light. It was well after midnight when I fell asleep.

4

I went into the office early to type up my initial notes for Nikki's file, indicating briefly what I'd been hired to do and the fact that a check for five thousand dollars had been paid on account. Then I called Charlie Scorsoni's office. His secretary said he had some time free midafternoon, so I set up an appointment for 3:15 and then used the rest of the morning to do a background check. When interviewing someone for the first time, it's always nice to have a little information up your sleeve. A visit to the county clerk's office, the credit bureau, and the newspaper morgue gave me sufficient facts to dash off a quick sketch of Laurence Fife's former law partner. Charlie Scorsoni was apparently single, owned his own home, paid his bills on time, did occasional public-speaking stints for worthy causes, had never been arrested or sued—in short, was a rather conservative, middle-aged man who didn't gamble, speculate on the stock market, or jeopardize himself in any way. I had caught glimpses of him at the trial and I remembered him as slightly overweight. His current office was within walking distance of mine.

The building itself looked like a Moorish castle: two stories of white adobe with windowsills two feet deep, inset with wrought-iron bars, and a corner tower that probably housed the rest rooms and floor mops. Scorsoni and Powers, Attorneys-at-Law, were on the second floor. I pushed through a massive carved wooden door and found myself in a small reception area with carpeting as soft underfoot as moss and about the same shade. The walls were white, hung with watercolors in various pastels, all abstract, and there were plants here and there; two plump sofas of asparagus green wide-wale corduroy sat at right angles under a row of narrow windows.

The firm's secretary looked to be in her early seventies, and I thought at first she might be out on loan from some geriatric agency. She was thin and energetic, with bobbed hair straight out of the twenties and "mod" glasses replete with a rhinestone butterfly on the lower portion of one lens. She was wearing a wool skirt and a pale mauve sweater, which she must have knit herself, as it was a masterpiece of cable stitches, wheat ears, twisted ribs, popcorn stitches, and picot appliqué. She and I became instant friends when I recognized the aforementioned—my aunt having raised me on a regimen of such accomplishments—and we were soon on a first-name basis. Hers was Ruth; nice biblical stuff.

She was a chatty little thing, full of pep, and I wondered if she wasn't about perfect for Henry Pitts. Since Charlie Scorsoni was keeping me waiting, I took my revenge by eliciting as much information from Ruth as I could manage without appearing too rude. She told me she had worked for Scorsoni and Powers since the formation of their partnership seven years ago. Her husband had left her for a younger woman (fifty-five) and Ruth, on her own for the first time in years, had despaired of ever finding a job, as she was then sixty-two years old, "though in perfect health," she said. She was quick, capable, and of course was being aced out at every turn by women one-third her age who were cute instead of competent.

"The only cleavage I got left, I sit on," she said and then hooted at herself. I gave Scorsoni and Powers several points for their perceptiveness. Ruth had nothing but raves for them both. Still her rhapsodizing hardly prepared me for the man who shook my hand across the desk when I was finally ushered into his office forty-five minutes late.

Charlie Scorsoni was big, but any excess weight I remembered was gone. He had thick, sandy hair, receding at the temples, a solid jaw, cleft chin, his blue eyes magnified by big rimless glasses. His collar was open, his tie askew, sleeves rolled up as far as his muscular forearms would permit. He was tilted back in his swivel chair with his feet propped up against the edge of the desk, and his smile was slow to form and smoldered with suppressed sexuality. His air was watchful, bemused, and he took in the sight of me with almost embarrassing attention to detail. He laced his hands across the top of his head. "Ruth tells me you have a few questions about Laurence Fife. What gives?"

"I don't know yet. I'm looking into his death and this seemed like the logical place to start. Mind if I sit down?"

He gestured with one hand almost carelessly, but his expression had changed. I sat down and Scorsoni eased himself into an upright position.

"I heard Nikki was out on parole," he said. "If she claims she didn't kill him, she's nuts."

"I didn't say I was working for her."

"Well it's for damn sure nobody else would bother."

"Maybe not. You don't sound too happy about the idea."

"Hey listen. Laurence was my best friend. I would have walked on nails for him." His gaze was direct and there was something bristly under the surface—grief, misdirected rage. It was hard to tell what.

"Did you know Nikki well?" I asked.

"Well enough I guess." The sense of sexuality that had seemed so apparent at first was seeping away and I wondered if he could turn it off and on like a heater. Certainly his manner was wary now.

"How did you meet Laurence?"

"We went to the University of Denver together. Same fraternity. Laurence was a playboy. Everything came easily to him. Law school, he went to Harvard, I went to Arizona State. His family had money. Mine had none. I lost track of him for a few years and then I heard he'd opened his own law firm here in town. So I came out and talked to him about going to work for him and he said fine. He made me a partner two years later."

"Was he married to his first wife then?"

"Yeah, Gwen. She's still around town someplace but I'd be a little careful with her. She ended up bitter as hell and I've heard she's got surly things to say about him. She has a dog-grooming place up on State Street somewhere if that's any help. I try to avoid running into her myself."

He was watching me steadily and I got the impression that he knew exactly how much he would tell me and exactly how much he would not.

"What about Sharon Napier? Did she work for him long?"

"She was here when I hired on, though she did precious little. I finally ended up hiring a girl of my own."

"She and Laurence got along okay?"

"As far as I know. She hung around until the trial was over and then she took off. She stiffed me for some money I'd advanced against her salary. If you run into her, I'd love to hear about it. Send her a bill or something just to let her know I haven't forgotten old times."

"Does the name Libby Glass mean anything to you?"

"Who?"

"She was the accountant who handled your business down in L.A. She worked for Haycraft and McNiece."

Scorsoni continued to look blank for a moment and then shook his head. "What's she got to do with it?"

"She was also killed with oleander right about the time Laurence died," I said. He didn't seem to react with any particular shock or dismay. He made a skeptical pull at his lower lip and then shrugged.

"It's a new one on me but I'll take your word for it," he said.

"You never met her yourself?"

"I must have. Laurence and I shared the paperwork but he had most of the actual contact with the business managers. I pitched in occasionally though, so I probably ran into her at some point."

"I've heard he was having an affair with her," I said.

"I don't like to gossip about the dead," Scorsoni said.

"Me neither, but he did play around," I said carefully. "I don't mean to push the point, but there were plenty of women who testified to that at the trial."

Scorsoni smiled at the box he was drawing on his legal pad. The look he gave me then was shrewd.

"Well, I'll say this. One, the guy never forced himself on anyone. And two, I don't believe he would get himself involved with a business associate. That was not his style."

"What about his clients? Didn't he get involved with them?"

"No comment."

"Would *you* get in bed with a female client?" I asked.

"Mine are all eighty years old so the answer is no. I do

estate planning. He did divorce." He glanced at his watch and then pushed his chair back. "I hate to cut this short but it's four-fifteen now and I have a brief to prepare."

"Sorry. I didn't mean to take up your time. It was nice of you to see me on such short notice."

Scorsoni walked me out toward the front, his big body exuding heat. He held the door open for me, his left arm extending up along the doorframe. Again, that barely suppressed male animal seemed to peer out through his eyes. "Good luck," he said. "I suspect you won't turn up much."

I picked up the eight-by-ten glossies of the sidewalk crack I'd photographed for California Fidelity. The six shots of the broken concrete were clear enough. The claimant, Marcia Threadgill, had filed for disability, asserting that she'd stumbled on the jutting slab of sidewalk that had been forced upward by a combination of tree roots and shifting soil. She was suing the owner of the craft shop whose property encompassed the errant walkway. The claim, a "slip and fall" case, wasn't a large one—maybe forty-eight hundred dollars, which included her medical bills and damages, along with compensation for the time she'd been off work. It looked like the insurance company would pay, but I had been instructed to give a cursory look on the off chance that the claim was trumped-up.

Ms. Threadgill's apartment was in a terraced building set into a hill overlooking the beach, not that far from my place. I parked my car about six doors down and got my binoculars out of the glove compartment. By slouching down on my spine, I could just bring her patio into focus, the view clear enough to disclose that she wasn't watering her ferns the way she ought. I don't know a lot about houseplants, but when all the green things turn brown, I'd take it as a hint. One of the ferns was that nasty kind that grow little gray hairy paws that begin, little by little, to creep right out of the pot. Anyone who'd own a thing like that probably had an inclination to defraud and I could just picture her hefting a twenty-five-pound sack of fern mulch with her alleged sprained back. I watched her place for an hour and a half but she didn't show. One of my old cohorts used to claim that men are the only suitable candidates for surveillance work because they can sit in a parked car and pee discreetly into a tennis-ball can, thus avoiding unnecessary absences. I was losing interest in Marcia Threadgill and in truth, I had to pee like crazy, so I put the binoculars away and found the nearest service station on my way back into town.

I stopped in at the credit bureau again and talked to my buddy who lets me peek into files not ordinarily made public. I asked him to see what he could find out about Sharon Napier and he said he'd get back to me. I did a couple of personal errands and then went home. It had not been a very satisfying day but then most of my days are the same: checking and cross-checking, filling in blanks, detail work that was absolutely essential to the job but scarcely dramatic stuff. The basic characteristics of any good investigator are a plodding nature and infinite patience. Society has inadvertently been grooming women to this end for years. I sat down at my desk and consigned Charlie Scorsoni to several index cards. It had been an unsettling interview and I had a feeling that I wasn't done with him.

5

Living with the climate in Santa Teresa is rather like functioning in a room with an overhead light fixture. The illumination is uniform—clear and bright enough—but the shadows are gone and there is a disturbing lack of dimension. The days are blanketed with sunlight. Often it is sixty-seven degrees and fair. The nights are consistently cool. Seasonally it does rain but the rest of the time, one day looks very much like the next and the constant, cloudless blue sky has a peculiar, disorienting effect, making it impossible to remember where one is in the year. Being in a building with no exterior windows gives the same impression: a subliminal suffocation, as though some, but not all, of the oxygen has been removed from the air.

I left my apartment at 9:00, heading north on Chapel. I stopped for gasoline, using the self-service pump and thinking, as I always do, what a simple but absurd pleasure it is to be able to do that sort of thing myself. By the time I found K-9 Korners, it was 9:15. The discreet sign in the window indicated that the place opened for business at eight. The grooming establishment was attached to a veterinarian's office on State Street just where it made the big bend. The building was painted flamingo pink, one wing of it housing a wilderness supply store with a mummy bag hanging in the window and a dummy, in a camping outfit, staring blankly at a tent pole.

I pushed my way into K-9 Korners to the accompaniment of many barking dogs. Dogs and I do not get along. They inevitably stick their snouts right in my crotch, sometimes clamping themselves around my leg as though to do some kind of two-legged dance. On certain occasions, I have limped gamely along, dog affixed, their masters swatting at them ineffectually, saying "Hamlet, get down! What's the matter with you!?" It is hard to look such a dog in the face, and I prefer to keep my distance from the lot of them.

There was a glass showcase full of dog-care products, and many photographs of dogs and cats affixed to the wall. To my right was a half door, the upper portion opening into a small office with several grooming rooms adjoining. By peering around the doorjamb, I could spot several dogs in various stages of being done up. Most were shivering, their eyes rolling piteously. One was having a little red bow put in its topknot, right between its ears. On a worktable were some little brown lumps I thought I could recognize. The groomer, a woman, looked up at me.

"Can I help you?"

"The dog just stepped on that brown lump," I said.

She looked down at the table. "Oh Dashiell, not again. Excuse me a minute," she said. Dashiell remained on the table, trembling, while she grabbed for some paper towels, deftly scooping up Dashiell's little accident. She seemed pretty good-natured about it. She was in her mid-forties with large brown eyes and shoulder-length gray hair, which was pulled back and secured with a scarf. She wore a dark wine-colored smock and I could see that she was tall and slim.

"Are you Gwen?"

She glanced up with a quick smile. "Yes, that's right."

"I'm Kinsey Millhone. I'm a private investigator."

Gwen laughed. "Oh Lord, what's this all about?" She disposed of the paper towel and moved over to the half door and opened it. "Come on in. I'll be right back."

She lifted Dashiell from the table and carried him into a back room just off to the left. More dogs began to bark and I could hear a blower being turned off. The air in the place was dense with heat, scented with the smell of damp hair, and the odd combination of flea syrup and dog perfume. The brown linoleum tile floor was covered with assorted clippings, like a barber shop. In the adjoining room, I could see a dog being bathed by a young girl who worked over an elevated bathtub. To my left several dogs, beribboned, were waiting in cages to be picked up. Another young woman was clipping a poodle on a second grooming table. She glanced at me with interest. Gwen returned with a little gray dog under her arm.

"This is Wuffles," she said, half clamping the dog's mouth shut. Wuffles gave her a few licks in the mouth. She pulled her head back, laughing, and made a face.

"I hope you don't mind if I finish this up. Have a seat," she said affably, indicating a metal stool nearby. I perched, wishing I didn't have to mention Laurence Fife's name. From what Charlie Scorsoni had told me, it would rather spoil her good humor.

Gwen began to clip Wuffles's toenails, tucking the dog against her body to prevent sudden moves. "You're local, I assume," she said.

"Yes, I have an office downtown here," I said, pulling out my I.D. automatically. I held it toward her so she could read it. She gave it a glance, apparently accepting it without much suspicion or concern. It always amazes me when people take me on faith.

"I understand you used to be married to Laurence Fife," I ventured.

"Yes, that's right. Is this about him? He's been dead for years."

"I know. His case is being opened up again."

"Oh, *that's* interesting. By whom?"

"Nikki. Who else?" I said. "The Homicide Department knows I'm looking into it and I have their cooperation, if that helps you any. Could you answer some questions for me?"

"All right," she said. Her tone was cautious but there was also a note of interest, as though she considered it a curious inquiry but not necessarily bad.

"You don't sound that surprised," I said.

"Actually I am. I thought that was finished business."

"Well, I'm just starting to look into it and I may come up with a blank. We don't have to talk here if it's inconvenient. I don't like to interrupt your work."

"This is fine with me, as long as you don't mind watching me clip a few dogs. I really can't afford a time-out right now. We're loaded today. Hold on," she said. "Kathy, could you hand me that flea spray? I think we missed a few here."

The dark-haired groomer left the poodle long enough to reach up for the flea spray, which was passed over to Gwen.

"That's Kathy, as you might have gathered," Gwen said. "The one up to her elbows in soapsuds is Jan."

Gwen began to spray Wuffles, turning her face away to avoid the fumes. "Sorry. Go ahead."

"How long were you married to Fife?"

"Thirteen years. We met in college, his third year, my first. I'd known him about six months I guess."

"Good years? Bad years?"

"Well I'm mellowing some on that," she said. "I used to think it was all a big waste but now I don't know. Did you know Laurence yourself?"

"I met him a couple of times," I said, "just superficially."

Gwen's look was wry. "He could be very charming if he wanted to, but at heart he was a real son of a bitch."

Kathy glanced over at Gwen and smiled. Gwen laughed. "These two have heard my version about a hundred times," she said by way of explanation. "Neither has ever been married so I tend to play devil's advocate. Anyway, in those days I was the dutiful wife, and I mean I played the part with a dedication few could match. I cooked elegant meals. I made lists. I cleaned the house. I raised the kids. I'm not saying I'm anything unique for that, except that I took it awfully to heart. I wore my hair up in this French roll, not a pin out of place, and I had these outfits to put on and take off, kind of like a Barbie doll." She stopped and laughed at the image of herself, pretending to pull a string from her neck. "Hello, I'm Gwen. I'm a good wife," she burbled in a kind of nasal parrot tone. Her manner was rather affectionate as though she, instead of Laurence, had died but was remembered fondly by dear friends. Part of the time she was looking at me, and part of the time she combed and clipped the dog on the table in front of her, but in any event her manner was friendly—hardly the bitter, withdrawn account I'd expected.

"When it was over, I was pretty angry—not so much at him as at myself for buying into the whole gig. I mean, don't get me wrong. I liked it at the time and it suited me fine, but there was also a form of sensory deprivation going on so that when the marriage blew up, I was totally unequipped to deal with the real world. He managed the money. He pulled the strings. He made the major decisions, especially where the kids were concerned. I bathed and dressed and fed them and he shaped their lives. I didn't realize it at the time because I was just running around anxious to please him, which was no easy task, but now that I look back on it, it was really fucked."

She glanced up at me to see if I'd react to the language, but I just smiled bak.

"So now I sound like all the other women who came out of marriages in that era. You know, we're all faintly grumpy about it because we think we've been had."

"You said you'd mellowed some," I said. "How did that come about?"

"Six thousand dollars' worth of therapy," she said flatly.

I smiled. "What made the marriage blow?"

Her cheeks tinted slightly at that but her gaze remained just as frank. "I'd rather save that for later if you're really interested."

"Sure, fine," I said. "I didn't mean to interrupt anyway."

"Well. It wasn't all his fault," she said. "But it wasn't all mine either and he hosed me with that divorce. I'm telling you, I got beat up."

"How?"

"How many ways are there? I was scared and I was also naïve. I wanted Laurence out of my life and I didn't care much what it cost. Except the kids. I fought him tooth and nail over them, but what can I tell you? I lost. I've never quite recovered from that."

I wanted to ask her about the grounds for the custody battle but I had the feeling it was touchy stuff. Better to let that slide for the moment and come back to it later if I could. "The kids must have come back to you after he died, though. Especially with his second wife going to prison."

Gwen pushed at a strand of gray hair with a capable-looking hand. "They were almost college age by then. In fact, Gregory had left that fall and Diane left the year after. But they were very messed-up kids. Laurence was a strict disciplinarian. Not that I have any quarrel with that—I think kids need structure—but he was a very controlling person, really out of touch with anything emotional, rather aggressive in his manner of dealing with anyone, the kids in particular. So the two of them, after five years of that regime, were both withdrawn and shut-down. Defensive, uncommunicative. From what I could tell, his relation to them was based on attack, being held accountable, much like what he had done with me. Of course, I'd been seeing them alternate weekends and that sort of thing, and I had the usual summer visitation. I just didn't have any idea how far it had gone. And his death was a kick in the head to them on top of that. I'm sure they both had a lot of feelings that were never resolved. Diane went straight into therapy. And Gregory's seen someone since, though not regularly." She paused a moment. "I feel like I've giving you case histories here."

"Oh no, I appreciate your candor," I said. "Are the kids here in town too?"

"Greg's living south of Palm Springs. Salton Sea. He has a boat down there."

"What sort of work does he do?"

"Well, he doesn't have to do anything. Laurence did provide for them financially. I don't know if you've checked on the insurance yet, but his estate was divided equally between the three kids—Greg, Diane, and Nikki's son, Colin."

"What about Diane? Where is she?"

"She's in Claremont, going to school. Working on another degree. She's interested in teaching deaf children and she seems to do very well. It worried me some at first because I suspect, in her mind, it was all tied up—my divorce, Nikki, Colin, and her responsibility—even though it had nothing to do with her."

"Wait a minute. I don't understand what you mean," I said.

Gwen glanced up at me with surprise. "I thought you'd already talked to Nikki."

"Well, I talked to her once," I said.

"Didn't she tell you Colin was deaf? He was deaf from birth. I don't really remember what caused it, but there was nothing they could do about it apparently. Diane was very upset. She was thirteen, I think, when the baby was born and maybe she resented the intrusion. I don't mean to be so analytical at every turn but some of this came out with her psychiatrist and it seems pertinent. I think now she can articulate most of it herself—in fact she does—so I don't think I'm violating any confidence."

She selected a couple of strands of ribbon from about twenty spools hung on pegboard on the wall above the grooming table. She laid a blue and an orange on Wuffles's head. "What do you think, Wuf? Blue or orange?"

Wuffles raised her (I assumed) eyes and panted happily, and Gwen chose the orange, which I must admit made a certain jaunty sense against Wuffles's silver-gray mop of hair. The dog was docile, full of trust, loving every move even though half of Gwen's attention was turned to me.

"Gregory was into drugs for a while," Gwen said conversationally. "That's what his generation seemed to do while mine was playing house. But he's a good kid and I think he's okay now. Or as okay as he'll ever be. He's happy, which is a lot more than most of us can say—I mean, *I'm* happy but I know a lot of people who aren't."

"Won't he get tired of boating?"

"I hope so," Gwen said lightly. "He can afford to do anything he wants, so if the leisure begins to pall, he'll find something useful to do. He's very smart and he's a very capable kid, in spite of the fact that he's idle right now. Sometimes I envy him that."

"Do you think it would distress the kids if I talked to them?"

Gwen was startled at that, the first time she'd seemed disconcerted by anything. "About their father?"

"I may have to at some point," I said. "I wouldn't like to do it without your knowledge, but it might really help."

"I suppose it would be all right," she said, but her tone was full of misgivings.

"We can talk about it later. It may not be necessary at all."

"Oh. Well. I don't see how it could hurt. I must say, I don't really understand why you're into this business again."

"To see if justice was done, I guess," I said. "It sounds melodramatic, but that's what it amounts to."

"Justice to whom. Laurence or Nikki?"

"Maybe you should tell me what you think. I'm assuming there was no love lost between you and them, but do you think he got his 'just desserts'?"

"Sure, why not? I don't know about her. I figure she had a fair trial and if that's the way it came out, well she must have done it. But there were times I'd have done it myself if I had thought of some way."

"So if she killed him, you wouldn't blame her?"

"Me and half a dozen others. Laurence alienated a lot of people," she said carelessly. "We could have formed a club and sent out a monthly newsletter. I still run into people who sidle up to me and say 'Thank god he's dead.' Literally. Out of the corner of their mouths." Gwen laughed again. "I'm sorry if that sounds irreverent but he was not a nice man."

"But who in particular?"

She put her hand on her hip and gave me a jaded look. "If you got an hour, I'll give you a list," she said.

I laughed then. Her humor seemed irrepressible or maybe she was only feeling ill at ease. Talking to a private eye is often unnerving to people.

Gwen put Wuffles in an empty cage and then went into the other room and led out a big English sheepdog. She lifted its front feet first, placing them on the table, and then she heaved its hind legs up while the dog whined uneasily.

"Oh come on, Duke," she snapped. "This one is such a sissy."

"Do you think we could talk again soon?" I asked.

"Sure, I'd like that. I close up here at six. If you're free then, we can have a drink. By the end of the day, I'm ready for one."

"Me too. I'll see you then," I said.

I hopped down off my stool and let myself out. When the door closed, she was already chatting with the dog. I wondered what else she knew and how much of it she was willing to share. I also hoped to hell I could look that good in another ten years.

6

I stopped off at a pay phone and gave Nikki a call. She picked up on the third ring.

"Nikki? This is Kinsey. I have a request. Is there any way I can get into the house where you and Laurence lived?"

"Sure. I still own it. I'm just leaving to drive up to Monterey to bring Colin back but it's en route. I can meet you there if you like."

She gave me the address and said she'd be there in fifteen minutes or so. I hung up and headed for my car. I wasn't sure what I was after but I wanted to walk through the place, to get a feel for what it was like, living as they lived. The house was in Montebello, a section of town where there are rumored to be more millionaires per square mile than in any other part of the country. Most of the houses are not even visible from the road. Occasionally you can catch a glimpse of a tiled roof hidden away in tangles of olive trees and live oak. Many parcels of land are bordered by winding walls of hand-hewn stone overgrown with wild roses and nasturtiums. Towering eucalyptus trees line the roads, with intermittent palms looking like Spanish exclamation points.

The Fifes' house was on the corner of two lanes, shielded from view by ten-foot hedges that parted at one point to admit a narrow brick driveway. The house was substantial: two stories of putty-colored stucco with white trim. The facade was plain and there was a portico to one side. The surrounding land was equally plain except for patches of California poppies in shades of peach and rich yellow, gold, and pink. Beyond the house, I could see a double garage with what I guessed was a caretaker's quarters above. The lawns were well tended and the house, while it had an unoccupied look, didn't seem neglected. I parked my car on the portion of the drive that circled back on itself to permit easy exit. In spite of the red-tiled roof, the house looked more French than Spanish: windows without cornices, the front door flush with the drive.

I got out of my car and walked around to the right, my footsteps making no sound on the pale rosy bricks. In the rear, I could see the outline of a swimming pool and for the first time, I felt something chill and out of place. The pool had been filled to the brim with dirt and trash. An aluminum lawn chair was half-sunk in the sod, weeds growing through the rungs. The diving board extended now over an irregular surface of grass clippings and dead leaves, as though the water had thickened and congealed. A set of steps with handholds disappeared into the depths and the surrounding concrete apron was riddled with dark splotches.

I found myself approaching with uneasiness and I was startled out of my concentration by the sound of malicious hissing. Waddling toward me with remarkable speed were two huge white geese, their heads thrust forward, mouths open like snakes with their tongues protruding, emitting a terrifying sound. I gave a low involuntary cry and began to backtrack toward my car, afraid to take my eyes off them. They covered the ground between us at a pace that forced me into a run. I barely reached my car before they caught up with me. I wrenched the door open and slammed it again with a panic I hadn't felt in years. I locked both doors, half expecting the viperous birds to batter at my windows until they gave way. For a moment they balanced, half lifted, wings flapping, black eyes bright with ill-will, their hissing faces even with mine. And then they lost interest and waddled off, honking and hissing, pecking savagely at the grass. Until that moment, it had never even occurred to me to include crazed geese among my fears, but they had suddenly shot straight to the top of the list along with worms and water bugs.

Nikki's car pulled in behind mine. She got out with perfect composure and approached as I rolled my window down. The two geese appeared again around the corner of the house, making their flat-footed beeline for the flesh of her calves. She gave them an idle glance and then laughed. Both raised up again, short wings flopping ineffectually, their manner suddenly benign. Nikki had a bread bag in her hand and she tossed them some crumbs.

"What the hell *are* those things?" I eased out of the car cautiously but neither paid the slightest attention to me.

"That's Hansel and Gretel," she said amicably. "They're Embden geese."

"The geese part I could tell. What happened? Did somebody train them to kill?"

"It keeps little kids off the property," she said. "Come on in." She inserted a key in the lock and the front door swung open. Nikki stooped to pick up some junk mail that had been pushed through the slot. "The mailman gives them saltines," she said as an afterthought. "They'll eat anything."

"Who else had keys to this place?" I asked. I noticed an alarm-system panel, which was apparently turned off.

She shrugged. "Laurence and me. Greg and Diane. I can't think of anyone else."

"Gardener? Maid?"

"Both have keys now but I don't think they did at the time. We did have a housekeeper. Mrs. Voss. She probably had one."

"Did you have a security system then?"

"We do now but that's only been in the last four years. I should have sold the place years ago but I didn't want to make decisions like that when I was in prison."

"It must be worth a lot."

"Oh sure. Real-estate values have tripled and we paid seven hundred and fifty thousand at the time. He picked it out. Put it in my name for business reasons, but it never did appeal to me much."

"Who did the decorating?" I asked.

Nikki smiled sheepishly. "I did. I don't think Laurence knew any better, but I took a subtle revenge. He insisted that we buy the place so I left all the color out."

The rooms were large, ceilings high, and plenty of light came in. The floors were dark-stained tongue and groove. The layout was very conventional: living room to the right, dining room to the left, with the kitchen behind. There was a sitting room beyond the living room and a long glassed-in porch along that side, running the length of the house. There was a curious air to the house, which I assumed was because no one had lived there for years, like a department-store display of especially elegant appointments. The furniture was still in place and there was no sign of dust. There were no plants and no magazines, no evidence of ongoing activity. Even the silence had a hollow tone, barren and lifeless.

The whole interior was done in neutral tones: grays and oyster whites, hazel and cinnamon. The couches and chairs were soft upholstered pieces with rounded arms and thick cushions, a sort of art deco look without any attempt at flash. There was a nice blend of modern and antique and it was clear that Nikki knew what she was doing even when she didn't care.

Upstairs, there were five bedrooms, all with fireplaces, all with bathrooms of remarkable size, deep closets, dressing rooms, the whole of it carpeted in thick fawn-colored wall-to-wall wool shag.

"This is the master suite?"

Nikki nodded. I followed her into the bathroom. Fat chocolate towels were stacked near the sink. There was a sunken tub, the surrounding ceramic tile a pale tobacco shade. There was a separate glassed-in shower that had been outfitted as a steam room. Soap, toilet paper, Kleenex.

"Do you stay here?" I asked as we came down the stairs.

"I haven't as yet, but I may. I have someone come in every two weeks to clean and of course there's a gardener on the premises all the time. I've been staying at the beach."

"You have another house out there?"

"Yes. Laurence's mother left it to me."

"Why you and not him?"

She smiled slightly. "Laurence and his mother didn't get along. Would you like some tea?"

"I thought you had to hit the road."

"I have time."

I followed her out to the kitchen. There was a cooking island in the center of the room with a big copper hood above the burners, a wide expanse of chopping block counter, and all manner of pans, baskets, and kitchen implements hanging on a circular metal rack that extended from the ceiling. All of the other counters were white ceramic tile; a double stainless-steel sink was sunk into one. There was a regular oven, a convection oven, a microwave, a refrigerator, two freezers, and impressive storage space.

Nikki put some water on to boil and perched herself on a wooden stool. I took up a stool across from her, the two of us sitting in the center of the room, which looked as much like a chem lab as a cook's dream.

"Who have you talked to so far?" she asked.

I told her about my conversation with Charlie Scorsoni.

"They seem like an odd pair of friends to me," I said. "My recollection of Laurence is a little hazy, but he always struck me as very elegant and cerebral. Scorsoni's very physical. He reminds me of a guy in an ad for chain saws."

"Oh Charlie's a real scrapper. From what I hear, he came up the hard way, bulldozing his way past all obstacles. Kind of like the blurb on a paperback: 'stepping over the bodies of those he loved . . .' Maybe Laurence liked that. He always talked about Charlie with grudging respect. Laurence had everything handed to him. Of course Charlie thought Laurence could do no wrong."

"That seemed clear enough," I said. "I don't suppose he had any motive for murder. Did you ever think he might have had a hand in it?"

Nikki smiled, getting up to take out cups, saucers, and tea bags. "At one time or another, I've considered everyone, but Charlie seems unlikely to me. He certainly didn't benefit financially or professionally . . ." She poured boiling water into both cups.

"As far as the eye can see," I said, dunking my tea bag.

"Well yes, that's true. I suppose there might have been some kind of hidden dividend, but surely that would have come to light at some point in the last eight years."

"One would think." I went on to tell her about my interview with Gwen. Nikki's cheeks went ever so faintly pink.

"I feel bad about her," she said. "By the time they divorced, Laurence really hated her and I tended to fan the flames a bit. He never could take any responsibility for the failure of that marriage and as a result, he had to blame her and punish her. I didn't help. At first I really believed what he was saying about her. I mean, I personally thought she seemed like a capable person and I knew Laurence had been very dependent on her but it was safer to wean him away by feeding his bad feelings. You know what I mean? In some ways, his hating her so strongly was no different from his loving her, but it made me feel more secure to widen the breach. I'm ashamed of that now. When I fell out of love with him myself and he began to turn on me, I suddenly recognized the process.''

"But I thought you were the downfall of that relationship," I said, looking at her carefully through the steam rising from my teacup.

Nikki ran both hands into her hair, lifting it away from her head and letting it fall again, giving her head a slight toss. "Oh no," she said, "I was his revenge. Never mind the fact that he'd been screwing around on her for years. He found out she was having an affair so he had me. Nice, huh? I didn't realize all this until much later, but that's how it was."

"Wait a minute. Let me see if I got this straight," I said. "He found out *she* was involved with someone, so he gets involved with you and then divorces her. From what I understand she got reamed."

"Oh yes. That's exactly what he did. The affair with me was his way of proving he didn't care. Taking the kids and the money was her punishment. He was very vindictive. It was one reason he made such a good attorney. He identified passionately with anyone who'd been wronged. He'd whip himself into a frenzy over the least little thing and then he'd use that as a driving force until he'd ground the opposition down. He was merciless. Absolutely merciless.''

"Who did Gwen have the affair with?"

"You'd have to ask her that. I'm not sure I ever knew. It was certainly something he never talked about."

I asked her about the night Laurence died and she filled me in on those details.

"What was he allergic to?"

"Animal hair. Mostly dogs but cat dander too. For a long time he wouldn't tolerate pets in the house but then when Colin was two, someone suggested that we get him a dog."

"I understand Colin's deaf."

"He was born deaf. They test newborns' hearing so we knew right away, but nothing could be done for him. Apparently I had a mild case of German measles before I even realized I was pregnant. Fortunately that was the only damage he seemed to suffer. We were lucky to that extent."

"And the dog was for him? Like a guard dog or something?"

"Something like that. You can't watch a kid night and day. That's why we had the pool filled in. Bruno was a big help too."

"A German shepherd."

"Yes," Nikki said and then hesitated slightly. "He's dead now. He got hit by a car right out there on the road, but he was a great dog. Very smart, very loving, very protective of Colin. Anyway, Laurence could see what it did for him, having a dog like Bruno, so he went back on the allergy medication. He really did love Colin. Whatever his faults, and he had lots of them, believe me, he did love that little boy."

Her smile faded and her face went through an odd alteration. She was suddenly gone, disengaged. Her eyes were blank and the look she gave me was empty of emotion.

"I'm sorry, Nikki. I wish we didn't have to go into all of this."

We finished our tea and then got up. She removed the cups and saucers, tucking them into the dishwasher. When she looked back at me, her eyes were that flat gun-metal gray again. "I hope you find out who killed him. I'll never be happy until I know."

The tone of her voice made my hands numb. There was a flash in her eyes like the one I'd seen in the eyes of the geese: malevolent, unreasoning. It was just a flicker and it quickly disappeared.

"You wouldn't try to get even, would you?" I asked.

She glanced away from me. "No. I used to think about that in prison a lot but now that I'm out, it doesn't seem that important to me. Right now, all I want is to have my son back. And I want to lie on the beach and drink Perrier and wear my own clothes. And eat in restaurants and when I'm not doing that, I want to cook. And sleep late and take bubble baths . . .'' She stopped and laughed at herself and then took a deep breath. ''So. No, I don't want to risk my freedom.''

Her eyes met mine and I smiled in response. ''You better hit the road,'' I said.

7

I stopped off at the Montebello Pharmacy while I was in the neighborhood. The pharmacist, whose name tag said "Carroll Sims," was in his fifties, medium height, with mild brown eyes behind mild tortoiseshell frames. He was in the midst of explaining to quite an old woman exactly what her medication was and how it should be taken. She was both puzzled and exasperated by the explanation but Sims was tactful, answering her flustered inquiries with a benign goodwill. I could imagine people showing him their warts and cat bites, describing chest pains and urinary symptoms across the counter. When it was my turn, I wished I had some little ill I could tell him about. Instead, I showed him my I.D.

"What can I do for you?"

"Did you happen to work here eight years ago when Laurence Fife was murdered?"

"Well I sure did. I own the place. Are you a friend of his?"

"No," I said, "I've been hired to look into the whole case again. I thought this was a logical place to start."

"I don't think I can be much help. I can tell you the medication he was taking, dosage, number of refills, the doctor who prescribed it, but I can't tell you how the switch was made. Well, I can tell you that. I just can't tell you who did it."

Most of the information Sims gave me I already knew. Laurence was taking an antihistamine called HistaDril, which he'd been on for years. He consulted an allergist about once a year and the rest of the time the refill on the medication was automatically okayed. The only thing Sims told me that I hadn't known was that HistaDril had recently been taken off the market because of possible carcinogenic side-effects.

"In other words, if Fife had just taken the medication for a few more years, he might have gotten cancer and died anyway."

"Maybe," the pharmacist said. We stared at one another for a moment.

"I don't suppose you have any idea who killed him," I said.

"Nope."

"Well, I guess that's that. Did you see any of the trial?"

"Just when I testified. I identified the pill bottle as one of ours. It had been pretty recently refilled but Fife himself had done that and we'd chitchatted at the time. He'd been taking HistaDril for so long we hardly needed to talk about that."

"Do you remember what you did talk about?"

"Oh, the usual thing. I think there was a fire burning across the backside of the city about that time and we talked about that. A lot of people with allergies were bothered by the increase in air pollution."

"Was it bothering him?"

"It bothered everyone a little bit but I don't remember him being any worse off than anyone else."

"Well," I said, "I thank you for your time. If you think of anything else, will you give me a buzz? I'm in the book."

"Sure, if I think of anything," he said.

It was midafternoon and I wasn't meeting Gwen again until 6:00. I felt restless and out of sorts. Bit by bit, I was putting together background information, but nothing was really happening yet, and as far as I knew nothing might ever come of it. As far as the state of California was concerned, justice had been served and only Nikki Fife stood in contradiction of this. Nikki and the nameless, faceless killer of Laurence Fife who had enjoyed eight years of immunity from prosecution, eight years of freedom that I was now being hired to violate. At some point, I was bound to tread on someone's toes and that someone was not going to be happy with me.

I decided to go spy on Marcia Threadgill. At the time she tripped on that crack in the sidewalk, she had just come from the craft shop, having purchased items necessary to make one ot those wooden purses covered with assorted shells. I imagined her decoupaging orange crates, making clever hanging ornaments out of egg cartons festooned with plastic sprigs of lily of the valley. Marcia Threadgill was twenty-six years old and she suffered from bad taste. The owner of the

craft shop had filled me in on the projects she had done and
every bit of it reminded me of my aunt. Marcia Threadgill was
cheap at heart. She turned common trash into Christmas gifts.
This is the mentality, in my opinion, that leads to cheating
insurance companies and other sly ruses. This is the kind of
person who would write to the Pepsi-Cola bottling plant
claiming to have found a mouse hair in her drink, trying to net
herself a free case of soda.

I parked a few doors down from her apartment and got out
my binoculars. I slouched, focusing on her patio, and then sat
up. "Well I'll be damned," I breathed.

In place of the nasty brown withered fern was a hanging
plant of mammoth proportions, which must have weighed
twenty pounds. Now how had she lifted that up to attach to a
hook high above her head? A neighbor? A boyfriend? Had she
done it herself perchance? I could even see the price tag stuck
to one side of the pot. She'd bought it at a Gateway
supermarket for $29.95, which was quite a price considering
that it was probably full of fruit flies.

"Shit," I said. Where was I when she hoisted that mama
up? Twenty pounds of glossy plant and moist soil on a chain at
shoulder height. Had she stood on a chair? I drove straight over
to the nearby Gateway supermarket and headed back to the
produce department. There were five or six such plants—
Dumbo ears or elephant tongues, whatever the damn things are
called. I lifted one. Oh my God. It was worse than I had
thought. Awkward and heavy, impossible to manage without
help. I picked up some film in the Ten Items or Less, No
Checks line and loaded my camera. "Marcia, you little
sweetheart," I cooed, "I'm gonna nail your ass."

I drove back to her apartment and got out my binoculars
again. I'd no more than settled down on my spine, glasses
trained on her patio, than Ms. Threadgill herself appeared,
trailing one of those long plastic hoses, which must have been
attached to her faucet inside. She misted and sprayed and
watered and carried on, poking a finger down into the dirt,
plucking a yellowing leaf from another potted plant on the
patio rail. A real obsessive type by the look of it, inspecting the
underside of leaves for God knows what pests. I studied her
face. She looked like she'd spent about forty-five dollars

having a free makeup demonstration in some department store. Mocha and caramel on her eyelids. Raspberry on her cheekbones. Lipstick the color of chocolate. Her fingernails were long and painted the approximate shade of cherry syrup in the sort of boxed candies you wish you hadn't bitten into so eagerly.

An old woman in a nylon jersey dress came out onto the patio above Marcia's and the two had a conversation. I guessed that it was some kind of complaint because neither looked happy and Marcia eventually flounced away. The old lady yelled something after her that looked dirty even in pantomime. I got out of the car and locked it, taking a clipboard and legal pad.

Marcia's apartment was listed on the register as 2-C. The apartment above hers was listed under the name Augusta White. I bypassed the elevator and took the stairs, pausing first outside Marcia's door. She was playing a Barry Manilow album full-blast, and even as I listened she cranked up the volume a notch or two. I went up another flight and tapped on Augusta's door. She was there in a flash, her face thrust forward through the crack like a Pekingese, complete with bulging eyes, pug nose, and chin whiskers. "Yes?" she snapped. She was eighty years old if a day.

"I'm in the building next door," I said. "We've had some complaints about the noise and the manager asked me to look into it. Could I talk to you?" I held up my official-looking clipboard.

"Hold on."

She moved away from the door and stomped back into her kitchen to get her broom. I heard her bang on the kitchen floor a few times. From below, there was a mighty thump, as though Marcia Threadgill had whacked on the ceiling with a combat boot.

Augusta White stomped back, squinting at me through the crack. "You look like a real-estate agent to me," she said suspiciously.

"Well, I'm not. Honest."

"You look like one anyway so just go on off with your papers. I know all the people next door and you aren't one." She slammed the door shut and shot the bolt into place.

So much for that. I shrugged and made my way back down
the stairs. Outside again, I made an eyeball assessment of the
terraces. The patios were staggered in a pyramid effect and I
had a quick flash of myself climbing up the outside of the
building like a second-story man to spy on Marcia Threadgill
at close range. I had really hoped I could enlist someone's aid
in getting a firsthand report of Ms. Threadgill, but I was going
to have to let it slide for a moment. I took some pictures of the
hanging plant from the vantage point of my car, hoping it
would soon wither and perish from a bad case of root rot. I
wanted to be there when she hung a new one into place.

I went back to my apartment and jotted down some notes.
It was 4:45 and I changed into my jogging clothes: a pair of
shorts and an old cotton turtleneck. I'm really not a physical
fitness advocate. I've been in shape maybe once in my life,
when I qualified for the police academy, but there's something
about running that satisfies a masochistic streak. It hurts and
I'm slow but I have good shoes and I like the smell of my own
sweat. I run on the mile and a half of sidewalk that tracks the
beach, and the air is usually slightly damp and very clean.
Palm trees line the wide grassy area between the sidewalk and
the sand and there are always other joggers, most of them
looking lots better than I.

I did two miles and then called it quits. My calves hurt. My
chest was burning. I huffed and puffed, bending from the
waist, imagining all kinds of toxic wastes pumping out through
my pores and lungs, a regular purge. I walked for half a block
and then I heard a car horn toot. I glanced over. Charlie
Scorsoni had pulled in at the curb in a pale blue 450 SL that
looked very good on him. I wiped the sweat trickling down my
face on an upraised shirt sleeve and crossed to his car.

"Your cheeks are bright pink," he said.

"I always look like I'm having an attack. You should see
the looks I get. What are you doing down here?"

"I felt guilty. Because I cut you short yesterday. Hop in."

"Oh no." I laughed, still trying to catch my breath. "I
don't want to get sweat all over your seats."

"Can I follow you back to your place?"

"Are you serious?"

"Sure," he said. "I thought I'd be especially winsome so you wouldn't put me on your 'possibly guilty' list."

"Won't help. I'm suspicious of everyone."

When I came out of the shower and stuck my head around the bathroom door, Scorsoni was looking at the books stacked up on my desk. "Did you have time to search through the drawers?" I asked.

He smiled benignly. "They were locked."

I smiled and closed the bathroom door again, getting dressed. I noticed that I was pleased to see him and that didn't sit well with me. I'm a real hard-ass when it comes to men. I don't often think of a forty-eight-year-old man as "cute" but that's how he struck me. He was big and his hair had a nice curl to it, his rimless glasses making his blue eyes look almost luminous. The dimple in his chin didn't hurt either.

I left the bathroom, moving toward the kitchenette in my bare feet. "Want a beer?"

He was sitting on the couch by then, leafing through a book about auto theft. "Very literate taste," he said. "Why don't you let me buy you a drink?"

"I have to be somewhere at six," I said.

"Beer's fine then."

I uncapped it and handed it to him, sitting down at the other end of the couch with my feet tucked up under me. "You must have left the office early. I'm flattered."

"I'll go back tonight. I have to go out of town for a couple of days and I'll have to get my briefcase packed, tidy up some loose ends for Ruth."

"Why take time out for me?"

Scorsoni gave me a quizzical smile with the barest hint of irritation. "God, so defensive. Why not take time out for you? If Nikki didn't kill Laurence, I'm as interested as anyone in finding out who did it, that's all."

"You don't believe she's innocent for a minute," I said.

"I believe you believe it," he said.

I looked at him carefully. "I can't give you information. I hope you understand that. I could use any help you've got and if you have a brainstorm, I'd love to hear it, but it can't be a two-way street."

"You want to lecture an attorney about client privilege, is that it? Jesus Christ, Millhone. Give me a break."

"Okay, okay. I'm sorry," I said. I looked down at his big hands and then up at his face again. "I just didn't want my brain picked, that's all."

His expression relaxed and his smile was lazy. "You said you didn't know anything anyway," he pointed out, "so what's to pick? You're such a goddamn *grouch*."

I smiled then. "Listen, I don't know what my chances are on this thing. I don't have a feel for it yet and it's making me nervous."

"Yeah and you've been working on it—what—two days?"

"About that."

"Then give yourself a break while you're at it." He took a sip of beer and then with a small tap set the bottle on the coffee table. "I wasn't very honest with you yesterday," he said.

"About what?"

"Libby Glass. I did know who she was and I suspected that he was into some kind of relationship with her. I just didn't think it was any of your business."

"I don't see how it could make any difference at this point," I said.

"That's what I decided. And maybe it's important to your case—who knows? I think since he died, I've tended to invest him with a purity he never really had. He played around a lot. But his taste usually ran to the moneyed class. Older women. Those slim elegant ones who marry aristocracy."

"What was Libby like?"

"I don't really know. I ran into her a couple of times when she was setting up our tax account. She seemed nice enough. Young. She couldn't have been more than twenty-five or twenty-six."

"Did he tell you he was having an affair with her?"

"Oh no, not him. I never knew him to kiss and tell."

"A real gentleman," I said.

Scorsoni shot me a warning look.

"I'm not being facetious," I said hastily. "I've heard he kept his mouth shut about the women in his life. That's all I meant."

"Yeah, he did. He played everything close to his chest.

That's what made him a good attorney too. He never tipped his hand, never telegraphed. The last six months before he died, he was odd though, protective. There were times when I almost thought he wasn't well, but it wasn't physical. It was some kind of psychic pain, if you'll excuse the phrase."

"You had drinks with him that night, didn't you?"

"We had dinner. Down at the Bistro. Nikki was off someplace and we played racquetball and then had a bite to eat. He was fine as far as I could tell."

"Did he have the allergy medication with him then?"

Scorsoni shook his head. "He wasn't much for pills anyway. Tylenol if he had a headache, but that was rare. Even Nikki admitted that he took the allergy cap after he got home. It had to be someone who had access to that."

"Had Libby Glass been up here?"

"Not for business as far as I know. She might have come up to see him but he never said anything to me. Why?"

"I don't know. I was just thinking that somebody might have dosed them both somehow at the same time. She didn't die until four days later but that's not hard to explain if the caps were self-administered."

"I never heard much about her death. I don't even think it hit the papers here. He was down in Los Angeles though, I do know that. About a week and a half before he died."

"That's interesting. I'm going down there anyway. Maybe I can check that out."

He glanced at his watch. "I better let you go," he said, getting up. I got up and ambled to the door with him, oddly reluctant to see him go.

"How'd you lose the weight?" I said.

"What, this?" he asked, slapping his midsection. He leaned toward me slightly as though he meant to confide some incredible regimen of denial and self-abuse.

"I gave up candy bars. I used to keep 'em in my desk drawer," he murmured conspiratorially. "Snickers and Three Musketeers, Hershey's Kisses, with the silver wrappers and the little paper wick at the top? A hundred a day . . ."

I could feel a laugh bubble up because his tone was caressing and he sounded like he was confessing to a secret addiction to wearing panty hose. Also because I knew if I turned my face, I'd be closer to him than I thought I could cope with at that point.

"Mars Bars? Baby Ruths?" I said.

"All the time," he said. I could almost feel the heat of his face and I slid a look up at him sideways. He laughed at himself then, breaking the spell, and his eyes held mine only a little longer than they should. "I'll see you," he said.

We shook hands as he left. I didn't know why—maybe just an excuse to touch. Even a contact that casual made the hairs stand up along my arm. My early-warning system was clanging away like crazy and I wasn't sure how to interpret it. It's the same sensation I have sometimes on the twenty-first floor when I open a window—a terrible attraction to the notion of tumbling out. I go a long time between men and maybe it was time again. Not good, I thought, not good.

8

When I pulled up in front of K-9 Korners at 6:00, Gwen was just locking up. I rolled down my car window and leaned across the seat. "You want to go in my car?"

"I better follow you," she said. "Do you know where the Palm Garden is? Is that all right with you?"

"Sure, that's fine."

She moved off toward the parking lot and a minute later she pulled out of the driveway in a bright yellow Saab. The restaurant was only a few blocks away and we pulled into the parking lot side by side. She had stripped off her smock and was brushing haphazardly at the lap of her skirt.

"Pardon the dog hair," she said. "Usually I head straight for a bath."

The Palm Garden is located in the heart of Santa Teresa, tucked back into a shopping complex, with tables outside and the requisite palms in big wooden tubs. We found a small table off to one side and I ordered white wine while she ordered Perrier.

"You don't drink?"

"Not much. I gave that up when I got divorced. Before that I was knocking back a *lot* of Scotch. How's your case?"

"It's hard to tell at this point," I said. "How long have you been in the dog-grooming business?"

"Longer than I'd like," she said and laughed.

We talked for a while about nothing in particular. I wanted time to study her, hoping to figure out what she and Nikki Fife had in common that both of them had ended up married to him. It was she who brought the conversation back around to the subject at hand. "So fire away," she said.

I curtsied mentally. She was very deft, making my job much easier than I'd thought she would. "I didn't think you'd be so cooperative."

"You've been talking to Charlie Scorsoni," she said.

"It seemed like a logical place to start," I said with a shrug. "Is he on your list?"

"Of people who might have killed Laurence? No. I don't think so. Am I on his?"

I shook my head.

"That's odd," she said.

"How so?"

She tilted her head, her expression composed. "He thinks I'm bitter. I've heard it from a lot of different sources. Small town. If you wait long enough, anyone's opinion about you will be reported back."

"It sounds like you'd be entitled to a little bitterness."

"I worked that through a long time ago. By the way, this is where you can reach Greg and Diane if you're interested." She pulled an index card out of her purse with the two names, addresses, and telephone numbers.

"Thanks. I appreciate that. Any advice about how they should be approached? I was serious when I said I didn't want to upset them."

"No, no. They're straight shooters, both of them. If anything, you might find them a little *too* up front."

"I understand they haven't kept in touch with Nikkie."

"Probably not, but that's too bad. Old business. I'd much rather see them let that go. She was very good to them." She reached back then and pulled the scarf out of her hair, shaking her hair slightly so that it would fall loose. It was shoulder-length, an interesting shade of gray that I didn't imagine had been tampered with. The contrast was nice . . . gray hair, brown eyes. She had strong cheekbones, nice lines around her mouth, good teeth, a tan that suggested health without vanity.

"What did you think of Nikki?" I asked, now that the subject had been broached.

"I'm not really sure. I mean, I resented the hell out of her back then but I'd like to talk to her sometime. I feel like we might understand each other a lot better. You want to know why I married him?"

"I'd be interested in that."

"He had a big cock," she said impishly and then laughed. "Sorry. I couldn't resist that. Actually he was awful in the sack. A regular screwing machine. Terrific if you like your sex depersonalized."

"I'm not crazy about that kind myself," I said dryly.

"Neither was I when I figured it out. I was a virgin when I married him."

"Jesus," I said. "That's a bore."

"It was an even bigger bore back then but it was all part of the message I was raised on. I always thought the failure was mine in terms of our sex life . . ." She trailed off and the faintest tint came to her cheeks.

"Until what," I ventured.

"Maybe I should have wine too," she said and signaled to the waitress. I ordered a second glass. Gwen turned to me.

"I had an affair when I turned thirty."

"Shows you had *some* sense."

"Well yes and no. It only lasted about six weeks but it was the best six weeks of my life. In a way, I was glad to see it end. It was powerful stuff and it would have turned my life around. I wasn't ready for that." She paused and I could see her reviewing the information in her head. "Laurence was always very critical of me and I believed I deserved it. Then I ran into a man who thought I could do no wrong. At first I resisted. I knew what I was feeling for this man but it went against the grain. Finally I just gave in. For a while I told myself it was good for my relationship with Laurence. I was suddenly getting something I'd needed for a long time and it made me feel very giving with him. And then the double life began to take its toll. I deceived Laurence for as long as I could but he began to suspect something was going on. I got so I couldn't tolerate his touch—too much tension, too much deceit. Too much good stuff somewhere else. He must have felt the change come over me because he began to probe and question, wanted to know where I was every minute of the day. Called at odd hours in the afternoon and of course I was out. Even when I was with Laurence, I was somewhere else. He threatened me with divorce and I got scared so I 'fessed up. That was the biggest mistake of my life because he divorced me anyway."

"As punishment."

"As only Laurence Fife knew how. In spades."

"Where is he now?"

"My lover? Why do you ask?"

Her tone was instantly guarded, her expression wary.

"Laurence must have known who he was. If he was punishing you, why not punish the other guy too?"

"I don't want to cast suspicion on him," she said. "That would be a lousy thing to do. He had nothing to do with Laurence's death. I'll give you a written guarantee."

"What makes you so sure? A lot of people were mistaken about a lot of things back then and Nikki paid a price for it."

"Hey," she said sharply, "Nikki was represented by the best lawyer in the state. Maybe she got a few bad breaks and maybe not, but there's no point in trying to lay the blame on someone who had nothing to do with it."

"I'm not trying to blame anyone. I'm just trying to come up with a direction on this thing. I can't force you to tell me who he is . . ."

"That's right and I think you'd have a hell of a time finding out from anyone else."

"Look, I'm not here to pick a fight. I'm sorry. Skip that for now."

Two patches of red appeared on her neck. She was fighting back anger, trying to get control of herself again. I thought, for a moment, she would bolt.

"I'm not going to press the point," I said. "That's a whole separate issue and I came here to talk to you. You don't want to talk about that then it's fine with me."

She still seemed poised for flight so I shut my mouth and let her work it out for herself. Finally I could see her relax a little and I realized then that I was as tense as she. This was too valuable a contact for me to blow.

"Let's go back to Laurence. Tell me about him," I said. "What were all the infidelities about?"

She laughed self-consciously then and took a sip of wine, shaking her head. "Sorry. I didn't mean to get upset but you took me by surprise."

"Yeah, well that happens now and then. Sometimes I surprise myself."

"I don't think he liked women. He was always expecting to be betrayed. Women were the people who did you in. He liked to get there first, or at least that's my guess. I suspect an affair for him was always a power relationship and he was top dog."

" 'Do unto others before they do unto you.' "

"Right."

"But who had an ax to grind with him? Who could have hated him that much?"

She shrugged and her composure seemed restored. "I've thought about that all afternoon and what's odd is that when it comes right down to it, I'm not sure. He had awful relationships with a lot of people. Divorce attorneys are never very popular, but most of them don't get murdered."

"Maybe it wasn't related to business," I suggested. "Maybe it wasn't an irate husband pissed off about alimony and child support. Maybe it was something else—'a woman scorned.' "

"Well there were a lot of those. But I think he was probably very slick about breaking things off. Or the women themselves were sufficiently recovered to recognize the limits of the relationship and move on. He did have an awful affair with the wife of a local judge, a woman named Charlotte Mercer. She'd have run him down in the street given half a chance. Or that's what I've heard since. She wasn't the type to let go gracefully."

"How'd you find out about it?"

"She called me up after he broke off with her."

"Before your divorce or afterwards?"

"Oh afterwards, because I remember thinking at the time that I wished she'd called sooner. I went into court with nothing."

"I don't understand," I said. "What good would it have done? You couldn't have gotten him on adultery even back then."

"He didn't get *me* on that either but it sure would have given me a psychological edge. I felt so guilty about what I'd done that I hardly put up a fight except when it came to the kids, and even then he beat me down. If she'd wanted to cause trouble, she could have been a big help. He still had his reputation to protect. Anyway, maybe Charlotte Mercer can fill you in."

"Wonderful. I'll tell her she's my number-one suspect."

Gwen laughed. "Feel free to mention my name if she wants to know who sent you. It's the least I can do."

After Gwen left, I looked up Charlotte Mercer's address in the telephone book by the pay phone in the rear. She and the judge lived up in the foothills above Santa Teresa in what turned out to be a sprawling one-story house with stables off to the right, the land all dust and scrub brush. The sun was just beginning to go down and the view was spectacular. The ocean looked like a wide lavender ribbon stitched up against a pink-and-blue sky.

A housekeeper in a black uniform answered the bell and I was left in a wide cool hallway while "the missus" was fetched. Light footsteps approached from the rear of the house and I thought at first the Mercers' teenage daughter (if there was one) had appeared in Charlotte's place.

"Yes, what is it?"

The voice was low and husky and rude and the initial impression of adolescence gave way rapidly.

"Charlotte Mercer?"

"Yes, that's right."

She was petite, probably five-four, maybe a hundred pounds if that. Sandals, tank top, white shorts, her legs tawny and shapely. Not a line on her face. Her hair was a dusty blond, cut short, her makeup subdued. She had to be fifty-five years old and there was no way she could have looked that good without a team of experts. There was an artificial firmness to her jaw and her cheeks had that sleek tucked-up look that only a face-lift can provide at that late date. Her neck was lined and the backs of her hands were knotted with veins but those were the only contradictions to the appearance of slim, cool youth. Her eyes were a pale blue, made vivid by the skillful application of mascara and an eye shadow in two shades of gray. Gold bracelets jangled on one arm.

"I'm Kinsey Millhone," I said. "I'm a private investigator."

"Goody for you. What brings you here?"

"I'm looking into Laurence Fife's death."

Her smile faltered, sinking from minimal good manners into something cruel. She gave me a cursory inspection, dismissing me in the same glance. "I hope it won't take long," she said, and looked back. "Come out to the patio. I've left my drink there."

I followed her toward the back of the house. The rooms we passed looked spacious and elegant and unused: windows sparkling, the thick powder-blue carpeting still furrowed with vacuum-cleaner tracks, fresh-cut flowers in professional arrangements on glossy tabletops. The wallpaper and drapes were endless repetitions of the same blue floral print and everything smelled of Lemon Pledge. I wondered if she used it to disguise the mild scent of bourbon on the rocks that wafted after her. As we passed the kitchen, I could smell roast lamb laced with garlic.

The patio was shaded by latticework. The furniture was white wicker with bright green canvas cushions. She took up her drink from a coffee table of glass and wrought iron, plunking herself down on a padded chaise. She reached automatically for her cigarettes and a slim gold Dunhill. She seemed amused, as though I'd arrived solely to entertain her during the cocktail hour.

"Who sent you up here? Nikki or little Gwen?" Her eyes slid away from mine and she seemed to require no response. She lit her cigarette, pulling the half-filled ashtray closer. She waved a hand at me. "Have a seat."

I chose a padded chair not far from hers. An egg-shaped swimming pool was visible beyond the shrubs surrounding the patio. Charlotte caught my look.

"You want to stop and have a swim or what?"

I decided not to take offense. I had the feeling that sarcasm came easily to her, an automatic reaction, like someone with a smoker's cough.

"So who sent you up here?" she said, repeating herself. It was the second hint I had that she wasn't as sober as she should have been, even at that hour of the day.

"Word gets around."

"Oh, I'll bet it does," she said with a snort of smoke. "Well, I'll tell you this, sweetie pie. I was more than a piece of ass to that man. I wasn't the first and I wasn't the last but I was the fucking *best*."

"Is that why he broke it off?"

"Don't be a bitch," she said with a quick sharp look, but she laughed at the same time, low in her throat, and I suspected I might have gone up in her estimation. She apparently played fast and loose and didn't object to a cut now and then in the interest of a fair game. "Sure he broke it off. Why should I have secrets these days? I had a little wingding with him before he divorced Gwen and then he came back around a few months before he died. He was like some old tomcat, always sniffin' around the same back porch."

"What happened this last time?"

She gave me a jaded look as if none of it seemed to matter much. "He got involved with somebody else. Very hush-hush. Very hot. Screw him. He discarded me like yesterday's underpants."

"I'm surprised you weren't a suspect," I said.

Her brows shot up. "Me?" She hooted. "The wife of a prominent judge? I never even testified and they knew damn well that I was involved with him. The cops tiptoed around me like I was a fussy baby taking an unexpected nap. And who asked 'em to? I would have told 'em anything. Hell, I didn't give a shit. Besides, they already had their suspect."

"Nikki?"

"Sure, Nikki," she said expansively. Her gestures were relaxed, the hand with the cigarette waving languidly as she spoke. "You ask me, she was way too prissy to kill anyone. Not that anyone cared much what I thought. I'm just your Mrs. Loud-Mouth Drunk. What does she know? Who's going to listen to her? I could tell you things about anybody in this town and who'd pay attention to me? And you know how I find out? I'll tell you this. You'll be interested in this because that's what you do, too, find out about people, right?"

"More or less," I murmured, trying not to interrupt the flow. Charlotte Mercer was the type who'd barge right on if she didn't get sidetracked. She took a long drag on her cigarette, blowing smoke through her nose in two fierce streams. She coughed, shaking her head.

"Pardon me while I choke to death," she said, pausing to cough again. "You tell secrets," she went on, taking up from where she left off. "You tell the dirtiest damn thing you know and nine times out of ten, you'll net yourself something worse. You can try it yourself. I say anything. I tell stories on myself just to see what I get back. You want gossip, honey, you came to the right place."

"What's the word out on Gwen?" I asked, testing the waters.

Charlotte laughed. "You don't trade," she said. "You got nothing to swap."

"Well no, that's true. I wouldn't be in business long if I didn't keep my mouth shut."

She laughed again. She seemed to like that. My guess about her was that it made her feel important to know what she knew. I was hoping she liked to show off a little bit too. She might well have heard about Gwen's affair but I couldn't ask without tipping my hand so I just waited her out, hoping to pick up what I could.

"Gwen was the biggest chump who ever lived," she said without much interest. "I don't like the type myself and I don't know how she held on to him as long as she did. Laurence Fife was one cold cookie, which was why I was so crazy about him if you haven't guessed. I can't stand a man who *fawns*, you know what I mean? I can't stand a man sucking up to me, but he was the kind who took you right on the floor and he didn't even look at you afterwards when he zipped up his pants."

"That sounds crude enough," I said.

"*Sex* is crude, which is why we all run around doing it, which is why I was such a good match for him. He was crude as he was mean and that's the truth about him. Nikki was too refined, too lah-de-dah. So was Gwen."

"So maybe he liked both extremes," I suggested.

"Well now, I don't doubt that. Probably so. Maybe he married the snooty ones and fooled around with flash."

"What about Libby Glass? Did you ever hear about her?"

"Nope. No dice. Who else?"

God, this woman made me wish I had a list. I thought fast, trying to milk her while she was in the mood. I had the feeling the moment would pass and she'd turn sullen again.

"Sharon Napier," I said, as though it were a parlor game.

"Oh yeah. I checked that one out myself. The first time I ever laid eyes on that little snake, I knew something was off."

"You think he was involved with her?"

"Oh no, it's better yet. Not her. Her *mother*. I hired a private dick to look that up. Ruined her life and Sharon knew about it, too, so up she pops years later and sticks it to him. Her parents broke up over him and Mommy had a nervous breakdown or turned to drink, some damn thing. I don't know all the details except he fucked everyone over but good and Sharon collected on that for *years*."

"Was she *blackmailing* him?"

"Not for bucks. For her livelihood. She couldn't *type*. She barely knew how to spell her own name. She just wanted revenge, so she shows up every day for work and she does what she feels like doing and thumbs her nose at him. He took anything she dished out."

"Could she have killed him?"

"Sure, why not? Maybe the gig wore thin or maybe just taking his pay from week to week wasn't good enough." She paused, pushing the ember out on her cigarette with a number of ineffectual stabs. She smiled over at me with cunning.

"I hope you don't think I'm rude," she said with a glance at the door. "But school's out. My esteemed husband, the good judge, is due home any second now and I don't want to sit and explain what you're doing in my house."

"Fair enough," I said. "I'll let myself out. You've been a big help."

"I'll bet." She got to her feet, setting her drink down on the glass-topped table with a resounding crack. There was no harm done and she recovered herself with a long slow look of relief.

She studied my face briefly. "You're gonna have to get your eyes done in a couple of years. Right now, you're okay," she pronounced.

I laughed. "I like lines," I said. "I earn mine. But thanks anyway."

I left her on the patio and went around the side of the house to where my car was parked. The conversation wasn't sitting that well with me and I was glad to be on my way. Charlotte Mercer was shrewd and perhaps not above using her drunkenness for its effect. Maybe she'd been telling the truth and maybe not. Somehow the revelation about Sharon Napier seemed too pat. As a solution, it seemed too obvious. On the other hand, the cops are sometimes right. Homicide usually isn't subtle and most of the time, you don't have that far to look.

9

It took me a day and a half to come up with an address on Sharon Napier. By means I'd just as soon not spell out, I tapped into the Department of Motor Vehicles computer and discovered that her driver's license had expired some six years back. I checked with the Auto Title Department, making a quick trip downtown, and found that a dark green Karmann Ghia was registered in her name with an address that matched the last-known address I had for her locally, but a side note indicated that the title had been transferred to Nevada, which probably meant that she'd left the state.

I placed a call to Bob Dietz, a Nevada investigator whose name I looked up in the National Directory. I told him what information I needed, and he said he'd call me back, which he did that afternoon. Sharon Napier had applied for and had been issued a Nevada driver's license; it showed a Reno address. His Reno sources, however, reported that she'd skipped out on a big string of creditors the previous March, which meant that she'd been gone for approximately fourteen months. He'd guessed that she was probably still in the state so he'd done some further nosing around. A small Reno credit company showed requests for information on her from Carson City and again from Las Vegas, which he thought was my best bet. I thanked him profusely for his efficiency and told him to bill me for his time but he said he'd just as soon trade tit for tat at some point, so I made sure he had my address and home phone if he needed it. I tried Information in Las Vegas, but there was no listing for her so I called a friend of mine down there and he said he'd check around. I told him I'd be driving to Los Angeles early in the week and gave him the number so he could reach me there in case it took him a while to pick up a lead on her.

The next day was Sunday and I devoted that to myself:

laundry, housecleaning, grocery shopping. I even shaved my legs just to show I still had some class. Monday morning I did clerical work. I typed up a report for Nikki and put in another call to the local credit bureau just to double-check. Sharon Napier had apparently left town with a lot of money owed and a lot of people mad. They had no forwarding address so I gave them the information I had. Then I had a long talk with California Fidelity on the subject of Marcia Threadgill. For forty-eight hundred dollars, the insurance company was almost ready to settle with her and move on, and I had to argue with as much cunning as I could muster. My services on that one weren't costing them anything out of pocket and it pissed me off that they were halfway inclined to look the other way. I even had to stoop so low as to mention principles, which never sits that well with the claims manager. "She's cheating your *ass*," I kept saying, but he just shook his head as though there were forces at work that I was too dim to grasp. I told him to check with his boss and I'd get back to him.

By 2:00, I was on the road to Los Angeles. The other piece of the puzzle was Libby Glass and I needed to know how she fit into all of this. When I reached L.A., I checked into the Hacienda Motor Lodge on Wilshire, near Bundy. The Hacienda is not even remotely hacienda-like—an L-shaped, two-story structure with a cramped parking lot and a swimming pool surrounded by a chain-link fence with a padlock. A very fat woman named Arlette doubles as manager and switchboard operator. I could see straight into her apartment from the desk. It's furnished, I'm told, from her profits as a Tupperware lady, a little hustling she does on the side. She leans toward Mediterranean-style furniture upholstered in red plush.

"Fat is beautiful, Kinsey," she said to me confidentially as I filled out the registration card. "Looka here."

I looked. She was holding out her arm so that I could admire the hefty downhang of excess flesh.

"I don't know, Arlette," I said dubiously. "I keep trying to avoid it myself."

"And look at all the time and energy it takes," she said. "The problem is that our society shuns tubbos. Fat people are heavily discriminated against. Worse than the handicapped. Why, they got it easy compared to us. Everywhere you go now,

there are signs out for them. Handicapped parking. Handicapped johns. You've seen those little stick figures in wheel-
chairs. Show me the international sign for the grossly
overweight. We got rights."

Her face was moon-shaped, surrounded by a girlish cap of
wispy blonde hair. Her cheeks were permanently flushed as
though vital supply lines were being dangerously squeezed.

"But it's so unhealthy, Arlette," I said. "I mean, don't you
have to worry about high blood pressure, heart attacks . . ."

"Well there's hazards to everything. All the more reason
we should be treated decently."

I gave her my credit card and after she made the imprint
she handed me the key to room #2. "That's right up here
close," she said. "I know how you hate being stuck out
back."

"Thanks."

I've been in room #2 about twenty times and it is always
dreary in a comforting sort of way. A double bed. Threadbare
wall-to-wall carpeting in a squirrel gray. A chair upholstered in
orange plastic with one gimpy leg. On the desk, there is a lamp
shaped like a football helmet with "UCLA" printed on the
side. The bathroom is small and the shower mat is paper. It is
the sort of place where you are likely to find someone else's
underpanties beneath the bed. It costs me $11.95 plus room tax
in the off-season and includes a "Continental" breakfast—
instant coffee and jelly doughnuts, most of which Arlette eats
herself. Once, at midnight, a drunk sat on my front step and
yelled for an hour and a half until the cops came and took him
away. I stay there because I'm cheap.

I set my suitcase on the bed and took out my jogging
clothes. I did a fast walk from Wilshire to San Vicente and then
headed west at a trot as far as Twenty-sixth Street, where I
tagged a stop sign and turned around, jogging back up to
Westgate and across to Wilshire again. The first mile is the one
that hurts. I was panting hard when I got back. Given the
exhaust fumes I'd taken in from passing motorists on San
Vicente, I figured I was about neck-and-neck with toxic
wastes. Back in room #2 again, I showered and dressed and
then checked back through my notes. Then I made some phone

calls. The first was to Lyle Abernathy's last-known work address, the Wonder Bread Company, down on Santa Monica. Not surprisingly, he had left and the personnel office had no idea where he was. A quick check in the phone book showed no listing for him locally, but a Raymond Glass still lived in Sherman Oaks and I verified the street number I had noted from the police files up in Santa Teresa. I placed another call to my friend in Vegas. He had a lead on Sharon Napier but said it would take him probably half a day to pin it down. I alerted Arlette that he might be calling and cautioned her to make sure the information, if she took it, was exact. She acted a little injured that I didn't trust her to take phone messages for me, but she'd been negligent before and it had cost me plenty last time around.

I called Nikki in Santa Teresa and told her where I was and what I was up to. Then I checked my answering service. Charlie Scorsoni had called but left no number. I figured if it was important he'd call back. I gave my service the number where I could be reached. Having tagged all those bases, I went next door to a restaurant that seems to change nationalities every time I'm there. Last time I was in town, it was Mexican fare, which is to say very hot plates of pale brown goo. This time it was Greek: turdlike lumps wrapped in leaves. I'd seen things in roadside parks that looked about that good but I washed them down with a glass of wine that tasted like lighter fluid and who knew the difference? It was now 7:15 and I didn't have anything to do. The television set in my room was on the fritz so I wandered down to the office and watched TV with Arlette while she ate a box of caramel Ayds.

In the morning, I drove over the mountain into the San Fernando Valley. At the crest of the hill, where the San Diego Freeway tips over into Sherman Oaks, I could see a layer of smog spread out like a mirage, a shimmering mist of pale yellow smoke through which a few tall buildings yearned as though for fresh air. Libby's parents lived in a four-unit apartment building set into the crook of the San Diego and Ventura freeways, a cumbersome structure of stucco and frame with bay windows bulging out along the front. There was an open corridor dividing the building in half, with the front doors

to the two downstairs apartments opening up just inside. On
the right, a stairway led to the second-floor landing. The
building itself affected no particular style and I guessed that it
had gone up in the thirties before anybody figured out that
California architecture should imitate southern mansions and
Italian villas. There was a pale lawn of crab and Bermuda
grasses intermixed. A short driveway along the left extended
back to a row of frame garages, with four green plastic garbage
cans chained to a wooden fence. The juniper bushes growing
along the front of the building were tall enough to obscure the
ground-floor windows and seemed to be suffering from some
peculiar molting process that made some of the branches turn
brown and the rest go bald. They looked like cut-rate
Christmas trees with the bad side facing out. The season to be
jolly, in this neighborhood, was long past.

Apartment #1 was on my left. When I rang the bell, it
sounded like the br-r-r-r of an alarm clock running down. The
door was opened by a woman with a row of pins in her mouth
that bobbed up and down when she spoke. I worried she would
swallow one.

"Yes?"

"Mrs. Glass?"

"That's right."

"My name is Kinsey Millhone. I'm a private investigator. I
work up in Santa Teresa. Could I talk to you?"

She took the pins out of her mouth one by one and stuck
them into a pin cushion that she wore on her wrist like a
bristling corsage. I handed her my identification and she
studied it with care, turning it over as though there might be
tricky messages written in fine print on the back. While she did
that, I studied her. She was in her early fifties. Her silky brown
hair was cut short, a careless style with strands anchored
behind her ears. Brown eyes, no makeup, bare-legged. She
wore a wraparound denim skirt, a washed-out Madras blouse
in bleeding shades of blue, and the kind of cotton slippers I've
seen in cellophane packs in grocery stores.

"It's about Elizabeth," she said, finally returning my I.D.

"Yes. It is."

She hesitated and then moved back into the living room,

making way for me. I picked my way across the living-room floor and took the one chair that wasn't covered with lengths of fabric or patterns. The ironing board was set up near the bay window, the iron plugged in a ticking as it heated. There were finished garments hanging on a rack near the sewing machine on the far wall. The air smelled of fabric sizing and hot metal.

In the archway to the dining room, a heavyset man in his sixties sat in a wheelchair, his expression blank, his pants undone in front, heavy paunch protruding. She crossed the room and turned his chair around so that it faced the television set. She put headphones on him and then plugged the jack into the TV, which she flipped on. He watched a game show whether he liked it or not. A couple were dressed up like a boy and girl chicken but I couldn't tell if they were winning anything.

"I'm Grace," she said. "That's her father. He was in an automobile accident three years ago last spring. He doesn't talk but he can hear and any mention of Elizabeth upsets him. Help yourself to coffee if you like."

There was a ceramic percolator on the coffee table, plugged into an extension cord that ran back under the couch. It looked as if all the other appliances in the room were radiating from the same power source. Grace eased down onto her knees. She had about four yards of dark green silk spread out on the hardwood floor and she was pinning a handmade pattern into place. She held a magazine out to me, opened to a page that showed a designer dress with a deep slit up one side and narrow sleeves. I poured myself a cup of coffee and watched her work.

"I'm running this up for a woman married to a television star," she said mildly. "Somebody's sidekick. He got famous overnight and she says he's recognized even in the car wash now. People asking for his autograph. Has facials. Him, not her. He was poor, I hear, for the last fifteen years and now they go to all these parties in Bel Air. I do her clothes. He buys his on Rodeo Drive. She could, too, on the money he makes but it makes her feel insecure, she says. She's much nicer than he is. I already read in the *Hollywood Reporter*, 'New Two You,' him and somebody else 'pulling up steaks at Stellini's.' She'd be smart to put an expensive wardrobe together before he leaves her if you ask me."

Grace seemed to be talking to herself, her tone distracted, a smile warming her face now and then. She picked up a pair of pinking shears and began to cut along the straight edge, the scissors making a crunching sound against the wood floor. For a while I didn't say anything. There was something hypnotic about the work and there seemed to be no compulsion to converse. The television flickered, and from an angle I could see the girl chicken jumping up and down, hands to her face. I knew the audience was urging her to do something—choose, pass, change boxes, take what was behind the curtain, give back the envelope, all of it taking place in silence while Libby's father looked on from his wheelchair incuriously. I thought she should consult her boy-chicken mate but he just stood there self-consciously like a kid who knew he was too old to be out in costume on Halloween. The tissue-paper pattern rustled as Grace removed it, folding it carefully before she laid it aside.

"I sewed for Elizabeth when she was young," she said. "Once she left home, of course, she only wanted store-bought. Sixty dollars for a skirt that only had twelve dollars' worth of wool at most, but she did have a good eye for color and she could afford to do as she pleased. Would you like to see a picture of her?" Grace's eyes strayed up to mine and her smile was wistful.

"Yes. I'd appreciate that."

She took the silk first and placed it on the ironing board, testing the iron with a wet index finger as she passed. The iron spat back and she turned the lever down to "wool." There were two snapshots of Libby in a double frame on the windowsill and she studied them herself before she handed them to me. In one, Libby was facing the camera but her head was bent, her right hand upraised as though she were hiding her face. Her blonde hair was sun-streaked, cut short like her mother's but feathered back across her ears. Her blue eyes were amused, her grin wide, embarrassed to be caught, I couldn't think why. I'd never seen a twenty-four-year-old look quite so young or quite so fresh. In the second snapshot, the smile was only partially formed, lips parted over a flash of white teeth, a dimple showing near the corner of her mouth. Her complexion was clear, tinted with gold, lashes dark so that her eyes were delicately outlined.

"She's lovely," I said. "Really."

Grace was standing at the ironing board, touching up folds of silk with the tip of the iron, which sailed across the asbestos board like a boat on a flat sea of dark green. She turned the iron off and wiped her hands briefly down along her skirt, then took the pieces of silk and began to pin them together.

"I named her after Queen Elizabeth," she said and then she laughed shyly. "She was born on November 14, the same day Prince Charles was born. I'd have named her Charles if she'd been a boy. Raymond thought it was silly but I didn't care."

"You never called her Libby?"

"Oh no. She did that herself in grade school. She always had such a sense of who she was and how her life should be. Even as a child. She was very tidy—not prissy, but neat. She would line her dresser drawers with pretty floral wrapping papers and everything would be arranged just so. She liked accounting for the same reason. Mathematics was orderly and if made sense. The answers were always there if you worked carefully enough, or that's what she said." Grace moved over to the rocking chair and sat down, laying the silk across her lap. She began to baste darts.

"I understand she worked as an accountant for Haycraft and McNiece. How long was she there?"

"About a year and a half. She had done the accounts for her father's company—he did small-appliance repair—but it really didn't interest her, working for him. She was ambitious. She passed her CPA exam when she was twenty-two. She took a couple of computer courses, too, in night school, after that. She made very good grades. She had two junior accountants working under her, you know."

"Was she happy there?"

"I'm sure she was," Grace said. "She spoke of going to law school at one point. She enjoyed business management and finance. She liked working with figures and I know she was impressed because that company represented very wealthy people. She said you could learn a lot about someone's character by the way they spent money, what they bought and where—whether they lived within their means, that kind of thing. She said it was a study of human nature." Grace's voice was tinged with pride. It was hard for me to reconcile the idea of this prim-sounding CPA with the girl in the photographs who looked pretty, animated, bashful, and rather sweet, hardly a woman with a hard-driving purpose in life.

"What about her old boyfriend? Do you have any idea where he is now?"

"Who, Lyle? Oh, he'll be around in a bit."

"Here?"

"Oh my, yes. He stops by every day at noon to help me with Raymond. He's a lovely boy but of course you probably knew she broke off her engagement with him a few months before . . . she passed on. She went with Lyle all through high school and they both attended Santa Monica City College together until he dropped out."

"Is that when he went to work for Wonder Bread?"

"Oh no, Lyle's had many jobs. At the time Lyle left school, Elizabeth was in her own apartment and she didn't confide much in me but I feel she was disappointed in him. He was going to be a lawyer and then he simply changed his mind. He said law was too dull and he didn't like details."

"Did they live together?"

Grace's cheeks tinted slightly. "No, they didn't. It may sound odd and Raymond thought it was very wrong of me, but I encouraged them to move in together. I sensed that they were drifting apart and I thought it would help. Raymond was like Elizabeth, disenchanted with Lyle for quitting school. He told her she could do much better for herself. But Lyle adored her. I thought that should count for something. He would have found himself. He had a restless nature, like many boys that age. He would have come to his senses and I told her so. He needed responsibility. She could have been a very good influence because she was so responsible herself. But Elizabeth said she didn't want to live with him and that was that. She was strong-willed when she wanted to be. And I don't mean that as criticism. She was as nearly perfect as a daughter could be. Naturally I wanted whatever she wanted but I couldn't bear to see Lyle hurt. He's very dear. You'll see when you meet him."

"And you have no idea what actually caused the breakup between them? I mean, could she possibly have been involved with someone else?"

"You're talking about that attorney up in Santa Teresa," she said.

"It's his death I'm looking into," I said. "Did she ever talk to you about him?"

"I never knew anything about him until the police came down from Santa Teresa to talk to us. Elizabeth didn't like to confide her personal affairs, but I don't believe Elizabeth would fall in love with a married man," Grace said. She began to fuss with the silk, her manner agitated. She closed her eyes and then pressed a hand to her forehead as though checking to see if she'd contracted a sudden fever. "I'm sorry. Sometimes I forget. Sometimes I pretend she got sick. The other makes me cringe, that someone might have done that to her, that someone could have hated her that much. The police here don't do anything. It isn't solved but no one cares anymore so I just . . . I simply tell myself she got sick and was taken. How could someone have done that to her?" Her eyes welled with tears. Her grief rolled across the space between us like a wash of salt water and I could feel tears form in my own eyes in response. I reached out and took her hand. For a moment, she clutched my fingers hard and then she seemed to catch herself, pulling back.

"It's been like a weight pressing on my heart. I will never recover from it. Never."

I phrased my next question with care. "Could it have been an accident?" I said. "The other man—Laurence Fife—died from oleander, which someone put in an allergy capsule. Suppose they'd been doing business together, going over accounts or something. Maybe she was sneezing or complaining about a stuffy nose and he just volunteered his own medication. People do that all the time."

She considered that for a moment uneasily. "I thought the police said the attorney died before she did. Days before."

"Maybe she didn't take the pill right away," I said, shrugging. "With something like that, you never know when someone will take a doctored capsule. Maybe she put it in her purse and swallowed it later without even realizing there was any jeopardy. Did she have allergies? Could she have been coming down with a cold?"

Grace began to weep, a small mewing sound. "I don't remember. I don't think so. She didn't have hay fever or anything like that. I don't even know who'd remember after all these years."

Grace looked at me then with those large, dark eyes. She had a good face, almost childlike, with a small nose, a sweet mouth. She took out a Kleenex and wiped her cheeks. "I don't think I can talk about it anymore. Stay for lunch. Meet Lyle. Maybe he can tell you something that would help."

10

I sat on a stool in the kitchen and watched Grace make tuna fish salad for lunch. She had seemed to shake herself, as though wakening from a brief but vital nap and then she had put on her apron and cleared the dining-room table of the rest of her sewing paraphernalia. She was a woman who worked with care, her movements restful as she assembled placemats and napkins. I set the table for her, feeling like a well-behaved kid again while she rinsed lettuce and patted it dry, placing a layer on each plate like a doilie. She neatly pared thin ribbons of skin from several tomatoes and coiled them like roses. She fluted a mushroom for each plate, added two thin spikes of asparagus so that the whole of it looked like a flower arrangement. She smiled at me timidly, taking pleasure in the picture she had created. "Do you cook?"

I shook my head.

"I don't have much occasion to myself except when Lyle's here. Raymond wouldn't notice and I probably wouldn't bother at all if it were just for me." She lifted her head. "There."

I hadn't heard the truck pull into the driveway but she must have been tuned to Lyle's arrival. Her hand strayed unconsciously to a strand of hair, which she tucked back. He came in through a utility room off to the left, pausing around the corner, apparently to take off his boots. I heard two thunks. "Hey, babe. What's for lunch?"

He came around into the dining room with a grin, giving her cheek a noisy buss before he caught sight of me. He halted, the animation flickering off and on, then draining out of his face. He looked at her hesitantly.

"This is Miss Millhone," she said to him.

"Kinsey," I filled in, holding out my hand. He reached out and shook my hand automatically, but the central question still hadn't been answered. I suspected that I was intruding on an occasion that ordinarily admitted no variation. "I'm a private investigator from Santa Teresa," I said.

Lyle moved over to Raymond without another glance at me.

"Hey, Pops. How's it going today? You feeling okay?"

The old man's face registered nothing, but his eyes came into focus. Lyle took the headphones off, turning the set off too. The change in Lyle had been immediate and I felt as if I'd just seen snapshots of two different personalities in the same body, one joyful, the other keeping watch. He was not much taller than me and his body was trim, his shoulders wide. He had his shirt pulled out, unbuttoned down the front. His chest muscles were spare but well formed like those of a man who's been lifting weights. I guessed him to be about my own age. His hair was blond, worn long and faintly tinted with the green of a chlorinated swimming pool and hot sun. His eyes were a washed-out blue, too pale for his tan, his lashes bleached, his chin too narrow for the breadth of his cheeks. The overall effect was of a face oddly off—good looks gone slightly askew, as though under the surface there were a hairline crack. Some subterranean tremor had caused the bones to shift minutely and the two halves of his face seemed not quite to match. He wore faded jeans slung low on his hips and I could see the silky line of darkish hair pointing like an arrow toward his crotch.

He went about his business, ignoring me completely, talking to Grace while he worked. She handed him a towel, which he tucked under Raymond's chin, and then he proceeded to lather and shave him with a safety razor, which he rinsed in a stainless-steel bowl. Grace was taking out bottles of beer, removing the caps, pouring liquid into tulip glasses which she set at each place. There was no plate prepared for Raymond at all. When the shaving process had been completed, Lyle brushed Raymond's thinning white hair and then fed him a jar of baby food. Grace shot me a satisfied look. See what a dear he is? Lyle reminded me of an older brother caring for a toddler so that Mom would approve. She did. She looked on affectionately while Lyle scraped Raymond's chin with the bowl of the spoon, easing the drooling vegetable puree back into Raymond's slack mouth. Even as I watched, a stain began to spread across the front of Raymond's pants.

"Hey, don't worry about it, Pops," Lyle crooned, "we'll get you cleaned up after lunch. How's that?"

I could feel the muscles in my face setting with distaste.

During lunch, Lyle ate quickly, saying nothing to me and very little to Grace.

"What sort of work do you do, Lyle?" I said.

"Lay brick."

I looked at his hands. His fingers were long and dusted with mortar gray that had seeped down into the crevices of his skin. At this range, I could smell sweat, overlaid with the delicate scent of dope. I wondered if Grace noticed at all or if, perhaps, she thought it might be some exotic aftershave.

"I've got to make a run up to Vegas," I said to Grace, "but I'd like to stop back on my way up to Santa Teresa. Do you have any of Libby's belongings?" I was relatively certain she did.

Grace consulted Lyle with a quick look but his eyes were lowered to his plate. "I believe so. There are some boxes in the basement, aren't there, Lyle? Elizabeth's books and papers?"

The old man made a sound at the mention of her name and Lyle wiped his mouth, tossing the napkin down as he got up. He wheeled Raymond down the hallway.

"I'm sorry. I shouldn't have mentioned Libby," I said.

"Well that's all right," she said. "If you'll call or come by when you get back to Los Angeles, I'm sure it'd be all right if you looked at Elizabeth's belongings. There isn't much."

"Lyle doesn't seem to be in a very good mood," I remarked. "I hope he doesn't think I'm intruding."

"Oh no. He's quiet around people he doesn't know," she said. "I don't know what I'd do without him. Raymond is too heavy for me to lift. I have a neighbor who stops by twice a day to help me get him in and out of his chair. His spine was crushed in the accident."

Her conversational tone gave me the willies. "Do you mind if I use the bathroom?" I said.

"It's down the hall. The second door on the right."

As I passed the bedroom, I could see that Lyle had already lifted Raymond into bed. There were two straight-backed wooden chairs pushed up against the side of the double bed to keep him from falling out. Lyle was standing between the two chairs, cleaning Raymond's bare ass. I went into the bathroom and closed the door.

I helped Grace clear the table and then I left, waiting in my car across the street. I made no attempt to conceal myself and no pretense at driving away. I could see Lyle's pickup truck still parked in the driveway. I checked my watch. It was ten minutes to one and I figured he must be on a limited lunch hour. Sure enough, the side door opened and Lyle stepped out onto the narrow porch, pausing to lace his boots. He glanced over at the street, spotting my car, and seemed to smile to himself. Ass, I thought. He got into his truck and backed out of the driveway rapidly. I wondered for a moment if he intended to back straight across the street and into the side of my car, crushing me. He wheeled at the last minute, though, and flung the truck into gear, taking off with a chirp of rubber. I thought maybe we were going to have a little impromptu car chase but it turned out he didn't have that far to go. He drove eight blocks and then pulled into the driveway of a modest-sized Sherman Oaks house that was being refaced with red brick. I guessed it was a status symbol of some sort because brick is very expensive on the West Coast. There probably aren't six brick houses in the whole city of L.A.

He got out of his truck and ambled around to the back, tucking in his shirt, his manner insolent. I parked on the street and locked my car, following him. I wondered idly if he intended to smash my head in with a brick and then mortar me into a wall. He was not pleased with my arrival on the scene and he made no bones about that. As I rounded the corner, I could see that the owner of the house was disguising his little cottage with a whole new facade. Instead of looking like a modest California bungalow, it would look like certain pet hospitals in the Midwest, real high-rent stuff. Lyle was already mixing up mortar in a wheelbarrow in the back. I picked my way across some two-by-fours with crooked rusty nails protruding. A little kid would have to have a lot of tetanus shots after falling on those.

"Why don't we start all over again, Lyle," I said conversationally.

He snorted, taking out a cigarette, which he tucked into the corner of his mouth. He lit it, cupping crusty hands around the match, and then blew out the first mouthful of smoke. His eyes were small and one of them squinted now as the smoke curled up across his face. He reminded me of early photographs of James Dean—that defensive hunched stance, the crooked smile, the pointed chin. I wondered if he was a secret admirer of *East of Eden* reruns, staying up late at night to watch on obscure channels piped in from Bakersfield.

"Hey, come on. Why don't you talk to me," I said.

"I don't have nothin' to say to you. Why stir up all that shit again?"

"Aren't you interested in who killed Libby?"

He took his time about answering. He picked up a brick, holding it upright while he applied a thick layer of mortar to one end with a trowel, beveling the soft cement as if it were a gritty gray cheese. He laid the brick on the chest-high line of bricks where he'd been working and gave it a few taps with a hammer, bending down then to pick up the next brick.

I cupped my right hand to my ear. "Hello?" I said, as if I might have gone temporarily deaf.

He smirked, cigarette bobbing in his mouth. "You think you're real hot shit, don't you?"

I smiled. "Listen, Lyle. There's no point in this. You don't have to tell me anything and you know what I can do? Spend about an hour and a half this afternoon finding out anything I want to know about you. I can do it in six phone calls from a motel room in West Los Angeles and I've even got someone paying me for my time, so it's nothing to me. It's fun, if you really want to know the truth. I can get your service records, credit rating. I can find out if you've ever been arrested for anything, job history, library books overdue . . ."

"Go right ahead. I got nothin' to hide."

"Why put us through all that stuff?" I said. "I mean, I can go check you out but I'll just come back around here tomorrow and if you don't like me now, you ain't gonna like me any better then. I might be in a bad mood. Why don't you just loosen up?"

"Aw, I'm real loose," he said.

"What happened to your plans to go to law school?"

"I dropped out," he said sullenly.

"Maybe the dope smoking got to you," I suggested mildly.

"Maybe you can go get fucked," he snapped. "Do I look like a lawyer to you? I lost interest, okay? That's no fuckin crime."

"I'm not accusing you of anything. I just want to figure ou what happened to Libby."

He flipped the ash off the cigarette and dropped it chunking it into the dirt with the toe of his boot. I sat down on a pile of bricks that had been covered with a tarp. Lyle glance over at me through lowered lids.

"What makes you think I smoke dope anyway?" he aske abruptly.

I tapped my nose, letting him know I'd smelled it on him "Also laying brick doesn't seem that interesting," I said. " figure if you're smart, you gotta do something to keep fron going nuts."

He looked at me, his body relaxing just a little bit. "Wha makes you think I'm smart?"

I shrugged. "You went with Libby Glass for ten years."

He thought about that for a while.

"I don't know anything," he said, almost gruffly.

"You know more than I do at this point."

He was beginning to relent, though his shoulders were stil tense. He shook his head, going back to his work. He took th trowel and moved the damp mass of mortar around like cak icing that has gone all granular. "She dumped me after she me that guy from up north. That attorney . . ."

"Laurence Fife?"

"Yeah, I guess it was. She wouldn't tell me anything abou him. At first, it was business—something about some ac counts. His law firm had just hooked up with the place sh worked and she had to get all this stuff on the computer, yo know? Set up to run smoothly from month to month. It was al real complicated, calls goin' back and forth, things like that He came down a few times and she'd have drinks when the finished up, sometimes dinner. She fell in love. That's all know."

He took out a small metal brace at right angles an hammered it into the wooden siding on the house, placing mortar-laden brick on top.

"What's that do?" I asked out of curiosity.

"What? Oh. That keeps the brick wall from falling away from the rest," he said.

I nodded, halfway tempted to try laying brick myself. "And she broke up with you after that?" I asked, getting back to the point.

"Pretty much. I'd see her now and again, but it was over and I knew it."

He was beginning to drop the tension in his tone and he sounded more resigned than angry. Lyle buttered another brick with soft mortar and set it in place. The sun felt good on my back and I settled on my elbows, leaning back on the tarp.

"What's your theory?" I asked.

He looked at me slyly. "Maybe she killed herself."

"Suicide?" The thought hadn't even crossed my mind.

"You asked. I'm just tellin' you what I thought at the time. She sure was hung up on him."

"Yeah, but enough to kill herself when he died?"

"Who knows?" He lifted one shoulder and let it drop.

"How did she find out about his death?"

"Someone called her and told her about it."

"How do you know that?"

"Because she called me up. At first she didn't know what to make of it."

"She was grieving for him? Tears? Shock?"

He seemed to think back. "She was just real confused and upset. I went over there. She asked me to come and then she changed her mind and said she didn't want to talk about it. She was shaky, couldn't concentrate. It kind of made me mad that she was jerking me around, so I left. Next thing I knew, she was dead."

"Who found her?"

"The apartment manager where she lived. She didn't show up for work for two days and didn't call in, so her boss got worried and went over to her place. The manager tried peeping in the windows but the drapes were shut. They knocked some, front and back, and finally got in with a passkey. She was lying on the bathroom floor in her robe. She'd been dead for three days."

"What about her bed? Had it been slept in?"

"I don't know. The police didn't give that out."

I thought about that for a minute. It sounded like she might have taken a capsule at night, just as Laurence Fife had. It still seemed to me it might have been the same medication—some kind of antihistamine capsule in which someone had substituted oleander.

"Did she have allergies, Lyle? Was she complaining of a head cold or anything like that when you saw her last?"

He shrugged. "She might have, I guess. I don't remember anything like that. I saw her Thursday night. Wednesday or Thursday of that week when she heard that attorney was dead. She died on Saturday night late, they said. That much they put in the paper when it happened."

"What about this attorney she was involved with? Do you know if he kept anything at her place? Toothbrush? Razor? Things like that? Maybe she took medication that was meant for him."

"How do I know?" he said testily. "I don't stick my nose where it doesn't belong."

"Did she have a girl friend? Someone she might have confided in?"

"Maybe from work. I don't remember anyone in particular. She didn't have 'girl friends.'"

I took out my notebook and jotted down the telephone number at my motel. "This is where I can be reached. Will you give me a call if you think of anything else?"

He took the slip of paper and tucked it carelessly into the back pocket of his jeans. "What's in Las Vegas?" he asked. "How does that tie in?"

"I don't know yet. There may be a woman down there who can fill in some blanks. I'll be back through Los Angeles toward the end of the week. Maybe I'll look you up again."

Lyle had already tuned me out, tapping the next brick into place, troweling away the excess mortar that had drooled out between the cracks. I glanced at my watch. I still had time to check out the place where Libby Glass had worked. I didn't think Lyle was telling the whole truth, but I had no way to be sure. So I let it slide—for the time being anyway.

11

Haycraft and McNiece was located in the Avco Embassy building in Westwood, not far from my motel. I parked in an expensive lot adjacent to the Westwood Village Mortuary and went into the entranceway near the Wells Fargo Bank, taking the elevator up. The office itself was just to the right as I got off. I pushed through a solid teak door, lettered in brass. The interior was done with polished uneven red-tile flooring, mirrors floor to ceiling, and panels of raw gray wood, hung here and there with clusters of dried corn. A receptionist sat behind a corral to my left. A placard reading "Allison, Receptionist" sat on the corral post, the letters burned into the wood as though by some charred stick. I gave her my card.

"I wonder if I might talk to a senior accountant," I said. "I'm looking into the murder of a CPA who used to work here."

"Oh yeah. I heard about her," Allison said. "Hang on."

She was in her twenties with long dark hair. She wore jeans and a string tie, her western-cut shirt looking like it had been stuffed with many handfuls of hay. Her belt buckle was shaped like a bucking mustang.

"What is this? A theme park or something?" I asked.

"Huh?"

I shook my head, not willing to pursue the point, and she clopped away in her high-heeled boots through some swinging doors. After a moment, she returned.

"Mr. McNiece isn't in but the man you probably want to talk to is Garry Steinberg with two r's."

"B-e-r-r-g?"

"No, G-a-r-r-y."

"Oh, I see. Excuse me."

"That's okay," she said. "Everybody makes that mistake."

"Would it be possible to see Mr. Steinberg? Just briefly."

"He's in New York this week," she said.

"What about Mr. Haycraft?"

"He's dead. I mean, you know, he's been dead for years," she said. "So actually now it's McNiece and McNiece but nobody wants to have all the stationery changed. The other McNiece is in a meeting."

"Is there anybody else who might remember her?"

"I don't think so. I'm sorry."

She handed me my card. I turned it over and jotted down my motel number and my answering service up in Santa Teresa.

"Could you give this to Garry Steinberg when he gets back? I'd really appreciate a call. He can make it collect if I'm not at the motel here."

"Sure," she said. She sat down and I could have sworn she eased the card straight into the trash. I watched her for a moment and she smiled at me sheepishly.

"Maybe you could just leave that on his desk with a note," I suggested.

She leaned over slightly and came up again, card in hand. She speared it on a vicious-looking metal spike near the phone.

I looked at her some more. She took the card off the spike and got up.

"I'll just put this on his desk," she said and clopped off again.

"Good plan," I said.

I went back to the motel and made some phone calls. Ruth, in Charlie Scorsoni's office, said that he was still out of town but she gave me the number of his hotel in Denver. I called but he wasn't in, so I left my number at the message desk. I called Nikki and brought her up to date and then I checked with my answering service. There were no messages. I put on my jogging clothes and drove down to the beach to run. Things did not seem to be falling into place very fast. So far, I felt like I had a lapful of confetti and the notion of piecing it all together to make a picture seemed very remote indeed. Time had shredded the facts like a big machine, leaving only slender paper threads with which to reconstruct reality. I felt clumsy and irritable and I needed to blow off steam.

I parked near the Santa Monica pier and jogged south along the promenade, a stretch of asphalt walk that parallels the beach. I trotted past the old men bent over their chess games, past thin black boys roller-skating with incredible grace, boogeying to the secret music of their padded headphones, past guitar players, dopers, and loiterers whose eyes followed me with scorn. This stretch of pavement is the last remnant of the sixties' drug culture—the barefoot, sag-eyed, and scruffy young, some looking thirty-seven now instead of seventeen, still mystical and remote. A dog took up company with me, running along beside me, his tongue hanging out, eyes rolling up at me now and then happily. His coat was thick and bristly, the color of caramel corn, and his tail curled up like a party favor. He was one of those mutant breeds with a large head, short body, and little bitty short legs, but he seemed quite self-possessed. Together, we trotted beyond the promenade, past Ozone, Dudley, Paloma, Sunset, Thornton, and Park; by the time we reached Wave Crest, he'd lost interest, veering off to participate in a game of Frisbee out on the beach. The last I saw of him, he had made an incredible leap, catching a Frisbee midflight, mouth turned up in a grin. I smiled back. He was one of the few dogs I'd met in years that I really liked.

At Venice Boulevard I turned back, running most of the way and then slowing to a walk as I reached the pier again. The ocean breeze served as a damper to my body heat. I found myself winded but not sweating much. My mouth felt dry and my cheeks were aflame. It hadn't been a long run but I'd pushed myself a little harder than I normally did and my lungs were burning: liquid combustion in my chest. I run for the same reasons I learned to drive a car with a stick shift and drink my coffee black, imagining that a day might come when some amazing emergency would require such a test. This run was for "good measure," too, since I'd already decided to take a day off for good behavior. Too much virtue has a corrupting effect. I got back in my car when I'd cooled down and I drove east on Wilshire, back to my motel.

As I unlocked the door to my room, the phone began to ring. It was my Las Vegas buddy with Sharon Napier's address.

"Fantastic," I said. "I really appreciate this. Let me know

how to get in touch when I get down there and I'll pay you for
your time."

"General delivery is fine. I never know where I'll be."

"You got it. How much?"

"Fifty bucks. A discount. For you. She's strictly unlisted
and it wasn't easy."

"Let me know when I can return the service," I said,
knowing full well that he would.

"Oh, and Kinsey," he said, "she's dealing blackjack at the
Fremont but she's also hustling some on the side, so I hear. I
watched her operate last night. She's very sharp but she's not
fooling anyone."

"Is she stepping on someone's toes?"

"Not quite, but she's comin' close. You know, in this town
no one cares what you do as long as you don't cheat. She
shouldn't call attention to herself."

"Thanks for the information," I said.

"For sure," he said and hung up.

I showered and put on a pair of slacks and a shirt, then
went across the street and ate fried clams drowned in ketchup
with an order of french fries on the side. I got two cups of
coffee to go and went back to my room. As soon as the door
shut behind me, the phone began to ring. This time it was
Charlie Scorsoni.

"How's Denver?" I asked as soon as he identified himself.

"Not bad. How's L.A.?"

"Fair. I'm driving up to Las Vegas tonight."

"Gambling fever?"

"Not a bit. I got a line on Sharon."

"Terrific. Tell her to pay me back my six hundred bucks."

"Yeah. Right. With interest. I'm trying to find out what she
knows about a murder and you want me to hassle her about a
bad debt."

"*I'll* never have occasion to, that's for sure. When will you
be back in Santa Teresa?"

"Maybe Saturday. When I come back through L.A. on
Friday, I want to see some boxes that belong to Libby Glass.
But I don't think it will take long. What makes you ask?"

"I want to buy you a drink," he said. "I'm leaving Denver

day after tomorrow, so I'll be in town before you. Will you call me when you get back?"

I hesitated ever so slightly. "Okay."

"I mean, don't put yourself out, Millhone," he said wryly.

I laughed. "I'll call. I swear."

"Great. See you then."

After I hung up, I could feel a silly smile linger on my face long after it should have. What was it about that man?

Las Vegas is about six hours from L.A. and I decided I might as well hit the road. It was just after 7:00 and not dark yet, so I threw my things in the backseat of my car and told Arlette I'd be gone for a couple of days.

"You want me to refer calls or what?" she said.

"I'll call you when I get there and let you know how I can be reached," I said.

I headed north on the San Diego Freeway, picking up the Ventura, which I followed east until it turned into the Colorado Freeway, one of the few benign roads in the whole of the L.A. freeway system. The Colorado is broad and sparsely traveled, cutting across the northern boundary of metropolitan Los Angeles. It is possible to change lanes on the Colorado without having an anxiety attack and the sturdy concrete divider that separates east- and westbound traffic is a comforting assurance that cars will not wantonly drift over and crash into your vehicle head-on. From the Colorado, I doglegged south, picking up the San Bernardino Freeway, taking 15 northeast on a long irregular diagonal toward Las Vegas. With any luck, I could talk to Sharon Napier and then head south to the Salton Sea, where Greg Fife was living. I could complete the circuit with a swing up to Claremont on my way back for a brief chat with his sister, Diane. At this point, I wasn't sure what the journey would net me but I needed to complete the basics of my investigation. And Sharon Napier was bound to prove interesting.

I like driving at night. I'm not a sightseer at heart and in travels across the country, I'm never tempted by detours to scenic wonders. I'm not interested in hundred-foot rocks shaped like crookneck squash. I'm not keen on staring down into gullies formed by rivers now defunct and I do not marvel at great holes in the ground where meteors once fell to earth. Driving anywhere looks much the same to me. I stare at the concrete roadway. I watch the yellow line. I keep track of large trucks and passenger vehicles with little children asleep in the backseat and I keep my foot pressed flat to the floor until I reach my destination.

12

By the time Las Vegas loomed up, twinkling on the horizon, it was well after midnight and I felt stiff. I was anxious to avoid the Strip. I would have avoided the whole town if I could. I don't gamble, having no instincts for the sport and even less curiosity. Life in Las Vegas exactly suits my notion of some eventual life in cities under the sea. Day and night mean nothing. People ebb and surge aimlessly as though pulled by invisible thermal currents that are swift and disagreeably close. Everything is made of plaster of paris, imitative, larger than life, profoundly impersonal. The whole town smells of $1.89 fried shrimp dinners.

I found a motel near the airport, on the outskirts of town. The Bagdad looked like a foreign legion post made of marzipan. The night manager was dressed in a gold satin vest and an orange satin shirt with full puffed sleeves. He wore a fez with a tassel. His breathing had a raspy quality that made me want to clear my throat.

"Are you an out-of-state married couple?" he asked, not looking up.

"No."

"There's fifty dollars' worth of coupons with a double if you're an out-of-state married couple. I'll put it down. Nobody checks."

I gave him my credit card, which he ran off while I filled out the registration form. He gave me my key and a small paper cup full of nickels for the slot machines near the door. I left them on the counter.

I parked in the space outside my door and left the car, taking a cab into town through the artificial daylight of Glitter Gulch. I paid the cabbie and took a moment to orient myself. There was a constant stream of traffic on East Fremont, the sidewalks crowded with tourists, hot yellow signs, and flashing lights—THE MINT, THE FOUR QUEENS—illuminating a complete catalogue of hustlers: pimps and prostitutes, pickpockets, corn-fed con artists from the Midwest who flock to Vegas with the conviction that the system can be beaten with sufficient cunning and industry. I went into the Fremont.

I could smell the Chinese food from the coffee shop and the odor of chicken chow mein mingled oddly with the perfumed jet trail left by a woman who passed me in a royal blue polyester print pantsuit that made her look like a piece of walking wallpaper. I watched idly as she began to feed quarters into a slot machine in the lobby. The blackjack tables were off to my left. I asked one of the pit bosses about Sharon Napier and was told she'd be in at 11:00 in the morning. I hadn't really expected to run into her that night, but I wanted to get a feel for the place.

The casino hummed, the croupiers at the craps tables shoveling chips back and forth with a stick like some kind of tabletop shuffleboard with rules of its own. I once made a tour of the Nevada Dice Company, watching with something close to reverence as the sixty-pound cellulose nitrate slabs, an inch thick, were cured and cut into cubes, slightly bigger than the finished size, hardened, buffed and drilled on all sides, a white resinous compound applied to the sunken dots with special brushes. The dice, in process, looked like tiny squares of cherry Jell-O that might have been served up like some sort of low-cal dessert. I watched people place their bets. The Pass line, the Don't Pass line, Come, Don't Come, the Field, the Big 6 and the Big 8 were mysteries of another kind and I couldn't, for the life of me, penetrate the catechism of wins, losses, numbers being rattled out in a low chant of intense concentration and surprise. Over it all there hung a pale cloud of cigarette smoke, infused with the smell of spilled Scotch. The darkened mirrors above the tables must have been scanned by countless pairs of eyes, restlessly raking the patrons below for telltale signs of chicanery. Nothing could escape notice. The atmosphere was that of a crowded Woolworth's at Christmas, where the throngs of frantic shoppers couldn't be trusted not to lift an item now and then. Even the employees might lie, cheat, and steal, and nothing could be left to chance. I felt a fleeting respect for the whole system of checks and balances that keeps so much money flowing freely and allows so little to slip back into the individual pockets from which it has been coaxed. A sudden feeling of exhaustion came over me. I walked back out to the street again and found a cab.

The "Middle Eastern" decor of the Bagdad halted abruptly at the door to my room. The carpet was dark green cotton shag, the wallpaper lime-green foil in a pattern of overlapping palms, flocked with small clumps that might have been dates or clusters of fruit bats. I locked the door, kicked off my shoes, and pulled down the chenille spread, crawling under the covers with relief. I put a quick call through to my answering service and another to a groggy Arlette, leaving my latest location with the number where I could be reached.

I woke up at 10:00 A.M., feeling the first faint stages of a headache—as though I had a hangover in the making before I'd even had a drink. Vegas tends to affect me that way, some combination of tension and dread to which my body responds with all the symptoms of incipient flu. I took two Tylenols and showered for a long time, trying to wash away the roiling whisper of nausea. I felt like I'd eaten a pound of cold buttered popcorn and washed it down with bulk saccharin.

I stepped out of my motel room, the light causing me to squint. The air, at least, was fresh and there was, by day, the sense of a town subdued and shrunken, flattened out again to its true proportions. The desert stretched away behind the motel in a haze of pale gray, fading to mauve at the horizon. The wind was mild and dry, the promise of summer heat only hinted at in the distant shimmering sunlight that sat on the desert floor in flat pools, evaporating on approach. Occasional patches of sagebrush, nearly silver with dust, broke up the long low lines of treeless wasteland fenced in by distant hills.

I stopped off at the post office and left a fifty-dollar money order for my friend and then I checked out the address he had given me. Sharon Napier lived in a two-story apartment complex on the far side of town, salmon-pink stucco eroding around the edges as though animals had crept up in the night to gnaw the corners away. The roof was nearly flat, peppered with rocks, the iron railings sending streaks of rust down the sides of the building. The landscaping was rock and yucca and cactus plants. There were only twenty units, arranged around a kidney-shaped pool that was separated from the parking area by a dun-colored cinder-block wall. A couple of young kids were splashing about in the pool and a middle-aged woman was standing in front of her apartment up on the landing, a grocery bag wedged between her hip and the door as she let herself in. A Chicano boy hosed down the walks. The buildings on either side of the complex were single-family dwellings. There was a vacant lot across the street in back.

Sharon's apartment was on the ground floor, her name was neatly embossed on the mailbox on a white plastic strip. Her drapes were drawn, but some of the hooks had come loose at the top, causing the lined fabric to bow inward and sag, forming a gap through which I could see a beige Formica table and two beige upholstered plastic kitchen chairs. The telephone sat on one corner of the table, resting on a pile of papers. Beside it was a coffee cup with a waxy crescent of hot-pink lipstick on the rim. A cigarette, also rimmed with pink, had been extinguished in the saucer. I glanced around. No one seemed to be paying any particular attention to me. I walked quickly through a passageway that connected the courtyard to the rear of the apartment building.

Sharon's apartment number was marked on the rear door, too, and there were four other back doors at intervals, the rear entrances emptying into little rectangles surrounded by shoulder-high cinder-block walls designed, I suspected, to create the illusion of small patios. The trash containers were lined up on the walkway outside the wall. Her kitchen curtains were drawn. I eased onto her little patio. She had arranged six geraniums in pots along the back step. There were two aluminum folding chairs stacked against the wall, a pile of old newspapers by the back door. There was a small window up on the right and a larger window beyond that. I couldn't judge whether it might be her bedroom or her neighbor's. I looked out across the vacant lot and then eased out of the patio, turning left along the walk, which opened out onto the street again. I got back in my car and headed for the Fremont.

I felt as if I'd never left. The lady in royal blue was still pasted to the quarter slot machine, her hair sculpted into a glossy mahogany scrollwork on top of her head. The same

crowd seemed to be pressed to the craps table as though by
magnetic force, the croupier pushing chips back and forth with
his little stick as if it were a flat-bottomed broom and someone
had made an expensive mess. Waitresses circulated with drinks
and a heavyset man, whom I guessed to be plainclothes
security, wandered about trying to look like a tourist whose
luck had gone bad. I could hear the sounds of a female vocalist
in the Carnival Lounge, singing a slightly flat but lusty medley
of Broadway show tunes. I caught a glimpse of her, emoting to
a half-deserted room, her face a bright powder pink under the
spotlight.

Sharon Napier was not hard to find. She was tall, maybe
five ten or better in her high-heeled shoes. She was the sort of
woman you noticed from the ground up: long shapely legs
looking slender in black mesh hose, a short black skirt flaring
slightly at the tops of her thighs. She had narrow hips, a flat
stomach, and her breasts were pushed together to form
pronounced mounds. The bodice of her black outfit was tight
and low-cut, her name stitched above her left breast. Her hair
was an ashen blonde, pallid under the houselights; her eyes an
eerie green, a luminous shade I guessed to be from tinted
contact lenses. Her skin was pale and unblemished, the oval of
her face as white as eggshell and as finely textured. Her lips
were full and wide, the bright pink lipstick emphasizing their
generous proportions. It was a mouth built for unnatural acts.
Something about her demeanor promised cool improvisational
sex for the right price and it would not be cheap.

She dealt cards mechanically, with remarkable speed.
Three men were perched on stools ranged around the table
where she worked. No one said a word. The communication
was by the slightest lift of a hand, cards turned over or placed
under substantial bets, a shoulder shrugged as the up card
showed. Two down, one up. Flick, flick. One man scraped the
edge of his up card against the surface of the table, asking for a
hit. On the second round, one man turned up a blackjack and
she paid off—two hundred and fifty dollars' worth of chips. I
could see his eyes take her in as she flicked the cards back,
shuffling quickly, dealing out cards again. He was thin, with a
narrow balding head and a dark mustache, shirt sleeves rolled
up, underarms stained with sweat. His gaze drifted down

across her body and back up again to the immaculate face, cold
and clean, the green eyes blazing. She paid no particular
attention to him, but I had the feeling the two of them might do
some private business later on. I retreated to another table,
watching her from an easy distance. At 1:30, she took a break.
Another dealer took her place and she crossed the casino,
heading toward the Fiesta Room, where she ordered a Coke
and lit up a cigarette. I followed.

"Are you Sharon Napier?" I asked.

She looked up. Her eyes were rimmed with dark lashes, the
green taking on an almost turquoise hue in the fluorescent light
overhead.

"I don't think we've met," she said.

"I'm Kinsey Millhone," I said. "May I sit down?"

She shrugged by way of consent. She took a compact out
of her pocket and checked her eye makeup, removing a slight
smudge of shadow from her upper lid. Her lashes were clearly
false, but the effect was flashy, giving her eyes an exotic slant.
She applied fresh lip gloss, using her little finger, which she
dipped into a tiny pot of pink. "What can I do for you?" she
asked, glancing up briefly from her compact mirror.

"I'm looking into the death of Laurence Fife."

That stopped her. She paused, her whole body going still.
If I'd been taking a picture, it would have been the perfect
pose. A second passed and she was in motion again. She
snapped the compact shut and tucked it away, taking up her
cigarette. She took a long drag, watching me all the while. She
flicked an ash. "He was a real shitheel," she said brusquely,
smoke wafting out with each word.

"So I've heard," I said. "Did you work for him long?"

She smiled. "Well, you've done your homework at any
rate. I bet you even know the answer to that."

"More or less," I said. "But there's lots I don't know.
Want to fill me in?"

"On what?"

I shrugged. "What it was like to work for him? How you
felt about his death . . ."

"He was a prick to work for. I felt terrific about his death,"
she said. "I hated secretarial work in case you haven't
guessed."

"This must suit you better," I said.

"Look, I got nothing to discuss with you," she said flatly. "Who sent you up here anyway?"

I took a flyer on that one. "Nikki."

She seemed startled. "She's still in prison. Isn't she?"

I shook my head. "She's out."

She took a moment to calculate and then her manner became somewhat more gracious. "She's got bucks, right?"

"She's not hurting, if that's what you mean."

She stubbed out her cigarette, bending the live ember under and mashing it flat. "I'm off at seven. Why don't you come out to my place and we can chat."

"Anything you'd care to mention now?"

"Not here," she said.

She rattled out her address and I dutifully jotted it down in my notebook. She glanced off to the left and I thought at first she was lifting a hand to greet a friend. Her smile flashed and then faltered and she glanced back at me with uncertainty, turning slightly so that my line of sight was blocked. I peered back over her shoulder automatically but she distracted my attention, touching the back of my hand with a fingernail. I looked at her. She towered over me, her expression remote.

"That was the pit boss. End of my break."

She told lies the way I do, with a certain breezy insolence that dares the listener to refute or contradict.

"I'll see you at seven then," I said.

"Make it seven forty-five," she said easily. "I need time to unwind from work."

I wrote out my name and the name of my motel, tearing a sheet from my notebook. She made a sharp crease and tucked the slip into her cigarette pack under the cellophane wrapper. She walked away without a backward glance, hips swaying gracefully.

The mashed butt of her cigarette was still sending up a drift of smoke and my stomach emitted a little message of protest. I was tempted to hang around, just to keep an eye on her, but my hands were feeling clammy and I longed to lie down. I didn't feel good at all and I was beginning to think that my flu symptoms might be more real than reactionary. The headache was creeping up again from the back of my neck. I walked out through the lobby. Fresh air helped me some but only momentarily.

I drove back to the Bagdad and bought a 7Up from the vending machine. I needed to eat but I wasn't sure anything would stay down. It was early afternoon and I didn't have to be anywhere until well after suppertime. I put the Do Not Disturb sign on my door and crawled back into my unmade bed, pulling the covers around me tightly. My bones had begun to ache. It was a long time before I got warm.

13

The telephone rang with startling shrillness and I awoke with a jolt. The room was dark. I had no idea what time it was, no idea what bed I was in. I groped for the phone, feeling flushed and hot, shoving the covers away from me as I propped myself up on one elbow. I flicked on the light, shading my eyes from the sudden harsh glare.

"Hello?"

"Kinsey, this is Sharon. Did you forget about me?"

I looked at my watch. It was 8:30. Shit. "God, I'm sorry," I said. "I fell asleep. Will you be there for a while? I can be right over."

"All right," she said coolly, as though she had better plans. "Oh, hang on. There's someone at my door."

She put the phone down with a clack and I pictured it resting on the hard Formica surface of the tabletop. I listened idly, waiting for her to come back. I couldn't believe I'd overslept and I was kicking myself for my stupidity. I heard the door open and her muffled exclamation of surprise. And then I heard a brief, nearly hollow report.

I squinted, sitting up abruptly. I pressed my ear to the phone, pressing my hand over the receiver. What was going on? The receiver was picked up on her end. I expected to hear her voice and I nearly spoke her name but some impulse made me clamp my mouth shut. There was the sound of breathing in my ear, the sexless hushed tones of someone slightly winded. There was a whispered "hello" that chilled me. I closed my eyes, willing myself to silence; an alarm had spread through my body in a rush that made my heart pound in my ears. There was a small breathy chuckle and then the line went dead. I slammed the phone down and reached for my shoes, grabbing my jacket as I left the room.

The jolt of adrenaline had washed my body clean of pain.

My hands were shaking but at least I was in motion. I locked the door and went out to the car, my keys jingling as I tried to hit the ignition switch. I started the car and backed out rapidly, heading toward Sharon's apartment. I reached for the flashlight in my glove compartment, checking it. The light was strong. I drove, anxiety mounting. She was either playing games or dead, and I suspected I knew which.

I pulled up across the street. The building showed no particular signs of activity. No one was moving about. There were no crowds gathered, no police cars parked at the street, no sirens wailing an approach. There were numerous cars parked in the slots, and the lights in the building had been turned on in almost every apartment that I could see. I reached around in the backseat, removing a pair of rubber gloves from my locked briefcase. My hand touched the short barrel of my little automatic and I desperately longed to tuck that in my windbreaker pocket. I wasn't sure what I'd find in her apartment, wasn't sure who might be waiting for me, but the notion of being discovered there in possession of a loaded gun wouldn't do at all if she was dead. I left the gun where it was and got out, locking my car, tucking the keys into my jeans.

I moved into the front courtyard. It was dark, but several outdoor spots were placed strategically along the walk, six more green and yellow spots shooting upward along the cactus plants. The effect was more gaudy than illuminating. Sharon's apartment was dark and the gap in the drapes had been pulled tight. I tapped at the door. "Sharon?" I kept my voice low, scanning the front of the place for any signs of lights coming on. I pulled on the rubber gloves and tried the knob. Locked. I tapped again, repeating her name. There was no sound from inside. What was I going to do if someone was in there?

I moved along the short stretch of walk that led around the building to the rear. I could hear a stereo playing somewhere in one of the upstairs apartments. The small of my back ached and my cheeks felt as hot as if I'd just gotten back from a run, though whether it was from flu or fear I couldn't say. I moved quickly and silently along the rear walkway. Sharon's kitchen was the only one of the five that was dark. There was an outside bulb burning above each back door, casting a shallow but clear light onto each small patio. I tried the back door. Locked. I tapped on the glass.

"Sharon?" I strained for sounds inside the apartment. All was quiet. I scanned the rear entrance. If she had an extra set of keys outside, they would be hidden someplace close. I glanced back at the small panes of glass in her back door. If all else failed, I could always break one out. I slid my fingers along the top of the doorframe. Too narrow for keys. All the flowerpots seemed straight and a quick search revealed nothing tucked down in the dirt. There was no doormat. I lifted the pile of old newspapers, giving them a little riff, but no keys clattered out. The surrounding cinder-block patio wall was made of one-foot-square decorative "bricks," each design of sufficient intricacy to provide an ample, if not original, hiding place for a key. I hoped I wasn't going to have to check every single one. I glanced back at the small panes of glass, wondering if it might not be more to the point to pop one out with a padded fist. I looked down. There was a green plastic watering can and a trowel in one corner right up against the wall. I crouched, sliding my right hand into each of the decorative whorls of concrete. There was a key in one.

I reached up and gave the bulb above her back door a quick twist to the left. The patio was immersed in shadow. I fitted the key into the knob lock and opened the door a crack. "Sharon!" I whispered hoarsely. I was tempted to leave the apartment in darkness but I had to know if I was alone. I held the flashlight like a club, groping to my right until I found a switch. The recessed light above the sink went on. I saw the switch to the overhead kitchen light on the opposite wall. I crossed the room and flipped it on, ducking down and out of sight. I hunkered, holding my breath, my back against the refrigerator. I listened intently. Nothing. I hoped like hell I wasn't making a colossal fool of myself. For all I knew, the noise I'd heard was the popping of a champagne cork and Sharon was in the darkened bedroom performing illicit sexual acts with a little show dog and a whip.

I peered into the living room. Sharon was sprawled out on the living-room floor in a kelly green velour robe. She was either dead or sound asleep and I still didn't know who else might be in that apartment with me. I crossed to the living room in two steps and pressed myself up against the wall, waiting a moment before I peered back out into the darkened hallway. I couldn't see shit. I found a light switch just to my left and flipped it on. The hall was ablaze with light and the portion of the bedroom I could see seemed unoccupied. I felt for the bedroom switch and flipped it on, peering around quickly. I guessed the open doorway off to my right was the bathroom. There was no indication that the place had been ransacked. The sliding closet doors were shut and I didn't like that. From the bathroom, there was a faint metallic sound. I froze. My heart gave a thud and a half and I crouched. Me and my flashlight. I wished like hell I'd brought the gun. The little metallic squeak picked up again, assuming a rhythm that suddenly took on a familiar tone. I crept over to the door and flashed the light in. There was a goddamn little mouse going round and round in an exercise wheel. The cage sat on the bathroom counter. I flipped the light on. The bathroom was empty.

I crossed to the closet doors and slid one open, half waiting to get my head bashed in. Both sides of the closet were empty of anything but clothing. I let out the long breath I'd been holding and then did a second quick search of the place. I made sure the back door was locked, pulling the kitchen curtains across the window above the sink. And then I went back to Sharon. I flipped on the lamp in the living room and knelt down beside her. She had a bullet hole at the base of her throat, looking like a little locket filled with raw flesh instead of a photograph. Blood had soaked into the carpet under her head and it had darkened now to the color of uncooked chicken liver. There were small slivers of bone in her hair. I guessed that her spine had been shattered by the bullet on impact. Nice for her. No pain. She seemed to have been knocked straight back, arms flung out on either side of her body, her hips turned slightly. Her eyes were half open, the luminous green color looking sour now. Her blonde hair looked gray in death. If I'd gotten there when I was supposed to, she might not be dead, and I wanted to apologize for my bad manners, for the delay, for being sick, for being too late. I wanted to hold her hand and coax her back to life again but there was no way and I knew, in a quick flash, that if I'd been there on time, I might be dead myself.

I ran my gaze around the room with care. The carpeting was a high-low, matted with wear, so there were no shoe prints. I crossed to the front window and readjusted the drapes, making sure no crack appeared to afford a view from outside now that the lights were turned on. I made a brief tour again, taking in details this time. The bed was unmade. The bathroom was littered with damp towels. Dirty clothing bulged out of the hamper. An ashtray sat on the rim of the tub with several cigarette butts stubbed out, folded over and mashed flat in the manner I'd seen her use. The apartment was basically only those three rooms—living room with the dining table near the front windows, kitchen, and bedroom. The furniture looked as if it had been ordered by the boxcarload, and I assumed that little of it was actually hers. Whatever the disorder on the premises, it seemed to be of her own making—dishes in the sink, trash unemptied. I glanced down at the papers under the phone, a collection of past-due notices and bills. Apparently her penchant for financial chaos hadn't changed since her days in Santa Teresa. I picked up the whole batch and shoved them into my jacket pocket.

I could hear the little metallic squeak again and I went back to the bathroom, staring down at that foolish little creature. He was small and brown, with bright red eyes, patiently making his way around and around, going nowhere. "I'm sorry," I whispered, and tears stung my lips briefly. I shook my head. It was misplaced sentiment and I knew it. His water bottle was full but the plastic food dish was empty. I filled it with little green pellets and then I went back to the phone and dialed the operator, asking for the Las Vegas police. Con Dolan's warning sounded dully in my memory. All I needed was the LVPD holding me for questioning. One of those gravelly officious voices came on the line after two rings.

"Oh hello," I said. My voice had a tremor in it and I had to clear my throat quickly. "I, uh, heard some noise in my neighbor's apartment a little while ago and now I can't seem to get her to answer my knock. I'm worried that she's hurt herself. Is there any way you could check that out?"

He sounded irritated and bored, but he took down Sharon's address and said he'd send someone.

I checked my watch. I'd been in the apartment less than thirty minutes, but it was time to get out of there. I didn't want the phone to ring. I didn't want somebody knocking at the door unexpectedly. I moved toward the back, turning out lights as I went, unconsciously listening for sounds of someone approaching. I didn't have a lot of time to spare.

I glanced back at Sharon. I didn't like to leave her that way but I couldn't see the point in waiting it out. I didn't want to be linked to her death and I didn't want to hang around Las Vegas waiting for the coroner's inquest. And I certainly didn't want Con Dolan to find out I'd been here. Maybe the Mafia had killed her, or maybe some pimp, or maybe the man at the casino who'd looked at her with such hunger when she counted out his two hundred and fifty bucks. Or maybe she knew something about Laurence Fife that she wasn't supposed to tell.

I moved past her. Her fingers were relaxed in death, looking graceful, each tipped with a long rose-polished nail. I caught my breath. She had taken the slip with my name and motel jotted on it and had tucked it into her cigarette pack. But where was it? I looked around quickly, heart racing. I didn't see it on the Formica tabletop, though there was a cigarette that had apparently burned down to nothing, leaving only a perfect column of ash. There was no cigarette pack on the arm of the couch, none on the counter. I checked the bathroom again, listening acutely for sounds of the police. I could have sworn I heard a siren some distance off and I felt a ripple of alarm. Shit. I had to find that note. The bathroom trash was full of Kleenex and a soap wrapper, old cigarette butts. No cigarette pack on the bedtable. None on the dresser top. I went back to the living room and looked down at her with distaste. There were two generous side pockets in the green velour robe. I gritted my teeth, feeling gingerly. The pack was on the right-hand side, with maybe six cigarettes left, the sharply creased slip of paper bearing my name still visible under the cellophane. I tucked it hastily into my jacket.

I turned out the remaining lights and slipped to the back door, opening it a crack. I could hear voices remarkably close. A garbage can lid clattered near the apartment to my right.

"You better tell the manager her light's burned out," a woman commented. She sounded as if she was standing right next to me.

"Why don't you tell *her*?" came the slightly annoyed reply.

"I don't think she's home. Her lights are off."

"Yes she is. I just saw the lights on a minute ago."

"Sherman, they're off. The whole place is dark. She must have gone out the front," the woman said. The wailing siren was very loud, its tone winding down like a phonograph.

My heart was pounding so hard it was making my chest burn. I eased out onto the darkened patio, pausing to tuck the keys back into the little crevice behind the plastic watering can. I hoped like hell it wasn't my car keys I was hiding there. I slipped out of the patio, turning left, moving toward the street again. I had to force myself to walk casually past the patrol car that was now parked out front. I unlocked my car and got in, pushing the lock down hastily as though someone were in pursuit. I stripped off the rubber gloves. My head was aching fiercely and I felt a flash of clammy sweat, bile rising up in my throat. I had to get out of there. I swallowed convulsively. The nausea welled up and I fought an almost irresistible urge to heave. My hands were shaking so badly I could hardly get my car started but I managed, finally, and pulled away from the curb with care.

As I drove past the entranceway, I could see a uniformed patrolman move around to the back of Sharon's apartment, hand on the gun at his hip. It seemed somewhat theatrical for a simple domestic complaint and I wondered, with a chill, if someone else had placed a call with a message more explicit than mine. Half a minute more and I'd have been trapped in that apartment with a lot of explaining to do. I didn't like that idea at all.

I went back to the Bagdad and packed, cleaning the place of fingerprints. I felt as if I were running a low-grade fever. All I really wanted to do was roll up in a blanket and go back to sleep. Head throbbing, I went into the office. The manager's wife was there this time, looking like a Turkish harem girl—if the word "girl" applied. She was probably sixty-five, with a finely wrinkled face, like something that had been left in the dryer too long. She wore a pale satin pillbox perched on her gray hair, veils draped provocatively over her ears.

"I'll be on the road at five in the morning and I thought I'd get my bill squared away tonight," I said.

I gave her my room number and she sorted through the upright file, coming up with my ledger card. I was feeling restless, anxious, and sick, and I wanted to be out on the road. Instead, I had to force myself, brightly, casually, to deal with this woman who moved in slow motion.

"Where you headed?" she asked idly, toting up the charges on the adding machine. She made a mistake and had to do it all over again.

"Reno," I said, lying automatically.

"Any luck?"

"What?"

"You win much?"

"Oh yeah, I'm doing pretty good," I said. "I really surprised myself."

"Better than most folk," she remarked. "You won't be making any long-distance calls before you leave?" She gave me a sharp look.

I shook my head. "I'm going to hit the sack."

"You look like you could use some sleep," she said. She filled out the credit-card charge slip, which I signed, taking my copy.

"I didn't use the fifty dollars' worth of coupons," I said. "You might as well have those back."

She put the unused coupons in the drawer without a word.

Within minutes, miraculously, I was out on Highway 93, heading southeast toward Boulder City, where I took 95 south. I got as far as Needles and then I had to have relief. I found a cheap motel and checked in, crawled under the covers again, and slept for ten hours straight. Even that far down in oblivion, I felt an awesome dread of what had been set in motion and a pointless, aching sense of apology to Sharon Napier for whatever part I'd played in her death.

14

In the morning, I felt whole again. I ate a big breakfast in a little diner across the road from the motel, washing down bacon, scrambled eggs, and rye toast with fresh orange juice and three cups of coffee. I had the car filled up with gas, the oil checked, and then hit the road again. After Las Vegas, the desert drive was a pleasure. The land was spare, the colors subdued: a mild very pale lavender overlaid with fine dust. The sky was a stark, cloudless blue, the mountain ridges like crushed velvet, wrinkled dark gray along the face. There was something appealing about all that country unconquered yet, miles and miles of terrain without neon signs. The population was reduced to races of kangaroo rat and ground squirrel, the rocky canyons inhabited by kit fox and desert lynx. Af fifty-five miles an hour, no wildlife was visible but I had heard the cries of tree frogs even in my sleep and I pictured now, from my speeding car, the clay and gravel washes filled with buff-colored lizards and millipedes, creatures whose adaption to their environment include the husbanding of moisture and an aversion to hot sun. There are parasol ants in the desert that cut off leaves and carry them as sunshades over their backs, storing them later like beach umbrellas in the subterranean chambers where they live. The idea made me smile, and I kept my mind resolutely from the recollection of Sharon Napier's death.

I found Greg Fife in a little gray humpbacked camper outside Durmid on the eastern shore of the Salton Sea. It had taken me a while to track him down. Gwen had said that he lived on his boat but the boat had been pulled out of the water for paint and repair and Greg was temporarily lodged in an aluminum trailer that looked like a roly-poly bug. The interior was compact with a folding table hooked flat against the wall, a padded bench that became a single bed, a canvas chair that completely blocked passage to the sink, a chemical toilet, and a hot plate. He opened two bottles of beer, which he'd taken from a refrigerator the size of a cardboard box, located under the sink.

He offered me the padded bench, unfolding the small table between us. A single leg flopped down to give it support. I was effectively hemmed in and could only get comfortable by turning sideways. Greg took the canvas chair, tilting back so he could study me while I studied him. He looked a lot like Laurence Fife—lank dark-brown hair, a square-cut smooth face that was clean-shaven, dark eyes, bold dark brows, square chin. He looked younger than twenty-five but his smile had the same touch of arrogance that I remembered from his father. He was darkly tanned, cheekbones tinted with sunburn. His shoulders were wide, his body lean, his feet bare. He wore a red cotton turtleneck and cutoffs that were ragged at the bottom, nearly ruffled with bleached threads. He took a sip of beer.

"You think I look like him?"

"Yes," I said. "Does that suit you?"

Greg shrugged. "Doesn't matter much at this point," he said. "We weren't anything alike."

"How so?"

"God," he said facetiously, "let's just skip over the preliminaries and get right down to the personal stuff, why don't we."

I smiled. "I'm not very polite."

"Neither am I," he said.

"So what do you want to talk about first? The weather?"

"Skip it," he said. "I know what you're here for so get to the point."

"You remember much about that time in your life?"

"Not if I can help it."

"Except for shrinks," I suggested.

"I did that to please my mom," he said and then smiled briefly as though he recognized the fact that the phrase "my mom" sounded too boyish for him at his age.

"I worked for your father a couple of times," I said.

He began to peel a strip of label with his thumbnail, feigning disinterest. I wondered what he'd heard about his

father and I decided, on impulse, not to give Laurence Fife any
posthumous pats lest I sound condescending or insincere.

I said, "I've heard he was a real bastard."

"No shit," Greg said.

I shrugged. "I didn't think he was that bad myself. He was
straight with me. I suspect he was a complicated man and I
don't think many people got close to him."

"Did you?"

"No," I said. I shifted slightly in my seat. "How'd you
feel about Nikki?"

"Not that good."

I smiled. "Try to keep your answers short so I can get 'em
on one line," I said. He didn't bite. I drank beer for a while,
then rested my chin on my fist. Sometimes I just really do get
sick of trying to coax information out of people who aren't in
the mood. "Why don't you fold up the table and we'll go
outside," I said.

"What for?"

"So I can get some fresh air, fucker, what do you think?"

He chuckled suddenly and moved his long legs out of my
way as I slid out of the seat.

I'd surprised myself, getting snappish with him, but I get
tired of people being cute or sullen or cautious or tight-lipped.
I wanted straight answers and a lot of them too. And I wanted a
relationship based, just once, on some sort of mutual exchange
instead of me always having to connive and manipulate. I
walked aimlessly, Greg at my heels, trying to cool myself
down. It wasn't his fault, I knew, and I'm suspicious of myself
anyway when I'm feeling righteous and misunderstood.

"Sorry I snapped at you," I said.

The trailer was about two hundred yards from the water's
edge. There were several larger trailers nearby, all facing the
sea, like a queer band of animals that had crept down to the
water to drink. I pulled off my tennis shoes and tied the laces
together, hanging them around my neck. The Salton Sea has a
mild to nonexistent surf, like an ocean that has been totally
tamed. There is no vegetation visible in the water and few if
any fish. It gives the shore a curious air, as though the tides had
been brought to heel, becalmed, the life forms leeched away.
What remains is familiar but subtly changed, like a glimpse

into the future where certain laws of nature have been altered by the passage of time. I placed a drop of water on my tongue. The taste of salt was fierce. "Is this ocean water?"

Greg smiled, apparently unperturbed by my former outburst. In fact he seemed friendlier. "You want a lesson in geology," he said, "I'll give you one." It was the first time his voice had contained any sign of enthusiasm.

"Sure, why not?"

He picked up a rock, using it like a piece of chalk as he drew a crude map in the wet sand. "This is the California coastline and this is Baja. Over here is Mexico. Right at the tip of the Gulf of California is Yuma—southeast of here, more or less. This is us here," he said, pointing. "The Colorado River curves right up through here and then up past Las Vegas. That's Hoover Dam. Then it goes up here and over into Utah and then to Colorado, but we can skip that part. Now," he said, tossing the rock aside. He began to draw with his fingertip, glancing up at me to see if I was listening. "This area in here is called the Salton Sink. Two hundred and seventy-three feet below sea level—something like that. If it weren't for the Colorado River forming a kind of natural dam right here, all this water from the Gulf of California would have spilled into the Salton Sink years ago—all the way up to Indio. God, that gives me the willies when I think of it. Anyway, the Salton Sea came from the Colorado River itself, so it was originally fresh water. Overflowed in 1905—the river did, billions of gallons of water pouring in over a two-year period. It was finally controlled with rock and brush dams. The salt, which has been gradually saturating the water, was probably from prehistoric times when all of this area was submerged." He stood up, brushing wet sand off his hands, apparently satisfied with his summary.

We began to walk—he on the beach side, me scuffling my bare feet through the shallows. He tucked his hands in his back pockets. "Sorry if I was a pissant before," he said lightly, "I've been in a bad mood with my boat out of the water. I was never meant to be on land."

"You sure snapped out of it quick enough," I remarked.

"Because you said 'fuck.' I always get tickled when women say that. Especially you. It was the last thing I expected to come out of your mouth."

"What do you do down here?" I asked. "Fish?"

"Some. Mostly sail. Read. Drink beer. Hang out."

"I'd go nuts."

Greg shrugged. "I started out nuts so I'm getting sane."

"Not really 'nuts,'" I said.

"Not certifiable, no."

"What kind then?"

"Don't make me tell all that stuff," he said mildly. "I get bored with myself. Ask me something else. Three questions. Like magic wishes."

"If I have to limit myself to three questions, I might as well go home," I said, but basically I was willing to play the game. I looked over at him. He was looking less like his father and more like himself. "What do you remember from the period just before he died?"

"You asked me that before."

"Yeah, and that's just about the time you turned all surly on me. I'll tell you why I'm asking. Maybe that will help. I'd like to reconstruct the events just before his death. Maybe as far back as the last six months before he was killed. I mean, maybe he was involved in some kind of legal hassle—a personal feud. Maybe he fought with a neighbor over a property line. Somebody did it, and there had to be a sequence of events."

"I wouldn't know about that stuff," he said. "I can tell you just family events, but the other I wouldn't know."

"That's okay."

"We came down here that fall. That's one of the reasons I came back."

I wanted to prompt him with another question but I was afraid he'd count it as one of my three so I kept my mouth shut. He went on.

"I was seventeen. God, I was such a jerk and I thought my father was so impossibly perfect. I didn't know what he expected of me but I figured I'd never measure up, so I was a pissant. He was supercritical and he hurt my feelings a lot, but I'd just stonewall him. Half the time I hung on his every word and the rest of the time I hated his guts. So when he died, I lost the chance to square myself with him. I mean, for all time, you know? That's it. I've got no way to take care of any old

business with him, so I'm stuck. I figured if I was stuck in
time, I might as well be stuck in place, too, so that's why
came here. We were out on the beach once—and he had to go
back to the car for something and I remember watching him
walk. Just looking at him. He had his head bent and he was
probably thinking about anything but me. I felt like I should
call him back, really tell him how much I loved him, but of
course I didn't. So that's the way I remember him. That whole
business really screwed me up."

"It was just the two of you?"

"What? No, the whole family. Except Diane. She got sick
and stayed with Mom. It was Labor Day weekend. We drove to
Palm Springs, first, just for the day, and then came on down
here."

"How'd you feel about Colin?"

"Okay I guess, but I didn't see why the whole family had
to revolve around him. The kid had a handicap and I felt bad
about that, but I didn't want my life to focus on his infirmity,
you know? I mean, Jesus, I would have had to develop a
terminal disease to compete with him. This is me at seventeen,
you understand. Now I'm a little more compassionate, but
back then, I couldn't cope with that stuff. I didn't see why I
should. Dad and I were never bosom buddies, but I needed
time with him too. I used to have these fantasies of what it
would be like. I'd really tell him something important and he'd
really listen to me. Instead, all we talked about was bullshit—
just *bull*shit. So six weeks later he's dead."

He glanced at me and then shook his head, smiling
sheepishly.

"Shakespeare should have done a play about this stuff," he
said. "I could have done the monologue."

"So he never talked to you about his personal life?"

"That's number three, you know," he remarked. "You
sneaked in that little question about whether it was just Dad
and me down here. But the answer is no. He never talked to me
about anything. I told you I couldn't be much help. Let's knock
it off for a while, okay?"

I smiled and tossed my shoes up on the beach, starting to
jog.

"Do you jog?" I called back over my shoulder.

"Yeah, some," he said, catching up. He began to trot at my side.

"What happens if I work up a sweat?" I asked. "Can we get cleaned up?"

"The neighbors let me use their shower."

"Great," I said and picked up the pace.

We ran, not exchanging a word, just taking in sun and sand and dry heat. The whole time, the same question came up over and over again. How could Sharon Napier fit into this scheme? What could she possibly have known that she didn't live long enough to tell? So far, none of it made sense. Not Fife's death, not Libby's, not Sharon's death eight years later. Unless she was blackmailing someone. I glanced back at the little trailer, still visible, looking remarkably close in the odd perspective of the flat desert landscape. There was no one else around. No sign of vehicles, no boogeymen on foot. I smiled at Greg. He wasn't even panting yet.

"You're in good shape," I said.

"So are you. How long do we keep this up?"

"Thirty minutes. Forty-five."

We chunked along for a while, the sand causing mild pains in my calves.

"How about I ask you three?" he said.

"Okay."

"How'd you get along with your old man?"

"Oh great," I said. "He died when I was five. Both of them did. In a car wreck. Up near Lompoc. Big rock rolled down the mountain and smashed the windshield. Took them six hours to pry me out of the back. My mother cried for a while and then she stopped. I still hear it sometimes in my sleep. Not the sobs. The silence after that. I was raised by my aunt. Her sister."

He digested that. "You married?"

"Was." I held up two fingers.

He smiled. "Is that for 'twice' or question number two?"

I laughed. "That's number three."

"Hey come on. You cheat."

"All right. One more. But make it count."

"You ever kill anyone?"

I glanced over at him with curiosity. It seemed like a strange follow-up. "Let's put it this way," I said. "I did my first homicide investigation when I was twenty-six. A job I did for the public defender's office. A woman accused of killing her own kids. Three of them. Girls. All under five. Taped their mouths, hands, and feet, then put them in garbage cans and let them suffocate. I had to look at the glossy eight-by-ten police photographs. I got cured of any homicidal urges. Also any desire for motherhood."

"Jesus," he said. "And she really did it?"

"Oh sure. She got off, of course. Pleaded temporary insanity. She might be back on the streets again for all I know."

"How do you keep from getting cynical?" he asked.

"Who says I'm not?"

While I showered in the trailer next door, I tried to think what else I might learn from Greg. I was feeling restless, anxious to be on the road again. If I could get to Claremont by dark, I could talk to Diane first thing in the morning and then drive back to Los Angeles after lunch. I toweled my hair dry and dressed. Greg had opened another beer for me, which I sipped while I waited for him to get cleaned up. I glanced at my watch. It was 3:15. Greg came into the trailer, leaving the door open, sliding the screen door shut. His dark hair was still damp and he smelled of soap.

"You look poised for flight," he said, getting himself a beer. He popped the cap.

"I'm thinking I should try to get to Claremont before dark," I said. "You have any messages for your sister?"

"She knows where I am. We talk now and then, often enough to keep caught up," he said. He sat down in the canvas chair, propping his feet up on the padded bench next to me. "Anything else you want to ask?"

"Couple of things if you don't mind," I said.

"Fire away."

"What do you remember about your father's allergies?"

"Dogs, cat dander, sometimes hay fever but I don't know what that consisted of exactly."

"He wasn't allergic to any kind of food? Eggs? Wheat?"

Greg shook his head. "Not that I ever heard. Just stuff in the air—pollens, things like that."

"Did he have his allergy capsules with him when the family came down here that weekend?"

"I don't remember that. I would guess no. He knew we'd be out in the desert and the air down here is usually pretty clear even in late summer, early fall. The dog wasn't with us. We left him at home, so Dad wouldn't have needed the allergy medication for that, and I don't think there was anything else he needed it for."

"I thought the dog got killed. I thought Nikki told me that," I said.

"Yeah, he was. While we were gone as a matter of fact."

I felt a sudden chill. There was something odd about that, something off. "How'd you find out about it?"

Greg shrugged. "When we got home," he said, apparently not attaching much to the fact. "Mom had taken Diane over to the house to pick something up. Sunday morning I guess. We didn't get back until Monday night. Anyway, they found Bruno lying out on the side of the road. I guess he was pretty badly mangled. Mom wouldn't even let Diane see him up close. She called the animal-shelter people and they came and picked him up. He'd been dead awhile. All of us felt bad about it. He was a great beast."

"Good watchdog?"

"The best," he said.

"What about Mrs. Voss, the housekeeper? What was she like?"

"Nice enough, I guess. She seemed to get along with everybody," he said. "I wish I knew more but that's about it as far as I can tell."

I finished my beer and got up, holding out my hand to him. "Thanks, Greg. I may need to talk to you again if that's okay."

He kissed the back of my hand, pretending to clown but meaning something else, I was almost sure. "Godspeed," he said softly.

I smiled with unexpected pleasure. "Did you ever see *Young Bess*? Jean Simmons and Stewart Granger? That's what he says to her. He was doomed, I think, or maybe she was—I forget. Ripped my heart out. You ought to watch for it on the late movie some night. It killed me when I was a kid."

"You're only five or six years older than me," he said.

"Seven," I replied.

"Same smell."

"I'll let you know what I find out," I said.

"Good luck."

As I pulled away, I glanced back out of the car window. Greg was standing in the trailer doorway, the screen creating the ghostly illusion of Laurence Fife again.

15

I reached Claremont at 6:00, driving through Ontario, Montclair, and Pomona; all townships without real towns, a peculiar California phenomenon in which a series of shopping malls and acres of tract houses acquire a zip code and become realities on the map. Claremont is an oddity in that it resembles a trim little midwestern hamlet with elms and picket fences. The annual Fourth of July parade is composed of kazoo bands, platoons of children on crepe-paper-decorated bikes, and a self-satirizing team of husbands dressed in Bermuda shorts, black socks, and business shoes doing close-order drills with power mowers. Except for the smog, Claremont could even be considered "picturesque" with Mount Baldy forming a raw backdrop.

I pulled into a gas station and called the number Gwen had given me for Diane. She was out, but her roommate said she'd be home at 8:00. I headed up Indian Hill Boulevard, turning left onto Baughman. My friends Gideon and Nell live two doors down in a house with two kids, three cats, and a hot tub. Nell I've known since my college days. She's a creature of high intellect and wry humor who's learned never to be too amazed by my appearances on her doorstep. She seemed pleased to see me nevertheless and I sat in her kitchen, watching her make soup while we talked. I called Diane again after supper and she agreed to meet me for lunch. After that, Nell and I stripped down and soaked in the hot tub out on the deck, with icy white wine and a lot more catching up to do. Gideon graciously kept the children at bay. I slept on the couch that night with a cat curled up on my chest, wondering if there was any way I could have such a life for myself.

I met Diane at one of those brown-bread-and-sprout restaurants that all look the same: lots of natural varnished wood and

healthy hanging plants, macrame and leaded-glass windows
and waiters who don't smoke cigarettes but would probably
toke on anything else you've got. Ours was thin with receding
hair and a dark mustache, which he stroked incessantly, taking
our order with an earnestness that I don't think any sandwich
ever deserved. Mine was avocado and bacon. Hers was a
"vegetarian delite" stuffed in pita bread.

"Greg says he really treated you like shit when you first got
down there," she said and laughed. Some sort of dressing was
leaking out through a crack in her pita bread and she lapped it
off.

"When did you talk to him? Last night?"

"Sure." She took another unwieldy mouthful and I
watched her lick her fingers and wipe her chin. She had Greg's
clean good looks but she carried more weight, wide rump
packed into a pair of faded jeans, and an unexpected
powdering of freckles on her face. Her dark hair was parted in
the center and pulled up on top with a broad leather band,
pierced through with a wooden skewer.

"Did you know Nikki was out on parole?" I asked.

"That's what Mom said. Is Colin back?"

"Nikki was just on her way up to get him when I talked to
her a couple of days ago," I said. I was struggling to keep my
sandwich intact, thick bread breaking with every bite, but I
caught the look in her eye. Colin interested her. Nikki did not.

"Did you meet Mom?"

"Yes. I liked her a lot."

Diane flashed a quick, proud smile. "Daddy was really an
asshole to dump her for Nikki if you ask me. I mean, Nikki's
okay, but she's kind of cold, don't you think?"

I murmured something noncommittal. Diane didn't seem to
be listening anyway. "Your mother said you went into therapy
right after your father died," I said.

Diane rolled her eyes, taking a sip of peppermint tea. "I've
been in therapy half my life and my head's still not on straight.
It's really a drag. The shrink I got now thinks I should go into
analysis but nobody does that anymore. He says I need to go
into my 'dark' side. He's into this real Freudian horseshit. All
those old guys are. You know, they want you to lie there and
tell 'em all your dreams and kinky fantasies so they can whack

off mentally at your expense. I did Reichian before that but I got sick of huffing and puffing and pulling on towels. That just felt dumb to me."

I took a big bite of sandwich, nodding as if I knew what she was talking about. "I've never been in therapy," I murmured.

"Not even *group*?"

I shook my head.

"God, you must really be neurotic," she said respectfully.

"Well I don't bite my nails or wet the bed."

"You're probably the compulsive type, avoiding commitments and shit like that. Daddy was like that some."

"Like how?" I said, skipping right over the reference to my character. After all, it was just a wild guess.

"Oh. You know. Fucking around all the time. Greg and I still compare notes on that. My shrink says he was just warding off pain. My granny used to manipulate the shit out of him so he turned around and manipulated everyone else, including Greg and me. And Mom. And Nikki, and I don't even know who else. I don't think he ever loved anybody in his life except Colin maybe. Too threatening."

She finished her sandwich and spent a few minutes wiping her face and hands. Then she folded the paper napkin carefully.

"Greg told me you missed the trip to Salton Sea," I said.

"What, before Daddy died? Yeah I did. I had the flu, really grisly stuff, so I stayed with Mom. She was great, really poured on the TLC. I never slept so much in my life."

"How did the dog get out?"

She put her hands in her lap. "What?"

"Bruno. Greg said he got hit by a car. I just wondered who let him out. Was Mrs. Voss staying at the house while the family was gone?"

Diane looked at me with care and then away. "I don't think so. She was on vacation, I think." Her eyes strayed to the clock on the wall behind me. "I've got a class," she said. Her face was suffused with pink.

"Are you okay?"

"Sure. Fine," she said, casually gathering up her purse and books. She seemed relieved to have something to do. "Oh, I nearly forgot. I've got something for Colin if you're going to see him." She held out a paper bag. "It's an album I

put together for him. We had all those pictures in a box." She
was all business now, her manner distracted, her attention
disengaged. She gave me a brief smile. "I'm sorry I don't have
any more time. How much is my part of the lunch?"

"I'll take care of it," I said. "Can I drop you someplace?"

"I've got a car," she said. All the animation had left her
face.

"Diane, what's going on?" I said.

She sat down again abruptly, staring straight ahead. Her
voice had dropped about six notes. "I let the dog out myself,"
she said, "the day they left. Nikki said to let him have a run
before Mom picked me up so I did but I just felt like shit. I lay
down on the couch in the living room to wait for Mom and
when she honked, I just grabbed my stuff and went out the
front. I never even thought about the dog. He must have been
running around for two days before I remembered. That's why
Mom and I drove over there. To fed him and let him in."

Her eyes finally met mine and she seemed close to tears.
"That poor thing," she whispered. The guilt seemed to take
possession of her totally. "It was my fault. That's why he got
hit. Because I forgot." She put a trembling hand against her
mouth, blinking. "I felt awful about it but I never told anyone
except Mom and nobody ever asked. You won't tell, will you?
They were so upset that he got killed that nobody ever even
asked me how he got out and I never said a word. I couldn't.
Nikki would have hated me."

"Nikki's not going to hate you because the dog got killed,
Diane," I said. "That was years ago. What difference does it
make now?"

Her eyes took on a haunted look and I had to lean forward
to hear what she was saying. "Because someone got in. While
the dog was out. Someone got into the house and switched the
medication. And that's why Daddy died," she said. She
fumbled in her purse for a Kleenex, her sobs sounding like a
series of gasps, involuntary, quick, her shoulders hunching
helplessly.

Two guys from the next table looked over at her with
curiosity.

"Oh God, oh God," she whispered, her voice hoarse with
grief.

"Let's get out of here," I said, grabbing up her belongings. I left too much money on the table for the check. I took her by the arm, propelling her toward the door.

By the time we got out to the parking lot, she was almost in control of herself. "God, I'm sorry. I can't believe I did that," she said. "I never fall apart that way."

"That's okay," I said. "I had no idea I'd set you off like that. It was just something that stuck in my mind after Greg mentioned it. I didn't mean to *accuse* you of anything."

"I couldn't believe you said it," she said, tears rising again. She looked at me earnestly. "I thought you knew. I thought you must have found out. I never would have admitted it otherwise. I've felt so awful about that for so long."

"How can you blame yourself? If someone wanted to get into the house, he would have let the dog loose anyway. Or killed it and made it look like an accident. I mean, who's going to get upstairs with a goddamn German shepherd barking and snarling?" I said.

"I don't know. Maybe so. It could be, I guess. I mean, he *was* a good watchdog. If he'd been in, nobody could have done anything."

She let out a deep breath, blowing her nose again on the damp twisted Kleenex. "I was so irresponsible in those days. They were always on my case, which just made things worse. I couldn't tell 'em. And nobody seemed to make the connection when Daddy died except me and I *couldn't* admit it then."

"Hey it's over," I said, "it's done. You can't beat yourself to death with it. It's not as if you did it deliberately."

"I know, I know. But the result was the same, you know?" Her voice lifted up and her eyes squeezed shut again, tears running down her cheeks. "He was such a shit and I loved him so much. I know Greg hated his guts, but I just thought he was great. I didn't care if he screwed around. That wasn't his fault. He was just so messed up all his life. He really was."

She wiped her eyes with the wad of Kleenex and then took another deep breath. She reached in her purse for a compact.

"Why don't you skip your class and go home?" I said.

"Maybe I will," she said. She looked at herself in the mirror. "God, I'm a wreck. I can't go anywhere looking like this."

"I'm sorry I triggered this. I think I feel worse than you," I said sheepishly.

"No, that's all right. It's not your fault. It's mine. I guess I'll even have to tell my shrink now. He'll think it's cathartic. He loves that shit. I guess everyone will know now. God, that's all I need."

"Hey, I may or may not have to mention it. I really don't know yet, but I don't think it matters now. If someone was determined to kill your father, it would have been done one way or the other. That's just a fact."

"I guess so. Anyway, it's nice of you to say that. I feel better. Really. I didn't even know it was still weighing on me, but it must have been."

"You're sure you're okay now?"

She nodded, giving me a little smile.

We said our good-byes, which took a few minutes more, and then she walked to her car. I watched while she drove off and then I tossed the album for Colin in the backseat of my car and pulled out. Actually, though I hated to admit it, she was probably right. If the dog had been in the house, no one could have messed with anything. With the dog in or out, dead or alive, it certainly wouldn't have protected Libby Glass. And at least one piece of the puzzle now fit. It didn't seem to mean much, but it did seem to establish the approximate date of entry to the house, if that's how the killer had effected the switch. It felt like the first blank I'd really filled in. Small progress but it made me feel good. I drove back to the San Bernardino Freeway and headed for L.A.

16

When I got back to the Hacienda, I went into the office to check for telephone messages. Arlette had four, but three of them turned out to be from Charlie Scorsoni. She leaned an elbow on the counter, munching on something sticky and dark brown enclosed in cookie dough.

"What is that thing?"

"Trimline Diet Snack Bar," she said. "Six calories each." Some of the filling seemed to be stuck to her teeth like dental putty and she ran a finger along her gums, popping goo into her mouth again. "Look at this label. I bet there's not one natural ingredient in this entire piece of food. Milk powder, hydrogenated fat, powdered egg, and a whole list of chemicals and additives. But you know what? I've noticed real food doesn't taste as good as fake. Have you noticed that? It's just a fact of life. Real food is bland, watered-down-tasting. You take a supermarket tomato. Now it's pathetic what that tastes like," she said and shuddered. I was trying to sort through my messages but she was making it hard.

"I bet this isn't even real flour in this thing," she said. "I mean, I've heard people say junk food just has empty calories, but who needs full ones? I like 'em empty. That way I figure I can't gain any more weight. That Charlie Scorsoni sure kept in touch, didn't he? He called once from Denver and then he called from Tucson and last night from Santa Teresa. Wonder what he wants. He sounded cute."

"I'll be in my room," I said.

"Well all right. Good enough. You want to return those calls, you just give me a buzz up here and I'll put you through."

"Thanks," I said.

"Oh yeah, and I gave your telephone number in Las Vegas

to a couple of people who didn't want to leave messages. I
hope that's okay. You didn't say I couldn't refer calls."

"No, that's fine," I said. "Any idea who it might have
been?"

"Male and female, one each," she said airily.

When I got to my room, I kicked my shoes off and called
Charlie Scorsoni's office and talked to Ruth.

"He was supposed to get back last night," she said. "But
he didn't plan to come in to the office. You might try him at
home."

"Well, if I don't get him there, will you tell him I'm back
in Los Angeles? He knows where to reach me here."

"Will do," she said.

The other message was a bonus. Apparently Garry Steinberg, the accountant at Haycraft and McNiece, had come back
from New York a few days early and was willing to talk to me
on Friday afternoon, which was today. I called and talked to
him briefly, telling him I'd be there within the hour. Then I
called Mrs. Glass and told her I should be out at her place
shortly after supper. There was one more call I felt I should
make, though I dreaded the necessity. I sat for a moment on the
edge of the bed, staring at the phone and then I said to hell with
it and dialed my friend in Las Vegas.

"Jesus, Kinsey," he said through his teeth. "I wish you
wouldn't do this to me. I get you the lowdown on Sharon
Napier and next thing I know she's dead."

I gave him the situation as succinctly as I could but it didn't
seem to ease his anxieties. Or mine. "It could have been
anyone," I said. "We don't *know* that she was shot because of
me."

"Yeah, but I got to cover myself anyway. Somebody
remembers that I was asking around after this lady and then
she's found with a bullet in her throat. I mean, how does that
look?"

I apologized profusely and told him to let me know
anything he found out. He didn't seem that eager to keep in
touch. I changed clothes, putting on a skirt, hose, and heels,
and then I drove to the Avco Embassy building and took the
elevator to the tenth floor. I was feeling bad about Sharon

Napier all over again, guilt sitting in my gut like a low-level colic. How could I have missed that appointment? How could that have happened to me? She knew *something* and if I'd gotten there on time, I might be wrapping this investigation up instead of being where I was—which was nowhere in particular. I made my way back into the imitation barnyard of Haycraft and McNiece, staring at the dried corn on the wall while I whipped myself some more.

Garry Steinberg turned out to be a very nice man. I guessed him to be in his early thirties, with dark curly hair, dark eyes, and a small gap between his front teeth. He was probably five feet, ten inches and his body looked soft, his waist puffing out like rising bread dough.

"You're noticing my waist, am I right?" he asked.

I shrugged somewhat sheepishly, wondering if he did or did not want me to comment. He motioned me into a chair and then sat down behind his desk.

"Let me show you something," he said, lifting a finger. He opened his top desk drawer and took out a snapshot, which he handed to me. I glanced at it.

"Who's this?"

"Perfect," he said. "That was the perfect response. That's me. When I weighed three hundred and ten pounds. Now I weigh two-sixteen."

"My God," I said and looked at the picture again. Actually I could see now that in the old days he had looked a bit like Arlette might if she decided to cross-dress. I'm crazy about "before-and-after" shots, an avid fan of all those magazine ads showing women pumped up like tires and then magically thin, one foot arranged in front of the other, as though weight loss also involved the upsurge of charm and modeling skills. I wondered if there was anyone left in California not obsessed with self-image.

"How'd you do it?" I asked, handing the snapshot back.

"Scarsdale," he said. "It was a real honest-to-God bitch but I did it. I only cheated once—well, twice. Once was when I turned thirty-five. I figured I was entitled to a bagel and cream cheese with a birthday candle. And one night I binged because my girl friend got mad at me and kicked me out. I

mean, lookit, when I was three-ten I never even had a girl.
Now I'm having fits when she throws me out. We made up
again though, so that turned out all right. I've got twenty-five
pounds to lose yet but I'm giving myself a break. Strictly
maintenance. Have you ever done Scarsdale?"

I shook my head apologetically. I was beginning to feel I'd
never done anything. No Scarsdale, no therapy.

"No alcohol," he said. "That's the hard part. On the
maintenance diet, you can have like a small glass of white
wine now and then, but that's it. I figure the first fifty pounds I
lost was from that. Giving up booze. You'd be surprised how
much weight that adds."

"Sounds a lot better for you," I said.

"I feel good about myself," he said. "That's the important
thing. So. Enough of that. What do you want to know about
Libby Glass? The receptionist says you came about her."

I explained what I was up to and how I came to be involved
in the matter of her death. He took it all in, asking occasional
questions. "What can I tell you?" he said, finally.

"How long had she handled Laurence Fife's account?"

"I'm glad you asked me that because that's one thing I
looked up when I knew you were coming over. We handled his
personal finances first for about a year. The law firm of Fife
and Scorsoni had only been with us six months. Actually a
little less. We were just putting in our own computer system
and Libby was trying to get all the records straightened out for
the changeover. She was a very good accountant by the way.
Real conscientious and real smart."

"Were you a good friend of hers?"

"Pretty good. I was El Blimpo back then but I had a crush
on her and we kind of had this brotherr-sister relationship—
platonic. We didn't date. Just had lunch together once a week,
something like that. Sometimes a drink after work."

"How many accounts did she handle?"

"All together? I'd say twenty-five, maybe thirty. She was a
very ambitious girl and she really knocked herself out . . .
for all the good it did."

"Meaning what?"

He got up and closed the door to his office, pointing
significantly to the wall of the office next door.

"Listen, old man Haycraft was a petty tyrant, the original male chauvinist pig. Libby thought if she worked hard, she'd get a promotion and a raise, but no such thing. And these guys aren't much better. You want to know how I get a raise? I threaten to quit. Libby didn't even do that."

"How much was she paid?"

"I don't know. I could maybe look that up. Not enough to suit her, I can tell you that. Fife and Scorsoni was a big account—not the biggest, but big. She didn't feel it was fair."

"She did more work for Fife than Scorsoni, I assume."

"At first. After that, it was half and half. A lot of the purpose of our taking over their business management was to keep track of all the estate work. That was a big part of their ongoing business from what she said. The dead guy, Fife, did a lot of messy divorce work, which paid big fees but didn't require that much in the way of bookkeeping. Also, we did accounts receivable for them, paid their office bills, kept track of profits from the firm, and made suggestions about investments. Well, at that point, we weren't doing much in the way of investment counseling because they hadn't been with us that long but that was the object of the exercise eventually. We like to hold off some until we see where our clients stand. Anyway, I can't go into details on that but I can probably answer any other general questions you might have."

"Do you know anything about where the money from the Fife's estate went?"

"The kids. It was divided equally among them. I never saw the will but I helped settle the estate in terms of disbursements after probate."

"You don't happen to represent Scorsoni's new law firm, do you?"

"Nope," Garry said. "I met him a couple of times after Fife died. He seemed like a nice man."

"Is there any way I could look at the old books?"

"Nope," he said. "You could do it if I had Scorsoni's written permission but I don't know what good that would do you anyway unless you're an accountant yourself. Our system isn't that complicated, but I don't think it'd make sense to you."

"Probably not," I said, trying to think what else I wanted to ask him about.

"You want coffee? I'm sorry, I should have asked you sooner."

"No thanks. I'm fine," I said. "What about Libby's personal affairs. Is there any chance that she was sleeping with Laurence Fife?"

Garry laughed. "Now that I don't know. She'd been going with some creepy little guy ever since high school, and I knew she'd broken up with him. On my advice, I might add."

"How come?"

"He came in to apply for a job here. I was in charge of screening all applicants. He was just supposed to messenger stuff back and forth but he didn't even look that smart. He was belligerent, too, and if you want my honest opinion, he was high."

"You wouldn't still have his application on file, would you?" I asked, feeling a faint surge of excitement.

Garry looked at me. "We're not having this conversation, am I right?"

"Right."

"I'll see what I can find," he said promptly. "It wouldn't be here. It'd be over in the warehouse. We have all the old records stored there. Accountants are real pack rats. We never throw anything away and everything gets written down."

"Thanks, Garry," I said. "I can't tell you how much I appreciate this."

He smiled happily. "And maybe I'll look for the old Fife files as long as I'm over there. It won't hurt to take a peek. And to answer your question about Libby, my guess would be no. I don't think she was having an affair with Laurence Fife." He glanced at his watch. "I got a meeting."

I shook his hand across the desk, feeling good. "Thanks again," I said.

"No problem. Stop by again. Anytime."

I got back to my hotel room at 3:30. I put a pillow on the plastic chair, set my typewriter up on the wobbly desk, and spent an hour and a half typing up my notes. It had been a long time since I sat down to do paperwork but it had to be caught up. By the time I pecked my way through the last paragraph, I had a pain in my lower back and another one right between my shoulder blades. I changed into my running clothes, my body heat resurrecting the smell of old sweat and car fumes. I was going to have to find a Laundromat soon. I jogged south on Wilshire, just for variety, cutting across to San Vicente at Twenty-sixth Street. Once I got on the wide grassy divider, I could feel myself hit stride. Running always hurts—I don't care what they say—but it does acquaint one with all of one's body parts. This time I could feel my thighs protest and I noticed a mild aching in my shins, which I ignored, plodding on gamely. For my bravery, I netted a few rude remarks from two guys in a pickup truck. When I got back to the motel, I showered and got back into my jeans and then I stopped by McDonald's and had a Quarter Pounder with cheese, fries, and a medium Coke. By then, it was 6:45. I filled up the car with gas and headed over the hill into Sherman Oaks.

17

Mrs. Glass answered the door after half a buzz. This time the living room had been picked up to some extent, her sewing confined now to a neatly folded pile of fabric on the arm of the couch. Raymond was nowhere in sight.

"He had a bad day," she said to me. "Lyle stopped by on his way home from work and we put him to bed."

Even the television set was turned off, and I wondered what she did with herself in the evenings.

"Elizabeth's things are in the basement," she murmured. "I'll just get the key to the storage bin."

She returned a moment later and I followed her out into the corridor. We turned left, past the stairway back to the basement door which was set into the right-hand wall. The door was locked and after she opened it, she flipped the light switch at the top of the stairs. I could already smell the dry musty scent of old window screens and half-empty cans of latex paint. I was about two steps behind her as we made our way down the narrow passageway, wooden stairs taking a sharp right-hand turn. At the landing, I caught a glimpse of concrete floor with bins of wooden lathing reaching to the low ceiling. Something wasn't right but the oddity didn't really register before the blast rang out. The light bulb on the landing shattered, spraying us both with thin flakes of glass and the basement was instantly blanketed in darkness. Grace shrieked and I grabbed her, pulling her back up the stairs. I lost my balance and she stumbled over me. There must have been an outside exit because I heard a wrenching of wood, a bang, and then someone taking the concrete steps outside two at a time. I struggled out from under Grace, jerking her up the stairs with me and then I left her in the corridor, racing out through the front and around the side of the building. Someone had left an old power mower in the driveway and I tripped in the darkness, sprawling forward on my hands and knees, cursing savagely as I scrambled back to my feet again. I reached the rear of the building, keeping low, my heart pounding in my ears. It was black-dark, my eyes just beginning to adjust. A vehicle started up one street over and I could hear it chirp out with a quick shift of gears. I ducked back, leaning against the building then, hearing nothing but the fading roar of a vehicle being driven away at high speed. My mouth was dry. I was drenched in sweat and belatedly I felt a shudder go through me. Both my palms stung where the gravel had bitten into the flesh. I trotted back to my car and got out my flashlight, tucking the little automatic into my windbreaker pocket. I didn't think there was anyone left to shoot but I was tired of being surprised.

Grace was sitting on the doorsill, her head hanging down between her knees. She was shaking from head to foot and she'd started to weep. I helped her to her feet, easing open the apartment door.

"Lyle knew I was picking the stuff up, right?" I snapped at her. She gave me a haunted, pleading look.

"It couldn't have been him. He wouldn't have done that to me," she whimpered.

"Your faith is touching," I said. "Now sit. I'll be back in a minute."

I went back to the basement stairs. The beam from the flashlight cut through the blackness. There was a second bulb at the bottom of the stairs and I pulled the chain. A flat dull light from the swinging bulb threw out a yellow arc that slowed to a halt. I turned off the flashlight. I knew which bin belonged to Mrs. Glass. It had been smashed open, the padlock dangling ineffectually where the lathing had been broken through. Cardboard boxes had been torn open, the contents strewn about in haste, forming an ankle-deep mess through which I picked my way. The emptied boxes all bore the name "Elizabeth," obligingly rendered in bold Magic Marker strokes. I wondered if we'd interrupted the intruder before or after he'd found what he was looking for. I heard a sound behind me and I whirled, raising the flashlight instantly like a club.

A man stood there staring at me with bewilderment.

"Got a problem down here?"

"Oh fuck. Who are you?"

He was middle-aged, hands in his pockets, his expression sheepish. "Frank Isenberg from apartment three," he said apologetically. "Did somebody break in? You want me to call the police?"

"No, don't do that yet. Let me check upstairs with Grace. This looks like the only bin that's been damaged. Maybe it was just kids," I said, heart still thudding. "You didn't have to sneak up on me."

"Sorry. I just thought you might need some help."

"Yeah, well thanks anyway. I'll let you know if I need anything."

He stood there surveying the chaos for a moment and then he shrugged and went back upstairs.

I checked the basement door at the rear. The glass had been broken out and someone had pulled back the bolt by reaching through. The door was wide open of course. I shut it, pushing the bolt back into place. When I turned around, Grace was creeping timidly down the stairs, her face still pale. She clung to the railing. "Elizabeth's things," she whispered. "They spoiled all of her boxes, all the things I saved."

She sank down on the steps, rubbing her temples. Her large dark eyes looked injured, perplexed, with a touch of something else that I could have sworn was guilt.

"Maybe we should call the police," I said, feeling mean, wondering just how protective of Lyle she intended to be.

"Do you really think?" she said. Her gaze flitted back and forth indecisively and she took out a handkerchief, pressing it against her forehead as though to remove beads of sweat. "Nothing might be missing," she said hopefully. "Maybe nothing's gone."

"Or maybe we won't know the difference," I said.

She pulled herself up and moved over to the bin, taking in the disastrous piles of papers, stuffed animals, cosmetics, underwear. She stopped, picking up papers randomly, trying to make stacks. Her hands still trembled but I didn't think she was afraid. Startled perhaps, and thinking rapidly.

"I take it Raymond is still asleep," I said.

She nodded, tears welling up as the extent of the vandalism became more and more apparent. I could feel myself relent.

Even if Lyle had done it, it was mean-spirited, a violation of something precious to Grace. She had already suffered enough without this. I set the flashlight aside and began to pile papers back into the boxes: costume jewelry, lingerie, old issues of *Seventeen* and *Vogue*, patterns for clothing that Libby had probably never made. "Do you mind if I take these boxes with me and go through them tonight?" I asked. "I can have them back to you by morning."

"All right. I suppose. I can't see what harm it would do now anyway," she murmured, not looking at me.

It seemed hopeless to me. In this jumble, who knew what might be missing? I'd have to go through the boxes and see if I could spot anything, but the chances weren't good. Lyle couldn't have been down there long—if it had been him. He knew I was coming back for the stuff and when he'd been there earlier, Grace probably told him exactly what time I expected to arrive. He'd had to wait until dark and he probably thought we'd spend more time upstairs before coming down. Still, he was cutting it close—unless he simply didn't care. And why didn't he break in during the three days I was gone? I thought back to his insolence and I suspected that he might take a certain satisfaction in thwarting me, even if he was caught at it.

Grace helped me cart the boxes to the car, six of them. I should have taken the stuff the first time I was there, I thought, but I couldn't picture driving to Vegas with the entire backseat filled with cardboard boxes. Still, the boxes would have been intact. It was my own damn fault, I thought sourly.

I told Grace I'd be back first thing in the morning and then I pulled out. It was going to be a long night.

I bought two containers of black coffee across the street, locked the door to my motel room, and closed the drapes. I emptied the first carton onto the bed and then I started making stacks. School papers in one pile. Personal letters. Magazines. Stuffed animals. Clothing. Cosmetics. Bills and receipts. Grace had apparently saved every article Elizabeth had touched since kindergarten. Report cards. School projects. Really, six cartons seemed modest when I realized how much there was. Blue books from college. Copies of applications for work. Tax returns. The accumulation of an entire life and it was really only so much trash. Who would ever need to refer to

any of this again? The original energy and spirit had all seeped
away. I did feel for her. I did get some sense of that young girl,
whose gropings and triumphs and little failures were piled
together now in a drab motel room. I didn't even know what I
was looking for. I flipped through a diary from the fifth
grade—the handwriting round and dutiful, the entries dull. I
tried to imagine myself dead, someone sorting carelessly
through my belongings. What was there really of my life?
Canceled checks. Reports all typewritten and filed. Everything
of value reduced to terse prose. I didn't keep much myself,
didn't hoard or save. Two divorce decrees. That was about the
sum of it for me. I collected more information about other
people's lives than I did about my own, as though, perhaps, in
poring over the facts about other people, I could discover
something about myself. My own mystery, unplumbed, unde-
tected, was sorted into files that were neatly labeled but really
didn't say much. I picked through the last of Elizabeth's boxes
but there was nothing of interest. It was 4:00 in the morning
when I finished. Nothing. If there had been anything there, it
was gone now and I was irritated with myself again, berating
myself for my own poor judgment. This was the second time
I'd arrived too late—the second time some vital piece of
information had slipped away from me.

I began to repack boxes, automatically rechecking as I
went, sorting. Clothes in one box, stuffed animals tucked into
the spaces along the sides. School papers, diaries, blue books
in the next box. Back it all went, neatly catalogued this time,
compulsively arranged, as thought I owed Elizabeth Glass
some kind of order after I'd pried into the hidden crevices of
her abandoned life. I riffed through magazines, held textbooks
by the spine, letting the pages fly loose. The stacks on the bed
diminished. There weren't that many personal letters and I felt
guilty reading them, but I did. Some from an aunt in Arizona.
Some from a girl named Judy whom Libby must have known
in high school. No one seemed to refer to anything intimate in
her life and I had to conclude that she confided little or else that
she had no tales to tell. The disappointment was acute. I was
down to the last pile of books, mostly paperbacks. Such taste.
Leon Uris and Irving Stone, Victoria Holt, Georgette Heyer, a
few more exotic samples that I guessed had been from some
literature survey course in college. The letter slipped out of the

pages of a dog-eared copy of *Pride and Prejudice*. I nearly
tossed it in the box with the rest of the stuff. The handwriting
was a tightly stroked cursive on two sides in dark blue ink. No
date. No envelope. No postmark. I picked it up by one corner
and read it, feeling a cold pinching sensation begin at the base
of my spine.

Darling Elizabeth . . . I'm writing this so you'll have something when you get back. I know these separations are hard for
you and I wish there were some way I could ease your pain.
You are so much more honest than I am, so much more open
about what you feel than I allow myself to be, but I do love you
and I don't want you to have any doubts about that. You're
right when you say that I'm conservative. I'm guilty as
charged, your Honor, but I'm not immune to suffering and as
often as I've been accused of being selfish, I'm not as reckless
of others as you might think. I would like to take our time
about this and be sure that it's something we both want. What
we have now is very dear to me and I'm not saying—please
believe me—that I wouldn't turn my life around for you if it
comes to that. On the other hand, I think we should both be
sure that we can survive the day-to-day absurdities of being
together. Right now, the intensity dazzles and it seems simple
enough for us both to chuck it all and make some kind of life,
but we haven't known each other that long or that well. I can't
afford to risk wife, kids, and career in the heat of the moment
though you know it tempts me. Please let's move slowly on
this. I love you more than I can say and I don't want to lose
you—which is selfish enough, I suppose, in itself. You're right
to push, but please don't lose sight of what's at stake, for you
as well as me. Tolerate my caution if you can. I love you.
Laurence

I didn't know what to make of it. I realized, in a flash, that it
wasn't just that I hadn't believed in an affair between Laurence
and Elizabeth. I hadn't *wanted* to believe. I wasn't sure I
believed it yet but why the resistance? It was so neat. So
convenient. It fit in so nicely with what I knew of the facts and
still I stared at the letter, holding it gingerly by one corner as I
read it again. I leaned back against the bed. What was the

matter with me? I was exhausted and I knew I'd been through
too much in the last few days but something nagged at me and I
wasn't sure it had so much to do with the letter as it did with
myself, with something in my nature—some little niggling
piece of self-illumination that I was fighting hard not to recognize. Either the letter was real or it was not, and there were
ways to verify that. I pulled myself together wearily. I found a
large envelope and slipped the letter inside, being careful not
to smudge fingerprints, already thinking ahead to Con Dolan,
who would love it since it confirmed all his nastiest suspicions
about what had been going on back then. Was this what Sharon
Napier had figured out? Was this what she could have
corroborated if she'd lived long enough?

I lay on the bed fully dressed, body tense, brain wired.
Who could she have hoped to blackmail with this information
if she'd known? It had to be what she was up to. It had to be
why she'd been killed. Someone had followed me to Las
Vegas, knowing that I would see her, knowing that she might
confirm what I hadn't wanted to believe. I couldn't prove it, of
course, but I wondered if I was getting close enough to the
truth to be in danger myself. I wanted to go home. I wanted to
retreat to the safety of my small room. I wasn't thinking clearly
yet, but I was getting close. For eight years, nothing happened
and now it was all beginning again. If Nikki was innocent,
then someone had been sitting pretty all this time, someone in
danger of exposure now.

I saw, for an instant, the look that had flashed in Nikki's
eyes, unreasoning malevolence, a harsh irrational rage. She
had set this all in motion. I had to consider the possibility that
Sharon Napier was blackmailing *her*, that Sharon knew
something that could link Nikki to Libby's death. If Sharon had
dropped out of sight, it was possible that Nikki had hired me to
flush her out and that Nikki had then eliminated any threat with
one quick shot. She might also have followed me back to
Sherman Oaks for a frantic search through Libby's belongings
for anything that might have linked Libby to Laurence Fife.
There were pieces missing yet but they would fall into place
and then maybe the whole of it would make sense. Assuming I
lived long enough myself to figure it out . . .

18

I dragged myself out of bed at 6:00 A.M. I
hadn't slept at all. My mouth felt stale and I
brushed my teeth. I showered and dressed.
I longed to run but I felt too vulnerable to jog down the middle
of San Vicente at that hour. I packed, closing up my
typewriter, shoving the pages of my report into my briefcase. I
loaded the boxes into my car again, along with my suitcase.
The lights in the office were on and I could see Arlette taking
jelly doughnuts out of a bakery box, putting them on a plastic
plate with a clear dome lid. Water was already heating for that
awful, flat instant coffee. She was licking powdered sugar
from her fingers when I went in.

"God, you're up awful early," she said. "You want
breakfast?"

I shook my head. Even with my penchant for junk food, I
wouldn't eat a jelly doughnut. "No, but thanks," I said. "I'm
checking out."

"Right now?"

I nodded, almost too tired to talk. She finally seemed to
sense that this was the wrong time to chat. She got my bill
ready and I signed it, not even bothering to add up the charges.
She usually made a mistake but I didn't care.

I got in my car and headed for Sherman Oaks. There was a
light on in Grace's kitchen, which I approached from around
the side of the building. I tapped on the window and after a
moment, she came into the service porch and opened the side
door. She looked small and precise this morning in an A-line
corduroy skirt and a coffee-colored cotton turtleneck. She kept
her voice low.

"Raymond's not awake yet but there's coffee if you like,"
she said.

"Thanks, but I've got a breakfast meeting at eight," I said,
lying without much thought. Whatever I said would be passed

on to Lyle and my whereabouts were none of his business—or
hers. "I just wanted to drop the boxes off."

"Did you find anything?" she asked. Her gaze met mine
briefly and then she blinked, glancing first at the floor and then
off to my left.

"Too late," I said, trying to ignore the flush of relief that
tinted her cheeks.

"That's unfortunate," she murmured, placing a hand
against her throat. "I'm . . . uh . . . sure it wasn't
Lyle . . ."

"It doesn't matter much anyway," I said. I felt sorry for her
in spite of myself. "I packed everything back as neatly as I
could. I'll just stack the boxes in the basement near the bin.
You'll probably want to have that repaired when you get the
basement door fixed."

She nodded. She moved to close the door and I stepped
back, watching her pad back into the kitchen in her soft-soled
slippers. I felt as if I'd personally violated her life somehow,
that everything was ending on a bad note. She'd been as
helpful as she knew how and she'd gotten little in return. I had
to shrug. There was nothing I could do at this point. I unloaded
the car, making several trips, stacking boxes just inside the
damaged bin. Unconsciously, I listened for Lyle. The light in
the basement was cold and gray by day, but aside from the
splintered lathework and the shattered window, there was no
other evidence of the intruder. I went out the back way on the
last trip up from the basement, checking idly for smashed
cigarette butts, bloody fingerprints, a small printed business
card perhaps, dropped by whoever broke in. I came up the
concrete stairs outside, looking off to the right at the path the
intruder had taken—across the patchy grass in the backyard,
over a sagging wire fence, and through a tangle of bushes. I
could see through to the next street where the car must have
been parked. It was early morning yet and the sunlight was flat
and still. I could hear heavy traffic on the Ventura Freeway,
which was visible in glimpses through the clumps of trees off
to the right. The ground wasn't even soft enough to absorb
footprints. I moved around the building to the driveway on my
left, noting with interest that the power mower had now been
pulled off to one side. My palms were still ripped up in places,

two-inch tracks where I'd skidded across the gravel on my hands. I hadn't even thought to use Bactine and I hoped I wouldn't be subject to raging gangrene, perilous infections, or blood poisoning—dangers my aunt had warned me about every time I skinned my knee.

I got back in my car and headed for Santa Teresa, stopping in Thousand Oaks for breakfast. I was home by 10:00 in the morning. I wrapped myself up in a quilt on the couch and slept for most of the day.

At 4:00, I drove out to Nikki's beach house. I had called to say I was back in town and she invited me out for a drink. I wasn't sure yet how much I would tell her or how much, if anything, I would hold back, but after my recent gnawing suspicions about her, I wanted to test my perceptions. There are moments in every investigation when my speculations about what's possible cloud and confuse any lingering sense I have of what's actually true. I wanted to check out my intuitions.

The house was situated on a bluff overlooking the ocean. The lot was small, irregular in shape, surrounded by eucalyptus trees. The house was tucked into the landscaping—laurel and yew, with pink and red geraniums planted along the path—its exterior made of cedar shingles, still a raw-looking wood brown, the roofline undulating like an ocean swell. There was a large oval window in the front, flanked by two bow windows, all undraped. The lawn was a pale green, tender blades of grass looking almost edible, curls of eucalyptus bark intermingled like wood shavings. White and yellow daisies grew in careless patches. The whole effect was of subtle neglect, a refined wilderness untended but subdued, curiously appealing with the thick scent of ocean overlaid and the dull thunder of waves crashing down below. The air was moist and smelled of salt, wind buffeting the ragged grass. Where the house in Montebello was boxy, substantial, conventional, plain, this was a whimsical cottage, all wide angles, windows, and unpainted wood. The front door had a tall oval leaded-glass window in it, filled with tulip shapes, and the doorbell sounded like wind chimes.

Nikki appeared at once. She was wearing a celery-green caftan, its bodice embroidered with mirrors the size of dimes,

the sleeves wide. Her hair was pulled up and away from her
face, tied with a pale-green velvet ribbon. She seemed relaxed,
her wide forehead unlined, the gray eyes looking light and
clear, her mouth faintly tinted with pink, curving upward as
though from some secret merriment. The languidness in her
manner was gone and she was animated, energetic. I had
brought the photograph album Diane had given me and I
handed it to her as she closed the door behind me.

"What's this?" she asked.

"Diane put it together for Colin," I said.

"Come see him," she said. "We're making bread."

I followed her through the house. There were no square
rooms at all. The spaces flowed into one another, connected by
gleaming pale wood floors and bright shag rugs. There were
windows everywhere, plants, skylights. A free-form fireplace
in the living room looked as if it had been constructed from
buff-colored boulders, piled up randomly like the entrance to a
cave. On the far wall, a crude ladder led up to a loft that
overlooked the ocean. Nikki smiled back at me happily,
placing the album on the glass coffee table as she passed.

The kitchen was a semicircle, wood and white Formica and
luscious healthy houseplants, windows on three sides looking
onto a deck with the ocean stretching out beyond, wide and
gray in the late afternoon. Colin was kneading bread, his back
to me, his concentration complete. His hair was the same pale
no-color shade as Nikki's, silky like hers where it curled down
on his neck. His arms looked wiry and strong, his hands
capable, fingers long. He gathered the edges of the dough,
pressing inward, turning it over again. He looked like he was
just on the verge of adolescence, beginning to shoot up in
height but not awkward yet. Nikki touched him and he turned
quickly, his gaze sliding over to me at once. I was startled. His
eyes were large, tilted slightly, an army-fatigue green, his
lashes thick and dark. His face was narrow, chin pointed, ears
coming to a delicate point, a pixie effect with the fine hair
forming a point on his forehead. The two of them looked like
an illustration from a faerie book—fragile and beautiful and
strange. His eyes were peaceful, empty, glowing with acute
intelligence. I have seen the same look in cats, their eyes wise,
aloof, grave.

When I spoke to Nikki, he watched our lips, his own lips parting breathlessly, so that the effect was oddly sexual.

"I think I just fell in love," I said and laughed. Nikki smiled, signing to Colin, her fingers graceful, succinct. Colin flashed a smile at me, much older than his years. I felt myself flush.

"I hope you didn't tell him that," I said. "We'd probably have to run off together."

"I told him you were my first friend after prison. I told him you needed a drink," she said, still signing, eyes resting on Colin's face. "Most of the time we don't sign this much. I'm just brushing up."

While Nikki opened a bottle of wine. I watched Colin work the bread dough. He offered to let me help and I shook my head, preferring to watch his agile hands, the dough developing a smooth skin almost magically as he worked. He made gruff, unintelligible sounds now and then without seeming aware of it.

Nikki gave me chilled white wine in a glass with a thin stem while she drank Perrier. "Here's to parole," she said.

"You look much more relaxed," I said.

"Oh I am. I feel great. It's so good to have him here. I follow him everywhere. I feel like a puppy dog. He gets no peace."

Her hands were moving automatically and I could see that she was translating for him simultaneously with her comments to me. It made me feel rude and clumsy that I couldn't sign too. I felt as if there were things I wanted to say to him myself, questions I wanted to ask about the silence in his head. It was like charades of some kind, Nikki using body, arms, face, her whole self totally involved, Colin signing back to her casually. He seemed to speak much more quickly than she, without deliberation. Sometimes Nikki would halt, struggling for a word, remembering, laughing at herself as she relayed to him her own forgetfulness. His smile in those moments was indulgent, full of affection, and I envied them this special world of secrets, of self-mockery, wherein Colin was the master and Nikki the apprentice. I couldn't imagine Nikki with any other kind of child.

Colin placed the smooth dough in the bowl, turning it once

to coat its pale surface with butter, covering it carefully then with a clean white towel. Nikki motioned him into the living room, where she showed him the photo album. Colin settled on the edge of the couch, leaning forward, elbows on his knees, the album open on the coffee table in front of him. His face was still but his eyes took in everything and he was already engrossed in the snapshots.

Nikki and I went out onto the deck. It was getting late but there was still enough sunlight to create the illusion of warmth. She stood at the railing, staring out at the ocean that rumbled below us. I could see tangles of kelp just under the surface in places, dark strands undulating in waves of paler green.

"Nikki, did you talk to anyone about where I was and what I was up to?" I asked.

"Not at all," she said, startled. "What makes you ask?"

I filled her in on the events of the last few days—Sharon Napier's death, my talks with Greg and Diane, the letter I'd found among Libby Glass's effects. My trust in her was instinctive.

"Would you recognize his handwriting?"

"Sure."

I took the manila envelope out of my purse, carefully removing the letter, which I unfolded for her. She glanced at it briefly.

"That's him," she said.

"I'd like you to read it," I said. "I want to see if it coincides with your intuitions about what was going on."

Reluctantly her gaze dropped back to the pale blue pages, when she finished, she seemed almost embarrassed. "I wouldn't have guessed it was that serious. His other affairs weren't."

"What about Charlotte Mercer?"

"She's a bitch. She's an alcoholic. She called me once. I hated her. And she hated him. You should have heard what she said."

I folded the letter carefully. "I didn't get it. From Charlotte Mercer to Libby Glass. That's quite a leap. I assumed he was a man of taste."

Nikki shrugged. "He was easily seduced. It was his own vanity. Charlotte *is* beautiful . . . in her own way."

"Was she in the process of divorcing? Is that how they met?"

Nikki shook her head. "We socialized with them. Judge Mercer was a sort of mentor of Laurence's at one point. I don't imagine he ever found out about the affair—it would have killed him, I think. He's the only decent judge we've got anyway. You know what the rest are like."

"I only talked to her a short time," I said, "but I can't see how she could be involved. It had to be somebody who knew where I was and how could she have come by that kind of information? Somebody had to have followed me up to Las Vegas. Sharon's murder was too closely timed to have been coincidence."

Colin appeared at Nikki's side, placing the open photograph album up on the railing. He pointed to one of the snapshots, saying something I couldn't understand at all, an indistinct blur of vowels. It was the first time I'd heard him speak. His voice was deeper than I would have imagined for a twelve-year-old.

"That's Diane's junior-high-school graduation," Nikki said to him. Colin looked at her for a moment and then pointed again more emphatically. He put his index finger in front of his mouth and moved it up and down rapidly. Nikki frowned.

" 'Who' what, honey?"

Colin placed his finger on the picture of a group of people.

"That's Diane and Greg and Diane's friend, Terri, and Diane's mother," she said to him, enunciating carefully and signing at the same time.

A puzzled smile formed on Colin's face. Colin spread his hands out, putting his thumb against his forehead and then his chin.

Nikki laughed this time, her expression as puzzled as his.

"No, *that's* Nana," she said, pointing to a snapshot one page back. "This is *Diane's* mother, not Daddy's. The mother of Greg and Diane. Don't you remember Nana? Oh God, how could he," she flashed at me. "She died when he was a year old." She looked back at him.

Colin made some guttural sounds, something negative and frustrated. I wondered what would happen to his temper when puberty really caught up with him. Again the thumb against the forehead, then the chin. Nikki shot me another look. "He keeps saying 'Daddy's mother' for Gwen. How do you explain 'ex-wife'?" She signed again patiently.

Colin shook his head slightly, suddenly unsure of himself. He watched her for a moment more as though some other explanation might be forthcoming. He took the album and backed away, eyes still fixed on Nikki's face. He signed once more, flushing uncomfortably. Apparently, he didn't want to look foolish in front of me.

"We'll go through those together in a minute," she signed to him, translating for me.

Colin moved slowly back through the sliding glass doors, pushing the screen door shut.

"Sorry for the interruption," she said briefly.

"That's all right, I've got to go anyway," I said.

"You can stay for supper if you like. I've made a big pot of beef bourguignon. It's great with Colin's bread."

"Thanks but I've got all kinds of things to do," I said.

Nikki walked me to the door, signing our final chitchat without even being aware of it.

I got in my car and sat for a moment, puzzled by Colin's puzzlement over Gwen. That was odd. Very odd.

19

When I got back to my apartment, Charlie Scorsoni was sitting on my doorstep. I felt grubby and unprepared and I realized with embarrassment that I'd been entertaining a fantasy of how we'd meet again and it wasn't like this.

"God, don't get all excited, Millhone," he said when he saw the expression on my face.

I got out my key. "I'm sorry," I said, "but you catch me at the worst possible times."

"You have a date," he said.

"No, I don't have a date. I look like shit." I unlocked the door and flipped on the desk lamp, letting him follow me in.

"At least I caught you in a good mood," he said, making himself at home. He sauntered out to the kitchen and got out the last beer. The familiarity in his manner made me cross.

"Look, I've got laundry to do. I haven't been to the grocery store for a week. My mail is piled up, the whole place is covered with dust. I haven't even shaved my legs since I saw you last."

"You need a haircut too," he said.

"No I don't. It always looks like this."

He smiled, shaking his head. "Get dressed. We'll go out."

"I don't want to go out. I want to get my life in shape."

"You can do that tomorrow. It's Sunday. I bet you always do shit like that on Sunday anyway."

I stared at him. It was true. "Wait a minute. Here's how it's supposed to go," I said patiently. "I get home. I do all my chores, get a good night's sleep, which I could sorely use, then tomorrow I call you and we see each other tomorrow night."

"I gotta be at the office tomorrow night. I have a client coming in."

"On Sunday night?"

"We've got a court appearance first thing Monday morning

and this is the only thing we could work out. I just got back into town myself Thursday night and I'm up to my ass.''

I stared at him some more, wavering. ''Where would we go? Would I have to dress up?''

''Well I'm not going to take you anywhere looking like *that*,'' he said.

I glanced down. I was still wearing jeans and the shirt I'd slept in but I wasn't ready to back down yet. ''What's wrong with this?'' I asked perversely.

''Take a shower and change clothes. I'll pick up some stuff at the grocery store if you give me a list. By the time I get that done, you'll be ready, yes?''

''I like to shop for my own stuff. Anyway, all I need is milk and beer.''

''Then I'll take you to a supermarket after we eat,'' he said, emphasizing every single word.

We drove down to the Ranch House in Ojai, one of those elegant restaurants where the waiter stands at your table and recites the menu like a narrative poem.

''Shall I order for us or would that offend your feminine sensibilities?''

''Go ahead,'' I said, feeling oddly relieved, ''I'd like that.'' While he and the waiter conferred, I studied Charlie's face surreptitiously. It was strong and square, good jawline, visible dent in his chin, full mouth. His nose looked like it might have been broken once but mended skillfully, leaving only the slightest trace just below the bridge. His glasses had large lenses, tinted a blue-gray, and behind them, his blue eyes were as clear as sky. Sandy lashes, sandy brows, his thick sandy hair only beginning to recede. He had big hands, big bones in his wrists, and I could see a feathering of sandy hair at the cuff. There was something else about him, too, smoldering and opaque, the same sense I'd had before of sexuality that surfaced now and then. Sometimes he seemed to emit an almost audible hum, like a line of power stations marching inexorably across a hillside, ominous and marked with danger signs. I was afraid of him.

The waiter was nodding and moving away. Charlie turned back to me, obscurely amused. I felt myself go mute, but he

pretended not to notice and I felt dimly grateful, faintly
flushed. I was overcome with the same self-consciousness I'd
felt once at a birthday party in the sixth grade when I realized
that all the other little girls had worn nylon stockings and I was
still wearing stupid white ankle socks.

The waiter returned with a bottle of wine and Charlie went
through the usual ritual. When our glasses were filled, he
touched his rim to mine, his eyes on my face. I sipped, startled
by the delicacy of the wine, which was pale and cool.

"So how's the investigation going?" he asked when the
waiter had left.

I shook my head, taking a moment to orient myself. "I
don't want to talk about it," I said shortly and then caught
myself. "I don't mean to be rude," I said in a softened tone. "I
just don't think talking about it will help. It's not going well."

"I'm sorry to hear that," he said. "It's bound to improve."

I shrugged and watched while he lit a cigarette and snapped
the lighter shut. "I didn't know you smoked," I said.

"Now and then," he said. He offered me the pack and I
shook my head again. He seemed relaxed, in possession of
himself, a man of sophistication and grace. I felt doltish and
tongue-tied, but he didn't seem to expect anything of me,
talking on about inconsequential things. He seemed to operate
at half speed, taking his own time about everything. It made
me aware of the usual tension with which I live, that keyed-up
state of raw nerve that makes me grind my teeth in my sleep.
Sometimes I get so wired that I forget to eat at all, only
remembering at night, even then not being hungry but wolfing
down food anyway as though the speed and quantity of
consumption might atone for the infrequency. With Charlie, I
could feel my time clock readjust, my pace slowing to match
his. When I finished the second glass of wine, I heaved a sigh
and only then did I realize that I'd been holding myself tensely,
like a joke snake ready to jump out of a box.

"Feel better?" he said.

"Yes."

"Good. Then we'll eat."

The meal that followed was one of the most sensual I ever
experienced: fresh, tender bread with a crust of flaky layers,
spread with a buttery pâté, Boston lettuce with a delicate

vinaigrette, sand dabs sautéed in butter and served with succulent green grapes. There were fresh raspberries for dessert with a dollop of tart cream, and all the time Charlie's face across the table from me, shadowed by that suggestion of caution, that hint of something stark and fearful held back, pulling me forward even while I felt myself kept in check.

"How'd you end up in law school?" I asked him when coffee arrived.

"Accident I guess. My father was a drunk and a bum, a real shit. Knocked me around a lot. Not seriously. More like a piece of furniture that got in his way. He beat my mother too."

"Doesn't do much for your self-esteem," I ventured.

Charlie shrugged. "It was good for me actually. Made me tough. Let me know I couldn't depend on anyone but myself, which is a lesson you might as well learn when you're ten. I took care of me."

"You worked your way through school?"

"Every nickel's worth. I picked up money ghosting papers for jocks, sitting in on tests, writing C minus answers so no one would suspect. You'd be surprised how tricky it is to miss just enough questions to look genuine. I had regular jobs, too, but after I watched half a fraternity get into law school on my smarts, I figured I might as well try it myself."

"What'd your father do when he didn't drink?"

"Construction till his health broke down. He finally died of cancer. Took him six years. Bad stuff. I didn't give a shit and he knew it. All that pain. Served him right," he said and shook his head. "My mother died four months after he did. I thought she'd be relieved he was gone. Turns out she was dependent on the abuse."

"Why do estate law? That doesn't seem like you. I picture you doing criminal law, something like that."

"Listen, my father pissed away everything he had. I ended up with nothing—less than nothing. It took me years to pay off his hospital bills and his fucking debts. I had to pay for my mother's death, too, which at least was quick, God bless her, but hardly cheap. So now I show people how to outwit the government even in death. A lot of my clients are dead so we get along very well and I make sure their greedy heirs get more than they deserve. Also when you're executor for somebody's estate, you get paid on time and nobody calls you up about your bill."

"Not a bad deal," I said.

"Not at all," he agreed.

"Have you ever been married?"

"Nope. I never had time for that. I work. That's the only thing that interests me. I don't like the idea of giving someone else the right to make demands. In exchange for what?"

I had to laugh. I felt the same way myself. His tone throughout was ironic and the look he laid on me then was oddly sexual, full of strange, compelling male heat as though money and power and sexuality were all somehow tangled up for him and fed on one another. There was really nothing open or loose or free about him, however candid he might seem, but I knew that it was precisely his opacity that appealed to me. Did he know that I was attracted to him? He gave little indication of his own feelings one way or the other.

When we finished our coffee, he signaled for the waiter without a word and paid the check. Conversation between us was dwindling anyway and I let it lie, feeling watchful, quiet, even wary of him again. We moved through the restaurant, our bodies close but our behavior polite, circumspect. He opened the door for me. I passed through. He'd made no gesture toward me, verbally or otherwise, and I was suddenly disconcerted, lest my sense of his pull turn out to be something generated in me and not reciprocal. Charlie took my arm briefly, guiding me up a shallow step but as soon as we were on smooth pavement again, he dropped his hand. We went around to my side of the car. He opened the door and I got in. I didn't think I'd said anything flirtatious and I was glad of that, curious still about his intentions toward me. He was so matter-of-fact, so removed.

We drove back to Santa Teresa, saying little. I was feeling mute again, not uncomfortable but languid. As we approached the outskirts of town, he reached over and took my hand noncommittally. It felt like a low-voltage current was suffusing my left side. He kept his left hand on the steering wheel. With his right hand, he was carelessly, casually rubbing my fingers, his attitude inattentive. I was trying to be as casual as he, trying to pretend there might be some other way to interpret those smoldering sexual signals that made the air crackle between us and caused my mouth to go dry. What if I was wrong, I thought. What if I fell on the man like a dog on a bone only to discover that his meaning was merely friendly, absentminded, or impersonal? I couldn't think about anything because there was no sound between us, nothing said, not anything I could react to or fix on—no way to divert myself. He was making it hard to breathe. I felt like a glass rod being rubbed on silk. Out of the corner of my eye, I thought I saw his face turn toward me. I glanced at him.

"Hey," he said softly. "Guess what we're going to do?"

Charlie shifted in his seat slightly and pressed my hand between his legs. A charge shot through me and I groaned involuntarily. Charlie laughed, a low excited sound, and then he looked back at the road.

Making love with Charlie was like being taken into a big warm machine. Nothing was required of me. Everything was attended to with such ease, such fluidity. There were no awkward moments. There was no holding back, no self-consciousness, no hesitation, no heed. It was as though a channel had been opened between us, sexual energy flowing back and forth without impediment. We made love more than once. At first, there was too much hunger, too much heat. We came at each other with a clash, an intensity that admitted of no tenderness. We crashed against one other like waves on a breakwater, surges of pleasure driving straight up, curling back again. All of the emotional images were of pounding assault, sensations of boom and buffet and battering ram until he had broken through to me, rolling down again and over me until all my walls were reduced to rubble and ash. He raised himself up on his elbow then and kissed me long and sweet and it began all over again, only this time at his pace, half speed, agonizingly slow like the gradual ripening of a peach on a limb. I could feel myself go all rosy, turn to honey and oil—a mellowing ease filtering through me like a sedative. We lay there afterward, laughing and sweaty and out of breath and then he encompassed me in sleep, the weight of his big arms pinning me to the bed. But far from feeling trapped, I felt comforted and safe, as though nothing could ever harm me as long as I stayed in the shadow of this man, this sheltering cave of flesh, where I was tucked away until morning without waking once.

At 7:00, I felt him kiss me lightly on the forehead, and after that the door closed softly. By the time I'd stirred myself awake, he was gone.

20

I got up at 9:00 and spent Sunday taking care of personal chores. I cleaned my place, did laundry, went to the supermarket, and had a nice visit in the afternoon with my landlord, who was sunning himself in the backyard. For a man of eighty-one, Henry Pitts has an amazing set of legs. He also has a wonderful beaky nose, a thin aristocratic face, shocking white hair, and eyes that are periwinkle blue. The overall effect is very sexy, electric, and the photographs I've seen of him in his youth don't even half compare. At twenty and thirty and forty, Henry's face seems too full, too unformed. As the decades pass, the pictures begin to reveal a man growing lean and fierce, until now he seems totally concentrated, like a basic stock boiled down to a rich elixir.

"Listen, Henry," I said, plunking down on the grass near his chaise. "You live entirely too idle a life."

"Sin and degradation," he said complacently, not even bothering to open his eyes. "You had company last night."

"A sleep-over date. Just like our mamas warned us about."

"How was it?"

"I'm not telling," I said. "What kind of crossword puzzle did you concoct this week?"

"An easy one. All doubles. Prefixes—'bi,' 'di,' 'bis,' 'dis.' Twin. Twain. Binary. Things like that. Try this one: six letters, 'double impression.'"

"Already, I give up."

"'Mackle.' It's a printer's term. Kind of a cheat but the fit was so nice. Try this. 'Double meaning.' Nine letters."

"Henry, would you *quit* that?"

"'Ambiguity.' I'll leave it on your doorstep."

"No, don't. I get those things in my head and I can't get 'em out."

He smiled. "You run yet?"

"No, but I'm on my way," I said, hopping up again. I crossed the grass, glancing back at him with a grin. He was putting suntan oil on his knees, which were already a gorgeous shade of caramel. I wondered how much it really mattered that there was a fifty-year difference in our ages. But then again, I had Charlie Scorsoni to think about. I changed clothes and did my run. And thought about him.

Monday morning, I went in to see Con Dolan at Homicide. He was talking on the phone when I got there, so I sat down at his desk. He was tipped back in his chair, feet jammed against the edge of the desk, the receiver laid loosely against his ear. He was saying, "uh-huh, uh-huh, uh-huh," looking bored. He scanned me with care, taking in every detail of my face, as though he were memorizing me all over again, running me through a computer file of known felons, looking for a match. I stared back at him. In moments, I could see the young man in his face, which was sagging now and worn, pouches beneath his eyes, hair slicked down, cheeks turning soft at the jawline as though the flesh were beginning to warm and melt. The skin on his neck had collapsed into a series of fine folds, reddened and bulging slightly over his starched shirt collar. I feel an ornery kind of kinship with him, which I never can quite identify. He's tough, emotionless, withdrawn, calculating, harsh. I've heard he's mean, too, but what I see in him is the overriding competence. He knows his business and he takes no guff and despite the fact he gives me a hard time whenever he can, I know he likes me, though grudgingly. I saw his attention sharpen. He focused on what was being said to him and it made his temper climb.

"All right now, you listen here, Mitch, because I've said all I intend to say. We're getting down to the short strokes on this and I don't want you fuckin' up my case. Yeah, I know that. Yeah, that's what you said. I just want it clear between us. I gave your boy all the breaks I mean to give so either he cooperates or we can put him right back where he was. Yeah, well you talk to him again!"

Con dropped the phone down from a height, not exactly slamming it but making his point. He was done. He looked at me through a haze of irritation. I put the manila envelope on his desk. He put his feet on the floor.

"What *is* this?" he said snappishly. He peered in through the flap, removing the letter I'd found in Libby Glass's effects. Even without knowing what it was, he held it by the edges, his eyes raking the contents once and then going back again with caution. He glanced up at me sharply. He tucked it back in the envelope.

"Where'd you get it?"

"Libby Glass's mother kept all her stuff. It was shoved in a paperback book. I picked it up Friday. Can you have it checked for fingerprints?"

The look he gave me was cold. "Why don't we talk about Sharon Napier first?"

I felt a spurt of fear, but I didn't hesitate. "She's dead," I said, reaching for the envelope. He smacked his fist down on it and I drew my hand back. We locked eyes. "A friend of mine in Vegas told me," I said. "That's how I knew."

"Horseshit. You drove up there."

"Wrong."

"God damn it, don't lie to me," he snapped.

I could feel my temper flare. "You want to read me my rights, Lieutenant Dolan? You want to hand me a certification of notification of my constitutional rights? Because I'll read it and sign it if you like. And then I'll call my attorney, and when he gets down here, we can chat. How's that?"

"You've been on this business two weeks and somebody shows up dead. You cross me up and I'll have your ass. Now you give it to me straight. I told you to keep out of this."

"Uh-uh. You told me to keep out of trouble, which I did. You said you'd like a little help making the connection between Libby Glass and Laurence Fife and I gave you that," I said, indicating the manila envelope.

He picked it up and tossed it in the trash. I knew it was just for effect. I tried another tack.

"Come on, Con," I said. "I had nothing to do with Sharon Napier's death. Not in any way, shape, or form. What do you think? That I'd run up there and kill somebody who might be of help? You're crazy! I never even went to Vegas. I was down at the Salton Sea talking to Greg Fife and if you doubt my word, call *him*!" I shut my mouth then and stared at him hotly, letting this bold admixture of truth and utter falsehood penetrate his darkened face.

"How'd you know where she was?"

"Because I spent a day and a half on a trace through a Nevada P.I. named Bob Dietz. I was going to drive to Vegas after I talked to Greg. I put a call through first and found out somebody'd put a bullet in her. How do you think *I* feel about that? She might have filled in a few blanks for me. I've got it tough enough as it is. This goddamn case is eight years old, now give me a break!"

"Who knew you intended to talk to her?"

"I don't know that. If you're implying that somebody killed her to keep her from talking to me, I think you're wrong but I couldn't swear to that. She was stepping on a lot of toes up there from what I hear. And don't ask me the particulars because I don't know. I just hear she was treading on somebody's turf."

He sat and stared at me then and I guessed that I must have hit a vein. The rumors my friend in Vegas had passed on must have lined up with whatever the Las Vegas Police Department had turned up. I was personally convinced that she'd been killed to shut her mouth, that someone had followed me and had gotten to her just in time, but I was damned if I was going to have a finger pointed at me. I couldn't see what purpose it would serve and it would only prevent me from getting on with my own inquiries. I still wasn't entirely easy about the fact that someone else had probably tipped off the Las Vegas PD about the shooting. One more minute in her apartment and I'd have been in a real jam, which might have closed down my investigation for good. Whatever regret I felt for my involvement with her death wasn't going to be expiated by my being caught up in the aftermath.

"What else have you found out about Libby Glass?" he asked me then, his tone shifting slightly along with the subject.

"Not a lot. Right now, I'm still trying to make a few pieces fall into place, and so far I'm not having much luck. If that letter really was written by Laurence Fife, then at least we can nail that down. Frankly, I hope it wasn't, but Nikki seems to

think the writing is his. There's something about it that doesn't
sit well with me. Can you let me know if the prints match?"

Con pushed impatiently at a stack of files on his desk. "I'll
think about that," he said. "I don't want us to get buddy-
buddy over this."

"Believe me, we will never be close friends," I said, and
for some reason his expression softened slightly and I almost
thought he might smile.

"Get out of here," he said gruffly.

I went.

I got in my car and left the downtown area, taking a left on
Anaconda down to the beach. It was a gorgeous day—sunny
and cool, with fat clouds squatting on the horizon. There were
sailboats here and there, probably planted by the Chamber of
Commerce to look picturesque for the tourists who straggled
along the sidewalk taking snapshots of other tourists who were
sitting in the grass.

At Ludlow Beach, I followed the hill upward and then
branched off onto the steep side street where Marcia Threadgill
lived. I parked and got out my binoculars, scanning her patio.
All of her plants were present and accounted for and they were
all looking healthier than I liked. There was no sign of Marcia
or the neighbor she feuded with. I wished she would move so I
could take pictures of her lugging fifty-pound cartons of books
down to a U-Haul van. I'd even settle for a glimpse of her
coming back from the grocery store with a big double bag of
canned goods ripping across the bottom from the weight. I
focused in on her patio again and noticed for the first time that
there were actually four plant hooks screwed into the wooden
overhang of the patio above. On the hook at the near corner
was the mammoth plant I'd seen before, but the other three
hooks were empty.

I put the binoculars away and went into the building,
pausing at the landing between the second and third floors. I
peered down through the stair railing. If I situated myself
correctly, I'd be able to focus my camera at just the right angle
to pick up a nice view of Marcia's front door. Having
ascertained that much, I went out to my car again and drove to
the Gateway supermarket. I hefted a few houseplants potted in

plastic and found one that was just right for my purposes—twenty-five pounds of sturdy trunk with a series of vicious swordlike leaves protruding at intervals. I picked up some prettied gift ribbons in a fire-engine red and a get-well card with a sentimental verse. All of this was taking up precious time that I would have preferred devoting to Nikki Fife's business, but I have my rent to account for and I felt like I owed California Fidelity for at least half a month.

I went back to Marcia's apartment and parked in front. I checked my camera, tore open the packaged ribbons, and stuck several of them to the plastic pot in a jaunty fashion and then tucked the card down inside with a signature scrawled on it that even I couldn't read. I hoisted plant, camera, and myself with a slightly thudding heart up the steep concrete stairs, into the building, and up to the second floor. I set the plant down near Marcia's doorsill and then went up to the landing, where I checked my light meter, set up the camera, and adjusted the focus on the lens. Nice angle, I thought. This was going to be a work of art. I trotted back down, took a deep breath and rang Ms. Threadgill's bell, racing back up the stairs again at breakneck speed. I picked up the camera and checked the focus again. My timing was perfect.

Marcia Threadgill opened her front door and stared down with surprise and puzzlement. She was wearing shorts and a crocheted halter and in the background the voice of Olivia Newton-John boomed out like an audible lollipop. I hesitated a moment and then peered over the rail. Marcia was leaning over to extract the card. She read it, turned it over, and then studied its face again, shrugging with bewilderment. She glanced down the stairwell as though she might catch sight of the delivery person. I began to click off pictures, the whir of the thirty-five-millimeter camera obscured by the record being played too loudly. Marcia padded back to her doorsill and bent casually from the waist, picking up twenty-five pounds of plant without even bothering to bend her knees as we've all been instructed to in the exercise manuals. As soon as she'd trucked the plant inside, I raced back down the stairs and out to the street, focusing again from the sidewalk below just as she appeared on the patio and placed the plant up on the rail. She disappeared. I backed up several yards, attaching the telephoto lens, waiting then with my breath held.

Back she came with what must have been a kitchen chair. I clicked off some nice shots of her climbing up. Sure enough, she picked up the plant by the wire, heaving it up to shoulder height, muscles straining until she caught the wire loop on the overhead hook. The effort was such that her halter hiked up and I got a nice shot of Marcia Threadgill's quite large bosom peeping out. I turned away just in time, I suspect, catching only the inkling of her quick look around to see if anyone else had spotted her exposure. When I glanced back casually she was gone.

I dropped the film off to be developed, making sure it was properly dated and identified. Still photographs were not going to be much good to us, especially without a witness to corroborate my testimony as to the date, time, and circumstance, but the pictures might at least persuade the claims manager at California Fidelity to pursue the case, which was the best I could hope for at this point. With his authorization, I could go back with a video outfit and a real photographer and pick up some footage that would stand up in court.

I should have know he wouldn't see it that way. Andy Motycka is in his early forties and he still bites his nails. He was working on his right hand that day, trying to gnaw off what remained of his thumb. It made me nervous just to look at him. I kept expecting him to rip loose a big triangle of flesh at the corner of his cuticle. I could feel my face set with distaste and I had to stare just over his shoulder to the left. Before I was even halfway through my explanation, he was shaking his head.

"Can't do it," he said bluntly. "This chick doesn't even have an attorney. We're supposed to get a signed release from the doctor next week. No deal. I don't want to mess this one up. Forty-eight hundred dollars is chicken feed. It'd cost us ten grand to go into court. You know that."

"Well, I know, but—"

"But nothing. The risk is too great. I don't even know why Mac had you check this one out. Look, I know it frosts your ass, but so what? You set her off and she'll go straight out and hire a lawyer and next thing you know, she'll sue us for a million bucks. Forget it.''

"She'll just do it again somewhere else," I said.

Andy shrugged.

"Why do I waste my time on this shit," I said, voice rising with frustration.

"Beats me," he said conversationally. "Let me see the pix, though, when you get 'em back. Her tits are huge."

"Screw you," I said and moved on into my office.

21

There were two messages on my answering service. The first was from Garry Steinberg. I called him back.

"Hey, Kinsey," he said when I'd been put through.

"Hi, Garry. How are you?"

"Not bad. I've got a little piece of information for you," he said. I could tell from his tone that he was feeling satisfied with himself, but what he said next still took me by surprise.

"I looked up that job application on Lyle Abernathy this morning. Apparently he worked for a while as an apprentice to a locksmith. Some old guy named Fears."

"A locksmith?"

"That's right. I called the guy this morning. You'd have loved it. I said Abernathy had applied for a job as a security guard and I was doing a background check. Fears hemmed and hawed some and finally said he'd had to fire the kid. Fears was getting a lot of complaints about missing cash on jobs where Lyle had worked and he began to suspect he was involved in petty thievery. He never could prove it, but he couldn't afford to take the chance, so he let Lyle go."

"Oh God, that's great," I said. "That means Lyle could have gotten into the Fifes' house anytime he wanted to. Libby's too."

"It looks that way. He worked for Fears for eight months and he sure picked up enough information to give it a try, judging from what Fears said. Unless they had burglar alarms or something like that."

"Listen, the only security system they had in effect was a big German shepherd that got hit by a car six weeks before Laurence Fife died. He and his wife and kids were away when the dog was killed."

"Nice," Garry said. "Nothing you could prove after all

this time, but it might put you on the right track at any rate. What about the application? You want a copy?"

"I'd love it. What about Fife's accounts?"

"I've got those at my place and I'll look at 'em when I can. It's a lot of stuff. In the meantime, I just thought you might want to know about that locksmith stint."

"I appreciate your help. Jesus, what a shmuck that guy is."

"I'll say. Hey, I got another call coming in. I'll be in touch." He gave me his home phone in case I needed him.

"You're terrific. Thanks."

The second message was from Gwen at K-9 Korners. One of her assistants answered and I listened to assorted dogs bark and whine while Gwen came to the phone.

"Kinsey?"

"Yeah, it's me. I got your call. What's happening?"

"Are you free for lunch?"

"Just a minute. I'll check my appointment book," I said. I put my palm against the mouth of the receiver and looked at my watch. It was 1:45. Had I *eaten* lunch? Had I even eaten breakfast today? "Yes, I'm free."

"Good. I'll meet you at the Palm Garden in fifteen minutes if that's okay for you."

"Sure. Fine. See you shortly."

My glass of white wine had just arrived when I glanced up to see Gwen approaching from across the courtyard: tall and lean, her gray hair slicked away from her face. The blouse she wore was a gray silk, long full sleeves nipped in at the wrist, the dark gray skirt emphasizing her trim waist and hips. She was stylish, confident—like Nikki in that—and I could see where both women must have appealed to Laurence Fife. I guessed that once upon a time Charlotte Mercer fit the same mold: a woman of stature, a woman of taste. I wondered idly if Libby Glass would have aged as well had she lived. She must have been much less secure at twenty-four, but bright—someone whose freshness and ambition might have appealed to Laurence as he neared the age of forty. God save us all from the consequences of male menopause, I thought.

"Hello. How are you," Gwen said briskly, sitting down.

She removed the napkin beside her plate and ordered wine as the waitress passed. Close up, her image softened, the angularity of her cheekbones offset by the large brown eyes, the purposeful mouth tinted with soft pink. Most of all, there was her manner: amused, intelligent, feminine, refined.

"How are all the dogs?" I said.

She laughed. "Filthy. Thank God. We're swamped today, but I wanted to talk to you. You've been out of town."

"I just got back Saturday. Have you been trying to get in touch?"

She nodded. "I called the office on Tuesday, I think. Your answering service said you were in Los Angeles so I tried to reach you there. Some total nitwit answered—"

"Arlette."

"Well, whoever it was, she got my name wrong twice so I hung up."

The waitress arrived with Gwen's wine.

"Have you ordered yet?"

I shook my head. "I was waiting for you."

The waitress got out her order card, glancing at me.

"I'll have the chef's salad," I said.

"Make that two."

"Dressing?"

"Blue cheese," I said.

"I'll have oil and vinegar," Gwen said and then handed both menus to the waitress, who moved away. Gwen turned her attention to me.

"I've decided I should level with you."

"About what?"

"My old lover," she said. Her cheeks had flushed mildly. "I realized that if I didn't tell you who he was, you'd be off on some wild-goose chase, wasting a lot of time trying to find out his name. It really amounts to more mystery than it's worth."

"How so?"

"He died a few months ago of a heart attack," she said, her manner turning brisk again. "After I talked to you, I tried tracking him down myself. His name was David Ray. He was a schoolteacher. Greg's, as a matter of fact, which is how we met. I thought he should know that you were asking questions about Laurence's death, or at any rate that your curiosity might lead you to him."

"How'd you find him?"

"I'd heard that he and his wife had moved to San Francisco. Apparently he was living in the Bay Area, where he was a principal of one of the Oakland public schools."

"Why not tell me before?"

She shrugged. "Misplaced loyalty. Protectiveness. That was a very important relationship and I didn't want him involved at this late date."

She looked at me and she must have read the skepticism in my face. The flush in her cheeks deepened almost imperceptibly.

"I know how it looks," she said. "First I refuse to give you his name and then he's dead and out of reach, but that's exactly the point. If he were still alive, I don't know that I'd be telling you this."

I thought that was probably true, but there was something else going on and I wasn't sure what it was. The waitress arrived with our salads and there was a merciful few minutes in which we busied ourselves with melba rounds. Gwen was rearranging her lettuce but she wasn't eating much. I was curious to hear what else she had to say and too hungry to worry about it much until I'd eaten some.

"Did you know he had heart trouble?" I asked finally.

"I had no idea, but I gather he was ill for years."

"Did he break off the relationship or did you?"

Gwen smiled bitterly. "Laurence did that but I wonder now if David might have engineered it to some extent. The whole affair must have complicated his life unbearably."

"He'd told his wife?"

"I think so. She was very gracious on the phone. I told her that Greg had asked me to get in touch and she played right along. When she told me that David was dead, I was . . . I didn't even know what to say to her but of course, I had to babble right on—how sorry, how sad . . . like some disinterested bystander making the right noises somehow. It was awful. Terrible."

"She didn't mention your relationship herself?"

"Oh no. She was much too cool for that, but she did know

exactly who I was. Anyway, I'm sorry I didn't tell you to begin with."

"No harm done," I said.

"How's it going otherwise?" she asked.

I felt myself hesitate. "Bits and pieces. Nothing concrete."

"Do you really expect to turn up anything after all this time?"

I smiled. "You never know. People get careless when they're feeling safe."

"I guess that's true."

We talked briefly about Greg and Diane and my visits with them, which I edited heavily. At 2:50 Gwen glanced at her watch.

"I've got to get back," she said, fishing in her purse for her billfold. She took out a five-dollar bill. "Will you keep in touch?"

"Sure," I said. I took a sip of wine, watching her get up. "When did you last see Colin?"

She focused abruptly on my face. "Colin?"

"I just met him Saturday," I said as though that explained it. "I thought maybe Diane might like to know he's back. She's fond of him."

"Yes, she is," Gwen said. "I don't know when I saw him last myself. Diane's graduation, I guess. Her junior-high-school graduation. What makes you ask?"

I shrugged. "Just curious," I said. I gave her what I hoped was my blandest look. A mild pink patch had appeared on her neck and I wondered if that could be introduced in court as a lie-detecting device. "I'll take care of the tip," I said.

"Let me know how it goes," she said, all casual again. She tucked the money under her plate and moved off at the same efficient pace that had brought her in. I watched her departure, thinking that something vital had gone unsaid. She could have told me about David Ray on the phone. And I wasn't entirely convinced she hadn't known about his death to begin with. Colin popped into my head.

I walked the two blocks to Charlie's office. Ruth was typing from a Dictaphone, fingers moving lightly across the keyboard. She was very fast.

"Is he in?"

She smiled and nodded me on back, not missing a word, gaze turned inward as she translated sound to paper with no lag time in between.

I stuck my head into his office. He was sitting at his desk, coat off, a law book open in front of him. Beige shirt, dark brown vest. When he saw me, a slow smile formed and he leaned back, tucking an arm up over the back of his swivel chair. He tossed the pencil on his desk.

"Are you free for dinner?" I said.

"What's up?"

"Nothing's up. It's a proposition," I said.

"Six-fifteen."

"I'll be back," I said and closed his office door again, still thinking about that pale shirt and the dark brown vest. Now *that* was sexy. A man in a nylon bikini, with that little knot sticking out in front, isn't half as interesting as a man in a good-looking business suit. Charlie's outfit reminded me of a Reese's Peanut Butter Cup with a bite taken out and I wanted the rest.

I drove out to Nikki's beach house.

22

Nikki answered the door in an old gray sweatshirt and a pair of faded jeans. She was barefoot, hair loose, a paintbrush in one hand, her fingers stained the color of pecan shells.

"Oh hi, Kinsey. Come on in," she said. She was already moving back toward the deck and I followed her through the house. On the other side of the sliding glass doors, I could see Colin, shirtless, in a pair of bib overalls sitting cross-legged in front of a chest of drawers, which the two were apparently refinishing. The drawers were out, leaning upright along the balcony, hardware removed. The air smelled of stripper and turpentine, which mingled not incompatibly with the smell of eucalyptus bark. Several sheets of fine sandpaper were folded and tossed aside, creases worn white with wood dust, looking soft from hard use. The sun was hot on the railings and newspapers were spread out under the chest to protect the deck.

Colin glanced up at me and smiled as I came out. His nose and cheeks were faintly pink with sunburn, his eyes green as sea water, bare arms rosy, there wasn't even a whisper of facial hair yet. He went back to his work.

"I want to ask Colin something but I thought I'd try it out on you first," I said to Nikki.

"Sure, fire away," she replied. I leaned against the railing while she dipped the tip of her brush back into a small can of stain, easing the excess off along the edge. Colin seemed more interested in the painting than he was in our exchange. I imagined that it was a bit of a strain to try to follow a conversation even if his lip-reading skills were good or maybe he thought adults were a bore.

"Can you remember offhand if you were out of town for any length of time in the four to six months before Laurence died?"

Nikki looked at me with surprise and blinked, apparently not expecting that. "I was gone once for a week. My father had a heart attack that June and I flew back to Connecticut," she said. She paused then and shook her head. "That was the only time, I think. What are you getting at?"

"I'm not sure. I mean, this is going to seem farfetched, but I've been bothered by Colin's calling Gwen 'Daddy's mother.' Has he mentioned that since?"

"Nope. Not a word."

"Well, I'm wondering if he didn't have occasion to see Gwen at some point while you were gone. He's too smart to get her mixed up with his own grandmother unless somebody identified her to him that way."

Nikki gave me a skeptical look. "Boy, that *is* a stretch. He couldn't have been more than three and a half years old."

"Yeah, I know, but a little while ago I asked Gwen when she saw him last and she claims it was at Diane's junior-high-school graduation."

"That's probably true," Nikki said.

"Nikki, Colin must have been fourteen months old at the time. I saw those snapshots myself. He was still a babe in arms."

"So?"

"So why did he remember her at all?"

Nikki applied a band of stain, giving that some thought. "Maybe she saw him in a supermarket or ran into him with Diane. She could have seen him or he could easily have seen her without any particular significance attached to it.

"Maybe. But I think Gwen lied to me about it when I asked. If it was no big deal, why not just say so. Why cover up?"

Nikki gave me a long look. "Maybe she just forgot."

"Mind if I ask him?"

"No, go ahead."

"Where's the album?"

She gestured over her shoulder and I went back into the living room. The photograph album was sitting on the coffee table and I flipped through until I found the snapshot of Gwen. I slipped it out of the four little corners holding it down and went back out to the deck. I held it out to him.

"Ask him if he can remember what was happening when he saw her last," I said.

Nikki reached over and gave him a tap. He looked at her and then at the snapshot, eyes meeting mine inquisitively. Nikki signed the question to him. His face closed up like a day lily when the sun goes down.

"Colin?"

He started to paint again, his face averted.

"The little shit," she said good-naturedly. She gave him a nudge and asked him again.

Colin shrugged her off. I studied his reaction with care.

"Ask him if she was here."

"Who, Gwen? Why would she be here?"

"I don't know. That's why we're asking him."

The look she gave me was half doubt, half disbelief. Reluctantly, she looked back at him. She signed to him, translating for my benefit. She didn't seem to like it much.

"Was Gwen ever here or at the other house?"

Colin watched her face, his own face a remarkable mirror of uncertainty and something else—uneasiness, secrecy, dismay.

"I don't know," he said aloud. The consonants blurred together like ink on a wet page, his tone conveying a sort of stubborn distrust.

His eyes slid over to me. I thought suddenly of the time in the sixth grade when I first heard the word *fuck*. One of my classmates told me I should go ask my aunt what it meant. I could sense the trap though I had no idea what it consisted of.

"Tell him it's okay," I said to her. "Tell him it doesn't matter to you."

"Well it certainly does," she snapped.

"Oh come on, Nikki. It's important and what difference does it make after all this time."

She got into a short discussion with him then, just the two of them, signing away like mad—a digital argument. "He doesn't want to talk about it," she said guardedly. "He made a mistake."

I didn't think so and I could feel excitement stir. He was watching us now, trying to get an emotional reading from our interchange.

"I know this sounds weird," I said to her tentatively, "but I wonder if Laurence told him that—that she was his mother."

"Why would he do that?"

I looked at her. "Maybe Colin caught them embracing or something like that."

Nikki's expression was blank for a moment and then she frowned. Colin waited uncertainly, looking from her to me. Nikki signed to him again. He seemed embarrassed now, head bent. She signed again more earnestly. Colin shook his head but the gesture seemed to come out of caution, not ignorance.

Nikki's expression underwent a change. "I just remembered something," she said. She blinked rapidly, color mounting in her face. "Laurence did come out here. He told me he brought Colin out the weekend I was back east. Greg and Diane stayed at the house with Mrs. Voss. Both had social plans or something, but Laurence said the two of them—he and Colin—came out to the beach to get away for a bit."

"Nice," I said with irony. "At three and a half, none of it would have made sense to him anyway. Let's just assume it's true. Let's assume she was out here—"

"I really don't care to go on with this."

"Just one more," I said. "Just ask him why he called her 'Daddy's mother.' Ask him why the 'Daddy's mother' bit."

She relayed the question to Colin reluctantly but his face brightened with relief. He signed back at once, grabbing his head.

"She had gray hair," she reported to me. "She *looked* like a grandmother to him when she was here."

I caught a glint of temper in her voice but she recovered herself, apparently for his sake. She tousled his hair affectionately.

"I love you," she said. "It's fine. It's okay."

Colin seemed to relax but the tension had darkened Nikki's eyes to a charcoal gray.

"Laurence hated her," she said. "He *couldn't* have—"

"I'm just making an educated guess," I said. "It might have been completely innocent. Maybe they met for drinks and talked about the kids' schoolwork. We really don't know anything for *sure*."

"My ass," she murmured. Her mood was sour.

"Don't get mad at me," I said. "I'm just trying to put this thing together so it makes some sense."

"Well I don't believe a word of it," she said tersely.

"You want to tell me he was too nice a man to do such a thing?"

She put the paintbrush on the paper and wiped her hands on a rag.

"Maybe I'd like to have a few illusions left."

"I don't blame you a bit," I said. "But I don't understand why it bothers you. Charlotte Mercer was the one who put it into my head. She said he was like a tomcat, always sniffing around the same back porch."

"All right, Kinsey. You've made your point."

"No, I don't think I have. You paid me five grand to find out what happened. You don't like the answers, I can give you your money back."

"No, never mind. Just skip it. You're right," she said.

"You want me to pursue it or not?"

"Yes," she said flatly, but she didn't really look at me again. I made my excuses and left soon after that, feeling almost depressed. She still cared about the man and I didn't know what to make of that. Except that nothing's ever cut-and-dried—especially where men and women are concerned. So why did I feel guilty of doing my job?

I went into Charlie's office building. He was waiting at the top of the stairs, coat over one shoulder, tie loose.

"What happened to you," he said when he saw my face.

"Don't ask," I said. "I'm going to try to get a scholarship to secretarial school. Something simple and nice. Something nine-to-five."

I came up level with him, tilting my face slightly to look at him. It was as though I had suddenly entered a magnetic field like those two little dog-magnets when I was a kid—one black, one white. At the positive poles, if you held them half an inch apart, they would suck together with a little click. His face was solemn, so close, eyes resting on my mouth as though he might will me forward. For a full ten seconds we seemed caught and then I pulled back slightly, unprepared for the intensity.

"Jesus," he said, almost with surprise, and then he chuckled, a sound I knew well.

"I need a drink," I said.

"That's not all you need," he said mildly.

I smiled, ignoring him. "I hope you know how to cook because I don't."

"Hey listen, there is one slight kink," he said. "I'm house-sitting for my partner. He's out of town and I've got his dogs to feed. We can grab a bite to eat out there."

"Fine with me," I said.

He locked the office then and we went down the back stairs to the small parking lot adjacent to his office building. He opened his car door but I was already moving toward mine, which was parked out on the street.

"Don't you trust me to drive?"

"I'm courting a ticket if I stay parked out here. I'll follow you. I don't like to be stuck without my own wheels."

"'Wheels'? Like in the sixties, you refer to your car as 'wheels'?"

"Yeah, I read that in a book," I said dryly.

He rolled his eyes and smiled indulgently, apparently resigned. He got in his car and waited pointedly until I had reached mine. Then he pulled out, driving slowly so that I could follow him without getting lost. Once in a while, I could see him watching me in his rearview mirror.

"You sexy bastard," I said to him under my breath and then I shivered involuntarily. He had that effect.

We proceeded to John Powers's house at the beach, Charlie driving at a leisurely pace. As usual, he was operating at half speed. The road began to wind and finally his car slowed and he turned left down a steep drive, a place not far from Nikki's beach house, if my calculations were correct. I pulled my car in beside his, nose down, hoping my handbrake would hold. Powers's house was tucked up against the hill to the right, with a carport dead ahead and parking space for two cars. The carport itself had a white picket fence across it, the two halves forming a gate, locked shut, with what I guessed to be his car parked inside.

Charlie got out, waiting as I came around the front of my car. As with Nikki's property, this was up on the bluff, proba-

bly sixty or seventy feet above the beach. Through the carport,
I could see a patchy apron of grass, a crescent of yard. We
went along a narrow walkway behind the house and Charlie let
us into the kitchen. John Powers's two dogs were of the kind I
hate: the jumping, barking, slavering sort with toenails like
sharks' teeth. They reeked of bad breath. One was black and
the other was the color of moldering whale washed up on the
beach for a month. Both were large and insisted on standing up
on their hind legs to stare into my face. I kept my head back,
lips shut lest wet, sloppy kisses be forthcoming.

"Charlie, could you help me with this?" I ventured
through clenched teeth. One licked me right in the mouth as I
spoke.

"Tootsie! Moe! Knock it off!" he snapped.

I wiped my lips. "Tootsie and Moe?"

Charlie laughed and dragged them both by neck chains to
the utility room, where he shut them in. One began to howl
while the other barked.

"Oh Jesus. Let 'em out," I said. He opened the door and
both bounded out, tongues flapping like slivers of corned beef.
One of the dogs galummoxed into the other room and came
trotting back with a leash in its mouth. This was supposed to be
cute. Charlie put leashes on both and they pranced, wetting the
floor in spots.

"If I walk them, they calm down," Charlie remarked.
"Sort of like you."

I made a face at him but there seemed to be no alternative
but to follow him out the front. There were various dog lumps
in the grass. A narrow wooden stairway angled down toward
the beach, giving way in places to bare ground and rock. It was
a hazardous descent, especially with two ninety-five-pound
lunkheads doing leaps and pirouettes at every turn.

"John comes home at lunch to give 'em a run," Charlie
said back over his shoulder.

"Good for him," I said, picking my way down the
cliffside, concentrating on my feet. Fortunately, I was wearing
tennis shoes, which provided no traction but at least didn't
have heels that would catch in the rotting steps and pitch me
headfirst into the Pacific.

The beach below was long and narrow, bounded by precipitious rocks. The dogs loped from one end to the other, the black one pausing to take a big steaming dump, backside hunched, eyes downcast modestly. Jesus, I thought, is that all dogs know how to do? I averted my gaze. Really, it was all so *rude*. I found a seat on a rock and tried to turn my brain off. I needed a break, a long stretch of time in which I didn't have to worry about anybody but myself. Charlie threw sticks, which the dogs invariably missed.

Finally, the dog romp at an end, we staggered back up the steps together. As soon as we were inside, the dogs flopped happily on a big oval rug in the living room and began to chew it to shreds. Charlie went into the kitchen and I could hear ice trays cracking.

"What do you want to drink?" he called.

I moved over to the kitchen doorway. "Wine if you have it."

"Great. There's some in the fridge."

"You do this often?" I asked, indicating the pups.

He shrugged, filling ice trays again. "Every three or four weeks. It depends," he said and then smiled over at me. "See? I'm a nicer guy than you thought."

I twirled an index finger in the air just to show how impressed I was, but I did, actually, think it was nice of him to sit the dogs. I couldn't imagine Powers finding a kennel to keep them. He'd have to take them to the zoo. Charlie handed me a glass of wine, pouring a bourbon on the rocks for himself. I leaned against the doorframe.

"Did you know that Laurence had an affair at one time with Sharon Napier's mother?"

He gave me a startled look. "You're making a joke."

"No I'm not. Apparently it happened some time before Sharon went to work for him. From what I gather, her 'employment' was a combination extortion and revenge. Which might explain the way she treated him."

"Who told you this stuff?"

"What difference does that make?"

"Because it sounds like crap," he said. "The name Napier never meant anything to me and I knew him for years."

I shrugged. "That's what you said about Libby Glass," I replied.

Charlie's face began to fade. "Jesus, you don't forgive a thing, do you?" He moved into the living room and I followed. He sat down in a wicker chair, which creaked beneath his weight.

"Is that why you're here? To work?" he asked.

"Actually, it's not. Actually, it's just the opposite."

"Meaning what?"

"I came out here to get away from it," I said.

"Then why the questions? Why the third-degree? You know how I feel about Laurence and I don't like to be used."

I felt my own smile fade, my face setting with embarrassment.

"Is that what you think?" I asked.

He looked down at his glass, speaking carefully. "I can appreciate the fact you have a job to do. That's fine with me and I'm not complaining about that. I'll help you where I can, but I can do without the interrogation at every step. I don't think you have any idea what it's like. You ought to see the change that comes over you when you start talking homicide."

"I'm sorry," I said stiffly. "I don't mean to do that to you. I get information and I need to have it verified. I can't afford to take things at face value."

"Not even me?"

"Why are you doing this?" I said, and my voice seemed to have dropped to a hush.

"I'm just trying to get a few things clarified."

"Hey. You were the one who came after me. Remember that?"

"Saturday. Yes. And you were the one who came after me today. And now you're pumping me and I don't like that."

I stared down at the floor, feeling fragile and mortified. I didn't like being smacked down and it was pissing me off. A lot. I began to shake my head. "I had a hard day," I said. "I really don't need this shit."

"I had a hard day too," he said. "So what?"

I set my wineglass on the table and grabbed up my purse.

"Fuck off," I said mildly. "Just go fuck yourself."

I moved toward the kitchen. The dogs raised their heads

and watched me pass. I was hot and they lowered their eyes meekly as though I had communicated that much at any rate. Charlie didn't move. I banged out the back door and got into my car, starting it up with energy, peeling back up the driveway with a chirp. As I backed out onto the road, I caught a glimpse of Charlie standing near the carport. I put the car into first and pulled away.

23

I've never been good at taking shit, especially from men. It was an hour after I got home before I cooled down. Eight o'clock and I still hadn't eaten anything. I poured myself a big glass of wine and sat down at my desk. I took out some blank index cards and began to work. At 10:00 I had dinner—a sliced hard-boiled-egg sandwich, which I ate hot on wheat bread with a lot of mayonnaise and salt, popping open a Pepsi and a package of corn chips. By then I'd consigned all the information I had to the index cards, which I'd tacked up on my bulletin board.

I sketched the story out, allowing myself to speculate. I mean, why now? I didn't have much else to go on at this point. It seemed likely that someone had broken into the Fifes' house the weekend the German shepherd was killed, while Nikki and Laurence were off at the Salton Sea with Colin and Greg. It also seemed likely that Sharon Napier had come up with something after Laurence died—which was (maybe) why she had gotten herself killed. I started making lists, systematizing the information I had, along with the half-formed ideas that were simmering at the back of my head. I typed up my sheets and arranged them in alphabetical order, starting with Lyle Abernathy and Gwen.

I didn't dismiss the idea that Diane and Greg were possibly involved, though I couldn't make any sense of the notion that either could have killed him, let alone Libby Glass. I included Charlotte Mercer on my list. She was spoiled and spiteful and I didn't think she would spare any energy or expense in seeing that the world was arranged exactly as she wanted it. She could have hired someone if she didn't want to go to the trouble of murdering him herself. And if she killed him, why not Libby Glass? Why not Sharon Napier, if Sharon had figured it out? I decided it might be smart to check with the airlines to see if her name appeared on any of the passenger lists for Las Vegas at the time Sharon died. That was one angle I hadn't thought of. I made a note to myself. Charlie Scorsoni was still on my list and the realization had a disturbing effect.

There was a knock at the door and I jerked involuntarily, adrenaline shooting through me. I glanced at my watch: 12:25. My heart was thumping so hard it made my hands shake. I crossed to the door and bent my head.

"Yes?"

"It's me," Charlie said. "Can I come in?"

I opened the door. Charlie was leaning against the frame. No jacket. No tie. Tennis shoes with no socks. His square handsome face looked solemn and subdued. He searched my face and then looked away. "I came down on you too hard and I'm sorry," he said.

I studied his face. "You had a legitimate complaint," I said. I knew that my tone of voice was unrelenting, regardless of the content, and I knew that my purpose was punitive. He only had time to look at me to guess my real attitude and it frosted him some.

"Jesus Christ, could we just talk?" he said.

I glanced at him briefly and then moved away from the door. He came in, closing it behind him. He leaned on the door, hands in his pockets, watching me prowl the room, circling back to my desk, where I began to take cards down, packing papers away.

"What do you want from me?" he said helplessly.

"What do you want from *me*?" I snapped back. I caught myself and raised a hand. "I'm sorry. I didn't mean to use that tone."

He stared down at the floor as though trying to figure out where to go next. I sat down in the upholstered chair near the couch, flinging my legs over the padded arm.

"Want a drink?" I asked.

He shook his head. He moved over to the couch and sat down heavily, leaning his head back. His face looked lined, his brow furrowed. His sandy hair looked as though he's run a hand through it more than once. "I don't know what to do with you," he said.

"What's to do?" I asked. "I know I'm a bitch sometimes,

but why not? I'm serious, Charlie. I'm too old to take any guff from anyone. And truly, in this case, I don't know who did what to whom. Did you generate that fight or did I?"

He smiled slightly. "Okay, so we're both touchy now and then. Is that fair enough?"

"I don't know from fair anymore. I don't know from any of this stuff."

"Haven't you ever heard of compromise?"

"Oh sure," I said. "That's when you give away half the things you want. That's when you give the other guy half of what's rightfully yours. I've done that lots of times. It sucks."

He shook his head, smiling wearily. I stared at him, feeling stubborn and belligerent. He'd already given more than I, and I still couldn't bend. He regarded me skeptically.

"Where do you go when you look at me that way?" he asked. I didn't know what to say so I kept my mouth shut. He reached over and waggled my bare foot as though to get my attention.

"You know you keep me at arm's length," he said.

"Really? Saturday night you think I did that?"

"Kinsey, sex was the only time you let me get close. What am I supposed to do with that? Chase around after you with my dick hanging out?"

I smiled inside, hoping it wouldn't show on my face. He read it anyway in my eyes. "Yeah, why not?" I said.

"I don't think you're used to men," he said, not making eye contact, and then he corrected himself. "Not men," he said. "I don't think you're used to having anyone in your life. I think you're used to being freewheeling. And that's okay. Essentially I live the same way, but this is different. I think we should be careful of this."

"This what?"

"This relationship," he said. "I don't want you shutting me out. You're not that hard to read. Sometimes you disappear like a shot and I can't cope with that. I will try to tread easy. I'll try not to be a horse's ass myself, I promise you that. Just don't run off. Don't back away. You do this kind of knee-jerk retreat, like a clam—" He broke off then.

I softened, wondering if I'd misjudged him. I was too tough, too quick. I am hard on people and I know that.

"I'm sorry," I said. I had to clear my throat. "I'm sorry. I know I do that. I don't know who was at fault, but you ticked me off and I blew."

I held my hand out and he took it, squeezing my fingers. He looked at me for a long time. He took my fingertips and kissed them lightly, casually, looking at me the whole time. I felt like a switch was being turned on at the base of my spine. He turned my hand over and pressed his mouth into my palm. I didn't want him to do that but I noticed I wasn't pulling my hand away. I watched him, hypnotically, my senses dulled by the heat that was raging way down, way deep. It was like a pile of rags beginning to smolder, some dark part of me hidden away under the stairs, something firemen had warned us about in grade school. Paint cans, jars of gasoline—fumes in compression. All it needed was a spark, sometimes not even that. I could feel my eyes close, mouth coming open against my will. I sensed that Charlie was moving but I couldn't take that in and the next thing I was aware of, he was on his knees between mine, pulling the neck of my T-shirt down, his mouth on my bare breast. I clutched at him convulsively, slid down and forward against him and he half lifted me, hands cupped under my ass. I hadn't known how much I wanted him until then, until that point, but the sound I made was primitive and his response was fierce and immediate and after that, in the half-light, with the table pushed aside, we made love on the floor. He did things to me that I'd only read about in books, and at the end of it, legs trembling, heart thudding, I laughed and he buried his face against my belly, laughing too.

He was gone again by 2:00 A.M. He had work to do the next day and so did I. Even so, I missed him as I brushed my teeth, smirking at my own reflection in the bathroom mirror. My chin was pink from whisker burn. My hair seemed to be standing straight up on end. There is nothing quite as smug as the self-congratulation that abounds when one has been thoroughly and proficiently screwed, but I was a little bit embarrassed with myself nevertheless. This was not good, not cool. As a rule, I scrupulously avoid personal contact with anyone connected with a case. My sexual wrangling with Charlie was foolish, unprofessional, and in theory, possibly dangerous. In some little nagging part of my head, it didn't feel right to me, but I did love his *moves*. I couldn't think when I'd last run into a man quite so inventive. My reaction to him was gut-level chemistry—like crystals of sodium flung in a swimming pool, throwing off sparks, dancing across the water like light. I had a friend once who said to me, "Wherever there is sex, we work to create a relationship that's worthy of it." I thought about that now, sensing that soon I would do that with him—start to bond, start to fantasize, start to throw out emotional tendrils like snow peas curling up a string. I was wary of it too. The sex was very good and very strong but the fact remained that I was still in the middle of an investigation and he still had not been crossed off my list. I didn't think our physical relationship had clouded my judgment about him, but how could I tell? I couldn't really afford to take the chance. Unless, of course, I was just rationalizing my own inclination to hold back. Was I *that* careful with myself these days? Was I really just sidestepping intimacy? Did I long to relegate him to the role of "possible suspect" in order to justify my own reluctance to take a risk? He was a nice man—smart, caring, responsible, attractive, perceptive. What in God's name did I want?

I turned the bathroom light out and made up my bed, which really just amounted to a quilt folded lengthways on the couch. I could have opened out the sofa bed and done it right—sheets, pillow case, a proper nightgown. Instead I'd pulled the same T-shirt over my head and tucked myself into the fold of the quilt. My body heat was making a sexual perfume waft up from between my legs. I turned out the lamp on the desk and smiled in the dark, shivering with the recollection of his mouth on me. Maybe this wasn't the time to get analytical, I thought. Maybe this was just a time to reflect and assimilate. I slept like the dead.

In the morning, I showered, skipping breakfast, reaching the office by 9:00. I let myself in and checked with the service. Con Dolan had called. I dialed the Santa Teresa Police Department and asked for him.

"What," he barked, already annoyed with the world.

"Kinsey Millhone here," I said.

"Oh yeah? What do you want?"

"Lieutenant, you called me!" I could hear him blink.

"Oh. Right. I got a report here from the lab on that letter. No prints. Just smudges, so that's no good."

"Rats. What about the handwriting? Does that match?"

"Enough to satisfy us," he said. "I had Jimmy go over it and he says it's legitimate. What else you got?"

"Nothing right now. I may come in and talk to you, though, in a couple of days if that's okay."

"Call first," he said.

"Trust me," I replied.

I went out on the balcony and stared down at the street. Something wasn't right. I'd been half convinced that letter was a fake but now it was confirmed and verified. I didn't like it. I went back in and sat down in my swivel chair, tipping back and forth slightly, listening to it creak. I shook my head. Couldn't figure it out. I glanced at the calendar. I'd been working for Nikki for two weeks. It felt like she'd hired me a minute ago and it felt like I'd been on the case all my life. I tilted forward and grabbed a scratch pad, totaling the time I'd put in, adding expenses on top of that. I typed it all up, made copies of my receipts, and stuck the whole batch in an envelope, which I mailed to her out at the beach. I went into the California Fidelity offices and shot the shit with Vera, who processes claims for them.

I skipped lunch and knocked off at 3:00. I stopped on the way home and picked up the eight-by-ten color photographs of Marcia Threadgill and I sat in my car for a moment to survey my handiwork. It isn't often that I have such a captivating spectacle of avarice and fraud. The best shot (which I might have called "Portrait of a Chiseler") was of Marcia standing up on her kitchen chair, shoulders strained by the weight of the plant as she lifted it up. Her boobs, in the crocheted halter top, sagged down like flesh melons bursting through the bottom of a string bag. The image was so clear that I could see where her mascara had left little black dots on her upper lids like tracks of some tiny beast. Such a jerk. I smiled to myself grimly. If that's the way the world works, then let me not forget. I was resigned by now to the fact that Ms. Threadgill would have her way. Cheaters win all the time. It wasn't big news but it was worth remembering. I slid all the pictures back into the manila envelope. I started the car and headed toward home. I didn't feel like running today. I wanted to sit and brood.

24

I pinned the photograph of Marcia Threadgill up on my bulletin board and stared at it.
I kicked my shoes off and walked around.
I'd been thinking all day and it was getting me nowhere, so I
took out the crossword puzzle Henry had left on my doorstep. I
stretched out on the couch, pencil in hand. I did manage to
guess 6 Down—"disloyal," eight letters, which was "two-
faced," and I got 14 Across, which was "double-reed
instrument," four letters—"oboe." What a whiz. I got stuck
on "double helix," three letters, which turned out later to be
"DNA," a cheat if you ask me. At 7:05, I had an idea that
jumped out of the dim recesses of my brain with a little jolt of
electricity.

I looked up Charlotte Mercer's telephone number and
dialed the house. The housekeeper answered and I asked for
Charlotte.

"The judge and Mrs. Mercer are having dinner," she said
disapprovingly.

"Well, would you mind interrupting please? I just have a
quick question. I'm sure she won't mind."

"Who shall I say is calling?" she asked. I gave her my
name.

"Just one moment." She put the receiver down.

I corrected her mentally. *Whom,* sweetheart. *Whom* shall I
say is calling . . .

Charlotte answered, sounding drunk. "I don't appreciate
this," she hissed.

"I'm sorry," I said. "But I need a piece of information."

"I told you what I know and I don't want you calling when
the judge is here."

"All right. All right. Just one thing," I said hurriedly
before she could hang up. "Do you happen to remember Mrs.
Napier's first name."

Silence. I could practically see her hold the receiver out to look at it.

"Elizabeth," she said and slammed down the phone.

I hung up. The piece I was looking for had just clicked into place. The letter wasn't written to Libby Glass at all. Laurence Fife had written it to Elizabeth Napier years ago. I was willing to bet on that. The real question now was how Libby Glass had gotten hold of it and who had wanted it back.

I took out my note cards and went back to work on my list. I had deliberately deleted Raymond and Grace Glass. I didn't believe either of them would have killed their own child, and if my guess about that letter could be verified, then it was possible that Libby and Laurence had never been romantically involved. Which meant that the reasons for their dying had to be something else. But what? Suppose, I said to myself, just suppose Laurence Fife and *Lyle* were involved in something. Maybe Libby stumbled on to it and Lyle killed them both to protect himself. Maybe Sharon got wind of it and he'd killed her too. It didn't quite make sense to me from that angle, but after eight years much of the real proof must have been lost or destroyed. Some of the obvious connections must have faded by now. I jotted down a couple of notes and checked the list.

When I came to Charlie Scorsoni's name, I felt the same uneasiness I'd felt before. I'd checked him out two weeks ago, before I'd even met with him and he was clean, but appearances are deceptive. As squeamish as it made me feel, I thought I'd better verify his whereabouts the night Sharon died. I knew he'd been in Denver because I'd called him there myself but I wasn't really sure where he'd gone after that. Arlette said he'd left messages from Tucson and again from Santa Teresa but she only had his word for that. When it came to Laurence Fife he did have opportunity. From the first, this had been a case where motive and alibi were oddly overlapped. Ordinarily, an alibi is an account of a suspect's whereabouts at the time a crime was committed and it's offered up as proof of innocence, but here it didn't matter where anyone was. With a poisoning, it only mattered if someone had *reason* to want someone else dead—access to the poison, access to the victim, and the intent to kill. That's what I was still sorting through. My impulse was simply to take Charlie off my list but I had to question myself on that. Did I really believe he was innocent or did I simply want to relieve myself of my own uneasiness? I tried to think about something else. I tried to move on, but my mind I kept drifting back to the same point. I didn't think I was being smart. I wasn't sure I was being honest with myself. And suddenly, I didn't like the idea that my thinking might not be clear. The whole setup gave me a sick feeling down in my bones. I looked up his home phone number in the telephone book. I hesitated and then I shook myself free and dialed. I had to do it.

The phone rang four times. I thought he might be out at Powers's house at the beach but I didn't have that number. I was rooting for him to be out, gone. He picked up on the fifth ring and I felt my stomach churn. There was no point in putting it off.

"Hi, it's Kinsey," I said.

"Well hello," he said softly. The pleasure in his voice was audible and I could picture his face. "God, I was hoping I'd hear from you. Are you free?"

"No, actually I'm not. Uh, listen, Charlie. I'm thinking I shouldn't see you for a while. Until I get this wrapped up."

The silence was profound.

"All right," he said finally.

"Look, it's nothing personal," I said. "It's just a matter of policy."

"I'm not arguing," he said. "Do what you want. It's too bad you didn't think about 'policy' before."

"Charlie, it's not like that," I said desperately. "It may work out fine and it's no big deal, but it's been bothering me. A lot. I don't do this. It's been one of my cardinal rules. I can't keep on seeing you until I understand how this thing ties up."

"Babe, I understand," he said. "If it doesn't feel right to you, then it's no good anyway. Call me if you ever change your mind."

"Wait," I said. "God damn it, don't do that to me. I'm not rejecting you."

"Oh really," he said, his tone flat with disbelief.

"I just wanted you to know."

"Well. Now I know. I appreciate your honesty," he said. "I'll be in touch when I can."

"Have a good life," he said and the phone clicked quietly in my ear.

I sat with a hand on the phone, doubts crowding in, wanting to call him back, wanting to erase everything I'd just said. I'd been looking for relief, looking for a way to escape the discomfort I felt. I think I'd even wanted him to give me a hard time so that I could resist and feel righteous. It was a question of my own integrity. Wasn't it? The injury in his voice had been awful after what we'd been through. And maybe he was right in his assumption that I was rejecting him. Maybe I was just being perverse, pushing him away because I needed space between me and the world. The job does provide such a perfect excuse. I meet most people in the course of my work and if I can't get emotionally involved there, then where else can I go? Private investigation is my whole life. It is why I get up in the morning and what puts me to bed at night. Most of the time I'm alone, but why not? I'm not unhappy and I'm not discontent. I had to free up until I knew what was going on. He would just have to misunderstand and to hell with him until I got this goddamn case nailed down and then maybe we could see where we stood—if it wasn't too late. Even if he was right, even if my breaking with him was an excess of conscience, a cover for something else—so what? There were no declarations between us, no commitments. I'd been to bed with him twice. What did I owe him? I don't know what love is about and I'm not sure I believe in it anyway. "Then why so defensive?" came a little voice in reply, but I ignored it.

I had to push on. There was no other way to get out of this now. I picked up the phone and called Gwen.

"Hello?"

"Gwen. This is Kinsey," I said, keeping my voice neutral. "Something's come up and I think we should talk."

"What is it?"

"I'd rather talk to you in person. Do you know where Rosie's is, down here at the beach?"

"Yes. I think I know the place," she said with uncertainty.

"Can you meet me there in half an hour? It's important."

"Well sure. Just let me get my shoes on. I'll be there as soon as I can."

"Thanks," I said.

I checked my watch. It was 7:45. I wanted her on my turf this time.

Rosie's was deserted, the lights dim, the whole place smelling of yesterday's cigarette smoke. I used to go to a movie theater when I was a kid and the ladies' rest room always smelled like that. Rosie was wearing a muumuu in a print fabric that depicted many flamingos standing on one leg. She was seated at the end of the bar, reading a newspaper by the light of a small television set, which she'd placed on the bar, sound off. She looked up as I came in and she set the paper aside.

"It's too late for dinner. The kitchen is closed. I gave myself the night off," she announced from across the room. "You want something to eat, you gotta fix it yourself at home. Ask Henry Pitts. He'll do you something good."

"I'm meeting someone for a drink," I said. "Big crowd you got."

She looked around as though maybe she'd missed someone. I went over to the bar. She looked as though she'd just redyed her hair because her scalp was faintly pink. She was using a Maybelline dark brown eyeliner pencil on her brows, which she seemed to draw closer together every time, coquettishly arched. Pretty soon, she could take care of the whole thing with one wavy line.

"You got a man yet?" she asked.

"Six or eight a week," I said. "Do you have any cold chablis?"

"Just the crummy stuff. Help yourself."

I went around behind the bar and got a glass, taking the big gallon jug of white wine out of the refrigerator under the bar. I poured a tumblerful, adding ice. I went over to my favorite booth and sat down, preparing myself mentally like an actor about to go on stage. It was time to stop being polite.

Gwen arrived forty minutes later, looking crisp and capable. Her greeting to me was pleasant enough, but under it I thought I could detect the tension, as though she had some inkling of what I was about to say. Rosie shuffled over, giving Gwen a brief appraising look. She must have thought Gwen looked okay because she honored her with a direct question.

"You want something to drink?"

"Scotch on the rocks. And could I have a glass of water, too, please?"

Rosie shrugged. She didn't care what people drank. "You want to run a tab?" she said to me.

I shook my head. "I'll take care of it now," I said. Rosie moved off toward the bar. The look Gwen and I exchanged inadvertently indicated that both of us remembered her first reference to drinking Scotch in the days long past, when she was married to Laurence Fife and playing the perfect wife. I wondered what she was playing now.

"I revert now and then to the hard stuff," she said, picking up my thought.

"Why not?" I replied.

She studied me briefly. "What's up?"

The question was brave. I didn't think she really wanted to know, but she'd always struck me as the type to plunge right in. She probably whipped off big pieces of adhesive tape, too, with the same decisive thrust, just to get it over with.

"I talked to Colin," I said. "He remembered you."

The modification in her manner was slight and a look, not of apprehension, but of wariness flickered in her eyes.

"Well that's nice," she said. "I haven't seen him for years, of course. I told you that." She reached into her purse and took out a compact, checking her reflection quickly in the mirror, running a hand through her hair. Rosie came back with her Scotch and a glass of water. I paid the tab. Rosie tucked the money in the pocket of her muumuu and wandered back to the bar while Gwen took a sip of water. She seemed to be holding herself in check, not trusting herself to pick up the conversation where we'd left off. I bumped her along for the sake of surprise.

"You never mentioned that you had an affair with Laurence," I said.

A laugh burbled out. "Who, me? With him? You can't be *serious*."

I had to interrupt her merriment. "Colin saw you out at the beach house that weekend when Nikki was out of town. I don't know all the details, but I can make a guess."

I watched her compute that and shift gears. She was a very good little actress herself, but the slick cover she'd constructed was getting shabby from disuse. It had been a long time since she'd had to play this game and her timing was slightly off. She knew all the right lines, but the pretense was hard to sustain after an eight-year gap. She didn't seem to recognize the bluff and I kept my mouth shut. I could almost see what was happening inside her head. The terrible need to confess and be done with it, the pressure to spill it all out was too tempting to resist. She'd gone a few rounds with me and she'd pulled it off beautifully but only because I hadn't known which buttons to push.

"All right," she blurted out rebelliously, "I went to bed with him once. So what? I ran into him at the Palm Garden as a matter of fact. I nearly told you the other day. He was the one who told me Nikki was out of town. I was shocked that he'd even speak to me." She switched to the Scotch, taking a big drink.

She was fabricating as fast as she could and it sounded nice but it was like listening to a record album. I decided to skip the cuts I didn't want to hear. I bumped her again.

"It was more than once, Gwen," I said. "You had a full-blown affair with him. Charlotte Mercer was screwing his head off back then but he broke it off with her. She says he was into something very hush-hush. 'Very hot,' to quote her. I think it was you."

"What difference does it make if we had an affair. He'd been doing that for years."

I let a little time elapse and when I spoke I kept my voice low, leaning forward slightly just to give her the full effect.

"I think you killed him."

The animation drained out of her face as though a plug had been pulled. She started to say something but she couldn't get it out. I could see her mind working, but she couldn't put anything together quickly enough. She was struggling and I pressed.

"You want to tell me about it?" I said. My own heart was pounding and I could feel damp rings of sweat forming under my arms.

She shook her head but that was all she could manage. She seemed transfixed. Her face had changed, taking on that look people get in their sleep when all the guards are down. Her eyes were luminous and dark and two bright patches of pink appeared now in the pale of her cheeks, a clownish effect, as though she'd applied too much blusher in an artificial light. She blinked back tears then, propping her chin on her fist, looking off beyond me, fighting for self-control, but the last defense was breached and the guilt was pushing against that gorgeous façade. I'd seen it happen before. People can hold out just so long and then they fold. She was really an amateur at heart.

"You got pushed too hard and you broke," I said, hoping I wasn't overplaying my hand. "You waited until he and Nikki left town and then you used Diane's keys to get into the house. You put the oleander capsules in his little plastic vial, being careful to leave no prints, and then you left."

"I hated him," she said, mouth trembling. She blinked and a tear splashed on her shirt like a drop of rain. She took a deep breath, words coming out in a rush. "He ruined my life, took my kids, robbed me blind, insulted, abused—oh my God, you have no idea. The *venom* in that man . . ."

She snatched up a napkin and pressed it to her eyes. Amazingly, Rosie didn't seem to notice her distress. She sat at the bar, probably reading Ann Landers, thinking At Wit's End should have turned hubby in for the obscene calls he made, while a customer confessed to murder right under her nose. To her right, the little television set flickered a Muppets rerun.

Gwen sighed, staring down at the tabletop. She reached over and picked up her glass, taking in a big slug of Scotch, which made her shudder as it went down. "I didn't even feel bad about it, except for the kids. They took it hard and that surprised me. They were far better off with him gone."

"Why the affair?" I probed.

"I don't know," she said, folding and refolding the paper napkin. "I guess it was my revenge. He was such an egotist. I knew he couldn't resist. After all, I'd insulted the hell out of him by having an affair with someone else. He couldn't tolerate that. I knew he'd want his own back. It wasn't even that hard to engineer. He wanted to prove something to himself. He wanted to show me what I'd passed up. There was even a certain amount of jazz to the sex for once. The hostility was so close to the surface that it gave us both a sick charge. God, I loathed him. I really did. And I'll tell you something else," she said harshly. "Killing him once just wasn't enough. I wish I could kill him again."

She looked at me fully then and the enormity of what she was saying began to sink in.

"What about Nikki? What did she ever do to you?"

"I thought they'd acquit her," she said. "I never thought she'd go to jail, and when the sentence was handed down I wasn't going to stand up and take her place. By then it was too late."

"So what else?" I said and I noticed that my tone was getting sullen. "Did you kill the dog too?"

"I had nothing to do with that. He got hit Sunday morning. I drove Diane over there because she'd remembered that she'd left him out and she was upset. He was already lying in the street. My God, I wouldn't run over a *dog*," she said emphatically, as though I should appreciate the delicacy of her sentiments.

"And the rest just fell into place? The oleander in the yard? The capsules upstairs?"

"One capsule. I doctored *one*."

"Bullshit, Gwen. That's bullshit."

"It's not. I'm telling the truth. I swear to it. I'd thought about it for a long time but I couldn't see a way to make it work. I wasn't even sure it would kill him. Diane was a wreck about the dog anyway so I drove her to my place and put her to bed. As soon as she was asleep, I took her keys and went back and that's all it was." She spoke with an edge of defiance, as though having opened up this far there was no point in mincing words.

"What about the other two?" I snapped. "What about Sharon and Libby Glass?"

She blinked at me, pulling back. "I don't know what you're talking about."

"Oh the hell you don't," I said, getting up. "You've lied to me since the first minute we met. I can't believe a goddamn word you say and you know it."

She seemed startled by my energy. "What are you going to do?"

"Give the information to Nikki," I said. "She paid for it. We'll let her decide."

I moved away from the table, heading toward the door. Gwen grabbed her jacket and purse, keeping pace with me.

Out on the street, she snatched at my arm and I shook her off.

"Kinsey wait . . ." Her face was remarkably pale.

"Blow it out your ass," I said. "You'd better hire yourself a hot attorney, babe, because you're going to need one."

I moved off down the street, leaving Gwen behind.

25

I locked the door to my place and tried dialing Nikki out at the beach. The phone rang eight times and I hung up, pacing the room after that with an unsettled sensation in my chest. There was something off. There was something not right and I couldn't put my finger on what was bothering me. There was no feeling of closure. None. This should have been the end of it. The big climax. I'd been hired to find out who killed Laurence Fife and I had. The end. Finis. But I was left with half a case and a lot of loose ends. Gwen's killing of Laurence had been part premeditation and part impulse, but the rest of it didn't seem to fit. Why wasn't everything falling into place? I couldn't picture Gwen killing Libby Glass. Gwen had hated Laurence Fife for years, titillating herself perhaps with ways of killing him, maybe never even dreaming that she'd actually do it, never imagining that she could actually pull it off. She'd come up with oleander scheme and suddenly she'd seen a way to make it work. A perfect opportunity had presented itself and she'd acted. Surely Libby Glass's death couldn't have been that easy to arrange. How did Gwen know about her? How did she know where she lived? How could she have gotten into that apartment? And how could she have counted on her taking medication of any kind? I couldn't picture Gwen driving to Vegas either. Couldn't imagine her shooting Sharon in cold blood. For what? What was the point? Killing Laurence had wiped out an old grudge, satisfied an ancient and bitter hatred between them, but why kill the other two? Blackmail? Threat of exposure? That might account for Sharon but why Libby Glass? Gwen had seemed truly self-righteous in her bewilderment. Like her denial of any responsibility for killing the dog. There was just that odd note of genuine outrage in her voice. It didn't make sense.

Unless there was someone else involved. Someone else who killed.

I felt a chill.

Oh my God. Lyle? Charlie? I sat down, blinking rapidly, hand across my mouth. I'd bought into the notion that one person killed all three, but maybe not. Maybe there was another possibility. I tried it out. Gwen had murdered Laurence Fife. Why couldn't someone else have spotted the opening and taken advantage of it? The timing was close, the method the same. Of course it was going to look like it was all part of the same setup.

I thought about Lyle. I thought about his face, the strange imperceptibly mismatched eyes: sullen, watchful, belligerent. He said he'd been with Libby three days before she died. I knew he'd heard about Laurence's death. He was not a man who possessed a giant intellect, but he could have managed that much, imitating the cunning of someone else—even stoned.

I called my answering service. "I'm going down to Los Angeles," I said. "If Nikki Fife calls, I want you to give her the telephone number of the Hacienda motel down there and tell her it's important that she get in touch. But no one else. I don't want it known that I'm out of town. I'll check in with you often enough to pick up whatever calls come in. Just say I'm tied up and you don't know where I am. You got that?"

"All right, Miss Millhone. Will do," she said cheerfully and then clicked off. God. If I'd said to her, "Hold the calls. I'm slitting my throat," she'd have responded with the same blank good will.

The drive to Los Angeles was good for me—soothing, uneventful. It was after nine and there wasn't that much traffic on the darkened road south. On my left, hills swelled and rolled, covered with low vegetation—no trees, no rocks. On my right, the ocean rumbled, almost at arm's length, looking very black except for a ruffle of white here and there. I passed Summerland, Carpinteria, passed the oil derricks and the power plant, which was garlanded with tiny lights like a decorative display at Christmastime. There was something restful about having nothing to worry about except having a wreck and getting killed. It freed my mind for other things.

I had made a mistake, a false assumption, and I felt like a novice. On the other hand, I'd made the very assumption that everyone else had made: same M.O., same murderer. But now I didn't think that was true. Now it seemed to me the only explanation that made any sense was that someone else had killed Libby Glass—and Sharon too. I drove through Ventura, Oxnard, Camarillo, where the state mental asylum was located. I've heard that there is less tendency to violence among the institutionalized insane than there is in the citizenry at large and I believe that. I thought about Gwen without surprise or dismay, my mind jumping forward and back randomly. Somehow I was more offended by the minor crimes of a Marcia Threadgill who tried for less, without any motivation at all beyond greed. I wondered if Marcia Threadgill was the new standard of morality against which I would now judge all other sins. Hatred, I could understand—the need for revenge, the payment of old debts. That's what the notion of "justice" was all about anyway: settling up.

I went over the big hill into Thousand Oaks, with traffic picking up; tract housing stretched out on either side of the road, then shopping malls packed end to end. The night air was damp and I kept the windows rolled down. I felt over into the backseat for my briefcase and fumbled with the catch. I tucked my little automatic into my jacket pocket, encountering a wad of papers. I pulled them out and glanced down. Sharon Napier's bills. I'd stuck them in my windbreaker on the way out of her place and I hadn't thought about them since. I'd have to go through them. I tossed them on the passenger seat and looked at my watch by the icy wash of highway light. It was 10:10—forty-five minutes of driving left, maybe more given traffic on the surface roads once I got off the freeway. I thought about Charlie, wondering if I'd blown a perfectly nice relationship. He didn't seem like the type to forgive and forget, but who knew. He was a lot more yielding than I was, that was for sure. My thoughts rambled on disjunctively. Lyle had known I was driving to Vegas. I wasn't sure how Sharon connected, but I'd figure that out. Blackmail still seemed like the best bet. The letter I couldn't figure at all. How had Libby

come by that? Or had she? Maybe Lyle and *Sharon* were in
cahoots. Maybe Lyle got the letter from her. Maybe he was
planting the letter among Libby's effects, not trying to take it
away. It was certainly to his advantage to reinforce the idea of
Libby's romantic tie to Laurence Fife. He had known I was
stopping back through to pick up her boxes. He could have
made it back to Los Angeles well in advance of me since I'd
stopped for the night to see Diane. Maybe he had deliberately
timed it closely to incite my curiosity about what might have
been tucked away there. My mind veered off that and I thought
about Lieutenant Dolan with a faint smile. He was so sure
Nikki had killed her husband, so satisfied with that. I'd have to
put a call through to him when I got back. I thought about Lyle
again. I didn't intend to see him that night. He wasn't as smart
as Gwen, but he might be dangerous. *If* it was him. I didn't
think I should jump to conclusions again.

I checked into the Hacienda at 11:05, went straight to room
#2, and put myself to bed. Arlette's mother was on the desk.
She is twice as fat.

In the morning, I showered and got back into the same
clothes, staggering out to the car to retrieve the overnight case
I kept in the crowded backseat. I went back to my room and
brushed my teeth—oh blessed relief—and ran a comb through
my hair. I went down to a delicatessen on the corner of
Wilshire and Bundy, where I ordered scrambled eggs, sausage
links, a toasted bagel with cream cheese, coffee, and fresh
orange juice. Whoever invented breakfast really did it good.

I walked back up to the Hacienda to find Arlette waving a
massive arm out the office door for me. Her round face was
flushed, her little cap of blonde curls in a flyaway state, her
eyes squeezed almost to invisibility by the heavy cheeks. I
wondered when she'd last seen her own neck. Still, I liked her,
irksome as she was at times.

"There's someone on the phone for you and she sounds
real upset. I told her you were out but I said I'd flag you down.
Thank goodness you're back," she said to me, out of breath
and wheezing hard.

I hadn't seen Arlette so excited since she found out that
panty hose came in queen-size. I went into the office with

Arlette hard on my heels, breathing heavily. The receiver was on the counter and I picked it up.

"Hello?"

"Kinsey, this is Nikki."

Why the dread in her voice, I thought automatically. "I tried calling you last night," I said. "What's the matter? Are you okay?"

"Gwen's dead."

"I just talked to her last night," I said blankly. Killed herself. She'd killed herself. Oh shit, I thought.

"It happened this morning. Hit-and-run driver. I just heard it on the news. She was jogging along Cabana Boulevard and someone ran her down and then skipped."

"I don't believe it. Are you sure?"

"Positive. I tried calling you and the service said you were out of town. What are you doing in L.A.?"

"I've got to check out something down here but I should be back tonight," I said, thinking fast. "Look, would you see if you can find out the details?"

"I can try."

"Call Lieutenant Dolan at Homicide. Tell him I told you to ask."

"Homicide," she said, startled.

"Nikki, he's a *cop*. He'll know what's going on. And it may not be an accident anyway, so see what he has to say and I'll call you as soon as I get back."

"Well, okay," she said dubiously, "I'll see what I can do."

"Thanks." I hung up the phone.

"Is someone dead?" Arlette asked. "Was it someone you knew?"

I looked right at her but I drew a blank. Why Gwen? What was happening?

She followed me out of the office and toward my room.

"Is there anything I can do to help? Do you need anything? You look awful, Kinsey. You're pale as a ghost."

I closed the door behind me. I thought about that last image of Gwen, standing on the street, her face white. *Could* it have been an accident? Coincidence? Things were moving too quickly. Someone was beginning to panic and for reasons I still couldn't quite understand.

A possibility flashed into my head and out. I stood stock-still, running it by me again like an old film clip. Maybe so. Maybe yes. It was all going to come together soon. It was all going to fit.

I threw everything into the backseat of my car, not even bothering to check out. I'd mail Arlette the damn twelve bucks.

The drive to the Valley was a blur, the car moving automatically, though I paid no attention whatever to road, sun, traffic, smog. When I reached the house in Sherman Oaks where Lyle was laying brick, I saw his battered truck parked out front. I didn't have any more time to waste and I didn't want to play games. I locked the car and went up the drive, going around the side of the house to the back. I caught sight of Lyle before he caught sight of me. He was bending over a pile of two-by-fours: faded jeans, work boots, no shirt, a cigarette in the corner of his mouth.

"Lyle."

He turned around. I had the gun out and trained on him. I held it with two hands, legs apart, meaning busines. He froze instantly where he stood, not saying a word.

I felt cold and my voice was tight, but the gun never wavered an inch. "I want some answers and I want them now," I said. I saw him glance to his right. There was a hammer lying on the ground but he made no move.

"Back up," I said, stepping forward slightly until I was between him and the hammer. He did as instructed, the pale blue eyes sliding back to mine, hands coming up.

"I don't want to shoot you, Lyle, but I will."

For once, he didn't look sullen or sly or arrogant. He stared straight at me with the first sign of respect I'd seen from him.

"You're the boss," he said.

"Don't fuckin' smart-mouth *me*," I snapped. "I'm not in the mood. Now sit down in the grass. Out there. And don't move a muscle unless I tell you to."

Obediently, he moved out to a small stretch of grass and sat down, eyes on me the whole time. It was quiet and I could hear birds chirping stupidly but we seemed to be alone and I liked it that way. I kept the gun pointed right at his chest, willing my hands not to shake. The sun was hot and it made him squint.

"Tell me about Libby Glass," I said.

"I didn't kill her," he shot back uneasily.

"That's not the point. I want to know what went on. I want to know what you haven't told me yet. When did you see her last?"

He shut his mouth.

"Tell me!"

He didn't have Gwen's poise and he didn't have her smarts. The sight of the gun seemed to help him make up his mind.

"Saturday."

"The day she died, right?"

"That's right, but I didn't do anything. I went over to see her and we had a big fight and she was upset."

"All right, all right. Skip the buildup. What else?"

He was silent.

"Lyle," I said warningly. The muscles in his face seemed to pull together like a drawstring purse and he started to weep. He put his hands up over his face pathetically. He'd kept it in for a long time. If I was wrong about this, I was wrong about everything. I couldn't let him off the hook.

"Just tell me," I said, tone dead, "I need to know."

I thought he was coughing but I knew what I heard were sobs. He might have been nine years old, looking squeezed up and frail and small.

"I gave her a *tranq*," he said with anguish. "She asked for one and I found this bottle in the medicine cabinet and gave it to her. God, I even gave her a glass of water. I loved her so much."

The first rush subsided and he dashed at the tears on his face with a grubby hand, leaving streaks of dirt. He hugged himself, rocking back and forth in misery, tears streaming down his bony cheeks again.

"Go on," I said.

"I left after that but I felt bad and I went back later and that's when I found her dead on the bathroom floor. I was afraid they'd find my fingerprints and think I'd done something to her so I wiped the whole place down."

"And you took the tranquilizers with you when you left?"

He nodded, pressing his fingers into his eye sockets as though he could force the tears back. "I flushed 'em down the toilet when I got home. I smashed up the bottle and threw it away."

"How'd you know that's what it was?"

"I don't know. I just knew. I remembered that guy, the one up north and I knew he'd died that way. She might not have taken the goddamn thing if it weren't for me, but we had that screaming fight and she was so mad, she shook. I didn't even know she had any tranqs till she asked for one and I didn't see anything wrong with that. I went back to apologize." The worst of it seemed to be over with and he sighed deeply, his voice almost normal again.

"What else?"

"I don't know. The phone was unplugged. I plugged it back in and wiped that down too," he said woodenly. "I didn't mean any harm. I just had to protect myself. I wouldn't poison her. I wouldn't have done that to her, I swear to God. I didn't have anything to do with that or anything else except I cleaned the place. In case there were fingerprints. I didn't want anything pointing to me. And I took the bottle the pills were in. I did that."

"But you didn't break into the storage bin," I said.

He shook his head.

I lowered the gun. I'd half known but I had to be sure.

"Are you going to turn me in?"

"No. Not you."

I went back to the car and sat blankly, wondering in some vague irrational way if I really would have used the gun. I didn't think so. Tough. I'm tough, scaring the shit out of some dumb kid. I shook my head, feeling tears of my own. I started the car and put it into gear, heading back over the hill toward West L.A. I had one more stop and then I could drive back to Santa Teresa and clean it up. I thought I knew now who it was.

26

I caught sight of my reflection in one of the mirrored walls across from the entrance to Haycraft and McNiece. I looked like I was ready for the last round-up: seedy, disheveled, mouth grim. Even Allison, in her buckskin shirt with the fringes on the sleeves, seemed alarmed by the sight of me, and her prerehearsed receptionist's smile dropped from sixty watts to twenty-five.

"I have to talk to Garry Steinberg," I said, my tone apparently indicating that I wouldn't take much shit.

"He's back in his office," she said timidly. "Do you know which one it is?"

I nodded and pushed through the swinging doors. I caught sight of Garry walking down the narrow interior corridor toward his office, slapping a batch of unopened mail against his thigh.

"Garry?"

He turned, his face lighting up at the sight of me and then turning hesitant. "Where'd you come from? You look exhausted."

"I drove down last night. Can we talk?"

"Sure. Come on in."

He turned left into his office, gathering up a stack of files on the chair in front of his desk. "You want some coffee? Can I get you anything?" He tossed the mail on the file cabinet.

"No, I'm fine but I need to check out a hunch."

"Fire away," he said, sitting down.

"Didn't you tell me once upon a time—"

"Last week," he inserted.

"Yeah, I guess it was. You mentioned that Fife's accounts were being put on computer."

"Sure, we were converting everything. Makes it a hell of a

lot easier on us and it's better for the client too. Especially at tax time.''

"Well what if the books had been fiddled with?''

"You mean embezzlement?''

"In a word,'' I said with irony. "Wouldn't that have shown up pretty quickly?''

"Absolutely. You think Fife was milking his own accounts?''

"No,'' I said slowly, "I think Charlie Scorsoni was. That's part of what I need to ask you about. Could he have skimmed money out of the estates he was representing back then?''

"Sure. It can be done and it's not that hard,'' Garry said appreciatively, "but it might be a bitch to track. It really depends on how he did it.'' He thought for a moment, apparently warming to the idea. He shrugged. "For instance, he could have set up some kind of special account or an escrow account for all his estates—maybe two or three phony accounts within this overall account. A large dividend check comes in, he diverts a percentage of the check from the estate it's supposed to be credited to, and he credits it to a phony account instead.''

"Could Libby have realized something was wrong?''

"She might have. She had a head for that kind of thing. She'd have had to trace the dividends through Moody's Dividend Book, which gives the amount of each dividend by company. Then if there was some kind of discrepancy, she might have asked for records or documentation—bank statements, canceled checks, stuff like that.''

"Yeah, well Lyle told me last week that there were lots of phone calls back and forth, some attorney driving down for dinner. It finally occurred to me that Charlie might have engineered an affair with her in the hopes that she'd cover for him . . .''

"Or maybe he offered her a cut,'' Garry said.

"Oh God, would she have done that?''

Garry shrugged. "Hey, who knows? Would *he*?''

I stared down at his desk top. "Yeah, I think so,'' I said. "You know, everybody kept saying that she was involved with some Santa Teresa attorney and we all assumed it was Fife because both died the same way. But if I'm right about this

embezzlement business then I need proof. Are the files still at
your place?"

"No, I've got 'em right here as a matter of fact. I thought
I'd take a look at 'em during my lunch hour. I've been having
cottage cheese but I don't think that counts as food so I thought
I'd do without. I brought 'em in yesterday and then I got tied
up. Now that you mention it, I do think she was working on
that account when she died, because the cops found her
briefcase at her place," he said. He gave me a curious look.
"How'd you fix on him?"

I shook my head. "I don't know. It just popped into my
brain and it fit. Charlie told me that Fife made a trip to Los
Angeles sometime in the week before he died, but I don't think
that's true. I think probably Charlie made the trip himself and it
would have been within a day or two after Laurence died.
Libby had a bottle of tranqs and I think he doctored some—
who knows, maybe all of 'em. We'll never know about that."

"Jesus. He kill Fife too?"

I shook my head. "No, I know who killed Fife. My guess
is that Charlie saw a way to bail himself out. Maybe Libby
wouldn't play ball with him or maybe she'd threatened to turn
him in. Not that I've got any evidence one way or the other."

"Hey, it'll come," he said soothingly. "If it's there, we'll
find it. I'll start on the files this afternoon."

"Good," I said, "I'd like that."

"Take care."

We shook hands across the desk.

I drove back to Santa Teresa, resolutely refusing to think of
Gwen. Thinking about Charlie Scorsoni was depressing
enough. I would have to check his whereabouts at the time
Sharon died, but he could easily have checked out of the hotel
in Denver and flown straight to Las Vegas, picking up my
location from the answering service, finding my motel, and
then following me to the Fremont. I thought about Sharon—
that moment in the coffee shop when I thought she'd seen
someone she knew. She'd said it was the pit boss signaling the
end of her break, but I was sure she was lying. Charlie may
have put in an appearance then, pulling back when he spotted
me. Maybe she thought he had shown up to pay her off. I was

relatively certain she'd been leaning on him for bucks, but then again, I'd have to pin that down. Sharon must have known that Fife was never involved with Libby Glass sexually. It was Charlie who'd been making the trips down to Los Angeles to discuss the accounts. Sharon must have kept her mouth shut during the trial, watching the whole tale unfold, biding her time, eventually cashing in on whatever information she had. It was also possible that Charlie Scorsoni hadn't known where she was—that I'd led him straight down the path to her door. I was aware, as I went over the sequence of events, that much of it sounded like a lot of fancy guesswork, but I felt I was headed in the right direction and I could probe now for corroborating evidence.

If Charlie had killed Gwen in that hit-and-run accident, there were bound to be ways to trace it back to him: hair and fibers on the fender of his car, which probably sustained some damage that would have to be repaired; paint flakes and glass fragments on Gwen's clothes. Maybe even a witness some-where. It would have been much wiser if Charlie'd never made a move—just held tight and kept his mouth shut, lying low. It probably would have been impossible to put a case together against him after all these years. There was an arrogance in his behavior, a hint that he considered himself too smart and too slick to get caught. No one was *that* good. Especially at the rate he'd been operating these days. He had to be making mistakes.

And why not just go down for the count on the original embezzlement? He must have been desperately trying to cover for himself in Laurence Fife's eyes. But even if he'd been exposed, even if he'd been caught, I didn't believe Laurence would have turned him in. As sleazy as Fife had been in his personal life, I knew he was scrupulously honest in business matters. Still, Charlie was his best friend and the two went a long way back together. He might have warned Charlie off or smacked his hand—perhaps even dissolved the partnership. But I didn't think Charlie would have gone to jail or been disbarred from the practice of law. His life probably wouldn't have been ruined and he probably wouldn't have lost what he'd worked so hard to achieve. He would have lost Laurence Fife's good opinion and his trust perhaps, but he must have known that when he first put his hand in the cookie jar. The ludicrous fact of the matter is that in this day and age, a white-collar criminal can become a celebrity, a hero, can go on talk shows and write bestselling books. So what was there to sweat? Society will forgive just about anything except homicide. It was hard to shrug that one off, hard to rationalize that one away and whereas before, Charlie might have come out somewhat tarnished but intact, he was in big trouble now and things just seemed to be getting worse.

I didn't even address myself to the matter of his relationship to me. He'd played me for a sucker, just as he'd done with Libby Glass, and she, in her innocence, at least had a better excuse for the tumble than I did. It had been too long since I'd cared about anyone, too long since I'd taken that risk and I'd already invested too much. I just had to slam the gate shut emotionally and move on, but it didn't sit well with me.

When I reached Santa Teresa, I went straight to the office, taking with me the sheaf of bills from Sharon Napier's apartment. For the first time, I was beginning to think those might be significant. I went through them with an abstract curiosity that felt ghoulish nevertheless. She was dead and it seemed obscene now to note that she'd bought lingerie that had gone unpaid for, cosmetics, shoes. Her utilities were a month behind, with dunning notices from several small businesses including her tax man, a chiropractor, and a health spa membership renewal. Visa and Mastercharge had gotten churlish and American Express wanted its card back in no uncertain terms, but it was her telephone bill that interested me. In the area code that included Santa Teresa, there were three calls in the month of March, not an excessive number but telling. Two of the calls were to Charlie Scorsoni's office—both on the same day, ten minutes apart. The third number she'd called I didn't immediately recognize but the Santa Teresa exchange was the same. I picked up my Cross-Reference Directory. The number was for John Powers's house at the beach.

I dialed Ruth, not allowing myself to hesitate. Surely Charlie hadn't told her I'd broken with him. I couldn't picture him confiding his personal affairs to anyone. If he was there, I'd have to think fast and I wasn't sure what I intended to say. The information I needed was from her.

"Scorsoni and Powers," she sang.

"Oh hi, Ruth. This is Kinsey Millhone," I said, heart in my throat. "Is Charlie there?"

"Oh hi, Kinsey. No he's not," she said with a hint of regret in my behalf. "He's in court up in Santa Maria for the next two days."

Thank God for that, I thought, and took a deep breath. "Well maybe you can help me instead," I said. "I was just going over some bills for a client and it looks like she was in touch with him. Do you happen to remember someone calling him a couple of times maybe six, eight weeks ago? Her name was Sharon Napier. Long-distance."

"Oh, the one who used to work for him. Yes, I remember that. What did you need to know?"

"Well I can't quite tell from this if she actually got through to him or not. It looks like she called on a Friday—the twenty-first of March. Does that ring a bell?"

"Oh yes. Absolutely," Ruth said efficiently. "She called asking for him and he was out at Mr. Powers's house. She was very insistent that I put her through but I didn't feel I should give out the number without checking with him, so I told her to call me back and then I checked with him out at the beach and he said it was fine. I hope that's all right. I hope she hasn't hired you to pester him or anything."

I laughed. "Oh heavens, Ruth, would I do that to him? I did see the number for John Powers and I just thought maybe she talked to him instead."

"Oh no. He was out of town that weekend. He's usually gone around the twenty-first for a couple of days. I have it right here on my calendar. Mr. Scorsoni was taking care of his dogs."

"Oh well, that would explain it," I said casually. "God, that's been a great help. Now the only other thing I need to check is that trip to Tucson."

"Tucson?" she said. Doubt was beginning to creep into her voice, that protective tone secretaries sometimes take when it suddenly occurs to them that someone wants something they're not supposed to get. "What is this about, Kinsey? Maybe I could be of more help if I understood what this has to do with a client of yours. Mr. Scorsoni's pretty strict about things like that."

"Oh no, that's something else. And I can check that out myself so don't worry about it. I can always give Charlie a buzz when he gets back and ask him."

"Well, I can give you his motel number in Santa Maria if you want to call him yourself," she said. She was trying to play it both ways—helpful to me if my questions were legitimate, helpful to Charlie if they weren't—but in any case, dumping the whole matter in his lap. For an old lady, she was adroit.

I jotted the number down dutifully, knowing I'd never call him but glad to get a fix on him anyway. I wanted to tell her not to mention my call but I didn't see how I could do it without tipping my hand. I just had to hope that Charlie wouldn't check in with her anytime soon. If she told him what I'd been asking about, he would know like a shot that I was on his tail and he wouldn't like that a bit.

I put in a call to Dolan at Homicide. He was out but I left a message, "important" underlined, that he should call me back when he got in. I tried Nikki at the beach and got her on the third ring.

"Hi, Nikki, it's me," I said. "Is everything okay?"

"Oh yeah. We're fine. I still haven't quite recovered from the shock of Gwen's death, but I don't know what to do about that. I never even knew the woman and it still seems a shame."

"Did you get any details from Dolan? I just tried to call him and he's out."

"Not a lot," she said. "He was awfully rude. Worse than I remember him and he wouldn't tell me much except the car that hit her was black."

"Black?" I said with disbelief. I was picturing Charlie's pale blue Mercedes and I'd fully expected some detail that would tie that in. "Are you sure?"

"That's what he said. I guess the detectives have been checking with the body shops and garages but so far nothing's turned up."

"That's odd," I said.

"Are you coming out for a drink? I'd love to hear what's going on."

"Maybe later. I'm trying to clean up a couple of loose ends. I'll tell you what else I need. Maybe you can answer this. Remember the letter I showed you that Laurence wrote—"

"Sure, the one to Libby Glass," she broke in quickly.

"Yeah, well I'm almost sure now that the letter was written to Elizabeth Napier instead."

"Who?"

"I'll fill you in on that later. I suspect that Elizabeth Napier was the one he got involved with when he was married to Gwen. Sharon Napier's mother."

"Oh, the *scandal*," she said, light breaking. "Oh sure, it could well be. He never would tell me much about that. Messy business. I know the story because Charlotte Mercer filled me in on that, but I was never really sure of the name. God, that would have been way back in Denver, just after his law-school days."

I hesitated. "Can you think who else would have known about that letter? Who could have had access to it? I mean, could Gwen?"

"I suppose so," she said. "Certainly Charlie would. He was working as a law clerk in the firm that represented the husband in that divorce and he lifted the letter from what I heard."

"He what?"

"Stole it. Oh I'm sure that's the one. Didn't I ever tell you the end of that? Charlie snitched the letter, just cleaned out all the evidence, and that's why they ended up settling out of court. She didn't do that well but at least it got Laurence off the hook."

"What happened to the letter? Could Charlie have kept the letter himself?"

"I don't know. I always assumed it had been destroyed but I guess he could have hung on to it. He never did get caught and I don't think the husband's attorney ever figured it out. You know how things disappear in offices. Probably some secretary got fired."

"Could Gwen have testified to any of this?"

"What *am* I, the district attorney's office?" she said with a laugh. "How do I know what Gwen knew?"

"Well, whatever it was, she's quiet now," I said.

"Oh," she said and I could tell her smile had faded fast. "Oh, I don't like that. That's a terrible thought."

"I'll tell you the rest when I see you. If I can get out there, I'll call first and make sure you're home."

"We'll be here. I take it you're making progress."

"Rapidly," I said.

Her good-byes were puzzled and mine were brief.

I hauled out my typewriter and committed everything I knew to paper in a lengthy and detailed report. Another piece had fallen into place. The night the storage bin was broken into, it was Charlie, not Lyle, who was planting the letter among Libby's belongings, hoping I'd find it, hoping he could shore up his own tale about Laurence Fife's "affair" with Libby Glass. Which probably also explained the key to her apartment that had been found on Laurence's key ring in the office. It wouldn't have been hard for Charlie to plant that one too. I typed on, feeling exhausted but determined to get it all down. In the back of my mind, I kept thinking of it as a safeguard, an insurance policy, but I wasn't sure what kind of coverage I needed. Maybe none. Maybe I didn't need protection, I thought. As it turned out, I was wrong.

27

I finished my report and locked it in my desk drawer. I went out to the parking lot and retrieved my car, heading north toward Charlie's house on Missile Avenue. Two doors down from his place was a house called Tranquility for reasons unknown. I parked in front of it and walked back. Charlie's house was a two-story structure with a painted-yellow-shingle exterior and a dark shingled roof, a bay window in front, a long narrow driveway to the left. It was the sort of house that might appear in an establishing shot for a television family show, something that might come on at 8:00 P.M., everything looking regular and wholesome and suitable for kids. There was no sign of his car in the drive, no sign of occupants. I eased along the driveway toward the garage, looking back over my shoulder as I went. There weren't even any nosy neighbors peering out at me. When I reached the one-car garage, I went around to the side, cupping my hands so that I could peer into the window. It was empty: a woodworking bench along the back wall, old lawn furniture, dust. I looked around, wondering whose black car it was and why the cops hadn't gotten a line on it yet. If I could fill in that blank, then I'd have something to talk to Con Dolan about. I was going to have something concrete.

I walked back up the drive to my car and sat, a favorite occupation of mine. It was getting dark. I glanced at my watch. It was 6:45 and that startled me. I desperately longed for a glass of wine and I decided to drive on out to Nikki's. She had said she'd be home. I turned the car around, making an illegal U, and drove back down Missile to the freeway, heading north. I got off at La Cuesta, heading toward the beach by way of Horton Ravine, a large sprawling expanse of land that is known as "a luxury residential development." Horton Ravine once belonged to one family, but it is now divided into million-dollar parcels to accommodate the housing of the nouveau riche. In Santa Teresa, Montebello is considered "old" money, Horton Ravine the "new"—but nobody really takes the distinction seriously. Rich is rich and we all know what that means. The roads through Horton Ravine are narrow and winding, overhung with trees, and the only difference I could see was that here, some houses are visible from the road whereas in Montebello, they are not. I came out at Ocean Way and swung left, the road running parallel now to the bluffs, with a number of elegant properties tucked into the selvage of land that lay between the road and the cliffs.

I passed John Powers's house, almost missing the place since I'd come at it before from the other direction. I caught a quick glimpse of the roof, which was almost level with the road. I had a sudden thought and I slammed on the brakes, pulling over to the side. I sat for a moment, heart thudding with excitement. I turned the key off and stuck my little automatic in my jeans, taking the flashlight out of the glove compartment. I flicked it on. The light was good. There were very few streetlamps along this stretch and those I could see were ornamental, as dim and misty-looking as a lithograph, casting ineffectual circles of light that scarcely penetrated the dark. I got out of the car and locked it.

There were no sidewalks, just tangles of ivy along the road. The houses were widely spaced with wooded lots in between, ratcheting now with crickets and other night-singing insects. I walked back along the road to the Powers place. There were no houses at all across from it. No cars in either direction. I paused. There were no lights visible in the house. I headed down the driveway, shining the light in front of me. I wondered if Powers was still out of town, and if so where the dogs were. If Charlie was going to be up in Santa Maria for two days he wouldn't have left them unattended.

The night was still, the ocean pounding, a recurrent thunder like a storm about to break. There was only a faint crust of moon against the hazy night sky. It was chilly, too, the air smelling lush and damp. The flashlight cut a narrow trail down the drive, illuminating in a sudden band of white the gateway across the carport. Beyond it was John Powers's car, face-in, and even from where I stood I could see that it was black. I wasn't surprised. The white picket fencing that comprised the gate was padlocked but I eased around to the left of the carport toward the front of the house. I shone the light on the car. It was a Lincoln. I couldn't tell what year but the car wasn't old. I checked the fender on the left-hand side and it was fine. I could feel my heart beginning to thump dully with dread. The right-hand fender was crumpled, the headlight broken out, metal rim crimped and pulled away, bumper indented slightly. I tried not to think of Gwen's body at the moment of impact. I could guess what it must have been like.

I heard an abrupt squealing of brakes on the road above, the high whine of a car backing up at high speed. There was a sudden wash of bright light as a car pulled into the drive. I ducked automatically, flicking out the flashlight. If it was Charlie, I was dead. I caught a glimpse of blue. Oh shit. He'd called Ruth. He was back. He knew. The Mercedes's headlights were directed straight into the carport, with only Powers's vehicle shielding me from complete exposure. I heard the car door slam and I ran.

I flew across the yard, fairly skimming the rough cut grass. Behind me, almost soundlessly, came the low scuffling of the dogs in long loping strides. I started down the narrow wooden steps to the beach, my vision inky after the harsh glare of the headlights. I missed a step and half slid my way down to the next, groping blindly. Above me, only yards away, the black dog grumbled and started down, panting, toenails scrambling on the steps. I glanced up and back. The black one was just above my head. Without even thinking about it, I reached back and grabbed at one of his long bony forelegs, yanking abruptly. The dog let out a yelp of surprise and I shoved it forward, half flinging it down the steep rocky embankment. The other dog was whining, a ninety-five-pound sissy, picking its way down the stairs with trepidation. I nearly lost my balance but I righted myself, loosened soil tumbling down into the darkness in front of me. I could hear the black dog lunging at the cliffside but he couldn't seem to get a purchase, prowling back and forth restlessly. I was nearly lying on my side as I slid down the last few feet, tumbling onto the soft sand. The gun popped out of my hand and I scrambled frantically until my fingers closed over the butt again. The flashlight was long gone. I didn't even remember when I'd lost my hold on it. The black dog was loping toward me again. I waited until he was almost on me and then I lifted a foot, kicking viciously, bringing the gun down on his head. He yelped. He'd clearly never been trained to attack. My advantage was that I knew he was a danger to me and he was just beginning to figure out how treacherous I was. He backed off, barking. I made a quick choice. North along the beach, the steep cliffs continued for miles, interrupted only by Harley's Beach, which was too isolated for sanctuary. North, the dog was blocking my path. The beach to my right would eventually straggle past the town and it couldn't be more than a couple of miles. I began to move backward, away from the dog. He stood there, head down, barking vigorously. The waves were already washing up over my shoes and I began to lift my feet, trudging backward through the surf. I turned, holding the gun up, beginning to wade. The dog paced back and forth, barking only occasionally now. The next big surge of waves crashed against my knees, drenching me to the waist. I gasped from the shock of cold, glancing back with a burble of fear as I caught sight of Charlie at the top of the cliff. The outside lights were on now, his big body sculptured in shadow, his face blank. He was staring straight down at me. I propelled myself forward, nearly flinging myself through the waist-high water, edging toward the rocks at the extreme southern limits of the beach. I reached the rocks, slippery and sharp, a mass of granite that had broken loose from the cliff and tumbled into the sea. I scrambled across, hampered by my soggy jeans, which clung to my legs, by my shoes weighted down with water, hampered by the gun, which I didn't dare relinquish. Jagged barnacles and slime alternated under me. I slipped once and something bit into my left knee, right through my jeans. I pushed on, reaching hard-packed sand again, the beach widening slightly.

There was no sign of the Powers house around the bend. No sign of either dog. I had known they couldn't follow this far even if they'd tried, but I wasn't sure about Charlie. I didn't know if he'd come down the wooden stairs and trail me along the beach or simply wait. I glanced back with dread, but the hill projected, obscuring even the light. All he had to do was get back in his car. If he took a parallel path to mine, he could intercept me easily on the other end. Eventually we'd both end up at Ludlow Beach, but I couldn't turn back. Harley's Beach was worse, too far from streetlights and residential help. I began to run in earnest, uncertain how far I had to go yet. My wet clothes stuck to me, clammy and cold, but my prime concern was the gun. I'd already dropped it once and I knew sea water had curled up toward it as I crossed the rocks. I didn't think it had gotten wet but I wasn't sure. I could see somewhat better now, but the beach was littered with rocks and kelp. I prayed I wouldn't twist an ankle. If I couldn't run, then Charlie could track me at his own pace and I'd have no way out. I glanced back: no sign of him, sound masked by the breaking surf. I didn't think he was there. Once I got to Ludlow Beach, there were bound to be other people, passing motorists. As long as I was running, the fear seemed contained, adrenaline driving out every sensation except the urge to flee. The wind was down, but it was cold and I was wet to the bone.

The beach narrowed again and I found myself running in shallow water, slogging my way through the churning surf. I tried to get my bearings but I'd never been up this far. I caught sight of a wooden stairway zigzagging up the cliff to my left, the wind-bleached railing showing white against the dark tangle of vegetation clinging to the cliff. I followed the line up with my eyes. I guessed that it was Sea Shore Park, which ran along the bluff. Parking lot. Houses across the road. I grabbed the rail and started up, knees aching as I climbed, chest heaving. I reached the top and peered over the rim, heart stopping again.

Charlie's 450 SL was parked above, headlights raking the fence. I ducked back and started down the stairs again, a mewing sound in my throat that I couldn't control. My breathing was ragged, my chest afire. I hit the sand again and ran on, accelerating my pace. The sand was sluggish now, too soft, and I cut to my right, searching out the wet sand that was packed hard. At least I was getting warmer now, wet clothes chafing, water dripping from strands of hair matted with salt. My left knee was stinging and I could feel something warm ooze through my pantleg. The beach was interrupted not by rocks this time but by the sheer fear of the cliff, jutting out like a pie-shaped wedge into the black of the sea. I waded out into

the waves, undercurrent tugging at me as I rounded the bend.
Ludlow Beach was visible just ahead. I nearly wept with relief.
Painfully, I began to run again, trying for a pace I could live
with. I could make out lights now, dark patches of palm against
gray sky. I slowed to a jog, trying to catch my breath. I stopped
finally, bending from the waist, my mouth dry, sweat or salt
water streaking down my face. My cheeks were hot and my
eyes stung. I wiped my mouth on the back of my hand and
moved on, walking this time, fear creeping up again until my
heart was battering my ribs.

This stretch of beach was gentle and clean, looking pale
gray, widening to the left where the high cliff finally dwindled
away into sloping hillside, slipping down to the flat of the
sand. Beyond, I could see the long stretch of parking lot and
beyond that, the street, well lighted, empty, and inviting. The
beach park closed at 8:00 and I thought the parking lot would
probably be chained and locked. Still the sight of Charlie's pale
blue 450 SL was a jolt—that single vehicle in the whole
expanse of empty asphalt. His car lights were on, slanting
forward into the palms. There was no way I could cut across
the sand to the street without his seeing me. The darkness,
which had seemed to lift before, now felt like a veil. I couldn't
see clearly. I couldn't pick out anything in that smoky wash of
darkness. The streetlights at that distance seemed pointless and
whimsical and cruel, illuminating nothing, marking a path to
safety that I couldn't reach. And where was he? Sitting in his
car, his eyes scanning the park, waiting for me to crash through
to him? Or out among the palms much closer to the beach?

I moved to the right again, wading out into the ocean. The
icy water was making my blood congeal but I crept on, waves
splashing against my knees. Out here, I would be harder to
spot and if I couldn't see him, at least he couldn't see me.
When I was out far enough, I sank down, half walking, half
drifting through the undulating depths beyond the breakers. It
cost me everything to keep the gun up. I was obsessed with
that, arm aching, fingers numb. My hair floated around my
face like wet gauze. I watched the beach, seeing little,
searching for Charlie. Car lights still on. Nothing. No one. I
had moved perhaps two hundred yards past the far-left extreme
of the parking lot, almost even now with the concession stand:

a small oasis of palms and picnic tables, trash cans, public telephones. I put my feet down, easing into a standing position, still angling to the right. He could be anywhere, standing in any shadow. I waded toward the shallows, waves curling at knee height, washing forward then across my shoes. Finally I was on wet sand again, moving quickly toward the lot, straining through the darkness for sight of him. He couldn't be looking everyplace at once. I crouched, shifting my gaze to the left. Now that I was forced into immobility, the fear took up where it had left me, ice spreading across my lungs, pulse beating in my throat. I slipped out of my wet jeans and shoes—lightly, quietly.

The concession stand was dead ahead: squat structure of cinder block, windows boarded over for the night. I moved to the right, through powdery sand, sinking down to my ankles, working harder on land than I had in water. I jumped. There he was—just a flash to my left. I dropped to a crouch again, wondering how visible I was. I eased down flat on my belly, pulled myself forward on my elbows. I reached the dark shade of the palms, which even at this hour cast clear shadows against the gray of night. I peered to the left, spotting him again. He wore a white shirt, darker pants. He disappeared into the shadows, passing into the grove of palm trees where the picnic tables were set out. Behind me, the ocean was hushed, a sibilant backdrop to our little cat-and-mouse. To my right, there was an oblong metal trash bin, chest-height with a hinged metal lid. I heard Charlie's car start up and I glanced back with surprise. Maybe he was leaving. Maybe he thought he had missed me and was moving now to intercept me farther down the beach. As he swung back to turn around, I darted toward the trash bin, lifted the lid with one thrust, and pulled myself over the metal lip into the crush of paper cups, discarded picnic sacks, debris. I wrestled out a place for myself with my backside, shifting my bare legs down into the garbage, wrinkling my nose with disgust. My right foot was touching something cold and gooey and the trash beneath me felt warm, like a compost heap, smoldering with bacteria. I pushed up slightly and peered over my shoulder through the crack, the metal lid tilted slightly ajar by the mountain of accumulated trash. Charlie's car was moving toward me, headlights slicing straight across my hiding place. I ducked down, heartbeat making my eyes bulge.

He got out of the car, leaving the lights on. I could still see a slice of light reflected from where I crouched. He slammed the car door. I could hear his footsteps scratch across the concrete.

"Kinsey, I know you're here someplace," he said.

I tried not to move. Tried not to breathe.

Silence.

"Kinsey, you don't have to be afraid of me. My God, don't you know that?" His tone was insistent, gentle, persuasive, hurt.

Was I just imagining everything? He sounded like he always did. Silence. I heard his footsteps moving away. I eased up slowly, peering out throught the crack. He was standing ten feet away from me, staring out toward the ocean, his body still, half turned away. He started back and I ducked down. I could hear footsteps approaching. I shrank, pulling the gun up, hands shaking. Maybe I was crazy. Maybe I was making a fool of myself. I hated hide-and-seek. I'd never been good at that as a kid. I always jumped right out when anyone got close because the tension made me want to wet my pants. I felt tears rising. Oh Jesus, not *now,* I thought feverishly. The fear was like a sharp pain. My heart hurt me every time it beat, making the blood pound in my ears. Surely he could hear that. Surely he knew now where I was.

He lifted the lid. The beams from his headlights shone against his golden cheek. He glanced over at me. In his right hand was a butcher knife with a ten-inch blade.

I blew him away.

The Santa Teresa police conducted a brief investigation but in the end no charges were filed. The folder on Laurence Fife contains the report I sent to the chief of the Bureau of Collection and Investigative Services regarding the discharge of my firearm "while acting within the course and scope" of my employment. There is also a copy of the refund check I sent to Nikki for the unused portion of the $5000 she advanced on account. All together, I was paid $2978.25 for services rendered in the course of that sixteen days and I suppose it was fair enough. The shooting disturbs me still. It has moved me into the same camp with soldiers and maniacs. I never set out to kill anyone. But maybe that's what Gwen would say, and Charlie too. I'll recover, of course. I'll be ready for business again in a week or two, but I'll never be the same. You try to keep life simple but it never works, and in the end all you have left is yourself.

Respectfully submitted,
Kinsey Millhone

ABOUT THE AUTHOR

SUE GRAFTON has written novels, articles, short fiction, a screenplay, and numerous teleplays. She has also lectured on writing at colleges and conferences in Southern California and the Midwest. Her first mystery, 'A' IS FOR ALIBI, won an award from the Cloak and Clue Society of Wisconsin. 'B' IS FOR BURGLAR won both the Anthony and the Shamus awards for best novel of 1985, and 'C' IS FOR CORPSE won the Anthony Award for Best Novel in 1986. "The Parker Shotgun" won a Macavity Award from the Mystery Readers of America and an Anthony for Best Short Story of 1986. Grafton, who was born in Louisville, Kentucky, now lives in Southern California with her husband, Steven Humphrey.